JACK LONDON

JACK LONDON

NOVELS AND SOCIAL WRITINGS

The People of the Abyss

The Road

The Iron Heel

Martin Eden

John Barleycorn

Essays

THE LIBRARY OF AMERICA

Library of Congress Catalog Card Number: 82–6940
For Cataloging in PublicationData, see end of *Notes* section.
ISBN: 0-940450-06-2
─────
Fifth Printing
The Library of America—7

Manufactured in the United States of America

DONALD PIZER
WROTE THE NOTES AND CHRONOLOGY
AND SELECTED THE TEXTS
FOR THIS VOLUME

Grateful acknowledgment is made to the National Endowment for the Humanities and the Ford Foundation for their generous financial support of this series.

Contents

Each section has its own table of contents.

The People of the Abyss I

The Road 185

The Iron Heel 315

Martin Eden 555

John Barleycorn 933

Essays 1113

Chronology 1167

Note on the Texts 1171

Notes 1175

THE PEOPLE OF
THE ABYSS

THE chief priests and rulers cry:—

"O Lord and Master, not ours the guilt,
We build but as our fathers built;
Behold thine images how they stand
Sovereign and sole through all our land.

"Our task is hard—with sword and flame,
To hold thine earth forever the same.
And with sharp crooks of steel to keep,
Still as thou leftest them, thy sheep."

Then Christ sought out an artisan,
A low-browed, stunted, haggard man,
And a motherless girl whose fingers thin
Crushed from her faintly want and sin.

These set he in the midst of them,
And as they drew back their garment hem
For fear of defilement, "Lo, here," said he,
"The images ye have made of me."

—JAMES RUSSELL LOWELL

Contents

Preface 5

I. *The Descent* 7

II. *Johnny Upright* 15

III. *My Lodging and Some Others* 19

IV. *A Man and the Abyss* 23

V. *Those on the Edge* 30

VI. *Frying-pan Alley and a Glimpse of Inferno* 35

VII. *A Winner of the Victoria Cross* 41

VIII. *The Carter and the Carpenter* 46

IX. *The Spike* 56

X. *Carrying the Banner* 69

XI. *The Peg* 73

XII. *Coronation Day* 82

XIII. *Dan Cullen, Docker* 93

XIV. *Hops and Hoppers* 97

XV. *The Sea Wife* 104

XVI. *Property* versus *Person* 108

XVII. *Inefficiency* 113

XVIII. *Wages* 119

XIX. *The Ghetto* 124

XX. *Coffee-houses and Doss-houses* 135

XXI. *The Precariousness of Life* 143

XXII. *Suicide* 152

XXIII. *The Children* 158

XXIV. *A Vision of the Night* 163

XXV. *The Hunger Wail* 166

XXVI. *Drink, Temperance, and Thrift* 173

XXVII. *The Management* 179

Preface

THE experiences related in this volume fell to me in the summer of 1902. I went down into the under-world of London with an attitude of mind which I may best liken to that of the explorer. I was open to be convinced by the evidence of my eyes, rather than by the teachings of those who had not seen, or by the words of those who had seen and gone before. Further, I took with me certain simple criteria with which to measure the life of the under-world. That which made for more life, for physical and spiritual health, was good; that which made for less life, which hurt, and dwarfed, and distorted life, was bad.

It will be readily apparent to the reader that I saw much that was bad. Yet it must not be forgotten that the time of which I write was considered "good times" in England. The starvation and lack of shelter I encountered constituted a chronic condition of misery which is never wiped out, even in the periods of greatest prosperity.

Following the summer in question came a hard winter. To such an extent did the suffering and positive starvation increase that society was unable to cope with it. Great numbers of the unemployed formed into processions, as many as a dozen at a time, and daily marched through the streets of London crying for bread. Mr. Justin McCarthy, writing in the month of January, 1903, to the New York *Independent*, briefly epitomizes the situation as follows:—

"The workhouses have no space left in which to pack the starving crowds who are craving every day and night at their doors for food and shelter. All the charitable institutions have exhausted their means in trying to raise supplies of food for the famishing residents of the garrets and cellars of London lanes and alleys. The quarters of the Salvation Army in various parts of London are nightly besieged by hosts of the unemployed and the hungry for whom neither shelter nor the means of sustenance can be provided."

It has been urged that the criticism I have passed on things as they are in England is too pessimistic. I must say, in extenuation, that of optimists I am the most optimistic. But I measure manhood less by political aggregations than by individuals. Society grows, while political machines rack to pieces and become "scrap." For the English, so far as manhood and womanhood and health and happiness go, I see a broad and smiling future. But for a great deal of the political machinery, which at present mismanages for them, I see nothing else than the scrap heap.

JACK LONDON.
Piedmont, California

I

The Descent

Christ look upon us in this city,
And keep our sympathy and pity
    Fresh, and our faces heavenward;
        Lest we grow hard.
            —THOMAS ASHE

"B UT you can't do it, you know," friends said, to whom I
applied for assistance in the matter of sinking myself
down into the East End of London. "You had better see the
police for a guide," they added, on second thought, painfully
endeavoring to adjust themselves to the psychological processes of a madman who had come to them with better cre-
dentials than brains.

"But I don't want to see the police," I protested. "What I
wish to do, is to go down into the East End and see things
for myself. I wish to know how those people are living there,
and why they are living there, and what they are living for. In
short, I am going to live there myself."

"You don't want to *live* down there!" everybody said, with
disapprobation writ large upon their faces. "Why, it is said
there are places where a man's life isn't worth tu'pence."

"The very places I wish to see," I broke in.

"But you can't, you know," was the unfailing rejoinder.

"Which is not what I came to see you about," I answered
brusquely, somewhat nettled by their incomprehension. "I am
a stranger here, and I want you to tell me what you know of
the East End, in order that I may have something to start
on."

"But we know nothing of the East End. It is over there,
somewhere." And they waved their hands vaguely in the direction where the sun on rare occasions may be seen to rise.

"Then I shall go to Cook's," I announced.

"Oh, yes," they said, with relief. "Cook's will be sure to
know."

But O Cook, O Thomas Cook & Son, pathfinders and
trail-clearers, living sign-posts to all the world and bestowers

7

of first aid to bewildered travellers—unhesitatingly and instantly, with ease and celerity, could you send me to Darkest Africa or Innermost Thibet, but to the East End of London, barely a stone's throw distant from Ludgate Circus, you know not the way!

"You can't do it, you know," said the human emporium of routes and fares at Cook's Cheapside branch. "It is so—ahem—so unusual."

"Consult the police," he concluded authoritatively, when I persisted. "We are not accustomed to taking travellers to the East End; we receive no call to take them there, and we know nothing whatsoever about the place at all."

"Never mind that," I interposed, to save myself from being swept out of the office by his flood of negations. "Here's something you can do for me. I wish you to understand in advance what I intend doing, so that in case of trouble you may be able to identify me."

"Ah, I see; should you be murdered, we would be in position to identify the corpse."

He said it so cheerfully and cold-bloodedly that on the instant I saw my stark and mutilated cadaver stretched upon a slab where cool waters trickle ceaselessly, and him I saw bending over and sadly and patiently identifying it as the body of the insane American who *would* see the East End.

"No, no," I answered; "merely to identify me in case I get into a scrape with the 'bobbies.'" This last I said with a thrill; truly, I was gripping hold of the vernacular.

"That," he said, "is a matter for the consideration of the Chief Office."

"It is so unprecedented, you know," he added apologetically.

The man at the Chief Office hemmed and hawed. "We make it a rule," he explained, "to give no information concerning our clients."

"But in this case," I urged, "it is the client who requests you to give the information concerning himself."

Again he hemmed and hawed.

"Of course," I hastily anticipated, "I know it is unprecedented, but—"

"As I was about to remark," he went on steadily, "it is unprecedented, and I don't think we can do anything for you."

However, I departed with the address of a detective who lived in the East End, and took my way to the American consul-general. And here, at last, I found a man with whom I could 'do business.' There was no hemming and hawing, no lifted brows, open incredulity, or blank amazement. In one minute I explained myself and my project, which he accepted as a matter of course. In the second minute he asked my age, height, and weight, and looked me over. And in the third minute, as we shook hands at parting, he said: "All right, Jack. I'll remember you and keep track."

I breathed a sigh of relief. Having built my ships behind me, I was now free to plunge into that human wilderness of which nobody seemed to know anything. But at once I encountered a new difficulty in the shape of my cabby, a gray-whiskered and eminently decorous personage, who had imperturbably driven me for several hours about the 'City.'

"Drive me down to the East End," I ordered, taking my seat.

"Where, sir?" he demanded with frank surprise.

"To the East End, anywhere. Go on."

The hansom pursued an aimless way for several minutes, then came to a puzzled stop. The aperture above my head was uncovered, and the cabman peered down perplexedly at me.

"I say," he said, "wot plyce yer wanter go?"

"East End," I repeated. "Nowhere in particular. Just drive me around, anywhere."

"But wot's the haddress, sir?"

"See here!" I thundered. "Drive me down to the East End, and at once!"

It was evident that he did not understand, but he withdrew his head and grumblingly started his horse.

Nowhere in the streets of London may one escape the sight of abject poverty, while five minutes' walk from almost any point will bring one to a slum; but the region my hansom was now penetrating was one unending slum. The streets were filled with a new and different race of people, short of stature, and of wretched or beer-sodden appearance. We rolled along through miles of bricks and squalor, and from each cross street and alley flashed long vistas of bricks and misery. Here and there lurched a drunken man or woman, and the air was obscene with sounds of jangling and squabbling. At a market, tottery old men and women were searching in the garbage thrown in the mud for rotten potatoes, beans, and vegetables, while little children clustered like flies around a festering mass of fruit, thrusting their arms to the shoulders into the liquid corruption, and drawing forth morsels, but partially decayed, which they devoured on the spot.

Not a hansom did I meet with in all my drive, while mine was like an apparition from another and better world, the way the children ran after it and alongside. And as far as I could see were the solid walls of brick, the slimy pavements, and the screaming streets; and for the first time in my life the fear of the crowd smote me. It was like the fear of the sea; and the miserable multitudes, street upon street, seemed so many waves of a vast and malodorous sea, lapping about me and threatening to well up and over me.

"Stepney, sir; Stepney Station," the cabby called down.

I looked about. It was really a railroad station, and he had driven desperately to it as the one familiar spot he had ever heard of in all that wilderness.

"Well?" I said.

He spluttered unintelligibly, shook his head, and looked very miserable. "I'm a strynger 'ere," he managed to articulate. "An' if yer don't want Stepney Station, I'm blessed if I know wotcher do want."

"I'll tell you what I want," I said. "You drive along and keep your eye out for a shop where old clothes are sold. Now, when you see such a shop, drive right on till you turn the corner, then stop and let me out."

I could see that he was growing dubious of his fare, but not long afterward he pulled up to the curb and informed me that an old clothes shop was to be found a bit of the way back.

"Won'tcher py me?" he pleaded. "There's seven an' six owin' me."

"Yes," I laughed, "and it would be the last I'd see of you."

"Lord lumme, but it'll be the last I see of you if yer don't py me," he retorted.

But a crowd of ragged onlookers had already gathered around the cab, and I laughed again and walked back to the old clothes shop.

Here the chief difficulty was in making the shopman understand that I really and truly wanted old clothes. But after fruitless attempts to press upon me new and impossible coats and trousers, he began to bring to light heaps of old ones, looking mysterious the while and hinting darkly. This he did with the palpable intention of letting me know that he had 'piped my lay,' in order to bulldose me, through fear of exposure, into paying heavily for my purchases. A man in trouble, or a high-class criminal from across the water, was what he took my measure for—in either case, a person anxious to avoid the police.

But I disputed with him over the outrageous difference between prices and values, till I quite disabused him of the notion, and he settled down to drive a hard bargain with a hard customer. In the end I selected a pair of stout though well-worn trousers, a frayed jacket with one remaining button, a pair of brogans which had plainly seen service where coal was shovelled, a thin leather belt, and a very dirty cloth cap. My underclothing and socks, however, were new and warm, but of the sort that any American waif, down in his luck, could acquire in the ordinary course of events.

"I must sy yer a sharp 'un," he said, with counterfeit admiration, as I handed over the ten shillings finally agreed upon for the outfit. "Blimey, if you ain't ben up an' down Petticut Lane afore now. Yer trouseys is wuth five bob to hany man, an' a docker 'ud give two an' six for the shoes, to sy nothin' of the coat an' cap an' new stoker's singlet an' hother things."

"How much will you give me for them?" I demanded suddenly. "I paid you ten bob for the lot, and I'll sell them back to you, right now, for eight. Come, it's a go!"

But he grinned and shook his head, and though I had made a good bargain, I was unpleasantly aware that he had made a better one.

I found the cabby and a policeman with their heads together, but the latter, after looking me over sharply and particularly scrutinizing the bundle under my arm, turned away and left the cabby to wax mutinous by himself. And not a step would he budge till I paid him the seven shillings and sixpence owing him. Whereupon he was willing to drive me to the ends of the earth, apologizing profusely for his insistence, and explaining that one ran across queer customers in London Town.

But he drove me only to Highbury Vale, in North London, where my luggage was waiting for me. Here, next day, I took off my shoes (not without regret for their lightness and comfort), and my soft, gray travelling suit, and, in fact, all my clothing; and proceeded to array myself in the clothes of the other and unimaginable men, who must have been indeed unfortunate to have had to part with such rags for the pitiable sums obtainable from a dealer.

Inside my stoker's singlet, in the armpit, I sewed a gold sovereign (an emergency sum certainly of modest proportions); and inside my stoker's singlet I put myself. And then I sat down and moralized upon the fair years and fat, which had made my skin soft and brought the nerves close to the surface; for the singlet was rough and raspy as a hair shirt, and I am confident that the most rigorous of ascetics suffer no more than did I in the ensuing twenty-four hours.

The remainder of my costume was fairly easy to put on, though the brogans, or brogues, were quite a problem. As stiff and hard as if made of wood, it was only after a prolonged pounding of the uppers with my fists that I was able to get my feet into them at all. Then, with a few shillings, a knife, a handkerchief, and some brown papers and flake tobacco stowed away in my pockets, I thumped down the stairs and said good-by to my foreboding friends. As I passed out the door, the 'help,' a comely, middle-aged woman, could not conquer a grin that twisted her lips and separated them till the throat, out of involuntary sympathy, made the uncouth animal noises we are wont to designate as 'laughter.'

No sooner was I out on the streets than I was impressed by the difference in status effected by my clothes. All servility vanished from the demeanor of the common people with whom I came in contact. Presto! in the twinkling of an eye, so to say, I had become one of them. My frayed and out-at-elbows jacket was the badge and advertisement of my class, which was their class. It made me of like kind, and in place of the fawning and too-respectful attention I had hitherto received, I now shared with them a comradeship. The man in corduroy and dirty neckerchief no longer addressed me as 'sir' or 'governor.' It was 'mate,' now—and a fine and hearty word, with a tingle to it, and a warmth and gladness, which the other term does not possess. Governor! It smacks of mastery, and power, and high authority—the tribute of the man who is under to the man on top, delivered in the hope that he will let up a bit and ease his weight. Which is another way of saying that it is an appeal for alms.

This brings me to a delight I experienced in my rags and tatters which is denied the average American abroad. The European traveller from the States, who is not a Crœsus, speedily finds himself reduced to a chronic state of self-conscious sordidness by the hordes of cringing robbers who clutter his steps from dawn till dark, and deplete his pocketbook in a way that puts compound interest to the blush.

In my rags and tatters I escaped the pestilence of tipping, and encountered men on a basis of equality. Nay, before the day was out I turned the tables, and said, most gratefully, "Thank you, sir," to a gentleman whose horse I held, and who dropped a penny into my eager palm.

Other changes I discovered were wrought in my condition by my new garb. In crossing crowded thoroughfares I found I had to be, if anything, more lively in avoiding vehicles, and it was strikingly impressed upon me that my life had cheapened in direct ratio with my clothes. When before, I inquired the way of a policeman, I was usually asked, "Buss or 'ansom, sir?" But now the query became, "Walk or ride?" Also, at the railway stations it was the rule to be asked, "First or second, sir?" Now I was asked nothing, a third-class ticket being shoved out to me as a matter of course.

But there was compensation for it all. For the first time I met the English lower classes face to face, and knew them for what they were. When loungers and workmen, on street corners and in public houses, talked with me, they talked as one man to another, and they talked as natural men should talk, without the least idea of getting anything out of me for what they talked or the way they talked.

And when at last I made into the East End, I was gratified to find that the fear of the crowd no longer haunted me. I had become a part of it. The vast and malodorous sea had welled up and over me, or I had slipped gently into it, and there was nothing fearsome about it—with the one exception of the stoker's singlet.

II

Johnny Upright

The people live in squalid dens, where there can be no health
and no hope, but dogged discontent at their own lot, and futile
discontent at the wealth which they see possessed by others.
—THOROLD ROGERS

I SHALL not give you the address of Johnny Upright. Let it
suffice that he lives on the most respectable street in the
East End—a street that would be considered very mean in
America, but a veritable oasis in the desert of East London.
It is surrounded on every side by close-packed squalor and
streets jammed by a young and vile and dirty generation; but
its own pavements are comparatively bare of the children who
have no other place to play, while it has an air of desertion,
so few are the people that come and go.

Each house on this street, as on all the streets, is shoulder
to shoulder with its neighbors. To each house there is but
one entrance, the front door, and each house is about eighteen feet wide, with a bit of a brick-walled yard behind,
where, when it is not raining, one may look at a slate-colored
sky. But it must be understood that this is East End opulence
we are now considering. Some of the people on this street are
even so well-to-do as to keep a 'slavey.' Johnny Upright keeps
one, as I well know, she being my first acquaintance in this
particular portion of the world.

To Johnny Upright's house I came, and to the door came
the 'slavey.' Now, mark you, her position in life was pitiable
and contemptible, but it was with pity and contempt that she
looked at me. She evinced a plain desire that our conversation
should be short. It was Sunday, and Johnny Upright was not
at home, and that was all there was to it. But I lingered, discussing whether or not it was all there was to it, till Mrs.
Johnny Upright was attracted to the door, where she scolded
the girl for not having closed it before turning her attention
to me.

No, Mr. Johnny Upright was not at home, and further, he
saw nobody on Sunday. It is too bad, said I. Was I looking

for work? No, quite to the contrary; in fact, I had come to see Johnny Upright on business which might be profitable to him.

A change came over the face of things at once. The gentleman in question was at church, but would be home in an hour or thereabouts, when no doubt he could be seen.

Would I kindly step in?—no, the lady did not ask me, though I fished for an invitation by stating that I would go down to the corner and wait in a public house. And down to the corner I went, but, it being church time, the 'pub' was closed. A miserable drizzle was falling, and, in lieu of better, I took a seat on a neighborly doorstep and waited.

And here to the doorstep came the 'slavey,' very frowzy and very perplexed, to tell me that the missus would let me come back and wait in the kitchen.

"So many people come 'ere lookin' for work," Mrs. Johnny Upright apologetically explained. "So I 'ope you won't feel bad the way I spoke."

"Not at all, not at all," I replied, in my grandest manner, for the nonce investing my rags with dignity. "I quite understand, I assure you. I suppose people looking for work almost worry you to death?"

"That they do," she answered, with an eloquent and expressive glance; and thereupon ushered me into, not the kitchen, but the dining room—a favor, I took it, in recompense for my grand manner.

This dining room, on the same floor as the kitchen, was about four feet below the level of the ground, and so dark (it was midday) that I had to wait a space for my eyes to adjust themselves to the gloom. Dirty light filtered in through a window, the top of which was on a level with the sidewalk, and in this light I found that I was able to read newspaper print.

And here, while waiting the coming of Johnny Upright, let me explain my errand. While living, eating, and sleeping with the people of the East End, it was my intention to have a port of refuge, not too far distant, into which I could run now and again to assure myself that good clothes and cleanliness still existed. Also in such port I could receive my mail, work up my notes, and sally forth occasionally in changed garb to civilization.

But this involved a dilemma. A lodging where my property would be safe implied a landlady apt to be suspicious of a gentleman leading a double life; while a landlady who would not bother her head over the double life of her lodgers would imply lodgings where property was unsafe. To avoid the dilemma was what had brought me to Johnny Upright. A detective of thirty-odd years' continuous service in the East End, known far and wide by a name given him by a convicted felon in the dock, he was just the man to find me an honest landlady, and make her rest easy concerning the strange comings and goings of which I might be guilty.

His two daughters beat him home from church,—and pretty girls they were in their Sunday dresses, withal it was the certain weak and delicate prettiness which characterizes the Cockney lasses, a prettiness which is no more than a promise with no grip on time, and doomed to fade quickly away like the color from a sunset sky.

They looked me over with frank curiosity, as though I were some sort of a strange animal, and then ignored me utterly for the rest of my wait. Then Johnny Upright himself arrived, and I was summoned upstairs to confer with him.

"Speak loud," he interrupted my opening words. "I've got a bad cold, and I can't hear well."

Shades of Old Sleuth and Sherlock Holmes! I wondered as to where the assistant was located whose duty it was to take down whatever information I might loudly vouchsafe. And to this day, much as I have seen of Johnny Upright and much as I have puzzled over the incident, I have never been quite able to make up my mind as to whether or not he had a cold, or had an assistant planted in the other room. But of one thing I am sure; though I gave Johnny Upright the facts concerning myself and project, he withheld judgment till next day, when I dodged into his street conventionally garbed and in a hansom. Then his greeting was cordial enough, and I went down into the dining room to join the family at tea.

"We are humble here," he said, "not given to the flesh, and you must take us for what we are, in our humble way."

The girls were flushed and embarrassed at greeting me, while he did not make it any the easier for them.

"Ha! ha!" he roared heartily, slapping the table with his open hand till the dishes rang. "The girls thought yesterday you had come to ask for a piece of bread! Ha! ha! ho! ho! ho!"

This they indignantly denied, with snapping eyes and guilty red cheeks, as though it were an essential of true refinement to be able to discern under his rags a man who had no need to go ragged.

And then, while I ate bread and marmalade, proceeded a play at cross purposes, the daughters deeming it an insult to me that I should have been mistaken for a beggar, and the father considering it as the highest compliment to my cleverness to succeed in being so mistaken. All of which I enjoyed, and the bread, the marmalade, and the tea, till the time came for Johnny Upright to find me a lodging, which he did, not half a dozen doors away, on his own respectable and opulent street, in a house as like to his own as a pea to its mate.

III

My Lodging and Some Others

> The poor, the poor, the poor, they stand,
> Wedged by the pressing of Trade's hand,
> Against an inward-opening door
> That pressure tightens evermore;
> They sigh a monstrous, foul-air sigh
> For the outside leagues of liberty,
> Where art, sweet lark, translates the sky
> Into a heavenly melody.
> —SIDNEY LANIER

FROM an East London standpoint, the room I rented for six shillings, or a dollar and a half, per week was a most comfortable affair. From the American standpoint, on the other hand, it was rudely furnished, uncomfortable, and small. By the time I had added an ordinary typewriter table to its scanty furnishing, I was hard put to turn around; at the best, I managed to navigate it by a sort of vermicular progression requiring great dexterity and presence of mind.

Having settled myself, or my property rather, I put on my knockabout clothes and went out for a walk. Lodgings being fresh in my mind, I began to look them up, bearing in mind the hypothesis that I was a poor young man with a wife and large family.

My first discovery was that empty houses were few and far between. So far between, in fact, that though I walked miles in irregular circles over a large area, I still remained between. Not one empty house could I find—a conclusive proof that the district was 'saturated.'

It being plain that as a poor young man with a family I could rent no houses at all in this most undesirable region, I next looked for rooms, unfurnished rooms, in which I could store my wife and babies and chattels. There were not many, but I found them, usually in the singular, for one appears to be considered sufficient for a poor man's family in which to cook and eat and sleep. When I asked for two rooms, the sublettees looked at me very much in the manner, I imagine, that a certain personage looked at Oliver Twist when he asked for more.

Not only was one room deemed sufficient for a poor man and his family, but I learned that many families, occupying single rooms, had so much space to spare as to be able to take in a lodger or two. When such rooms can be rented for from 75 cents to $1.50 per week, it is a fair conclusion that a lodger with references should obtain floor space for, say from 15 to 25 cents. He may even be able to board with the sublettees for a few shillings more. This, however, I failed to inquire into—a reprehensible error on my part, considering that I was working on the basis of a hypothetical family.

Not only did the houses I investigated have no bath-tubs, but I learned that there were no bath-tubs in all the thousands of houses I had seen. Under the circumstances, with my wife and babies and a couple of lodgers suffering from the too-great spaciousness of one room, taking a bath in a tin wash basin would be an unfeasible undertaking. But, it seems, the compensation comes in with the saving of soap, so all's well, and God's still in heaven. Besides, so beautiful is the adjustment of all things in this world, here in East London it rains nearly every day, and, willy-nilly, our baths would be on tap upon the street.

True, the sanitation of the places I visited was wretched. From the imperfect sewage and drainage, defective traps, poor ventilation, dampness, and general foulness, I might expect my wife and babies speedily to be attacked by diphtheria, croup, typhoid, erysipelas, blood poisoning, bronchitis, pneumonia, consumption, and various kindred disorders. Certainly the death-rate would be exceedingly high. But observe again the beauty of the adjustment. The most rational act for a poor man in East London with a large family is to get rid of it; the conditions in East London are such that they will get rid of the large family for him. Of course, there is the chance that he may perish in the process. Adjustment is not so apparent in this event; but it is there, somewhere, I am sure. And when discovered it will prove to be a very beautiful and subtle adjustment, or else the whole scheme goes awry and something is wrong.

However, I rented no rooms, but returned to my own

Johnny Upright's street. What with my wife, and babies, and lodgers, and the various cubby-holes into which I had fitted them, my mind's eye had become narrow-angled, and I could not quite take in all of my own room at once. The immensity of it was awe-inspiring. Could this be the room I had rented for six shillings a week? Impossible! But my landlady, knocking at the door to learn if I were comfortable, dispelled my doubts.

"Oh, yes, sir," she said, in reply to a question. "This street is the very last. All the other streets were like this eight or ten years ago, and all the people were very respectable. But the others have driven our kind out. Those on this street are the only ones left. It's shocking, sir!"

And then she explained the process of saturation, by which the rental value of a neighborhood went up while its tone went down.

"You see, sir, our kind are not used to crowding in the way the others do. We need more room. The others, the foreigners and lower-class people, can get five and six families into this house, where we only get one. So they can pay more rent for the house than we can afford. It *is* shocking, sir; and just to think, only a few years ago all this neighborhood was just as nice as it could be."

I looked at her. Here was a woman, of the finest grade of the English working class, with numerous evidences of refinement, being slowly engulfed by that noisome and rotten tide of humanity which the powers that be are pouring eastward out of London Town. Bank, factory, hotel, and office building must go up, and the city poor folk are a nomadic breed; so they migrate eastward, wave upon wave, saturating and degrading neighborhood by neighborhood, driving the better class of workers before them to pioneer on the rim of the city, or dragging them down, if not in the first generation, surely in the second and third.

It is only a question of months when Johnny Upright's street must go. He realizes it himself.

"In a couple of years," he says, "my lease expires. My landlord is one of our kind. He has not put up the rent on any of his houses here, and this has enabled us to stay. But any day he may sell, or any day he may die, which is the same thing so far as we are concerned. The house is bought by a money breeder, who builds a sweat shop on the patch of ground at the rear where my grapevine is, adds to the house, and rents it a room to a family. There you are, and Johnny Upright's gone!"

And truly I saw Johnny Upright, and his good wife and fair daughters, and frowzy slavey, like so many ghosts, flitting eastward through the gloom, the monster city roaring at their heels.

But Johnny Upright is not alone in his flitting. Far, far out, on the fringe of the city, live the small business men, little managers, and successful clerks. They dwell in cottages and semidetached villas, with bits of flower garden, and elbow room, and breathing space. They inflate themselves with pride and throw chests when they contemplate the Abyss from which they have escaped, and they thank God that they are not as other men. And lo! down upon them comes Johnny Upright and the monster city at his heels. Tenements spring up like magic, gardens are built upon, villas are divided and subdivided into many dwellings, and the black night of London settles down in a greasy pall.

IV

A Man and the Abyss

After a momentary silence spake
Some vessel of a more ungainly make;
    They sneer at me for leaning all awry:
What! did the hand then of the Potter shake?
                                    —OMAR KHAYYAM

I SAY, can you let a lodging?"
    These words I discharged carelessly over my shoulder at a stout and elderly woman, of whose fare I was partaking in a greasy coffee-house down near the Pool and not very far from Limehouse.

"Oh, yus," she answered shortly, my appearance possibly not approximating the standard of affluence required by her house.

I said no more, consuming my rasher of bacon and pint of sickly tea in silence. Nor did she take further interest in me till I came to pay my reckoning (fourpence), when I pulled all of ten shillings out of my pocket. The expected result was produced.

"Yus, sir," she at once volunteered; "I 'ave nice lodgin's you'd likely tyke a fancy to. Back from a voyage, sir?"

"How much for a room?" I inquired, ignoring her curiosity.

She looked me up and down with frank surprise. "I don't let rooms, not to my reg'lar lodgers, much less casuals."

"Then I'll have to look along a bit," I said, with marked disappointment.

But the sight of my ten shillings had made her keen. "I can let you 'ave a nice bed in with two hother men," she urged. "Good respectable men, an' steady."

"But I don't want to sleep with two other men," I objected.

"You don't 'ave to. There's three beds in the room, an' hit's not a very small room."

"How much?" I demanded.

"Arf a crown a week, two an' six, to a regular lodger. You'll fancy the men, I'm sure. One works in the ware'ouse, an' 'e's

23

bin with me two years, now. An' the hother's bin with me six. Six years, sir, an' two months comin' nex' Saturday.

" 'E's a scene-shifter," she went on. "A steady, respectable man, never missin' a night's work in the time 'e's bin with me. An' 'e likes the 'ouse; 'e says as it's the best 'e can do in the w'y of lodgin's. I board 'im, an' the hother lodgers too."

"I suppose he's saving money right along," I insinuated innocently.

"Bless you, no! Nor can 'e do as well helsewhere with 'is money."

And I thought of my own spacious West, with room under its sky and unlimited air for a thousand Londons; and here was this man, a steady and reliable man, never missing a night's work, frugal and honest, lodging in one room with two other men, paying two dollars and a half per month for it, and out of his experience adjudging it to be the best he could do! And here was I, on the strength of the ten shillings in my pocket, able to enter in with my rags and take up my bed with him. The human soul is a lonely thing, but it must be very lonely sometimes when there are three beds to a room, and casuals with ten shillings are admitted.

"How long have you been here?" I asked.

"Thirteen years, sir; an' don't you think you'll fancy the lodgin'?"

The while she talked she was shuffling ponderously about the small kitchen in which she cooked the food for her lodgers who were also boarders. When I first entered, she had been hard at work, nor had she let up once throughout the conversation. Undoubtedly she was a busy woman. "Up at half-past five," "to bed the last thing at night," "workin' fit ter drop," thirteen years of it, and for reward, gray hairs, frowzy clothes, stooped shoulders, slatternly figure, unending toil in a foul and noisome coffee-house that faced on an alley ten feet between the walls, and a waterside environment that was ugly and sickening to say the least.

"You'll be hin hagain to 'ave a look?" she questioned wistfully, as I went out of the door.

And as I turned and looked at her, I realized to the full the deeper truth underlying that very wise old maxim: 'Virtue is its own reward.'

I went back to her. "Have you ever taken a vacation?" I asked.

"Vycytion!"

"A trip to the country for a couple of days, fresh air, a day off, you know, a rest."

"Lor' lumme!" she laughed, for the first time stopping from her work. "A vycytion, eh? for the likes o' me? Just fancy, now!—Mind yer feet!"—this last sharply, and to me, as I stumbled over the rotten threshold.

Down near the West India Dock I came upon a young fellow staring disconsolately at the muddy water. A fireman's cap was pulled down across his eyes, and the fit and sag of his clothes whispered unmistakably of the sea.

"Hello, mate," I greeted him, sparring for a beginning. "Can you tell me the way to Wapping?"

"Worked yer way over on a cattle boat?" he countered, fixing my nationality on the instant.

And thereupon we entered upon a talk that extended itself to a public house and a couple of pints of 'arf an' arf.' This led to closer intimacy, so that when I brought to light all of a shilling's worth of coppers (ostensibly my all), and put aside sixpence for a bed, and sixpence for more arf an' arf, he generously proposed that we drink up the whole shilling.

"My mate, 'e cut up rough las' night," he explained. "An' the bobbies got 'm, so you can bunk in wi' me. Wotcher say?"

I said yes, and by the time we had soaked ourselves in a whole shilling's worth of beer, and slept the night on a miserable bed in a miserable den, I knew him pretty fairly for what he was. And that in one respect he was representative of a large body of the lower-class London workman, my later experience substantiates.

He was London-born, his father a fireman and a drinker before him. As a child, his home was the streets and the docks. He had never learned to read, and had never felt the need for it—a vain and useless accomplishment, he held, at least for a man of his station in life.

He had had a mother and numerous squalling brothers and sisters, all crammed into a couple of rooms and living on poorer and less regular food than he could ordinarily rustle for himself. In fact, he never went home except at periods when he was unfortunate in procuring his own food. Petty pilfering and begging along the streets and docks, a trip or two to sea as mess-boy, a few trips more as coal-trimmer, and then, a full-fledged fireman, he had reached the top of his life.

And in the course of this he had also hammered out a philosophy of life, an ugly and repulsive philosophy, but withal a very logical and sensible one from his point of view. When I asked him what he lived for, he immediately answered, "Booze." A voyage to sea (for a man must live and get the wherewithal), and then the paying off and the big drunk at the end. After that, haphazard little drunks, sponged in the 'pubs' from mates with a few coppers left, like myself, and when sponging was played out another trip to sea and a repetition of the beastly cycle.

"But women," I suggested, when he had finished proclaiming booze the sole end of existence.

"Wimmen!" He thumped his pot upon the bar and orated eloquently. "Wimmen is a thing my edication 'as learnt me t' let alone. It don't pay, matey; it don't pay. Wot's a man like me want o' wimmen, eh? jest you tell me. There was my mar, she was enough, a-bangin' the kids about an' makin' the ole man mis'rable when 'e come 'ome, w'ich was seldom, I grant. An' fer w'y? Becos o' mar! She didn't make 'is 'ome 'appy, that was w'y. Then, there's the other wimmen, 'ow do they treat a pore stoker with a few shillin's in 'is trouseys? A good drunk is wot 'e's got in 'is pockits, a good long drunk, an' the wimmen skin 'im out of 'is money so quick 'e ain't 'ad 'ardly a glass. I know. I've 'ad my fling an' I know wot's wot.

"An' I tell you, where's wimmen is trouble—screechin' an' carryin' on, fightin', cuttin', bobbies, magistrates, an' a month's 'ard labor back of it all, an' no pay-day when you come out."

"But a wife and children," I insisted. "A home of your own, and all that. Think of it, back from a voyage, little children climbing on your knee, and the wife happy and smiling, and a kiss for you when she lays the table, and a kiss all around from the babies when they go to bed, and the kettle singing and the long talk afterward of where you've been and what you've seen, and of her and all the little happenings at home while you've been away, and—"

"Garn!" he cried, with a playful shove of his fist on my shoulder. "Wot's yer game, eh? A missus kissin', an' kids clim'in', an' kettle singin', all on four poun' ten a month w'en you 'ave a ship, an' four nothin' w'en you 'aven't. I'll tell you wot I'd get on four poun' ten—a missus rowin', kids squallin', no coal t' make the kettle sing, an' the kettle up the spout, that's wot I'd get. Enough t' make a bloke bloomin' well glad to be back t' sea. A missus! Wot for? T' make you mis'rable? Kids? Jest take my counsel, matey, an' don't 'ave 'em. Look at me! I can 'ave my beer w'en I like, an' no blessed missus an' kids a-cryin' for bread. I'm 'appy, I am, with my beer an' mates like you, an' a good ship comin', an' another trip to sea. So I say, let's 'ave another pint. Arf an' arf's good enough fer me."

Without going further with the speech of this young fellow of two and twenty, I think I have sufficiently indicated his philosophy of life and the underlying economic reason for it. Home life he had never known. The word 'home' aroused nothing but unpleasant associations. In the low wages of his father, and of other men in the same walk in life, he found sufficient reason for branding wife and children as encumbrances and causes of masculine misery. An unconscious hedonist, utterly unmoral and materialistic, he sought the greatest possible happiness for himself, and found it in drink.

A young sot; a premature wreck; physical inability to do a stoker's work; the gutter or the workhouse; and the end,— he saw it all, as clearly as I, but it held no terrors for him. From the moment of his birth, all the forces of his environment had tended to harden him, and he viewed his wretched, inevitable future with a callousness and unconcern I could not shake.

And yet he was not a bad man. He was not inherently vicious and brutal. He had normal mentality, and a more than average physique. His eyes were blue and round, shaded by long lashes, and wide apart. And there was a laugh in them, and a fund of humor behind. The brow and general features were good, the mouth and lips sweet, though already developing a harsh twist. The chin was weak, but not too weak; I have seen men sitting in the high places with weaker.

His head was shapely, and so gracefully was it poised upon

a perfect neck that I was not surprised by his body that night when he stripped for bed. I have seen many men strip, in gymnasium and training quarters, men of good blood and upbringing, but I have never seen one who stripped to better advantage than this young sot of two and twenty, this young god doomed to rack and ruin in four or five short years, and to pass hence without posterity to receive the splendid heritage it was his to bequeath.

It seemed sacrilege to waste such life, and yet I was forced to confess that he was right in not marrying on four pound ten in London Town. Just as the scene-shifter was happier in making both ends meet in a room shared with two other men, than he would have been had he packed a feeble family along with a couple of men into a cheaper room, and failed in making both ends meet.

And day by day I became convinced that not only is it unwise, but it is criminal for the people of the Abyss to marry. They are the stones by the builder rejected. There is no place for them in the social fabric, while all the forces of society drive them downward till they perish. At the bottom of the Abyss they are feeble, besotted, and imbecile. If they reproduce, the life is so cheap that perforce it perishes of itself. The work of the world goes on above them, and they do not care to take part in it, nor are they able. Moreover, the work of the world does not need them. There are plenty, far fitter than they, clinging to the steep slope above, and struggling frantically to slide no more.

In short, the London Abyss is a vast shambles. Year by year, and decade after decade, rural England pours in a flood of vigorous strong life, that not only does not renew itself, but perishes by the third generation. Competent authorities aver that the London workman whose parents and grandparents were born in London is so remarkable a specimen that he is rarely found.

Mr. A. C. Pigou has said that the aged poor and the residuum which compose the 'submerged tenth,' constitute $7^1/_2$ per cent of the population of London. Which is to say that last year, and yesterday, and to-day, at this very moment, 450,000 of these creatures are dying miserably at the bottom of the social pit called "London." As to how they die, I shall take an instance from this morning's paper.

Self-neglect

Yesterday Dr. Wynn Westcott held an inquest at Shoreditch, respecting the death of Elizabeth Crews, aged 77 years, of 32 East Street, Holborn, who died on Wednesday last. Alice Mathieson stated that she was landlady of the house where deceased lived. Witness last saw her alive on the previous Monday. She lived quite alone. Mr. Francis Birch, relieving officer for the Holborn district, stated that deceased had occupied the room in question for 35 years. When witness was called, on the 1st, he found the old woman in a terrible state, and the ambulance and coachman had to be disinfected after the removal. Dr. Chase Fennell said death was due to blood-poisoning from bed-sores, due to self-neglect and filthy surroundings, and the jury returned a verdict to that effect.

The most startling thing about this little incident of a woman's death is the smug complacency with which the officials looked upon it and rendered judgment. That an old woman of seventy-seven years of age should die of SELF-NEGLECT is the most optimistic way possible of looking at it. It was the old dead woman's fault that she died, and having located the responsibility, society goes contentedly on about its own affairs.

Of the 'submerged tenth,' Mr. Pigou has said: "Either through lack of bodily strength, or of intelligence, or of fibre, or of all three, they are inefficient or unwilling workers, and consequently unable to support themselves. . . . They are so often degraded in intellect as to be incapable of distinguishing their right from their left hand, or of recognizing the numbers of their own houses; their bodies are feeble and without stamina, their affections are warped, and they scarcely know what family life means."

Four hundred and fifty thousand is a whole lot of people. The young fireman was only one, and it took him some time to say his little say. I should not like to hear them all talk at once. I wonder if God hears them?

V

Those on the Edge

I assure you I found nothing worse, nothing more degrading,
nothing so hopeless, nothing nearly so intolerably dull and miserable as the life I left behind me in the East End of London.
— HUXLEY

M Y FIRST impression of East London was naturally a general one. Later the details began to appear, and here
and there in the chaos of misery I found little spots where a
fair measure of happiness reigned,—sometimes whole rows
of houses in little out-of-the-way streets, where artisans dwell
and where a rude sort of family life obtains. In the evenings
the men can be seen at the doors, pipes in their mouths and
children on their knees, wives gossiping, and laughter and fun
going on. The content of these people is manifestly great, for,
relative to the wretchedness that encompasses them, they are
well off.

But at the best, it is a dull, animal happiness, the content
of the full belly. The dominant note of their lives is materialistic. They are stupid and heavy, without imagination. The
Abyss seems to exude a stupefying atmosphere of torpor,
which wraps about them and deadens them. Religion passes
them by. The Unseen holds for them neither terror nor delight. They are unaware of the Unseen; and the full belly and
the evening pipe, with their regular 'arf an' arf,' is all they
demand, or dream of demanding, from existence.

This would not be so bad if it were all; but it is not all.
The satisfied torpor in which they are sunk is the deadly in-
ertia that precedes dissolution. There is no progress, and with
them not to progress is to fall back and into the Abyss. In
their own lives they may only start to fall, leaving the fall to
be completed by their children and their children's children.
Man always gets less than he demands from life; and so little
do they demand, that the less than little they get cannot save
them.

At the best, city life is an unnatural life for the human; but
the city life of London is so utterly unnatural that the average

workman or workwoman cannot stand it. Mind and body are sapped by the undermining influences ceaselessly at work. Moral and physical stamina are broken, and the good workman, fresh from the soil, becomes in the first city generation a poor workman; and by the second city generation, devoid of push and go and initiative, and actually unable physically to perform the labor his father did, he is well on the way to the shambles at the bottom of the Abyss.

If nothing else, the air he breathes, and from which he never escapes, is sufficient to weaken him mentally and physically, so that he becomes unable to compete with the fresh virile life from the country hastening on to London Town to destroy and be destroyed.

Leaving out the disease germs that fill the air of the East End, consider but the one item of smoke. Sir William Thistleton-Dyer, curator of Kew Gardens, has been studying smoke deposits on vegetation, and, according to his calculations, no less than six tons of solid matter, consisting of soot and tarry hydrocarbons, are deposited every week on every quarter of a square mile in and about London. This is equivalent to twenty-four tons per week to the square mile, or 1248 tons per year to the square mile. From the cornice below the dome of St. Paul's Cathedral was recently taken a solid deposit of crystallized sulphate of lime. This deposit had been formed by the action of the sulphuric acid in the atmosphere upon the carbonate of lime in the stone. And this sulphuric acid in the atmosphere is constantly being breathed by the London workmen through all the days and nights of their lives.

It is incontrovertible that the children grow up into rotten adults, without virility or stamina, a weak-kneed, narrow-chested, listless breed, that crumples up and goes down in the brute struggle for life with the invading hordes from the country. The railway men, carriers, omnibus drivers, corn and timber porters, and all those who require physical stamina, are largely drawn from the country; while in the Metropolitan Police there are, roughly, 12,000 country-born as against 3000 London-born.

So one is forced to conclude that the Abyss is literally a huge man-killing machine, and when I pass along the little out-of-the-way streets with the full-bellied artisans at the

doors, I am aware of a greater sorrow for them than for the
450,000 lost and hopeless wretches dying at the bottom of
the pit. They, at least, are dying, that is the point; while these
have yet to go through the slow and preliminary pangs extending through two and even three generations.

And yet the quality of the life is good. All human poten-
tialities are in it. Given proper conditions, it could live
through the centuries, and great men, heroes and masters,
spring from it and make the world better by having lived.

I talked with a woman who was representative of that type
which has been jerked out of its little out-of-the-way streets
and has started on the fatal fall to the bottom. Her husband
was a fitter and a member of the Engineers' Union. That he
was a poor engineer was evidenced by his inability to get regular employment. He did not have the energy and enterprise
necessary to obtain or hold a steady position.

The pair had two daughters, and the four of them lived in
a couple of holes, called 'rooms' by courtesy, for which they
paid seven shillings per week. They possessed no stove, managing their cooking on a single gas-ring in the fireplace. Not
being persons of property, they were unable to obtain an unlimited supply of gas; but a clever machine had been installed
for their benefit. By dropping a penny in the slot, the gas was
forthcoming, and when a penny's worth had forthcome the
supply was automatically shut off. "A penny gawn in no
time," she explained, "an' the cookin' not arf done!"

Incipient starvation had been their portion for years.
Month in and month out, they had arisen from the table able
and willing to eat more. And when once on the downward
slope, chronic innutrition is an important factor in sapping
vitality and hastening the descent.

Yet this woman was a hard worker. From 4.30 in the morning till the last light at night, she said, she had toiled at making cloth dress-skirts, lined up and with two flounces, for
seven shillings a dozen. Cloth dress-skirts, mark you, lined up
and with two flounces, for seven shillings a dozen! This is
equal to $1.75 per dozen, or $14^3/4$ cents per skirt.

The husband, in order to obtain employment, had to belong to the union, which collected one shilling and sixpence

from him each week. Also, when strikes were afoot and he chanced to be working, he had at times been compelled to pay as high as seventeen shillings into the union's coffers for the relief fund.

One daughter, the elder, had worked as green hand for a dressmaker, for one shilling and sixpence per week—$37\frac{1}{2}$ cents per week, or a fraction over 5 cents per day. However, when the slack season came she was discharged, though she had been taken on at such low pay with the understanding that she was to learn the trade and work up. After that she had been employed in a bicycle store for three years, for which she received five shillings per week, walking two miles to her work, and two back, and being fined for tardiness.

As far as the man and woman were concerned, the game was played. They had lost handhold and foothold, and were falling into the pit. But what of the daughters? Living like swine, enfeebled by chronic innutrition, being sapped mentally, morally, and physically, what chance have they to crawl up and out of the Abyss into which they were born falling?

As I write this, and for an hour past, the air had been made hideous by a free-for-all, rough-and-tumble fight going on in the yard that is back to back with my yard. When the first sounds reached me I took it for the barking and snarling of dogs, and some minutes were required to convince me that human beings, and women at that, could produce such a fearful clamor.

Drunken women fighting! It is not nice to think of; it is far worse to listen to. Something like this it runs:—

Incoherent babble, shrieked at the top of the lungs of several women; a lull, in which is heard a child crying and a young girl's voice pleading tearfully; a woman's voice rises, harsh and grating, "You 'it me! Jest you 'it me!" then, swat! challenge accepted and fight rages afresh.

The back windows of the houses commanding the scene are lined with enthusiastic spectators, and the sound of blows, and of oaths that make one's blood run cold, are borne to my ears.

A lull; "You let that child alone!" child, evidently of few years, screaming in downright terror; "Awright," repeated insistently and at top pitch twenty times straight running; "You'll git this rock on the 'ead!" and then rock evidently on the head from the shriek that goes up.

A lull; apparently one combatant temporarily disabled and being resuscitated; child's voice audible again, but now sunk to a lower note of terror and growing exhaustion.

Voices begin to go up the scale, something like this:—

"Yes?"

"Yes!"

"Yes?"

"Yes!"

"Yes?"

"Yes!"

"Yes?"

"Yes!"

Sufficient affirmation on both sides, conflict again precipitated. One combatant gets overwhelming advantage, and follows it up from the way other combatant screams bloody murder. Bloody murder gurgles and dies out, undoubtedly throttled by a strangle hold.

Entrance of new voices; a flank attack; strangle hold suddenly broken from way bloody murder goes up half an octave higher than before; general hullaballoo, everybody fighting.

Lull; new voice, young girl's, "I'm goin' ter tyke my mother's part"; dialogue, repeated about five times, "I'll do as I like, blankety, blank, blank!" "I'd like ter see yer, blankety, blank, blank!" renewed conflict, mothers, daughters, everybody, during which my landlady calls her young daughter in from the back steps, while I wonder what will be the effect of all that she has heard upon her moral fibre.

VI

Frying-pan Alley and a Glimpse of Inferno

The beasts they hunger, and eat, and die,
And so do we, and the world's a sty.
"Swinehood hath no remedy,"
Say many men, and hasten by.
—SIDNEY LANIER

THREE of us walked down Mile End Road, and one was a hero. He was a slender lad of nineteen, so slight and frail, in fact, that, like Fra Lippo Lippi, a puff of wind might double him up and turn him over. He was a burning young socialist, in the first throes of enthusiasm and ripe for martyrdom. As platform speaker or chairman he had taken an active and dangerous part in the many indoor and outdoor pro-Boer meetings which have vexed the serenity of Merry England these several years back. Little items he had been imparting to me as he walked along; of being mobbed in parks and on tram-cars; of climbing on the platform to lead the forlorn hope, when brother speaker after brother speaker had been dragged down by the angry crowd and cruelly beaten; of a siege in a church, where he and three others had taken sanctuary, and where, amid flying missiles and the crashing of stained glass, they had fought off the mob till rescued by platoons of constables; of pitched and giddy battles on stairways, galleries, and balconies; of smashed windows, collapsed stairways, wrecked lecture halls, and broken heads and bones—and then, with a regretful sigh, he looked at me and said: "How I envy you big, strong men! I'm such a little mite I can't do much when it comes to fighting."

And I, walking a head and shoulders above my two companions, remembered my own husky West and the stalwart men it had been my custom, in turn, to envy there. Also, as I looked at the mite of a youth with the heart of a lion, I thought, this is the type that on occasion rears barricades and shows the world that men have not forgotten how to die.

But up spoke my other companion, a man of twenty-eight who eked out a precarious existence in a sweating den.

"I'm a 'earty man, I am," he announced. "Not like the other chaps at my shop, I ain't. They consider me a fine specimen of manhood. W'y, d' ye know, I weigh one hundred and forty pounds!"

I was ashamed to tell him that I weighed one hundred and seventy, so I contented myself with taking his measure. Poor, misshapen little man! His skin an unhealthy color, body gnarled and twisted out of all decency, contracted chest, shoulders bent prodigiously from long hours of toil, and head hanging heavily forward and out of place! A " 'earty man," 'e was!

"How tall are you?"

"Five foot two," he answered proudly; "an' the chaps at the shop . . ."

"Let me see that shop," I said.

The shop was idle just then, but I still desired to see it. Passing Leman Street, we cut off to the left into Spital-fields, and dived into Frying-pan Alley. A spawn of children cluttered the slimy pavement, for all the world like tadpoles just turned frogs on the bottom of a dry pond. In a narrow doorway, so narrow that perforce we stepped over her, sat a woman with a young babe nursing at breasts grossly naked and libelling all the sacredness of motherhood. In the black and narrow hall behind her we waded through a mess of young life, and essayed an even narrower and fouler stairway. Up we went, three flights, each landing two feet by three in area, and heaped with filth and refuse.

There were seven rooms in this abomination called a house. In six of the rooms, twenty-odd people, of both sexes and all ages, cooked, ate, slept, and worked. In size the rooms averaged eight feet by eight, or possibly nine. The seventh room we entered. It was the den in which five men 'sweated.' It was seven feet wide by eight long, and the table at which the work was performed took up the major portion of the space. On this table were five lasts, and there was barely room for the men to stand to their work, for the rest of the space was heaped with cardboard, leather, bundles of shoe uppers, and a miscellaneous assortment of materials used in attaching the uppers of shoes to their soles.

In the adjoining room lived a woman and six children. In another vile hole lived a widow, with an only son of sixteen who was dying of consumption. The woman hawked sweetmeats on the street, I was told, and more often failed than not in supplying her son with the three quarts of milk he daily required. Further, this son, weak and dying, did not taste meat oftener than once a week; and the kind and quality of this meat cannot possibly be imagined by people who have never watched human swine eat.

"The w'y 'e coughs is somethin' terrible," volunteered my sweated friend, referring to the dying boy. "We 'ear 'im 'ere, w'ile we're workin', an' it's terrible, I say, terrible!"

And, what of the coughing and the sweetmeats, I found another menace added to the hostile environment of the children of the slum.

My sweated friend, when work was to be had, toiled with four other men in this eight-by-seven room. In winter a lamp burned nearly all the day and added its fumes to the overloaded air, which was breathed, and breathed, and breathed again.

In good times, when there was a rush of work, this man told me that he could earn as high as 'thirty bob a week.'— Thirty shillings! Seven dollars and a half!

"But it's only the best of us can do it," he qualified. "An' then we work twelve, thirteen, and fourteen hours a day, just as fast as we can. An' you should see us sweat! Just running from us! If you could see us, it'd dazzle your eyes—tacks flyin' out of mouth like from a machine. Look at my mouth."

I looked. The teeth were worn down by the constant friction of the metallic brads, while they were coal-black and rotten.

"I clean my teeth," he added, "else they'd be worse."

After he had told me that the workers had to furnish their own tools, brads, "grindery," cardboard, rent, light, and what not, it was plain that his thirty bob was a diminishing quantity.

"But how long does the rush season last, in which you receive this high wage of thirty bob?" I asked.

"Four months," was the answer; and for the rest of the year, he informed me, they average from 'half a quid' to a 'quid' a week, which is equivalent to from two dollars and a half to five dollars. The present week was half gone, and he had earned four bob, or one dollar. And yet I was given to understand that this was one of the better grades of sweating.

I looked out of the window, which should have commanded the back yards of the neighboring buildings. But there were no back yards, or, rather, they were covered with one-story hovels, cowsheds, in which people lived. The roofs of these hovels were covered with deposits of filth, in some places a couple of feet deep—the contributions from the back windows of the second and third stories. I could make out fish and meat bones, garbage, pestilential rags, old boots, broken earthenware, and all the general refuse of a human sty.

"This is the last year of this trade; they're getting machines to do away with us," said the sweated one mournfully, as we stepped over the woman with the breasts grossly naked and waded anew through the cheap young life.

We next visited the municipal dwellings erected by the London County Council on the site of the slums where lived Arthur Morrison's "Child of the Jago." While the buildings housed more people than before, it was much healthier. But the dwellings were inhabited by the better-class workmen and artisans. The slum people had simply drifted on to crowd other slums or to form new slums.

"An' now," said the sweated one, the 'earty man who worked so fast as to dazzle one's eyes, "I'll show you one of London's lungs. This is Spitalfields Garden." And he mouthed the word 'garden' with scorn.

The shadow of Christ's Church falls across Spitalfields Garden, and in the shadow of Christ's Church, at three o'clock in the afternoon, I saw a sight I never wish to see again. There are no flowers in this garden, which is smaller than my own rose garden at home. Grass only grows here, and it is surrounded by sharp-spiked iron fencing, as are all the parks of London Town, so that homeless men and women may not come in at night and sleep upon it.

As we entered the garden, an old woman, between fifty and sixty, passed us, striding with sturdy intention if somewhat rickety action, with two bulky bundles, covered with sacking, slung fore and aft upon her. She was a woman tramp, a houseless soul, too independent to drag her failing carcass through the workhouse door. Like the snail, she carried her home with her. In the two sacking-covered bundles were her household goods, her wardrobe, linen, and dear feminine possessions.

We went up the narrow gravelled walk. On the benches on either side was arrayed a mass of miserable and distorted humanity, the sight of which would have impelled Doré to more diabolical flights of fancy than he ever succeeded in achieving. It was a welter of rags and filth, of all manner of loathsome skin diseases, open sores, bruises, grossness, indecency, leering monstrosities, and bestial faces. A chill, raw wind was blowing, and these creatures huddled there in their rags, sleeping for the most part, or trying to sleep. Here were a dozen women, ranging in age from twenty years to seventy. Next a babe, possibly of nine months, lying asleep, flat on the hard bench, with neither pillow nor covering, nor with any one looking after it. Next, half a dozen men, sleeping bolt upright or leaning against one another in their sleep. In one place a family group, a child asleep in its sleeping mother's arms, and the husband (or male mate) clumsily mending a dilapidated shoe. On another bench a woman trimming the frayed strips of her rags with a knife, and another woman, with thread and needle, sewing up rents. Adjoining, a man holding a sleeping woman in his arms. Farther on, a man, his clothing caked with gutter mud, asleep with head in the lap of a woman, not more than twenty-five years old, and also asleep.

It was this sleeping that puzzled me. Why were nine out of ten of them asleep or trying to sleep? But it was not till afterward that I learned. *It is a law of the powers that be that the homeless shall not sleep by night.* On the pavement, by the portico of Christ's Church, where the stone pillars rise toward the sky in a stately row, were whole rows of men lying asleep or drowsing, and all too deep sunk in torpor to rouse or be made curious by our intrusion.

"A lung of London," I said; "nay, an abscess, a great putrescent sore."

"Oh, why did you bring me here?" demanded the burning young socialist, his delicate face white with sickness of soul and stomach sickness.

"Those women there," said our guide, "will sell themselves for thru'pence, or tu'pence, or a loaf of stale bread."

He said it with a cheerful sneer.

But what more he might have said I do not know, for the sick man cried, "For heaven's sake, let us get out of this."

VII

A Winner of the Victoria Cross

From out of the populous city men groan, and the soul of the
wounded crieth out.

—JOB

I HAVE found that it is not easy to get into the casual ward
of the workhouse. I have made two attempts now, and I
shall shortly make a third. The first time I started out at seven
o'clock in the evening with four shillings in my pocket.
Herein I committed two errors. In the first place, the appli-
cant for admission to the casual ward must be destitute, and
as he is subjected to a rigorous search, he must really be destitute; and fourpence, much less four shillings, is sufficient
affluence to disqualify him. In the second place, I made the
mistake of tardiness. Seven o'clock in the evening is too late
in the day for a pauper to get a pauper's bed.

For the benefit of gently nurtured and innocent folk, let me
explain what a casual ward is. It is a building where the
homeless, bedless, penniless man, if he be lucky, may *casually*
rest his weary bones, and then work like a navvy next day to
pay for it.

My second attempt to break into the casual ward began
more auspiciously. I started in the middle of the afternoon,
accompanied by the burning young socialist and another
friend, and all I had in my pocket was thru'pence. They pi-
loted me to the Whitechapel Workhouse, at which I peered
from around a friendly corner. It was a few minutes past five
in the afternoon, but already a long and melancholy line was
formed, which strung out around the corner of the building
and out of sight.

It was a most woful picture, men and women waiting in
the cold gray end of the day for a pauper's shelter from the
night, and I confess it almost unnerved me. Like the boy before the dentist's door, I suddenly discovered a multitude of
reasons for being elsewhere. Some hints of the struggle going
on within must have shown in my face, for one of my companions said, "Don't funk; you can do it."

41

Of course I could do it, but I became aware that even thru'pence in my pocket was too lordly a treasure for such a throng; and, in order that all invidious distinctions might be removed, I emptied out the coppers. Then I bade good-by to my friends, and with my heart going pit-a-pat, slouched down the street and took my place at the end of the line. Woful it looked, this line of poor folk tottering on the steep pitch to death; how woful it was I did not dream.

Next to me stood a short, stout man. Hale and hearty, though aged, strong-featured, with the tough and leathery skin produced by long years of sunbeat and weatherbeat, his was the unmistakable sea face and eyes; and at once there came to me a bit of Kipling's "Galley Slave": —

> "By the brand upon my shoulder, by the gall of
> clinging steel;
> By the welt the whips have left me, by the scars
> that never heal;
> By eyes grown old with staring through the
> sun-wash on the brine,
> I am paid in full for service. . . ."

How correct I was in my surmise, and how peculiarly appropriate the verse was, you shall learn.

"I won't stand it much longer, I won't," he was complaining to the man on the other side of him. "I'll smash a windy, a big 'un, an' get run in for fourteen days. Then I'll have a good place to sleep, never fear, an' better grub than you get here. Though I'd miss my bit of baccy"—this as an afterthought, and said regretfully and resignedly.

"I've been out two nights, now," he went on; "wet to the skin night before last, an' I can't stand it much longer. I'm gettin' old, an' some mornin' they'll pick me up dead."

He whirled with fierce passion on me: "Don't you ever let yourself grow old, lad. Die when you're young, or you'll come to this. I'm tellin' you sure. Seven an' eighty years am I, an' served my country like a man. Three good conduct stripes and the Victoria Cross, an' this is what I get for it. I wish I was dead, I wish I was dead. Can't come any too quick for me, I tell you."

The moisture rushed into his eyes, but, before the other man could comfort him, he began to hum a lilting sea song as though there was no such thing as heartbreak in the world.

Given encouragement, this is the story he told while waiting in line at the workhouse after two nights of exposure in the streets.

As a boy he had enlisted in the British navy, and for two score years and more served faithfully and well. Names, dates, commanders, ports, ships, engagements, and battles, rolled from his lips in a steady stream, but it is beyond me to remember them all, for it is not quite in keeping to take notes at the poorhouse door. He had been through the 'First War in China,' as he termed it; had enlisted in the East India Company and served ten years in India; was back in India again, in the English navy, at the time of the Mutiny; had served in the Burmese War and in the Crimea; and all this in addition to having fought and toiled for the English flag pretty well over the rest of the globe.

Then the thing happened. A little thing, if it could only be traced back to first causes: perhaps the lieutenant's breakfast had not agreed with him; or he had been up late the night before; or his debts were pressing; or the commander had spoken brusquely to him. The point is, that on this particular day the lieutenant was irritable. The sailor, with others, was 'setting up' the fore rigging.

Now, mark you, the sailor had been over forty years in the navy, had three good conduct stripes, and possessed the Victoria Cross for distinguished service in battle; so he could not have been such an altogether bad sort of a sailorman. The lieutenant was irritable; the lieutenant called him a name— well, not a nice sort of name. It referred to his mother. When I was a boy it was our boys' code to fight like little demons should such an insult be given our mothers; and many men have died in my part of the world for calling other men this name.

However, the lieutenant called the sailor this name. At that moment it chanced the sailor had an iron lever or bar in his hands. He promptly struck the lieutenant over the head with it, knocking him out of the rigging and overboard.

And then, in the man's own words: "I saw what I had

done. I knew the Regulations, and I said to myself, 'It's all up with you, Jack, my boy; so here goes.' An' I jumped over after him, my mind made up to drown us both. An' I'd ha' done it, too, only the pinnace from the flagship was just comin' alongside. Up we came to the top, me a hold of him an' punchin' him. This was what settled for me. If I hadn't ben strikin' him, I could have claimed that, seein' what I had done, I jumped over to save him."

Then came the court-martial, or whatever name a sea trial goes by. He recited his sentence, word for word, as though memorized and gone over in bitterness many times. And here it is, for the sake of discipline and respect to officers not always gentlemen, the punishment of a man who was guilty of manhood. To be reduced to the rank of ordinary seaman; to be debarred all prize money due him; to forfeit all rights to pension; to resign the Victoria Cross; to be discharged from the navy with a good character (this being his first offence); to receive fifty lashes; and to serve two years in prison.

"I wish I had drowned that day, I wish to God I had," he concluded, as the line moved up and we passed around the corner.

At last the door came in sight, through which the paupers were being admitted in bunches. And here I learned a surprising thing: *this being Wednesday, none of us would be released till Friday morning.* Furthermore, and oh, you tobacco users, take heed: *we would not be permitted to take in any tobacco.* This we would have to surrender as we entered. Sometimes, I was told, it was returned on leaving, and sometimes it was destroyed.

The old man-of-war's man gave me a lesson. Opening his pouch, he emptied the tobacco (a pitiful quantity) into a piece of paper. This, snugly and flatly wrapped, went down his sock inside his shoe. Down went my piece of tobacco inside my sock, for forty hours without tobacco is a hardship all tobacco users will understand.

Again and again the line moved up, and we were slowly but surely approaching the wicket. At the moment we happened to be standing on an iron grating, and a man appearing underneath, the old sailor called down to him:—

"How many more do they want?"

"Twenty-four," came the answer.

We looked ahead anxiously and counted. Thirty-four were ahead of us. Disappointment and consternation dawned upon the faces about me. It is not a nice thing, hungry and penniless, to face a sleepless night in the streets. But we hoped against hope, till, when ten stood outside the wicket, the porter turned us away.

"Full up," was what he said, as he banged the door.

Like a flash, for all his eighty-seven years, the old sailor was speeding away on the desperate chance of finding shelter elsewhere. I stood and debated with two other men, wise in the knowledge of casual wards, as to where we should go. They decided on the Poplar Workhouse, three miles away, and we started off.

As we rounded the corner, one of them said, "I could a' got in 'ere to-day. I come by at one o'clock, an' the line was beginnin' to form then—pets, that's what they are. They let 'm in, the same ones, night upon night."

VIII

The Carter and the Carpenter

It is not to die, nor even to die of hunger, that makes a man
wretched. Many men have died; all men must die. But it is to
live miserable, we know not why; to work sore, and yet gain
nothing; to be heart-worn, weary, yet isolated, unrelated, girt
in with a cold, universal *Laissez-faire*.

—CARLYLE

T HE CARTER, with his clean-cut face, chin beard, and
shaved upper lip, I should have taken in the United
States for anything from a master workman to a well-to-do
farmer. The Carpenter—well, I should have taken him for
a carpenter. He looked it, lean and wiry, with shrewd, observant eyes, and hands that had grown twisted to the handles of tools through forty-seven years' work at the trade.
The chief difficulty with these men was that they were old,
and that their children, instead of growing up to take care
of them, had died. Their years had told on them, and they
had been forced out of the whirl of industry by the
younger and stronger competitors who had taken their
places.

These two men, turned away from the casual ward of
Whitechapel Workhouse, were bound with me for Poplar
Workhouse. Not much of a show, they thought, but to
chance it was all that remained to us. It was Poplar, or the
streets and night. Both men were anxious for a bed, for they
were 'about gone,' as they phrased it. The Carter, fifty-eight
years of age, had spent the last three nights without shelter or
sleep, while the Carpenter, sixty-five years of age, had been
out five nights.

But, O dear, soft people, full of meat and blood, with
white beds and airy rooms waiting you each night, how can
I make you know what it is to suffer as you would suffer if
you spent a weary night on London's streets? Believe me, you
would think a thousand centuries had come and gone before
the east paled into dawn; you would shiver till you were
ready to cry aloud with the pain of each aching muscle; and

you would marvel that you could endure so much and live. Should you rest upon a bench, and your tired eyes close, depend upon it the policeman would rouse you and gruffly order you to 'move on.' You may rest upon the bench, and benches are few and far between; but if rest means sleep, on you must go, dragging your tired body through the endless streets. Should you, in desperate slyness, seek some forlorn alley or dark passageway and lie down, the omnipresent policeman will rout you out just the same. It is his business to rout you out. It is a law of the powers that be that you shall be routed out.

But when the dawn came, the nightmare over, you would hale you home to refresh yourself, and until you died you would tell the story of your adventure to groups of admiring friends. It would grow into a mighty story. Your little eight-hour night would become an Odyssey and you a Homer.

Not so with these homeless ones who walked to Poplar Workhouse with me. And there are thirty-five thousand of them, men and women, in London Town this night. Please don't remember it as you go to bed; if you are as soft as you ought to be, you may not rest so well as usual. But for old men of sixty, seventy, and eighty, ill-fed, with neither meat nor blood, to greet the dawn unrefreshed, and to stagger through the day in mad search for crusts, with relentless night rushing down upon them again, and to do this five nights and days—O dear, soft people, full of meat and blood, how can you ever understand?

I walked up Mile End Road between the Carter and the Carpenter. Mile End Road is a wide thoroughfare, cutting the heart of East London, and there were tens of thousands of people abroad on it. I tell you this so that you may fully appreciate what I shall describe in the next paragraph. As I say, we walked along, and when they grew bitter and cursed the land, I cursed with them, cursed as an American waif would curse, stranded in a strange and terrible land. And, as I tried to lead them to believe, and succeeded in making them believe, they took me for a 'seafaring man,' who had spent his money in riotous living, lost his clothes (no unusual occurrence with seafaring men ashore), and was temporarily broke while looking for a ship. This accounted for my ignorance of

English ways in general and casual wards in particular, and my curiosity concerning the same.

The Carter was hard put to keep the pace at which we walked (he told me that he had eaten nothing that day), but the Carpenter, lean and hungry, his gray and ragged overcoat flapping mournfully in the breeze, swung on in a long and tireless stride which reminded me strongly of the plains coyote. Both kept their eyes upon the pavement as they walked and talked, and every now and then one or the other would stoop and pick something up, never missing the stride the while. I thought it was cigar and cigarette stumps they were collecting, and for some time took no notice. Then I did notice.

From the slimy sidewalk, they were picking up bits of orange peel, apple skin, and grape stems, and they were eating them. The pits of green gage plums they cracked between their teeth for the kernels inside. They picked up stray crumbs of bread the size of peas, apple cores so black and dirty one would not take them to be apple cores, and these things these two men took into their mouths, and chewed them, and swallowed them; and this, between six and seven o'clock in the evening of August 20, year of our Lord 1902, in the heart of the greatest, wealthiest, and most powerful empire the world has ever seen.

These two men talked. They were not fools. They were merely old. And, naturally, their guts a-reek with pavement offal, they talked of bloody revolution. They talked as anarchists, fanatics, and madmen would talk. And who shall blame them? In spite of my three good meals that day, and the snug bed I could occupy if I wished, and my social philosophy, and my evolutionary belief in the slow development and metamorphosis of things—in spite of all this, I say, I felt impelled to talk rot with them or hold my tongue. Poor fools! Not of their sort are revolutions bred. And when they are dead and dust, which will be shortly, other fools will talk bloody revolution as they gather offal from the spittle-drenched sidewalk along Mile End Road to Poplar Workhouse.

Being a foreigner, and a young man, the Carter and the Carpenter explained things to me and advised me. Their advice, by the way, was brief and to the point; it was to get out of the country. "As fast as God'll let me," I assured them; "I'll hit only the high places, till you won't be able to see my trail for smoke." They felt the force of my figures, rather than understood them, and they nodded their heads approvingly.

"Actually make a man a criminal against 'is will," said the Carpenter. " 'Ere I am, old, younger men takin' my place, my clothes gettin' shabbier an' shabbier, an' makin' it 'arder every day to get a job. I go to the casual ward for a bed. Must be there by two or three in the afternoon or I won't get in. You saw what happened to-day. What chance does that give me to look for work? S'pose I do get into the casual ward? Keep me in all day to-morrow, let me out mornin' o' next day. What then? The law sez I can't get in another casual ward that night less'n ten miles distant. Have to hurry an' walk to be there in time that day. What chance does that give me to look for a job? S'pose I don't walk. S'pose I look for a job? In no time there's night come, an' no bed. No sleep all night, nothin' to eat, what shape am I in in the mornin' to look for work? Got to make up my sleep in the park somehow" (the vision of Christ's Church, Spitalfields, was strong on me) "an' get something to eat. An' there I am! Old, down, an' no chance to get up."

"Used to be a toll-gate 'ere," said the Carter. "Many's the time I've paid my toll 'ere in my cartin' days."

"I've 'ad three 'a'penny rolls in two days," the Carpenter announced, after a long pause in the conversation.

"Two of them I ate yesterday, an' the third to-day," he concluded, after another long pause.

"I ain't 'ad anything to-day," said the Carter. "An' I'm fagged out. My legs is hurtin' me something fearful."

"The roll you get in the 'spike' is that 'ard you can't eat it nicely with less'n a pint of water," said the Carpenter, for my benefit. And, on asking him what the 'spike' was, he answered, "The casual ward. It's a cant word, you know."

But what surprised me was that he should have the word 'cant' in his vocabulary, a vocabulary that I found was no mean one before we parted.

I asked them what I might expect in the way of treatment, if we succeeded in getting into the Poplar Workhouse, and between them I was supplied with much information. Having taken a cold bath on entering, I would be given for supper six ounces of bread and 'three parts of skilly.' 'Three parts' means three-quarters of a pint, and 'skilly' is a fluid concoction of three quarts of oatmeal stirred into three buckets and a half of hot water.

"Milk and sugar, I suppose, and a silver spoon?" I queried.

"No fear. Salt's what you'll get, an' I've seen some places where you'd not get any spoon. 'Old 'er up an' let 'er run down, that's 'ow they do it."

"You do get good skilly at 'Ackney," said the Carter.

"Oh, wonderful skilly, that," praised the Carpenter, and each looked eloquently at the other.

"Flour an' water at St. George's in the East," said the Carter.

The Carpenter nodded. He had tried them all.

"Then what?" I demanded.

And I was informed that I was sent directly to bed. "Call you at half after five in the mornin', an' you get up an' take a 'sluice'—if there's any soap. Then breakfast, same as supper, three parts o' skilly an' a six-ounce loaf."

"'Tisn't always six ounces," corrected the Carter.

"'Tisn't, no; an' often that sour you can 'ardly eat it. When first I started I couldn't eat the skilly nor the bread, but now I can eat my own an' another man's portion."

"I could eat three other men's portions," said the Carter. "I 'aven't 'ad a bit this blessed day."

"Then what?"

"Then you've got to do your task, pick four pounds of oakum, or clean an' scrub, or break ten to eleven hundredweight o' stones. I don't 'ave to break stones; I'm past sixty, you see. They'll make you do it, though. You're young an' strong."

"What I don't like," grumbled the Carter, "is to be locked up in a cell to pick oakum. It's too much like prison."

"But suppose, after you've had your night's sleep, you refuse to pick oakum, or break stones, or do any work at all?" I asked.

"No fear you'll refuse the second time; they'll run you in," answered the Carpenter. "Wouldn't advise you to try it on, my lad."

"Then comes dinner," he went on. "Eight ounces of bread, one and a arf ounces of cheese, an' cold water. Then you finish your task an' 'ave supper, same as before, three parts o' skilly an' six ounces o' bread. Then to bed, six o'clock, an' next mornin' you're turned loose, provided you've finished your task."

We had long since left Mile End Road, and after traversing a gloomy maze of narrow, winding streets, we came to Poplar Workhouse. On a low stone wall we spread our handkerchiefs, and each in his handkerchief put all his worldly possessions with the exception of the 'bit o' baccy' down his sock. And then, as the last light was fading from the drab-colored sky, the wind blowing cheerless and cold, we stood, with our pitiful little bundles in our hands, a forlorn group at the workhouse door.

Three working girls came along, and one looked pityingly at me; as she passed I followed her with my eyes, and she still looked pityingly back at me. The old men she did not notice. Dear Christ, she pitied me, young and vigorous and strong, but she had no pity for the two old men who stood by my side! She was a young woman, and I was a young man, and what vague sex promptings impelled her to pity me put her sentiment on the lowest plane. Pity for old men is an altruistic feeling, and besides, the workhouse door is the accustomed place for old men. So she showed no pity for them, only for me, who deserved it least or not at all. Not in honor do gray hairs go down to the grave in London Town.

On one side the door was a bell handle, on the other side a press button.

"Ring the bell," said the Carter to me.

And just as I ordinarily would at anybody's door, I pulled out the handle and rang a peal.

"Oh! Oh!" they cried in one terrified voice. "Not so 'ard!"

I let go, and they looked reproachfully at me, as though I had imperilled their chance for a bed and three parts of skilly. Nobody came. Luckily, it was the wrong bell, and I felt better.

"Press the button," I said to the Carpenter.

"No, no, wait a bit," the Carter hurriedly interposed.

From all of which I drew the conclusion that a poorhouse

porter, who commonly draws a yearly salary of from thirty to forty dollars, is a very finicky and important personage, and cannot be treated too fastidiously by—paupers.

So we waited, ten times a decent interval, when the Carter stealthily advanced a timid forefinger to the button, and gave it the faintest, shortest possible push. I have looked at waiting men where life and death was in the issue; but anxious suspense showed less plainly on their faces than it showed on the faces of these two men as they waited for the coming of the porter.

He came. He barely looked at us. "Full up," he said, and shut the door.

"Another night of it," groaned the Carpenter. In the dim light the Carter looked wan and gray.

Indiscriminate charity is vicious, say the professional philanthropists. Well, I resolved to be vicious.

"Come on; get your knife out and come here," I said to the Carter, drawing him into a dark alley.

He glared at me in a frightened manner, and tried to draw back. Possibly he took me for a latter day Jack-the-Ripper, with a penchant for elderly male paupers. Or he may have thought I was inveigling him into the commission of some desperate crime. Anyway, he was frightened.

It will be remembered, at the outset, that I sewed a pound inside my stoker's singlet under the armpit. This was my emergency fund, and I was now called upon to use it for the first time.

Not until I had gone through the acts of a contortionist, and shown the round coin sewed in, did I succeed in getting the Carter's help. Even then his hand was trembling so that I was afraid he would cut me instead of the stitches, and I was forced to take the knife away and do it myself. Out rolled the gold piece, a fortune in their hungry eyes; and away we stampeded for the nearest coffee-house.

Of course I had to explain to them that I was merely an investigator, a social student, seeking to find out how the other half lived. And at once they shut up like clams. I was not of their kind; my speech had changed, the tones of my voice were different, in short, I was a superior, and they were superbly class conscious.

"What will you have?" I asked, as the waiter came for the order.

"Two slices an' a cup of tea," meekly said the Carter.

"Two slices an' a cup of tea," meekly said the Carpenter.

Stop a moment, and consider the situation. Here were two men, invited by me into the coffee-house. They had seen my gold piece, and they could understand that I was no pauper. One had eaten a ha'penny roll that day, the other had eaten nothing. And they called for "two slices an' a cup of tea!" Each man had given a tu'penny order. 'Two slices,' by the way, means two slices of bread and butter.

This was the same degraded humility that had characterized their attitude toward the poorhouse porter. But I wouldn't have it. Step by step I increased their orders,—eggs, rashers of bacon, more eggs, more bacon, more tea, more slices, and so forth,—they denying wistfully all the while that they cared for anything more, and devouring it ravenously as fast as it arrived.

"First cup o' tea I've 'ad in a fortnight," said the Carter.

"Wonderful tea, that," said the Carpenter.

They each drank two pints of it, and I assure you that it was slops. It resembled tea less than lager beer resembles champagne. Nay, it was 'water-bewitched,' and did not resemble tea at all.

It was curious, after the first shock, to notice the effect the food had on them. At first they were melancholy, and talked of the divers times they had contemplated suicide. The Carter, not a week before, had stood on the bridge and looked at the water, and pondered the question. Water, the Carpenter insisted with heat, was a bad route. He, for one, he knew, would struggle. A bullet was ''andier,' but how under the sun was he to get hold of a revolver? That was the rub.

They grew more cheerful as the hot 'tea' soaked in, and talked more about themselves. The Carter had buried his wife and children, with the exception of one son, who grew to manhood and helped him in his little business. Then the thing happened. The son, a man of thirty-one, died of the smallpox. No sooner was this over than the father came down with fever and went to the hospital for three months. Then he was done for. He came out weak, debilitated, no strong

young son to stand by him, his little business gone glimmering, and not a farthing. The thing had happened, and the
game was up. No chance for an old man to start again.
Friends all poor and unable to help. He had tried for work
when they were putting up the stands for the first Coronation
parade. "An' I got fair sick of the answer; 'No! no! no!' It
rang in my ears at night when I tried to sleep, always the
same, 'No! no! no!' " Only the past week he had answered an
advertisement in Hackney, and on giving his age was told,
"Oh, too old, too old by far."

The Carpenter had been born in the army, where his father
had served twenty-two years. Likewise, his two brothers had
gone into the army; one, troop sergeant-major of the Seventh
Hussars, dying in India after the Mutiny; the other, after nine
years under Roberts in the East, had been lost in Egypt. The
Carpenter had not gone into the army, so here he was, still
on the planet.

"But 'ere, give me your 'and," he said, ripping open his
ragged shirt. "I'm fit for the anatomist, that's all. I'm wastin'
away, sir, actually wastin' away for want of food. Feel my ribs
an' you'll see."

I put my hand under his shirt and felt. The skin was
stretched like parchment over the bones, and the sensation
produced was for all the world like running one's hand over
a washboard.

"Seven years o' bliss I 'ad," he said. "A good missus and
three bonnie lassies. But they all died. Scarlet fever took the
girls inside a fortnight."

"After this, sir," said the Carter, indicating the spread, and
desiring to turn the conversation into more cheerful channels;
"after this, I wouldn't be able to eat a workhouse breakfast in
the morning."

"Nor I," agreed the Carpenter, and they fell to discussing
belly delights and the fine dishes their respective wives had
cooked in the old days.

"I've gone three days and never broke my fast," said the
Carter.

"And I, five," his companion added, turning gloomy with
the memory of it. "Five days once, with nothing on my stomach but a bit of orange peel, an' outraged nature wouldn't

stand it, sir, an' I near died. Sometimes, walkin' the streets at night, I've ben that desperate I've made up my mind to win the horse or lose the saddle. You know what I mean, sir—to commit some big robbery. But when mornin' come, there was I, too weak from 'unger an' cold to 'arm a mouse."

As their poor vitals warmed to the food, they began to expand and wax boastful, and to talk politics. I can only say that they talked politics as well as the average middle-class man, and a great deal better than some of the middle-class men I have heard. What surprised me was the hold they had on the world, its geography and peoples, and on recent and contemporaneous history. As I say, they were not fools, these two men. They were merely old, and their children had undutifully failed to grow up and give them a place by the fire.

One last incident, as I bade them good-by on the corner, happy with a couple of shillings in their pockets and the certain prospect of a bed for the night. Lighting a cigarette, I was about to throw away the burning match when the Carter reached for it. I proffered him the box, but he said, "Never mind, won't waste it, sir." And while he lighted the cigarette I had given him, the Carpenter hurried with the filling of his pipe in order to have a go at the same match.

"It's wrong to waste," said he.

"Yes," I said, but I was thinking of the washboard ribs over which I had run my hand.

IX

The Spike

The old Spartans had a wiser method; and went out and hunted
down their Helots, and speared and spitted them, when they
grew too numerous. With our improved fashions of hunting,
now after the invention of firearms and standing armies, how
much easier were such a hunt! Perhaps in the most thickly peo-
pled country, some three days annually might suffice to shoot all
the able-bodied paupers that had accumulated within the year.
— CARLYLE

F IRST of all, I must beg forgiveness of my body for the
vileness through which I have dragged it, and forgiveness
of my stomach for the vileness which I have thrust into it. I
have been to the spike, and slept in the spike, and eaten in
the spike; also, I have run away from the spike.

After my two unsuccessful attempts to penetrate the Whitechapel casual ward, I started early, and joined the desolate
line before three o'clock in the afternoon. They did not 'let
in' till six, but at that early hour I was number 20, while the
news had gone forth that only twenty-two were to be admitted. By four o'clock there were thirty-four in line, the last ten
hanging on in the slender hope of getting in by some kind of
a miracle. Many more came, looked at the line, and went
away, wise to the bitter fact that the spike would be 'full up.'

Conversation was slack at first, standing there, till the man
on one side of me and the man on the other side of me discovered that they had been in the smallpox hospital at the
same time, though a full house of sixteen hundred patients
had prevented their becoming acquainted. But they made up
for it, discussing and comparing the more loathsome features
of their disease in the most cold-blooded, matter-of-fact way.
I learned that the average mortality was one in six, that one
of them had been in three months and the other three months
and a half, and that they had been 'rotten wi' it.' Whereat my
flesh began to creep and crawl, and I asked them how long
they had been out. One had been out two weeks, and the

other three weeks. Their faces were badly pitted (though each assured the other that this was not so), and further, they showed me in their hands and under the nails the smallpox 'seeds' still working out. Nay, one of them worked a seed out for my edification, and pop it went, right out of his flesh into the air. I tried to shrink up smaller inside my clothes, and I registered a fervent though silent hope that it had not popped on me.

In both instances, I found that the smallpox was the cause of their being 'on the doss,' which means on the tramp. Both had been working when smitten by the disease, and both had emerged from the hospital 'broke,' with the gloomy task before them of hunting for work. So far, they had not found any, and they had come to the spike for a 'rest up' after three days and nights on the street.

It seems that not only the man who becomes old is punished for his involuntary misfortune, but likewise the man who is struck by disease or accident. Later on, I talked with another man,—'Ginger' we called him,—who stood at the head of the line—a sure indication that he had been waiting since one o'clock. A year before, one day, while in the employ of a fish dealer, he was carrying a heavy box of fish which was too much for him. Result: 'something broke,' and there was the box on the ground, and he on the ground beside it.

At the first hospital, whither he was immediately carried, they said it was a rupture, reduced the swelling, gave him some vaseline to rub on it, kept him four hours, and told him to get along. But he was not on the streets more than two or three hours when he was down on his back again. This time he went to another hospital and was patched up. But the point is, the employer did nothing, positively nothing, for the man injured in his employment, and even refused him 'a light job now and again,' when he came out. As far as Ginger is concerned, he is a broken man. His only chance to earn a living was by heavy work. He is now incapable of performing heavy work, and from now until he dies, the spike, the peg, and the streets are all he can look forward to in the way of food and shelter. The thing happened—that is all. He put his back under too great a load of fish, and his chance for happiness in life was crossed off the books.

Several men in the line had been to the United States, and they were wishing that they had remained there, and were cursing themselves for their folly in ever having left. England had become a prison to them, a prison from which there was no hope of escape. It was impossible for them to get away. They could neither scrape together the passage money, nor get a chance to work their passage. The country was too over-run by poor devils on that 'lay.'

I was on the seafaring-man-who-had-lost-his-clothes-and-money tack, and they all condoled with me and gave me much sound advice. To sum it up, the advice was something like this: To keep out of all places like the spike. There was nothing good in it for me. To head for the coast and bend every effort to get away on a ship. To go to work, if possible, and scrape together a pound or so, with which I might bribe some steward or underling to give me chance to work my passage. They envied me my youth and strength, which would sooner or later get me out of the country. These they no longer possessed. Age and English hardship had broken them, and for them the game was played and up.

There was one, however, who was still young, and who, I am sure, will in the end make it out. He had gone to the United States as a young fellow, and in fourteen years' resi-dence the longest period he had been out of work was twelve hours. He had saved his money, grown too prosperous, and returned to the mother country. Now he was standing in line at the spike.

For the past two years, he told me, he had been working as a cook. His hours had been from 7 A.M. to 10.30 P.M., and on Saturday to 12.30 P.M.—ninety-five hours per week, for which he had received twenty shillings, or five dollars.

"But the work and the long hours was killing me," he said, "and I had to chuck the job. I had a little money saved, but I spent it living and looking for another place."

This was his first night in the spike, and he had come in only to get rested. As soon as he emerged he intended to start for Bristol, a one-hundred-and-ten-mile walk, where he thought he would eventually get a ship for the States.

But the men in the line were not all of this caliber. Some were poor, wretched beasts, inarticulate and callous, but for all of that, in many ways very human. I remember a carter, evidently returning home after the day's work, stopping his cart before us so that his young hopeful, who had run to meet him, could climb in. But the cart was big, the young hopeful little, and he failed in his several attempts to swarm up. Whereupon one of the most degraded-looking men stepped out of the line and hoisted him in. Now the virtue and the joy of this act lies in that it was service of love, not hire. The carter was poor, and the man knew it; and the man was standing in the spike line, and the carter knew it; and the man had done the little act, and the carter had thanked him, even as you and I would have done and thanked.

Another beautiful touch was that displayed by the 'Hopper' and his 'ole woman.' He had been in line about half an hour when the 'ole woman' (his mate) came up to him. She was fairly clad, for her class, with a weatherworn bonnet on her gray head and a sacking covered bundle in her arms. As she talked to him, he reached forward, caught the one stray wisp of the white hair that was flying wild, deftly twirled it between his fingers, and tucked it back properly behind her ear. From all of which one may conclude many things. He certainly liked her well enough to wish her to be neat and tidy. He was proud of her, standing there in the spike line, and it was his desire that she should look well in the eyes of the other unfortunates who stood in the spike line. But last and best, and underlying all these motives, it was a sturdy affection he bore her; for man is not prone to bother his head over neatness and tidiness in a woman for whom he does not care, nor is he likely to be proud of such a woman.

And I found myself questioning why this man and his mate, hard workers I knew from their talk, should have to seek a pauper lodging. He had pride, pride in his old woman and pride in himself. When I asked him what he thought I, a greenhorn, might expect to earn at 'hopping,' he sized me up, and said that it all depended. Plenty of people were too slow to pick hops and made a failure of it. A man, to succeed, must use his head and be quick with his fingers, must be exceeding quick with his fingers. Now he and his old woman could do very well at it, working the one bin between them and not going to sleep over it; but then, they had been at it for years.

"I 'ad a mate as went down last year," spoke up a man. "It was 'is fust time, but 'e come back wi' two poun' ten in 'is pockit, an' 'e was only gone a month."

"There you are," said the Hopper, a wealth of admiration in his voice. " 'E was quick. 'E was jest nat'rally born to it, 'e was."

Two pound ten—twelve dollars and a half—for a month's work when one is 'jest nat'rally born to it'! And in addition, sleeping out without blankets and living the Lord knows how. There are moments when I am thankful that I was not 'jest nat'rally born' a genius for anything, not even hop-picking.

In the matter of getting an outfit for 'the hops,' the Hopper gave me some sterling advice, to which same give heed, you soft and tender people, in case you should ever be stranded in London Town.

"If you ain't got tins an' cookin' things, all as you can get'll be bread and cheese. No bloody good that! You must 'ave 'ot tea, an' wegetables, an' a bit o' meat, now an' again, if you're goin' to do work as is work. Cawn't do it on cold wittles. Tell you wot you do, lad. Run around in the mornin' an' look in the dust pans. You'll find plenty o' tins to cook in. Fine tins, wonderful good some o' them. Me an' the ole woman got ours that way." (He pointed at the bundle she held, while she nodded proudly, beaming on me with good nature and consciousness of success and prosperity.) "This overcoat is as good as a blanket," he went on, advancing the skirt of it that I might feel its thickness. "An' 'oo knows, I may find a blanket before long."

Again the old woman nodded and beamed, this time with the dead certainty that he *would* find a blanket before long.

"I call it a 'oliday, 'oppin'," he concluded rapturously. "A tidy way o' gettin' two or three pounds together an' fixin' up for winter. The only thing I don't like"—and here was the rift within the lute—"is paddin' the 'oof down there."

It was plain the years were telling on this energetic pair, and while they enjoyed the quick work with the fingers, 'paddin' the 'oof,' which is walking, was beginning to bear heavily upon them. And I looked at their gray hairs, and ahead into the future ten years, and wondered how it would be with them.

I noticed another man and his old woman join the line, both of them past fifty. The woman, because she was a woman, was admitted into the spike; but he was too late, and, separated from his mate, was turned away to tramp the streets all night.

The street on which we stood, from wall to wall, was barely twenty feet wide. The sidewalks were three feet wide. It was a residence street. At least workmen and their families existed in some sort of fashion in the houses across from us. And each day and every day, from one in the afternoon till six, our ragged spike line is the principal feature of the view commanded by their front doors and windows. One workman sat in his door directly opposite us, taking his rest and a breath of air after the toil of the day. His wife came to chat with him. The doorway was too small for two, so she stood up. Their babes sprawled before them. And here was the spike line, less than a score of feet away—neither privacy for the workman, nor privacy for the pauper. About our feet played the children of the neighborhood. To them our presence was nothing unusual. We were not an intrusion. We were as natural and ordinary as the brick walls and stone curbs of their environment. They had been born to the sight of the spike line, and all their brief days they had seen it.

At six o'clock the line moved up, and we were admitted in groups of three. Name, age, occupation, place of birth, condition of destitution, and the previous night's 'doss,' were taken with lightning-like rapidity by the superintendent; and as I turned I was startled by a man's thrusting into my hand something that felt like a brick, and shouting into my ear, "Any knives, matches, or tobacco?" "No, sir," I lied, as lied every man who entered. As I passed downstairs to the cellar, I looked at the brick in my hand, and saw that by doing violence to the language it might be called 'bread.' By its weight and hardness it certainly must have been unleavened.

The light was very dim down in the cellar, and before I knew it some other man had thrust a pannikin into my other hand. Then I stumbled on to a still darker room, where were benches and tables and men. The place smelled vilely, and the sombre gloom, and the mumble of voices from out of the obscurity, made it seem more like some anteroom to the infernal regions.

Most of the men were suffering from tired feet, and they prefaced the meal by removing their shoes and unbinding the filthy rags with which their feet were wrapped. This added to the general noisomeness, while it took away from my appetite.

In fact, I found that I had made a mistake. I had eaten a hearty dinner five hours before, and to have done justice to the fare before me I should have fasted for a couple of days. The pannikin contained skilly, three-quarters of a pint, a mixture of Indian corn and hot water. The men were dipping their bread into heaps of salt scattered over the dirty tables. I attempted the same, but the bread seemed to stick in my mouth, and I remembered the words of the Carpenter: "You need a pint of water to eat the bread nicely."

I went over into a dark corner where I had observed other men going, and found the water. Then I returned and attacked the skilly. It was coarse of texture, unseasoned, gross, and bitter. This bitterness which lingered persistently in the mouth after the skilly had passed on, I found especially repulsive. I struggled manfully, but was mastered by my qualms, and half a dozen mouthfuls of skilly and bread was the measure of my success. The man beside me ate his own share, and mine to boot, scraped the pannikins, and looked hungrily for more.

"I met a 'towny,' and he stood me too good a dinner," I explained.

"An' I 'aven't 'ad a bite since yesterday mornin'," he replied.

"How about tobacco?" I asked. "Will the bloke bother with a fellow now?"

"Oh, no," he answered me. "No bloody fear. This is the easiest spike goin'. Y'oughto see some of them. Search you to the skin."

The pannikins scraped clean, conversation began to spring up. "This super'tendent 'ere is always writin' to the papers 'bout us mugs," said the man on the other side of me.

"What does he say?" I asked.

"Oh, 'e sez we're no good, a lot o' blackguards an' scoundrels as won't work. Tells all the ole tricks I've bin 'earin' for twenty years an' w'ich I never seen a mug ever do. Las' thing of 'is I see, 'e was tellin' 'ow a mug gets out o' the spike, wi' a crust in 'is pockit. An' w'en 'e sees a nice ole gentleman comin' along the street 'e chucks the crust into the drain, an' borrows the old gent's stick to poke it out. An' then the ole gent gi'es 'im a tanner" [sixpence].

A roar of applause greeted the time-honored yarn, and from somewhere over in the deeper darkness came another voice, orating angrily: —

"Talk o' the country bein' good for tommy [food]. I'd like to see it. I jest came up from Dover, an' blessed little tommy I got. They won't gi' ye a drink o' water, they won't, much less tommy."

"There's mugs never go out of Kent," spoke a second voice, "an' they live bloomin' fat all along."

"I come through Kent," went on the first voice, still more angrily, "an' Gawd blimey if I see any tommy. An' I always notices as the blokes as talks about 'ow much they can get, w'en they're in the spike can eat my share o' skilly as well as their bleedin' own."

"There's chaps in London," said a man across the table from me, "that get all the tommy they want, an' they never think o' goin' to the country. Stay in London the year 'round. Nor do they think of lookin' for a kip [place to sleep], till nine or ten o'clock at night."

A general chorus verified this statement.

"But they're bloody clever, them chaps," said an admiring voice.

"Course they are," said another voice. "But it's not the likes of me an' you can do it. You got to be born to it, I say. Them chaps 'ave ben openin' cabs an' sellin' papers since the day they was born, an' their fathers an' mothers before 'em. It's all in the trainin', I say, an' the likes of me an' you 'ud starve at it."

This also was verified by the general chorus, and likewise the statement that there were "mugs as lives the twelvemonth 'round in the spike an' never get a blessed bit o' tommy other than spike skilly an' bread."

"I once got arf a crown in the Stratford spike," said a new voice. Silence fell on the instant, and all listened to the wonderful tale. "There was three of us breakin' stones. Wintertime, an' the cold was cruel. T'other two said they'd be blessed if they do it, an' they didn't; but I kept wearin' into mine to warm up, you know. An' then the guardians come, an' t'other chaps got run in for fourteen days, an' the guardians, w'en they see wot I'd been doin', gives me a tanner each, five o' them, an' turns me up."

The majority of these men, nay, all of them, I found, do not like the spike, and only come to it when driven in. After the 'rest up' they are good for two or three days and nights on the streets, when they are driven in again for another rest. Of course, this continuous hardship quickly breaks their constitutions, and they realize it, though only in a vague way; while it is so much the common run of things that they do not worry about it.

'On the doss,' they call vagabondage here, which corresponds to 'on the road' in the United States. The agreement is that kipping, or dossing, or sleeping, is the hardest problem they have to face, harder even than that of food. The inclement weather and the harsh laws are mainly responsible for this, while the men themselves ascribe their homelessness to foreign immigration, especially of Polish and Russian Jews, who take their places at lower wages and establish the sweating system.

By seven o'clock we were called away to bathe and go to bed. We stripped our clothes, wrapping them up in our coats and buckling our belts about them, and deposited them in a heaped rack and on the floor—a beautiful scheme for the spread of vermin. Then, two by two, we entered the bathroom. There were two ordinary tubs, and this I know: the two men preceding had washed in that water, we washed in the same water, and it was not changed for the two men that followed us. This I know; but I am quite certain that the twenty-two of us washed in the same water.

I did no more than make a show of splashing some of this dubious liquid at myself, while I hastily brushed it off with a towel wet from the bodies of other men. My equanimity was not restored by seeing the back of one poor wretch a mass of blood from attacks of vermin and retaliatory scratching.

A shirt was handed me—which I could not help but wonder how many other men had worn; and with a couple of blankets under my arm I trudged off to the sleeping apartment. This was a long, narrow room, traversed by two low iron rails. Between these rails were stretched, not hammocks, but pieces of canvas, six feet long and less than two feet wide. These were the beds, and they were six inches apart and about eight inches above the floor. The chief difficulty was that the head was somewhat higher than the feet, which caused the body constantly to slip down. Being slung to the same rails, when one man moved, no matter how slightly, the rest were set rocking; and whenever I dozed somebody was sure to struggle back to the position from which he had slipped, and arouse me again.

Many hours passed before I won to sleep. It was only seven in the evening, and the voices of children, in shrill outcry, playing in the street, continued till nearly midnight. The smell was frightful and sickening, while my imagination broke loose, and my skin crept and crawled till I was nearly frantic. Grunting, groaning, and snoring arose like the sounds emitted by some sea monster, and several times, afflicted by nightmare, one or another, by his shrieks and yells, aroused the lot of us. Toward morning I was awakened by a rat or some similar animal on my breast. In the quick transition from sleep to waking, before I was completely myself, I raised a shout to wake the dead. At any rate, I woke the living, and they cursed me roundly for my lack of manners.

But morning came, with a six o'clock breakfast of bread and skilly, which I gave away; and we were told off to our various tasks. Some were set to scrubbing and cleaning, others to picking oakum, and eight of us were convoyed across the street to the Whitechapel Infirmary, where we were set at scavenger work. This was the method by which we paid for our skilly and canvas, and I, for one, know that I paid in full many times over.

Though we had most revolting tasks to perform, our allotment was considered the best, and the other men deemed themselves lucky in being chosen to perform it.

"Don't touch it, mate, the nurse sez it's deadly," warned my working partner, as I held open a sack into which he was emptying a garbage can.

It came from the sick wards, and I told him that I purposed neither to touch *it*, nor to allow *it* to touch me. Nevertheless, I had to carry the sack, and other sacks, down five flights of stairs and empty them in a receptacle where the corruption was speedily sprinkled with strong disinfectant.

Perhaps there is a wise mercy in all this. These men of the spike, the peg, and the street, are encumbrances. They are of no good or use to any one, nor to themselves. They clutter the earth with their presence, and are better out of the way. Broken by hardship, ill fed, and worse nourished, they are always the first to be struck down by disease, as they are likewise the quickest to die.

They feel, themselves, that the forces of society tend to hurl them out of existence. We were sprinkling disinfectant by the mortuary, when the dead wagon drove up and five bodies were packed into it. The conversation turned to the 'white potion' and 'black jack,' and I found they were all agreed that the poor person, man or woman, who in the Infirmary gave too much trouble or was in a bad way, was 'polished off.' That is to say, the incurables and the obstreperous were given a dose of 'black jack' or the 'white potion,' and sent over the divide. It does not matter in the least whether this be actually so or not. The point is, they have the feeling that it is so, and they have created the language with which to express that feeling—'black jack,' 'white potion,' 'polishing off.'

At eight o'clock we went down into a cellar under the Infirmary, where tea was brought to us, and the hospital scraps. These were heaped high on a huge platter in an indescribable mess—pieces of bread, chunks of grease and fat pork, the burnt skin from the outside of roasted joints, bones, in short, all the leavings from the fingers and mouths of the sick ones suffering from all manner of diseases. Into this mess the men plunged their hands, digging, pawing, turning over, examining, rejecting, and scrambling for. It wasn't pretty. Pigs couldn't have done worse. But the poor devils were hungry, and they ate ravenously of the swill, and when they could eat no more they bundled what was left into their handkerchiefs and thrust it inside their shirts.

"Once, w'en I was 'ere before, wot did I find out there but a 'ole lot of pork-ribs," said Ginger to me. By 'out there' he meant the place where the corruption was dumped and sprinkled with strong disinfectant. "They was a prime lot, no end o' meat on 'em, an' I 'ad 'em into my arms an' was out the gate an' down the street, a-lookin' for some 'un to gi' 'em to. Couldn't see a soul, an' I was runnin' 'round clean crazy, the bloke runnin' after me an' thinkin' I was 'slingin' my 'ook' [running away]. But jest before 'e got me, I got a ole woman an' poked 'em into 'er apron."

O Charity, O Philanthropy, descend to the spike and take a lesson from Ginger. At the bottom of the Abyss he performed as purely an altruistic act as was ever performed outside the Abyss. It was fine of Ginger, and if the old woman caught some contagion from the 'no end o' meat' on the pork-ribs, it was still fine, though not so fine. But the most salient thing in this incident, it seems to me, is poor Ginger, 'clean crazy' at sight of so much food going to waste.

It is the rule of the casual ward that a man who enters must stay two nights and a day; but I had seen sufficient for my purpose, had paid for my skilly and canvas, and was preparing to run for it.

"Come on, let's sling it," I said to one of my mates, pointing toward the open gate through which the dead wagon had come.

"An' get fourteen days?"

"No; get away."

"Aw, I come 'ere for a rest," he said complacently. "An' another night's kip won't 'urt me none."

They were all of this opinion, so I was forced to 'sling it' alone.

"You cawn't ever come back 'ere again for a doss," they warned me.

"No bloody fear," said I, with an enthusiasm they could not comprehend; and, dodging out the gate, I sped down the street.

Straight to my room I hurried, changed my clothes, and

less than an hour from my escape, in a Turkish bath, I was sweating out whatever germs and other things had penetrated my epidermis, and wishing that I could stand a temperature of three hundred and twenty rather than two hundred and twenty.

X

Carrying the Banner

I would not have the laborer sacrificed to the result. I would
not have the laborer sacrificed to my convenience and pride, nor
to that of a great class of such as me. Let there be worse cotton
and better men. The weaver should not be bereaved of his superiority to his work.

—EMERSON

To carry the banner' means to walk the streets all night;
and I, with the figurative emblem hoisted, went out to
see what I could see. Men and women walk the streets at
night all over this great city, but I selected the West End,
making Leicester Square my base, and scouting about from
the Thames Embankment to Hyde Park.

The rain was falling heavily when the theatres let out, and
the brilliant throng which poured from the places of amusement was hard put to find cabs. The streets were so many
wild rivers of cabs, most of which were engaged, however;
and here I saw the desperate attempts of ragged men and
boys to get a shelter from the night by procuring cabs for the
cabless ladies and gentlemen. I use the word 'desperate' ad-
visedly; for these wretched homeless ones were gambling a
soaking against a bed; and most of them, I took notice, got
the soaking and missed the bed. Now, to go through a
stormy night with wet clothes, and, in addition, to be ill-
nourished and not to have tasted meat for a week or a month,
is about as severe a hardship as a man can undergo. Well-fed
and well-clad, I have travelled all day with the spirit thermometer down to seventy-four degrees below zero; and
though I suffered, it was a mere nothing compared with carrying the banner for a night, ill-fed, ill-clad, and soaking wet.

The streets grew very quiet and lonely after the theatre
crowd had gone home. Only were to be seen the ubiquitous
policemen, flashing their dark lanterns into doorways and alleys, and men and women and boys taking shelter in the lee
of buildings from the wind and rain. Piccadilly, however, was
not quite so deserted. Its pavements were brightened by well-

dressed women without escort, and there was more life and
action there than elsewhere, due to the process of finding escort. But by three o'clock the last of them had vanished, and
it was then indeed lonely.

At half-past one the steady downpour ceased, and only
showers fell thereafter. The homeless folk came away from the
protection of the buildings, and slouched up and down and
everywhere, in order to rush up the circulation and keep
warm.

One old woman, between fifty and sixty, a sheer wreck, I
had noticed, earlier in the night, standing in Piccadilly, not
far from Leicester Square. She seemed to have neither the
sense nor the strength to get out of the rain or keep walking,
but stood stupidly, whenever she got the chance, meditating
on past days, I imagine, when life was young and blood was
warm. But she did not get the chance often. She was moved
on by every policeman, and it required an average of six
moves to send her doddering off one man's beat and on to
another's. By three o'clock she had progressed as far as St.
James Street, and as the clocks were striking four I saw her
sleeping soundly against the iron railings of Green Park. A
brisk shower was falling at the time, and she must have been
drenched to the skin.

Now, said I, at one o'clock, to myself; consider that you
are a poor young man, penniless, in London Town, and that
to-morrow you must look for work. It is necessary, therefore,
that you get some sleep in order that you may have strength
to look for work and to do work in case you find it.

So I sat down on the stone steps of a building. Five minutes later, a policeman was looking at me. My eyes were wide
open, so he only grunted and passed on. Ten minutes later
my head was on my knees, I was dozing, and the same policeman was saying gruffly, "'Ere, you, get outa that!"

I got. And, like the old woman, I continued to get; for
every time I dozed, a policeman was there to rout me along
again. Not long after, when I had given this up, I was walking with a young Londoner (who had been out to the colonies and wished he were out to them again), when I noticed
an open passage leading under a building and disappearing in
darkness. A low iron gate barred the entrance.

"Come on," I said. "Let's climb over and get a good sleep."

"Wot?" he answered, recoiling from me. "An' get run in fer three months! Blimey if I do!"

Later on, I was passing Hyde Park with a young boy of fourteen or fifteen, a most wretched-looking youth, gaunt and hollow-eyed and sick.

"Let's go over the fence," I proposed, "and crawl into the shrubbery for a sleep. The bobbies couldn't find us there."

"No fear," he answered. "There's the park guardians, and they'd run you in for six months."

Times have changed, alas! When I was a youngster I used to read of homeless boys sleeping in doorways. Already the thing has become a tradition. As a stock situation it will doubtlessly linger in literature for a century to come, but as a cold fact it has ceased to be. Here are the doorways, and here are the boys, but happy conjunctions are no longer effected. The doorways remain empty, and the boys keep awake and carry the banner.

"I was down under the arches," grumbled another young fellow. By 'arches' he meant the shore arches where begin the bridges that span the Thames. "I was down under the arches, w'en it was ryning its 'ardest, an' a bobby comes in an' chyses me out. But I come back, an' 'e come too. ''Ere,' sez 'e, 'wot you doin' 'ere?' An' out I goes, but I sez, 'Think I want ter pinch [steal] the bleedin' bridge?' "

Among those who carry the banner, Green Park has the reputation of opening its gates earlier than the other parks, and at quarter-past four in the morning, I, and many more, entered Green Park. It was raining again, but they were worn out with the night's walking, and they were down on the benches and asleep at once. Many of the men stretched out full length on the dripping wet grass, and, with the rain falling steadily upon them, were sleeping the sleep of exhaustion.

And now I wish to criticise the powers that be. They *are* the powers, therefore they may decree whatever they please; so I make bold only to criticise the ridiculousness of their decrees. All night long they make the homeless ones walk up and down. They drive them out of doors and passages, and lock them out of the parks. The evident intention of all this is to deprive them of sleep. Well and good, the powers have the power to deprive them of sleep, or of anything else for that matter; but why under the sun do they open the gates of the parks at five o'clock in the morning and let the homeless ones go inside and sleep? If it is their intention to deprive them of sleep, why do they let them sleep after five in the morning? And if it is not their intention to deprive them of sleep, why don't they let them sleep earlier in the night?

In this connection, I will say that I came by Green Park that same day, at one in the afternoon, and that I counted scores of the ragged wretches asleep in the grass. It was Sunday afternoon, the sun was fitfully appearing, and the well-dressed West Enders, with their wives and progeny, were out by thousands, taking the air. It was not a pleasant sight for them, those horrible, unkempt, sleeping vagabonds; while the vagabonds themselves, I know, would rather have done their sleeping the night before.

And so, dear soft people, should you ever visit London Town, and see these men asleep on the benches and in the grass, please do not think they are lazy creatures, preferring sleep to work. Know that the powers that be have kept them walking all the night long, and that in the day they have nowhere else to sleep.

XI

The Peg

And I believe that this claim for a healthy body for all of us
carries with it all other due claims; for who knows where the
seeds of disease, which even rich people suffer from, were first
sown? From the luxury of an ancestor, perhaps; yet often, I
suspect, from his poverty.

—WILLIAM MORRIS

B UT, after carrying the banner all night, I did not sleep in
Green Park when morning dawned. I was wet to the
skin, it is true, and I had had no sleep for twenty-four hours;
but, still adventuring as a penniless man looking for work, I
had to look about me, first for a breakfast, and next for the
work.

During the night I had heard of a place over on the Surrey
side of the Thames, where the Salvation Army every Sunday
morning gave away a breakfast to the unwashed. (And, by
the way, the men who carry the banner *are* unwashed in the
morning, and unless it is raining they do not have much show
for a wash, either.) This, thought I, is the very thing,—breakfast in the morning, and then the whole day in which to look
for work.

It was a weary walk. Down St. James Street I dragged my
tired legs, along Pall Mall, past Trafalgar Square, to the
Strand. I crossed the Waterloo Bridge to the Surrey side, cut
across to Blackfriars Road, coming out near the Surrey Theatre, and arrived at the Salvation Army barracks before seven
o'clock. This was 'the peg.' And by 'the peg,' in the argot, is
meant the place where a free meal may be obtained.

Here was a motley crowd of woebegone wretches who had
spent the night in the rain. Such prodigious misery! and so
much of it! Old men, young men, all manner of men, and
boys to boot, and all manner of boys. Some were drowsing
standing up; half a score of them were stretched out on the
stone steps in most painful postures, all of them sound asleep,
the skin of their bodies showing red through the holes and
rents in their rags. And up and down the street and across the

73

street for a block either way, each doorstep had from two to three occupants, all asleep, their heads bent forward on their knees. And, it must be remembered, these are not hard times in England. Things are going on very much as they ordinarily do, and times are neither hard nor easy.

And then came the policeman. "Get outa that, you bloody swine! Eigh! eigh! Get out now!" And like swine he drove them from the doorways and scattered them to the four winds of Surrey. But when he encountered the crowd asleep on the steps he was astounded. "Shocking!" he exclaimed. "Shocking! And of a Sunday morning! A pretty sight! Eigh! eigh! Get outa that, you bleeding nuisances!"

Of course it was a shocking sight. I was shocked myself. And I should not care to have my own daughter pollute her eyes with such a sight, or come within half a mile of it; but— and there we were, and there you are, and 'but' is all that can be said.

The policeman passed on, and back we clustered, like flies around a honey jar. For was there not that wonderful thing, a breakfast, awaiting us? We could not have clustered more persistently and desperately had they been giving away mil-lion-dollar bank-notes. Some were already off to sleep, when back came the policeman and away we scattered, only to re-turn again as soon as the coast was clear.

At half-past seven a little door opened, and a Salvation Army soldier stuck out his head. "Ayn't no sense blockin' the wy up that wy," he said. "Those as 'as tickets cawn come hin now, an' those as 'asn't cawn't come hin till nine."

Oh, that breakfast! Nine o'clock! An hour and a half longer! The men who held tickets were greatly envied. They were permitted to go inside, have a wash, and sit down and rest until breakfast, while we waited for the same breakfast on the street. The tickets had been distributed the previous night on the streets and along the Embankment, and the possession of them was not a matter of merit, but of chance.

At eight-thirty, more men with tickets were admitted, and by nine the little gate was opened to us. We crushed through somehow, and found ourselves packed in a courtyard like sar-dines. On more occasions than one, as a Yankee tramp in Yankeeland, I have had to work for my breakfast; but for no breakfast did I ever work so hard as for this one. For over two hours I had waited outside, and for over another hour I waited in this packed courtyard. I had had nothing to eat all night, and I was weak and faint, while the smell of the soiled clothes and unwashed bodies, steaming from pent animal heat, and blocked solidly about me, nearly turned my stomach. So tightly were we packed, that a number of the men took advantage of the opportunity and went soundly asleep standing up.

Now, about the Salvation Army in general I know nothing, and whatever criticism I shall make here is of that particular portion of the Salvation Army which does business on Blackfriars Road near the Surrey Theatre. In the first place, this forcing of men who have been up all night to stand on their feet for hours longer, is as cruel as it is needless. We were weak, famished, and exhausted from our night's hardship and lack of sleep, and yet there we stood, and stood, and stood, without rhyme or reason.

Sailors were very plentiful in this crowd. It seemed to me that one man in four was looking for a ship, and I found at least a dozen of them to be American sailors. In accounting for their being 'on the beach,' I received the same story from each and all, and from my knowledge of sea affairs this story rang true. English ships sign their sailors for the voyage, which means the round trip, sometimes lasting as long as three years; and they cannot sign off and receive their discharges until they reach the home port, which is England. Their wages are low, their food is bad, and their treatment worse. Very often they are really forced by their captains to desert in the New World or the colonies, leaving a handsome sum of wages behind them,—a distinct gain, either to the captain or the owners, or to both. But whether for this reason alone or not, it is a fact that large numbers of them desert. Then, for the home voyage, the ship engages whatever sailors it can find on the beach. These men are engaged at the somewhat higher wages that obtain in other portions of the world, under the agreement that they shall sign off on reaching England. The reason for this is obvious; for it would be poor business policy to sign them for any longer time, since seamen's wages are low in England, and England is always crowded with sailormen on the beach. So this fully accounted for the American seamen at the Salvation Army barracks. To get off the beach in other outlandish places they had come to England, and gone on the beach in the most outlandish place of all.

There were fully a score of Americans in the crowd, the non-sailors being 'tramps royal,' the men whose 'mate is the wind that tramps the world.' They were all cheerful, facing things with the pluck which is their chief characteristic and which seems never to desert them, withal they were cursing the country with lurid metaphors quite refreshing after a month of unimaginative, monotonous Cockney swearing. The Cockney has one oath, and one oath only, the most in-decent in the language, which he uses on any and every oc-casion. Far different is the luminous and varied Western swearing, which runs to blasphemy rather than indecency. And after all, since men will swear, I think I prefer blasphemy to indecency; there is an audacity about it, an adventurous-ness and defiance that is far finer than sheer filthiness.

There was one American tramp royal whom I found partic-ularly enjoyable. I first noticed him on the street, asleep in a doorway, his head on his knees, but a hat on his head that one does not meet this side of the Western Ocean. When the policeman routed him out, he got up slowly and deliberately, looked at the policeman, yawned and stretched himself, looked at the policeman again as much as to say he didn't know whether he would or wouldn't, and then sauntered lei-surely down the sidewalk. At the outset I was sure of the hat, but this made me sure of the wearer of the hat.

In the jam inside I found myself alongside of him, and we had quite a chat. He had been through Spain, Italy, Switzer-land, and France, and had accomplished the practically im-possible feat of beating his way three hundred miles on a French railway without being caught at the finish. Where was I hanging out? he asked. And how did I manage for 'kip-ping'?—which means sleeping. Did I know the rounds yet? He was getting on, though the country was 'horstyl' and the cities were 'bum.' Fierce, wasn't it? Couldn't 'batter' (beg) anywhere without being 'pinched.' But he wasn't going to quit it. Buffalo Bill's Show was coming over soon, and a man who could drive eight horses was sure of a job any time. These mugs over here didn't know beans about driving anything more than a span. What was the matter with me hanging on and waiting for Buffalo Bill? He was sure I could ring in somehow.

And so, after all, blood is thicker than water. We were fellow-countrymen and strangers in a strange land. I had warmed to his battered old hat at sight of it, and he was as solicitous for my welfare as if we were blood brothers. We swapped all manner of useful information concerning the country and the ways of its people, methods by which to obtain food and shelter and what not, and we parted genuinely sorry at having to say good-by.

One thing particularly conspicuous in this crowd was the shortness of stature. I, who am but of medium height, looked over the heads of nine out of ten. The natives were all short, as were the foreign sailors. There were only five or six in the crowd who could be called fairly tall, and they were Scandinavians and Americans. The tallest man there, however, was an exception. He was an Englishman, though not a Londoner. "Candidate for the Life Guards," I remarked to him. "You've hit it, mate," was his reply; "I've served my bit in that same, and the way things are I'll be back at it before long."

For an hour we stood quietly in this packed courtyard. Then the men began to grow restless. There was pushing and shoving forward, and a mild hubbub of voices. Nothing rough, however, or violent; merely the restlessness of weary and hungry men. At this juncture forth came the adjutant. I did not like him. His eyes were not good. There was nothing of the lowly Galilean about him, but a great deal of the centurion who said: "For I am a man in authority, having soldiers under me; and I say to this man, Go, and he goeth; and to another, Come, and he cometh; and to my servant, Do this, and he doeth it."

Well, he looked at us in just that way, and those nearest to him quailed. Then he lifted his voice.

"Stop this 'ere, now, or I'll turn you the other wy, an' march you out, an' you'll get no breakfast."

I cannot convey by printed speech the insufferable way in

which he said this, the self-consciousness of superiority, the brutal gluttony of power. He revelled in that he was a man in authority, able to say to half a thousand ragged wretches, "You may eat or go hungry, as I elect."

To deny us our breakfast after standing for hours! It was an awful threat, and the pitiful, abject silence which instantly fell attested its awfulness. And it was a cowardly threat, a foul blow, struck below the belt. We could not strike back, for we were starving; and it is the way of the world that when one man feeds another he is that man's master. But the centurion—I mean the adjutant—was not satisfied. In the dead silence he raised his voice again, and repeated the threat, and amplified it, and glared ferociously.

At last we were permitted to enter the feasting hall, where we found the 'ticket men' washed but unfed. All told, there must have been nearly seven hundred of us who sat down— not to meat or bread, but to speech, song, and prayer. From all of which I am convinced that Tantalus suffers in many guises this side of the infernal regions. The adjutant made the prayer, but I did not take note of it, being too engrossed with the massed picture of misery before me. But the speech ran something like this: "You will feast in paradise. No matter how you starve and suffer here, you will feast in paradise, that is, if you will follow the directions." And so forth and so forth. A clever bit of propaganda, I took it, but rendered of no avail for two reasons. First, the men who received it were unimaginative and materialistic, unaware of the existence of any Unseen, and too inured to hell on earth to be frightened by hell to come. And second, weary and exhausted from the night's sleeplessness and hardship, suffering from the long wait upon their feet, and faint from hunger, they were yearning, not for salvation, but for grub. The 'soul-snatchers' (as these men call all religious propagandists) should study the physiological basis of psychology a little, if they wish to make their efforts more effective.

All in good time, about eleven o'clock, breakfast arrived. It arrived, not on plates, but in paper parcels. I did not have all I wanted, and I am sure that no man there had all he wanted, or half of what he wanted or needed. I gave part of my bread to the tramp royal who was waiting for Buffalo Bill, and he was as ravenous at the end as he was in the beginning. This is the breakfast: two slices of bread, one small piece of bread with raisins in it and called 'cake,' a wafer of cheese, and a mug of 'water bewitched.' Numbers of the men had been waiting since five o'clock for it, while all of us had waited at least four hours; and in addition, we had been herded like swine, packed like sardines, and treated like curs, and been preached at, and sung to, and prayed for. Nor was that all.

No sooner was breakfast over (and it was over almost as quickly as it takes to tell) than the tired heads began to nod and droop, and in five minutes half of us were sound asleep. There were no signs of our being dismissed, while there were unmistakable signs of preparation for a meeting. I looked at a small clock hanging on the wall. It indicated twenty-five minutes to twelve. Heigh ho, thought I, time is flying, and I have yet to look for work.

"I want to go," I said to a couple of waking men near me.

"Got ter sty fer the service," was the answer.

"Do you want to stay?" I asked.

They shook their heads.

"Then let us go up and tell them we want to get out," I continued. "Come on."

But the poor creatures were aghast. So I left them to their fate, and went up to the nearest Salvation Army man.

"I want to go," I said. "I came here for breakfast in order that I might be in shape to look for work. I didn't think it would take so long to get breakfast. I think I have a chance for work in Stepney, and the sooner I start, the better chance I'll have of getting it."

He was really a good fellow, though he was startled by my request. "Why," he said, "we're goin' to 'old services, and you'd better sty."

"But that will spoil my chances for work," I urged. "And work is the most important thing for me just now."

As he was only a private, he referred me to the adjutant, and to the adjutant I repeated my reasons for wishing to go, and politely requested that he let me go.

"But it cawn't be done," he said, waxing virtuously indignant at such ingratitude. "The idea!" he snorted. "The idea!"

"Do you mean to say that I can't get out of here?" I demanded. "That you will keep me here against my will?"

"Yes," he snorted.

I do not know what might have happened, for I was waxing indignant myself; but the 'congregation' had 'piped' the situation, and he drew me over to a corner of the room, and then into another room. Here he again demanded my reasons for wishing to go.

"I want to go," I said, "because I wish to look for work over in Stepney, and every hour lessens my chance of finding work. It is now twenty-five minutes to twelve. I did not think when I came in that it would take so long to get a breakfast."

"You 'ave business, eh?" he sneered. "A man of business you are, eh? Then wot did you come 'ere for?"

"I was out all night, and I needed a breakfast in order to strengthen me to find work. That is why I came here."

"A nice thing to do," he went on, in the same sneering manner. "A man with business shouldn't come 'ere. You've tyken some poor man's breakfast 'ere this morning, that's wot you've done."

Which was a lie, for every mother's son of us had come in.

Now I submit, was this Christian-like, or even honest?— after I had plainly stated that I was homeless and hungry, and that I wished to look for work, for him to call my looking for work 'business,' to call me therefore a business man, and to draw the corollary that a man of business, and well off, did not require a charity breakfast, and that by taking a charity breakfast I had robbed some hungry waif who was not a man of business.

I kept my temper, but I went over the facts again and clearly and concisely demonstrated to him how unjust he was and how he had perverted the facts. As I manifested no signs of backing down (and I am sure my eyes were beginning to snap), he led me to the rear of the building, where, in an open court, stood a tent. In the same sneering tone he informed a couple of privates standing there that "'ere is a fellow that 'as business an' 'e wants to go before services."

They were duly shocked, of course, and they looked unutterable horror while he went into the tent and brought out the major. Still in the same sneering manner, laying particular stress on the 'business,' he brought my case before the commanding officer. The major was of a different stamp of man. I liked him as soon as I saw him, and to him I stated my case in the same fashion as before.

"Didn't you know you had to stay for services?" he asked.

"Certainly not," I answered, "or I should have gone without my breakfast. You have no placards posted to that effect, nor was I so informed when I entered the place."

He mediated a moment. "You can go," he said.

It was twelve o'clock when I gained the street, and I couldn't quite make up my mind whether I had been in the army or in prison. The day was half gone, and it was a far fetch to Stepney. And besides, it was Sunday, and why should even a starving man look for work on Sunday? Furthermore, it was my judgment that I had done a hard night's work walking the streets, and a hard day's work getting my breakfast; so I disconnected myself from my working hypothesis of a starving young man in search of employment, hailed a bus, and climbed aboard.

After a shave and a bath, with my clothes all off, I got in between clean white sheets and went to sleep. It was six in the evening when I closed my eyes. When they opened again, the clocks were striking nine next morning. I had slept fifteen straight hours. And as I lay there drowsily, my mind went back to the seven hundred unfortunates I had left waiting for services. No bath, no shave for them, no clean white sheets and all clothes off, and fifteen hours straight sleep. Services over, it was the weary streets again, the problem of a crust of bread ere night, and the long sleepless night in the streets, and the pondering of the problem of how to obtain a crust at dawn.

XII

Coronation Day

O thou that sea-walls sever
From lands unwalled by seas!
Wilt thou endure forever,
O Milton's England, these?
Thou that wast his Republic,
Wilt thou clasp their knees?
These royalties rust-eaten,
These worm-corroded lies
That keep thy head storm-beaten,
And sun-like strength of eyes
From the open air and heaven
Of intercepted skies!

—SWINBURNE

VIVAT Rex Eduardus! They crowned a king this day, and there has been great rejoicing and elaborate tomfoolery, and I am perplexed and saddened. I never saw anything to compare with the pageant, except Yankee circuses and Alhambra ballets; nor did I ever see anything so hopeless and so tragic.

To have enjoyed the Coronation procession, I should have come straight from America to the Hotel Cecil, and straight from the Hotel Cecil to a five-guinea seat among the washed. My mistake was in coming from the unwashed of the East End. There were not many who came from that quarter. The East End, as a whole, remained in the East End and got drunk. The Socialists, Democrats, and Republicans went off to the country for a breath of fresh air, quite unaffected by the fact that forty millions of people were taking to themselves a crowned and anointed ruler. Six thousand five hundred prelates, priests, statesmen, princes, and warriors beheld the crowning and anointing and the rest of us the pageant as it passed.

I saw it at Trafalgar Square, 'the most splendid site in Europe,' and the very uttermost heart of the empire. There were many thousands of us, all checked and held in order by a

superb display of armed power. The line of march was dou-
ble-walled with soldiers. The base of the Nelson Column was
triple-fringed with blue-jackets. Eastward, at the entrance to
the square, stood the Royal Marine Artillery. In the triangle
of Pall Mall and Cockspur, the statue of George III was buttressed on either side by the Lancers and Hussars. To the
west were the red coats of the Royal Marines, and from the
Union Club to the embouchure of Whitehall swept the glittering, massive curve of the 1st Life Guards—gigantic men
mounted on gigantic chargers, steel-breastplated, steel-hel-
meted, steel-caparisoned, a great war-sword of steel ready to
the hand of the powers that be. And further, throughout the
crowd, were flung long lines of the Metropolitan Constabulary, while in the rear were the reserves—tall, well-fed men,
with weapons to wield and muscles to wield them in case of
need.

And as it was thus at Trafalgar Square, so was it along the
whole line of march—force, overpowering force; myriads of
men, splendid men, the pick of the people, whose sole function in life is blindly to obey, and blindly to kill and destroy
and stamp out life. And that they should be well fed, well
clothed, and well armed, and have ships to hurl them to the
ends of the earth, the East End of London, and the 'East End'
of all England, toils and rots and dies.

There is a Chinese proverb that if one man lives in laziness
another will die of hunger; and Montesquieu has said, "The
fact that many men are occupied in making clothes for one
individual is the cause of there being many people without
clothes." So one explains the other. We cannot understand
the starved and runty toiler of the East End (living with
his family in a one-room den, and letting out the floor
space for lodgings to other starved and runty toilers) till
we look at the strapping Life Guardsmen of the West End,
and come to know that the one must feed and clothe and
groom the other.

And while in Westminster Abbey the people were taking
unto themselves a king, I, jammed between the Life Guards
and Constabulary of Trafalgar Square, was dwelling upon the
time when the people of Israel first took unto themselves a
king. You all know how it runs. The elders came to the

Prophet Samuel, and said: "Make us a king to judge us like all the nations."

And the Lord said unto Samuel: Now therefore hearken unto their voice; howbeit thou shalt show them the manner of the king that shall reign over them.

And Samuel told all the words of the Lord unto the people that asked of him a king, and he said:

This will be the manner of the king that shall reign over you; he will take your sons, and appoint them unto him, for his chariots, and to be his horsemen, and they shall run before his chariots.

And he will appoint them unto him for captains of thousands, and captains of fifties; and he will set some to plough his ground, and to reap his harvest, and to make his instruments of war, and the instruments of his chariots.

And he will take your daughters to be confectionaries, and to be cooks, and to be bakers.

And he will take your fields, and your vineyards, and your oliveyards, even the best of them, and give them to his servants.

And he will take a tenth of your seed, and of your vineyards, and give to his officers, and to his servants.

And he will take your menservants, and your maidservants, and your goodliest young men, and your asses, and put them to his work.

He will take a tenth of your flocks; and ye shall be his servants.

And ye shall call out in that day because of your king which ye shall have chosen you; and the Lord will not answer you in that day.

All of which came to pass in that ancient day, and they did cry out to Samuel, saying: "Pray for thy servants unto the Lord thy God, that we die not; for we have added unto all our sins this evil, to ask us a king." And after Saul and David came Solomon, who "answered the people roughly, saying: My father made your yoke heavy, but I will add to your yoke; my father chastised you with whips, but I will chastise you with scorpions."

And in these latter days, five hundred hereditary peers own

one-fifth of England; and they, and the officers and servants under the King, and those who go to compose the powers that be, yearly spend in wasteful luxury $1,850,000,000, which is thirty-two per cent of the total wealth produced by all the toilers of the country.

At the Abbey, clad in wonderful golden raiment, amid fanfare of trumpets and throbbing of music, surrounded by a brilliant throng of masters, lords, and rulers, the King was being invested with the insignia of his sovereignty. The spurs were placed to his heels by the Lord Great Chamberlain, and a sword of state, in purple scabbard, was presented him by the Archbishop of Canterbury, with these words:—

> Receive this kingly sword brought now from the altar of God, and delivered to you by the hands of the bishops and servants of God, though unworthy.

Whereupon, being girded, he gave heed to the Archbishop's exhortation:—

> With this sword do justice, stop the growth of iniquity, protect the Holy Church of God, help and defend widows and orphans, restore the things that are gone to decay, maintain the things that are restored, punish and reform what is amiss, and confirm what is in good order.

But hark! There is cheering down Whitehall; the crowd sways, the double walls of soldiers come to attention, and into view swing the King's watermen, in fantastic mediæval garbs of red, for all the world like the van of a circus parade. Then a royal carriage, filled with ladies and gentlemen of the household, with powdered footmen and coachmen most gorgeously arrayed. More carriages, lords, and chamberlains, viscounts, mistresses of the robes—lackeys all. Then the warriors, a kingly escort, generals, bronzed and worn, from the ends of the earth come up to London Town; volunteer officers, officers of the militia and regular forces; Spens and Plumer, Broadwood and Cooper who relieved Ookiep, Malthias of Dargai, Dixon of Vlakfontein; General Gaselee and Admiral Seymour of China; Kitchener of Khartoum; Lord Roberts of India and all the world—the fighting men of England, masters of destruction, engineers of death! Another race of men from those of the shops and slums, a totally different race of men.

But here they come, in all the pomp and certitude of power, and still they come, these men of steel, these war lords and world harnessers. Pell-mell, peers and commoners, princes and maharajahs, Equerries to the King and Yeomen of the Guard. And here the colonials, lithe and hardy men; and here all the breeds of all the world—soldiers from Canada, Australia, New Zealand; from Bermuda, Borneo, Fiji, and the Gold Coast; from Rhodesia, Cape Colony, Natal, Sierra Leone and Gambia, Nigeria, and Uganda; from Ceylon, Cyprus, Hong-Kong, Jamaica, and Wei-Hai-Wei; from Lagos, Malta, St. Lucia, Singapore, Straits Settlements, Trinidad. And here the conquered men of Ind, swarthy horsemen and sword wielders, fiercely barbaric, blazing in crimson and scarlet, Sikhs, Rajputs, Burmese, province by province, and caste by caste.

And now the Horse Guards, a glimpse of beautiful cream ponies, and a golden panoply, a hurricane of cheers, the crashing of bands—"The King! the King! God save the King!" Everybody has gone mad. The contagion is sweeping me off my feet. I, too, want to shout, "The King! God save the King!" Ragged men about me, tears in their eyes, are tossing up their hats and crying ecstatically, "Bless 'em! Bless 'em! Bless 'em!" See, there he is, in that wondrous golden coach, the great crown flashing on his head, the woman in white beside him likewise crowned.

And I check myself with a rush, striving to convince myself that it is all real and rational, and not some glimpse of fairyland. This I cannot succeed in doing, and it is better so. I much prefer to believe that all this pomp, and vanity, and show, and mumbo-jumbo foolery has come from fairyland, than to believe it the performance of sane and sensible people who have mastered matter, and solved the secrets of the stars.

Princes and princelings, dukes, duchesses, and all manner of coroneted folk of the royal train are flashing past; more warriors, and lackeys, and conquered peoples, and the pageant is over. I drift with the crowd out of the square into a tangle of narrow streets, where the public houses are a-roar with drunkenness, men, women, and children mixed together

in colossal debauch. And on every side is rising the favorite
song of the Coronation:—

Oh! on Coronation Day, on Coronation Day,
We'll have a spree, a jubilee, and shout, Hip, hip, hooray,
For we'll all be merry, drinking whiskey, wine, and sherry,
We'll be merry on Coronation Day.

The rain is pouring down in torrents. Up the street come
troops of the auxiliaries, black Africans and yellow Asiatics,
beturbaned and befezed, and coolies swinging along with machine guns and mountain batteries on their heads, and the
bare feet of all, in quick rhythm, going *slish*, *slish*, *slish*
through the pavement mud. The public houses empty by
magic, and the swarthy allegiants are cheered by their British
brothers, who return at once to the carouse.

"And how did you like the procession, mate?" I asked an
old man on a bench in Green Park.

" 'Ow did I like it? A bloody good chawnce, sez I to myself, for a sleep, wi' all the coppers aw'y, so I turned into the
corner there, along wi' fifty others. But I couldn't sleep, a-
lyin' there 'ungry an' thinkin' 'ow I'd worked all the years o'
my life an' now 'ad no plyce to rest my 'ead; an' the music
comin' to me, an' the cheers an' cannon, till I got almost a
hanarchist an' wanted to blow out the brains o' the Lord
Chamberlain."

Why the Lord Chamberlain, I could not precisely see, nor
could he, but that was the way he felt, he said conclusively,
and there was no more discussion.

As night drew on, the city became a blaze of light.
Splashes of color, green, amber, and ruby, caught the eye
at every point, and "E. R.," in great cut-crystal letters and
backed by flaming gas, was everywhere. The crowds in the
streets increased by hundreds of thousands, and though the
police sternly put down mafficking, drunkenness and rough
play abounded. The tired workers seemed to have gone
mad with the relaxation and excitement, and they surged
and danced down the streets, men and women, old and
young, with linked arms and in long rows, singing, "I may
be crazy, but I love you," "Dolly Gray," and "The Honey-

suckle and the Bee,"—the last rendered something like
this:—

> Yew aw the enny, ennyseckle, Oi em ther bee,
> Oi'd like ter sip ther enny from those red lips, yew see.

I sat on a bench on the Thames Embankment, looking
across the illuminated water. It was approaching midnight,
and before me poured the better class of merrymakers, shun-
ning the more riotous streets and returning home. On the
bench beside me sat two ragged creatures, a man and a
woman, nodding and dozing. The woman sat with her arms
clasped across the breast, holding tightly, her body in constant play,—now dropping forward till it seemed its balance
would be overcome and she would fall to the pavement; now
inclining to the left, sideways, till her head rested on the
man's shoulder; and now to the right, stretched and strained,
till the pain of it awoke her and she sat bolt upright. Whereupon the dropping forward would begin again and go
through its cycle till she was aroused by the strain and stretch.

Every little while, boys and young men stopped long
enough to go behind the bench and give vent to sudden and
fiendish shouts. This always jerked the man and woman
abruptly from their sleep; and at sight of the startled woe
upon their faces the crowd would roar with laughter as it
flooded past.

This was the most striking thing, the general heartlessness
exhibited on every hand. It is a commonplace, the homeless
on the benches, the poor miserable folk who may be teased
and are harmless. Fifty thousand people must have passed the
bench while I sat upon it, and not one, on such a jubilee
occasion as the crowning of the King, felt his heart-strings
touched sufficiently to come up and say to the woman:
"Here's sixpence; go and get a bed." But the women, especially the young women, made witty remarks upon the
woman nodding, and invariably set their companions laughing.

To use a Briticism, it was 'cruel'; the corresponding Americanism was more appropriate—it was 'fierce.' I confess I began to grow incensed at this happy crowd streaming by, and

to extract a sort of satisfaction from the London statistics which demonstrate that one in every four adults is destined to die on public charity, either· in the workhouse, the infirmary, or the asylum.

I talked with the man. He was fifty-four and a broken-down docker. He could only find odd work when there was a large demand for labor, for the younger and stronger men were preferred when times were slack. He had spent a week, now, on the benches of the Embankment; but things looked brighter for next week, and he might possibly get in a few days' work and have a bed in some doss-house. He had lived all his life in London, save for five years, when, in 1878, he saw foreign service in India.

Of course he would eat; so would the girl. Days like this were uncommon hard on such as they, though the coppers were so busy poor folk could get in more sleep. I awoke the girl, or woman rather, for she was "Eyght an' twenty, sir"; and we started for a coffee-house.

"Wot a lot o' work, puttin' up the lights," said the man at sight of some building superbly illuminated. This was the keynote of his being. All his life he had worked, and the whole objective universe, as well as his own soul, he could express in terms only of work. "Coronations is some good," he went on. "They give work to men."

"But your belly is empty," I said.

"Yes," he answered. "I tried, but there wasn't any chawnce. My age is against me. Wot do you work at? Seafarin' chap, eh? I knew it from yer clothes."

"I know wot you are," said the girl, "an Eyetalian."

"No 'e ayn't," the man cried heatedly. "'E's a Yank, that's wot 'e is. I know."

"Lord lumme, look a' that," she exclaimed as we debouched upon the Strand, choked with the roaring, reeling Coronation crowd, the men bellowing and the girls singing in high throaty notes: —

Oh! on Coronation D'y, on Coronation D'y,
We'll 'ave a spree, a jubilee, an' shout 'Ip, 'ip, 'ooray.
For we'll all be merry, drinkin' whiskey, wine, and sherry,
We'll be merry on Coronation D'y.

"'Ow dirty I am, bein' around the w'y I 'ave," the woman said, as she sat down in a coffee-house, wiping the sleep and grime from the corners of her eyes. "An' the sights I 'ave seen this d'y, an' I enjoyed it, though it was lonesome by myself. An' the duchesses an' the lydies 'ad sich gran' w'ite dresses. They was jest bu'ful, bu'ful."

"I'm Irish," she said, in answer to a question. "My nyme's Eyethorne."

"What?" I asked.

"Eyethorne, sir; Eyethorne."

"Spell it."

"H-a-y-t-h-o-r-n-e, Eyethorne."

"Oh," I said, "Irish Cockney."

"Yes, sir, London-born."

She had lived happily at home till her father died, killed in accident, when she had found herself on the world. One brother was in the army, and the other brother, engaged in keeping a wife and eight children on twenty shillings a week and unsteady employment, could do nothing for her. She had been out of London once in her life, to a place in Essex, twelve miles away, where she had picked fruit for three weeks—"An' I was as brown as a berry w'en I come back. You won't b'lieve it, but I was."

The last place in which she had worked was a coffee-house, hours from seven in the morning till eleven at night, and for which she had received five shillings a week and her food. Then she had fallen sick, and since emerging from the hospital had been unable to find anything to do. She wasn't feeling up to much, and the last two nights had been spent in the street.

Between them they stowed away a prodigious amount of food, this man and woman, and it was not till I had duplicated and triplicated their original orders that they showed signs of easing down.

Once she reached across and felt the texture of my coat and shirt, and remarked upon the good clothes the Yanks wore. My rags good clothes! It put me to the blush; but, on inspecting them more closely and on examining the clothes worn by the man and woman, I began to feel quite well-dressed and respectable.

"What do you expect to do in the end?" I asked them. "You know you're growing older every day."

"Work'ouse," said he.

"Gawd blimey if I do," said she. "There's no 'ope for me, I know, but I'll die on the streets. No work'ouse for me, thank you."

"No, indeed," she sniffed in the silence that fell.

"After you have been out all night in the streets," I asked, "what do you do in the morning for something to eat?"

"Try to get a penny, if you 'aven't one saved over," the man explained. "Then go to a coffee-'ouse an' get a mug o' tea."

"But I don't see how that is to feed you," I objected.

The pair smiled knowingly.

"You drink your tea in little sips," he went on, "making it last its longest. An' you look sharp, an' there's some as leaves a bit be'ind 'em."

"It's s'prisin', the food wot some people leaves," the woman broke in.

"The thing," said the man judicially, as the trick dawned upon me, "is to get 'old o' the penny."

As we started to leave, Miss Haythorne gathered up a couple of crusts from the neighboring tables and thrust them somewhere into her rags.

"Cawn't wyste 'em, you know," said she, to which the docker nodded, tucking away a couple of crusts himself.

At three in the morning I strolled up the Embankment. It was a gala night for the homeless, for the police were elsewhere; and each bench was jammed with sleeping occupants. There were as many women as men, and the great majority of them, male and female, were old. Occasionally a boy was to be seen. On one bench I noticed a family, a man sitting upright with a sleeping babe in his arms, his wife asleep, her head on his shoulder, and in her lap the head of a sleeping youngster. The man's eyes were wide open. He was staring out over the water and thinking, which is not a good thing for a shelterless man with a family to do. It would not be a pleasant thing to speculate upon his thoughts; but this I know, and all London knows, that the cases of out-of-works killing their wives and babies is not an uncommon happening.

One cannot walk along the Thames Embankment, in the small hours of morning, from the Houses of Parliament, past Cleopatra's Needle, to Waterloo Bridge, without being reminded of the sufferings, seven and twenty centuries old, recited by the author of 'Job': —

> There are that remove the landmarks; they violently take away flocks and feed them.
>
> They drive away the ass of the fatherless, they take the widow's ox for a pledge.
>
> They turn the needy out of the way; the poor of the earth hide themselves together.
>
> Behold, as wild asses in the desert they go forth to their work, seeking diligently for meat; the wilderness yieldeth them food for their children.
>
> They cut their provender in the field, and they glean the vintage of the wicked.
>
> They lie all night naked without clothing, and have no covering in the cold.
>
> They are wet with the showers of the mountains, and embrace the rock for want of a shelter.
>
> There are that pluck the fatherless from the breast, and take a pledge of the poor.
>
> So that they go about naked without clothing, and being an hungered they carry the sheaves.—Job xxiv. 2–10.

Seven and twenty centuries agone! And it is all as true and apposite to-day in the innermost centre of this Christian civilization whereof Edward VII is king.

XIII

Dan Cullen, Docker

Life scarce can tread majestically
Foul court and fever-stricken alley.
—THOMAS ASHE

I STOOD, yesterday, in a room in one of the 'Municipal Dwellings,' not far from Leman Street. If I looked into a dreary future and saw that I would have to live in such a room until I died, I should immediately go down, plump into the Thames, and cut the tenancy short.

It was not a room. Courtesy to the language will no more permit it to be called a room than it will permit a hovel to be called a mansion. It was a den, a lair. Seven feet by eight were its dimensions, and the ceiling was so low as not to give the cubic air space required by a British soldier in barracks. A crazy couch, with ragged coverlets, occupied nearly half the room. A rickety table, a chair, and a couple of boxes left little space in which to turn around. Five dollars would have purchased everything in sight. The floor was bare, while the walls and ceiling were literally covered with blood marks and splotches. Each mark represented a violent death—of a bedbug, with which vermin the building swarmed, a plague with which no person could cope single-handed.

The man who had occupied this hole, one Dan Cullen, docker, was dying in hospital. Yet he had impressed his personality on his miserable surroundings sufficiently to give an inkling as to what sort of a man he was. On the walls were cheap pictures of Garibaldi, Engels, Dan Burns, and other labor leaders, while on the table lay one of Walter Besant's novels. He knew his Shakespeare, I was told, and had read history, sociology, and economics. And he was self-educated.

On the table, amidst a wonderful disarray, lay a sheet of paper on which was scrawled: *Mr. Cullen, please return the large white jug and corkscrew I lent you,*—articles loaned, during the first stages of his sickness, by a woman neighbor, and demanded back in anticipation of his death. A large white jug and a corkscrew are far too valuable to a creature of the Abyss to permit another creature to die in peace. To the last, Dan Cullen's soul must be harrowed by the sordidness out of which it strove vainly to rise.

It is a brief little story, the story of Dan Cullen, but there is much to read between the lines. He was born lowly in a city and land where the lines of caste are tightly drawn. All his days he toiled hard with his body; and because he had opened the books, and been caught up by the fires of the spirit, and could 'write a letter like a lawyer,' he had been selected by his fellows to toil hard for them with his brain. He became a leader of the fruit-porters, represented the dockers on the London Trades Council, and wrote trenchant articles for the labor journals.

He did not cringe to other men, even though they were his economic masters and controlled the means whereby he lived, and he spoke his mind freely, and fought the good fight. In the 'Great Dock Strike' he was guilty of taking a leading part. And that was the end of Dan Cullen. From that day he was a marked man, and every day, for ten years and more, he was 'paid off' for what he had done.

A docker is a casual laborer. Work ebbs and flows, and he works or does not work according to the amount of goods on hand to be moved. Dan Cullen was discriminated against. While he was not absolutely turned away (which would have caused trouble, and which would certainly have been more merciful), he was called in by the foreman to do not more than two or three days' work per week. This is what is called being 'disciplined,' or 'drilled.' It means being starved. There is no politer word. Ten years of it broke his heart, and broken-hearted men cannot live.

He took to his bed in his terrible den, which grew more terrible with his helplessness. He was without kith or kin, a lonely old man, embittered and pessimistic, fighting vermin the while and looking at Garibaldi, Engels, and Dan Burns gazing down at him from the blood-bespattered walls. No one came to see him in that crowded municipal barracks (he had made friends with none of them), and he was left to rot.

But from the far-reaches of the East End came a cobbler and his son, his sole friends. They cleansed his room, brought fresh linen from home, and took from off his limbs the sheets, grayish-black with dirt. And they brought to him one of the Queen's Bounty nurses from Aldgate.

She washed his face, shook up his couch, and talked with him. It was interesting to talk with him—until he learned her name. Oh, yes, Blank was her name, she replied innocently, and Sir George Blank was her brother. Sir George Blank, eh? thundered old Dan Cullen on his death-bed; Sir George Blank, solicitor to the docks at Cardiff, who, more than any other man, had broken up the Docker's Union of Cardiff, and was knighted? And she was his sister? Thereupon Dan Cullen sat up on his crazy couch and pronounced anathema upon her and all her breed; and she fled, to return no more, strongly impressed with the ungratefulness of the poor.

Dan Cullen's feet became swollen with dropsy. He sat up all day on the side of the bed (to keep the water out of his body), no mat on the floor, a thin blanket on his legs, and an old coat around his shoulders. A missionary brought him a pair of paper slippers, worth fourpence (I saw them), and proceeded to offer up fifty prayers or so for the good of Dan Cullen's soul. But Dan Cullen was the sort of a man that wanted his soul left alone. He did not care to have Tom, Dick, or Harry, on the strength of fourpenny slippers, tampering with it. He asked the missionary kindly to open the window, so that he might toss the slippers out. And the missionary went away, to return no more, likewise impressed with the ungratefulness of the poor.

The cobbler, a brave old hero himself, though unannaled and unsung, went privily to the head office of the big fruit brokers for whom Dan Cullen had worked as a casual laborer for thirty years. Their system was such that the work was almost entirely done by casual hands. The cobbler told them the man's desperate plight, old, broken, dying, without help or money, reminded them that he had worked for them thirty years, and asked them to do something for him.

"Oh," said the manager, remembering Dan Cullen without having to refer to the books, "you see, we make it a rule never to help casuals, and we can do nothing."

Nor did they do anything, not even sign a letter asking for Dan Cullen's admission to a hospital. And it is not so easy to get into a hospital in London Town. At Hampstead, if he passed the doctors, at least four months would elapse before he could get in, there were so many on the books ahead of him. The cobbler finally got him into the Whitechapel Infirmary, where he visited him frequently. Here he found that Dan Cullen had succumbed to the prevalent feeling, that, being hopeless, they were hurrying him out of the way. A fair and logical conclusion, one must agree, for an old and broken man to arrive at, who has been resolutely 'disciplined' and 'drilled' for ten years. When they sweated him for Bright's disease to remove the fat from the kidneys, Dan Cullen contended that the sweating was hastening his death; while Bright's disease, being a wasting away of the kidneys, there was therefore no fat to remove and the doctor's excuse was a palpable lie. Whereupon the doctor became wroth, and did not come near him for nine days.

Then his bed was tilted up so that his feet and legs were elevated. At once dropsy appeared in the body, and Dan Cullen contended that the thing was done in order to run the water down into his body from his legs and kill him more quickly. He demanded his discharge, though they told him he would die on the stairs, and dragged himself more dead than alive to the cobbler's shop. At the moment of writing this, he is dying at the Temperance Hospital, into which place his stanch friend, the cobbler, moved heaven and earth to have him admitted.

Poor Dan Cullen! A Jude the Obscure, who reached out after knowledge; who toiled with his body in the day and studied in the watches of the night; who dreamed his dream and struck valiantly for the Cause; a patriot, a lover of human freedom, and a fighter unafraid; and in the end, not gigantic enough to beat down the conditions which baffled and stifled him, a cynic and a pessimist, gasping his final agony on a pauper's couch in a charity ward.—"For a man to have died who might have been wise and was not, this I call a tragedy."

XIV

Hops and Hoppers

Ill fares the land, to hastening ills a prey,
Where wealth accumulates and men decay:
Princes and lords may flourish, or may fade,
A breath can make them, as a breath is made;
But a bold peasantry, their country's pride,
When once destroyed, can never be supplied.
— GOLDSMITH

S O FAR has the divorcement of the worker from the soil proceeded, that the farming districts, the civilized world over, are dependent upon the cities for the gathering of the harvests. Then it is, when the land is spilling its ripe wealth to waste, that the street folk, who have been driven away from the soil, are called back to it again. But in England they return, not as prodigals, but as outcasts still, as vagrants and pariahs, to be doubted and flouted by their country brethren, to sleep in jails and casual wards, or under the hedges, and to live the Lord knows how.

It is estimated that Kent alone requires eighty thousand of the street people to pick her hops. And out they come, obedient to the call, which is the call of their bellies and of the lingering dregs of adventure-lust still in them. Slum, stews, and ghetto pour them forth, and the festering contents of slum, stews, and ghetto are undiminished. Yet they overrun the country like an army of ghouls, and the country does not want them. They are out of place. As they drag their squat, misshapen bodies along the highways and byways, they resemble some vile spawn from underground. Their very presence, the fact of their existence, is an outrage to the fresh bright sun and the green and growing things. The clean, upstanding trees cry shame upon them and their withered crookedness, and their rottenness is a slimy desecration of the sweetness and purity of nature.

Is the picture overdrawn? It all depends. For one who sees and thinks life in terms of shares and coupons, it is certainly overdrawn. But for one who sees and thinks life in terms of manhood and womanhood, it cannot be overdrawn. Such hordes of beastly wretchedness and inarticulate misery are no compensation for a millionnaire brewer who lives in a West End palace, sates himself with the sensuous delights of London's golden theatres, hobnobs with lordlings and princelings, and is knighted by the king. Wins his spurs—God forbid! In old time the great blonde beasts rode in the battle's van and won their spurs by cleaving men from pate to chine. And, after all, it is far finer to kill a strong man with a clean-slicing blow of singing steel than to make a beast of him, and of his seed through the generations, by the artful and spidery manipulation of industry and politics.

But to return to the hops. Here the divorcement from the soil is as apparent as in every other agricultural line in England. While the manufacture of beer steadily increases, the growth of hops steadily decreases. In 1835 the acreage under hops was 71,327. To-day it stands at 48,024, a decrease of 3103 from the acreage of last year.

Small as the acreage is this year, a poor summer and terrible storms reduced the yield. This misfortune is divided between the people who own hops and the people who pick hops. The owners perforce must put up with less of the nicer things of life, the pickers with less grub, of which, in the best of times, they never get enough. For weary weeks headlines like the following have appeared in the London papers:—

TRAMPS PLENTIFUL, BUT THE HOPS ARE FEW
AND NOT YET READY.

Then there have been numberless paragraphs like this:—

From the neighborhood of the hop fields comes news of a distressing nature. The bright outburst of the last two days has sent many hundreds of hoppers into Kent, who will have to wait till the fields are ready for them. At Dover the number of vagrants in the workhouse is treble the number there last year at this time, and in other towns the lateness of the season is responsible for a large increase in the number of casuals.

To cap their wretchedness, when at last the picking had begun, hops and hoppers were well-nigh swept away by a

frightful storm of wind, rain, and hail. The hops were
stripped clean from the poles and pounded into the earth,
while the hoppers, seeking shelter from the stinging hail,
were close to drowning in their huts and camps on the low-
lying ground. Their condition after the storm was pitiable,
their state of vagrancy more pronounced than ever; for, poor
crop that it was, its destruction had taken away the chance of
earning a few pennies, and nothing remained for thousands
of them but to 'pad the hoof' back to London.

"We ayn't crossin'-sweepers," they said, turning away from
the ground, carpeted ankle-deep with hops.

Those that remained grumbled savagely among the half-
stripped poles at the seven bushels for a shilling—a rate paid
in good seasons when the hops are in prime condition, and a
rate likewise paid in bad seasons by the growers because they
cannot afford more.

I passed through Teston and East and West Farleigh
shortly after the storm, and listened to the grumbling of the
hoppers and saw the hops rotting on the ground. At the
hothouses of Barham Court, thirty thousand panes of glass
had been broken by the hail, while peaches, plums, pears, ap-
ples, rhubarb, cabbages, mangolds,—everything, had been
pounded to pieces and torn to shreds.

All of which was too bad for the owners, certainly; but at
the worst, not one of them, for one meal, would have to go
short of food or drink. Yet it was to them that the newspapers
devoted columns of sympathy, their pecuniary losses being
detailed at harrowing length. "Mr. Herbert Leney calculates
his loss at £8000;" "Mr. Fremlin, of brewery fame, who rents
all the land in this parish, loses £10,000;" and "Mr. Leney,
the Wateringbury brewer, brother to Mr. Herbert Leney, is
another heavy loser." As for the hoppers, they did not count.
Yet I venture to assert that the several almost square meals
lost by underfed William Buggles, and underfed Mrs. Buggles, and the underfed Buggles kiddies, was a greater tragedy
than the £10,000 lost by Mr. Fremlin. And in addition, underfed William Buggles' tragedy might be multiplied by thousands where Mr. Fremlin's could not be multiplied by five.

To see how William Buggles and his kind fared, I donned
my seafaring togs and started out to get a job. With me was

a young East London cobbler, Bert, who had yielded to the lure of adventure and joined me for the trip. Acting on my advice, he had brought his 'worst rags,' and as we hiked up the London Road out of Maidstone he was worrying greatly for fear we had come too ill-dressed for the business.

Nor was he to be blamed. When we stopped in a tavern the publican eyed us gingerly, nor did his demeanor brighten till we flashed the color of our cash. The natives along the road were all dubious; and 'bean-feasters' from London, dashing past in coaches, cheered and jeered and shouted insulting things after us. But before we were done with the Maidstone district my friend found that we were as well clad, if not better, than the average hopper. Some of the bunches of rags we chanced upon were marvellous.

"The tide is out," called a gypsy-looking woman to her mates, as we came up a long row of bins into which the pickers were stripping the hops.

"Do you twig?" Bert whispered. "She's on to you."

I twigged. And it must be confessed the figure was an apt one. When the tide is out boats are left on the beach and do not sail, and a sailor, when the tide is out, does not sail either. My seafaring togs and my presence in the hop field proclaimed that I was a seaman without a ship, a man on the beach, and very like a craft at low water.

"Can yer give us a job, governor?" Bert asked the bailiff, a kindly faced and elderly man who was very busy.

His "No," was decisively uttered; but Bert clung on and followed him about, and I followed after, pretty well all over the field. Whether our persistency struck the bailiff as anxiety to work, or whether he was affected by our hard-luck appearance and tale, neither Bert nor I succeeded in making out; but in the end he softened his heart and found us the one unoccupied bin in the place—a bin deserted by two other men, from what I could learn, because of inability to make living wages.

"No bad conduct, mind ye," warned the bailiff, as he left us at work in the midst of the women.

It was Saturday afternoon, and we knew quitting time would come early; so we applied ourselves earnestly to the task, desiring to learn if we could at least make our salt. It was simple work, woman's work, in fact, and not man's. We sat on the edge of the bin, between the standing hops, while a pole-puller supplied us with great fragrant branches. In an hour's time we became as expert as it is possible to become. As soon as the fingers became accustomed automatically to differentiate between hops and leaves and to strip half a dozen blossoms at a time there was no more to learn.

We worked nimbly, and as fast as the women themselves, though their bins filled more rapidly because of their swarming children each of which picked with two hands almost as fast as we picked.

"Don'tcher pick too clean, it's against the rules," one of the women informed us; and we took the tip and were grateful.

As the afternoon wore along, we realized that living wages could not be made—by men. Women could pick as much as men, and children could do almost as well as women; so it was impossible for a man to compete with a woman and half a dozen children. For it is the woman and the half-dozen children who count as a unit and by their combined capacity determine the unit's pay.

"I say, matey, I'm beastly hungry," said I to Bert. We had not had any dinner.

"Blimey, but I could eat the 'ops," he replied.

Whereupon we both lamented our negligence in not rearing up a numerous progeny to help us in this day of need. And in such fashion we whiled away the time and talked for the edification of our neighbors. We quite won the sympathy of the pole-puller, a young country yokel, who now and again emptied a few picked blossoms into our bin, it being part of his business to gather up the stray clusters torn off in the process of pulling.

With him we discussed how much we could 'sub,' and were informed that while we were being paid a shilling for seven bushels, we could only 'sub,' or have advanced to us, a shilling for every twelve bushels. Which is to say that the pay for five out of every twelve bushels was withheld—a method of the grower to hold the hopper to his work whether the crop runs good or bad, and especially if it runs bad.

After all, it was pleasant sitting there in the bright sunshine, the golden pollen showering from our hands, the pungent, aromatic odor of the hops biting our nostrils, and the while remembering dimly the sounding cities whence these people came. Poor street people! Poor gutter folk! Even they grow earth-hungry, and yearn vaguely for the soil from which they have been driven, and for the free life in the open, and the wind and rain and sun all undefiled by city smirches. As the sea calls to the sailor, so calls the land to them; and, deep down in their aborted and decaying carcasses, they are stirred strangely by the peasant memories of their forbears who lived before cities were. And in incomprehensible ways they are made glad by the earth smells and sights and sounds which their blood has not forgotten though unremembered by them.

"No more 'ops, matey," Bert complained.

It was five o'clock, and the pole-pullers had knocked off, so that everything could be cleaned up, there being no work on Sunday. For an hour we were forced idly to wait the coming of the measurers, our feet tingling with the frost which came on the heels of the setting sun. In the adjoining bin, two women and half a dozen children had picked nine bushels; so that the five bushels the measurers found in our bin demonstrated that we had done equally well, for the half-dozen children had ranged from nine to fourteen years of age.

Five bushels! We worked it out to eight pence ha'penny, or seventeen cents, for two men working three hours and a half. Eight and one-half cents apiece, a rate of two and three-sevenths cents per hour! But we were allowed only to 'sub' fivepence of the total sum, though the tally-keeper, short of change, gave us sixpence. Entreaty was in vain. A hard luck story could not move him. He proclaimed loudly that we had received a penny more than our due, and went his way.

Granting, for the sake of the argument, that we were what we represented ourselves to be, namely, poor men and broke, then here was our position: night was coming on; we had had no supper, much less dinner; and we possessed sixpence between us. I was hungry enough to eat three sixpenn'orths of food, and so was Bert. One thing was patent. By doing $16^2/_3$ per cent justice to our stomachs, we would expend the sixpence, and our stomachs would still be gnawing under $83^1/_3$ per cent injustice. Being broke again, we could sleep under a hedge, which was not so bad, though the cold would sap an undue portion of what we had eaten. But the morrow was Sunday, on which we could do no work, though our silly stomachs would not knock off on that account. Here, then, was the problem: how to get three meals on Sunday, and two on Monday (for we could not make another 'sub' till Monday evening). We knew that the casual wards were overcrowded; also, that if we begged from farmer or villager, there was a large likelihood of our going to jail for fourteen days. What was to be done? We looked at each other in despair—

—Not a bit of it. We joyfully thanked God that we were not as other men, especially hoppers, and went down the road to Maidstone, jingling in our pockets the half-crowns and florins we had brought from London.

XV
The Sea Wife

These stupid peasants, who, throughout the world, hold poten-
tates on their thrones, make statesmen illustrious, provide generals with lasting victories, all with ignorance, indifference, or
half-witted hatred, moving the world with the strength of their
arms, and getting their heads knocked together in the name of
God, the king, or the stock exchange—immortal, dreaming,
hopeless asses, who surrender their reason to the care of a shining puppet, and persuade some toy to carry their lives in his
purse.

—STEPHEN CRANE

Y OU might not expect to find the Sea Wife in the heart of
Kent, but that is where I found her, on a mean street, in
the poor quarter of Maidstone. In her window she had no
sign of lodgings to let, and persuasion was necessary before
she could bring herself to let me sleep in her front room. In
the evening I descended to the semi-subterranean kitchen,
and talked with her and her old man, Thomas Mugridge by
name.

And as I talked to them, all the subtleties and complexities
of this tremendous machine civilization vanished away. It
seemed that I went down through the skin and the flesh to
the naked soul of it, and in Thomas Mugridge and his old
woman gripped hold of the essence of this remarkable English breed. I found there the spirit of the wander-lust which
has lured Albion's sons across the zones; and I found there
the colossal unreckoning which has tricked the English into
foolish squabblings and preposterous fights, and the dogged-
ness and stubbornness which have brought them blindly
through to empire and greatness; and likewise I found that
vast, incomprehensible patience which has enabled the home
population to endure under the burden of it all, to toil without complaint through the weary years, and docilely to yield
the best of its sons to fight and colonize to the ends of the
earth.

Thomas Mugridge was seventy-one years old and a little

man. It was because he was little that he had not gone for a soldier. He had remained at home and worked. His first recollections were connected with work. He knew nothing else but work. He had worked all his days, and at seventy-one he still worked. Each morning saw him up with the lark and afield, a day laborer, for as such he had been born. Mrs. Mugridge was seventy-three. From seven years of age she had worked in the fields, doing a boy's work at first, and later, a man's. She still worked, keeping the house shining, washing, boiling, and baking, and, with my advent, cooking for me and shaming me by making my bed. At the end of threescore years and more of work they possessed nothing, had nothing to look forward to save more work. And they were contented. They expected nothing else, desired nothing else.

They lived simply. Their wants were few,—a pint of beer at the end of the day, sipped in the semi-subterranean kitchen, a weekly paper to pore over for seven nights hand-running, and conversation as meditative and vacant as the chewing of a heifer's cud. From a wood engraving on the wall a slender, angelic girl looked down upon them, and underneath was the legend: "Our Future Queen." And from a highly colored lithograph alongside looked down a stout and elderly lady, with underneath: "Our Queen—Diamond Jubilee."

"What you earn is sweetest," quoth Mrs. Mugridge, when I suggested that it was about time they took a rest.

"No, an' we don't want help," said Thomas Mugridge, in reply to my question as to whether the children lent them a hand.

"We'll work till we dry up and blow away, mother an' me," he added; and Mrs. Mugridge nodded her head in vigorous indorsement.

Fifteen children she had borne, and all were away and gone, or dead. The 'baby,' however, lived in Maidstone, and she was twenty-seven. When the children married they had their hands full with their own families and troubles, like their fathers and mothers before them.

Where were the children? Ah, where were they not? Lizzie was in Australia; Mary was in Buenos Ayres; Poll was in New York; Joe had died in India,—and so they called them up, the living and the dead, soldier and sailor, and colonist's wife, for the traveller's sake who sat in their kitchen.

They passed me a photograph. A trim young fellow in soldier's garb looked out at me.

"And which son is this?" I asked.

They laughed a hearty chorus. Son! Nay, grandson, just back from Indian service and a soldier-trumpeter to the King. His brother was in the same regiment with him. And so it ran, sons and daughters, and grand sons and daughters, world-wanderers and empire-builders, all of them, while the old folks stayed at home and worked at building empire too.

> There dwells a wife by the Northern Gate,
>   And a wealthy wife is she;
> She breeds a breed o' rovin' men
>   And casts them over sea.
>
> And some are drowned in deep water,
>   And some in sight of shore;
> And word goes back to the weary wife,
>   And ever she sends more.

But the Sea Wife's childbearing is about done. The stock is running out, and the planet is filling up. The wives of her sons may carry on the breed, but her work is past. The erstwhile men of England are now the men of Australia, of Africa, of America. England has sent forth 'the best she breeds' for so long, and has destroyed those that remained so fiercely, that little remains for her to do but to sit down through the long nights and gaze at royalty on the wall.

The true British merchant seaman has passed away. The merchant service is no longer a recruiting ground for such sea dogs as fought with Nelson at Trafalgar and the Nile. Foreigners largely man the merchant ships, though Englishmen still continue to officer them and to prefer foreigners for'ard. In South Africa the colonial teaches the Islander how to shoot, and the officers muddle and blunder; while at home the street people play hysterically at mafficking, and the War Office lowers the stature for enlistment.

It could not be otherwise. The most complacent Britisher

cannot hope to draw off the life blood, and underfeed, and keep it up forever. The average Mrs. Thomas Mugridge has been driven into the city, and she is not breeding very much of anything save an anæmic and sickly progeny which cannot find enough to eat. The strength of the English-speaking race to-day is not in the tight little island, but in the New World overseas, where are the sons and daughters of Mrs. Thomas Mugridge. The Sea Wife by the Northern Gate has just about done her work in the world, though she does not realize it. She must sit down and rest her tired loins for a space; and if the casual ward and the workhouse do not await her, it is because of the sons and daughters she has reared up against the day of her feebleness and decay.

XVI

Property versus *Person*

The rights of property have been so much extended that the rights of the community have almost altogether disappeared, and it is hardly too much to say that the prosperity and the comfort and the liberties of a great proportion of the population has been laid at the feet of a small number of proprietors, who neither toil nor spin.

—JOSEPH CHAMBERLAIN

IN A CIVILIZATION frankly materialistic and based upon property, not soul, it is inevitable that property shall be exalted over soul, that crimes against property shall be considered far more serious than crimes against the person. To pound one's wife to a jelly and break a few of her ribs is a trivial offence compared with sleeping out under the naked stars because one has not the price of a doss. The lad who steals a few pears from a wealthy railway corporation is a greater menace to society than the young brute who commits an unprovoked assault upon an old man over seventy years of age. While the young girl who takes a lodging under the pretence that she has work commits so dangerous an offence, that, were she not severely punished, she and her kind might bring the whole fabric of property clattering to the ground. Had she unholily tramped Piccadilly and the Strand after midnight, the police would not have interfered with her, and she would have been able to pay for her lodging.

The following illustrative cases are culled from the police court reports for a single week:—

Widnes Police Court. Before Aldermen Gossage and Neil. Thomas Lynch, charged with being drunk and disorderly and with assaulting a constable. Defendant rescued a woman from custody, kicked the constable, and threw stones at him. Fined 3s. 6d. for the first offence, and 10s. and costs for the assault.

Glasgow Queen's Park Police Court. Before Bailie Norman Thompson. John Kane pleaded guilty to assaulting his wife. There were five previous convictions. Fined £2 2s.

Taunton County Petty Sessions. John Painter, a big, burly fellow, described as a laborer, charged with assaulting his wife. The woman received two severe black eyes, and her face was badly swollen. Fined £1 8s. including costs, and bound over to keep the peace.

Widnes Police Court. Richard Bestwick and George Hunt, charged with trespassing in search of game. Hunt fined £1 and costs, Bestwick £2 and costs; in default one month.

Shaftesbury Police Court. Before the Mayor (Mr. A. T. Carpenter). Thomas Baker, charged with sleeping out. Fourteen days.

Glasgow Central Police Court. Before Bailie Dunlop. Edward Morrison, a lad, convicted of stealing fifteen pears from a lorry at the railroad station. Seven days.

Doncaster Borough Police Court. Before Alderman Clark and other magistrates. James M'Gowan, charged under the Poaching Prevention Act with being found in possession of poaching implements and a number of rabbits. Fined £2 and costs, or one month.

Dunfermline Sheriff Court. Before Sheriff Gillespie. John Young, a pit-head worker, pleaded guilty to assaulting Alexander Storrar by beating him about the head and body with his fists, throwing him on the ground, and also striking him with a pit prop. Fined £1.

Kirkcaldy Police Court. Before Bailie Dishart. Simon Walker pleaded guilty to assaulting a man by striking and knocking him down. It was an unprovoking assault, and the magistrate described the accused as a perfect danger to the community. Fined 30s.

Mansfield Police Court. Before the Mayor, Messrs. F. J. Turner, J. Whitaker, F. Tidsbury, E. Holmes, and Dr. R. Nesbitt. Joseph Jackson, charged with assaulting Charles Nunn. Without any provocation, defendant struck the complainant a violent blow in the face, knocking him down, and then kicked him on the side of the head. He was rendered unconscious, and he remained under medical treatment for a fortnight. Fined 21*s*.

Perth Sheriff Court. Before Sheriff Sym. David Mitchell, charged with poaching. There were two previous convictions, the last being three years ago. The sheriff was asked to deal leniently with Mitchell, who was sixty-two years of age, and who offered no resistance to the gamekeeper. Four months.

Dundee Sheriff Court. Before Hon. Sheriff substitute R. C. Walker. John Murray, Donald Craig, and James Parkes, charged with poaching. Craig and Parkes fined £1 each or fourteen days; Murray £5 or one month.

Reading Borough Police Court. Before Messrs. W. B. Monck, F. B. Parfitt, H. M. Wallis, and G. Gillagan. Alfred Masters, aged sixteen, charged with sleeping out on a waste piece of ground and having no visible means of subsistence. Seven days.

Salisbury City Petty Sessions. Before the Mayor, Messrs. C. Hoskins, G. Fullford, E. Alexander, and W. Marlow. James Moore, charged with stealing a pair of boots from outside a shop. Twenty-one days.

Horncastle Police Court. Before the Rev. W. P. Massingberd, the Rev. J. Graham, and Mr. N. Lucas Calcraft. George Brackenbury, a young laborer, convicted of what the magistrates characterized as an altogether unprovoked and brutal assault upon James Sargeant Foster, a man over seventy years of age. Fined £1 and 5*s*. 6*d*. costs.

Worksop Petty Sessions. Before Messrs. F. J. S. Foljambe, R. Eddison, and S. Smith. John Priestley, charged with assaulting the Rev. Leslie Graham. Defendant, who was drunk, was wheeling a perambulator and pushed it in front of a lorry, with the result that the perambulator was overturned and the baby in it thrown out. The lorry passed over the perambulator, but the baby was uninjured. Defendant then attacked the driver of the lorry, and afterwards assaulted the complainant, who remonstrated with him upon his conduct. In consequence of the injuries defendant inflicted, complainant had to consult a doctor. Fined 40*s.* and costs.

Rotherham West Riding Police Court. Before Messrs. C. Wright and G. Pugh and Colonel Stoddart. Benjamin Storey, Thomas Brammer, and Samuel Wilcock, charged with poaching. One month each.

Southampton County Police Court. Before Admiral J. C. Rowley, Mr. H. H. Culme-Seymour, and other magistrates. Henry Thorrington, charged with sleeping out. Seven days.

Eckington Police Court. Before Major L. B. Bowden, Messrs. R. Eyre, and H. A. Fowler, and Dr. Court. Joseph Watts, charged with stealing nine ferns from a garden. One month.

Ripley Petty Sessions. Before Messrs. J. B. Wheeler, W. D. Bembridge, and M. Hooper. Vincent Allen and George Hall, charged under the Poaching Prevention Act with being found in possession of a number of rabbits, and John Sparham, charged with aiding and abetting them. Hall and Sparham fined £1 17*s.* 4*d.*, and Allen £2 17*s.* 4*d.*, including costs; the former committed for fourteen days and the latter for one month in default of payment.

South-western Police Court, London. Before Mr. Rose. John Probyn, charged with doing grievous bodily harm to a constable. Prisoner had been kicking his wife, and also assaulting another woman who protested against his brutality. The constable tried to persuade him to go inside his house, but prisoner suddenly turned upon him, knocking him down by a blow on the face, kicking him as he lay on the ground, and attempting to strangle him. Finally the prisoner deliberately kicked the officer in a dangerous part, inflicting an injury which will keep him off duty for a long time to come. Six weeks.

Lambeth Police Court, London. Before Mr. Hopkins. 'Baby' Stuart, aged nineteen, described as a chorus girl, charged with obtaining food and lodging to the value of 5s., by false pretences, and with intent to defraud Emma Brasier. Emma Brasier, complainant, lodging-house keeper of Atwell Road. Prisoner took apartments at her house on the representation that she was employed at the Crown Theatre. After prisoner had been in her house two or three days, Mrs. Brasier made inquiries, and, finding the girl's story untrue, gave her into custody. Prisoner told the magistrate that she would have worked had she not had such bad health. Six weeks hard labor.

XVII

Inefficiency

I'd rather die on the high road under the open blue. I'd rather starve to death in the sweet air, or drown in the brave, salt sea, or have one fierce glad hour of battle, and then a bullet, than lead the life of a brute in a stinking hell, and gasp out my broken breath at last on a pauper's pallet.

— ROBERT BLATCHFORD

I STOPPED a moment to listen to an argument on the Mile End Waste. It was night-time, and they were all workmen of the better class. They had surrounded one of their number, a pleasant-faced man of thirty, and were giving it to him rather heatedly.

"But 'ow about this 'ere cheap immigration?" one of them demanded. "The Jews of Whitechapel, say, a-cuttin' our throats right along?"

"You can't blame them," was the answer. "They're just like us, and they've got to live. Don't blame the man who offers to work cheaper than you and gets your job."

"But 'ow about the wife an' kiddies?" his interlocutor demanded.

"There you are," came the answer. "How about the wife and kiddies of the man who works cheaper than you and gets your job? Eh? How about his wife and kiddies? He's more interested in them than in yours, and he can't see them starve. So he cuts the price of labor and out you go. But you mustn't blame him, poor devil. He can't help it. Wages always come down when two men are after the same job. That's the fault of competition, not of the man who cuts the price."

"But wyges don't come down where there's a union," the objection was made.

"And there you are again, right on the head. The union checks competition among the laborers, but makes it harder where there are no unions. There's where your cheap labor of Whitechapel comes in. They're unskilled, and have no unions, and cut each other's throats, and ours in the bargain, if we don't belong to a strong union."

Without going further into the argument, this man on the
Mile End Waste pointed the moral that when two men were
after the one job wages were bound to fall. Had he gone
deeper into the matter, he would have found that even the
union, say twenty thousand strong, could not hold up wages
if twenty thousand idle men were trying to displace the union
men. This is admirably instanced, just now, by the return and
disbandment of the soldiers from South Africa. They find
themselves, by tens of thousands, in desperate straits in the
army of the unemployed. There is a general decline in wages
throughout the land, which, giving rise to labor disputes and
strikes, is taken advantage of by the unemployed, who gladly
pick up the tools thrown down by the strikers.

Sweating, starvation wages, armies of unemployed, and
great numbers of the homeless and shelterless are inevitable
when there are more men to do work than there is work for
men to do. The men and women I have met upon the streets,
and in the spikes and pegs, are not there because as a mode
of life it may be considered a 'soft snap.' I have sufficiently
outlined the hardships they undergo to demonstrate that their
existence is anything but 'soft.'

It is a matter of sober calculation, here in England, that it
is softer to work for twenty shillings ($5) a week, and have
regular food, and a bed at night, than it is to walk the streets.
The man who walks the streets suffers more, and works
harder, for far less return. I have depicted the nights they
spend, and how, driven in by physical exhaustion, they go to
the casual ward for a 'rest up.' Nor is the casual ward a soft
snap. To pick four pounds of oakum, break twelve hundredweight of stones, or perform the most revolting tasks, in return for the miserable food and shelter they receive, is an
unqualified extravagance on the part of the men who are
guilty of it. On the part of the authorities, it is sheer robbery.
They give the men far less for their labor than do the capitalistic employers. The wage for the same amount of labor,
performed for a private employer, would buy them better
beds, better food, more good cheer, and, above all, greater
freedom.

As I say, it is an extravagance for a man to patronize a
casual ward. And that they know it themselves is shown by

the way these men shun it till driven in by physical exhaustion. Then why do they do it? Not because they are discouraged workers. The very opposite is true; they are discouraged vagabonds. In the United States the tramp is almost invariably a discouraged worker. He finds tramping a softer mode of life than working. But this is not true in England. Here the powers that be do their utmost to discourage the tramp and vagabond, and he is, in all truth, a mightily discouraged creature. He knows that two shillings a day, which is only fifty cents, will buy him three fair meals, a bed at night, and leave him a couple of pennies for pocket money. He would rather work for those two shillings, than for the charity of the casual ward; for he knows that he would not have to work so hard and that he would not be so abominably treated. He does not do so, however, because there are more men to do work than there is work for men to do.

When there are more men than there is work to be done, a sifting-out process must obtain. In every branch of industry the less efficient are crowded out. Being crowded out because of inefficiency, they cannot go up, but must descend, and continue to descend, until they reach their proper level, a place in the industrial fabric where they are efficient. It follows, therefore, and it is inexorable, that the least efficient must descend to the very bottom, which is the shambles wherein they perish miserably.

A glance at the confirmed inefficients at the bottom demonstrates that they are, as a rule, mental, physical, and moral wrecks. The exceptions to the rule are the late arrivals, who are merely very inefficient, and upon whom the wrecking process is just beginning to operate. All the forces here, it must be remembered, are destructive. The good body (which is there because its brain is not quick and capable) is speedily wrenched and twisted out of shape; the clean mind (which is there because of its weak body) is speedily fouled and contaminated. The mortality is excessive, but, even then, they die far too lingering deaths.

Here, then, we have the construction of the Abyss and the shambles. Throughout the whole industrial fabric a constant elimination is going on. The inefficient are weeded out and flung downward. Various things constitute inefficiency. The engineer who is irregular or irresponsible will sink down until he finds his place, say as a casual laborer, an occupation irregular in its very nature and in which there is little or no responsibility. Those who are slow and clumsy, who suffer from weakness of body or mind, or who lack nervous, mental, and physical stamina, must sink down, sometimes rapidly, sometimes step by step, to the bottom. Accident, by disabling an efficient worker, will make him inefficient, and down he must go. And the worker who becomes aged, with failing energy and numbing brain, must begin the frightful descent which knows no stopping-place short of the bottom and death.

In this last instance, the statistics of London tell a terrible tale. The population of London is one-seventh of the total population of the United Kingdom, and in London, year in and year out, one adult in every four dies on public charity, either in the workhouse, the hospital, or the asylum. When the fact that the well-to-do do not end thus is taken into consideration, it becomes manifest that it is the fate of at least one in every three adult workers to die on public charity.

As an illustration of how a good worker may suddenly become inefficient, and what then happens to him, I am tempted to give the case of M'Garry, a man thirty-two years of age, and an inmate of the workhouse. The extracts are quoted from the annual report of the trade union:—

> I worked at Sullivan's place in Widnes, better known as the British Alkali Chemical Works. I was working in a shed, and I had to cross the yard. It was ten o'clock at night, and there was no light about. While crossing the yard I felt something take hold of my leg and screw it off. I became unconscious; I didn't know what became of me for a day or two. On the following Sunday night I came to my senses, and found myself in the hospital. I asked the nurse what was to do with my legs, and she told me both legs were off.
>
> There was a stationary crank in the yard, let into the ground; the hole was 18 inches long, 15 inches deep, and 15 inches wide. The crank revolved in the hole three revolutions a minute. There was no fence or covering over the hole. Since my accident they have stopped it altogether,

and have covered the hole up with a piece of sheet iron. . . . They gave me £25. They didn't reckon that as compensation; they said it was only for charity's sake. Out of that I paid £9 for a machine by which to wheel myself about.

I was laboring at the time I got my legs off. I got twenty-four shillings a week, rather better pay than the other men, because I used to take shifts. When there was heavy work to be done I used to be picked out to do it. Mr. Manton, the manager, visited me at the hospital several times. When I was getting better, I asked him if he would be able to find me a job. He told me not to trouble myself, as the firm was not cold-hearted. I would be right enough in any case. . . . Mr. Manton stopped coming to see me; and the last time, he said he thought of asking the directors to give me a fifty-pound note, so I could go home to my friends in Ireland.

Poor M'Garry! He received rather better pay than the other men because he was ambitious and took shifts, and when heavy work was to be done he was the man picked out to do it. And then the thing happened, and he went into the workhouse. The alternative to the workhouse is to go home to Ireland and burden his friends for the rest of his life. Comment is superfluous.

It must be understood that efficiency is not determined by the workers themselves, but is determined by the demand for labor. If three men seek one position, the most efficient man will get it. The other two, no matter how capable they may be, will none the less be inefficients. If Germany, Japan, and the United States should capture the entire world market for iron, coal, and textiles, at once the English workers would be thrown idle by hundreds of thousands. Some would emigrate, but the rest would rush their labor into the remaining industries. A general shaking up of the workers from top to bottom would result; and when equilibrium had been restored, the number of the inefficients at the bottom of the Abyss would have been increased by hundreds of thousands. On the other hand, conditions remaining constant and all the workers doubling their efficiency, there would still be as many inefficients, though each inefficient were twice as capable as he had been and more capable than many of the efficients had previously been.

When there are more men to work than there is work for men to do, just as many men as are in excess of work will be inefficients, and as inefficients they are doomed to lingering and painful destruction. It shall be the aim of future chapters to show, by their work and manner of living, not only how the inefficients are weeded out and destroyed, but to show how inefficients are being constantly and wantonly created by the forces of industrial society as it exists to-day.

XVIII
Wages

Some sell their lives for bread;
   Some sell their souls for gold;
Some seek the river bed;
   Some seek the workhouse mold.

Such is proud England's sway,
   Where wealth may work its will;
White flesh is cheap to-day,
   White souls are cheaper still.
                              —FANTASIAS

W HEN I learned that in Lesser London there were 1,292,737 people who received 21 shillings or less a week per family, I became interested as to how the wages could best be spent in order to maintain the physical efficiency of such families. Families of six, seven, eight, or ten being beyond consideration, I have based the following table upon a family of five, a father, mother, and three children; while I have made 21 shillings equivalent to $5.25, though actually, 21 shillings are equivalent to about $5.11.

Rent	$1.50
Bread	1.00
Meat	.87$^{1}/_{2}$
Vegetables	.62$^{1}/_{2}$
Coals	.25
Tea	.18
Oil	.16
Sugar	.18
Milk	.12
Soap	.08
Butter	.20
Firewood	.08
Total	$5.25

An analysis of one item alone will show how little room there is for waste. *Bread*, $1: for a family of five, for seven

days, one dollar's worth of bread will give each a daily ration
of 2⁶/₇ cents; and if they eat three meals a day, each may consume per meal 9½ mills' worth of bread, a little less than one
cent's worth. Now bread is the heaviest item. They will get
less of meat per mouth each meal, and still less of vegetables;
while the smaller items become too microscopic for consideration. On the other hand, these food articles are all bought
at small retail, the most expensive and wasteful method of
purchasing.

While the table given above will permit no extravagance,
no overloading of stomachs, it will be noticed that there is no
surplus. The whole $5.25 is spent for food and rent. There is
no pocket money left over. Does the man buy a glass of beer,
the family must eat that much less; and in so far as it eats less,
just that far will it impair its physical efficiency. The members
of this family cannot ride in busses or trams, cannot write
letters, take outings, go to a 'tu'penny gaff' for cheap vaude-
ville, join social or benefit clubs, nor can they buy sweetmeats,
tobacco, books, or newspapers.

And further, should one child (and there are three) require
a pair of shoes, the family must strike meat for a week
from its bill of fare. And, since there are five pairs of feet requiring shoes, and five heads requiring hats, and five bodies
requiring clothes, and since there are laws regulating indecency, the family must constantly impair its physical
efficiency in order to keep warm and out of jail. For notice,
when rent, coals, oil, soap, and firewood are extracted from
the weekly income, there remains a daily allowance for food
of 9 cents to each person; and that 9 cents cannot be lessened
by buying clothes without impairing the physical efficiency.

All of which is hard enough. But the thing happens; the
husband and father breaks his leg or his neck. No 9 cents a
day per mouth for food is coming in; no 9½ mills' worth of
bread per meal; and, at the end of the week, no $1.50 for rent.
So out they must go, to the streets or the workhouse, or to
a miserable den, somewhere, in which the mother will desperately endeavor to hold the family together on the 10 shillings she may possibly be able to earn.

While in Lesser London there are 1,292,737 people who receive 21 shillings or less a week per family, it must be remem-

bered that we have investigated a family of five living on a 21-shillings basis. There are larger families, there are many families that live on less than 21 shillings, and there is much irregular employment. The question naturally arises, How do *they* live? The answer is that they do not live. They do not know what life is. They drag out a subter-bestial existence until mercifully released by death.

Before descending to the fouler depths, let the case of the telegraph girls be cited. Here are clean, fresh, English maids, for whom a higher standard of living than that of the beasts is absolutely necessary. Otherwise they cannot remain clean, fresh English maids. On entering the service, a telephone girl receives a weekly wage of $2.75. If she be quick and clever, she may, at the end of five years, attain a maximum wage of $5.00. Recently a table of such a girl's weekly expenditure was furnished to Lord Londonderry. Here it is:—

Rent, fire, and light	1.87\frac{1}{2}$
Board at home	.87$\frac{1}{2}$
Board at the office	1.12$\frac{1}{2}$
Street car fare	.37$\frac{1}{2}$
Laundry	.25
Total	$4.50

This leaves nothing for clothes, recreation, or sickness. And yet many of the girls are receiving, not $4.50, but $2.75, $3, and $3.50 per week. They must have clothes and recreation, and—

> Man to Man so oft unjust,
> Is always so to Woman.

At the Trades Union Congress now being held in London, the Gasworkers' Union moved that instructions be given the Parliamentary Committee to introduce a bill to prohibit the employment of children under fifteen years of age. Mr. Shackleton, Member of Parliament and a representative of the Northern Counties' Weavers, opposed the resolution on behalf of the textile workers, who, he said, could not dispense with the earnings of their children and live on the scale of wages which obtained. The representatives of 514,000 workers voted against the resolution, while the representatives of

535,000 workers voted in favor of it. When 514,000 workers oppose a resolution prohibiting child-labor under fifteen, it is evident that a less-than-living wage is being paid to an immense number of the adult workers of the country.

I have spoken with women in Whitechapel who receive right along less than 25 cents for a twelve-hour day in the coat-making sweat shops; and with women trousers finishers who receive an average princely and weekly wage of 75 cents to $1.

A case recently cropped up of men, in the employ of a wealthy business house, receiving their board and $1.50 per week for six working days of sixteen hours each. The sandwich men get 27 cents per day and find themselves. The average weekly earnings of the hawkers and costermongers are not more than $2.50 to $3. The average of all common laborers, outside the dockers, is less than $4 per week, while the dockers average from $2 to $2.25. These figures are taken from a royal commission report and are authentic.

Conceive of an old woman, broken and dying, supporting herself and four children, and paying 75 cents per week rent, by making match boxes at $4\frac{1}{2}$ cents per gross. Twelve dozen boxes for $4\frac{1}{2}$ cents, and, in addition, finding her own paste and thread! She never knew a day off, either for sickness, rest, or recreation. Each day and every day, Sundays as well, she toiled fourteen hours. Her day's stint was seven gross, for which she received $31\frac{1}{2}$ cents. In the week of ninety-eight hours' work, she made 7066 match boxes, and earned $2.20\frac{1}{2}$, less her paste and thread.

Last year, Mr. Thomas Holmes, a police court missionary of note, after writing about the condition of the women workers, received the following letter, dated April 18, 1901: —

> SIR: Pardon the liberty I am taking, but, having read what you said about poor women working fourteen hours a day for ten shillings per week, I beg to state my case. I am a tie-maker, who, after working all the week, cannot earn more than five shillings, and I have a poor afflicted husband to keep who hasn't earned a penny for more than ten years.

Imagine a woman, capable of writing such a clear, sensible,

grammatical letter, supporting her husband and self on 5 shillings ($1.25) per week! Mr. Holmes visited her. He had to squeeze to get into the room. There lay her sick husband; there she worked all day long; there she cooked, ate, washed, and slept; and there her husband and she performed all the functions of living and dying. There was no space for the missionary to sit down, save on the bed, which was partially covered with ties and silk. The sick man's lungs were in the last stages of decay. He coughed and expectorated constantly, the woman ceasing from her work to assist him in his paroxysms. The silken fluff from the ties was not good for his sickness; nor was his sickness good for the ties, and the handlers and wearers of the ties yet to come.

Another case Mr. Holmes visited was that of a young girl, twelve years of age, charged in the police court with stealing food. He found her the deputy mother of a boy of nine, a crippled boy of seven, and a younger child. Her mother was a widow and a blouse-maker. She paid $1.25 a week rent. Here are the last items in her housekeeping account: *Tea*, 1 *cent*; *sugar*, 1 *cent*; *bread*, 1/2 *cent*; *margarine*, 2 *cents*; *oil*, 3 *cents*; *and firewood*, 1 *cent*. Good housewives of the soft and tender folk, imagine yourselves marketing and keeping house on such a scale, setting a table for five, and keeping an eye on your deputy mother of twelve to see that she did not steal food for her little brothers and sisters, the while you stitched, stitched, stitched at a nightmare line of blouses, which stretched away into the gloom and down to the pauper's coffin a-yawn for you.

XIX
The Ghetto

Is it well that while we range with Science, glorying in the time,
City children soak and blacken soul and sense in city slime?
There among the gloomy alleys Progress halts on palsied feet,
Crime and hunger cast our maidens by the thousand on the street;

There the master scrimps his haggard seamstress of her daily bread;
There a single sordid attic holds the living and the dead;
There the smouldering fire of fever creeps across the rotted floor,
And the crowded couch of incest, in the warrens of the poor.

—TENNYSON

AT ONE TIME the nations of Europe confined the undesirable Jews in city ghettos. But to-day the dominant economic class, by less arbitrary but none the less rigorous methods, has confined the undesirable yet necessary workers into ghettos of remarkable meanness and vastness. East London is such a ghetto, where the rich and the powerful do not dwell, and the traveller cometh not, and where two million workers swarm, procreate, and die.

It must not be supposed that all the workers of London are crowded into the East End, but the tide is setting strongly in that direction. The poor quarters of the city proper are constantly being destroyed, and the main stream of the unhoused is toward the east. In the last twelve years, one district, "London over the Border," as it is called, which lies well beyond Aldgate, Whitechapel, and Mile End, has increased 260,000, or over sixty per cent. The churches in this district, by the way, can seat but one in every thirty-seven of the added population.

The City of Dreadful Monotony the East End is often called, especially by well-fed, optimistic sightseers, who look over the surface of things and are merely shocked by the intolerable sameness and meanness of it all. If the East End is worthy of no worse title than The City of Dreadful Monotony, and if working people are unworthy of variety and beauty and surprise, it would not be such a bad place in which to live. But the East End does merit a worse title. It should be called The City of Degradation.

While it is not a city of slums, as some people imagine, it may well be said to be one gigantic slum. From the standpoint of simple decency and clean manhood and womanhood, any mean street, of all its mean streets, is a slum. Where sights and sounds abound which neither you nor I would care to have our children see and hear is a place where no man's children should live, and see and hear. Where you and I would not care to have our wives pass their lives is a place where no other man's wife should have to pass her life. For here, in the East End, the obscenities and brute vulgarities of life are rampant. There is no privacy. The bad corrupts the good, and all fester together. Innocent childhood is sweet and beautiful; but in East London innocence is a fleeting thing, and you must catch them before they crawl out of the cradle, or you will find the very babes as unholily wise as you.

The application of the Golden Rule determines that East London is an unfit place in which to live. Where you would not have your own babe live, and develop, and gather to itself knowledge of life and the things of life, is not a fit place for the babes of other men to live, and develop, and gather to themselves knowledge of life and the things of life. It is a simple thing, this Golden Rule, and all that is required. Political economy and the survival of the fittest can go hang if they say otherwise. What is not good enough for you is not good enough for other men, and there's no more to be said.

There are 300,000 people in London, divided into families, that live in one-room tenements. Far, far more live in two and three rooms and are as badly crowded, regardless of sex, as those that live in one room. The law demands 400 cubic feet of space for each person. In army barracks each soldier is allowed 600 cubic feet. Professor Huxley, at one time himself a medical officer in East London, always held that each person should have 800 cubic feet of space, and that it should be well ventilated with pure air. Yet in London there are 900,000 people living in less than the 400 cubic feet prescribed by the law.

Mr. Charles Booth, who engaged in a systematic work of years in charting and classifying the toiling city population, estimates that there are 1,800,000 people in London who are *poor* and *very poor*. It is of interest to mark what he terms *poor*. By *poor* he means families which have a total weekly income of from $4.50 to $5.25. The *very poor* fall greatly below this standard.

The workers, as a class, are being more and more segregated by their economic masters; and this process, with its jamming and overcrowding, tends not so much toward immorality as unmorality. Here is an extract from a recent meeting of the London County Council, terse and bald, but with a wealth of horror to be read between the lines: —

Mr. Bruce asked the Chairman of the Public Health Committee whether his attention had been called to a number of cases of serious overcrowding in the East End. In St. Georges-in-the-East a man and his wife and their family of eight occupied one small room. This family consisted of five daughters, aged twenty, seventeen, eight, four, and an infant, and three sons, aged fifteen, thirteen, and twelve. In Whitechapel a man and his wife and their three daughters, aged sixteen, eight, and four, and two sons, aged ten and twelve years, occupied a smaller room. In Bethnal Green a man and his wife, with four sons, aged twenty-three, twenty-one, nineteen, and sixteen, and two daughters, aged fourteen and seven, were also found in one room. He asked whether it was not the duty of the various local authorities to prevent such serious overcrowding.

But with 900,000 people actually living under illegal conditions, the authorities have their hands full. When the overcrowded folk are ejected they stray off into some other hole; and, as they move their belongings by night, on hand-barrows (one hand-barrow accommodating the entire household goods and the sleeping children), it is next to impossible to keep track of them. If the Public Health Act of 1891 were suddenly and completely enforced, 900,000 people would receive notice to clear out of their houses and go on to the streets, and 500,000 rooms would have to be built before they were all legally housed again.

The mean streets merely look mean from the outside, but inside the walls are to be found squalor, misery, and tragedy.

While the following tragedy may be revolting to read, it must not be forgotten that the existence of it is far more revolting. In Devonshire Place, Lisson Grove, a short while back died an old woman of seventy-five years of age. At the inquest the coroner's officer stated that "all he found in the room was a lot of old rags covered with vermin. He had got himself smothered with the vermin. The room was in a shocking condition, and he had never seen anything like it. Everything was absolutely covered with vermin."

The doctor said: "He found deceased lying across the fender on her back. She had one garment and her stockings on. The body was quite alive with vermin, and all the clothes in the room were absolutely gray with insects. Deceased was very badly nourished and was very emaciated. She had extensive sores on her legs, and her stockings were adherent to those sores. The sores were the result of vermin."

A man present at the inquest wrote: "I had the evil fortune to see the body of the unfortunate woman as it lay in the mortuary; and even now the memory of that grewsome sight makes me shudder. There she lay in the mortuary shell, so starved and emaciated that she was a mere bundle of skin and bones. Her hair, which was matted with filth, was simply a nest of vermin. Over her bony chest leaped and rolled hundreds, thousands, myriads of vermin."

If it is not good for your mother and my mother so to die, then it is not good for this woman, whosoever's mother she might be, so to die.

Bishop Wilkinson, who has lived in Zululand, recently said, "No headman of an African village would allow such a promiscuous mixing of young men and women, boys and girls." He had reference to the children of the overcrowded folk, who at five have nothing to learn and much to unlearn which they will never unlearn.

It is notorious that here in the Ghetto the houses of the poor are greater profit earners than the mansions of the rich. Not only does the poor worker have to live like a beast, but he pays proportionately more for it than does the rich man for his spacious comfort. A class of house-sweaters has been made possible by the competition of the poor for houses. There are more people than there is room, and numbers are in the workhouse because they cannot find shelter elsewhere. Not only are houses let, but they are sublet, and sub-sublet down to the very rooms.

"A part of a room to let." This notice was posted a short while ago in a window not five minutes' walk from St. James's Hall. The Rev. Hugh Price Hughes is authority for the statement that beds are let on the three-relay system— that is, three tenants to a bed, each occupying it eight hours, so that it never grows cold; while the floor space underneath the bed is likewise let on the three-relay system. Health officers are not at all unused to finding such cases as the following: in one room having a cubic capacity of 1000 feet, three adult females in the bed, and two adult females under the bed; and in one room of 1650 cubic feet, one adult male and two children in the bed, and two adult females under the bed.

Here is a typical example of a room on the more respectable two-relay system. It is occupied in the daytime by a young woman employed all night in a hotel. At seven o'clock in the evening she vacates the room, and a bricklayer's laborer comes in. At seven in the morning he vacates, and goes to his work, at which time she returns from hers.

The Rev. W. N. Davies, rector of Spitalfields, took a census of some of the alleys in his parish. He says:—

> In one alley there are 10 houses—51 rooms, nearly all about 8 feet by 9 feet—and 254 people. In six instances only do 2 people occupy one room; and in others the number varied from 3 to 9. In another court with 6 houses and 22 rooms were 84 people—again, 6, 7, 8, and 9 being the number living in one room, in several instances. In one house with 8 rooms are 45 people—one room containing 9 persons, one 8, two 7, and another 6.

This Ghetto crowding is not through inclination, but compulsion. Nearly fifty per cent of the workers pay from one-fourth to one-half of their earnings for rent. The average rent in the larger part of the East End is from $1.00 to $1.50 per week for one room, while skilled mechanics, earning $8.75 per week, are forced to part with $3.75 of it for two or three pokey little dens, in which they strive desperately to obtain some semblance of home life. And rents are going up all the time.

In one street in Stepney the increase in only two years has been from $3.25 to $4.50; in another street from $2.75 to $4; and in another street, from $2.75 to $3.75; while in Whitechapel, two-room houses that recently rented for $2.50 are now costing $5.25. East, west, north, and south, the rents are going up. When land is worth from $100,000 to $150,000 an acre, some one must pay the landlord.

Mr. W. C. Steadman, in the House of Commons, in a speech concerning his constituency in Stepney, related the following:—

> This morning, not a hundred yards from where I am myself living, a widow stopped me. She has six children to support, and the rent of her house was 14 shillings per week. She gets her living by letting the house to lodgers and doing a day's washing or charing. That woman, with tears in her eyes, told me that the landlord had increased the rent from 14 shillings to 18 shillings. What could the woman do? There is no accommodation in Stepney. Every place is taken up and overcrowded.

Class supremacy can rest only on class degradation; and when the workers are segregated in the Ghetto, they cannot escape the consequent degradation. A short and stunted people is created,—a breed strikingly differentiated from their masters' breed, a pavement folk, as it were, lacking stamina and strength. The men become caricatures of what physical men ought to be, and their women and children are pale and anæmic, with eyes ringed darkly, who stoop and slouch, and are early twisted out of all shapeliness and beauty.

To make matters worse, the men of the Ghetto are the men who are left, a deteriorated stock left to undergo still further deterioration. For a hundred and fifty years, at least, they have been drained of their best. The strong men, the men of pluck, initiative, and ambition, have been faring forth to the fresher and freer portions of the globe, to make new lands and nations. Those who are lacking, the weak of heart and head and hand, as well as the rotten and hopeless, have remained to carry on the breed. And year by year, in turn, the best they breed are taken from them. Wherever a man of vigor and stature manages to grow up, he is haled forthwith into the army. A soldier, as Bernard Shaw has said, "ostensibly a heroic and patriotic defender of his country, is really an unfortunate man driven by destitution to offer himself as food for powder for the sake of regular rations, shelter, and clothing."

This constant selection of the best from the workers has impoverished those who are left, a sadly degraded remainder, for the great part, which, in the Ghetto, sinks to the deepest depths. The wine of life has been drawn off to spill itself in blood and progeny over the rest of the earth. Those that remain are the lees, and they are segregated and steeped in themselves. They become indecent and bestial. When they kill, they kill with their hands, and then stupidly surrender themselves to the executioners. There is no splendid audacity about their transgressions. They gouge a mate with a dull knife, or beat his head in with an iron pot, and then sit down and wait for the police. Wife-beating is the masculine prerogative of matrimony. They wear remarkable boots of brass and iron, and when they have polished off the mother of their children with a black eye or so, they knock her down and proceed to trample her very much as a Western stallion tramples a rattlesnake.

A woman of the lower Ghetto classes is as much the slave of her husband as is the Indian squaw. And I, for one, were I a woman and had but the two choices, should prefer being the squaw. The men are economically dependent on their masters, and the women are economically dependent on the men. The result is, the woman gets the beating the man should give his master, and she can do nothing. There are the kiddies, and he is the breadwinner, and she dare not send him to jail and leave herself and children to starve. Evidence to convict can rarely be obtained when such cases come into the courts; as a rule the trampled wife and mother is weeping and hysterically beseeching the magistrate to let her husband off for the kiddies' sakes.

The wives become screaming harridans or broken-spirited and doglike, lose what little decency and self-respect they have remaining over from their maiden days, and all sink together, unheeding, in their degradation and dirt.

Sometimes I become afraid of my own generalizations

upon the massed misery of this Ghetto life, and feel that my
impressions are exaggerated, that I am too close to the picture
and lack perspective. At such moments I find it well to turn
to the testimony of other men to prove to myself that I am
not becoming overwrought and addle-pated. Frederick Har-
rison has always struck me as being a level-headed, well-con-
trolled man, and he says:—

> To me, at least, it would be enough to condemn modern
> society as hardly an advance on slavery or serfdom, if the
> permanent condition of industry were to be that which we
> behold, that ninety per cent of the actual producers of
> wealth have no home that they can call their own beyond
> the end of the week; have no bit of soil, or so much as a
> room that belongs to them; have nothing of value of any
> kind, except as much old furniture as will go into a cart;
> have the precarious chance of weekly wages, which barely
> suffice to keep them in health; are housed, for the most
> part, in places that no man thinks fit for his horse; are sep-
> arated by so narrow a margin from destitution that a
> month of bad trade, sickness, or unexpected loss brings
> them face to face with hunger and pauperism. . . . But
> below this normal state of the average workman in town
> and country, there is found the great band of destitute out-
> casts—the camp followers of the army of industry—at
> least one-tenth of the whole proletarian population, whose
> normal condition is one of sickening wretchedness. If this
> is to be the permanent arrangement of modern society, civ-
> ilization must be held to bring a curse on the great majority
> of mankind.

Ninety per cent! The figures are appalling, yet the Rev.
Stopford Brooke, after drawing a frightful London picture,
finds himself compelled to multiply it by half a million. Here
it is:—

> I often used to meet, when I was curate at Kensington,
> families drifting into London along the Hammersmith
> Road. One day there came along a laborer and his wife, his
> son and two daughters. Their family had lived for a long
> time on an estate in the country, and managed, with the

help of the common-land and their labor, to get on. But the time came when the common was encroached upon, and their labor was not needed on the estate, and they were quietly turned out of their cottage. Where should they go? Of course to London, where work was thought to be plentiful. They had a little savings, and they thought they could get two decent rooms to live in. But the inexorable land question met them in London. They tried the decent courts for lodgings, and found that two rooms would cost ten shillings a week. Food was dear and bad, water was bad, and in a short time their health suffered. Work was hard to get, and its wage was so low that they were soon in debt. They became more ill and more despairing with the poisonous surroundings, the darkness, and the long hours of work; and they were driven forth to seek a cheaper lodging. They found it in a court I knew well—a hotbed of crime and nameless horrors. In this they got a single room at a cruel rent, and work was more difficult for them to get now, as they came from a place of such bad repute, and they fell into the hands of those who sweat the last drop out of man and woman and child, for wages which are the food only of despair. And the darkness and the dirt, the bad food and the sickness, and the want of water was worse than before; and the crowd and the companionship of the court robbed them of the last shreds of self-respect. The drink demon seized upon them. Of course there was a public house at both ends of the court. There they fled, one and all, for shelter, and warmth, and society, and forgetfulness. And they came out in deeper debt, with inflamed senses and burning brains, and an unsatisfied craving for drink they would do anything to satiate. And in a few months the father was in prison, the wife dying, the son a criminal, and the daughters on the street. *Multiply this by half a million, and you will be beneath the truth*.

No more dreary spectacle can be found on this earth than the whole of the 'awful East,' with its Whitechapel, Hoxton, Spitalfields, Bethnal Green, and Wapping to the East India Docks. The color of life is gray and drab. Everything is helpless, hopeless, unrelieved, and dirty. Bath-tubs are a thing totally unknown, as mythical as the ambrosia of the gods. The people themselves are dirty, while any attempt at cleanliness becomes howling farce, when it is not pitiful and tragic. Strange, vagrant odors come drifting along the greasy wind, and the rain, when it falls, is more like grease than water from heaven. The very cobblestones are scummed with grease. In brief, a vast and complacent dirtiness obtains, which could be done away with by nothing short of a Vesuvius or Mount Pelée.

Here lives a population as dull and unimaginative as its long gray miles of dingy brick. Religion has virtually passed it by, and a gross and stupid materialism reigns, fatal alike to the things of the spirit and the finer instincts of life.

It used to be the proud boast that every Englishman's home was his castle. But to-day it is an anachronism. The Ghetto folk have no homes. They do not know the significance and the sacredness of home life. Even the municipal dwellings, where live the better-class workers, are over-crowded barracks. They have no home life. The very language proves it. The father returning from work asks his child in the street where her mother is; and back the answer comes, "In the buildings."

A new race has sprung up, a street people. They pass their lives at work and in the streets. They have dens and lairs into which to crawl for sleeping purposes, and that is all. One cannot travesty the word by calling such dens and lairs 'homes.' The traditional silent and reserved Englishman has passed away. The pavement folk are noisy, voluble, high-strung, excitable—when they are yet young. As they grow older they become steeped and stupefied in beer. When they have nothing else to do, they ruminate as a cow ruminates. They are to be met with everywhere, standing on curbs and corners, and staring into vacancy. Watch one of them. He will stand there, motionless, for hours, and when you go away you will leave him still staring into vacancy. It is most absorbing. He has no money for beer, and his lair is only for sleeping purposes, so what else remains for him to do? He has already solved the mysteries of girl's love, and wife's love, and child's love, and found them delusions and shams, vain and fleeting as dewdrops, quick-vanishing before the ferocious facts of life.

As I say, the young are high-strung, nervous, excitable; the middle-aged are empty-headed, stolid, and stupid. It is absurd to think for an instant that they can compete with the workers of the New World. Brutalized, degraded, and dull, the Ghetto folk will be unable to render efficient service to England in the world struggle for industrial supremacy which economists declare has already begun. Neither as workers nor as soldiers can they come up to the mark when England, in her need, calls upon them, her forgotten ones; and if England be flung out of the world's industrial orbit, they will perish like flies at the end of summer. Or, with England critically situated, and with them made desperate as wild beasts are made desperate, they may become a menace and go 'swelling' down to the West End to return the 'slumming' the West End has done in the East. In which case, before rapid-fire guns and the modern machinery of warfare, they will perish the more swiftly and easily.

XX

Coffee-houses and Doss-houses

Why should we be packed, head and tail, like canned sardines?
— ROBERT BLATCHFORD

ANOTHER PHRASE gone glimmering, shorn of romance and
tradition and all that goes to make phrases worth keeping! For me, henceforth, 'coffee-house' will possess anything
but an agreeable connotation. Over on the other side of the
world, the mere mention of the word was sufficient to conjure up whole crowds of its historic frequenters, and to send
trooping through my imagination endless groups of wits and
dandies, pamphleteers and bravos, and bohemians of Grub
Street.

But here, on this side of the world, alas and alack, the very
name is a misnomer. Coffee-house: a place where people
drink coffee. Not at all. You cannot obtain coffee in such a
place for love or money. True, you may call for coffee, and
you will have brought you something in a cup purporting to
be coffee, and you will taste it and be disillusioned, for coffee
it certainly is not.

And what is true of the coffee is true of the coffee-house.
Working-men, in the main, frequent these places, and greasy,
dirty places they are, without one thing about them to cherish
decency in a man or put self-respect into him. Tablecloths and
napkins are unknown. A man eats in the midst of the débris
left by his predecessor, and dribbles his own scraps about him
and on the floor. In rush times, in such places, I have positively waded through the muck and mess that covered the
floor and I have managed to eat because I was abominably
hungry and capable of eating anything.

This seems to be the normal condition of the working-man,
from the zest with which he addresses himself to the board.
Eating is a necessity, and there are no frills about it. He
brings in with him a primitive voraciousness, and, I am confident, carries away with him a fairly healthy appetite. When
you see such a man, on his way to work in the morning,

order a pint of tea, which is no more tea than it is ambrosia, pull a hunk of dry bread from his pocket, and wash the one down with the other, depend upon it, that man has not the right sort of stuff in his belly, nor enough of the wrong sort of stuff, to fit him for his day's work. And further, depend upon it, he and a thousand of his kind will not turn out the quantity or quality of work that a thousand men will who have eaten heartily of meat and potatoes and drunk coffee that is coffee.

A pint of tea, kipper (or bloater), and 'two slices' (bread and butter) are a very good breakfast for a London workman. I have looked in vain for him to order a five-penny or six-penny steak (the cheapest to be had); while, when I ordered one for myself, I have usually had to wait till the proprietor could send out to the nearest butchershop and buy one.

As a vagrant in the 'Hobo' of a California jail, I have been served better food and drink than the London workman receives in his coffee-houses; while as an American laborer I have eaten a breakfast for twelvepence such as the British laborer would not dream of eating. Of course, he will pay only three or four pence for his; which is, however, as much as I paid, for I would be earning six shillings to his two or two and a half. On the other hand, though, and in return, I would turn out an amount of work in the course of the day that would put to shame the amount he turned out. So there are two sides to it. The man with the high standard of living will always do more work and better than the man with the low standard of living.

There is a comparison which sailormen make between the English and American merchant services. In an English ship, they say, it is poor grub, poor pay, and easy work; in an American ship, good grub, good pay, and hard work. And this is applicable to the working populations of both countries. The ocean greyhounds have to pay for speed and steam, and so does the workman. But if the workman is not able to pay for it, he will not have the speed and steam, that is all. The proof of it is when the English workman comes to America. He will lay more bricks in New York than he will in London, still more bricks in St. Louis, and still more bricks when he gets to San Francisco.[1] His standard of living has been rising all the time.

Early in the morning, along the streets frequented by workmen on the way to work, many women sit on the sidewalk with sacks of bread beside them. No end of workmen purchase these, and eat them as they walk along. They do not even wash the dry bread down with the tea to be obtained for a penny in the coffee-houses. It is incontestable that a man is not fit to begin his day's work on a meal like that; and it is equally incontestable that the loss will fall upon his employer and upon the nation. For some time, now, statesmen have been crying, "Wake up, England!" It would show more hardheaded common sense if they changed the tune to "Feed up, England!"

Not only is the worker poorly fed, but he is filthily fed. I have stood outside a butchershop and watched a horde of speculative housewives turning over the trimmings and scraps and shreds of beef and mutton—dog-meat in the States. I would not vouch for the clean fingers of these housewives, no more than I would vouch for the cleanliness of the single rooms in which many of them and their families lived; yet they raked, and pawed, and scraped the mess about in their anxiety to get the worth of their coppers. I kept my eye on one particularly offensive-looking bit of meat, and followed it through the clutches of over twenty women, till it fell to the lot of a timid-appearing little woman whom the butcher bulldosed into taking it. All day long this heap of scraps was added to and taken away from, the dust and dirt of the street falling upon it, flies settling on it, and the dirty fingers turning it over and over.

The costers wheel loads of specked and decaying fruit around in the barrows all day, and very often store it in their one living and sleeping room for the night. There it is exposed to the sickness and disease, the effluvia and vile exhalations of overcrowded and rotten life, and next day it is carted about again to be sold.

The poor worker of the East End never knows what it is to eat good wholesome meat or fruit—in fact, he rarely eats

[1] The San Francisco bricklayer receives twenty shillings per day, and at present is on strike for twenty-four shillings.

meat or fruit at all; while the skilled workman has nothing to boast of in the way of what he eats. Judging from the coffee-houses, which is a fair criterion, they never know in all their lives what tea, coffee, or cocoa taste like. The slops and water-witcheries of the coffee-houses, varying only in sloppiness and witchery, never even approximate or suggest what you and I are accustomed to drink as tea and coffee.

A little incident comes to me, connected with a coffee-house not far from Jubilee Street on the Mile End Road.

"Cawn yer let me 'ave somethin' for this, daughter? Anythin', Hi don't mind. Hi 'aven't 'ad a bite the blessed dy, an Hi'm that fynt. . . ."

She was an old woman, clad in decent black rags, and in her hand she held a penny. The one she had addressed as 'daughter' was a care-worn woman of forty, proprietress and waitress of the house.

I waited, possibly as anxiously as the old woman, to see how the appeal would be received. It was four in the afternoon, and she looked faint and sick. The woman hesitated an instant, then brought a large plate of 'stewed lamb and young peas.' I was eating a plate of it myself, and it is my judgment that the lamb was mutton and that the peas might have been younger without being youthful. However, the point is, the dish was sold at sixpence, and the proprietress gave it for a penny, demonstrating anew the old truth that the poor are the most charitable.

The old woman, profuse in her gratitude, took a seat on the other side of the narrow table and ravenously attacked the smoking stew. We ate steadily and silently, the pair of us, when suddenly, explosively and most gleefully, she cried out to me: —

"Hi sold a box o' matches!"

"Yus," she confirmed, if anything with greater and more explosive glee. "Hi sold a box o' matches! That's 'ow Hi got the penny."

"You must be getting along in years," I suggested.

"Seventy-four yesterday," she replied, and returned with gusto to her plate.

"Blimey, I'd like to do something for the old girl, that I would, but this is the first I've 'ad to-dy," the young fellow alongside volunteered to me. "An' I only 'ave this because I 'appened to make an odd shilling washin' out, Lord lumme! I don't know 'ow many pots."

"No work at my own tryde for six weeks," he said further, in reply to my questions; "nothin' but odd jobs a blessed long wy between."

One meets with all sorts of adventures in coffee-houses, and I shall not soon forget a Cockney Amazon in a place near Trafalgar Square, to whom I tendered a sovereign when paying my score. (By the way, one is supposed to pay before he begins to eat, and if he be poorly dressed he is compelled to pay before he eats.)

The girl bit the gold piece between her teeth, rang it on the counter, and then looked me and my rags witheringly up and down.

"Where'd you find it?" she at length demanded.

"Some mug left it on the table when he went out, eh, don't you think?" I retorted.

"Wot's yer gyme?" she queried, looking me calmly in the eyes.

"I makes 'em," quoth I.

She sniffed superciliously and gave me the change in small silver, and I had my revenge by biting and ringing every piece of it.

"I'll give you ha'penny for another lump of sugar in the tea," I said.

"I'll see you in 'ell first," came the retort courteous. Also, she amplified the retort courteous in divers vivid and unprintable ways.

I never had much talent for repartee, but she knocked silly what little I had, and I gulped down my tea a beaten man, while she gloated after me even as I passed out to the street.

While 300,000 people of London live in one-room tenements, and 900,000 are illegally and viciously housed, 38,000 more are registered as living in common lodging-houses—known in the vernacular as 'doss-houses.' There are many kinds of doss-houses, but in one thing they are all alike, from the filthy little ones to the monster big ones paying five per cent and blatantly lauded by smug middle-class men who know nothing about them, and that one thing is their uninhabitableness. By this I do not mean that the roofs leak or the walls are draughty; but what I do mean is that life in them is degrading and unwholesome.

'The poor man's hotel,' they are often called, but the phrase is caricature. Not to possess a room to one's self, in which sometimes to sit alone; to be forced out of bed willy-nilly, the first thing in the morning; to engage and pay anew for a bed each night; and never to have any privacy, surely is a mode of existence quite different from that of hotel life.

This must not be considered a sweeping condemnation of the big private and municipal lodging-houses and working-men's homes. Far from it. They have remedied many of the atrocities attendant upon the irresponsible small doss-houses, and they give the workman more for his money than he ever received before; but that does not make them as habitable or wholesome as the dwelling-place of a man should be who does his work in the world.

The little private doss-houses, as a rule, are unmitigated horrors. I have slept in them, and I know; but let me pass them by and confine myself to the bigger and better ones. Not far from Middlesex Street, Whitechapel, I entered such a house, a place inhabited almost entirely by working-men. The entrance was by way of a flight of steps descending from the sidewalk to what was properly the cellar of the building. Here were two large and gloomily lighted rooms, in which men cooked and ate. I had intended to do some cooking myself, but the smell of the place stole away my appetite, or, rather, wrested it from me; so I contented myself with watching other men cook and eat.

One workman, home from work, sat down opposite me at the rough wooden table, and began his meal. A handful of salt on the not over-clean table constituted his butter. Into it he dipped his bread, mouthful by mouthful, and washed it down with tea from a big mug. A piece of fish completed his bill of fare. He ate silently, looking neither to right nor left nor across at me. Here and there, at the various tables, other men were eating, just as silently. In the whole room there was hardly a note of conversation. A feeling of gloom pervaded the ill-lighted place. Many of them sat and brooded over the crumbs of their repast, and made me wonder, as Childe

Roland wondered, what evil they had done that they should be punished so.

From the kitchen came the sounds of more genial life, and I ventured in to the range where the men were cooking. But the smell I had noticed on entering was stronger here, and a rising nausea drove me into the street for fresh air.

On my return I paid fivepence for a 'cabin,' took my receipt for the same in the form of a huge brass check, and went upstairs to the smoking-room. Here, a couple of small billiard tables and several checkerboards were being used by young working-men, who waited in relays for their turn at the games, while many men were sitting around, smoking, reading, and mending their clothes. The young men were hilarious, the old men were gloomy. In fact, there were two types of men, the cheerful and the sodden or blue, and age seemed to determine the classification.

But no more than the two cellar rooms, did this room convey the remotest suggestion of home. Certainly there could be nothing homelike about it to you and me, who know what home really is. On the walls were the most preposterous and insulting notices regulating the conduct of the guests, and at ten o'clock the lights were put out, and nothing remained but bed. This was gained by descending again to the cellar, by surrendering the brass check to a burly doorkeeper, and by climbing a long flight of stairs into the upper regions. I went to the top of the building and down again, passing several floors filled with sleeping men. The 'cabins' were the best accommodation, each cabin allowing space for a tiny bed and room alongside of it in which to undress. The bedding was clean, and with neither it nor the bed do I find any fault. But there was no privacy about it, no being alone.

To get an adequate idea of a floor filled with cabins, you have merely to magnify a layer of the pasteboard pigeon-holes of an egg-crate till each pigeon-hole is seven feet in height and otherwise properly dimensioned, then place the magnified layer on the floor of a large, barnlike room, and there you have it. There are no ceilings to the pigeon-holes, the walls are thin, and the snores from all the sleepers and every move and turn of your nearer neighbors come plainly to your ears. And this cabin is yours only for a little while. In the morning out you go. You cannot put your trunk in it, or come and go when you like, or lock the door behind you, or anything of the sort. In fact, there is no door at all, only a doorway. If you care to remain a guest in this poor man's hotel, you must put up with all this, and with prison regulations which impress upon you constantly that you are nobody, with little soul of your own and less to say about it.

Now I contend that the least a man who does his day's work should have, is a room to himself, where he can lock the door and be safe in his possessions; where he can sit down and read by a window or look out; where he can come and go whenever he wishes; where he can accumulate a few personal belongings other than those he carries about with him on his back and in his pockets; where he can hang up pictures of his mother, sister, sweetheart, ballet dancers, or bulldogs, as his heart listeth—in short, one place of his own on the earth of which he can say: "This is mine, my castle; the world stops at the threshold; here am I lord and master." He will be a better citizen, this man; and he will do a better day's work.

I stood on one floor of the poor man's hotel and listened. I went from bed to bed and looked at the sleepers. They were young men, from twenty to forty, most of them. Old men cannot afford the working-man's home. They go to the workhouse. But I looked at the young men, scores of them, and they were not bad-looking fellows. Their faces were made for women's kisses, their necks for women's arms. They were lovable, as men are lovable. They were capable of love. A woman's touch redeems and softens, and they needed such redemption and softening instead of each day growing harsh and harsher. And I wondered where these women were, and heard a 'harlot's ginny laugh.' Leman Street, Waterloo Road, Piccadilly, The Strand, answered me, and I knew where they were.

XXI

The Precariousness of Life

What do you work at? You look ill.
It's me lungs. I make sulphuric acid.

You are a salt-cake man?
Yes.
Is it hard work?
It is damned hard work.

Why do you work at such a slavish trade?
I am married. I have children. Am I to starve and let them?

Why do you lead this life?
I am married. There's a terrible lot of men out of work in St.
    Helen's.

What do you call hard work?
My work. *You* come and heave them three-hundredweight
    lumps with a fifty-pound bar, in that heat at the furnace
    door, and try it.
I will not. I am a philosopher.
Oh! Well, thee stick to t' job. Ours is t' vary devil.
    — *From interviews with workmen by* ROBERT BLATCHFORD

I WAS TALKING with a very vindictive man. In his opinion,
his wife had wronged him and the law had wronged him.
The merits and morals of the case are immaterial. The meat
of the matter is that she had obtained a separation, and he
was compelled to pay ten shillings each week for the support
of her and the five children. "But look you," said he to me,
"wot'll 'appen to 'er if I don't py up the ten shillings?
S'posin', now, just s'posin' a accident 'appens to me, so I
cawn't work. S'posin' I get a rupture, or the rheumatics, or
the cholera. Wot's she goin' to do, eh? Wot's she goin' to
do?"

He shook his head sadly. "No 'ope for 'er. The best she
cawn do is the work'ouse, an' that's 'ell. An' if she don't go
to the work'ouse, it'll be worse 'ell. Come along 'ith me an'

I'll show you women sleepin' in a passage, a dozen of 'em. An' I'll show you worse, wot she'll come to if anythin' 'appens to me and the ten shillings."

The certitude of this man's forecast is worthy of consideration. He knew conditions sufficiently to know the precariousness of his wife's grasp on food and shelter. For her the game was up when his working capacity was impaired or destroyed. And when this state of affairs is looked at in its larger aspect, the same will be found true of hundreds of thousands and even millions of men and women living amicably together and coöperating in the pursuit of food and shelter.

The figures are appalling; 1,800,000 people in London live on the poverty line and below it, and another 1,000,000 live with one week's wages between them and pauperism. In all England and Wales, eighteen per cent of the whole population are driven to the parish for relief, and in London, according to the statistics of the London County Council, twenty-one per cent of the whole population are driven to the parish for relief. Between being driven to the parish for relief and being an out-and-out pauper there is a great difference, yet London supports 123,000 paupers, quite a city of folk in themselves. One in every four in London dies on public charity, while 939 out of every 1000 in the United Kingdom die in poverty; 8,000,000 simply struggle on the ragged edge of starvation, and 20,000,000 more are not comfortable in the simple and clean sense of the word.

It is interesting to go more into detail concerning the London people who die on charity. In 1886, and up to 1893, the percentage of pauperism to population was less in London than in all England; but since 1893, and for every succeeding year, the percentage of pauperism to population has been greater in London than in all England. Yet, from the Registrar General's Report for 1886, the following figures are taken:—

Out of 81,951 deaths in London (1884)—

In workhouses	9,909
In hospitals	6,559
In lunatic asylums	278
Total in public refuges	16,746

Commenting on these figures, a Fabian writer says: "Considering that comparatively few of these are children, it is probable that one in every three London adults will be driven into one of these refuges to die, and the proportion in the case of the manual labor class must of course be still larger."

These figures serve somewhat to indicate the proximity of the average worker to pauperism. Various things make pauperism. An advertisement, for instance, such as this, appearing in yesterday morning's paper: "Clerk wanted, with knowledge of shorthand, typewriting, and invoicing; wages ten shillings ($2.50) a week. Apply by letter," etc. And in to-day's paper I read of a clerk, thirty-five years of age and an inmate of a London workhouse, brought before a magistrate for non-performance of task. He claimed that he had done his various tasks since he had been an inmate; but when the master set him to breaking stones, his hands blistered, and he could not finish the task. He had never been used to an implement heavier than a pen, he said. The magistrate sentenced him and his blistered hands to seven days' hard labor.

Old age, of course, makes pauperism. And then there is the accident, the thing happening, the death or disablement of the husband, father, and bread-winner. Here is a man, with a wife and three children, living on the ticklish security of twenty shillings ($5.00) per week—and there are hundreds of thousands of such families in London. Perforce, to even half exist, they must live up to the last penny of it, so that a week's wages, $5.00, is all that stands between this family and pauperism or starvation. The thing happens, the father is struck down, and what then? A mother with three children can do little or nothing. Either she must hand her children over to society as juvenile paupers, in order to be free to do something adequate for herself, or she must go to the sweat-shops for work which she can perform in the vile den possible to her reduced income. But with the sweat-shops, married women who eke out their husband's earnings, and single women who have but themselves miserably to support, determine the scale of wages. And this scale of wages, so determined, is so low that the mother and her three children can live only in positive beastliness and semi-starvation, till decay and death end their suffering.

To show that this mother, with her three children to support, cannot compete in the sweating industries, I instance from the current newspapers the two following cases. A father indignantly writes that his daughter and a girl companion receive 17 cents per gross for making boxes. They made each day four gross. Their expenses were 16 cents for carfare, 4 cents for stamps, 5 cents for glue, and 2 cents for string, so that all they earned between them was 42 cents, or a daily wage each of 21 cents. In the second case, before the Luton Guardians a few days ago, an old woman of seventy-two appeared, asking for relief. "She was a straw hat maker, but had been compelled to give up the work owing to the price she obtained for them—namely, $4^{1}/_{2}$ cents each. For that price she had to provide plait trimmings and make and finish the hats."

Yet this mother and her three children we are considering, have done no wrong that they should be so punished. They have not sinned. The thing happened, that is all; the husband, father, and bread-winner, was struck down. There is no guarding against it. It is fortuitous. A family stands so many chances of escaping the bottom of the Abyss, and so many chances of falling plump down to it. The chance is reducible to cold, pitiless figures, and a few of these figures will not be out of place.

Sir A. Forwood calculates that,—

1 of every 1400 workmen is killed annually.
1 of every 2500 workmen is totally disabled.
1 of every 300 workmen is permanently partially disabled.
1 of every 8 workmen is temporarily disabled 3 or 4 weeks.

But these are only the accidents of industry. The high mortality of the people who live in the Ghetto plays a terrible part. The average age at death among the people of the West End is fifty-five years; the average age at death among the people of the East End is thirty years. That is to say, the person in the West End has twice the chance for life that the person has in the East End. Talk of war! The mortality in South Africa and the Philippines fades away to insignificance. Here, in the heart of peace, is where the blood is being shed; and here not even the civilized rules of warfare obtain, for the women and children and babes in the arms are killed just as ferociously as the men are killed. War! In England, every year, 500,000 men, women, and children, engaged in the various industries, are killed and disabled, or are injured to disablement by disease.

In the West End eighteen per cent of the children die before five years of age; in the East End fifty-five per cent of the children die before five years of age. And there are streets in London where, out of every one hundred children born in a year, fifty die during the next year; and of the fifty that remain, twenty-five die before they are five years old. Slaughter! Herod did not do quite so badly—his was a mere fifty per cent bagatelle mortality.

That industry causes greater havoc with human life than battle does no better substantiation can be given than the following extract from a recent report of the Liverpool Medical Officer, which is not applicable to Liverpool alone:—

> In many instances little if any sunlight could get to the courts, and the atmosphere within the dwellings was always foul, owing largely to the saturated condition of the walls and ceilings, which for so many years had absorbed the exhalations of the occupants into their porous material. Singular testimony to the absence of sunlight in these courts was furnished by the action of the Parks and Gardens Committee, who desired to brighten the homes of the poorest class by gifts of growing flowers and window-boxes; but these gifts could not be made in courts such as these, *as flowers and plants were susceptible to the unwholesome surroundings, and would not live*.

Mr. George Haw has compiled the following table on the three St. George's parishes (London parishes):—

	Percentage of Population Overcrowded	Death Rate per 1000
St. George's West	10	13.2
St. George's South	35	23.7
St. George's East	40	26.4

Then there are the 'dangerous trades,' in which countless workers are employed. Their hold on life is indeed precarious—far, far more precarious than the hold of the twentieth-century soldier on life. In the linen trade, in the preparation of the flax, wet feet and wet clothes cause an unusual amount of bronchitis, pneumonia, and severe rheumatism; while in the carding and spinning departments the fine dust produces lung-disease in the majority of cases, and the woman who starts carding at seventeen or eighteen begins to break up and go to pieces at thirty. The chemical laborers, picked from the strongest and most splendidly built men to be found, live, on an average, less than forty-eight years.

Says Dr. Arlidge, of the potter's trade: "Potter's dust does not kill suddenly, but settles, year after year, a little more firmly into the lungs, until at length a case of plaster is formed. Breathing becomes more and more difficult and depressed, and finally ceases."

Steel dust, stone dust, clay dust, alkali dust, fluff dust, fibre dust—all these things kill, and they are more deadly than machine-guns and pom-poms. Worst of all is the lead dust in the white lead trades. Here is a description of the typical dissolution of a young, healthy, well-developed girl who goes to work in a white lead factory:—

Here, after a varying degree of exposure, she becomes anæmic. It may be that her gums show a very faint blue line, or perchance her teeth and gums are perfectly sound, and no blue line is discernible. Coincidently with the anæmia she has been getting thinner, but so gradually as scarcely to impress itself upon her or her friends. Sickness, however, ensues, and headaches, growing in intensity, are developed. These are frequently attended by obscuration of vision or temporary blindness. Such a girl passes into what appears to her friends and medical adviser as ordinary hysteria. This gradually deepens without warning, until she is suddenly seized with a convulsion, beginning in one-half of the face, then involving the arm, next the leg of the same side of the body, until the convulsion, violent and purely epileptic form in character, becomes universal. This is attended by loss of consciousness, out of which she passes into a series of convulsions, gradually increasing in severity, in one of which she dies—or consciousness, partial or perfect, is regained, either, it may be, for a few minutes, a few hours, or days, during which violent headache is complained of, or she is delirious and excited, as in acute mania, or dull and sullen as in melancholia, and requires to be roused, when she is found wandering, and her speech is somewhat imperfect. Without further warning, save that the pulse, which has become soft, with nearly the normal number of beats, all at once becomes low and hard; she is suddenly seized with another convulsion, in which she dies, or passes into a state of coma from which she never rallies. In another case the convulsions will gradually subside, the headache disappears and the patient recovers, only to find that she has completely lost her eyesight, a loss that may be temporary or permanent.

And here are a few specific cases of white lead poisoning:—

Charlotte Rafferty, a fine, well-grown young woman with a splendid constitution—who had never had a day's illness in her life—became a white lead worker. Convulsions seized her at the foot of the ladder in the works. Dr. Oliver examined her, found the blue line along her gums, which shows that the system is under the influence of the lead. He knew that the convulsions would shortly return. They did so, and she died.

Mary Ann Toler—a girl of seventeen, who had never had a fit in her life—three times became ill and had to leave off work in the factory. Before she was nineteen she showed symptoms of lead poisoning—had fits, frothed at the mouth, and died.

Mary A., an unusually vigorous woman, was able to work in the lead factory for *twenty years*, having colic once only during that time. Her eight children all died in early infancy from convulsions. One morning, whilst brushing her hair, this woman suddenly lost all power in both her wrists.

Eliza H., aged twenty-five, *after five months* at lead works, was seized with colic. She entered another factory (after being refused by the first one) and worked on uninterruptedly for two years. Then the former symptoms returned, she was seized with convulsions, and died in two days of acute lead poisoning.

Mr. Vaughan Nash, speaking of the unborn generation, says: "The children of the white lead worker enter the world, as a rule, only to die from the convulsions of lead poisoning—they are either born prematurely, or die within the first year."

And, finally, let me instance the case of Harriet A. Walker, a young girl of seventeen, killed while leading a forlorn hope on the industrial battlefield. She was employed as an enamelled ware brusher, wherein lead poisoning is encountered. Her father and brother were both out of employment. She concealed her illness, walked six miles a day to and from work, earned her seven or eight shillings per week, and died, at seventeen.

Depression in trade also plays an important part in hurling the workers into the Abyss. With a week's wages between a family and pauperism, a month's enforced idleness means hardship and misery almost undescribable, and from the ravages of which the victims do not always recover when work is to be had again. Just now the daily papers contain the report of a meeting of the Carlisle Branch of the Docker's Union, wherein it is stated that many of the men, for months past, have not averaged a weekly income of more than $1.00 to $1.25. The stagnated state of the shipping industry in the port of London is held accountable for this condition of affairs.

To the young working-man or working-woman, or married couple, there is no assurance of happy or healthy middle life, nor of solvent old age. Work as they will, they cannot make their future secure. It is all a matter of chance. Everything depends upon the thing happening, the thing with which they have nothing to do. Precaution cannot fend it off, nor can wiles evade it. If they remain on the industrial battlefield they must face it and take their chance against heavy odds. Of course, if they are favorably made and are not tied by kinship duties, they may run away from the industrial battlefield. In which event, the safest thing the man can do is to join the army; and for the woman, possibly, to become a Red Cross nurse or go into a nunnery. In either case they must forego home and children and all that makes life worth living and old age other than a nightmare.

XXII

Suicide

England is the paradise of the rich, the purgatory of the wise, and the hell of the poor.

—THEODORE PARKER

WITH LIFE so precarious, and opportunity for the happiness of life so remote, it is inevitable that life shall be cheap and suicide common. So common is it, that one cannot pick up a daily paper without running across it; while an attempt-at-suicide case in a police court excites no more interest than an ordinary 'drunk,' and is handled with the same rapidity and unconcern.

I remember such a case in the Thames Police Court. I pride myself that I have good eyes and ears, and a fair working knowledge of men and things; but I confess, as I stood in that courtroom, that I was half-bewildered by the amazing despatch with which drunks, disorderlies, vagrants, brawlers, wife-beaters, thieves, fences, gamblers, and women of the street went through the machine of justice. The dock stood in the centre of the court (where the light is best), and into it and out again stepped men, women, and children, in a stream as steady as the stream of sentences which fell from the magistrate's lips.

I was still pondering over a consumptive 'fence' who had pleaded inability to work and necessity for supporting wife and children, and who had received a year at hard labor, when a young boy of about twenty appeared in the dock. 'Alfred Freeman.' I caught his name, but failed to catch the charge. A stout and motherly-looking woman bobbed up in the witness-box and began her testimony. Wife of the Britannia lock-keeper, I learned she was. Time, night; a splash; she ran to the lock and found the prisoner in the water.

I flashed my gaze from her to him. So that was the charge, self-murder. He stood there dazed and unheeding, his bonny brown hair rumpled down his forehead, his face haggard and care-worn and boyish still.

"Yes, sir," the lock-keeper's wife was saying. "As fast as I pulled to get 'im out, 'e crawled back. Then I called for 'elp, and some workmen 'appened along, and we got 'im out and turned 'im over to the constable."

The magistrate complimented the woman on her muscular powers, and the courtroom laughed; but all I could see was a boy on the threshold of life, passionately crawling to muddy death, and there was no laughter in it.

A man was now in the witness-box, testifying to the boy's good character and giving extenuating evidence. He was the boy's foreman, or had been. Alfred was a good boy, but he had had lots of trouble at home, money matters. And then his mother was sick. He was given to worrying, and he worried over it till he laid himself out and wasn't fit for work. He (the foreman), for the sake of his own reputation, the boy's work being bad, had been forced to ask him to resign.

"Anything to say?" the magistrate demanded abruptly.

The boy in the dock mumbled something indistinctly. He was still dazed.

"What does he say, constable?" the magistrate asked impatiently.

The stalwart man in blue bent his ear to the prisoner's lips, and then replied loudly, "He says he's very sorry, your Worship."

"Remanded," said his Worship; and the next case was under way, the first witness already engaged in taking the oath. The boy, dazed and unheeding, passed out with the jailer. That was all, five minutes from start to finish; and two hulking brutes in the dock were trying strenuously to shift the responsibility of the possession of a stolen fishing-pole, worth probably ten cents.

The chief trouble with these poor folk is that they do not know how to commit suicide, and usually have to make two or three attempts before they succeed. This, very naturally, is a horrid nuisance to the constables and magistrates, and gives them no end of trouble. Sometimes, however, the magistrates are frankly outspoken about the matter, and censure the prisoners for the slackness of their attempts. For instance, Mr. R. Sykes, chairman of the Stalybridge magistrates, in the case the other day of Ann Wood, who tried to make away with herself in the canal: "If you wanted to do it, why didn't you do it and get it done with?" demanded the indignant Mr. Sykes. "Why did you not get under the water and make an end of it, instead of giving us all this trouble and bother?"

Poverty, misery, and fear of the workhouse, are the principal causes of suicide among the working classes. "I'll drown myself before I go into the workhouse," said Ellen Hughes Hunt, aged fifty-two. Last Wednesday they held an inquest on her body at Shoreditch. Her husband came from the Islington Workhouse to testify. He had been a cheesemonger, but failure in business and poverty had driven him into the workhouse, whither his wife had refused to accompany him.

She was last seen at one in the morning. Three hours later her hat and jacket were found on the towing path by the Regent's Canal, and later her body was fished from the water. *Verdict: Suicide during temporary insanity.*

Such verdicts are crimes against truth. The Law is a lie, and through it men lie most shamelessly. For instance, a disgraced woman, forsaken and spat upon by kith and kin, doses herself and her baby with laudanum. The baby dies; but she pulls through after a few weeks in hospital, is charged with murder, convicted, and sentenced to ten years' penal servitude. Recovering, the Law holds her responsible for her actions; yet, had she died, the same Law would have rendered a verdict of temporary insanity.

Now, considering the case of Ellen Hughes Hunt, it is as fair and logical to say that her husband was suffering from temporary insanity when he went into the Islington Workhouse, as it is to say that she was suffering from temporary insanity when she went into the Regent's Canal. As to which is the preferable sojourning place is a matter of opinion, of intellectual judgment. I, for one, from what I know of canals and workhouses, should choose the canal, were I in a similar position. And I make bold to contend that I am no more insane than Ellen Hughes Hunt, her husband, and the rest of the human herd.

Man no longer follows instinct with the old natural fidelity. He has developed into a reasoning creature, and can intellectually cling to life or discard life just as life happens to promise great pleasure or pain. I dare to assert that Ellen Hughes

Hunt, defrauded and bilked of all the joys of life which fifty-two years' service in the world had earned, with nothing but the horrors of the workhouse before her, was very rational and level-headed when she elected to jump into the canal. And I dare to assert, further, that the jury had done a wiser thing to bring in a verdict charging society with temporary insanity for allowing Ellen Hughes Hunt to be defrauded and bilked of all the joys of life which fifty-two years' service in the world had earned.

Temporary insanity! Oh, these cursed phrases, these lies of language, under which people with meat in their bellies and whole shirts on their backs shelter themselves, and evade the responsibility of their brothers and sisters, empty of belly and without whole shirts on their backs.

From one issue of the *Observer*, an East End paper, I quote the following commonplace events: —

A ship's fireman, named Johnny King, was charged with attempting to commit suicide. On Wednesday defendant went to Bow Police Station and stated that he had swallowed a quantity of phosphor paste, as he was hard up and unable to obtain work. King was taken inside and an emetic administered, when he vomited up a quantity of the poison. Defendant now said he was very sorry. Although he had sixteen years' good character, he was unable to obtain work of any kind. Mr. Dickinson had defendant put back for the court missionary to see him.

Timothy Warner, thirty-two, was remanded for a similar offence. He jumped off Limehouse Pier, and when rescued, said, "I intended to do it."

A decent-looking young woman, named Ellen Gray, was remanded on a charge of attempting to commit suicide. About half-past eight on Sunday morning Constable 834 K found defendant lying in a doorway in Benworth Street, and she was in a very drowsy condition. She was holding an empty bottle in one hand, and stated that some two or three hours previously she had swallowed a quantity of laudanum. As she was evidently very ill, the divisional surgeon was sent for, and having administered some coffee, ordered

that she was to be kept awake. When defendant was
charged, she stated that the reason why she attempted to
take her life was she had neither home nor friends.

I do not say that all people who commit suicide are sane,
no more than I say that all people who do not commit suicide
are sane. Insecurity of food and shelter, by the way, is a great
cause of insanity among the living. Costermongers, hawkers,
and pedlars, a class of workers who live from hand to mouth
more than those of any other class, form the highest percentage of those in the lunatic asylums. Among the males each
year, 26.9 per 10,000 go insane, and among the women, 36.9.
On the other hand, of soldiers, who are at least sure of food
and shelter, 13 per 10,000 go insane; and of farmers and gra-
ziers, only 5.1. So a coster is twice as likely to lose his reason
as a soldier, and five times as likely as a farmer.

Misfortune and misery are very potent in turning people's
heads, and drive one person to the lunatic asylum, and another to the morgue or the gallows. When the thing happens,
and the father and husband, for all of his love for wife and
children and his willingness to work, can get no work to do,
it is a simple matter for his reason to totter and the light
within his brain go out. And it is especially simple when it is
taken into consideration that his body is ravaged by innutrition and disease, in addition to his soul being torn by the
sight of his suffering wife and little ones.

"He is a good-looking man, with a mass of black hair, dark,
expressive eyes, delicately chiselled nose and chin, and wavy,
fair moustache." This is the reporter's description of Frank
Cavilla as he stood in court, this dreary month of September,
"dressed in a much worn gray suit, and wearing no collar."

Frank Cavilla lived and worked as a house decorator in
London. He is described as a good workman, a steady fellow,
and not given to drink, while all his neighbors unite in testifying that he was a gentle and affectionate husband and
father.

His wife, Hannah Cavilla, was a big, handsome, light-
hearted woman. She saw to it that his children were sent
neat and clean (the neighbors all remarked the fact) to the
Childeric Road Board School. And so, with such a man, so

blessed, working steadily and living temperately, all went well, and the goose hung high.

Then the thing happened. He worked for a Mr. Beck, builder, and lived in one of his master's houses in Trundley Road. Mr. Beck was thrown from his trap and killed. The thing was an unruly horse, and, as I say, it happened. Cavilla had to seek fresh employment and find another house.

This occurred eighteen months ago. For eighteen months he fought the big fight. He got rooms in a little house on Batavia Road, but could not make both ends meet. Steady work could not be obtained. He struggled manfully at casual employment of all sorts, his wife and four children starving before his eyes. He starved himself, and grew weak, and fell ill. This was three months ago, and then there was absolutely no food at all. They made no complaint, spoke no word; but poor folk know. The housewives of Batavia Road sent them food, but so respectable were the Cavillas that the food was sent anonymously, mysteriously, so as not to hurt their pride.

The thing had happened. He had fought, and starved, and suffered for eighteen months. He got up one September morning, early. He opened his pocket-knife. He cut the throat of his wife, Hannah Cavilla, aged thirty-three. He cut the throat of his first-born, Frank, aged twelve. He cut the throat of his son, Walter, aged eight. He cut the throat of his daughter, Nellie, aged four. He cut the throat of his youngest-born, Ernest, aged sixteen months. Then he watched beside the dead all day until the evening, when the police came, and he told them to put a penny in the slot of the gas-meter in order that they might have light to see.

Frank Cavilla stood in court, dressed in a much worn gray suit, and wearing no collar. He was a good-looking man, with a mass of black hair, dark, expressive eyes, delicately chiselled nose and chin, and wavy, fair moustache.

XXIII

The Children

Where home is a hovel, and dull we grovel,
Forgetting the world is fair.

THERE is one beautiful sight in the East End, and only
one, and it is the children dancing in the street when the
organ-grinder goes his round. It is fascinating to watch them,
the new-born, the next generation, swaying and stepping,
with pretty little mimicries and graceful inventions all their
own, with muscles that move swiftly and easily, and bodies
that leap airily, weaving rhythms never taught in dancing
school.

I have talked with these children, here, there, and everywhere, and they struck me as being bright as other children,
and in many ways even brighter. They have most active little
imaginations. Their capacity for projecting themselves into
the realm of romance and fantasy is remarkable. A joyous life
is romping in their blood. They delight in music, and motion,
and color, and very often they betray a startling beauty of face
and form under their filth and rags.

But there is a Pied Piper of London Town who steals them
all away. They disappear. One never sees them again, or anything that suggests them. You may look for them in vain
amongst the generation of grown-ups. Here you will find
stunted forms, ugly faces, and blunt and stolid minds. Grace,
beauty, imagination, all the resiliency of mind and muscle, are
gone. Sometimes, however, you may see a woman, not necessarily old, but twisted and deformed out of all womanhood,
bloated and drunken, lift her draggled skirts and execute a
few grotesque and lumbering steps upon the pavement. It is
a hint that she was once one of those children who danced to
the organ-grinder. Those grotesque and lumbering steps are
all that is left of the promise of childhood. In the befogged
recesses of her brain has arisen a fleeting memory that she was
once a girl. The crowd closes in. Little girls are dancing beside her, about her, with all the pretty graces she dimly rec-

ollects, but can no more than parody with her body. Then she pants for breath, exhausted, and stumbles out through the circle. But the little girls dance on.

The children of the Ghetto possess all the qualities which make for noble manhood and womanhood; but the Ghetto itself, like an infuriated tigress turning on its young, turns upon and destroys all these qualities, blots out the light and laughter, and moulds those it does not kill into sodden and forlorn creatures, uncouth, degraded and wretched below the beasts of the field.

As to the manner in which this is done, I have in previous chapters described at length; here let Professor Huxley describe in brief: "Any one who is acquainted with the state of the population of all great industrial centres, whether in this or other countries, is aware that amidst a large and increasing body of that population there reigns supreme . . . that condition which the French call *la misère*, a word for which I do not think there is any exact English equivalent. It is a condition in which the food, warmth, and clothing which are necessary for the mere maintenance of the functions of the body in their normal state cannot be obtained; in which men, women, and children are forced to crowd into dens wherein decency is abolished, and the most ordinary conditions of healthful existence are impossible of attainment; in which the pleasures within reach are reduced to brutality and drunkenness; in which the pains accumulate at compound interest in the shape of starvation, disease, stunted development, and moral degradation; in which the prospect of even steady and honest industry is a life of unsuccessful battling with hunger, rounded by a pauper's grave."

In such conditions, the outlook for children is hopeless. They die like flies, and those that survive, survive because they possess excessive vitality and a capacity of adaptation to the degradation with which they are surrounded. They have no home life. In the dens and lairs in which they live they are exposed to all that is obscene and indecent. And as their minds are made rotten, so are their bodies made rotten by bad sanitation, overcrowding, and underfeeding. When a father and mother live with three or four children in a room where the children take turn about in sitting up to drive the

rats away from the sleepers, when those children never have
enough to eat and are preyed upon and made miserable and
weak by swarming vermin, the sort of men and women the
survivors will make can readily be imagined.

> Dull despair and misery
> Lie about them from their birth;
> Ugly curses, uglier mirth,
> Are their earliest lullaby.

A man and a woman marry and set up housekeeping in one
room. Their income does not increase with the years, though
their family does, and the man is exceedingly lucky if he can
keep his health and his job. A baby comes, and then another.
This means that more room should be obtained; but these
little mouths and bodies mean additional expense and make it
absolutely impossible to get more spacious quarters. More babies come. There is not room in which to turn around. The
youngsters run the streets, and by the time they are twelve or
fourteen the room-issue comes to a head, and out they go on
the streets for good. The boy, if he be lucky, can manage to
make the common lodging-houses, and he may have any one
of several ends. But the girl of fourteen or fifteen, forced in
this manner to leave the one room called home, and able to
earn at the best a paltry five or six shillings per week, can have
but one end. And the bitter end of that one end is such as
that of the woman whose body the police found this morning
in a doorway on Dorset Street, Whitechapel. Homeless, shelterless, sick, with no one with her in her last hour, she had
died in the night of exposure. She was sixty-two years old and
a match vender. She died as a wild animal dies.

Fresh in my mind is the picture of a boy in the dock of an
East End police court. His head was barely visible above the
railing. He was being proved guilty of stealing two shillings
from a woman, which he had spent, not for candy and cakes
and a good time, but for food.

"Why didn't you ask the woman for food?" the magistrate
demanded, in a hurt sort of tone. "She would surely have
given you something to eat."

"If I 'ad arsked 'er, I'd got locked up for beggin'," was the boy's reply.

The magistrate knitted his brows and accepted the rebuke. Nobody knew the boy, nor his father or mother. He was without beginning or antecedents, a waif, a stray, a young cub seeking his food in the jungle of empire, preying upon the weak and being preyed upon by the strong.

The people who try to help gather up the Ghetto children and send them away on a day's outing to the country. They believe that not very many children reach the age of ten without having had at least one day there. Of this, a writer says: "The mental change caused by one day so spent must not be undervalued. Whatever the circumstances, the children learn the meaning of fields and woods, so that descriptions of country scenery in the books they read, which before conveyed no impression, become now intelligible."

One day in the fields and woods, if they are lucky enough to be picked up by the people who try to help! And they are being born faster every day than they can be carted off to the fields and woods for the one day in their lives. One day! In all their lives, one day! And for the rest of the days, as the boy told a certain bishop, "At ten we 'ops the wag; at thirteen we nicks things; an' at sixteen we bashes the copper." Which is to say, at ten they play truant, at thirteen steal, and at sixteen are sufficiently developed hooligans to smash the policemen.

The Rev. J. Cartmel Robinson tells of a boy and girl of his parish, who set out to walk to the forest. They walked and walked through the never-ending streets, expecting always to see it by and by; until they sat down at last, faint and despairing, and were rescued by a kind woman who brought them back. Evidently they had been overlooked by the people who try to help.

The same gentleman is authority for the statement that in a street in Hoxton (a district of the vast East End), over seven hundred children, between five and thirteen years, live in eighty small houses. And he adds: "It is because London has largely shut her children in a maze of streets and houses and robbed them of their rightful inheritance in sky and field and brook, that they grow up to be men and women physically unfit."

He tells of a member of his congregation who let a basement room to a married couple. "They said they had two children; when they got possession it turned out that they had four. After a while a fifth appeared, and the landlord gave them notice to quit. They paid no attention to it. Then the sanitary inspector, who has to wink at the law so often, came in and threatened my friend with legal proceedings. He pleaded that he could not get them out. They pleaded that nobody would have them with so many children at a rental within their means, which is one of the commonest complaints of the poor, by the bye. What was to be done? The landlord was between two millstones. Finally he applied to the magistrate, who sent up an officer to inquire into the case. Since that time about twenty days have elapsed, and nothing has yet been done. Is this a singular case? By no means; it is quite common."

Last week the police raided a disorderly house. In one room were found two young children. They were arrested and charged with being inmates the same as the women had been. Their father appeared at the trial. He stated that himself and wife and two older children, besides the two in the dock, occupied that room; he stated also that he occupied it because he could get no other room for the half-crown a week he paid for it. The magistrate discharged the two juvenile offenders and warned the father that he was bringing his children up unhealthily.

But there is need further to multiply instances. In London the slaughter of the innocents goes on on a scale more stupendous than any before in the history of the world. And equally stupendous is the callousness of the people who believe in Christ, acknowledge God, and go to church regularly on Sunday. For the rest of the week they riot about on the rents and profits which come to them from the East End stained with the blood of the children. Also, at times, so peculiarly are they made, they will take half a million of these rents and profits and send it away to educate the black boys of the Soudan.

XXIV

A Vision of the Night

All these were years ago little red-colored, pulpy infants, capable
of being kneaded, baked, into any social form you chose.

—CARLYLE

LATE LAST NIGHT I walked along Commercial Street from
Spitalfields to Whitechapel, and still continuing south,
down Leman Street to the docks. And as I walked I smiled at
the East End papers, which, filled with civic pride, boastfully
proclaim that there is nothing the matter with the East End
as a living place for men and women.

It is rather hard to tell a tithe of what I saw. Much of it is
untellable. But in a general way I may say that I saw a nightmare, a fearful slime that quickened the pavement with life, a
mess of unmentionable obscenity that put into eclipse the
'nightly horror' of Piccadilly and the Strand. It was a menagerie of garmented bipeds that looked something like humans
and more like beasts, and to complete the picture, brass-buttoned keepers kept order among them when they snarled too
fiercely.

I was glad the keepers were there, for I did not have on my
'seafaring' clothes, and I was what is called a 'mark' for the
creatures of prey that prowled up and down. At times, between keepers, these males looked at me sharply, hungrily,
gutter-wolves that they were, and I was afraid of their hands,
of their naked hands, as one may be afraid of the paws of a
gorilla. They reminded me of gorillas. Their bodies were
small, ill-shaped, and squat. There were no swelling muscles,
no abundant thews and wide-spreading shoulders. They exhibited, rather, an elemental economy of nature, such as the
cave-men must have exhibited. But there was strength in
those meagre bodies, the ferocious, primordial strength to
clutch and gripe and tear and rend. When they spring upon
their human prey they are known even to bend the victim
backward and double its body till the back is broken. They
possess neither conscience nor sentiment, and they will kill

for a half-sovereign, without fear or favor, if they are given but half a chance. They are a new species, a breed of city savages. The streets and houses, alleys and courts, are their hunting grounds. As valley and mountain are to the natural savage, street and building are valley and mountain to them. The slum is their jungle, and they live and prey in the jungle.

The dear soft people of the golden theatres and wonder-mansions of the West End do not see these creatures, do not dream that they exist. But they are here, alive, very much alive in their jungle. And woe the day, when England is fighting in her last trench, and her able-bodied men are on the firing-line! For on that day they will crawl out of their dens and lairs, and the people of the West End will see them, as the dear soft aristocrats of Feudal France saw them and asked one another, "Whence came they?" "Are they men?"

But they were not the only beasts that ranged the menagerie. They were only here and there, lurking in dark courts and passing like gray shadows along the walls; but the women from whose rotten loins they spring were everywhere. They whined insolently, and in maudlin tones begged me for pennies, and worse. They held carouse in every boozing ken, slatternly, unkempt, bleary-eyed, and tousled, leering and gibbering, overspilling with foulness and corruption, and, gone in debauch, sprawling across benches and bars, unspeakably repulsive, fearful to look upon.

And there were others, strange, weird faces and forms and twisted monstrosities that shouldered me on every side, inconceivable types of sodden ugliness, the wrecks of society, the perambulating carcasses, the living deaths—women, blasted by disease and drink till their shame brought not tu'pence in the open mart; and men, in fantastic rags, wrenched by hardship and exposure out of all semblance of men, their faces in a perpetual writhe of pain, grinning idiotically, shambling like apes, dying with every step they took and each breath they drew. And there were young girls, of eighteen and twenty, with trim bodies and faces yet untouched with twist and bloat, who had fetched the bottom of the Abyss plump, in one swift fall. And I remember a lad of fourteen, and one of six or seven, white-faced and sickly, homeless, the pair of them, who sat upon the pavement with their backs against a railing and watched it all.

The unfit and the unneeded! Industry does not clamor for them. There are no jobs going begging through lack of men and women. The dockers crowd at the entrance gate, and curse and turn away when the foreman does not give them a call. The engineers who have work pay six shillings a week to their brother engineers who can find nothing to do; 514,000 textile workers oppose a resolution condemning the employment of children under fifteen. Women, and plenty to spare, are found to toil under the sweat-shop masters for tenpence a day of fourteen hours. Alfred Freeman crawls to muddy death because he loses his job. Ellen Hughes Hunt prefers Regent's Canal to Islington Workhouse. Frank Cavilla cuts the throats of his wife and children because he cannot find work enough to give them food and shelter.

The unfit and the unneeded! The miserable and despised and forgotten, dying in the social shambles. The progeny of prostitution—of the prostitution of men and women and children, of flesh and blood, and sparkle and spirit; in brief, the prostitution of labor. If this is the best that civilization can do for the human, then give us howling and naked savagery. Far better to be a people of the wilderness and desert, of the cave and the squatting-place, than to be a people of the machine and the Abyss.

XXV

The Hunger Wail

I hold, if the Almighty had ever made a set of men to do all of
the eating and none of the work, he would have made them
with mouths only, and no hands; and if he had ever made another set that he had intended should do all of the work and
none of the eating, he would have made them without mouths
and with all hands.

—ABRAHAM LINCOLN

M Y FATHER has more stamina than I, for he is country-
born."

The speaker, a bright young East Ender, was lamenting his
poor physical development.

"Look at my scrawny arm, will you." He pulled up his
sleeve. "Not enough to eat, that's what's the matter with it.
Oh, not now. I have what I want to eat these days. But it's
too late. It can't make up for what I didn't have to eat when
I was a kiddy. Dad came up to London from the Fen Country. Mother died, and there were six of us kiddies and dad
living in two small rooms.

"He had hard times, dad did. He might have chucked us,
but he didn't. He slaved all day, and at night he came home
and cooked and cared for us. He was father and mother,
both. He did his best, but we didn't have enough to eat. We
rarely saw meat, and then of the worst. And it is not good
for growing kiddies to sit down to a dinner of bread and a
bit of cheese, and not enough of it.

"And what's the result? I am undersized, and I haven't the
stamina of my dad. It was starved out of me. In a couple of
generations there'll be no more of me here in London. Yet
there's my younger brother; he's bigger and better developed.
You see, dad and we children held together, and that accounts for it."

"But I don't see," I objected. "I should think, under such
conditions, that the vitality should decrease and the younger
children be born weaker and weaker."

"Not when they hold together," he replied. "Whenever you

come along in the East End and see a child of from eight to twelve, good-sized, well-developed, and healthy-looking, just you ask, and you will find that it is the youngest in the family, or at least is one of the younger. The way of it is this: the older children starve more than the younger ones. By the time the younger ones come along, the older ones are starting to work, and there is more money coming in, and more food to go around."

He pulled down his sleeve, a concrete instance of where chronic semi-starvation kills not, but stunts. His voice was but one among the myriads that raise the cry of the hunger wail in the greatest empire in the world. On any one day, over 1,000,000 people are in receipt of poor-law relief in the United Kingdom. One in eleven of the whole working-class receive poor-law relief in the course of the year; 37,500,000 people receive less than $60 per month, per family; and a constant army of 8,000,000 lives on the border of starvation.

A committee of the London County school board makes this declaration: "At times, *when there is no special distress*, 55,000 children in a state of hunger, which makes it useless to attempt to teach them, are in the schools of London alone." The italics are mine. "When there is no special distress" means good times in England; for the people of England have come to look upon starvation and suffering, which they call "distress," as part of the social order. Chronic starvation is looked upon as a matter of course. It is only when acute starvation makes its appearance on a large scale that they think something is unusual.

I shall never forget the bitter wail of a blind man in a little East End shop at the close of a murky day. He had been the eldest of five children, with a mother and no father. Being the eldest, he had starved and worked as a child to put bread into the mouths of his little brothers and sisters. Not once in three months did he ever taste meat. He never knew what it was to have his hunger thoroughly appeased. And he claimed that this chronic starvation of his childhood had robbed him of his sight. To support the claim, he quoted from the report of the Royal Commission on the Blind, "Blindness is most prevalent in poor districts, and poverty accelerates this dreadful affliction."

But he went further, this blind man, and in his voice was the bitterness of an afflicted man to whom society did not give enough to eat. He was one of an army of six million blind in London, and he said that in the blind homes they did not receive half enough to eat. He gave the diet for a day:—

> Breakfast—³/₄ pint of skilly and dry bread.
> Dinner—3 oz. meat.
>   1 slice of bread.
>   ¹/₂ lb. potatoes.
> Supper—³/₄ pint of skilly and dry bread.

Oscar Wilde, God rest his soul, voices the cry of the prison child, which, in varying degree, is the cry of the prison man and woman: "The second thing from which a child suffers in prison is hunger. The food that is given to it consists of a piece of usually bad-baked prison bread and a tin of water for breakfast at half-past seven. At twelve o'clock it gets dinner, composed of a tin of coarse Indian meal stirabout (skilly), and at half-past five it gets a piece of dry bread and a tin of water for its supper. This diet in the case of a strong grown man is always productive of illness of some kind, chiefly of course diarrhœa, with its attendant weakness. In fact, in a big prison astringent medicines are served out regularly by the warders as a matter of course. In the case of a child, the child is, as a rule, incapable of eating the food at all. Any one who knows anything about children knows how easily a child's digestion is upset by a fit of crying, or trouble and mental distress of any kind. A child who has been crying all day long, and per-haps half the night, in a lonely dim-lit cell, and is preyed upon by terror, simply cannot eat food of this coarse, horrible kind. In the case of the little child to whom warden Martin gave the biscuits, the child was crying with hunger on Tuesday morning, and utterly unable to eat the bread and water served to it for its breakfast. Martin went out after the breakfasts had been served and bought the few sweet biscuits for the child rather than see it starving. It was a beautiful action on his part, and was so recognized by the child, who, utterly uncon-scious of the regulations of the Prison Board, told one of the senior wardens how kind this junior warden had been to him. The result was, of course, a report and a dismissal."

Robert Blatchford compares the workhouse pauper's daily diet with the soldier's, which, when he was a soldier, was not considered liberal enough, and yet is twice as liberal as the pauper's.

PAUPER	DIET	SOLDIER
$3^{1}/_{4}$ oz.	Meat	12 oz.
$15^{1}/_{2}$ oz.	Bread	24 oz.
6 oz.	Vegetables	8 oz.

The adult male pauper gets meat (outside of soup) but once a week, and the paupers "have nearly all that pallid, pasty complexion which is the sure mark of starvation."

Here is a table, comparing the workhouse pauper's weekly allowance with the workhouse officer's weekly allowance: —

OFFICER	DIET	PAUPER
7 lb.	Bread	$6^{3}/_{4}$ lb.
5 lb.	Meat	1 lb. 2 oz.
12 oz.	Bacon	$2^{1}/_{2}$ oz.
8 oz.	Cheese	2 oz.
7 lb.	Potatoes	$1^{1}/_{2}$ lb.
6 lb.	Vegetables	none
1 lb.	Flour	none
2 oz.	Lard	none
12 oz.	Butter	7 oz.
none	Rice pudding	1 lb.

And as the same writer remarks: "The officer's diet is still more liberal than the pauper's; but evidently it is not considered liberal enough, for a footnote is added to the officer's table saying that 'a cash payment of two shillings sixpence a week is also made to each resident officer and servant.' If the pauper has ample food, why does the officer have more? And if the officer has not too much, can the pauper be properly fed on less than half the amount?"

But it is not alone the Ghetto-dweller, the prisoner, and

the pauper that starve. Hodge, of the country, does not know
what it is always to have a full belly. In truth, it is his empty
belly which has driven him to the city in such great numbers.
Let us investigate the way of living of a laborer from a parish
in the Bradfield Poor Law Union, Berks. Supposing him to
have two children, steady work, a rent-free cottage, and an
average weekly wage of thirteen shillings, which is equivalent
to $3.25, then here is his weekly budget: —

	s.	d.
Bread (5 quarterns)	1	10
Flour (½ gallon)	0	4
Tea (¼ lb.)	0	6
Butter (1 lb.)	1	3
Lard (1 lb.)	0	6
Sugar (6 lb.)	1	0
Bacon or other meat (about 4 lb.)	2	8
Cheese (1 lb.)	0	8
Milk (half-tin condensed)	0	3¼
Oil, candles, blue, soap, salt, pepper, etc.	1	0
Coal	1	6
Beer	none	
Tobacco	none	
Insurance ("Prudential")	0	3
Laborers' Union	0	1
Wood, tools, dispensary, etc.	0	6
Insurance ("Foresters") and margin for clothes	1	1¾
Total	13s.	0d.

The guardians of the workhouse in the above Union pride
themselves on their rigid economy. It costs per pauper per
week: —

	s.	d.
Men	6	1½
Women	5	6½
Children	5	1¼

If the laborer whose budget has been described, should
quit his toil and go into the workhouse, he would cost the
guardians for

	s.	d.
Himself	6	1¹/₂
Wife	5	6¹/₂
Two children	10	2¹/₂
Total	21s.	10¹/₂d.

Or, roughly, $5.46

It would require $5.46 for the workhouse to care for him and his family, which he, somehow, manages to do on $3.25. And in addition, it is an understood fact that it is cheaper to cater for a large number of people—buying, cooking, and serving wholesale—than it is to cater for a small number of people, say a family.

Nevertheless, at the time this budget was compiled, there was in that parish another family, not of four, but *eleven* persons, who had to live on an income, not of thirteen shillings, but of twelve shillings per week (eleven shillings in winter), and which had, not a rent-free cottage, but a cottage for which it paid three shillings per week.

This must be understood, and understood clearly: *Whatever is true of London in the way of poverty and degradation, is true of all England.* While Paris is not by any means France, the city of London is England. The frightful conditions which mark London an inferno likewise mark the United Kingdom an inferno. The argument that the decentralization of London would ameliorate conditions is a vain thing and false. If the 6,000,000 people of London were separated into one hundred cities each with a population of 60,000, misery would be decentralized but not diminished. The sum of it would remain as large.

In this instance, Mr. B. S. Rowntree, by an exhaustive analysis, has proved for the country town what Mr. Charles Booth has proved for the metropolis, that fully one-fourth of the dwellers are condemned to a poverty which destroys them physically and spiritually; that fully one-fourth of the dwellers do not have enough to eat, are inadequately clothed, sheltered, and warmed in a rigorous climate, and are doomed to a moral degeneracy which puts them lower than the savage in cleanliness and decency.

After listening to the wail of an old Irish peasant in Kerry, Robert Blatchford asked him what he wanted. "The old man leaned upon his spade and looked out across the black peat fields at the lowering skies. 'What is it that I'm wantun?' he said; then in a deep plaintive tone he continued, more to himself than to me, 'All our brave bhoys and dear gurrls is away an' over the says, an' the agent has taken the pig off me, an' the wet has spiled the praties, an' I'm an owld man, *an' I want the Day av Judgment.*'"

The Day of Judgment! More than he want it. From all the land rises the hunger wail, from Ghetto and countryside, from prison and casual ward, from asylum and workhouse— the cry of the people who have not enough to eat. Millions of people, men, women, children, little babes, the blind, the deaf, the halt, the sick, vagabonds and toilers, prisoners and paupers, the people of Ireland, England, Scotland, Wales, who have not enough to eat. And this, in face of the fact that five men can produce bread for a thousand; that one workman can produce cotton cloth for 250 people, woollens for 300, and boots and shoes for 1000. It would seem that 40,000,000 people are keeping a big house, and that they are keeping it badly. The income is all right, but there is something criminally wrong with the management. And who dares to say that it is not criminally mismanaged, this big house, when five men can produce bread for a thousand, and yet millions have not enough to eat?

XXVI
Drink, Temperance, and Thrift

Sometimes the poor are praised for being thrifty. But to recommend thrift to the poor is both grotesque and insulting. It is
like advising a man who is starving to eat less. For a town or
country laborer to practice thrift would be absolutely immoral.
Man should not be ready to show that he can live like a badly-
fed animal.

—OSCAR WILDE

THE English working classes may be said to be soaked in
beer. They are made dull and sodden by it. Their efficiency is sadly impaired, and they lose whatever imagination,
invention, and quickness may be theirs by right of race. It
may hardly be called an acquired habit, for they are accustomed to it from their earliest infancy. Children are begotten
in drunkenness, saturated in drink before they draw their first
breath, born to the smell and taste of it, and brought up in
the midst of it.

The public house is ubiquitous. It flourishes on every corner and between corners, and it is frequented almost as much
by women as by men. Children are to be found in it as well,
waiting till their fathers and mothers are ready to go home,
sipping from the glasses of their elders, listening to the coarse
language and degrading conversation, catching the contagion
of it, familiarizing themselves with licentiousness and de-
bauchery.

Mrs. Grundy rules as supremely over the workers as she
does over the bourgeoisie; but in the case of the workers, the
one thing she does not frown upon is the public house. No
disgrace or shame attaches to it, nor to the young woman or
girl who makes a practice of entering it.

I remember a girl in a coffee-house saying, "I never drink
spirits when in a public 'ouse." She was a young and pretty
waitress, and she was laying down to another waitress her
preëminent respectability and discretion. Mrs. Grundy drew
the line at spirits, but allowed that it was quite proper for a

clean young girl to drink beer and to go into a public house to drink it.

Not only is this beer unfit for the people to drink it, but too often the men and women are unfit to drink it. On the other hand, it is their very unfitness that drives them to drink it. Ill-fed, suffering from innutrition and the evil effects of overcrowding and squalor, their constitutions develop a morbid craving for the drink, just as the sickly stomach of the over-strung Manchester factory operative hankers after excessive quantities of pickles and similar weird foods. Unhealthy working and living engenders unhealthy appetites and desires. Man cannot be worked worse than a horse is worked, and be housed and fed as a pig is housed and fed, and at the same time have clean and wholesome ideals and aspirations.

As home-life vanishes, the public house appears. Not only do men and women abnormally crave drink, who are overworked, exhausted, suffering from deranged stomachs and bad sanitation, and deadened by the ugliness and monotony of existence; but the gregarious men and women who have no home-life flee to the bright and clattering public house in a vain attempt to express their gregariousness. And when a family is housed in one small room, home-life is impossible.

A brief examination of such a dwelling will serve to bring to light one important cause of drunkenness. Here the family arises in the morning, dresses, and makes its toilet, father, mother, sons, and daughters, and in the same room, shoulder to shoulder (for the room is small), the wife and mother cooks the breakfast. And in the same room, heavy and sickening with the exhalations of their packed bodies throughout the night, that breakfast is eaten. The father goes to work, the elder children go to school or on to the street, and the mother remains with her crawling, toddling youngsters to do her housework—still in the same room. Here she washes the clothes, filling the pent space with soapsuds and the smell of dirty clothes, and overhead she hangs the wet linen to dry.

Here, in the evening, amid the manifold smells of the day, the family goes to its virtuous couch. That is to say, as many as possible pile into the one bed (if bed they have), and the surplus turns in on the floor. And this is the round of their existence, month after month, year after year, for they never get a vacation save when they are evicted. When a child dies, and some are always bound to die since fifty-five per cent of the East End children die before they are five years old, the body is laid out in the same room. And if they are very poor, it is kept for some time until they can bury it. During the day it lies on the bed; during the night, when the living take the bed, the dead occupies the table, from which, in the morning, when the dead is put back into the bed, they eat their breakfast. Sometimes the body is placed on the shelf which serves as pantry for their food. Only a couple of weeks ago, an East End woman was in trouble, because, in this fashion, being unable to bury it, she had kept her dead child three weeks.

Now such a room as I have described, is not home but horror; and the men and women who flee away from it to the public house are to be pitied, not blamed. There are 300,000 people, in London, divided into families that live in single rooms, while there are 900,000 who are illegally housed according to the Public Health Act of 1891—a respectable recruiting ground for the drink traffic.

Then there are the insecurity of happiness, the precariousness of existence, the well-founded fear of the future—potent factors in driving people to drink. Wretchedness squirms for alleviation, and in the public house its pain is eased and forgetfulness is obtained. It is unhealthy. Certainly it is, but everything else about their lives is unhealthy, while this brings the oblivion that nothing else in their lives can bring. It even exalts them, and makes them feel that they are finer and better, though at the same time it drags them down and makes them more beastly than ever. For the unfortunate man or woman, it is a race between miseries that ends with death.

It is of no avail to preach temperance and teetotalism to these people. The drink habit may be the cause of many miseries; but it is, in turn, the effect of other and prior miseries. The temperance advocates may preach their hearts out over the evils of drink, but until the evils that cause people to drink are abolished, drink and its evils will remain.

Until the people who try to help, realize this, their well-intentioned efforts will be futile, and they will present a spectacle fit only to set Olympus laughing. I have gone through an exhibition of Japanese art, got up for the poor of White-

chapel with the idea of elevating them, of begetting in them
yearnings for the Beautiful and True and Good. Granting
(what is not so) that the poor folk are thus taught to know
and yearn after the Beautiful and True and Good, the foul
facts of their existence and the social law that dooms one in
three to a public-charity death, demonstrates that this knowledge and yearning will be only so much of an added curse to
them. They will have so much more to forget than if they had
never known and yearned. Did Destiny to-day bind me down
to the life of an East End slave for the rest of my years, and
did Destiny grant me but one wish, I should ask that I might
forget all about the Beautiful and True and Good; that I
might forget all I had learned from the open books, and forget the people I had known, the things I had heard, and the
lands I had seen. And if Destiny didn't grant it, I am pretty
confident that I should get drunk and forget it as often as
possible.

These people who try to help! Their college settlements,
missions, charities, and what not, are failures. In the nature
of things they cannot but be failures. They are wrongly,
though sincerely, conceived. They approach life through a
misunderstanding of life, these good folk. They do not understand the West End, yet they come down to the East End
as teachers and savants. They do not understand the simple
sociology of Christ, yet they come to the miserable and the
despised with the pomp of social redeemers. They have
worked faithfully, but beyond relieving an infinitesimal fraction of misery and collecting a certain amount of data which
might otherwise have been more scientifically and less expen-
sively collected, they have achieved nothing.

As some one has said, they do everything for the poor except get off their backs. The very money they dribble out in
their child's schemes has been wrung from the poor. They
come from a race of successful and predatory bipeds who
stand between the worker and his wages, and they try to tell
the worker what he shall do with the pitiful balance left to
him. Of what use, in the name of God, is it to establish nurseries for women workers, in which, for instance, a child is
taken while the mother makes violets in Islington at three
farthings a gross, when more children and violet-makers than

they can cope with are being born right along? This violet-maker handles each flower four times, 576 handlings for three farthings, and in the day she handles the flowers 6912 times for a wage of eighteen cents. She is being robbed. Somebody is on her back, and a yearning for the Beautiful and True and Good will not lighten her burden. They do nothing for her, these dabblers; and what they do not do for the mother, un-does at night, when the child comes home, all that they have done for the child in the day.

And one and all, they join in teaching a fundamental lie. They do not know it is a lie, but their ignorance does not make it more of a truth. And the lie they preach is 'thrift.' An instance will demonstrate it. In overcrowded London, the struggle for a chance to work is keen, and because of this struggle wages sink to the lowest means of subsistence. To be thrifty means for a worker to spend less than his income—in other words, to live on less. This is equivalent to a lowering of the standard of living. In the competition for a chance to work, the man with a lower standard of living will underbid the man with a higher standard. And a small group of such thrifty workers in any overcrowded industry will permanently lower the wages of that industry. And the thrifty ones will no longer be thrifty, for their income will have been reduced till it balances their expenditure.

In short, thrift negates thrift. If every worker in England should heed the preachers of thrift and cut expenditure in half, the condition of there being more men to work than there is work to do would swiftly cut wages in half. And then none of the workers of England would be thrifty, for they would be living up to their diminished incomes. The short-sighted thrift-preachers would naturally be astounded at the outcome. The measure of their failure would be precisely the measure of the success of their propaganda. And, anyway, it is sheer bosh and nonsense to preach thrift to the 1,800,000 London workers who are divided into families which have a total income of less than \$5.25 per week, one-quarter to one-half of which must be paid for rent.

Concerning the futility of the people who try to help, I wish to make one notable, noble exception, namely, the Dr. Barnardo Homes. Dr. Barnardo is a child-catcher. First, he

catches them when they are young, before they are set, hardened, in the vicious social mould; and then he sends them
away to grow up and be formed in another and better social
mould. Up to date he has sent out of the country 13,340 boys,
most of them to Canada, and not one in fifty has failed. A
splendid record, when it is considered that these lads are waifs
and strays, homeless and parentless, jerked out from the very
bottom of the Abyss, and forty-nine out of fifty of them made
into men.

Every twenty-four hours in the year Dr. Barnardo snatches
nine waifs from the streets; so the enormous field he has to
work in may be comprehended. The people who try to help
have something to learn from him. He does not play with
palliatives. He traces social viciousness and misery to their
sources. He removes the progeny of the gutter-folk from their
pestilential environment, and gives them a healthy, wholesome environment in which to be pressed and prodded and
moulded into men.

When the people who try to help cease their playing and
dabbling with day nurseries and Japanese art exhibits, and go
back and learn their West End and the sociology of Christ,
they will be in better shape to buckle down to the work they
ought to be doing in the world. And if they do buckle down
to the work, they will follow Dr. Barnardo's lead, only on a
scale as large as the nation is large. They won't cram yearnings for the Beautiful and True and Good down the throat of
the woman making violets for three farthings a gross, but
they will make somebody get off her back and quit cramming
himself till, like the Romans, he must go to a bath and sweat
it out. And to their consternation, they will find that they will
have to get off that woman's back themselves, as well as the
backs of a few other women and children they did not dream
they were riding upon.

XXVII

The Management

Seven men working sixteen hours could produce food by best
improved machinery to support one thousand men.
                                                    —EDWARD ATKINSON

IN THIS final chapter it were well to look at the Social Abyss
in its widest aspect, and to put certain questions to Civilization, by the answers to which Civilization must stand or
fall. For instance, has Civilization bettered the lot of man?
"Man" I use in its democratic sense, meaning the average
man. So the question reshapes itself: *Has Civilization bettered
the lot of the average man?*

Let us see. In Alaska, along the banks of the Yukon River,
near its mouth, live the Innuit folk. They are a very primitive
people, manifesting but mere glimmering adumbrations of
that tremendous artifice, Civilization. Their capital amounts
possibly to $10 per head. They hunt and fish for their food
with bone-headed spears and arrows. They never suffer from
lack of shelter. Their clothes, largely made from the skins of
animals, are warm. They always have fuel for their fires, likewise timber for their houses, which they build partly underground, and in which they lie snugly during the periods of
intense cold. In the summer they live in tents, open to every
breeze and cool. They are healthy, and strong, and happy.
Their one problem is food. They have their times of plenty
and times of famine. In good times they feast; in bad times
they die of starvation. But starvation, as a chronic condition,
present with a large number of them all the time, is a thing
unknown. Further, they have no debts.

In the United Kingdom, on the rim of the Western Ocean,
live the English folk. They are a consummately civilized people. Their capital amounts to at least $1500 per head. They
gain their food, not by hunting and fishing, but by toil at
colossal artifices. For the most part, they suffer from lack of
shelter. The greater number of them are vilely housed, do not
have enough fuel to keep them warm, and are insufficiently

clothed. A constant number never have any houses at all, and sleep shelterless under the stars. Many are to be found, winter and summer, shivering on the streets in their rags. They have good times and bad. In good times most of them manage to get enough to eat, in bad times they die of starvation. They are dying now, they were dying yesterday and last year, they will die to-morrow and next year, of starvation; for they, unlike the Innuit, suffer from a chronic condition of starvation. There are 40,000,000 of the English folk, and 939 out of every 1000 of them die in poverty, while a constant army of 8,000,000 struggles on the ragged edge of starvation. Further, each babe that is born, is born in debt to the sum of $110. This is because of an artifice called the National Debt.

In a fair comparison of the average Innuit and the average Englishman, it will be seen that life is less rigorous for the Innuit; that while the Innuit suffers only during bad times from starvation, the Englishman suffers during good times as well; that no Innuit lacks fuel, clothing, or housing, while the Englishman is in perpetual lack of these three essentials. In this connection it is well to instance the judgment of a man such as Huxley. From the knowledge gained as a medical officer in the East End of London, and as a scientist pursuing investigations among the most elemental savages, he concludes, "Were the alternative presented to me I would deliberately prefer the life of the savage to that of those people of Christian London."

The creature comforts man enjoys are the products of man's labor. Since Civilization has failed to give the average Englishman food and shelter equal to that enjoyed by the Innuit, the question arises: *Has Civilization increased the producing power of the average man?* If it has not increased man's producing power, then Civilization cannot stand.

But, it will be instantly admitted, Civilization *has* increased man's producing power. Five men can produce bread for a thousand. One man can produce cotton cloth for 250 people, woollens for 300, and boots and shoes for 1000. Yet it has been shown throughout the pages of this book that English folk by the millions do not receive enough food, clothes, and boots. Then arises the third and inexorable question: *If*

Civilization has increased the producing power of the average man, why has it not bettered the lot of the average man?

There can be one answer only—MISMANAGEMENT. Civilization has made possible all manner of creature comforts and heart's delights. In these the average Englishman does not participate. If he shall be forever unable to participate, then Civilization falls. There is no reason for the continued existence of an artifice so avowed a failure. But it is impossible that men should have reared this tremendous artifice in vain. It stuns the intellect. To acknowledge so crushing a defeat is to give the death-blow to striving and progress.

One other alternative, and one other only, presents itself. *Civilization must be compelled to better the lot of the average man.* This accepted, it becomes at once a question of business management. Things profitable must be continued; things unprofitable must be eliminated. Either the Empire is a profit to England or it is a loss. If it is a loss, it must be done away with. If it is a profit, it must be managed so that the average man comes in for a share of the profit.

If the struggle for commercial supremacy is profitable, continue it. If it is not, if it hurts the worker and makes his lot worse than the lot of a savage, then fling foreign markets and industrial empire overboard. For it is a patent fact that if 40,000,000 people, aided by Civilization, possess a greater individual producing power than the Innuit, then those 40,000,000 people should enjoy more creature comforts and heart's delights than the Innuits enjoy.

If the 400,000 English gentlemen, "of no occupation," according to their own statement in the Census of 1881, are unprofitable, do away with them. Set them to work ploughing game preserves and planting potatoes. If they are profitable, continue them by all means, but let it be seen to that the average Englishman shares somewhat in the profits they produce by working at no occupation.

In short, society must be reorganized, and a capable management put at the head. That the present management is incapable, there can be no discussion. It has drained the United Kingdom of its life-blood. It has enfeebled the stay-at-home folk till they are unable longer to struggle in the van of the competing nations. It has built up a West End and an East End as large as the Kingdom is large, in which one end is riotous and rotten, the other end sickly and underfed.

A vast empire is foundering on the hands of this incapable management. And by empire is meant the political machinery which holds together the English-speaking people of the world outside of the United States. Nor is this charged in a pessimistic spirit. Blood empire is greater than political empire, and the English of the New World and the Antipodes are strong and vigorous as ever. But the political empire under which they are nominally assembled is perishing. The political machine known as the British Empire is running down. In the hands of its management it is losing momentum every day.

It is inevitable that this management, which has grossly and criminally mismanaged, shall be swept away. Not only has it been wasteful and inefficient, but it has misappropriated the funds. Every worn-out, pasty-faced pauper, every blind man, every prison babe, every man, woman, and child whose belly is gnawing with hunger pangs, is hungry because the funds have been misappropriated by the management.

Nor can one member of this managing class plead not guilty before the judgment bar of Man. "The living in their houses, and in their graves the dead," are challenged by every babe that dies of innutrition, by every girl that flees the sweater's den to the nightly promenade of Piccadilly, by every worked-out toiler that plunges into the canal. The food this managing class eats, the wine it drinks, the shows it makes, and the fine clothes it wears, are challenged by eight million mouths which have never had enough to fill them, and by twice eight million bodies which have never been sufficiently clothed and housed.

There can be no mistake. Civilization has increased man's producing power an hundred fold, and through mismanagement the men of Civilization live worse than the beasts, and have less to eat and wear and protect them from the elements than the savage Innuit in a frigid climate who lives today as he lived in the stone age ten thousand years ago.

CHALLENGE

I have a vague remembrance
  Of a story that is told
In some ancient Spanish legend
  Or chronicle of old.

It was when brave King Sanchez
  Was before Zamora slain,
And his great besieging army
  Lay encamped upon the plain.

Don Diego de Ordenez
  Sallied forth in front of all,
And shouted loud his challenge
  To the warders on the wall.

All the people of Zamora,
  Both the born and the unborn,
As traitors did he challenge
  With taunting words of scorn.

The living in their houses,
  And in their graves the dead,
And the waters in their rivers,
  And their wine, and oil, and bread.

There is a greater army
  That besets us round with strife,
A starving, numberless army
  At all the gates of life.

The poverty-stricken millions
  Who challenge our wine and bread,
And impeach us all as traitors,
  Both the living and the dead.

And whenever I sit at the banquet,
  Where the feast and song are high,

Amid the mirth and music
  I can hear that fearful cry.

And hollow and haggard faces
  Look into the lighted hall,
And wasted hands are extended
  To catch the crumbs that fall.

And within there is light and plenty,
  And odors fill the air;
But without there is cold and darkness,
  And hunger and despair.

And there in the camp of famine,
  In wind, and cold, and rain,
Christ, the great Lord of the Army,
  Lies dead upon the plain.
                              —LONGFELLOW

THE ROAD

Contents

Confession 189

Holding Her Down 202

Pictures 218

"Pinched" 230

The Pen 244

Hoboes That Pass in the Night 257

Road-Kids and Gay-Cats 274

Two Thousand Stiffs 287

Bulls 299

"Speakin' in general, I 'ave tried 'em all,
The 'appy roads that take you o'er the world.
Speakin' in general, I 'ave found them good
For such as cannot use one bed too long,
But must get 'ence, the same as I 'ave done,
An' go observin' matters till they die."
                              —*Sestina of the Tramp-Royal*

Confession

THERE IS a woman in the state of Nevada to whom I once lied continuously, consistently, and shamelessly, for the matter of a couple of hours. I don't want to apologize to her. Far be it from me. But I do want to explain. Unfortunately, I do not know her name, much less her present address. If her eyes should chance upon these lines, I hope she will write to me.

It was in Reno, Nevada, in the summer of 1892. Also, it was fair-time, and the town was filled with petty crooks and tin-horns, to say nothing of a vast and hungry horde of hoboes. It was the hungry hoboes that made the town a "hungry" town. They "battered" the back doors of the homes of the citizens until the back doors became unresponsive.

A hard town for "scoffings," was what the hoboes called it at that time. I know that I missed many a meal, in spite of the fact that I could "throw my feet" with the next one when it came to "slamming a gate" for a "poke-out" or a "set-down," or hitting for a "light piece" on the street. Why, I was so hard put in that town, one day, that I gave the porter the slip and invaded the private car of some itinerant millionnaire. The train started as I made the platform, and I headed for the aforesaid millionnaire with the porter one jump behind and reaching for me. It was a dead heat, for I reached the millionnaire at the same instant that the porter reached me. I had no time for formalities. "Gimme a quarter to eat on," I blurted out. And as I live, that millionnaire dipped into his pocket and gave me . . . just . . . precisely . . . a quarter. It is my conviction that he was so flabbergasted that he obeyed automatically, and it has been a matter of keen regret ever since, on my part, that I didn't ask him for a dollar. I know that I'd have got it. I swung off the platform of that private car with the porter manœuvring to kick me in the face. He missed me. One is at a terrible disadvantage when trying to swing off the lowest step of a car and not break his neck on the right of way, with, at the same time, an irate Ethiopian on the plat-

form above trying to land him in the face with a number
eleven. But I got the quarter! I got it!

But to return to the woman to whom I so shamelessly lied.
It was in the evening of my last day in Reno. I had been out
to the race-track watching the ponies run, and had missed my
dinner (*i.e.* the mid-day meal). I was hungry, and, furthermore, a committee of public safety had just been organized
to rid the town of just such hungry mortals as I. Already a lot
of my brother hoboes had been gathered in by John Law,
and I could hear the sunny valleys of California calling to me
over the cold crests of the Sierras. Two acts remained for me
to perform before I shook the dust of Reno from my feet.
One was to catch the blind baggage on the westbound overland that night. The other was first to get something to eat.
Even youth will hesitate at an all-night ride, on an empty
stomach, outside a train that is tearing the atmosphere
through the snow-sheds, tunnels, and eternal snows of
heaven-aspiring mountains.

But that something to eat was a hard proposition. I was
"turned down" at a dozen houses. Sometimes I received insulting remarks and was informed of the barred domicile that
should be mine if I had my just deserts. The worst of it was
that such assertions were only too true. That was why I was
pulling west that night. John Law was abroad in the town,
seeking eagerly for the hungry and homeless, for by such was
his barred domicile tenanted.

At other houses the doors were slammed in my face, cutting short my politely and humbly couched request for something to eat. At one house they did not open the door. I
stood on the porch and knocked, and they looked out at me
through the window. They even held one sturdy little boy
aloft so that he could see over the shoulders of his elders the
tramp who wasn't going to get anything to eat at their house.

It began to look as if I should be compelled to go to the
very poor for my food. The very poor constitute the last sure
recourse of the hungry tramp. The very poor can always be
depended upon. They never turn away the hungry. Time and
again, all over the United States, have I been refused food
by the big house on the hill; and always have I received
food from the little shack down by the creek or marsh,

with its broken windows stuffed with rags and its tired-faced mother broken with labor. Oh, you charity-mongers! Go to the poor and learn, for the poor alone are the charitable. They neither give nor withhold from their excess. They have no excess. They give, and they withhold never, from what they need for themselves, and very often from what they cruelly need for themselves. A bone to the dog is not charity. Charity is the bone shared with the dog when you are just as hungry as the dog.

There was one house in particular where I was turned down that evening. The porch windows opened on the dining room, and through them I saw a man eating pie—a big meat-pie. I stood in the open door, and while he talked with me, he went on eating. He was prosperous, and out of his prosperity had been bred resentment against his less fortunate brothers.

He cut short my request for something to eat, snapping out, "I don't believe you want to work."

Now this was irrelevant. I hadn't said anything about work. The topic of conversation I had introduced was "food." In fact, I didn't want to work. I wanted to take the westbound overland that night.

"You wouldn't work if you had a chance," he bullied.

I glanced at his meek-faced wife, and knew that but for the presence of this Cerberus I'd have a whack at that meat-pie myself. But Cerberus sopped himself in the pie, and I saw that I must placate him if I were to get a share of it. So I sighed to myself and accepted his work-morality.

"Of course I want work," I bluffed.

"Don't believe it," he snorted.

"Try me," I answered, warming to the bluff.

"All right," he said. "Come to the corner of blank and blank streets"—(I have forgotten the address)—"to-morrow morning. You know where that burned building is, and I'll put you to work tossing bricks."

"All right, sir; I'll be there."

He grunted and went on eating. I waited. After a couple of minutes he looked up with an I-thought-you-were-gone expression on his face, and demanded:—

"Well?"

"I . . . I am waiting for something to eat," I said gently.

"I knew you wouldn't work!" he roared.

He was right, of course; but his conclusion must have been reached by mind-reading, for his logic wouldn't bear it out. But the beggar at the door must be humble, so I accepted his logic as I had accepted his morality.

"You see, I am now hungry," I said still gently. "To-morrow morning I shall be hungrier. Think how hungry I shall be when I have tossed bricks all day without anything to eat. Now if you will give me something to eat, I'll be in great shape for those bricks."

He gravely considered my plea, at the same time going on eating, while his wife nearly trembled into propitiatory speech, but refrained.

"I'll tell you what I'll do," he said between mouthfuls. "You come to work to-morrow, and in the middle of the day I'll advance you enough for your dinner. That will show whether you are in earnest or not."

"In the meantime—" I began; but he interrupted.

"If I gave you something to eat now, I'd never see you again. Oh, I know your kind. Look at me. I owe no man. I have never descended so low as to ask any one for food. I have always earned my food. The trouble with you is that you are idle and dissolute. I can see it in your face. I have worked and been honest. I have made myself what I am. And you can do the same, if you work and are honest."

"Like you?" I queried.

Alas, no ray of humor had ever penetrated the sombre work-sodden soul of that man.

"Yes, like me," he answered.

"All of us?" I queried.

"Yes, all of you," he answered, conviction vibrating in his voice.

"But if we all became like you," I said, "allow me to point out that there'd be nobody to toss bricks for you."

I swear there was a flicker of a smile in his wife's eye. As for him, he was aghast—but whether at the awful possibility of a reformed humanity that would not enable him to get anybody to toss bricks for him, or at my impudence, I shall never know.

"I'll not waste words on you," he roared. "Get out of here, you ungrateful whelp!"

I scraped my feet to advertise my intention of going, and queried: —

"And I don't get anything to eat?"

He arose suddenly to his feet. He was a large man. I was a stranger in a strange land, and John Law was looking for me. I went away hurriedly. "But why ungrateful?" I asked myself as I slammed his gate. "What in the dickens did he give me to be ungrateful about?" I looked back. I could still see him through the window. He had returned to his pie.

By this time I had lost heart. I passed many houses by without venturing up to them. All houses looked alike, and none looked "good." After walking half a dozen blocks I shook off my despondency and gathered my "nerve." This begging for food was all a game, and if I didn't like the cards, I could always call for a new deal. I made up my mind to tackle the next house. I approached it in the deepening twilight, going around to the kitchen door.

I knocked softly, and when I saw the kind face of the middle-aged woman who answered, as by inspiration came to me the "story" I was to tell. For know that upon his ability to tell a good story depends the success of the beggar. First of all, and on the instant, the beggar must "size up" his victim. After that, he must tell a story that will appeal to the peculiar personality and temperament of that particular victim. And right here arises the great difficulty: in the instant that he is sizing up the victim he must begin his story. Not a minute is allowed for preparation. As in a lightning flash he must divine the nature of the victim and conceive a tale that will hit home. The successful hobo must be an artist. He must create spontaneously and instantaneously—and not upon a theme selected from the plenitude of his own imagination, but upon the theme he reads in the face of the person who opens the door, be it man, woman, or child, sweet or crabbed, generous or miserly, good-natured or cantankerous, Jew or Gentile, black or white, race-prejudiced or brotherly, provincial or universal, or whatever else it may be. I have often thought that to this training of my tramp days is due much of my success as a story-writer. In order to get the food whereby I lived, I was compelled to tell tales that rang true. At the back door, out of inexorable necessity, is developed the convincingness and sincerity laid down by all authorities on the art of the short-story. Also, I quite believe it was my tramp-apprenticeship that made a realist out of me. Realism constitutes the only goods one can exchange at the kitchen door for grub.

After all, art is only consummate artfulness, and artfulness saves many a "story." I remember lying in a police station at Winnipeg, Manitoba. I was bound west over the Canadian Pacific. Of course, the police wanted my story, and I gave it to them—on the spur of the moment. They were landlubbers, in the heart of the continent, and what better story for them than a sea story? They could never trip me up on that. And so I told a tearful tale of my life on the hell-ship *Glenmore*. (I had once seen the *Glenmore* lying at anchor in San Francisco Bay.)

I was an English apprentice, I said. And they said that I didn't talk like an English boy. It was up to me to create on the instant. I had been born and reared in the United States. On the death of my parents, I had been sent to England to my grandparents. It was they who had apprenticed me on the *Glenmore*. I hope the captain of the *Glenmore* will forgive me, for I gave him a character that night in the Winnipeg police station. Such cruelty! Such brutality! Such diabolical ingenuity of torture! It explained why I had deserted the *Glenmore* at Montreal.

But why was I in the middle of Canada going west, when my grandparents lived in England? Promptly I created a married sister who lived in California. She would take care of me. I developed at length her loving nature. But they were not done with me, those hard-hearted policemen. I had joined the *Glenmore* in England; in the two years that had elapsed before my desertion at Montreal, what had the *Glenmore* done and where had she been? And thereat I took those landlubbers around the world with me. Buffeted by pounding seas and stung with flying spray, they fought a typhoon with me off the coast of Japan. They loaded and unloaded cargo with me in all the ports of the Seven Seas. I took them to India, and Rangoon, and China, and had them hammer ice with me around the Horn and at last come to moorings at Montreal.

And then they said to wait a moment, and one policeman went forth into the night while I warmed myself at the stove, all the while racking my brains for the trap they were going to spring on me.

I groaned to myself when I saw him come in the door at the heels of the policeman. No gypsy prank had thrust those tiny hoops of gold through the ears; no prairie winds had beaten that skin into wrinkled leather; nor had snow-drift and mountain-slope put in his walk that reminiscent roll. And in those eyes, when they looked at me, I saw the unmistakable sun-wash of the sea. Here was a theme, alas! with half a dozen policemen to watch me read—I who had never sailed the China seas, nor been around the Horn, nor looked with my eyes upon India and Rangoon.

I was desperate. Disaster stalked before me incarnate in the form of that gold-ear-ringed, weather-beaten son of the sea. Who was he? What was he? I must solve him ere he solved me. I must take a new orientation, or else those wicked policemen would orientate me to a cell, a police court, and more cells. If he questioned me first, before I knew how much he knew, I was lost.

But did I betray my desperate plight to those lynx-eyed guardians of the public welfare of Winnipeg? Not I. I met that aged sailorman glad-eyed and beaming, with all the simulated relief at deliverance that a drowning man would display on finding a life-preserver in his last despairing clutch. Here was a man who understood and who would verify my true story to the faces of those sleuth-hounds who did not understand, or, at least, such was what I endeavored to play-act. I seized upon him; I volleyed him with questions about himself. Before my judges I would prove the character of my savior before he saved me.

He was a kindly sailorman—an "easy mark." The policemen grew impatient while I questioned him. At last one of them told me to shut up. I shut up; but while I remained shut up, I was busy creating, busy sketching the scenario of the next act. I had learned enough to go on with. He was a Frenchman. He had sailed always on French merchant vessels, with the one exception of a voyage on a "lime-juicer." And last of all—blessed fact!—he had not been on the sea for twenty years.

The policeman urged him on to examine me.

"You called in at Rangoon?" he queried.

I nodded. "We put our third mate ashore there. Fever."

If he had asked me what kind of fever, I should have answered, "Enteric," though for the life of me I didn't know what enteric was. But he didn't ask me. Instead, his next question was:—

"And how is Rangoon?"

"All right. It rained a whole lot when we were there."

"Did you get shore-leave?"

"Sure," I answered. "Three of us apprentices went ashore together."

"Do you remember the temple?"

"Which temple?" I parried.

"The big one, at the top of the stairway."

If I remembered that temple, I knew I'd have to describe it. The gulf yawned for me.

I shook my head.

"You can see it from all over the harbor," he informed me. "You don't need shore-leave to see that temple."

I never loathed a temple so in my life. But I fixed that particular temple at Rangoon.

"You can't see it from the harbor," I contradicted. "You can't see it from the town. You can't see it from the top of the stairway. Because—" I paused for the effect. "Because there isn't any temple there."

"But I saw it with my own eyes!" he cried.

"That was in—?" I queried.

"Seventy-one."

"It was destroyed in the great earthquake of 1887," I explained. "It was very old."

There was a pause. He was busy reconstructing in his old eyes the youthful vision of that fair temple by the sea.

"The stairway is still there," I aided him. "You can see it from all over the harbor. And you remember that little island on the right-hand side coming into the harbor?" I guess there must have been one there (I was prepared to shift it over to the left-hand side), for he nodded. "Gone," I said. "Seven fathoms of water there now."

I had gained a moment for breath. While he pondered on time's changes, I prepared the finishing touches of my story.

"You remember the custom-house at Bombay?"

He remembered it.

"Burned to the ground," I announced.

"Do you remember Jim Wan?" he came back at me.

"Dead," I said; but who the devil Jim Wan was I hadn't the slightest idea.

I was on thin ice again.

"Do you remember Billy Harper, at Shanghai?" I queried back at him quickly.

That aged sailorman worked hard to recollect, but the Billy Harper of my imagination was beyond his faded memory.

"Of course you remember Billy Harper," I insisted. "Everybody knows him. He's been there forty years. Well, he's still there, that's all."

And then the miracle happened. The sailorman remembered Billy Harper. Perhaps there was a Billy Harper, and perhaps he had been in Shanghai for forty years and was still there; but it was news to me.

For fully half an hour longer, the sailorman and I talked on in similar fashion. In the end he told the policemen that I was what I represented myself to be, and after a night's lodging and a breakfast I was released to wander on westward to my married sister in San Francisco.

But to return to the woman in Reno who opened her door to me in the deepening twilight. At the first glimpse of her kindly face I took my cue. I became a sweet, innocent, unfortunate lad. I couldn't speak. I opened my mouth and closed it again. Never in my life before had I asked any one for food. My embarrassment was painful, extreme. I was ashamed. I, who looked upon begging as a delightful whimsicality, thumbed myself over into a true son of Mrs. Grundy, burdened with all her bourgeois morality. Only the harsh pangs of the belly-need could compel me to do so degraded and ignoble a thing as beg for food. And into my face I strove to throw all the wan wistfulness of famished and ingenuous youth unused to mendicancy.

"You are hungry, my poor boy," she said.

I had made her speak first.

I nodded my head and gulped.

"It is the first time I have ever . . . asked," I faltered.

"Come right in." The door swung open. "We have already finished eating, but the fire is burning and I can get something up for you."

She looked at me closely when she got me into the light.

"I wish my boy were as healthy and strong as you," she said. "But he is not strong. He sometimes falls down. He just fell down this afternoon and hurt himself badly, the poor dear."

She mothered him with her voice, with an ineffable tenderness in it that I yearned to appropriate. I glanced at him. He sat across the table, slender and pale, his head swathed in bandages. He did not move, but his eyes, bright in the lamplight, were fixed upon me in a steady and wondering stare.

"Just like my poor father," I said. "He had the falling sickness. Some kind of vertigo. It puzzled the doctors. They never could make out what was the matter with him."

"He is dead?" she queried gently, setting before me half a dozen soft-boiled eggs.

"Dead," I gulped. "Two weeks ago. I was with him when it happened. We were crossing the street together. He fell right down. He was never conscious again. They carried him into a drug-store. He died there."

And thereat I developed the pitiful tale of my father—how, after my mother's death, he and I had gone to San Francisco from the ranch; how his pension (he was an old soldier), and the little other money he had, was not enough; and how he had tried book-canvassing. Also, I narrated my own woes during the few days after his death that I had spent alone and forlorn on the streets of San Francisco. While that good woman warmed up biscuits, fried bacon, and cooked more eggs, and while I kept pace with her in taking care of all that she placed before me, I enlarged the picture of that poor orphan boy and filled in the details. I became that poor boy. I believed in him as I believed in the beautiful eggs I was devouring. I could have wept for myself. I know the tears did get into my voice at times. It was very effective.

In fact, with every touch I added to the picture, that kind soul gave me something also. She made up a lunch for me to carry away. She put in many boiled eggs, pepper and salt, and other things, and a big apple. She provided me with three pairs of thick red woollen socks. She gave me clean handkerchiefs and other things which I have since forgotten. And all the time she cooked more and more and I ate more and more. I gorged like a savage; but then it was a far cry across the Sierras on a blind baggage, and I knew not when nor where I should find my next meal. And all the while, like a death's-head at the feast, silent and motionless, her own unfortunate boy sat and stared at me across the table. I suppose I represented to him mystery, and romance, and adventure—all that was denied the feeble flicker of life that was in him. And yet I could not forbear, once or twice, from wondering if he saw through me down to the bottom of my mendacious heart.

"But where are you going to?" she asked me.

"Salt Lake City," said I. "I have a sister there—a married sister." (I debated if I should make a Mormon out of her, and decided against it.) "Her husband is a plumber—a contracting plumber."

Now I knew that contracting plumbers were usually credited with making lots of money. But I had spoken. It was up to me to qualify.

"They would have sent me the money for my fare if I had asked for it," I explained, "but they have had sickness and business troubles. His partner cheated him. And so I wouldn't write for the money. I knew I could make my way there somehow. I let them think I had enough to get me to Salt Lake City. She is lovely, and so kind. She was always kind to me. I guess I'll go into the shop and learn the trade. She has two daughters. They are younger than I. One is only a baby."

Of all my married sisters that I have distributed among the cities of the United States, that Salt Lake sister is my favorite. She is quite real, too. When I tell about her, I can see her, and her two little girls, and her plumber husband. She is a large, motherly woman, just verging on beneficent stoutness—the kind, you know, that always cooks nice things and that never gets angry. She is a brunette. Her husband is a quiet, easy-going fellow. Sometimes I almost know him quite well. And who knows but some day I may meet him? If that aged sailorman could remember Billy Harper, I see no reason why I should not some day meet the husband of my sister who lives in Salt Lake City.

On the other hand, I have a feeling of certitude within me that I shall never meet in the flesh my many parents and grandparents—you see, I invariably killed them off. Heart disease was my favorite way of getting rid of my mother, though on occasion I did away with her by means of consumption, pneumonia, and typhoid fever. It is true, as the Winnipeg policemen will attest, that I have grandparents living in England; but that was a long time ago and it is a fair assumption that they are dead by now. At any rate, they have never written to me.

I hope that woman in Reno will read these lines and forgive me my gracelessness and unveracity. I do not apologize, for I am unashamed. It was youth, delight in life, zest for experience, that brought me to her door. It did me good. It taught me the intrinsic kindliness of human nature. I hope it did her good. Anyway, she may get a good laugh out of it now that she learns the real inwardness of the situation.

To her my story was "true." She believed in me and all my family, and she was filled with solicitude for the dangerous journey I must make ere I won to Salt Lake City. This solicitude nearly brought me to grief. Just as I was leaving, my arms full of lunch and my pockets bulging with fat woollen socks, she bethought herself of a nephew, or uncle, or relative of some sort, who was in the railway mail service, and who, moreover, would come through that night on the very train on which I was going to steal my ride. The very thing! She would take me down to the depot, tell him my story, and get him to hide me in the mail car. Thus, without danger or hardship, I would be carried straight through to Ogden. Salt Lake City was only a few miles farther on. My heart sank. She grew excited as she developed the plan and with my sinking heart I had to feign unbounded gladness and enthusiasm at this solution of my difficulties.

Solution! Why I was bound west that night, and here was I being trapped into going east. It *was* a trap, and I hadn't the heart to tell her that it was all a miserable lie. And while I made believe that I was delighted, I was busy cudgelling my brains for some way to escape. But there was no way. She would see me into the mail-car—she said so herself—and then that mail-clerk relative of hers would carry me to Ogden. And then I would have to beat my way back over all those hundreds of miles of desert.

But luck was with me that night. Just about the time she was getting ready to put on her bonnet and accompany me, she discovered that she had made a mistake. Her mail-clerk relative was not scheduled to come through that night. His run had been changed. He would not come through until two nights afterward. I was saved, for of course my boundless youth would never permit me to wait those two days. I optimistically assured her that I'd get to Salt Lake City quicker if I started immediately, and I departed with her blessings and best wishes ringing in my ears.

But those woollen socks were great. I know. I wore a pair of them that night on the blind baggage of the overland, and that overland went west.

Holding Her Down

BARRING ACCIDENTS, a good hobo, with youth and agility, can hold a train down despite all the efforts of the
train-crew to "ditch" him—given, of course, night-time as an
essential condition. When such a hobo, under such conditions, makes up his mind that he is going to hold her down,
either he does hold her down, or chance trips him up. There
is no legitimate way, short of murder, whereby the train-crew
can ditch him. That train-crews have not stopped short of
murder is a current belief in the tramp world. Not having had
that particular experience in my tramp days I cannot vouch
for it personally.

But this I have heard of the "bad" roads. When a tramp
has "gone underneath," on the rods, and the train is in motion, there is apparently no way of dislodging him until the
train stops. The tramp, snugly ensconced inside the truck,
with the four wheels and all the framework around him, has
the "cinch" on the crew—or so he thinks, until some day he
rides the rods on a bad road. A bad road is usually one on
which a short time previously one or several trainmen have
been killed by tramps. Heaven pity the tramp who is caught
"underneath" on such a road—for caught he is, though the
train be going sixty miles an hour.

The "shack" (brakeman) takes a coupling-pin and a length
of bell-cord to the platform in front of the truck in which the
tramp is riding. The shack fastens the coupling-pin to the
bell-cord, drops the former down between the platforms, and
pays out the latter. The coupling-pin strikes the ties between
the rails, rebounds against the bottom of the car, and again
strikes the ties. The shack plays it back and forth, now to this
side, now to the other, lets it out a bit and hauls it in a bit,
giving his weapon opportunity for every variety of impact
and rebound. Every blow of that flying coupling-pin is
freighted with death, and at sixty miles an hour it beats a
veritable tattoo of death. The next day the remains of that
tramp are gathered up along the right of way, and a line in
the local paper mentions the unknown man, undoubtedly a

tramp, assumably drunk, who had probably fallen asleep on the track.

As a characteristic illustration of how a capable hobo can hold her down, I am minded to give the following experience. I was in Ottawa, bound west over the Canadian Pacific. Three thousand miles of that road stretched before me; it was the fall of the year, and I had to cross Manitoba and the Rocky Mountains. I could expect "crimpy" weather, and every moment of delay increased the frigid hardships of the journey. Furthermore, I was disgusted. The distance between Montreal and Ottawa is one hundred and twenty miles. I ought to know, for I had just come over it and it had taken me six days. By mistake I had missed the main line and come over a small "jerk" with only two locals a day on it. And during these six days I had lived on dry crusts, and not enough of them, begged from the French peasants.

Furthermore, my disgust had been heightened by the one day I had spent in Ottawa trying to get an outfit of clothing for my long journey. Let me put it on record right here that Ottawa, with one exception, is the hardest town in the United States and Canada to beg clothes in; the one exception is Washington, D.C. The latter fair city is the limit. I spent two weeks there trying to beg a pair of shoes, and then had to go on to Jersey City before I got them.

But to return to Ottawa. At eight sharp in the morning I started out after clothes. I worked energetically all day. I swear I walked forty miles. I interviewed the housewives of a thousand homes. I did not even knock off work for dinner. And at six in the afternoon, after ten hours of unremitting and depressing toil, I was still shy one shirt, while the pair of trousers I had managed to acquire was tight and, moreover, was showing all the signs of an early disintegration.

At six I quit work and headed for the railroad yards, expecting to pick up something to eat on the way. But my hard luck was still with me. I was refused food at house after house. Then I got a "hand-out." My spirits soared, for it was the largest hand-out I had ever seen in a long and varied experience. It was a parcel wrapped in newspapers and as big as a mature suit-case. I hurried to a vacant lot and opened it. First, I saw cake, then more cake, all kinds and makes of cake, and then some. It was all cake. No bread and butter with thick firm slices of meat between—nothing but cake; and I who of all things abhorred cake most! In another age and clime they sat down by the waters of Babylon and wept. And in a vacant lot in Canada's proud capital, I, too, sat down and wept . . . over a mountain of cake. As one looks upon the face of his dead son, so looked I upon that multitudinous pastry. I suppose I was an ungrateful tramp, for I refused to partake of the bounteousness of the house that had had a party the night before. Evidently the guests hadn't liked cake either.

That cake marked the crisis in my fortunes. Than it nothing could be worse; therefore things must begin to mend. And they did. At the very next house I was given a "set-down." Now a "set-down" is the height of bliss. One is taken inside, very often is given a chance to wash, and is then "set-down" at a table. Tramps love to throw their legs under a table. The house was large and comfortable, in the midst of spacious grounds and fine trees, and sat well back from the street. They had just finished eating, and I was taken right into the dining room—in itself a most unusual happening, for the tramp who is lucky enough to win a set-down usually receives it in the kitchen. A grizzled and gracious Englishman, his matronly wife, and a beautiful young Frenchwoman talked with me while I ate.

I wonder if that beautiful young Frenchwoman would remember, at this late day, the laugh I gave her when I uttered the barbaric phrase, "two-bits." You see, I was trying delicately to hit them for a "light piece." That was how the sum of money came to be mentioned. "What?" she said. "Two-bits," said I. Her mouth was twitching as she again said, "What?" "Two-bits," said I. Whereat she burst into laughter. "Won't you repeat it?" she said, when she had regained control of herself. "Two-bits," said I. And once more she rippled into uncontrollable silvery laughter. "I beg your pardon," said she; "but what . . . what was it you said?" "Two-bits," said I; "is there anything wrong about it?" "Not that I know of," she gurgled between gasps; "but what does it mean?" I explained, but I do not remember now whether or not I got that two-bits out of her; but I have often wondered since as to which of us was the provincial.

When I arrived at the depot, I found, much to my disgust, a bunch of at least twenty tramps that were waiting to ride out the blind baggages of the overland. Now two or three tramps on the blind baggage are all right. They are inconspicuous. But a score! That meant trouble. No train-crew would ever let all of us ride.

I may as well explain here what a blind baggage is. Some mail-cars are built without doors in the ends; hence, such a car is "blind." The mail-cars that possess end doors, have those doors always locked. Suppose, after the train has started, that a tramp gets on to the platform of one of these blind cars. There is no door, or the door is locked. No conductor or brakeman can get to him to collect fare or throw him off. It is clear that the tramp is safe until the next time the train stops. Then he must get off, run ahead in the darkness, and when the train pulls by, jump on to the blind again. But there are ways and ways, as you shall see.

When the train pulled out, those twenty tramps swarmed upon the three blinds. Some climbed on before the train had run a car-length. They were awkward dubs, and I saw their speedy finish. Of course, the train-crew was "on," and at the first stop the trouble began. I jumped off and ran forward along the track. I noticed that I was accompanied by a number of the tramps. They evidently knew their business. When one is beating an overland, he must always keep well ahead of the train at the stops. I ran ahead, and as I ran, one by one those that accompanied me dropped out. This dropping out was the measure of their skill and nerve in boarding a train.

For this is the way it works. When the train starts, the shack rides out the blind. There is no way for him to get back into the train proper except by jumping off the blind and catching a platform where the car-ends are not "blind." When the train is going as fast as the shack cares to risk, he therefore jumps off the blind, lets several cars go by, and gets on to the train. So it is up to the tramp to run so far ahead that before the blind is opposite him the shack will have already vacated it.

I dropped the last tramp by about fifty feet, and waited. The train started. I saw the lantern of the shack on the first blind. He was riding her out. And I saw the dubs stand forlornly by the track as the blind went by. They made no attempt to get on. They were beaten by their own inefficiency at the very start. After them, in the line-up, came the tramps that knew a little something about the game. They let the first blind, occupied by the shack, go by, and jumped on the second and third blinds. Of course, the shack jumped off the first and on to the second as it went by, and scrambled around there, throwing off the men who had boarded it. But the point is that I was so far ahead that when the first blind came opposite me, the shack had already left it and was tangled up with the tramps on the second blind. A half dozen of the more skilful tramps, who had run far enough ahead, made the first blind, too.

At the next stop, as we ran forward along the track, I counted but fifteen of us. Five had been ditched. The weeding-out process had begun nobly, and it continued station by station. Now we were fourteen, now twelve, now eleven, now nine, now eight. It reminded me of the ten little niggers of the nursery rhyme. I was resolved that I should be the last little nigger of all. And why not? Was I not blessed with strength, agility, and youth? (I was eighteen, and in perfect condition.) And didn't I have my "nerve" with me? And furthermore, was I not a tramp-royal? Were not these other tramps mere dubs and "gay-cats" and amateurs alongside of me? If I weren't the last little nigger, I might as well quit the game and get a job on an alfalfa farm somewhere.

By the time our number had been reduced to four, the whole train-crew had become interested. From then on it was a contest of skill and wits, with the odds in favor of the crew. One by one the three other survivors turned up missing, until I alone remained. My, but I was proud of myself! No Crœsus was ever prouder of his first million. I was holding her down in spite of two brakemen, a conductor, a fireman, and an engineer.

And here are a few samples of the way I held her down. Out ahead, in the darkness,—so far ahead that the shack riding out the blind must perforce get off before it reaches me,—I get on. Very well. I am good for another station. When that station is reached, I dart ahead again to repeat the manœuvre. The train pulls out. I watch her coming. There is no light of a lantern on the blind. Has the crew abandoned the fight? I do not know. One never knows, and one must be prepared every moment for anything. As the first blind comes opposite me, and I run to leap aboard, I strain my eyes to see if the shack is on the platform. For all I know he may be there, with his lantern doused, and even as I spring upon the steps that lantern may smash down upon my head. I ought to know. I have been hit by lanterns two or three times.

But no, the first blind is empty. The train is gathering speed. I am safe for another station. But am I? I feel the train slacken speed. On the instant I am alert. A manœuvre is being executed against me, and I do not know what it is. I try to watch on both sides at once, not forgetting to keep track of the tender in front of me. From any one, or all, of these three directions, I may be assailed.

Ah, there it comes. The shack has ridden out the engine. My first warning is when his feet strike the steps of the right-hand side of the blind. Like a flash I am off the blind to the left and running ahead past the engine. I lose myself in the darkness. The situation is where it has been ever since the train left Ottawa. I am ahead, and the train must come past me if it is to proceed on its journey. I have as good a chance as ever for boarding her.

I watch carefully. I see a lantern come forward to the engine, and I do not see it go back from the engine. It must therefore be still on the engine, and it is a fair assumption that attached to the handle of that lantern is a shack. That shack was lazy, or else he would have put out his lantern instead of trying to shield it as he came forward. The train pulls out. The first blind is empty, and I gain it. As before the train slackens, the shack from the engine boards the blind from one side, and I go off the other side and run forward.

As I wait in the darkness I am conscious of a big thrill of pride. The overland has stopped twice for me—for me, a poor hobo on the bum. I alone have twice stopped the overland with its many passengers and coaches, its government mail, and its two thousand steam horses straining in the engine. And I weigh only one hundred and sixty pounds, and I haven't a five-cent piece in my pocket!

Again I see the lantern come forward to the engine. But this time it comes conspicuously. A bit too conspicuously to suit me, and I wonder what is up. At any rate I have something else to be afraid of than the shack on the engine. The train pulls by. Just in time, before I make my spring, I see the dark form of a shack, without a lantern, on the first blind. I let it go by, and prepare to board the second blind. But the shack on the first blind has jumped off and is at my heels. Also, I have a fleeting glimpse of the lantern of the shack who rode out the engine. He has jumped off, and now both shacks are on the ground on the same side with me. The next moment the second blind comes by and I am aboard it. But I do not linger. I have figured out my countermove. As I dash across the platform I hear the impact of the shack's feet against the steps as he boards. I jump off the other side and run forward with the train. My plan is to run forward and get on the first blind. It is nip and tuck, for the train is gathering speed. Also, the shack is behind me and running after me. I guess I am the better sprinter, for I make the first blind. I stand on the steps and watch my pursuer. He is only about ten feet back and running hard; but now the train has approximated his own speed, and, relative to me, he is standing still. I encourage him, hold out my hand to him; but he explodes in a mighty oath, gives up and makes the train several cars back.

The train is speeding along, and I am still chuckling to myself, when, without warning, a spray of water strikes me. The fireman is playing the hose on me from the engine. I step forward from the car-platform to the rear of the tender, where I am sheltered under the overhang. The water flies harmlessly over my head. My fingers itch to climb up on the tender and lam that fireman with a chunk of coal; but I know if I do that, I'll be massacred by him and the engineer, and I refrain.

At the next stop I am off and ahead in the darkness. This time, when the train pulls out, both shacks are on the first blind. I divine their game. They have blocked the repetition of my previous play. I cannot again take the second blind, cross over, and run forward to the first. As soon as the first blind passes and I do not get on, they swing off, one on each side of the train. I board the second blind, and as I do so I know that a moment later, simultaneously, those two shacks will arrive on both sides of me. It is like a trap. Both ways are blocked. Yet there is another way out, and that way is up.

So I do not wait for my pursuers to arrive. I climb upon the upright ironwork of the platform and stand upon the wheel of the hand-brake. This has taken up the moment of grace and I hear the shacks strike the steps on either side. I don't stop to look. I raise my arms overhead until my hands rest against the down-curving ends of the roofs of the two cars. One hand, of course, is on the curved roof of one car, the other hand on the curved roof of the other car. By this time both shacks are coming up the steps. I know it, though I am too busy to see them. All this is happening in the space of only several seconds. I make a spring with my legs and "muscle" myself up with my arms. As I draw up my legs, both shacks reach for me and clutch empty air. I know this, for I look down and see them. Also I hear them swear.

I am now in a precarious position, riding the ends of the down-curving roofs of two cars at the same time. With a quick, tense movement, I transfer both legs to the curve of one roof and both hands to the curve of the other roof. Then, gripping the edge of that curving roof, I climb over the curve to the level roof above, where I sit down to catch my breath, holding on the while to a ventilator that projects above the surface. I am on top of the train—on the "decks," as the tramps call it, and this process I have described is by them called "decking her." And let me say right here that only a young and vigorous tramp is able to deck a passenger train, and also, that the young and vigorous tramp must have his nerve with him as well.

The train goes on gathering speed, and I know I am safe until the next stop—but only until the next stop. If I remain on the roof after the train stops, I know those shacks will fusillade me with rocks. A healthy shack can "dewdrop" a pretty heavy chunk of stone on top of a car—say anywhere from five to twenty pounds. On the other hand, the chances are large that at the next stop the shacks will be waiting for me to descend at the place I climbed up. It is up to me to climb down at some other platform.

Registering a fervent hope that there are no tunnels in the next half mile, I rise to my feet and walk down the train half a dozen cars. And let me say that one must leave timidity behind him on such a *passear*. The roofs of passenger coaches are not made for midnight promenades. And if any one thinks they are, let me advise him to try it. Just let him walk along the roof of a jolting, lurching car, with nothing to hold on to but the black and empty air, and when he comes to the down-curving end of the roof, all wet and slippery with dew, let him accelerate his speed so as to step across to the next roof, down-curving and wet and slippery. Believe me, he will learn whether his heart is weak or his head is giddy.

As the train slows down for a stop, half a dozen platforms from where I had decked her I come down. No one is on the platform. When the train comes to a standstill, I slip off to the ground. Ahead, and between me and the engine, are two moving lanterns. The shacks are looking for me on the roofs of the cars. I note that the car beside which I am standing is a "four-wheeler"—by which is meant that it has only four wheels to each truck. (When you go underneath on the rods, be sure to avoid the "six-wheelers,"—they lead to disasters.)

I duck under the train and make for the rods, and I can tell you I am mighty glad that the train is standing still. It is the first time I have ever gone underneath on the Canadian Pacific, and the internal arrangements are new to me. I try to crawl over the top of the truck, between the truck and the bottom of the car. But the space is not large enough for me to squeeze through. This is new to me. Down in the United States I am accustomed to going underneath on rapidly moving trains, seizing a gunnel and swinging my feet under to the brake-beam, and from there crawling over the top of the truck and down inside the truck to a seat on the cross-rod.

Feeling with my hands in the darkness, I learn that there is room between the brake-beam and the ground. It is a tight squeeze. I have to lie flat and worm my way through. Once inside the truck, I take my seat on the rod and wonder what the shacks are thinking has become of me. The train gets under way. They have given me up at last.

But have they? At the very next stop, I see a lantern thrust under the next truck to mine at the other end of the car. They are searching the rods for me. I must make my get-away pretty lively. I crawl on my stomach under the brake-beam. They see me and run for me, but I crawl on hands and knees across the rail on the opposite side and gain my feet. Then away I go for the head of the train. I run past the engine and hide in the sheltering darkness. It is the same old situation. I am ahead of the train, and the train must go past me.

The train pulls out. There is a lantern on the first blind. I lie low, and see the peering shack go by. But there is also a lantern on the second blind. That shack spots me and calls to the shack who has gone past on the first blind. Both jump off. Never mind, I'll take the third blind and deck her. But heavens, there is a lantern on the third blind, too. It is the conductor. I let it go by. At any rate I have now the full train-crew in front of me. I turn and run back in the opposite direction to what the train is going. I look over my shoulder. All three lanterns are on the ground and wobbling along in pursuit. I sprint. Half the train has gone by, and it is going quite fast, when I spring aboard. I know that the two shacks and the conductor will arrive like ravening wolves in about two seconds. I spring upon the wheel of the hand-brake, get my hands on the curved ends of the roofs, and muscle myself up to the decks; while my disappointed pursuers, clustering on the platform beneath like dogs that have treed a cat, howl curses up at me and say unsocial things about my ancestors.

But what does that matter? It is five to one, including the engineer and fireman, and the majesty of the law and the might of a great corporation are behind them, and I am beating them out. I am too far down the train, and I run ahead over the roofs of the coaches until I am over the fifth or sixth platform from the engine. I peer down cautiously. A shack is on that platform. That he has caught sight of me, I know from the way he makes a swift sneak inside the car; and I know, also, that he is waiting inside the door, all ready to pounce out on me when I climb down. But I make believe that I don't know, and I remain there to encourage him in his error. I do not see him, yet I know that he opens the door once and peeps up to assure himself that I am still there.

The train slows down for a station. I dangle my legs down in a tentative way. The train stops. My legs are still dangling. I hear the door unlatch softly. He is all ready for me. Suddenly I spring up and run forward over the roof. This is right over his head, where he lurks inside the door. The train is standing still; the night is quiet, and I take care to make plenty of noise on the metal roof with my feet. I don't know, but my assumption is that he is now running forward to catch me as I descend at the next platform. But I don't descend there. Halfway along the roof of the coach, I turn, retrace my way softly and quickly to the platform both the shack and I have just abandoned. The coast is clear. I descend to the ground on the off-side of the train and hide in the darkness. Not a soul has seen me.

I go over to the fence, at the edge of the right of way, and watch. Ah, ha! What's that? I see a lantern on top of the train, moving along from front to rear. They think I haven't come down, and they are searching the roofs for me. And better than that—on the ground on each side of the train, moving abreast with the lantern on top, are two other lanterns. It is a rabbit-drive, and I am the rabbit. When the shack on top flushes me, the ones on each side will nab me. I roll a cigarette and watch the procession go by. Once past me, I am safe to proceed to the front of the train. She pulls out, and I make the front blind without opposition. But before she is fully under way and just as I am lighting my cigarette, I am aware that the fireman has climbed over the coal to the back of the tender and is looking down at me. I am filled with apprehension. From his position he can mash me to a jelly with lumps of coal. Instead of which he addresses me, and I note with relief the admiration in his voice.

"You son-of-a-gun," is what he says.

It is a high compliment, and I thrill as a schoolboy thrills on receiving a reward of merit.

"Say," I call up to him, "don't you play the hose on me any more."

"All right," he answers, and goes back to his work.

I have made friends with the engine, but the shacks are still looking for me. At the next stop, the shacks ride out all three blinds, and as before, I let them go by and deck in the middle of the train. The crew is on its mettle by now, and the train stops. The shacks are going to ditch me or know the reason why. Three times the mighty overland stops for me at that station, and each time I elude the shacks and make the decks. But it is hopeless, for they have finally come to an understanding of the situation. I have taught them that they cannot guard the train from me. They must do something else.

And they do it. When the train stops that last time, they take after me hot-footed. Ah, I see their game. They are trying to run me down. At first they herd me back toward the rear of the train. I know my peril. Once to the rear of the train, it will pull out with me left behind. I double, and twist, and turn, dodge through my pursuers, and gain the front of the train. One shack still hangs on after me. All right, I'll give him the run of his life, for my wind is good. I run straight ahead along the track. It doesn't matter. If he chases me ten miles, he'll nevertheless have to catch the train, and I can board her at any speed that he can.

So I run on, keeping just comfortably ahead of him and straining my eyes in the gloom for cattle-guards and switches that may bring me to grief. Alas! I strain my eyes too far ahead, and trip over something just under my feet, I know not what, some little thing, and go down to earth in a long, stumbling fall. The next moment I am on my feet, but the shack has me by the collar. I do not struggle. I am busy with breathing deeply and with sizing him up. He is narrow-shouldered, and I have at least thirty pounds the better of him in weight. Besides, he is just as tired as I am, and if he tries to slug me, I'll teach him a few things.

But he doesn't try to slug me, and that problem is settled. Instead, he starts to lead me back toward the train, and another possible problem arises. I see the lanterns of the conductor and the other shack. We are approaching them. Not for nothing have I made the acquaintance of the New York police. Not for nothing, in box-cars, by water-tanks, and in prison-cells, have I listened to bloody tales of man-handling. What if these three men are about to man-handle me? Heaven knows I have given them provocation enough. I think quickly. We are drawing nearer and nearer to the other two trainmen. I line up the stomach and the jaw of my captor, and plan the right and left I'll give him at the first sign of trouble.

Pshaw! I know another trick I'd like to work on him, and I almost regret that I did not do it at the moment I was captured. I could make him sick, what of his clutch on my collar. His fingers, tight-gripping, are buried inside my collar. My coat is tightly buttoned. Did you ever see a tourniquet? Well, this is one. All I have to do is to duck my head under his arm and begin to twist. I must twist rapidly—very rapidly. I know how to do it; twisting in a violent, jerky way, ducking my head under his arm with each revolution. Before he knows it, those detaining fingers of his will be detained. He will be unable to withdraw them. It is a powerful leverage. Twenty seconds after I have started revolving, the blood will be bursting out of his finger-ends, the delicate tendons will be rupturing, and all the muscles and nerves will be mashing and crushing together in a shrieking mass. Try it sometime when somebody has you by the collar. But be quick—quick as lightning. Also, be sure to hug yourself while you are revolving—hug your face with your left arm and your abdomen with your right. You see, the other fellow might try to stop you with a punch from his free arm. It would be a good idea, too, to revolve away from that free arm rather than toward it. A punch going is never so bad as a punch coming.

That shack will never know how near he was to being made very, very sick. All that saves him is that it is not in their plan to man-handle me. When we draw near enough, he calls out that he has me, and they signal the train to come on. The engine passes us, and the three blinds. After that, the conductor and the other shack swing aboard. But still my captor holds on to me. I see the plan. He is going to hold me until the rear of the train goes by. Then he will hop on, and I shall be left behind—ditched.

But the train has pulled out fast, the engineer trying to make up for lost time. Also, it is a long train. It is going very lively, and I know the shack is measuring its speed with apprehension.

"Think you can make it?" I query innocently.

He releases my collar, makes a quick run, and swings

aboard. A number of coaches are yet to pass by. He knows it, and remains on the steps, his head poked out and watching me. In that moment my next move comes to me. I'll make the last platform. I know she's going fast and faster, but I'll only get a roll in the dirt if I fail, and the optimism of youth is mine. I do not give myself away. I stand with a dejected droop of shoulder, advertising that I have abandoned hope. But at the same time I am feeling with my feet the good gravel. It is perfect footing. Also I am watching the poked-out head of the shack. I see it withdrawn. He is confident that the train is going too fast for me ever to make it.

And the train *is* going fast—faster than any train I have ever tackled. As the last coach comes by I sprint in the same direction with it. It is a swift, short sprint. I cannot hope to equal the speed of the train, but I can reduce the difference of our speed to the minimum, and, hence, reduce the shock of impact, when I leap on board. In the fleeting instant of darkness I do not see the iron hand-rail of the last platform; nor is there time for me to locate it. I reach for where I think it ought to be, and at the same instant my feet leave the ground. It is all in the toss. The next moment I may be rolling in the gravel with broken ribs, or arms, or head. But my fingers grip the hand-hold, there is a jerk on my arms that slightly pivots my body, and my feet land on the steps with sharp violence.

I sit down, feeling very proud of myself. In all my hoboing it is the best bit of train-jumping I have done. I know that late at night one is always good for several stations on the last platform, but I do not care to trust myself at the rear of the train. At the first stop I run forward on the off-side of the train, pass the Pullmans, and duck under and take a rod under a day-coach. At the next stop I run forward again and take another rod.

I am now comparatively safe. The shacks think I am ditched. But the long day and the strenuous night are beginning to tell on me. Also, it is not so windy nor cold underneath, and I begin to doze. This will never do. Sleep on the rods spells death, so I crawl out at a station and go forward to the second blind. Here I can lie down and sleep; and here I do sleep—how long I do not know—for I am awakened by a lantern thrust into my face. The two shacks are staring at me. I scramble up on the defensive, wondering as to which one is going to make the first "pass" at me. But slugging is far from their minds.

"I thought you was ditched," says the shack who had held me by the collar.

"If you hadn't let go of me when you did, you'd have been ditched along with me," I answer.

"How's that?" he asks.

"I'd have gone into a clinch with you, that's all," is my reply.

They hold a consultation, and their verdict is summed up in:—

"Well, I guess you can ride, Bo. There's no use trying to keep you off."

And they go away and leave me in peace to the end of their division.

I have given the foregoing as a sample of what "holding her down" means. Of course, I have selected a fortunate night out of my experiences, and said nothing of the nights—and many of them—when I was tripped up by accident and ditched.

In conclusion, I want to tell of what happened when I reached the end of the division. On single-track, transcontinental lines, the freight trains wait at the divisions and follow out after the passenger trains. When the division was reached, I left my train, and looked for the freight that would pull out behind it. I found the freight, made up on a side-track and waiting. I climbed into a box-car half full of coal and lay down. In no time I was asleep.

I was awakened by the sliding open of the door. Day was just dawning, cold and gray, and the freight had not yet started. A "con" (conductor) was poking his head inside the door.

"Get out of that, you blankety-blank-blank!" he roared at me.

I got, and outside I watched him go down the line inspecting every car in the train. When he got out of sight I thought to myself that he would never think I'd have the nerve to

climb back into the very car out of which he had fired me. So
back I climbed and lay down again.

Now that con's mental processes must have been paralleling
mine, for he reasoned that it was the very thing I would do.
For back he came and fired me out.

Now, surely, I reasoned, he will never dream that I'd do it
a third time. Back I went, into the very same car. But I decided to make sure. Only one side-door could be opened. The
other side-door was nailed up. Beginning at the top of the
coal, I dug a hole alongside of that door and lay down in it.
I heard the other door open. The con climbed up and looked
in over the top of the coal. He couldn't see me. He called to
me to get out. I tried to fool him by remaining quiet. But
when he began tossing chunks of coal into the hole on top of
me, I gave up and for the third time was fired out. Also, he
informed me in warm terms of what would happen to me if
he caught me in there again.

I changed my tactics. When a man is paralleling your mental processes, ditch him. Abruptly break off your line of reasoning, and go off on a new line. This I did. I hid between
some cars on an adjacent side-track, and watched. Sure
enough, that con came back again to the car. He opened the
door, he climbed up, he called, he threw coal into the hole I
had made. He even crawled over the coal and looked into the
hole. That satisfied him. Five minutes later the freight was
pulling out, and he was not in sight. I ran alongside the car,
pulled the door open, and climbed in. He never looked for
me again, and I rode that coal-car precisely one thousand and
twenty-two miles, sleeping most of the time and getting out
at divisions (where the freights always stop for an hour or so)
to beg my food. And at the end of the thousand and twenty-
two miles I lost that car through a happy incident. I got a
"set-down," and the tramp doesn't live who won't miss a train
for a set-down any time.

Pictures

"What do it matter where or 'ow we die,
So long as we've our 'ealth to watch it all?"
— *Sestina of the Tramp-Royal*

PERHAPS the greatest charm of tramp-life is the absence of monotony. In Hobo Land the face of life is protean—an ever changing phantasmagoria, where the impossible happens and the unexpected jumps out of the bushes at every turn of the road. The hobo never knows what is going to happen the next moment; hence, he lives only in the present moment. He has learned the futility of telic endeavor, and knows the delight of drifting along with the whimsicalities of Chance.

Often I think over my tramp days, and ever I marvel at the swift succession of pictures that flash up in my memory. It matters not where I begin to think; any day of all the days is a day apart, with a record of swift-moving pictures all its own. For instance, I remember a sunny summer morning in Harrisburg, Pennsylvania, and immediately comes to my mind the auspicious beginning of the day—a "set-down" with two maiden ladies, and not in their kitchen, but in their dining room, with them beside me at the table. We ate eggs, out of egg-cups! It was the first time I had ever seen egg-cups, or heard of egg-cups! I was a bit awkward at first, I'll confess; but I was hungry and unabashed. I mastered the egg-cup, and I mastered the eggs in a way that made those two maiden ladies sit up.

Why, they ate like a couple of canaries, dabbling with the one egg each they took, and nibbling at tiny wafers of toast. Life was low in their bodies; their blood ran thin; and they had slept warm all night. I had been out all night, consuming much fuel of my body to keep warm, beating my way down from a place called Emporium, in the northern part of the state. Wafers of toast! Out of sight! But each wafer was no more than a mouthful to me—nay, no more than a bite. It is tedious to have to reach for another piece of toast each bite when one is potential with many bites.

When I was a very little lad, I had a very little dog called Punch. I saw to his feeding myself. Some one in the household had shot a lot of ducks, and we had a fine meat dinner. When I had finished, I prepared Punch's dinner—a large plateful of bones and tidbits. I went outside to give it to him. Now it happened that a visitor had ridden over from a neighboring ranch, and with him had come a Newfoundland dog as big as a calf. I set the plate on the ground. Punch wagged his tail and began. He had before him a blissful half-hour at least. There was a sudden rush. Punch was brushed aside like a straw in the path of a cyclone, and that Newfoundland swooped down upon the plate. In spite of his huge maw he must have been trained to quick lunches, for, in the fleeting instant before he received the kick in the ribs I aimed at him, he completely engulfed the contents of the plate. He swept it clean. One last lingering lick of his tongue removed even the grease stains.

As that big Newfoundland behaved at the plate of my dog Punch, so behaved I at the table of those two maiden ladies of Harrisburg. I swept it bare. I didn't break anything, but I cleaned out the eggs and the toast and the coffee. The servant brought more, but I kept her busy, and ever she brought more and more. The coffee was delicious, but it needn't have been served in such tiny cups. What time had I to eat when it took all my time to prepare the many cups of coffee for drinking?

At any rate, it gave my tongue time to wag. Those two maiden ladies, with their pink-and-white complexions and gray curls, had never looked upon the bright face of adventure. As the "Tramp-Royal" would have it, they had worked all their lives "on one same shift." Into the sweet scents and narrow confines of their uneventful existence I brought the large airs of the world, freighted with the lusty smells of sweat and strife, and with the tangs and odors of strange lands and soils. And right well I scratched their soft palms with the callous on my own palms—the half-inch horn that comes of pull-and-haul of rope and long and arduous hours of caressing shovel-handles. This I did, not merely in the braggadocio of youth, but to prove, by toil performed, the claim I had upon their charity.

Ah, I can see them now, those dear, sweet ladies, just as I sat at their breakfast table twelve years ago, discoursing upon the way of my feet in the world, brushing aside their kindly counsel as a real devilish fellow should, and thrilling them, not alone with my own adventures, but with the adventures of all the other fellows with whom I had rubbed shoulders and exchanged confidences. I appropriated them all, the adventures of the other fellows, I mean; and if those maiden ladies had been less trustful and guileless, they could have tangled me up beautifully in my chronology. Well, well, and what of it? It was fair exchange. For their many cups of coffee, and eggs, and bites of toast, I gave full value. Right royally I gave them entertainment. My coming to sit at their table was their adventure, and adventure is beyond price anyway.

Coming along the street, after parting from the maiden ladies, I gathered in a newspaper from the doorway of some late-riser, and in a grassy park lay down to get in touch with the last twenty-four hours of the world. There, in the park, I met a fellow-hobo who told me his life-story and who wrestled with me to join the United States Army. He had given in to the recruiting officer and was just about to join, and he couldn't see why I shouldn't join with him. He had been a member of Coxey's Army in the march to Washington several months before, and that seemed to have given him a taste for army life. I, too, was a veteran, for had I not been a private in Company L of the Second Division of Kelly's Industrial Army?—said Company L being commonly known as the "Nevada push." But my army experience had had the opposite effect on me; so I left that hobo to go his way to the dogs of war, while I "threw my feet" for dinner.

This duty performed, I started to walk across the bridge over the Susquehanna to the west shore. I forget the name of the railroad that ran down that side, but while lying in the grass in the morning the idea had come to me to go to Baltimore; so to Baltimore I was going on that railroad, whatever its name was. It was a warm afternoon, and part way across the bridge I came to a lot of fellows who were in swimming off one of the piers. Off went my clothes and in went I.

The water was fine; but when I came out and dressed, I found I had been robbed. Some one had gone through my clothes. Now I leave it to you if being robbed isn't in itself adventure enough for one day. I have known men who have been robbed and who have talked all the rest of their lives about it. True, the thief that went through my clothes didn't get much—some thirty or forty cents in nickels and pennies, and my tobacco and cigarette papers; but it was all I had, which is more than most men can be robbed of, for they have something left at home, while I had no home. It was a pretty tough gang in swimming there. I sized up, and knew better than to squeal. So I begged "the makings," and I could have sworn it was one of my own papers I rolled the tobacco in.

Then on across the bridge I hiked to the west shore. Here ran the railroad I was after. No station was in sight. How to catch a freight without walking to a station was the problem. I noticed that the track came up a steep grade, culminating at the point where I had tapped it, and I knew that a heavy freight couldn't pull up there any too lively. But how lively? On the opposite side of the track rose a high bank. On the edge, at the top, I saw a man's head sticking up from the grass. Perhaps he knew how fast the freights took the grade, and when the next one went south. I called out my questions to him, and he motioned to me to come up.

I obeyed, and when I reached the top, I found four other men lying in the grass with him. I took in the scene and knew them for what they were—American gypsies. In the open space that extended back among the trees from the edge of the bank were several nondescript wagons. Ragged, half-naked children swarmed over the camp, though I noticed that they took care not to come near and bother the men-folk. Several lean, unbeautiful, and toil-degraded women were pottering about with camp-chores, and one I noticed who sat by herself on the seat of one of the wagons, her head drooped forward, her knees drawn up to her chin and clasped limply by her arms. She did not look happy. She looked as if she did not care for anything—in this I was wrong, for later I was to learn that there was something for which she did care. The full measure of human suffering was in her face, and, in addition, there was the tragic expression of incapacity for further suffering. Nothing could hurt any more, was what her face seemed to portray; but in this, too, I was wrong.

I lay in the grass on the edge of the steep and talked with the men-folk. We were kin—brothers. I was the American hobo, and they were the American gypsy. I knew enough of their argot for conversation, and they knew enough of mine. There were two more in their gang, who were across the river "mushing" in Harrisburg. A "musher" is an itinerant fakir. This word is not to be confounded with the Klondike "musher," though the origin of both terms may be the same; namely, the corruption of the French *marche ons*, to march, to walk, to "mush." The particular graft of the two mushers who had crossed the river was umbrella-mending; but what real graft lay behind their umbrella-mending, I was not told, nor would it have been polite to ask.

It was a glorious day. Not a breath of wind was stirring, and we basked in the shimmering warmth of the sun. From everywhere arose the drowsy hum of insects, and the balmy air was filled with scents of the sweet earth and the green growing things. We were too lazy to do more than mumble on in intermittent conversation. And then, all abruptly, the peace and quietude was jarred awry by man.

Two bare-legged boys of eight or nine in some minor way broke some rule of the camp—what it was I did not know; and a man who lay beside me suddenly sat up and called to them. He was chief of the tribe, a man with narrow forehead and narrow-slitted eyes, whose thin lips and twisted sardonic features explained why the two boys jumped and tensed like startled deer at the sound of his voice. The alertness of fear was in their faces, and they turned, in a panic, to run. He called to them to come back, and one boy lagged behind reluctantly, his meagre little frame portraying in pantomime the struggle within him between fear and reason. He wanted to come back. His intelligence and past experience told him that to come back was a lesser evil than to run on; but lesser evil that it was, it was great enough to put wings to his fear and urge his feet to flight.

Still he lagged and struggled until he reached the shelter of the trees, where he halted. The chief of the tribe did not pursue. He sauntered over to a wagon and picked up a heavy whip. Then he came back to the centre of the open space and stood still. He did not speak. He made no gestures. He was the Law, pitiless and omnipotent. He merely stood there and waited. And I knew, and all knew, and the two boys in the shelter of the trees knew, for what he waited.

The boy who had lagged slowly came back. His face was stamped with quivering resolution. He did not falter. He had made up his mind to take his punishment. And mark you, the punishment was not for the original offence, but for the offence of running away. And in this, that tribal chieftain but behaved as behaves the exalted society in which he lived. We punish our criminals, and when they escape and run away, we bring them back and add to their punishment.

Straight up to the chief the boy came, halting at the proper distance for the swing of the lash. The whip hissed through the air, and I caught myself with a start of surprise at the weight of the blow. The thin little leg was so very thin and little. The flesh showed white where the lash had curled and bitten, and then, where the white had shown, sprang up the savage welt, with here and there along its length little scarlet oozings where the skin had broken. Again the whip swung, and the boy's whole body winced in anticipation of the blow, though he did not move from the spot. His will held good. A second welt sprang up, and a third. It was not until the fourth landed that the boy screamed. Also, he could no longer stand still, and from then on, blow after blow, he danced up and down in his anguish, screaming; but he did not attempt to run away. If his involuntary dancing took him beyond the reach of the whip, he danced back into range again. And when it was all over—a dozen blows—he went away, whimpering and squealing, among the wagons.

The chief stood still and waited. The second boy came out from the trees. But he did not come straight. He came like a cringing dog, obsessed by little panics that made him turn and dart away for half a dozen steps. But always he turned and came back, circling nearer and nearer to the man, whimpering, making inarticulate animal-noises in his throat. I saw that he never looked at the man. His eyes always were fixed upon the whip, and in his eyes was a terror that made me sick—the frantic terror of an inconceivably maltreated child. I have seen strong men dropping right and left out of battle and squirming in their death-throes, I have seen them by scores blown into the air by bursting shells and their bodies torn asunder; believe me, the witnessing was as merrymaking and laughter and song to me in comparison with the way the sight of that poor child affected me.

The whipping began. The whipping of the first boy was as play compared with this one. In no time the blood was running down his thin little legs. He danced and squirmed and doubled up till it seemed almost that he was some grotesque marionette operated by strings. I say "seemed," for his screaming gave the lie to the seeming and stamped it with reality. His shrieks were shrill and piercing; within them no hoarse notes, but only the thin sexlessness of the voice of a child. The time came when the boy could stand it no more. Reason fled, and he tried to run away. But now the man followed up, curbing his flight, herding him with blows back always into the open space.

Then came interruption. I heard a wild smothered cry. The woman who sat in the wagon seat had got out and was running to interfere. She sprang between the man and boy.

"You want some, eh?" said he with the whip. "All right, then."

He swung the whip upon her. Her skirts were long, so he did not try for her legs. He drove the lash for her face, which she shielded as best she could with her hands and forearms, drooping her head forward between her lean shoulders, and on the lean shoulders and arms receiving the blows. Heroic mother! She knew just what she was doing. The boy, still shrieking, was making his get-away to the wagons.

And all the while the four men lay beside me and watched and made no move. Nor did I move, and without shame I say it; though my reason was compelled to struggle hard against my natural impulse to rise up and interfere. I knew life. Of what use to the woman, or to me, would be my being beaten to death by five men there on the bank of the Susquehanna? I once saw a man hanged, and though my whole soul cried protest, my mouth cried not. Had it cried, I should most likely have had my skull crushed by the butt of a revolver, for it was the law that the man should hang. And here, in this gypsy group, it was the law that the woman should be whipped.

Even so, the reason in both cases that I did not interfere was not that it was the law, but that the law was stronger than I. Had it not been for those four men beside me in the grass, right gladly would I have waded into the man with the whip. And, barring the accident of the landing on me with a knife or a club in the hands of some of the various women of the camp, I am confident that I should have beaten him into a mess. But the four men *were* beside me in the grass. They made their law stronger than I.

Oh, believe me, I did my own suffering. I had seen women beaten before, often, but never had I seen such a beating as this. Her dress across the shoulders was cut into shreds. One blow that had passed her guard, had raised a bloody welt from cheek to chin. Not one blow, nor two, not one dozen, nor two dozen, but endlessly, infinitely, that whip-lash smote and curled about her. The sweat poured from me, and I breathed hard, clutching at the grass with my hands until I strained it out by the roots. And all the time my reason kept whispering, "Fool! Fool!" That welt on the face nearly did for me. I started to rise to my feet; but the hand of the man next to me went out to my shoulder and pressed me down.

"Easy, pardner, easy," he warned me in a low voice. I looked at him. His eyes met mine unwaveringly. He was a large man, broad-shouldered and heavy-muscled; and his face was lazy, phlegmatic, slothful, withal kindly, yet without passion, and quite soulless—a dim soul, unmalicious, unmoral, bovine, and stubborn. Just an animal he was, with no more than a faint flickering of intelligence, a good-natured brute with the strength and mental caliber of a gorilla. His hand pressed heavily upon me, and I knew the weight of the muscles behind. I looked at the other brutes, two of them unperturbed and incurious, and one of them that gloated over the spectacle; and my reason came back to me, my muscles relaxed, and I sank down in the grass.

My mind went back to the two maiden ladies with whom I had had breakfast that morning. Less than two miles, as the crow flies, separated them from this scene. Here, in the windless day, under a beneficent sun, was a sister of theirs being beaten by a brother of mine. Here was a page of life they could never see—and better so, though for lack of seeing they would never be able to understand their sisterhood, nor themselves, nor know the clay of which they were made. For it is not given to woman to live in sweet-scented, narrow rooms and at the same time be a little sister to all the world.

The whipping was finished, and the woman, no longer screaming, went back to her seat in the wagon. Nor did the other women come to her—just then. They were afraid. But they came afterward, when a decent interval had elapsed. The man put the whip away and rejoined us, flinging himself down on the other side of me. He was breathing hard from his exertions. He wiped the sweat from his eyes on his coat-sleeve, and looked challengingly at me. I returned his look carelessly; what he had done was no concern of mine. I did not go away abruptly. I lay there half an hour longer, which, under the circumstances, was tact and etiquette. I rolled cig-arettes from tobacco I borrowed from them, and when I slipped down the bank to the railroad, I was equipped with the necessary information for catching the next freight bound south.

Well, and what of it? It was a page out of life, that's all; and there are many pages worse, far worse, that I have seen. I have sometimes held forth (facetiously, so my listeners be-lieved) that the chief distinguishing trait between man and the other animals is that man is the only animal that maltreats the females of his kind. It is something of which no wolf nor cowardly coyote is ever guilty. It is something that even the dog, degenerated by domestication, will not do. The dog still retains the wild instinct in this matter, while man has lost most of his wild instincts—at least, most of the good ones.

Worse pages of life than what I have described? Read the reports on child labor in the United States,—east, west, north, and south, it doesn't matter where,—and know that all of us, profit-mongers that we are, are typesetters and print-ers of worse pages of life than that mere page of wife-beating on the Susquehanna.

I went down the grade a hundred yards to where the foot-ing beside the track was good. Here I could catch my freight

as it pulled slowly up the hill, and here I found half a dozen
hoboes waiting for the same purpose. Several were playing
seven-up with an old pack of cards. I took a hand. A coon
began to shuffle the deck. He was fat, and young, and moon-
faced. He beamed with good-nature. It fairly oozed from
him. As he dealt the first card to me, he paused and said:—

"Say, Bo, ain't I done seen you befo'?"

"You sure have," I answered. "An' you didn't have those
same duds on, either."

He was puzzled.

"D'ye remember Buffalo?" I queried.

Then he knew me, and with laughter and ejaculation hailed
me as a comrade; for at Buffalo his clothes had been striped
while he did his bit of time in the Erie County Penitentiary.
For that matter, my clothes had been likewise striped, for I
had been doing my bit of time, too.

The game proceeded, and I learned the stake for which we
played. Down the bank toward the river descended a steep
and narrow path that led to a spring some twenty-five feet
beneath. We played on the edge of the bank. The man who
was "stuck" had to take a small condensed-milk can, and with
it carry water to the winners.

The first game was played and the coon was stuck. He took
the small milk-tin and climbed down the bank, while we sat
above and guyed him. We drank like fish. Four round trips
he had to make for me alone, and the others were equally
lavish with their thirst. The path was very steep, and sometimes the coon slipped when part way up, spilled the water,
and had to go back for more. But he didn't get angry. He
laughed as heartily as any of us; that was why he slipped so
often. Also, he assured us of the prodigious quantities of water he would drink when some one else got stuck.

When our thirst was quenched, another game was started.
Again the coon was stuck, and again we drank our fill. A
third game and a fourth ended the same way, and each time
that moon-faced darky nearly died with delight at appreciation of the fate that Chance was dealing out to him. And we
nearly died with him, what of our delight. We laughed like
careless children, or gods, there on the edge of the bank. I
know that I laughed till it seemed the top of my head would

come off, and I drank from the milk-tin till I was nigh water-logged. Serious discussion arose as to whether we could successfully board the freight when it pulled up the grade, what of the weight of water secreted on our persons. This particular phase of the situation just about finished the coon. He had to break off from water-carrying for at least five minutes while he lay down and rolled with laughter.

The lengthening shadows stretched farther and farther across the river, and the soft, cool twilight came on, and ever we drank water, and ever our ebony cup-bearer brought more and more. Forgotten was the beaten woman of the hour before. That was a page read and turned over; I was busy now with this new page, and when the engine whistled on the grade, this page would be finished and another begun; and so the book of life goes on, page after page and pages without end—when one is young.

And then we played a game in which the coon failed to be stuck. The victim was a lean and dyspeptic-looking hobo, the one who had laughed least of all of us. We said we didn't want any water—which was the truth. Not the wealth of Ormuz and of Ind, nor the pressure of a pneumatic ram, could have forced another drop into my saturated carcass. The coon looked disappointed, then rose to the occasion and guessed he'd have some. He meant it, too. He had some, and then some, and then some. Ever the melancholy hobo climbed down and up the steep bank, and ever the coon called for more. He drank more water than all the rest of us put together. The twilight deepened into night, the stars came out, and he still drank on. I do believe that if the whistle of the freight hadn't sounded, he'd be there yet, swilling water and revenge while the melancholy hobo toiled down and up.

But the whistle sounded. The page was done. We sprang to our feet and strung out alongside the track. There she came, coughing and spluttering up the grade, the headlight turning night into day and silhouetting us in sharp relief. The engine passed us, and we were all running with the train, some boarding on the side-ladders, others "springing" the side-doors of empty box-cars and climbing in. I caught a flat-car loaded with mixed lumber and crawled away into a comfortable nook. I lay on my back with a newspaper under my head for a pillow. Above me the stars were winking and wheeling in squadrons back and forth as the train rounded the curves, and watching them I fell asleep. The day was done—one day of all my days. To-morrow would be another day, and I was young.

"Pinched"

I RODE into Niagara Falls in a "side-door Pullman," or, in common parlance, a box-car. A flat-car, by the way, is known amongst the fraternity as a "gondola," with the second syllable emphasized and pronounced long. But to return. I arrived in the afternoon and headed straight from the freight train to the falls. Once my eyes were filled with that wonder-vision of down-rushing water, I was lost. I could not tear myself away long enough to "batter" the "privates" (domiciles) for my supper. Even a "set-down" could not have lured me away. Night came on, a beautiful night of moonlight, and I lingered by the falls until after eleven. Then it was up to me to hunt for a place to "kip."

"Kip," "doss," "flop," "pound your ear," all mean the same thing; namely, to sleep. Somehow, I had a "hunch" that Niagara Falls was a "bad" town for hoboes, and I headed out into the country. I climbed a fence and "flopped" in a field. John Law would never find me there, I flattered myself. I lay on my back in the grass and slept like a babe. It was so balmy warm that I woke up not once all night. But with the first gray daylight my eyes opened, and I remembered the wonderful falls. I climbed the fence and started down the road to have another look at them. It was early—not more than five o'clock—and not until eight o'clock could I begin to batter for my breakfast. I could spend at least three hours by the river. Alas! I was fated never to see the river nor the falls again.

The town was asleep when I entered it. As I came along the quiet street, I saw three men coming toward me along the sidewalk. They were walking abreast. Hoboes, I decided, like myself, who had got up early. In this surmise I was not quite correct. I was only sixty-six and two-thirds per cent correct. The men on each side were hoboes all right, but the man in the middle wasn't. I directed my steps to the edge of the sidewalk in order to let the trio go by. But it didn't go by. At some word from the man in the centre, all three halted, and he of the centre addressed me.

I piped the lay on the instant. He was a "fly-cop" and the two hoboes were his prisoners. John Law was up and out after the early worm. I was a worm. Had I been richer by the experiences that were to befall me in the next several months, I should have turned and run like the very devil. He might have shot at me, but he'd have had to hit me to get me. He'd have never run after me, for two hoboes in the hand are worth more than one on the get-away. But like a dummy I stood still when he halted me. Our conversation was brief.

"What hotel are you stopping at?" he queried.

He had me. I wasn't stopping at any hotel, and, since I did not know the name of a hotel in the place, I could not claim residence in any of them. Also, I was up too early in the morning. Everything was against me.

"I just arrived," I said.

"Well, you turn around and walk in front of me, and not too far in front. There's somebody wants to see you."

I was "pinched." I knew who wanted to see me. With that "fly-cop" and the two hoboes at my heels, and under the direction of the former, I led the way to the city jail. There we were searched and our names registered. I have forgotten, now, under which name I was registered. I gave the name of Jack Drake, but when they searched me, they found letters addressed to Jack London. This caused trouble and required explanation, all of which has passed from my mind, and to this day I do not know whether I was pinched as Jack Drake or Jack London. But one or the other, it should be there to-day in the prison register of Niagara Falls. Reference can bring it to light. The time was somewhere in the latter part of June, 1894. It was only a few days after my arrest that the great railroad strike began.

From the office we were led to the "Hobo" and locked in. The "Hobo" is that part of a prison where the minor offenders are confined together in a large iron cage. Since hoboes constitute the principal division of the minor offenders, the aforesaid iron cage is called the Hobo. Here we met several hoboes who had already been pinched that morning, and every little while the door was unlocked and two or three more were thrust in on us. At last, when we totalled sixteen, we were led upstairs into the court-room. And now I shall faithfully describe what took place in that court-room, for know that my patriotic American citizenship there received a shock from which it has never fully recovered.

In the court-room were the sixteen prisoners, the judge, and two bailiffs. The judge seemed to act as his own clerk. There were no witnesses. There were no citizens of Niagara Falls present to look on and see how justice was administered in their community. The judge glanced at the list of cases before him and called out a name. A hobo stood up. The judge glanced at a bailiff. "Vagrancy, your Honor," said the bailiff. "Thirty days," said his Honor. The hobo sat down, and the judge was calling another name and another hobo was rising to his feet.

The trial of that hobo had taken just about fifteen seconds. The trial of the next hobo came off with equal celerity. The bailiff said, "Vagrancy, your Honor," and his Honor said, "Thirty days." Thus it went like clockwork, fifteen seconds to a hobo—and thirty days.

They are poor dumb cattle, I thought to myself. But wait till my turn comes; I'll give his Honor a "spiel." Part way along in the performance, his Honor, moved by some whim, gave one of us an opportunity to speak. As chance would have it, this man was not a genuine hobo. He bore none of the ear-marks of the professional "stiff." Had he approached the rest of us, while waiting at a water-tank for a freight, should have unhesitatingly classified him as a "gay-cat." Gay-cat is the synonym for tenderfoot in Hobo Land. This gay-cat was well along in years—somewhere around forty-five, I should judge. His shoulders were humped a trifle, and his face was seamed by weather-beat.

For many years, according to his story, he had driven team for some firm in (if I remember rightly) Lockport, New York. The firm had ceased to prosper, and finally, in the hard times of 1893, had gone out of business. He had been kept on to the last, though toward the last his work had been very irregular. He went on and explained at length his difficulties in getting work (when so many were out of work) during the succeeding months. In the end, deciding that he would find better opportunities for work on the Lakes, he had started for

Buffalo. Of course he was "broke," and there he was. That was all.

"Thirty days," said his Honor, and called another hobo's name.

Said hobo got up. "Vagrancy, your Honor," said the bailiff, and his Honor said, "Thirty days."

And so it went, fifteen seconds and thirty days to each hobo. The machine of justice was grinding smoothly. Most likely, considering how early it was in the morning, his Honor had not yet had his breakfast and was in a hurry.

But my American blood was up. Behind me were the many generations of my American ancestry. One of the kinds of liberty those ancestors of mine had fought and died for was the right of trial by jury. This was my heritage, stained sacred by their blood, and it devolved upon me to stand up for it. All right, I threatened to myself; just wait till he gets to me.

He got to me. My name, whatever it was, was called, and I stood up. The bailiff said, "Vagrancy, your Honor," and I began to talk. But the judge began talking at the same time, and he said, "Thirty days." I started to protest, but at that moment his Honor was calling the name of the next hobo on the list. His Honor paused long enough to say to me, "Shut up!" The bailiff forced me to sit down. And the next moment that next hobo had received thirty days and the succeeding hobo was just in process of getting his.

When we had all been disposed of, thirty days to each stiff, his Honor, just as he was about to dismiss us, suddenly turned to the teamster from Lockport—the one man he had allowed to talk.

"Why did you quit your job?" his Honor asked.

Now the teamster had already explained how his job had quit him, and the question took him aback.

"Your Honor," he began confusedly, "isn't that a funny question to ask?"

"Thirty days more for quitting your job," said his Honor, and the court was closed. That was the outcome. The teamster got sixty days all together, while the rest of us got thirty days.

We were taken down below, locked up, and given breakfast. It was a pretty good breakfast, as prison breakfasts go, and it was the best I was to get for a month to come.

As for me, I was dazed. Here was I, under sentence, after a farce of a trial wherein I was denied not only my right of trial by jury, but my right to plead guilty or not guilty. Another thing my fathers had fought for flashed through my brain—habeas corpus. I'd show them. But when I asked for a lawyer, I was laughed at. Habeas corpus was all right, but of what good was it to me when I could communicate with no one outside the jail? But I'd show them. They couldn't keep me in jail forever. Just wait till I got out, that was all. I'd make them sit up. I knew something about the law and my own rights, and I'd expose their maladministration of justice. Visions of damage suits and sensational newspaper headlines were dancing before my eyes when the jailers came in and began hustling us out into the main office.

A policeman snapped a handcuff on my right wrist. (Ah, ha, thought I, a new indignity. Just wait till I get out.) On the left wrist of a negro he snapped the other handcuff of that pair. He was a very tall negro, well past six feet—so tall was he that when we stood side by side his hand lifted mine up a trifle in the manacles. Also, he was the happiest and the raggedest negro I have ever seen.

We were all handcuffed similarly, in pairs. This accomplished, a bright nickel-steel chain was brought forth, run down through the links of all the handcuffs, and locked at front and rear of the double-line. We were now a chain-gang. The command to march was given, and out we went upon the street, guarded by two officers. The tall negro and I had the place of honor. We led the procession.

After the tomb-like gloom of the jail, the outside sunshine was dazzling. I had never known it to be so sweet as now, a prisoner with clanking chains, I knew that I was soon to see the last of it for thirty days. Down through the streets of Niagara Falls we marched to the railroad station, stared at by curious passers-by, and especially by a group of tourists on the veranda of a hotel that we marched past.

There was plenty of slack in the chain, and with much rattling and clanking we sat down, two and two, in the seats of the smoking-car. Afire with indignation as I was at the outrage that had been perpetrated on me and my forefathers, I was nevertheless too prosaically practical to lose my head over it. This was all new to me. Thirty days of mystery were before me, and I looked about me to find somebody who knew the ropes. For I had already learned that I was not bound for a petty jail with a hundred or so prisoners in it, but for a full-grown penitentiary with a couple of thousand prisoners in it, doing anywhere from ten days to ten years.

In the seat behind me, attached to the chain by his wrist, was a squat, heavily-built, powerfully-muscled man. He was somewhere between thirty-five and forty years of age. I sized him up. In the corners of his eyes I saw humor and laughter and kindliness. As for the rest of him, he was a brute-beast, wholly unmoral, and with all the passion and turgid violence of the brute-beast. What saved him, what made him possible for me, were those corners of his eyes—the humor and laughter and kindliness of the beast when unaroused.

He was my "meat." I "cottoned" to him. While my cuff-mate, the tall negro, mourned with chucklings and laughter over some laundry he was sure to lose through his arrest, and while the train rolled on toward Buffalo, I talked with the man in the seat behind me. He had an empty pipe. I filled it for him with my precious tobacco—enough in a single filling to make a dozen cigarettes. Nay, the more we talked the surer I was that he was my meat, and I divided all my tobacco with him.

Now it happens that I am a fluid sort of an organism, with sufficient kinship with life to fit myself in 'most anywhere. I laid myself out to fit in with that man, though little did I dream to what extraordinary good purpose I was succeeding. He had never been in the particular penitentiary to which we were going, but he had done "one-," "two-," and "five-spots" in various other penitentiaries (a "spot" is a year), and he was filled with wisdom. We became pretty chummy, and my heart bounded when he cautioned me to follow his lead. He called me "Jack," and I called him "Jack."

The train stopped at a station about five miles from Buffalo, and we, the chain-gang, got off. I do not remember the name of this station, but I am confident that it is some one of the following: Rocklyn, Rockwood, Black Rock, Rockcastle, or Newcastle. But whatever the name of the place, we were walked a short distance and then put on a street-car. It was an old-fashioned car, with a seat, running the full length, on each side. All the passengers who sat on one side were asked to move over to the other side, and we, with a great clanking of chain, took their places. We sat facing them, I remember, and I remember, too, the awed expression on the faces of the women, who took us, undoubtedly, for convicted murderers and bank-robbers. I tried to look my fiercest, but that cuff-mate of mine, the too happy negro, insisted on rolling his eyes, laughing, and reiterating, "O Lawdy! Lawdy!"

We left the car, walked some more, and were led into the office of the Erie County Penitentiary. Here we were to register, and on that register one or the other of my names will be found. Also, we were informed that we must leave in the office all our valuables: money, tobacco, matches, pocket-knives, and so forth.

My new pal shook his head at me.

"If you do not leave your things here, they will be confiscated inside," warned the official.

Still my pal shook his head. He was busy with his hands, hiding his movements behind the other fellows. (Our hand-cuffs had been removed.) I watched him, and followed suit, wrapping up in a bundle in my handkerchief all the things I wanted to take in. These bundles the two of us thrust into our shirts. I noticed that our fellow-prisoners, with the exception of one or two who had watches, did not turn over their belongings to the man in the office. They were determined to smuggle them in somehow, trusting to luck; but they were not so wise as my pal, for they did not wrap their things in bundles.

Our erstwhile guardians gathered up the handcuffs and chain and departed for Niagara Falls, while we, under new guardians, were led away into the prison. While we were in the office, our number had been added to by other squads of newly arrived prisoners, so that we were now a procession forty or fifty strong.

Know, ye unimprisoned, that traffic is as restricted inside a large prison as commerce was in the Middle Ages. Once inside a penitentiary, one cannot move about at will. Every few steps are encountered great steel doors or gates which are always kept locked. We were bound for the barber-shop, but we encountered delays in the unlocking of doors for us. We were thus delayed in the first "hall" we entered. A "hall" is not a corridor. Imagine an oblong cube, built out of bricks and rising six stories high, each story a row of cells, say fifty cells in a row—in short, imagine a cube of colossal honeycomb. Place this cube on the ground and enclose it in a building with a roof overhead and walls all around. Such a cube and encompassing building constitute a "hall" in the Erie County Penitentiary. Also, to complete the picture, see a narrow gallery, with steel railing, running the full length of each tier of cells and at the ends of the oblong cube see all these galleries, from both sides, connected by a fire-escape system of narrow steel stairways.

We were halted in the first hall, waiting for some guard to unlock a door. Here and there, moving about, were convicts, with close-cropped heads and shaven faces, and garbed in prison stripes. One such convict I noticed above us on the gallery of the third tier of cells. He was standing on the gallery and leaning forward, his arms resting on the railing, himself apparently oblivious of our presence. He seemed staring into vacancy. My pal made a slight hissing noise. The convict glanced down. Motioned signals passed between them. Then through the air soared the handkerchief bundle of my pal. The convict caught it, and like a flash it was out of sight in his shirt and he was staring into vacancy. My pal had told me to follow his lead. I watched my chance when the guard's back was turned, and my bundle followed the other one into the shirt of the convict.

A minute later the door was unlocked, and we filed into the barber-shop. Here were more men in convict stripes. They were the prison barbers. Also, there were bath-tubs, hot water, soap, and scrubbing-brushes. We were ordered to strip and bathe, each man to scrub his neighbor's back—a needless precaution, this compulsory bath, for the prison swarmed with vermin. After the bath, we were each given a canvas clothes-bag.

"Put all your clothes in the bags," said the guard. "It's no good trying to smuggle anything in. You've got to line up naked for inspection. Men for thirty days or less keep their shoes and suspenders. Men for more than thirty days keep nothing."

This announcement was received with consternation. How could naked men smuggle anything past an inspection? Only my pal and I were safe. But it was right here that the convict barbers got in their work. They passed among the poor new-comers, kindly volunteering to take charge of their precious little belongings, and promising to return them later in the day. Those barbers were philanthropists—to hear them talk. As in the case of Fra Lippo Lippi, never was there such prompt disemburdening. Matches, tobacco, rice-paper, pipes, knives, money, everything, flowed into the capacious shirts of the barbers. They fairly bulged with the spoil, and the guards made believe not to see. To cut the story short, nothing was ever returned. The barbers never had any intention of return-ing what they had taken. They considered it legitimately theirs. It was the barber-shop graft. There were many grafts in that prison, as I was to learn; and I, too, was destined to become a grafter—thanks to my new pal.

There were several chairs, and the barbers worked rapidly. The quickest shaves and hair-cuts I have ever seen were given in that shop. The men lathered themselves, and the barbers shaved them at the rate of a minute to a man. A hair-cut took a trifle longer. In three minutes the down of eighteen was scraped from my face, and my head was as smooth as a bil-liard-ball just sprouting a crop of bristles. Beards, mustaches, like our clothes and everything, came off. Take my word for it, we were a villainous-looking gang when they got through with us. I had not realized before how really altogether bad we were.

Then came the line-up, forty or fifty of us, naked as Kip-ling's heroes who stormed Lungtungpen. To search us was easy. There were only our shoes and ourselves. Two or three rash spirits, who had doubted the barbers, had the goods found on them—which goods, namely, tobacco, pipes, matches, and small change, were quickly confiscated. This over, our new clothes were brought to us—stout prison shirts, and coats and trousers conspicuously striped. I had always lingered under the impression that the convict

stripes were put on a man only after he had been convicted of a felony. I lingered no longer, but put on the
insignia of shame and got my first taste of marching the
lock-step.

In single file, close together, each man's hands on the
shoulders of the man in front, we marched on into another
large hall. Here we were ranged up against the wall in a long
line and ordered to strip our left arms. A youth, a medical
student who was getting in his practice on cattle such as we,
came down the line. He vaccinated just about four times as
rapidly as the barbers shaved. With a final caution to avoid
rubbing our arms against anything, and to let the blood dry
so as to form the scab, we were led away to our cells. Here
my pal and I parted, but not before he had time to whisper
to me, "Suck it out."

As soon as I was locked in, I sucked my arm clean. And
afterward I saw men who had not sucked and who had horrible holes in their arms into which I could have thrust my
fist. It was their own fault. They could have sucked.

In my cell was another man. We were to be cell-mates. He
was a young, manly fellow, not talkative, but very capable,
indeed as splendid a fellow as one could meet with in a day's
ride, and this in spite of the fact that he had just recently
finished a two-year term in some Ohio penitentiary.

Hardly had we been in our cell half an hour, when a convict sauntered down the gallery and looked in. It was my pal.
He had the freedom of the hall, he explained. He was unlocked at six in the morning and not locked up again till nine
at night. He was in with the "push" in that hall, and had been
promptly appointed a trusty of the kind technically known as
"hall-man." The man who had appointed him was also a prisoner and a trusty, and was known as "First Hall-man." There
were thirteen hall-men in that hall. Ten of them had charge
each of a gallery of cells, and over them were the First, Second, and Third Hall-men.

We newcomers were to stay in our cells for the rest of the
day, my pal informed me, so that the vaccine would have a
chance to take. Then next morning we would be put to hard
labor in the prison-yard.

"But I'll get you out of the work as soon as I can," he

promised. "I'll get one of the hall-men fired and have you put in his place."

He put his hand into his shirt, drew out the handkerchief containing my precious belongings, passed it in to me through the bars, and went on down the gallery.

I opened the bundle. Everything was there. Not even a match was missing. I shared the makings of a cigarette with my cell-mate. When I started to strike a match for a light, he stopped me. A flimsy, dirty comforter lay in each of our bunks for bedding. He tore off a narrow strip of the thin cloth and rolled it tightly and telescopically into a long and slender cylinder. This he lighted with a precious match. The cylinder of tight-rolled cotton cloth did not flame. On the end a coal of fire slowly smouldered. It would last for hours, and my cell-mate called it a "punk." And when it burned short, all that was necessary was to make a new punk, put the end of it against the old, blow on them, and so transfer the glowing coal. Why, we could have given Prometheus pointers on the conserving of fire.

At twelve o'clock dinner was served. At the bottom of our cage door was a small opening like the entrance of a runway in a chicken-yard. Through this were thrust two hunks of dry bread and two pannikins of "soup." A portion of soup consisted of about a quart of hot water with floating on its surface a lonely drop of grease. Also, there was some salt in that water.

We drank the soup, but we did not eat the bread. Not that we were not hungry, and not that the bread was uneatable. It was fairly good bread. But we had reasons. My cell-mate had discovered that our cell was alive with bed-bugs. In all the cracks and interstices between the bricks where the mortar had fallen out flourished great colonies. The natives even ventured out in the broad daylight and swarmed over the walls and ceiling by hundreds. My cell-mate was wise in the ways of the beasts. Like Childe Roland, dauntless the slug-horn to his lips he bore. Never was there such a battle. It lasted for hours. It was shambles. And when the last survivors fled to their brick-and-mortar fastnesses, our work was only half done. We chewed mouthfuls of our bread until it was reduced to the consistency of putty. When a fleeing belligerent escaped into a crevice between the bricks, we promptly walled him in with a daub of the chewed bread. We toiled on until the light grew dim and until every hole, nook, and cranny was closed. I shudder to think of the tragedies of starvation and cannibalism that must have ensued behind those bread-plastered ramparts.

We threw ourselves on our bunks, tired out and hungry, to wait for supper. It was a good day's work well done. In the weeks to come we at least should not suffer from the hosts of vermin. We had foregone our dinner, saved our hides at the expense of our stomachs; but we were content. Alas for the futility of human effort! Scarcely was our long task completed when a guard unlocked our door. A redistribution of prisoners was being made, and we were taken to another cell and locked in two galleries higher up.

Early next morning our cells were unlocked, and down in the hall the several hundred prisoners of us formed the lock-step and marched out into the prison-yard to go to work. The Erie Canal runs right by the back yard of the Erie County Penitentiary. Our task was to unload canal-boats, carrying huge stay-bolts on our shoulders, like railroad ties, into the prison. As I worked I sized up the situation and studied the chances for a get-away. There wasn't the ghost of a show. Along the tops of the walls marched guards armed with repeating rifles, and I was told, furthermore, that there were machine-guns in the sentry-towers.

I did not worry. Thirty days were not so long. I'd stay those thirty days, and add to the store of material I intended to use, when I got out, against the harpies of justice. I'd show what an American boy could do when his rights and privileges had been trampled on the way mine had. I had been denied my right of trial by jury; I had been denied my right to plead guilty or not guilty; I had been denied a trial even (for I couldn't consider that what I had received at Niagara Falls was a trial); I had not been allowed to communicate with a lawyer nor any one, and hence had been denied my right of suing for a writ of habeas corpus; my face had been shaved, my hair cropped close, convict stripes had been put upon my body; I was forced to toil hard on a diet of bread and water and to march the shameful lock-step with armed guards over me—and all for what? What had I done? What crime had I committed against the good citizens of Niagara Falls that all this vengeance should be wreaked upon me? I had not even violated their "sleeping-out" ordinance. I had slept outside their jurisdiction, in the country, that night. I had not even begged for a meal, or battered for a "light piece" on their streets. All that I had done was to walk along their sidewalk and gaze at their picayune waterfall. And what crime was there in that? Technically I was guilty of no misdemeanor. All right, I'd show them when I got out.

The next day I talked with a guard. I wanted to send for a lawyer. The guard laughed at me. So did the other guards. I really was *incommunicado* so far as the outside world was concerned. I tried to write a letter out, but I learned that all letters were read, and censured or confiscated, by the prison authorities, and that "short-timers" were not allowed to write letters anyway. A little later I tried smuggling letters out by men who were released, but I learned that they were searched and the letters found and destroyed. Never mind. It all helped to make it a blacker case when I did get out.

But as the prison days went by (which I shall describe in the next chapter), I "learned a few." I heard tales of the police, and police-courts, and lawyers, that were unbelievable and monstrous. Men, prisoners, told me of personal experiences with the police of great cities that were awful. And more awful were the hearsay tales they told me concerning men who had died at the hands of the police and who therefore could not testify for themselves. Years afterward, in the report of the Lexow Committee, I was to read tales true and more awful than those told to me. But in the meantime, during the first days of my imprisonment, I scoffed at what I heard.

As the days went by, however, I began to grow convinced. I saw with my own eyes, there in that prison, things unbelievable and monstrous. And the more convinced I became, the profounder grew the respect in me for the sleuth-hounds of the law and for the whole institution of criminal justice.

My indignation ebbed away, and into my being rushed the tides of fear. I saw at last, clear-eyed, what I was up against. I grew meek and lowly. Each day I resolved more emphatically to make no rumpus when I got out. All I asked, when I got out, was a chance to fade away from the landscape. And that was just what I did do when I was released. I kept my tongue between my teeth, walked softly, and sneaked for Pennsylvania, a wiser and a humbler man.

The Pen

F OR TWO DAYS I toiled in the prison-yard. It was heavy work, and, in spite of the fact that I malingered at every opportunity, I was played out. This was because of the food. No man could work hard on such food. Bread and water, that was all that was given us. Once a week we were supposed to get meat; but this meat did not always go around, and since all nutriment had first been boiled out of it in the making of soup, it didn't matter whether one got a taste of it once a week or not.

Furthermore, there was one vital defect in the bread-and-water diet. While we got plenty of water, we did not get enough of the bread. A ration of bread was about the size of one's two fists, and three rations a day were given to each prisoner. There was one good thing, I must say, about the water—it was hot. In the morning it was called "coffee," at noon it was dignified as "soup," and at night it masqueraded as "tea." But it was the same old water all the time. The prisoners called it "water bewitched." In the morning it was black water, the color being due to boiling it with burnt bread-crusts. At noon it was served minus the color, with salt and a drop of grease added. At night it was served with a purplish-auburn hue that defied all speculation; it was darn poor tea, but it was dandy hot water.

We were a hungry lot in the Erie County Pen. Only the "long-timers" knew what it was to have enough to eat. The reason for this was that they would have died after a time on the fare we "short-timers" received. I know that the long-timers got more substantial grub, because there was a whole row of them on the ground floor in our hall, and when I was a trusty, I used to steal from their grub while serving them. Man cannot live on bread alone and not enough of it.

My pal delivered the goods. After two days of work in the yard I was taken out of my cell and made a trusty, a "hall-man." At morning and night we served the bread to the prisoners in their cells; but at twelve o'clock a different method was used. The convicts marched in from work in a long line.

244

As they entered the door of our hall, they broke the lock-step and took their hands down from the shoulders of their line-mates. Just inside the door were piled trays of bread, and here also stood the First Hall-man and two ordinary hall-men. I was one of the two. Our task was to hold the trays of bread as the line of convicts filed past. As soon as the tray, say, that I was holding was emptied, the other hall-man took my place with a full tray. And when his was emptied, I took his place with a full tray. Thus the line tramped steadily by, each man reaching with his right hand and taking one ration of bread from the extended tray.

The task of the First Hall-man was different. He used a club. He stood beside the tray and watched. The hungry wretches could never get over the delusion that sometime they could manage to get two rations of bread out of the tray. But in my experience that sometime never came. The club of the First Hall-man had a way of flashing out—quick as the stroke of a tiger's claw—to the hand that dared ambitiously. The First Hall-man was a good judge of distance, and he had smashed so many hands with that club that he had become infallible. He never missed, and he usually punished the of-fending convict by taking his one ration away from him and sending him to his cell to make his meal off of hot water.

And at times, while all these men lay hungry in their cells, I have seen a hundred or so extra rations of bread hidden away in the cells of the hall-men. It would seem absurd, our retaining this bread. But it was one of our grafts. We were economic masters inside our hall, turning the trick in ways quite similar to the economic masters of civilization. We con-trolled the food-supply of the population, and, just like our brother bandits outside, we made the people pay through the nose for it. We peddled the bread. Once a week, the men who worked in the yard received a five-cent plug of chewing tobacco. This chewing tobacco was the coin of the realm. Two or three rations of bread for a plug was the way we exchanged, and they traded, not because they loved tobacco less, but because they loved bread more. Oh, I know, it was like taking candy from a baby, but what would you? We had to live. And certainly there should be some reward for initia-tive and enterprise. Besides, we but patterned ourselves after

our betters outside the walls, who, on a larger scale, and under the respectable disguise of merchants, bankers, and captains of industry, did precisely what we were doing. What
awful things would have happened to those poor wretches if
it hadn't been for us, I can't imagine. Heaven knows we put
bread into circulation in the Erie County Pen. Ay, and we
encouraged frugality and thrift . . . in the poor devils who
forewent their tobacco. And then there was our example. In
the breast of every convict there we implanted the ambition
to become even as we and run a graft. Saviours of society—
I guess yes.

Here was a hungry man without any tobacco. Maybe he
was a profligate and had used it all up on himself. Very good;
he had a pair of suspenders. I exchanged half a dozen rations
of bread for it—or a dozen rations if the suspenders were
very good. Now I never wore suspenders, but that didn't
matter. Around the corner lodged a long-timer, doing ten
years for manslaughter. He wore suspenders, and he wanted
a pair. I could trade them to him for some of his meat. Meat
was what I wanted. Or perhaps he had a tattered, paper-cov-
ered novel. That was treasure-trove. I could read it and then
trade it off to the bakers for cake, or to the cooks for meat
and vegetables, or to the firemen for decent coffee, or to some
one or other for the newspaper that occasionally filtered in,
heaven alone knows how. The cooks, bakers, and firemen
were prisoners like myself, and they lodged in our hall in the
first row of cells over us.

In short, a full-grown system of barter obtained in the
Erie County Pen. There was even money in circulation.
This money was sometimes smuggled in by the short-
timers, more frequently came from the barber-shop graft,
where the newcomers were mulcted, but most of all flowed
from the cells of the long-timers—though how they got it
I don't know.

What of his preëminent position, the First Hall-man was
reputed to be quite wealthy. In addition to his miscellaneous
grafts, he grafted on us. We farmed the general wretchedness,
and the First Hall-man was Farmer-General over all of us. We
held our particular grafts by his permission, and we had to
pay for that permission. As I say, he was reputed to be

wealthy; but we never saw his money, and he lived in a cell all to himself in solitary grandeur.

But that money was made in the Pen I had direct evidence, for I was cell-mate quite a time with the Third Hall-man. He had over sixteen dollars. He used to count his money every night after nine o'clock, when we were locked in. Also, he used to tell me each night what he would do to me if I gave away on him to the other hall-men. You see, he was afraid of being robbed, and danger threatened him from three different directions. There were the guards. A couple of them might jump upon him, give him a good beating for alleged insubordination, and throw him into the "solitaire" (the dungeon); and in the mix-up that sixteen dollars of his would take wings. Then again, the First Hall-man could have taken it all away from him by threatening to dismiss him and fire him back to hard labor in the prison-yard. And yet again, there were the ten of us who were ordinary hall-men. If we got an inkling of his wealth, there was a large liability, some quiet day, of the whole bunch of us getting him into a corner and dragging him down. Oh, we were wolves, believe me—just like the fellows who do business in Wall Street.

He had good reason to be afraid of us, and so had I to be afraid of him. He was a huge, illiterate brute, an ex-Chesapeake-Bay-oyster-pirate, an "ex-con" who had done five years in Sing Sing, and a general all-around stupidly carnivorous beast. He used to trap sparrows that flew into our hall through the open bars. When he made a capture, he hurried away with it into his cell, where I have seen him crunching bones and spitting out feathers as he bolted it raw. Oh, no, I never gave away on him to the other hall-men. This is the first time I have mentioned his sixteen dollars.

But I grafted on him just the same. He was in love with a woman prisoner who was confined in the "female department." He could neither read nor write, and I used to read her letters to him and write his replies. And I made him pay for it, too. But they were good letters. I laid myself out on them, put in my best licks, and furthermore, I won her for him; though I shrewdly guess that she was in love, not with him, but with the humble scribe. I repeat, those letters were great.

Another one of our grafts was "passing the punk." We were the celestial messengers, the fire-bringers, in that iron world of bolt and bar. When the men came in from work at night and were locked in their cells, they wanted to smoke. Then it was that we restored the divine spark, running the galleries, from cell to cell, with our smouldering punks. Those who were wise, or with whom we did business, had their punks all ready to light. Not every one got divine sparks, however. The guy who refused to dig up, went sparkless and smokeless to bed. But what did we care? We had the immortal cinch on him, and if he got fresh, two or three of us would pitch on him and give him "what-for."

You see, this was the working-theory of the hall-men. There were thirteen of us. We had something like half a thousand prisoners in our hall. We were supposed to do the work, and to keep order. The latter was the function of the guards, which they turned over to us. It was up to us to keep order; if we didn't, we'd be fired back to hard labor, most probably with a taste of the dungeon thrown in. But so long as we maintained order, that long could we work our own particular grafts.

Bear with me a moment and look at the problem. Here were thirteen beasts of us over half a thousand other beasts. It was a living hell, that prison, and it was up to us thirteen there to rule. It was impossible, considering the nature of the beasts, for us to rule by kindness. We ruled by fear. Of course, behind us, backing us up, were the guards. In extremity we called upon them for help; but it would bother them if we called upon them too often, in which event we could depend upon it that they would get more efficient trusties to take our places. But we did not call upon them often, except in a quiet sort of way, when we wanted a cell unlocked in order to get at a refractory prisoner inside. In such cases all the guard did was to unlock the door and walk away so as not to be a witness of what happened when half a dozen hall-men went inside and did a bit of man-handling.

As regards the details of this man-handling I shall say nothing. And after all, man-handling was merely one of the very minor unprintable horrors of the Erie County Pen. I say "unprintable"; and in justice I must also say "unthinkable." They were unthinkable to me until I saw them, and I was no spring chicken in the ways of the world and the awful abysses of human degradation. It would take a deep plummet to reach bottom in the Erie County Pen, and I do but skim lightly and facetiously the surface of things as I there saw them.

At times, say in the morning when the prisoners came down to wash, the thirteen of us would be practically alone in the midst of them, and every last one of them had it in for us. Thirteen against five hundred, and we ruled by fear. We could not permit the slightest infraction of rules, the slightest insolence. If we did, we were lost. Our own rule was to hit a man as soon as he opened his mouth—hit him hard, hit him with anything. A broom-handle, end-on, in the face, had a very sobering effect. But that was not all. Such a man must be made an example of; so the next rule was to wade right in and follow him up. Of course, one was sure that every hall-man in sight would come on the run to join in the chastise-ment; for this also was a rule. Whenever any hall-man was in trouble with a prisoner, the duty of any other hall-man who happened to be around was to lend a fist. Never mind the merits of the case—wade in and hit, and hit with anything; in short, lay the man out.

I remember a handsome young mulatto of about twenty who got the insane idea into his head that he should stand for his rights. And he did have the right of it, too; but that didn't help him any. He lived on the topmost gallery. Eight hall-men took the conceit out of him in just about a minute and a half—for that was the length of time required to travel along his gallery to the end and down five flights of steel stairs. He travelled the whole distance on every portion of his anatomy except his feet, and the eight hall-men were not idle. The mulatto struck the pavement where I was standing watching it all. He regained his feet and stood upright for a moment. In that moment he threw his arms wide apart and omitted an awful scream of terror and pain and heartbreak. At the same instant, as in a transformation scene, the shreds of his stout prison clothes fell from him, leaving him wholly naked and streaming blood from every portion of the surface of his body. Then he collapsed in a heap, unconscious. He had learned his lesson, and every convict within those walls who heard him scream had learned a lesson. So had I learned mine. It is not a nice thing to see a man's heart broken in a minute and a half.

The following will illustrate how we drummed up business in the graft of passing the punk. A row of newcomers is installed in your cells. You pass along before the bars with your punk. "Hey, Bo, give us a light," some one calls to you. Now this is an advertisement that that particular man has tobacco on him. You pass in the punk and go your way. A little later you come back and lean up casually against the bars. "Say, Bo, can you let us have a little tobacco?" is what you say. If he is not wise to the game, the chances are that he solemnly avers that he hasn't any more tobacco. All very well. You condole with him and go your way. But you know that his punk will last him only the rest of that day. Next day you come by, and he says again, "Hey, Bo, give us a light." And you say, "You haven't any tobacco and you don't need a light." And you don't give him any, either. Half an hour after, or an hour or two or three hours, you will be passing by and the man will call out to you in mild tones, "Come here, Bo." And you come. You thrust your hand between the bars and have it filled with precious tobacco. Then you give him a light.

Sometimes, however, a newcomer arrives, upon whom no grafts are to be worked. The mysterious word is passed along that he is to be treated decently. Where this word originated I could never learn. The one thing patent is that the man has a "pull." It may be with one of the superior hall-men; it may be with one of the guards in some other part of the prison; it may be that good treatment has been purchased from grafters higher up; but be it as it may, we know that it is up to us to treat him decently if we want to avoid trouble.

We hall-men were middle-men and common carriers. We arranged trades between convicts confined in different parts of the prison, and we put through the exchange. Also, we took our commissions coming and going. Sometimes the objects traded had to go through the hands of half a dozen middle-men, each of whom took his whack, or in some way or another was paid for his service.

Sometimes one was in debt for services, and sometimes one had others in his debt. Thus, I entered the prison in debt to the convict who smuggled in my things for me. A week or so afterward, one of the firemen passed a letter into my hand. It had been given to him by a barber. The barber had received it from the convict who had smuggled in my things. Because of my debt to him I was to carry the letter on. But he had not written the letter. The original sender was a long-timer in his hall. The letter was for a woman prisoner in the female department. But whether it was intended for her, or whether she, in turn, was one of the chain of go-betweens, I did not know. All that I knew was her description, and that it was up to me to get it into her hands.

Two days passed, during which time I kept the letter in my possession; then the opportunity came. The women did the mending of all the clothes worn by the convicts. A number of our hall-men had to go to the female department to bring back huge bundles of clothes. I fixed it with the First Hall-man that I was to go along. Door after door was unlocked for us as we threaded our way across the prison to the women's quarters. We entered a large room where the women sat working at their mending. My eyes were peeled for the woman who had been described to me. I located her and worked near to her. Two eagle-eyed matrons were on watch. I held the letter in my palm, and I looked my intention at the woman. She knew I had something for her; she must have been expecting it, and had set herself to divining, at the moment we entered, which of us was the messenger. But one of the matrons stood within two feet of her. Already the hall-men were picking up the bundles they were to carry away. The moment was passing. I delayed with my bundle, making believe that it was not tied securely. Would that matron ever look away? Or was I to fail? And just then another woman cut up playfully with one of the hall-men—stuck out her foot and tripped him, or pinched him, or did something or other. The matron looked that way and reprimanded the woman sharply. Now I do not know whether or not this was all planned to distract the matron's attention, but I did know that it was my opportunity. My particular woman's hand dropped from her lap down by her side. I stooped to pick up my bundle. From my stooping position I slipped the letter into her hand, and received another in exchange. The next moment the bundle was on my shoulder, the matron's gaze had returned to me because I was the last hall-man, and I was hastening to catch up with my companions. The letter I had received from the woman I turned over to the fireman, and thence it passed through the hands of the barber, of the convict who had smuggled in my things, and on to the long-timer at the other end.

Often we conveyed letters, the chain of communication of which was so complex that we knew neither sender nor sendee. We were but links in the chain. Somewhere, some-how, a convict would thrust a letter into my hand with the instruction to pass it on to the next link. All such acts were favors to be reciprocated later on, when I should be acting directly with a principal in transmitting letters, and from whom I should be receiving my pay. The whole prison was covered by a network of lines of communication. And we who were in control of the system of communication, natu-rally, since we were modelled after capitalistic society, exacted heavy tolls from our customers. It was service for profit with a vengeance, though we were at times not above giving ser-vice for love.

And all the time I was in the Pen I was making myself solid with my pal. He had done much for me, and in return he expected me to do as much for him. When we got out, we were to travel together, and, it goes without saying, pull off "jobs" together. For my pal was a criminal—oh, not a jewel of the first water, merely a petty criminal who would steal and rob, commit burglary, and, if cornered, not stop short of murder. Many a quiet hour we sat and talked together. He had two or three jobs in view for the immediate future, in which my work was cut out for me, and in which I joined in planning the details. I had been with and seen much of crim-inals, and my pal never dreamed that I was only fooling him, giving him a string thirty days long. He thought I was the real goods, liked me because I was not stupid, and liked me a bit, too, I think, for myself. Of course I had not the slight-est intention of joining him in a life of sordid, petty crime; but I'd have been an idiot to throw away all the good things his friendship made possible. When one is on the hot lava of hell, he cannot pick and choose his path, and so it was with me in the Erie County Pen. I had to stay in with the "push," or do hard labor on bread and water; and to stay in with the push I had to make good with my pal.

Life was not monotonous in the Pen. Every day something was happening: men were having fits, going crazy, fighting, or the hall-men were getting drunk. Rover Jack, one of the ordinary hall-men, was our star "oryide." He was a true "profesh," a "blowed-in-the-glass" stiff, and as such received all kinds of latitude from the hall-men in authority. Pittsburg Joe, who was Second Hall-man, used to join Rover Jack in his jags; and it was a saying of the pair that the Erie County Pen was the only place where a man could get "slopped" and not be arrested. I never knew, but I was told that bromide of potassium, gained in devious ways from the dispensary, was the dope they used. But I do know, whatever their dope was, that they got good and drunk on occasion.

Our hall was a common stews, filled with the ruck and the filth, the scum and dregs, of society—hereditary inefficients, degenerates, wrecks, lunatics, addled intelligences, epileptics, monsters, weaklings, in short, a very nightmare of humanity. Hence, fits flourished with us. These fits seemed contagious. When one man began throwing a fit, others followed his lead. I have seen seven men down with fits at the same time, making the air hideous with their cries, while as many more lunatics would be raging and gibbering up and down. Nothing was ever done for the men with fits except to throw cold water on them. It was useless to send for the medical student or the doctor. They were not to be bothered with such trivial and frequent occurrences.

There was a young Dutch boy, about eighteen years of age, who had fits most frequently of all. He usually threw one every day. It was for that reason that we kept him on the ground floor farther down in the row of cells in which we lodged. After he had had a few fits in the prison-yard, the guards refused to be bothered with him any more, and so he remained locked up in his cell all day with a Cockney cellmate, to keep him company. Not that the Cockney was of any use. Whenever the Dutch boy had a fit, the Cockney became paralyzed with terror.

The Dutch boy could not speak a word of English. He was

a farmer's boy, serving ninety days as punishment for having
got into a scrap with some one. He prefaced his fits with
howling. He howled like a wolf. Also, he took his fits standing up, which was very inconvenient for him, for his fits always culminated in a headlong pitch to the floor. Whenever
I heard the long wolf-howl rising, I used to grab a broom
and run to his cell. Now the trusties were not allowed keys to
the cells, so I could not get in to him. He would stand up in
the middle of his narrow cell, shivering convulsively, his eyes
rolled backward till only the whites were visible, and howling
like a lost soul. Try as I would, I could never get the Cockney
to lend him a hand. While he stood and howled, the Cockney crouched and trembled in the upper bunk, his terror-
stricken gaze fixed on that awful figure, with eyes rolled back,
that howled and howled. It was hard on him, too, the poor
devil of a Cockney. His own reason was not any too firmly
seated, and the wonder is that he did not go mad.

All that I could do was my best with the broom. I would
thrust it through the bars, train it on Dutchy's chest, and
wait. As the crisis approached he would begin swaying back
and forth. I followed this swaying with the broom, for there
was no telling when he would take that dreadful forward
pitch. But when he did, I was there with the broom, catching
him and easing him down. Contrive as I would, he never
came down quite gently, and his face was usually bruised by
the stone floor. Once down and writhing in convulsions, I'd
throw a bucket of water over him. I don't know whether cold
water was the right thing or not, but it was the custom in the
Erie County Pen. Nothing more than that was ever done for
him. He would lie there, wet, for an hour or so, and then
crawl into his bunk. I knew better than to run to a guard for
assistance. What was a man with a fit, anyway?

In the adjoining cell lived a strange character—a man who
was doing sixty days for eating swill out of Barnum's swill-
barrel, or at least that was the way he put it. He was a badly
addled creature, and, at first, very mild and gentle. The facts
of his case were as he had stated them. He had strayed out to
the circus ground, and, being hungry, had made his way to
the barrel that contained the refuse from the table of the circus people. "And it *was* good bread," he often assured me;

"and the meat was out of sight." A policeman had seen him and arrested him, and there he was.

Once I passed his cell with a piece of stiff thin wire in my hand. He asked me for it so earnestly that I passed it through the bars to him. Promptly, and with no tool but his fingers, he broke it into short lengths and twisted them into half a dozen very creditable safety pins. He sharpened the points on the stone floor. Thereafter I did quite a trade in safety pins. I furnished the raw material and peddled the finished product, and he did the work. As wages, I paid him extra rations of bread, and once in a while a chunk of meat or a piece of soup-bone with some marrow inside.

But his imprisonment told on him, and he grew violent day by day. The hall-men took delight in teasing him. They filled his weak brain with stories of a great fortune that had been left him. It was in order to rob him of it that he had been arrested and sent to jail. Of course, as he himself knew, there was no law against eating out of a barrel. Therefore he was wrongly imprisoned. It was a plot to deprive him of his fortune.

The first I knew of it, I heard the hall-men laughing about the string they had given him. Next he held a serious conference with me, in which he told me of his millions and the plot to deprive him of them, and in which he appointed me his detective. I did my best to let him down gently, speaking vaguely of a mistake, and that it was another man with a similar name who was the rightful heir. I left him quite cooled down; but I couldn't keep the hall-men away from him, and they continued to string him worse than ever. In the end, after a most violent scene, he threw me down, revoked my private detectiveship, and went on strike. My trade in safety pins ceased. He refused to make any more safety pins, and he peppered me with raw material through the bars of his cell when I passed by.

I could never make it up with him. The other hall-men told him that I was a detective in the employ of the conspirators. And in the meantime the hall-men drove him mad with their stringing. His fictitious wrongs preyed upon his mind, and at last he became a dangerous and homicidal lunatic. The guards refused to listen to his tale of stolen millions, and he accused them of being in the plot. One day he threw a pannikin of hot tea over one of them, and then his case was investigated. The warden talked with him a few minutes through the bars of his cell. Then he was taken away for examination before the doctors. He never came back, and I often wonder if he is dead, or if he still gibbers about his millions in some asylum for the insane.

At last came the day of days, my release. It was the day of release for the Third Hall-man as well, and the short-timer girl I had won for him was waiting for him outside the wall. They went away blissfully together. My pal and I went out together, and together we walked down into Buffalo. Were we not to be together always? We begged together on the "main-drag" that day for pennies, and what we received was spent for "shupers" of beer—I don't know how they are spelled, but they are pronounced the way I have spelled them, and they cost three cents. I was watching my chance all the time for a get-away. From some bo on the drag I managed to learn what time a certain freight pulled out. I calculated my time accordingly. When the moment came, my pal and I were in a saloon. Two foaming shupers were before us. I'd have liked to say good-by. He had been good to me. But I did not dare. I went out through the rear of the saloon and jumped the fence. It was a swift sneak, and a few minutes later I was on board a freight and heading south on the Western New York and Pennsylvania Railroad.

Hoboes That Pass in the Night

IN THE COURSE of my tramping I encountered hundreds of hoboes, whom I hailed or who hailed me, and with whom I waited at water-tanks, "boiled-up," cooked "mulligans," "battered" the "drag" or "privates," and beat trains, and who passed and were seen never again. On the other hand, there were hoboes who passed and repassed with amazing frequency, and others, still, who passed like ghosts, close at hand, unseen, and never seen.

It was one of the latter that I chased clear across Canada over three thousand miles of railroad, and never once did I lay eyes on him. His "monica" was Skysail Jack. I first ran into it at Montreal. Carved with a jack-knife was the skysail-yard of a ship. It was perfectly executed. Under it was "Skysail Jack." Above was "B.W. 9–15–94." This latter conveyed the information that he had passed through Montreal bound west, on October 15, 1894. He had one day the start of me. "Sailor Jack" was my monica at that particular time, and promptly I carved it alongside of his, along with the date and the information that I, too, was bound west.

I had misfortune in getting over the next hundred miles, and eight days later I picked up Skysail Jack's trail three hundred miles west of Ottawa. There it was, carved on a water-tank, and by the date I saw that he likewise had met with delay. He was only two days ahead of me. I was a "comet" and "tramp-royal," so was Skysail Jack; and it was up to my pride and reputation to catch up with him. I "railroaded" day and night, and I passed him; then turn about he passed me. Sometimes he was a day or so ahead, and sometimes I was. From hoboes, bound east, I got word of him occasionally, when he happened to be ahead; and from them I learned that he had become interested in Sailor Jack and was making inquiries about me.

We'd have made a precious pair, I am sure, if we'd ever got together; but get together we couldn't. I kept ahead of him clear across Manitoba, but he led the way across Alberta, and early one bitter gray morning, at the end of a division just east of Kicking Horse Pass, I learned that he had been seen the night before between Kicking Horse Pass and Rogers' Pass. It was rather curious the way the information came to me. I had been riding all night in a "side-door Pullman" (box-car), and nearly dead with cold had crawled out at the division to beg for food. A freezing fog was drifting past, and I "hit" some firemen I found in the round-house. They fixed me up with the leavings from their lunch-pails, and in addition I got out of them nearly a quart of heavenly "Java" (coffee). I heated the latter, and, as I sat down to eat, a freight pulled in from the west. I saw a side-door open and a road-kid climb out. Through the drifting fog he limped over to me. He was stiff with cold, his lips blue. I shared my Java and grub with him, learned about Skysail Jack, and then learned about him. Behold, he was from my own town, Oakland, California, and he was a member of the celebrated Boo Gang—a gang with which I had affiliated at rare intervals. We talked fast and bolted the grub in the half-hour that followed. Then my freight pulled out, and I was on it, bound west on the trail of Skysail Jack.

I was delayed between the passes, went two days without food, and walked eleven miles on the third day before I got any, and yet I succeeded in passing Skysail Jack along the Fraser River in British Columbia. I was riding "passengers" then and making time; but he must have been riding passengers, too, and with more luck or skill than I, for he got into Mission ahead of me.

Now Mission was a junction, forty miles east of Vancouver. From the junction one could proceed south through Washington and Oregon over the Northern Pacific. I wondered which way Skysail Jack would go, for I thought I was ahead of him. As for myself I was still bound west to Vancouver. I proceeded to the water-tank to leave that information, and there, freshly carved, with that day's date upon it, was Skysail Jack's monica. I hurried on into Vancouver. But he was gone. He had taken ship immediately and was still flying west on his world-adventure. Truly, Skysail Jack, you were a tramp-royal, and your mate was the "wind that tramps the world." I take off my hat to you. You were "blowed-in-the-glass" all right. A week later I, too, got my ship, and on board the steamship *Umatilla*, in the forecastle, was working my way down the coast to San Francisco. Skysail Jack and Sailor Jack—gee! if we'd ever got together.

Water-tanks are tramp directories. Not all in idle wantonness do tramps carve their monicas, dates, and courses. Often and often have I met hoboes earnestly inquiring if I had seen anywhere such and such a "stiff" or his monica. And more than once I have been able to give the monica of recent date, the water-tank, and the direction in which he was then bound. And promptly the hobo to whom I gave the information lit out after his pal. I have met hoboes who, in trying to catch a pal, had pursued clear across the continent and back again, and were still going.

"Monicas" are the *nom-de-rails* that hoboes assume or accept when thrust upon them by their fellows. Leary Joe, for instance, was timid, and was so named by his fellows. No self-respecting hobo would select Stew Bum for himself. Very few tramps care to remember their pasts during which they ignobly worked, so monicas based upon trades are very rare, though I remember having met the following: Moulder Blackey, Painter Red, Chi Plumber, Boiler-maker, Sailor Boy, and Printer Bo. "Chi" (pronounced *shy*), by the way, is the argot for "Chicago."

A favorite device of hoboes is to base their monicas on the localities from which they hail, as: New York Tommy, Pacific Slim, Buffalo Smithy, Canton Tim, Pittsburg Jack, Syracuse Shine, Troy Mickey, K. L. Bill, and Connecticut Jimmy. Then there was "Slim Jim from Vinegar Hill, who never worked and never will." A "shine" is always a negro, so called, possibly, from the high lights on his countenance. Texas Shine or Toledo Shine convey both race and nativity.

Among those that incorporated their race, I recollect the following: Frisco Sheeny, New York Irish, Michigan French, English Jack, Cockney Kid, and Milwaukee Dutch. Others seem to take their monicas in part from the color-schemes stamped upon them at birth, such as: Chi Whitey, New Jersey Red, Boston Blackey, Seattle Browney, and Yellow Dick and Yellow Belly—the last a Creole from Mississippi, who, I suspect, had his monica thrust upon him.

Texas Royal, Happy Joe, Bust Connors, Burley Bo, Tornado Blackey, and Touch McCall used more imagination in rechristening themselves. Others, with less fancy, carry the names of their physical peculiarities, such as: Vancouver Slim, Detroit Shorty, Ohio Fatty, Long Jack, Big Jim, Little Joe, New York Blink, Chi Nosey, and Broken-backed Ben.

By themselves come the road-kids, sporting an infinite variety of monicas. For example, the following, whom here and there I have encountered: Buck Kid, Blind Kid, Midget Kid, Holy Kid, Bat Kid, Swift Kid, Cookey Kid, Monkey Kid, Iowa Kid, Corduroy Kid, Orator Kid (who could tell how it happened), and Lippy Kid (who was insolent, depend upon it).

On the water-tank at San Marcial, New Mexico, a dozen years ago, was the following hobo bill of fare: —

(1) Main-drag fair.
(2) Bulls not hostile.
(3) Round-house good for kipping.
(4) North-bound trains no good.
(5) Privates no good.
(6) Restaurants good for cooks only.
(7) Railroad House good for night-work only.

Number one conveys the information that begging for money on the main street is fair; number two, that the police will not bother hoboes; number three, that one can sleep in the round-house. Number four, however, is ambiguous. The north-bound trains may be no good to beat, and they may be no good to beg. Number five means that the residences are not good to beggars, and number six means that only hoboes that have been cooks can get grub from the restaurants. Number seven bothers me. I cannot make out whether the Railroad House is a good place for any hobo to beg at night, or whether it is good only for hobo-cooks to beg at night, or whether any hobo, cook or non-cook, can lend a hand at night, helping the cooks of the Railroad House with their dirty work and getting something to eat in payment.

But to return to the hoboes that pass in the night. I remember one I met in California. He was a Swede, but he had lived so long in the United States that one couldn't guess his nationality. He had to tell it on himself. In fact, he had come to the United States when no more than a baby. I ran into him first at the mountain town of Truckee. "Which way, Bo?" was our greeting, and "Bound east" was the answer each of us gave. Quite a bunch of "stiffs" tried to ride out the overland that night, and I lost the Swede in the shuffle. Also, I lost the overland.

I arrived in Reno, Nevada, in a box-car that was promptly side-tracked. It was Sunday morning, and after I threw my feet for breakfast, I wandered over to the Piute camp to watch the Indians gambling. And there stood the Swede, hugely interested. Of course we got together. He was the only acquaintance I had in that region, and I was his only acquaintance. We rushed together like a couple of dissatisfied hermits, and together we spent the day, threw our feet for dinner, and late in the afternoon tried to "nail" the same freight. But he was ditched, and I rode her out alone, to be ditched myself in the desert twenty miles beyond.

Of all desolate places, the one at which I was ditched was the limit. It was called a flag-station, and it consisted of a shanty dumped inconsequentially into the sand and sagebrush. A chill wind was blowing, night was coming on, and the solitary telegraph operator who lived in the shanty was afraid of me. I knew that neither grub nor bed could I get out of him. It was because of his manifest fear of me that I did not believe him when he told me that east-bound trains never stopped there. Besides, hadn't I been thrown off of an east-bound train right at that very spot not five minutes before? He assured me that it had stopped under orders, and that a year might go by before another was stopped under orders. He advised me that it was only a dozen or fifteen miles on to Wadsworth and that I'd better hike. I elected to wait, however, and I had the pleasure of seeing two west-bound freights go by without stopping, and one east-bound freight. I wondered if the Swede was on the latter. It was up to me to hit the ties to Wadsworth, and hit them I did, much to the telegraph operator's relief, for I neglected to burn his shanty and murder him. Telegraph operators have much to be thankful for. At the end of half a dozen miles, I had to get off the ties and let the east-bound overland go by. She was going fast, but I caught sight of a dim form on the first "blind" that looked like the Swede.

That was the last I saw of him for weary days. I hit the high places across those hundreds of miles of Nevada desert, riding the overlands at night, for speed, and in the day-time riding in box-cars and getting my sleep. It was early in the year, and it was cold in those upland pastures. Snow lay here and there on the level, all the mountains were shrouded in white, and at night the most miserable wind imaginable blew off from them. It was not a land in which to linger. And remember, gentle reader, the hobo goes through such a land, without shelter, without money, begging his way and sleeping at night without blankets. This last is something that can be realized only by experience.

In the early evening I came down to the depot at Ogden. The overland of the Union Pacific was pulling east, and I was bent on making connections. Out in the tangle of tracks ahead of the engine I encountered a figure slouching through the gloom. It was the Swede. We shook hands like long-lost brothers, and discovered that our hands were gloved. "Where'd ye glahm 'em?" I asked. "Out of an engine-cab," he answered; "and where did you?" "They belonged to a fireman," said I; "he was careless."

We caught the blind as the overland pulled out, and mighty cold we found it. The way led up a narrow gorge between snow-covered mountains, and we shivered and shook and exchanged confidences about how we had covered the ground between Reno and Ogden. I had closed my eyes for only an hour or so the previous night, and the blind was not comfortable enough to suit me for a snooze. At a stop, I went forward to the engine. We had on a "double-header" (two engines) to take us over the grade.

The pilot of the head engine, because it "punched the wind," I knew would be too cold; so I selected the pilot of the second engine, which was sheltered by the first engine. I stepped on the cowcatcher and found the pilot occupied. In the darkness I felt out the form of a young boy. He was sound asleep. By squeezing, there was room for two on the pilot, and I made the boy hudge over and crawled up beside him. It was a "good" night; the "shacks" (brakemen) didn't bother us, and in no time we were asleep. Once in a while hot cinders or heavy jolts aroused me, when I snuggled closer to the boy and dozed off to the coughing of the engines and the screeching of the wheels.

The overland made Evanston, Wyoming, and went no farther. A wreck ahead blocked the line. The dead engineer had been brought in, and his body attested the peril of the way. A tramp, also, had been killed, but his body had not been brought in. I talked with the boy. He was thirteen years old. He had run away from his folks in some place in Oregon, and was heading east to his grandmother. He had a tale of cruel treatment in the home he had left that rang true; besides, there was no need for him to lie to me, a nameless hobo on the track.

And that boy was going some, too. He couldn't cover the ground fast enough. When the division superintendents decided to send the overland back over the way it had come, then up on a cross "jerk" to the Oregon Short Line, and back along that road to tap the Union Pacific the other side of the wreck, that boy climbed upon the pilot and said he was going to stay with it. This was too much for the Swede and me. It meant travelling the rest of that frigid night in order to gain no more than a dozen miles or so. We said we'd wait till the wreck was cleared away, and in the meantime get a good sleep.

Now it is no snap to strike a strange town, broke, at midnight, in cold weather, and find a place to sleep. The Swede hadn't a penny. My total assets consisted of two dimes and a nickel. From some of the town boys we learned that beer was five cents, and that the saloons kept open all night. There was our meat. Two glasses of beer would cost ten cents, there would be a stove and chairs, and we could sleep it out till morning. We headed for the lights of a saloon, walking briskly, the snow crunching under our feet, a chill little wind blowing through us.

Alas, I had misunderstood the town boys. Beer was five cents in one saloon only in the whole burg, and we didn't strike that saloon. But the one we entered was all right. A blessed stove was roaring white-hot; there were cosey, cane-bottomed arm-chairs, and a none-too-pleasant-looking bar-keeper who glared suspiciously at us as we came in. A man cannot spend continuous days and nights in his clothes, beating trains, fighting soot and cinders, and sleeping anywhere, and maintain a good "front." Our fronts were decidedly against us; but what did we care? I had the price in my jeans.

"Two beers," said I nonchalantly to the barkeeper, and while he drew them, the Swede and I leaned against the bar and yearned secretly for the arm-chairs by the stove.

The barkeeper set the two foaming glasses before us, and with pride I deposited the ten cents. Now I was dead game. As soon as I learned my error in the price I'd have dug up another ten cents. Never mind if it did leave me only a nickel to my name, a stranger in a strange land. I'd have paid it all right. But that barkeeper never gave me a chance. As soon as his eyes spotted the dime I had laid down, he seized the two glasses, one in each hand, and dumped the beer into the sink behind the bar. At the same time, glaring at us malevolently, he said:—

"You've got scabs on your nose. You've got scabs on your nose. You've got scabs on your nose. See!"

I hadn't either, and neither had the Swede. Our noses were all right. The direct bearing of his words was beyond our comprehension, but the indirect bearing was clear as print: he didn't like our looks, and beer was evidently ten cents a glass.

I dug down and laid another dime on the bar, remarking carelessly, "Oh, I thought this was a five-cent joint."

"Your money's no good here," he answered, shoving the two dimes across the bar to me.

Sadly I dropped them back into my pocket, sadly we yearned toward the blessed stove and the arm-chairs, and sadly we went out the door into the frosty night.

But as we went out the door, the barkeeper, still glaring, called after us, "You've got scabs on your nose, see!"

I have seen much of the world since then, journeyed among strange lands and peoples, opened many books, sat in many lecture-halls; but to this day, though I have pondered long and deep, I have been unable to divine the meaning in the cryptic utterance of that barkeeper in Evanston, Wyoming. Our noses *were* all right.

We slept that night over the boilers in an electric-lighting plant. How we discovered that "kipping" place I can't remember. We must have just headed for it, instinctively, as horses head for water or carrier-pigeons head for the home-cote. But it was a night not pleasant to remember. A dozen hoboes were ahead of us on top the boilers, and it was too hot for all of us. To complete our misery, the engineer would not let us stand around down below. He gave us our choice of the boilers or the outside snow.

"You said you wanted to sleep, and so, damn you, sleep," said he to me, when, frantic and beaten out by the heat, I came down into the fire-room.

"Water," I gasped, wiping the sweat from my eyes, "water."

He pointed out of doors and assured me that down there somewhere in the blackness I'd find the river. I started for the river, got lost in the dark, fell into two or three drifts, gave it up, and returned half-frozen to the top of the boilers. When I had thawed out, I was thirstier than ever. Around me the hoboes were moaning, groaning, sobbing, sighing, gasping, panting, rolling and tossing and floundering heavily in their torment. We were so many lost souls toasting on a griddle in hell, and the engineer, Satan Incarnate, gave us the sole alternative of freezing in the outer cold. The Swede sat up and anathematized passionately the wanderlust in man that sent him tramping and suffering hardships such as that.

"When I get back to Chicago," he perorated, "I'm going to get a job and stick to it till hell freezes over. Then I'll go tramping again."

And, such is the irony of fate, next day, when the wreck ahead was cleared, the Swede and I pulled out of Evanston in the ice-boxes of an "orange special," a fast freight laden with fruit from sunny California. Of course, the ice-boxes were empty on account of the cold weather, but that didn't make them any warmer for us. We entered them through hatchways in the top of the car; the boxes were constructed of galvanized iron, and in that biting weather were not pleasant to the touch. We lay there, shivered and shook, and with chattering teeth held a council wherein we decided that we'd stay by the ice-boxes day and night till we got out of the inhospitable plateau region and down into the Mississippi Valley.

But we must eat, and we decided that at the next division

we would throw our feet for grub and make a rush back to our ice-boxes. We arrived in the town of Green River late in the afternoon, but too early for supper. Before meal-time is the worst time for "battering" back-doors; but we put on our nerve, swung off the side-ladders as the freight pulled into the yards, and made a run for the houses. We were quickly separated; but we had agreed to meet in the ice-boxes. I had bad luck at first; but in the end, with a couple of "hand-outs" poked into my shirt, I chased for the train. It was pulling out and going fast. The particular refrigerator-car in which we were to meet had already gone by, and half a dozen cars down the train from it I swung on to the side-ladders, went up on top hurriedly, and dropped down into an ice-box.

But a shack had seen me from the caboose, and at the next stop a few miles farther on, Rock Springs, the shack stuck his head into my box and said: "Hit the grit, you son of a toad! Hit the grit!" Also he grabbed me by the heels and dragged me out. I hit the grit all right, and the orange special and the Swede rolled on without me.

Snow was beginning to fall. A cold night was coming on. After dark I hunted around in the railroad yards until I found an empty refrigerator car. In I climbed—not into the ice-boxes, but into the car itself. I swung the heavy doors shut, and their edges, covered with strips of rubber, sealed the car air-tight. The walls were thick. There was no way for the outside cold to get in. But the inside was just as cold as the outside. How to raise the temperature was the problem. But trust a "profesh" for that. Out of my pockets I dug up three or four newspapers. These I burned, one at a time, on the floor of the car. The smoke rose to the top. Not a bit of the heat could escape, and, comfortable and warm, I passed a beautiful night. I didn't wake up once.

In the morning it was still snowing. While throwing my feet for breakfast, I missed an east-bound freight. Later in the day I nailed two other freights and was ditched from both of them. All afternoon no east-bound trains went by. The snow was falling thicker than ever, but at twilight I rode out on the first blind of the overland. As I swung aboard the blind from one side, somebody swung aboard from the other. It was the boy who had run away from Oregon.

Now the first blind of a fast train in a driving snow-storm is no summer picnic. The wind goes right through one, strikes the front of the car, and comes back again. At the first stop, darkness having come on, I went forward and interviewed the fireman. I offered to "shove" coal to the end of his run, which was Rawlins, and my offer was accepted. My work was out on the tender, in the snow, breaking the lumps of coal with a sledge and shovelling it forward to him in the cab. But as I did not have to work all the time, I could come into the cab and warm up now and again.

"Say," I said to the fireman, at my first breathing spell, "there's a little kid back there on the first blind. He's pretty cold."

The cabs on the Union Pacific engines are quite spacious, and we fitted the kid into a warm nook in front of the high seat of the fireman, where the kid promptly fell asleep. We arrived at Rawlins at midnight. The snow was thicker than ever. Here the engine was to go into the round-house, being replaced by a fresh engine. As the train came to a stop, I dropped off the engine steps plump into the arms of a large man in a large overcoat. He began asking me questions, and I promptly demanded who he was. Just as promptly he informed me that he was the sheriff. I drew in my horns and listened and answered.

He began describing the kid who was still asleep in the cab. I did some quick thinking. Evidently the family was on the trail of the kid, and the sheriff had received telegraphed instructions from Oregon. Yes, I had seen the kid. I had met him first in Ogden. The date tallied with the sheriff's information. But the kid was still behind somewhere, I explained, for he had been ditched from that very overland that night when it pulled out of Rock Springs. And all the time I was praying that the kid wouldn't wake up, come down out of the cab, and put the "kibosh" on me.

The sheriff left me in order to interview the shacks, but before he left he said:—

"Bo, this town is no place for you. Understand? You ride this train out, and make no mistake about it. If I catch you after it's gone . . ."

I assured him that it was not through desire that I was in

his town; that the only reason I was there was that the train had stopped there; and that he wouldn't see me for smoke the way I'd get out of his darn town.

While he went to interview the shacks, I jumped back into the cab. The kid was awake and rubbing his eyes. I told him the news and advised him to ride the engine into the round-house. To cut the story short, the kid made the same overland out, riding the pilot, with instructions to make an appeal to the fireman at the first stop for permission to ride in the engine. As for myself, I got ditched. The new fireman was young and not yet lax enough to break the rules of the Company against having tramps in the engine; so he turned down my offer to shove coal. I hope the kid succeeded with him, for all night on the pilot in that blizzard would have meant death.

Strange to say, I do not at this late day remember a detail of how I was ditched at Rawlins. I remember watching the train as it was immediately swallowed up in the snow-storm, and of heading for a saloon to warm up. Here was light and warmth. Everything was in full blast and wide open. Faro, roulette, craps, and poker tables were running, and some mad cow-punchers were making the night merry. I had just succeeded in fraternizing with them and was downing my first drink at their expense, when a heavy hand descended on my shoulder. I looked around and sighed. It was the sheriff.

Without a word he led me out into the snow.

"There's an orange special down there in the yards," said he.

"It's a damn cold night," said I.

"It pulls out in ten minutes," said he.

That was all. There was no discussion. And when that orange special pulled out, I was in the ice-boxes. I thought my feet would freeze before morning, and the last twenty miles into Laramie I stood upright in the hatchway and danced up and down. The snow was too thick for the shacks to see me, and I didn't care if they did.

My quarter of a dollar bought me a hot breakfast at Laramie, and immediately afterward I was on board the blind baggage of an overland that was climbing to the pass through the backbone of the Rockies. One does not ride blind baggages in the daytime; but in this blizzard at the top of the Rocky Mountains I doubted if the shacks would have the heart to put me off. And they didn't. They made a practice of coming forward at every stop to see if I was frozen yet.

At Ames' Monument, at the summit of the Rockies,—I forget the altitude,—the shack came forward for the last time.

"Say, Bo," he said, "you see that freight side-tracked over there to let us go by?"

I saw. It was on the next track, six feet away. A few feet more in that storm and I could not have seen it.

"Well, the 'after-push' of Kelly's Army is in one of them cars. They've got two feet of straw under them, and there's so many of them that they keep the car warm."

His advice was good, and I followed it, prepared, however, if it was a "con game" the shack had given me, to take the blind as the overland pulled out. But it was straight goods. I found the car—a big refrigerator car with the leeward door wide open for ventilation. Up I climbed and in. I stepped on a man's leg, next on some other man's arm. The light was dim, and all I could make out was arms and legs and bodies inextricably confused. Never was there such a tangle of humanity. They were all lying in the straw, and over, and under, and around one another. Eighty-four husky hoboes take up a lot of room when they are stretched out. The men I stepped on were resentful. Their bodies heaved under me like the waves of the sea, and imparted an involuntary forward movement to me. I could not find any straw to step upon, so I stepped upon more men. The resentment increased, so did my forward movement. I lost my footing and sat down with sharp abruptness. Unfortunately, it was on a man's head. The next moment he had risen on his hands and knees in wrath, and I was flying through the air. What goes up must come down, and I came down on another man's head.

What happened after that is very vague in my memory. It was like going through a threshing-machine. I was bandied about from one end of the car to the other. Those eighty-four hoboes winnowed me out till what little was left of me, by some miracle, found a bit of straw to rest upon. I was initiated, and into a jolly crowd. All the rest of that day we rode through the blizzard, and to while the time away it was decided that each man was to tell a story. It was stipulated that each story must be a good one, and, furthermore, that it must be a story no one had ever heard before. The penalty for failure was the threshing-machine. Nobody failed. And I want to say right here that never in my life have I sat at so marvellous a story-telling debauch. Here were eighty-four men from all the world—I made eighty-five; and each man told a masterpiece. It had to be, for it was either masterpiece or threshing-machine.

Late in the afternoon we arrived in Cheyenne. The blizzard was at its height, and though the last meal of all of us had been breakfast, no man cared to throw his feet for supper. All night we rolled on through the storm, and next day found us down on the sweet plains of Nebraska and still rolling. We were out of the storm and the mountains. The blessed sun was shining over a smiling land, and we had eaten nothing for twenty-four hours. We found out that the freight would arrive about noon at a town, if I remember right, that was called Grand Island.

We took up a collection and sent a telegram to the authorities of that town. The text of the message was that eighty-five healthy, hungry hoboes would arrive about noon and that it would be a good idea to have dinner ready for them. The authorities of Grand Island had two courses open to them. They could feed us, or they could throw us in jail. In the latter event they'd have to feed us anyway, and they decided wisely that one meal would be the cheaper way.

When the freight rolled into Grand Island at noon, we were sitting on the tops of the cars and dangling our legs in the sunshine. All the police in the burg were on the reception committee. They marched us in squads to the various hotels and restaurants, where dinners were spread for us. We had been thirty-six hours without food, and we didn't have to be taught what to do. After that we were marched back to the railroad station. The police had thoughtfully compelled the freight to wait for us. She pulled out slowly, and the eighty-five of us, strung out along the track, swarmed up the side-ladders. We "captured" the train.

We had no supper that evening—at least the "push" didn't, but I did. Just at supper time, as the freight was pulling out of a small town, a man climbed into the car where I was playing pedro with three other stiffs. The man's shirt was bulging suspiciously. In his hand he carried a battered quart-measure from which arose steam. I smelled "Java." I turned my cards over to one of the stiffs who was looking on, and excused myself. Then, in the other end of the car, pursued by envious glances, I sat down with the man who had climbed aboard and shared his "Java" and the hand-outs that had bulged his shirt. It was the Swede.

At about ten o'clock in the evening, we arrived at Omaha.

"Let's shake the push," said the Swede to me.

"Sure," said I.

As the freight pulled into Omaha, we made ready to do so. But the people of Omaha were also ready. The Swede and I hung upon the side-ladders, ready to drop off. But the freight did not stop. Furthermore, long rows of policemen, their brass buttons and stars glittering in the electric lights, were lined up on each side of the track. The Swede and I knew what would happen to us if we ever dropped off into their arms. We stuck by the side-ladders, and the train rolled on across the Missouri River to Council Bluffs.

"General" Kelly, with an army of two thousand hoboes, lay in camp at Chautauqua Park, several miles away. The after-push we were with was General Kelly's rearguard, and, de-training at Council Bluffs, it started to march to camp. The night had turned cold, and heavy wind-squalls, accompanied by rain, were chilling and wetting us. Many police were guarding us and herding us to the camp. The Swede and I watched our chance and made a successful get-away.

The rain began coming down in torrents, and in the darkness, unable to see our hands in front of our faces, like a pair of blind men we fumbled about for shelter. Our instinct served us, for in no time we stumbled upon a saloon—not a saloon that was open and doing business, not merely a saloon that was closed for the night, and not even a saloon with a permanent address, but a saloon propped up on big timbers, with rollers underneath, that was being moved from some-where to somewhere. The doors were locked. A squall of wind and rain drove down upon us. We did not hesitate. Smash went the door, and in we went.

I have made some tough camps in my time, "carried the banner" in infernal metropolises, bedded in pools of water, slept in the snow under two blankets when the spirit thermometer registered seventy-four degrees below zero (which is a mere trifle of one hundred and six degrees of frost); but I want to say right here that never did I make a tougher camp, pass a more miserable night, than that night I passed with the Swede in the itinerant saloon at Council Bluffs. In the first place, the building, perched up as it was in the air, had exposed a multitude of openings in the floor through which the wind whistled. In the second place, the bar was empty; there was no bottled fire-water with which we could warm ourselves and forget our misery. We had no blankets, and in our wet clothes, wet to the skin, we tried to sleep. I rolled under the bar, and the Swede rolled under the table. The holes and crevices in the floor made it impossible, and at the end of half an hour I crawled up on top the bar. A little later the Swede crawled up on top his table.

And there we shivered and prayed for daylight. I know, for one, that I shivered until I could shiver no more, till the shivering muscles exhausted themselves and merely ached horribly. The Swede moaned and groaned, and every little while, through chattering teeth, he muttered, "Never again; never again." He muttered this phrase repeatedly, ceaselessly, a thousand times; and when he dozed, he went on muttering it in his sleep.

At the first gray of dawn we left our house of pain, and outside, found ourselves in a mist, dense and chill. We stumbled on till we came to the railroad track. I was going back to Omaha to throw my feet for breakfast; my companion was going on to Chicago. The moment for parting had come. Our palsied hands went out to each other. We were both shivering. When we tried to speak, our teeth chattered us back into silence. We stood alone, shut off from the world; all that we could see was a short length of railroad track, both ends of which were lost in the driving mist. We stared dumbly at each other, our clasped hands shaking sympathetically. The Swede's face was blue with the cold, and I know mine must have been.

"Never again what?" I managed to articulate.

Speech strove for utterance in the Swede's throat; then, faint and distant, in a thin whisper from the very bottom of his frozen soul, came the words:—

"Never again a hobo."

He paused, and, as he went on again, his voice gathered strength and huskiness as it affirmed his will.

"Never again a hobo. I'm going to get a job. You'd better do the same. Nights like this make rheumatism."

He wrung my hand.

"Good-by, Bo," said he.

"Good-by, Bo," said I.

The next we were swallowed up from each other by the mist. It was our final passing. But here's to you, Mr. Swede, wherever you are. I hope you got that job.

Road-Kids and Gay-Cats

EVERY once in a while, in newspapers, magazines, and bio-graphical dictionaries, I run upon sketches of my life, wherein, delicately phrased, I learn that it was in order to study sociology that I became a tramp. This is very nice and thoughtful of the biographers, but it is inaccurate. I became a tramp—well, because of the life that was in me, of the wan-derlust in my blood that would not let me rest. Sociology was merely incidental; it came afterward, in the same manner that a wet skin follows a ducking. I went on "The Road" because I couldn't keep away from it; because I hadn't the price of the railroad fare in my jeans; because I was so made that I couldn't work all my life on "one same shift"; because—well, just because it was easier to than not to.

It happened in my own town, in Oakland, when I was six-teen. At that time I had attained a dizzy reputation in my chosen circle of adventurers, by whom I was known as the Prince of the Oyster Pirates. It is true, those immediately out-side my circle, such as honest bay-sailors, longshoremen, yachtsmen, and the legal owners of the oysters, called me "tough," "hoodlum," "smoudge," "thief," "robber," and var-ious other not nice things—all of which was complimentary and but served to increase the dizziness of the high place in which I sat. At that time I had not read "Paradise Lost," and later, when I read Milton's "Better to reign in hell than serve in heaven," I was fully convinced that great minds run in the same channels.

It was at this time that the fortuitous concatenation of events sent me upon my first adventure on The Road. It hap-pened that there was nothing doing in oysters just then; that at Benicia, forty miles away, I had some blankets I wanted to get; and that at Port Costa, several miles from Benicia, a sto-len boat lay at anchor in charge of the constable. Now this boat was owned by a friend of mine, by name Dinny McCrea. It had been stolen and left at Port Costa by Whiskey Bob, another friend of mine. (Poor Whiskey Bob! Only last winter his body was picked up on the beach shot full of holes by nobody knows whom.) I had come down from "up river" some time before, and reported to Dinny McCrea the whereabouts of his boat; and Dinny McCrea had promptly offered ten dollars to me if I should bring it down to Oakland to him.

Time was heavy on my hands. I sat on the dock and talked it over with Nickey the Greek, another idle oyster pirate. "Let's go," said I, and Nickey was willing. He was "broke." I possessed fifty cents and a small skiff. The former I invested and loaded into the latter in the form of crackers, canned corned beef, and a ten-cent bottle of French mustard. (We were keen on French mustard in those days.) Then, late in the afternoon, we hoisted our small spritsail and started. We sailed all night, and next morning, on the first of a glorious flood-tide, a fair wind behind us, we came booming up the Carquinez Straits to Port Costa. There lay the stolen boat, not twenty-five feet from the wharf. We ran alongside and doused our little spritsail. I sent Nickey forward to lift the anchor, while I began casting off the gaskets.

A man ran out on the wharf and hailed us. It was the constable. It suddenly came to me that I had neglected to get a written authorization from Dinny McCrea to take possession of his boat. Also, I knew that constable wanted to charge at least twenty-five dollars in fees for capturing the boat from Whiskey Bob and subsequently taking care of it. And my last fifty cents had been blown in for corned beef and French mustard, and the reward was only ten dollars anyway. I shot a glance forward to Nickey. He had the anchor up-and-down and was straining at it. "Break her out," I whispered to him, and turned and shouted back to the constable. The result was that he and I were talking at the same time, our spoken thoughts colliding in mid-air and making gibberish.

The constable grew more imperative, and perforce I had to listen. Nickey was heaving on the anchor till I thought he'd burst a blood-vessel. When the constable got done with his threats and warnings, I asked him who he was. The time he lost in telling me enabled Nickey to break out the anchor. I was doing some quick calculating. At the feet of the constable a ladder ran down the dock to the water, and to the ladder was moored a skiff. The oars were in it. But it was padlocked.

I gambled everything on that padlock. I felt the breeze on my cheek, saw the surge of the tide, looked at the remaining gaskets that confined the sail, ran my eyes up the halyards to the blocks and knew that all was clear, and then threw off all dissimulation.

"In with her!" I shouted to Nickey, and sprang to the gaskets, casting them loose and thanking my stars that Whiskey Bob had tied them in square-knots instead of "grannies."

The constable had slid down the ladder and was fumbling with a key at the padlock. The anchor came aboard and the last gasket was loosed at the same instant that the constable freed the skiff and jumped to the oars.

"Peak-halyards!" I commanded my crew, at the same time swinging on to the throat-halyards. Up came the sail on the run. I belayed and ran aft to the tiller.

"Stretch her!" I shouted to Nickey at the peak. The constable was just reaching for our stern. A puff of wind caught us, and we shot away. It was great. If I'd had a black flag, I know I'd have run it up in triumph. The constable stood up in the skiff, and paled the glory of the day with the vividness of his language. Also, he wailed for a gun. You see, that was another gamble we had taken.

Anyway, we weren't stealing the boat. It wasn't the constable's. We were merely stealing his fees, which was his particular form of graft. And we weren't stealing the fees for ourselves, either; we were stealing them for my friend, Dinny McCrea.

Benicia was made in a few minutes, and a few minutes later my blankets were aboard. I shifted the boat down to the far end of Steamboat Wharf, from which point of vantage we could see anybody coming after us. There was no telling. Maybe the Port Costa constable would telephone to the Benicia constable. Nickey and I held a council of war. We lay on deck in the warm sun, the fresh breeze on our cheeks, the flood-tide rippling and swirling past. It was impossible to start back to Oakland till afternoon, when the ebb would begin to run. But we figured that the constable would have an eye out on the Carquinez Straits when the ebb started, and that nothing remained for us but to wait for the following ebb, at two o'clock next morning, when we could slip by Cerberus in the darkness.

So we lay on deck, smoked cigarettes, and were glad that we were alive. I spat over the side and gauged the speed of the current.

"With this wind, we could run this flood clear to Rio Vista," I said.

"And it's fruit-time on the river," said Nickey.

"And low water on the river," said I. "It's the best time of the year to make Sacramento."

We sat up and looked at each other. The glorious west wind was pouring over us like wine. We both spat over the side and gauged the current. Now I contend that it was all the fault of that flood-tide and fair wind. They appealed to our sailor instinct. If it had not been for them, the whole chain of events that was to put me upon The Road would have broken down.

We said no word, but cast off our moorings and hoisted sail. Our adventures up the Sacramento River are no part of this narrative. We subsequently made the city of Sacramento and tied up at a wharf. The water was fine, and we spent most of our time in swimming. On the sand-bar above the railroad bridge we fell in with a bunch of boys likewise in swimming. Between swims we lay on the bank and talked. They talked differently from the fellows I had been used to herding with. It was a new vernacular. They were road-kids, and with every word they uttered the lure of The Road laid hold of me more imperiously.

"When I was down in Alabama," one kid would begin; or, another, "Coming up on the C. & A. from K.C."; whereat, a third kid, "On the C. & A. there ain't no steps to the 'blinds.'" And I would lie silently in the sand and listen. "It was at a little town in Ohio on the Lake Shore and Michigan Southern," a kid would start; and another, "Ever ride the Cannonball on the Wabash?"; and yet another, "Nope, but I've been on the White Mail out of Chicago." "Talk about railroadin'—wait till you hit the Pennsylvania, four tracks, no water tanks, take water on the fly, that's goin' some." "The Northern Pacific's a bad road now." "Salinas is on the 'hog,' the 'bulls' is 'horstile.'" "I got 'pinched' at El Paso, along with Moke Kid." "Talkin' of 'poke-outs,' wait till you hit the French country out of Montreal—not a word of English— you say, '*Mongee, Madame, mongee, no spika da French*,' an' rub your stomach an' look hungry, an' she gives you a slice of sow-belly an' a chunk of dry 'punk.'"

And I continued to lie in the sand and listen. These wanderers made my oyster-piracy look like thirty cents. A new world was calling to me in every word that was spoken—a world of rods and gunnels, blind baggages and "side-door Pullmans," "bulls" and "shacks," "floppings" and "chewin's," "pinches" and "get-aways," "strong arms" and "bindle-stiffs," "punks" and "profesh." And it all spelled Adventure. Very well; I would tackle this new world. I "lined" myself up alongside those road-kids. I was just as strong as any of them, just as quick, just as nervy, and my brain was just as good.

After the swim, as evening came on, they dressed and went up town. I went along. The kids began "battering" the "main-stem" for "light pieces," or, in other words, begging for money on the main street. I had never begged in my life, and this was the hardest thing for me to stomach when I first went on The Road. I had absurd notions about begging. My philosophy, up to that time, was that it was finer to steal than to beg; and that robbery was finer still because the risk and the penalty were proportionately greater. As an oyster pirate I had already earned convictions at the hands of justice, which, if I had tried to serve them, would have required a thousand years in state's prison. To rob was manly; to beg was sordid and despicable. But I developed in the days to come all right, all right, till I came to look upon begging as a joyous prank, a game of wits, a nerve-exerciser.

That first night, however, I couldn't rise to it; and the result was that when the kids were ready to go to a restaurant and eat, I wasn't. I was broke. Meeny Kid, I think it was, gave me the price, and we all ate together. But while I ate, I meditated. The receiver, it was said, was as bad as the thief; Meeny Kid had done the begging, and I was profiting by it. I decided that the receiver was a whole lot worse than the thief, and that it shouldn't happen again. And it didn't. I turned out next day and threw my feet as well as the next one.

Nickey the Greek's ambition didn't run to The Road. He was not a success at throwing his feet, and he stowed away one night on a barge and went down river to San Francisco. I met him, only a week ago, at a pugilistic carnival. He has progressed. He sat in a place of honor at the ring-side. He is now a manager of prize-fighters and proud of it. In fact, in a small way, in local sportdom, he is quite a shining light.

"No kid is a road-kid until he has gone over 'the hill' "— such was the law of The Road I heard expounded in Sacramento. All right, I'd go over the hill and matriculate. "The hill," by the way, was the Sierra Nevadas. The whole gang was going over the hill on a jaunt, and of course I'd go along. It was French Kid's first adventure on The Road. He had just run away from his people in San Francisco. It was up to him and me to deliver the goods. In passing, I may remark that my old title of "Prince" had vanished. I had received my "monica." I was now "Sailor Kid," later to be known as " 'Frisco Kid," when I had put the Rockies between me and my native state.

At 10.20 P.M. the Central Pacific overland pulled out of the depot at Sacramento for the East—that particular item of time-table is indelibly engraved on my memory. There were about a dozen in our gang, and we strung out in the darkness ahead of the train ready to take her out. All the local road-kids that we knew came down to see us off—also, to "ditch" us if they could. That was their idea of a joke, and there were only about forty of them to carry it out. Their ring-leader was a crackerjack road-kid named Bob. Sacramento was his home town, but he'd hit The Road pretty well everywhere over the whole country. He took French Kid and me aside and gave us advice something like this: "We're goin' to try an' ditch your bunch, see? Youse two are weak. The rest of the push can take care of itself. So, as soon as youse two nail a blind, deck her. An' stay on the decks till youse pass Roseville Junction, at which burg the constables are horstile, sloughin' in everybody on sight."

The engine whistled and the overland pulled out. There were three blinds on her—room for all of us. The dozen of us who were trying to make her out would have preferred to slip aboard quietly; but our forty friends crowded on with the most amazing and shameless publicity and advertisement. Following Bob's advice, I immediately "decked her," that is, climbed up on top of the roof of one of the mail-cars. There I lay down, my heart jumping a few extra beats, and listened to the fun. The whole train crew was forward, and the ditching went on fast and furious. After the train had run half a mile, it stopped, and the crew came forward again and ditched the survivors. I, alone, had made the train out.

Back at the depot, about him two or three of the push that had witnessed the accident, lay French Kid with both legs off. French Kid had slipped or stumbled—that was all, and the wheels had done the rest. Such was my initiation to The Road. It was two years afterward when I next saw French Kid and examined his "stumps." This was an act of courtesy. "Cripples" always like to have their stumps examined. One of the entertaining sights on The Road is to witness the meeting of two cripples. Their common disability is a fruitful source of conversation; and they tell how it happened, describe what they know of the amputation, pass critical judgment on their own and each other's surgeons, and wind up by withdrawing to one side, taking off bandages and wrappings, and comparing stumps.

But it was not until several days later, over in Nevada, when the push caught up with me, that I learned of French Kid's accident. The push itself arrived in bad condition. It had gone through a train-wreck in the snow-sheds; Happy Joe was on crutches with two mashed legs, and the rest were nursing skins and bruises.

In the meantime, I lay on the roof of the mail-car, trying to remember whether Roseville Junction, against which burg Bob had warned me, was the first stop or the second stop. To make sure, I delayed descending to the platform of the blind until after the second stop. And then I didn't descend. I was new to the game, and I felt safer where I was. But I never told the push that I held down the decks the whole night, clear across the Sierras, through snow-sheds and tunnels, and down to Truckee on the other side, where I arrived at seven in the morning. Such a thing was disgraceful, and I'd have been a common laughing-stock. This is the first time I have confessed the truth about that first ride over the hill. As for the push, it decided that I was all right, and when I came back over the hill to Sacramento, I was a full-fledged road-kid.

Yet I had much to learn. Bob was my mentor, and he was all right. I remember one evening (it was fair-time in Sacramento, and we were knocking about and having a good time) when I lost my hat in a fight. There was I bare-headed in the street, and it was Bob to the rescue. He took me to one side from the push and told me what to do. I was a bit timid of his advice. I had just come out of jail, where I had been three days, and I knew that if the police "pinched" me again, I'd get good and "soaked." On the other hand, I couldn't show the white feather. I'd been over the hill, I was running full-fledged with the push, and it was up to me to deliver the goods. So I accepted Bob's advice, and he came along with me to see that I did it up brown.

We took our position on K Street, on the corner, I think, of Fifth. It was early in the evening and the street was crowded. Bob studied the head-gear of every Chinaman that passed. I used to wonder how the road-kids all managed to wear "five-dollar Stetson stiff-rims," and now I knew. They got them, the way I was going to get mine, from the Chinese. I was nervous—there were so many people about; but Bob was cool as an iceberg. Several times, when I started forward toward a Chinaman, all nerved and keyed up, Bob dragged me back. He wanted me to get a good hat, and one that fitted. Now a hat came by that was the right size but not new; and, after a dozen impossible hats, along would come one that was new but not the right size. And when one did come by that was new and the right size, the rim was too large or not large enough. My, Bob was finicky. I was so wrought up that I'd have snatched any kind of a head-covering.

At last came the hat, the one hat in Sacramento for me. I knew it was a winner as soon as I looked at it. I glanced at Bob. He sent a sweeping look-about for police, then nodded his head. I lifted the hat from the Chinaman's head and pulled it down on my own. It was a perfect fit. Then I started. I heard Bob crying out, and I caught a glimpse of him blocking the irate Mongolian and tripping him up. I ran on. I turned

up the next corner, and around the next. This street was not
so crowded as K, and I walked along in quietude, catching
my breath and congratulating myself upon my hat and my
get-away.

And then, suddenly, around the corner at my back, came
the bare-headed Chinaman. With him were a couple more
Chinamen, and at their heels were half a dozen men and boys.
I sprinted to the next corner, crossed the street, and rounded
the following corner. I decided that I had surely played him
out, and I dropped into a walk again. But around the corner
at my heels came that persistent Mongolian. It was the old
story of the hare and the tortoise. He could not run so fast as
I, but he stayed with it, plodding along at a shambling and
deceptive trot, and wasting much good breath in noisy impre-
cations. He called all Sacramento to witness the dishonor that
had been done him, and a goodly portion of Sacramento
heard and flocked at his heels. And I ran on like the hare, and
ever that persistent Mongolian, with the increasing rabble,
overhauled me. But finally, when a policeman had joined his
following, I let out all my links. I twisted and turned, and I
swear I ran at least twenty blocks on the straight away. And
I never saw that Chinaman again. The hat was a dandy, a
brand-new Stetson, just out of the shop, and it was the envy
of the whole push. Furthermore, it was the symbol that I had
delivered the goods. I wore it for over a year.

Road-kids are nice little chaps—when you get them alone
and they are telling you "how it happened"; but take my
word for it, watch out for them when they run in pack. Then
they are wolves, and like wolves they are capable of dragging
down the strongest man. At such times they are not cowardly.
They will fling themselves upon a man and hold on with
every ounce of strength in their wiry bodies, till he is thrown
and helpless. More than once have I seen them do it, and I
know whereof I speak. Their motive is usually robbery. And
watch out for the "strong arm." Every kid in the push I travelled with was expert at it. Even French Kid mastered it before he lost his legs.

I have strong upon me now a vision of what I once saw in
"The Willows." The Willows was a clump of trees in a waste
piece of land near the railway depot and not more than five

minutes walk from the heart of Sacramento. It is night-time, and the scene is illumined by the thin light of stars. I see a husky laborer in the midst of a pack of road-kids. He is infuriated and cursing them, not a bit afraid, confident of his own strength. He weighs about one hundred and eighty pounds, and his muscles are hard; but he doesn't know what he is up against. The kids are snarling. It is not pretty. They make a rush from all sides, and he lashes out and whirls. Barber Kid is standing beside me. As the man whirls, Barber Kid leaps forward and does the trick. Into the man's back goes his knee; around the man's neck, from behind, passes his right hand, the bone of the wrist pressing against the jugular vein. Barber Kid throws his whole weight backward. It is a powerful leverage. Besides, the man's wind has been shut off. It is the strong arm.

The man resists, but he is already practically helpless. The road-kids are upon him from every side, clinging to arms and legs and body, and like a wolf at the throat of a moose Barber Kid hangs on and drags backward. Over the man goes, and down under the heap. Barber Kid changes the position of his own body, but never lets go. While some of the kids are "going through" the victim, others are holding his legs so that he cannot kick and thresh about. They improve the opportunity by taking off the man's shoes. As for him, he has given in. He is beaten. Also, what of the strong arm at his throat, he is short of wind. He is making ugly choking noises, and the kids hurry. They really don't want to kill him. All is done. At a word all holds are released at once, and the kids scatter, one of them lugging the shoes—he knows where he can get half a dollar for them. The man sits up and looks about him, dazed and helpless. Even if he wanted to, barefooted pursuit in the darkness would be hopeless. I linger a moment and watch him. He is feeling at his throat, making dry, hawking noises, and jerking his head in a quaint way as though to assure himself that the neck is not dislocated. Then I slip away to join the push, and see that man no more— though I shall always see him, sitting there in the starlight, somewhat dazed, a bit frightened, greatly dishevelled, and making quaint jerking movements of head and neck.

Drunken men are the especial prey of the road-kids. Rob-

bing a drunken man they call "rolling a stiff"; and wherever
they are, they are on the constant lookout for drunks. The
drunk is their particular meat, as the fly is the particular meat
of the spider. The rolling of a stiff is ofttimes an amusing
sight, especially when the stiff is helpless and when interference is unlikely. At the first swoop the stiff's money and jew-
ellery go. Then the kids sit around their victim in a sort of
pow-wow. A kid generates a fancy for the stiff's necktie. Off
it comes. Another kid is after underclothes. Off they come,
and a knife quickly abbreviates arms and legs. Friendly hoboes may be called in to take the coat and trousers, which are
too large for the kids. And in the end they depart, leaving
beside the stiff the heap of their discarded rags.

Another vision comes to me. It is a dark night. My push is
coming along the sidewalk in the suburbs. Ahead of us, under
an electric light, a man crosses the street diagonally. There is
something tentative and desultory in his walk. The kids scent
the game on the instant. The man is drunk. He blunders
across the opposite sidewalk and is lost in the darkness as he
takes a short-cut through a vacant lot. No hunting cry is
raised, but the pack flings itself forward in quick pursuit. In
the middle of the vacant lot it comes upon him. But what is
this?—snarling and strange forms, small and dim and menacing, are between the pack and its prey. It is another pack of
road-kids, and in the hostile pause we learn that it is their
meat, that they have been trailing it a dozen blocks and more
and that we are butting in. But it is the world primeval. These
wolves are baby wolves. (As a matter of fact, I don't think
one of them was over twelve or thirteen years of age. I met
some of them afterward, and learned that they had just arrived that day over the hill, and that they hailed from Denver
and Salt Lake City.) Our pack flings forward. The baby
wolves squeal and screech and fight like little demons. All
about the drunken man rages the struggle for the possession
of him. Down he goes in the thick of it, and the combat rages
over his body after the fashion of the Greeks and Trojans over
the body and armor of a fallen hero. Amid cries and tears and
wailings the baby wolves are dispossessed, and my pack rolls
the stiff. But always I remember the poor stiff and his befuddled amazement at the abrupt eruption of battle in the vacant

lot. I see him now, dim in the darkness, titubating in stupid wonder, good-naturedly essaying the rôle of peacemaker in that multitudinous scrap the significance of which he did not understand, and the really hurt expression on his face when he, unoffending he, was clutched at by many hands and dragged down in the thick of the press.

"Bindle-stiffs" are favorite prey of the road-kids. A bindle-stiff is a working tramp. He takes his name from the roll of blankets he carries, which is known as a "bindle." Because he does work, a bindle-stiff is expected usually to have some small change about him, and it is after that small change that the road-kids go. The best hunting-ground for bindle-stiffs is in the sheds, barns, lumber-yards, railroad-yards, etc., on the edges of a city, and the time for hunting is the night, when the bindle-stiff seeks these places to roll up in his blankets and sleep.

"Gay-cats" also come to grief at the hands of the road-kid. In more familiar parlance, gay-cats are short-horns, *chechaquos*, new chums, or tenderfeet. A gay-cat is a newcomer on The Road who is man-grown, or, at least, youth-grown. A boy on The Road, on the other hand, no matter how green he is, is never a gay-cat; he is a road-kid or a "punk," and if he travels with a "profesh," he is known possessively as a "prushun." I was never a prushun, for I did not take kindly to possession. I was first a road-kid and then a profesh. Because I started in young, I practically skipped my gay-cat apprenticeship. For a short period, during the time I was exchanging my 'Frisco Kid monica for that of Sailor Jack, I labored under the suspicion of being a gay-cat. But closer acquaintance on the part of those that suspected me quickly disabused their minds, and in a short time I acquired the unmistakable airs and ear-marks of the blowed-in-the-glass profesh. And be it known, here and now, that the profesh are the aristocracy of The Road. They are the lords and masters, the aggressive men, the primordial noblemen, the *blond beasts* so beloved of Nietzsche.

When I came back over the hill from Nevada, I found that some river pirate had stolen Dinny McCrea's boat. (A funny thing at this day is that I cannot remember what became of the skiff in which Nickey the Greek and I sailed from Oakland to Port Costa. I know that the constable didn't get it, and I know that it didn't go with us up the Sacramento River, and that is all I do know.) With the loss of Dinny McCrea's boat, I was pledged to The Road; and when I grew tired of Sacramento, I said good-by to the push (which, in its friendly way, tried to ditch me from a freight as I left town) and started on a *passear* down the valley of the San Joaquin. The Road had gripped me and would not let me go; and later, when I had voyaged to sea and done one thing and another, I returned to The Road to make longer flights, to be a "comet" and a profesh, and to plump into the bath of sociology that wet me to the skin.

Two Thousand Stiffs

A "STIFF" is a tramp. It was once my fortune to travel a few weeks with a "push" that numbered two thousand. This was known as "Kelly's Army." Across the wild and woolly West, clear from California, General Kelly and his heroes had captured trains; but they fell down when they crossed the Missouri and went up against the effete East. The East hadn't the slightest intention of giving free transportation to two thousand hoboes. Kelly's Army lay helplessly for some time at Council Bluffs. The day I joined it, made desperate by delay, it marched out to capture a train.

It was quite an imposing sight. General Kelly sat a magnificent black charger, and with waving banners, to the martial music of fife and drum corps, company by company, in two divisions, his two thousand stiffs countermarched before him and hit the wagon-road to the little burg of Weston, seven miles away. Being the latest recruit, I was in the last company, of the last regiment, of the Second Division, and, furthermore, in the last rank of the rear-guard. The army went into camp at Weston beside the railroad track—beside the tracks, rather, for two roads went through: the Chicago, Milwaukee, and St. Paul, and the Rock Island.

Our intention was to take the first train out, but the railroad officials "coppered" our play—and won. There was no first train. They tied up the two lines and stopped running trains. In the meantime, while we lay by the dead tracks, the good people of Omaha and Council Bluffs were bestirring themselves. Preparations were making to form a mob, capture a train in Council Bluffs, run it down to us, and make us a present of it. The railroad officials coppered that play, too. They didn't wait for the mob. Early in the morning of the second day, an engine, with a single private car attached, arrived at the station and side-tracked. At this sign that life had renewed in the dead roads, the whole army lined up beside the track.

But never did life renew so monstrously on a dead railroad as it did on those two roads. From the west came the whistle

of a locomotive. It was coming in our direction, bound east.
We were bound east. A stir of preparation ran down our
ranks. The whistle tooted fast and furiously, and the train
thundered at top speed. The hobo didn't live that could have
boarded it. Another locomotive whistled, and another train
came through at top speed, and another, and another, train
after train, train after train, till toward the last the trains were
composed of passenger coaches, box-cars, flat-cars, dead engines, cabooses, mail-cars, wrecking appliances, and all the
riff-raff of worn-out and abandoned rolling-stock that collects
in the yards of great railways. When the yards at Council
Bluffs had been completely cleaned, the private car and engine
went east, and the tracks died for keeps.

That day went by, and the next, and nothing moved, and
in the meantime, pelted by sleet, and rain, and hail, the two
thousand hoboes lay beside the track. But that night the good
people of Council Bluffs went the railroad officials one better.
A mob formed in Council Bluffs, crossed the river to Omaha,
and there joined with another mob in a raid on the Union
Pacific yards. First they captured an engine, next they
knocked a train together, and then the united mobs piled
aboard, crossed the Missouri, and ran down the Rock Island
right of way to turn the train over to us. The railway officials
tried to copper this play, but fell down, to the mortal terror
of the section boss and one member of the section gang at
Weston. This pair, under secret telegraphic orders, tried to
wreck our train-load of sympathizers by tearing up the track.
It happened that we were suspicious and had our patrols out.
Caught red-handed at train-wrecking, and surrounded by
twenty hundred infuriated hoboes, that section-gang boss and
assistant prepared to meet death. I don't remember what
saved them, unless it was the arrival of the train.

It was our turn to fall down, and we did, hard. In their
haste, the two mobs had neglected to make up a sufficiently
long train. There wasn't room for two thousand hoboes to
ride. So the mobs and the hoboes had a talkfest, fraternized,
sang songs, and parted, the mobs going back on their captured train to Omaha, the hoboes pulling out next morning
on a hundred-and-forty-mile march to Des Moines. It was
not until Kelly's Army crossed the Missouri that it began to

walk, and after that it never rode again. It cost the railroads slathers of money, but they were acting on principle, and they won.

Underwood, Leola, Menden, Avoca, Walnut, Marno, Atlantic, Wyoto, Anita, Adair, Adam, Casey, Stuart, Dexter, Carlham, De Soto, Van Meter, Booneville, Commerce, Valley Junction—how the names of the towns come back to me as I con the map and trace our route through the fat Iowa country! And the hospitable Iowa farmer-folk! They turned out with their wagons and carried our baggage; gave us hot lunches at noon by the wayside; mayors of comfortable little towns made speeches of welcome and hastened us on our way; deputations of little girls and maidens came out to meet us, and the good citizens turned out by hundreds, locked arms, and marched with us down their main streets. It was circus day when we came to town, and every day was circus day, for there were many towns.

In the evenings our camps were invaded by whole populations. Every company had its campfire, and around each fire something was doing. The cooks in my company, Company L, were song-and-dance artists and contributed most of our entertainment. In another part of the encampment the glee club would be singing—one of its star voices was the "Dentist," drawn from Company L, and we were mighty proud of him. Also, he pulled teeth for the whole army, and, since the extractions usually occurred at meal-time, our digestions were stimulated by variety of incident. The Dentist had no anæsthetics, but two or three of us were always on tap to volunteer to hold down the patient. In addition to the stunts of the companies and the glee club, church services were usually held, local preachers officiating, and always there was a great making of political speeches. All these things ran neck and neck; it was a full-blown Midway. A lot of talent can be dug out of two thousand hoboes. I remember we had a picked baseball nine, and on Sundays we made a practice of putting it all over the local nines. Sometimes we did it twice on Sundays.

Last year, while on a lecturing trip, I rode into Des Moines in a Pullman—I don't mean a "side-door Pullman," but the real thing. On the outskirts of the city I saw the old stove-works, and my heart leaped. It was there, at the stove-works, a dozen years before, that the Army lay down and swore a mighty oath that its feet were sore and that it would walk no more. We took possession of the stove-works and told Des Moines that we had come to stay—that we'd walked in, but we'd be blessed if we'd walk out. Des Moines was hospitable, but this was too much of a good thing. Do a little mental arithmetic, gentle reader. Two thousand hoboes, eating three square meals, make six thousand meals per day, forty-two thousand meals per week, or one hundred and sixty-eight thousand meals per shortest month in the calendar. That's going some. We had no money. It was up to Des Moines.

Des Moines was desperate. We lay in camp, made political speeches, held sacred concerts, pulled teeth, played baseball and seven-up, and ate our six thousand meals per day, and Des Moines paid for it. Des Moines pleaded with the railroads, but they were obdurate; they had said we shouldn't ride, and that settled it. To permit us to ride would be to establish a precedent, and there weren't going to be any precedents. And still we went on eating. That was the terrifying factor in the situation. We were bound for Washington, and Des Moines would have had to float municipal bonds to pay all our railroad fares, even at special rates, and if we remained much longer, she'd have to float bonds anyway to feed us.

Then some local genius solved the problem. We wouldn't walk. Very good. We should ride. From Des Moines to Keokuk on the Mississippi flowed the Des Moines River. This particular stretch of river was three hundred miles long. We could ride on it, said the local genius; and, once equipped with floating stock, we could ride on down the Mississippi to the Ohio, and thence up the Ohio, winding up with a short portage over the mountains to Washington.

Des Moines took up a subscription. Public-spirited citizens contributed several thousand dollars. Lumber, rope, nails, and cotton for calking were bought in large quantities, and on the banks of the Des Moines was inaugurated a tremendous era of shipbuilding. Now the Des Moines is a picayune stream, unduly dignified by the appellation of "river." In our spacious western land it would be called a "creek." The oldest inhabitants shook their heads and said we couldn't make it, that there wasn't enough water to float us. Des Moines didn't care, so long as it got rid of us, and we were such well-fed optimists that we didn't care either.

On Wednesday, May 9, 1894, we got under way and started on our colossal picnic. Des Moines had got off pretty easily, and she certainly owes a statue in bronze to the local genius who got her out of her difficulty. True, Des Moines had to pay for our boats; we had eaten sixty-six thousand meals at the stove-works; and we took twelve thousand additional meals along with us in our commissary—as a precaution against famine in the wilds; but then, think what it would have meant if we had remained at Des Moines eleven months instead of eleven days. Also, when we departed, we promised Des Moines we'd come back if the river failed to float us.

It was all very well having twelve thousand meals in the commissary, and no doubt the commissary "ducks" enjoyed them; for the commissary promptly got lost, and my boat, for one, never saw it again. The company formation was hopelessly broken up during the river-trip. In any camp of men there will always be found a certain percentage of shirks, of helpless, of just ordinary, and of hustlers. There were ten men in my boat, and they were the cream of Company L. Every man was a hustler. For two reasons I was included in the ten. First, I was as good a hustler as ever "threw his feet," and next, I was "Sailor Jack." I understood boats and boating. The ten of us forgot the remaining forty men of Company L, and by the time we had missed one meal we promptly forgot the commissary. We were independent. We went down the river "on our own," hustling our "chewin's," beating every boat in the fleet, and, alas that I must say it, sometimes taking possession of the stores the farmer-folk had collected for the Army.

For a good part of the three hundred miles we were from half a day to a day or so in advance of the Army. We had managed to get hold of several American flags. When we approached a small town, or when we saw a group of farmers gathered on the bank, we ran up our flags, called ourselves the "advance boat," and demanded to know what provisions had been collected for the Army. We represented the Army, of course, and the provisions were turned over to us. But there wasn't anything small about us. We never took more than we could get away with. But we did take the cream of everything. For instance, if some philanthropic farmer had donated several dollars' worth of tobacco, we took it. So, also, we took butter and sugar, coffee and canned goods; but when the stores consisted of sacks of beans and flour, or two or three slaughtered steers, we resolutely refrained and went our way, leaving orders to turn such provisions over to the commissary boats whose business was to follow behind us.

My, but the ten of us did live on the fat of the land! For a long time General Kelly vainly tried to head us off. He sent two rowers, in a light, round-bottomed boat, to overtake us and put a stop to our piratical careers. They overtook us all right, but they were two and we were ten. They were empowered by General Kelly to make us prisoners, and they told us so. When we expressed disinclination to become prisoners, they hurried ahead to the next town to invoke the aid of the authorities. We went ashore immediately and cooked an early supper; and under the cloak of darkness we ran by the town and its authorities.

I kept a diary on part of the trip, and as I read it over now I note one persistently recurring phrase, namely, "Living fine." We did live fine. We even disdained to use coffee boiled in water. We made our coffee out of milk, calling the wonderful beverage, if I remember rightly, "pale Vienna."

While we were ahead, skimming the cream, and while the commissary was lost far behind, the main Army, coming along in the middle, starved. This was hard on the Army, I'll allow; but then, the ten of us were individualists. We had initiative and enterprise. We ardently believed that the grub was to the man who got there first, the pale Vienna to the strong. On one stretch the Army went forty-eight hours without grub; and then it arrived at a small village of some three hundred inhabitants, the name of which I do not remember, though I think it was Red Rock. This town, following the practice of all towns through which the Army passed, had appointed a committee of safety. Counting five to a family, Red Rock consisted of sixty households. Her committee of safety was scared stiff by the eruption of two thousand hungry hoboes who lined their boats two and three deep along the river bank. General Kelly was a fair man. He had no intention of working a hardship on the village. He did not expect sixty households to furnish two thousand meals. Besides, the Army had its treasure-chest.

But the committee of safety lost its head. "No encouragement to the invader" was its programme, and when General Kelly wanted to buy food, the committee turned him down. It had nothing to sell; General Kelly's money was "no good" in their burg. And then General Kelly went into action. The bugles blew. The Army left the boats and on top of the bank formed in battle array. The committee was there to see. General Kelly's speech was brief.

"Boys," he said, "when did you eat last?"

"Day before yesterday," they shouted.

"Are you hungry?"

A mighty affirmation from two thousand throats shook the atmosphere. Then General Kelly turned to the committee of safety: —

"You see, gentlemen, the situation. My men have eaten nothing in forty-eight hours. If I turn them loose upon your town, I'll not be responsible for what happens. They are desperate. I offered to buy food for them, but you refused to sell. I now withdraw my offer. Instead, I shall demand. I give you five minutes to decide. Either kill me six steers and give me four thousand rations, or I turn the men loose. Five minutes, gentlemen."

The terrified committee of safety looked at the two thousand hungry hoboes and collapsed. It didn't wait the five minutes. It wasn't going to take any chances. The killing of the steers and the collecting of the requisition began forthwith, and the Army dined.

And still the ten graceless individualists soared along ahead and gathered in everything in sight. But General Kelly fixed us. He sent horsemen down each bank, warning farmers and townspeople against us. They did their work thoroughly, all right. The erstwhile hospitable farmers met us with the icy mit. Also, they summoned the constables when we tied up to the bank, and loosed the dogs. I know. Two of the latter caught me with a barbed-wire fence between me and the river. I was carrying two buckets of milk for the pale Vienna.

I didn't damage the fence any; but we drank plebian coffee boiled with vulgar water, and it was up to me to throw my feet for another pair of trousers. I wonder, gentle reader, if you ever essayed hastily to climb a barbed-wire fence with a bucket of milk in each hand. Ever since that day I have had a prejudice against barbed wire, and I have gathered statistics on the subject.

Unable to make an honest living so long as General Kelly kept his two horsemen ahead of us, we returned to the Army and raised a revolution. It was a small affair, but it devastated Company L of the Second Division. The captain of Company L refused to recognize us; said we were deserters, and traitors, and scalawags; and when he drew rations for Company L from the commissary, he wouldn't give us any. That captain didn't appreciate us, or he wouldn't have refused us grub. Promptly we intrigued with the first lieutenant. He joined us with the ten men in his boat, and in return we elected him captain of Company M. The captain of Company L raised a roar. Down upon us came General Kelly, Colonel Speed, and Colonel Baker. The twenty of us stood firm, and our revolution was ratified.

But we never bothered with the commissary. Our hustlers drew better rations from the farmers. Our new captain, however, doubted us. He never knew when he'd see the ten of us again, once we got under way in the morning, so he called in a blacksmith to clinch his captaincy. In the stern of our boat, one on each side, were driven two heavy eye-bolts of iron. Correspondingly, on the bow of his boat, were fastened two huge iron hooks. The boats were brought together, end on, the hooks dropped into the eye-bolts, and there we were, hard and fast. We couldn't lose that captain. But we were irrepressible. Out of our very manacles we wrought an invincible device that enabled us to put it all over every other boat in the fleet.

Like all great inventions, this one of ours was accidental. We discovered it the first time we ran on a snag in a bit of a rapid. The head-boat hung up and anchored, and the tail-boat swung around in the current, pivoting the head-boat on the snag. I was at the stern of the tail-boat, steering. In vain we tried to shove off. Then I ordered the men from the head-boat into the tail-boat. Immediately the head-boat floated clear, and its men returned into it. After that, snags, reefs, shoals, and bars had no terrors for us. The instant the head-boat struck, the men in it leaped into the tail-boat. Of course, the head-boat floated over the obstruction and the tail-boat then struck. Like automatons, the twenty men now in the tail-boat leaped into the head-boat, and the tail-boat floated past.

The boats used by the Army were all alike, made by the mile and sawed off. They were flat-boats, and their lines were rectangles. Each boat was six feet wide, ten feet long, and a foot and a half deep. Thus, when our two boats were hooked together, I sat at the stern steering a craft twenty feet long, containing twenty husky hoboes who "spelled" each other at the oars and paddles, and loaded with blankets, cooking outfit, and our own private commissary.

Still we caused General Kelly trouble. He had called in his horsemen, and substituted three police-boats that travelled in the van and allowed no boats to pass them. The craft containing Company M crowded the police-boats hard. We could have passed them easily, but it was against the rules. So we kept a respectful distance astern and waited. Ahead we knew was virgin farming country, unbegged and generous; but we waited. White water was all we needed, and when we rounded a bend and a rapid showed up we knew what would happen. Smash! Police-boat number one goes on a boulder and hangs up. Bang! Police-boat number two follows suit. Whop! Police-boat number three encounters the common fate of all. Of course our boat does the same things; but one, two, the men are out of the head-boat and into the tail-boat; one, two, they are out of the tail-boat and into the head-boat; and one, two, the men who belong in the tail-boat are back in it and we are dashing on. "Stop! you blankety-blank-blanks!" shriek the police-boats. "How can we?—blank the blankety-blank river, anyway!" we wail plaintively as we surge past, caught in that remorseless current that sweeps us on out of sight and into the hospitable farmer-country that replenishes our private commissary with the cream of its contributions. Again we drink pale Vienna and realize that the grub is to the man who gets there.

Poor General Kelly! He devised another scheme. The whole fleet started ahead of us. Company M of the Second Division started in its proper place in the line, which was last. And it took us only one day to put the "kibosh" on that particular scheme. Twenty-five miles of bad water lay before us—all rapids, shoals, bars, and boulders. It was over that stretch of water that the oldest inhabitants of Des Moines had shaken their heads. Nearly two hundred boats entered the bad water ahead of us, and they piled up in the most astounding manner. We went through that stranded fleet like hemlock through the fire. There was no avoiding the boulders, bars, and snags except by getting out on the bank. We didn't avoid them. We went right over them, one, two, one, two, head-boat, tail-boat, head-boat, tail-boat, all hands back and forth and back again. We camped that night alone, and loafed in camp all of next day while the Army patched and repaired its wrecked boats and straggled up to us.

There was no stopping our cussedness. We rigged up a mast, piled on the canvas (blankets), and travelled short hours while the Army worked over-time to keep us in sight. Then General Kelly had recourse to diplomacy. No boat could touch us in the straight-away. Without discussion, we were the hottest bunch that ever came down the Des Moines. The ban of the police-boats was lifted. Colonel Speed was put aboard, and with this distinguished officer we had the honor of arriving first at Keokuk on the Mississippi. And right here I want to say to General Kelly and Colonel Speed that here's my hand. You were heroes, both of you, and you were men. And I'm sorry for at least ten per cent of the trouble that was given you by the head-boat of Company M.

At Keokuk the whole fleet was lashed together in a huge raft, and, after being wind-bound a day, a steamboat took us in tow down the Mississippi to Quincy, Illinois, where we camped across the river on Goose Island. Here the raft idea was abandoned, the boats being joined together in groups of four and decked over. Somebody told me that Quincy was the richest town of its size in the United States. When I heard this, I was immediately overcome by an irresistible impulse to throw my feet. No "blowed-in-the-glass profesh" could possibly pass up such a promising burg. I crossed the river to

Quincy in a small dug-out; but I came back in a large river-boat, down to the gunwales with the results of my thrown feet. Of course I kept all the money I had collected, though I paid the boat-hire; also I took my pick of the underwear, socks, cast-off clothes, shirts, "kicks," and "sky-pieces"; and when Company M had taken all it wanted there was still a respectable heap that was turned over to Company L. Alas, I was young and prodigal in those days! I told a thousand "stories" to the good people of Quincy, and every story was "good"; but since I have come to write for the magazines I have often regretted the wealth of story, the fecundity of fiction, I lavished that day in Quincy, Illinois.

It was at Hannibal, Missouri, that the ten invincibles went to pieces. It was not planned. We just naturally flew apart. The Boiler-Maker and I deserted secretly. On the same day Scotty and Davy made a swift sneak for the Illinois shore; also McAvoy and Fish achieved their get-away. This accounts for six of the ten; what became of the remaining four I do not know. As a sample of life on The Road, I make the following quotation from my diary of the several days following my desertion.

"Friday, May 25th. Boiler-Maker and I left the camp on the island. We went ashore on the Illinois side in a skiff and walked six miles on the C.B. & Q. to Fell Creek. We had gone six miles out of our way, but we got on a hand-car and rode six miles to Hull's, on the Wabash. While there, we met McAvoy, Fish, Scotty, and Davy, who had also pulled out from the Army.

"Saturday, May 26th. At 2.11 A.M. we caught the Cannon-ball as she slowed up at the crossing. Scotty and Davy were ditched. The four of us were ditched at the Bluffs, forty miles farther on. In the afternoon Fish and McAvoy caught a freight while Boiler-Maker and I were away getting something to eat.

"Sunday, May 27th. At 3.21 A.M. we caught the Cannon-ball and found Scotty and Davy on the blind. We were all ditched at daylight at Jacksonville. The C. & A. runs through here, and we're going to take that. Boiler-Maker went off, but didn't return. Guess he caught a freight.

"Monday, May 28th. Boiler-Maker didn't show up. Scotty

and Davy went off to sleep somewhere, and didn't get back
in time to catch the K.C. passenger at 3.30 A.M. I caught her
and rode her till after sunrise to Masson City, 25,000 inhabitants. Caught a cattle train and rode all night.

"Tuesday, May 29th. Arrived in Chicago at 7 A.M. . . ."

*   *   *

And years afterward, in China, I had the grief of learning
that the device we employed to navigate the rapids of the Des
Moines—the one-two-one-two, head-boat-tail-boat proposition—was not originated by us. I learned that the Chinese
river-boatmen had for thousands of years used a similar device to negotiate "bad water." It is a good stunt all right, even
if we don't get the credit. It answers Dr. Jordan's test of
truth: "Will it work? Will you trust your life to it?"

Bulls

IF THE TRAMP were suddenly to pass away from the United States, widespread misery for many families would follow. The tramp enables thousands of men to earn honest livings, educate their children, and bring them up God-fearing and industrious. I know. At one time my father was a constable and hunted tramps for a living. The community paid him so much per head for all the tramps he could catch, and also, I believe, he got mileage fees. Ways and means was always a pressing problem in our household, and the amount of meat on the table, the new pair of shoes, the day's outing, or the text-book for school, were dependent upon my father's luck in the chase. Well I remember the suppressed eagerness and the suspense with which I waited to learn each morning what the results of his past night's toil had been—how many tramps he had gathered in and what the chances were for convicting them. And so it was, when later, as a tramp, I succeeded in eluding some predatory constable, I could not but feel sorry for the little boys and girls at home in that constable's house; it seemed to me in a way that I was defrauding those little boys and girls of some of the good things of life.

But it's all in the game. The hobo defies society, and society's watch-dogs make a living out of him. Some hoboes like to be caught by the watch-dogs—especially in winter-time. Of course, such hoboes select communities where the jails are "good," wherein no work is performed and the food is substantial. Also, there have been, and most probably still are, constables who divide their fees with the hoboes they arrest. Such a constable does not have to hunt. He whistles, and the game comes right up to his hand. It is surprising, the money that is made out of stone-broke tramps. All through the South—at least when I was hoboing—are convict camps and plantations, where the time of convicted hoboes is bought by the farmers, and where the hoboes simply have to work. Then there are places like the quarries at Rutland, Vermont, where the hobo is exploited, the unearned energy in his body, which he has accumulated by "battering on the drag" or "slamming gates," being extracted for the benefit of that particular community.

Now I don't know anything about the quarries at Rutland, Vermont. I'm very glad that I don't, when I remember how near I was to getting into them. Tramps pass the word along, and I first heard of those quarries when I was in Indiana. But when I got into New England, I heard of them continually, and always with danger-signals flying. "They want men in the quarries," the passing hoboes said; "and they never give a 'stiff' less than ninety days." By the time I got into New Hampshire I was pretty well keyed up over those quarries, and I fought shy of railroad cops, "bulls," and constables as I never had before.

One evening I went down to the railroad yards at Concord and found a freight train made up and ready to start. I located an empty box-car, slid open the side-door, and climbed in. It was my hope to win across to White River by morning; that would bring me into Vermont and not more than a thousand miles from Rutland. But after that, as I worked north, the distance between me and the point of danger would begin to increase. In the car I found a "gay-cat," who displayed unusual trepidation at my entrance. He took me for a "shack" (brakeman), and when he learned I was only a stiff, he began talking about the quarries at Rutland as the cause of the fright I had given him. He was a young country fellow, and had beaten his way only over local stretches of road.

The freight got under way, and we lay down in one end of the box-car and went to sleep. Two or three hours afterward, at a stop, I was awakened by the noise of the right-hand door being softly slid open. The gay-cat slept on. I made no movement, though I veiled my eyes with my lashes to a little slit through which I could see out. A lantern was thrust in through the doorway, followed by the head of a shack. He discovered us, and looked at us for a moment. I was prepared for a violent expression on his part, or the customary "Hit the grit, you son of a toad!" Instead of this he cautiously withdrew the lantern and very, very softly slid the door to. This struck me as eminently unusual and suspicious. I listened, and softly I heard the hasp drop into place. The door was latched on the outside. We could not open it from the inside. One way of sudden exit from that car was blocked. It would never do. I waited a few seconds, then crept to the left-hand door and tried it. It was not yet latched. I opened it, dropped to the ground, and closed it behind me. Then I passed across the bumpers to the other side of the train. I opened the door the shack had latched, climbed in, and closed it behind me. Both exits were available again. The gay-cat was still asleep.

The train got under way. It came to the next stop. I heard footsteps in the gravel. Then the left-hand door was thrown open noisily. The gay-cat awoke, I made believe to awake; and we sat up and stared at the shack and his lantern. He didn't waste any time getting down to business.

"I want three dollars," he said.

We got on our feet and came nearer to him to confer. We expressed an absolute and devoted willingness to give him three dollars, but explained our wretched luck that compelled our desire to remain unsatisfied. The shack was incredulous. He dickered with us. He would compromise for two dollars. We regretted our condition of poverty. He said uncomplimentary things, called us sons of toads, and damned us from hell to breakfast. Then he threatened. He explained that if we didn't dig up, he'd lock us in and carry us on to White River and turn us over to the authorities. He also explained all about the quarries at Rutland.

Now that shack thought he had us dead to rights. Was not he guarding the one door, and had he not himself latched the opposite door but a few minutes before? When he began talking about quarries, the frightened gay-cat started to sidle across to the other door. The shack laughed loud and long. "Don't be in a hurry," he said; "I locked that door on the outside at the last stop." So implicitly did he believe the door to be locked that his words carried conviction. The gay-cat believed and was in despair.

The shack delivered his ultimatum. Either we should dig up two dollars, or he would lock us in and turn us over to the constable at White River—and that meant ninety days and the quarries. Now, gentle reader, just suppose that the other door had been locked. Behold the precariousness of human life. For lack of a dollar, I'd have gone to the quarries and served three months as a convict slave. So would the gay-cat. Count me out, for I was hopeless; but consider the gay-cat. He might have come out, after those ninety days, pledged to a life of crime. And later he might have broken your skull, even your skull, with a blackjack in an endeavor to take possession of the money on your person—and if not your skull, then some other poor and unoffending creature's skull.

But the door was unlocked, and I alone knew it. The gay-cat and I begged for mercy. I joined in the pleading and wailing out of sheer cussedness, I suppose. But I did my best. I told a "story" that would have melted the heart of any mug; but it didn't melt the heart of that sordid money-grasper of a shack. When he became convinced that we didn't have any money, he slid the door shut and latched it, then lingered a moment on the chance that we had fooled him and that we would now offer him the two dollars.

Then it was that I let out a few links. I called *him* a son of a toad. I called him all the other things he had called me. And then I called him a few additional things. I came from the West, where men knew how to swear, and I wasn't going to let any mangy shack on a measly New England "jerk" put it over me in vividness and vigor of language. At first the shack tried to laugh it down. Then he made the mistake of attempting to reply. I let out a few more links, and I cut him to the raw and therein rubbed winged and flaming epithets. Nor was my fine frenzy all whim and literary; I was indignant at this vile creature, who, in default of a dollar, would consign me to three months of slavery. Furthermore, I had a sneaking idea that he got a "drag" out of the constable fees.

But I fixed him. I lacerated his feelings and pride several dollars' worth. He tried to scare me by threatening to come in after me and kick the stuffing out of me. In return, I promised to kick him in the face while he was climbing in. The advantage of position was with me, and he saw it. So he kept the door shut and called for help from the rest of the train-crew. I could hear them answering and crunching through the gravel to him. And all the time the other door was un-latched, and they didn't know it; and in the meantime the gay-cat was ready to die with fear.

Oh, I was a hero—with my line of retreat straight behind me. I slanged the shack and his mates till they threw the door open and I could see their infuriated faces in the shine of the lanterns. It was all very simple to them. They had us cornered in the car, and they were going to come in and man-handle us. They started. I didn't kick anybody in the face. I jerked the opposite door open, and the gay-cat and I went out. The train-crew took after us.

We went over—if I remember correctly—a stone fence. But I have no doubts of recollection about where we found ourselves. In the darkness I promptly fell over a grave-stone. The gay-cat sprawled over another. And then we got the chase of our lives through that graveyard. The ghosts must have thought we were going some. So did the train-crew, for when we emerged from the graveyard and plunged across a road into a dark wood, the shacks gave up the pursuit and went back to their train. A little later that night the gay-cat and I found ourselves at the well of a farmhouse. We were after a drink of water, but we noticed a small rope that ran down one side of the well. We hauled it up and found on the end of it a gallon-can of cream. And that is as near as I got to the quarries of Rutland, Vermont.

When hoboes pass the word along, concerning a town, that "the bulls is horstile," avoid that town, or, if you must, go through softly. There are some towns that one must always go through softly. Such a town was Cheyenne, on the Union Pacific. It had a national reputation for being "horstile,"— and it was all due to the efforts of one Jeff Carr (if I remember his name aright). Jeff Carr could size up the "front" of a hobo on the instant. He never entered into discussion. In the one moment he sized up the hobo, and in the next he struck out with both fists, a club, or anything else he had handy. After he had man-handled the hobo, he started him out of town with a promise of worse if he ever saw him again. Jeff Carr knew the game. North, south, east, and west to the ut-termost confines of the United States (Canada and Mexico included), the man-handled hoboes carried the word that Cheyenne was "horstile." Fortunately, I never encountered Jeff Carr. I passed through Cheyenne in a blizzard. There were eighty-four hoboes with me at the time. The strength of numbers made us pretty nonchalant on most things, but not on Jeff Carr. The connotation of "Jeff Carr" stunned our imagination, numbed our virility, and the whole gang was mortally scared of meeting him.

It rarely pays to stop and enter into explanations with bulls when they look "horstile." A swift get-away is the thing to do. It took me some time to learn this; but the finishing touch was put upon me by a bull in New York City. Ever since that time it has been an automatic process with me to make a run for it when I see a bull reaching for me. This automatic process has become a mainspring of conduct in me, wound up and ready for instant release. I shall never get over it. Should I be eighty years old, hobbling along the street on crutches, and should a policeman suddenly reach out for me, I know I'd drop the crutches and run like a deer.

The finishing touch to my education in bulls was received on a hot summer afternoon in New York City. It was during a week of scorching weather. I had got into the habit of throwing my feet in the morning, and of spending the afternoon in the little park that is hard by Newspaper Row and the City Hall. It was near there that I could buy from push-cart men current books (that had been injured in the making or binding) for a few cents each. Then, right in the park itself, were little booths where one could buy glorious, ice-cold, sterilized milk and buttermilk at a penny a glass. Every afternoon I sat on a bench and read, and went on a milk debauch. I got away with from five to ten glasses each afternoon. It was dreadfully hot weather.

So here I was, a meek and studious milk-drinking hobo, and behold what I got for it. One afternoon I arrived at the park, a fresh book-purchase under my arm and a tremendous buttermilk thirst under my shirt. In the middle of the street, in front of the City Hall, I noticed, as I came along heading for the buttermilk booth, that a crowd had formed. It was right where I was crossing the street, so I stopped to see the cause of the collection of curious men. At first I could see nothing. Then, from the sounds I heard and from a glimpse I caught, I knew that it was a bunch of gamins playing pee-wee. Now pee-wee is not permitted in the streets of New

York. I didn't know that, but I learned pretty lively. I had paused possibly thirty seconds, in which time I had learned the cause of the crowd, when I heard a gamin yell "Bull!" The gamins knew their business. They ran. I didn't.

The crowd broke up immediately and started for the sidewalk on both sides of the street. I started for the sidewalk on the park-side. There must have been fifty men, who had been in the original crowd, who were heading in the same direction. We were loosely strung out. I noticed the bull, a strapping policeman in a gray suit. He was coming along the middle of the street, without haste, merely sauntering. I noticed casually that he changed his course, and was heading obliquely for the same sidewalk that I was heading for directly. He sauntered along, threading the strung-out crowd, and I noticed that his course and mine would cross each other. I was so innocent of wrong-doing that, in spite of my education in bulls and their ways, I apprehended nothing. I never dreamed that bull was after me. Out of my respect for the law I was actually all ready to pause the next moment and let him cross in front of me. The pause came all right, but it was not of my volition; also it was a backward pause. Without warning, that bull had suddenly launched out at me on the chest with both hands. At the same moment, verbally, he cast the bar sinister on my genealogy.

All my free American blood boiled. All my liberty-loving ancestors clamored in me. "What do you mean?" I demanded. You see, I wanted an explanation. And I got it. Bang! His club came down on top of my head, and I was reeling backward like a drunken man, the curious faces of the onlookers billowing up and down like the waves of the sea, my precious book falling from under my arm into the dirt, the bull advancing with the club ready for another blow. And in that dizzy moment I had a vision. I saw that club descending many times upon my head; I saw myself, bloody and battered and hard-looking, in a police-court; I heard a charge of disorderly conduct, profane language, resisting an officer, and a few other things, read by a clerk; and I saw myself across in Blackwell's Island. Oh, I knew the game. I lost all interest in explanations. I didn't stop to pick up my precious, unread book. I turned and ran. I was pretty sick, but I ran. And run I shall, to my dying day, whenever a bull begins to explain with a club.

Why, years after my tramping days, when I was a student in the University of California, one night I went to the circus. After the show and the concert I lingered on to watch the working of the transportation machinery of a great circus. The circus was leaving that night. By a bonfire I came upon a bunch of small boys. There were about twenty of them, and as they talked with one another I learned that they were going to run away with the circus. Now the circus-men didn't want to be bothered with this mess of urchins, and a telephone to police headquarters had "coppered" the play. A squad of ten policemen had been despatched to the scene to arrest the small boys for violating the nine o'clock curfew ordinance. The policemen surrounded the bonfire, and crept up close to it in the darkness. At the signal, they made a rush, each policeman grabbing at the youngsters as he would grab into a basket of squirming eels.

Now I didn't know anything about the coming of the police; and when I saw the sudden eruption of brass-buttoned, helmeted bulls, each of them reaching with both hands, all the forces and stability of my being were overthrown. Remained only the automatic process to run. And I ran. I didn't know I was running. I didn't know anything. It was, as I have said, automatic. There was no reason for me to run. I was not a hobo. I was a citizen of that community. It was my home town. I was guilty of no wrong-doing. I was a college man. I had even got my name in the papers, and I wore good clothes that had never been slept in. And yet I ran—blindly, madly, like a startled deer, for over a block. And when I came to myself, I noted that I was still running. It required a positive effort of will to stop those legs of mine.

No, I'll never get over it. I can't help it. When a bull reaches, I run. Besides, I have an unhappy faculty for getting into jail. I have been in jail more times since I was a hobo than when I was one. I start out on a Sunday morning with a young lady on a bicycle ride. Before we can get outside the city limits we are arrested for passing a pedestrian on the sidewalk. I resolve to be more careful. The next time I am on a

bicycle it is night-time and my acetylene-gas-lamp is misbe-
having. I cherish the sickly flame carefully, because of the ordinance. I am in a hurry, but I ride at a snail's pace so as not
to jar out the flickering flame. I reach the city limits; I am
beyond the jurisdiction of the ordinance; and I proceed to
scorch to make up for lost time. And half a mile farther on I
am "pinched" by a bull, and the next morning I forfeit my
bail in the police court. The city had treacherously extended
its limits into a mile of the country, and I didn't know, that
was all. I remember my inalienable right of free speech and
peaceable assemblage, and I get up on a soap-box to trot out
the particular economic bees that buzz in my bonnet, and a
bull takes me off that box and leads me to the city prison, and
after that I get out on bail. It's no use. In Korea I used to be
arrested about every other day. It was the same thing in Manchuria. The last time I was in Japan I broke into jail under
the pretext of being a Russian spy. It wasn't my pretext, but
it got me into jail just the same. There is no hope for me.
I am fated to do the Prisoner-of-Chillon stunt yet. This is
prophecy.

I once hypnotized a bull on Boston Common. It was past
midnight and he had me dead to rights; but before I got done
with him he had ponied up a silver quarter and given me the
address of an all-night restaurant. Then there was a bull in
Bristol, New Jersey, who caught me and let me go, and
heaven knows he had provocation enough to put me in jail.
I hit him the hardest I'll wager he was ever hit in his life. It
happened this way. About midnight I nailed a freight out of
Philadelphia. The shacks ditched me. She was pulling out
slowly through the maze of tracks and switches of the freight-
yards. I nailed her again, and again I was ditched. You see, I
had to nail her "outside," for she was a through freight with
every door locked and sealed.

The second time I was ditched the shack gave me a lecture.
He told me I was risking my life, that it was a fast freight and
that she went some. I told him I was used to going some
myself, but it was no go. He said he wouldn't permit me to
commit suicide, and I hit the grit. But I nailed her a third
time, getting in between on the bumpers. They were the most
meagre bumpers I had ever seen—I do not refer to the real

bumpers, the iron bumpers that are connected by the coupling-link and that pound and grind on each other; what I refer to are the beams, like huge cleats, that cross the ends of freight cars just above the bumpers. When one rides the bumpers, he stands on these cleats, one foot on each, the bumpers between his feet and just beneath.

But the beams or cleats I found myself on were not the broad, generous ones that at that time were usually on box-cars. On the contrary, they were very narrow—not more than an inch and a half in breadth. I couldn't get half of the width of my sole on them. Then there was nothing to which to hold with my hands. True, there were the ends of the two box-cars; but those ends were flat, perpendicular surfaces. There were no grips. I could only press the flats of my palms against the car-ends for support. But that would have been all right if the cleats for my feet had been decently wide.

As the freight got out of Philadelphia she began to hit up speed. Then I understood what the shack had meant by suicide. The freight went faster and faster. She was a through freight, and there was nothing to stop her. On that section of the Pennsylvania four tracks run side by side, and my east-bound freight didn't need to worry about passing west-bound freights, nor about being overtaken by east-bound expresses. She had the track to herself, and she used it. I was in a precarious situation. I stood with the mere edges of my feet on the narrow projections, the palms of my hands pressing desperately against the flat, perpendicular ends of each car. And those cars moved, and moved individually, up and down and back and forth. Did you ever see a circus rider, standing on two running horses, with one foot on the back of each horse? Well, that was what I was doing, with several differences. The circus rider had the reins to hold on to, while I had nothing; he stood on the broad soles of his feet, while I stood on the edges of mine; he bent his legs and body, gaining the strength of the arch in his posture and achieving the stability of a low centre of gravity, while I was compelled to stand upright and keep my legs straight; he rode face forward, while I was riding sidewise; and also, if he fell off, he'd get only a roll in the sawdust, while I'd have been ground to pieces beneath the wheels.

And that freight was certainly going some, roaring and shrieking, swinging madly around curves, thundering over trestles, one car-end bumping up when the other was jarring down, or jerking to the right at the same moment the other was lurching to the left, and with me all the while praying and hoping for the train to stop. But she didn't stop. She didn't have to. For the first, last, and only time on The Road, I got all I wanted. I abandoned the bumpers and managed to get out on a side-ladder; it was ticklish work, for I had never encountered car-ends that were so parsimonious of hand-holds and foot-holds as those car-ends were.

I heard the engine whistling, and I felt the speed easing down. I knew the train wasn't going to stop, but my mind was made up to chance it if she slowed down sufficiently. The right of way at this point took a curve, crossed a bridge over a canal, and cut through the town of Bristol. This combination compelled slow speed. I clung on to the side-ladder and waited. I didn't know it was the town of Bristol we were approaching. I did not know what necessitated slackening in speed. All I knew was that I wanted to get off. I strained my eyes in the darkness for a street-crossing on which to land. I was pretty well down the train, and before my car was in the town the engine was past the station and I could feel her making speed again.

Then came the street. It was too dark to see how wide it was or what was on the other side. I knew I needed all of that street if I was to remain on my feet after I struck. I dropped off on the near side. It sounds easy. By "dropped off" I mean just this: I first of all, on the side-ladder, thrust my body forward as far as I could in the direction the train was going—this to give as much space as possible in which to gain backward momentum when I swung off. Then I swung, swung out and backward, backward with all my might, and let go—at the same time throwing myself backward as if I intended to strike the ground on the back of my head. The whole effort was to overcome as much as possible the primary forward momentum the train had imparted to my body. When my feet hit the grit, my body was lying backward on the air at an angle of forty-five degrees. I had reduced the forward momentum some, for when my feet

struck, I did not immediately pitch forward on my face. Instead, my body rose to the perpendicular and began to incline
forward. In point of fact, my body proper still retained much
momentum, while my feet, through contact with the earth,
had lost all their momentum. This momentum the feet had
lost I had to supply anew by lifting them as rapidly as I could
and running them forward in order to keep them under my
forward-moving body. The result was that my feet beat a
rapid and explosive tattoo clear across the street. I didn't dare
stop them. If I had, I'd have pitched forward. It was up to
me to keep on going.

I was an involuntary projectile, worrying about what was
on the other side of the street and hoping that it wouldn't be
a stone wall or a telegraph pole. And just then I hit something. Horrors! I saw it just the instant before the disaster—
of all things, a bull, standing there in the darkness. We went
down together, rolling over and over; and the automatic process was such in that miserable creature that in the moment
of impact he reached out and clutched me and never let go.
We were both knocked out, and he held on to a very lamb-
like hobo while he recovered.

If that bull had any imagination, he must have thought me
a traveller from other worlds, the man from Mars just arriving; for in the darkness he hadn't seen me swing from the
train. In fact, his first words were: "Where did you come
from?" His next words, and before I had time to answer,
were: "I've a good mind to run you in." This latter, I am
convinced, was likewise automatic. He was a really good bull
at heart, for after I had told him a "story" and helped brush
off his clothes, he gave me until the next freight to get out of
town. I stipulated two things: first, that the freight be east-
bound, and second, that it should not be a through freight
with all doors sealed and locked. To this he agreed, and thus,
by the terms of the Treaty of Bristol, I escaped being pinched.

I remember another night, in that part of the country,
when I just missed another bull. If I had hit him, I'd have
telescoped him, for I was coming down from above, all holds
free, with several other bulls one jump behind and reaching
for me. This is how it happened. I had been lodging in a
livery stable in Washington. I had a box-stall and unnum-

bered horse-blankets all to myself. In return for such sumptuous accommodation I took care of a string of horses each
morning. I might have been there yet, if it hadn't been for
the bulls.

One evening, about nine o'clock, I returned to the stable
to go to bed, and found a crap game in full blast. It had been
a market day, and all the negroes had money. It would be
well to explain the lay of the land. The livery stable faced on
two streets. I entered the front, passed through the office, and
came to the alley between two rows of stalls that ran the
length of the building and opened out on the other street.
Midway along this alley, beneath a gas-jet and between the
rows of horses, were about forty negroes. I joined them as an
onlooker. I was broke and couldn't play. A coon was making
passes and not dragging down. He was riding his luck, and
with each pass the total stake doubled. All kinds of money lay
on the floor. It was fascinating. With each pass, the chances
increased tremendously against the coon making another
pass. The excitement was intense. And just then there came a
thundering smash on the big doors that opened on the back
street.

A few of the negroes bolted in the opposite direction. I
paused from my flight a moment to grab at the all kinds of
money on the floor. This wasn't theft: it was merely custom.
Every man who hadn't run was grabbing. The doors crashed
open and swung in, and through them surged a squad of
bulls. We surged the other way. It was dark in the office, and
the narrow door would not permit all of us to pass out to the
street at the same time. Things became congested. A coon
took a dive through the window, taking the sash along with
him and followed by other coons. At our rear, the bulls were
nailing prisoners. A big coon and myself made a dash at the
door at the same time. He was bigger than I, and he pivoted
me and got through first. The next instant a club swatted him
on the head and he went down like a steer. Another squad of
bulls was waiting outside for us. They knew they couldn't
stop the rush with their hands, and so they were swinging
their clubs. I stumbled over the fallen coon who had pivoted
me, ducked a swat from a club, dived between a bull's legs,
and was free. And then how I ran! There was a lean mulatto

just in front of me, and I took his pace. He knew the town better than I did, and I knew that in the way he ran lay safety. But he, on the other hand, took me for a pursuing bull. He never looked around. He just ran. My wind was good, and I hung on to his pace and nearly killed him. In the end he stumbled weakly, went down on his knees, and surrendered to me. And when he discovered I wasn't a bull, all that saved me was that he didn't have any wind left in him.

That was why I left Washington—not on account of the mulatto, but on account of the bulls. I went down to the depot and caught the first blind out on a Pennsylvania Railroad express. After the train got good and under way and I noted the speed she was making, a misgiving smote me. This was a four-track railroad, and the engines took water on the fly. Hoboes had long since warned me never to ride the first blind on trains where the engines took water on the fly. And now let me explain. Between the tracks are shallow metal troughs. As the engine, at full speed, passes above, a sort of chute drops down into the trough. The result is that all the water in the trough rushes up the chute and fills the tender.

Somewhere along between Washington and Baltimore, as I sat on the platform of the blind, a fine spray began to fill the air. It did no harm. Ah, ha, thought I; it's all a bluff, this taking water on the fly being bad for the bo on the first blind. What does this little spray amount to? Then I began to marvel at the device. This *was* railroading! Talk about your primitive Western railroading—and just then the tender filled up, and it hadn't reached the end of the trough. A tidal wave of water poured over the back of the tender and down upon me. I was soaked to the skin, as wet as if I had fallen overboard.

The train pulled into Baltimore. As is the custom in the great Eastern cities, the railroad ran beneath the level of the streets on the bottom of a big "cut." As the train pulled into the lighted depot, I made myself as small as possible on the blind. But a railroad bull saw me, and gave chase. Two more joined him. I was past the depot, and I ran straight on down the track. I was in a sort of trap. On each side of me rose the steep walls of the cut, and if I ever essayed them and failed, I knew that I'd slide back into the clutches of the bulls. I ran on and on, studying the walls of the cut for a favorable place

to climb up. At last I saw such a place. It came just after I
had passed under a bridge that carried a level street across the
cut. Up the steep slope I went, clawing hand and foot. The
three railroad bulls were clawing up right after me.

At the top, I found myself in a vacant lot. On one side was
a low wall that separated it from the street. There was no
time for minute investigation. They were at my heels. I
headed for the wall and vaulted it. And right there was where
I got the surprise of my life. One is used to thinking that one
side of a wall is just as high as the other side. But that wall
was different. You see, the vacant lot was much higher than
the level of the street. On my side the wall was low, but on
the other side—well, as I came soaring over the top, all holds
free, it seemed to me that I was falling feet-first, plump into
an abyss. There beneath me, on the sidewalk, under the light
of a street-lamp was a bull. I guess it was nine or ten feet
down to the sidewalk; but in the shock of surprise in mid-air
it seemed twice that distance.

I straightened out in the air and came down. At first I
thought I was going to land on the bull. My clothes did
brush him as my feet struck the sidewalk with explosive impact. It was a wonder he didn't drop dead, for he hadn't
heard me coming. It was the man-from-Mars stunt over
again. The bull did jump. He shied away from me like a horse
from an auto; and then he reached for me. I didn't stop to
explain. I left that to my pursuers, who were dropping over
the wall rather gingerly. But I got a chase all right. I ran up
one street and down another, dodged around corners, and at
last got away.

After spending some of the coin I'd got from the crap game
and killing off an hour of time, I came back to the railroad
cut, just outside the lights of the depot, and waited for a
train. My blood had cooled down, and I shivered miserably,
what of my wet clothes. At last a train pulled into the station.
I lay low in the darkness, and successfully boarded her when
she pulled out, taking good care this time to make the second
blind. No more water on the fly in mine. The train ran forty
miles to the first stop. I got off in a lighted depot that was
strangely familiar. I was back in Washington. In some way,
during the excitement of the get-away in Baltimore, running

through strange streets, dodging and turning and retracing, I had got turned around. I had taken the train out the wrong way. I had lost a night's sleep, I had been soaked to the skin, I had been chased for my life; and for all my pains I was back where I had started. Oh, no, life on The Road is not all beer and skittles. But I didn't go back to the livery stable. I had done some pretty successful grabbing, and I didn't want to reckon up with the coons. So I caught the next train out, and ate my breakfast in Baltimore.

THE IRON HEEL

"At first, this Earth, a stage so gloomed with woe
  You almost sicken at the shifting of the scenes.
And yet be patient. Our Playwright may show
  In some fifth act what this Wild Drama means."

Contents

FOREWORD 319

I *My Eagle* 323

II *Challenges* 337

III *Jackson's Arm* 350

IV *Slaves of the Machine* 360

V *The Philomaths* 368

VI *Adumbrations* 386

VII *The Bishop's Vision* 393

VIII *The Machine Breakers* 399

IX *The Mathematics of a Dream* 413

X *The Vortex* 428

XI *The Great Adventure* 437

XII *The Bishop* 444

XIII *The General Strike* 454

XIV *The Beginning of the End* 463

XV *Last Days* 471

XVI *The End* 477

XVII *The Scarlet Livery* 486

XVIII *In the Shadow of Sonoma* 494

XIX *Transformation* 502

XX *A Lost Oligarch* 510

XXI *The Roaring Abysmal Beast* 517

XXII *The Chicago Commune* 523

XXIII *The People of the Abyss* 534

XXIV *Nightmare* 546

XXV *The Terrorists* 552

Foreword

IT CANNOT be said that the Everhard Manuscript is an important historical document. To the historian it bristles with errors—not errors of fact, but errors of interpretation. Looking back across the seven centuries that have lapsed since Avis Everhard completed her manuscript, events, and the bearings of events, that were confused and veiled to her, are clear to us. She lacked perspective. She was too close to the events she writes about. Nay, she was merged in the events she has described.

Nevertheless, as a personal document, the Everhard Manuscript is of inestimable value. But here again enter error of perspective, and vitiation due to the bias of love. Yet we smile, indeed, and forgive Avis Everhard for the heroic lines upon which she modelled her husband. We know to-day that he was not so colossal, and that he loomed among the events of his times less largely than the Manuscript would lead us to believe.

We know that Ernest Everhard was an exceptionally strong man, but not so exceptional as his wife thought him to be. He was, after all, but one of a large number of heroes who, throughout the world, devoted their lives to the Revolution; though it must be conceded that he did unusual work, especially in his elaboration and interpretation of working-class philosophy. "Proletarian science" and "proletarian philosophy" were his phrases for it, and therein he shows the provincialism of his mind—a defect, however, that was due to the times and that none in that day could escape.

But to return to the Manuscript. Especially valuable is it in communicating to us the *feel* of those terrible times. Nowhere do we find more vividly portrayed the psychology of the persons that lived in that turbulent period embraced between the years 1912 and 1932—their mistakes and ignorance, their doubts and fears and misapprehensions, their ethical delusions, their violent passions, their inconceivable sordidness and selfishness. These are the things that are so hard for us of this enlightened age to understand. History tells us that these things were, and biology and psychology tell us why they were; but history and biology and psychology do not make these things alive. We accept them as facts, but we are left without sympathetic comprehension of them.

This sympathy comes to us, however, as we peruse the Everhard Manuscript. We enter into the minds of the actors in that long-ago world-drama, and for the time being their mental processes are our mental processes. Not alone do we understand Avis Everhard's love for her hero-husband, but we feel, as he felt, in those first days, the vague and terrible loom of the Oligarchy. The Iron Heel (well named) we feel descending upon and crushing mankind.

And in passing we note that that historic phrase, the Iron Heel, originated in Ernest Everhard's mind. This, we may say, is the one moot question that this new-found document clears up. Previous to this, the earliest-known use of the phrase occurred in the pamphlet, "Ye Slaves," written by George Milford and published in December, 1912. This George Milford was an obscure agitator about whom nothing is known, save the one additional bit of information gained from the Manuscript, which mentions that he was shot in the Chicago Commune. Evidently he had heard Ernest Everhard make use of the phrase in some public speech, most probably when he was running for Congress in the fall of 1912. From the Manuscript we learn that Everhard used the phrase at a private dinner in the spring of 1912. This is, without discussion, the earliest-known occasion on which the Oligarchy was so designated.

The rise of the Oligarchy will always remain a cause of secret wonder to the historian and the philosopher. Other great historical events have their place in social evolution. They were inevitable. Their coming could have been predicted with the same certitude that astronomers to-day predict the outcome of the movements of stars. Without these other great historical events, social evolution could not have proceeded. Primitive communism, chattel slavery, serf slavery, and wage slavery were necessary stepping-stones in the evolution of society. But it were ridiculous to assert that the Iron Heel was a necessary stepping-stone. Rather, to-day, is it adjudged a step aside, or a step backward, to the social tyrannies that made the early world a hell, but that were as necessary as the Iron Heel was unnecessary.

Black as Feudalism was, yet the coming of it was inevitable. What else than Feudalism could have followed upon the breakdown of that great centralized governmental machine known as the Roman Empire? Not so, however, with the Iron Heel. In the orderly procedure of social evolution there was no place for it. It was not necessary, and it was not inevitable. It must always remain the great curiosity of history—a whim, a fantasy, an apparition, a thing unexpected and undreamed; and it should serve as a warning to those rash political theorists of to-day who speak with certitude of social processes.

Capitalism was adjudged by the sociologists of the time to be the culmination of bourgeois rule, the ripened fruit of the bourgeois revolution. And we of to-day can but applaud that judgment. Following upon Capitalism, it was held, even by such intellectual and antagonistic giants as Herbert Spencer, that Socialism would come. Out of the decay of self-seeking capitalism, it was held, would arise that flower of the ages, the Brotherhood of Man. Instead of which, appalling alike to us who look back and to those that lived at the time, capitalism, rotten-ripe, sent forth that monstrous offshoot, the Oligarchy.

Too late did the socialist movement of the early twentieth century divine the coming of the Oligarchy. Even as it was divined, the Oligarchy was there—a fact established in blood, a stupendous and awful reality. Nor even then, as the Everhard Manuscript well shows, was any permanence attributed to the Iron Heel. Its overthrow was a matter of a few short years, was the judgment of the revolutionists. It is true, they realized that the Peasant Revolt was unplanned, and that the First Revolt was premature; but they little realized that the Second Revolt, planned and mature, was doomed to equal futility and more terrible punishment.

It is apparent that Avis Everhard completed the Manuscript during the last days of preparation for the Second Revolt; hence the fact that there is no mention of the disastrous outcome of the Second Revolt. It is quite clear that she intended the Manuscript for immediate publication, as soon as the Iron

Heel was overthrown, so that her husband, so recently dead, should receive full credit for all that he had ventured and accomplished. Then came the frightful crushing of the Second Revolt, and it is probable that in the moment of danger, ere she fled or was captured by the Mercenaries, she hid the Manuscript in the hollow oak at Wake Robin Lodge.

Of Avis Everhard there is no further record. Undoubtedly she was executed by the Mercenaries; and, as is well known, no record of such executions was kept by the Iron Heel. But little did she realize, even then, as she hid the Manuscript and prepared to flee, how terrible had been the breakdown of the Second Revolt. Little did she realize that the tortuous and distorted evolution of the next three centuries would compel a Third Revolt and a Fourth Revolt, and many Revolts, all drowned in seas of blood, ere the world-movement of labor should come into its own. And little did she dream that for seven long centuries the tribute of her love to Ernest Everhard would repose undisturbed in the heart of the ancient oak at Wake Robin Lodge.

ANTHONY MEREDITH.

Ardis,
November 27, 419 B.O.M.

I

My Eagle

THE soft summer wind stirs the redwoods, and Wild-Water ripples sweet cadences over its mossy stones. There are butterflies in the sunshine, and from everywhere arises the drowsy hum of bees. It is so quiet and peaceful, and I sit here, and ponder, and am restless. It is the quiet that makes me restless. It seems unreal. All the world is quiet, but it is the quiet before the storm. I strain my ears, and all my senses, for some betrayal of that impending storm. Oh, that it may not be premature! That it may not be premature![1]

Small wonder that I am restless. I think, and think, and I cannot cease from thinking. I have been in the thick of life so long that I am oppressed by the peace and quiet, and I cannot forbear from dwelling upon that mad maelstrom of death and destruction so soon to burst forth. In my ears are the cries of the stricken; and I can see, as I have seen in the past,[2] all the marring and mangling of the sweet, beautiful flesh, and the souls torn with violence from proud bodies and hurled to God. Thus do we poor humans attain our ends, striving through carnage and destruction to bring lasting peace and happiness upon the earth.

And then I am lonely. When I do not think of what is to come, I think of what has been and is no more—my Eagle, beating with tireless wings the void, soaring toward what was ever his sun, the flaming ideal of human freedom. I cannot sit idly by and wait the great event that is his making, though he is not here to see. He devoted all the years of his manhood

[1] The Second Revolt was largely the work of Ernest Everhard, though he coöperated, of course, with the European leaders. The capture and secret execution of Everhard was the great event of the spring of 1932 A.D. Yet so thoroughly had he prepared for the revolt, that his fellow-conspirators were able, with little confusion or delay, to carry out his plans. It was after Everhard's execution that his wife went to Wake Robin Lodge, a small bungalow in the Sonoma Hills of California.

[2] Without doubt she here refers to the Chicago Commune.

to it, and for it he gave his life. It is his handiwork. He made it.[1]

And so it is, in this anxious time of waiting, that I shall write of my husband. There is much light that I alone of all persons living can throw upon his character, and so noble a character cannot be blazoned forth too brightly. His was a great soul, and, when my love grows unselfish, my chiefest regret is that he is not here to witness to-morrow's dawn. We cannot fail. He has built too stoutly and too surely for that. Woe to the Iron Heel! Soon shall it be thrust back from off prostrate humanity. When the word goes forth, the labor hosts of all the world shall rise. There has been nothing like it in the history of the world. The solidarity of labor is assured, and for the first time will there be an international revolution wide as the world is wide.[2]

You see, I am full of what is impending. I have lived it day and night utterly and for so long that it is ever present in my mind. For that matter, I cannot think of my husband without thinking of it. He was the soul of it, and how can I possibly separate the two in thought?

As I have said, there is much light that I alone can throw upon his character. It is well known that he toiled hard for liberty and suffered sore. How hard he toiled and how greatly he suffered, I well know; for I have been with him during these twenty anxious years and I know his patience, his untiring effort, his infinite devotion to the Cause for which, only two months gone, he laid down his life.

I shall try to write simply and to tell here how Ernest Ever-

---

[1] With all respect to Avis Everhard, it must be pointed out that Everhard was but one of many able leaders who planned the Second Revolt. And we, to-day, looking back across the centuries, can safely say that even had he lived, the Second Revolt would not have been less calamitous in its outcome than it was.

[2] The Second Revolt was truly international. It was a colossal plan—too colossal to be wrought by the genius of one man alone. Labor, in all the oligarchies of the world, was prepared to rise at the signal. Germany, Italy, France, and all Australasia were labor countries—socialist states. They were ready to lend aid to the revolution. Gallantly they did; and it was for this reason, when the Second Revolt was crushed, that they, too, were crushed by the united oligarchies of the world, their socialist governments being replaced by oligarchical governments.

hard entered my life—how I first met him, how he grew until I became a part of him, and the tremendous changes he wrought in my life. In this way may you look at him through my eyes and learn him as I learned him—in all save the things too secret and sweet for me to tell.

It was in February, 1912, that I first met him, when, as a guest of my father's[1] at dinner, he came to our house in Berkeley. I cannot say that my very first impression of him was favorable. He was one of many at dinner, and in the drawing-room where we gathered and waited for all to arrive, he made a rather incongruous appearance. It was "preacher's night," as my father privately called it, and Ernest was certainly out of place in the midst of the churchmen.

In the first place, his clothes did not fit him. He wore a ready-made suit of dark cloth that was ill adjusted to his body. In fact, no ready-made suit of clothes ever could fit his body. And on this night, as always, the cloth bulged with his muscles, while the coat between the shoulders, what of the heavy shoulder-development, was a maze of wrinkles. His neck was the neck of a prize-fighter,[2] thick and strong. So this was the social philosopher and ex-horseshoer my father had discovered, was my thought. And he certainly looked it with those bulging muscles and that bull-throat. Immediately I classified him—a sort of prodigy, I thought, a Blind Tom[3] of the working class.

And then, when he shook hands with me! His handshake

[1] John Cunningham, Avis Everhard's father, was a professor at the State University at Berkeley, California. His chosen field was physics, and in addition he did much original research and was greatly distinguished as a scientist. His chief contribution to science was his studies of the electron and his monumental work on the "Identification of Matter and Energy," wherein he established, beyond cavil and for all time, that the ultimate unit of matter and the ultimate unit of force were identical. This idea had been earlier advanced, but not demonstrated, by Sir Oliver Lodge and other students in the new field of radio-activity.

[2] In that day it was the custom of men to compete for purses of money. They fought with their hands. When one was beaten into insensibility or killed, the survivor took the money.

[3] This obscure reference applies to a blind negro musician who took the world by storm in the latter half of the nineteenth century of the Christian Era.

was firm and strong, but he looked at me boldly with his black eyes—too boldly, I thought. You see, I was a creature of environment, and at that time had strong class instincts. Such boldness on the part of a man of my own class would have been almost unforgivable. I know that I could not avoid dropping my eyes, and I was quite relieved when I passed him on and turned to greet Bishop Morehouse—a favorite of mine, a sweet and serious man of middle age, Christ-like in appearance and goodness, and a scholar as well.

But this boldness that I took to be presumption was a vital clew to the nature of Ernest Everhard. He was simple, direct, afraid of nothing, and he refused to waste time on conventional mannerisms. "You pleased me," he explained long afterward; "and why should I not fill my eyes with that which pleases me?" I have said that he was afraid of nothing. He was a natural aristocrat—and this in spite of the fact that he was in the camp of the non-aristocrats. He was a superman, a blond beast such as Nietzsche[1] has described, and in addition he was aflame with democracy.

In the interest of meeting the other guests, and what of my unfavorable impression, I forgot all about the working-class philosopher, though once or twice at table I noticed him—especially the twinkle in his eye as he listened to the talk first of one minister and then of another. He has humor, I thought, and I almost forgave him his clothes. But the time went by, and the dinner went by, and he never opened his mouth to speak, while the ministers talked interminably about the working class and its relation to the church, and what the church had done and was doing for it. I noticed that my father was annoyed because Ernest did not talk. Once father took advantage of a lull and asked him to say something; but Ernest shrugged his shoulders and with an "I have nothing to say" went on eating salted almonds.

But father was not to be denied. After a while he said:

"We have with us a member of the working class. I am sure

[1] Friedrich Nietzsche, the mad philosopher of the nineteenth century of the Christian Era, who caught wild glimpses of truth, but who, before he was done, reasoned himself around the great circle of human thought and off into madness.

that he can present things from a new point of view that will
be interesting and refreshing. I refer to Mr. Everhard."

The others betrayed a well-mannered interest, and urged
Ernest for a statement of his views. Their attitude toward him
was so broadly tolerant and kindly that it was really patronizing. And I saw that Ernest noted it and was amused. He
looked slowly about him, and I saw the glint of laughter in
his eyes.

"I am not versed in the courtesies of ecclesiastical controversy," he began, and then hesitated with modesty and indecision.

"Go on," they urged, and Dr. Hammerfield said: "We do
not mind the truth that is in any man. If it is sincere," he
amended.

"Then you separate sincerity from truth?" Ernest laughed
quickly.

Dr. Hammerfield gasped, and managed to answer, "The
best of us may be mistaken, young man, the best of us."

Ernest's manner changed on the instant. He became another man.

"All right, then," he answered; "and let me begin by saying
that you are all mistaken. You know nothing, and worse than
nothing, about the working class. Your sociology is as vicious
and worthless as is your method of thinking."

It was not so much what he said as how he said it. I roused
at the first sound of his voice. It was as bold as his eyes. It
was a clarion-call that thrilled me. And the whole table was
aroused, shaken alive from monotony and drowsiness.

"What is so dreadfully vicious and worthless in our method
of thinking, young man?" Dr. Hammerfield demanded, and
already there was something unpleasant in his voice and manner of utterance.

"You are metaphysicians. You can prove anything by metaphysics; and having done so, every metaphysician can prove
every other metaphysician wrong—to his own satisfaction.
You are anarchists in the realm of thought. And you are mad
cosmos-makers. Each of you dwells in a cosmos of his own
making, created out of his own fancies and desires. You do
not know the real world in which you live, and your thinking

has no place in the real world except in so far as it is phenomena of mental aberration.

"Do you know what I was reminded of as I sat at table and listened to you talk and talk? You reminded me for all the world of the scholastics of the Middle Ages who gravely and learnedly debated the absorbing question of how many angels could dance on the point of a needle. Why, my dear sirs, you are as remote from the intellectual life of the twentieth century as an Indian medicine-man making incantation in the primeval forest ten thousand years ago."

As Ernest talked he seemed in a fine passion; his face glowed, his eyes snapped and flashed, and his chin and jaw were eloquent with aggressiveness. But it was only a way he had. It always aroused people. His smashing, sledge-hammer manner of attack invariably made them forget themselves. And they were forgetting themselves now. Bishop Morehouse was leaning forward and listening intently. Exasperation and anger were flushing the face of Dr. Hammerfield. And others were exasperated, too, and some were smiling in an amused and superior way. As for myself, I found it most enjoyable. I glanced at father, and I was afraid he was going to giggle at the effect of this human bombshell he had been guilty of launching amongst us.

"Your terms are rather vague," Dr. Hammerfield interrupted. "Just precisely what do you mean when you call us metaphysicians?"

"I call you metaphysicians because you reason metaphysically," Ernest went on. "Your method of reasoning is the opposite to that of science. There is no validity to your conclusions. You can prove everything and nothing, and no two of you can agree upon anything. Each of you goes into his own consciousness to explain himself and the universe. As well may you lift yourselves by your own bootstraps as to explain consciousness by consciousness."

"I do not understand," Bishop Morehouse said. "It seems to me that all things of the mind are metaphysical. That most exact and convincing of all sciences, mathematics, is sheerly metaphysical. Each and every thought-process of the scientific reasoner is metaphysical. Surely you will agree with me?"

"As you say, you do not understand," Ernest replied. "The

metaphysician reasons deductively out of his own subjectivity. The scientist reasons inductively from the facts of experience. The metaphysician reasons from theory to facts, the scientist reasons from facts to theory. The metaphysician explains the universe by himself, the scientist explains himself by the universe."

"Thank God we are not scientists," Dr. Hammerfield murmured complacently.

"What are you then?" Ernest demanded.

"Philosophers."

"There you go," Ernest laughed. "You have left the real and solid earth and are up in the air with a word for a flying machine. Pray come down to earth and tell me precisely what you do mean by philosophy."

"Philosophy is—" (Dr. Hammerfield paused and cleared his throat)—"something that cannot be defined comprehensively except to such minds and temperaments as are philosophical. The narrow scientist with his nose in a test-tube cannot understand philosophy."

Ernest ignored the thrust. It was always his way to turn the point back upon an opponent, and he did it now, with a beaming brotherliness of face and utterance.

"Then you will undoubtedly understand the definition I shall now make of philosophy. But before I make it, I shall challenge you to point out error in it or to remain a silent metaphysician. Philosophy is merely the widest science of all. Its reasoning method is the same as that of any particular science and of all particular sciences. And by that same method of reasoning, the inductive method, philosophy fuses all particular sciences into one great science. As Spencer says, the data of any particular science are partially unified knowledge. Philosophy unifies the knowledge that is contributed by all the sciences. Philosophy is the science of science, the master science, if you please. How do you like my definition?"

"Very creditable, very creditable," Dr. Hammerfield muttered lamely.

But Ernest was merciless.

"Remember," he warned, "my definition is fatal to metaphysics. If you do not now point out a flaw in my definition, you are disqualified later on from advancing metaphysical arguments. You must go through life seeking that flaw and remaining metaphysically silent until you have found it."

Ernest waited. The silence was painful. Dr. Hammerfield was pained. He was also puzzled. Ernest's sledge-hammer attack disconcerted him. He was not used to the simple and direct method of controversy. He looked appealingly around the table, but no one answered for him. I caught father grinning into his napkin.

"There is another way of disqualifying the metaphysicians," Ernest said, when he had rendered Dr. Hammerfield's discomfiture complete. "Judge them by their works. What have they done for mankind beyond the spinning of airy fancies and the mistaking of their own shadows for gods? They have added to the gayety of mankind, I grant; but what tangible good have they wrought for mankind? They philosophized, if you will pardon my misuse of the word, about the heart as the seat of the emotions, while the scientists were formulating the circulation of the blood. They declaimed about famine and pestilence as being scourges of God, while the scientists were building granaries and draining cities. They builded gods in their own shapes and out of their own desires, while the scientists were building roads and bridges. They were describing the earth as the centre of the universe, while the scientists were discovering America and probing space for the stars and the laws of the stars. In short, the metaphysicians have done nothing, absolutely nothing, for mankind. Step by step, before the advance of science, they have been driven back. As fast as the ascertained facts of science have overthrown their subjective explanations of things, they have made new subjective explanations of things, including explanations of the latest ascertained facts. And this, I doubt not, they will go on doing to the end of time. Gentlemen, a metaphysician is a medicine man. The difference between you and the Eskimo who makes a fur-clad blubber-eating god is merely a difference of several thousand years of ascertained facts. That is all."

"Yet the thought of Aristotle ruled Europe for twelve centuries," Dr. Ballingford announced pompously. "And Aristotle was a metaphysician."

Dr. Ballingford glanced around the table and was rewarded by nods and smiles of approval.

"Your illustration is most unfortunate," Ernest replied. "You refer to a very dark period in human history. In fact, we call that period the Dark Ages. A period wherein science was raped by the metaphysicians, wherein physics became a search for the Philosopher's Stone, wherein chemistry became alchemy, and astronomy became astrology. Sorry the domination of Aristotle's thought!"

Dr. Ballingford looked pained, then he brightened up and said:

"Granted this horrible picture you have drawn, yet you must confess that metaphysics was inherently potent in so far as it drew humanity out of this dark period and on into the illumination of the succeeding centuries."

"Metaphysics had nothing to do with it," Ernest retorted.

"What?" Dr. Hammerfield cried. "It was not the thinking and the speculation that led to the voyages of discovery?"

"Ah, my dear sir," Ernest smiled, "I thought you were disqualified. You have not yet picked out the flaw in my definition of philosophy. You are now on an unsubstantial basis. But it is the way of the metaphysicians, and I forgive you. No, I repeat, metaphysics had nothing to do with it. Bread and butter, silks and jewels, dollars and cents, and, incidentally, the closing up of the overland trade-routes to India, were the things that caused the voyages of discovery. With the fall of Constantinople, in 1453, the Turks blocked the way of the caravans to India. The traders of Europe had to find another route. Here was the original cause for the voyages of discovery. Columbus sailed to find a new route to the Indies. It is so stated in all the history books. Incidentally, new facts were learned about the nature, size, and form of the earth, and the Ptolemaic system went glimmering."

Dr. Hammerfield snorted.

"You do not agree with me?" Ernest queried. "Then wherein am I wrong?"

"I can only reaffirm my position," Dr. Hammerfield retorted tartly. "It is too long a story to enter into now."

"No story is too long for the scientist," Ernest said sweetly. "That is why the scientist gets to places. That is why he got to America."

I shall not describe the whole evening, though it is a joy to me to recall every moment, every detail, of those first hours of my coming to know Ernest Everhard.

Battle royal raged, and the ministers grew red-faced and excited, especially at the moments when Ernest called them romantic philosophers, shadow-projectors, and similar things. And always he checked them back to facts. "The fact, man, the irrefragable fact!" he would proclaim triumphantly, when he had brought one of them a cropper. He bristled with facts. He tripped them up with facts, ambuscaded them with facts, bombarded them with broadsides of facts.

"You seem to worship at the shrine of fact," Dr. Hammerfield taunted him.

"There is no God but Fact, and Mr. Everhard is its prophet," Dr. Ballingford paraphrased.

Ernest smilingly acquiesced.

"I'm like the man from Texas," he said. And, on being solicited, he explained. "You see, the man from Missouri always says, 'You've got to show me.' But the man from Texas says, 'You've got to put it in my hand.' From which it is apparent that he is no metaphysician."

Another time, when Ernest had just said that the metaphysical philosophers could never stand the test of truth, Dr. Hammerfield suddenly demanded:

"What is the test of truth, young man? Will you kindly explain what has so long puzzled wiser heads than yours?"

"Certainly," Ernest answered. His cocksureness irritated them. "The wise heads have puzzled so sorely over truth because they went up into the air after it. Had they remained on the solid earth, they would have found it easily enough—ay, they would have found that they themselves were precisely testing truth with every practical act and thought of their lives."

"The test, the test," Dr. Hammerfield repeated impatiently. "Never mind the preamble. Give us that which we have sought so long—the test of truth. Give it us, and we will be as gods."

There was an impolite and sneering scepticism in his words and manner that secretly pleased most of them at the table, though it seemed to bother Bishop Morehouse.

"Dr. Jordan[1] has stated it very clearly," Ernest said. "His test of truth is: 'Will it work? Will you trust your life to it?'"

"Pish!" Dr. Hammerfield sneered. "You have not taken Bishop Berkeley[2] into account. He has never been answered."

"The noblest metaphysician of them all," Ernest laughed. "But your example is unfortunate. As Berkeley himself attested, his metaphysics didn't work."

Dr. Hammerfield was angry, righteously angry. It was as though he had caught Ernest in a theft or a lie.

"Young man," he trumpeted, "that statement is on a par with all you have uttered to-night. It is a base and unwarranted assumption."

"I am quite crushed," Ernest murmured meekly. "Only I don't know what hit me. You'll have to put it in my hand, Doctor."

"I will, I will," Dr. Hammerfield spluttered. "How do you know? You do not know that Bishop Berkeley attested that his metaphysics did not work. You have no proof. Young man, they have always worked."

"I take it as proof that Berkeley's metaphysics did not work, because—" Ernest paused calmly for a moment. "Because Berkeley made an invariable practice of going through doors instead of walls. Because he trusted his life to solid bread and butter and roast beef. Because he shaved himself with a razor that worked when it removed the hair from his face."

"But those are actual things!" Dr. Hammerfield cried. "Metaphysics is of the mind."

[1] A noted educator of the late nineteenth and early twentieth centuries of the Christian Era. He was president of the Stanford University, a private benefaction of the times.

[2] An idealistic monist who long puzzled the philosophers of that time with his denial of the existence of matter, but whose clever argument was finally demolished when the new empiric facts of science were philosophically generalized.

"And they work—in the mind?" Ernest queried softly.

The other nodded.

"And even a multitude of angels can dance on the point of a needle—in the mind," Ernest went on reflectively. "And a blubber-eating, fur-clad god can exist and work—in the mind; and there are no proofs to the contrary—in the mind. I suppose, Doctor, you live in the mind?"

"My mind to me a kingdom is," was the answer.

"That's another way of saying that you live up in the air. But you come back to earth at meal-time, I am sure, or when an earthquake happens along. Or, tell me, Doctor, do you have no apprehension in an earthquake that that incorporeal body of yours will be hit by an immaterial brick?"

Instantly, and quite unconsciously, Dr. Hammerfield's hand shot up to his head, where a scar disappeared under the hair. It happened that Ernest had blundered on an apposite illustration. Dr. Hammerfield had been nearly killed in the Great Earthquake[1] by a falling chimney. Everybody broke out into roars of laughter.

"Well?" Ernest asked, when the merriment had subsided. "Proofs to the contrary?"

And in the silence he asked again, "Well?" Then he added, "Still well, but not so well, that argument of yours."

But Dr. Hammerfield was temporarily crushed, and the battle raged on in new directions. On point after point, Ernest challenged the ministers. When they affirmed that they knew the working class, he told them fundamental truths about the working class that they did not know, and challenged them for disproofs. He gave them facts, always facts, checked their excursions into the air, and brought them back to the solid earth and its facts.

How the scene comes back to me! I can hear him now, with that war-note in his voice, flaying them with his facts, each fact a lash that stung and stung again. And he was merciless. He took no quarter,[2] and gave none. I can never forget the flaying he gave them at the end:

[1] The Great Earthquake of 1906 A.D. that destroyed San Francisco.

[2] This figure arises from the customs of the times. When, among men fighting to the death in their wild-animal way, a beaten man threw down his weapons, it was at the option of the victor to slay him or spare him.

"You have repeatedly confessed to-night, by direct avowal or ignorant statement, that you do not know the working class. But you are not to be blamed for this. How can you know anything about the working class? You do not live in the same locality with the working class. You herd with the capitalist class in another locality. And why not? It is the capitalist class that pays you, that feeds you, that puts the very clothes on your backs that you are wearing here to-night. And in return you preach to your employers the brands of metaphysics that are especially acceptable to them; and the especially acceptable brands are acceptable because they do not menace the established order of society."

Here there was a stir of dissent around the table.

"Oh, I am not challenging your sincerity," Ernest continued. "You are sincere. You preach what you believe. There lies your strength and your value—to the capitalist class. But should you change your belief to something that menaces the established order, your preaching would be unacceptable to your employers, and you would be discharged. Every little while some one or another of you is so discharged.[2] Am I not right?"

This time there was no dissent. They sat dumbly acquiescent, with the exception of Dr. Hammerfield, who said:

"It is when their thinking is wrong that they are asked to resign."

"Which is another way of saying when their thinking is unacceptable," Ernest answered, and then went on. "So I say to you, go ahead and preach and earn your pay, but for goodness' sake leave the working class alone. You belong in the enemy's camp. You have nothing in common with the working class. Your hands are soft with the work others have performed for you. Your stomachs are round with the plenitude of eating." (Here Dr. Ballingford winced, and every eye glanced at his prodigious girth. It was said he had not seen his own feet in years.) "And your minds are filled with doctrines that are buttresses of the established order. You are as much mercenaries (sincere mercenaries, I grant) as were the

[2] During this period there were many ministers cast out of the church for preaching unacceptable doctrine. Especially were they cast out when their preaching became tainted with socialism.

men of the Swiss Guard.[1] Be true to your salt and your hire; guard, with your preaching, the interests of your employers; but do not come down to the working class and serve as false leaders. You cannot honestly be in the two camps at once. The working class has done without you. Believe me, the working class will continue to do without you. And, furthermore, the working class can do better without you than with you."

[1] The hired foreign palace guards of Louis XVI., a king of France that was beheaded by his people.

II

Challenges

AFTER THE GUESTS had gone, father threw himself into a chair and gave vent to roars of Gargantuan laughter. Not since the death of my mother had I known him to laugh so heartily.

"I'll wager Dr. Hammerfield was never up against anything like it in his life," he laughed. " 'The courtesies of ecclesiastical controversy!' Did you notice how he began like a lamb—Everhard, I mean, and how quickly he became a roaring lion? He has a splendidly disciplined mind. He would have made a good scientist if his energies had been directed that way."

I need scarcely say that I was deeply interested in Ernest Everhard. It was not alone what he had said and how he had said it, but it was the man himself. I had never met a man like him. I suppose that was why, in spite of my twenty-four years, I had not married. I liked him; I had to confess it to myself. And my like for him was founded on things beyond intellect and argument. Regardless of his bulging muscles and prize-fighter's throat, he impressed me as an ingenuous boy. I felt that under the guise of an intellectual swashbuckler was a delicate and sensitive spirit. I sensed this, in ways I knew not, save that they were my woman's intuitions.

There was something in that clarion-call of his that went to my heart. It still rang in my ears, and I felt that I should like to hear it again—and to see again that glint of laughter in his eyes that belied the impassioned seriousness of his face. And there were further reaches of vague and indeterminate feelings that stirred in me. I almost loved him then, though I am confident, had I never seen him again, that the vague feelings would have passed away and that I should easily have forgotten him.

But I was not destined never to see him again. My father's new-born interest in sociology and the dinner parties he gave would not permit. Father was not a sociologist. His marriage with my mother had been very happy, and in the researches

of his own science, physics, he had been very happy. But
when mother died, his own work could not fill the emptiness.
At first, in a mild way, he had dabbled in philosophy; then,
becoming interested, he had drifted on into economics and
sociology. He had a strong sense of justice, and he soon became fired with a passion to redress wrong. It was with gratitude that I hailed these signs of a new interest in life, though
I little dreamed what the outcome would be. With the enthusiasm of a boy he plunged excitedly into these new pursuits,
regardless of whither they led him.

He had been used always to the laboratory, and so it was
that he turned the dining room into a sociological laboratory.
Here came to dinner all sorts and conditions of men,—scientists, politicians, bankers, merchants, professors, labor leaders, socialists, and anarchists. He stirred them to discussion,
and analyzed their thoughts on life and society.

He had met Ernest shortly prior to the "preacher's night."
And after the guests were gone, I learned how he had met
him, passing down a street at night and stopping to listen to
a man on a soap-box who was addressing a crowd of workingmen. The man on the box was Ernest. Not that he was a
mere soap-box orator. He stood high in the councils of the
socialist party, was one of the leaders, and was the acknowledged leader in the philosophy of socialism. But he had a
certain clear way of stating the abstruse in simple language,
was a born expositor and teacher, and was not above the
soap-box as a means of interpreting economics to the workingmen.

My father stopped to listen, became interested, effected a
meeting, and, after quite an acquaintance, invited him to the
ministers' dinner. It was after the dinner that father told me
what little he knew about him. He had been born in the
working class, though he was a descendant of the old line of
Everhards that for over two hundred years had lived in America.[1] At ten years of age he had gone to work in the mills,
and later he served his apprenticeship and became a horse-
shoer. He was self-educated, had taught himself German and

---

[1] The distinction between being native born and foreign born was sharp
and invidious in those days.

French, and at that time was earning a meagre living by translating scientific and philosophical works for a struggling socialist publishing house in Chicago. Also, his earnings were
added to by the royalties from the small sales of his own economic and philosophic works.

This much I learned of him before I went to bed, and I lay
long awake, listening in memory to the sound of his voice. I
grew frightened at my thoughts. He was so unlike the men of
my own class, so alien and so strong. His masterfulness delighted me and terrified me, for my fancies wantonly roved
until I found myself considering him as a lover, as a husband.
I had always heard that the strength of men was an irresistible
attraction to women; but he was too strong. "No! no!" I
cried out. "It is impossible, absurd!" And on the morrow I
awoke to find in myself a longing to see him again. I wanted
to see him mastering men in discussion, the war-note in his
voice; to see him, in all his certitude and strength, shattering
their complacency, shaking them out of their ruts of thinking.
What if he did swashbuckle? To use his own phrase, "it
worked," it produced effects. And, besides, his swashbuckling
was a fine thing to see. It stirred one like the onset of battle.

Several days passed during which I read Ernest's books,
borrowed from my father. His written word was as his spoken word, clear and convincing. It was its absolute simplicity
that convinced even while one continued to doubt. He had
the gift of lucidity. He was the perfect expositor. Yet, in spite
of his style, there was much that I did not like. He laid too
great stress on what he called the class struggle, the antagonism between labor and capital, the conflict of interest.

Father reported with glee Dr. Hammerfield's judgment of
Ernest, which was to the effect that he was "an insolent
young puppy, made bumptious by a little and very inadequate
learning." Also, Dr. Hammerfield declined to meet Ernest
again.

But Bishop Morehouse turned out to have become interested in Ernest, and was anxious for another meeting. "A
strong young man," he said; "and very much alive, very much
alive. But he is too sure, too sure."

Ernest came one afternoon with father. The Bishop had

already arrived, and we were having tea on the veranda. Ernest's continued presence in Berkeley, by the way, was accounted for by the fact that he was taking special courses in biology at the university, and also that he was hard at work on a new book entitled "Philosophy and Revolution."[1]

The veranda seemed suddenly to have become small when Ernest arrived. Not that he was so very large—he stood only five feet nine inches; but that he seemed to radiate an atmosphere of largeness. As he stopped to meet me, he betrayed a certain slight awkwardness that was strangely at variance with his bold-looking eyes and his firm, sure hand that clasped for a moment in greeting. And in that moment his eyes were just as steady and sure. There seemed a question in them this time, and as before he looked at me over long.

"I have been reading your 'Working-class Philosophy,'" I said, and his eyes lighted in a pleased way.

"Of course," he answered, "you took into consideration the audience to which it was addressed."

"I did, and it is because I did that I have a quarrel with you," I challenged.

"I, too, have a quarrel with you, Mr. Everhard," Bishop Morehouse said.

Ernest shrugged his shoulders whimsically and accepted a cup of tea.

The Bishop bowed and gave me precedence.

"You foment class hatred," I said. "I consider it wrong and criminal to appeal to all that is narrow and brutal in the working class. Class hatred is anti-social, and, it seems to me, anti-socialistic."

"Not guilty," he answered. "Class hatred is neither in the text nor in the spirit of anything I have ever written."

"Oh!" I cried reproachfully, and reached for his book and opened it.

He sipped his tea and smiled at me while I ran over the pages.

"Page one hundred and thirty-two," I read aloud: "'The class struggle, therefore, presents itself in the present stage of

[1] This book continued to be secretly printed throughout the three centuries of the Iron Heel. There are several copies of various editions in the National Library of Ardis.

social development between the wage-paying and the wage-paid classes.' "

I looked at him triumphantly.

"No mention there of class hatred," he smiled back.

"But," I answered, "you say 'class struggle.' "

"A different thing from class hatred," he replied. "And, believe me, we foment no hatred. We say that the class struggle is a law of social development. We are not responsible for it. We do not make the class struggle. We merely explain it, as Newton explained gravitation. We explain the nature of the conflict of interest that produces the class struggle."

"But there should be no conflict of interest!" I cried.

"I agree with you heartily," he answered. "That is what we socialists are trying to bring about,—the abolition of the conflict of interest. Pardon me. Let me read an extract." He took his book and turned back several pages. "Page one hundred and twenty-six: 'The cycle of class struggles which began with the dissolution of rude, tribal communism and the rise of private property will end with the passing of private property in the means of social existence.' "

"But I disagree with you," the Bishop interposed, his pale, ascetic face betraying by a faint glow the intensity of his feelings. "Your premise is wrong. There is no such thing as a conflict of interest between labor and capital—or, rather, there ought not to be."

"Thank you," Ernest said gravely. "By that last statement you have given me back my premise."

"But why should there be a conflict?" the Bishop demanded warmly.

Ernest shrugged his shoulders. "Because we are so made, I guess."

"But we are not so made!" cried the other.

"Are you discussing the ideal man?" Ernest asked, "—unselfish and godlike, and so few in numbers as to be practically non-existent, or are you discussing the common and ordinary average man?"

"The common and ordinary man," was the answer.

"Who is weak and fallible, prone to error?"

Bishop Morehouse nodded.

"And petty and selfish?"

Again he nodded.

"Watch out!" Ernest warned. "I said 'selfish.' "

"The average man *is* selfish," the Bishop affirmed valiantly.

"Wants all he can get?"

"Wants all he can get—true but deplorable."

"Then I've got you." Ernest's jaw snapped like a trap. "Let me show you. Here is a man who works on the street railways."

"He couldn't work if it weren't for capital," the Bishop interrupted.

"True, and you will grant that capital would perish if there were no labor to earn the dividends."

The Bishop was silent.

"Won't you?" Ernest insisted.

The Bishop nodded.

"Then our statements cancel each other," Ernest said in a matter-of-fact tone, "and we are where we were. Now to begin again. The workingmen on the street railway furnish the labor. The stockholders furnish the capital. By the joint effort of the workingmen and the capital, money is earned.[1] They divide between them this money that is earned. Capital's share is called 'dividends.' Labor's share is called 'wages.' "

"Very good," the Bishop interposed. "And there is no reason that the division should not be amicable."

"You have already forgotten what we had agreed upon," Ernest replied. "We agreed that the average man is selfish. He is the man that is. You have gone up in the air and are arranging a division between the kind of men that ought to be but are not. But to return to the earth, the workingman, being selfish, wants all he can get in the division. The capitalist, being selfish, wants all he can get in the division. When there is only so much of the same thing, and when two men want all they can get of the same thing, there is a conflict of interest. This is the conflict of interest between labor and capital. And it is an irreconcilable conflict. As long as workingmen and capitalists exist, they will continue to quarrel over the division. If you were in San

[1] In those days, groups of predatory individuals controlled all the means of transportation, and for the use of same levied toll upon the public.

Francisco this afternoon, you'd have to walk. There isn't a street car running."

"Another strike?"[1] the Bishop queried with alarm.

"Yes, they're quarrelling over the division of the earnings of the street railways."

Bishop Morehouse became excited.

"It is wrong!" he cried. "It is so short-sighted on the part of the workingmen. How can they hope to keep our sympathy—"

"When we are compelled to walk," Ernest said slyly.

But Bishop Morehouse ignored him and went on:

"Their outlook is too narrow. Men should be men, not brutes. There will be violence and murder now, and sorrowing widows and orphans. Capital and labor should be friends. They should work hand in hand and to their mutual benefit."

"Ah, now you are up in the air again," Ernest remarked dryly. "Come back to earth. Remember, we agreed that the average man is selfish."

"But he ought not to be!" the Bishop cried.

"And there I agree with you," was Ernest's rejoinder. "He ought not to be selfish, but he will continue to be selfish as long as he lives in a social system that is based on pig-ethics."

The Bishop was aghast, and my father chuckled.

"Yes, pig-ethics," Ernest went on remorselessly. "That is the meaning of the capitalist system. And that is what your church is standing for, what you are preaching for every time you get up in the pulpit. Pig-ethics! There is no other name for it."

Bishop Morehouse turned appealingly to my father, but he laughed and nodded his head.

"I'm afraid Mr. Everhard is right," he said. "*Laissez-faire*, the let-alone policy of each for himself and devil take the hindmost. As Mr. Everhard said the other night, the function

[1]These quarrels were very common in those irrational and anarchic times. Sometimes the laborers refused to work. Sometimes the capitalists refused to let the laborers work. In the violence and turbulence of such disagreements much property was destroyed and many lives lost. All this is inconceivable to us—as inconceivable as another custom of that time, namely, the habit the men of the lower classes had of breaking the furniture when they quarrelled with their wives.

you churchmen perform is to maintain the established order of society, and society is established on that foundation."

"But that is not the teaching of Christ!" cried the Bishop.

"The Church is not teaching Christ these days," Ernest put in quickly. "That is why the workingmen will have nothing to do with the Church. The Church condones the frightful brutality and savagery with which the capitalist class treats the working class."

"The Church does not condone it," the Bishop objected.

"The Church does not protest against it," Ernest replied. "And in so far as the Church does not protest, it condones, for remember the Church is supported by the capitalist class."

"I had not looked at it in that light," the Bishop said naïvely. "You must be wrong. I know that there is much that is sad and wicked in this world. I know that the Church has lost the—what you call the proletariat."[1]

"You never had the proletariat," Ernest cried. "The proletariat has grown up outside the Church and without the Church."

"I do not follow you," the Bishop said faintly.

"Then let me explain. With the introduction of machinery and the factory system in the latter part of the eighteenth century, the great mass of the working people was separated from the land. The old system of labor was broken down. The working people were driven from their villages and herded in factory towns. The mothers and children were put to work at the new machines. Family life ceased. The conditions were frightful. It is a tale of blood."

"I know, I know," Bishop Morehouse interrupted with an agonized expression on his face. "It was terrible. But it occurred a century and a half ago."

"And there, a century and a half ago, originated the modern proletariat," Ernest continued. "And the Church ignored it. While a slaughter-house was made of the nation

[1] *Proletariat*: Derived originally from the Latin *proletarii*, the name given in the census of Servius Tullius to those who were of value to the state only as the rearers of offspring (*proles*); in other words, they were of no importance either for wealth, or position, or exceptional ability.

by the capitalists, the Church was dumb. It did not protest, as to-day it does not protest. As Austin Lewis[1] says, speaking of that time, those to whom the command 'Feed my lambs' had been given, saw those lambs sold into slavery and worked to death without a protest.[2] The Church was dumb, then, and before I go on I want you either flatly to agree with me or flatly to disagree with me. Was the Church dumb then?"

Bishop Morehouse hesitated. Like Dr. Hammerfield, he was unused to this fierce "infighting," as Ernest called it.

"The history of the eighteenth century is written," Ernest prompted. "If the Church was not dumb, it will be found not dumb in the books."

"I am afraid the Church was dumb," the Bishop confessed.

"And the Church is dumb to-day."

"There I disagree," said the Bishop.

Ernest paused, looked at him searchingly, and accepted the challenge.

"All right," he said. "Let us see. In Chicago there are women who toil all the week for ninety cents. Has the Church protested?"

"This is news to me," was the answer. "Ninety cents per week! It is horrible!"

"Has the Church protested?" Ernest insisted.

"The Church does not know." The Bishop was struggling hard.

"Yet the command to the Church was, 'Feed my lambs,' " Ernest sneered. And then, the next moment, "Pardon my sneer, Bishop. But can you wonder that we lose patience with you? When have you protested to your capitalistic congregations at the working of children in the Southern cotton

[1] Candidate for Governor of California on the Socialist ticket in the fall election of 1906 Christian Era. An Englishman by birth, a writer of many books on political economy and philosophy, and one of the Socialist leaders of the times.

[2] There is no more horrible page in history than the treatment of the child and women slaves in the English factories in the latter half of the eighteenth century of the Christian Era. In such industrial hells arose some of the proudest fortunes of that day.

mills?[1] Children, six and seven years of age, working every
night at twelve-hour shifts? They never see the blessed sunshine. They die like flies. The dividends are paid out of their
blood. And out of the dividends magnificent churches are
builded in New England, wherein your kind preaches pleasant platitudes to the sleek, full-bellied recipients of those dividends."

"I did not know," the Bishop murmured faintly. His face
was pale, and he seemed suffering from nausea.

"Then you have not protested?"

The Bishop shook his head.

"Then the Church is dumb to-day, as it was in the eighteenth century?"

[1]Everhard might have drawn a better illustration from the Southern
Church's outspoken defence of chattel slavery prior to what is known as the
"War of the Rebellion." Several such illustrations, culled from the documents
of the times, are here appended. In 1835 A.D., the General Assembly of the
Presbyterian Church resolved that: "*slavery is recognized in both the Old and
the New Testaments, and is not condemned by the authority of God.*" The Charleston Baptist Association issued the following, in an address, in 1835 A.D.: "*The
right of masters to dispose of the time of their slaves has been distinctly recognized
by the Creator of all things, who is surely at liberty to vest the right of property over
any object whomsoever He pleases.*" The Rev. E. D. Simon, Doctor of Divinity
and professor in the Randolph-Macon Methodist College of Virginia, wrote:
"*Extracts from Holy Writ unequivocally assert the right of property in slaves, together with the usual incidents to that right. The right to buy and sell is clearly
stated. Upon the whole, then, whether we consult the Jewish policy instituted by
God himself, or the uniform opinion and practice of mankind in all ages, or the
injunctions of the New Testament and the moral law, we are brought to the conclusion that slavery is not immoral. Having established the point that the first
African slaves were legally brought into bondage, the right to detain their children
in bondage follows as an indispensable consequence. Thus we see that the slavery
that exists in America was founded in right.*"

It is not at all remarkable that this same note should have been struck by
the Church a generation or so later in relation to the defence of capitalistic
property. In the great museum at Asgard there is a book entitled "Essays in
Application," written by Henry van Dyke. The book was published in 1905
of the Christian Era. From what we can make out, Van Dyke must have been
a Churchman. The book is a good example of what Everhard would have
called bourgeois thinking. Note the similarity between the utterance of the
Charleston Baptist Association quoted above, and the following utterance of
Van Dyke seventy years later: "*The Bible teaches that God owns the world. He
distributes to every man according to His own good pleasure, conformably to general
laws.*"

The Bishop was silent, and for once Ernest forbore to press the point.

"And do not forget, whenever a churchman does protest, that he is discharged."

"I hardly think that is fair," was the objection.

"Will you protest?" Ernest demanded.

"Show me evils, such as you mention, in our own community, and I will protest."

"I'll show you," Ernest said quietly. "I am at your disposal. I will take you on a journey through hell."

"And I shall protest." The Bishop straightened himself in his chair, and over his gentle face spread the harshness of the warrior. "The Church shall not be dumb!"

"You will be discharged," was the warning.

"I shall prove the contrary," was the retort. "I shall prove, if what you say is so, that the Church has erred through ignorance. And, furthermore, I hold that whatever is horrible in industrial society is due to the ignorance of the capitalist class. It will mend all that is wrong as soon as it receives the message. And this message it shall be the duty of the Church to deliver."

Ernest laughed. He laughed brutally, and I was driven to the Bishop's defence.

"Remember," I said, "you see but one side of the shield. There is much good in us, though you give us credit for no good at all. Bishop Morehouse is right. The industrial wrong, terrible as you say it is, is due to ignorance. The divisions of society have become too widely separated."

"The wild Indian is not so brutal and savage as the capitalist class," he answered; and in that moment I hated him.

"You do not know us," I answered. "We are not brutal and savage."

"Prove it," he challenged.

"How can I prove it . . . to you?" I was growing angry.

He shook his head. "I do not ask you to prove it to me. I ask you to prove it to yourself."

"I know," I said.

"You know nothing," was his rude reply.

"There, there, children," father said soothingly.

"I don't care—" I began indignantly, but Ernest interrupted.

"I understand you have money, or your father has, which is the same thing—money invested in the Sierra Mills."

"What has that to do with it?" I cried.

"Nothing much," he began slowly, "except that the gown you wear is stained with blood. The food you eat is a bloody stew. The blood of little children and of strong men is dripping from your very roof-beams. I can close my eyes, now, and hear it drip, drop, drip, drop, all about me."

And suiting the action to the words, he closed his eyes and leaned back in his chair. I burst into tears of mortification and hurt vanity. I had never been so brutally treated in my life. Both the Bishop and my father were embarrassed and perturbed. They tried to lead the conversation away into easier channels; but Ernest opened his eyes, looked at me, and waved them aside. His mouth was stern, and his eyes too; and in the latter there was no glint of laughter. What he was about to say, what terrible castigation he was going to give me, I never knew; for at that moment a man, passing along the sidewalk, stopped and glanced in at us. He was a large man, poorly dressed, and on his back was a great load of rattan and bamboo stands, chairs, and screens. He looked at the house as if debating whether or not he should come in and try to sell some of his wares.

"That man's name is Jackson," Ernest said.

"With that strong body of his he should be at work, and not peddling,"[1] I answered curtly.

"Notice the sleeve of his left arm," Ernest said gently.

I looked, and saw that the sleeve was empty.

"It was some of the blood from that arm that I heard dripping from your roof-beams," Ernest said with continued gentleness. "He lost his arm in the Sierra Mills, and like a broken-down horse you turned him out on the highway to die. When I say 'you,' I mean the superintendent and the officials that you and the other stockholders pay to manage the

[1]In that day there were many thousands of these poor merchants called *pedlers*. They carried their whole stock in trade from door to door. It was a most wasteful expenditure of energy. Distribution was as confused and irrational as the whole general system of society.

mills for you. It was an accident. It was caused by his trying to save the company a few dollars. The toothed drum of the picker caught his arm. He might have let the small flint that he saw in the teeth go through. It would have smashed out a double row of spikes. But he reached for the flint, and his arm was picked and clawed to shreds from the finger tips to the shoulder. It was at night. The mills were working overtime. They paid a fat dividend that quarter. Jackson had been working many hours, and his muscles had lost their resiliency and snap. They made his movements a bit slow. That was why the machine caught him. He had a wife and three children."

"And what did the company do for him?" I asked.

"Nothing. Oh, yes, they did do something. They successfully fought the damage suit he brought when he came out of hospital. The company employs very efficient lawyers, you know."

"You have not told the whole story," I said with conviction. "Or else you do not know the whole story. Maybe the man was insolent."

"Insolent! Ha! ha!" His laughter was Mephistophelian. "Great God! Insolent! And with his arm chewed off! Nevertheless he was a meek and lowly servant, and there is no record of his having been insolent."

"But the courts," I urged. "The case would not have been decided against him had there been no more to the affair than you have mentioned."

"Colonel Ingram is leading counsel for the company. He is a shrewd lawyer." Ernest looked at me intently for a moment, then went on. "I'll tell you what you do, Miss Cunningham. You investigate Jackson's case."

"I had already determined to," I said coldly.

"All right," he beamed good-naturedly, "and I'll tell you where to find him. But I tremble for you when I think of all you are to prove by Jackson's arm."

And so it came about that both the Bishop and I accepted Ernest's challenges. They went away together, leaving me smarting with a sense of injustice that had been done me and my class. The man was a beast. I hated him, then, and consoled myself with the thought that his behavior was what was to be expected from a man of the working class.

III

Jackson's Arm

L ITTLE did I dream the fateful part Jackson's arm was to
play in my life. Jackson himself did not impress me
when I hunted him out. I found him in a crazy, ramshackle[1]
house down near the bay on the edge of the marsh. Pools of
stagnant water stood around the house, their surfaces covered
with a green and putrid-looking scum, while the stench that
arose from them was intolerable.

I found Jackson the meek and lowly man he had been described. He was making some sort of rattan-work, and he
toiled on stolidly while I talked with him. But in spite of his
meekness and lowliness, I fancied I caught the first note of a
nascent bitterness in him when he said:

"They might a-given me a job as watchman,[2] anyway."

I got little out of him. He struck me as stupid, and yet the
deftness with which he worked with his one hand seemed to
belie his stupidity. This suggested an idea to me.

"How did you happen to get your arm caught in the machine?" I asked.

He looked at me in a slow and pondering way, and shook
his head. "I don't know. It just happened."

"Carelessness?" I prompted.

"No," he answered, "I ain't for callin' it that. I was workin'
overtime, an' I guess I was tired out some. I worked seven-

[1] An adjective descriptive of ruined and dilapidated houses in which great
numbers of the working people found shelter in those days. They invariably
paid rent, and, considering the value of such houses, enormous rent, to the
landlords.

[2] In those days thievery was incredibly prevalent. Everybody stole property
from everybody else. The lords of society stole legally or else legalized their
stealing, while the poorer classes stole illegally. Nothing was safe unless
guarded. Enormous numbers of men were employed as watchmen to protect
property. The houses of the well-to-do were a combination of safe deposit
vault and fortress. The appropriation of the personal belongings of others by
our own children of to-day is looked upon as a rudimentary survival of the
theft-characteristic that in those early times was universal.

teen years in them mills, an' I've took notice that most of the accidents happens just before whistle-blow.[1] I'm willin' to bet that more accidents happens in the hour before whistle-blow than in all the rest of the day. A man ain't so quick after workin' steady for hours. I've seen too many of 'em cut up an' gouged an' chawed not to know."

"Many of them?" I queried.

"Hundreds an' hundreds, an' children, too."

With the exception of the terrible details, Jackson's story of his accident was the same as that I had already heard. When I asked him if he had broken some rule of working the machinery, he shook his head.

"I chucked off the belt with my right hand," he said, "an' made a reach for the flint with my left. I didn't stop to see if the belt was off. I thought my right hand had done it—only it didn't. I reached quick, and the belt wasn't all the way off. And then my arm was chewed off."

"It must have been painful," I said sympathetically.

"The crunchin' of the bones wasn't nice," was his answer.

His mind was rather hazy concerning the damage suit. Only one thing was clear to him, and that was that he had not got any damages. He had a feeling that the testimony of the foremen and the superintendent had brought about the adverse decision of the court. Their testimony, as he put it, "wasn't what it ought to have ben." And to them I resolved to go.

One thing was plain, Jackson's situation was wretched. His wife was in ill health, and he was unable to earn, by his rattan-work and peddling, sufficient food for the family. He was back in his rent, and the oldest boy, a lad of eleven, had started to work in the mills.

"They might a-given me that watchman's job," were his last words as I went away.

By the time I had seen the lawyer who had handled Jackson's case, and the two foremen and the superintendent at the mills who had testified, I began to feel that there was something after all in Ernest's contention.

He was a weak and inefficient-looking man, the lawyer, and

[1] The laborers were called to work and dismissed by savage, screaming, nerve-racking steam-whistles.

at sight of him I did not wonder that Jackson's case had been lost. My first thought was that it had served Jackson right for getting such a lawyer. But the next moment two of Ernest's statements came flashing into my consciousness: "The company employs very efficient lawyers" and "Colonel Ingram is a shrewd lawyer." I did some rapid thinking. It dawned upon me that of course the company could afford finer legal talent than could a workingman like Jackson. But this was merely a minor detail. There was some very good reason, I was sure, why Jackson's case had gone against him.

"Why did you lose the case?" I asked.

The lawyer was perplexed and worried for a moment, and I found it in my heart to pity the wretched little creature. Then he began to whine. I do believe his whine was congenital. He was a man beaten at birth. He whined about the testimony. The witnesses had given only the evidence that helped the other side. Not one word could he get out of them that would have helped Jackson. They knew which side their bread was buttered on. Jackson was a fool. He had been brow-beaten and confused by Colonel Ingram. Colonel Ingram was brilliant at cross-examination. He had made Jackson answer damaging questions.

"How could his answers be damaging if he had the right on his side?" I demanded.

"What's right got to do with it?" he demanded back. "You see all those books." He moved his hand over the array of volumes on the walls of his tiny office. "All my reading and studying of them has taught me that law is one thing and right is another thing. Ask any lawyer. You go to Sunday-school to learn what is right. But you go to those books to learn . . . law."

"Do you mean to tell me that Jackson had the right on his side and yet was beaten?" I queried tentatively. "Do you mean to tell me that there is no justice in Judge Caldwell's court?"

The little lawyer glared at me a moment, and then the belligerence faded out of his face.

"I hadn't a fair chance," he began whining again. "They made a fool out of Jackson and out of me, too. What chance had I? Colonel Ingram is a great lawyer. If he wasn't great, would he have charge of the law business of the Sierra Mills, of the Erston Land Syndicate, of the Berkeley Consolidated, of the Oakland, San Leandro, and Pleasanton Electric? He's a corporation lawyer, and corporation lawyers are not paid for being fools.[1] What do you think the Sierra Mills alone give him twenty thousand dollars a year for? Because he's worth twenty thousand dollars a year to them, that's what for. I'm not worth that much. If I was, I wouldn't be on the outside, starving and taking cases like Jackson's. What do you think I'd have got if I'd won Jackson's case?"

"You'd have robbed him, most probably,"[2] I answered.

"Of course I would," he cried angrily. "I've got to live, haven't I?"[2]

"He has a wife and children," I chided.

"So have I a wife and children," he retorted. "And there's not a soul in this world except myself that cares whether they starve or not."

His face suddenly softened, and he opened his watch and showed me a small photograph of a woman and two little girls pasted inside the case.

"There they are. Look at them. We've had a hard time, a hard time. I had hoped to send them away to the country if I'd won Jackson's case. They're not healthy here, but I can't afford to send them away."

When I started to leave, he dropped back into his whine.

"I hadn't the ghost of a chance. Colonel Ingram and Judge Caldwell are pretty friendly. I'm not saying that if I'd got the right kind of testimony out of their witnesses on cross-examination, that friendship would have decided the case.

[1] The function of the corporation lawyer was to serve, by corrupt methods, the money-grabbing propensities of the corporations. It is on record that Theodore Roosevelt, at that time President of the United States, said in 1905 A.D., in his address at Harvard Commencement: *"We all know that, as things actually are, many of the most influential and most highly remunerated members of the Bar in every centre of wealth, make it their special task to work out bold and ingenious schemes by which their wealthy clients, individual or corporate, can evade the laws which were made to regulate, in the interests of the public, the uses of great wealth."*

[2] A typical illustration of the internecine strife that permeated all society. Men preyed upon one another like ravening wolves. The big wolves ate the little wolves, and in the social pack Jackson was one of the least of the little wolves.

And yet I must say that Judge Caldwell did a whole lot to prevent my getting that very testimony. Why, Judge Caldwell and Colonel Ingram belong to the same lodge and the same club. They live in the same neighborhood—one I can't afford. And their wives are always in and out of each other's houses. They're always having whist parties and such things back and forth."

"And yet you think Jackson had the right of it?" I asked, pausing for the moment on the threshold.

"I don't think; I know it," was his answer. "And at first I thought he had some show, too. But I didn't tell my wife. I didn't want to disappoint her. She had her heart set on a trip to the country hard enough as it was."

"Why did you not call attention to the fact that Jackson was trying to save the machinery from being injured?" I asked Peter Donnelly, one of the foremen who had testified at the trial.

He pondered a long time before replying. Then he cast an anxious look about him and said:

"Because I've a good wife an' three of the sweetest children ye ever laid eyes on, that's why."

"I do not understand," I said.

"In other words, because it wouldn't a-ben healthy," he answered.

"You mean—" I began.

But he interrupted passionately.

"I mean what I said. It's long years I've worked in the mills. I began as a little lad on the spindles. I worked up ever since. It's by hard work I got to my present exalted position. I'm a foreman, if you please. An' I doubt me if there's a man in the mills that'd put out a hand to drag me from drownin'. I used to belong to the union. But I've stayed by the company through two strikes. They called me 'scab.' There's not a man among 'em to-day to take a drink with me if I asked him. D'ye see the scars on me head where I was struck with flying bricks? There ain't a child at the spindles but what would curse me name. Me only friend is the company. It's not me duty, but me bread an' butter an' the life of me children to stand by the mills. That's why."

"Was Jackson to blame?" I asked.

"He should a-got the damages. He was a good worker an' never made trouble."

"Then you were not at liberty to tell the whole truth, as you had sworn to do?"

He shook his head.

"The truth, the whole truth, and nothing but the truth?" I said solemnly.

Again his face became impassioned, and he lifted it, not to me, but to heaven.

"I'd let me soul an' body burn in everlastin' hell for them children of mine," was his answer.

Henry Dallas, the superintendent, was a vulpine-faced creature who regarded me insolently and refused to talk. Not a word could I get from him concerning the trial and his testimony. But with the other foreman I had better luck. James Smith was a hard-faced man, and my heart sank as I encountered him. He, too, gave me the impression that he was not a free agent, and as we talked I began to see that he was mentally superior to the average of his kind. He agreed with Peter Donnelly that Jackson should have got damages, and he went farther and called the action heartless and cold-blooded that had turned the worker adrift after he had been made helpless by the accident. Also, he explained that there were many accidents in the mills, and that the company's policy was to fight to the bitter end all consequent damage suits.

"It means hundreds of thousands a year to the stockholders," he said; and as he spoke I remembered the last dividend that had been paid my father, and the pretty gown for me and the books for him that had been bought out of that dividend. I remembered Ernest's charge that my gown was stained with blood, and my flesh began to crawl underneath my garments.

"When you testified at the trial, you didn't point out that Jackson received his accident through trying to save the machinery from damage?" I said.

"No, I did not," was the answer, and his mouth set bitterly. "I testified to the effect that Jackson injured himself by neglect and carelessness, and that the company was not in any way to blame or liable."

"Was it carelessness?" I asked.

"Call it that, or anything you want to call it. The fact is, a man gets tired after he's been working for hours."

I was becoming interested in the man. He certainly was of a superior kind.

"You are better educated than most workingmen," I said.

"I went through high school," he replied. "I worked my way through doing janitor-work. I wanted to go through the university. But my father died, and I came to work in the mills.

"I wanted to become a naturalist," he explained shyly, as though confessing a weakness. "I love animals. But I came to work in the mills. When I was promoted to foreman I got married, then the family came, and . . . well, I wasn't my own boss any more."

"What do you mean by that?" I asked.

"I was explaining why I testified at the trial the way I did—why I followed instructions."

"Whose instructions?"

"Colonel Ingram. He outlined the evidence I was to give."

"And it lost Jackson's case for him."

He nodded, and the blood began to rise darkly in his face.

"And Jackson had a wife and two children dependent on him."

"I know," he said quietly, though his face was growing darker.

"Tell me," I went on, "was it easy to make yourself over from what you were, say in high school, to the man you must have become to do such a thing at the trial?"

The suddenness of his outburst startled and frightened me. He ripped[1] out a savage oath, and clenched his fist as though about to strike me.

"I beg your pardon," he said the next moment. "No, it was not easy. And now I guess you can go away. You've got all you wanted out of me. But let me tell you this before you go. It won't do you any good to repeat anything I've said. I'll deny it, and there are no witnesses. I'll deny

[1] It is interesting to note the virilities of language that were common speech in that day, as indicative of the life, 'red of claw and fang,' that was then lived. Reference is here made, of course, not to the oath of Smith, but to the verb *ripped* used by Avis Everhard.

every word of it; and if I have to, I'll do it under oath on the witness stand."

After my interview with Smith I went to my father's office in the Chemistry Building and there encountered Ernest. It was quite unexpected, but he met me with his bold eyes and firm hand-clasp, and with that curious blend of his awkwardness and ease. It was as though our last stormy meeting was forgotten; but I was not in the mood to have it forgotten.

"I have been looking up Jackson's case," I said abruptly.

He was all interested attention, and waited for me to go on, though I could see in his eyes the certitude that my convictions had been shaken.

"He seems to have been badly treated," I confessed. "I—I—think some of his blood is dripping from our roof-beams."

"Of course," he answered. "If Jackson and all his fellows were treated mercifully, the dividends would not be so large."

"I shall never be able to take pleasure in pretty gowns again," I added.

I felt humble and contrite, and was aware of a sweet feeling that Ernest was a sort of father confessor. Then, as ever after, his strength appealed to me. It seemed to radiate a promise of peace and protection.

"Nor will you be able to take pleasure in sackcloth," he said gravely. "There are the jute mills, you know, and the same thing goes on there. It goes on everywhere. Our boasted civilization is based upon blood, soaked in blood, and neither you nor I nor any of us can escape the scarlet stain. The men you talked with—who were they?"

I told him all that had taken place.

"And not one of them was a free agent," he said. "They were all tied to the merciless industrial machine. And the pathos of it and the tragedy is that they are tied by their heart-strings. Their children—always the young life that it is their instinct to protect. This instinct is stronger than any ethic they possess. My father! He lied, he stole, he did all sorts of dishonorable things to put bread into my mouth and into the mouths of my brothers and sisters. He was a slave to the industrial machine, and it stamped his life out, worked him to death."

"But you," I interjected. "You are surely a free agent."

"Not wholly," he replied. "I am not tied by my heart-strings. I am often thankful that I have no children, and I dearly love children. Yet if I married I should not dare to have any."

"That surely is bad doctrine," I cried.

"I know it is," he said sadly. "But it is expedient doctrine. I am a revolutionist, and it is a perilous vocation."

I laughed incredulously.

"If I tried to enter your father's house at night to steal his dividends from the Sierra Mills, what would he do?"

"He sleeps with a revolver on the stand by the bed," I answered. "He would most probably shoot you."

"And if I and a few others should lead a million and a half of men[1] into the houses of all the well-to-do, there would be a great deal of shooting, wouldn't there?"

"Yes, but you are not doing that," I objected.

"It is precisely what I am doing. And we intend to take, not the mere wealth in the houses, but all the sources of that wealth, all the mines, and railroads, and factories, and banks, and stores. That is the revolution. It is truly perilous. There will be more shooting, I am afraid, than even I dream of. But as I was saying, no one to-day is a free agent. We are all caught up in the wheels and cogs of the industrial machine. You found that you were, and that the men you talked with were. Talk with more of them. Go and see Colonel Ingram. Look up the reporters that kept Jackson's case out of the papers, and the editors that run the papers. You will find them all slaves of the machine."

A little later in our conversation I asked him a simple little question about the liability of workingmen to accidents, and received a statistical lecture in return.

"It is all in the books," he said. "The figures have been gathered, and it has been proved conclusively that accidents rarely occur in the first hours of the morning work, but that they increase rapidly in the succeeding hours as the workers

[1]This reference is to the socialist vote cast in the United States in 1910. The rise of this vote clearly indicates the swift growth of the party of revolution. Its voting strength in the United States in 1888 was 2068; in 1902, 127,713; in 1904, 435,040; in 1908, 1,108,427; and in 1910, 1,688,211.

grow tired and slower in both their muscular and mental processes.

"Why, do you know that your father has three times as many chances for safety of life and limb than has a workingman? He has. The insurance[1] companies know. They will charge him four dollars and twenty cents a year on a thousand-dollar accident policy, and for the same policy they will charge a laborer fifteen dollars."

"And you?" I asked; and in the moment of asking I was aware of a solicitude that was something more than slight.

"Oh, as a revolutionist, I have about eight chances to the workingman's one of being injured or killed," he answered carelessly. "The insurance companies charge the highly trained chemists that handle explosives eight times what they charge the workingmen. I don't think they'd insure me at all. Why did you ask?"

My eyes fluttered, and I could feel the blood warm in my face. It was not that he had caught me in my solicitude, but that I had caught myself, and in his presence.

Just then my father came in and began making preparations to depart with me. Ernest returned some books he had borrowed, and went away first. But just as he was going, he turned and said:

"Oh, by the way, while you are ruining your own peace of mind and I am ruining the Bishop's, you'd better look up Mrs. Wickson and Mrs. Pertonwaithe. Their husbands, you know, are the two principal stockholders in the Mills. Like all the rest of humanity, those two women are tied to the machine, but they are so tied that they sit on top of it."

[1] In the terrible wolf-struggle of those centuries, no man was permanently safe, no matter how much wealth he amassed. Out of fear for the welfare of their families, men devised the scheme of insurance. To us, in this intelligent age, such a device is laughably absurd and primitive. But in that age insurance was a very serious matter. The amusing part of it is that the funds of the insurance companies were frequently plundered and wasted by the very officials who were intrusted with the management of them.

IV

Slaves of the Machine

T HE MORE I thought of Jackson's arm, the more shaken I
was. I was confronted by the concrete. For the first time
I was seeing life. My university life, and study and culture,
had not been real. I had learned nothing but theories of life
and society that looked all very well on the printed page, but
now I had seen life itself. Jackson's arm was a fact of life.
"The fact, man, the irrefragable fact!" of Ernest's was ringing
in my consciousness.

It seemed monstrous, impossible, that our whole society
was based upon blood. And yet there was Jackson. I could
not get away from him. Constantly my thought swung back
to him as the compass to the Pole. He had been monstrously
treated. His blood had not been paid for in order that a larger
dividend might be paid. And I knew a score of happy complacent families that had received those dividends and by that
much had profited by Jackson's blood. If one man could be
so monstrously treated and society move on its way unheeding, might not many men be so monstrously treated? I remembered Ernest's women of Chicago who toiled for ninety
cents a week, and the child slaves of the Southern cotton mills
he had described. And I could see their wan white hands,
from which the blood had been pressed, at work upon the
cloth out of which had been made my gown. And then I
thought of the Sierra Mills and the dividends that had been
paid, and I saw the blood of Jackson upon my gown as well.
Jackson I could not escape. Always my meditations led me
back to him.

Down in the depths of me I had a feeling that I stood on
the edge of a precipice. It was as though I were about to see
a new and awful revelation of life. And not I alone. My whole
world was turning over. There was my father. I could see the
effect Ernest was beginning to have on him. And then there
was the Bishop. When I had last seen him he had looked a
sick man. He was at high nervous tension, and in his eyes

there was unspeakable horror. From the little I learned I knew that Ernest had been keeping his promise of taking him through hell. But what scenes of hell the Bishop's eyes had seen, I knew not, for he seemed too stunned to speak about them.

Once, the feeling strong upon me that my little world and all the world was turning over, I thought of Ernest as the cause of it; and also I thought, "We were so happy and peaceful before he came!" And the next moment I was aware that the thought was a treason against truth, and Ernest rose before me transfigured, the apostle of truth, with shining brows and the fearlessness of one of God's own angels, battling for the truth and the right, and battling for the succor of the poor and lonely and oppressed. And then there arose before me another figure, the Christ! He, too, had taken the part of the lowly and oppressed, and against all the established power of priest and pharisee. And I remembered his end upon the cross, and my heart contracted with a pang as I thought of Ernest. Was he, too, destined for a cross?—he, with his clarion call and war-noted voice, and all the fine man's vigor of him!

And in that moment I knew that I loved him, and that I was melting with desire to comfort him. I thought of his life. A sordid, harsh, and meagre life it must have been. And I thought of his father, who had lied and stolen for him and been worked to death. And he himself had gone into the mills when he was ten! All my heart seemed bursting with desire to fold my arms around him, and to rest his head on my breast—his head that must be weary with so many thoughts; and to give him rest—just rest—and easement and forgetfulness for a tender space.

I met Colonel Ingram at a church reception. Him I knew well and had known well for many years. I trapped him behind large palms and rubber plants, though he did not know he was trapped. He met me with the conventional gayety and gallantry. He was ever a graceful man, diplomatic, tactful, and considerate. And as for appearance, he was the most distinguished-looking man in our society. Beside him even the venerable head of the university looked tawdry and small.

And yet I found Colonel Ingram situated the same as the

unlettered mechanics. He was not a free agent. He, too, was bound upon the wheel. I shall never forget the change in him when I mentioned Jackson's case. His smiling good-nature vanished like a ghost. A sudden, frightful expression distorted his well-bred face. I felt the same alarm that I had felt when James Smith broke out. But Colonel Ingram did not curse. That was the slight difference that was left between the workingman and him. He was famed as a wit, but he had no wit now. And, unconsciously, this way and that he glanced for avenues of escape. But he was trapped amid the palms and rubber trees.

Oh, he was sick of the sound of Jackson's name. Why had I brought the matter up? He did not relish my joke. It was poor taste on my part, and very inconsiderate. Did I not know that in his profession personal feelings did not count? He left his personal feelings at home when he went down to the office. At the office he had only professional feelings.

"Should Jackson have received damages?" I asked.

"Certainly," he answered. "That is, personally, I have a feeling that he should. But that has nothing to do with the legal aspects of the case."

He was getting his scattered wits slightly in hand.

"Tell me, has right anything to do with the law?" I asked.

"You have used the wrong initial consonant," he smiled in answer.

"Might?" I queried; and he nodded his head. "And yet we are supposed to get justice by means of the law?"

"That is the paradox of it," he countered. "We do get justice."

"You are speaking professionally now, are you not?" I asked.

Colonel Ingram blushed, actually blushed, and again he looked anxiously about him for a way of escape. But I blocked his path and did not offer to move.

"Tell me," I said, "when one surrenders his personal feelings to his professional feelings, may not the action be defined as a sort of spiritual mayhem?"

I did not get an answer. Colonel Ingram had ingloriously bolted, overturning a palm in his flight.

Next I tried the newspapers. I wrote a quiet, restrained,

dispassionate account of Jackson's case. I made no charges against the men with whom I had talked, nor, for that matter, did I even mention them. I gave the actual facts of the case, the long years Jackson had worked in the mills, his effort to save the machinery from damage and the consequent accident, and his own present wretched and starving condition. The three local newspapers rejected my communication, likewise did the two weeklies.

I got hold of Percy Layton. He was a graduate of the university, had gone in for journalism, and was then serving his apprenticeship as reporter on the most influential of the three newspapers. He smiled when I asked him the reason the newspapers suppressed all mention of Jackson or his case.

"Editorial policy," he said. "We have nothing to do with that. It's up to the editors."

"But why is it policy?" I asked.

"We're all solid with the corporations," he answered. "If you paid advertising rates, you couldn't get any such matter into the papers. A man who tried to smuggle it in would lose his job. You couldn't get it in if you paid ten times the regular advertising rates."

"How about your own policy?" I questioned. "It would seem your function is to twist truth at the command of your employers, who, in turn, obey the behests of the corporations."

"I haven't anything to do with that." He looked uncomfortable for the moment, then brightened as he saw his way out. "I, myself, do not write untruthful things. I keep square all right with my own conscience. Of course, there's lots that's repugnant in the course of the day's work. But then, you see, that's all part of the day's work," he wound up boyishly.

"Yet you expect to sit at an editor's desk some day and conduct a policy."

"I'll be case-hardened by that time," was his reply.

"Since you are not yet case-hardened, tell me what you think right now about the general editorial policy."

"I don't think," he answered quickly. "One can't kick over the ropes if he's going to succeed in journalism. I've learned that much, at any rate."

And he nodded his young head sagely.

"But the right?" I persisted.

"You don't understand the game. Of course it's all right, because it comes out all right, don't you see?"

"Delightfully vague," I murmured; but my heart was aching for the youth of him, and I felt that I must either scream or burst into tears.

I was beginning to see through the appearances of the society in which I had always lived, and to find the frightful realities that were beneath. There seemed a tacit conspiracy against Jackson, and I was aware of a thrill of sympathy for the whining lawyer who had ingloriously fought his case. But this tacit conspiracy grew large. Not alone was it aimed against Jackson. It was aimed against every workingman who was maimed in the mills. And if against every man in the mills, why not against every man in all the other mills and factories? In fact, was it not true of all the industries?

And if this was so, then society was a lie. I shrank back from my own conclusions. It was too terrible and awful to be true. But there was Jackson, and Jackson's arm, and the blood that stained my gown and dripped from my own roof-beams. And there were many Jacksons—hundreds of them in the mills alone, as Jackson himself had said. Jackson I could not escape.

I saw Mr. Wickson and Mr. Pertonwaithe, the two men who held most of the stock in the Sierra Mills. But I could not shake them as I had shaken the mechanics in their employ. I discovered that they had an ethic superior to that of the rest of society. It was what I may call the aristocratic ethic or the master ethic.[1] They talked in large ways of policy, and they identified policy and right. And to me they talked in fatherly ways, patronizing my youth and inexperience. They were the most hopeless of all I had encountered in my quest. They believed absolutely that their conduct was right. There was no question about it, no discussion. They were convinced that they were the saviours of society, and that it was they who made happiness for the many. And they drew pathetic

[1] Before Avis Everhard was born, John Stuart Mill, in his essay, *On Liberty*, wrote: "Wherever there is an ascendant class, a large portion of the morality emanates from its class interests and its class feelings of superiority."

pictures of what would be the sufferings of the working class were it not for the employment that they, and they alone, by their wisdom, provided for it.

Fresh from these two masters, I met Ernest and related my experience. He looked at me with a pleased expression, and said:

"Really, this is fine. You are beginning to dig truth for yourself. It is your own empirical generalization, and it is correct. No man in the industrial machine is a free-will agent, except the large capitalist, and he isn't, if you'll pardon the Irishism.[1] You see, the masters are quite sure that they are right in what they are doing. That is the crowning absurdity of the whole situation. They are so tied by their human nature that they can't do a thing unless they think it is right. They must have a sanction for their acts.

"When they want to do a thing, in business of course, they must wait till there arises in their brains, somehow, a religious, or ethical, or scientific, or philosophic, concept that the thing is right. And then they go ahead and do it, unwitting that one of the weaknesses of the human mind is that the wish is parent to the thought. No matter what they want to do, the sanction always comes. They are superficial casuists. They are Jesuitical. They even see their way to doing wrong that right may come of it. One of the pleasant and axiomatic fictions they have created is that they are superior to the rest of mankind in wisdom and efficiency. Therefrom comes their sanction to manage the bread and butter of the rest of mankind. They have even resurrected the theory of the divine right of kings—commercial kings in their case.[2]

"The weakness in their position lies in that they are merely business men. They are not philosophers. They are not biologists nor sociologists. If they were, of course all would be well. A business man who was also a biologist and a sociolo-

[1] Verbal contradictions, called *bulls*, were long an amiable weakness of the ancient Irish.

[2] The newspapers, in 1902 of that era, credited the president of the Anthracite Coal Trust, George F. Baer, with the enunciation of the following principle: "*The rights and interests of the laboring man will be protected by the Christian men to whom God in His infinite wisdom has given the property interests of the country.*"

gist would know, approximately, the right thing to do for humanity. But, outside the realm of business, these men are stupid. They know only business. They do not know mankind nor society, and yet they set themselves up as arbiters of the fates of the hungry millions and all the other millions thrown in. History, some day, will have an excruciating laugh at their expense."

I was not surprised when I had my talk out with Mrs. Wickson and Mrs. Pertonwaithe. They were society women.[1] Their homes were palaces. They had many homes scattered over the country, in the mountains, on lakes, and by the sea. They were tended by armies of servants, and their social activities were bewildering. They patronized the university and the churches, and the pastors especially bowed at their knees in meek subservience.[2] They were powers, these two women, what of the money that was theirs. The power of subsidization of thought was theirs to a remarkable degree, as I was soon to learn under Ernest's tuition.

They aped their husbands, and talked in the same large ways about policy, and the duties and responsibilities of the rich. They were swayed by the same ethic that dominated their husbands—the ethic of their class; and they uttered glib phrases that their own ears did not understand.

Also, they grew irritated when I told them of the deplorable condition of Jackson's family, and when I wondered that they had made no voluntary provision for the man. I was told that they thanked no one for instructing them in their social duties. When I asked them flatly to assist Jackson, they as flatly refused. The astounding thing about it was that they refused in almost identically the same language, and this in face of the fact that I interviewed them separately and that one did not know that I had seen or was going to see the other. Their common reply was that they were glad of the

---

[1] *Society* is here used in a restricted sense, a common usage of the times to denote the gilded drones that did no labor, but only glutted themselves at the honey-vats of the workers. Neither the business men nor the laborers had time or opportunity for *society*. *Society* was the creation of the idle rich who toiled not and who in this way played.

[2] "Bring on your tainted money," was the expressed sentiment of the Church during this period.

opportunity to make it perfectly plain that no premium would ever be put on carelessness by them; nor would they, by paying for accident, tempt the poor to hurt themselves in the machinery.[1]

And they were sincere, these two women. They were drunk with conviction of the superiority of their class and of themselves. They had a sanction, in their own class-ethic, for every act they performed. As I drove away from Mrs. Pertonwaithe's great house, I looked back at it, and I remembered Ernest's expression that they were bound to the machine, but that they were so bound that they sat on top of it.

[1] In the files of the *Outlook*, a critical weekly of the period, in the number dated August 18, 1906, is related the circumstance of a workingman losing his arm, the details of which are quite similar to those of Jackson's case as related by Avis Everhard.

V

The Philomaths

ERNEST WAS often at the house. Nor was it my father, merely, nor the controversial dinners, that drew him there. Even at that time I flattered myself that I played some part in causing his visits, and it was not long before I learned the correctness of my surmise. For never was there such a lover as Ernest Everhard. His gaze and his hand-clasp grew firmer and steadier, if that were possible; and the question that had grown from the first in his eyes, grew only the more imperative.

My impression of him, the first time I saw him, had been unfavorable. Then I had found myself attracted toward him. Next came my repulsion, when he so savagely attacked my class and me. After that, as I saw that he had not maligned my class, and that the harsh and bitter things he said about it were justified, I had drawn closer to him again. He became my oracle. For me he tore the sham from the face of society and gave me glimpses of reality that were as unpleasant as they were undeniably true.

As I have said, there was never such a lover as he. No girl could live in a university town till she was twenty-four and not have love experiences. I had been made love to by beardless sophomores and gray professors, and by the athletes and the football giants. But not one of them made love to me as Ernest did. His arms were around me before I knew. His lips were on mine before I could protest or resist. Before his earnestness conventional maiden dignity was ridiculous. He swept me off my feet by the splendid invincible rush of him. He did not propose. He put his arms around me and kissed me and took it for granted that we should be married. There was no discussion about it. The only discussion—and that arose afterward—was when we should be married.

It was unprecedented. It was unreal. Yet, in accordance with Ernest's test of truth, it worked. I trusted my life to it. And fortunate was the trust. Yet during those first days of

our love, fear of the future came often to me when I thought
of the violence and impetuosity of his love-making. Yet such
fears were groundless. No woman was ever blessed with a
gentler, tenderer husband. This gentleness and violence on his
part was a curious blend similar to the one in his carriage of
awkwardness and ease. That slight awkwardness! He never
got over it, and it was delicious. His behavior in our drawing-
room reminded me of a careful bull in a china shop.[1]

It was at this time that vanished my last doubt of the completeness of my love for him (a subconscious doubt, at most).
It was at the Philomath Club—a wonderful night of battle,
wherein Ernest bearded the masters in their lair. Now the
Philomath Club was the most select on the Pacific Coast. It
was the creation of Miss Brentwood, an enormously wealthy
old maid; and it was her husband, and family, and toy. Its
members were the wealthiest in the community, and the
strongest-minded of the wealthy, with, of course, a sprinkling
of scholars to give it intellectual tone.

The Philomath had no club house. It was not that kind of
a club. Once a month its members gathered at some one of
their private houses to listen to a lecture. The lecturers were
usually, though not always, hired. If a chemist in New York
made a new discovery in say radium, all his expenses across
the continent were paid, and as well he received a princely fee
for his time. The same with a returning explorer from the
polar regions, or the latest literary or artistic success. No visitors were allowed, while it was the Philomath's policy to permit none of its discussions to get into the papers. Thus great
statesmen—and there had been such occasions—were able
fully to speak their minds.

I spread before me a wrinkled letter, written to me by Ernest twenty years ago, and from it I copy the following:

"Your father is a member of the Philomath, so you are able
to come. Therefore come next Tuesday night. I promise you
that you will have the time of your life. In your recent en-

[1] In those days it was still the custom to fill the living rooms with bric-a-
brac. They had not discovered simplicity of living. Such rooms were mu-
seums, entailing endless labor to keep clean. The dust-demon was the lord of
the household. There were a myriad devices for catching dust, and only a few
devices for getting rid of it.

counters, you failed to shake the masters. If you come, I'll
shake them for you. I'll make them snarl like wolves. You
merely questioned their morality. When their morality is
questioned, they grow only the more complacent and superior. But I shall menace their money-bags. That will shake
them to the roots of their primitive natures. If you can come,
you will see the cave-man, in evening dress, snarling and
snapping over a bone. I promise you a great caterwauling and
an illuminating insight into the nature of the beast.

"They've invited me in order to tear me to pieces. This is
the idea of Miss Brentwood. She clumsily hinted as much
when she invited me. She's given them that kind of fun before. They delight in getting trustful-souled gentle reformers
before them. Miss Brentwood thinks I am as mild as a kitten
and as good-natured and stolid as the family cow. I'll not
deny that I helped to give her that impression. She was very
tentative at first, until she divined my harmlessness. I am to
receive a handsome fee—two hundred and fifty dollars—as
befits the man who, though a radical, once ran for governor.
Also, I am to wear evening dress. This is compulsory. I never
was so apparelled in my life. I suppose I'll have to hire one
somewhere. But I'd do more than that to get a chance at the
Philomaths."

Of all places, the Club gathered that night at the Pertonwaithe house. Extra chairs had been brought into the great
drawing-room, and in all there must have been two hundred
Philomaths that sat down to hear Ernest. They were truly
lords of society. I amused myself with running over in my
mind the sum of the fortunes represented, and it ran well into
the hundreds of millions. And the possessors were not of the
idle rich. They were men of affairs who took most active parts
in industrial and political life.

We were all seated when Miss Brentwood brought Ernest
in. They moved at once to the head of the room, from where
he was to speak. He was in evening dress, and, what of his
broad shoulders and kingly head, he looked magnificent. And
then there was that faint and unmistakable touch of awkwardness in his movements. I almost think I could have loved him
for that alone. And as I looked at him I was aware of a great
joy. I felt again the pulse of his palm on mine, the touch of

his lips; and such pride was mine that I felt I must rise up and cry out to the assembled company: "He is mine! He has held me in his arms, and I, mere I, have filled that mind of his to the exclusion of all his multitudinous and kingly thoughts!"

At the head of the room, Miss Brentwood introduced him to Colonel Van Gilbert, and I knew that the latter was to preside. Colonel Van Gilbert was a great corporation lawyer. In addition, he was immensely wealthy. The smallest fee he would deign to notice was a hundred thousand dollars. He was a master of law. The law was a puppet with which he played. He moulded it like clay, twisted and distorted it like a Chinese puzzle into any design he chose. In appearance and rhetoric he was old-fashioned, but in imagination and knowledge and resource he was as young as the latest statute. His first prominence had come when he broke the Shardwell will.[1] His fee for this one act was five hundred thousand dollars. From then on he had risen like a rocket. He was often called the greatest lawyer in the country—corporation lawyer, of course; and no classification of the three greatest lawyers in the United States could have excluded him.

He arose and began, in a few well-chosen phrases that carried an undertone of faint irony, to introduce Ernest. Colonel Van Gilbert was subtly facetious in his introduction of the social reformer and member of the working class, and the audience smiled. It made me angry, and I glanced at Ernest. The sight of him made me doubly angry. He did not seem to resent the delicate slurs. Worse than that, he did not seem to be aware of them. There he sat, gentle, and stolid, and somnolent. He really looked stupid. And for a moment the thought rose in my mind, What if he were overawed by this

[1] This breaking of wills was a peculiar feature of the period. With the accumulation of vast fortunes, the problem of disposing of these fortunes after death was a vexing one to the accumulators. Will-making and will-breaking became complementary trades, like armor-making and gun-making. The shrewdest will-making lawyers were called in to make wills that could not be broken. But these wills were always broken, and very often by the very lawyers that had drawn them up. Nevertheless the delusion persisted in the wealthy class that an absolutely unbreakable will could be cast; and so, through the generations, clients and lawyers pursued the illusion. It was a pursuit like unto that of the Universal Solvent of the mediæval alchemists.

imposing array of power and brains? Then I smiled. He couldn't fool me. But he fooled the others, just as he had fooled Miss Brentwood. She occupied a chair right up to the front, and several times she turned her head toward one or another of her *confrères* and smiled her appreciation of the remarks.

Colonel Van Gilbert done, Ernest arose and began to speak. He began in a low voice, haltingly and modestly, and with an air of evident embarrassment. He spoke of his birth in the working class, and of the sordidness and wretchedness of his environment, where flesh and spirit were alike starved and tormented. He described his ambitions and ideals, and his conception of the paradise wherein lived the people of the upper classes. As he said:

"Up above me, I knew, were unselfishnesses of the spirit, clean and noble thinking, keen intellectual living. I knew all this because I read 'Seaside Library'[1] novels, in which, with the exception of the villains and adventuresses, all men and women thought beautiful thoughts, spoke a beautiful tongue, and performed glorious deeds. In short, as I accepted the rising of the sun, I accepted that up above me was all that was fine and noble and gracious, all that gave decency and dignity to life, all that made life worth living and that remunerated one for his travail and misery."

He went on and traced his life in the mills, the learning of the horseshoeing trade, and his meeting with the socialists. Among them, he said, he had found keen intellects and brilliant wits, ministers of the Gospel who had been broken because their Christianity was too wide for any congregation of mammon-worshippers, and professors who had been broken on the wheel of university subservience to the ruling class. The socialists were revolutionists, he said, struggling to overthrow the irrational society of the present and out of the material to build the rational society of the future. Much more he said that would take too long to write, but I shall never forget how he described the life among the revolutionists. All halting utterance vanished. His voice grew strong and confi-

---

[1] A curious and amazing literature that served to make the working class utterly misapprehend the nature of the leisure class.

dent, and it glowed as he glowed, and as the thoughts glowed that poured out from him. He said:

"Amongst the revolutionists I found, also, warm faith in the human, ardent idealism, sweetnesses of unselfishness, renunciation, and martyrdom—all the splendid, stinging things of the spirit. Here life was clean, noble, and alive. I was in touch with great souls who exalted flesh and spirit over dollars and cents, and to whom the thin wail of the starved slum child meant more than all the pomp and circumstance of commercial expansion and world empire. All about me were nobleness of purpose and heroism of effort, and my days and nights were sunshine and starshine, all fire and dew, with before my eyes, ever burning and blazing, the Holy Grail, Christ's own Grail, the warm human, long-suffering and maltreated but to be rescued and saved at the last."

As before I had seen him transfigured, so now he stood transfigured before me. His brows were bright with the divine that was in him, and brighter yet shone his eyes from the midst of the radiance that seemed to envelop him as a mantle. But the others did not see this radiance, and I assumed that it was due to the tears of joy and love that dimmed my vision. At any rate, Mr. Wickson, who sat behind me, was unaffected, for I heard him sneer aloud, "Utopian."[1]

Ernest went on to his rise in society, till at last he came in touch with members of the upper classes, and rubbed shoulders with the men who sat in the high places. Then came his disillusionment, and this disillusionment he described in terms that did not flatter his audience. He was surprised at the commonness of the clay. Life proved not to be fine and gracious. He was appalled by the selfishness he encountered, and what had surprised him even more than that was the absence of intellectual life. Fresh from his revolutionists, he was

[1] The people of that age were phrase slaves. The abjectness of their servitude is incomprehensible to us. There was a magic in words greater than the conjurer's art. So befuddled and chaotic were their minds that the utterance of a single word could negative the generalizations of a lifetime of serious research and thought. Such a word was the adjective *Utopian*. The mere utterance of it could damn any scheme, no matter how sanely conceived, of economic amelioration or regeneration. Vast populations grew frenzied over such phrases as "an honest dollar" and "a full dinner pail." The coinage of such phrases was considered strokes of genius.

shocked by the intellectual stupidity of the master class. And then, in spite of their magnificent churches and well-paid preachers, he had found the masters, men and women, grossly material. It was true that they prattled sweet little ideals and dear little moralities, but in spite of their prattle the dominant key of the life they lived was materialistic. And they were without real morality—for instance, that which Christ had preached but which was no longer preached.

"I met men," he said, "who invoked the name of the Prince of Peace in their diatribes against war, and who put rifles in the hands of Pinkertons[1] with which to shoot down strikers in their own factories. I met men incoherent with indignation at the brutality of prize-fighting, and who, at the same time, were parties to the adulteration of food that killed each year more babes than even red-handed Herod had killed.

"This delicate, aristocratic-featured gentleman was a dummy director and a tool of corporations that secretly robbed widows and orphans. This gentleman, who collected fine editions and was a patron of literature, paid blackmail to a heavy-jowled, black-browed boss of a municipal machine. This editor, who published patent medicine advertisements, called me a scoundrelly demagogue because I dared him to print in his paper the truth about patent medicines.[2] This man, talking soberly and earnestly about the beauties of idealism and the goodness of God, had just betrayed his comrades in a business deal. This man, a pillar of the church and heavy contributor to foreign missions, worked his shop girls ten hours a day on a starvation wage and thereby directly encouraged prostitution. This man, who endowed chairs in universities and erected magnificent chapels, perjured himself in courts of law over dollars and cents. This railroad magnate broke his word as a citizen, as a gentleman, and as a Christian, when he granted a secret rebate, and he granted many

[1] Originally, they were private detectives; but they quickly became hired fighting men of the capitalists, and ultimately developed into the Mercenaries of the Oligarchy.

[2] *Patent medicines* were patent lies, but, like the charms and indulgences of the Middle Ages, they deceived the people. The only difference lay in that the patent medicines were more harmful and more costly.

secret rebates. This senator was the tool and the slave, the little puppet, of a brutal uneducated machine boss;[1] so was this governor and this supreme court judge; and all three rode on railroad passes; and, also, this sleek capitalist owned the machine, the machine boss, and the railroads that issued the passes.

"And so it was, instead of in paradise, that I found myself in the arid desert of commercialism. I found nothing but stupidity, except for business. I found none clean, noble, and alive, though I found many who were alive—with rottenness. What I did find was monstrous selfishness and heartlessness, and a gross, gluttonous, practised, and practical materialism."

Much more Ernest told them of themselves and of his disillusionment. Intellectually they had bored him; morally and spiritually they had sickened him; so that he was glad to go back to his revolutionists, who were clean, noble, and alive, and all that the capitalists were not.

"And now," he said, "let me tell you about that revolution."

But first I must say that his terrible diatribe had not touched them. I looked about me at their faces and saw that they remained complacently superior to what he had charged. And I remembered what he had told me: that no indictment of their morality could shake them. However, I could see that the boldness of his language had affected Miss Brentwood. She was looking worried and apprehensive.

Ernest began by describing the army of revolution, and as he gave the figures of its strength (the votes cast in the various countries), the assemblage began to grow restless. Concern showed in their faces, and I noticed a tightening of lips. At last the gage of battle had been thrown down. He described the international organization of the socialists that united the million and a half in the United States with the twenty-three millions and a half in the rest of the world.

[1] Even as late as 1912, A.D., the great mass of the people still persisted in the belief that they ruled the country by virtue of their ballots. In reality, the country was ruled by what were called *political machines*. At first the machine bosses charged the master capitalists extortionate tolls for legislation; but in a short time the master capitalists found it cheaper to own the political machines themselves and to hire the machine bosses.

"Such an army of revolution," he said, "twenty-five millions strong, is a thing to make rulers and ruling classes pause and consider. The cry of this army is: 'No quarter! We want all that you possess. We will be content with nothing less than all that you possess. We want in our hands the reins of power and the destiny of mankind. Here are our hands. They are strong hands. We are going to take your governments, your palaces, and all your purpled ease away from you, and in that day you shall work for your bread even as the peasant in the field or the starved and runty clerk in your metropolises. Here are our hands. They are strong hands!' "

And as he spoke he extended from his splendid shoulders his two great arms, and the horseshoer's hands were clutching the air like eagle's talons. He was the spirit of regnant labor as he stood there, his hands outreaching to rend and crush his audience. I was aware of a faintly perceptible shrinking on the part of the listeners before this figure of revolution, concrete, potential, and menacing. That is, the women shrank, and fear was in their faces. Not so with the men. They were of the active rich, and not the idle, and they were fighters. A low, throaty rumble arose, lingered on the air a moment, and ceased. It was the forerunner of the snarl, and I was to hear it many times that night—the token of the brute in man, the earnest of his primitive passions. And they were unconscious that they had made this sound. It was the growl of the pack, mouthed by the pack, and mouthed in all unconsciousness. And in that moment, as I saw the harshness form in their faces and saw the fight-light flashing in their eyes, I realized that not easily would they let their lordship of the world be wrested from them.

Ernest proceeded with his attack. He accounted for the existence of the million and a half of revolutionists in the United States by charging the capitalist class with having mismanaged society. He sketched the economic condition of the cave-man and of the savage peoples of to-day, pointing out that they possessed neither tools nor machines, and possessed only a natural efficiency of one in producing power. Then he traced the development of machinery and social organization so that to-day the producing power of civilized man was a thousand times greater than that of the savage.

"Five men," he said, "can produce bread for a thousand. One man can produce cotton cloth for two hundred and fifty people, woollens for three hundred, and boots and shoes for a thousand. One would conclude from this that under a capable management of society modern civilized man would be a great deal better off than the cave-man. But is he? Let us see. In the United States to-day there are fifteen million[1] people living in poverty; and by poverty is meant that condition in life in which, through lack of food and adequate shelter, the mere standard of working efficiency cannot be maintained. In the United States to-day, in spite of all your so-called labor legislation, there are three millions of child laborers.[2] In twelve years their numbers have been doubled. And in passing I will ask you managers of society why you did not make public the census figures of 1910? And I will answer for you, that you were afraid. The figures of misery would have precipitated the revolution that even now is gathering.

"But to return to my indictment. If modern man's producing power is a thousand times greater than that of the cave-man, why then, in the United States to-day, are there fifteen million people who are not properly sheltered and properly fed? Why then, in the United States to-day, are there three million child laborers? It is a true indictment. The capitalist class has mismanaged. In face of the facts that modern man lives more wretchedly than the cave-man, and that his producing power is a thousand times greater than that of the cave-man, no other conclusion is possible than that the capitalist class has mismanaged, that you have mismanaged, my masters, that you have criminally and selfishly mismanaged. And on this count you cannot answer me here to-night, face to face, any more than can your whole class answer the million and a half of revolutionists in the United States. You cannot answer. I challenge you to answer. And furthermore, I dare to say to you now that when I have finished you will

[1] Robert Hunter, in 1906, in a book entitled "Poverty," pointed out that at that time there were ten millions in the United States living in poverty.

[2] In the United States Census of 1900 (the last census the figures of which were made public), the number of child laborers was placed at 1,752,187.

not answer. On that point you will be tongue-tied, though you will talk wordily enough about other things.

"You have failed in your management. You have made a shambles of civilization. You have been blind and greedy. You have risen up (as you to-day rise up), shamelessly, in our legislative halls, and declared that profits were impossible without the toil of children and babes. Don't take my word for it. It is all in the records against you. You have lulled your conscience to sleep with prattle of sweet ideals and dear moralities. You are fat with power and possession, drunken with success; and you have no more hope against us than have the drones, clustered about the honey-vats, when the worker-bees spring upon them to end their rotund existence. You have failed in your management of society, and your management is to be taken away from you. A million and a half of the men of the working class say that they are going to get the rest of the working class to join with them and take the management away from you. This is the revolution, my masters. Stop it if you can."

For an appreciable lapse of time Ernest's voice continued to ring through the great room. Then arose the throaty rumble I had heard before, and a dozen men were on their feet clamoring for recognition from Colonel Van Gilbert. I noticed Miss Brentwood's shoulders moving convulsively, and for the moment I was angry, for I thought that she was laughing at Ernest. And then I discovered that it was not laughter, but hysteria. She was appalled by what she had done in bringing this firebrand before her blessed Philomath Club.

Colonel Van Gilbert did not notice the dozen men, with passion-wrought faces, who strove to get permission from him to speak. His own face was passion-wrought. He sprang to his feet, waving his arms, and for a moment could utter only incoherent sounds. Then speech poured from him. But it was not the speech of a one-hundred-thousand-dollar lawyer, nor was the rhetoric old-fashioned.

"Fallacy upon fallacy!" he cried. "Never in all my life have I heard so many fallacies uttered in one short hour. And besides, young man, I must tell you that you have said nothing new. I learned all that at college before you were born. Jean Jacques Rousseau enunciated your socialistic theory nearly two centuries ago. A return to the soil, forsooth! Reversion! Our biology teaches the absurdity of it. It has been truly said that a little learning is a dangerous thing, and you have exemplified it to-night with your madcap theories. Fallacy upon fallacy! I was never so nauseated in my life with overplus of fallacy. That for your immature generalizations and childish reasonings!"

He snapped his fingers contemptuously and proceeded to sit down. There were lip-exclamations of approval on the part of the women, and hoarser notes of confirmation came from the men. As for the dozen men who were clamoring for the floor, half of them began speaking at once. The confusion and babel was indescribable. Never had Mrs. Pertonwaithe's spacious walls beheld such a spectacle. These, then, were the cool captains of industry and lords of society, these snarling, growling savages in evening clothes. Truly Ernest had shaken them when he stretched out his hands for their money-bags, his hands that had appeared in their eyes as the hands of the fifteen hundred thousand revolutionists.

But Ernest never lost his head in a situation. Before Colonel Van Gilbert had succeeded in sitting down, Ernest was on his feet and had sprung forward.

"One at a time!" he roared at them.

The sound arose from his great lungs and dominated the human tempest. By sheer compulsion of personality he commanded silence.

"One at a time," he repeated softly. "Let me answer Colonel Van Gilbert. After that the rest of you can come at me— but one at a time, remember. No mass-plays here. This is not a football field.

"As for you," he went on, turning toward Colonel Van Gilbert, "you have replied to nothing I have said. You have merely made a few excited and dogmatic assertions about my mental caliber. That may serve you in your business, but you can't talk to me like that. I am not a workingman, cap in hand, asking you to increase my wages or to protect me from the machine at which I work. You cannot be dogmatic with truth when you deal with me. Save that for dealing with your wage-slaves. They will not dare reply to you because you hold their bread and butter, their lives, in your hands.

"As for this return to nature that you say you learned at college before I was born, permit me to point out that on the face of it you cannot have learned anything since. Socialism has no more to do with the state of nature than has differential calculus with a Bible class. I have called your class stupid when outside the realm of business. You, sir, have brilliantly exemplified my statement."

This terrible castigation of her hundred-thousand-dollar lawyer was too much for Miss Brentwood's nerves. Her hysteria became violent, and she was helped, weeping and laughing, out of the room. It was just as well, for there was worse to follow.

"Don't take my word for it," Ernest continued, when the interruption had been led away. "Your own authorities with one unanimous voice will prove you stupid. Your own hired purveyors of knowledge will tell you that you are wrong. Go to your meekest little assistant instructor of sociology and ask him what is the difference between Rousseau's theory of the return to nature and the theory of socialism; ask your greatest orthodox bourgeois political economists and sociologists; question through the pages of every text-book written on the subject and stored on the shelves of your subsidized libraries; and from one and all the answer will be that there is nothing congruous between the return to nature and socialism. On the other hand, the unanimous affirmative answer will be that the return to nature and socialism are diametrically opposed to each other. As I say, don't take my word for it. The record of your stupidity is there in the books, your own books that you never read. And so far as your stupidity is concerned, you are but the exemplar of your class.

"You know law and business, Colonel Van Gilbert. You know how to serve corporations and increase dividends by twisting the law. Very good. Stick to it. You are quite a figure. You are a very good lawyer, but you are a poor historian, you know nothing of sociology, and your biology is contemporaneous with Pliny."

Here Colonel Van Gilbert writhed in his chair. There was perfect quiet in the room. Everybody sat fascinated—paralyzed, I may say. Such fearful treatment of the great Colonel Van Gilbert was unheard of, undreamed of, impossible to believe—the great Colonel Van Gilbert before whom judges trembled when he arose in court. But Ernest never gave quarter to an enemy.

"This is, of course, no reflection on you," Ernest said. "Every man to his trade. Only you stick to your trade, and I'll stick to mine. You have specialized. When it comes to a knowledge of the law, of how best to evade the law or make new law for the benefit of thieving corporations, I am down in the dirt at your feet. But when it comes to sociology—my trade—you are down in the dirt at my feet. Remember that. Remember, also, that your law is the stuff of a day, and that you are not versatile in the stuff of more than a day. Therefore your dogmatic assertions and rash generalizations on things historical and sociological are not worth the breath you waste on them."

Ernest paused for a moment and regarded him thoughtfully, noting his face dark and twisted with anger, his panting chest, his writhing body, and his slim white hands nervously clenching and unclenching.

"But it seems you have breath to use, and I'll give you a chance to use it. I indicted your class. Show me that my indictment is wrong. I pointed out to you the wretchedness of modern man—three million child slaves in the United States, without whose labor profits would not be possible, and fifteen million under-fed, ill-clothed, and worse-housed people. I pointed out that modern man's producing power through social organization and the use of machinery was a thousand times greater than that of the cave-man. And I stated that from these two facts no other conclusion was possible than that the capitalist class had mismanaged. This was my indictment, and I specifically and at length challenged you to answer it. Nay, I did more. I prophesied that you would not answer. It remains for your breath to smash my prophecy. You called my speech fallacy. Show the fallacy, Colonel Van Gilbert. Answer the indictment that I and my fifteen hundred thousand comrades have brought against your class and you."

Colonel Van Gilbert quite forgot that he was presiding, and that in courtesy he should permit the other clamorers to speak. He was on his feet, flinging his arms, his rhetoric, and his control to the winds, alternately abusing Ernest for his

youth and demagoguery, and savagely attacking the working
class, elaborating its inefficiency and worthlessness.

"For a lawyer, you are the hardest man to keep to a point
I ever saw," Ernest began his answer to the tirade. "My youth
has nothing to do with what I have enunciated. Nor has the
worthlessness of the working class. I charged the capitalist
class with having mismanaged society. You have not answered. You have made no attempt to answer. Why? Is it
because you have no answer? You are the champion of this
whole audience. Every one here, except me, is hanging on
your lips for that answer. They are hanging on your lips for
that answer because they have no answer themselves. As for
me, as I said before, I know that you not only cannot answer,
but that you will not attempt an answer."

"This is intolerable!" Colonel Van Gilbert cried out. "This
is insult!"

"That you should not answer is intolerable," Ernest replied
gravely. "No man can be intellectually insulted. Insult, in its
very nature, is emotional. Recover yourself. Give me an intellectual answer to my intellectual charge that the capitalist class
has mismanaged society."

Colonel Van Gilbert remained silent, a sullen, superior
expression on his face, such as will appear on the face of a
man who will not bandy words with a ruffian.

"Do not be downcast," Ernest said. "Take consolation in
the fact that no member of your class has ever yet answered
that charge." He turned to the other men who were anxious
to speak. "And now it's your chance. Fire away, and do not
forget that I here challenge you to give the answer that Colonel Van Gilbert has failed to give."

It would be impossible for me to write all that was said in
the discussion. I never realized before how many words could
be spoken in three short hours. At any rate, it was glorious.
The more his opponents grew excited, the more Ernest deliberately excited them. He had an encyclopædic command
of the field of knowledge, and by a word or a phrase, by
delicate rapier thrusts, he punctured them. He named the
points of their illogic. This was a false syllogism, that conclusion had no connection with the premise, while that
next premise was an impostor because it had cunningly

hidden in it the conclusion that was being attempted to be proved. This was an error, that was an assumption, and the next was an assertion contrary to ascertained truth as printed in all the text-books.

And so it went. Sometimes he exchanged the rapier for the club and went smashing amongst their thoughts right and left. And always he demanded facts and refused to discuss theories. And his facts made for them a Waterloo. When they attacked the working class, he always retorted, "The pot calling the kettle black; that is no answer to the charge that your own face is dirty." And to one and all he said: "Why have you not answered the charge that your class has mismanaged? You have talked about other things and things concerning other things, but you have not answered. Is it because you have no answer?"

It was at the end of the discussion that Mr. Wickson spoke. He was the only one that was cool, and Ernest treated him with a respect he had not accorded the others.

"No answer is necessary," Mr. Wickson said with slow deliberation. "I have followed the whole discussion with amazement and disgust. I am disgusted with you, gentlemen, members of my class. You have behaved like foolish little schoolboys, what with intruding ethics and the thunder of the common politician into such a discussion. You have been outgeneralled and outclassed. You have been very wordy, and all you have done is buzz. You have buzzed like gnats about a bear. Gentlemen, there stands the bear" (he pointed at Ernest), "and your buzzing has only tickled his ears.

"Believe me, the situation is serious. That bear reached out his paws to-night to crush us. He has said there are a million and a half of revolutionists in the United States. That is a fact. He has said that it is their intention to take away from us our governments, our palaces, and all our purpled ease. That, also, is a fact. A change, a great change, is coming in society; but, haply, it may not be the change the bear anticipates. The bear has said that he will crush us. What if we crush the bear?"

The throat-rumble arose in the great room, and man nodded to man with indorsement and certitude. Their faces were set hard. They were fighters, that was certain.

"But not by buzzing will we crush the bear," Mr. Wickson went on coldly and dispassionately. "We will hunt the bear. We will not reply to the bear in words. Our reply shall be couched in terms of lead. We are in power. Nobody will deny it. By virtue of that power we shall remain in power."

He turned suddenly upon Ernest. The moment was dramatic.

"This, then, is our answer. We have no words to waste on you. When you reach out your vaunted strong hands for our palaces and purpled ease, we will show you what strength is. In roar of shell and shrapnel and in whine of machine-guns will our answer be couched.[1] We will grind you revolutionists down under our heel, and we shall walk upon your faces. The world is ours, we are its lords, and ours it shall remain. As for the host of labor, it has been in the dirt since history began, and I read history aright. And in the dirt it shall remain so long as I and mine and those that come after us have the power. There is the word. It is the king of words— Power. Not God, not Mammon, but Power. Pour it over your tongue till it tingles with it. Power."

"I am answered," Ernest said quietly. "It is the only answer that could be given. Power. It is what we of the working class preach. We know, and well we know by bitter experience, that no appeal for the right, for justice, for humanity, can ever touch you. Your hearts are hard as your heels with which you tread upon the faces of the poor. So we have preached power. By the power of our ballots on election day will we take your government away from you—"

"What if you do get a majority, a sweeping majority, on election day?" Mr. Wickson broke in to demand. "Suppose we refuse to turn the government over to you after you have captured it at the ballot-box?"

"That, also, have we considered," Ernest replied. "And we shall give you an answer in terms of lead. Power, you have proclaimed the king of words. Very good. Power it shall be.

---

[1] To show the tenor of thought, the following definition is quoted from "The Cynic's Word Book" (1906 A.D.), written by one Ambrose Bierce, an avowed and confirmed misanthrope of the period: "Grapeshot, *n. An argument which the future is preparing in answer to the demands of American Socialism.*"

And in the day that we sweep to victory at the ballot-box, and you refuse to turn over to us the government we have constitutionally and peacefully captured, and you demand what we are going to do about it—in that day, I say, we shall answer you; and in roar of shell and shrapnel and in whine of machine-guns shall our answer be couched.

"You cannot escape us. It is true that you have read history aright. It is true that labor has from the beginning of history been in the dirt. And it is equally true that so long as you and yours and those that come after you have power, that labor shall remain in the dirt. I agree with you. I agree with all that you have said. Power will be the arbiter, as it always has been the arbiter. It is a struggle of classes. Just as your class dragged down the old feudal nobility, so shall it be dragged down by my class, the working class. If you will read your biology and your sociology as clearly as you do your history, you will see that this end I have described is inevitable. It does not matter whether it is in one year, ten, or a thousand—your class shall be dragged down. And it shall be done by power. We of the labor hosts have conned that word over till our minds are all a-tingle with it. Power. It is a kingly word."

And so ended the night with the Philomaths.

VI

Adumbrations

I<small>T</small> <small>WAS</small> about this time that the warnings of coming events began to fall about us thick and fast. Ernest had already questioned father's policy of having socialists and labor leaders at his house, and of openly attending socialist meetings; and father had only laughed at him for his pains. As for myself, I was learning much from this contact with the working-class leaders and thinkers. I was seeing the other side of the shield. I was delighted with the unselfishness and high idealism I encountered, though I was appalled by the vast philosophic and scientific literature of socialism that was opened up to me. I was learning fast, but I learned not fast enough to realize then the peril of our position.

There were warnings, but I did not heed them. For instance, Mrs. Pertonwaithe and Mrs. Wickson exercised tremendous social power in the university town, and from them emanated the sentiment that I was a too-forward and self-assertive young woman with a mischievous penchant for officiousness and interference in other persons' affairs. This I thought no more than natural, considering the part I had played in investigating the case of Jackson's arm. But the effect of such a sentiment, enunciated by two such powerful social arbiters, I underestimated.

True, I noticed a certain aloofness on the part of my general friends, but this I ascribed to the disapproval that was prevalent in my circles of my intended marriage with Ernest. It was not till some time afterward that Ernest pointed out to me clearly that this general attitude of my class was something more than spontaneous, that behind it were the hidden springs of an organized conduct. "You have given shelter to an enemy of your class," he said. "And not alone shelter, for you have given your love, yourself. This is treason to your class. Think not that you will escape being penalized."

But it was before this that father returned one afternoon. Ernest was with me, and we could see that father was angry—philosophically angry. He was rarely really angry; but a certain measure of controlled anger he allowed himself. He called it a tonic. And we could see that he was tonic-angry when he entered the room.

"What do you think?" he demanded. "I had luncheon with Wilcox."

Wilcox was the superannuated president of the university, whose withered mind was stored with generalizations that were young in 1870, and which he had since failed to revise.

"I was invited," father announced. "I was sent for."

He paused, and we waited.

"Oh, it was done very nicely, I'll allow; but I was reprimanded. I! And by that old fossil!"

"I'll wager I know what you were reprimanded for," Ernest said.

"Not in three guesses," father laughed.

"One guess will do," Ernest retorted. "And it won't be a guess. It will be a deduction. You were reprimanded for your private life."

"The very thing!" father cried. "How did you guess?"

"I knew it was coming. I warned you before about it."

"Yes, you did," father meditated. "But I couldn't believe it. At any rate, it is only so much more clinching evidence for my book."

"It is nothing to what will come," Ernest went on, "if you persist in your policy of having these socialists and radicals of all sorts at your house, myself included."

"Just what old Wilcox said. And of all unwarranted things! He said it was in poor taste, utterly profitless, anyway, and not in harmony with university traditions and policy. He said much more of the same vague sort, and I couldn't pin him down to anything specific. I made it pretty awkward for him, and he could only go on repeating himself and telling me how much he honored me, and all the world honored me, as a scientist. It wasn't an agreeable task for him. I could see he didn't like it."

"He was not a free agent," Ernest said. "The leg-bar[1] is not always worn graciously."

"Yes. I got that much out of him. He said the university needed ever so much more money this year than the state was willing to furnish; and that it must come from wealthy personages who could not but be offended by the swerving of the university from its high ideal of the passionless pursuit of passionless intelligence. When I tried to pin him down to what my home life had to do with swerving the university from its high ideal, he offered me a two years' vacation, on full pay, in Europe, for recreation and research. Of course I couldn't accept it under the circumstances."

"It would have been far better if you had," Ernest said gravely.

"It was a bribe," father protested; and Ernest nodded.

"Also, the beggar said that there was talk, tea-table gossip and so forth, about my daughter being seen in public with so notorious a character as you, and that it was not in keeping with university tone and dignity. Not that he personally objected—oh, no; but that there was talk and that I would understand."

Ernest considered this announcement for a moment, and then said, and his face was very grave, withal there was a sombre wrath in it:

"There is more behind this than a mere university ideal. Somebody has put pressure on President Wilcox."

"Do you think so?" father asked, and his face showed that he was interested rather than frightened.

"I wish I could convey to you the conception that is dimly forming in my own mind," Ernest said. "Never in the history of the world was society in so terrific flux as it is right now. The swift changes in our industrial system are causing equally swift changes in our religious, political, and social structures. An unseen and fearful revolution is taking place in the fibre and structure of society. One can only dimly feel these things. But they are in the air, now, to-day. One can feel the loom of them—things vast, vague, and terrible. My mind recoils from

[1] *Leg-bar*—the African slaves were so manacled; also criminals. It was not until the coming of the Brotherhood of Man that the leg-bar passed out of use.

contemplation of what they may crystallize into. You heard Wickson talk the other night. Behind what he said were the same nameless, formless things that I feel. He spoke out of a superconscious apprehension of them."

"You mean . . . ?" father began, then paused.

"I mean that there is a shadow of something colossal and menacing that even now is beginning to fall across the land. Call it the shadow of an oligarchy, if you will; it is the nearest I dare approximate it. What its nature may be I refuse to imagine.[1] But what I wanted to say was this: You are in a perilous position—a peril that my own fear enhances because I am not able even to measure it. Take my advice and accept the vacation."

"But it would be cowardly," was the protest.

"Not at all. You are an old man. You have done your work in the world, and a great work. Leave the present battle to youth and strength. We young fellows have our work yet to do. Avis will stand by my side in what is to come. She will be your representative in the battle-front."

"But they can't hurt me," father objected. "Thank God I am independent. Oh, I assure you, I know the frightful persecution they can wage on a professor who is economically dependent on his university. But I am independent. I have not been a professor for the sake of my salary. I can get along very comfortably on my own income, and the salary is all they can take away from me."

"But you do not realize," Ernest answered. "If all that I fear be so, your private income, your principal itself, can be taken from you just as easily as your salary."

Father was silent for a few minutes. He was thinking

[1] Though, like Everhard, they did not dream of the nature of it, there were men, even before his time, who caught glimpses of the shadow. John C. Calhoun said: "*A power has risen up in the government greater than the people themselves, consisting of many and various and powerful interests, combined into one mass, and held together by the cohesive power of the vast surplus in the banks.*" And that great humanist, Abraham Lincoln, said, just before his assassination: "*I see in the near future a crisis approaching that unnerves me and causes me to tremble for the safety of my country. . . . Corporations have been enthroned, an era of corruption in high places will follow, and the money-power of the country will endeavor to prolong its reign by working upon the prejudices of the people until the wealth is aggregated in a few hands and the Republic is destroyed.*"

deeply, and I could see the lines of decision forming in his face. At last he spoke.

"I shall not take the vacation." He paused again. "I shall go on with my book.[1] You may be wrong, but whether you are wrong or right, I shall stand by my guns."

"All right," Ernest said. "You are travelling the same path that Bishop Morehouse is, and toward a similar smash-up. You'll both be proletarians before you're done with it."

The conversation turned upon the Bishop, and we got Ernest to explain what he had been doing with him.

"He is soul-sick from the journey through hell I have given him. I took him through the homes of a few of our factory workers. I showed him the human wrecks cast aside by the industrial machine, and he listened to their life stories. I took him through the slums of San Francisco, and in drunkenness, prostitution, and criminality he learned a deeper cause than innate depravity. He is very sick, and, worse than that, he has got out of hand. He is too ethical. He has been too severely touched. And, as usual, he is unpractical. He is up in the air with all kinds of ethical delusions and plans for mission work among the cultured. He feels it is his bounden duty to resurrect the ancient spirit of the Church and to deliver its message to the masters. He is overwrought. Sooner or later he is going to break out, and then there's going to be a smash-up. What form it will take I can't even guess. He is a pure, exalted soul, but he is so unpractical. He's beyond me. I can't keep his feet on the earth. And through the air he is rushing on to his Gethsemane. And after this his crucifixion. Such high souls are made for crucifixion."

"And you?" I asked; and beneath my smile was the seriousness of the anxiety of love.

"Not I," he laughed back. "I may be executed, or assassi-

[1] This book, "Economics and Education," was published in that year. Three copies of it are extant; two at Ardis, and one at Asgard. It dealt, in elaborate detail, with one factor in the persistence of the established, namely, the capitalistic bias of the universities and common schools. It was a logical and crushing indictment of the whole system of education that developed in the minds of the students only such ideas as were favorable to the capitalistic régime, to the exclusion of all ideas that were inimical and subversive. The book created a furor, and was promptly suppressed by the Oligarchy.

nated, but I shall never be crucified. I am planted too solidly and stolidly upon the earth."

"But why should you bring about the crucifixion of the Bishop?" I asked. "You will not deny that you are the cause of it."

"Why should I leave one comfortable soul in comfort when there are millions in travail and misery?" he demanded back.

"Then why did you advise father to accept the vacation?"

"Because I am not a pure, exalted soul," was the answer. "Because I am solid and stolid and selfish. Because I love you and, like Ruth of old, thy people are my people. As for the Bishop, he has no daughter. Besides, no matter how small the good, nevertheless his little inadequate wail will be productive of some good in the revolution, and every little bit counts."

I could not agree with Ernest. I knew well the noble nature of Bishop Morehouse, and I could not conceive that his voice raised for righteousness would be no more than a little inadequate wail. But I did not yet have the harsh facts of life at my fingers' ends as Ernest had. He saw clearly the futility of the Bishop's great soul, as coming events were soon to show as clearly to me.

It was shortly after this day that Ernest told me, as a good story, the offer he had received from the government, namely, an appointment as United States Commissioner of Labor. I was overjoyed. The salary was comparatively large, and would make safe our marriage. And then it surely was congenial work for Ernest, and, furthermore, my jealous pride in him made me hail the proffered appointment as a recognition of his abilities.

Then I noticed the twinkle in his eyes. He was laughing at me.

"You are not going to . . . to decline?" I quavered.

"It is a bribe," he said. "Behind it is the fine hand of Wickson, and behind him the hands of greater men than he. It is an old trick, old as the class struggle is old—stealing the captains from the army of labor. Poor betrayed labor! If you but knew how many of its leaders have been bought out in similar ways in the past. It is cheaper, so much cheaper, to buy a general than to fight him and his whole army. There was—

but I'll not call any names. I'm bitter enough over it as it is. Dear heart, I am a captain of labor. I could not sell out. If for no other reason, the memory of my poor old father and the way he was worked to death would prevent."

The tears were in his eyes, this great, strong hero of mine. He never could forgive the way his father had been mal-formed—the sordid lies and the petty thefts he had been compelled to, in order to put food in his children's mouths.

"My father was a good man," Ernest once said to me. "The soul of him was good, and yet it was twisted, and maimed, and blunted by the savagery of his life. He was made into a broken-down beast by his masters, the arch-beasts. He should be alive to-day, like your father. He had a strong constitution. But he was caught in the machine and worked to death—for profit. Think of it. For profit—his life blood transmuted into a wine-supper, or a jewelled gewgaw, or some similar sense-orgy of the parasitic and idle rich, his masters, the arch-beasts."

VII

The Bishop's Vision

T HE BISHOP is out of hand," Ernest wrote me. "He is clear up in the air. To-night he is going to begin putting to rights this very miserable world of ours. He is going to deliver his message. He has told me so, and I cannot dissuade him. To-night he is chairman of the I. P. H., and he will embody his message in his introductory remarks.

"May I bring you to hear him? Of course, he is foredoomed to futility. It will break your heart—it will break his; but for you it will be an excellent object lesson. You know, dear heart, how proud I am because you love me. And because of that I want you to know my fullest value, I want to redeem, in your eyes, some small measure of my unworthiness. And so it is that my pride desires that you shall know my thinking is correct and right. My views are harsh; the futility of so noble a soul as the Bishop will show you the compulsion for such harshness. So come to-night. Sad though this night's happening will be, I feel that it will but draw you more closely to me."

The I. P. H.[1] held its convention that night in San Francisco.[2] This convention had been called to consider public immorality and the remedy for it. Bishop Morehouse presided. He was very nervous as he sat on the platform, and I could see the high tension he was under. By his side were Bishop Dickinson; H. H. Jones, the head of the ethical department in the University of California; Mrs. W. W. Hurd, the great charity organizer; Philip Ward, the equally great philanthropist; and several lesser luminaries in the field of morality and charity. Bishop Morehouse arose and abruptly began:

"I was in my brougham, driving through the streets. It was night-time. Now and then I looked through the carriage win-

[1] There is no clew to the name of the organization for which these initials stand.

[2] It took but a few minutes to cross by ferry from Berkeley to San Francisco. These, and the other bay cities, practically composed one community.

dows, and suddenly my eyes seemed to be opened, and I saw things as they really are. At first I covered my eyes with my hands to shut out the awful sight, and then, in the darkness, the question came to me: What is to be done? What is to be done? A little later the question came to me in another way: What would the Master do? And with the question a great light seemed to fill the place, and I saw my duty sun-clear, as Saul saw his on the way to Damascus.

"I stopped the carriage, got out, and, after a few minutes' conversation, persuaded two of the public women to get into the brougham with me. If Jesus was right, then these two unfortunates were my sisters, and the only hope of their purification was in my affection and tenderness.

"I live in one of the loveliest localities of San Francisco. The house in which I live cost a hundred thousand dollars, and its furnishings, books, and works of art cost as much more. The house is a mansion. No, it is a palace, wherein there are many servants. I never knew what palaces were good for. I had thought they were to live in. But now I know. I took the two women of the street to my palace, and they are going to stay with me. I hope to fill every room in my palace with such sisters as they."

The audience had been growing more and more restless and unsettled, and the faces of those that sat on the platform had been betraying greater and greater dismay and consternation. And at this point Bishop Dickinson arose, and, with an expression of disgust on his face, fled from the platform and the hall. But Bishop Morehouse, oblivious to all, his eyes filled with his vision, continued:

"Oh, sisters and brothers, in this act of mine I find the solution of all my difficulties. I didn't know what broughams were made for, but now I know. They are made to carry the weak, the sick, and the aged; they are made to show honor to those who have lost the sense even of shame.

"I did not know what palaces were made for, but now I have found a use for them. The palaces of the Church should be hospitals and nurseries for those who have fallen by the wayside and are perishing."

He made a long pause, plainly overcome by the thought that was in him, and nervous how best to express it.

"I am not fit, dear brethren, to tell you anything about morality. I have lived in shame and hypocrisies too long to be able to help others; but my action with those women, sisters of mine, shows me that the better way is easy to find. To those who believe in Jesus and his gospel there can be no other relation between man and man than the relation of affection. Love alone is stronger than sin—stronger than death. I therefore say to the rich among you that it is their duty to do what I have done and am doing. Let each one of you who is prosperous take into his house some thief and treat him as his brother, some unfortunate and treat her as his sister, and San Francisco will need no police force and no magistrates; the prisons will be turned into hospitals, and the criminal will disappear with his crime.

"We must give ourselves and not our money alone. We must do as Christ did; that is the message of the Church today. We have wandered far from the Master's teaching. We are consumed in our own flesh-pots. We have put mammon in the place of Christ. I have here a poem that tells the whole story. I should like to read it to you. It was written by an erring soul who yet saw clearly.[1] It must not be mistaken for an attack upon the Catholic Church. It is an attack upon all churches, upon the pomp and splendor of all churches that have wandered from the Master's path and hedged themselves in from his lambs. Here it is:

"The silver trumpets rang across the Dome;
    The people knelt upon the ground with awe;
    And borne upon the necks of men I saw,
Like some great God, the Holy Lord of Rome.

"Priest-like, he wore a robe more white than foam,
    And, king-like, swathed himself in royal red,
    Three crowns of gold rose high upon his head;
In splendor and in light the Pope passed home.

"My heart stole back across wide wastes of years
    To One who wandered by a lonely sea;

[1] Oscar Wilde, one of the lords of language of the nineteenth century of the Christian Era.

And sought in vain for any place of rest:
'Foxes have holes, and every bird its nest,
    I, only I, must wander wearily,
And bruise my feet, and drink wine salt with tears.' "

The audience was agitated, but unresponsive. Yet Bishop
Morehouse was not aware of it. He held steadily on his way.

"And so I say to the rich among you, and to all the rich,
that bitterly you oppress the Master's lambs. You have hardened your hearts. You have closed your ears to the voices that
are crying in the land—the voices of pain and sorrow that
you will not hear but that some day will be heard. And so I
say—"

But at this point H. H. Jones and Philip Ward, who had
already risen from their chairs, led the Bishop off the platform, while the audience sat breathless and shocked.

Ernest laughed harshly and savagely when he had gained
the street. His laughter jarred upon me. My heart seemed
ready to burst with suppressed tears.

"He has delivered his message," Ernest cried. "The manhood and the deep-hidden, tender nature of their Bishop
burst out, and his Christian audience, that loved him, concluded that he was crazy! Did you see them leading him so
solicitously from the platform? There must have been laughter in hell at the spectacle."

"Nevertheless, it will make a great impression, what the
Bishop did and said to-night," I said.

"Think so?" Ernest queried mockingly.

"It will make a sensation," I asserted. "Didn't you see the
reporters scribbling like mad while he was speaking?"

"Not a line of which will appear in to-morrow's papers."

"I can't believe it," I cried.

"Just wait and see," was the answer. "Not a line, not a
thought that he uttered. The daily press? The daily suppres-
sage!"

"But the reporters," I objected. "I saw them."

"Not a word that he uttered will see print. You have forgotten the editors. They draw their salaries for the policy they
maintain. Their policy is to print nothing that is a vital menace to the established. The Bishop's utterance was a violent

assault upon the established morality. It was heresy. They led him from the platform to prevent him from uttering more heresy. The newspapers will purge his heresy in the oblivion of silence. The press of the United States? It is a parasitic growth that battens on the capitalist class. Its function is to serve the established by moulding public opinion, and right well it serves it.

"Let me prophesy. To-morrow's papers will merely mention that the Bishop is in poor health, that he has been working too hard, and that he broke down last night. The next mention, some days hence, will be to the effect that he is suffering from nervous prostration and has been given a vacation by his grateful flock. After that, one of two things will happen: either the Bishop will see the error of his way and return from his vacation a well man in whose eyes there are no more visions, or else he will persist in his madness, and then you may expect to see in the papers, couched pathetically and tenderly, the announcement of his insanity. After that he will be left to gibber his visions to padded walls."

"Now there you go too far!" I cried out.

"In the eyes of society it will truly be insanity," he replied. "What honest man, who is not insane, would take lost women and thieves into his house to dwell with him sisterly and brotherly? True, Christ died between two thieves, but that is another story. Insanity? The mental processes of the man with whom one disagrees, are always wrong. Therefore the mind of the man is wrong. Where is the line between wrong mind and insane mind? It is inconceivable that any sane man can radically disagree with one's most sane conclusions.

"There is a good example of it in this evening's paper. Mary McKenna lives south of Market Street. She is a poor but honest woman. She is also patriotic. But she has erroneous ideas concerning the American flag and the protection it is supposed to symbolize. And here's what happened to her. Her husband had an accident and was laid up in hospital three months. In spite of taking in washing, she got behind in her rent. Yesterday they evicted her. But first, she hoisted an American flag, and from under its folds she announced that by virtue of its protection they could not turn her out on to the cold street. What was done? She was arrested and arraigned for insanity. To-day she was examined by the regular insanity experts. She was found insane. She was consigned to the Napa Asylum."

"But that is far-fetched," I objected. "Suppose I should disagree with everybody about the literary style of a book. They wouldn't send me to an asylum for that."

"Very true," he replied. "But such divergence of opinion would constitute no menace to society. Therein lies the difference. The divergence of opinion on the parts of Mary McKenna and the Bishop do menace society. What if all the poor people should refuse to pay rent and shelter themselves under the American flag? Landlordism would go crumbling. The Bishop's views are just as perilous to society. Ergo, to the asylum with him."

But still I refused to believe.

"Wait and see," Ernest said, and I waited.

Next morning I sent out for all the papers. So far Ernest was right. Not a word that Bishop Morehouse had uttered was in print. Mention was made in one or two of the papers that he had been overcome by his feelings. Yet the platitudes of the speakers that followed him were reported at length.

Several days later the brief announcement was made that he had gone away on a vacation to recover from the effects of overwork. So far so good, but there had been no hint of insanity, nor even of nervous collapse. Little did I dream the terrible road the Bishop was destined to travel—the Gethsemane and crucifixion that Ernest had pondered about.

VIII

The Machine Breakers

IT WAS just before Ernest ran for Congress, on the socialist ticket, that father gave what he privately called his
"Profit and Loss" dinner. Ernest called it the dinner of the
Machine Breakers. In point of fact, it was merely a dinner
for business men—small business men, of course. I doubt
if one of them was interested in any business the total capitalization of which exceeded a couple of hundred thousand
dollars. They were truly representative middle-class business
men.

There was Owen, of Silverberg, Owen & Company—a
large grocery firm with several branch stores. We bought our
groceries from them. There were both partners of the big
drug firm of Kowalt & Washburn, and Mr. Asmunsen, the
owner of a large granite quarry in Contra Costa County. And
there were many similar men, owners or part-owners in small
factories, small businesses and small industries—small capitalists, in short.

They were shrewd-faced, interesting men, and they talked
with simplicity and clearness. Their unanimous complaint
was against the corporations and trusts. Their creed was,
"Bust the Trusts." All oppression originated in the trusts,
and one and all told the same tale of woe. They advocated
government ownership of such trusts as the railroads and
telegraphs, and excessive income taxes, graduated with ferocity, to destroy large accumulations. Likewise they advocated, as a cure for local ills, municipal ownership of such
public utilities as water, gas, telephones, and street railways.

Especially interesting was Mr. Asmunsen's narrative of
his tribulations as a quarry owner. He confessed that he
never made any profits out of his quarry, and this, in spite
of the enormous volume of business that had been caused
by the destruction of San Francisco by the big earthquake.
For six years the rebuilding of San Francisco had been

going on, and his business had quadrupled and octupled, and yet he was no better off.

"The railroad knows my business just a little bit better than I do," he said. "It knows my operating expenses to a cent, and it knows the terms of my contracts. How it knows these things I can only guess. It must have spies in my employ, and it must have access to the parties to all my contracts. For look you, when I place a big contract, the terms of which favor me a goodly profit, the freight rate from my quarry to market is promptly raised. No explanation is made. The railroad gets my profit. Under such circumstances I have never succeeded in getting the railroad to reconsider its raise. On the other hand, when there have been accidents, increased expenses of operating, or contracts with less profitable terms, I have always succeeded in getting the railroad to lower its rate. What is the result? Large or small, the railroad always gets my profits."

"What remains to you over and above," Ernest interrupted to ask, "would roughly be the equivalent of your salary as a manager did the railroad own the quarry."

"The very thing," Mr. Asmunsen replied. "Only a short time ago I had my books gone through for the past ten years. I discovered that for those ten years my gain was just equivalent to a manager's salary. The railroad might just as well have owned my quarry and hired me to run it."

"But with this difference," Ernest laughed; "the railroad would have had to assume all the risk which you so obligingly assumed for it."

"Very true," Mr. Asmunsen answered sadly.

Having let them have their say, Ernest began asking questions right and left. He began with Mr. Owen.

"You started a branch store here in Berkeley about six months ago?"

"Yes," Mr. Owen answered.

"And since then I've noticed that three little corner groceries have gone out of business. Was your branch store the cause of it?"

Mr. Owen affirmed with a complacent smile. "They had no chance against us."

"Why not?"

"We had greater capital. With a large business there is always less waste and greater efficiency."

"And your branch store absorbed the profits of the three small ones. I see. But tell me, what became of the owners of the three stores?"

"One is driving a delivery wagon for us. I don't know what happened to the other two."

Ernest turned abruptly on Mr. Kowalt.

"You sell a great deal at cut-rates.[1] What have become of the owners of the small drug stores that you forced to the wall?"

"One of them, Mr. Haasfurther, has charge now of our prescription department," was the answer.

"And you absorbed the profits they had been making?"

"Surely. That is what we are in business for."

"And you?" Ernest said suddenly to Mr. Asmunsen. "You are disgusted because the railroad has absorbed your profits?"

Mr. Asmunsen nodded.

"What you want is to make profits yourself?"

Again Mr. Asmunsen nodded.

"Out of others?"

There was no answer.

"Out of others?" Ernest insisted.

"That is the way profits are made," Mr. Asmunsen replied curtly.

"Then the business game is to make profits out of others, and to prevent others from making profits out of you. That's it, isn't it?"

Ernest had to repeat his question before Mr. Asmunsen gave an answer, and then he said:

"Yes, that's it, except that we do not object to the others making profits so long as they are not extortionate."

"By extortionate you mean large; yet you do not object to making large profits yourself? . . . Surely not?"

And Mr. Asmunsen amiably confessed to the weakness. There was one other man who was quizzed by Ernest at this

[1] A lowering of selling price to cost, and even to less than cost. Thus, a large company could sell at a loss for a longer period than a small company, and so drive the small company out of business. A common device of competition.

juncture, a Mr. Calvin, who had once been a great dairy-owner.

"Some time ago you were fighting the Milk Trust," Ernest said to him; "and now you are in Grange politics.[1] How did it happen?"

"Oh, I haven't quit the fight," Mr. Calvin answered, and he looked belligerent enough. "I'm fighting the Trust on the only field where it is possible to fight—the political field. Let me show you. A few years ago we dairymen had everything our own way."

"But you competed among yourselves?" Ernest interrupted.

"Yes, that was what kept the profits down. We did try to organize, but independent dairymen always broke through us. Then came the Milk Trust."

"Financed by surplus capital from Standard Oil,"[2] Ernest said.

"Yes," Mr. Calvin acknowledged. "But we did not know it at the time. Its agents approached us with a club. 'Come in and be fat,' was their proposition, 'or stay out and starve.' Most of us came in. Those that didn't, starved. Oh, it paid us . . . at first. Milk was raised a cent a quart. One-quarter of this cent came to us. Three-quarters of it went to the Trust. Then milk was raised another cent, only we didn't get any of that cent. Our complaints were useless. The Trust was in control. We discovered that we were pawns. Finally, the additional quarter of a cent was denied us. Then the Trust began to squeeze us out. What could we do? We were squeezed out. There were no dairymen, only a Milk Trust."

"But with milk two cents higher, I should think you could have competed," Ernest suggested slyly.

"So we thought. We tried it." Mr. Calvin paused a moment. "It broke us. The Trust could put milk upon the market more cheaply than we. It could sell still at a slight profit when we were selling at actual loss. I dropped fifty thousand

[1]Many efforts were made during this period to organize the perishing farmer class into a political party, the aim of which was to destroy the trusts and corporations by drastic legislation. All such attempts ended in failure.

[2]The first successful great trust—almost a generation in advance of the rest.

dollars in that venture. Most of us went bankrupt.[1] The dairy-men were wiped out of existence."

"So the Trust took your profits away from you," Ernest said, "and you've gone into politics in order to legislate the Trust out of existence and get the profits back?"

Mr. Calvin's face lighted up. "That is precisely what I say in my speeches to the farmers. That's our whole idea in a nutshell."

"And yet the Trust produces milk more cheaply than could the independent dairymen?" Ernest queried.

"Why shouldn't it, with the splendid organization and new machinery its large capital makes possible?"

"There is no discussion," Ernest answered. "It certainly should, and, furthermore, it does."

Mr. Calvin here launched out into a political speech in ex-position of his views. He was warmly followed by a number of the others, and the cry of all was to destroy the trusts.

"Poor simple folk," Ernest said to me in an undertone. "They see clearly as far as they see, but they see only to the ends of their noses."

A little later he got the floor again, and in his characteristic way controlled it for the rest of the evening.

"I have listened carefully to all of you," he began, "and I see plainly that you play the business game in the ortho-dox fashion. Life sums itself up to you in profits. You have a firm and abiding belief that you were created for the sole purpose of making profits. Only there is a hitch. In the midst of your own profit-making along comes the trust and takes your profits away from you. This is a dilemma that interferes somehow with the aim of creation, and the only way out, as it seems to you, is to destroy that which takes from you your profits.

"I have listened carefully, and there is only one name that will epitomize you. I shall call you that name. You are machine-breakers. Do you know what a machine-breaker is? Let me tell you. In the eighteenth century, in England,

---

[1]Bankruptcy—a peculiar institution that enabled an individual, who had failed in competitive industry, to forego paying his debts. The effect was to ameliorate the too savage conditions of the fang-and-claw social struggle.

men and women wove cloth on hand-looms in their own
cottages. It was a slow, clumsy, and costly way of weaving
cloth, this cottage system of manufacture. Along came the
steam-engine and labor-saving machinery. A thousand
looms assembled in a large factory, and driven by a central
engine wove cloth vastly more cheaply than could the cottage weavers on their hand-looms. Here in the factory was
combination, and before it competition faded away. The
men and women who had worked the hand-looms for
themselves now went into the factories and worked the
machine-looms, not for themselves, but for the capitalist
owners. Furthermore, little children went to work on the
machine-looms, at lower wages, and displaced the men.
This made hard times for the men. Their standard of living
fell. They starved. And they said it was all the fault of the
machines. Therefore, they proceeded to break the machines.
They did not succeed, and they were very stupid.

"Yet you have not learned their lesson. Here are you, a
century and a half later, trying to break machines. By your
own confession the trust machines do the work more efficiently and more cheaply than you can. That is why you
cannot compete with them. And yet you would break those
machines. You are even more stupid than the stupid workmen
of England. And while you maunder about restoring competition, the trusts go on destroying you.

"One and all you tell the same story,—the passing away of
competition and the coming on of combination. You, Mr.
Owen, destroyed competition here in Berkeley when your
branch store drove the three small groceries out of business.
Your combination was more effective. Yet you feel the pressure of other combinations on you, the trust combinations,
and you cry out. It is because you are not a trust. If you were
a grocery trust for the whole United States, you would be
singing another song. And the song would be, 'Blessed are
the trusts.' And yet again, not only is your small combination
not a trust, but you are aware yourself of its lack of strength.
You are beginning to divine your own end. You feel yourself
and your branch stores a pawn in the game. You see the powerful interests rising and growing more powerful day by day;
you feel their mailed hands descending upon your profits and

taking a pinch here and a pinch there—the railroad trust, the oil trust, the steel trust, the coal trust; and you know that in the end they will destroy you, take away from you the last per cent of your little profits.

"You, sir, are a poor gamester. When you squeezed out the three small groceries here in Berkeley by virtue of your superior combination, you swelled out your chest, talked about efficiency and enterprise, and sent your wife to Europe on the profits you had gained by eating up the three small groceries. It is dog eat dog, and you ate them up. But, on the other hand, you are being eaten up in turn by the bigger dogs, wherefore you squeal. And what I say to you is true of all of you at this table. You are all squealing. You are all playing the losing game, and you are all squealing about it.

"But when you squeal you don't state the situation flatly, as I have stated it. You don't say that you like to squeeze profits out of others, and that you are making all the row because others are squeezing your profits out of you. No, you are too cunning for that. You say something else. You make small-capitalist political speeches such as Mr. Calvin made. What did he say? Here are a few of his phrases I caught: 'Our original principles are all right,' 'What this country requires is a return to fundamental American methods—free opportunity for all,' 'The spirit of liberty in which this nation was born,' 'Let us return to the principles of our forefathers.'

"When he says 'free opportunity for all,' he means free opportunity to squeeze profits, which freedom of opportunity is now denied him by the great trusts. And the absurd thing about it is that you have repeated these phrases so often that you believe them. You want opportunity to plunder your fellow-men in your own small way, but you hypnotize yourselves into thinking you want freedom. You are piggish and acquisitive, but the magic of your phrases leads you to believe that you are patriotic. Your desire for profits, which is sheer selfishness, you metamorphose into altruistic solicitude for suffering humanity. Come on now, right here amongst ourselves, and be honest for once. Look the matter in the face and state it in direct terms."

There were flushed and angry faces at the table, and withal a measure of awe. They were a little frightened at this smooth-faced young fellow, and the swing and smash of his words, and his dreadful trait of calling a spade a spade. Mr. Calvin promptly replied.

"And why not?" he demanded. "Why can we not return to the ways of our fathers when this republic was founded? You have spoken much truth, Mr. Everhard, unpalatable though it has been. But here amongst outselves let us speak out. Let us throw off all disguise and accept the truth as Mr. Everhard has flatly stated it. It is true that we smaller capitalists are after profits, and that the trusts are taking our profits away from us. It is true that we want to destroy the trusts in order that our profits may remain to us. And why can we not do it? Why not? I say, why not?"

"Ah, now we come to the gist of the matter," Ernest said with a pleased expression. "I'll try to tell you why not, though the telling will be rather hard. You see, you fellows have studied business, in a small way, but you have not studied social evolution at all. You are in the midst of a transition stage now in economic evolution, but you do not understand it, and that's what causes all the confusion. Why cannot you return? Because you can't. You can no more make water run up hill than can you cause the tide of economic evolution to flow back in its channel along the way it came. Joshua made the sun stand still upon Gibeon, but you would outdo Joshua. You would make the sun go backward in the sky. You would have time retrace its steps from noon to morning.

"In the face of labor-saving machinery, of organized production, of the increased efficiency of combination, you would set the economic sun back a whole generation or so to the time when there were no great capitalists, no great machinery, no railroads—a time when a host of little capitalists warred with each other in economic anarchy, and when production was primitive, wasteful, unorganized, and costly. Believe me, Joshua's task was easier, and he had Jehovah to help him. But God has forsaken you small capitalists. The sun of the small capitalists is setting. It will never rise again. Nor is it in your power even to make it stand still. You are perishing, and you are doomed to perish utterly from the face of society.

"This is the fiat of evolution. It is the word of God. Combination is stronger than competition. Primitive man was a puny creature hiding in the crevices of the rocks. He combined and made war upon his carnivorous enemies. They were competitive beasts. Primitive man was a combinative beast, and because of it he rose to primacy over all the animals. And man has been achieving greater and greater combinations ever since. It is combination *versus* competition, a thousand centuries long struggle, in which competition has always been worsted. Whoso enlists on the side of competition perishes."

"But the trusts themselves arose out of competition," Mr. Calvin interrupted.

"Very true," Ernest answered. "And the trusts themselves destroyed competition. That, by your own word, is why you are no longer in the dairy business."

The first laughter of the evening went around the table, and even Mr. Calvin joined in the laugh against himself.

"And now, while we are on the trusts," Ernest went on, "let us settle a few things. I shall make certain statements, and if you disagree with them, speak up. Silence will mean agreement. Is it not true that a machine-loom will weave more cloth and weave more cheaply than a hand-loom?" He paused, but nobody spoke up. "Is it not then highly irrational to break the machine-loom and go back to the clumsy and more costly hand-loom method of weaving?" Heads nodded in acquiescence. "Is it not true that that combination known as a trust produces more efficiently and cheaply than can a thousand competing small concerns?" Still no one objected. "Then is it not irrational to destroy that cheap and efficient combination?"

No one answered for a long time. Then Mr. Kowalt spoke.

"What are we to do, then?" he demanded. "To destroy the trusts is the only way we can see to escape their domination."

Ernest was all fire and aliveness on the instant.

"I'll show you another way!" he cried. "Let us not destroy those wonderful machines that produce efficiently and cheaply. Let us control them. Let us profit by their effi-

ciency and cheapness. Let us run them for ourselves. Let
us oust the present owners of the wonderful machines, and
let us own the wonderful machines ourselves. That, gentlemen, is socialism, a greater combination than the trusts, a
greater economic and social combination than any that has
as yet appeared on the planet. It is in line with evolution.
We meet combination with greater combination. It is the
winning side. Come on over with us socialists and play on
the winning side."

Here arose dissent. There was a shaking of heads, and mutterings arose.

"All right, then, you prefer to be anachronisms," Ernest
laughed. "You prefer to play atavistic rôles. You are doomed to
perish as all atavisms perish. Have you ever asked what will happen to you when greater combinations than even the present
trusts arise? Have you ever considered where you will stand
when the great trusts themselves combine into the combination
of combinations—into the social, economic, and political
trust?"

He turned abruptly and irrelevantly upon Mr. Calvin.

"Tell me," Ernest said, "if this is not true. You are compelled to form a new political party because the old parties
are in the hands of the trusts. The chief obstacle to your
Grange propaganda is the trusts. Behind every obstacle you
encounter, every blow that smites you, every defeat that you
receive, is the hand of the trusts. Is this not so? Tell me."

Mr. Calvin sat in uncomfortable silence.

"Go ahead," Ernest encouraged.

"It is true," Mr. Calvin confessed. "We captured the state
legislature of Oregon and put through splendid protective
legislation, and it was vetoed by the governor, who was a
creature of the trusts. We elected a governor of Colorado,
and the legislature refused to permit him to take office. Twice
we have passed a national income tax, and each time the supreme court smashed it as unconstitutional. The courts are in
the hands of the trusts. We, the people, do not pay our judges
sufficiently. But there will come a time—"

"When the combination of the trusts will control all legislation, when the combination of the trusts will itself be the
government," Ernest interrupted.

"Never! never!" were the cries that arose. Everybody was excited and belligerent.

"Tell me," Ernest demanded, "what will you do when such a time comes?"

"We will rise in our strength!" Mr. Asmunsen cried, and many voices backed his decision.

"That will be civil war," Ernest warned them.

"So be it, civil war," was Mr. Asmunsen's answer, with the cries of all the men at the table behind him. "We have not forgotten the deeds of our forefathers. For our liberties we are ready to fight and die."

Ernest smiled.

"Do not forget," he said, "that we had tacitly agreed that liberty in your case, gentlemen, means liberty to squeeze profits out of others."

The table was angry, now, fighting angry; but Ernest controlled the tumult and made himself heard.

"One more question. When you rise in your strength, remember, the reason for your rising will be that the government is in the hands of the trusts. Therefore, against your strength the government will turn the regular army, the navy, the militia, the police—in short, the whole organized war machinery of the United States. Where will your strength be then?"

Dismay sat on their faces, and before they could recover, Ernest struck again.

"Do you remember, not so long ago, when our regular army was only fifty thousand? Year by year it has been increased until to-day it is three hundred thousand."

Again he struck.

"Nor is that all. While you diligently pursued that favorite phantom of yours, called profits, and moralized about that favorite fetich of yours, called competition, even greater and more direful things have been accomplished by combination. There is the militia."

"It is our strength!" cried Mr. Kowalt. "With it we would repel the invasion of the regular army."

"You would go into the militia yourself," was Ernest's retort, "and be sent to Maine, or Florida, or the Philippines, or anywhere else, to drown in blood your own comrades civil-warring for their liberties. While from Kansas, or Wisconsin, or any other state, your own comrades would go into the militia and come here to California to drown in blood your own civil-warring."

Now they were really shocked, and they sat wordless, until Mr. Owen murmured:

"We would not go into the militia. That would settle it. We would not be so foolish."

Ernest laughed outright.

"You do not understand the combination that has been effected. You could not help yourself. You would be drafted into the militia."

"There is such a thing as civil law," Mr. Owen insisted.

"Not when the government suspends civil law. In that day when you speak of rising in your strength, your strength would be turned against yourself. Into the militia you would go, willy-nilly. Habeas corpus, I heard some one mutter just now. Instead of habeas corpus you would get post mortems. If you refused to go into the militia, or to obey after you were in, you would be tried by drumhead court martial and shot down like dogs. It is the law."

"It is not the law!" Mr. Calvin asserted positively. "There is no such law. Young man, you have dreamed all this. Why, you spoke of sending the militia to the Philippines. That is unconstitutional. The Constitution especially states that the militia cannot be sent out of the country."

"What's the Constitution got to do with it?" Ernest demanded. "The courts interpret the Constitution, and the courts, as Mr. Asmunsen agreed, are the creatures of the trusts. Besides, it is as I have said, the law. It has been the law for years, for nine years, gentlemen."

"That we can be drafted into the militia?" Mr. Calvin asked incredulously. "That they can shoot us by drumhead court martial if we refuse?"

"Yes," Ernest answered, "precisely that."

"How is it that we have never heard of this law?" my father asked, and I could see that it was likewise new to him.

"For two reasons," Ernest said. "First, there has been no need to enforce it. If there had, you'd have heard of it soon enough. And secondly, the law was rushed through Congress and the Senate secretly, with practically no discussion. Of course, the newspapers made no mention of it. But we socialists knew about it. We published it in our papers. But you never read our papers."

"I still insist you are dreaming," Mr. Calvin said stubbornly. "The country would never have permitted it."

"But the country did permit it," Ernest replied. "And as for my dreaming—" he put his hand in his pocket and drew out a small pamphlet—"tell me if this looks like dream-stuff."

He opened it and began to read:

" 'Section One, be it enacted, and so forth and so forth, that the militia shall consist of every able-bodied male citizen of the respective states, territories, and District of Columbia, who is more than eighteen and less than forty-five years of age.'

" 'Section Seven, that any officer or enlisted man'—remember Section One, gentlemen, you are all enlisted men—'that any enlisted man of the militia who shall refuse or neglect to present himself to such mustering officer upon being called forth as herein prescribed, shall be subject to trial by court martial, and shall be punished as such court martial shall direct.'

" 'Section Eight, that courts martial, for the trial of officers or men of the militia, shall be composed of militia officers only.'

" 'Section Nine, that the militia, when called into the actual service of the United States, shall be subject to the same rules and articles of war as the regular troops of the United States.'

"There you are, gentlemen, American citizens, and fellow-militiamen. Nine years ago we socialists thought that law was aimed against labor. But it would seem that it was aimed against you, too. Congressman Wiley, in the brief discussion that was permitted, said that the bill 'provided for a reserve force to take the mob by the throat'—you're the mob, gentlemen—'and protect at all hazards life, liberty, and property.' And in the time to come, when you rise in your strength, remember that you will be rising against the property of the trusts, and the liberty of the trusts, according to the law, to squeeze you. Your teeth are pulled, gentlemen. Your claws are trimmed. In the day you rise in your strength, toothless and clawless, you will be as harmless as an army of clams."

"I don't believe it!" Kowalt cried. "There is no such law. It is a canard got up by you socialists."

"This bill was introduced in the House of Representatives on July 30, 1902," was the reply. "It was introduced by Representative Dick of Ohio. It was rushed through. It was passed unanimously by the Senate on January 14, 1903. And just seven days afterward was approved by the President of the United States."[1]

[1] Everhard was right in the essential particulars, though his date of the introduction of the bill is in error. The bill was introduced on June 30, and not on July 30. The *Congressional Record* is here in Ardis, and a reference to it shows mention of the bill on the following dates: June 30, December 9, 15, 16, and 17, 1902, and January 7 and 14, 1903. The ignorance evidenced by the business men at the dinner was nothing unusual. Very few people knew of the existence of this law. E. Untermann, a revolutionist, in July, 1903, published a pamphlet at Girard, Kansas, on the "Militia Bill." This pamphlet had a small circulation among workingmen; but already had the segregation of classes proceeded so far, that the members of the middle class never heard of the pamphlet at all, and so remained in ignorance of the law.

IX

The Mathematics of a Dream

IN THE MIDST of the consternation his revelation had produced, Ernest began again to speak.

"You have said, a dozen of you to-night, that socialism is impossible. You have asserted the impossible, now let me demonstrate the inevitable. Not only is it inevitable that you small capitalists shall pass away, but it is inevitable that the large capitalists, and the trusts also, shall pass away. Remember, the tide of evolution never flows backward. It flows on and on, and it flows from competition to combination, and from little combination to large combination, and from large combination to colossal combination, and it flows on to socialism, which is the most colossal combination of all.

"You tell me that I dream. Very good. I'll give you the mathematics of my dream; and here, in advance, I challenge you to show that my mathematics are wrong. I shall develop the inevitability of the breakdown of the capitalist system, and I shall demonstrate mathematically why it must break down. Here goes, and bear with me if at first I seem irrelevant.

"Let us, first of all, investigate a particular industrial process, and whenever I state something with which you disagree, please interrupt me. Here is a shoe factory. This factory takes leather and makes it into shoes. Here is one hundred dollars' worth of leather. It goes through the factory and comes out in the form of shoes, worth, let us say, two hundred dollars. What has happened? One hundred dollars has been added to the value of the leather. How was it added? Let us see.

"Capital and labor added this value of one hundred dollars. Capital furnished the factory, the machines, and paid all the expenses. Labor furnished labor. By the joint effort of capital and labor one hundred dollars of value was added. Are you all agreed so far?"

Heads nodded around the table in affirmation.

"Labor and capital having produced this one hundred dollars, now proceed to divide it. The statistics of this division are fractional; so let us, for the sake of convenience, make them roughly approximate. Capital takes fifty dollars as its share, and labor gets in wages fifty dollars as its share. We will not enter into the squabbling over the division.[1] No matter how much squabbling takes place, in one percentage or another the division is arranged. And take notice here, that what is true of this particular industrial process is true of all industrial processes. Am I right?"

Again the whole table agreed with Ernest.

"Now, suppose labor, having received its fifty dollars, wanted to buy back shoes. It could only buy back fifty dollars' worth. That's clear, isn't it?

"And now we shift from this particular process to the sum total of all industrial processes in the United States, which includes the leather itself, raw material, transportation, selling, everything. We will say, for the sake of round figures, that the total production of wealth in the United States in one year is four billion dollars. Then labor has received in wages, during the same period, two billion dollars. Four billion dollars has been produced. How much of this can labor buy back? Two billions. There is no discussion of this, I am sure. For that matter, my percentages are mild. Because of a thousand capitalistic devices, labor cannot buy back even half of the total product.

"But to return. We will say labor buys back two billions. Then it stands to reason that labor can consume only two billions. There are still two billions to be accounted for, which labor cannot buy back and consume."

"Labor does not consume its two billions, even," Mr. Kowalt spoke up. "If it did, it would not have any deposits in the savings banks."

"Labor's deposits in the savings banks are only a sort of reserve fund that is consumed as fast as it accumulates. These

[1]Everhard here clearly develops the cause of all the labor troubles of that time. In the division of the joint-product, capital wanted all it could get, and labor wanted all it could get. This quarrel over the division was irreconcilable. So long as the system of capitalistic production existed, labor and capital continued to quarrel over the division of the joint-product. It is a ludicrous spectacle to us, but we must not forget that we have seven centuries' advantage over those that lived in that time.

deposits are saved for old age, for sickness and accident, and for funeral expenses. The savings bank deposit is simply a piece of the loaf put back on the shelf to be eaten next day. No, labor consumes all of the total product that its wages will buy back.

"Two billions are left to capital. After it has paid its expenses, does it consume the remainder? Does capital consume all of its two billions?"

Ernest stopped and put the question point blank to a number of the men. They shook their heads.

"I don't know," one of them frankly said.

"Of course you do," Ernest went on. "Stop and think a moment. If capital consumed its share, the sum total of capital could not increase. It would remain constant. If you will look at the economic history of the United States, you will see that the sum total of capital has continually increased. Therefore capital does not consume its share. Do you remember when England owned so much of our railroad bonds? As the years went by, we bought back those bonds. What does that mean? That part of capital's unconsumed share bought back the bonds. What is the meaning of the fact that to-day the capitalists of the United States own hundreds and hundreds of millions of dollars of Mexican bonds, Russian bonds, Italian bonds, Grecian bonds? The meaning is that those hundreds and hundreds of millions were part of capital's share which capital did not consume. Furthermore, from the very beginning of the capitalist system, capital has never consumed all of its share.

"And now we come to the point. Four billion dollars of wealth is produced in one year in the United States. Labor buys back and consumes two billions. Capital does not consume the remaining two billions. There is a large balance left over unconsumed. What is done with this balance? What can be done with it? Labor cannot consume any of it, for labor has already spent all its wages. Capital will not consume this balance, because, already, according to its nature, it has consumed all it can. And still remains the balance. What can be done with it? What is done with it?"

"It is sold abroad," Mr. Kowalt volunteered.

"The very thing," Ernest agreed. "Because of this balance

arises our need for a foreign market. This is sold abroad. It has to be sold abroad. There is no other way of getting rid of it. And that unconsumed surplus, sold abroad, becomes what we call our favorable balance of trade. Are we all agreed so far?"

"Surely it is a waste of time to elaborate these A B C's of commerce," Mr. Calvin said tartly. "We all understand them."

"And it is by these A B C's I have so carefully elaborated that I shall confound you," Ernest retorted. "There's the beauty of it. And I'm going to confound you with them right now. Here goes.

"The United States is a capitalist country that has developed its resources. According to its capitalist system of industry, it has an unconsumed surplus that must be got rid of, and that must be got rid of abroad.[1] What is true of the United States is true of every other capitalist country with developed resources. Every one of such countries has an unconsumed surplus. Don't forget that they have already traded with one another, and that these surpluses yet remain. Labor in all these countries has spent its wages, and cannot buy any of the surpluses. Capital in all these countries has already consumed all it is able according to its nature. And still remain the surpluses. They cannot dispose of these surpluses to one another. How are they going to get rid of them?"

"Sell them to countries with undeveloped resources," Mr. Kowalt suggested.

"The very thing. You see, my argument is so clear and simple that in your own minds you carry it on for me. And now for the next step. Suppose the United States disposes of its surplus to a country with undeveloped resources like, say, Brazil. Remember this surplus is over and above trade, which

[1] Theodore Roosevelt, President of the United States a few years prior to this time, made the following public declaration: *"A more liberal and extensive reciprocity in the purchase and sale of commodities is necessary, so that the overproduction of the United States can be satisfactorily disposed of to foreign countries."* Of course, this overproduction he mentions was the profits of the capitalist system over and beyond the consuming power of the capitalists. It was at this time that Senator Mark Hanna said: *"The production of wealth in the United States is one-third larger annually than its consumption."* Also a fellow-Senator, Chauncey Depew, said: *"The American people produce annually two billions more wealth than they consume."*

articles of trade have been consumed. What, then, does the United States get in return from Brazil?"

"Gold," said Mr. Kowalt.

"But there is only so much gold, and not much of it, in the world," Ernest objected.

"Gold in the form of securities and bonds and so forth," Mr. Kowalt amended.

"Now you've struck it," Ernest said. "From Brazil the United States, in return for her surplus, gets bonds and securities. And what does that mean? It means that the United States is coming to own railroads in Brazil, factories, mines, and lands in Brazil. And what is the meaning of that in turn?"

Mr. Kowalt pondered and shook his head.

"I'll tell you," Ernest continued. "It means that the resources of Brazil are being developed. And now, the next point. When Brazil, under the capitalist system, has developed her resources, she will herself have an unconsumed surplus. Can she get rid of this surplus to the United States? No, because the United States has herself a surplus. Can the United States do what she previously did—get rid of her surplus to Brazil? No, for Brazil now has a surplus, too.

"What happens? The United States and Brazil must both seek out other countries with undeveloped resources, in order to unload the surpluses on them. But by the very process of unloading the surpluses, the resources of those countries are in turn developed. Soon they have surpluses, and are seeking other countries on which to unload. Now, gentlemen, follow me. The planet is only so large. There are only so many countries in the world. What will happen when every country in the world, down to the smallest and last, with a surplus in its hands, stands confronting every other country with surpluses in their hands?"

He paused and regarded his listeners. The bepuzzlement in their faces was delicious. Also, there was awe in their faces. Out of abstractions Ernest had conjured a vision and made them see it. They were seeing it then, as they sat there, and they were frightened by it.

"We started with A B C, Mr. Calvin," Ernest said slyly. "I have now given you the rest of the alphabet. It is very simple. That is the beauty of it. You surely have the answer forthcoming. What, then, when every country in the world has an unconsumed surplus? Where will your capitalist system be then?"

But Mr. Calvin shook a troubled head. He was obviously questing back through Ernest's reasoning in search of an error.

"Let me briefly go over the ground with you again," Ernest said. "We began with a particular industrial process, the shoe factory. We found that the division of the joint product that took place there was similar to the division that took place in the sum total of all industrial processes. We found that labor could buy back with its wages only so much of the product, and that capital did not consume all of the remainder of the product. We found that when labor had consumed to the full extent of its wages, and when capital had consumed all it wanted, there was still left an unconsumed surplus. We agreed that this surplus could only be disposed of abroad. We agreed, also, that the effect of unloading this surplus on another country would be to develop the resources of that country, and that in a short time that country would have an unconsumed surplus. We extended this process to all the countries on the planet, till every country was producing every year, and every day, an unconsumed surplus, which it could dispose of to no other country. And now I ask you again, what are we going to do with those surpluses?"

Still no one answered.

"Mr. Calvin?" Ernest queried.

"It beats me," Mr. Calvin confessed.

"I never dreamed of such a thing," Mr. Asmunsen said. "And yet it does seem clear as print."

It was the first time I had ever heard Karl Marx's[1] doctrine of surplus value elaborated, and Ernest had done it so simply that I, too, sat puzzled and dumfounded.

[1] Karl Marx—the great intellectual hero of Socialism. A German Jew of the nineteenth century. A contemporary of John Stuart Mill. It seems incredible to us that whole generations should have elapsed after the enunciation of Marx's economic discoveries, in which time he was sneered at by the world's accepted thinkers and scholars. Because of his discoveries he was banished from his native country, and he died an exile in England.

"I'll tell you a way to get rid of the surplus," Ernest said. "Throw it into the sea. Throw every year hundreds of millions of dollars' worth of shoes and wheat and clothing and all the commodities of commerce into the sea. Won't that fix it?"

"It will certainly fix it," Mr. Calvin answered. "But it is absurd for you to talk that way."

Ernest was upon him like a flash.

"Is it a bit more absurd than what you advocate, you machine-breaker, returning to the antediluvian ways of your forefathers? What do you propose in order to get rid of the surplus? You would escape the problem of the surplus by not producing any surplus. And how do you propose to avoid producing a surplus? By returning to a primitive method of production, so confused and disorderly and irrational, so wasteful and costly, that it will be impossible to produce a surplus."

Mr. Calvin swallowed. The point had been driven home. He swallowed again and cleared his throat.

"You are right," he said. "I stand convicted. It is absurd. But we've got to do something. It is a case of life and death for us of the middle class. We refuse to perish. We elect to be absurd and to return to the truly crude and wasteful methods of our forefathers. We will put back industry to its pre-trust stage. We will break the machines. And what are you going to do about it?"

"But you can't break the machines," Ernest replied. "You cannot make the tide of evolution flow backward. Opposed to you are two great forces, each of which is more powerful than you of the middle class. The large capitalists, the trusts, in short, will not let you turn back. They don't want the machines destroyed. And greater than the trusts, and more powerful, is labor. It will not let you destroy the machines. The ownership of the world, along with the machines, lies between the trusts and labor. That is the battle alignment. Neither side wants the destruction of the machines. But each side wants to possess the machines. In this battle the middle class has no place. The middle class is a pygmy between two giants. Don't you see, you poor perishing middle class, you are caught between the upper and nether millstones, and even now has the grinding begun.

"I have demonstrated to you mathematically the inevitable breakdown of the capitalist system. When every country stands with an unconsumed and unsalable surplus on its hands, the capitalist system will break down under the terrific structure of profits that it itself has reared. And in that day there won't be any destruction of the machines. The struggle then will be for the ownership of the machines. If labor wins, your way will be easy. The United States, and the whole world for that matter, will enter upon a new and tremendous era. Instead of being crushed by the machines, life will be made fairer, and happier, and nobler by them. You of the destroyed middle class, along with labor—there will be nothing but labor then; so you, and all the rest of labor, will participate in the equitable distribution of the products of the wonderful machines. And we, all of us, will make new and more wonderful machines. And there won't be any unconsumed surplus, because there won't be any profits."

"But suppose the trusts win in this battle over the ownership of the machines and the world?" Mr. Kowalt asked.

"Then," Ernest answered, "you, and labor, and all of us, will be crushed under the iron heel of a despotism as relentless and terrible as any despotism that has blackened the pages of the history of man. That will be a good name for that despotism, the Iron Heel."[1]

There was a long pause, and every man at the table meditated in ways unwonted and profound.

"But this socialism of yours is a dream," Mr. Calvin said; and repeated, "a dream."

"I'll show you something that isn't a dream, then," Ernest answered. "And that something I shall call the Oligarchy. You call it the Plutocracy. We both mean the same thing, the large capitalists or the trusts. Let us see where the power lies to-day. And in order to do so, let us apportion society into its class divisions.

"There are three big classes in society. First comes the Plu-

[1] The earliest known use of that name to designate the Oligarchy.

tocracy, which is composed of wealthy bankers, railway magnates, corporation directors, and trust magnates. Second, is
the middle class, your class, gentlemen, which is composed of
farmers, merchants, small manufacturers, and professional
men. And third and last comes my class, the proletariat,
which is composed of the wage-workers.[1]

"You cannot but grant that the ownership of wealth constitutes essential power in the United States to-day. How is
this wealth owned by these three classes? Here are the figures.
The Plutocracy owns sixty-seven billions of wealth. Of the
total number of persons engaged in occupations in the
United States, only nine-tenths of one per cent are from
the Plutocracy, yet the Plutocracy owns seventy per cent
of the total wealth. The middle class owns twenty-four billions. Twenty-nine per cent of those in occupations are from
the middle class, and they own twenty-five per cent of the
total wealth. Remains the proletariat. It owns four billions.
Of all persons in occupations, seventy per cent come from the
proletariat; and the proletariat owns four per cent of the total
wealth. Where does the power lie, gentlemen?"

"From your own figures, we of the middle class are more
powerful than labor," Mr. Asmunsen remarked.

"Calling us weak does not make you stronger in the face of
the strength of the Plutocracy," Ernest retorted. "And furthermore, I'm not done with you. There is a greater strength
than wealth, and it is greater because it cannot be taken
away. Our strength, the strength of the proletariat, is in our
muscles, in our hands to cast ballots, in our fingers to pull
triggers. This strength we cannot be stripped of. It is the
primitive strength, it is the strength that is to life germane, it
is the strength that is stronger than wealth, and that wealth
cannot take away.

"But your strength is detachable. It can be taken away from
you. Even now the Plutocracy is taking it away from you. In
the end it will take it all away from you. And then you will

[1] This division of society made by Everhard is in accordance with that made
by Lucien Sanial, one of the statistical authorities of that time. His calculation of the membership of these divisions by occupations, from the United
States Census of 1900, is as follows: Plutocratic class, 250,251; Middle class,
8,429,845; and Proletariat class, 20,393,137.

cease to be the middle class. You will descend to us. You will become proletarians. And the beauty of it is that you will then add to our strength. We will hail you brothers, and we will fight shoulder to shoulder in the cause of humanity.

"You see, labor has nothing concrete of which to be despoiled. Its share of the wealth of the country consists of clothes and household furniture, with here and there, in very rare cases, an unencumbered home. But you have the concrete wealth, twenty-four billions of it, and the Plutocracy will take it away from you. Of course, there is the large likelihood that the proletariat will take it away first. Don't you see your position, gentlemen? The middle class is a wobbly little lamb between a lion and a tiger. If one doesn't get you, the other will. And if the Plutocracy gets you first, why it's only a matter of time when the Proletariat gets the Plutocracy.

"Even your present wealth is not a true measure of your power. The strength of your wealth at this moment is only an empty shell. That is why you are crying out your feeble little battle-cry, 'Return to the ways of our fathers.' You are aware of your impotency. You know that your strength is an empty shell. And I'll show you the emptiness of it.

"What power have the farmers? Over fifty per cent are thralls by virtue of the fact that they are merely tenants or are mortgaged. And all of them are thralls by virtue of the fact that the trusts already own or control (which is the same thing only better)—own and control all the means of marketing the crops, such as cold storage, railroads, elevators, and steamship lines. And, furthermore, the trusts control the markets. In all this the farmers are without power. As regards their political and governmental power, I'll take that up later, along with the political and governmental power of the whole middle class.

"Day by day the trusts squeeze out the farmers as they squeezed out Mr. Calvin and the rest of the dairymen. And day by day are the merchants squeezed out in the same way. Do you remember how, in six months, the Tobacco Trust squeezed out over four hundred cigar stores in New York City alone? Where are the old-time owners of the coal fields? You know to-day, without my telling you, that the Railroad Trust owns or controls the entire anthracite and bituminous coal fields. Doesn't the Standard Oil Trust[1] own a score of the ocean lines? And does it not also control copper, to say nothing of running a smelter trust as a little side enterprise? There are ten thousand cities in the United States to-night lighted by the companies owned or controlled by Standard Oil, and in as many cities all the electric transportation,—urban, suburban, and interurban,—is in the hands of Standard Oil. The small capitalists who were in these thousands of enterprises are gone. You know that. It's the same way that you are going.

"The small manufacturer is like the farmer; and small manufacturers and farmers to-day are reduced, to all intents and purposes, to feudal tenure. For that matter, the professional men and the artists are at this present moment villeins in everything but name, while the politicians are henchmen. Why do you, Mr. Calvin, work all your nights and days to organize the farmers, along with the rest of the middle class, into a new political party? Because the politicians of the old parties will have nothing to do with your atavistic ideas; and with your atavistic ideas, they will have nothing to do because they are what I said they are, henchmen, retainers of the Plutocracy.

"I spoke of the professional men and the artists as villeins. What else are they? One and all, the professors, the preachers, and the editors, hold their jobs by serving the Plutocracy, and their service consists of propagating only such ideas as are either harmless to or commendatory of the Plutocracy. Whenever they propagate ideas that menace the Plutocracy, they lose their jobs, in which case, if they have not provided for the rainy day, they descend into the proletariat and either perish or become working-class agitators. And don't forget that it is the press, the pulpit, and the university that mould public opinion, set the thought-pace of the nation. As for the artists, they merely pander to the little less than ignoble tastes of the Plutocracy.

"But after all, wealth in itself is not the real power; it is the means to power, and power is governmental. Who controls the government to-day? The proletariat with its

[1] Standard Oil and Rockefeller—see footnote on page 425.

twenty millions engaged in occupations? Even you laugh at
the idea. Does the middle class, with its eight million occupied members? No more than the proletariat. Who, then,
controls the government? The Plutocracy, with its paltry
quarter of a million of occupied members. But this quarter
of a million does not control the government, though it
renders yeoman service. It is the brain of the Plutocracy
that controls the government, and this brain consists of
seven[1] small and powerful groups of men. And do not forget that these groups are working to-day practically in uni-
son.

"Let me point out the power of but one of them, the
railroad group. It employs forty thousand lawyers to defeat
the people in the courts. It issues countless thousands of
free passes to judges, bankers, editors, ministers, university
men, members of state legislatures, and of Congress. It
maintains luxurious lobbies[2] at every state capital, and at
the national capital; and in all the cities and towns of the
land it employs an immense army of pettifoggers and small
politicians whose business is to attend primaries, pack conventions, get on juries, bribe judges, and in every way to
work for its interests.[3]

"Gentlemen, I have merely sketched the power of one of

[1]Even as late as 1907, it was considered that eleven groups dominated the
country, but this number was reduced by the amalgamation of the five railroad groups into a supreme combination of all the railroads. These five
groups so amalgamated, along with their financial and political allies, were
(1) James J. Hill with his control of the Northwest; (2) the Pennsylvania
railway group, Schiff financial manager, with big banking firms of Philadelphia and New York; (3) Harriman, with Frick for counsel and Odell as political lieutenant, controlling the central continental, Southwestern and
Southern Pacific Coast lines of transportation; (4) the Gould family railway
interests; and (5) Moore, Reid, and Leeds, known as the "Rock Island
crowd." These strong oligarchs arose out of the conflict of competition and
travelled the inevitable road toward combination.

[2]*Lobby*—a peculiar institution for bribing, bulldozing, and corrupting the
legislators who were supposed to represent the people's interests.

[3]A decade before this speech of Everhard's, the New York Board of Trade
issued a report from which the following is quoted: *"The railroads control
absolutely the legislatures of a majority of the states of the Union; they make and
unmake United States Senators, congressmen, and governors, and are practically
dictators of the governmental policy of the United States."*

the seven groups that constitute the brain of the Plutocracy.[1]
Your twenty-four billions of wealth does not give you
twenty-five cents' worth of governmental power. It is an
empty shell, and soon even the empty shell will be taken away
from you. The Plutocracy has all power in its hands to-day.
It to-day makes the laws, for it owns the Senate, Congress,

[1]Rockefeller began as a member of the proletariat, and through thrift and
cunning succeeded in developing the first perfect trust, namely that known as
Standard Oil. We cannot forbear giving the following remarkable page from
the history of the times, to show how the need for reinvestment of the Standard Oil surplus crushed out small capitalists and hastened the breakdown of
the capitalist system. David Graham Phillips was a radical writer of the period, and the quotation, by him, is taken from a copy of the *Saturday Evening
Post*, dated October 4, 1902 A.D. This is the only copy of this publication that
has come down to us, and yet, from its appearance and content, we cannot
but conclude that it was one of the popular periodicals with a large circulation. The quotation here follows:

*"About ten years ago Rockefeller's income was given as thirty millions by an
excellent authority. He had reached the limit of profitable investment of profits in
the oil industry. Here, then, were these enormous sums in cash pouring in —more
than $2,000,000 a month for John Davison Rockefeller alone. The problem of
reinvestment became more serious. It became a nightmare. The oil income was
swelling, swelling, and the number of sound investments limited, even more limited
than it is now. It was through no special eagerness for more gains that the Rockefellers began to branch out from oil into other things. They were forced, swept on
by this inrolling tide of wealth which their monopoly magnet irresistibly attracted.
They developed a staff of investment seekers and investigators. It is said that the
chief of this staff has a salary of $125,000 a year.*

*"The first conspicuous excursion and incursion of the Rockefellers was into the
railway field. By 1895 they controlled one-fifth of the railway mileage of the country.
What do they own or, through dominant ownership, control to-day? They are powerful in all the great railways of New York, north, east, and west, except one,
where their share is only a few millions. They are in most of the great railways
radiating from Chicago. They dominate in several of the systems that extend to the
Pacific. It is their votes that make Mr. Morgan so potent, though, it may be added,
they need his brains more than he needs their votes —at present, and the combination of the two constitutes in large measure the 'community of interest.'*

*"But railways could not alone absorb rapidly enough those mighty floods of gold.
Presently John D. Rockefeller's $2,500,000 a month had increased to four, to five,
to six millions a month, to $75,000,000 a year. Illuminating oil was becoming all
profit. The reinvestments of income were adding their mite of many annual millions.*

*"The Rockefellers went into gas and electricity when those industries had devel-
oped to the safe investment stage. And now a large part of the American people
must begin to enrich the Rockefellers as soon as the sun goes down, no matter what
form of illuminant they use. They went into farm mortgages. It is said that when
prosperity a few years ago enabled the farmers to rid themselves of their mortgages,*

the courts, and the state legislatures. And not only that. Behind law must be force to execute the law. To-day the Plutocracy makes the law, and to enforce the law it has at its
beck and call the police, the army, the navy, and, lastly, the
militia, which is you, and me, and all of us."

Little discussion took place after this, and the dinner soon
broke up. All were quiet and subdued, and leave-taking was
done with low voices. It seemed almost that they were scared
by the vision of the times they had seen.

"The situation is, indeed, serious," Mr. Calvin said to Er-
nest. "I have little quarrel with the way you have depicted it.
Only I disagree with you about the doom of the middle class.
We shall survive, and we shall overthrow the trusts."

"And return to the ways of your fathers," Ernest finished
for him.

"Even so," Mr. Calvin answered gravely. "I know it's a sort
of machine-breaking, and that it is absurd. But then life seems

----

*John D. Rockefeller was moved almost to tears; eight millions which he had thought
taken care of for years to come at a good interest were suddenly dumped upon his
doorstep and there set up a-squawking for a new home. This unexpected addition
to his worriments in finding places for the progeny of his petroleum and their progeny and their progeny's progeny was too much for the equanimity of a man without
a digestion. . . .*

*"The Rockefellers went into mines—iron and coal and copper and lead; into
other industrial companies; into street railways, into national, state, and municipal
bonds; into steamships and steamboats and telegraphy; into real estate, into sky
scrapers and residences and hotels and business blocks; into life insurance, into
banking. There was soon literally no field of industry where their millions were not
at work. . . .*

*"The Rockefeller bank—the National City Bank—is by itself far and away the
biggest bank in the United States. It is exceeded in the world only by the Bank of
England and the Bank of France. The deposits average more than one hundred
millions a day; and it dominates the call loan market on Wall Street and the stock
market. But it is not alone; it is the head of the Rockefeller chain of banks, which
includes fourteen banks and trust companies in New York City, and banks of great
strength and influence in every large money center in the country.*

*"John D. Rockefeller owns Standard Oil stock worth between four and five
hundred millions at the market quotations. He has a hundred millions in the steel
trust, almost as much in a single western railway system, half as much in a second,
and so on and on and on until the mind wearies of the cataloguing. His income
last year was about $100,000,000—it is doubtful if the incomes of all
the Rothschilds together make a greater sum. And it is going up by leaps and
bounds."*

absurd to-day, what of the machinations of the Plutocracy. And at any rate, our sort of machine-breaking is at least practical and possible, which your dream is not. Your socialistic dream is . . . well, a dream. We cannot follow you."

"I only wish you fellows knew a little something about evolution and sociology," Ernest said wistfully, as they shook hands. "We would be saved so much trouble if you did."

X

The Vortex

FOLLOWING like thunder claps upon the Business Men's dinner, occurred event after event of terrifying moment; and I, little I, who had lived so placidly all my days in the quiet university town, found myself and my personal affairs drawn into the vortex of the great world-affairs. Whether it was my love for Ernest, or the clear sight he had given me of the society in which I lived, that made me a revolutionist, I know not; but a revolutionist I became, and I was plunged into a whirl of happenings that would have been inconceivable three short months before.

The crisis in my own fortunes came simultaneously with great crises in society. First of all, father was discharged from the university. Oh, he was not technically discharged. His resignation was demanded, that was all. This, in itself, did not amount to much. Father, in fact, was delighted. He was especially delighted because his discharge had been precipitated by the publication of his book, "Economics and Education." It clinched his argument, he contended. What better evidence could be advanced to prove that education was dominated by the capitalist class?

But this proof never got anywhere. Nobody knew he had been forced to resign from the university. He was so eminent a scientist that such an announcement, coupled with the reason for his enforced resignation, would have created somewhat of a furor all over the world. The newspapers showered him with praise and honor, and commended him for having given up the drudgery of the lecture room in order to devote his whole time to scientific research.

At first father laughed. Then he became angry—tonic angry. Then came the suppression of his book. This suppression was performed secretly, so secretly that at first we could not comprehend. The publication of the book had immediately caused a bit of excitement in the country. Father had been politely abused in the capitalist press, the tone of the abuse being to the effect that it was a pity so great a scientist should leave his field and invade the realm of sociology, about which he knew nothing and wherein he had promptly become lost. This lasted for a week, while father chuckled and said the book had touched a sore spot on capitalism. And then, abruptly, the newspapers and the critical magazines ceased saying anything about the book at all. Also, and with equal suddenness, the book disappeared from the market. Not a copy was obtainable from any bookseller. Father wrote to the publishers and was informed that the plates had been accidentally injured. An unsatisfactory correspondence followed. Driven finally to an unequivocal stand, the publishers stated that they could not see their way to putting the book into type again, but that they were willing to relinquish their rights in it.

"And you won't find another publishing house in the country to touch it," Ernest said. "And if I were you, I'd hunt cover right now. You've merely got a foretaste of the Iron Heel."

But father was nothing if not a scientist. He never believed in jumping to conclusions. A laboratory experiment was no experiment if it were not carried through in all its details. So he patiently went the round of the publishing houses. They gave a multitude of excuses, but not one house would consider the book.

When father became convinced that the book had actually been suppressed, he tried to get the fact into the newspapers; but his communications were ignored. At a political meeting of the socialists, where many reporters were present, father saw his chance. He arose and related the history of the suppression of the book. He laughed next day when he read the newspapers, and then he grew angry to a degree that eliminated all tonic qualities. The papers made no mention of the book, but they misreported him beautifully. They twisted his words and phrases away from the context, and turned his subdued and controlled remarks into a howling anarchistic speech. It was done artfully. One instance, in particular, I remember. He had used the phrase "social revolution." The reporter merely dropped out "social." This was sent out all over the country in an Associated Press despatch, and from

all over the country arose a cry of alarm. Father was branded
as a nihilist and an anarchist, and in one cartoon that was
copied widely he was portrayed waving a red flag at the head
of a mob of long-haired, wild-eyed men who bore in their
hands torches, knives, and dynamite bombs.

He was assailed terribly in the press, in long and abusive
editorials, for his anarchy, and hints were made of mental
breakdown on his part. This behavior, on the part of the capitalist press, was nothing new, Ernest told us. It was the custom, he said, to send reporters to all the socialist meetings for
the express purpose of misreporting and distorting what was
said, in order to frighten the middle class away from any possible affiliation with the proletariat. And repeatedly Ernest
warned father to cease fighting and to take to cover.

The socialist press of the country took up the fight, however, and throughout the reading portion of the working class
it was known that the book had been suppressed. But this
knowledge stopped with the working class. Next, the "Appeal
to Reason," a big socialist publishing house, arranged with
father to bring out the book. Father was jubilant, but Ernest
was alarmed.

"I tell you we are on the verge of the unknown," he insisted. "Big things are happening secretly all around us. We
can feel them. We do not know what they are, but they are
there. The whole fabric of society is a-tremble with them.
Don't ask me. I don't know myself. But out of this flux of
society something is about to crystallize. It is crystallizing
now. The suppression of the book is a precipitation. How
many books have been suppressed? We haven't the least idea.
We are in the dark. We have no way of learning. Watch out
next for the suppression of the socialist press and socialist
publishing houses. I'm afraid it's coming. We are going to be
throttled."

Ernest had his hand on the pulse of events even more
closely than the rest of the socialists, and within two days the
first blow was struck. The *Appeal to Reason* was a weekly, and
its regular circulation amongst the proletariat was seven
hundred and fifty thousand. Also, it very frequently got out
special editions of from two to five millions. These great editions were paid for and distributed by the small army of vol-

untary workers who had marshalled around the *Appeal*. The first blow was aimed at these special editions, and it was a crushing one. By an arbitrary ruling of the Post Office, these editions were decided to be not the regular circulation of the paper, and for that reason were denied admission to the mails.

A week later the Post Office Department ruled that the paper was seditious, and barred it entirely from the mails. This was a fearful blow to the socialist propaganda. The *Appeal* was desperate. It devised a plan of reaching its subscribers through the express companies, but they declined to handle it. This was the end of the *Appeal*. But not quite. It prepared to go on with its book publishing. Twenty thousand copies of father's book were in the bindery, and the presses were turning off more. And then, without warning, a mob arose one night, and, under a waving American flag, singing patriotic songs, set fire to the great plant of the *Appeal* and totally destroyed it.

Now Girard, Kansas, was a quiet, peaceable town. There had never been any labor troubles there. The *Appeal* paid union wages; and, in fact, was the backbone of the town, giving employment to hundreds of men and women. It was not the citizens of Girard that composed the mob. This mob had risen up out of the earth apparently, and to all intents and purposes, its work done, it had gone back into the earth. Ernest saw in the affair the most sinister import.

"The Black Hundreds[1] are being organized in the United States," he said. "This is the beginning. There will be more of it. The Iron Heel is getting bold."

And so perished father's book. We were to see much of the Black Hundreds as the days went by. Week by week more of the socialist papers were barred from the mails, and in a number of instances the Black Hundreds destroyed the socialist presses. Of course, the newspapers of the land lived up to the reactionary policy of the ruling class, and the destroyed socialist press was misrepresented and vilified, while the Black

---

[1] The Black Hundreds were reactionary mobs organized by the perishing Autocracy in the Russian Revolution. These reactionary groups attacked the revolutionary groups, and also, at needed moments, rioted and destroyed property so as to afford the Autocracy the pretext of calling out the Cossacks.

Hundreds were represented as true patriots and saviours of society. So convincing was all this misrepresentation that even sincere ministers in the pulpit praised the Black Hundreds while regretting the necessity of violence.

History was making fast. The fall elections were soon to occur, and Ernest was nominated by the socialist party to run for Congress. His chance for election was most favorable. The street-car strike in San Francisco had been broken. And following upon it the teamsters' strike had been broken. These two defeats had been very disastrous to organized labor. The whole Water Front Federation, along with its allies in the structural trades, had backed up the teamsters, and all had smashed down ingloriously. It had been a bloody strike. The police had broken countless heads with their riot clubs; and the death list had been augmented by the turning loose of a machine-gun on the strikers from the barns of the Marsden Special Delivery Company.

In consequence, the men were sullen and vindictive. They wanted blood, and revenge. Beaten on their chosen field, they were ripe to seek revenge by means of political action. They still maintained their labor organization, and this gave them strength in the political struggle that was on. Ernest's chance for election grew stronger and stronger. Day by day unions and more unions voted their support to the socialists, until even Ernest laughed when the Undertakers' Assistants and the Chicken Pickers fell into line. Labor became mulish. While it packed the socialist meetings with mad enthusiasm, it was impervious to the wiles of the old-party politicians. The old-party orators were usually greeted with empty halls, though occasionally they encountered full halls where they were so roughly handled that more than once it was necessary to call out the police reserves.

History was making fast. The air was vibrant with things happening and impending. The country was on the verge of hard times,[1] caused by a series of prosperous years wherein the difficulty of disposing abroad of the unconsumed surplus had become increasingly difficult. Industries were working

[1] Under the capitalist régime these periods of hard times were as inevitable as they were absurd. Prosperity always brought calamity. This, of course, was due to the excess of unconsumed profits that was piled up.

short time; many great factories were standing idle against the time when the surplus should be gone; and wages were being cut right and left.

Also, the great machinist strike had been broken. Two hundred thousand machinists, along with their five hundred thousand allies in the metal-working trades, had been defeated in as bloody a strike as had ever marred the United States. Pitched battles had been fought with the small armies of armed strike-breakers[1] put in the field by the employers' associations; the Black Hundreds, appearing in scores of wide-scattered places, had destroyed property; and, in consequence, a hundred thousand regular soldiers of the United States had been called out to put a frightful end to the whole affair. A number of the labor leaders had been executed; many others had been sentenced to prison, while thousands of the rank and file of the strikers had been herded into bull-pens[2] and abominably treated by the soldiers.

The years of prosperity were now to be paid for. All markets were glutted; all markets were falling; and amidst the general crumble of prices the price of labor crumbled fastest of all. The land was convulsed with industrial dissensions. Labor was striking here, there, and everywhere; and where it was not striking, it was being turned out by the capitalists. The papers were filled with tales of violence and blood. And through it all the Black Hundreds played their part. Riot, arson, and wanton destruction of property was their function,

---

[1] *Strike-breakers*—these were, in purpose and practice and everything except name, the private soldiers of the capitalists. They were thoroughly organized and well armed, and they were held in readiness to be hurled in special trains to any part of the country where labor went out on strike or was locked out by the employers. Only those curious times could have given rise to the amazing spectacle of one, Farley, a notorious commander of strike-breakers, who, in 1906, swept across the United States in special trains from New York to San Francisco with an army of twenty-five hundred men, fully armed and equipped, to break a strike of the San Francisco street-car men. Such an act was in direct violation of the laws of the land. The fact that this act, and thousands of similar acts, went unpunished, goes to show how completely the judiciary was the creature of the Plutocracy.

[2] *Bull-pen*—in a miners' strike in Idaho, in the latter part of the nineteenth century, it happened that many of the strikers were confined in a bull-pen by the troops. The practice and the name continued in the twentieth century.

and well they performed it. The whole regular army was in
the field, called there by the actions of the Black Hundreds.[1]
All cities and towns were like armed camps, and laborers were
shot down like dogs. Out of the vast army of the unemployed
the strike-breakers were recruited; and when the strike-breakers were worsted by the labor unions, the troops always appeared and crushed the unions. Then there was the militia. As
yet, it was not necessary to have recourse to the secret militia
law. Only the regularly organized militia was out, and it was
out everywhere. And in this time of terror, the regular army
was increased an additional hundred thousand by the government.

Never had labor received such an all-around beating. The
great captains of industry, the oligarchs, had for the first time
thrown their full weight into the breach the struggling employers' associations had made. These associations were practically middle-class affairs, and now, compelled by hard times
and crashing markets, and aided by the great captains of industry, they gave organized labor an awful and decisive defeat. It was an all-powerful alliance, but it was an alliance of
the lion and the lamb, as the middle class was soon to learn.

Labor was bloody and sullen, but crushed. Yet its defeat
did not put an end to the hard times. The banks, themselves
constituting one of the most important forces of the Oligarchy, continued to call in credits. The Wall Street[2] group
turned the stock market into a maelstrom where the values of

[1] The name only, and not the idea, was imported from Russia. The Black
Hundreds were a development out of the secret agents of the capitalists, and
their use arose in the labor struggles of the nineteenth century. There is no
discussion of this. No less an authority of the times than Carroll D. Wright,
United States Commissioner of Labor, is responsible for the statement. From
his book, entitled "The Battles of Labor," is quoted the declaration that "*in
some of the great historic strikes the employers themselves have instigated acts of
violence*;" that manufacturers have deliberately provoked strikes in order to
get rid of surplus stock; and that freight cars have been burned by employers'
agents during railroad strikes in order to increase disorder. It was out of
these secret agents of the employers that the Black Hundreds arose; and it
was they, in turn, that later became that terrible weapon of the Oligarchy,
the agents-provocateurs.

[2] *Wall Street*—so named from a street in ancient New York, where was
situated the stock exchange, and where the irrational organization of society
permitted underhanded manipulation of all the industries of the country.

all the land crumbled away almost to nothingness. And out of all the rack and ruin rose the form of the nascent Oligarchy, imperturbable, indifferent, and sure. Its serenity and certitude was terrifying. Not only did it use its own vast power, but it used all the power of the United States Treasury to carry out its plans.

The captains of industry had turned upon the middle class. The employers' associations, that had helped the captains of industry to tear and rend labor, were now torn and rent by their quondam allies. Amidst the crashing of the middle men, the small business men and manufacturers, the trusts stood firm. Nay, the trusts did more than stand firm. They were active. They sowed wind, and wind, and ever more wind; for they alone knew how to reap the whirlwind and make a profit out of it. And such profits! Colossal profits! Strong enough themselves to weather the storm that was largely their own brewing, they turned loose and plundered the wrecks that floated about them. Values were pitifully and inconceivably shrunken, and the trusts added hugely to their holdings, even extending their enterprises into many new fields—and always at the expense of the middle class.

Thus the summer of 1912 witnessed the virtual death-thrust to the middle class. Even Ernest was astounded at the quickness with which it had been done. He shook his head ominously and looked forward without hope to the fall elections.

"It's no use," he said. "We are beaten. The Iron Heel is here. I had hoped for a peaceable victory at the ballot-box. I was wrong. Wickson was right. We shall be robbed of our few remaining liberties; the Iron Heel will walk upon our faces; nothing remains but a bloody revolution of the working class. Of course we will win, but I shudder to think of it."

And from then on Ernest pinned his faith in revolution. In this he was in advance of his party. His fellow-socialists could not agree with him. They still insisted that victory could be gained through the elections. It was not that they were stunned. They were too cool-headed and courageous for that. They were merely incredulous, that was all. Ernest could not get them seriously to fear the coming of the Oligarchy. They were stirred by him, but they were too sure of their own

strength. There was no room in their theoretical social evolution for an oligarchy, therefore the Oligarchy could not be.

"We'll send you to Congress and it will be all right," they
told him at one of our secret meetings.

"And when they take me out of Congress," Ernest replied
coldly, "and put me against a wall, and blow my brains out—
what then?"

"Then we'll rise in our might," a dozen voices answered at
once.

"Then you'll welter in your gore," was his retort. "I've
heard that song sung by the middle class, and where is it now
in its might?"

XI

The Great Adventure

M R. WICKSON did not send for father. They met by chance on the ferry-boat to San Francisco, so that the warning he gave father was not premeditated. Had they not met accidentally, there would not have been any warning. Not that the outcome would have been different, however. Father came of stout old *Mayflower*[1] stock, and the blood was imperative in him.

"Ernest was right," he told me, as soon as he had returned home. "Ernest is a very remarkable young man, and I'd rather see you his wife than the wife of Rockefeller himself or the King of England."

"What's the matter?" I asked in alarm.

"The Oligarchy is about to tread upon our faces—yours and mine. Wickson as much as told me so. He was very kind—for an oligarch. He offered to reinstate me in the university. What do you think of that? He, Wickson, a sordid money-grabber, has the power to determine whether I shall or shall not teach in the university of the state. But he offered me even better than that—offered to make me president of some great college of physical sciences that is being planned—the Oligarchy must get rid of its surplus somehow, you see.

" 'Do you remember what I told that socialist lover of your daughter's?' he said. 'I told him that we would walk upon the faces of the working class. And so we shall. As for you, I have for you a deep respect as a scientist; but if you throw your fortunes in with the working class—well, watch out for your face, that is all.' And then he turned and left me."

"It means we'll have to marry earlier than you planned," was Ernest's comment when we told him.

---

[1] One of the first ships that carried colonies to America, after the discovery of the New World. Descendants of these original colonists were for a while inordinately proud of their genealogy; but in time the blood became so widely diffused that it ran in the veins practically of all Americans.

I could not follow his reasoning, but I was soon to learn it. It was at this time that the quarterly dividend of the Sierra Mills was paid—or, rather, should have been paid, for father did not receive his. After waiting several days, father wrote to the secretary. Promptly came the reply that there was no record on the books of father's owning any stock, and a polite request for more explicit information.

"I'll make it explicit enough, confound him," father declared, and departed for the bank to get the stock in question from his safe-deposit box.

"Ernest is a very remarkable man," he said when he got back and while I was helping him off with his overcoat. "I repeat, my daughter, that young man of yours is a very remarkable young man."

I had learned, whenever he praised Ernest in such fashion, to expect disaster.

"They have already walked upon my face," father explained. "There was no stock. The box was empty. You and Ernest will have to get married pretty quickly."

Father insisted on laboratory methods. He brought the Sierra Mills into court, but he could not bring the books of the Sierra Mills into court. He did not control the courts, and the Sierra Mills did. That explained it all. He was thoroughly beaten by the law, and the bare-faced robbery held good.

It is almost laughable now, when I look back on it, the way father was beaten. He met Wickson accidentally on the street in San Francisco, and he told Wickson that he was a damned scoundrel. And then father was arrested for attempted assault, fined in the police court, and bound over to keep the peace. It was all so ridiculous that when he got home he had to laugh himself. But what a furor was raised in the local papers! There was grave talk about the bacillus of violence that infected all men who embraced socialism; and father, with his long and peaceful life, was instanced as a shining example of how the bacillus of violence worked. Also, it was asserted by more than one paper that father's mind had weakened under the strain of scientific study, and confinement in a state asylum for the insane was suggested. Nor was this merely talk. It was an imminent peril. But father was wise enough to see it. He had the Bishop's experience to lesson from, and he lessoned well. He kept quiet no matter what injustice was perpetrated on him, and really, I think, surprised his enemies.

There was the matter of the house—our home. A mortgage was foreclosed on it, and we had to give up possession. Of course there wasn't any mortgage, and never had been any mortgage. The ground had been bought outright, and the house had been paid for when it was built. And house and lot had always been free and unencumbered. Nevertheless there was the mortgage, properly and legally drawn up and signed, with a record of the payments of interest through a number of years. Father made no outcry. As he had been robbed of his money, so was he now robbed of his home. And he had no recourse. The machinery of society was in the hands of those who were bent on breaking him. He was a philosopher at heart, and he was no longer even angry.

"I am doomed to be broken," he said to me; "but that is no reason that I should not try to be shattered as little as possible. These old bones of mine are fragile, and I've learned my lesson. God knows I don't want to spend my last days in an insane asylum."

Which reminds me of Bishop Morehouse, whom I have neglected for many pages. But first let me tell of my marriage. In the play of events, my marriage sinks into insignificance, I know, so I shall barely mention it.

"Now we shall become real proletarians," father said, when we were driven from our home. "I have often envied that young man of yours for his actual knowledge of the proletariat. Now I shall see and learn for myself."

Father must have had strong in him the blood of adventure. He looked upon our catastrophe in the light of an adventure. No anger nor bitterness possessed him. He was too philosophic and simple to be vindictive, and he lived too much in the world of mind to miss the creature comforts we were giving up. So it was, when we moved to San Francisco into four wretched rooms in the slum south of Market Street, that he embarked upon the adventure with the joy and enthusiasm of a child—combined with the clear sight and mental grasp of an extraordinary intellect. He really never crystallized mentally. He had no false sense of values. Conventional or habitual values meant nothing to him. The only values he recognized were mathematical and scientific facts. My father was a great man. He had the mind and the soul that only great men have. In ways he was even greater than Ernest, than whom I have known none greater.

Even I found some relief in our change of living. If nothing else, I was escaping from the organized ostracism that had been our increasing portion in the university town ever since the enmity of the nascent Oligarchy had been incurred. And the change was to me likewise adventure, and the greatest of all, for it was love-adventure. The change in our fortunes had hastened my marriage, and it was as a wife that I came to live in the four rooms on Pell Street, in the San Francisco slum.

And this out of all remains: I made Ernest happy. I came into his stormy life, not as a new perturbing force, but as one that made toward peace and repose. I gave him rest. It was the guerdon of my love for him. It was the one infallible token that I had not failed. To bring forgetfulness, or the light of gladness, into those poor tired eyes of his—what greater joy could have blessed me than that?

Those dear tired eyes. He toiled as few men ever toiled, and all his lifetime he toiled for others. That was the measure of his manhood. He was a humanist and a lover. And he, with his incarnate spirit of battle, his gladiator body and his eagle spirit—he was as gentle and tender to me as a poet. He was a poet. A singer in deeds. And all his life he sang the song of man. And he did it out of sheer love of man, and for man he gave his life and was crucified.

And all this he did with no hope of future reward. In his conception of things there was no future life. He, who fairly burnt with immortality, denied himself immortality—such was the paradox of him. He, so warm in spirit, was dominated by that cold and forbidding philosophy, materialistic monism. I used to refute him by telling him that I measured his immortality by the wings of his soul, and that I should have to live endless æons in order to achieve the full measurement. Whereat he would laugh, and his arms would leap out to me, and he would call me his sweet metaphysician; and the tiredness would pass out of his eyes, and into them would flood the happy love-light that was in itself a new and sufficient advertisement of his immortality.

Also, he used to call me his dualist, and he would explain how Kant, by means of pure reason, had abolished reason, in order to worship God. And he drew the parallel and included me guilty of a similar act. And when I pleaded guilty, but defended the act as highly rational, he but pressed me closer and laughed as only one of God's own lovers could laugh. I was wont to deny that heredity and environment could explain his own originality and genius, any more than could the cold groping finger of science catch and analyze and classify that elusive essence that lurked in the constitution of life itself.

I held that space was an apparition of God, and that soul was a projection of the character of God; and when he called me his sweet metaphysician, I called him my immortal materialist. And so we loved and were happy; and I forgave him his materialism because of his tremendous work in the world, performed without thought of soul-gain thereby, and because of his so exceeding modesty of spirit that prevented him from having pride and regal consciousness of himself and his soul.

But he had pride. How could he have been an eagle and not have pride? His contention was that it was finer for a finite mortal speck of life to feel Godlike, than for a god to feel godlike; and so it was that he exalted what he deemed his mortality. He was fond of quoting a fragment from a certain poem. He had never seen the whole poem, and he had tried vainly to learn its authorship. I here give the fragment, not alone because he loved it, but because it epitomized the paradox that he was in the spirit of him, and his conception of his spirit. For how can a man, with thrilling, and burning, and exaltation, recite the following and still be mere mortal earth, a bit of fugitive force, an evanescent form? Here it is:

"Joy upon joy and gain upon gain
  Are the destined rights of my birth,
  And I shout the praise of my endless days
  To the echoing edge of the earth.
  Though I suffer all deaths that a man can die
  To the uttermost end of time,
  I have deep-drained this, my cup of bliss,
  In every age and clime—

The froth of Pride, the tang of Power,
The sweet of Womanhood!
I drain the lees upon my knees,
For oh, the draught is good;
I drink to Life, I drink to Death,
And smack my lips with song,
For when I die, another 'I' shall pass the cup along.

"The man you drove from Eden's grove
    Was I, my Lord, was I,
And I shall be there when the earth and the air
    Are rent from sea to sky;
For it is my world, my gorgeous world,
    The world of my dearest woes,
From the first faint cry of the newborn
    To the rack of the woman's throes.

"Packed with the pulse of an unborn race,
Torn with a world's desire,
The surging flood of my wild young blood
Would quench the judgment fire.
I am Man, Man, Man, from the tingling flesh
To the dust of my earthly goal,
From the nestling gloom of the pregnant womb
To the sheen of my naked soul.
Bone of my bone and flesh of my flesh
The whole world leaps to my will,
And the unslaked thirst of an Eden cursed
Shall harrow the earth for its fill.
Almighty God, when I drain life's glass
Of all its rainbow gleams,
The hapless plight of eternal night
Shall be none too long for my dreams.

"The man you drove from Eden's grove
    Was I, my Lord, was I,
And I shall be there when the earth and the air
    Are rent from sea to sky;
For it is my world, my gorgeous world,
    The world of my dear delight,

From the brightest gleam of the Arctic stream
To the dusk of my own love-night."

Ernest always overworked. His wonderful constitution kept him up; but even that constitution could not keep the tired look out of his eyes. His dear, tired eyes! He never slept more than four and one-half hours a night; yet he never found time to do all the work he wanted to do. He never ceased from his activities as a propagandist, and was always scheduled long in advance for lectures to workingmen's organizations. Then there was the campaign. He did a man's full work in that alone. With the suppression of the socialist publishing houses, his meagre royalties ceased, and he was hard-put to make a living; for he had to make a living in addition to all his other labor. He did a great deal of translating for the magazines on scientific and philosophic subjects; and, coming home late at night, worn out from the strain of the campaign, he would plunge into his translating and toil on well into the morning hours. And in addition to everything, there was his studying. To the day of his death he kept up his studies, and he studied prodigiously.

And yet he found time in which to love me and make me happy. But this was accomplished only through my merging my life completely into his. I learned shorthand and typewriting, and became his secretary. He insisted that I succeeded in cutting his work in half; and so it was that I schooled myself to understand his work. Our interests became mutual, and we worked together and played together.

And then there were our sweet stolen moments in the midst of our work—just a word, or caress, or flash of love-light; and our moments were sweeter for being stolen. For we lived on the heights, where the air was keen and sparkling, where the toil was for humanity, and where sordidness and selfishness never entered. We loved love, and our love was never smirched by anything less than the best. And this out of all remains: I did not fail. I gave him rest—he who worked so hard for others, my dear, tired-eyed mortalist.

XII

The Bishop

I T WAS after my marriage that I chanced upon Bishop
Morehouse. But I must give the events in their proper sequence. After his outbreak at the I.P.H. Convention, the
Bishop, being a gentle soul, had yielded to the friendly pressure brought to bear upon him, and had gone away on a
vacation. But he returned more fixed than ever in his determination to preach the message of the Church. To the consternation of his congregation, his first sermon was quite
similar to the address he had given before the Convention.
Again he said, and at length and with distressing detail, that
the Church had wandered away from the Master's teaching,
and that Mammon had been instated in the place of Christ.

And the result was, willy-nilly, that he was led away to a
private sanitarium for mental disease, while in the newspapers
appeared pathetic accounts of his mental breakdown and of
the saintliness of his character. He was held a prisoner in the
sanitarium. I called repeatedly, but was denied access to him;
and I was terribly impressed by the tragedy of a sane, normal,
saintly man being crushed by the brutal will of society. For
the Bishop was sane, and pure, and noble. As Ernest said, all
that was the matter with him was that he had incorrect notions of biology and sociology, and because of his incorrect
notions he had not gone about it in the right way to rectify
matters.

What terrified me was the Bishop's helplessness. If he persisted in the truth as he saw it, he was doomed to an insane
ward. And he could do nothing. His money, his position, his
culture, could not save him. His views were perilous to society, and society could not conceive that such perilous views
could be the product of a sane mind. Or, at least, it seems to
me that such was society's attitude.

But the Bishop, in spite of the gentleness and purity of his
spirit, was possessed of guile. He apprehended clearly his danger. He saw himself caught in the web, and he tried to escape

444

from it. Denied help from his friends, such as father and Ernest and I could have given, he was left to battle for himself alone. And in the enforced solitude of the sanitarium he recovered. He became again sane. His eyes ceased to see visions; his brain was purged of the fancy that it was the duty of society to feed the Master's lambs.

As I say, he became well, quite well, and the newspapers and the church people hailed his return with joy. I went once to his church. The sermon was of the same order as the ones he had preached long before his eyes had seen visions. I was disappointed, shocked. Had society then beaten him into submission? Was he a coward? Had he been bulldozed into recanting? Or had the strain been too great for him, and had he meekly surrendered to the Juggernaut of the established?

I called upon him in his beautiful home. He was wofully changed. He was thinner, and there were lines on his face which I had never seen before. He was manifestly distressed by my coming. He plucked nervously at his sleeve as we talked; and his eyes were restless, fluttering here, there, and everywhere, and refusing to meet mine. His mind seemed preoccupied, and there were strange pauses in his conversation, abrupt changes of topic, and an inconsecutiveness that was bewildering. Could this, then, be the firm-poised, Christlike man I had known, with pure, limpid eyes and a gaze steady and unfaltering as his soul? He had been man-handled; he had been cowed into subjection. His spirit was too gentle. It had not been mighty enough to face the organized wolfpack of society.

I felt sad, unutterably sad. He talked ambiguously, and was so apprehensive of what I might say that I had not the heart to catechise him. He spoke in a far-away manner of his illness, and we talked disjointedly about the church, the alterations in the organ, and about petty charities; and he saw me depart with such evident relief that I should have laughed had not my heart been so full of tears.

The poor little hero! If I had only known! He was battling like a giant, and I did not guess it. Alone, all alone, in the midst of millions of his fellow-men, he was fighting his fight. Torn by his horror of the asylum and his fidelity to truth and the right, he clung steadfastly to truth and the right; but so alone was he that he did not dare to trust even me. He had learned his lesson well—too well.

But I was soon to know. One day the Bishop disappeared. He had told nobody that he was going away; and as the days went by and he did not reappear, there was much gossip to the effect that he had committed suicide while temporarily deranged. But this idea was dispelled when it was learned that he had sold all his possessions,—his city mansion, his country house at Menlo Park, his paintings, and collections, and even his cherished library. It was patent that he had made a clean and secret sweep of everything before he disappeared.

This happened during the time when calamity had overtaken us in our own affairs; and it was not till we were well settled in our new home that we had opportunity really to wonder and speculate about the Bishop's doings. And then, everything was suddenly made clear. Early one evening, while it was yet twilight, I had run across the street and into the butcher-shop to get some chops for Ernest's supper. We called the last meal of the day "supper" in our new environment.

Just at the moment I came out of the butcher-shop, a man emerged from the corner grocery that stood alongside. A queer sense of familiarity made me look again. But the man had turned and was walking rapidly away. There was something about the slope of the shoulders and the fringe of silver hair between coat collar and slouch hat that aroused vague memories. Instead of crossing the street, I hurried after the man. I quickened my pace, trying not to think the thoughts that formed unbidden in my brain. No, it was impossible. It could not be—not in those faded overalls, too long in the legs and frayed at the bottoms.

I paused, laughed at myself, and almost abandoned the chase. But the haunting familiarity of those shoulders and that silver hair! Again I hurried on. As I passed him, I shot a keen look at his face; then I whirled around abruptly and confronted—the Bishop.

He halted with equal abruptness, and gasped. A large paper bag in his right hand fell to the sidewalk. It burst, and about his feet and mine bounced and rolled a flood of potatoes. He looked at me with surprise and alarm, then he seemed to wilt away; the shoulders drooped with dejection, and he uttered a deep sigh.

I held out my hand. He shook it, but his hand felt clammy. He cleared his throat in embarrassment, and I could see the sweat starting out on his forehead. It was evident that he was badly frightened.

"The potatoes," he murmured faintly. "They are precious."

Between us we picked them up and replaced them in the broken bag, which he now held carefully in the hollow of his arm. I tried to tell him my gladness at meeting him and that he must come right home with me.

"Father will be rejoiced to see you," I said. "We live only a stone's throw away."

"I can't," he said, "I must be going. Good-by."

He looked apprehensively about him, as though dreading discovery, and made an attempt to walk on.

"Tell me where you live, and I shall call later," he said, when he saw that I walked beside him and that it was my intention to stick to him now that he was found.

"No," I answered firmly. "You must come now."

He looked at the potatoes spilling on his arm, and at the small parcels on his other arm.

"Really, it is impossible," he said. "Forgive me for my rudeness. If you only knew."

He looked as if he were going to break down, but the next moment he had himself in control.

"Besides, this food," he went on. "It is a sad case. It is terrible. She is an old woman. I must take it to her at once. She is suffering from want of it. I must go at once. You understand. Then I will return. I promise you."

"Let me go with you," I volunteered. "Is it far?"

He sighed again, and surrendered.

"Only two blocks," he said. "Let us hasten."

Under the Bishop's guidance I learned something of my own neighborhood. I had not dreamed such wretchedness and misery existed in it. Of course, this was because I did not concern myself with charity. I had become convinced that Ernest was right when he sneered at charity as a poulticing of an ulcer. Remove the ulcer, was his remedy; give to the worker his product; pension as soldiers those who grow honorably old in their toil, and there will be no need for charity. Convinced of this, I toiled with him at the revolution, and did not exhaust my energy in alleviating the social ills that continuously arose from the injustice of the system.

I followed the Bishop into a small room, ten by twelve, in a rear tenement. And there we found a little old German woman—sixty-four years old, the Bishop said. She was surprised at seeing me, but she nodded a pleasant greeting and went on sewing on the pair of men's trousers in her lap. Beside her, on the floor, was a pile of trousers. The Bishop discovered there was neither coal nor kindling, and went out to buy some.

I took up a pair of trousers and examined her work.

"Six cents, lady," she said, nodding her head gently while she went on stitching. She stitched slowly, but never did she cease from stitching. She seemed mastered by the verb "to stitch."

"For all that work?" I asked. "Is that what they pay? How long does it take you?"

"Yes," she answered, "that is what they pay. Six cents for finishing. Two hours' sewing on each pair.

"But the boss doesn't know that," she added quickly, betraying a fear of getting him into trouble. "I'm slow. I've got the rheumatism in my hands. Girls work much faster. They finish in half that time. The boss is kind. He lets me take the work home, now that I am old and the noise of the machine bothers my head. If it wasn't for his kindness, I'd starve.

"Yes, those who work in the shop get eight cents. But what can you do? There is not enough work for the young. The old have no chance. Often one pair is all I can get. Sometimes, like to-day, I am given eight pair to finish before night."

I asked her the hours she worked, and she said it depended on the season.

"In the summer, when there is a rush order, I work from five in the morning to nine at night. But in the winter it is too cold. The hands do not early get over the stiffness. Then you must work later—till after midnight sometimes.

"Yes, it has been a bad summer. The hard times. God must be angry. This is the first work the boss has given me in a week. It is true, one cannot eat much when there is no work. I am used to it. I have sewed all my life, in the old country and here in San Francisco—thirty-three years.

"If you are sure of the rent, it is all right. The houseman is very kind, but he must have his rent. It is fair. He only charges three dollars for this room. That is cheap. But it is not easy for you to find all of three dollars every month."

She ceased talking, and, nodding her head, went on stitching.

"You have to be very careful as to how you spend your earnings," I suggested.

She nodded emphatically.

"After the rent it's not so bad. Of course you can't buy meat. And there is no milk for the coffee. But always there is one meal a day, and often two."

She said this last proudly. There was a smack of success in her words. But as she stitched on in silence, I noticed the sadness in her pleasant eyes and the droop of her mouth. The look in her eyes became far away. She rubbed the dimness hastily out of them; it interfered with her stitching.

"No, it is not the hunger that makes the heart ache," she explained. "You get used to being hungry. It is for my child that I cry. It was the machine that killed her. It is true she worked hard, but I cannot understand. She was strong. And she was young—only forty; and she worked only thirty years. She began young, it is true; but my man died. The boiler exploded down at the works. And what were we to do? She was ten, but she was very strong. But the machine killed her. Yes, it did. It killed her, and she was the fastest worker in the shop. I have thought about it often, and I know. That is why I cannot work in the shop. The machine bothers my head. Always I hear it saying, 'I did it, I did it.' And it says that all day long. And then I think of my daughter, and I cannot work."

The moistness was in her old eyes again, and she had to wipe it away before she could go on stitching.

I heard the Bishop stumbling up the stairs, and I opened the door. What a spectacle he was. On his back he carried half a sack of coal, with kindling on top. Some of the coal dust had coated his face, and the sweat from his exertions was running in streaks. He dropped his burden in the corner by the stove and wiped his face on a coarse bandana handkerchief. I could scarcely accept the verdict of my senses. The Bishop, black as a coal-heaver, in a workingman's cheap cotton shirt (one button was missing from the throat), and in overalls! That was the most incongruous of all—the overalls, frayed at the bottoms, dragged down at the heels, and held up by a narrow leather belt around the hips such as laborers wear.

Though the Bishop was warm, the poor swollen hands of the old woman were already cramping with the cold; and before we left her, the Bishop had built the fire, while I had peeled the potatoes and put them on to boil. I was to learn, as time went by, that there were many cases similar to hers, and many worse, hidden away in the monstrous depths of the tenements in my neighborhood.

We got back to find Ernest alarmed by my absence. After the first surprise of greeting was over, the Bishop leaned back in his chair, stretched out his overall-covered legs, and actually sighed a comfortable sigh. We were the first of his old friends he had met since his disappearance, he told us; and during the intervening weeks he must have suffered greatly from loneliness. He told us much, though he told us more of the joy he had experienced in doing the Master's bidding.

"For truly now," he said, "I am feeding his lambs. And I have learned a great lesson. The soul cannot be ministered to till the stomach is appeased. His lambs must be fed bread and butter and potatoes and meat; after that, and only after that, are their spirits ready for more refined nourishment."

He ate heartily of the supper I cooked. Never had he had such an appetite at our table in the old days. We spoke of it, and he said that he had never been so healthy in his life.

"I walk always now," he said, and a blush was on his cheek at the thought of the time when he rode in his carriage, as though it were a sin not lightly to be laid.

"My health is better for it," he added hastily. "And I am very happy—indeed, most happy. At last I am a consecrated spirit."

And yet there was in his face a permanent pain, the pain of the world that he was now taking to himself. He was seeing life in the raw, and it was a different life from what he had known within the printed books of his library.

"And you are responsible for all this, young man," he said directly to Ernest.

Ernest was embarrassed and awkward.

"I—I warned you," he faltered.

"No, you misunderstand," the Bishop answered. "I speak not in reproach, but in gratitude. I have you to thank for showing me my path. You led me from theories about life to life itself. You pulled aside the veils from the social shams. You were light in my darkness, but now I, too, see the light. And I am very happy, only . . ." he hesitated painfully, and in his eyes fear leaped large. "Only the persecution. I harm no one. Why will they not let me alone? But it is not that. It is the nature of the persecution. I shouldn't mind if they cut my flesh with stripes, or burned me at the stake, or crucified me head-downward. But it is the asylum that frightens me. Think of it! Of me—in an asylum for the insane! It is revolting. I saw some of the cases at the sanitarium. They were violent. My blood chills when I think of it. And to be imprisoned for the rest of my life amid scenes of screaming madness! No! no! Not that! Not that!"

It was pitiful. His hands shook, his whole body quivered and shrank away from the picture he had conjured. But the next moment he was calm.

"Forgive me," he said simply. "It is my wretched nerves. And if the Master's work leads there, so be it. Who am I to complain?"

I felt like crying aloud as I looked at him: "Great Bishop! O hero! God's hero!"

As the evening wore on we learned more of his doings.

"I sold my house—my houses, rather," he said, "and all my other possessions. I knew I must do it secretly, else they would have taken everything away from me. That would have been terrible. I often marvel these days at the immense quantity of potatoes two or three hundred thousand dollars will buy, or bread, or meat, or coal and kindling." He turned to Ernest. "You are right, young man. Labor is dreadfully underpaid. I never did a bit of work in my life, except to appeal æsthetically to Pharisees—I thought I was preaching the message—and yet I was worth half a million dollars. I never knew what half a million dollars meant until I realized how much potatoes and bread and butter and meat it could buy. And then I realized something more. I realized that all those potatoes and that bread and butter and meat were mine, and that I had not worked to make them. Then it was clear to me, some one else had worked and made them and been robbed of them. And when I came down amongst the poor I found those who had been robbed and who were hungry and wretched because they had been robbed."

We drew him back to his narrative.

"The money? I have it deposited in many different banks under different names. It can never be taken away from me, because it can never be found. And it is so good, that money. It buys so much food. I never knew before what money was good for."

"I wish we could get some of it for the propaganda," Ernest said wistfully. "It would do immense good."

"Do you think so?" the Bishop said. "I do not have much faith in politics. In fact, I am afraid I do not understand politics."

Ernest was delicate in such matters. He did not repeat his suggestion, though he knew only too well the sore straits the Socialist Party was in through lack of money.

"I sleep in cheap lodging houses," the Bishop went on. "But I am afraid, and I never stay long in one place. Also, I rent two rooms in workingmen's houses in different quarters of the city. It is a great extravagance, I know, but it is necessary. I make up for it in part by doing my own cooking, though sometimes I get something to eat in cheap coffee-houses. And I have made a discovery. Tamales[1] are very good when the air grows chilly late at night. Only they are so expensive. But I have discovered a place where I can get three for ten cents. They are not so good as the others, but they are very warming.

"And so I have at last found my work in the world, thanks to you, young man. It is the Master's work." He looked at

[1]A Mexican dish, referred to occasionally in the literature of the times. It is supposed that it was warmly seasoned. No recipe of it has come down to us.

me, and his eyes twinkled. "You caught me feeding his lambs, you know. And of course you will all keep my secret."

He spoke carelessly enough, but there was real fear behind the speech. He promised to call upon us again. But a week later we read in the newspaper of the sad case of Bishop Morehouse, who had been committed to the Napa Asylum and for whom there were still hopes held out. In vain we tried to see him, to have his case reconsidered or investigated. Nor could we learn anything about him except the reiterated statements that slight hopes were still held for his recovery.

"Christ told the rich young man to sell all he had," Ernest said bitterly. "The Bishop obeyed Christ's injunction and got locked up in a madhouse. Times have changed since Christ's day. A rich man to-day who gives all he has to the poor is crazy. There is no discussion. Society has spoken."

XIII

The General Strike

O F COURSE Ernest was elected to Congress in the great socialist landslide that took place in the fall of 1912. One great factor that helped to swell the socialist vote was the destruction of Hearst.[1] This the Plutocracy found an easy task. It cost Hearst eighteen million dollars a year to run his various papers, and this sum, and more, he got back from the middle class in payment for advertising. The source of his financial strength lay wholly in the middle class. The trusts did not advertise.[2] To destroy Hearst, all that was necessary was to take away from him his advertising.

The whole middle class had not yet been exterminated. The sturdy skeleton of it remained; but it was without power. The small manufacturers and small business men who still survived were at the complete mercy of the Plutocracy. They had no economic nor political souls of their own. When the fiat of the Plutocracy went forth, they withdrew their advertisements from the Hearst papers.

Hearst made a gallant fight. He brought his papers out at a loss of a million and a half each month. He continued to publish the advertisements for which he no longer received pay. Again the fiat of the Plutocracy went forth, and the small business men and manufacturers swamped him with a flood

[1] *William Randolph Hearst*—a young California millionaire who became the most powerful newspaper owner in the country. His newspapers were published in all the large cities, and they appealed to the perishing middle class and to the proletariat. So large was his following that he managed to take possession of the empty shell of the old Democratic Party. He occupied an anomalous position, preaching an emasculated socialism combined with a nondescript sort of petty bourgeois capitalism. It was oil and water, and there was no hope for him, though for a short period he was a source of serious apprehension to the Plutocrats.

[2] The cost of advertising was amazing in those helter-skelter times. Only the small capitalists competed, and therefore they did the advertising. There being no competition where there was a trust, there was no need for the trusts to advertise.

of notices that he must discontinue running their old advertisements. Hearst persisted. Injunctions were served on him.
Still he persisted. He received six months' imprisonment for
contempt of court in disobeying the injunctions, while he was
bankrupted by countless damage suits. He had no chance.
The Plutocracy had passed sentence on him. The courts were
in the hands of the Plutocracy to carry the sentence out. And
with Hearst crashed also to destruction the Democratic Party
that he had so recently captured.

With the destruction of Hearst and the Democratic Party,
there were only two paths for his following to take. One was
into the Socialist Party; the other was into the Republican
Party. Then it was that we socialists reaped the fruit of
Hearst's pseudo-socialistic preaching; for the great majority
of his followers came over to us.

The expropriation of the farmers that took place at this
time would also have swelled our vote had it not been for the
brief and futile rise of the Grange Party. Ernest and the socialist leaders fought fiercely to capture the farmers; but the
destruction of the socialist press and publishing houses constituted too great a handicap, while the mouth-to-mouth
propaganda had not yet been perfected. So it was that politicians like Mr. Calvin, who were themselves farmers long since
expropriated, captured the farmers and threw their political
strength away in a vain campaign.

"The poor farmers," Ernest once laughed savagely; "the
trusts have them both coming and going."

And that was really the situation. The seven great trusts,
working together, had pooled their enormous surpluses and
made a farm trust. The railroads, controlling rates, and the
bankers and stock exchange gamesters, controlling prices,
had long since bled the farmers into indebtedness. The bankers, and all the trusts for that matter, had likewise long
since loaned colossal amounts of money to the farmers. The
farmers were in the net. All that remained to be done
was the drawing in of the net. This the farm trust proceeded
to do.

The hard times of 1912 had already caused a frightful slump
in the farm markets. Prices were now deliberately pressed
down to bankruptcy, while the railroads, with extortionate

rates, broke the back of the farmer-camel. Thus the farmers were compelled to borrow more and more, while they were prevented from paying back old loans. Then ensued the great foreclosing of mortgages and enforced collection of notes. The farmers simply surrendered the land to the farm trust. There was nothing else for them to do. And having surrendered the land, the farmers next went to work for the farm trust, becoming managers, superintendents, foremen, and common laborers. They worked for wages. They became villeins, in short—serfs bound to the soil by a living wage. They could not leave their masters, for their masters composed the Plutocracy. They could not go to the cities, for there, also, the Plutocracy was in control. They had but one alternative,—to leave the soil and become vagrants, in brief, to starve. And even there they were frustrated, for stringent vagrancy laws were passed and rigidly enforced.

Of course, here and there, farmers, and even whole communities of farmers, escaped expropriation by virtue of exceptional conditions. But they were merely strays and did not count, and they were gathered in anyway during the following year.[1]

Thus it was that in the fall of 1912 the socialist leaders, with the exception of Ernest, decided that the end of capitalism had come. What of the hard times and the consequent vast army of the unemployed; what of the destruction of the farmers and the middle class; and what of the decisive defeat administered all along the line to the labor unions; the socialists

[1] The destruction of the Roman yeomanry proceeded far less rapidly than the destruction of the American farmers and small capitalists. There was momentum in the twentieth century, while there was practically none in ancient Rome.

Numbers of the farmers, impelled by an insane lust for the soil, and willing to show what beasts they could become, tried to escape expropriation by withdrawing from any and all market-dealing. They sold nothing. They bought nothing. Among themselves a primitive barter began to spring up. Their privation and hardships were terrible, but they persisted. It became quite a movement, in fact. The manner in which they were beaten was unique and logical and simple. The Plutocracy, by virtue of its possession of the government, raised their taxes. It was the weak joint in their armor. Neither buying nor selling, they had no money, and in the end their land was sold to pay the taxes.

were really justified in believing that the end of capitalism had come and in themselves throwing down the gauntlet to the Plutocracy.

Alas, how we underestimated the strength of the enemy! Everywhere the socialists proclaimed their coming victory at the ballot-box, while, in unmistakable terms, they stated the situation. The Plutocracy accepted the challenge. It was the Plutocracy, weighing and balancing, that defeated us by dividing our strength. It was the Plutocracy, through its secret agents, that raised the cry that socialism was sacrilegious and atheistic; it was the Plutocracy that whipped the churches, and especially the Catholic Church, into line, and robbed us of a portion of the labor vote. And it was the Plutocracy, through its secret agents of course, that encouraged the Grange Party and even spread it to the cities into the ranks of the dying middle class.

Nevertheless the socialist landslide occurred. But, instead of a sweeping victory with chief executive officers and majorities in all legislative bodies, we found ourselves in the minority. It is true, we elected fifty Congressmen; but when they took their seats in the spring of 1913, they found themselves without power of any sort. Yet they were more fortunate than the Grangers, who captured a dozen state governments, and who, in the spring, were not permitted to take possession of the captured offices. The incumbents refused to retire, and the courts were in the hands of the Oligarchy. But this is too far in advance of events. I have yet to tell of the stirring times of the winter of 1912.

The hard times at home had caused an immense decrease in consumption. Labor, out of work, had no wages with which to buy. The result was that the Plutocracy found a greater surplus than ever on its hands. This surplus it was compelled to dispose of abroad, and, what of its colossal plans, it needed money. Because of its strenuous efforts to dispose of the surplus in the world market, the Plutocracy clashed with Germany. Economic clashes were usually succeeded by wars, and this particular clash was no exception. The great German war-lord prepared, and so did the United States prepare.

The war-cloud hovered dark and ominous. The stage was set for a world-catastrophe, for in all the world were hard times, labor troubles, perishing middle classes, armies of unemployed, clashes of economic interests in the world-market, and mutterings and rumblings of the socialist revolution.[1]

The Oligarchy wanted the war with Germany. And it wanted the war for a dozen reasons. In the juggling of events such a war would cause, in the reshuffling of the international cards and the making of new treaties and alliances, the Oligarchy had much to gain. And, furthermore, the war would consume many national surpluses, reduce the armies of unemployed that menaced all countries, and give the Oligarchy a breathing space in which to perfect its plans and carry them out. Such a war would virtually put the Oligarchy in possession of the world-market. Also, such a war would create a large standing army that need never be disbanded, while in the minds of the people would be substituted the issue, "America *versus* Germany," in place of "Socialism *versus* Oligarchy."

And truly the war would have done all these things had it not been for the socialists. A secret meeting of the Western leaders was held in our four tiny rooms in Pell Street. Here was first considered the stand the socialists were to take. It

[1]For a long time these mutterings and rumblings had been heard. As far back as 1906 A.D., Lord Avebury, an Englishman, uttered the following in the House of Lords: "*The unrest in Europe, the spread of socialism, and the ominous rise of Anarchism, are warnings to the governments and the ruling classes that the condition of the working classes in Europe is becoming intolerable, and that if a revolution is to be avoided some steps must be taken to increase wages, reduce the hours of labor, and lower the prices of the necessaries of life.*" The *Wall Street Journal*, a stock gamesters' publication, in commenting upon Lord Avebury's speech, said: "*These words were spoken by an aristocrat and a member of the most conservative body in all Europe. That gives them all the more significance. They contain more valuable political economy than is to be found in most of the books. They sound a note of warning. Take heed, gentlemen of the war and navy departments!*"

At the same time, Sydney Brooks, writing in America, in *Harper's Weekly*, said: "*You will not hear the socialists mentioned in Washington. Why should you? The politicians are always the last people in this country to see what is going on under their noses. They will jeer at me when I prophesy, and prophesy with the utmost confidence, that at the next presidential election the socialists will poll over a million votes.*"

was not the first time we had put our foot down upon war,[1] but it was the first time we had done so in the United States. After our secret meeting we got in touch with the national organization, and soon our code cables were passing back and forth across the Atlantic between us and the International Bureau.

The German socialists were ready to act with us. There were over five million of them, many of them in the standing army, and, in addition, they were on friendly terms with the labor unions. In both countries the socialists came out in bold declaration against the war and threatened the general strike. And in the meantime they made preparation for the general strike. Furthermore, the revolutionary parties in all countries gave public utterance to the socialist principle of international peace that must be preserved at all hazards, even to the extent of revolt and revolution at home.

The general strike was the one great victory we American socialists won. On the 4th of December the American minister was withdrawn from the German capital. That night a German fleet made a dash on Honolulu, sinking three American cruisers and a revenue cutter, and bombarding the city. Next day both Germany and the United States declared war, and within an hour the socialists called the general strike in both countries.

For the first time the German war-lord faced the men of his empire who made his empire go. Without them he could not run his empire. The novelty of the situation lay in that their revolt was passive. They did not fight. They did nothing. And by doing nothing they tied their war-lord's hands. He would have asked for nothing better than an opportunity

[1]It was at the very beginning of the twentieth century A.D., that the international organization of the socialists finally formulated their long-maturing policy on war. Epitomized, their doctrine was: *"Why should the workingmen of one country fight with the workingmen of another country for the benefit of their capitalist masters?"*

On May 21, 1905 A.D., when war threatened between Austria and Italy, the socialists of Italy, Austria, and Hungary held a conference at Trieste, and threatened a general strike of the workingmen of both countries in case war was declared. This was repeated the following year, when the "Morocco Affair" threatened to involve France, Germany, and England.

to loose his war-dogs on his rebellious proletariat. But this was denied him. He could not loose his war-dogs. Neither could he mobilize his army to go forth to war, nor could he punish his recalcitrant subjects. Not a wheel moved in his empire. Not a train ran, not a telegraphic message went over the wires, for the telegraphers and railroad men had ceased work along with the rest of the population.

And as it was in Germany, so it was in the United States. At last organized labor had learned its lesson. Beaten decisively on its own chosen field, it had abandoned that field and come over to the political field of the socialists; for the general strike was a political strike. Besides, organized labor had been so badly beaten that it did not care. It joined in the general strike out of sheer desperation. The workers threw down their tools and left their tasks by the millions. Especially notable were the machinists. Their heads were bloody, their organization had apparently been destroyed, yet out they came, along with their allies in the metal-working trades.

Even the common laborers and all unorganized labor ceased work. The strike had tied everything up so that nobody could work. Besides, the women proved to be the strongest promoters of the strike. They set their faces against the war. They did not want their men to go forth to die. Then, also, the idea of the general strike caught the mood of the people. It struck their sense of humor. The idea was infectious. The children struck in all the schools, and such teachers as came, went home again from deserted class rooms. The general strike took the form of a great national picnic. And the idea of the solidarity of labor, so evidenced, appealed to the imagination of all. And, finally, there was no danger to be incurred by the colossal frolic. When everybody was guilty, how was anybody to be punished?

The United States was paralyzed. No one knew what was happening. There were no newspapers, no letters, no despatches. Every community was as completely isolated as though ten thousand miles of primeval wilderness stretched between it and the rest of the world. For that matter, the world had ceased to exist. And for a week this state of affairs was maintained.

In San Francisco we did not know what was happening even across the bay in Oakland or Berkeley. The effect on one's sensibilities was weird, depressing. It seemed as though some great cosmic thing lay dead. The pulse of the land had ceased to beat. Of a truth the nation had died. There were no wagons rumbling on the streets, no factory whistles, no hum of electricity in the air, no passing of street cars, no cries of news-boys—nothing but persons who at rare intervals went by like furtive ghosts, themselves oppressed and made unreal by the silence.

And during that week of silence the Oligarchy was taught its lesson. And well it learned the lesson. The general strike was a warning. It should never occur again. The Oligarchy would see to that.

At the end of the week, as had been prearranged, the telegraphers of Germany and the United States returned to their posts. Through them the socialist leaders of both countries presented their ultimatum to the rulers. The war should be called off, or the general strike would continue. It did not take long to come to an understanding. The war was declared off, and the populations of both countries returned to their tasks.

It was this renewal of peace that brought about the alliance between Germany and the United States. In reality, this was an alliance between the Emperor and the Oligarchy, for the purpose of meeting their common foe, the revolutionary proletariat of both countries. And it was this alliance that the Oligarchy afterward so treacherously broke when the German socialists rose and drove the war-lord from his throne. It was the very thing the Oligarchy had played for—the destruction of its great rival in the world-market. With the German Emperor out of the way, Germany would have no surplus to sell abroad. By the very nature of the socialist state, the German population would consume all that it produced. Of course, it would trade abroad certain things it produced for things it did not produce; but this would be quite different from an unconsumable surplus.

"I'll wager the Oligarchy finds justification," Ernest said, when its treachery to the German Emperor became known. "As usual, the Oligarchy will believe it has done right."

And sure enough. The Oligarchy's public defence for the act was that it had done it for the sake of the American people whose interests it was looking out for. It had flung its hated rival out of the world-market and enabled us to dispose of our surplus in that market.

"And the howling folly of it is that we are so helpless that such idiots really are managing our interests," was Ernest's comment. "They have enabled us to sell more abroad, which means that we'll be compelled to consume less at home."

XIV
The Beginning of the End

A S EARLY as January, 1913, Ernest saw the true trend of affairs, but he could not get his brother leaders to see the vision of the Iron Heel that had arisen in his brain. They were too confident. Events were rushing too rapidly to culmination. A crisis had come in world affairs. The American Oligarchy was practically in possession of the world-market, and scores of countries were flung out of that market with unconsumable and unsalable surpluses on their hands. For such countries nothing remained but reorganization. They could not continue their method of producing surpluses. The capitalistic system, so far as they were concerned, had hopelessly broken down.

The reorganization of these countries took the form of revolution. It was a time of confusion and violence. Everywhere institutions and governments were crashing. Everywhere, with the exception of two or three countries, the erstwhile capitalist masters fought bitterly for their possessions. But the governments were taken away from them by the militant proletariat. At last was being realized Karl Marx's classic: "The knell of private capitalist property sounds. The expropriators are expropriated." And as fast as capitalistic governments crashed, coöperative commonwealths arose in their place.

"Why does the United States lag behind?"; "Get busy, you American revolutionists!"; "What's the matter with America?"—were the messages sent to us by our successful comrades in other lands. But we could not keep up. The Oligarchy stood in the way. Its bulk, like that of some huge monster, blocked our path.

"Wait till we take office in the spring," we answered. "Then you'll see."

Behind this lay our secret. We had won over the Grangers, and in the spring a dozen states would pass into their hands by virtue of the elections of the preceding fall. At once would be instituted a dozen coöperative commonwealth states. After that, the rest would be easy.

"But what if the Grangers fail to get possession?" Ernest demanded. And his comrades called him a calamity howler.

But this failure to get possession was not the chief danger that Ernest had in mind. What he foresaw was the defection of the great labor unions and the rise of the castes.

"Ghent has taught the oligarchs how to do it," Ernest said. "I'll wager they've made a text-book out of his 'Benevolent Feudalism.' "[1]

Never shall I forget the night when, after a hot discussion with half a dozen labor leaders, Ernest turned to me and said quietly: "That settles it. The Iron Heel has won. The end is in sight."

This little conference in our home was unofficial; but Ernest, like the rest of his comrades, was working for assurances from the labor leaders that they would call out their men in the next general strike. O'Connor, the president of the Association of Machinists, had been foremost of the six leaders present in refusing to give such assurance.

"You have seen that you were beaten soundly at your old tactics of strike and boycott," Ernest urged.

O'Connor and the others nodded their heads.

"And you saw what a general strike would do," Ernest went on. "We stopped the war with Germany. Never was there so fine a display of the solidarity and the power of labor. Labor can and will rule the world. If you continue to stand with us, we'll put an end to the reign of capitalism. It is your only hope. And what is more, you know it. There is no other way out. No matter what you do under your old tactics, you are doomed to defeat, if for no other reason because the masters control the courts."[2]

---

[1] "Our Benevolent Feudalism," a book published in 1902 A.D., by W. J. Ghent. It has always been insisted that Ghent put the idea of the Oligarchy into the minds of the great capitalists. This belief persists throughout the literature of the three centuries of the Iron Heel, and even in the literature of the first century of the Brotherhood of Man. To-day we know better, but our knowledge does not overcome the fact that Ghent remains the most abused innocent man in all history.

[2] As a sample of the decisions of the courts adverse to labor, the following instances are given. In the coal-mining regions the employment of children was notorious. In 1905 A.D., labor succeeded in getting a law passed in Pennsylvania providing that proof of the age of the child and of certain educa-

"You run ahead too fast," O'Connor answered. "You don't know all the ways out. There is another way out. We know what we're about. We're sick of strikes. They've got us beaten that way to a frazzle. But I don't think we'll ever need to call our men out again."

"What is your way out?" Ernest demanded bluntly.

O'Connor laughed and shook his head. "I can tell you this much: We've not been asleep. And we're not dreaming now."

"There's nothing to be afraid of, or ashamed of, I hope," Ernest challenged.

"I guess we know our business best," was the retort.

"It's a dark business, from the way you hide it," Ernest said with growing anger.

"We've paid for our experience in sweat and blood, and we've earned all that's coming to us," was the reply. "Charity begins at home."

"If you're afraid to tell me your way out, I'll tell it to you." Ernest's blood was up. "You're going in for grab-sharing. You've made terms with the enemy, that's what you've done. You've sold out the cause of labor, of all labor. You are leaving the battle-field like cowards."

"I'm not saying anything," O'Connor answered sullenly. "Only I guess we know what's best for us a little bit better than you do."

"And you don't care a cent for what is best for the rest of labor. You kick it into the ditch."

"I'm not saying anything," O'Connor replied, "except that

---

tional qualifications must accompany the oath of the parent. This was promptly declared unconstitutional by the Luzerne County Court, on the ground that it violated the Fourteenth Amendment in that it discriminated between individuals of the same class—namely, children above fourteen years of age and children below. The state court sustained the decision. The New York Court of Special Sessions, in 1905 A.D., declared unconstitutional the law prohibiting minors and women from working in factories after nine o'clock at night, the ground taken being that such a law was "class legislation." Again, the bakers of that time were terribly overworked. The New York Legislature passed a law restricting work in bakeries to ten hours a day. In 1906 A.D., the Supreme Court of the United States declared this law to be unconstitutional. In part the decision read: "*There is no reasonable ground for interfering with the liberty of persons or the right of free contract by determining the hours of labor in the occupation of a baker.*"

I'm president of the Machinists' Association, and it's my business to consider the interests of the men I represent, that's all."

And then, when the labor leaders had left, Ernest, with the calmness of defeat, outlined to me the course of events to come.

"The socialists used to foretell with joy," he said, "the coming of the day when organized labor, defeated on the industrial field, would come over on to the political field. Well, the Iron Heel has defeated the labor unions on the industrial field and driven them over to the political field; and instead of this being joyful for us, it will be a source of grief. The Iron Heel learned its lesson. We showed it our power in the general strike. It has taken steps to prevent another general strike."

"But how?" I asked.

"Simply by subsidizing the great unions. They won't join in the next general strike. Therefore it won't be a general strike."

"But the Iron Heel can't maintain so costly a programme forever," I objected.

"Oh, it hasn't subsidized all of the unions. That's not necessary. Here is what is going to happen. Wages are going to be advanced and hours shortened in the railroad unions, the iron and steel workers unions, and the engineer and machinist unions. In these unions more favorable conditions will continue to prevail. Membership in these unions will become like seats in Paradise."

"Still I don't see," I objected. "What is to become of the other unions? There are far more unions outside of this combination than in it."

"The other unions will be ground out of existence—all of them. For, don't you see, the railway men, machinists and engineers, iron and steel workers, do all of the vitally essential work in our machine civilization. Assured of their faithfulness, the Iron Heel can snap its fingers at all the rest of labor. Iron, steel, coal, machinery, and transportation constitute the backbone of the whole industrial fabric."

"But coal?" I queried. "There are nearly a million coal miners."

"They are practically unskilled labor. They will not count.

Their wages will go down and their hours will increase. They will be slaves like all the rest of us, and they will become about the most bestial of all of us. They will be compelled to work, just as the farmers are compelled to work now for the masters who robbed them of their land. And the same with all the other unions outside the combination. Watch them wobble and go to pieces, and their members become slaves driven to toil by empty stomachs and the law of the land.

"Do you know what will happen to Farley[1] and his strike-breakers? I'll tell you. Strike-breaking as an occupation will cease. There won't be any more strikes. In place of strikes will be slave revolts. Farley and his gang will be promoted to slave-driving. Oh, it won't be called that; it will be called enforcing the law of the land that compels the laborers to work. It simply prolongs the fight, this treachery of the big unions. Heaven only knows now where and when the Revolution will triumph."

"But with such a powerful combination as the Oligarchy and the big unions, is there any reason to believe that the Revolution will ever triumph?" I queried. "May not the combination endure forever?"

He shook his head. "One of our generalizations is that every system founded upon class and caste contains within itself the germs of its own decay. When a system is founded upon class, how can caste be prevented? The Iron Heel will not be able to prevent it, and in the end caste will destroy the Iron Heel. The oligarchs have already developed caste among themselves; but wait until the favored unions develop caste. The Iron Heel will use all its power to prevent it, but it will fail.

"In the favored unions are the flower of the American workingmen. They are strong, efficient men. They have become members of those unions through competition for place. Every fit workman in the United States will be possessed by the ambition to become a member of the favored

[1] James Farley—a notorious strike-breaker of the period. A man more courageous than ethical, and of undeniable ability. He rose high under the rule of the Iron Heel and finally was translated into the oligarch class. He was assassinated in 1932 by Sarah Jenkins, whose husband, thirty years before, had been killed by Farley's strike-breakers.

unions. The Oligarchy will encourage such ambition and the consequent competition. Thus will the strong men, who might else be revolutionists, be won away and their strength used to bolster the Oligarchy.

"On the other hand, the labor castes, the members of the favored unions, will strive to make their organizations into close corporations. And they will succeed. Membership in the labor castes will become hereditary. Sons will succeed fathers, and there will be no inflow of new strength from that eternal reservoir of strength, the common people. This will mean deterioration of the labor castes, and in the end they will become weaker and weaker. At the same time, as an institution, they will become temporarily all-powerful. They will be like the guards of the palace in old Rome, and there will be palace revolutions whereby the labor castes will seize the reins of power. And there will be counter-palace revolutions of the oligarchs, and sometimes the one, and sometimes the other, will be in power. And through it all the inevitable caste-weakening will go on, so that in the end the common people will come into their own."

This foreshadowing of a slow social evolution was made when Ernest was first depressed by the defection of the great unions. I never agreed with him in it, and I disagree now, as I write these lines, more heartily than ever; for even now, though Ernest is gone, we are on the verge of the revolt that will sweep all oligarchies away. Yet I have here given Ernest's prophecy because it was his prophecy. In spite of his belief in it, he worked like a giant against it, and he, more than any man, has made possible the revolt that even now waits the signal to burst forth.[1]

"But if the Oligarchy persists," I asked him that evening, "what will become of the great surpluses that will fall to its share every year?"

"The surpluses will have to be expended somehow," he answered; "and trust the oligarchs to find a way. Magnificent roads will be built. There will be great achievements in sci-

[1]Everhard's social foresight was remarkable. As clearly as in the light of past events, he saw the defection of the favored unions, the rise and the slow decay of the labor castes, and the struggle between the decaying oligarchs and labor castes for control of the great governmental machine.

ence, and especially in art. When the oligarchs have completely mastered the people, they will have time to spare for other things. They will become worshippers of beauty. They will become art-lovers. And under their direction, and generously rewarded, will toil the artists. The result will be great art; for no longer, as up to yesterday, will the artists pander to the bourgeois taste of the middle class. It will be great art, I tell you, and wonder cities will arise that will make tawdry and cheap the cities of old time. And in these cities will the oligarchs dwell and worship beauty.[1]

"Thus will the surplus be constantly expended while labor does the work. The building of these great works and cities will give a starvation ration to millions of common laborers, for the enormous bulk of the surplus will compel an equally enormous expenditure, and the oligarchs will build for a thousand years—ay, for ten thousand years. They will build as the Egyptians and the Babylonians never dreamed of building; and when the oligarchs have passed away, their great roads and their wonder cities will remain for the brotherhood of labor to tread upon and dwell within.[2]

"These things the oligarchs will do because they cannot help doing them. These great works will be the form their expenditure of the surplus will take, and in the same way that the ruling classes of Egypt of long ago expended the surplus they robbed from the people by the building of temples and pyramids. Under the oligarchs will flourish, not a priest class, but an artist class. And in place of the merchant class of bourgeoisie will be the labor castes. And beneath will be the abyss, wherein will fester and starve and rot, and ever renew itself, the common people, the great bulk of the population. And in the end, who knows in what day, the common people will

[1] We cannot but marvel at Everhard's foresight. Before ever the thought of wonder cities like Ardis and Asgard entered the minds of the oligarchs, Everhard saw those cities and the inevitable necessity for their creation.

[2] And since that day of prophecy, have passed away the three centuries of the Iron Heel and the four centuries of the Brotherhood of Man, and to-day we tread the roads and dwell in the cities that the oligarchs built. It is true, we are even now building still more wonderful wonder cities, but the wonder cities of the oligarchs endure, and I write these lines in Ardis, one of the most wonderful of them all.

rise up out of the abyss; the labor castes and the Oligarchy will crumble away; and then, at last, after the travail of the centuries, will it be the day of the common man. I had thought to see that day; but now I know that I shall never see it."

He paused and looked at me, and added:

"Social evolution is exasperatingly slow, isn't it, sweetheart?"

My arms were about him, and his head was on my breast.

"Sing me to sleep," he murmured whimsically. "I have had a visioning, and I wish to forget."

XV
Last Days

IT WAS near the end of January, 1913, that the changed attitude of the Oligarchy toward the favored unions was made public. The newspapers published information of an unprecedented rise in wages and shortening of hours for the railroad employees, the iron and steel workers, and the engineers and machinists. But the whole truth was not told. The oligarchs did not dare permit the telling of the whole truth. In reality, the wages had been raised much higher, and the privileges were correspondingly greater. All this was secret, but secrets will out. Members of the favored unions told their wives, and the wives gossiped, and soon all the labor world knew what had happened.

It was merely the logical development of what in the nineteenth century had been known as grab-sharing. In the industrial warfare of that time, profit-sharing had been tried. That is, the capitalists had striven to placate the workers by interesting them financially in their work. But profit-sharing, as a system, was ridiculous and impossible. Profit-sharing could be successful only in isolated cases in the midst of a system of industrial strife; for if all labor and all capital shared profits, the same conditions would obtain as did obtain when there was no profit-sharing.

So, out of the unpractical idea of profit-sharing, arose the practical idea of grab-sharing. "Give us more pay and charge it to the public," was the slogan of the strong unions. And here and there this selfish policy worked successfully. In charging it to the public, it was charged to the great mass of unorganized labor and of weakly organized labor. These workers actually paid the increased wages of their stronger brothers who were members of unions that were labor monopolies. This idea, as I say, was merely carried to its logical conclusion, on a large scale, by the combination of the oligarchs and the favored unions.[1]

---

[1] All the railroad unions entered into this combination with the oligarchs, and it is of interest to note that the first definite application of the policy of

471

As soon as the secret of the defection of the favored unions leaked out, there were rumblings and mutterings in the labor world. Next, the favored unions withdrew from the international organizations and broke off all affiliations. Then came trouble and violence. The members of the favored unions were branded as traitors, and in saloons and brothels, on the streets and at work, and, in fact, everywhere, they were assaulted by the comrades they had so treacherously deserted.

Countless heads were broken, and there were many killed. No member of the favored unions was safe. They gathered together in bands in order to go to work or to return from work. They walked always in the middle of the street. On the sidewalk they were liable to have their skulls crushed by bricks and cobblestones thrown from windows and house-tops. They were permitted to carry weapons, and the authorities aided them in every way. Their persecutors were sentenced to long terms in prison, where they were harshly treated; while no man, not a member of the favored unions, was permitted to carry weapons. Violation of this law was made a high misdemeanor and punished accordingly.

Outraged labor continued to wreak vengeance on the traitors. Caste lines formed automatically. The children of the traitors were persecuted by the children of the workers who had been betrayed, until it was impossible for the former to play on the streets or to attend the public schools. Also, the wives and families of the traitors were ostracized, while the corner groceryman who sold provisions to them was boycotted.

As a result, driven back upon themselves from every side,

---

profit-grabbing was made by a railroad union in the nineteenth century A.D., namely, the Brotherhood of Locomotive Engineers. P. M. Arthur was for twenty years Grand Chief of the Brotherhood. After the strike on the Pennsylvania Railroad in 1877, he broached a scheme to have the Locomotive Engineers make terms with the railroads and to "go it alone" so far as the rest of the labor unions were concerned. This scheme was eminently successful. It was as successful as it was selfish, and out of it was coined the word "arthurization," to denote grab-sharing on the part of labor unions. This word "arthurization" has long puzzled the etymologists, but its derivation, I hope, is now made clear.

the traitors and their families became clannish. Finding it impossible to dwell in safety in the midst of the betrayed proletariat, they moved into new localities inhabited by themselves alone. In this they were favored by the oligarchs. Good dwellings, modern and sanitary, were built for them, surrounded by spacious yards, and separated here and there by parks and playgrounds. Their children attended schools especially built for them, and in these schools manual training and applied science were specialized upon. Thus, and unavoidably, at the very beginning, out of this segregation arose caste. The members of the favored unions became the aristocracy of labor. They were set apart from the rest of labor. They were better housed, better clothed, better fed, better treated. They were grab-sharing with a vengeance.

In the meantime, the rest of the working class was more harshly treated. Many little privileges were taken away from it, while its wages and its standard of living steadily sank down. Incidentally, its public schools deteriorated, and education slowly ceased to be compulsory. The increase in the younger generation of children who could not read nor write was perilous.

The capture of the world-market by the United States had disrupted the rest of the world. Institutions and governments were everywhere crashing or transforming. Germany, Italy, France, Australia, and New Zealand were busy forming coöperative commonwealths. The British Empire was falling apart. England's hands were full. In India revolt was in full swing. The cry in all Asia was, "Asia for the Asiatics!" And behind this cry was Japan, ever urging and aiding the yellow and brown races against the white. And while Japan dreamed of continental empire and strove to realize the dream, she suppressed her own proletarian revolution. It was a simple war of the castes, Coolie *versus* Samurai, and the coolie socialists were executed by tens of thousands. Forty thousand were killed in the street-fighting of Tokio and in the futile assault on the Mikado's palace. Kobe was a shambles; the slaughter of the cotton operatives by machine-guns became classic as the most terrific execution ever achieved by modern war machines. Most savage of all was the Japanese Oligarchy that arose. Japan dominated the East, and took to herself the whole Asiatic portion of the world-market, with the exception of India.

England managed to crush her own proletarian revolution and to hold on to India, though she was brought to the verge of exhaustion. Also, she was compelled to let her great colonies slip away from her. So it was that the socialists succeeded in making Australia and New Zealand into coöperative commonwealths. And it was for the same reason that Canada was lost to the mother country. But Canada crushed her own socialist revolution, being aided in this by the Iron Heel. At the same time, the Iron Heel helped Mexico and Cuba to put down revolt. The result was that the Iron Heel was firmly established in the New World. It had welded into one compact political mass the whole of North America from the Panama Canal to the Arctic Ocean.

And England, at the sacrifice of her great colonies, had succeeded only in retaining India. But this was no more than temporary. The struggle with Japan and the rest of Asia for India was merely delayed. England was destined shortly to lose India, while behind that event loomed the struggle between a united Asia and the world.

And while all the world was torn with conflict, we of the United States were not placid and peaceful. The defection of the great unions had prevented our proletarian revolt, but violence was everywhere. In addition to the labor troubles, and the discontent of the farmers and of the remnant of the middle class, a religious revival had blazed up. An offshoot of the Seventh Day Adventists sprang into sudden prominence, proclaiming the end of the world.

"Confusion thrice confounded!" Ernest cried. "How can we hope for solidarity with all these cross purposes and conflicts?"

And truly the religious revival assumed formidable proportions. The people, what of their wretchedness, and of their disappointment in all things earthly, were ripe and eager for a heaven where industrial tyrants entered no more than camels passed through needle-eyes. Wild-eyed itinerant preachers swarmed over the land; and despite the prohibition of the civil authorities, and the persecution for disobedience, the flames of religious frenzy were fanned by countless camp-meetings.

It was the last days, they claimed, the beginning of the end of the world. The four winds had been loosed. God had stirred the nations to strife. It was a time of visions and miracles, while seers and prophetesses were legion. The people ceased work by hundreds of thousands and fled to the mountains, there to await the imminent coming of God and the rising of the hundred and forty and four thousand to heaven. But in the meantime God did not come, and they starved to death in great numbers. In their desperation they ravaged the farms for food, and the consequent tumult and anarchy in the country districts but increased the woes of the poor expropriated farmers.

Also, the farms and warehouses were the property of the Iron Heel. Armies of troops were put into the field, and the fanatics were herded back at the bayonet point to their tasks in the cities. There they broke out in ever recurring mobs and riots. Their leaders were executed for sedition or confined in madhouses. Those who were executed went to their deaths with all the gladness of martyrs. It was a time of madness. The unrest spread. In the swamps and deserts and waste places, from Florida to Alaska, the small groups of Indians that survived were dancing ghost dances and waiting the coming of a Messiah of their own.

And through it all, with a serenity and certitude that was terrifying, continued to rise the form of that monster of the ages, the Oligarchy. With iron hand and iron heel it mastered the surging millions, out of confusion brought order, out of the very chaos wrought its own foundation and structure.

"Just wait till we get in," the Grangers said—Calvin said it to us in our Pell Street quarters. "Look at the states we've captured. With you socialists to back us, we'll make them sing another song when we take office."

"The millions of the discontented and the impoverished are ours," the socialists said. "The Grangers have come over to us, the farmers, the middle class, and the laborers. The capitalist system will fall to pieces. In another month we send fifty men to Congress. Two years hence every office will be ours, from the President down to the local dog-catcher."

To all of which Ernest would shake his head and say:

"How many rifles have you got? Do you know where you can get plenty of lead? When it comes to powder, chemical mixtures are better than mechanical mixtures, you take my word."

XVI

The End

WHEN it came time for Ernest and me to go to Washington, father did not accompany us. He had become enamoured of proletarian life. He looked upon our slum neighborhood as a great sociological laboratory, and he had embarked upon an apparently endless orgy of investigation. He chummed with the laborers, and was an intimate in scores of homes. Also, he worked at odd jobs, and the work was play as well as learned investigation, for he delighted in it and was always returning home with copious notes and bubbling over with new adventures. He was the perfect scientist.

There was no need for his working at all, because Ernest managed to earn enough from his translating to take care of the three of us. But father insisted on pursuing his favorite phantom, and a protean phantom it was, judging from the jobs he worked at. I shall never forget the evening he brought home his street pedler's outfit of shoe-laces and suspenders, nor the time I went into the little corner grocery to make some purchase and had him wait on me. After that I was not surprised when he tended bar for a week in the saloon across the street. He worked as a night watchman, hawked potatoes on the street, pasted labels in a cannery warehouse, was utility man in a paper-box factory, and water-carrier for a street railway construction gang, and even joined the Dishwashers' Union just before it fell to pieces.

I think the Bishop's example, so far as wearing apparel was concerned, must have fascinated father, for he wore the cheap cotton shirt of the laborer and the overalls with the narrow strap about the hips. Yet one habit remained to him from the old life; he always dressed for dinner, or supper, rather.

I could be happy anywhere with Ernest; and father's happiness in our changed circumstances rounded out my own happiness.

"When I was a boy," father said, "I was very curious. I wanted to know why things were and how they came to pass.

That was why I became a physicist. The life in me to-day is just as curious as it was in my boyhood, and it's the being curious that makes life worth living."

Sometimes he ventured north of Market Street into the shopping and theatre district, where he sold papers, ran errands, and opened cabs. There, one day, closing a cab, he encountered Mr. Wickson. In high glee father described the incident to us that evening.

"Wickson looked at me sharply when I closed the door on him, and muttered, 'Well, I'll be damned.' Just like that he said it, 'Well, I'll be damned.' His face turned red and he was so confused that he forgot to tip me. But he must have recovered himself quickly, for the cab hadn't gone fifty feet before it turned around and came back. He leaned out of the door.

" 'Look here, Professor,' he said, 'this is too much. What can I do for you?'

" 'I closed the cab door for you,' I answered. 'According to common custom you might give me a dime.'

" 'Bother that!' he snorted. 'I mean something substantial.'

"He was certainly serious—a twinge of ossified conscience or something; and so I considered with grave deliberation for a moment.

"His face was quite expectant when I began my answer, but you should have seen it when I finished.

" 'You might give me back my home,' I said, 'and my stock in the Sierra Mills.' "

Father paused.

"What did he say?" I questioned eagerly.

"What could he say? He said nothing. But I said, 'I hope you are happy.' He looked at me curiously. 'Tell me, are you happy?' I asked.

"He ordered the cabman to drive on, and went away swearing horribly. And he didn't give me the dime, much less the home and stock; so you see, my dear, your father's street-arab career is beset with disappointments."

And so it was that father kept on at our Pell Street quarters, while Ernest and I went to Washington. Except for the final consummation, the old order had passed away, and the final consummation was nearer than I dreamed. Contrary to our expectation, no obstacles were raised to prevent the socialist

Congressmen from taking their seats. Everything went smoothly, and I laughed at Ernest when he looked upon the very smoothness as something ominous.

We found our socialist comrades confident, optimistic of their strength and of the things they would accomplish. A few Grangers who had been elected to Congress increased our strength, and an elaborate programme of what was to be done was prepared by the united forces. In all of which Ernest joined loyally and energetically, though he could not forbear, now and again, from saying, apropos of nothing in particular, "When it comes to powder, chemical mixtures are better than mechanical mixtures, you take my word."

The trouble arose first with the Grangers in the various states they had captured at the last election. There were a dozen of these states, but the Grangers who had been elected were not permitted to take office. The incumbents refused to get out. It was very simple. They merely charged illegality in the elections and wrapped up the whole situation in the interminable red tape of the law. The Grangers were powerless. The courts were the last recourse, and the courts were in the hands of their enemies.

This was the moment of danger. If the cheated Grangers became violent, all was lost. How we socialists worked to hold them back! There were days and nights when Ernest never closed his eyes in sleep. The big leaders of the Grangers saw the peril and were with us to a man. But it was all of no avail. The Oligarchy wanted violence, and it set its agents-provocateurs to work. Without discussion, it was the agents-provocateurs who caused the Peasant Revolt.

In a dozen states the revolt flared up. The expropriated farmers took forcible possession of the state governments. Of course this was unconstitutional, and of course the United States put its soldiers into the field. Everywhere the agents-provocateurs urged the people on. These emissaries of the Iron Heel disguised themselves as artisans, farmers, and farm laborers. In Sacramento, the capital of California, the Grangers had succeeded in maintaining order. Thousands of secret agents were rushed to the devoted city. In mobs composed wholly of themselves, they fired and looted buildings and factories. They worked the people up until they joined them in the pillage. Liquor in large quantities was distributed among the slum classes further to inflame their minds. And then, when all was ready, appeared upon the scene the soldiers of the United States, who were, in reality, the soldiers of the Iron Heel. Eleven thousand men, women, and children were shot down on the streets of Sacramento or murdered in their houses. The national government took possession of the state government, and all was over for California.

And as with California, so elsewhere. Every Granger state was ravaged with violence and washed in blood. First, disorder was precipitated by the secret agents and the Black Hundreds, then the troops were called out. Rioting and mob-rule reigned throughout the rural districts. Day and night the smoke of burning farms, warehouses, villages, and cities filled the sky. Dynamite appeared. Railroad bridges and tunnels were blown up and trains were wrecked. The poor farmers were shot and hanged in great numbers. Reprisals were bitter, and many plutocrats and army officers were murdered. Blood and vengeance were in men's hearts. The regular troops fought the farmers as savagely as had they been Indians. And the regular troops had cause. Twenty-eight hundred of them had been annihilated in a tremendous series of dynamite explosions in Oregon, and in a similar manner, a number of train loads, at different times and places, had been destroyed. So it was that the regular troops fought for their lives as well as did the farmers.

As for the militia, the militia law of 1903 was put into effect, and the workers of one state were compelled, under pain of death, to shoot down their comrade-workers in other states. Of course, the militia law did not work smoothly at first. Many militia officers were murdered, and many militiamen were executed by drumhead court martial. Ernest's prophecy was strikingly fulfilled in the cases of Mr. Kowalt and Mr. Asmunsen. Both were eligible for the militia, and both were drafted to serve in the punitive expedition that was despatched from California against the farmers of Missouri. Mr. Kowalt and Mr. Asmunsen refused to serve. They were given short shrift. Drumhead court martial was their portion, and military execution their end. They were shot with their backs to the firing squad.

Many young men fled into the mountains to escape serving in the militia. There they became outlaws, and it was not until more peaceful times that they received their punishment. It was drastic. The government issued a proclamation for all law-abiding citizens to come in from the mountains for a period of three months. When the proclaimed date arrived, half a million soldiers were sent into the mountainous districts everywhere. There was no investigation, no trial. Wherever a man was encountered, he was shot down on the spot. The troops operated on the basis that no man not an outlaw remained in the mountains. Some bands, in strong positions, fought gallantly, but in the end every deserter from the militia met death.

A more immediate lesson, however, was impressed on the minds of the people by the punishment meted out to the Kansas militia. The great Kansas Mutiny occurred at the very beginning of military operations against the Grangers. Six thousand of the militia mutinied. They had been for several weeks very turbulent and sullen, and for that reason had been kept in camp. Their open mutiny, however, was without doubt precipitated by the agents-provocateurs.

On the night of the 22d of April they arose and murdered their officers, only a small remnant of the latter escaping. This was beyond the scheme of the Iron Heel, for the agents-provocateurs had done their work too well. But everything was grist to the Iron Heel. It had prepared for the outbreak, and the killing of so many officers gave it justification for what followed. As by magic, forty thousand soldiers of the regular army surrounded the malcontents. It was a trap. The wretched militiamen found that their machine-guns had been tampered with, and that the cartridges from the captured magazines did not fit their rifles. They hoisted the white flag of surrender, but it was ignored. There were no survivors. The entire six thousand were annihilated. Common shell and shrapnel were thrown in upon them from a distance, and, when, in their desperation, they charged the encircling lines, they were mowed down by the machine-guns. I talked with an eye-witness, and he said that the nearest any militiaman approached the machine-guns was a hundred and fifty yards. The earth was carpeted with the slain, and a final charge of cavalry, with trampling of horses' hoofs, revolvers, and sabres, crushed the wounded into the ground.

Simultaneously with the destruction of the Grangers came the revolt of the coal miners. It was the expiring effort of organized labor. Three-quarters of a million of miners went out on strike. But they were too widely scattered over the country to advantage from their own strength. They were segregated in their own districts and beaten into submission. This was the first great slave-drive. Pocock[1] won his spurs as a slave-driver and earned the undying hatred of the proletariat. Countless attempts were made upon his life, but he seemed to bear a charmed existence. It was he who was responsible for the introduction of the Russian passport system among the miners, and the denial of their right of removal from one part of the country to another.

In the meantime, the socialists held firm. While the Grangers expired in flame and blood, and organized labor was disrupted, the socialists held their peace and perfected their secret organization. In vain the Grangers pleaded with us. We rightly contended that any revolt on our part was virtually suicide for the whole Revolution. The Iron Heel, at first dubious about dealing with the entire proletariat at one time, had found the work easier than it had expected, and would have asked nothing better than an uprising on our part. But we avoided the issue, in spite of the fact that agents-provocateurs swarmed in our midst. In those early days, the agents of the Iron Heel were clumsy in their methods. They had much to learn and in the meantime our Fighting Groups

[1]Albert Pocock, another of the notorious strike-breakers of earlier years, who, to the day of his death, successfully held all the coal-miners of the country to their task. He was succeeded by his son, Lewis Pocock, and for five generations this remarkable line of slave-drivers handled the coal mines. The elder Pocock, known as Pocock I., has been described as follows: "A long, lean head, semicircled by a fringe of brown and gray hair, with big cheek-bones and a heavy chin, . . . a pale face, lustreless gray eyes, a metallic voice, and a languid manner." He was born of humble parents, and began his career as a bartender. He next became a private detective for a street railway corporation, and by successive steps developed into a professional strike-breaker. Pocock V., the last of the line, was blown up in a pump-house by a bomb during a petty revolt of the miners in the Indian Territory. This occurred in 2073 A.D.

weeded them out. It was bitter, bloody work, but we were
fighting for life and for the Revolution, and we had to fight
the enemy with its own weapons. Yet we were fair. No agent
of the Iron Heel was executed without a trial. We may have
made mistakes, but if so, very rarely. The bravest, and the
most combative and self-sacrificing of our comrades went into
the Fighting Groups. Once, after ten years had passed, Ernest
made a calculation from figures furnished by the chiefs of the
Fighting Groups, and his conclusion was that the average life
of a man or woman after becoming a member was five years.
The comrades of the Fighting Groups were heroes all, and
the peculiar thing about it was that they were opposed to the
taking of life. They violated their own natures, yet they loved
liberty and knew of no sacrifice too great to make for the
Cause.[1]

The task we set ourselves was threefold. First, the weeding
out from our circles of the secret agents of the Oligarchy.
Second, the organizing of the Fighting Groups, and, outside
of them, of the general secret organization of the Revolution.
And third, the introduction of our own secret agents into
every branch of the Oligarchy—into the labor castes and especially among the telegraphers and secretaries and clerks,

[1] These Fighting groups were modelled somewhat after the Fighting Organization of the Russian Revolution, and, despite the unceasing efforts of
the Iron Heel, these groups persisted throughout the three centuries of its
existence. Composed of men and women actuated by lofty purpose and unafraid to die, the Fighting Groups exercised tremendous influence and tempered the savage brutality of the rulers. Not alone was their work confined
to unseen warfare with the secret agents of the Oligarchy. The oligarchs
themselves were compelled to listen to the decrees of the Groups, and often,
when they disobeyed, were punished by death—and likewise with the sub-
ordinates of the oligarchs, with the officers of the army and the leaders of the
labor castes.

Stern justice was meted out by these organized avengers, but most remarkable was their passionless and judicial procedure. There were no snap judgments. When a man was captured he was given fair trial and opportunity for
defence. Of necessity, many men were tried and condemned by proxy, as in
the case of General Lampton. This occurred in 2138 A.D. Possibly the most
bloodthirsty and malignant of all the mercenaries that ever served the Iron
Heel, he was informed by the Fighting Groups that they had tried him,
found him guilty, and condemned him to death—and this, after three warnings for him to cease from his ferocious treatment of the proletariat. After

into the army, the agents-provocateurs, and the slave-drivers. It was slow work, and perilous, and often were our efforts rewarded with costly failures.

The Iron Heel had triumphed in open warfare, but we held our own in the new warfare, strange and awful and subterranean, that we instituted. All was unseen, much was unguessed; the blind fought the blind; and yet through it all was order, purpose, control. We permeated the entire organization of the Iron Heel with our agents, while our own organization was permeated with the agents of the Iron Heel. It was warfare dark and devious, replete with intrigue and conspiracy, plot and counterplot. And behind all, ever menacing, was death, violent and terrible. Men and women disappeared, our nearest and dearest comrades. We saw them to-day. To-morrow they were gone; we never saw them again, and we knew that they had died.

There was no trust, no confidence anywhere. The man who plotted beside us, for all we knew, might be an agent of the Iron Heel. We mined the organization of the Iron Heel with our secret agents, and the Iron Heel countermined with its secret agents inside its own organization. And it was the same

his condemnation he surrounded himself with a myriad protective devices. Years passed, and in vain the Fighting Groups strove to execute their decree. Comrade after comrade, men and women, failed in their attempts, and were cruelly executed by the Oligarchy. It was the case of General Lampton that revived crucifixion as a legal method of execution. But in the end the condemned man found his executioner in the form of a slender girl of seventeen, Madeline Provence, who, to accomplish her purpose, served two years in his palace as a seamstress to the household. She died in solitary confinement after horrible and prolonged torture; but to-day she stands in imperishable bronze in the Pantheon of Brotherhood in the wonder city of Serles.

We, who by personal experience know nothing of bloodshed, must not judge harshly the heroes of the Fighting Groups. They gave up their lives for humanity, no sacrifice was too great for them to accomplish, while inexorable necessity compelled them to bloody expression in an age of blood. The Fighting Groups constituted the one thorn in the side of the Iron Heel that the Iron Heel could never remove. Everhard was the father of this curious army, and its accomplishments and successful persistence for three hundred years bear witness to the wisdom with which he organized and the solid foundation he laid for the succeeding generations to build upon. In some respects, despite his great economic and sociological contributions, and his work as a general leader in the Revolution, his organization of the Fighting Groups must be regarded as his greatest achievement.

with our organization. And despite the absence of confidence and trust we were compelled to base our every effort on confidence and trust. Often were we betrayed. Men were weak. The Iron Heel could offer money, leisure, the joys and pleasures that waited in the repose of the wonder cities. We could offer nothing but the satisfaction of being faithful to a noble ideal. As for the rest, the wages of those who were loyal were unceasing peril, torture, and death.

Men were weak, I say, and because of their weakness we were compelled to make the only other reward that was within our power. It was the reward of death. Out of necessity we had to punish our traitors. For every man who betrayed us, from one to a dozen faithful avengers were loosed upon his heels. We might fail to carry out our decrees against our enemies, such as the Pococks, for instance; but the one thing we could not afford to fail in was the punishment of our own traitors. Comrades turned traitor by permission, in order to win to the wonder cities and there execute our sentences on the real traitors. In fact, so terrible did we make ourselves, that it became a greater peril to betray us than to remain loyal to us.

The Revolution took on largely the character of religion. We worshipped at the shrine of the Revolution, which was the shrine of liberty. It was the divine flashing through us. Men and women devoted their lives to the Cause, and newborn babes were sealed to it as of old they had been sealed to the service of God. We were lovers of Humanity.

XVII

The Scarlet Livery

WITH THE DESTRUCTION of the Granger states, the Grangers in Congress disappeared. They were being tried for high treason, and their places were taken by the creatures of the Iron Heel. The socialists were in a pitiful minority, and they knew that their end was near. Congress and the Senate were empty pretences, farces. Public questions were gravely debated and passed upon according to the old forms, while in reality all that was done was to give the stamp of constitutional procedure to the mandates of the Oligarchy.

Ernest was in the thick of the fight when the end came. It was in the debate on the bill to assist the unemployed. The hard times of the preceding year had thrust great masses of the proletariat beneath the starvation line, and the continued and wide-reaching disorder had but sunk them deeper. Millions of people were starving, while the oligarchs and their supporters were surfeiting on the surplus.[1] We called these wretched people the people of the abyss,[2] and it was to alleviate their awful suffering that the socialists had introduced the unemployed bill. But this was not to the fancy of the Iron

[1] The same conditions obtained in the nineteenth century A.D., under British rule in India. The natives died of starvation by the million, while their rulers robbed them of the fruits of their toil and expended it on magnificent pageants and mumbo-jumbo fooleries. Perforce, in this enlightened age, we have much to blush for in the acts of our ancestors. Our only consolation is philosophic. We must accept the capitalistic stage in social evolution as about on a par with the earlier monkey stage. The human had to pass through those stages in its rise from the mire and slime of low organic life. It was inevitable that much of the mire and slime should cling and be not easily shaken off.

[2] *The people of the abyss*—this phrase was struck out by the genius of H. G. Wells in the late nineteenth century A.D. Wells was a sociological seer, sane and normal as well as warm human. Many fragments of his work have come down to us, while two of his greatest achievements, "Anticipations" and "Mankind in the Making," have come down intact. Before the oligarchs, and before Everhard, Wells speculated upon the building of the wonder cities, though in his writings they are referred to as "pleasure cities."

Heel. In its own way it was preparing to set these millions to work, but the way was not our way, wherefore it had issued its orders that our bill should be voted down. Ernest and his fellows knew that their effort was futile, but they were tired of the suspense. They wanted something to happen. They were accomplishing nothing, and the best they hoped for was the putting of an end to the legislative farce in which they were unwilling players. They knew not what end would come, but they never anticipated a more disastrous end than the one that did come.

I sat in the gallery that day. We all knew that something terrible was imminent. It was in the air, and its presence was made visible by the armed soldiers drawn up in lines in the corridors, and by the officers grouped in the entrances to the House itself. The Oligarchy was about to strike. Ernest was speaking. He was describing the sufferings of the unemployed, as if with the wild idea of in some way touching their hearts and consciences; but the Republican and Democratic members sneered and jeered at him, and there was uproar and confusion. Ernest abruptly changed front.

"I know nothing that I may say can influence you," he said. "You have no souls to be influenced. You are spineless, flaccid things. You pompously call yourselves Republicans and Democrats. There is no Republican Party. There is no Democratic Party. There are no Republicans nor Democrats in this House. You are lick-spittlers and panderers, the creatures of the Plutocracy. You talk verbosely in antiquated terminology of your love of liberty, and all the while you wear the scarlet livery of the Iron Heel."

Here the shouting and the cries of "Order! order!" drowned his voice, and he stood disdainfully till the din had somewhat subsided. He waved his hand to include all of them, turned to his own comrades, and said:

"Listen to the bellowing of the well-fed beasts."

Pandemonium broke out again. The Speaker rapped for order and glanced expectantly at the officers in the doorways. There were cries of "Sedition!" and a great, rotund New York member began shouting "Anarchist!" at Ernest. And Ernest was not pleasant to look at. Every fighting fibre of him was quivering, and his face was the face of a fighting animal, withal he was cool and collected.

"Remember," he said, in a voice that made itself heard above the din, "that as you show mercy now to the proletariat, some day will that same proletariat show mercy to you."

The cries of "Sedition!" and "Anarchist!" redoubled.

"I know that you will not vote for this bill," Ernest went on. "You have received the command from your masters to vote against it. And yet you call me anarchist. You, who have destroyed the government of the people, and who shamelessly flaunt your scarlet shame in public places, call me anarchist. I do not believe in hell-fire and brimstone; but in moments like this I regret my unbelief. Nay, in moments like this I almost do believe. Surely there must be a hell, for in no less place could it be possible for you to receive punishment adequate to your crimes. So long as you exist, there is a vital need for hell-fire in the Cosmos."

There was movement in the doorways. Ernest, the Speaker, all the members turned to see.

"Why do you not call your soldiers in, Mr. Speaker, and bid them do their work?" Ernest demanded. "They should carry out your plan with expedition."

"There are other plans afoot," was the retort. "That is why the soldiers are present."

"Our plans, I suppose," Ernest sneered. "Assassination or something kindred."

But at the word "assassination" the uproar broke out again. Ernest could not make himself heard, but he remained on his feet waiting for a lull. And then it happened. From my place in the gallery I saw nothing except the flash of the explosion. The roar of it filled my ears and I saw Ernest reeling and falling in a swirl of smoke, and the soldiers rushing up all the aisles. His comrades were on their feet, wild with anger, capable of any violence. But Earnest steadied himself for a moment, and waved his arms for silence.

"It is a plot!" his voice rang out in warning to his comrades. "Do nothing, or you will be destroyed."

Then he slowly sank down, and the soldiers reached him. The next moment soldiers were clearing the galleries and I saw no more.

Though he was my husband, I was not permitted to get to him. When I announced who I was, I was promptly placed under arrest. And at the same time were arrested all socialist Congressmen in Washington, including the unfortunate Simpson, who lay ill with typhoid fever in his hotel.

The trial was prompt and brief. The men were fore-doomed. The wonder was that Ernest was not executed. This was a blunder on the part of the Oligarchy, and a costly one. But the Oligarchy was too confident in those days. It was drunk with success, and little did it dream that that small handful of heroes had within them the power to rock it to its foundations. To-morrow, when the Great Revolt breaks out and all the world resounds with the tramp, tramp of the millions, the Oligarchy will realize, and too late, how mightily that band of heroes has grown.[1]

As a revolutionist myself, as one on the inside who knew the hopes and fears and secret plans of the revolutionists, I am fitted to answer, as very few are, the charge that they were guilty of exploding the bomb in Congress. And I can say flatly, without qualification or doubt of any sort, that the socialists, in Congress and out, had no hand in the affair. Who threw the bomb we do not know, but the one thing we are absolutely sure of is that we did not throw it.

On the other hand, there is evidence to show that the Iron

[1] Avis Everhard took for granted that her narrative would be read in her own day, and so omits to mention the outcome of the trial for high treason. Many other similar disconcerting omissions will be noticed in the Manuscript. Fifty-two socialist Congressmen were tried, and all were found guilty. Strange to relate, not one received the death sentence. Everhard and eleven others, among whom were Theodore Donnelson and Matthew Kent, received life imprisonment. The remaining forty received sentences varying from thirty to forty-five years; while Arthur Simpson, referred to in the Manuscript as being ill of typhoid fever at the time of the explosion, received only fifteen years. It is the tradition that he died of starvation in solitary confinement, and this harsh treatment is explained as having been caused by his uncompromising stubbornness and his fiery and tactless hatred for all men that served the despotism. He died in Cabanas in Cuba, where three of his comrades were also confined. The fifty-two socialist Congressmen were confined in military fortresses scattered all over the United States. Thus, Du Bois and Woods were held in Porto Rico, while Everhard and Merryweather were placed in Alcatraz, an island in San Francisco Bay that had already seen long service as a military prison.

Heel was responsible for the act. Of course, we cannot prove this. Our conclusion is merely presumptive. But here are such facts as we do know. It had been reported to the Speaker of the House, by secret-service agents of the government, that the socialist Congressmen were about to resort to terroristic tactics, and that they had decided upon the day when their tactics would go into effect. This day was the very day of the explosion. Wherefore the Capitol had been packed with troops in anticipation. Since we knew nothing about the bomb, and since a bomb actually was exploded, and since the authorities had prepared in advance for the explosion, it is only fair to conclude that the Iron Heel did know. Furthermore, we charge that the Iron Heel was guilty of the outrage, and that the Iron Heel planned and perpetrated the outrage for the purpose of foisting the guilt on our shoulders and so bringing about our destruction.

From the Speaker the warning leaked out to all the creatures in the House that wore the scarlet livery. They knew, while Ernest was speaking, that some violent act was to be committed. And to do them justice, they honestly believed that the act was to be committed by the socialists. At the trial, and still with honest belief, several testified to having seen Ernest prepare to throw the bomb, and that it exploded prematurely. Of course they saw nothing of the sort. In the fevered imagination of fear they thought they saw, that was all.

As Ernest said at the trial: "Does it stand to reason, if I were going to throw a bomb, that I should elect to throw a feeble little squib like the one that was thrown? There wasn't enough powder in it. It made a lot of smoke, but hurt no one except me. It exploded right at my feet, and yet it did not kill me. Believe me, when I get to throwing bombs, I'll do damage. There'll be more than smoke in my petards."

In return it was argued by the prosecution that the weakness of the bomb was a blunder on the part of the socialists, just as its premature explosion, caused by Ernest's losing his nerve and dropping it, was a blunder. And to clinch the argument, there were the several Congressmen who testified to having seen Ernest fumble and drop the bomb.

As for ourselves, not one of us knew how the bomb was

thrown. Ernest told me that the fraction of an instant before it exploded he both heard and saw it strike at his feet. He testified to this at the trial, but no one believed him. Besides, the whole thing, in popular slang, was "cooked up." The Iron Heel had made up its mind to destroy us, and there was no withstanding it.

There is a saying that truth will out. I have come to doubt that saying. Nineteen years have elapsed, and despite our untiring efforts, we have failed to find the man who really did throw the bomb. Undoubtedly he was some emissary of the Iron Heel, but he has escaped detection. We have never got the slightest clew to his identity. And now, at this late date, nothing remains but for the affair to take its place among the mysteries of history.[1]

[1]Avis Everhard would have had to live for many generations ere she could have seen the clearing up of this particular mystery. A little less than a hundred years ago, and a little more than six hundred years after her death, the confession of Pervaise was discovered in the secret archives of the Vatican. It is perhaps well to tell a little something about this obscure document, which, in the main, is of interest to the historian only.

Pervaise was an American, of French descent, who, in 1913 A.D., was lying in the Tombs Prison, New York City, awaiting trial for murder. From his confession we learn that he was not a criminal. He was warm-blooded, passionate, emotional. In an insane fit of jealousy he killed his wife—a very common act in those times. Pervaise was mastered by the fear of death, all of which is recounted at length in his confession. To escape death he would have done anything, and the police agents prepared him by assuring him that he could not possibly escape conviction of murder in the first degree when his trial came off. In those days, murder in the first degree was a capital offense. The guilty man or woman was placed in a specially constructed death-chair, and, under the supervision of competent physicians, was destroyed by a current of electricity. This was called electrocution, and it was very popular during that period. Anæsthesia, as a mode of compulsory death, was not introduced until later.

This man, good at heart but with a ferocious animalism close at the surface of his being, lying in jail and expectant of nothing less than death, was prevailed upon by the agents of the Iron Heel to throw the bomb in the House of Representatives. In his confession he states explicitly that he was informed that the bomb was to be a feeble thing and that no lives would be lost. This is directly in line with the fact that the bomb was lightly charged, and that its explosion at Everhard's feet was not deadly.

Pervaise was smuggled into one of the galleries ostensibly closed for repairs. He was to select the moment for the throwing of the bomb, and he naïvely confesses that in his interest in Everhard's tirade and the general commotion raised thereby, he nearly forgot his mission.

Not only was he released from prison in reward for his deed, but he was granted an income for life. This he did not long enjoy. In 1914 A.D., in September, he was stricken with rheumatism of the heart and lived for three days. It was then that he sent for the Catholic priest, Father Peter Durban, and to him made confession. So important did it seem to the priest, that he had the confession taken down in writing and sworn to. What happened after this we can only surmise. The document was certainly important enough to find its way to Rome. Powerful influences must have been brought to bear, hence its suppression. For centuries no hint of its existence reached the world. It was not until in the last century that Lorbia, the brilliant Italian scholar, stumbled upon it quite by chance during his researches in the Vatican.

There is to-day no doubt whatever that the Iron Heel was responsible for the bomb that exploded in the House of Representatives in 1913 A.D. Even though the Pervaise confession had never come to light, no reasonable doubt could obtain; for the act in question, that sent fifty-two Congressmen to prison, was on a par with countless other acts committed by the oligarchs, and, before them, by the capitalists.

There is the classic instance of the ferocious and wanton judicial murder of the innocent and so-called Haymarket Anarchists in Chicago in the penultimate decade of the nineteenth century A.D. In a category by itself is the deliberate burning and destruction of capitalist property by the capitalists themselves—see first footnote on page 434. For such destruction of property innocent men were frequently punished—"railroaded" in the parlance of the times.

In the labor troubles of the first decade of the twentieth century A.D., between the capitalists and the Western Federation of Miners, similar but more bloody tactics were employed. The railroad station at Independence was blown up by the agents of the capitalists. Thirteen men were killed, and many more were wounded. And then the capitalists, controlling the legislative and judicial machinery of the state of Colorado, charged the miners with the crime and came very near to convicting them. Romaines, one of the tools in this affair, like Pervaise, was lying in jail in another state, Kansas, awaiting trial, when he was approached by the agents of the capitalists. But, unlike Pervaise, the confession of Romaines was made public in his own time.

Then, during this same period, there was the case of Moyer and Haywood, two strong, fearless leaders of labor. One was president and the other was secretary of the Western Federation of Miners. The ex-governor of Idaho had been mysteriously murdered. The crime, at the time, was openly charged to the mine owners by the socialists and miners. Nevertheless, in violation of the national and state constitutions, and by means of conspiracy on the parts of the governors of Idaho and Colorado, Moyer and Haywood were kidnapped, thrown into jail, and charged with the murder. It was this instance that provoked from Eugene V. Debs, national leader of the American socialists at the time, the following words: *"The labor leaders that cannot be bribed nor bullied, must be ambushed and murdered. The only crime of Moyer and Hay-*

wood is that they have been unswervingly true to the working class. The capitalists have stolen our country, debauched our politics, defiled our judiciary, and ridden over us rough-shod, and now they propose to murder those who will not abjectly surrender to their brutal dominion. The governors of Colorado and Idaho are but executing the mandates of their masters, the Plutocracy. The issue is the Workers versus the Plutocracy. If they strike the first violent blow, we will strike the last."

XVIII

In the Shadow of Sonoma

O F MYSELF, during this period, there is not much to say. For six months I was kept in prison, though charged with no crime. I was a *suspect*—a word of fear that all revolutionists were soon to come to know. But our own nascent secret service was beginning to work. By the end of my second month in prison, one of the jailers made himself known as a revolutionist in touch with the organization. Several weeks later, Joseph Parkhurst, the prison doctor who had just been appointed, proved himself to be a member of one of the Fighting Groups.

Thus, throughout the organization of the Oligarchy, our own organization, weblike and spidery, was insinuating itself. And so I was kept in touch with all that was happening in the world without. And furthermore, every one of our imprisoned leaders was in contact with brave comrades who masqueraded in the livery of the Iron Heel. Though Ernest lay in prison three thousand miles away, on the Pacific Coast, I was in unbroken communication with him, and our letters passed regularly back and forth.

The leaders, in prison and out, were able to discuss and direct the campaign. It would have been possible, within a few months, to have effected the escape of some of them; but since imprisonment proved no bar to our activities, it was decided to avoid anything premature. Fifty-two Congressmen were in prison, and fully three hundred more of our leaders. It was planned that they should be delivered simultaneously. If part of them escaped, the vigilance of the oligarchs might be aroused so as to prevent the escape of the remainder. On the other hand, it was held that a simultaneous jail-delivery all over the land would have immense psychological influence on the proletariat. It would show our strength and give confidence.

So it was arranged, when I was released at the end of six months, that I was to disappear and prepare a secure hiding-place for Ernest. To disappear was in itself no easy thing. No sooner did I get my freedom than my footsteps began to be dogged by the spies of the Iron Heel. It was necessary that they should be thrown off the track, and that I should win to California. It is laughable, the way this was accomplished.

Already the passport system, modelled on the Russian, was developing. I dared not cross the continent in my own character. It was necessary that I should be completely lost if ever I was to see Ernest again, for by trailing me after he escaped, he would be caught once more. Again, I could not disguise myself as a proletarian and travel. There remained the disguise of a member of the Oligarchy. While the arch-oligarchs were no more than a handful, there were myriads of lesser ones of the type, say, of Mr. Wickson—men, worth a few millions, who were adherents of the arch-oligarchs. The wives and daughters of these lesser oligarchs were legion, and it was decided that I should assume the disguise of such a one. A few years later this would have been impossible, because the passport system was to become so perfect that no man, woman, nor child in all the land was unregistered and unaccounted for in his or her movements.

When the time was ripe, the spies were thrown off my track. An hour later Avis Everhard was no more. At that time one Felice Van Verdighan, accompanied by two maids and a lap-dog, with another maid for the lap-dog,[1] entered a drawing-room on a Pullman,[2] and a few minutes later was speeding west.

The three maids who accompanied me were revolutionists. Two were members of the Fighting Groups, and the third, Grace Holbrook, entered a group the following year, and six months later was executed by the Iron Heel. She it was who waited upon the dog. Of the other two, Bertha Stole disap-

[1] This ridiculous picture well illustrates the heartless conduct of the masters. While people starved, lap-dogs were waited upon by maids. This was a serious masquerade on the part of Avis Everhard. Life and death and the Cause were in the issue; therefore the picture must be accepted as a true picture. It affords a striking commentary of the times.

[2] *Pullman*—the designation of the more luxurious railway cars of the period and so named from the inventor.

peared twelve years later, while Anna Roylston still lives and plays an increasingly important part in the Revolution.[1]

Without adventure we crossed the United States to California. When the train stopped at Sixteenth Street Station, in Oakland, we alighted, and there Felice Van Verdighan, with her two maids, her lap-dog, and her lap-dog's maid, disappeared forever. The maids, guided by trusty comrades, were led away. Other comrades took charge of me. Within half an hour after leaving the train I was on board a small fishing boat and out on the waters of San Francisco Bay. The winds baffled, and we drifted aimlessly the greater part of the night. But I saw the lights of Alcatraz where Ernest lay, and found comfort in the thought of nearness to him. By dawn, what with the rowing of the fishermen, we made the Marin Islands. Here we lay in hiding all day, and on the following night, swept on by a flood tide and a fresh wind, we crossed San Pablo Bay in two hours and ran up Petaluma Creek.

Here horses were ready and another comrade, and without delay we were away through the starlight. To the north I could see the loom of Sonoma Mountain, toward which we rode. We left the old town of Sonoma to the right and rode up a canyon that lay between outlying buttresses of the mountain. The wagon-road became a wood-road, the wood-road became a cow-path, and the cow-path dwindled away and ceased among the upland pastures. Straight over Sonoma Mountain we rode. It was the safest route. There was no one to mark our passing.

Dawn caught us on the northern brow, and in the gray light we dropped down through chaparral into redwood canyons deep and warm with the breath of passing summer. It was old country to me that I knew and loved, and soon I became the guide. The hiding-place was mine. I had selected

[1]Despite continual and almost inconceivable hazards, Anna Roylston lived to the royal age of ninety-one. As the Pococks defied the executioners of the Fighting Groups, so she defied the executioners of the Iron Heel. She bore a charmed life and prospered amid dangers and alarms. She herself was an executioner for the Fighting Groups, and, known as the Red Virgin, she became one of the inspired figures of the Revolution. When she was an old woman of sixty-nine she shot "Bloody" Halcliffe down in the midst of his armed escort and got away unscathed. In the end she died peaceably of old age in a secret refuge of the revolutionists in the Ozark mountains.

it. We let down the bars and crossed an upland meadow.
Next, we went over a low, oak-covered ridge and descended
into a smaller meadow. Again we climbed a ridge, this time
riding under red-limbed madroños and manzanitas of deeper
red. The first rays of the sun streamed upon our backs as we
climbed. A flight of quail thrummed off through the thickets.
A big jack-rabbit crossed our path, leaping swiftly and silently
like a deer. And then a deer, a many-pronged buck, the sun
flashing red-gold from neck and shoulders, cleared the crest
of the ridge before us and was gone.

We followed in his wake a space, then dropped down a
zigzag trail that he disdained into a group of noble redwoods that stood about a pool of water murky with minerals from the mountain side. I knew every inch of the
way. Once a writer friend of mine had owned the ranch;
but he, too, had become a revolutionist, though more di-
sastrously than I, for he was already dead and gone, and
none knew where nor how. He alone, in the days he had
lived, knew the secret of the hiding-place for which I was
bound. He had bought the ranch for beauty, and paid a
round price for it, much to the disgust of the local farmers. He used to tell with great glee how they were wont to
shake their heads mournfully at the price, to accomplish
ponderously a bit of mental arithmetic, and then to say,
"But you can't make six per cent on it."

But he was dead now, nor did the ranch descend to his
children. Of all men, it was now the property of Mr. Wickson, who owned the whole eastern and northern slopes of
Sonoma Mountain, running from the Spreckels estate to the
divide of Bennett Valley. Out of it he had made a magnificent
deer-park, where, over thousands of acres of sweet slopes and
glades and canyons, the deer ran almost in primitive wildness.
The people who had owned the soil had been driven away. A
state home for the feeble-minded had also been demolished
to make room for the deer.

To cap it all, Wickson's hunting lodge was a quarter of a
mile from my hiding-place. This, instead of being a danger,
was an added security. We were sheltered under the very ægis
of one of the minor oligarchs. Suspicion, by the nature of the
situation, was turned aside. The last place in the world the

spies of the Iron Heel would dream of looking for me, and for Ernest when he joined me, was Wickson's deer-park.

We tied our horses among the redwoods at the pool. From a cache behind a hollow rotting log my companion brought out a variety of things,—a fifty-pound sack of flour, tinned foods of all sorts, cooking utensils, blankets, a canvas tarpaulin, books and writing material, a great bundle of letters, a five-gallon can of kerosene, an oil stove, and, last and most important, a large coil of stout rope. So large was the supply of things that a number of trips would be necessary to carry them to the refuge.

But the refuge was very near. Taking the rope and leading the way, I passed through a glade of tangled vines and bushes that ran between two wooded knolls. The glade ended abruptly at the steep bank of a stream. It was a little stream, rising from springs, and the hottest summer never dried it up. On every hand were tall wooded knolls, a group of them, with all the seeming of having been flung there from some careless Titan's hand. There was no bed-rock in them. They rose from their bases hundreds of feet, and they were composed of red volcanic earth, the famous wine-soil of Sonoma. Through these the tiny stream had cut its deep and precipitous channel.

It was quite a scramble down to the stream bed, and, once on the bed, we went down stream perhaps for a hundred feet. And then we came to the great hole. There was no warning of the existence of the hole, nor was it a hole in the common sense of the word. One crawled through tight-locked briers and branches, and found oneself on the very edge, peering out and down through a green screen. A couple of hundred feet in length and width, it was half of that in depth. Possibly because of some fault that had occurred when the knolls were flung together, and certainly helped by freakish erosion, the hole had been scooped out in the course of centuries by the wash of water. Nowhere did the raw earth appear. All was garmented by vegetation, from tiny maiden-hair and gold-back ferns to mighty redwoods and Douglas spruces. These great trees even sprang out from the walls of the hole. Some leaned over at angles as great as forty-five degrees, though the majority towered straight up from the soft and almost perpendicular earth walls.

It was a perfect hiding-place. No one ever came there, not even the village boys of Glen Ellen. Had this hole existed in the bed of a canyon a mile long, or several miles long, it would have been well known. But this was no canyon. From beginning to end the length of the stream was no more than five hundred yards. Three hundred yards above the hole the stream took its rise in a spring at the foot of a flat meadow. A hundred yards below the hole the stream ran out into open country, joining the main stream and flowing across rolling and grass-covered land.

My companion took a turn of the rope around a tree, and with me fast on the other end lowered away. In no time I was on the bottom. And in but a short while he had carried all the articles from the cache and lowered them down to me. He hauled the rope up and hid it, and before he went away called down to me a cheerful parting.

Before I go on I want to say a word for this comrade, John Carlson, a humble figure of the Revolution, one of the count-less faithful ones in the ranks. He worked for Wickson, in the stables near the hunting lodge. In fact, it was on Wickson's horses that we had ridden over Sonoma Mountain. For nearly twenty years now John Carlson has been custodian of the ref-uge. No thought of disloyalty, I am sure, has ever entered his mind during all that time. To betray his trust would have been in his mind a thing undreamed. He was phlegmatic, stolid to such a degree that one could not but wonder how the Revolution had any meaning to him at all. And yet love of freedom glowed sombrely and steadily in his dim soul. In ways it was indeed good that he was not flighty and imagi-native. He never lost his head. He could obey orders, and he was neither curious nor garrulous. Once I asked how it was that he was a revolutionist.

"When I was a young man I was a soldier," was his answer. "It was in Germany. There all young men must be in the army. So I was in the army. There was another soldier there, a young man, too. His father was what you call an agitator, and his father was in jail for lese majesty—what you call speaking the truth about the Emperor. And the young man, the son, talked with me much about people, and work, and the robbery of the people by the capitalists. He made me see things in new ways, and I became a socialist. His talk was very true and good, and I have never forgotten. When I came to the United States I hunted up the socialists. I became a member of a section—that was in the day of the S. L. P. Then later, when the split came, I joined the local of the S. P. I was working in a livery stable in San Francisco then. That was before the Earthquake. I have paid my dues for twenty-two years. I am yet a member, and I yet pay my dues, though it is very secret now. I will always pay my dues, and when the coöperative commonwealth comes, I will be glad."

Left to myself, I proceeded to cook breakfast on the oil stove and to prepare my home. Often, in the early morning, or in the evening after dark, Carlson would steal down to the refuge and work for a couple of hours. At first my home was the tarpaulin. Later, a small tent was put up. And still later, when we became assured of the perfect security of the place, a small house was erected. This house was completely hidden from any chance eye that might peer down from the edge of the hole. The lush vegetation of that sheltered spot made a natural shield. Also, the house was built against the perpendicular wall; and in the wall itself, shored by strong timbers, well drained and ventilated, we excavated two small rooms. Oh, believe me, we had many comforts. When Biedenbach, the German terrorist, hid with us some time later, he installed a smoke-consuming device that enabled us to sit by crackling wood fires on winter nights.

And here I must say a word for that gentle-souled terrorist, than whom there is no comrade in the Revolution more fearfully misunderstood. Comrade Biedenbach did not betray the Cause. Nor was he executed by the comrades as is commonly supposed. This canard was circulated by the creatures of the Oligarchy. Comrade Biedenbach was absent-minded, forgetful. He was shot by one of our lookouts at the cave-refuge at Carmel, through failure on his part to remember the secret signals. It was all a sad mistake. And that he betrayed his Fighting Group is an absolute lie. No truer, more loyal man ever labored for the Cause.[1]

[1] Search as we may through all the material of those times that has come down to us, we can find no clew to the Biedenbach here referred to. No mention is made of him anywhere save in the Everhard Manuscript.

For nineteen years now the refuge that I selected has been almost continuously occupied, and in all that time, with one exception, it has never been discovered by an outsider. And yet it was only a quarter of a mile from Wickson's hunting-lodge, and a short mile from the village of Glen Ellen. I was able, always, to hear the morning and evening trains arrive and depart, and I used to set my watch by the whistle at the brickyards.[1]

[1]If the curious traveller will turn south from Glen Ellen, he will find himself on a boulevard that is identical with the old county road of seven centuries ago. A quarter of a mile from Glen Ellen, after the second bridge is passed, to the right will be noticed a barranca that runs like a scar across the rolling land toward a group of wooded knolls. The barranca is the site of the ancient right of way that in the time of private property in land ran across the holding of one Chauvet, a French pioneer of California who came from his native country in the fabled days of gold. The wooded knolls are the same knolls referred to by Avis Everhard.

The Great Earthquake of 2368 A.D. broke off the side of one of these knolls and toppled it into the hole where the Everhards made their refuge. Since the finding of the Manuscript excavations have been made, and the house, the two cave rooms, and all the accumulated rubbish of long occupancy have been brought to light. Many valuable relics have been found, among which, curious to relate, is the smoke-consuming device of Biedenbach's mentioned in the narrative. Students interested in such matters should read the brochure of Arnold Bentham soon to be published.

A mile northwest from the wooded knolls brings one to the site of Wake Robin Lodge at the junction of Wild-Water and Sonoma Creeks. It may be noticed, in passing, that Wild-Water was originally called Graham Creek and was so named on the early local maps. But the later name sticks. It was at Wake Robin Lodge that Avis Everhard later lived for short periods, when, disguised as an agent-provocateur of the Iron Heel, she was enabled to play with impunity her part among men and events. The official permission to occupy Wake Robin Lodge is still on the records, signed by no less a man than Wickson, the minor oligarch of the Manuscript.

XIX
Transformation

"Y OU MUST make yourself over again," Ernest wrote to me. "You must cease to be. You must become another woman—and not merely in the clothes you wear, but inside your skin under the clothes. You must make yourself over again so that even I would not know you—your voice, your gestures, your mannerisms, your carriage, your walk, everything."

This command I obeyed. Every day I practised for hours in burying forever the old Avis Everhard beneath the skin of another woman whom I may call my other self. It was only by long practice that such results could be obtained. In the mere detail of voice intonation I practised almost perpetually till the voice of my new self became fixed, automatic. It was this automatic assumption of a rôle that was considered imperative. One must become so adept as to deceive oneself. It was like learning a new language, say the French. At first speech in French is self-conscious, a matter of the will. The student thinks in English and then transmutes into French, or reads in French but transmutes into English before he can understand. Then later, becoming firmly grounded, automatic, the student reads, writes, and *thinks* in French, without any recourse to English at all.

And so with our disguises. It was necessary for us to practise until our assumed rôles became real; until to be our original selves would require a watchful and strong exercise of will. Of course, at first, much was mere blundering experiment. We were creating a new art, and we had much to discover. But the work was going on everywhere; masters in the art were developing, and a fund of tricks and expedients was being accumulated. This fund became a sort of text-book that was passed on, a part of the curriculum, as it were, of the school of Revolution.[1]

[1]Disguise did become a veritable art during that period. The revolutionists maintained schools of acting in all their refuges. They scorned accessories,

It was at this time that my father disappeared. His letters, which had come to me regularly, ceased. He no longer appeared at our Pell Street quarters. Our comrades sought him everywhere. Through our secret service we ransacked every prison in the land. But he was lost as completely as if the earth had swallowed him up, and to this day no clew to his end has ever been discovered.[1]

Six lonely months I spent in the refuge, but they were not idle months. Our organization went on apace, and there were mountains of work always waiting to be done. Ernest and his fellow-leaders, from their prisons, decided what should be done; and it remained for us on the outside to do it. There was the organization of the mouth-to-mouth propaganda; the organization, with all its ramifications, of our spy system; the establishment of our secret printing-presses; and the establishment of our underground railways, which meant the knitting together of all our myriads of places of refuge, and the formation of new refuges where links were missing in the chains we ran over all the land.

So I say, the work was never done. At the end of six months my loneliness was broken by the arrival of two comrades. They were young girls, brave souls and passionate lovers of liberty: Lora Peterson, who disappeared in 1922, and Kate Bierce, who later married Du Bois,[2] and who is still with

---

such as wigs and beards, false eyebrows, and such aids of the theatrical actors. The game of revolution was a game of life and death, and mere accessories were traps. Disguise had to be fundamental, intrinsic, part and parcel of one's being, second nature. The Red Virgin is reported to have been one of the most adept in the art, to which must be ascribed her long and successful career.

[1]Disappearance was one of the horrors of the time. As a motif, in song and story, it constantly crops up. It was an inevitable concomitant of the subterranean warfare that raged through those three centuries. This phenomenon was almost as common in the oligarch class and the labor castes, as it was in the ranks of the revolutionists. Without warning, without trace, men and women, and even children, disappeared and were seen no more, their ends shrouded in mystery.

[2]Du Bois, the present librarian of Ardis, is a lineal descendant of this revolutionary pair.

us with eyes lifted to to-morrow's sun, that heralds in the new age.

The two girls arrived in a flurry of excitement, danger, and sudden death. In the crew of the fishing boat that conveyed them across San Pablo Bay was a spy. A creature of the Iron Heel, he had successfully masqueraded as a revolutionist and penetrated deep into the secrets of our organization. Without doubt he was on my trail, for we had long since learned that my disappearance had been cause of deep concern to the secret service of the Oligarchy. Luckily, as the outcome proved, he had not divulged his discoveries to any one. He had evidently delayed reporting, preferring to wait until he had brought things to a successful conclusion by discovering my hiding-place and capturing me. His information died with him. Under some pretext, after the girls had landed at Petaluma Creek and taken to the horses, he managed to get away from the boat.

Part way up Sonoma Mountain, John Carlson let the girls go on, leading his horse, while he went back on foot. His suspicions had been aroused. He captured the spy, and as to what then happened, Carlson gave us a fair idea.

"I fixed him," was Carlson's unimaginative way of describing the affair. "I fixed him," he repeated, while a sombre light burnt in his eyes, and his huge, toil-distorted hands opened and closed eloquently. "He made no noise. I hid him, and to-night I will go back and bury him deep."

During that period I used to marvel at my own metamorphosis. At times it seemed impossible, either that I had ever lived a placid, peaceful life in a college town, or else that I had become a revolutionist inured to scenes of violence and death. One or the other could not be. One was real, the other was a dream, but which was which? Was this present life of a revolutionist, hiding in a hole, a nightmare? or was I a revolutionist who had somewhere, somehow, dreamed that in some former existence I had lived in Berkeley and never known of life more violent than teas and dances, debating societies, and lecture rooms? But then I suppose this was a common experience of all of us who had rallied under the red banner of the brotherhood of man.

I often remembered figures from that other life, and, curiously enough, they appeared and disappeared, now and again, in my new life. There was Bishop Morehouse. In vain we searched for him after our organization had developed. He had been transferred from asylum to asylum. We traced him from the state hospital for the insane at Napa to the one in Stockton, and from there to the one in the Santa Clara Valley called Agnews, and there the trail ceased. There was no record of his death. In some way he must have escaped. Little did I dream of the awful manner in which I was to see him once again—the fleeting glimpse of him in the whirlwind carnage of the Chicago Commune.

Jackson, who had lost his arm in the Sierra Mills and who had been the cause of my own conversion into a revolutionist, I never saw again; but we all knew what he did before he died. He never joined the revolutionists. Embittered by his fate, brooding over his wrongs, he became an anarchist—not a philosophic anarchist, but a mere animal, mad with hate and lust for revenge. And well he revenged himself. Evading the guards, in the night-time while all were asleep, he blew the Pertonwaithe palace into atoms. Not a soul escaped, not even the guards. And in prison, while awaiting trial, he suffocated himself under his blankets.

Dr. Hammerfield and Dr. Ballingford achieved quite different fates from that of Jackson. They have been faithful to their salt, and they have been correspondingly rewarded with ecclesiastical palaces wherein they dwell at peace with the world. Both are apologists for the Oligarchy. Both have grown very fat. "Dr. Hammerfield," as Ernest once said, "has succeeded in modifying his metaphysics so as to give God's sanction to the Iron Heel, and also to include much worship of beauty and to reduce to an invisible wraith the gaseous vertebrate described by Haeckel—the difference between Dr. Hammerfield and Dr. Ballingford being that the latter has made the God of the oligarchs a little more gaseous and a little less vertebrate."

Peter Donnelly, the scab foreman at the Sierra Mills whom I encountered while investigating the case of Jackson, was a surprise to all of us. In 1918 I was present at a meeting of the 'Frisco Reds. Of all our Fighting Groups this one was the most formidable, ferocious, and merciless. It was really not a part of our organization. Its members were fanatics, madmen. We dared not encourage such a spirit. On the other hand, though they did not belong to us, we remained on friendly terms with them. It was a matter of vital importance that brought me there that night. I, alone in the midst of a score of men, was the only person unmasked. After the business that brought me there was transacted, I was led away by one of them. In a dark passage this guide struck a match, and, holding it close to his face, slipped back his mask. For a moment I gazed upon the passion-wrought features of Peter Donnelly. Then the match went out.

"I just wanted you to know it was me," he said in the darkness. "D'you remember Dallas, the superintendent?"

I nodded at recollection of the vulpine-faced superintendent of the Sierra Mills.

"Well, I got him first," Donnelly said with pride. " 'Twas after that I joined the Reds."

"But how comes it that you are here?" I queried. "Your wife and children?"

"Dead," he answered. "That's why. No," he went on hastily, " 'tis not revenge for them. They died easily in their beds—sickness, you see, one time and another. They tied my arms while they lived. And now that they're gone, 'tis revenge for my blasted manhood I'm after. I was once Peter Donnelly, the scab foreman. But to-night I'm Number 27 of the 'Frisco Reds. Come on now, and I'll get you out of this."

More I heard of him afterward. In his own way he had told the truth when he said all were dead. But one lived, Timothy, and him his father considered dead because he had taken service with the Iron Heel in the Mercenaries.[1] A member of the 'Frisco Reds pledged himself to twelve annual executions. The penalty for failure was death. A member who failed to complete his number committed suicide. These executions were not haphazard. This group of madmen met frequently

[1] In addition to the labor castes, there arose another caste, the military. A standing army of professional soldiers was created, officered by members of the Oligarchy and known as the Mercenaries. This institution took the place of the militia, which had proved impracticable under the new régime. Outside the regular secret service of the Iron Heel, there was further established a secret service of the Mercenaries, this latter forming a connecting link between the police and the military.

and passed wholesale judgments upon offending members and servitors of the Oligarchy. The executions were afterward apportioned by lot.

In fact, the business that brought me there the night of my visit was such a trial. One of our own comrades, who for years had successfully maintained himself in a clerical position in the local bureau of the secret service of the Iron Heel, had fallen under the ban of the 'Frisco Reds and was being tried. Of course he was not present, and of course his judges did not know that he was one of our men. My mission had been to testify to his identity and loyalty. It may be wondered how we came to know of the affair at all. The explanation is simple. One of our secret agents was a member of the 'Frisco Reds. It was necessary for us to keep an eye on friend as well as foe, and this group of madmen was not too unimportant to escape our surveillance.

But to return to Peter Donnelly and his son. All went well with Donnelly until, in the following year, he found among the sheaf of executions that fell to him the name of Timothy Donnelly. Then it was that that family clannishness, which was his to so extraordinary a degree, asserted itself. To save his son, he betrayed his comrades. In this he was partially blocked, but a dozen of the 'Frisco Reds were executed, and the group was well-nigh destroyed. In retaliation, the survivors meted out to Donnelly the death he had earned by his treason.

Nor did Timothy Donnelly long survive. The 'Frisco Reds pledged themselves to his execution. Every effort was made by the Oligarchy to save him. He was transferred from one part of the country to another. Three of the Reds lost their lives in vain efforts to get him. The Group was composed only of men. In the end they fell back on a woman, one of our comrades, and none other than Anna Roylston. Our Inner Circle forbade her, but she had ever a will of her own and disdained discipline. Furthermore, she was a genius and lovable, and we could never discipline her anyway. She is in a class by herself and not amenable to the ordinary standards of the revolutionists.

Despite our refusal to grant permission to do the deed, she went on with it. Now Anna Roylston was a fascinating woman. All she had to do was to beckon a man to her. She broke the hearts of scores of our young comrades, and scores of others she captured, and by their heart-strings led into our organization. Yet she steadfastly refused to marry. She dearly loved children, but she held that a child of her own would claim her from the Cause, and that it was the Cause to which her life was devoted.

It was an easy task for Anna Roylston to win Timothy Donnelly. Her conscience did not trouble her, for at that very time occurred the *Nashville Massacre*, when the Mercenaries, Donnelly in command, literally murdered eight hundred weavers of that city. But she did not kill Donnelly. She turned him over, a prisoner, to the 'Frisco Reds. This happened only last year, and now she has been renamed. The revolutionists everywhere are calling her the "Red Virgin."[1]

Colonel Ingram and Colonel Van Gilbert are two more familiar figures that I was later to encounter. Colonel Ingram rose high in the Oligarchy and became Minister to Germany. He was cordially detested by the proletariat of both countries. It was in Berlin that I met him, where, as an accredited international spy of the Iron Heel, I was received by him and afforded much assistance. Incidentally, I may state that in my dual rôle I managed a few important things for the Revolution.

Colonel Van Gilbert became known as "Snarling" Van Gilbert. His important part was played in drafting the new code after the Chicago Commune. But before that, as trial judge, he had earned sentence of death by his fiendish malignancy. I was one of those that tried him and passed sentence upon him. Anna Roylston carried out the execution.

Still another figure arises out of the old life—Jackson's lawyer. Least of all would I have expected again to meet this man, Joseph Hurd. It was a strange meeting. Late at night, two years after the Chicago Commune, Ernest and I arrived

---

[1] It was not until the Second Revolt was crushed, that the 'Frisco Reds flourished again. And for two generations the Group flourished. Then an agent of the Iron Heel managed to become a member, penetrated all its secrets, and brought about its total annihilation. This occurred in 2002 A.D. The members were executed one at a time, at intervals of three weeks, and their bodies exposed in the labor-ghetto of San Francisco.

together at the Benton Harbor refuge. This was in Michigan, across the lake from Chicago. We arrived just at the conclusion of the trial of a spy. Sentence of death had been passed, and he was being led away. Such was the scene as we came upon it. The next moment the wretched man had wrenched free from his captors and flung himself at my feet, his arms clutching me about the knees in a vicelike grip as he prayed in a frenzy for mercy. As he turned his agonized face up to me, I recognized him as Joseph Hurd. Of all the terrible things I have witnessed, never have I been so unnerved as by this frantic creature's pleading for life. He was mad for life. It was pitiable. He refused to let go of me, despite the hands of a dozen comrades. And when at last he was dragged shrieking away, I sank down fainting upon the floor. It is far easier to see brave men die than to hear a coward beg for life.[1]

[1] The Benton Harbor refuge was a catacomb, the entrance of which was cunningly contrived by way of a well. It has been maintained in a fair state of preservation, and the curious visitor may to-day tread its labyrinths to the assembly hall, where, without doubt, occurred the scene described by Avis Everhard. Farther on are the cells where the prisoners were confined, and the death chamber where the executions took place. Beyond is the cemetery— long, winding galleries hewn out of the solid rock, with recesses on either hand, wherein, tier above tier, lie the revolutionists just as they were laid away by their comrades long years agone.

XX

A Lost Oligarch

B UT IN REMEMBERING the old life I have run ahead of my story into the new life. The wholesale jail delivery did not occur until well along into 1915. Complicated as it was, it was carried through without a hitch, and as a very creditable achievement it cheered us on in our work. From Cuba to California, out of scores of jails, military prisons, and fortresses, in a single night, we delivered fifty-one of our fifty-two Congressmen, and in addition over three hundred other leaders. There was not a single instance of miscarriage. Not only did they escape, but every one of them won to the refuges as planned. The one comrade Congressman we did not get was Arthur Simpson, and he had already died in Cabañas after cruel tortures.

The eighteen months that followed was perhaps the happiest period of my life with Ernest. During that time we were never apart. Later, when we went back into the world, we were separated much. Not more impatiently do I await the flame of to-morrow's revolt than did I that night await the coming of Ernest. I had not seen him for so long, and the thought of a possible hitch or error in our plans that would keep him still in his island prison almost drove me mad. The hours passed like ages. I was all alone. Biedenbach, and three young men who had been living in the refuge, were out and over the mountain, heavily armed and prepared for anything. The refuges all over the land were quite empty, I imagine, of comrades that night.

Just as the sky paled with the first warning of dawn, I heard the signal from above and gave the answer. In the darkness I almost embraced Biedenbach, who came down first; but the next moment I was in Ernest's arms. And in that moment, so complete had been my transformation, I discovered it was only by an effort of will that I could be the old Avis Everhard, with the old mannerisms and smiles, phrases and intonations of voice. It was by strong effort only that I was able to maintain my old identity; I could not allow myself to forget for an instant, so automatically imperative had become the new personality I had created.

Once inside the little cabin, I saw Ernest's face in the light. With the exception of the prison pallor, there was no change in him—at least, not much. He was my same lover-husband and hero. And yet there was a certain ascetic lengthening of the lines of his face. But he could well stand it, for it seemed to add a certain nobility of refinement to the riotous excess of life that had always marked his features. He might have been a trifle graver than of yore, but the glint of laughter still was in his eyes. He was twenty pounds lighter, but in splendid physical condition. He had kept up exercise during the whole period of confinement, and his muscles were like iron. In truth, he was in better condition than when he had entered prison. Hours passed before his head touched pillow and I had soothed him off to sleep. But there was no sleep for me. I was too happy, and the fatigue of jail-breaking and riding horseback had not been mine.

While Ernest slept, I changed my dress, arranged my hair differently, and came back to my new automatic self. Then, when Biedenbach and the other comrades awoke, with their aid I concocted a little conspiracy. All was ready, and we were in the cave-room that served for kitchen and dining room when Ernest opened the door and entered. At that moment Biedenbach addressed me as Mary, and I turned and answered him. Then I glanced at Ernest with curious interest, such as any young comrade might betray on seeing for the first time so noted a hero of the Revolution. But Ernest's glance took me in and questioned impatiently past and around the room. The next moment I was being introduced to him as Mary Holmes.

To complete the deception, an extra plate was laid, and when we sat down to table one chair was not occupied. I could have cried out with joy as I noted Ernest's increasing uneasiness and impatience. Finally he could stand it no longer.

"Where's my wife?" he demanded bluntly.

"She is still asleep," I answered.

It was the crucial moment. But my voice was a strange voice, and in it he recognized nothing familiar. The meal went on. I talked a great deal, and enthusiastically, as a hero-worshipper might talk, and it was obvious that he was my hero. I rose to a climax of enthusiasm and worship, and, before he could guess my intention, threw my arms around his neck and kissed him on the lips. He held me from him at arm's length and stared about in annoyance and perplexity. The four men greeted him with roars of laughter, and explanations were made. At first he was sceptical. He scrutinized me keenly and was half convinced, then shook his head and would not believe. It was not until I became the old Avis Everhard and whispered secrets in his ear that none knew but he and Avis Everhard, that he accepted me as his really, truly wife.

It was later in the day that he took me in his arms, manifesting great embarrassment and claiming polygamous emotions.

"You are my Avis," he said, "and you are also some one else. You are two women, and therefore you are my harem. At any rate, we are safe now. If the United States becomes too hot for us, why, I have qualified for citizenship in Turkey."[1]

Life became for me very happy in the refuge. It is true, we worked hard and for long hours; but we worked together. We had each other for eighteen precious months, and we were not lonely, for there was always a coming and going of leaders and comrades—strange voices from the under-world of intrigue and revolution, bringing stranger tales of strife and war from all our battle-line. And there was much fun and delight. We were not mere gloomy conspirators. We toiled hard and suffered greatly, filled the gaps in our ranks and went on, and through all the labor and the play and interplay of life and death we found time to laugh and love. There were artists, scientists, scholars, musicians, and poets among us; and in that hole in the ground culture was higher and finer than in the palaces or wonder-cities of the oligarchs. In truth,

[1]At that time polygamy was still practised in Turkey.

many of our comrades toiled at making beautiful those same palaces and wonder-cities.[1]

Nor were we confined to the refuge itself. Often at night we rode over the mountains for exercise, and we rode on Wickson's horses. If only he knew how many revolutionists his horses have carried! We even went on picnics to isolated spots we knew, where we remained all day, going before daylight and returning after dark. Also, we used Wickson's cream and butter;[2] and Ernest was not above shooting Wickson's quail and rabbits, and, on occasion, his young bucks.

Indeed, it was a safe refuge. I have said that it was discovered only once, and this brings me to the clearing up of the mystery of the disappearance of young Wickson. Now that he is dead, I am free to speak. There was a nook on the bottom of the great hole where the sun shone for several hours and which was hidden from above. Here we had carried many loads of gravel from the creek-bed, so that it was dry and warm, a pleasant basking place; and here, one afternoon, I was drowsing, half asleep, over a volume of Mendenhall.[3] I was so comfortable and secure that even his flaming lyrics failed to stir me.

I was aroused by a clod of earth striking at my feet. Then, from above, I heard a sound of scrambling. The next moment a young man, with a final slide down the crumbling wall, alighted at my feet. It was Philip Wickson, though I did not know him at the time. He looked at me coolly and uttered a low whistle of surprise.

---

[1] This is not braggadocio on the part of Avis Everhard. The flower of the artistic and intellectual world were revolutionists. With the exception of a few of the musicians and singers, and of a few of the oligarchs, all the great creators of the period whose names have come down to us, were revolutionists.

[2] Even as late as that period, cream and butter were still crudely extracted from cow's milk. The laboratory preparation of foods had not yet begun.

[3] In all the extant literature and documents of that period, continual reference is made to the poems of Rudolph Mendenhall. By his comrades he was called "The Flame." He was undoubtedly a great genius; yet, beyond weird and haunting fragments of his verse, quoted in the writings of others, nothing of his has come down to us. He was executed by the Iron Heel in 1928 A.D.

"Well," he said; and the next moment, cap in hand, he was saying, "I beg your pardon. I did not expect to find any one here."

I was not so cool. I was still a tyro so far as concerned knowing how to behave in desperate circumstances. Later on, when I was an international spy, I should have been less clumsy, I am sure. As it was, I scrambled to my feet and cried out the danger call.

"Why did you do that?" he asked, looking at me searchingly.

It was evident that he had had no suspicion of our presence when making the descent. I recognized this with relief.

"For what purpose do you think I did it?" I countered. I was indeed clumsy in those days.

"I don't know," he answered, shaking his head. "Unless you've got friends about. Anyway, you've got some explanations to make. I don't like the look of it. You are trespassing. This is my father's land, and—"

But at that moment, Biedenbach, ever polite and gentle, said from behind him in a low voice, "Hands up, my young sir."

Young Wickson put his hands up first, then turned to confront Biedenbach, who held a thirty-thirty automatic rifle on him. Wickson was imperturbable.

"Oh, ho," he said, "a nest of revolutionists—and quite a hornet's nest it would seem. Well, you won't abide here long, I can tell you."

"Maybe you'll abide here long enough to reconsider that statement," Biedenbach said quietly. "And in the meanwhile I must ask you to come inside with me."

"Inside?" The young man was genuinely astonished. "Have you a catacomb here? I have heard of such things."

"Come on and see," Biedenbach answered with his adorable accent.

"But it is unlawful," was the protest.

"Yes, by your law," the terrorist replied significantly. "But by our law, believe me, it is quite lawful. You must accustom yourself to the fact that you are in another world than the one of oppression and brutality in which you have lived."

"There is room for argument there," Wickson muttered.

"Then stay with us and discuss it."

The young fellow laughed and followed his captor into the house. He was led into the inner cave-room, and one of the young comrades left to guard him, while we discussed the situation in the kitchen.

Biedenbach, with tears in his eyes, held that Wickson must die, and was quite relieved when we outvoted him and his horrible proposition. On the other hand, we could not dream of allowing the young oligarch to depart.

"I'll tell you what to do," Ernest said. "We'll keep him and give him an education."

"I bespeak the privilege, then, of enlightening him in jurisprudence," Biedenbach cried.

And so a decision was laughingly reached. We would keep Philip Wickson a prisoner and educate him in our ethics and sociology. But in the meantime there was work to be done. All trace of the young oligarch must be obliterated. There were the marks he had left when descending the crumbling wall of the hole. This task fell to Biedenbach, and, slung on a rope from above, he toiled cunningly for the rest of the day till no sign remained. Back up the canyon from the lip of the hole all marks were likewise removed. Then, at twilight, came John Carlson, who demanded Wickson's shoes.

The young man did not want to give up his shoes, and even offered to fight for them, till he felt the horse-shoer's strength in Ernest's hands. Carlson afterward reported several blisters and much grievous loss of skin due to the smallness of the shoes, but he succeeded in doing gallant work with them. Back from the lip of the hole, where ended the young man's obliterated trial, Carlson put on the shoes and walked away to the left. He walked for miles, around knolls, over ridges and through canyons, and finally covered the trail in the running water of a creek-bed. Here he removed the shoes, and, still hiding trail for a distance, at last put on his own shoes. A week later Wickson got back his shoes.

That night the hounds were out, and there was little sleep in the refuge. Next day, time and again, the baying hounds came down the canyon, plunged off to the left on the trail Carlson had made for them, and were lost to ear in the farther canyons high up the mountain. And all the time our men waited in the refuge, weapons in hand—automatic revolvers and rifles, to say nothing of half a dozen infernal machines of Biedenbach's manufacture. A more surprised party of rescuers could not be imagined, had they ventured down into our hiding-place.

I have now given the true disappearance of Philip Wickson, one-time oligarch, and, later, comrade in the Revolution. For we converted him in the end. His mind was fresh and plastic, and by nature he was very ethical. Several months later we rode him, on one of his father's horses, over Sonoma Mountain to Petaluma Creek and embarked him in a small fishing-launch. By easy stages we smuggled him along our underground railway to the Carmel refuge.

There he remained eight months, at the end of which time, for two reasons, he was loath to leave us. One reason was that he had fallen in love with Anna Roylston, and the other was that he had become one of us. It was not until he became convinced of the hopelessness of his love affair that he acceded to our wishes and went back to his father. Ostensibly an oligarch until his death, he was in reality one of the most valuable of our agents. Often and often has the Iron Heel been dumfounded by the miscarriage of its plans and operations against us. If it but knew the number of its own members who are our agents, it would understand. Young Wickson never wavered in his loyalty to the Cause. In truth, his very death was incurred by his devotion to duty. In the great storm of 1927, while attending a meeting of our leaders, he contracted the pneumonia of which he died.[1]

---

[1] The case of this young man was not unusual. Many young men of the Oligarchy, impelled by sense of right conduct, or their imaginations captured by the glory of the Revolution, ethically or romantically devoted their lives to it. In similar way, many sons of the Russian nobility played their parts in the earlier and protracted revolution in that country.

XXI

The Roaring Abysmal Beast

D URING the long period of our stay in the refuge, we
were kept closely in touch with what was happening in
the world without, and we were learning thoroughly the
strength of the Oligarchy with which we were at war. Out of
the flux of transition the new institutions were forming more
definitely and taking on the appearance and attributes of permanence. The oligarchs had succeeded in devising a governmental machine, as intricate as it was vast, that worked—and
this despite all our efforts to clog and hamper.

This was a surprise to many of the revolutionists. They
had not conceived it possible. Nevertheless the work of the
country went on. The men toiled in the mines and fields—
perforce they were no more than slaves. As for the vital industries, everything prospered. The members of the great labor castes were contented and worked on merrily. For the
first time in their lives they knew industrial peace. No more
were they worried by slack times, strike and lockout, and the
union label. They lived in more comfortable homes and in
delightful cities of their own—delightful compared with the
slums and ghettos in which they had formerly dwelt. They
had better food to eat, less hours of labor, more holidays, and
a greater amount and variety of interests and pleasures. And
for their less fortunate brothers and sisters, the unfavored laborers, the driven people of the abyss, they cared nothing. An
age of selfishness was dawning upon mankind. And yet this is
not altogether true. The labor castes were honeycombed by
our agents—men whose eyes saw, beyond the belly-need, the
radiant figure of liberty and brotherhood.

Another great institution that had taken form and was
working smoothly was the Mercenaries. This body of soldiers
had been evolved out of the old regular army and was now a
million strong, to say nothing of the colonial forces. The
Mercenaries constituted a race apart. They dwelt in cities of
their own which were practically self-governed, and they were

granted many privileges. By them a large portion of the per-
plexing surplus was consumed. They were losing all touch
and sympathy with the rest of the people, and, in fact, were
developing their own class morality and consciousness. And
yet we had thousands of our agents among them.[1]

The oligarchs themselves were going through a remarkable
and, it must be confessed, unexpected development. As a
class, they disciplined themselves. Every member had his
work to do in the world, and this work he was compelled to
do. There were no more idle-rich young men. Their strength
was used to give united strength to the Oligarchy. They
served as leaders of troops and as lieutenants and captains of
industry. They found careers in applied science, and many of
them became great engineers. They went into the multitudinous divisions of the government, took service in the colonial
possessions, and by tens of thousands went into the various
secret services. They were, I may say, apprenticed to education, to art, to the church, to science, to literature; and in
those fields they served the important function of moulding
the thought-processes of the nation in the direction of the
perpetuity of the Oligarchy.

They were taught, and later they in turn taught, that what
they were doing was right. They assimilated the aristocratic
idea from the moment they began, as children, to receive
impressions of the world. The aristocratic idea was woven
into the making of them until it became bone of them and
flesh of them. They looked upon themselves as wild-animal
trainers, rulers of beasts. From beneath their feet rose always
the subterranean rumbles of revolt. Violent death ever stalked
in their midst; bomb and knife and bullet were looked upon
as so many fangs of the roaring abysmal beast they must dominate if humanity were to persist. They were the saviours of
humanity, and they regarded themselves as heroic and sacrificing laborers for the highest good.

They, as a class, believed that they alone maintained civilization. It was their belief that if ever they weakened, the great

---

[1] The Mercenaries, in the last days of the Iron Heel, played an important
rôle. They constituted the balance of power in the struggles between the
labor castes and the oligarchs, and now to one side and now to the other,
threw their strength according to the play of intrigue and conspiracy.

beast would ingulf them and everything of beauty and wonder and joy and good in its cavernous and slime-dripping
maw. Without them, anarchy would reign and humanity
would drop backward into the primitive night out of which
it had so painfully emerged. The horrid picture of anarchy
was held always before their child's eyes until they, in turn,
obsessed by this cultivated fear, held the picture of anarchy
before the eyes of the children that followed them. This was
the beast to be stamped upon, and the highest duty of the
aristocrat was to stamp upon it. In short, they alone, by their
unremitting toil and sacrifice, stood between weak humanity
and the all-devouring beast; and they believed it, firmly believed it.

I cannot lay too great stress upon this high ethical righteousness of the whole oligarch class. This has been the
strength of the Iron Heel, and too many of the comrades have
been slow or loath to realize it. Many of them have ascribed
the strength of the Iron Heel to its system of reward and
punishment. This is a mistake. Heaven and hell may be the
prime factors of zeal in the religion of a fanatic; but for the
great majority of the religious, heaven and hell are incidental
to right and wrong. Love of the right, desire for the right,
unhappiness with anything less than the right—in short,
right conduct, is the prime factor of religion. And so with the
Oligarchy. Prisons, banishment and degradation, honors and
palaces and wonder-cities, are all incidental. The great driving
force of the oligarchs is the belief that they are doing right.
Never mind the exceptions, and never mind the oppression
and injustice in which the Iron Heel was conceived. All is
granted. The point is that the strength of the Oligarchy to-
day lies in its satisfied conception of its own righteousness.[1]

For that matter, the strength of the Revolution, during

[1] Out of the ethical incoherency and inconsistency of capitalism, the oligarchs emerged with a new ethics, coherent and definite, sharp and severe as
steel, the most absurd and unscientific and at the same time the most potent
ever possessed by any tyrant class. The oligarchs believed their ethics, in spite
of the fact that biology and evolution gave them the lie; and, because of their
faith, for three centuries they were able to hold back the mighty tide of human progress—a spectacle, profound, tremendous, puzzling to the metaphysical moralist, and one that to the materialist is the cause of many doubts
and reconsiderations.

these frightful twenty years, has resided in nothing else
than the sense of righteousness. In no other way can be
explained our sacrifices and martyrdoms. For no other reason did Rudolph Mendenhall flame out his soul for the
Cause and sing his wild swan-song that last night of life.
For no other reason did Hurlbert die under torture, refusing to the last to betray his comrades. For no other reason
has Anna Roylston refused blessed motherhood. For no
other reason has John Carlson been the faithful and unre-
warded custodian of the Glen Ellen Refuge. It does not
matter, young or old, man or woman, high or low, genius
or clod, go where one will among the comrades of the
Revolution, the motor-force will be found to be a great
and abiding desire for the right.

But I have run away from my narrative. Ernest and I well
understood, before we left the refuge, how the strength of
the Iron Heel was developing. The labor castes, the Mercenaries, and the great hordes of secret agents and police of
various sorts were all pledged to the Oligarchy. In the main,
and ignoring the loss of liberty, they were better off than they
had been. On the other hand, the great helpless mass of the
population, the people of the abyss, was sinking into a brutish
apathy of content with misery. Whenever strong proletarians
asserted their strength in the midst of the mass, they were
drawn away from the mass by the oligarchs and given better
conditions by being made members of the labor castes or of
the Mercenaries. Thus discontent was lulled and the proletariat robbed of its natural leaders.

The condition of the people of the abyss was pitiable.
Common school education, so far as they were concerned,
had ceased. They lived like beasts in great squalid labor-
ghettos, festering in misery and degradation. All their old liberties were gone. They were labor-slaves. Choice of work was
denied them. Likewise was denied them the right to move
from place to place, or the right to bear or possess arms. They
were not land-serfs like the farmers. They were machine-serfs
and labor-serfs. When unusual needs arose for them, such as
the building of the great highways and air-lines, of canals,
tunnels, subways, and fortifications, levies were made on the
labor-ghettos, and tens of thousands of serfs, willy-nilly, were

transported to the scene of operations. Great armies of them are toiling now at the building of Ardis, housed in wretched barracks where family life cannot exist, and where decency is displaced by dull bestiality. In all truth, there in the labor-ghettos is the roaring abysmal beast the oligarchs fear so dreadfully—but it is the beast of their own making. In it they will not let the ape and tiger die.

And just now the word has gone forth that new levies are being imposed for the building of Asgard, the projected won-der-city that will far exceed Ardis when the latter is com-pleted.[1] We of the Revolution will go on with that great work, but it will not be done by the miserable serfs. The walls and towers and shafts of that fair city will arise to the sound of singing, and into its beauty and wonder will be woven, not sighs and groans, but music and laughter.

Ernest was madly impatient to be out in the world and doing, for our ill-fated First Revolt, that miscarried in the Chicago Commune, was ripening fast. Yet he possessed his soul with patience, and during the time of his torment, when Hadly, who had been brought for the purpose from Illinois, made him over into another man,[2] he revolved great plans in his head for the organization of the learned proletariat, and for the maintenance of at least the rudiments of education

[1]Ardis was completed in 1942 A.D., while Asgard was not completed until 1984 A.D. It was fifty-two years in the building, during which time a perma-nent army of half a million serfs was employed. At times these numbers swelled to over a million—without any account being taken of the hundreds of thousands of the labor castes and the artists.

[2]Among the Revolutionists were many surgeons, and in vivisection they attained marvellous proficiency. In Avis Everhard's words, they could literally make a man over. To them the elimination of scars and disfigurements was a trivial detail. They changed the features with such microscopic care that no traces were left of their handiwork. The nose was a favorite organ to work upon. Skin-grafting and hair-transplanting were among their commonest de-vices. The changes in expression they accomplished were wizardlike. Eyes and eyebrows, lips, mouths, and ears, were radically altered. By cunning op-erations on tongue, throat, larynx, and nasal cavities a man's whole enuncia-tion and manner of speech could be changed. Desperate times give need for desperate remedies, and the surgeons of the Revolution rose to the need. Among other things, they could increase an adult's stature by as much as four or five inches and decrease it by one or two inches. What they did is to-day a lost art. We have no need for it.

amongst the people of the abyss—all this, of course, in the event of the First Revolt being a failure.

It was not until January, 1917, that we left the refuge. All had been arranged. We took our place at once as agents-provocateurs in the scheme of the Iron Heel. I was supposed to be Ernest's sister. By oligarchs and comrades on the inside who were high in authority, place had been made for us, we were in possession of all necessary documents, and our pasts were accounted for. With help on the inside, this was not difficult, for in that shadow-world of secret service identity was nebulous. Like ghosts the agents came and went, obeying commands, fulfilling duties, following clews, making their reports often to officers they never saw or coöperating with other agents they had never seen before and would never see again.

XXII

The Chicago Commune

As AGENTS-PROVOCATEURS, not alone were we able to travel a great deal, but our very work threw us in contact with the proletariat and with our comrades, the revolutionists. Thus we were in both camps at the same time, ostensibly serving the Iron Heel and secretly working with all our might for the Cause. There were many of us in the various secret services of the Oligarchy, and despite the shakings-up and reorganizations the secret services have undergone, they have never been able to weed all of us out.

Ernest had largely planned the First Revolt, and the date set had been somewhere early in the spring of 1918. In the fall of 1917 we were not ready; much remained to be done, and when the Revolt was precipitated, of course it was doomed to failure. The plot of necessity was frightfully intricate, and anything premature was sure to destroy it. This the Iron Heel foresaw and laid its schemes accordingly.

We had planned to strike our first blow at the nervous system of the Oligarchy. The latter had remembered the general strike, and had guarded against the defection of the telegraphers by installing wireless stations, in the control of the Mercenaries. We, in turn, had countered this move. When the signal was given, from every refuge, all over the land, and from the cities, and towns, and barracks, devoted comrades were to go forth and blow up the wireless stations. Thus at the first shock would the Iron Heel be brought to earth and lie practically dismembered.

At the same moment, other comrades were to blow up the bridges and tunnels and disrupt the whole network of railroads. Still further, other groups of comrades, at the signal, were to seize the officers of the Mercenaries and the police, as well as all Oligarchs of unusual ability or who held executive positions. Thus would the leaders of the enemy be removed from the field of the local battles that would inevitably be fought all over the land.

Many things were to occur simultaneously when the signal went forth. The Canadian and Mexican patriots, who were far stronger than the Iron Heel dreamed, were to duplicate our tactics. Then there were comrades (these were the women, for the men would be busy elsewhere) who were to post the proclamations from our secret presses. Those of us in the higher employ of the Iron Heel were to proceed immediately to make confusion and anarchy in all our departments. Inside the Mercenaries were thousands of our comrades. Their work was to blow up the magazines and to destroy the delicate mechanism of all the war machinery. In the cities of the Mercenaries and of the labor castes similar programmes of disruption were to be carried out.

In short, a sudden, colossal, stunning blow was to be struck. Before the paralyzed Oligarchy could recover itself, its end would have come. It would have meant terrible times and great loss of life, but no revolutionist hesitates at such things. Why, we even depended much, in our plan, on the unorganized people of the abyss. They were to be loosed on the palaces and cities of the masters. Never mind the destruction of life and property. Let the abysmal brute roar and the police and Mercenaries slay. The abysmal brute would roar anyway, and the police and Mercenaries would slay anyway. It would merely mean that various dangers to us were harmlessly destroying one another. In the meantime we would be doing our own work, largely unhampered, and gaining control of all the machinery of society.

Such was our plan, every detail of which had to be worked out in secret, and, as the day drew near, communicated to more and more comrades. This was the danger point, the stretching of the conspiracy. But that danger-point was never reached. Through its spy-system the Iron Heel got wind of the Revolt and prepared to teach us another of its bloody lessons. Chicago was the devoted city selected for the instruction, and well were we instructed.

Chicago[1] was the ripest of all—Chicago which of old time

---

[1] Chicago was the industrial inferno of the nineteenth century A.D. A curious anecdote has come down to us of John Burns, a great English labor leader and one time member of the British Cabinet. In Chicago, while on a visit to the United States, he was asked by a newspaper reporter for his opin-

was the city of blood and which was to earn anew its name. There the revolutionary spirit was strong. Too many bitter strikes had been curbed there in the days of capitalism for the workers to forget and forgive. Even the labor castes of the city were alive with revolt. Too many heads had been broken in the early strikes. Despite their changed and favorable conditions, their hatred for the master class had not died. This spirit had infected the Mercenaries, of which three regiments in particular were ready to come over to us *en masse*.

Chicago had always been the storm-centre of the conflict between labor and capital, a city of street-battles and violent death, with a class-conscious capitalist organization and a class-conscious workman organization, where, in the old days, the very school-teachers were formed into labor unions and affiliated with the hod-carriers and brick-layers in the American Federation of Labor. And Chicago became the storm-centre of the premature First Revolt.

The trouble was precipitated by the Iron Heel. It was cleverly done. The whole population, including the favored labor castes, was given a course of outrageous treatment. Promises and agreements were broken, and most drastic punishments visited upon even petty offenders. The people of the abyss were tormented out of their apathy. In fact, the Iron Heel was preparing to make the abysmal beast roar. And hand in hand with this, in all precautionary measures in Chicago, the Iron Heel was inconceivably careless. Discipline was relaxed among the Mercenaries that remained, while many regiments had been withdrawn and sent to various parts of the country.

It did not take long to carry out this programme—only several weeks. We of the Revolution caught vague rumors of the state of affairs, but had nothing definite enough for an understanding. In fact, we thought it was a spontaneous spirit of revolt that would require careful curbing on our part, and never dreamed that it was deliberately manufactured—and it had been manufactured so secretly, from the very innermost

---

ion of that city. "Chicago," he answered, "is a pocket edition of hell." Some time later, as he was going aboard his steamer to sail to England, he was approached by another reporter, who wanted to know if he had changed his opinion of Chicago. "Yes, I have," was his reply. "My present opinion is that hell is a pocket edition of Chicago."

circle of the Iron Heel, that we had got no inkling. The counter-plot was an able achievement, and ably carried out.

I was in New York when I received the order to proceed immediately to Chicago. The man who gave me the order was one of the oligarchs, I could tell that by his speech, though I did not know his name nor see his face. His instructions were too clear for me to make a mistake. Plainly I read between the lines that our plot had been discovered, that we had been countermined. The explosion was ready for the flash of powder, and countless agents of the Iron Heel, including me, either on the ground or being sent there, were to supply that flash. I flatter myself that I maintained my composure under the keen eye of the oligarch, but my heart was beating madly. I could almost have shrieked and flown at his throat with my naked hands before his final, cold-blooded instructions were given.

Once out of his presence, I calculated the time. I had just the moments to spare, if I were lucky, to get in touch with some local leader before catching my train. Guarding against being trailed, I made a rush of it for the Emergency Hospital. Luck was with me, and I gained access at once to comrade Galvin, the surgeon-in-chief. I started to gasp out my information, but he stopped me.

"I already know," he said quietly, though his Irish eyes were flashing. "I knew what you had come for. I got the word fifteen minutes ago, and I have already passed it along. Everything shall be done here to keep the comrades quiet. Chicago is to be sacrificed, but it shall be Chicago alone."

"Have you tried to get word to Chicago?" I asked.

He shook his head. "No telegraphic communication. Chicago is shut off. It's going to be hell there."

He paused a moment, and I saw his white hands clinch. Then he burst out:

"By God! I wish I were going to be there!"

"There is yet a chance to stop it," I said, "if nothing happens to the train and I can get there in time. Or if some of the other secret-service comrades who have learned the truth can get there in time."

"You on the inside were caught napping this time," he said.

I nodded my head humbly.

"It was very secret," I answered. "Only the inner chiefs could have known up to to-day. We haven't yet penetrated that far, so we couldn't escape being kept in the dark. If only Ernest were here. Maybe he is in Chicago now, and all is well."

Dr. Galvin shook his head. "The last news I heard of him was that he had been sent to Boston or New Haven. This secret service for the enemy must hamper him a lot, but it's better than lying in a refuge."

I started to go, and Galvin wrung my hand.

"Keep a stout heart," were his parting words. "What if the First Revolt is lost? There will be a second, and we will be wiser then. Good-by and good luck. I don't know whether I'll ever see you again. It's going to be hell there, but I'd give ten years of my life for your chance to be in it."

The Twentieth Century[1] left New York at six in the evening, and was supposed to arrive at Chicago at seven next morning. But it lost time that night. We were running behind another train. Among the travellers in my Pullman was comrade Hartman, like myself in the secret service of the Iron Heel. He it was who told me of the train that immediately preceded us. It was an exact duplicate of our train, though it contained no passengers. The idea was that the empty train should receive the disaster were an attempt made to blow up the Twentieth Century. For that matter there were very few people on the train—only a baker's dozen in our car.

"There must be some big men on board," Hartman concluded. "I noticed a private car on the rear."

Night had fallen when we made our first change of engine, and I walked down the platform for a breath of fresh air and to see what I could see. Through the windows of the private car I caught a glimpse of three men whom I recognized. Hartman was right. One of the men was General Altendorff; and the other two were Mason and Vanderbold, the brains of the inner circle of the Oligarchy's secret service.

It was a quiet moonlight night, but I tossed restlessly and

[1] This was reputed to be the fastest train in the world then. It was quite a famous train.

could not sleep. At five in the morning I dressed and abandoned my bed.

I asked the maid in the dressing-room how late the train was, and she told me two hours. She was a mulatto woman, and I noticed that her face was haggard, with great circles under the eyes, while the eyes themselves were wide with some haunting fear.

"What is the matter?" I asked.

"Nothing, miss; I didn't sleep well, I guess," was her reply.

I looked at her closely, and tried her with one of our signals. She responded, and I made sure of her.

"Something terrible is going to happen in Chicago," she said. "There's that fake[1] train in front of us. That and the troop-trains have made us late."

"Troop-trains?" I queried.

She nodded her head. "The line is thick with them. We've been passing them all night. And they're all heading for Chicago. And bringing them over the air-line—that means business.

"I've a lover in Chicago," she added apologetically. "He's one of us, and he's in the Mercenaries, and I'm afraid for him."

Poor girl. Her lover was in one of the three disloyal regiments.

Hartman and I had breakfast together in the dining car, and I forced myself to eat. The sky had clouded, and the train rushed on like a sullen thunderbolt through the gray pall of advancing day. The very negroes that waited on us knew that something terrible was impending. Oppression sat heavily upon them; the lightness of their natures had ebbed out of them; they were slack and absent-minded in their service, and they whispered gloomily to one another in the far end of the car next to the kitchen. Hartman was hopeless over the situation.

"What can we do?" he demanded for the twentieth time, with a helpless shrug of the shoulders.

He pointed out of the window. "See, all is ready. You can depend upon it that they're holding them like this, thirty or forty miles outside the city, on every road."

[1]False.

He had reference to troop-trains on the side-track. The soldiers were cooking their breakfasts over fires built on the ground beside the track, and they looked up curiously at us as we thundered past without slackening our terrific speed.

All was quiet as we entered Chicago. It was evident nothing had happened yet. In the suburbs the morning papers came on board the train. There was nothing in them, and yet there was much in them for those skilled in reading between the lines that it was intended the ordinary reader should read into the text. The fine hand of the Iron Heel was apparent in every column. Glimmerings of weakness in the armor of the Oligarchy were given. Of course, there was nothing definite. It was intended that the reader should feel his way to these glimmerings. It was cleverly done. As fiction, those morning papers of October 27th were masterpieces.

The local news was missing. This in itself was a masterstroke. It shrouded Chicago in mystery, and it suggested to the average Chicago reader that the Oligarchy did not dare give the local news. Hints that were untrue, of course, were given of insubordination all over the land, crudely disguised with complacent references to punitive measures to be taken. There were reports of numerous wireless stations that had been blown up, with heavy rewards offered for the detection of the perpetrators. Of course no wireless stations had been blown up. Many similar outrages, that dovetailed with the plot of the revolutionists, were given. The impression to be made on the minds of the Chicago comrades was that the general Revolt was beginning, albeit with a confusing miscarriage in many details. It was impossible for one uninformed to escape the vague yet certain feeling that all the land was ripe for the revolt that had already begun to break out.

It was reported that the defection of the Mercenaries in California had become so serious that half a dozen regiments had been disbanded and broken, and that their members with their families had been driven from their own city and on into the labor-ghettos. And the California Mercenaries were in reality the most faithful of all to their salt! But how was Chicago, shut off from the rest of the world, to know? Then there was a ragged telegram describing an outbreak of the populace in New York City, in which the labor castes were joining, concluding with the statement (intended to be accepted as a bluff[1]) that the troops had the situation in hand.

And as the oligarchs had done with the morning papers, so had they done in a thousand other ways. These we learned afterward, as, for example, the secret messages of the oligarchs, sent with the express purpose of leaking to the ears of the revolutionists, that had come over the wires, now and again, during the first part of the night.

"I guess the Iron Heel won't need our services," Hartman remarked, putting down the paper he had been reading, when the train pulled into the central depot. "They wasted their time sending us here. Their plans have evidently prospered better than they expected. Hell will break loose any second now."

He turned and looked down the train as we alighted.

"I thought so," he muttered. "They dropped that private car when the papers came aboard."

Hartman was hopelessly depressed. I tried to cheer him up, but he ignored my effort and suddenly began talking very hurriedly, in a low voice, as we passed through the station. At first I could not understand.

"I have not been sure," he was saying, "and I have told no one. I have been working on it for weeks, and I cannot make sure. Watch out for Knowlton. I suspect him. He knows the secrets of a score of our refuges. He carries the lives of hundreds of us in his hands, and I think he is a traitor. It's more a feeling on my part than anything else. But I thought I marked a change in him a short while back. There is the danger that he has sold us out, or is going to sell us out. I am almost sure of it. I wouldn't whisper my suspicions to a soul, but, somehow, I don't think I'll leave Chicago alive. Keep your eye on Knowlton. Trap him. Find out. I don't know anything more. It is only an intuition, and so far I have failed to find the slightest clew." We were just stepping out upon the sidewalk. "Remember," Hartman concluded earnestly. "Keep your eyes upon Knowlton."

And Hartman was right. Before a month went by Knowlton paid for his treason with his life. He was formally executed by the comrades in Milwaukee.

[1] A lie.

All was quiet on the streets—too quiet. Chicago lay dead. There was no roar and rumble of traffic. There were not even cabs on the streets. The surface cars and the elevated were not running. Only occasionally, on the sidewalks, were there stray pedestrians, and these pedestrians did not loiter. They went their ways with great haste and definiteness, withal there was a curious indecision in their movements, as though they expected the buildings to topple over on them or the sidewalks to sink under their feet or fly up in the air. A few gamins, however, were around, in their eyes a suppressed eagerness in anticipation of wonderful and exciting things to happen.

From somewhere, far to the south, the dull sound of an explosion came to our ears. That was all. Then quiet again, though the gamins had startled and listened, like young deer, at the sound. The doorways to all the buildings were closed; the shutters to the shops were up. But there were many police and watchmen in evidence, and now and again automobile patrols of the Mercenaries slipped swiftly past.

Hartman and I agreed that it was useless to report ourselves to the local chiefs of the secret service. Our failure so to report would be excused, we knew, in the light of subsequent events. So we headed for the great labor-ghetto on the South Side in the hope of getting in contact with some of the comrades. Too late! We knew it. But we could not stand still and do nothing in those ghastly, silent streets. Where was Ernest? I was wondering. What was happening in the cities of the labor castes and Mercenaries? In the fortresses?

As if in answer, a great screaming roar went up, dim with distance, punctuated with detonation after detonation.

"It's the fortresses," Hartman said. "God pity those three regiments!"

At a crossing we noticed, in the direction of the stockyards, a gigantic pillar of smoke. At the next crossing several similar smoke pillars were rising skyward in the direction of the West Side. Over the city of the Mercenaries we saw a great captive war-balloon that burst even as we looked at it, and fell in flaming wreckage toward the earth. There was no clew to that tragedy of the air. We could not determine whether the balloon had been manned by comrades or enemies. A vague sound came to our ears, like the bubbling of a gigantic caldron a long way off, and Hartman said it was machine-guns and automatic rifles.

And still we walked in immediate quietude. Nothing was happening where we were. The police and the automobile patrols went by, and once half a dozen fire-engines, returning evidently from some conflagration. A question was called to the fireman by an officer in an automobile, and we heard one shout in reply: "No water! They've blown up the mains!"

"We've smashed the water supply," Hartman cried excitedly to me. "If we can do all this in a premature, isolated, abortive attempt, what can't we do in a concerted, ripened effort all over the land?"

The automobile containing the officer who had asked the question darted on. Suddenly there was a deafening roar. The machine, with its human freight, lifted in an upburst of smoke, and sank down a mass of wreckage and death.

Hartman was jubilant. "Well done! well done!" he was repeating, over and over, in a whisper. "The proletariat gets its lesson to-day, but it gives one, too."

Police were running for the spot. Also, another patrol machine had halted. As for myself, I was in a daze. The suddenness of it was stunning. How had it happened? I knew not how, and yet I had been looking directly at it. So dazed was I for the moment that I was scarcely aware of the fact that we were being held up by the police. I abruptly saw that a policeman was in the act of shooting Hartman. But Hartman was cool and was giving the proper passwords. I saw the levelled revolver hesitate, then sink down, and heard the disgusted grunt of the policeman. He was very angry, and was cursing the whole secret service. It was always in the way, he was averring, while Hartman was talking back to him and with fitting secret-service pride explaining to him the clumsiness of the police.

The next moment I knew how it had happened. There was quite a group about the wreck, and two men were just lifting up the wounded officer to carry him to the other machine. A panic seized all of them, and they scattered in every direction, running in blind terror, the wounded officer, roughly dropped, being left behind. The cursing policeman alongside of me also ran, and Hartman and I ran, too, we knew not why, obsessed with the same blind terror to get away from that particular spot.

Nothing really happened then, but everything was explained. The flying men were sheepishly coming back, but all the while their eyes were raised apprehensively to the many-windowed, lofty buildings that towered like the sheer walls of a canyon on each side of the street. From one of those countless windows the bomb had been thrown, but which window? There had been no second bomb, only a fear of one.

Thereafter we looked with speculative comprehension at the windows. Any of them contained possible death. Each building was a possible ambuscade. This was warfare in that modern jungle, a great city. Every street was a canyon, every building a mountain. We had not changed much from primitive man, despite the war automobiles that were sliding by.

Turning a corner, we came upon a woman. She was lying on the pavement, in a pool of blood. Hartman bent over and examined her. As for myself, I turned deathly sick. I was to see many dead that day, but the total carnage was not to affect me as did this first forlorn body lying there at my feet abandoned on the pavement. "Shot in the breast," was Hartman's report. Clasped in the hollow of her arm, as a child might be clasped, was a bundle of printed matter. Even in death she seemed loath to part with that which had caused her death; for when Hartman had succeeded in withdrawing the bundle, we found that it consisted of large printed sheets, the proclamations of the revolutionists.

"A comrade," I said.

But Hartman only cursed the Iron Heel, and we passed on. Often we were halted by the police and patrols, but our passwords enabled us to proceed. No more bombs fell from the windows, the last pedestrians seemed to have vanished from the streets, and our immediate quietude grew more profound; though the gigantic caldron continued to bubble in the distance, dull roars of explosions came to us from all directions, and the smoke-pillars were towering more ominously in the heavens.

XXIII

The People of the Abyss

S UDDENLY a change came over the face of things. A tingle
of excitement ran along the air. Automobiles fled past,
two, three, a dozen, and from them warnings were shouted
to us. One of the machines swerved wildly at high speed half
a block down, and the next moment, already left well behind
it, the pavement was torn into a great hole by a bursting
bomb. We saw the police disappearing down the cross-streets
on the run, and knew that something terrible was coming.
We could hear the rising roar of it.

"Our brave comrades are coming," Hartman said.

We could see the front of their column filling the street
from gutter to gutter, as the last war-automobile fled past.
The machine stopped for a moment just abreast of us. A soldier leaped from it, carrying something carefully in his hands.
This, with the same care, he deposited in the gutter. Then he
leaped back to his seat and the machine dashed on, took the
turn at the corner, and was gone from sight. Hartman ran to
the gutter and stooped over the object.

"Keep back," he warned me.

I could see he was working rapidly with his hands. When
he returned to me the sweat was heavy on his forehead.

"I disconnected it," he said, "and just in the nick of time.
The soldier was clumsy. He intended it for our comrades, but
he didn't give it enough time. It would have exploded prematurely. Now it won't explode at all."

Everything was happening rapidly now. Across the street
and half a block down, high up in a building, I could see
heads peering out. I had just pointed them out to Hartman,
when a sheet of flame and smoke ran along that portion of
the face of the building where the heads had appeared, and
the air was shaken by the explosion. In places the stone facing
of the building was torn away, exposing the iron construction
beneath. The next moment similar sheets of flame and smoke
smote the front of the building across the street opposite it.

534

Between the explosions we could hear the rattle of the automatic pistols and rifles. For several minutes this mid-air battle continued, then died out. It was patent that our comrades were in one building, that Mercenaries were in the other, and that they were fighting across the street. But we could not tell which was which—which building contained our comrades and which the Mercenaries.

By this time the column on the street was almost on us. As the front of it passed under the warring buildings, both went into action again—one building dropping bombs into the street, being attacked from across the street, and in return replying to that attack. Thus we learned which building was held by our comrades, and they did good work, saving those in the street from the bombs of the enemy.

Hartman gripped my arm and dragged me into a wide entrance.

"They're not our comrades," he shouted in my ear.

The inner doors to the entrance were locked and bolted. We could not escape. The next moment the front of the column went by. It was not a column, but a mob, an awful river that filled the street, the people of the abyss, mad with drink and wrong, up at last and roaring for the blood of their masters. I had seen the people of the abyss before, gone through its ghettos, and thought I knew it; but I found that I was now looking on it for the first time. Dumb apathy had vanished. It was now dynamic—a fascinating spectacle of dread. It surged past my vision in concrete waves of wrath, snarling and growling, carnivorous, drunk with whiskey from pillaged warehouses, drunk with hatred, drunk with lust for blood—men, women, and children, in rags and tatters, dim ferocious intelligences with all the godlike blotted from their features and all the fiendlike stamped in, apes and tigers, anæmic consumptives and great hairy beasts of burden, wan faces from which vampire society had sucked the juice of life, bloated forms swollen with physical grossness and corruption, withered hags and death's-heads bearded like patriarchs, festering youth and festering age, faces of fiends, crooked, twisted, misshapen monsters blasted with the ravages of disease and all the horrors of chronic innutrition—the refuse and the scum of life, a raging, screaming, screeching, demoniacal horde.

And why not? The people of the abyss had nothing to lose but the misery and pain of living. And to gain?—nothing, save one final, awful glut of vengeance. And as I looked the thought came to me that in that rushing stream of human lava were men, comrades and heroes, whose mission had been to rouse the abysmal beast and to keep the enemy occupied in coping with it.

And now a strange thing happened to me. A transformation came over me. The fear of death, for myself and for others, left me. I was strangely exalted, another being in another life. Nothing mattered. The Cause for this one time was lost, but the Cause would be here to-morrow, the same Cause, ever fresh and ever burning. And thereafter, in the orgy of horror that raged through the succeeding hours, I was able to take a calm interest. Death meant nothing, life meant nothing. I was an interested spectator of events, and, sometimes swept on by the rush, was myself a curious participant. For my mind had leaped to a star-cool altitude and grasped a passionless transvaluation of values. Had it not done this, I know that I should have died.

Half a mile of the mob had swept by when we were discovered. A woman in fantastic rags, with cheeks cavernously hollow and with narrow black eyes like burning gimlets, caught a glimpse of Hartman and me. She let out a shrill shriek and bore in upon us. A section of the mob tore itself loose and surged in after her. I can see her now, as I write these lines, a leap in advance, her gray hair flying in thin tangled strings, the blood dripping down her forehead from some wound in the scalp, in her right hand a hatchet, her left hand, lean and wrinkled, a yellow talon, gripping the air convulsively. Hartman sprang in front of me. This was no time for explanations. We were well dressed, and that was enough. His fist shot out, striking the woman between her burning eyes. The impact of the blow drove her backward, but she struck the wall of her on-coming fellows and bounced forward again, dazed and helpless, the brandished hatchet falling feebly on Hartman's shoulder.

The next moment I knew not what was happening. I was overborne by the crowd. The confined space was filled with shrieks and yells and curses. Blows were falling on me. Hands were ripping and tearing at my flesh and garments. I felt that I was being torn to pieces. I was being borne down, suffocated. Some strong hand gripped my shoulder in the thick of the press and was dragging fiercely at me. Between pain and pressure I fainted. Hartman never came out of that entrance. He had shielded me and received the first brunt of the attack. This had saved me, for the jam had quickly become too dense for anything more than the mad gripping and tearing of hands.

I came to in the midst of wild movement. All about me was the same movement. I had been caught up in a monstrous flood that was sweeping me I knew not whither. Fresh air was on my cheek and biting sweetly in my lungs. Faint and dizzy, I was vaguely aware of a strong arm around my body under the arms, and half-lifting me and dragging me along. Feebly my own limbs were helping me. In front of me I could see the moving back of a man's coat. It had been slit from top to bottom along the centre seam, and it pulsed rhythmically, the slit opening and closing regularly with every leap of the wearer. This phenomenon fascinated me for a time, while my senses were coming back to me. Next I became aware of stinging cheeks and nose, and could feel blood dripping on my face. My hat was gone. My hair was down and flying, and from the stinging of the scalp I managed to recollect a hand in the press of the entrance that had torn at my hair. My chest and arms were bruised and aching in a score of places.

My brain grew clearer, and I turned as I ran and looked at the man who was holding me up. He it was who had dragged me out and saved me. He noticed my movement.

"It's all right!" he shouted hoarsely. "I knew you on the instant."

I failed to recognize him, but before I could speak I trod upon something that was alive and that squirmed under my foot. I was swept on by those behind and could not look down and see, and yet I knew that it was a woman who had fallen and who was being trampled into the pavement by thousands of successive feet.

"It's all right," he repeated. "I'm Garthwaite."

He was bearded and gaunt and dirty, but I succeeded in

remembering him as the stalwart youth that had spent several months in our Glen Ellen refuge three years before. He passed me the signals of the Iron Heel's secret service, in token that he, too, was in its employ.

"I'll get you out of this as soon as I can get a chance," he assured me. "But watch your footing. On your life don't stumble and go down."

All things happened abruptly on that day, and with an abruptness that was sickening the mob checked itself. I came in violent collision with a large woman in front of me (the man with the split coat had vanished), while those behind collided against me. A devilish pandemonium reigned,— shrieks, curses, and cries of death, while above all rose the churning rattle of machine-guns and the put-a-put, put-a-put of rifles. At first I could make out nothing. People were falling about me right and left. The woman in front doubled up and went down, her hands on her abdomen in a frenzied clutch. A man was quivering against my legs in a death-struggle.

It came to me that we were at the head of the column. Half a mile of it had disappeared—where or how I never learned. To this day I do not know what became of that half-mile of humanity—whether it was blotted out by some frightful bolt of war, whether it was scattered and destroyed piecemeal, or whether it escaped. But there we were, at the head of the column instead of in its middle, and we were being swept out of life by a torrent of shrieking lead.

As soon as death had thinned the jam, Garthwaite, still grasping my arm, led a rush of survivors into the wide entrance of an office building. Here, at the rear, against the doors, we were pressed by a panting, gasping mass of creatures. For some time we remained in this position without a change in the situation.

"I did it beautifully," Garthwaite was lamenting to me. "Ran you right into a trap. We had a gambler's chance in the street, but in here there is no chance at all. It's all over but the shouting. Vive la Revolution!"

Then, what he expected, began. The Mercenaries were killing without quarter. At first, the surge back upon us was crushing, but as the killing continued the pressure was eased.

The dead and dying went down and made room. Garthwaite put his mouth to my ear and shouted, but in the frightful din I could not catch what he said. He did not wait. He seized me and threw me down. Next he dragged a dying woman over on top of me, and, with much squeezing and shoving, crawled in beside me and partly over me. A mound of dead and dying began to pile up over us, and over this mound, pawing and moaning, crept those that still survived. But these, too, soon ceased, and a semi-silence settled down, broken by groans and sobs and sounds of strangulation.

I should have been crushed had it not been for Garthwaite. As it was, it seemed inconceivable that I could bear the weight I did and live. And yet, outside of pain, the only feeling I possessed was one of curiosity. How was it going to end? What would death be like? Thus did I receive my red baptism in that Chicago shambles. Prior to that, death to me had been a theory; but ever afterward death has been a simple fact that does not matter, it is so easy.

But the Mercenaries were not content with what they had done. They invaded the entrance, killing the wounded and searching out the unhurt that, like ourselves, were playing dead. I remember one man they dragged out of a heap, who pleaded abjectly until a revolver shot cut him short. Then there was a woman who charged from a heap, snarling and shooting. She fired six shots before they got her, though what damage she did we could not know. We could follow these tragedies only by the sound. Every little while flurries like this occurred, each flurry culminating in the revolver shot that put an end to it. In the intervals we could hear the soldiers talking and swearing as they rummaged among the carcasses, urged on by their officers to hurry up.

At last they went to work on our heap, and we could feel the pressure diminish as they dragged away the dead and wounded. Garthwaite began uttering aloud the signals. At first he was not heard. Then he raised his voice.

"Listen to that," we heard a soldier say. And next the sharp voice of an officer. "Hold on there! Careful as you go!"

Oh, that first breath of air as we were dragged out! Garthwaite did the talking at first, but I was compelled to undergo a brief examination to prove service with the Iron Heel.

"Agents-provocateurs all right," was the officer's conclusion. He was a beardless young fellow, a cadet, evidently, of some great oligarch family.

"It's a hell of a job," Garthwaite grumbled. "I'm going to try and resign and get into the army. You fellows have a snap."

"You've earned it," was the young officer's answer. "I've got some pull, and I'll see if it can be managed. I can tell them how I found you."

He took Garthwaite's name and number, then turned to me.

"And you?"

"Oh, I'm going to be married," I answered lightly, "and then I'll be out of it all."

And so we talked, while the killing of the wounded went on. It is all a dream, now, as I look back on it; but at the time it was the most natural thing in the world. Garthwaite and the young officer fell into an animated conversation over the difference between so-called modern warfare and the present street-fighting and sky-scraper fighting that was taking place all over the city. I followed them intently, fixing up my hair at the same time and pinning together my torn skirts. And all the time the killing of the wounded went on. Sometimes the revolver shots drowned the voices of Garthwaite and the officer, and they were compelled to repeat what they had been saying.

I lived through three days of the Chicago Commune, and the vastness of it and of the slaughter may be imagined when I say that in all that time I saw practically nothing outside the killing of the people of the abyss and the mid-air fighting between sky-scrapers. I really saw nothing of the heroic work done by the comrades. I could hear the explosions of their mines and bombs, and see the smoke of their conflagrations, and that was all. The mid-air part of one great deed I saw, however, and that was the balloon attacks made by our comrades on the fortresses. That was on the second day. The three disloyal regiments had been destroyed in the fortresses to the last man. The fortresses were crowded with Mercenaries, the wind blew in the right direction, and up went our balloons from one of the office buildings in the city.

Now Biedenbach, after he left Glen Ellen, had invented a most powerful explosive—"expedite" he called it. This was the weapon the balloons used. They were only hot-air balloons, clumsily and hastily made, but they did the work. I saw it all from the top of an office building. The first balloon missed the fortresses completely and disappeared into the country; but we learned about it afterward. Burton and O'Sullivan were in it. As they were descending they swept across a railroad directly over a troop-train that was heading at full speed for Chicago. They dropped their whole supply of expedite upon the locomotive. The resulting wreck tied the line up for days. And the best of it was that, released from the weight of expedite, the balloon shot up into the air and did not come down for half a dozen miles, both heroes escaping unharmed.

The second balloon was a failure. Its flight was lame. It floated too low and was shot full of holes before it could reach the fortresses. Herford and Guinness were in it, and they were blown to pieces along with the field into which they fell. Biedenbach was in despair—we heard all about it afterward—and he went up alone in the third balloon. He, too, made a low flight, but he was in luck, for they failed seriously to puncture his balloon. I can see it now as I did then, from the lofty top of the building—that inflated bag drifting along the air, and that tiny speck of a man clinging on beneath. I could not see the fortress, but those on the roof with me said he was directly over it. I did not see the expedite fall when he cut it loose. But I did see the balloon suddenly leap up into the sky. An appreciable time after that the great column of the explosion towered in the air, and after that, in turn, I heard the roar of it. Biedenbach the gentle had destroyed a fortress. Two other balloons followed at the same time. One was blown to pieces in the air, the expedite exploding, and the shock of it disrupted the second balloon, which fell prettily into the remaining fortress. It couldn't have been better planned, though the two comrades in it sacrificed their lives.

But to return to the people of the abyss. My experiences were confined to them. They raged and slaughtered and destroyed all over the city proper, and were in turn destroyed; but never once did they succeed in reaching the city of the oligarchs over on the west side. The oligarchs had protected themselves well. No matter what destruction was wreaked in the heart of the city, they, and their womenkind and children, were to escape hurt. I am told that their children played in the parks during those terrible days and that their favorite game was an imitation of their elders stamping upon the proletariat.

But the Mercenaries found it no easy task to cope with the people of the abyss and at the same time fight with the comrades. Chicago was true to her traditions, and though a generation of revolutionists was wiped out, it took along with it pretty close to a generation of its enemies. Of course, the Iron Heel kept the figures secret, but, at a very conservative estimate, at least one hundred and thirty thousand Mercenaries were slain. But the comrades had no chance. Instead of the whole country being hand in hand in revolt, they were all alone, and the total strength of the Oligarchy could have been directed against them if necessary. As it was, hour after hour, day after day, in endless train-loads, by hundreds of thousands, the Mercenaries were hurled into Chicago.

And there were so many of the people of the abyss! Tiring of the slaughter, a great herding movement was begun by the soldiers, the intent of which was to drive the street mobs, like cattle, into Lake Michigan. It was at the beginning of this movement that Garthwaite and I had encountered the young officer. This herding movement was practically a failure, thanks to the splendid work of the comrades. Instead of the great host the Mercenaries had hoped to gather together, they succeeded in driving no more than forty thousand of the wretches into the lake. Time and again, when a mob of them was well in hand and being driven along the streets to the water, the comrades would create a diversion, and the mob would escape through the consequent hole torn in the encircling net.

Garthwaite and I saw an example of this shortly after meeting with the young officer. The mob of which we had been a part, and which had been put in retreat, was prevented from escaping to the south and east by strong bodies of troops. The troops we had fallen in with had held it back on the west. The only outlet was north, and north it went toward the lake, driven on from east and west and south by machine-gun fire and automatics. Whether it divined that it was being driven toward the lake, or whether it was merely a blind squirm of the monster, I do not know; but at any rate the mob took a cross street to the west, turned down the next street, and came back upon its track, heading south toward the great ghetto.

Garthwaite and I at that time were trying to make our way westward to get out of the territory of street-fighting, and we were caught right in the thick of it again. As we came to the corner we saw the howling mob bearing down upon us. Garthwaite seized my arm and we were just starting to run, when he dragged me back from in front of the wheels of half a dozen war automobiles, equipped with machine-guns, that were rushing for the spot. Behind them came the soldiers with their automatic rifles. By the time they took position, the mob was upon them, and it looked as though they would be overwhelmed before they could get into action.

Here and there a soldier was discharging his rifle, but this scattered fire had no effect in checking the mob. On it came, bellowing with brute rage. It seemed the machine-guns could not get started. The automobiles on which they were mounted blocked the street, compelling the soldiers to find positions in, between, and on the sidewalks. More and more soldiers were arriving, and in the jam we were unable to get away. Garthwaite held me by the arm, and we pressed close against the front of a building.

The mob was no more than twenty-five feet away when the machine-guns opened up; but before that flaming sheet of death nothing could live. The mob came on, but it could not advance. It piled up in a heap, a mound, a huge and growing wave of dead and dying. Those behind urged on, and the column, from gutter to gutter, telescoped upon itself. Wounded creatures, men and women, were vomited over the top of that awful wave and fell squirming down the face of it till they threshed about under the automobiles and against the legs of the soldiers. The latter bayoneted the struggling wretches, though one I saw who gained his feet and flew at a soldier's throat with his teeth. Together they went down, soldier and slave, into the welter.

The firing ceased. The work was done. The mob had been stopped in its wild attempt to break through. Orders were being given to clear the wheels of the war-machines. They could not advance over that wave of dead, and the idea was to run them down the cross street. The soldiers were dragging the bodies away from the wheels when it happened. We learned afterward how it happened. A block distant a hundred of our comrades had been holding a building. Across roofs and through buildings they made their way, till they found themselves looking down upon the close-packed soldiers. Then it was counter-massacre.

Without warning, a shower of bombs fell from the top of the building. The automobiles were blown to fragments, along with many soldiers. We, with the survivors, swept back in mad retreat. Half a block down another building opened fire on us. As the soldiers had carpeted the street with dead slaves, so, in turn, did they themselves become carpet. Garthwaite and I bore charmed lives. As we had done before, so again we sought shelter in an entrance. But he was not to be caught napping this time. As the roar of the bombs died away, he began peering out.

"The mob's coming back!" he called to me. "We've got to get out of this!"

We fled, hand in hand, down the bloody pavement, slipping and sliding, and making for the corner. Down the cross street we could see a few soldiers still running. Nothing was happening to them. The way was clear. So we paused a moment and looked back. The mob came on slowly. It was busy arming itself with the rifles of the slain and killing the wounded. We saw the end of the young officer who had rescued us. He painfully lifted himself on his elbow and turned loose with his automatic pistol.

"There goes my chance of promotion," Garthwaite laughed, as a woman bore down on the wounded man, brandishing a butcher's cleaver. "Come on. It's the wrong direction, but we'll get out somehow."

And we fled eastward through the quiet streets, prepared at every cross street for anything to happen. To the south a monster conflagration was filling the sky, and we knew that the great ghetto was burning. At last I sank down on the sidewalk. I was exhausted and could go no farther. I was bruised and sore and aching in every limb; yet I could not escape smiling at Garthwaite, who was rolling a cigarette and saying:

"I know I'm making a mess of rescuing you, but I can't get head nor tail of the situation. It's all a mess. Every time we try to break out, something happens and we're turned back. We're only a couple of blocks now from where I got you out of that entrance. Friend and foe are all mixed up. It's chaos. You can't tell who is in those darned buildings. Try to find out, and you get a bomb on your head. Try to go peaceably on your way, and you run into a mob and are killed by machine-guns, or you run into the Mercenaries and are killed by your own comrades from a roof. And on the top of it all the mob comes along and kills you, too."

He shook his head dolefully, lighted his cigarette, and sat down beside me.

"And I'm that hungry," he added, "I could eat cobble-stones."

The next moment he was on his feet again and out in the street prying up a cobblestone. He came back with it and assaulted the window of a store behind us.

"It's ground floor and no good," he explained as he helped me through the hole he had made; "but it's the best we can do. You get a nap and I'll reconnoitre. I'll finish this rescue all right, but I want time, time, lots of it—and something to eat."

It was a harness store we found ourselves in, and he fixed me up a couch of horse blankets in the private office well to the rear. To add to my wretchedness a splitting headache was coming on, and I was only too glad to close my eyes and try to sleep.

"I'll be back," were his parting words. "I don't hope to get an auto, but I'll surely bring some grub,[1] anyway."

And that was the last I saw of Garthwaite for three years. Instead of coming back, he was carried away to a hospital with a bullet through his lungs and another through the fleshy part of his neck.

[1]Food.

XXIV

Nightmare

I HAD not closed my eyes the night before on the Twentieth Century, and what of that and of my exhaustion I slept soundly. When I first awoke, it was night. Garthwaite had not returned. I had lost my watch and had no idea of the time. As I lay with my eyes closed, I heard the same dull sound of distant explosions. The inferno was still raging. I crept through the store to the front. The reflection from the sky of vast conflagrations made the street almost as light as day. One could have read the finest print with ease. From several blocks away came the crackle of small hand-bombs and the churning of machine-guns, and from a long way off came a long series of heavy explosions. I crept back to my horse blankets and slept again.

When next I awoke, a sickly yellow light was filtering in on me. It was dawn of the second day. I crept to the front of the store. A smoke pall, shot through with lurid gleams, filled the sky. Down the opposite side of the street tottered a wretched slave. One hand he held tightly against his side, and behind him he left a bloody trail. His eyes roved everywhere, and they were filled with apprehension and dread. Once he looked straight across at me, and in his face was all the dumb pathos of the wounded and hunted animal. He saw me, but there was no kinship between us, and with him, at least, no sympathy of understanding; for he cowered perceptibly and dragged himself on. He could expect no aid in all God's world. He was a helot in the great hunt of helots that the masters were making. All he could hope for, all he sought, was some hole to crawl away in and hide like any animal. The sharp clang of a passing ambulance at the corner gave him a start. Ambulances were not for such as he. With a groan of pain he threw himself into a doorway. A minute later he was out again and desperately hobbling on.

I went back to my horse blankets and waited an hour for Garthwaite. My headache had not gone away. On the contrary, it was increasing. It was by an effort of will only that I was able to open my eyes and look at objects. And with the opening of my eyes and the looking came intolerable torment. Also, a great pulse was beating in my brain. Weak and reeling, I went out through the broken window and down the street, seeking to escape, instinctively and gropingly, from the awful shambles. And thereafter I lived nightmare. My memory of what happened in the succeeding hours is the memory one would have of nightmare. Many events are focussed sharply on my brain, but between these indelible pictures I retain are intervals of unconsciousness. What occurred in those intervals I know not, and never shall know.

I remember stumbling at the corner over the legs of a man. It was the poor hunted wretch that had dragged himself past my hiding-place. How distinctly do I remember his poor, pitiful, gnarled hands as he lay there on the pavement—hands that were more hoof and claw than hands, all twisted and distorted by the toil of all his days, with on the palms a horny growth of callous a half inch thick. And as I picked myself up and started on, I looked into the face of the thing and saw that it still lived; for the eyes, dimly intelligent, were looking at me and seeing me.

After that came a kindly blank. I knew nothing, saw nothing, merely tottered on in my quest for safety. My next nightmare vision was a quiet street of the dead. I came upon it abruptly, as a wanderer in the country would come upon a flowing stream. Only this stream I gazed upon did not flow. It was congealed in death. From pavement to pavement, and covering the sidewalks, it lay there, spread out quite evenly, with only here and there a lump or mound of bodies to break the surface. Poor driven people of the abyss, hunted helots— they lay there as the rabbits in California after a drive.[1] Up the street and down I looked. There was no movement, no sound. The quiet buildings looked down upon the scene from their many windows. And once, and once only, I saw an arm

[1]In those days, so sparsely populated was the land that wild animals often became pests. In California the custom of rabbit-driving obtained. On a given day all the farmers in a locality would assemble and sweep across the country in converging lines, driving the rabbits by scores of thousands into a prepared enclosure, where they were clubbed to death by men and boys.

that moved in that dead stream. I swear I saw it move, with a strange writhing gesture of agony, and with it lifted a head, gory with nameless horror, that gibbered at me and then lay down again and moved no more.

I remember another street, with quiet buildings on either side, and the panic that smote me into consciousness as again I saw the people of the abyss, but this time in a stream that flowed and came on. And then I saw there was nothing to fear. The stream moved slowly, while from it arose groans and lamentations, cursings, babblings of senility, hysteria, and insanity; for these were the very young and the very old, the feeble and the sick, the helpless and the hopeless, all the wreckage of the ghetto. The burning of the great ghetto on the South Side had driven them forth into the inferno of the street-fighting, and whither they wended and whatever became of them I did not know and never learned.[1]

I have faint memories of breaking a window and hiding in some shop to escape a street mob that was pursued by soldiers. Also, a bomb burst near me, once, in some still street, where, look as I would, up and down, I could see no human being. But my next sharp recollection begins with the crack of a rifle and an abrupt becoming aware that I am being fired at by a soldier in an automobile. The shot missed, and the next moment I was screaming and motioning the signals. My memory of riding in the automobile is very hazy, though this ride, in turn, is broken by one vivid picture. The crack of the rifle of the soldier sitting beside me made me open my eyes, and I saw George Milford, whom I had known in the Pell Street days, sinking slowly down to the sidewalk. Even as he sank the soldier fired again, and Milford doubled in, then flung his body out, and fell sprawling. The soldier chuckled, and the automobile sped on.

The next I knew after that I was awakened out of a

---

[1] It was long a question of debate, whether the burning of the South Side ghetto was accidental, or whether it was done by the Mercenaries; but it is definitely settled now that the ghetto was fired by the Mercenaries under orders from their chiefs.

sound sleep by a man who walked up and down close beside me. His face was drawn and strained, and the sweat rolled down his nose from his forehead. One hand was clutched tightly against his chest by the other hand, and blood dripped down upon the floor as he walked. He wore the uniform of the Mercenaries. From without, as through thick walls, came the muffled roar of bursting bombs. I was in some building that was locked in combat with some other building.

A surgeon came in to dress the wounded soldier, and I learned that it was two in the afternoon. My headache was no better, and the surgeon paused from his work long enough to give me a powerful drug that would depress the heart and bring relief. I slept again, and the next I knew I was on top of the building. The immediate fighting had ceased, and I was watching the balloon attack on the fortresses. Some one had an arm around me and I was leaning close against him. It came to me quite as a matter of course that this was Ernest, and I found myself wondering how he had got his hair and eyebrows so badly singed.

It was by the merest chance that we had found each other in that terrible city. He had had no idea that I had left New York, and, coming through the room where I lay asleep, could not at first believe that it was I. Little more I saw of the Chicago Commune. After watching the balloon attack, Ernest took me down into the heart of the building, where I slept the afternoon out and the night. The third day we spent in the building, and on the fourth, Ernest having got permission and an automobile from the authorities, we left Chicago.

My headache was gone, but, body and soul, I was very tired. I lay back against Ernest in the automobile, and with apathetic eyes watched the soldiers trying to get the machine out of the city. Fighting was still going on, but only in isolated localities. Here and there whole districts were still in possession of the comrades, but such districts were surrounded and guarded by heavy bodies of troops. In a hundred segregated traps were the comrades thus held while the work of subjugating them went on. Subjugation meant death, for no quarter was given, and they fought heroically to the last man.[1]

Whenever we approached such localities, the guards turned us back and sent us around. Once, the only way past two strong positions of the comrades was through a burnt section that lay between. From either side we could hear the rattle and roar of war, while the automobile picked its way through smoking ruins and tottering walls. Often the streets were blocked by mountains of débris that compelled us to go around. We were in a labyrinth of ruin, and our progress was slow.

The stockyards (ghetto, plant, and everything) were smouldering ruins. Far off to the right a wide smoke haze dimmed the sky,—the town of Pullman, the soldier chauffeur told us, or what had been the town of Pullman, for it was utterly destroyed. He had driven the machine out there, with despatches, on the afternoon of the third day. Some of the heaviest fighting had occurred there, he said, many of the streets being rendered impassable by the heaps of the dead.

Swinging around the shattered walls of a building, in the stockyards district, the automobile was stopped by a wave of dead. It was for all the world like a wave tossed up by the sea. It was patent to us what had happened. As the mob charged past the corner, it had been swept, at right angles and point-blank range, by the machine-guns drawn up on the cross street. But disaster had come to the soldiers. A chance bomb must have exploded among them, for the mob, checked until its dead and dying formed the wave, had white-capped and flung forward its foam of living, fighting slaves. Soldiers and slaves lay together, torn and mangled, around and over the wreckage of the automobiles and guns.

Ernest sprang out. A familiar pair of shoulders in a cotton shirt and a familiar fringe of white hair had caught his eye. I

[1]Numbers of the buildings held out over a week, while one held out eleven days. Each building had to be stormed like a fort, and the Mercenaries fought their way upward floor by floor. It was deadly fighting. Quarter was neither given nor taken, and in the fighting the revolutionists had the advantage of being above. While the revolutionists were wiped out, the loss was not one-sided. The proud Chicago proletariat lived up to its ancient boast. For as many of itself as were killed, it killed that many of the enemy.

did not watch him, and it was not until he was back beside me and we were speeding on that he said:

"It was Bishop Morehouse."

Soon we were in the green country, and I took one last glance back at the smoke-filled sky. Faint and far came the low thud of an explosion. Then I turned my face against Ernest's breast and wept softly for the Cause that was lost. Ernest's arm about me was eloquent with love.

"For this time lost, dear heart," he said, "but not forever. We have learned. To-morrow the Cause will rise again, strong with wisdom and discipline."

The automobile drew up at a railroad station. Here we would catch a train to New York. As we waited on the platform, three trains thundered past, bound west to Chicago. They were crowded with ragged, unskilled laborers, people of the abyss.

"Slave-levies for the rebuilding of Chicago," Ernest said. "You see, the Chicago slaves are all killed."

XXV

The Terrorists

IT WAS not until Ernest and I were back in New York, and after weeks had elapsed, that we were able to comprehend thoroughly the full sweep of the disaster that had befallen the Cause. The situation was bitter and bloody. In many places, scattered over the country, slave revolts and massacres had occurred. The roll of the martyrs increased mightily. Countless executions took place everywhere. The mountains and waste regions were filled with outlaws and refugees who were being hunted down mercilessly. Our own refuges were packed with comrades who had prices on their heads. Through information furnished by its spies, scores of our refuges were raided by the soldiers of the Iron Heel.

Many of the comrades were disheartened, and they retaliated with terroristic tactics. The set-back to their hopes made them despairing and desperate. Many terrorist organizations unaffiliated with us sprang into existence and caused us much trouble.[1] These misguided people sacrificed their own lives

[1] The annals of this short-lived era of despair make bloody reading. Revenge was the ruling motive, and the members of the terroristic organizations were careless of their own lives and hopeless about the future. The Danites, taking their name from the avenging angels of the Mormon mythology, sprang up in the mountains of the Great West and spread over the Pacific Coast from Panama to Alaska. The Valkyries were women. They were the most terrible of all. No woman was eligible for membership who had not lost near relatives at the hands of the Oligarchy. They were guilty of torturing their prisoners to death. Another famous organization of women was The Widows of War. A companion organization to the Valkyries was the Berserkers. These men placed no value whatever upon their own lives, and it was they who totally destroyed the great Mercenary city of Bellona along with its population of over a hundred thousand souls. The Bedlamites and the Helldamites were twin slave organizations, while a new religious sect that did not flourish long was called The Wrath of God. Among others, to show the whimsicality of their deadly seriousness, may be mentioned the following: The Bleeding Hearts, Sons of the Morning, the Morning Stars, The Flamingoes, The Triple Triangles, The Three Bars, The Rubonics, The Vindicators, The Comanches, and The Erebusites.

wantonly, very often made our own plans go astray, and retarded our organization.

And through it all moved the Iron Heel, impassive and deliberate, shaking up the whole fabric of the social structure in its search for the comrades, combing out the Mercenaries, the labor castes, and all its secret services, punishing without mercy and without malice, suffering in silence all retaliations that were made upon it, and filling the gaps in its fighting line as fast as they appeared. And hand in hand with this, Ernest and the other leaders were hard at work reorganizing the forces of the Revolution. The magnitude of the task may be understood when it is taken into[1]

[1] This is the end of the Everhard Manuscript. It breaks off abruptly in the middle of a sentence. She must have received warning of the coming of the Mercenaries, for she had time safely to hide the Manuscript before she fled or was captured. It is to be regretted that she did not live to complete her narrative, for then, undoubtedly, would have been cleared away the mystery that has shrouded for seven centuries the execution of Ernest Everhard.

MARTIN EDEN

"Let me live out my years in heat of blood!
    Let me lie drunken with the dreamer's wine!
Let me not see this soul-house built of mud
    Go toppling to the dust a vacant shrine!"

Chapter I

THE ONE opened the door with a latch-key and went in, followed by a young fellow who awkwardly removed his cap. He wore rough clothes that smacked of the sea, and he was manifestly out of place in the spacious hall in which he found himself. He did not know what to do with his cap, and was stuffing it into his coat pocket when the other took it from him. The act was done quietly and naturally, and the awkward young fellow appreciated it. "He understands," was his thought. "He'll see me through all right."

He walked at the other's heels with a swing to his shoulders, and his legs spread unwittingly, as if the level floors were tilting up and sinking down to the heave and lunge of the sea. The wide rooms seemed too narrow for his rolling gait, and to himself he was in terror lest his broad shoulders should collide with the doorways or sweep the bric-a-brac from the low mantel. He recoiled from side to side between the various objects and multiplied the hazards that in reality lodged only in his mind. Between a grand piano and a centre-table piled high with books was space for a half a dozen to walk abreast, yet he essayed it with trepidation. His heavy arms hung loosely at his sides. He did not know what to do with those arms and hands, and when, to his excited vision, one arm seemed liable to brush against the books on the table, he lurched away like a frightened horse, barely missing the piano stool. He watched the easy walk of the other in front of him, and for the first time realized that his walk was different from that of other men. He experienced a momentary pang of shame that he should walk so uncouthly. The sweat burst through the skin of his forehead in tiny beads, and he paused and mopped his bronzed face with his handkerchief.

"Hold on, Arthur, my boy," he said, attempting to mask his anxiety with facetious utterance. "This is too much all at once for yours truly. Give me a chance to get my nerve. You know I didn't want to come, an' I guess your fam'ly ain't hankerin' to see me neither."

"That's all right," was the reassuring answer. "You mustn't be frightened at us. We're just homely people—Hello, there's a letter for me."

He stepped back to the table, tore open the envelope, and began to read, giving the stranger an opportunity to recover himself. And the stranger understood and appreciated. His was the gift of sympathy, understanding; and beneath his alarmed exterior that sympathetic process went on. He mopped his forehead dry and glanced about him with a controlled face, though in the eyes there was an expression such as wild animals betray when they fear the trap. He was surrounded by the unknown, apprehensive of what might happen, ignorant of what he should do, aware that he walked and bore himself awkwardly, fearful that every attribute and power of him was similarly afflicted. He was keenly sensitive, hopelessly self-conscious, and the amused glance that the other stole privily at him over the top of the letter burned into him like a dagger-thrust. He saw the glance, but he gave no sign, for among the things he had learned was discipline. Also, that dagger-thrust went to his pride. He cursed himself for having come, and at the same time resolved that, happen what would, having come, he would carry it through. The lines of his face hardened, and into his eyes came a fighting light. He looked about more unconcernedly, sharply observant, every detail of the pretty interior registering itself on his brain. His eyes were wide apart; nothing in their field of vision escaped; and as they drank in the beauty before them the fighting light died out and a warm glow took its place. He was responsive to beauty, and here was cause to respond.

An oil painting caught and held him. A heavy surf thundered and burst over an outjutting rock; lowering storm-clouds covered the sky; and, outside the line of surf, a pilot-schooner, close-hauled, heeled over till every detail of her deck was visible, was surging along against a stormy sunset sky. There was beauty, and it drew him irresistibly. He forgot his awkward walk and came closer to the painting, very close. The beauty faded out of the canvas. His face expressed his bepuzzlement. He stared at what seemed a careless daub of paint, then stepped away. Immediately all the beauty flashed back into the canvas. "A trick picture," was his thought, as he dismissed it, though in the midst of the multitudinous impressions he was receiving he found time to feel a prod of indignation that so much beauty should be sacrificed to make a trick. He did not know painting. He had been brought up on chromos and lithographs that were always definite and sharp, near or far. He had seen oil paintings, it was true, in the show windows of shops, but the glass of the windows had prevented his eager eyes from approaching too near.

He glanced around at his friend reading the letter and saw the books on the table. Into his eyes leaped a wistfulness and a yearning as promptly as the yearning leaps into the eyes of a starving man at sight of food. An impulsive stride, with one lurch to right and left of the shoulders, brought him to the table, where he began affectionately handling the books. He glanced at the titles and the authors' names, read fragments of text, caressing the volumes with his eyes and hands, and, once, recognized a book he had read. For the rest, they were strange books and strange authors. He chanced upon a volume of Swinburne and began reading steadily, forgetful of where he was, his face glowing. Twice he closed the book on his forefinger to look at the name of the author. Swinburne! he would remember that name. That fellow had eyes, and he had certainly seen color and flashing light. But who was Swinburne? Was he dead a hundred years or so, like most of the poets? Or was he alive still, and writing? He turned to the title-page . . . yes, he had written other books; well, he would go to the free library the first thing in the morning and try to get hold of some of Swinburne's stuff. He went back to the text and lost himself. He did not notice that a young woman had entered the room. The first he knew was when he heard Arthur's voice saying: —

"Ruth, this is Mr. Eden."

The book was closed on his forefinger, and before he turned he was thrilling to the first new impression, which was not of the girl, but of her brother's words. Under that muscled body of his he was a mass of quivering sensibilities. At the slightest impact of the outside world upon his consciousness, his thoughts, sympathies, and emotions leapt and played like lambent flame. He was extraordinarily receptive and responsive, while his imagination, pitched high, was ever at work establishing relations of likeness and difference. "Mr. Eden," was what he had thrilled to—he who had been called "Eden," or "Martin Eden," or just "Martin," all his life. And *"Mister!"* It was certainly going some, was his internal comment. His mind seemed to turn, on the instant, into a vast camera obscura, and he saw arrayed around his consciousness endless pictures from his life, of stoke-holes and forecastles, camps and beaches, jails and boozing-kens, fever-hospitals and slum streets, wherein the thread of association was the fashion in which he had been addressed in those various situations.

And then he turned and saw the girl. The phantasmagoria of his brain vanished at sight of her. She was a pale, ethereal creature, with wide, spiritual blue eyes and a wealth of golden hair. He did not know how she was dressed, except that the dress was as wonderful as she. He likened her to a pale gold flower upon a slender stem. No, she was a spirit, a divinity, a goddess; such sublimated beauty was not of the earth. Or perhaps the books were right, and there were many such as she in the upper walks of life. She might well be sung by that chap Swinburne. Perhaps he had had somebody like her in mind when he painted that girl, Iseult, in the book there on the table. All this plethora of sight, and feeling, and thought occurred on the instant. There was no pause of the realities wherein he moved. He saw her hand coming out to his, and she looked him straight in the eyes as she shook hands, frankly, like a man. The women he had known did not shake hands that way. For that matter, most of them did not shake hands at all. A flood of associations, visions of various ways he had made the acquaintance of women, rushed into his mind and threatened to swamp it. But he shook them aside and looked at her. Never had he seen such a woman. The women he had known! Immediately, beside her, on either hand, ranged the women he had known. For an eternal second he stood in the midst of a portrait gallery, wherein she occupied the central place, while about her were limned many women, all to be weighed and measured by a fleeting glance, herself the unit of weight and measure. He saw the weak and sickly faces of the girls of the factories, and the simpering, boisterous girls from the south of Market. There were women of the cattle camps, and swarthy cigarette-smoking women of Old Mexico. These, in turn, were crowded out by Japanese women, doll-like, stepping mincingly on wooden clogs; by Eurasians, delicate featured, stamped with degeneracy; by full-bodied South-Sea-Island women, flower-crowned and brown-skinned. All these were blotted out by a grotesque and terrible nightmare brood—frowsy, shuffling creatures from the pavements of Whitechapel, gin-bloated hags of the stews, and all the vast hell's following of harpies, vile-mouthed and filthy, that under the guise of monstrous female form prey upon sailors, the scrapings of the ports, the scum and slime of the human pit.

"Won't you sit down, Mr. Eden?" the girl was saying. "I have been looking forward to meeting you ever since Arthur told us. It was brave of you—"

He waved his hand deprecatingly and muttered that it was nothing at all, what he had done, and that any fellow would have done it. She noticed that the hand he waved was covered with fresh abrasions, in the process of healing, and a glance at the other loose-hanging hand showed it to be in the same condition. Also, with quick, critical eye, she noted a scar on his cheek, another that peeped out from under the hair of the forehead, and a third that ran down and disappeared under the starched collar. She repressed a smile at sight of the red line that marked the chafe of the collar against the bronzed neck. He was evidently unused to stiff collars. Likewise her feminine eye took in the clothes he wore, the cheap and unæsthetic cut, the wrinkling of the coat across the shoulders, and the series of wrinkles in the sleeves that advertised bulging biceps muscles.

While he waved his hand and muttered that he had done nothing at all, he was obeying her behest by trying to get into a chair. He found time to admire the ease with which she sat down, then lurched toward a chair facing her, overwhelmed with consciousness of the awkward figure he was cutting. This was a new experience for him. All his life, up to then, he had been unaware of being either graceful or awkward. Such thoughts of self had never entered his mind. He sat down gingerly on the edge of the chair, greatly worried by his hands. They were in the way wherever he put them.

Arthur was leaving the room, and Martin Eden followed his exit with longing eyes. He felt lost, alone there in the room with that pale spirit of a woman. There was no barkeeper upon whom to call for drinks, no small boy to send around the corner for a can of beer and by means of that social fluid start the amenities of friendship flowing.

"You have such a scar on your neck, Mr. Eden," the girl was saying. "How did it happen? I am sure it must have been some adventure."

"A Mexican with a knife, miss," he answered, moistening his parched lips and clearing his throat. "It was just a fight. After I got the knife away, he tried to bite off my nose."

Baldly as he had stated it, in his eyes was a rich vision of that hot, starry night at Salina Cruz, the white strip of beach, the lights of the sugar steamers in the harbor, the voices of the drunken sailors in the distance, the jostling stevedores, the flaming passion in the Mexican's face, the glint of the beast-eyes in the starlight, the sting of the steel in his neck, and the rush of blood, the crowd and the cries, the two bodies, his and the Mexican's, locked together, rolling over and over and tearing up the sand, and from away off somewhere the mellow tinkling of a guitar. Such was the picture, and he thrilled to the memory of it, wondering if the man could paint it who had painted the pilot-schooner on the wall. The white beach, the stars, and the lights of the sugar steamers would look great, he thought, and midway on the sand the dark group of figures that surrounded the fighters. The knife occupied a place in the picture, he decided, and would show well, with a sort of gleam, in the light of the stars. But of all this no hint had crept into his speech. "He tried to bite off my nose," he concluded.

"Oh," the girl said, in a faint, far voice, and he noticed the shock in her sensitive face.

He felt a shock himself, and a blush of embarrassment shone faintly on his sunburned cheeks, though to him it burned as hotly as when his cheeks had been exposed to the open furnace-door in the fire-room. Such sordid things as stabbing affrays were evidently not fit subjects for conversation with a lady. People in the books, in her walk of life, did not talk about such things—perhaps they did not know about them, either.

There was a brief pause in the conversation they were trying to get started. Then she asked tentatively about the scar on his cheek. Even as she asked, he realized that she was making an effort to talk his talk, and he resolved to get away from it and talk hers.

"It was just an accident," he said, putting his hand to his cheek. "One night, in a calm, with a heavy sea running, the main-boom-lift carried away, an' next the tackle. The lift was wire, an' it was threshin' around like a snake. The whole watch was tryin' to grab it, an' I rushed in an' got swatted."

"Oh," she said, this time with an accent of comprehension, though secretly his speech had been so much Greek to her and she was wondering what a *lift* was and what *swatted* meant.

"This man Swineburne," he began, attempting to put his plan into execution and pronouncing the *i* long.

"Who?"

"Swineburne," he repeated, with the same mispronunciation. "The poet."

"Swinburne," she corrected.

"Yes, that's the chap," he stammered, his cheeks hot again. "How long since he died?"

"Why, I haven't heard that he was dead." She looked at him curiously. "Where did you make his acquaintance?"

"I never clapped eyes on him," was the reply. "But I read some of his poetry out of that book there on the table just before you come in. How do you like his poetry?"

And thereat she began to talk quickly and easily upon the subject he had suggested. He felt better, and settled back slightly from the edge of the chair, holding tightly to its arms with his hands, as if it might get away from him and buck him to the floor. He had succeeded in making her talk her talk, and while she rattled on, he strove to follow her, marvelling at all the knowledge that was stowed away in that pretty head of hers, and drinking in the pale beauty of her face. Follow her he did, though bothered by unfamiliar words that fell glibly from her lips and by critical phrases and thought-processes that were foreign to his mind, but that nevertheless stimulated his mind and set it tingling. Here was intellectual life, he thought, and here was beauty, warm and wonderful as he had never dreamed it could be. He forgot himself and stared at her with hungry eyes. Here was something to live for, to win to, to fight for—ay, and die for. The books were true. There were such women in the world. She was one of them. She lent wings to his imagination, and great, luminous canvases spread themselves before him, whereon loomed vague, gigantic figures of love and romance, and of heroic deeds for woman's sake—for a pale woman, a flower of gold. And through the swaying, palpitant vision, as through a fairy mirage, he stared at the real woman, sitting there and talking of literature and art. He listened as well, but he stared, unconscious of the fixity of his gaze or of the fact that all that was essentially masculine in his nature was shining in his eyes. But she, who knew little of the world of men, being a woman, was keenly aware of his burning eyes. She had never had men look at her in such fashion, and it embarrassed her. She stumbled and halted in her utterance. The thread of argument slipped from her. He frightened her, and at the same time it was strangely pleasant to be so looked upon. Her training warned her of peril and of wrong, subtle, mysterious, luring; while her instincts rang clarion-voiced through her being, impelling her to hurdle caste and place and gain to this traveller from another world, to this uncouth young fellow with lacerated hands and a line of raw red caused by the unaccustomed linen at his throat, who, all too evidently, was soiled and tainted by ungracious existence. She was clean, and her cleanness revolted; but she was woman, and she was just beginning to learn the paradox of woman.

"As I was saying—what was I saying?" She broke off abruptly and laughed merrily at her predicament.

"You was saying that this man Swinburne failed bein' a great poet because—an' that was as far as you got, miss," he prompted, while to himself he seemed suddenly hungry, and delicious little thrills crawled up and down his spine at the sound of her laughter. Like silver, he thought to himself, like tinkling silver bells; and on the instant, and for an instant, he was transported to a far land, where under pink cherry blossoms, he smoked a cigarette and listened to the bells of the peaked pagoda calling straw-sandalled devotees to worship.

"Yes, thank you," she said. "Swinburne fails, when all is said, because he is, well, indelicate. There are many of his poems that should never be read. Every line of the really great poets is filled with beautiful truth, and calls to all that is high and noble in the human. Not a line of the great poets can be spared without impoverishing the world by that much."

"I thought it was great," he said hesitatingly, "the little I read. I had no idea he was such a—a scoundrel. I guess that crops out in his other books."

"There are many lines that could be spared from the book you were reading," she said, her voice primly firm and dogmatic.

"I must 'a' missed 'em," he announced. "What I read was the real goods. It was all lighted up an' shining, an' it shun right into me an' lighted me up inside, like the sun or a searchlight. That's the way it landed on me, but I guess I ain't up much on poetry, miss."

He broke off lamely. He was confused, painfully conscious of his inarticulateness. He had felt the bigness and glow of life in what he had read, but his speech was inadequate. He could not express what he felt, and to himself he likened himself to a sailor, in a strange ship, on a dark night, groping about in the unfamiliar running rigging. Well, he decided, it was up to him to get acquainted in this new world. He had never seen anything that he couldn't get the hang of when he wanted to and it was about time for him to want to learn to talk the things that were inside of him so that she could understand. *She* was bulking large on his horizon.

"Now Longfellow—" she was saying.

"Yes, I've read 'm," he broke in impulsively, spurred on to exhibit and make the most of his little store of book knowledge, desirous of showing her that he was not wholly a stupid clod. " 'The Psalm of Life,' 'Excelsior,' an'. . . . I guess that's all."

She nodded her head and smiled, and he felt, somehow, that her smile was tolerant, pitifully tolerant. He was a fool to attempt to make a pretence that way. That Longfellow chap most likely had written countless books of poetry.

"Excuse me, miss, for buttin' in that way. I guess the real facts is that I don't know nothin' much about such things. It ain't in my class. But I'm goin' to make it in my class."

It sounded like a threat. His voice was determined, his eyes were flashing, the lines of his face had grown harsh. And to her it seemed that the angle of his jaw had changed; its pitch had become unpleasantly aggressive. At the same time a wave of intense virility seemed to surge out from him and impinge upon her.

"I think you could make it in—in your class," she finished with a laugh. "You are very strong."

Her gaze rested for a moment on the muscular neck, heavy corded, almost bull-like, bronzed by the sun, spilling over with rugged health and strength. And though he sat there, blushing and humble, again she felt drawn to him. She was surprised by a wanton thought that rushed into her mind. It seemed to her that if she could lay her two hands upon that neck that all its strength and vigor would flow out to her. She was shocked by this thought. It seemed to reveal to her an undreamed depravity in her nature. Besides, strength to her was a gross and brutish thing. Her ideal of masculine beauty had always been slender gracefulness. Yet the thought still persisted. It bewildered her that she should desire to place her hands on that sunburned neck. In truth, she was far from robust, and the need of her body and mind was for strength. But she did not know it. She knew only that no man had ever affected her before as this one had, who shocked her from moment to moment with his awful grammar.

"Yes, I ain't no invalid," he said. "When it comes down to hard-pan, I can digest scrap-iron. But just now I've got dyspepsia. Most of what you was sayin' I can't digest. Never trained that way, you see. I like books and poetry, and what time I've had I've read 'em, but I've never thought about 'em the way you have. That's why I can't talk about 'em. I'm like a navigator adrift on a strange sea without chart or compass. Now I want to get my bearin's. Mebbe you can put me right. How did you learn all this you've ben talkin'?"

"By going to school, I fancy, and by studying," she answered.

"I went to school when I was a kid," he began to object.

"Yes; but I mean high school, and lectures, and the university."

"You've gone to the university?" he demanded in frank amazement. He felt that she had become remoter from him by at least a million miles.

"I'm going there now. I'm taking special courses in English."

He did not know what "English" meant, but he made a mental note of that item of ignorance and passed on.

"How long would I have to study before I could go to the university?" he asked.

She beamed encouragement upon his desire for knowledge, and said: "That depends upon how much studying you have already done. You have never attended high school? Of course not. But did you finish grammar school?"

"I had two years to run, when I left," he answered. "But I was always honorably promoted at school."

The next moment, angry with himself for the boast, he had gripped the arms of the chair so savagely that every finger-end was stinging. At the same moment he became aware that a woman was entering the room. He saw the girl leave her chair and trip swiftly across the floor to the newcomer. They kissed each other, and, with arms around each other's waists, they advanced toward him. That must be her mother, he thought. She was a tall, blond woman, slender, and stately, and beautiful. Her gown was what he might expect in such a house. His eyes delighted in the graceful lines of it. She and her dress together reminded him of women on the stage. Then he remembered seeing similar grand ladies and gowns entering the London theatres while he stood and watched and the policemen shoved him back into the drizzle beyond the awning. Next his mind leaped to the Grand Hotel at Yokohama, where, too, from the sidewalk, he had seen grand ladies. Then the city and the harbor of Yokohama, in a thousand pictures, began flashing before his eyes. But he swiftly dismissed the kaleidoscope of memory, oppressed by the urgent need of the present. He knew that he must stand up to be introduced, and he struggled painfully to his feet, where he stood with trousers bagging at the knees, his arms loose-hanging and ludicrous, his face set hard for the impending ordeal.

Chapter II

THE PROCESS of getting into the dining room was a
nightmare to him. Between halts and stumbles, jerks and
lurches, locomotion had at times seemed impossible. But at
last he had made it, and was seated alongside of Her. The
array of knives and forks frightened him. They bristled with
unknown perils, and he gazed at them, fascinated, till their
dazzle became a background across which moved a succession
of forecastle pictures, wherein he and his mates sat eating salt
beef with sheath-knives and fingers, or scooping thick pea-
soup out of pannikins by means of battered iron spoons. The
stench of bad beef was in his nostrils, while in his ears, to the
accompaniment of creaking timbers and groaning bulkheads,
echoed the loud mouth-noises of the eaters. He watched them
eating, and decided that they ate like pigs. Well, he would be
careful here. He would make no noise. He would keep his
mind upon it all the time.

He glanced around the table. Opposite him was Arthur,
and Arthur's brother, Norman. They were her brothers, he
reminded himself, and his heart warmed toward them. How
they loved each other, the members of this family! There
flashed into his mind the picture of her mother, of the kiss of
greeting, and of the pair of them walking toward him with
arms entwined. Not in his world were such displays of affection between parents and children made. It was a revelation
of the heights of existence that were attained in the world
above. It was the finest thing yet that he had seen in this small
glimpse of that world. He was moved deeply by appreciation
of it, and his heart was melting with sympathetic tenderness.
He had starved for love all his life. His nature craved love. It
was an organic demand of his being. Yet he had gone without, and hardened himself in the process. He had not known
that he needed love. Nor did he know it now. He merely saw
it in operation, and thrilled to it, and thought it fine, and
high, and splendid.

He was glad that Mr. Morse was not there. It was difficult
enough getting acquainted with her, and her mother, and her

brother, Norman. Arthur he already knew somewhat. The father would have been too much for him, he felt sure. It
seemed to him that he had never worked so hard in his life.
The severest toil was child's play compared with this. Tiny
nodules of moisture stood out on his forehead, and his shirt
was wet with sweat from the exertion of doing so many unaccustomed things at once. He had to eat as he had never
eaten before, to handle strange tools, to glance surreptitiously
about and learn how to accomplish each new thing, to receive
the flood of impressions that was pouring in upon him and
being mentally annotated and classified; to be conscious of a
yearning for her that perturbed him in the form of a dull,
aching restlessness; to feel the prod of desire to win to the
walk in life whereon she trod, and to have his mind ever and
again straying off in speculation and vague plans of how to
reach to her. Also, when his secret glance went across to Norman opposite him, or to any one else, to ascertain just what
knife or fork was to be used in any particular occasion, that
person's features were seized upon by his mind, which automatically strove to appraise them and to divine what they
were—all in relation to her. Then he had to talk, to hear
what was said to him and what was said back and forth, and
to answer, when it was necessary, with a tongue prone to
looseness of speech that required a constant curb. And to add
confusion to confusion, there was the servant, an unceasing
menace, that appeared noiselessly at his shoulder, a dire
Sphinx that propounded puzzles and conundrums demanding
instantaneous solution. He was oppressed throughout the
meal by the thought of finger-bowls. Irrelevantly, insistently,
scores of times, he wondered when they would come on and
what they looked like. He had heard of such things, and now,
sooner or later, somewhere in the next few minutes, he would
see them, sit at table with exalted beings who used them—
ay, and he would use them himself. And most important of
all, far down and yet always at the surface of his thought, was
the problem of how he should comport himself toward these
persons. What should his attitude be? He wrestled continually
and anxiously with the problem. There were cowardly suggestions that he should make believe, assume a part; and there
were still more cowardly suggestions that warned him he

would fail in such course, that his nature was not fitted to live up to it, and that he would make a fool of himself.

It was during the first part of the dinner, struggling to decide upon his attitude, that he was very quiet. He did not know that his quietness was giving the lie to Arthur's words of the day before, when that brother of hers had announced that he was going to bring a wild man home to dinner and for them not to be alarmed, because they would find him an interesting wild man. Martin Eden could not have found it in him, just then, to believe that her brother could be guilty of such treachery—especially when he had been the means of getting this particular brother out of an unpleasant row. So he sat at table, perturbed by his own unfitness and at the same time charmed by all that went on about him. For the first time he realized that eating was something more than a utilitarian function. He was unaware of what he ate. It was merely food. He was feasting his love of beauty at this table where eating was an æsthetic function. It was an intellectual function, too. His mind was stirred. He heard words spoken that were meaningless to him, and other words that he had seen only in books and that no man or woman he had known was of large enough mental caliber to pronounce. When he heard such words dropping carelessly from the lips of the members of this marvellous family, her family, he thrilled with delight. The romance, and beauty, and high vigor of the books were coming true. He was in that rare and blissful state wherein a man sees his dreams stalk out from the crannies of fantasy and become fact.

Never had he been at such an altitude of living, and he kept himself in the background, listening, observing, and pleasuring, replying in reticent monosyllables, saying "Yes, miss," and "No, miss," to her, and "Yes, ma'am," and "No, ma'am," to her mother. He curbed the impulse, arising out of his sea-training, to say "Yes, sir," and "No, sir," to her brothers. He felt that it would be inappropriate and a confession of inferiority on his part—which would never do if he was to win to her. Also, it was a dictate of his pride. "By God!" he cried to himself, once; "I'm just as good as them, and if they do know lots that I don't, I could learn 'm a few myself, all the same!" And the next moment, when she or her mother addressed him as "Mr. Eden," his aggressive pride was forgotten, and he was glowing and warm with delight. He was a civilized man, that was what he was, shoulder to shoulder, at dinner, with people he had read about in books. He was in the books himself, adventuring through the printed pages of bound volumes.

But while he belied Arthur's description, and appeared a gentle lamb rather than a wild man, he was racking his brains for a course of action. He was no gentle lamb, and the part of second fiddle would never do for the high-pitched dominance of his nature. He talked only when he had to, and then his speech was like his walk to the table, filled with jerks and halts as he groped in his polyglot vocabulary for words, debating over words he knew were fit but which he feared he could not pronounce, rejecting other words he knew would not be understood or would be raw and harsh. But all the time he was oppressed by the consciousness that this carefulness of diction was making a booby of him, preventing him from expressing what he had in him. Also, his love of freedom chafed against the restriction in much the same way his neck chafed against the starched fetter of a collar. Besides, he was confident that he could not keep it up. He was by nature powerful of thought and sensibility, and the creative spirit was restive and urgent. He was swiftly mastered by the concept or sensation in him that struggled in birth-throes to receive expression and form, and then he forgot himself and where he was, and the old words—the tools of speech he knew—slipped out.

Once, he declined something from the servant who interrupted and pestered at his shoulder, and he said, shortly and emphatically, "Pow!"

On the instant those at the table were keyed up and expectant, the servant was smugly pleased, and he was wallowing in mortification. But he recovered himself quickly.

"It's the Kanaka for 'finish,'" he explained, "and it just come out naturally. It's spelt p-a-u."

He caught her curious and speculative eyes fixed on his hands, and, being in explanatory mood, he said:—

"I just come down the Coast on one of the Pacific mail steamers. She was behind time, an' around the Puget Sound ports we worked like niggers, storing cargo—mixed freight, if you know what that means. That's how the skin got knocked off."

"Oh, it wasn't that," she hastened to explain, in turn. "Your hands seemed too small for your body."

His cheeks were hot. He took it as an exposure of another of his deficiencies.

"Yes," he said depreciatingly. "They ain't big enough to stand the strain. I can hit like a mule with my arms and shoulders. They are too strong, an' when I smash a man on the jaw the hands get smashed, too."

He was not happy at what he had said. He was filled with disgust at himself. He had loosed the guard upon his tongue and talked about things that were not nice.

"It was brave of you to help Arthur the way you did—and you a stranger," she said tactfully, aware of his discomfiture though not of the reason for it.

He, in turn, realized what she had done, and in the consequent warm surge of gratefulness that overwhelmed him forgot his loose-worded tongue.

"It wasn't nothin' at all," he said. "Any guy 'ud do it for another. That bunch of hoodlums was lookin' for trouble, an' Arthur wasn't botherin' 'em none. They butted in on 'm, an' then I butted in on them an' poked a few. That's where some of the skin off my hands went, along with some of the teeth of the gang. I wouldn't 'a' missed it for anything. When I seen—"

He paused, open-mouthed, on the verge of the pit of his own depravity and utter worthlessness to breathe the same air she did. And while Arthur took up the tale, for the twentieth time, of his adventure with the drunken hoodlums on the ferry-boat and of how Martin Eden had rushed in and rescued him, that individual, with frowning brows, meditated upon the fool he had made of himself, and wrestled more determinedly with the problem of how he should conduct himself toward these people. He certainly had not succeeded so far. He wasn't of their tribe, and he couldn't talk their lingo, was the way he put it to himself. He couldn't fake being their kind. The masquerade would fail, and besides, masquerade was foreign to his nature. There was no room in him for sham or artifice. Whatever happened, he must be real. He couldn't talk their talk just yet, though in time he would. Upon that he was resolved. But in the meantime, talk he must, and it must be his own talk, toned down, of course, so as to be comprehensible to them and so as not to shock them too much. And furthermore, he wouldn't claim, not even by tacit acceptance, to be familiar with anything that was unfamiliar. In pursuance of this decision, when the two brothers, talking university shop, had used "trig" several times, Martin Eden demanded:—

"What is *trig*?"

"Trigonometry," Norman said; "a higher form of math."

"And what is *math*?" was the next question, which, somehow, brought the laugh on Norman.

"Mathematics, arithmetic," was the answer.

Martin Eden nodded. He had caught a glimpse of the apparently illimitable vistas of knowledge. What he saw took on tangibility. His abnormal power of vision made abstractions take on concrete form. In the alchemy of his brain, trigonometry and mathematics and the whole field of knowledge which they betokened were transmuted into so much landscape. The vistas he saw were vistas of green foliage and forest glades, all softly luminous or shot through with flashing lights. In the distance, detail was veiled and blurred by a purple haze, but behind this purple haze, he knew, was the glamour of the unknown, the lure of romance. It was like wine to him. Here was adventure, something to do with head and hand, a world to conquer—and straightway from the back of his consciousness rushed the thought, *conquering, to win to her, that lily-pale spirit sitting beside him.*

The glimmering vision was rent asunder and dissipated by Arthur, who, all evening, had been trying to draw his wild man out. Martin Eden remembered his decision. For the first time he became himself, consciously and deliberately at first, but soon lost in the joy of creating, in making life as he knew it appear before his listeners' eyes. He had been a member of the crew of the smuggling schooner *Halcyon* when she was captured by a revenue cutter. He saw with wide eyes, and he could tell what he saw. He brought the pulsing sea before them, and the men and the ships upon the sea. He commu-

nicated his power of vision, till they saw with his eyes what
he had seen. He selected from the vast mass of detail with an
artist's touch, drawing pictures of life that glowed and
burned with light and color, injecting movement so that his
listeners surged along with him on the flood of rough elo-
quence, enthusiasm, and power. At times he shocked them
with the vividness of the narrative and his terms of speech,
but beauty always followed fast upon the heels of violence,
and tragedy was relieved by humor, by interpretations of the
strange twists and quirks of sailors' minds.

And while he talked, the girl looked at him with startled
eyes. His fire warmed her. She wondered if she had been cold
all her days. She wanted to lean toward this burning, blazing
man that was like a volcano spouting forth strength, robust-
ness, and health. She felt that she must lean toward him, and
resisted by an effort. Then, too, there was the counter impulse to shrink away from him. She was repelled by those
lacerated hands, grimed by toil so that the very dirt of life
was ingrained in the flesh itself, by that red chafe of the collar
and those bulging muscles. His roughness frightened her;
each roughness of speech was an insult to her ear, each rough
phase of his life an insult to her soul. And ever and again
would come the draw of him, till she thought he must be evil
to have such power over her. All that was most firmly established in her mind was rocking. His romance and adventure
were battering at the conventions. Before his facile perils and
ready laugh, life was no longer an affair of serious effort and
restraint, but a toy, to be played with and turned topsy-turvy,
carelessly to be lived and pleasured in, and carelessly to be
flung aside. "Therefore, play!" was the cry that rang through
her. "Lean toward him, if so you will, and place your two
hands upon his neck!" She wanted to cry out at the recklessness of the thought, and in vain she appraised her own cleanness and culture and balanced all that she was against what he
was not. She glanced about her and saw the others gazing at
him with rapt attention; and she would have despaired had
not she seen horror in her mother's eyes—fascinated horror,
it was true, but none the less horror. This man from outer
darkness was evil. Her mother saw it, and her mother was
right. She would trust her mother's judgment in this as she

had always trusted it in all things. The fire of him was no longer warm, and the fear of him was no longer poignant.

Later, at the piano, she played for him, and at him, aggressively, with the vague intent of emphasizing the impassableness of the gulf that separated them. Her music was a club that she swung brutally upon his head; and though it stunned him and crushed him down, it incited him. He gazed upon her in awe. In his mind, as in her own, the gulf widened; but faster than it widened, towered his ambition to win across it. But he was too complicated a plexus of sensibilities to sit staring at a gulf a whole evening, especially when there was music. He was remarkably susceptible to music. It was like strong drink, firing him to audacities of feeling,—a drug that laid hold of his imagination and went cloud-soaring through the sky. It banished sordid fact, flooded his mind with beauty, loosed romance and to its heels added wings. He did not understand the music she played. It was different from the dance-hall piano-banging and blatant brass bands he had heard. But he had caught hints of such music from the books, and he accepted her playing largely on faith, patiently waiting, at first, for the lilting measures of pronounced and simple rhythm, puzzled because those measures were not long continued. Just as he caught the swing of them and started, his imagination attuned in flight, always they vanished away in a chaotic scramble of sounds that was meaningless to him, and that dropped his imagination, an inert weight, back to earth.

Once, it entered his mind that there was a deliberate rebuff in all this. He caught her spirit of antagonism and strove to divine the message that her hands pronounced upon the keys. Then he dismissed the thought as unworthy and impossible, and yielded himself more freely to the music. The old delightful condition began to be induced. His feet were no longer clay, and his flesh became spirit; before his eyes and behind his eyes shone a great glory; and then the scene before him vanished and he was away, rocking over the world that was to him a very dear world. The known and the unknown were commingled in the dream-pageant that thronged his vision. He entered strange ports of sun-washed lands, and trod market-places among barbaric peoples that no man had ever seen. The scent of the spice islands was in his nostrils as he had known it on warm, breathless nights at sea, or he beat up against the southeast trades through long tropic days, sinking palm-tufted coral islets in the turquoise sea behind and lifting palm-tufted coral islets in the turquoise sea ahead. Swift as thought the pictures came and went. One instant he was astride a broncho and flying through the fairy-colored Painted Desert country; the next instant he was gazing down through shimmering heat into the whited sepulchre of Death Valley, or pulling an oar on a freezing ocean where great ice islands towered and glistened in the sun. He lay on a coral beach where the cocoanuts grew down to the mellow-sounding surf. The hulk of an ancient wreck burned with blue fires, in the light of which danced the *hula* dancers to the barbaric love-calls of the singers, who chanted to tinkling *ukuleles* and rumbling tom-toms. It was a sensuous, tropic night. In the background a volcano crater was silhouetted against the stars. Overhead drifted a pale crescent moon, and the Southern Cross burned low in the sky.

He was a harp; all life that he had known and that was his consciousness was the strings; and the flood of music was a wind that poured against those strings and set them vibrating with memories and dreams. He did not merely feel. Sensation invested itself in form and color and radiance, and what his imagination dared, it objectified in some sublimated and magic way. Past, present, and future mingled; and he went on oscillating across the broad, warm world, through high adventure and noble deeds to Her—ay, and with her, winning her, his arm about her, and carrying her on in flight through the empery of his mind.

And she, glancing at him across her shoulder, saw something of all this in his face. It was a transfigured face, with great shining eyes that gazed beyond the veil of sound and saw behind it the leap and pulse of life and the gigantic phantoms of the spirit. She was startled. The raw, stumbling lout was gone. The ill-fitting clothes, battered hands, and sunburned face remained; but these seemed the prison-bars through which she saw a great soul looking forth, inarticulate and dumb because of those feeble lips that would not give it speech. Only for a flashing moment did she see this, then she saw the lout returned, and she laughed at the whim of her fancy. But the impression of that fleeting glimpse lingered, and when the time came for him to beat a stumbling retreat and go, she lent him the volume of Swinburne, and another of Browning—she was studying Browning in one of her English courses. He seemed such a boy, as he stood blushing and stammering his thanks, that a wave of pity, maternal in its prompting, welled up in her. She did not remember the lout, nor the imprisoned soul, nor the man who had stared at her in all masculineness and delighted and frightened her. She saw before her only a boy, who was shaking her hand with a hand so calloused that it felt like a nutmeg-grater and rasped her skin, and who was saying jerkily:—

"The greatest time of my life. You see, I ain't used to things. . . ." He looked about him helplessly. "To people and houses like this. It's all new to me, and I like it."

"I hope you'll call again," she said, as he was saying good night to her brothers.

He pulled on his cap, lurched desperately through the doorway, and was gone.

"Well, what do you think of him?" Arthur demanded.

"He is most interesting, a whiff of ozone," she answered. "How old is he?"

"Twenty—almost twenty-one. I asked him this afternoon. I didn't think he was that young."

And I am three years older, was the thought in her mind as she kissed her brothers good night.

Chapter III

As Martin Eden went down the steps, his hand dropped into his coat pocket. It came out with a brown rice paper and a pinch of Mexican tobacco, which were deftly rolled together into a cigarette. He drew the first whiff of smoke deep into his lungs and expelled it in a long and lingering exhalation. "By God!" he said aloud, in a voice of awe and wonder. "By God!" he repeated. And yet again he murmured, "By God!" Then his hand went to his collar, which he ripped out of the shirt and stuffed into his pocket. A cold drizzle was falling, but he bared his head to it and unbuttoned his vest, swinging along in splendid unconcern. He was only dimly aware that it was raining. He was in an ecstasy, dreaming dreams and reconstructing the scenes just past.

He had met the woman at last—the woman that he had thought little about, not being given to thinking about women, but whom he had expected, in a remote way, he would sometime meet. He had sat next to her at table. He had felt her hand in his, he had looked into her eyes and caught a vision of a beautiful spirit;—but no more beautiful than the eyes through which it shone, nor than the flesh that gave it expression and form. He did not think of her flesh as flesh,—which was new to him; for of the women he had known that was the only way he thought. Her flesh was somehow different. He did not conceive of her body as a body, subject to the ills and frailties of bodies. Her body was more than the garb of her spirit. It was an emanation of her spirit, a pure and gracious crystallization of her divine essence. This feeling of the divine startled him. It shocked him from his dreams to sober thought. No word, no clew, no hint, of the divine had ever reached him before. He had never believed in the divine. He had always been irreligious, scoffing good-naturedly at the sky-pilots and their immortality of the soul. There was no life beyond, he had contended; it was here and now, then darkness everlasting. But what he had seen in her eyes was soul—immortal soul that could never die. No man he had known, nor any woman, had given him the message of immortality. But she had. She had whispered it to him the first moment she looked at him. Her face shimmered before his eyes as he walked along,—pale and serious, sweet and sensitive, smiling with pity and tenderness as only a spirit could smile, and pure as he had never dreamed purity could be. Her purity smote him like a blow. It startled him. He had known good and bad; but purity, as an attribute of existence, had never entered his mind. And now, in her, he conceived purity to be the superlative of goodness and of cleanness, the sum of which constituted eternal life.

And promptly urged his ambition to grasp at eternal life. He was not fit to carry water for her—he knew that; it was a miracle of luck and a fantastic stroke that had enabled him to see her and be with her and talk with her that night. It was accidental. There was no merit in it. He did not deserve such fortune. His mood was essentially religious. He was humble and meek, filled with self-disparagement and abasement. In such frame of mind sinners come to the penitent form. He was convicted of sin. But as the meek and lowly at the penitent form catch splendid glimpses of their future lordly existence, so did he catch similar glimpses of the state he would gain to by possessing her. But this possession of her was dim and nebulous and totally different from possession as he had known it. Ambition soared on mad wings, and he saw himself climbing the heights with her, sharing thoughts with her, pleasuring in beautiful and noble things with her. It was a soul-possession he dreamed, refined beyond any grossness, a free comradeship of spirit that he could not put into definite thought. He did not think it. For that matter, he did not think at all. Sensation usurped reason, and he was quivering and palpitant with emotions he had never known, drifting deliciously on a sea of sensibility where feeling itself was exalted and spiritualized and carried beyond the summits of life.

He staggered along like a drunken man, murmuring fervently aloud: "By God! By God!"

A policeman on a street corner eyed him suspiciously, then noted his sailor roll.

"Where did you get it?" the policeman demanded.

Martin Eden came back to earth. His was a fluid organism,

swiftly adjustable, capable of flowing into and filling all sorts of nooks and crannies. With the policeman's hail he was immediately his ordinary self, grasping the situation clearly.

"It's a beaut, ain't it?" he laughed back. "I didn't know I was talkin' out loud."

"You'll be singing next," was the policeman's diagnosis.

"No, I won't. Gimme a match an' I'll catch the next car home."

He lighted his cigarette, said good night, and went on. "Now wouldn't that rattle you?" he ejaculated under his breath. "That copper thought I was drunk." He smiled to himself and meditated. "I guess I was," he added; "but I didn't think a woman's face'd do it."

He caught a Telegraph Avenue car that was going to Berkeley. It was crowded with youths and young men who were singing songs and ever and again barking out college yells. He studied them curiously. They were university boys. They went to the same university that she did, were in her class socially, could know her, could see her every day if they wanted to. He wondered that they did not want to, that they had been out having a good time instead of being with her that evening, talking with her, sitting around her in a worshipful and adoring circle. His thoughts wandered on. He noticed one with narrow-slitted eyes and a loose-lipped mouth. That fellow was vicious, he decided. On shipboard he would be a sneak, a whiner, a tattler. He, Martin Eden, was a better man than that fellow. The thought cheered him. It seemed to draw him nearer to Her. He began comparing himself with the students. He grew conscious of the muscled mechanism of his body and felt confident that he was physically their master. But their heads were filled with knowledge that enabled them to talk her talk,—the thought depressed him. But what was a brain for? he demanded passionately. What they had done, he could do. They had been studying about life from the books while he had been busy living life. His brain was just as full of knowledge as theirs, though it was a different kind of knowledge. How many of them could tie a lanyard knot, or take a wheel or a lookout? His life spread out before him in a series of pictures of danger and daring, hardship and toil. He remembered his failures and scrapes in the process of learning. He was that much to the good, anyway. Later on they would have to begin living life and going through the mill as he had gone. Very well. While they were busy with that, he could be learning the other side of life from the books.

As the car crossed the zone of scattered dwellings that separated Oakland from Berkeley, he kept a lookout for a familiar, two-story building along the front of which ran the proud sign, HIGGINBOTHAM'S CASH STORE. Martin Eden got off at this corner. He stared up for a moment at the sign. It carried a message to him beyond its mere wording. A personality of smallness and egotism and petty underhandedness seemed to emanate from the letters themselves. Bernard Higginbotham had married his sister, and he knew him well. He let himself in with a latch-key and climbed the stairs to the second floor. Here lived his brother-in-law. The grocery was below. There was a smell of stale vegetables in the air. As he groped his way across the hall he stumbled over a toy-cart, left there by one of his numerous nephews and nieces, and brought up against a door with a resounding bang. "The pincher," was his thought; "too miserly to burn two cents' worth of gas and save his boarders' necks."

He fumbled for the knob and entered a lighted room, where sat his sister and Bernard Higginbotham. She was patching a pair of his trousers, while his lean body was distributed over two chairs, his feet dangling in dilapidated carpet-slippers over the edge of the second chair. He glanced across the top of the paper he was reading, showing a pair of dark, insincere, sharp-staring eyes. Martin Eden never looked at him without experiencing a sense of repulsion. What his sister had seen in the man was beyond him. The other affected him as so much vermin, and always aroused in him an impulse to crush him under his foot. "Some day I'll beat the face off of him," was the way he often consoled himself for enduring the man's existence. The eyes, weasel-like and cruel, were looking at him complainingly.

"Well," Martin demanded. "Out with it."

"I had that door painted only last week," Mr. Higginbotham half whined, half bullied; "and you know what union wages are. You should be more careful."

Martin had intended to reply, but he was struck by the hopelessness of it. He gazed across the monstrous sordidness of soul to a chromo on the wall. It surprised him. He had always liked it, but it seemed that now he was seeing it for the first time. It was cheap, that was what it was, like everything else in this house. His mind went back to the house he had just left, and he saw, first, the paintings, and next, Her, looking at him with melting sweetness as she shook his hand at leaving. He forgot where he was and Bernard Higginbotham's existence, till that gentleman demanded: —

"Seen a ghost?"

Martin came back and looked at the beady eyes, sneering, truculent, cowardly, and there leaped into his vision, as on a screen, the same eyes when their owner was making a sale in the store below—subservient eyes, smug, and oily, and flattering.

"Yes," Martin answered. "I seen a ghost. Good night. Good night, Gertrude."

He started to leave the room, tripping over a loose seam in the slatternly carpet.

"Don't bang the door," Mr. Higginbotham cautioned him.

He felt the blood crawl in his veins, but controlled himself and closed the door softly behind him.

Mr. Higginbotham looked at his wife exultantly.

"He's ben drinkin'," he proclaimed in a hoarse whisper. "I told you he would."

She nodded her head resignedly.

"His eyes was pretty shiny," she confessed; "and he didn't have no collar, though he went away with one. But mebbe he didn't have more'n a couple of glasses."

"He couldn't stand up straight," asserted her husband. "I watched him. He couldn't walk across the floor without stumblin'. You heard 'm yourself almost fall down in the hall."

"I think it was over Alice's cart," she said. "He couldn't see it in the dark."

Mr. Higginbotham's voice and wrath began to rise. All day he effaced himself in the store, reserving for the evening, with his family, the privilege of being himself.

"I tell you that precious brother of yours was drunk."

His voice was cold, sharp, and final, his lips stamping the enunciation of each word like the die of a machine. His wife sighed and remained silent. She was a large, stout woman, always dressed slatternly and always tired from the burdens of her flesh, her work, and her husband.

"He's got it in him, I tell you, from his father," Mr. Higginbotham went on accusingly. "An' he'll croak in the gutter the same way. You know that."

She nodded, sighed, and went on stitching. They were agreed that Martin had come home drunk. They did not have it in their souls to know beauty or they would have known that those shining eyes and that glowing face betokened youth's first vision of love.

"Settin' a fine example to the children," Mr. Higginbotham snorted, suddenly, in the silence for which his wife was responsible and which he resented. Sometimes he almost wished she would oppose him more. "If he does it again, he's got to get out. Understand! I won't put up with his shinanigan—debotchin' innocent children with his boozing." Mr. Higginbotham liked the word, which was a new one in his vocabulary, recently gleaned from a newspaper column. "That's what it is, debotchin'—there ain't no other name for it."

Still his wife sighed, shook her head sorrowfully, and stitched on. Mr. Higginbotham resumed the newspaper.

"Has he paid last week's board?" he shot across the top of the newspaper.

She nodded, then added, "He still has some money."

"When is he goin' to sea again?"

"When his pay-day's spent, I guess," she answered. "He was over to San Francisco yesterday looking for a ship. But he's got money, yet, an' he's particular about the kind of ship he signs for."

"It's not for a deck-swab like him to put on airs," Mr. Higginbotham snorted. "Particular! Him!"

"He said something about a schooner that's gettin' ready to go off to some outlandish place to look for buried treasure, that he'd sail on her if his money held out."

"If he only wanted to steady down, I'd give him a job drivin' the wagon," her husband said, but with no trace of benevolence in his voice. "Tom's quit."

His wife looked alarm and interrogation.

"Quit to-night. Is goin' to work for Carruthers. They paid 'm more'n I could afford."

"I told you you'd lose 'm," she cried out. "He was worth more'n you was giving him."

"Now look here, old woman," Higginbotham bullied, "for the thousandth time I've told you to keep your nose out of the business. I won't tell you again."

"I don't care," she sniffled. "Tom was a good boy."

Her husband glared at her. This was unqualified defiance.

"If that brother of yours was worth his salt, he could take the wagon," he snorted.

"He pays his board, just the same," was the retort. "An' he's my brother, an' so long as he don't owe you money you've got no right to be jumping on him all the time. I've got some feelings, if I have been married to you for seven years."

"Did you tell 'm you'd charge him for gas if he goes on readin' in bed?" he demanded.

Mrs. Higginbotham made no reply. Her revolt faded away, her spirit wilting down into her tired flesh. Her husband was triumphant. He had her. His eyes snapped vindictively, while his ears joyed in the sniffles she emitted. He extracted great happiness from squelching her, and she squelched easily these days, though it had been different in the first years of their married life, before the brood of children and his incessant nagging had sapped her energy.

"Well, you tell 'm to-morrow, that's all," he said. "An' I just want to tell you, before I forget it, that you'd better send for Marian to-morrow to take care of the children. With Tom quit, I'll have to be out on the wagon, an' you can make up your mind to it to be down below waitin' on the counter."

"But to-morrow's wash day," she objected weakly.

"Get up early, then, an' do it first. I won't start out till ten o'clock."

He crinkled the paper viciously and resumed his reading.

Chapter IV

MARTIN EDEN, with blood still crawling from contact with his brother-in-law, felt his way along the unlighted back hall and entered his room, a tiny cubbyhole with space for a bed, a wash-stand, and one chair. Mr. Higginbotham was too thrifty to keep a servant when his wife could do the work. Besides, the servant's room enabled them to take in two boarders instead of one. Martin placed the Swinburne and Browning on the chair, took off his coat, and sat down on the bed. A screeching of asthmatic springs greeted the weight of his body, but he did not notice them. He started to take off his shoes, but fell to staring at the white plaster wall opposite him, broken by long streaks of dirty brown where rain had leaked through the roof. On this befouled background visions began to flow and burn. He forgot his shoes and stared long, till his lips began to move and he murmured, "Ruth."

"Ruth." He had not thought a simple sound could be so beautiful. It delighted his ear, and he grew intoxicated with the repetition of it. "Ruth." It was a talisman, a magic word to conjure with. Each time he murmured it, her face shimmered before him, suffusing the foul wall with a golden radiance. This radiance did not stop at the wall. It extended on into infinity, and through its golden depths his soul went questing after hers. The best that was in him was pouring out in splendid flood. The very thought of her ennobled and purified him, made him better, and made him want to be better. This was new to him. He had never known women who had made him better. They had always had the counter effect of making him beastly. He did not know that many of them had done their best, bad as it was. Never having been conscious of himself, he did not know that he had that in his being that drew love from women and which had been the cause of their reaching out for his youth. Though they had often bothered him, he had never bothered about them; and he would never have dreamed that there were women who had been better because of him. Always in sublime carelessness had he lived, till now, and now it seemed to him that they had always reached out and dragged at him with vile hands. This was not just to them, nor to himself. But he, who for the first time was becoming conscious of himself, was in no condition to judge, and he burned with shame as he stared at the vision of his infamy.

He got up abruptly and tried to see himself in the dirty looking-glass over the wash-stand. He passed a towel over it and looked again, long and carefully. It was the first time he had ever really seen himself. His eyes were made for seeing, but up to that moment they had been filled with the ever changing panorama of the world, at which he had been too busy gazing, ever to gaze at himself. He saw the head and face of a young fellow of twenty, but, being unused to such appraisement, he did not know how to value it. Above a square-domed forehead he saw a mop of brown hair, nut-brown, with a wave to it and hints of curls that were a delight to any woman, making hands tingle to stroke it and fingers tingle to pass caresses through it. But he passed it by as without merit, in Her eyes, and dwelt long and thoughtfully on the high, square forehead,—striving to penetrate it and learn the quality of its content. What kind of a brain lay behind there? was his insistent interrogation. What was it capable of? How far would it take him? Would it take him to her?

He wondered if there was soul in those steel-gray eyes that were often quite blue of color and that were strong with the briny airs of the sun-washed deep. He wondered, also, how his eyes looked to her. He tried to imagine himself she, gazing into those eyes of his, but failed in the jugglery. He could successfully put himself inside other men's minds, but they had to be men whose ways of life he knew. He did not know her way of life. She was wonder and mystery, and how could he guess one thought of hers? Well, they were honest eyes, he concluded, and in them was neither smallness nor meanness. The brown sunburn of his face surprised him. He had not dreamed he was so black. He rolled up his shirt-sleeve and compared the white underside of the arm with his face. Yes, he was a white man, after all. But the arms were sunburned, too. He twisted his arm, rolled the biceps over with his other hand, and gazed underneath where he was least touched by the sun. It was very white. He laughed at his bronzed face in the glass at the thought that it was once as white as the underside of his arm; nor did he dream that in the world there were few pale spirits of women who could boast fairer or smoother skins than he—fairer than where he had escaped the ravages of the sun.

His might have been a cherub's mouth, had not the full, sensuous lips a trick, under stress, of drawing firmly across the teeth. At times, so tightly did they draw, the mouth became stern and harsh, even ascetic. They were the lips of a fighter and of a lover. They could taste the sweetness of life with relish, and they could put the sweetness aside and command life. The chin and jaw, strong and just hinting of square aggressiveness, helped the lips to command life. Strength balanced sensuousness and had upon it a tonic effect, compelling him to love beauty that was healthy and making him vibrate to sensations that were wholesome. And between the lips were teeth that had never known nor needed the dentist's care. They were white and strong and regular, he decided, as he looked at them. But as he looked, he began to be troubled. Somewhere, stored away in the recesses of his mind and vaguely remembered, was the impression that there were people who washed their teeth every day. They were the people from up above—people in her class. She must wash her teeth every day, too. What would she think if she learned that he had never washed his teeth in all the days of his life? He resolved to get a tooth-brush and form the habit. He would begin at once, to-morrow. It was not by mere achievement that he could hope to win to her. He must make a personal reform in all things, even to tooth-washing and neck-gear, though a starched collar affected him as a renunciation of freedom.

He held up his hand, rubbing the ball of the thumb over the calloused palm and gazing at the dirt that was ingrained in the flesh itself and which no brush could scrub away. How different was her palm! He thrilled deliciously at the remembrance. Like a rose-petal, he thought; cool and soft as a snow-flake. He had never thought that a mere woman's hand could be so sweetly soft. He caught himself imagining the wonder of a caress from such a hand, and flushed guiltily. It was too

gross a thought for her. In ways it seemed to impugn her
high spirituality. She was a pale, slender spirit, exalted far beyond the flesh; but nevertheless the softness of her palm persisted in his thoughts. He was used to the harsh callousness
of factory girls and working women. Well he knew why their
hands were rough; but this hand of hers . . . It was soft
because she had never used it to work with. The gulf yawned
between her and him at the awesome thought of a person
who did not have to work for a living. He suddenly saw the
aristocracy of the people who did not labor. It towered before
him on the wall, a figure in brass, arrogant and powerful. He
had worked himself; his first memories seemed connected
with work, and all his family had worked. There was Gertrude. When her hands were not hard from the endless housework, they were swollen and red like boiled beef, what of the
washing. And there was his sister Marian. She had worked in
the cannery the preceding summer, and her slim, pretty hands
were all scarred with the tomato-knives. Besides, the tips of
two of her fingers had been left in the cutting machine at the
paper-box factory the preceding winter. He remembered the
hard palms of his mother as she lay in her coffin. And his
father had worked to the last fading gasp; the horned growth
on his hands must have been half an inch thick when he died.
But Her hands were soft, and her mother's hands, and her
brothers'. This last came to him as a surprise; it was tremendously indicative of the highness of their caste, of the enormous distance that stretched between her and him.

He sat back on the bed with a bitter laugh, and finished
taking off his shoes. He was a fool; he had been made drunk-
en by a woman's face and by a woman's soft, white hands.
And then, suddenly, before his eyes, on the foul plaster-wall
appeared a vision. He stood in front of a gloomy tenement
house. It was night-time, in the East End of London, and
before him stood Margey, a little factory girl of fifteen. He
had seen her home after the bean-feast. She lived in that
gloomy tenement, a place not fit for swine. His hand was
going out to hers as he said good night. She had put her lips
up to be kissed, but he wasn't going to kiss her. Somehow he
was afraid of her. And then her hand closed on his and
pressed feverishly. He felt her callouses grind and grate on

his, and a great wave of pity welled over him. He saw her yearning, hungry eyes, and her ill-fed female form which had been rushed from childhood into a frightened and ferocious maturity; then he put his arms about her in large tolerance and stooped and kissed her on the lips. Her glad little cry rang in his ears, and he felt her clinging to him like a cat. Poor little starveling! He continued to stare at the vision of what had happened in the long ago. His flesh was crawling as it had crawled that night when she clung to him, and his heart was warm with pity. It was a gray scene, greasy gray, and the rain drizzled greasily on the pavement stones. And then a radiant glory shone on the wall, and up through the other vision, displacing it, glimmered Her pale face under its crown of golden hair, remote and inaccessible as a star.

He took the Browning and the Swinburne from the chair and kissed them. Just the same, she told me to call again, he thought. He took another look at himself in the glass, and said aloud, with great solemnity: —

"Martin Eden, the first thing to-morrow you go to the free library an' read up on etiquette. Understand!"

He turned off the gas, and the springs shrieked under his body.

"But you've got to quit cussin', Martin, old boy; you've got to quit cussin'," he said aloud.

Then he dozed off to sleep and to dream dreams that for madness and audacity rivalled those of poppy-eaters.

Chapter V

HE AWOKE next morning from rosy scenes of dream to a steamy atmosphere that smelled of soapsuds and dirty clothes, and that was vibrant with the jar and jangle of tormented life. As he came out of his room he heard the slosh of water, a sharp exclamation, and a resounding smack as his sister visited her irritation upon one of her numerous progeny. The squall of the child went through him like a knife. He was aware that the whole thing, the very air he breathed, was repulsive and mean. How different, he thought, from the atmosphere of beauty and repose of the house wherein Ruth dwelt. There it was all spiritual. Here it was all material, and meanly material.

"Come here, Alfred," he called to the crying child, at the same time thrusting his hand into his trousers pocket, where he carried his money loose in the same large way that he lived life in general. He put a quarter in the youngster's hand and held him in his arms a moment, soothing his sobs. "Now run along and get some candy, and don't forget to give some to your brothers and sisters. Be sure and get the kind that lasts longest."

His sister lifted a flushed face from the wash-tub and looked at him.

"A nickel'd ha' ben enough," she said. "It's just like you, no idea of the value of money. The child'll eat himself sick."

"That's all right, sis," he answered jovially. "My money'll take care of itself. If you weren't so busy, I'd kiss you good morning."

He wanted to be affectionate to this sister, who was good, and who, in her way, he knew, loved him. But, somehow, she grew less herself as the years went by, and more and more baffling. It was the hard work, the many children, and the nagging of her husband, he decided, that had changed her. It came to him, in a flash of fancy, that her nature seemed taking on the attributes of stale vegetables, smelly soapsuds, and of the greasy dimes, nickels, and quarters she took in over the counter of the store.

"Go along an' get your breakfast," she said roughly, though secretly pleased. Of all her wandering brood of brothers he had always been her favorite. "I declare I *will* kiss you," she said, with a sudden stir at her heart.

With thumb and forefinger she swept the dripping suds first from one arm and then from the other. He put his arms round her massive waist and kissed her wet, steamy lips. The tears welled into her eyes—not so much from strength of feeling as from the weakness of chronic overwork. She shoved him away from her, but not before he caught a glimpse of her moist eyes.

"You'll find breakfast in the oven," she said hurriedly. "Jim ought to be up now. I had to get up early for the washing. Now get along with you and get out of the house early. It won't be nice to-day, what of Tom quittin' an' nobody but Bernard to drive the wagon."

Martin went into the kitchen with a sinking heart, the image of her red face and slatternly form eating its way like acid into his brain. She might love him if she only had some time, he concluded. But she was worked to death. Bernard Higginbotham was a brute to work her so hard. But he could not help but feel, on the other hand, that there had not been anything beautiful in that kiss. It was true, it was an unusual kiss. For years she had kissed him only when he returned from voyages or departed on voyages. But this kiss had tasted of soapsuds, and the lips, he had noticed, were flabby. There had been no quick, vigorous lip-pressure such as should accompany any kiss. Hers was the kiss of a tired woman who had been tired so long that she had forgotten how to kiss. He remembered her as a girl, before her marriage, when she would dance with the best, all night, after a hard day's work at the laundry, and think nothing of leaving the dance to go to another day's hard work. And then he thought of Ruth and the cool sweetness that must reside in her lips as it resided in all about her. Her kiss would be like her hand-shake or the way she looked at one, firm and frank. In imagination he dared to think of her lips on his, and so vividly did he imagine that he went dizzy at the thought and seemed to rift through clouds of rose-petals, filling his brain with their perfume.

In the kitchen he found Jim, the other boarder, eating mush very languidly, with a sick, far-away look in his eyes. Jim was a plumber's apprentice whose weak chin and hedonistic temperament, coupled with a certain nervous stupidity, promised to take him nowhere in the race for bread and butter.

"Why don't you eat?" he demanded, as Martin dipped dolefully into the cold, half-cooked oatmeal mush. "Was you drunk again last night?"

Martin shook his head. He was oppressed by the utter squalidness of it all. Ruth Morse seemed farther removed than ever.

"I was," Jim went on with a boastful, nervous giggle. "I was loaded right to the neck. Oh, she was a daisy. Billy brought me home."

Martin nodded that he heard,—it was a habit of nature with him to pay heed to whoever talked to him,—and poured a cup of lukewarm coffee.

"Goin' to the Lotus Club dance to-night?" Jim demanded. "They're goin' to have beer, an' if that Temescal bunch comes, there'll be a rough-house. I don't care, though. I'm takin' my lady friend just the same. Cripes, but I've got a taste in my mouth!"

He made a wry face and attempted to wash the taste away with coffee.

"D'ye know Julia?"

Martin shook his head.

"She's my lady friend," Jim explained, "and she's a peach. I'd introduce you to her, only you'd win her. I don't see what the girls see in you, honest I don't; but the way you win them away from the fellers is sickenin'."

"I never got any away from you," Martin answered uninterestedly. The breakfast had to be got through somehow.

"Yes, you did, too," the other asserted warmly. "There was Maggie."

"Never had anything to do with her. Never danced with her except that one night."

"Yes, an' that's just what did it," Jim cried out. "You just danced with her an' looked at her, an' it was all off. Of course you didn't mean nothin' by it, but it settled me for keeps. Wouldn't look at me again. Always askin' about you. She'd have made fast dates enough with you if you'd wanted to."

"But I didn't want to."

"Wasn't necessary. I was left at the pole." Jim looked at him admiringly. "How d'ye do it, anyway, Mart?"

"By not carin' about 'em," was the answer.

"You mean makin' b'lieve you don't care about them?" Jim queried eagerly.

Martin considered for a moment, then answered, "Perhaps that will do, but with me I guess it's different. I never have cared—much. If you can put it on, it's all right, most likely."

"You should 'a' ben up at Riley's barn last night," Jim announced inconsequently. "A lot of the fellers put on the gloves. There was a peach from West Oakland. They called 'm 'The Rat.' Slick as silk. No one could touch 'm. We was all wishin' you was there. Where was you anyway?"

"Down in Oakland," Martin replied.

"To the show?"

Martin shoved his plate away and got up.

"Comin' to the dance to-night?" the other called after him.

"No, I think not," he answered.

He went downstairs and out into the street, breathing great breaths of air. He had been suffocating in that atmosphere, while the apprentice's chatter had driven him frantic. There had been times when it was all he could do to refrain from reaching over and mopping Jim's face in the mush-plate. The more he had chattered, the more remote had Ruth seemed to him. How could he, herding with such cattle, ever become worthy of her? He was appalled at the problem confronting him, weighted down by the incubus of his working-class station. Everything reached out to hold him down—his sister, his sister's house and family, Jim the apprentice, everybody he knew, every tie of life. Existence did not taste good in his mouth. Up to then he had accepted existence, as he had lived it with all about him, as a good thing. He had never questioned it, except when he read books; but then, they were only books, fairy stories of a fairer and impossible world. But now he had seen that world, possible and real, with a flower of a woman called Ruth in the midmost centre of it; and thenceforth he must know bitter tastes, and longings sharp as pain, and hopelessness that tantalized because it fed on hope.

He had debated between the Berkeley Free Library and the Oakland Free Library, and decided upon the latter because Ruth lived in Oakland. Who could tell?—a library was a most likely place for her, and he might see her there. He did not know the way of libraries, and he wandered through end-less rows of fiction, till the delicate-featured French-looking girl who seemed in charge, told him that the reference de-partment was upstairs. He did not know enough to ask the man at the desk, and began his adventures in the philosophy alcove. He had heard of book philosophy, but had not imag-ined there had been so much written about it. The high, bulging shelves of heavy tomes humbled him and at the same time stimulated him. Here was work for the vigor of his brain. He found books on trigonometry in the mathematics section, and ran the pages, and stared at the meaningless for-mulas and figures. He could read English, but he saw there an alien speech. Norman and Arthur knew that speech. He had heard them talking it. And they were her brothers. He left the alcove in despair. From every side the books seemed to press upon him and crush him. He had never dreamed that the fund of human knowledge bulked so big. He was fright-ened. How could his brain ever master it all? Later, he re-membered that there were other men, many men, who had mastered it; and he breathed a great oath, passionately, under his breath, swearing that his brain could do what theirs had done.

And so he wandered on, alternating between depression and elation as he stared at the shelves packed with wisdom. In one miscellaneous section he came upon a "Norrie's Epit-ome." He turned the pages reverently. In a way, it spoke a kindred speech. Both he and it were of the sea. Then he found a "Bowditch" and books by Lecky and Marshall. There it was; he would teach himself navigation. He would quit drinking, work up, and become a captain. Ruth seemed very near to him in that moment. As a captain, he could marry her (if she would have him). And if she wouldn't, well—he would live a good life among men, because of Her, and he would quit drinking anyway. Then he remembered the underwriters and the owners, the two masters a captain must serve, either of which could and would break him and whose interests were diametrically opposed. He cast his eyes about the room and closed the lids down on a vision of ten thousand books. No; no more of the sea for him. There was power in all that wealth of books, and if he would do great things, he must do them on the land. Besides, captains were not allowed to take their wives to sea with them.

Noon came, and afternoon. He forgot to eat, and sought on for the books on etiquette; for, in addition to career, his mind was vexed by a simple and very concrete problem: *When you meet a young lady and she asks you to call, how soon can you call?* was the way he worded it to himself. But when he found the right shelf, he sought vainly for the answer. He was appalled at the vast edifice of etiquette, and lost himself in the mazes of visiting-card conduct between persons in polite society. He abandoned his search. He had not found what he wanted, though he had found that it would take all of a man's time to be polite, and that he would have to live a preliminary life in which to learn how to be polite.

"Did you find what you wanted?" the man at the desk asked him as he was leaving.

"Yes, sir," he answered. "You have a fine library here."

The man nodded. "We should be glad to see you here often. Are you a sailor?"

"Yes, sir," he answered. "And I'll come again."

Now, how did he know that? he asked himself as he went down the stairs.

And for the first block along the street he walked very stiff and straight and awkwardly, until he forgot himself in his thoughts, whereupon his rolling gait gracefully returned to him.

Chapter VI

$\mathbf{A}$ TERRIBLE RESTLESSNESS that was akin to hunger afflicted Martin Eden. He was famished for a sight of the girl whose slender hands had gripped his life with a giant's grasp. He could not steel himself to call upon her. He was afraid that he might call too soon, and so be guilty of an awful breach of that awful thing called etiquette. He spent long hours in the Oakland and Berkeley libraries, and made out application blanks for membership for himself, his sisters Gertrude and Marian, and Jim, the latter's consent being obtained at the expense of several glasses of beer. With four cards permitting him to draw books, he burned the gas late in the servant's room, and was charged fifty cents a week for it by Mr. Higginbotham.

The many books he read but served to whet his unrest. Every page of every book was a peep-hole into the realm of knowledge. His hunger fed upon what he read, and increased. Also, he did not know where to begin, and continually suffered from lack of preparation. The commonest references, that he could see plainly every reader was expected to know, he did not know. And the same was true of the poetry he read which maddened him with delight. He read more of Swinburne than was contained in the volume Ruth had lent him; and "Dolores" he understood thoroughly. But surely Ruth did not understand it, he concluded. How could she, living the refined life she did? Then he chanced upon Kipling's poems, and was swept away by the lilt and swing and glamour with which familiar things had been invested. He was amazed at the man's sympathy with life and at his incisive psychology. *Psychology* was a new word in Martin's vocabulary. He had bought a dictionary, which deed had decreased his supply of money and brought nearer the day on which he must sail in search of more. Also, it incensed Mr. Higginbotham, who would have preferred the money taking the form of board.

He dared not go near Ruth's neighborhood in the daytime, but night found him lurking like a thief around the Morse home, stealing glimpses at the windows and loving the very walls that sheltered her. Several times he barely escaped being caught by her brothers, and once he trailed Mr. Morse down town and studied his face in the lighted streets, longing all the while for some quick danger of death to threaten so that he might spring in and save her father. On another night, his vigil was rewarded by a glimpse of Ruth through a second-story window. He saw only her head and shoulders, and her arms raised as she fixed her hair before a mirror. It was only for a moment, but it was a long moment to him, during which his blood turned to wine and sang through his veins. Then she pulled down the shade. But it was her room—he had learned that; and thereafter he strayed there often, hiding under a dark tree on the opposite side of the street and smoking countless cigarettes. One afternoon he saw her mother coming out of a bank, and received another proof of the enormous distance that separated Ruth from him. She was of the class that dealt with banks. He had never been inside a bank in his life, and he had an idea that such institutions were frequented only by the very rich and the very powerful.

In one way, he had undergone a moral revolution. Her cleanness and purity had reacted upon him, and he felt in his being a crying need to be clean. He must be that if he were ever to be worthy of breathing the same air with her. He washed his teeth, and scrubbed his hands with a kitchen scrub-brush till he saw a nail-brush in a drug-store window and divined its use. While purchasing it, the clerk glanced at his nails, suggested a nail-file, and so he became possessed of an additional toilet-tool. He ran across a book in the library on the care of the body, and promptly developed a penchant for a cold-water bath every morning, much to the amazement of Jim, and to the bewilderment of Mr. Higginbotham, who was not in sympathy with such high-fangled notions and who seriously debated whether or not he should charge Martin extra for the water. Another stride was in the direction of creased trousers. Now that Martin was aroused in such matters, he swiftly noted the difference between the baggy knees of the trousers worn by the working class and the straight line from knee to foot of those worn by the men above the working class. Also, he learned the reason why, and invaded his sister's kitchen in search of irons and ironing-board. He had misadventures at first, hopelessly burning one pair and buying another, which expenditure again brought nearer the day on which he must put to sea.

But the reform went deeper than mere outward appearance. He still smoked, but he drank no more. Up to that time, drinking had seemed to him the proper thing for men to do, and he had prided himself on his strong head which enabled him to drink most men under the table. Whenever he encountered a chance shipmate, and there were many in San Francisco, he treated them and was treated in turn, as of old, but he ordered for himself root beer or ginger ale and good-naturedly endured their chaffing. And as they waxed maudlin he studied them, watching the beast rise and master them and thanking God that he was no longer as they. They had their limitations to forget, and when they were drunk, their dim, stupid spirits were even as gods, and each ruled in his heaven of intoxicated desire. With Martin the need for strong drink had vanished. He was drunken in new and more profound ways—with Ruth, who had fired him with love and with a glimpse of higher and eternal life; with books, that had set a myriad maggots of desire gnawing in his brain; and with the sense of personal cleanliness he was achieving, that gave him even more superb health than what he had enjoyed and that made his whole body sing with physical well-being.

One night he went to the theatre, on the blind chance that he might see her there, and from the second balcony he did see her. He saw her come down the aisle, with Arthur and a strange young man with a football mop of hair and eye-glasses, the sight of whom spurred him to instant apprehension and jealousy. He saw her take her seat in the orchestra circle, and little else than her did he see that night—a pair of slender white shoulders and a mass of pale gold hair, dim with distance. But there were others who saw, and now and again, glancing at those about him, he noted two young girls who looked back from the row in front, a dozen seats along, and who smiled at him with bold eyes. He had always been easy-going. It was not in his nature to give rebuff. In the old days he would have smiled back, and gone further and en-couraged smiling. But now it was different. He did smile back, then looked away, and looked no more deliberately. But several times, forgetting the existence of the two girls, his eyes caught their smiles. He could not re-thumb himself in a day, nor could he violate the intrinsic kindliness of his nature; so, at such moments, he smiled at the girls in warm human friendliness. It was nothing new to him. He knew they were reaching out their woman's hands to him. But it was different now. Far down there in the orchestra circle was the one woman in all the world, so different, so terrifically different, from these two girls of his class, that he could feel for them only pity and sorrow. He had it in his heart to wish that they could possess, in some small measure, her goodness and glory. And not for the world could he hurt them because of their outreaching. He was not flattered by it; he even felt a slight shame at his lowliness that permitted it. He knew, did he belong in Ruth's class, that there would be no overtures from these girls; and with each glance of theirs he felt the fingers of his own class clutching at him to hold him down.

He left his seat before the curtain went down on the last act, intent on seeing Her as she passed out. There were always numbers of men who stood on the sidewalk outside, and he could pull his cap down over his eyes and screen himself behind some one's shoulder so that she should not see him. He emerged from the theatre with the first of the crowd; but scarcely had he taken his position on the edge of the sidewalk when the two girls appeared. They were looking for him, he knew; and for the moment he could have cursed that in him which drew women. Their casual edging across the sidewalk to the curb, as they drew near, apprised him of discovery. They slowed down, and were in the thick of the crowd as they came up with him. One of them brushed against him and apparently for the first time noticed him. She was a slender, dark girl, with black, defiant eyes. But they smiled at him, and he smiled back.

"Hello," he said.

It was automatic; he had said it so often before under similar circumstances of first meetings. Besides, he could do no less. There was that large tolerance and sympathy in his nature that would permit him to do no less. The black-eyed girl smiled gratification and greeting, and showed signs of stop-

ping, while her companion, arm linked in arm, giggled and
likewise showed signs of halting. He thought quickly. It
would never do for Her to come out and see him talking
there with them. Quite naturally, as a matter of course, he
swung in alongside the dark-eyed one and walked with her.
There was no awkwardness on his part, no numb tongue. He
was at home here, and he held his own royally in the badinage, bristling with slang and sharpness, that was always the
preliminary to getting acquainted in these swift-moving affairs. At the corner where the main stream of people flowed
onward, he started to edge out into the cross street. But the
girl with the black eyes caught his arm, following him and
dragging her companion after her, as she cried:—

"Hold on, Bill! What's yer rush? You're not goin' to shake
us so sudden as all that?"

He halted with a laugh, and turned, facing them. Across
their shoulders he could see the moving throng passing under
the street lamps. Where he stood it was not so light, and,
unseen, he would be able to see Her as she passed by. She
would certainly pass by, for that way led home.

"What's her name?" he asked of the giggling girl, nodding
at the dark-eyed one.

"You ask her," was the convulsed response.

"Well, what is it?" he demanded, turning squarely on the
girl in question.

"You ain't told me yours, yet," she retorted.

"You never asked it," he smiled. "Besides, you guessed the
first rattle. It's Bill, all right, all right."

"Aw, go 'long with you." She looked him in the eyes, her
own sharply passionate and inviting. "What is it, honest?"

Again she looked. All the centuries of woman since sex began were eloquent in her eyes. And he measured her in a
careless way, and knew, bold now, that she would begin to
retreat, coyly and delicately, as he pursued, ever ready to reverse the game should he turn faint-hearted. And, too, he was
human, and could feel the draw of her, while his ego could
not but appreciate the flattery of her kindness. Oh, he knew
it all, and knew them well, from A to Z. Good, as goodness
might be measured in their particular class, hard-working for
meagre wages and scorning the sale of self for easier ways,

nervously desirous for some small pinch of happiness in the desert of existence, and facing a future that was a gamble between the ugliness of unending toil and the black pit of more terrible wretchedness, the way whereto being briefer though better paid.

"Bill," he answered, nodding his head. "Sure, Pete, Bill an' no other."

"No joshin'?" she queried.

"It ain't Bill at all," the other broke in.

"How do you know?" he demanded. "You never laid eyes on me before."

"No need to, to know you're lyin'," was the retort.

"Straight, Bill, what is it?" the first girl asked.

"Bill'll do," he confessed.

She reached out to his arm and shook him playfully. "I knew you was lyin', but you look good to me just the same."

He captured the hand that invited, and felt on the palm familiar markings and distortions.

"When'd you chuck the cannery?" he asked.

"How'd yeh know?" and "My, ain't cheh a mind-reader!" the girls chorussed.

And while he exchanged the stupidities of stupid minds with them, before his inner sight towered the book-shelves of the library, filled with the wisdom of the ages. He smiled bitterly at the incongruity of it, and was assailed by doubts. But between inner vision and outward pleasantry he found time to watch the theatre crowd streaming by. And then he saw Her, under the lights, between her brother and the strange young man with glasses, and his heart seemed to stand still. He had waited long for this moment. He had time to note the light, fluffy something that hid her queenly head, the tasteful lines of her wrapped figure, the gracefulness of her carriage and of the hand that caught up her skirts; and then she was gone and he was left staring at the two girls of the cannery, at their tawdry attempts at prettiness of dress, their tragic efforts to be clean and trim, the cheap cloth, the cheap ribbons, and the cheap rings on the fingers. He felt a tug at his arm, and heard a voice saying:—

"Wake up, Bill! What's the matter with you?"

"What was you sayin'?" he asked.

"Oh, nothin'," the dark girl answered, with a toss of her head. "I was only remarkin'—"

"What?"

"Well, I was whisperin' it'd be a good idea if you could dig up a gentleman friend—for her" (indicating her companion), "and then, we could go off an' have ice-cream soda somewhere, or coffee, or anything."

He was afflicted by a sudden spiritual nausea. The transition from Ruth to this had been too abrupt. Ranged side by side with the bold, defiant eyes of the girl before him, he saw Ruth's clear, luminous eyes, like a saint's, gazing at him out of unplumbed depths of purity. And, somehow, he felt within him a stir of power. He was better than this. Life meant more to him than it meant to these two girls whose thoughts did not go beyond ice-cream and a gentleman friend. He remembered that he had led always a secret life in his thoughts. These thoughts he had tried to share, but never had he found a woman capable of understanding—nor a man. He had tried, at times, but had only puzzled his listeners. And as his thoughts had been beyond them, so, he argued now, he must be beyond them. He felt power move in him, and clenched his fists. If life meant more to him, then it was for him to demand more from life, but he could not demand it from such companionship as this. Those bold black eyes had nothing to offer. He knew the thoughts behind them—of ice-cream and of something else. But those saint's eyes alongside—they offered all he knew and more than he could guess. They offered books and painting, beauty and repose, and all the fine elegance of higher existence. Behind those black eyes he knew every thought process. It was like clockwork. He could watch every wheel go around. Their bid was low pleasure, narrow as the grave, that palled, and the grave was at the end of it. But the bid of the saint's eyes was mystery, and wonder unthinkable, and eternal life. He had caught glimpses of the soul in them, and glimpses of his own soul, too.

"There's only one thing wrong with the programme," he said aloud. "I've got a date already."

The girl's eyes blazed her disappointment.

"To sit up with a sick friend, I suppose?" she sneered.

"No, a real, honest date with—" he faltered, "with a girl."

"You're not stringin' me?" she asked earnestly.

He looked her in the eyes and answered: "It's straight, all right. But why can't we meet some other time? You ain't told me your name yet. An' where d'ye live?"

"Lizzie," she replied, softening toward him, her hand pressing his arm, while her body leaned against his. "Lizzie Connolly. And I live at Fifth an' Market."

He talked on a few minutes before saying good night. He did not go home immediately; and under the tree where he kept his vigils he looked up at a window and murmured: "That date was with you, Ruth. I kept it for you."

Chapter VII

A WEEK of heavy reading had passed since the evening he first met Ruth Morse, and still he dared not call. Time and again he nerved himself up to call, but under the doubts that assailed him his determination died away. He did not know the proper time to call, nor was there any one to tell him, and he was afraid of committing himself to an irretrievable blunder. Having shaken himself free from his old companions and old ways of life, and having no new companions, nothing remained for him but to read, and the long hours he devoted to it would have ruined a dozen pairs of ordinary eyes. But his eyes were strong, and they were backed by a body superbly strong. Furthermore, his mind was fallow. It had lain fallow all his life so far as the abstract thought of the books was concerned, and it was ripe for the sowing. It had never been jaded by study, and it bit hold of the knowledge in the books with sharp teeth that would not let go.

It seemed to him, by the end of the week, that he had lived centuries, so far behind were the old life and outlook. But he was baffled by lack of preparation. He attempted to read books that required years of preliminary specialization. One day he would read a book of antiquated philosophy, and the next day one that was ultra-modern, so that his head would be whirling with the conflict and contradiction of ideas. It was the same with the economists. On the one shelf at the library he found Karl Marx, Ricardo, Adam Smith, and Mill, and the abstruse formulas of the one gave no clew that the ideas of another were obsolete. He was bewildered, and yet he wanted to know. He had become interested, in a day, in economics, industry, and politics. Passing through the City Hall Park, he had noticed a group of men, in the centre of which were half a dozen, with flushed faces and raised voices, earnestly carrying on a discussion. He joined the listeners, and heard a new, alien tongue in the mouths of the philosophers of the people. One was a tramp, another was a labor agitator, a third was a law-school student, and the remainder was composed of wordy workingmen. For the first time he heard of socialism, anarchism, and single tax, and learned that there were warring social philosophies. He heard hundreds of technical words that were new to him, belonging to fields of thought that his meagre reading had never touched upon. Because of this he could not follow the arguments closely, and he could only guess at and surmise the ideas wrapped up in such strange expressions. Then there was a black-eyed restaurant waiter who was a theosophist, a union baker who was an agnostic, an old man who baffled all of them with the strange philosophy that *what is is right*, and another old man who discoursed interminably about the cosmos and the father-atom and the mother-atom.

Martin Eden's head was in a state of addlement when he went away after several hours, and he hurried to the library to look up the definitions of a dozen unusual words. And when he left the library, he carried under his arm four volumes: Madam Blavatsky's "Secret Doctrine," "Progress and Poverty," "The Quintessence of Socialism," and "Warfare of Religion and Science." Unfortunately, he began on the "Secret Doctrine." Every line bristled with many-syllabled words he did not understand. He sat up in bed, and the dictionary was in front of him more often than the book. He looked up so many new words that when they recurred, he had forgotten their meaning and had to look them up again. He devised the plan of writing the definitions in a note-book, and filled page after page with them. And still he could not understand. He read until three in the morning, and his brain was in a turmoil, but not one essential thought in the text had he grasped. He looked up, and it seemed that the room was lifting, heeling, and plunging like a ship upon the sea. Then he hurled the "Secret Doctrine" and many curses across the room, turned off the gas, and composed himself to sleep. Nor did he have much better luck with the other three books. It was not that his brain was weak or incapable; it could think these thoughts were it not for lack of training in thinking and lack of the thought-tools with which to think. He guessed this, and for a while entertained the idea of reading nothing but the dictionary until he had mastered every word in it.

Poetry, however, was his solace, and he read much of it, finding his greatest joy in the simpler poets, who were more understandable. He loved beauty, and there he found beauty. Poetry, like music, stirred him profoundly, and, though he did not know it, he was preparing his mind for the heavier work that was to come. The pages of his mind were blank, and, without effort, much he read and liked, stanza by stanza, was impressed upon those pages, so that he was soon able to extract great joy from chanting aloud or under his breath the music and the beauty of the printed words he had read. Then he stumbled upon Gayley's "Classic Myths" and Bulfinch's "Age of Fable," side by side on a library shelf. It was illumination, a great light in the darkness of his ignorance, and he read poetry more avidly than ever.

The man at the desk in the library had seen Martin there so often that he had become quite cordial, always greeting him with a smile and a nod when he entered. It was because of this that Martin did a daring thing. Drawing out some books at the desk, and while the man was stamping the cards, Martin blurted out:—

"Say, there's something I'd like to ask you."

The man smiled and paid attention.

"When you meet a young lady an' she asks you to call, how soon can you call?"

Martin felt his shirt press and cling to his shoulders, what of the sweat of the effort.

"Why I'd say any time," the man answered.

"Yes, but this is different," Martin objected. "She—I—well, you see, it's this way: maybe she won't be there. She goes to the university."

"Then call again."

"What I said ain't what I meant," Martin confessed falteringly, while he made up his mind to throw himself wholly upon the other's mercy. "I'm just a rough sort of a fellow, an' I ain't never seen anything of society. This girl is all that I ain't, an' I ain't anything that she is. You don't think I'm playin' the fool, do you?" he demanded abruptly.

"No, no; not at all, I assure you," the other protested. "Your request is not exactly in the scope of the reference department, but I shall be only too pleased to assist you."

Martin looked at him admiringly.

"If I could tear it off that way, I'd be all right," he said.

"I beg pardon?"

"I mean if I could talk easy that way, an' polite, an' all the rest."

"Oh," said the other, with comprehension.

"What is the best time to call? The afternoon?—not too close to meal-time? Or the evening? Or Sunday?"

"I'll tell you," the librarian said with a brightening face. "You call her up on the telephone and find out."

"I'll do it," he said, picking up his books and starting away. He turned back and asked:—

"When you're speakin' to a young lady—say, for instance, Miss Lizzie Smith—do you say 'Miss Lizzie'? or 'Miss Smith'?"

"Say 'Miss Smith,'" the librarian stated authoritatively. "Say 'Miss Smith' always—until you come to know her better."

So it was that Martin Eden solved the problem.

"Come down any time; I'll be at home all afternoon," was Ruth's reply over the telephone to his stammered request as to when he could return the borrowed books.

She meet him at the door herself, and her woman's eyes took in immediately the creased trousers and the certain slight but indefinable change in him for the better. Also, she was struck by his face. It was almost violent, this health of his, and it seemed to rush out of him and at her in waves of force. She felt the urge again of the desire to lean toward him for warmth, and marvelled again at the effect his presence produced upon her. And he, in turn, knew again the swimming sensation of bliss when he felt the contact of her hand in greeting. The difference between them lay in that she was cool and self-possessed while his face flushed to the roots of the hair. He stumbled with his old awkwardness after her, and his shoulders swung and lurched perilously.

Once they were seated in the living-room, he began to get on easily—more easily by far than he had expected. She made it easy for him; and the gracious spirit with which she did it made him love her more madly than ever. They talked first of the borrowed books, of the Swinburne he was devoted to, and of the Browning he did not understand; and she led the conversation on from subject to subject, while she pondered the problem of how she could be of help to him. She had thought of this often since their first meeting. She wanted to help him. He made a call upon her pity and tenderness that no one had ever made before, and the pity was not so much derogatory of him as maternal in her. Her pity could not be of the common sort, when the man who drew it was so much man as to shock her with maidenly fears and set her mind and pulse thrilling with strange thoughts and feelings. The old fascination of his neck was there, and there was sweetness in the thought of laying her hands upon it. It seemed still a wanton impulse, but she had grown more used to it. She did not dream that in such guise new-born love would epitomize itself. Nor did she dream that the feeling he excited in her was love. She thought she was merely interested in him as an unusual type possessing various potential excellencies, and she even felt philanthropic about it.

She did not know she desired him; but with him it was different. He knew that he loved her, and he desired her as he had never before desired anything in his life. He had loved poetry for beauty's sake; but since he met her the gates to the vast field of love-poetry had been opened wide. She had given him understanding even more than Bulfinch and Gayley. There was a line that a week before he would not have favored with a second thought—"God's own mad lover dying on a kiss"; but now it was ever insistent in his mind. He marvelled at the wonder of it and the truth; and as he gazed upon her he knew that he could die gladly upon a kiss. He felt himself God's own mad lover, and no accolade of knighthood could have given him greater pride. And at last he knew the meaning of life and why he had been born.

As he gazed at her and listened, his thoughts grew daring. He reviewed all the wild delight of the pressure of her hand in his at the door, and longed for it again. His gaze wandered often toward her lips, and he yearned for them hungrily. But there was nothing gross or earthly about this yearning. It gave him exquisite delight to watch every movement and play of those lips as they enunciated the words she spoke; yet they were not ordinary lips such as all men and women had. Their substance was not mere human clay. They were lips of pure spirit, and his desire for them seemed absolutely different from the desire that had led him to other women's lips. He could kiss her lips, rest his own physical lips upon them, but it would be with the lofty and awful fervor with which one would kiss the robe of God. He was not conscious of this transvaluation of values that had taken place in him, and was unaware that the light that shone in his eyes when he looked at her was quite the same light that shines in all men's eyes when the desire of love is upon them. He did not dream how ardent and masculine his gaze was, nor that the warm flame of it was affecting the alchemy of her spirit. Her penetrative virginity exalted and disguised his own emotions, elevating his thoughts to a star-cool chastity, and he would have been startled to learn that there was that shining out of his eyes, like warm waves, that flowed through her and kindled a kindred warmth. She was subtly perturbed by it, and more than once, though she knew not why, it disrupted her train of thought with its delicious intrusion and compelled her to grope for the remainder of ideas partly uttered. Speech was always easy with her, and these interruptions would have puzzled her had she not decided that it was because he was a remarkable type. She was very sensitive to impressions, and it was not strange, after all, that this aura of a traveller from another world should so affect her.

The problem in the background of her consciousness was how to help him, and she turned the conversation in that direction; but it was Martin who came to the point first.

"I wonder if I can get some advice from you," he began, and received an acquiescence of willingness that made his heart bound. "You remember the other time I was here I said I couldn't talk about books an' things because I didn't know how? Well, I've ben doin' a lot of thinkin' ever since. I've ben to the library a whole lot, but most of the books I've tackled have ben over my head. Mebbe I'd better begin at the beginnin'. I ain't never had no advantages. I've worked pretty hard ever since I was a kid, an' since I've ben to the library, lookin' with new eyes at books—an' lookin' at new books, too—I've just about concluded that I ain't ben reading the right kind. You know the books you find in cattle-camps an' fo'c's'ls ain't the same you've got in this house, for instance. Well, that's the sort of readin' matter I've ben accustomed to. And yet—

an' I ain't just makin' a brag of it—I've ben different from the people I've herded with. Not that I'm any better than the sailors an' cow-punchers I travelled with,—I was cow-punchin' for a short time, you know,—but I always liked books, read everything I could lay hands on, an'—well, I guess I think differently from most of 'em.

"Now, to come to what I'm drivin' at. I was never inside a house like this. When I come a week ago, an' saw all this, an' you, an' your mother, an' brothers, an' everything—well, I liked it. I'd heard about such things an' read about such things in some of the books, an' when I looked around at your house, why, the books come true. But the thing I'm after is I liked it. I wanted it. I want it now. I want to breathe air like you get in this house—air that is filled with books, and pictures, and beautiful things, where people talk in low voices an' are clean, an' their thoughts are clean. The air I always breathed was mixed up with grub an' house-rent an' scrappin' an' booze an' that's all they talked about, too. Why, when you was crossin' the room to kiss your mother, I thought it was the most beautiful thing I ever seen. I've seen a whole lot of life, an' somehow I've seen a whole lot more of it than most of them that was with me. I like to see, an' I want to see more, an' I want to see it different.

"But I ain't got to the point yet. Here it is. I want to make my way to the kind of life you have in this house. There's more in life than booze, an' hard work, an' knockin' about. Now, how am I goin' to get it? Where do I take hold an' begin? I'm willin' to work my passage, you know, an' I can make most men sick when it comes to hard work. Once I get started, I'll work night an' day. Mebbe you think it's funny, me askin' you about all this. I know you're the last person in the world I ought to ask, but I don't know anybody else I could ask—unless it's Arthur. Mebbe I ought to ask him. If I was—"

His voice died away. His firmly planned intention had come to a halt on the verge of the horrible probability that he should have asked Arthur and that he had made a fool of himself. Ruth did not speak immediately. She was too absorbed in striving to reconcile the stumbling, uncouth speech and its simplicity of thought with what she saw in his face. She had never looked in eyes that expressed greater power. Here was a man who could do anything, was the message she read there, and it accorded ill with the weakness of his spoken thought. And for that matter so complex and quick was her own mind that she did not have a just appreciation of simplicity. And yet she had caught an impression of power in the very groping of this mind. It had seemed to her like a giant writhing and straining at the bonds that held him down. Her face was all sympathy when she did speak.

"What you need, you realize yourself, and it is education. You should go back and finish grammar school, and then go through the high school and university."

"But that takes money," he interrupted.

"Oh!" she cried. "I had not thought of that. But then you have relatives, somebody who could assist you?"

He shook his head.

"My father and mother are dead. I've two sisters, one married, an' the other'll get married soon, I suppose. Then I've a string of brothers,—I'm the youngest,—but they never helped nobody. They've just knocked around over the world, lookin' out for number one. The oldest died in India. Two are in South Africa now, an' another's on a whaling voyage, an' one's travellin' with a circus—he does trapeze work. An' I guess I'm just like them. I've taken care of myself since I was eleven—that's when my mother died. I've got to study by myself, I guess, an' what I want to know is where to begin."

"I should say the first thing of all would be to get a grammar. Your grammar is—" She had intended saying "awful," but she amended it to "is not particularly good."

He flushed and sweated.

"I know I must talk a lot of slang an' words you don't understand. But then they're the only words I know—how to speak. I've got other words in my mind, picked 'em up from books, but I can't pronounce 'em, so I don't use 'em."

"It isn't what you say, so much as how you say it. You don't mind my being frank, do you? I don't want to hurt you."

"No, no," he cried, while he secretly blessed her for her kindness. "Fire away. I've got to know, an' I'd sooner know from you than anybody else."

"Well, then, you say, 'You was'; it should be, 'You were.' You say 'I seen' for 'I saw.' You use the double negative—"

"What's the double negative?" he demanded; then added humbly, "You see, I don't even understand your explanations."

"I'm afraid I didn't explain that," she smiled. "A double negative is—let me see—well, you say, 'never helped nobody.' 'Never' is a negative. 'Nobody' is another negative. It is a rule that two negatives make a positive. 'Never helped nobody' means that, not helping nobody, they must have helped somebody."

"That's pretty clear," he said. "I never thought of it before. But it don't mean they *must* have helped somebody, does it? Seems to me that 'never helped nobody' just naturally fails to say whether or not they helped somebody. I never thought of it before, and I'll never say it again."

She was pleased and surprised with the quickness and surety of his mind. As soon as he had got the clew he not only understood but corrected her error.

"You'll find it all in the grammar," she went on. "There's something else I noticed in your speech. You say 'don't' when you shouldn't. 'Don't' is a contraction and stands for two words. Do you know them?"

He thought a moment, then answered, " 'Do not.' "

She nodded her head, and said, "And you use 'don't' when you mean 'does not.' "

He was puzzled over this, and did not get it so quickly.

"Give me an illustration," he asked.

"Well—" She puckered her brows and pursed up her mouth as she thought, while he looked on and decided that her expression was most adorable. " 'It don't do to be hasty.' Change 'don't' to 'do not,' and it reads, 'It do not do to be hasty,' which is perfectly absurd."

He turned it over in his mind and considered.

"Doesn't it jar on your ear?" she suggested.

"Can't say that it does," he replied judicially.

"Why didn't you say, 'Can't say that it do'?" she queried.

"That sounds wrong," he said slowly. "As for the other I can't make up my mind. I guess my ear ain't had the trainin' yours has."

"There is no such word as 'ain't,'" she said, prettily emphatic.

Martin flushed again.

"And you say 'ben' for 'been,'" she continued; "'I come' for 'I came'; and the way you chop your endings is something dreadful."

"How do you mean?" He leaned forward, feeling that he ought to get down on his knees before so marvellous a mind. "How do I chop?"

"You don't complete the endings. 'A-n-d' spells 'and.' You pronounce it 'an'.' 'I-n-g' spells 'ing.' Sometimes you pronounce it 'ing' and sometimes you leave off the 'g.' And then you slur by dropping initial letters and diphthongs. 'T-h-e-m' spells 'them.' You pronounce it—oh, well, it is not necessary to go over all of them. What you need is the grammar. I'll get one and show you how to begin."

As she arose, there shot through his mind something that he had read in the etiquette books, and he stood up awkwardly, worrying as to whether he was doing the right thing, and fearing that she might take it as a sign that he was about to go.

"By the way, Mr. Eden," she called back, as she was leaving the room. "What is *booze*? You used it several times, you know."

"Oh, booze," he laughed. "It's slang. It means whiskey an' beer—anything that will make you drunk."

"And another thing," she laughed back. "Don't use 'you' when you are impersonal. 'You' is very personal, and your use of it just now was not precisely what you meant."

"I don't just see that."

"Why, you said just now, to me, 'whiskey and beer—anything that will make you drunk'—make *me* drunk, don't you see?"

"Well, it would, wouldn't it?"

"Yes, of course," she smiled. "But it would be nicer not to bring me into it. Substitute 'one' for 'you' and see how much better it sounds."

When she returned with the grammar, she drew a chair near his—he wondered if he should have helped her with the chair—and sat down beside him. She turned the pages of the grammar, and their heads were inclined toward each other. He could hardly follow her outlining of the work he must do, so amazed was he by her delightful propinquity. But when she began to lay down the importance of conjugation, he forgot all about her. He had never heard of conjugation, and was fascinated by the glimpse he was catching into the tieribs of language. He leaned closer to the page, and her hair touched his cheek. He had fainted but once in his life, and he thought he was going to faint again. He could scarcely breathe, and his heart was pounding the blood up into his throat and suffocating him. Never had she seemed so accessible as now. For the moment the great gulf that separated them was bridged. But there was no diminution in the loftiness of his feeling for her. She had not descended to him. It was he who had been caught up into the clouds and carried to her. His reverence for her, in that moment, was of the same order as religious awe and fervor. It seemed to him that he had intruded upon the holy of holies, and slowly and carefully he moved his head aside from the contact which thrilled him like an electric shock and of which she had not been aware.

Chapter VIII

SEVERAL WEEKS went by, during which Martin Eden studied his grammar, reviewed the books on etiquette, and
read voraciously the books that caught his fancy. Of his own
class he saw nothing. The girls of the Lotus Club wondered
what had become of him and worried Jim with questions,
and some of the fellows who put on the glove at Riley's were
glad that Martin came no more. He made another discovery
of treasure-trove in the library. As the grammar had shown
him the tie-ribs of language, so that book showed him the
tie-ribs of poetry, and he began to learn metre and construction and form, beneath the beauty he loved finding
the why and wherefore of that beauty. Another modern
book he found treated poetry as a representative art,
treated it exhaustively, with copious illustrations from the
best in literature. Never had he read fiction with so keen
zest as he studied these books. And his fresh mind, un-
taxed for twenty years and impelled by maturity of desire,
gripped hold of what he read with a virility unusual to the
student mind.

When he looked back now from his vantage-ground, the
old world he had known, the world of land and sea and ships,
of sailor-men and harpy-women, seemed a very small world;
and yet it blended in with this new world and expanded. His
mind made for unity, and he was surprised when at first he
began to see points of contact between the two worlds. And
he was ennobled, as well, by the loftiness of thought and
beauty he found in the books. This led him to believe more
firmly than ever that up above him, in society like Ruth and
her family, all men and women thought these thoughts and
lived them. Down below where he lived was the ignoble,
and he wanted to purge himself of the ignoble that had soiled
all his days, and to rise to that sublimated realm where dwelt
the upper classes. All his childhood and youth had been troubled by a vague unrest; he had never known what he wanted,
but he had wanted something that he had hunted vainly for
until he met Ruth. And now his unrest had become sharp

and painful, and he knew at last, clearly and definitely, that it was beauty, and intellect, and love that he must have.

During those several weeks he saw Ruth half a dozen times, and each time was an added inspiration. She helped him with his English, corrected his pronunciation, and started him on arithmetic. But their intercourse was not all devoted to elementary study. He had seen too much of life, and his mind was too matured, to be wholly content with fractions, cube root, parsing, and analysis; and there were times when their conversation turned on other themes—the last poetry he had read, the latest poet she had studied. And when she read aloud to him her favorite passages, he ascended to the topmost heaven of delight. Never, in all the women he had heard speak, had he heard a voice like hers. The least sound of it was a stimulus to his love, and he thrilled and throbbed with every word she uttered. It was the quality of it, the repose, and the musical modulation—the soft, rich, indefinable product of culture and a gentle soul. As he listened to her, there rang in the ears of his memory the harsh cries of barbarian women and of hags, and, in lesser degrees of harshness, the strident voices of working women and of the girls of his own class. Then the chemistry of vision would begin to work, and they would troop in review across his mind, each, by contrast, multiplying Ruth's glories. Then, too, his bliss was heightened by the knowledge that her mind was comprehending what she read and was quivering with appreciation of the beauty of the written thought. She read to him much from "The Princess," and often he saw her eyes swimming with tears, so finely was her æsthetic nature strung. At such moments her own emotions elevated him till he was as a god, and, as he gazed at her and listened, he seemed gazing on the face of life and reading its deepest secrets. And then, becoming aware of the heights of exquisite sensibility he attained, he decided that this was love and that love was the greatest thing in the world. And in review would pass along the corridors of memory all previous thrills and burnings he had known,—the drunkenness of wine, the caresses of women, the rough play and give and take of physical contests,—and they seemed trivial and mean compared with this sublime ardor he now enjoyed.

The situation was obscured to Ruth. She had never had any experiences of the heart. Her only experiences in such matters were of the books, where the facts of ordinary day were translated by fancy into a fairy realm of unreality; and she little knew that this rough sailor was creeping into her heart and storing there pent forces that would some day burst forth and surge through her in waves of fire. She did not know the actual fire of love. Her knowledge of love was purely theoretical, and she conceived of it as lambent flame, gentle as the fall of dew or the ripple of quiet water, and cool as the velvet-dark of summer nights. Her idea of love was more that of placid affection, serving the loved one softly in an atmosphere, flower-scented and dim-lighted, of ethereal calm. She did not dream of the volcanic convulsions of love, its scorching heat and sterile wastes of parched ashes. She knew neither her own potencies, nor the potencies of the world; and the deeps of life were to her seas of illusion. The conjugal affection of her father and mother constituted her ideal of love-affinity, and she looked forward some day to emerging, without shock or friction, into that same quiet sweetness of existence with a loved one.

So it was that she looked upon Martin Eden as a novelty, a strange individual, and she identified with novelty and strangeness the effects he produced upon her. It was only natural. In similar ways she had experienced unusual feelings when she looked at wild animals in the menagerie, or when she witnessed a storm of wind, or shuddered at the bright-ribbed lightning. There was something cosmic in such things, and there was something cosmic in him. He came to her breathing of large airs and great spaces. The blaze of tropic suns was in his face, and in his swelling, resilient muscles was the primordial vigor of life. He was marred and scarred by that mysterious world of rough men and rougher deeds, the outposts of which began beyond her horizon. He was untamed, wild, and in secret ways her vanity was touched by the fact that he came so mildly to her hand. Likewise she was stirred by the common impulse to tame the wild thing. It was an unconscious impulse, and farthest from her thoughts that her desire was to re-thumb the clay of him into a likeness of her father's image, which image she believed to be the finest in the world. Nor was there any way, out of her inexperience, for her to know that the cosmic feel she caught of him was that most cosmic of things, love, which with equal power drew men and women together across the world, compelled stags to kill each other in the rutting season, and drove even the elements irresistibly to unite.

His swift development was a source of surprise and interest. She detected unguessed finenesses in him that seemed to bud, day by day, like flowers in congenial soil. She read Browning aloud to him, and was often puzzled by the strange interpretations he gave to mooted passages. It was beyond her to realize that, out of his experience of men and women and life, his interpretations were far more frequently correct than hers. His conceptions seemed naïve to her, though she was often fired by his daring flights of comprehension, whose orbit-path was so wide among the stars that she could not follow and could only sit and thrill to the impact of unguessed power. Then she played to him—no longer at him—and probed him with music that sank to depths beyond her plumb-line. His nature opened to music as a flower to the sun, and the transition was quick from his working-class ragtime and jingles to her classical display pieces that she knew nearly by heart. Yet he betrayed a democratic fondness for Wagner, and the "Tannhäuser" overture, when she had given him the clew to it, claimed him as nothing else she played. In an immediate way it personified his life. All his past was the *Venusburg* motif, while her he identified somehow with the *Pilgrim's Chorus* motif; and from the exalted state this elevated him to, he swept onward and upward into that vast shadow-realm of spirit-groping, where good and evil war eternally.

Sometimes he questioned, and induced in her mind temporary doubts as to the correctness of her own definitions and conceptions of music. But her singing he did not question. It was too wholly her, and he sat always amazed at the divine melody of her pure soprano voice. And he could not help but contrast it with the weak pipings and shrill quaverings of factory girls, ill-nourished and untrained, and with the raucous shriekings from gin-cracked throats of the women of the seaport towns. She enjoyed singing and playing to him. In truth, it was the first time she had ever had a human soul to play with, and the plastic clay of him was a delight to mould; for she thought she was moulding it, and her intentions were good. Besides, it was pleasant to be with him. He did not repel her. That first repulsion had been really a fear of her undiscovered self, and the fear had gone to sleep. Though she did not know it, she had a feeling in him of proprietary right. Also, he had a tonic effect upon her. She was studying hard at the university, and it seemed to strengthen her to emerge from the dusty books and have the fresh sea-breeze of his personality blow upon her. Strength! Strength was what she needed, and he gave it to her in generous measure. To come into the same room with him, or to meet him at the door, was to take heart of life. And when he had gone, she would return to her books with a keener zest and fresh store of energy.

She knew her Browning, but it had never sunk into her that it was an awkward thing to play with souls. As her interest in Martin increased, the remodelling of his life became a passion with her.

"There is Mr. Butler," she said one afternoon, when grammar and arithmetic and poetry had been put aside. "He had comparatively no advantages at first. His father had been a bank cashier, but he lingered for years, dying of consumption in Arizona, so that when he was dead, Mr. Butler, Charles Butler he was called, found himself alone in the world. His father had come from Australia, you know, and so he had no relatives in California. He went to work in a printing-office,—I have heard him tell of it many times,—and he got three dollars a week, at first. His income to-day is at least thirty thousand a year. How did he do it? He was honest, and faithful, and industrious, and economical. He denied himself the enjoyments that most boys indulge in. He made it a point to save so much every week, no matter what he had to do without in order to save it. Of course, he was soon earning more than three dollars a week, and as his wages increased he saved more and more.

"He worked in the daytime, and at night he went to night school. He had his eyes fixed always on the future. Later on he went to night high school. When he was only seventeen, he was earning excellent wages at setting type, but he was ambitious. He wanted a career, not a livelihood, and he was content to make immediate sacrifices for his ultimate gain. He decided upon the law, and he entered father's office as an office boy—think of that!—and got only four dollars a week. But he had learned how to be economical, and out of that four dollars he went on saving money."

She paused for breath, and to note how Martin was receiving it. His face was lighted up with interest in the youthful struggles of Mr. Butler; but there was a frown upon his face as well.

"I'd say they was pretty hard lines for a young fellow," he remarked. "Four dollars a week! How could he live on it? You can bet he didn't have any frills. Why, I pay five dollars a week for board now, an' there's nothin' excitin' about it, you can lay to that. He must have lived like a dog. The food he ate—"

"He cooked for himself," she interrupted, "on a little kerosene stove."

"The food he ate must have been worse than what a sailor gets on the worst-feedin' deep-water ships, than which there ain't much that can be possibly worse."

"But think of him now!" she cried enthusiastically. "Think of what his income affords him. His early denials are paid for a thousand-fold."

Martin looked at her sharply.

"There's one thing I'll bet you," he said, "and it is that Mr. Butler is nothin' gay-hearted now in his fat days. He fed himself like that for years an' years, on a boy's stomach, an' I bet his stomach's none too good now for it."

Her eyes dropped before his searching gaze.

"I'll bet he's got dyspepsia right now!" Martin challenged.

"Yes, he has," she confessed; "but—"

"An' I bet," Martin dashed on, "that he's solemn an' serious as an old owl, an' doesn't care a rap for a good time, for all his thirty thousand a year. An' I'll bet he's not particularly joyful at seein' others have a good time. Ain't I right?"

She nodded her head in agreement, and hastened to explain:—

"But he is not that type of man. By nature he is sober and serious. He always was that."

"You can bet he was," Martin proclaimed. "Three dollars a week, an' four dollars a week, an' a young boy cookin' for himself on an oil-burner an' layin' up money, workin' all day an' studyin' all night, just workin' an' never playin', never havin' a good time, an' never learnin' how to have a good time—of course his thirty thousand came along too late."

His sympathetic imagination was flashing upon his inner sight all the thousands of details of the boy's existence and of his narrow spiritual development into a thirty-thousand-dollar-a-year man. With the swiftness and wide-reaching of multitudinous thought Charles Butler's whole life was telescoped upon his vision.

"Do you know," he added, "I feel sorry for Mr. Butler. He was too young to know better, but he robbed himself of life for the sake of thirty thousand a year that's clean wasted upon him. Why, thirty thousand, lump sum, wouldn't buy for him right now what ten cents he was layin' up would have bought him, when he was a kid, in the way of candy an' peanuts or a seat in nigger heaven."

It was just such uniqueness of points of view that startled Ruth. Not only were they new to her, and contrary to her own beliefs, but she always felt in them germs of truth that threatened to unseat or modify her own convictions. Had she been fourteen instead of twenty-four, she might have been changed by them; but she was twenty-four, conservative by nature and upbringing, and already crystallized into the cranny of life where she had been born and formed. It was true, his bizarre judgments troubled her in the moments they were uttered, but she ascribed them to his novelty of type and strangeness of living, and they were soon forgotten. Nevertheless, while she disapproved of them, the strength of their utterance, and the flashing of eyes and earnestness of face that accompanied them, always thrilled her and drew her toward him. She would never have guessed that this man who had come from beyond her horizon, was, in such moments, flashing on beyond her horizon with wider and deeper concepts. Her own limits were the limits of her horizon; but limited minds can recognize limitations only in others. And so she felt that her outlook was very wide indeed, and that where his conflicted with hers marked his limitations; and she dreamed of helping him to see as she saw, of widening his horizon until it was identified with hers.

"But I have not finished my story," she said. "He worked, so father says, as no other office boy he ever had. Mr. Butler was always eager to work. He never was late, and he was usually at the office a few minutes before his regular time. And yet he saved his time. Every spare moment was devoted to study. He studied book-keeping and type-writing, and he paid for lessons in shorthand by dictating at night to a court reporter who needed practice. He quickly became a clerk, and he made himself invaluable. Father appreciated him and saw that he was bound to rise. It was on father's suggestion that he went to law college. He became a lawyer, and hardly was he back in the office when father took him in as junior partner. He is a great man. He refused the United States Senate several times, and father says he could become a justice of the Supreme Court any time a vacancy occurs, if he wants to. Such a life is an inspiration to all of us. It shows us that a man with will may rise superior to his environment."

"He is a great man," Martin said sincerely.

But it seemed to him there was something in the recital that jarred upon his sense of beauty and life. He could not find an adequate motive in Mr. Butler's life of pinching and privation. Had he done it for love of a woman, or for attainment of beauty, Martin would have understood. God's own mad lover should do anything for the kiss, but not for thirty thousand dollars a year. He was dissatisfied with Mr. Butler's career. There was something paltry about it, after all. Thirty thousand a year was all right, but dyspepsia and inability to be humanly happy robbed such princely income of all its value.

Much of this he strove to express to Ruth, and shocked her and made it clear that more remodelling was necessary. Hers was that common insularity of mind that makes human creatures believe that their color, creed, and politics are best and right and that other human creatures scattered over the world are less fortunately placed than they. It was the same insu-

larity of mind that made the ancient Jew thank God he was
not born a woman, and sent the modern missionary god-
substituting to the ends of the earth; and it made Ruth desire
to shape this man from other crannies of life into the likeness
of the men who lived in her particular cranny of life.

Chapter IX

BACK FROM SEA Martin Eden came, homing for California with a lover's desire. His store of money exhausted, he had shipped before the mast on the treasure-hunting schooner; and the Solomon Islands, after eight months of failure to find treasure, had witnessed the breaking up of the expedition. The men had been paid off in Australia, and Martin had immediately shipped on a deep-water vessel for San Francisco. Not alone had those eight months earned him enough money to stay on land for many weeks, but they had enabled him to do a great deal of studying and reading.

His was the student's mind, and behind his ability to learn was the indomitability of his nature and his love for Ruth. The grammar he had taken along he went through again and again until his unjaded brain had mastered it. He noticed the bad grammar used by his shipmates, and made a point of mentally correcting and reconstructing their crudities of speech. To his great joy he discovered that his ear was becoming sensitive and that he was developing grammatical nerves. A double negative jarred him like a discord, and often, from lack of practice, it was from his own lips that the jar came. His tongue refused to learn new tricks in a day.

After he had been through the grammar repeatedly, he took up the dictionary and added twenty words a day to his vocabulary. He found that this was no light task, and at wheel or lookout he steadily went over and over his lengthening list of pronunciations and definitions, while he invariably memorized himself to sleep. "Never did anything," "if I were," and "those things," were phrases, with many variations, that he repeated under his breath in order to accustom his tongue to the language spoken by Ruth. "And" and "ing," with the "d" and "g" pronounced emphatically, he went over thousands of times; and to his surprise he noticed that he was beginning to speak cleaner and more correct English than the officers themselves and the gentleman-adventurers in the cabin who had financed the expedition.

The captain was a fishy-eyed Norwegian who somehow

had fallen into possession of a complete Shakespeare, which he never read, and Martin had washed his clothes for him and in return been permitted access to the precious volumes. For a time, so steeped was he in the plays and in the many favorite passages that impressed themselves almost without effort on his brain, that all the world seemed to shape itself into forms of Elizabethan tragedy or comedy and his very thoughts were in blank verse. It trained his ear and gave him a fine appreciation for noble English; withal it introduced into his mind much that was archaic and obsolete.

The eight months had been well spent, and, in addition to what he had learned of right speaking and high thinking, he had learned much of himself. Along with his humbleness because he knew so little, there arose a conviction of power. He felt a sharp gradation between himself and his shipmates, and was wise enough to realize that the difference lay in potentiality rather than achievement. What he could do, they could do; but within him he felt a confused ferment working that told him there was more in him than he had done. He was tortured by the exquisite beauty of the world, and wished that Ruth were there to share it with him. He decided that he would describe to her many of the bits of South Sea beauty. The creative spirit in him flamed up at the thought and urged that he recreate this beauty for a wider audience than Ruth. And then, in splendor and glory, came the great idea. He would write. He would be one of the eyes through which the world saw, one of the ears through which it heard, one of the hearts through which it felt. He would write—everything—poetry and prose, fiction and description, and plays like Shakespeare. There was career and the way to win to Ruth. The men of literature were the world's giants, and he conceived them to be far finer than the Mr. Butlers who earned thirty thousand a year and could be Supreme Court justices if they wanted to.

Once the idea had germinated, it mastered him, and the return voyage to San Francisco was like a dream. He was drunken with unguessed power and felt that he could do anything. In the midst of the great and lonely sea he gained perspective. Clearly, and for the first time, he saw Ruth and her world. It was all visualized in his mind as a concrete thing

which he could take up in his two hands and turn around and
about and examine. There was much that was dim and nebulous in that world, but he saw it as a whole and not in detail,
and he saw, also, the way to master it. To write! The thought
was fire in him. He would begin as soon as he got back. The
first thing he would do would be to describe the voyage of
the treasure-hunters. He would sell it to some San Francisco
newspaper. He would not tell Ruth anything about it, and
she would be surprised and pleased when she saw his name in
print. While he wrote, he could go on studying. There were
twenty-four hours in each day. He was invincible. He knew
how to work, and the citadels would go down before him.
He would not have to go to sea again—as a sailor; and for
the instant he caught a vision of a steam yacht. There were
other writers who possessed steam yachts. Of course, he cautioned himself, it would be slow succeeding at first, and for a
time he would be content to earn enough money by his writing to enable him to go on studying. And then, after some
time,—a very indeterminate time,—when he had learned and
prepared himself, he would write the great things and his
name would be on all men's lips. But greater than that, infinitely greater and greatest of all, he would have proved himself worthy of Ruth. Fame was all very well, but it was for
Ruth that his splendid dream arose. He was not a fame-mon-
ger, but merely one of God's mad lovers.

Arrived in Oakland, with his snug pay-day in his pocket,
he took up his old room at Bernard Higginbotham's and set
to work. He did not even let Ruth know he was back. He
would go and see her when he finished the article on the
treasure-hunters. It was not so difficult to abstain from seeing
her, because of the violent heat of creative fever that burned
in him. Besides, the very article he was writing would bring
her nearer to him. He did not know how long an article he
should write, but he counted the words in a double-page article in the Sunday supplement of the *San Francisco Examiner*,
and guided himself by that. Three days, at white heat, completed his narrative; but when he had copied it carefully, in a
large scrawl that was easy to read, he learned from a rhetoric
he picked up in the library that there were such things as
paragraphs and quotation marks. He had never thought of

such things before; and he promptly set to work writing the article over, referring continually to the pages of the rhetoric and learning more in a day about composition than the average schoolboy in a year. When he had copied the article a second time and rolled it up carefully, he read in a newspaper an item on hints to beginners, and discovered the iron law that manuscripts should never be rolled and that they should be written on one side of the paper. He had violated the law on both counts. Also, he learned from the item that first-class papers paid a minimum of ten dollars a column. So, while he copied the manuscript a third time, he consoled himself by multiplying ten columns by ten dollars. The product was always the same, one hundred dollars, and he decided that that was better than seafaring. If it hadn't been for his blunders, he would have finished the article in three days. One hundred dollars in three days! It would have taken him three months and longer on the sea to earn a similar amount. A man was a fool to go to sea when he could write, he concluded, though the money in itself meant nothing to him. Its value was in the liberty it would get him, the presentable garments it would buy him, all of which would bring him nearer, swiftly nearer, to the slender, pale girl who had turned his life back upon itself and given him inspiration.

He mailed the manuscript in a flat envelope, and addressed it to the editor of the *San Francisco Examiner*. He had an idea that anything accepted by a paper was published immediately, and as he had sent the manuscript in on Friday he expected it to come out on the following Sunday. He conceived that it would be fine to let that event apprise Ruth of his return. Then, Sunday afternoon, he would call and see her. In the meantime he was occupied by another idea, which he prided himself upon as being a particularly sane, careful, and modest idea. He would write an adventure story for boys and sell it to *The Youth's Companion*. He went to the free reading-room and looked through the files of *The Youth's Companion*. Serial stories, he found, were usually published in that weekly in five instalments of about three thousand words each. He discovered several serials that ran to seven instalments, and decided to write one of that length.

He had been on a whaling voyage in the Arctic, once—a

voyage that was to have been for three years and which had
terminated in shipwreck at the end of six months. While his
imagination was fanciful, even fantastic at times, he had a
basic love of reality that compelled him to write about the
things he knew. He knew whaling, and out of the real materials of his knowledge he proceeded to manufacture the fictitious adventures of the two boys he intended to use as joint
heroes. It was easy work, he decided on Saturday evening.
He had completed on that day the first instalment of three
thousand words—much to the amusement of Jim, and to the
open derision of Mr. Higginbotham, who sneered throughout meal-time at the "litery" person they had discovered in
the family.

Martin contented himself by picturing his brother-in-law's
surprise on Sunday morning when he opened his *Examiner*
and saw the article on the treasure-hunters. Early that morning he was out himself to the front door, nervously racing
through the many-sheeted newspaper. He went through it a
second time, very carefully, then folded it up and left it where
he had found it. He was glad he had not told any one about
his article. On second thought he concluded that he had been
wrong about the speed with which things found their way
into newspaper columns. Besides, there had not been any
news value in his article, and most likely the editor would
write to him about it first.

After breakfast he went on with his serial. The words
flowed from his pen, though he broke off from the writing
frequently to look up definitions in the dictionary or to refer
to the rhetoric. He often read or re-read a chapter at a time,
during such pauses; and he consoled himself that while he
was not writing the great things he felt to be in him, he was
learning composition, at any rate, and training himself to
shape up and express his thoughts. He toiled on till dark,
when he went out to the reading-room and explored magazines and weeklies until the place closed at ten o'clock. This
was his programme for a week. Each day he did three thousand words, and each evening he puzzled his way through the
magazines, taking note of the stories, articles, and poems that
editors saw fit to publish. One thing was certain: What these

multitudinous writers did he could do, and only give him time and he would do what they could not do. He was cheered to read in *Book News*, in a paragraph on the payment of magazine writers, not that Rudyard Kipling received a dollar per word, but that the minimum rate paid by first-class magazines was two cents a word. *The Youth's Companion* was certainly first class, and at that rate the three thousand words he had written that day would bring him sixty dollars—two months' wages on the sea!

On Friday night he finished the serial, twenty-one thousand words long. At two cents a word, he calculated, that would bring him four hundred and twenty dollars. Not a bad week's work. It was more money than he had ever possessed at one time. He did not know how he could spend it all. He had tapped a gold mine. Where this came from he could always get more. He planned to buy some more clothes, to subscribe to many magazines, and to buy dozens of reference books that at present he was compelled to go to the library to consult. And still there was a large portion of the four hundred and twenty dollars unspent. This worried him until the thought came to him of hiring a servant for Gertrude and of buying a bicycle for Marian.

He mailed the bulky manuscript to *The Youth's Companion*, and on Saturday afternoon, after having planned an article on pearl-diving, he went to see Ruth. He had telephoned, and she went herself to greet him at the door. The old familiar blaze of health rushed out from him and struck her like a blow. It seemed to enter into her body and course through her veins in a liquid glow, and to set her quivering with its imparted strength. He flushed warmly as he took her hand and looked into her blue eyes, but the fresh bronze of eight months of sun hid the flush, though it did not protect the neck from the gnawing chafe of the stiff collar. She noted the red line of it with amusement which quickly vanished as she glanced at his clothes. They really fitted him,—it was his first made-to-order suit,—and he seemed slimmer and better modelled. In addition, his cloth cap had been replaced by a soft hat, which she commanded him to put on and then complimented him on his appearance. She did not remember when she had felt so happy. This change in him was her handiwork, and she was proud of it and fired with ambition further to help him.

But the most radical change of all, and the one that pleased her most, was the change in his speech. Not only did he speak more correctly, but he spoke more easily, and there were many new words in his vocabulary. When he grew excited or enthusiastic, however, he dropped back into the old slurring and the dropping of final consonants. Also, there was an awkward hesitancy, at times, as he essayed the new words he had learned. On the other hand, along with his ease of expression, he displayed a lightness and facetiousness of thought that delighted her. It was his old spirit of humor and badinage that had made him a favorite in his own class, but which he had hitherto been unable to use in her presence through lack of words and training. He was just beginning to orientate himself and to feel that he was not wholly an intruder. But he was very tentative, fastidiously so, letting Ruth set the pace of sprightliness and fancy, keeping up with her but never daring to go beyond her.

He told her of what he had been doing, and of his plan to write for a livelihood and of going on with his studies. But he was disappointed at her lack of approval. She did not think much of his plan.

"You see," she said frankly, "writing must be a trade, like anything else. Not that I know anything about it, of course. I only bring common judgment to bear. You couldn't hope to be a blacksmith without spending three years at learning the trade—or is it five years! Now writers are so much better paid than blacksmiths that there must be ever so many more men who would like to write, who—try to write."

"But then, may not I be peculiarly constituted to write?" he queried, secretly exulting at the language he had used, his swift imagination throwing the whole scene and atmosphere upon a vast screen along with a thousand other scenes from his life—scenes that were rough and raw, gross and bestial.

The whole composite vision was achieved with the speed of light, producing no pause in the conversation, nor interrupting his calm train of thought. On the screen of his imagination he saw himself and this sweet and beautiful girl, facing each other and conversing in good English, in a room of books and paintings and tone and culture, and all illuminated by a bright light of steadfast brilliance; while ranged about and fading away to the remote edges of the screen were antithetical scenes, each scene a picture, and he the onlooker, free to look at will upon what he wished. He saw these other scenes through drifting vapors and swirls of sullen fog dissolving before shafts of red and garish light. He saw cowboys at the bar, drinking fierce whiskey, the air filled with obscenity and ribald language, and he saw himself with them, drinking and cursing with the wildest, or sitting at table with them, under smoking kerosene lamps, while the chips clicked and clattered and the cards were dealt around. He saw himself, stripped to the waist, with naked fists, fighting his great fight with Liverpool Red in the forecastle of the *Susquehanna*; and he saw the bloody deck of the *John Rogers*, that gray morning of attempted mutiny, the mate kicking in death-throes on the main-hatch, the revolver in the old man's hand spitting fire and smoke, the men with passion-wrenched faces, of brutes screaming vile blasphemies and falling about him—and then he returned to the central scene, calm and clean in the steadfast light, where Ruth sat and talked with him amid books and paintings; and he saw the grand piano upon which she would later play to him; and he heard the echoes of his own selected and correct words, "But then, may I not be peculiarly constituted to write?"

"But no matter how peculiarly constituted a man may be for blacksmithing," she was laughing, "I never heard of one becoming a blacksmith without first serving his apprenticeship."

"What would you advise?" he asked. "And don't forget that I feel in me this capacity to write—I can't explain it; I just know that it is in me."

"You must get a thorough education," was the answer, "whether or not you ultimately become a writer. This education is indispensable for whatever career you select, and it must not be slipshod or sketchy. You should go to high school."

"Yes—" he began; but she interrupted with an afterthought:—

"Of course, you could go on with your writing, too."

"I would have to," he said grimly.

"Why?" She looked at him, prettily puzzled, for she did not quite like the persistence with which he clung to his notion.

"Because, without writing there wouldn't be any high school. I must live and buy books and clothes, you know."

"I'd forgotten that," she laughed. "Why weren't you born with an income?"

"I'd rather have good health and imagination," he answered. "I can make good on the income, but the other things have to be made good for—" He almost said "you," then amended his sentence to, "have to be made good for one."

"Don't say 'make good,'" she cried, sweetly petulant. "It's slang, and it's horrid."

He flushed, and stammered, "That's right, and I only wish you'd correct me every time."

"I—I'd like to," she said haltingly. "You have so much in you that is good that I want to see you perfect."

He was clay in her hands immediately, as passionately desirous of being moulded by her as she was desirous of shaping him into the image of her ideal of man. And when she pointed out the opportuneness of the time, that the entrance examinations to high school began on the following Monday, he promptly volunteered that he would take them.

Then she played and sang to him, while he gazed with hungry yearning at her, drinking in her loveliness and marvelling that there should not be a hundred suitors listening there and longing for her as he listened and longed.

Chapter X

H E STOPPED to dinner that evening, and, much to Ruth's satisfaction, made a favorable impression on her father. They talked about the sea as a career, a subject which Martin had at his finger-ends, and Mr. Morse remarked afterward that he seemed a very clear-headed young man. In his avoidance of slang and his search after right words, Martin was compelled to talk slowly, which enabled him to find the best thoughts that were in him. He was more at ease than that first night at dinner, nearly a year before, and his shyness and modesty even commended him to Mrs. Morse, who was pleased at his manifest improvement.

"He is the first man that ever drew passing notice from Ruth," she told her husband. "She has been so singularly backward where men are concerned that I have been worried greatly."

Mr. Morse looked at his wife curiously.

"You mean to use this young sailor to wake her up?" he questioned.

"I mean that she is not to die an old maid if I can help it," was the answer. "If this young Eden can arouse her interest in mankind in general, it will be good thing."

"A very good thing," he commented. "But suppose,—and we must suppose, sometimes, my dear,—suppose he arouses her interest too particularly in him?"

"Impossible," Mrs. Morse laughed. "She is three years older than he, and, besides, it is impossible. Nothing will ever come of it. Trust that to me."

And so Martin's rôle was arranged for him, while he, led on by Arthur and Norman, was meditating an extravagance. They were going out for a ride into the hills Sunday morning on their wheels, which did not interest Martin until he learned that Ruth, too, rode a wheel and was going along. He did not ride, nor own a wheel, but if Ruth rode, it was up to him to begin, was his decision; and when he said good night, he stopped in at a cyclery on his way home and spent forty dollars for a wheel. It was more than a month's hard-earned wages, and it reduced his stock of money amazingly; but when he added the hundred dollars he was to receive from the *Examiner* to the four hundred and twenty dollars that was the least *The Youth's Companion* could pay him, he felt that he had reduced the perplexity the unwonted amount of money had caused him. Nor did he mind, in the course of learning to ride the wheel home, the fact that he ruined his suit of clothes. He caught the tailor by telephone that night from Mr. Higginbotham's store and ordered another suit. Then he carried the wheel up the narrow stairway that clung like a fire-escape to the rear wall of the building, and when he had moved his bed out from the wall, found there was just space enough in the small room for himself and the wheel.

Sunday he had intended to devote to studying for the high school examination, but the pearl-diving article lured him away, and he spent the day in the white-hot fever of re-creating the beauty and romance that burned in him. The fact that the *Examiner* of that morning had failed to publish his treasure-hunting article did not dash his spirits. He was at too great a height for that, and having been deaf to a twice-repeated summons, he went without the heavy Sunday dinner with which Mr. Higginbotham invariably graced his table. To Mr. Higginbotham such a dinner was advertisement of his worldly achievement and prosperity, and he honored it by delivering platitudinous sermonettes upon American institutions and the opportunity said institutions gave to any hard-working man to rise—the rise, in his case, which he pointed out unfailingly, being from a grocer's clerk to the ownership of Higginbotham's Cash Store.

Martin Eden looked with a sigh at his unfinished "Pearl-diving" on Monday morning, and took the car down to Oakland to the high school. And when, days later, he applied for the results of his examinations, he learned that he had failed in everything save grammar.

"Your grammar is excellent," Professor Hilton informed him, staring at him through heavy spectacles; "but you know nothing, positively nothing, in the other branches, and your United States history is abominable—there is no other word for it, abominable. I should advise you—"

Professor Hilton paused and glared at him, unsympathetic

and unimaginative as one of his own test-tubes. He was professor of physics in the high school, possessor of a large family, a meagre salary, and a select fund of parrot-learned knowledge.

"Yes, sir," Martin said humbly, wishing somehow that the man at the desk in the library was in Professor Hilton's place just then.

"And I should advise you to go back to the grammar school for at least two years. Good day."

Martin was not deeply affected by his failure, though he was surprised at Ruth's shocked expression when he told her Professor Hilton's advice. Her disappointment was so evident that he was sorry he had failed, but chiefly so for her sake.

"You see I was right," she said. "You know far more than any of the students entering high school, and yet you can't pass the examinations. It is because what education you have is fragmentary, sketchy. You need the discipline of study, such as only skilled teachers can give you. You must be thoroughly grounded. Professor Hilton is right, and if I were you, I'd go to night school. A year and a half of it might enable you to catch up that additional six months. Besides, that would leave you your days in which to write, or, if you could not make your living by your pen, you would have your days in which to work in some position."

But if my days are taken up with work and my nights with school, when am I going to see you?—was Martin's first thought, though he refrained from uttering it. Instead, he said:—

"It seems so babyish for me to be going to night school. But I wouldn't mind that if I thought it would pay. But I don't think it will pay. I can do the work quicker than they can teach me. It would be a loss of time—" he thought of her and his desire to have her—"and I can't afford the time. I haven't the time to spare, in fact."

"There is so much that is necessary." She looked at him gently, and he felt that he was a brute to oppose her. "Physics and chemistry—you can't do them without laboratory study; and you'll find algebra and geometry almost hopeless without instruction. You need the skilled teachers, the specialists in the art of imparting knowledge."

He was silent for a minute, casting about for the least vainglorious way in which to express himself.

"Please don't think I'm bragging," he began. "I don't intend it that way at all. But I have a feeling that I am what I may call a natural student. I can study by myself. I take to it kindly, like a duck to water. You see yourself what I did with grammar. And I've learned much of other things—you would never dream how much. And I'm only getting started. Wait till I get—" He hesitated and assured himself of the pronunciation before he said "momentum. I'm getting my first real feel of things now. I'm beginning to size up the situation—"

"Please don't say 'size up,' " she interrupted.

"To get a line on things," he hastily amended.

"That doesn't mean anything in correct English," she objected.

He floundered for a fresh start.

"What I'm driving at is that I'm beginning to get the lay of the land."

Out of pity she forebore, and he went on.

"Knowledge seems to me like a chart-room. Whenever I go into the library, I am impressed that way. The part played by teachers is to teach the student the contents of the chart-room in a systematic way. The teachers are guides to the chart-room, that's all. It's not something that they have in their own heads. They don't make it up, don't create it. It's all in the chart-room and they know their way about in it, and it's their business to show the place to strangers who might else get lost. Now I don't get lost easily. I have the bump of location. I usually know where I'm at— What's wrong now?"

"Don't say 'where I'm at.' "

"That's right," he said gratefully, "where I am. But where am I at—I mean, where am I? Oh, yes, in the chart-room. Well, some people—"

"Persons," she corrected.

"Some persons need guides, most persons do; but I think I can get along without them. I've spent a lot of time in the chart-room now, and I'm on the edge of knowing my way about, what charts I want to refer to, what coasts I want to explore. And from the way I line it up, I'll explore a whole lot more quickly by myself. The speed of a fleet, you know, is the speed of the slowest ship, and the speed of the teachers is affected the same way. They can't go any faster than the ruck of their scholars, and I can set a faster pace for myself than they set for a whole schoolroom."

" 'He travels the fastest who travels alone,' " she quoted at him.

But I'd travel faster with you just the same, was what he wanted to blurt out, as he caught a vision of a world without end of sunlit spaces and starry voids through which he drifted with her, his arm around her, her pale gold hair blowing about his face. In the same instant he was aware of the pitiful inadequacy of speech. God! If he could so frame words that she could see what he then saw! And he felt the stir in him, like a throe of yearning pain, of the desire to paint these visions that flashed unsummoned on the mirror of his mind. Ah, that was it! He caught at the hem of the secret. It was the very thing that the great writers and master-poets did. That was why they were giants. They knew how to express what they thought, and felt, and saw. Dogs asleep in the sun often whined and barked, but they were unable to tell what they saw that made them whine and bark. He had often wondered what it was. And that was all he was, a dog asleep in the sun. He saw noble and beautiful visions, but he could only whine and bark at Ruth. But he would cease sleeping in the sun. He would stand up, with open eyes, and he would struggle and toil and learn until, with eyes unblinded and tongue untied, he could share with her his visioned wealth. Other men had discovered the trick of expression, of making words obedient servitors, and of making combinations of words mean more than the sum of their separate meanings. He was stirred profoundly by the passing glimpse at the secret, and he was again caught up in the vision of sunlit spaces and starry voids—until it came to him that it was very quiet, and he saw Ruth regarding him with an amused expression and a smile in her eyes.

"I have had a great visioning," he said, and at the sound of his words in his own ears his heart gave a leap. Where had those words come from? They had adequately expressed the pause his vision had put in the conversation. It was a miracle.

Never had he so loftily framed a lofty thought. But never had
he attempted to frame lofty thoughts in words. That was it.
That explained it. He had never tried. But Swinburne had,
and Tennyson, and Kipling, and all the other poets. His mind
flashed on to his "Pearl-diving." He had never dared the big
things, the spirit of the beauty that was a fire in him. That
article would be a different thing when he was done with it.
He was appalled by the vastness of the beauty that rightfully
belonged in it, and again his mind flashed and dared, and he
demanded of himself why he could not chant that beauty in
noble verse as the great poets did. And there was all the mysterious delight and spiritual wonder of his love for Ruth.
Why could he not chant that, too, as the poets did? They had
sung of love. So would he. By God!—

And in his frightened ears he heard his exclamation echoing. Carried away, he had breathed it aloud. The blood
surged into his face, wave upon wave, mastering the bronze
of it till the blush of shame flaunted itself from collar-rim to
the roots of his hair.

"I—I—beg your pardon," he stammered. "I was thinking."

"It sounded as if you were praying," she said bravely, but
she felt herself inside to be withering and shrinking. It was
the first time she had heard an oath from the lips of a man
she knew, and she was shocked, not merely as a matter of
principle and training, but shocked in spirit by this rough
blast of life in the garden of her sheltered maidenhood.

But she forgave, and with surprise at the ease of her forgiveness. Somehow it was not so difficult to forgive him anything. He had not had a chance to be as other men, and he
was trying so hard, and succeeding, too. It never entered her
head that there could be any other reason for her being kindly
disposed toward him. She was tenderly disposed toward him,
but she did not know it. She had no way of knowing it. The
placid poise of twenty-four years without a single love affair
did not fit her with a keen perception of her own feelings,
and she who had never warmed to actual love was unaware
that she was warming now.

Chapter XI

MARTIN went back to his pearl-diving article, which would have been finished sooner if it had not been broken in upon so frequently by his attempts to write poetry. His poems were love poems, inspired by Ruth, but they were never completed. Not in a day could he learn to chant in noble verse. Rhyme and metre and structure were serious enough in themselves, but there was, over and beyond them, an intangible and evasive something that he caught in all great poetry, but which he could not catch and imprison in his own. It was the elusive spirit of poetry itself that he sensed and sought after but could not capture. It seemed a glow to him, a warm and trailing vapor, ever beyond his reaching, though sometimes he was rewarded by catching at shreds of it and weaving them into phrases that echoed in his brain with haunting notes or drifted across his vision in misty wafture of unseen beauty. It was baffling. He ached with desire to express and could but gibber prosaically as everybody gibbered. He read his fragments aloud. The metre marched along on perfect feet, and the rhyme pounded a longer and equally faultless rhythm, but the glow and high exaltation that he felt within were lacking. He could not understand, and time and again, in despair, defeated and depressed, he returned to his article. Prose was certainly an easier medium.

Following the "Pearl-diving," he wrote an article on the sea as a career, another on turtle-catching, and a third on the northeast trades. Then he tried, as an experiment, a short story, and before he broke his stride he had finished six short stories and despatched them to various magazines. He wrote prolifically, intensely, from morning till night, and late at night, except when he broke off to go to the reading-room, draw books from the library, or to call on Ruth. He was profoundly happy. Life was pitched high. He was in a fever that never broke. The joy of creation that is supposed to belong to the gods was his. All the life about him—the odors of stale vegetables and soapsuds, the slatternly form of his sister, and the jeering face of Mr. Higginbotham—was a dream. The real world was in his mind, and the stories he wrote were so many pieces of reality out of his mind.

The days were too short. There was so much he wanted to study. He cut his sleep down to five hours and found that he could get along upon it. He tried four hours and a half, and regretfully came back to five. He could joyfully have spent all his waking hours upon any one of his pursuits. It was with regret that he ceased from writing to study, that he ceased from study to go to the library, that he tore himself away from that chart-room of knowledge or from the magazines in the reading-room that were filled with the secrets of writers who succeeded in selling their wares. It was like severing heart-strings, when he was with Ruth, to stand up and go; and he scorched through the dark streets so as to get home to his books at the least possible expense of time. And hardest of all was it to shut up the algebra or physics, put note-book and pencil aside, and close his tired eyes in sleep. He hated the thought of ceasing to live, even for so short a time, and his sole consolation was that the alarm clock was set five hours ahead. He would lose only five hours anyway, and then the jangling bell would jerk him out of unconsciousness and he would have before him another glorious day of nineteen hours.

In the meantime the weeks were passing, his money was ebbing low, and there was no money coming in. A month after he had mailed it, the adventure serial for boys was returned to him by *The Youth's Companion*. The rejection slip was so tactfully worded that he felt kindly toward the editor. But he did not feel so kindly toward the editor of the *San Francisco Examiner*. After waiting two whole weeks, Martin had written to him. A week later he wrote again. At the end of the month, he went over to San Francisco and personally called upon the editor. But he did not meet that exalted personage, thanks to a Cerberus of an office boy, of tender years and red hair, who guarded the portals. At the end of the fifth week the manuscript came back to him, by mail, without comment. There was no rejection slip, no explanation, nothing. In the same way his other articles were tied up with the other leading San Francisco papers. When he recovered them, he sent them to the magazines in the East, from which they were returned more promptly, accompanied always by the printed rejection slips.

The short stories were returned in similar fashion. He read them over and over, and liked them so much that he could not puzzle out the cause of their rejection, until, one day, he read in a newspaper that manuscripts should always be type-written. That explained it. Of course editors were so busy that they could not afford the time and strain of reading hand-writing. Martin rented a typewriter and spent a day mastering the machine. Each day he typed what he composed, and he typed his earlier manuscripts as fast as they were returned him. He was surprised when the typed ones began to come back. His jaw seemed to become squarer, his chin more ag-gressive, and he bundled the manuscripts off to new editors.

The thought came to him that he was not a good judge of his own work. He tried it out on Gertrude. He read his sto-ries aloud to her. Her eyes glistened, and she looked at him proudly as she said: —

"Ain't it grand, you writin' those sort of things."

"Yes, yes," he demanded impatiently. "But the story—how did you like it?"

"Just grand," was the reply. "Just grand, an' thrilling, too. I was all worked up."

He could see that her mind was not clear. The perplexity was strong in her good-natured face. So he waited.

"But, say, Mart," after a long pause, "how did it end? Did that young man who spoke so highfalutin' get her?"

And, after he had explained the end, which he thought he had made artistically obvious, she would say: —

"That's what I wanted to know. Why didn't you write that way in the story?"

One thing he learned, after he had read her a number of stories, namely, that she liked happy endings.

"That story was perfectly grand," she announced, straight-ening up from the wash-tub with a tired sigh and wiping the sweat from her forehead with a red, steamy hand; "but it makes me sad. I want to cry. There is too many sad things in the world anyway. It makes me happy to think about happy things. Now if he'd married her, and— You don't mind, Mart?" she queried apprehensively. "I just happen to feel that

way, because I'm tired, I guess. But the story was grand just
the same, perfectly grand. Where are you goin' to sell it?"

"That's a horse of another color," he laughed.

"But if you *did* sell it, what do you think you'd get for it?"

"Oh, a hundred dollars. That would be the least, the way
prices go."

"My! I do hope you'll sell it!"

"Easy money, eh?" Then he added proudly: "I wrote it in
two days. That's fifty dollars a day."

He longed to read his stories to Ruth, but did not dare.
He would wait till some were published, he decided, then she
would understand what he had been working for. In the
meantime he toiled on. Never had the spirit of adventure
lured him more strongly than on this amazing exploration of
the realm of mind. He bought the text-books on physics and
chemistry, and, along with his algebra, worked out problems
and demonstrations. He took the laboratory proofs on faith,
and his intense power of vision enabled him to see the reactions of chemicals more understandingly than the average
student saw them in the laboratory. Martin wandered on
through the heavy pages, overwhelmed by the clews he was
getting to the nature of things. He had accepted the world as
the world, but now he was comprehending the organization
of it, the play and interplay of force and matter. Spontaneous
explanations of old matters were continually arising in his
mind. Levers and purchases fascinated him, and his mind
roved backward to hand-spikes and blocks and tackles at sea.
The theory of navigation, which enabled the ships to travel
unerringly their courses over the pathless ocean, was made
clear to him. The mysteries of storm, and rain, and tide were
revealed, and the reason for the existence of trade-winds made
him wonder whether he had written his article on the northeast trade too soon. At any rate he knew he could write it
better now. One afternoon he went out with Arthur to the
University of California, and, with bated breath and a feeling
of religious awe, went through the laboratories, saw demonstrations, and listened to a physics professor lecturing to his
classes.

But he did not neglect his writing. A stream of short stories
flowed from his pen, and he branched out into the easier

forms of verse—the kind he saw printed in the magazines—
though he lost his head and wasted two weeks on a tragedy
in blank verse, the swift rejection of which, by half a dozen
magazines, dumfounded him. Then he discovered Henley and
wrote a series of sea-poems on the model of "Hospital
Sketches." They were simple poems, of light and color, and
romance and adventure. "Sea Lyrics," he called them, and he
judged them to be the best work he had yet done. There were
thirty, and he completed them in a month, doing one a day
after having done his regular day's work on fiction, which
day's work was the equivalent to a week's work of the average
successful writer. The toil meant nothing to him. It was not
toil. He was finding speech, and all the beauty and wonder
that had been pent for years behind his inarticulate lips was
now pouring forth in a wild and virile flood.

He showed the "Sea Lyrics" to no one, not even to the
editors. He had become distrustful of editors. But it was not
distrust that prevented him from submitting the "Lyrics."
They were so beautiful to him that he was impelled to save
them to share with Ruth in some glorious, far-off time when
he would dare to read to her what he had written. Against
that time he kept them with him, reading them aloud, going
over them until he knew them by heart.

He lived every moment of his waking hours, and he lived
in his sleep, his subjective mind rioting through his five hours
of surcease and combining the thoughts and events of the day
into grotesque and impossible marvels. In reality, he never
rested, and a weaker body or a less firmly poised brain would
have been prostrated in a general break-down. His late afternoon calls on Ruth were rarer now, for June was approaching, when she would take her degree and finish with the
university. Bachelor of Arts!—when he thought of her
degree, it seemed she fled beyond him faster than he could
pursue.

One afternoon a week she gave to him, and arriving late,
he usually stayed for dinner and for music afterward. Those
were his red-letter days. The atmosphere of the house, in such
contrast with that in which he lived, and the mere nearness to
her, sent him forth each time with a firmer grip on his resolve
to climb the heights. In spite of the beauty in him, and the

aching desire to create, it was for her that he struggled. He
was a lover first and always. All other things he subordinated
to love. Greater than his adventure in the world of thought
was his love-adventure. The world itself was not so amazing
because of the atoms and molecules that composed it according to the propulsions of irresistible force; what made it
amazing was the fact that Ruth lived in it. She was the most
amazing thing he had ever known, or dreamed, or guessed.

But he was oppressed always by her remoteness. She was
so far from him, and he did not know how to approach her.
He had been a success with girls and women in his own class;
but he had never loved any of them, while he did love her,
and besides, she was not merely of another class. His very
love elevated her above all classes. She was a being apart, so
far apart that he did not know how to draw near to her as a
lover should draw near. It was true, as he acquired knowledge
and language, that he was drawing nearer, talking her speech,
discovering ideas and delights in common; but this did not
satisfy his lover's yearning. His lover's imagination had made
her holy, too holy, too spiritualized, to have any kinship with
him in the flesh. It was his own love that thrust her from him
and made her seem impossible for him. Love itself denied
him the one thing that it desired.

And then, one day, without warning, the gulf between
them was bridged for a moment, and thereafter, though the
gulf remained, it was ever narrower. They had been eating
cherries—great, luscious, black cherries with a juice of the
color of dark wine. And later, as she read aloud to him from
"The Princess," he chanced to notice the stain of the cherries
on her lips. For the moment her divinity was shattered. She
was clay, after all, mere clay, subject to the common law of
clay as his clay was subject, or anybody's clay. Her lips were
flesh like his, and cherries dyed them as cherries dyed his.
And if so with her lips, then was it so with all of her. She was
woman, all woman, just like any woman. It came upon him
abruptly. It was a revelation that stunned him. It was as if he
had seen the sun fall out of the sky, or had seen worshipped
purity polluted.

Then he realized the significance of it, and his heart began
pounding and challenging him to play the lover with this

woman who was not a spirit from other worlds but a mere woman with lips a cherry could stain. He trembled at the audacity of his thought; but all his soul was singing, and reason, in a triumphant pæan, assured him he was right. Something of this change in him must have reached her, for she paused from her reading, looked up at him, and smiled. His eyes dropped from her blue eyes to her lips, and the sight of the stain maddened him. His arms all but flashed out to her and around her, in the way of his old careless life. She seemed to lean toward him, to wait, and all his will fought to hold him back.

"You were not following a word," she pouted.

Then she laughed at him, delighting in his confusion, and as he looked into her frank eyes and knew that she had divined nothing of what he felt, he became abashed. He had indeed in thought dared too far. Of all the women he had known there was no woman who would not have guessed— save her. And she had not guessed. There was the difference. She *was* different. He was appalled by his own grossness, awed by her clear innocence, and he gazed again at her across the gulf. The bridge had broken down.

But still the incident had brought him nearer. The memory of it persisted, and in the moments when he was most cast down, he dwelt upon it eagerly. The gulf was never again so wide. He had accomplished a distance vastly greater than a bachelorship of arts, or a dozen bachelorships. She was pure, it was true, as he had never dreamed of purity; but cherries stained her lips. She was subject to the laws of the universe just as inexorably as he was. She had to eat to live, and when she got her feet wet, she caught cold. But that was not the point. If she could feel hunger and thirst, and heat and cold, then could she feel love—and love for a man. Well, he was a man. And why could he not be *the* man? "It's up to me to make good," he would murmur fervently. "I will be *the* man. I will make myself *the* man. I will make good."

Chapter XII

EARLY ONE EVENING, struggling with a sonnet that twisted all awry the beauty and thought that trailed in glow and vapor through his brain, Martin was called to the telephone.

"It's a lady's voice, a fine lady's," Mr. Higginbotham, who had called him, jeered.

Martin went to the telephone in the corner of the room, and felt a wave of warmth rush through him as he heard Ruth's voice. In his battle with the sonnet he had forgotten her existence, and at the sound of her voice his love for her smote him like a sudden blow. And such a voice!—delicate and sweet, like a strain of music heard far off and faint, or, better, like a bell of silver, a perfect tone, crystal-pure. No mere woman had a voice like that. There was something celestial about it, and it came from other worlds. He could scarcely hear what it said, so ravished was he, though he controlled his face, for he knew that Mr. Higginbotham's ferret eyes were fixed upon him.

It was not much that Ruth wanted to say—merely that Norman had been going to take her to a lecture that night, but that he had a headache, and she was so disappointed, and she had the tickets, and that if he had no other engagement, would he be good enough to take her?

Would he! He fought to suppress the eagerness in his voice. It was amazing. He had always seen her in her own house. And he had never dared to ask her to go anywhere with him. Quite irrelevantly, still at the telephone and talking with her, he felt an overpowering desire to die for her, and visions of heroic sacrifice shaped and dissolved in his whirling brain. He loved her so much, so terribly, so hopelessly. In that moment of mad happiness that she should go out with him, go to a lecture with him—with him, Martin Eden—she soared so far above him that there seemed nothing else for him to do than die for her. It was the only fit way in which he could express the tremendous and lofty emotion he felt for her. It was the sublime abnegation of true love that comes to all lovers, and it came to him there, at the telephone, in a whirlwind of fire and glory; and to die for her, he felt, was to have lived and loved well. And he was only twenty-one, and he had never been in love before.

His hand trembled as he hung up the receiver, and he was weak from the organ which had stirred him. His eyes were shining like an angel's, and his face was transfigured, purged of all earthly dross, and pure and holy.

"Makin' dates outside, eh?" his brother-in-law sneered. "You know what that means. You'll be in the police court yet."

But Martin could not come down from the height. Not even the bestiality of the allusion could bring him back to earth. Anger and hurt were beneath him. He had seen a great vision and was as a god, and he could feel only profound and awful pity for this maggot of a man. He did not look at him, and though his eyes passed over him, he did not see him; and as in a dream he passed out of the room to dress. It was not until he had reached his own room and was tying his necktie that he became aware of a sound that lingered unpleasantly in his ears. On investigating this sound he identified it as the final snort of Bernard Higginbotham, which somehow had not penetrated to his brain before.

As Ruth's front door closed behind them and he came down the steps with her, he found himself greatly perturbed. It was not unalloyed bliss, taking her to the lecture. He did not know what he ought to do. He had seen, on the streets, with persons of her class, that the women took the men's arms. But then, again, he had seen them when they didn't; and he wondered if it was only in the evening that arms were taken, or only between husbands and wives and relatives.

Just before he reached the sidewalk, he remembered Minnie. Minnie had always been a stickler. She had called him down the second time she walked out with him, because he had gone along on the inside, and she had laid the law down to him that a gentleman always walked on the outside—when he was with a lady. And Minnie had made a practice of kicking his heels, whenever they crossed from one side of the street to the other, to remind him to get over on the outside. He wondered where she had got that

item of etiquette, and whether it had filtered down from
above and was all right.

It wouldn't do any harm to try it, he decided, by the time
they had reached the sidewalk; and he swung behind Ruth
and took up his station on the outside. Then the other problem presented itself. Should he offer her his arm? He had
never offered anybody his arm in his life. The girls he had
known never took the fellows' arms. For the first several times
they walked freely, side by side, and after that it was arms
around the waists, and heads against the fellows' shoulders
where the streets were unlighted. But this was different. She
wasn't that kind of a girl. He must do something.

He crooked the arm next to her—crooked it very slightly
and with secret tentativeness, not invitingly, but just casually,
as though he was accustomed to walk that way. And then the
wonderful thing happened. He felt her hand upon his arm.
Delicious thrills ran through him at the contact, and for a few
sweet moments it seemed that he had left the solid earth and
was flying with her through the air. But he was soon back
again, perturbed by a new complication. They were crossing
the street. This would put him on the inside. He should be
on the outside. Should he therefore drop her arm and change
over? And if he did so, would he have to repeat the
manœuvre the next time? And the next? There was something
wrong about it, and he resolved not to caper about and play
the fool. Yet he was not satisfied with his conclusion, and
when he found himself on the inside, he talked quickly and
earnestly, making a show of being carried away by what he
was saying, so that, in case he was wrong in not changing
sides, his enthusiasm would seem the cause for his carelessness.

As they crossed Broadway, he came face to face with a new
problem. In the blaze of the electric lights, he saw Lizzie
Connolly and her giggly friend. Only for an instant he hesitated, then his hand went up and his hat came off. He could
not be disloyal to his kind, and it was to more than Lizzie
Connolly that his hat was lifted. She nodded and looked at
him boldly, not with soft and gentle eyes like Ruth's, but
with eyes that were handsome and hard, and that swept on
past him to Ruth and itemized her face and dress and station.

And he was aware that Ruth looked, too, with quick eyes that were timid and mild as a dove's, but which saw, in a look that was a flutter on and past, the working-class girl in her cheap finery and under the strange hat that all working-class girls were wearing just then.

"What a pretty girl!" Ruth said a moment later.

Martin could have blessed her, though he said: —

"I don't know. I guess it's all a matter of personal taste, but she doesn't strike me as being particularly pretty."

"Why, there isn't one woman in ten thousand with features as regular as hers. They are splendid. Her face is as clear-cut as a cameo. And her eyes are beautiful."

"Do you think so?" Martin queried absently, for to him there was only one beautiful woman in the world, and she was beside him, her hand upon his arm.

"Do I think so? If that girl had proper opportunity to dress, Mr. Eden, and if she were taught how to carry herself, you would be fairly dazzled by her, and so would all men."

"She would have to be taught how to speak," he commented, "or else most of the men wouldn't understand her. I'm sure you couldn't understand a quarter of what she said if she just spoke naturally."

"Nonsense! You are as bad as Arthur when you try to make your point."

"You forget how I talked when you first met me. I have learned a new language since then. Before that time I talked as that girl talks. Now I can manage to make myself understood sufficiently in your language to explain that you do not know that other girl's language. And do you know why she carries herself the way she does? I think about such things now, though I never used to think about them, and I am beginning to understand—much."

"But why does she?"

"She has worked long hours for years at machines. When one's body is young, it is very pliable, and hard work will mould it like putty according to the nature of the work. I can tell at a glance the trades of many workingmen I meet on the street. Look at me. Why am I rolling all about the shop? Because of the years I put in on the sea. If I'd put in the same years cow-punching, with my body young and pliable, I

wouldn't be rolling now, but I'd be bow-legged. And so with
that girl. You noticed that her eyes were what I might call
hard. She has never been sheltered. She has had to take care
of herself, and a young girl can't take care of herself and keep
her eyes soft and gentle like—like yours, for example."

"I think you are right," Ruth said in a low voice. "And it
is too bad. She is such a pretty girl."

He looked at her and saw her eyes luminous with pity. And
then he remembered that he loved her and was lost in amazement at his fortune that permitted him to love her and to take
her on his arm to a lecture.

Who are you, Martin Eden? he demanded of himself in the
looking-glass, that night when he got back to his room. He
gazed at himself long and curiously. Who are you? What are
you? Where do you belong? You belong by rights to girls like
Lizzie Connolly. You belong with the legions of toil, with all
that is low, and vulgar, and unbeautiful. You belong with the
oxen and the drudges, in dirty surroundings among smells
and stenches. There are the stale vegetables now. Those potatoes are rotting. Smell them, damn you, smell them. And
yet you dare to open the books, to listen to beautiful music,
to learn to love beautiful paintings, to speak good English, to
think thoughts that none of your own kind thinks, to tear
yourself away from the oxen and the Lizzie Connollys and to
love a pale spirit of a woman who is a million miles beyond
you and who lives in the stars! Who are you? and what are
you? damn you! And are you going to make good?

He shook his fist at himself in the glass, and sat down on
the edge of the bed to dream for a space with wide eyes. Then
he got out note-book and algebra and lost himself in quadratic equations, while the hours slipped by, and the stars
dimmed, and the gray of dawn flooded against his window.

Chapter XIII

IT WAS the knot of wordy socialists and working-class philosophers that held forth in the City Hall Park on warm afternoons that was responsible for the great discovery. Once or twice in the month, while riding through the park on his way to the library, Martin dismounted from his wheel and listened to the arguments, and each time he tore himself away reluctantly. The tone of discussion was much lower than at Mr. Morse's table. The men were not grave and dignified. They lost their tempers easily and called one another names, while oaths and obscene allusions were frequent on their lips. Once or twice he had seen them come to blows. And yet, he knew not why, there seemed something vital about the stuff of these men's thoughts. Their logomachy was far more stimulating to his intellect than the reserved and quiet dogmatism of Mr. Morse. These men, who slaughtered English, gesticulated like lunatics, and fought one another's ideas with primitive anger, seemed somehow to be more alive than Mr. Morse and his crony, Mr. Butler.

Martin had heard Herbert Spencer quoted several times in the park, but one afternoon a disciple of Spencer's appeared, a seedy tramp with a dirty coat buttoned tightly at the throat to conceal the absence of a shirt. Battle royal was waged, amid the smoking of many cigarettes and the expectoration of much tobacco-juice, wherein the tramp successfully held his own, even when a socialist workman sneered, "There is no god but the Unknowable, and Herbert Spencer is his prophet." Martin was puzzled as to what the discussion was about, but when he rode on to the library he carried with him a new-born interest in Herbert Spencer, and because of the frequency with which the tramp had mentioned "First Principles," Martin drew out that volume.

So the great discovery began. Once before he had tried Spencer, and choosing the "Principles of Psychology" to begin with, he had failed as abjectly as he had failed with Madam Blavatsky. There had been no understanding the book, and he had returned it unread. But this night, after

algebra and physics, and an attempt at a sonnet, he got into
bed and opened "First Principles." Morning found him still
reading. It was impossible for him to sleep. Nor did he write
that day. He lay on the bed till his body grew tired, when he
tried the hard floor, reading on his back, the book held in the
air above him, or changing from side to side. He slept that
night, and did his writing next morning, and then the book
tempted him and he fell, reading all afternoon, oblivious to
everything and oblivious to the fact that that was the afternoon Ruth gave to him. His first consciousness of the immediate world about him was when Bernard Higginbotham
jerked open the door and demanded to know if he thought
they were running a restaurant.

Martin Eden had been mastered by curiosity all his days.
He wanted to know, and it was this desire that had sent him
adventuring over the world. But he was now learning from
Spencer that he never had known, and that he never could
have known had he continued his sailing and wandering forever. He had merely skimmed over the surface of things, observing detached phenomena, accumulating fragments of
facts, making superficial little generalizations—and all and
everything quite unrelated in a capricious and disorderly
world of whim and chance. The mechanism of the flight of
birds he had watched and reasoned about with understanding; but it had never entered his head to try to explain the
process whereby birds, as organic flying mechanisms, had
been developed. He had never dreamed there was such a process. That birds should have come to be, was unguessed. They
always had been. They just happened.

And as it was with birds, so had it been with everything.
His ignorant and unprepared attempts at philosophy had
been fruitless. The mediæval metaphysics of Kant had given
him the key to nothing, and had served the sole purpose of
making him doubt his own intellectual powers. In similar
manner his attempt to study evolution had been confined to
a hopelessly technical volume by Romanes. He had understood nothing, and the only idea he had gathered was that
evolution was a dry-as-dust theory, of a lot of little men possessed of huge and unintelligible vocabularies. And now he
learned that evolution was no mere theory but an accepted

process of development; that scientists no longer disagreed about it, their only differences being over the method of evolution.

And here was the man Spencer, organizing all knowledge for him, reducing everything to unity, elaborating ultimate realities, and presenting to his startled gaze a universe so concrete of realization that it was like the model of a ship such as sailors make and put into glass bottles. There was no caprice, no chance. All was law. It was in obedience to law that the bird flew, and it was in obedience to the same law that fermenting slime had writhed and squirmed and put out legs and wings and become a bird.

Martin had ascended from pitch to pitch of intellectual living, and here he was at a higher pitch than ever. All the hidden things were laying their secrets bare. He was drunken with comprehension. At night, asleep, he lived with the gods in colossal nightmare; and awake, in the day, he went around like a somnambulist, with absent stare, gazing upon the world he had just discovered. At table he failed to hear the conversation about petty and ignoble things, his eager mind seeking out and following cause and effect in everything before him. In the meat on the platter he saw the shining sun and traced its energy back through all its transformations to its source a hundred million miles away, or traced its energy ahead to the moving muscles in his arms that enabled him to cut the meat, and to the brain wherewith he willed the muscles to move to cut the meat, until, with inward gaze, he saw the same sun shining in his brain. He was entranced by illumination, and did not hear the "Bughouse," whispered by Jim, nor see the anxiety on his sister's face, nor notice the rotary motion of Bernard Higginbotham's finger, whereby he imparted the suggestion of wheels revolving in his brother-in-law's head.

What, in a way, most profoundly impressed Martin, was the correlation of knowledge—of all knowledge. He had been curious to know things, and whatever he acquired he had filed away in separate memory compartments in his brain. Thus, on the subject of sailing he had an immense store. On the subject of woman he had a fairly large store. But these two subjects had been unrelated. Between the two memory compartments there had been no connection. That, in the fabric of knowledge, there should be any connection whatever between a woman with hysterics and a schooner carrying a weather-helm or heaving to in a gale, would have struck him as ridiculous and impossible. But Herbert Spencer had shown him not only that it was not ridiculous, but that it was impossible for there to be no connection. All things were related to all other things from the farthermost star in the wastes of space to the myriads of atoms in the grain of sand under one's foot. This new concept was a perpetual amazement to Martin, and he found himself engaged continually in tracing the relationship between all things under the sun and on the other side of the sun. He drew up lists of the most incongruous things and was unhappy until he succeeded in establishing kinship between them all—kinship between love, poetry, earthquake, fire, rattlesnakes, rainbows, precious gems, monstrosities, sunsets, the roaring of lions, illuminating gas, cannibalism, beauty, murder, lovers, fulcrums, and tobacco. Thus, he unified the universe and held it up and looked at it, or wandered through its byways and alleys and jungles, not as a terrified traveller in the thick of mysteries seeking an unknown goal, but observing and charting and becoming familiar with all there was to know. And the more he knew, the more passionately he admired the universe, and life, and his own life in the midst of it all.

"You fool!" he cried at his image in the looking-glass. "You wanted to write, and you tried to write, and you had nothing in you to write about. What did you have in you?—some childish notions, a few half-baked sentiments, a lot of undigested beauty, a great black mass of ignorance, a heart filled to bursting with love, and an ambition as big as your love and as futile as your ignorance. And you wanted to write! Why, you're just on the edge of beginning to get something in you to write about. You wanted to create beauty, but how could you when you knew nothing about the nature of beauty? You wanted to write about life when you knew nothing of the essential characteristics of life. You wanted to write about the world and the scheme of existence when the world was a Chinese puzzle to you and all that you could have written would have been about what you did not know of the scheme of existence. But cheer up, Martin, my boy. You'll write yet. You know a little, a very little, and you're on the right road now to know more. Some day, if you're lucky, you may come pretty close to knowing all that may be known. Then you will write."

He brought his great discovery to Ruth, sharing with her all his joy and wonder in it. But she did not seem to be so enthusiastic over it. She tacitly accepted it and, in a way, seemed aware of it from her own studies. It did not stir her deeply, as it did him, and he would have been surprised had he not reasoned it out that it was not new and fresh to her as it was to him. Arthur and Norman, he found, believed in evolution and had read Spencer, though it did not seem to have made any vital impression upon them, while the young fellow with the glasses and the mop of hair, Will Olney, sneered disagreeably at Spencer and repeated the epigram, "There is no god but the Unknowable, and Herbert Spencer is his prophet."

But Martin forgave him the sneer, for he had begun to discover that Olney was not in love with Ruth. Later, he was dumfounded to learn from various little happenings not only that Olney did not care for Ruth, but that he had a positive dislike for her. Martin could not understand this. It was a bit of phenomena that he could not correlate with all the rest of the phenomena in the universe. But nevertheless he felt sorry for the young fellow because of the great lack in his nature that prevented him from a proper appreciation of Ruth's fineness and beauty. They rode out into the hills several Sundays on their wheels, and Martin had ample opportunity to observe the armed truce that existed between Ruth and Olney. The latter chummed with Norman, throwing Arthur and Martin into company with Ruth, for which Martin was duly grateful.

Those Sundays were great days for Martin, greatest because he was with Ruth, and great, also, because they were putting him more on a par with the young men of her class. In spite of their long years of disciplined education, he was finding himself their intellectual equal, and the hours spent with them in conversation was so much practice for him in the use of the grammar he had studied so hard. He had abandoned the

etiquette books, falling back upon observation to show him
the right things to do. Except when carried away by his enthusiasm, he was always on guard, keenly watchful of their
actions and learning their little courtesies and refinements of
conduct.

The fact that Spencer was very little read was for some time
a source of surprise to Martin. "Herbert Spencer," said the
man at the desk in the library, "oh, yes, a great mind." But
the man did not seem to know anything of the content of
that great mind. One evening, at dinner, when Mr. Butler
was there, Martin turned the conversation upon Spencer. Mr.
Morse bitterly arraigned the English philosopher's agnosticism, but confessed that he had not read "First Principles";
while Mr. Butler stated that he had no patience with Spencer,
had never read a line of him, and had managed to get along
quite well without him. Doubts arose in Martin's mind, and
had he been less strongly individual he would have accepted
the general opinion and given Herbert Spencer up. As it was,
he found Spencer's explanation of things convincing; and, as
he phrased it to himself, to give up Spencer would be equivalent to a navigator throwing the compass and chronometer
overboard. So Martin went on into a thorough study of evolution, mastering more and more the subject himself, and
being convinced by the corroborative testimony of a thousand independent writers. The more he studied, the more vistas he caught of fields of knowledge yet unexplored, and the
regret that days were only twenty-four hours long became a
chronic complaint with him.

One day, because the days were so short, he decided to
give up algebra and geometry. Trigonometry he had not even
attempted. Then he cut chemistry from his study-list, retaining only physics.

"I am not a specialist," he said, in defence, to Ruth. "Nor
am I going to try to be a specialist. There are too many special fields for any one man, in a whole lifetime, to master a
tithe of them. I must pursue general knowledge. When I need
the work of specialists, I shall refer to their books."

"But that is not like having the knowledge yourself," she
protested.

"But it is unnecessary to have it. We profit from the work

of the specialists. That's what they are for. When I came in, I noticed the chimney-sweeps at work. They're specialists, and when they get done, you will enjoy clean chimneys without knowing anything about the construction of chimneys."

"That's far-fetched, I am afraid."

She looked at him curiously, and he felt a reproach in her gaze and manner. But he was convinced of the rightness of his position.

"All thinkers on general subjects, the greatest minds in the world, in fact, rely on the specialists. Herbert Spencer did that. He generalized upon the findings of thousands of investigators. He would have had to live a thousand lives in order to do it all himself. And so with Darwin. He took advantage of all that had been learned by the florists and cattle-breeders."

"You're right, Martin," Olney said. "You know what you're after, and Ruth doesn't. She doesn't know what she is after for herself even.

"—Oh, yes," Olney rushed on, heading off her objection, "I know you call it general culture. But it doesn't matter what you study if you want general culture. You can study French, or you can study German, or cut them both out and study Esperanto, you'll get the culture tone just the same. You can study Greek or Latin, too, for the same purpose, though it will never be any use to you. It will be culture, though. Why, Ruth studied Saxon, became clever in it,—that was two years ago,—and all that she remembers of it now is 'Whan that sweet Aprile with his schowers soote'—isn't that the way it goes?

"But it's given you the culture tone just the same," he laughed, again heading her off. "I know. We were in the same classes."

"But you speak of culture as if it should be a means to something," Ruth cried out. Her eyes were flashing, and in her cheeks were two spots of color. "Culture is the end in itself."

"But that is not what Martin wants."

"How do you know?"

"What do you want, Martin?" Olney demanded, turning squarely upon him.

Martin felt very uncomfortable, and looked entreaty at Ruth.

"Yes, what do you want?" Ruth asked. "That will settle it."

"Yes, of course, I want culture," Martin faltered. "I love beauty, and culture will give me a finer and keener appreciation of beauty."

She nodded her head and looked triumph.

"Rot, and you know it," was Olney's comment. "Martin's after career, not culture. It just happens that culture, in his case, is incidental to career. If he wanted to be a chemist, culture would be unnecessary. Martin wants to write, but he's afraid to say so because it will put you in the wrong.

"And why does Martin want to write?" he went on. "Because he isn't rolling in wealth. Why do you fill your head with Saxon and general culture? Because you don't have to make your way in the world. Your father sees to that. He buys your clothes for you, and all the rest. What rotten good is our education, yours and mine and Arthur's and Norman's? We're soaked in general culture, and if our daddies went broke to-day, we'd be falling down to-morrow on teachers' examinations. The best job you could get, Ruth, would be a country school or music teacher in a girls' boarding-school."

"And pray what would you do?" she asked.

"Not a blessed thing. I could earn a dollar and a half a day, common labor, and I might get in as instructor in Hanley's cramming joint—I say might, mind you, and I might be chucked out at the end of the week for sheer inability."

Martin followed the discussion closely, and while he was convinced that Olney was right, he resented the rather cavalier treatment he accorded Ruth. A new conception of love formed in his mind as he listened. Reason had nothing to do with love. It mattered not whether the woman he loved reasoned correctly or incorrectly. Love was above reason. If it just happened that she did not fully appreciate his necessity for a career, that did not make her a bit less lovable. She was all lovable, and what she thought had nothing to do with her lovableness.

"What's that?" he replied to a question from Olney that broke in upon his train of thought.

"I was saying that I hoped you wouldn't be fool enough to tackle Latin."

"But Latin is more than culture," Ruth broke in. "It is equipment."

"Well, are you going to tackle it?" Olney persisted.

Martin was sore beset. He could see that Ruth was hanging eagerly upon his answer.

"I am afraid I won't have time," he said finally. "I'd like to, but I won't have time."

"You see Martin's not seeking culture," Olney exulted. "He's trying to get somewhere, to do something."

"Oh, but it's mental training. It's mind discipline. It's what makes disciplined minds." Ruth looked expectantly at Martin, as if waiting for him to change his judgment. "You know, the foot-ball players have to train before the big game. And that is what Latin does for the thinker. It trains."

"Rot and bosh! That's what they told us when we were kids. But there is one thing they didn't tell us then. They let us find it out for ourselves afterwards." Olney paused for effect, then added, "And what they didn't tell us was that every gentleman should have studied Latin, but that no gentleman should know Latin."

"Now that's unfair," Ruth cried. "I knew you were turning the conversation just in order to get off something."

"It's clever all right," was the retort, "but it's fair, too. The only men who know their Latin are the apothecaries, the lawyers, and the Latin professors. And if Martin wants to be one of them, I miss my guess. But what's all that got to do with Herbert Spencer anyway? Martin's just discovered Spencer, and he's wild over him. Why? Because Spencer is taking him somewhere. Spencer couldn't take me anywhere, nor you. We haven't got anywhere to go. You'll get married some day, and I'll have nothing to do but keep track of the lawyers and business agents who will take care of the money my father's going to leave me."

Olney got up to go, but turned at the door and delivered a parting shot.

"You leave Martin alone, Ruth. He knows what's best for himself. Look at what he's done already. He makes me sick sometimes, sick and ashamed of myself. He knows more now about the world, and life, and man's place, and all the rest, than Arthur, or Norman, or I, or you, too, for that matter, and in spite of all our Latin, and French, and Saxon, and culture."

"But Ruth is my teacher," Martin answered chivalrously. "She is responsible for what little I have learned."

"Rats!" Olney looked at Ruth, and his expression was malicious. "I suppose you'll be telling me next that you read Spencer on her recommendation—only you didn't. And she doesn't know anything more about Darwin and evolution than I do about King Solomon's mines. What's that jawbreaker definition about something or other, of Spencer's, that you sprang on us the other day—that indefinite, incoherent homogeneity thing? Spring it on her, and see if she understands a word of it. That isn't culture, you see. Well, tra la, and if you tackle Latin, Martin, I won't have any respect for you."

And all the while, interested in the discussion, Martin had been aware of an irk in it as well. It was about studies and lessons, dealing with the rudiments of knowledge, and the schoolboyish tone of it conflicted with the big things that were stirring in him—with the grip upon life that was even then crooking his fingers like eagle's talons, with the cosmic thrills that made him ache, and with the inchoate consciousness of mastery of it all. He likened himself to a poet, wrecked on the shores of a strange land, filled with power of beauty, stumbling and stammering and vainly trying to sing in the rough, barbaric tongue of his brethren in the new land. And so with him. He was alive, painfully alive, to the great universal things, and yet he was compelled to potter and grope among schoolboy topics and debate whether or not he should study Latin.

"What in hell has Latin to do with it?" he demanded before his mirror that night. "I wish dead people would stay dead. Why should I and the beauty in me be ruled by the dead? Beauty is alive and everlasting. Languages come and go. They are the dust of the dead."

And his next thought was that he had been phrasing his ideas very well, and he went to bed wondering why he could not talk in similar fashion when he was with Ruth. He was only a schoolboy, with a schoolboy's tongue, when he was in her presence.

"Give me time," he said aloud. "Only give me time."

Time! Time! Time! was his unending plaint.

Chapter XIV

IT WAS not because of Olney, but in spite of Ruth, and his
love for Ruth, that he finally decided not to take up Latin.
His money meant time. There was so much that was more
important than Latin, so many studies that clamored with imperious voices. And he must write. He must earn money. He
had had no acceptances. Twoscore of manuscripts were travelling the endless round of the magazines. How did the others do it? He spent long hours in the free reading-room,
going over what others had written, studying their work eagerly and critically, comparing it with his own, and wondering, wondering, about the secret trick they had discovered
which enabled them to sell their work.

He was amazed at the immense amount of printed stuff
that was dead. No light, no life, no color, was shot through
it. There was no breath of life in it, and yet it sold, at two
cents a word, twenty dollars a thousand—the newspaper clipping had said so. He was puzzled by countless short stories,
written lightly and cleverly he confessed, but without vitality
or reality. Life was so strange and wonderful, filled with an
immensity of problems, of dreams, and of heroic toils, and
yet these stories dealt only with the commonplaces of life. He
felt the stress and strain of life, its fevers and sweats and wild
insurgences—surely this was the stuff to write about! He
wanted to glorify the leaders of forlorn hopes, the mad lovers,
the giants that fought under stress and strain, amid terror and
tragedy, making life crackle with the strength of their endeavor. And yet the magazine short stories seemed intent on
glorifying the Mr. Butlers, the sordid dollar-chasers, and the
commonplace little love affairs of commonplace little men and
women. Was it because the editors of the magazines were
commonplace? he demanded. Or were they afraid of life,
these writers and editors and readers?

But his chief trouble was that he did not know any editors
or writers. And not merely did he not know any writers, but
he did not know anybody who had ever attempted to write.
There was nobody to tell him, to hint to him, to give him the

least word of advice. He began to doubt that editors were real men. They seemed cogs in a machine. That was what it was, a machine. He poured his soul into stories, articles, and poems, and intrusted them to the machine. He folded them just so, put the proper stamps inside the long envelope along with the manuscript, sealed the envelope, put more stamps outside, and dropped it into the mail-box. It travelled across the continent, and after a certain lapse of time the postman returned him the manuscript in another long envelope, on the outside of which were the stamps he had enclosed. There was no human editor at the other end, but a mere cunning arrangement of cogs that changed the manuscript from one envelope to another and stuck on the stamps. It was like the slot machines wherein one dropped pennies, and, with a metallic whirl of machinery had delivered to him a stick of chewing-gum or a tablet of chocolate. It depended upon which slot one dropped the penny in, whether he got chocolate or gum. And so with the editorial machine. One slot brought checks and the other brought rejection slips. So far he had found only the latter slot.

It was the rejection slips that completed the horrible machinelikeness of the process. These slips were printed in stereotyped forms and he had received hundreds of them—as many as a dozen or more on each of his earlier manuscripts. If he had received one line, one personal line, along with one rejection of all his rejections, he would have been cheered. But not one editor had given that proof of existence. And he could conclude only that there were no warm human men at the other end, only mere cogs, well oiled and running beautifully in the machine.

He was a good fighter, whole-souled and stubborn, and he would have been content to continue feeding the machine for years; but he was bleeding to death, and not years but weeks would determine the fight. Each week his board bill brought him nearer destruction, while the postage on forty manuscripts bled him almost as severely. He no longer bought books, and he economized in petty ways and sought to delay the inevitable end; though he did not know how to economize, and brought the end nearer by a week when he gave his sister Marian five dollars for a dress.

He struggled in the dark, without advice, without encouragement, and in the teeth of discouragement. Even Gertrude was beginning to look askance. At first she had tolerated with sisterly fondness what she conceived to be his foolishness; but now, out of sisterly solicitude, she grew anxious. To her it seemed that his foolishness was becoming a madness. Martin knew this and suffered more keenly from it than from the open and nagging contempt of Bernard Higginbotham. Martin had faith in himself, but he was alone in this faith. Not even Ruth had faith. She had wanted him to devote himself to study, and, though she had not openly disapproved of his writing, she had never approved.

He had never offered to show her his work. A fastidious delicacy had prevented him. Besides, she had been studying heavily at the university, and he felt averse to robbing her of her time. But when she had taken her degree, she asked him herself to let her see something of what he had been doing. Martin was elated and diffident. Here was a judge. She was a bachelor of arts. She had studied literature under skilled instructors. Perhaps the editors were capable judges, too. But she would be different from them. She would not hand him a stereotyped rejection slip, nor would she inform him that lack of preference for his work did not necessarily imply lack of merit in his work. She would talk, a warm human being, in her quick, bright way, and, most important of all, she would catch glimpses of the real Martin Eden. In his work she would discern what his heart and soul were like, and she would come to understand something, a little something, of the stuff of his dreams and the strength of his power.

Martin gathered together a number of carbon copies of his short stories, hesitated a moment, then added his "Sea Lyrics." They mounted their wheels on a late June afternoon and rode for the hills. It was the second time he had been out with her alone, and as they rode along through the balmy warmth, just chilled by the sea-breeze to refreshing coolness, he was profoundly impressed by the fact that it was a very beautiful and well-ordered world and that it was good to be alive and to love. They left their wheels by the roadside and climbed to the brown top of an open knoll where the sunburnt grass breathed a harvest breath of dry sweetness and content.

"Its work is done," Martin said, as they seated themselves, she upon his coat, and he sprawling close to the warm earth. He sniffed the sweetness of the tawny grass, which entered his brain and set his thoughts whirling on from the particular to the universal. "It has achieved its reason for existence," he went on, patting the dry grass affectionately. "It quickened with ambition under the dreary downpour of last winter, fought the violent early spring, flowered, and lured the insects and the bees, scattered its seeds, squared itself with its duty and the world, and—"

"Why do you always look at things with such dreadfully practical eyes?" she interrupted.

"Because I've been studying evolution, I guess. It's only recently that I got my eyesight, if the truth were told."

"But it seems to me you lose sight of beauty by being so practical, that you destroy beauty like the boys who catch butterflies and rub the down off their beautiful wings."

He shook his head.

"Beauty has significance, but I never knew its significance before. I just accepted beauty as something meaningless, as something that was just beautiful without rhyme or reason. I did not know anything about beauty. But now I know, or, rather, am just beginning to know. This grass is more beautiful to me now that I know why it is grass, and all the hidden chemistry of sun and rain and earth that makes it become grass. Why, there is romance in the life-history of any grass, yes, and adventure, too. The very thought of it stirs me. When I think of the play of force and matter, and all the tremendous struggle of it, I feel as if I could write an epic on the grass."

"How well you talk," she said absently, and he noted that she was looking at him in a searching way.

He was all confusion and embarrassment on the instant, the blood flushing red on his neck and brow.

"I hope I am learning to talk," he stammered. "There seems to be so much in me I want to say. But it is all so big. I can't find ways to say what is really in me. Sometimes it seems to me that all the world, all life, everything, had taken up residence inside of me and was clamoring for me to be the spokesman. I feel—oh, I can't describe it—I feel the bigness of it, but when I speak, I babble like a little child. It is a great task to transmute feeling and sensation into speech, written or spoken, that will, in turn, in him who reads or listens, transmute itself back into the selfsame feeling and sensation. It is a lordly task. See, I bury my face in the grass, and the breath I draw in through my nostrils sets me quivering with a thousand thoughts and fancies. It is a breath of the universe I have breathed. I know song and laughter, and success and pain, and struggle and death; and I see visions that arise in my brain somehow out of the scent of the grass, and I would like to tell them to you, to the world. But how can I? My tongue is tied. I have tried, by the spoken word, just now, to describe to you the effect on me of the scent of the grass. But I have not succeeded. I have no more than hinted in awkward speech. My words seem gibberish to me. And yet I am stifled with desire to tell. Oh!—" he threw up his hands with a despairing gesture—"it is impossible! It is not understandable! It is incommunicable!"

"But you do talk well," she insisted. "Just think how you have improved in the short time I have known you. Mr. Butler is a noted public speaker. He is always asked by the State Committee to go out on stump during campaign. Yet you talked just as well as he the other night at dinner. Only he was more controlled. You get too excited; but you will get over that with practice. Why, you would make a good public speaker. You can go far—if you want to. You are masterly. You can lead men, I am sure, and there is no reason why you should not succeed at anything you set your hand to, just as you have succeeded with grammar. You would make a good lawyer. You should shine in politics. There is nothing to prevent you from making as great a success as Mr. Butler has made. And minus the dyspepsia," she added with a smile.

They talked on; she, in her gently persistent way, returning always to the need of thorough grounding in education and to the advantages of Latin as part of the foundation for any career. She drew her ideal of the successful man, and it was largely in her father's image, with a few unmistakable lines and touches of color from the image of Mr. Butler. He lis-

tened eagerly, with receptive ears, lying on his back and looking up and joying in each movement of her lips as she talked.
But his brain was not receptive. There was nothing alluring
in the pictures she drew, and he was aware of a dull pain of
disappointment and of a sharper ache of love for her. In all
she said there was no mention of his writing, and the manuscripts he had brought to read lay neglected on the ground.

At last, in a pause, he glanced at the sun, measured its
height above the horizon, and suggested his manuscripts by
picking them up.

"I had forgotten," she said quickly. "And I am so anxious
to hear."

He read to her a story, one that he flattered himself was
among his very best. He called it "The Wine of Life," and the
wine of it, that had stolen into his brain when he wrote it,
stole into his brain now as he read it. There was a certain
magic in the original conception, and he had adorned it with
more magic of phrase and touch. All the old fire and passion
with which he had written it were reborn in him, and he was
swayed and swept away so that he was blind and deaf to the
faults of it. But it was not so with Ruth. Her trained ear
detected the weaknesses and exaggerations, the overemphasis
of the tyro, and she was instantly aware each time the sen-
tence-rhythm tripped and faltered. She scarcely noted the
rhythm otherwise, except when it became too pompous, at
which moments she was disagreeably impressed with its amateurishness. That was her final judgment on the story as a
whole—amateurish, though she did not tell him so. Instead,
when he had done, she pointed out the minor flaws and said
that she liked the story.

But he was disappointed. Her criticism was just. He acknowledged that, but he had a feeling that he was not sharing
his work with her for the purpose of schoolroom correction.
The details did not matter. They could take care of themselves. He could mend them, he could learn to mend them.
Out of life he had captured something big and attempted to
imprison it in the story. It was the big thing out of life he
had read to her, not sentence-structure and semicolons. He
wanted her to feel with him this big thing that was his, that
he had seen with his own eyes, grappled with his own brain,

and placed there on the page with his own hands in printed words. Well, he had failed, was his secret decision. Perhaps the editors were right. He had felt the big thing, but he had failed to transmute it. He concealed his disappointment, and joined so easily with her in her criticism that she did not realize that deep down in him was running a strong undercurrent of disagreement.

"This next thing I've called 'The Pot'," he said, unfolding the manuscript. "It has been refused by four or five magazines now, but still I think it is good. In fact, I don't know what to think of it, except that I've caught something there. Maybe it won't affect you as it does me. It's a short thing—only two thousand words."

"How dreadful!" she cried, when he had finished. "It is horrible, unutterably horrible!"

He noted her pale face, her eyes wide and tense, and her clenched hands, with secret satisfaction. He had succeeded. He had communicated the stuff of fancy and feeling from out of his brain. It had struck home. No matter whether she liked it or not, it had gripped her and mastered her, made her sit there and listen and forget details.

"It is life," he said, "and life is not always beautiful. And yet, perhaps because I am strangely made, I find something beautiful there. It seems to me that the beauty is tenfold enhanced because it is there—"

"But why couldn't the poor woman—" she broke in disconnectedly. Then she left the revolt of her thought unexpressed to cry out: "Oh! It is degrading! It is not nice! It is nasty!"

For the moment it seemed to him that his heart stood still. *Nasty!* He had never dreamed it. He had not meant it. The whole sketch stood before him in letters of fire, and in such blaze of illumination he sought vainly for nastiness. Then his heart began to beat again. He was not guilty.

"Why didn't you select a nice subject?" she was saying. "We know there are nasty things in the world, but that is no reason—"

She talked on in her indignant strain, but he was not following her. He was smiling to himself as he looked up into her virginal face, so innocent, so penetratingly innocent, that its purity seemed always to enter into him, driving out of him all dross and bathing him in some ethereal effulgence that was as cool and soft and velvety as starshine. *We know there are nasty things in the world!* He cuddled to him the notion of her knowing, and chuckled over it as a love joke. The next moment, in a flashing vision of multitudinous detail, he sighted the whole sea of life's nastiness that he had known and voyaged over and through, and he forgave her for not understanding the story. It was through no fault of hers that she could not understand. He thanked God that she had been born and sheltered to such innocence. But he knew life, its foulness as well as its fairness, its greatness in spite of the slime that infested it, and by God he was going to have his say on it to the world. Saints in heaven—how could they be anything but fair and pure? No praise to them. But saints in slime—ah, that was the everlasting wonder! That was what made life worth while. To see moral grandeur rising out of cesspools of iniquity; to rise himself and first glimpse beauty, faint and far, through mud-dripping eyes; to see out of weakness, and frailty, and viciousness, and all abysmal brutishness, arising strength, and truth, and high spiritual endowment—

He caught a stray sequence of sentences she was uttering.

"The tone of it all is low. And there is so much that is high. Take 'In Memoriam.'"

He was impelled to suggest "Locksley Hall," and would have done so, had not his vision gripped him again and left him staring at her, the female of his kind, who, out of the primordial ferment, creeping and crawling up the vast ladder of life for a thousand thousand centuries, had emerged on the topmost rung, having become one Ruth, pure, and fair, and divine, and with power to make him know love, and to aspire toward purity, and to desire to taste divinity—him, Martin Eden, who, too, had come up in some amazing fashion from out of the ruck and the mire and the countless mistakes and abortions of unending creation. There was the romance, and the wonder, and the glory. There was the stuff to write, if he could only find speech. Saints in heaven!—They were only saints and could not help themselves. But he was a man.

"You have strength," he could hear her saying, "but it is untutored strength."

"Like a bull in a china shop," he suggested, and won a smile.

"And you must develop discrimination. You must consult taste, and fineness, and tone."

"I dare too much," he muttered.

She smiled approbation, and settled herself to listen to another story.

"I don't know what you'll make of this," he said apologetically. "It's a funny thing. I'm afraid I got beyond my depth in it, but my intentions were good. Don't bother about the little features of it. Just see if you catch the feel of the big thing in it. It is big, and it is true, though the chance is large that I have failed to make it intelligible."

He read, and as he read he watched her. At last he had reached her, he thought. She sat without movement, her eyes steadfast upon him, scarcely breathing, caught up and out of herself, he thought, by the witchery of the thing he had created. He had entitled the story "Adventure," and it was the apotheosis of adventure—not of the adventure of the storybooks, but of real adventure, the savage taskmaster, awful of punishment and awful of reward, faithless and whimsical, demanding terrible patience and heartbreaking days and nights of toil, offering the blazing sunlight glory or dark death at the end of thirst and famine or of the long drag and monstrous delirium of rotting fever, through blood and sweat and stinging insects leading up by long chains of petty and ignoble contacts to royal culminations and lordly achievements.

It was this, all of it, and more, that he had put into his story, and it was this, he believed, that warmed her as she sat and listened. Her eyes were wide, color was in her pale cheeks, and before he finished it seemed to him that she was almost panting. Truly, she was warmed; but she was warmed, not by the story, but by him. She did not think much of the story; it was Martin's intensity of power, the old excess of strength that seemed to pour from his body and on and over her. The paradox of it was that it was the story itself that was freighted with his power, that was the channel, for the time being, through which his strength poured out to her. She was aware only of the strength, and not of the medium, and when she seemed most carried away by what he had written, in reality she had been carried away by something quite foreign to it—by a thought, terrible and perilous, that had formed itself unsummoned in her brain. She had caught herself wondering what marriage was like, and the becoming conscious of the waywardness and ardor of the thought had terrified her. It was unmaidenly. It was not like her. She had never been tormented by womanhood, and she had lived in a dreamland of Tennysonian poesy, dense even to the full significance of that delicate master's delicate allusions to the grossnesses that intrude upon the relations of queens and knights. She had been asleep, always, and now life was thundering imperatively at all her doors. Mentally she was in a panic to shoot the bolts and drop the bars into place, while wanton instincts urged her to throw wide her portals and bid the deliciously strange visitor to enter in.

Martin waited with satisfaction for her verdict. He had no doubt of what it would be, and he was astounded when he heard her say:—

"It is beautiful."

"It *is* beautiful," she repeated, with emphasis, after a pause.

Of course it was beautiful; but there was something more than mere beauty in it, something more stingingly splendid which had made beauty its handmaiden. He sprawled silently on the ground, watching the grisly form of a great doubt rising before him. He had failed. He was inarticulate. He had seen one of the greatest things in the world, and he had not expressed it.

"What did you think of the—" He hesitated, abashed at his first attempt to use a strange word. "Of the *motif*?" he asked.

"It was confused," she answered. "That is my only criticism in the large way. I followed the story, but there seemed so much else. It is too wordy. You clog the action by introducing so much extraneous material."

"That was the major *motif*," he hurriedly explained, "the big underrunning *motif*, the cosmic and universal thing. I tried to make it keep time with the story itself, which was only superficial after all. I was on the right scent, but I guess I did it badly. I did not succeed in suggesting what I was driving at. But I'll learn in time."

She did not follow him. She was a bachelor of arts, but he had gone beyond her limitations. This she did not comprehend, attributing her incomprehension to his incoherence.

"You were too voluble," she said. "But it was beautiful, in places."

He heard her voice as from far off, for he was debating whether he would read her the "Sea Lyrics." He lay in dull despair, while she watched him searchingly, pondering again upon unsummoned and wayward thoughts of marriage.

"You want to be famous?" she asked abruptly.

"Yes, a little bit," he confessed. "That is part of the adventure. It is not the being famous, but the process of becoming so, that counts. And after all, to be famous would be, for me, only a means to something else. I want to be famous very much, for that matter, and for that reason."

"For your sake," he wanted to add, and might have added had she proved enthusiastic over what he had read to her.

But she was too busy in her mind, carving out a career for him that would at least be possible, to ask what the ultimate something was which he had hinted at. There was no career for him in literature. Of that she was convinced. He had proved it to-day, with his amateurish and sophomoric productions. He could talk well, but he was incapable of expressing himself in a literary way. She compared Tennyson, and Browning, and her favorite prose masters with him, and to his hopeless discredit. Yet she did not tell him her whole mind. Her strange interest in him led her to temporize. His desire to write was, after all, a little weakness which he would grow out of in time. Then he would devote himself to the more serious affairs of life. And he would succeed, too. She knew that. He was so strong that he could not fail—if only he would drop writing.

"I wish you would show me all you write, Mr. Eden," she said.

He flushed with pleasure. She was interested, that much was sure. And at least she had not given him a rejection slip. She had called certain portions of his work beautiful, and that was the first encouragement he had ever received from any one.

"I will," he said passionately. "And I promise you, Miss

Morse, that I will make good. I have come far, I know that; and I have far to go, and I will cover it if I have to do it on my hands and knees." He held up a bunch of manuscript. "Here are the 'Sea Lyrics.' When you get home, I'll turn them over to you to read at your leisure. And you must be sure to tell me just what you think of them. What I need, you know, above all things, is criticism. And do, please, be frank with me."

"I will be perfectly frank," she promised, with an uneasy conviction that she had not been frank with him and with a doubt if she could be quite frank with him the next time.

Chapter XV

"THE FIRST BATTLE, fought and finished," Martin said to the looking-glass ten days later. "But there will be a second battle, and a third battle, and battles to the end of time, unless—"

He had not finished the sentence, but looked about the mean little room and let his eyes dwell sadly upon a heap of returned manuscripts, still in their long envelopes, which lay in a corner on the floor. He had no stamps with which to continue them on their travels, and for a week they had been piling up. More of them would come in on the morrow, and on the next day, and the next, till they were all in. And he would be unable to start them out again. He was a month's rent behind on the type-writer, which he could not pay, having barely enough for the week's board which was due and for the employment office fees.

He sat down and regarded the table thoughtfully. There were ink stains upon it, and he suddenly discovered that he was fond of it.

"Dear old table," he said, "I've spent some happy hours with you, and you've been a pretty good friend when all is said and done. You never turned me down, never passed me out a reward-of-unmerit rejection slip, never complained about working overtime."

He dropped his arms upon the table and buried his face in them. His throat was aching, and he wanted to cry. It reminded him of his first fight, when he was six years old, when he punched away with the tears running down his cheeks while the other boy, two years his elder, had beaten and pounded him into exhaustion. He saw the ring of boys, howling like barbarians as he went down at last, writhing in the throes of nausea, the blood streaming from his nose and the tears from his bruised eyes.

"Poor little shaver," he murmured. "And you're just as badly licked now. You're beaten to a pulp. You're down and out."

But the vision of that first fight still lingered under his eyelids, and as he watched he saw it dissolve and reshape into the series of fights which had followed. Six months later Cheese-Face (that was the boy) had whipped him again. But he had blacked Cheese-Face's eye that time. That was going some. He saw them all, fight after fight, himself always whipped and Cheese-Face exulting over him. But he had never run away. He felt strengthened by the memory of that. He had always stayed and taken his medicine. Cheese-Face had been a little fiend at fighting, and had never once shown mercy to him. But he had stayed! He had stayed with it!

Next, he saw a narrow alley, between ramshackle frame buildings. The end of the alley was blocked by a one-story brick building, out of which issued the rhythmic thunder of the presses, running off the first edition of the *Enquirer*. He was eleven, and Cheese-Face was thirteen, and they both carried the *Enquirer*. That was why they were there, waiting for their papers. And, of course, Cheese-Face had picked on him again, and there was another fight that was indeterminate, because at quarter to four the door of the press-room was thrown open and the gang of boys crowded in to fold their papers.

"I'll lick you to-morrow," he heard Cheese-Face promise; and he heard his own voice, piping and trembling with unshed tears, agreeing to be there on the morrow.

And he had come there the next day, hurrying from school to be there first, and beating Cheese-Face by two minutes. The other boys said he was all right, and gave him advice, pointing out his faults as a scrapper and promising him victory if he carried out their instructions. The same boys gave Cheese-Face advice, too. How they had enjoyed the fight! He paused in his recollections long enough to envy them the spectacle he and Cheese-Face had put up. Then the fight was on, and it went on, without rounds, for thirty minutes, until the press-room door was opened.

He watched the youthful apparition of himself, day after day, hurrying from school to the *Enquirer* alley. He could not walk very fast. He was stiff and lame from the incessant fighting. His forearms were black and blue from wrist to elbow, what of the countless blows he had warded off, and here and there the tortured flesh was beginning to fester. His head and arms and shoulders ached, the small of his back ached,—he ached all over, and his brain was heavy and dazed. He did not play at school. Nor did he study. Even to sit still all day at his desk, as he did, was a torment. It seemed centuries since he had begun the round of daily fights, and time stretched away into a nightmare and infinite future of daily fights. Why couldn't Cheese-Face be licked? he often thought; that would put him, Martin, out of his misery. It never entered his head to cease fighting, to allow Cheese-Face to whip him.

And so he dragged himself to the *Enquirer* alley, sick in body and soul, but learning the long patience, to confront his eternal enemy, Cheese-Face, who was just as sick as he, and just a bit willing to quit if it were not for the gang of newsboys that looked on and made pride painful and necessary. One afternoon, after twenty minutes of desperate efforts to annihilate each other according to set rules that did not permit kicking, striking below the belt, nor hitting when one was down, Cheese-Face, panting for breath and reeling, offered to call it quits. And Martin, head on arms, thrilled at the picture he caught of himself, at that moment in the afternoon of long ago, when he reeled and panted and choked with the blood that ran into his mouth and down his throat from his cut lips; when he tottered toward Cheese-Face, spitting out a mouthful of blood so that he could speak, crying out that he would never quit, though Cheese-Face could give in if he wanted to. And Cheese-Face did not give in, and the fight went on.

The next day and the next, days without end, witnessed the afternoon fight. When he put up his arms, each day, to begin, they pained exquisitely, and the first few blows, struck and received, racked his soul; after that things grew numb, and he fought on blindly, seeing as in a dream, dancing and wavering, the large features and burning, animal-like eyes of Cheese-Face. He concentrated upon that face; all else about him was a whirling void. There was nothing else in the world but that face, and he would never know rest, blessed rest, until he had beaten that face into a pulp with his bleeding knuckles, or until the bleeding knuckles that somehow belonged to that face had beaten him into a pulp. And then, one way or the other, he would have rest. But to quit,—for him, Martin, to quit,—that was impossible!

Came the day when he dragged himself into the *Enquirer* alley, and there was no Cheese-Face. Nor did Cheese-Face come. The boys congratulated him, and told him that he had licked Cheese-Face. But Martin was not satisfied. He had not licked Cheese-Face, nor had Cheese-Face licked him. The problem had not been solved. It was not until afterward that they learned that Cheese-Face's father had died suddenly that very day.

Martin skipped on through the years to the night in the nigger heaven at the Auditorium. He was seventeen and just back from sea. A row started. Somebody was bullying somebody, and Martin interfered, to be confronted by Cheese-Face's blazing eyes.

"I'll fix you after de show," his ancient enemy hissed.

Martin nodded. The nigger-heaven bouncer was making his way toward the disturbance.

"I'll meet you outside, after the last act," Martin whispered, the while his face showed undivided interest in the buck-and-wing dancing on the stage.

The bouncer glared and went away.

"Got a gang?" he asked Cheese-Face, at the end of the act.

"Sure."

"Then I got to get one," Martin announced.

Between the acts he mustered his following—three fellows he knew from the nail works, a railroad fireman, and half a dozen of the Boo Gang, along with as many more from the dread Eighteen-and-Market Gang.

When the theatre let out, the two gangs strung along inconspicuously on opposite sides of the street. When they came to a quiet corner, they united and held a council of war.

"Eighth Street Bridge is the place," said a red-headed fellow belonging to Cheese-Face's gang. "You kin fight in the middle, under the electric light, an' whichever way the bulls come in we kin sneak the other way."

"That's agreeable to me," Martin said, after consulting with the leaders of his own gang.

The Eighth Street Bridge, crossing an arm of San Antonio Estuary, was the length of three city blocks. In the middle of

the bridge, and at each end, were electric lights. No policeman could pass those end-lights unseen. It was the safe place
for the battle that revived itself under Martin's eyelids. He
saw the two gangs, aggressive and sullen, rigidly keeping
apart from each other and backing their respective champi-
ons; and he saw himself and Cheese-Face stripping. A short
distance away lookouts were set, their task being to watch the
lighted ends of the bridge. A member of the Boo Gang held
Martin's coat, and shirt, and cap, ready to race with them into
safety in case the police interfered. Martin watched himself go
into the centre, facing Cheese-Face, and he heard himself say,
as he held up his hand warningly:—

"They ain't no hand-shakin' in this. Understand? They ain't
nothin' but scrap. No throwin' up the sponge. This is a
grudge-fight an' it's to a finish. Understand? Somebody's
goin' to get licked."

Cheese-Face wanted to demur,—Martin could see that,—
but Cheese-Face's old perilous pride was touched before the
two gangs.

"Aw, come on," he replied. "Wot's the good of chewin' de
rag about it? I'm wit' cheh to de finish."

Then they fell upon each other, like young bulls, in all the
glory of youth, with naked fists, with hatred, with desire to
hurt, to maim, to destroy. All the painful, thousand years'
gains of man in his upward climb through creation were lost.
Only the electric light remained, a milestone on the path of
the great human adventure. Martin and Cheese-Face were
two savages, of the stone age, of the squatting place and the
tree refuge. They sank lower and lower into the muddy abyss,
back into the dregs of the raw beginnings of life, striving
blindly and chemically, as atoms strive, as the star-dust of the
heavens strives, colliding, recoiling, and colliding again and
eternally again.

"God! We are animals! Brute-beasts!" Martin muttered
aloud, as he watched the progress of the fight. It was to him,
with his splendid power of vision, like gazing into a kineto-
scope. He was both onlooker and participant. His long
months of culture and refinement shuddered at the sight;
then the present was blotted out of his consciousness and the
ghosts of the past possessed him, and he was Martin Eden,

just returned from sea and fighting Cheese-Face on the Eighth Street Bridge. He suffered and toiled and sweated and bled, and exulted when his naked knuckles smashed home.

They were twin whirlwinds of hatred, revolving about each other monstrously. The time passed, and the two hostile gangs became very quiet. They had never witnessed such intensity of ferocity, and they were awed by it. The two fighters were greater brutes than they. The first splendid velvet edge of youth and condition wore off, and they fought more cautiously and deliberately. There had been no advantage gained either way. "It's anybody's fight," Martin heard some one saying. Then he followed up a feint, right and left, was fiercely countered, and felt his cheek laid open to the bone. No bare knuckle had done that. He heard mutters of amazement at the ghastly damage wrought, and was drenched with his own blood. But he gave no sign. He became immensely wary, for he was wise with knowledge of the low cunning and foul vileness of his kind. He watched and waited, until he feigned a wild rush, which he stopped midway, for he had seen the glint of metal.

"Hold up yer hand!" he screamed. "Them's brass knuckles, an' you hit me with 'em!"

Both gangs surged forward, growling and snarling. In a second there would be a free-for-all fight, and he would be robbed of his vengeance. He was beside himself.

"You guys keep out!" he screamed hoarsely. "Understand? Say, d'ye understand?"

They shrank away from him. They were brutes, but he was the arch-brute, a thing of terror that towered over them and dominated them.

"This is my scrap, an' they ain't goin' to be no buttin' in. Gimme them knuckles."

Cheese-Face, sobered and a bit frightened, surrendered the foul weapon.

"You passed 'em to him, you red-head sneakin' in behind the push there," Martin went on, as he tossed the knuckles into the water. "I seen you, an' I was wonderin' what you was up to. If you try anything like that again, I'll beat cheh to death. Understand?"

They fought on, through exhaustion and beyond, to ex-

haustion immeasurable and inconceivable, until the crowd of
brutes, its blood-lust sated, terrified by what it saw, begged
them impartially to cease. And Cheese-Face, ready to drop
and die, or to stay on his legs and die, a grisly monster out of
whose features all likeness to Cheese-Face had been beaten,
wavered and hesitated; but Martin sprang in and smashed
him again and again.

Next, after a seeming century or so, with Cheese-Face
weakening fast, in a mix-up of blows there was a loud snap,
and Martin's right arm dropped to his side. It was a broken
bone. Everybody heard it and knew; and Cheese-Face knew,
rushing like a tiger in the other's extremity and raining blow
on blow. Martin's gang surged forward to interfere. Dazed
by the rapid succession of blows, Martin warned them back
with vile and earnest curses sobbed out and groaned in ultimate desolation and despair.

He punched on, with his left hand only, and as he
punched, doggedly, only half-conscious, as from a remote distance he heard murmurs of fear in the gangs, and one who
said with shaking voice: "This ain't a scrap, fellows. It's murder, an' we ought to stop it."

But no one stopped it, and he was glad, punching on wearily and endlessly with his one arm, battering away at a
bloody something before him that was not a face but a horror, an oscillating, hideous, gibbering, nameless thing that
persisted before his wavering vision and would not go away.
And he punched on and on, slower and slower, as the last
shreds of vitality oozed from him, through centuries and
æons and enormous lapses of time, until, in a dim way, he
became aware that the nameless thing was sinking, slowly
sinking down to the rough board-planking of the bridge. And
the next moment he was standing over it, staggering and
swaying on shaky legs, clutching at the air for support, and
saying in a voice he did not recognize:—

"D'ye want any more? Say, d'ye want any more?"

He was still saying it, over and over,—demanding, entreating, threatening, to know if it wanted any more,—when he
felt the fellows of his gang laying hands on him, patting him
on the back and trying to put his coat on him. And then came
a sudden rush of blackness and oblivion.

The tin alarm-clock on the table ticked on, but Martin Eden, his face buried on his arms, did not hear it. He heard nothing. He did not think. So absolutely had he relived life that he had fainted just as he fainted years before on the Eighth Street Bridge. For a full minute the blackness and the blankness endured. Then, like one from the dead, he sprang upright, eyes flaming, sweat pouring down his face, shouting:—

"I licked you, Cheese-Face! It took me eleven years, but I licked you!"

His knees were trembling under him, he felt faint, and he staggered back to the bed, sinking down and sitting on the edge of it. He was still in the clutch of the past. He looked about the room, perplexed, alarmed, wondering where he was, until he caught sight of the pile of manuscripts in the corner. Then the wheels of memory slipped ahead through four years of time, and he was aware of the present, of the books he had opened and the universe he had won from their pages, of his dreams and ambitions, and of his love for a pale wraith of a girl, sensitive and sheltered and ethereal, who would die of horror did she witness but one moment of what he had just lived through—one moment of all the muck of life through which he had waded.

He arose to his feet and confronted himself in the looking-glass.

"And so you arise from the mud, Martin Eden," he said solemnly. "And you cleanse your eyes in a great brightness, and thrust your shoulders among the stars, doing what all life has done, letting the 'ape and tiger die' and wresting highest heritage from all powers that be."

He looked more closely at himself and laughed.

"A bit of hysteria and melodrama, eh?" he queried. "Well, never mind. You licked Cheese-Face, and you'll lick the editors if it takes twice eleven years to do it in. You can't stop here. You've got to go on. It's to a finish, you know."

Chapter XVI

THE ALARM-CLOCK went off, jerking Martin out of sleep with a suddenness that would have given headache to one with less splendid constitution. Though he slept soundly, he awoke instantly, like a cat, and he awoke eagerly, glad that the five hours of unconsciousness were gone. He hated the oblivion of sleep. There was too much to do, too much of life to live. He grudged every moment of life sleep robbed him of, and before the clock had ceased its clattering he was head and ears in the wash-basin and thrilling to the cold bite of the water.

But he did not follow his regular programme. There was no unfinished story waiting his hand, no new story demanding articulation. He had studied late, and it was nearly time for breakfast. He tried to read a chapter in Fiske, but his brain was restless and he closed the book. To-day witnessed the beginning of the new battle, wherein for some time there would be no writing. He was aware of a sadness akin to that with which one leaves home and family. He looked at the manuscripts in the corner. That was it. He was going away from them, his pitiful, dishonored children that were welcome nowhere. He went over and began to rummage among them, reading snatches here and there, his favorite portions. "The Pot" he honored with reading aloud, as he did "Adventure." "Joy," his latest-born, completed the day before and tossed into the corner for lack of stamps, won his keenest approbation.

"I can't understand," he murmured. "Or maybe it's the editors who can't understand. There's nothing wrong with that. They publish worse every month. Everything they publish is worse—nearly everything, anyway."

After breakfast he put the type-writer in its case and carried it down into Oakland.

"I owe a month on it," he told the clerk in the store. "But you tell the manager I'm going to work and that I'll be in in a month or so and straighten up."

He crossed on the ferry to San Francisco and made his way

to an employment office. "Any kind of work, no trade," he told the agent; and was interrupted by a newcomer, dressed rather foppishly, as some workingmen dress who have instincts for finer things. The agent shook his head despondently.

"Nothin' doin', eh?" said the other. "Well, I got to get somebody to-day."

He turned and stared at Martin, and Martin, staring back, noted the puffed and discolored face, handsome and weak, and knew that he had been making a night of it.

"Lookin' for a job?" the other queried. "What can you do?"

"Hard labor, sailorizing, run a type-writer, no shorthand, can sit on a horse, willing to do anything and tackle anything," was the answer.

The other nodded.

"Sounds good to me. My name's Dawson, Joe Dawson, an' I'm tryin' to scare up a laundryman."

"Too much for me." Martin caught an amusing glimpse of himself ironing fluffy white things that women wear. But he had taken a liking to the other, and he added: "I might do the plain washing. I learned that much at sea."

Joe Dawson thought visibly for a moment.

"Look here, let's get together an' frame it up. Willin' to listen?"

Martin nodded.

"This is a small laundry, up country, belongs to Shelly Hot Springs,—hotel, you know. Two men do the work, boss and assistant. I'm the boss. You don't work for me, but you work under me. Think you'd be willin' to learn?"

Martin paused to think. The prospect was alluring. A few months of it, and he would have time to himself for study. He could work hard and study hard.

"Good grub an' a room to yourself," Joe said.

That settled it. A room to himself where he could burn the midnight oil unmolested.

"But work like hell," the other added.

Martin caressed his swelling shoulder-muscles significantly. "That came from hard work."

"Then let's get to it." Joe held his hand to his head for a moment. "Gee, but it's a stem-winder. Can hardly see. I went down the line last night—everything—everything. Here's the frame-up. The wages for two is a hundred and board. I've ben drawin' down sixty, the second man forty. But he knew the biz. You're green. If I break you in, I'll be doing plenty of your work at first. Suppose you begin at thirty, an' work up to the forty. I'll play fair. Just as soon as you can do your share you get the forty."

"I'll go you," Martin announced, stretching out his hand, which the other shook. "Any advance?—for railroad ticket and extras?"

"I blew it in," was Joe's sad answer, with another reach at his aching head. "All I got is a return ticket."

"And I'm broke—when I pay my board."

"Jump it," Joe advised.

"Can't. Owe it to my sister."

Joe whistled a long, perplexed whistle, and racked his brains to little purpose.

"I've got the price of the drinks," he said desperately. "Come on, an' mebbe we'll cook up something."

Martin declined.

"Water-wagon?"

This time Martin nodded, and Joe lamented, "Wish I was.

"But I somehow just can't," he said in extenuation. "After I've ben workin' like hell all week I just got to booze up. If I didn't, I'd cut my throat or burn up the premises. But I'm glad you're on the wagon. Stay with it."

Martin knew of the enormous gulf between him and this man—the gulf the books had made; but he found no difficulty in crossing back over that gulf. He had lived all his life in the working-class world, and the *camaraderie* of labor was second nature with him. He solved the difficulty of transportation that was too much for the other's aching head. He would send his trunk up to Shelly Hot Springs on Joe's ticket. As for himself, there was his wheel. It was seventy miles, and he could ride it on Sunday and be ready for work Monday morning. In the meantime he would go home and pack up. There was no one to say good-by to. Ruth and her whole family were spending the long summer in the Sierras, at Lake Tahoe.

He arrived at Shelly Hot Springs, tired and dusty, on Sunday night. Joe greeted him exuberantly. With a wet towel bound about his aching brow, he had been at work all day.

"Part of last week's washin' mounted up, me bein' away to get you," he explained. "Your box arrived all right. It's in your room. But it's a hell of a thing to call a trunk. An' what's in it? Gold bricks?"

Joe sat on the bed while Martin unpacked. The box was a packing-case for breakfast food, and Mr. Higginbotham had charged him half a dollar for it. Two rope handles, nailed on by Martin, had technically transformed it into a trunk eligible for the baggage-car. Joe watched, with bulging eyes, a few shirts and several changes of underclothes come out of the box, followed by books, and more books.

"Books clean to the bottom?" he asked.

Martin nodded, and went on arranging the books on a kitchen table which served in the room in place of a wash-stand.

"Gee!" Joe exploded, then waited in silence for the deduction to arise in his brain. At last it came.

"Say, you don't care for the girls—much?" he queried.

"No," was the answer. "I used to chase a lot before I tackled the books. But since then there's no time."

"And there won't be any time here. All you can do is work an' sleep."

Martin thought of his five hours' sleep a night, and smiled. The room was situated over the laundry and was in the same building with the engine that pumped water, made electricity, and ran the laundry machinery. The engineer, who occupied the adjoining room, dropped in to meet the new hand and helped Martin rig up an electric bulb, on an extension wire, so that it travelled along a stretched cord from over the table to the bed.

The next morning, at quarter-past six, Martin was routed out for a quarter-to-seven breakfast. There happened to be a bath-tub for the servants in the laundry building, and he electrified Joe by taking a cold bath.

"Gee, but you're a hummer!" Joe announced, as they sat down to breakfast in a corner of the hotel kitchen.

With them was the engineer, the gardener, and the assistant gardener, and two or three men from the stable. They ate

hurriedly and gloomily, with but little conversation, and as
Martin ate and listened he realized how far he had travelled
from their status. Their small mental caliber was depressing
to him, and he was anxious to get away from them. So he
bolted his breakfast, a sickly, sloppy affair, as rapidly as they,
and heaved a sigh of relief when he passed out through the
kitchen door.

It was a perfectly appointed, small steam laundry, wherein
the most modern machinery did everything that was possible
for machinery to do. Martin, after a few instructions, sorted
the great heaps of soiled clothes, while Joe started the masher
and made up fresh supplies of soft-soap, compounded of biting chemicals that compelled him to swathe his mouth and
nostrils and eyes in bath-towels till he resembled a mummy.
Finished the sorting, Martin lent a hand in wringing the
clothes. This was done by dumping them into a spinning receptacle that went at a rate of a few thousand revolutions a
minute, tearing the water from the clothes by centrifugal
force. Then Martin began to alternate between the dryer and
the wringer, between times "shaking out" socks and stockings. By the afternoon, one feeding and one stacking up, they
were running socks and stockings through the mangle while
the irons were heating. Then it was hot irons and underclothes till six o'clock, at which time Joe shook his head dubiously.

"Way behind," he said. "Got to work after supper."

And after supper they worked until ten o'clock, under the
blazing electric lights, until the last piece of underclothing
was ironed and folded away in the distributing room. It was
a hot California night, and though the windows were thrown
wide, the room, with its red-hot ironing-stove, was a furnace.
Martin and Joe, down to undershirts, bare armed, sweated
and panted for air.

"Like trimming cargo in the tropics," Martin said, when
they went upstairs.

"You'll do," Joe answered. "You take hold like a good fellow. If you keep up the pace, you'll be on thirty dollars only
one month. The second month you'll be gettin' your forty.
But don't tell me you never ironed before. I know better."

"Never ironed a rag in my life, honestly, until to-day," Martin protested.

He was surprised at his weariness when he got into his room, forgetful of the fact that he had been on his feet and working without let up for fourteen hours. He set the alarm at six, and measured back five hours to one o'clock. He could read until then. Slipping off his shoes, to ease his swollen feet, he sat down at the table with his books. He opened Fiske, where he had left off two days before, and began to read. But he found trouble with the first paragraph and began to read it through a second time. Then he awoke, in pain from his stiffened muscles and chilled by the mountain wind that had begun to blow in through the window. He looked at the clock. It marked two. He had been asleep four hours. He pulled off his clothes and crawled into bed, where he was asleep the moment after his head touched the pillow.

Tuesday was a day of similar unremitting toil. The speed with which Joe worked won Martin's admiration. Joe was a dozen of demons for work. He was keyed up to concert pitch, and there was never a moment in the long day when he was not fighting for moments. He concentrated himself upon his work and upon how to save time, pointing out to Martin where he did in five motions what could be done in three, or in three motions what could be done in two. "Elimination of waste motion," Martin phrased it as he watched and patterned after. He was a good workman himself, quick and deft, and it had always been a point of pride with him that no man should do any of his work for him or outwork him. As a result, he concentrated with a similar singleness of purpose, greedily snapping up the hints and suggestions thrown out by his working mate. He "rubbed out" collars and cuffs, rubbing the starch out from between the double thicknesses of linen so that there would be no blisters when it came to the ironing, and doing it at a pace that elicited Joe's praise.

There was never an interval when something was not at hand to be done. Joe waited for nothing, waited on nothing, and went on the jump from task to task. They starched two hundred white shirts, with a single gathering movement seizing a shirt so that the wristbands, neckband, yoke, and bosom

protruded beyond the circling right hand. At the same moment the left hand held up the body of the shirt so that it
would not enter the starch, and at the same moment the right
hand dipped into the starch—starch so hot that, in order to
wring it out, their hands had to be thrust, and thrust continually, into a bucket of cold water. And that night they worked
till half-past ten, dipping "fancy starch"—all the frilled and
airy, delicate wear of ladies.

"Me for the tropics and no clothes," Martin laughed.

"And me out of a job," Joe answered seriously. "I don't
know nothin' but laundrying."

"And you know it well."

"I ought to. Began in the Contra Costa in Oakland when
I was eleven, shakin' out for the mangle. That was eighteen
years ago, an' I've never done a tap of anything else. But this
job is the fiercest I ever had. Ought to be one more man on
it at least. We work to-morrow night. Always run the mangle
Wednesday nights—collars an' cuffs."

Martin set his alarm, drew up to the table, and opened
Fiske. He did not finish the first paragraph. The lines blurred
and ran together and his head nodded. He walked up and
down, batting his head savagely with his fists, but he could
not conquer the numbness of sleep. He propped the book
before him, and propped his eyelids with his fingers, and fell
asleep with his eyes wide open. Then he surrendered, and,
scarcely conscious of what he did, got off his clothes and into
bed. He slept seven hours of heavy, animal-like sleep, and
awoke by the alarm, feeling that he had not had enough.

"Doin' much readin'?" Joe asked.

Martin shook his head.

"Never mind. We got to run the mangle to-night, but
Thursday we'll knock off at six. That'll give you a chance."

Martin washed woollens that day, by hand, in a large barrel, with strong soft-soap, by means of a hub from a wagon
wheel, mounted on a plunger-pole that was attached to a
spring-pole overhead.

"My invention," Joe said proudly. "Beats a wash-board an'
your knuckles, and, besides, it saves at least fifteen minutes in
the week, an' fifteen minutes ain't to be sneezed at in this
shebang."

Running the collars and cuffs through the mangle was also Joe's idea. That night, while they toiled on under the electric lights, he explained it.

"Something no laundry ever does, except this one. An' I got to do it if I'm goin' to get done Saturday afternoon at three o'clock. But I know how, an' that's the difference. Got to have right heat, right pressure, and run 'em through three times. Look at that!" He held a cuff aloft. "Couldn't do it better by hand or on a tiler."

Thursday, Joe was in a rage. A bundle of extra "fancy starch" had come in.

"I'm goin' to quit," he announced. "I won't stand for it. I'm goin' to quit it cold. What's the good of me workin' like a slave all week, a-savin' minutes, an' them a-comin' an' ringin' in fancy-starch extras on me? This is a free country, an' I'm goin' to tell that fat Dutchman what I think of him. An' I won't tell 'm in French. Plain United States is good enough for me. Him a-ringin' in fancy starch extras!"

"We got to work to-night," he said the next moment, reversing his judgment and surrendering to fate.

And Martin did no reading that night. He had seen no daily paper all week, and, strangely to him, felt no desire to see one. He was not interested in the news. He was too tired and jaded to be interested in anything, though he planned to leave Saturday afternoon, if they finished at three, and ride on his wheel to Oakland. It was seventy miles, and the same distance back on Sunday afternoon would leave him anything but rested for the second week's work. It would have been easier to go on the train, but the round trip was two dollars and a half, and he was intent on saving money.

Chapter XVII

MARTIN LEARNED to do many things. In the course of the first week, in one afternoon, he and Joe accounted for the two hundred white shirts. Joe ran the tiler, a machine wherein a hot iron was hooked on a steel string which furnished the pressure. By this means he ironed the yoke, wristbands, and neckband, setting the latter at right angles to the shirt, and put the glossy finish on the bosom. As fast as he finished them, he flung the shirts on a rack between him and Martin, who caught them up and "backed" them. This task consisted of ironing all the unstarched portions of the shirts.

It was exhausting work, carried on, hour after hour, at top speed. Out on the broad verandas of the hotel, men and women, in cool white, sipped iced drinks and kept their circulation down. But in the laundry the air was sizzling. The huge stove roared red hot and white hot, while the irons, moving over the damp cloth, sent up clouds of steam. The heat of these irons was different from that used by housewives. An iron that stood the ordinary test of a wet finger was too cold for Joe and Martin, and such test was useless. They went wholly by holding the irons close to their cheeks, gauging the heat by some secret mental process that Martin admired but could not understand. When the fresh irons proved too hot, they hooked them on iron rods and dipped them into cold water. This again required a precise and subtle judgment. A fraction of a second too long in the water and the fine and silken edge of the proper heat was lost, and Martin found time to marvel at the accuracy he developed—an automatic accuracy, founded upon criteria that were machinelike and unerring.

But there was little time in which to marvel. All Martin's consciousness was concentrated in the work. Ceaselessly active, head and hand, an intelligent machine, all that constituted him a man was devoted to furnishing that intelligence. There was no room in his brain for the universe and its mighty problems. All the broad and spacious corridors of his mind were closed and hermetically sealed. The echoing cham-

ber of his soul was a narrow room, a conning tower, whence
were directed his arm and shoulder muscles, his ten nimble
fingers, and the swift-moving iron along its steaming path in
broad, sweeping strokes, just so many strokes and no more,
just so far with each stroke and not a fraction of an inch farther, rushing along interminable sleeves, sides, backs, and
tails, and tossing the finished shirts, without rumpling, upon
the receiving frame. And even as his hurrying soul tossed, it
was reaching for another shirt. This went on, hour after hour,
while outside all the world swooned under the overhead California sun. But there was no swooning in that superheated
room. The cool guests on the verandas needed clean linen.

The sweat poured from Martin. He drank enormous quantities of water, but so great was the heat of the day and of his
exertions, that the water sluiced through the interstices of his
flesh and out at all his pores. Always, at sea, except at rare
intervals, the work he performed had given him ample opportunity to commune with himself. The master of the ship had
been lord of Martin's time; but here the manager of the hotel
was lord of Martin's thoughts as well. He had no thoughts
save for the nerve-racking, body-destroying toil. Outside of
that it was impossible to think. He did not know that he
loved Ruth. She did not even exist, for his driven soul had no
time to remember her. It was only when he crawled to bed at
night, or to breakfast in the morning, that she asserted herself
to him in fleeting memories.

"This is hell, ain't it?" Joe remarked once.

Martin nodded, but felt a rasp of irritation. The statement
had been obvious and unnecessary. They did not talk while
they worked. Conversation threw them out of their stride, as
it did this time, compelling Martin to miss a stroke of his iron
and to make two extra motions before he caught his stride
again.

On Friday morning the washer ran. Twice a week they had
to put through hotel linen,—the sheets, pillow-slips, spreads,
table-cloths, and napkins. This finished, they buckled down
to "fancy starch." It was slow work, fastidious and delicate,
and Martin did not learn it so readily. Besides, he could not
take chances. Mistakes were disastrous.

"See that," Joe said, holding up a filmy corset-cover that he could have crumpled from view in one hand. "Scorch that an' it's twenty dollars out of your wages."

So Martin did not scorch that, and eased down on his muscular tension, though nervous tension rose higher than ever, and he listened sympathetically to the other's blasphemies as he toiled and suffered over the beautiful things that women wear when they do not have to do their own laundrying. "Fancy starch" was Martin's nightmare, and it was Joe's, too. It was "fancy starch" that robbed them of their hard-won minutes. They toiled at it all day. At seven in the evening they broke off to run the hotel linen through the mangle. At ten o'clock, while the hotel guests slept, the two laundrymen sweated on at "fancy starch" till midnight, till one, till two. At half-past two they knocked off.

Saturday morning it was "fancy starch," and odds and ends, and at three in the afternoon the week's work was done.

"You ain't a-goin' to ride them seventy miles into Oakland on top of this?" Joe demanded, as they sat on the stairs and took a triumphant smoke.

"Got to," was the answer.

"What are you goin' for?—a girl?"

"No; to save two and a half on the railroad ticket. I want to renew some books at the library."

"Why don't you send 'em down an' up by express? That'll cost only a quarter each way."

Martin considered it.

"An' take a rest to-morrow," the other urged. "You need it. I know I do. I'm plumb tuckered out."

He looked it. Indomitable, never resting, fighting for seconds and minutes all week, circumventing delays and crushing down obstacles, a fount of resistless energy, a high-driven human motor, a demon for work, now that he had accomplished the week's task he was in a state of collapse. He was worn and haggard, and his handsome face drooped in lean exhaustion. He puffed his cigarette spiritlessly, and his voice was peculiarly dead and monotonous. All the snap and fire had gone out of him. His triumph seemed a sorry one.

"An' next week we got to do it all over again," he said sadly. "An' what's the good of it all, hey? Sometimes I wish I was a hobo. They don't work, an' they get their livin'. Gee!

I wish I had a glass of beer; but I can't get up the gumption to go down to the village an' get it. You'll stay over, an' send your books down by express, or else you're a damn fool."

"But what can I do here all day Sunday?" Martin asked.

"Rest. You don't know how tired you are. Why, I'm that tired Sunday I can't even read the papers. I was sick once—typhoid. In the hospital two months an' a half. Didn't do a tap of work all that time. It was beautiful.

"It was beautiful," he repeated dreamily, a minute later.

Martin took a bath, after which he found that the head laundryman had disappeared. Most likely he had gone for the glass of beer, Martin decided, but the half-mile walk down to the village to find out seemed a long journey to him. He lay on his bed with his shoes off, trying to make up his mind. He did not reach out for a book. He was too tired to feel sleepy, and he lay, scarcely thinking, in a semi-stupor of weariness, until it was time for supper. Joe did not appear for that function, and when Martin heard the gardener remark that most likely he was ripping the slats off the bar, Martin understood. He went to bed immediately afterward, and in the morning decided that he was greatly rested. Joe being still absent, Martin procured a Sunday paper and lay down in a shady nook under the trees. The morning passed, he knew not how. He did not sleep, nobody disturbed him, and he did not finish the paper. He came back to it in the afternoon, after dinner, and fell asleep over it.

So passed Sunday, and Monday morning he was hard at work, sorting clothes, while Joe, a towel bound tightly around his head, with groans and blasphemies, was running the washer and mixing soft-soap.

"I simply can't help it," he explained. "I got to drink when Saturday night comes around."

Another week passed, a great battle that continued under the electric lights each night and that culminated on Saturday afternoon at three o'clock, when Joe tasted his moment of wilted triumph and then drifted down to the village to forget. Martin's Sunday was the same as before. He slept in the shade of the trees, toiled aimlessly through the newspaper, and spent long hours lying on his back, doing nothing, thinking nothing. He was too dazed to think, though he was aware that he did not like himself. He was self-repelled, as though he had undergone some degradation or was intrinsically foul. All that was god-like in him was blotted out. The spur of ambition was blunted; he had no vitality with which to feel the prod of it. He was dead. His soul seemed dead. He was a beast, a work-beast. He saw no beauty in the sunshine sifting down through the green leaves, nor did the azure vault of the sky whisper as of old and hint of cosmic vastness and secrets trembling to disclosure. Life was intolerably dull and stupid, and its taste was bad in his mouth. A black screen was drawn across his mirror of inner vision, and fancy lay in a darkened sick-room where entered no ray of light. He envied Joe, down in the village, rampant, tearing the slats off the bar, his brain gnawing with maggots, exulting in maudlin ways over maudlin things, fantastically and gloriously drunk and forgetful of Monday morning and the week of deadening toil to come.

A third week went by, and Martin loathed himself, and loathed life. He was oppressed by a sense of failure. There was reason for the editors refusing his stuff. He could see that clearly now, and laugh at himself and the dreams he had dreamed. Ruth returned his "Sea Lyrics" by mail. He read her letter apathetically. She did her best to say how much she liked them and that they were beautiful. But she could not lie, and she could not disguise the truth from herself. She knew they were failures, and he read her disapproval in every perfunctory and unenthusiastic line of her letter. And she was right. He was firmly convinced of it as he read the poems over. Beauty and wonder had departed from him, and as he read the poems he caught himself puzzling as to what he had had in mind when he wrote them. His audacities of phrase struck him as grotesque, his felicities of expression were monstrosities, and everything was absurd, unreal, and impossible. He would have burned the "Sea Lyrics" on the spot, had his will been strong enough to set them aflame. There was the engine-room, but the exertion of carrying them to the furnace was not worth while. All his exertion was used in washing other persons' clothes. He did not have any left for private affairs.

He resolved that when Sunday came he would pull himself

together and answer Ruth's letter. But Saturday afternoon, after work was finished and he had taken a bath, the desire to forget overpowered him. "I guess I'll go down and see how Joe's getting on," was the way he put it to himself; and in the same moment he knew that he lied. But he did not have the energy to consider the lie. If he had had the energy, he would have refused to consider the lie, because he wanted to forget. He started for the village slowly and casually, increasing his pace in spite of himself as he neared the saloon.

"I thought you was on the water-wagon," was Joe's greeting.

Martin did not deign to offer excuses, but called for whiskey, filling his own glass brimming before he passed the bottle.

"Don't take all night about it," he said roughly.

The other was dawdling with the bottle, and Martin refused to wait for him, tossing the glass off in a gulp and refilling it.

"Now, I can wait for you," he said grimly; "but hurry up."

Joe hurried, and they drank together.

"The work did it, eh?" Joe queried.

Martin refused to discuss the matter.

"It's fair hell, I know," the other went on, "but I kind of hate to see you come off the wagon, Mart. Well, here's how!"

Martin drank on silently, biting out his orders and invitations and awing the barkeeper, an effeminate country youngster with watery blue eyes and hair parted in the middle.

"It's something scandalous the way they work us poor devils," Joe was remarking. "If I didn't bowl up, I'd break loose an' burn down the shebang. My bowlin' up is all that saves 'em, I can tell you that."

But Martin made no answer. A few more drinks, and in his brain he felt the maggots of intoxication beginning to crawl. Ah, it was living, the first breath of life he had breathed in three weeks. His dreams came back to him. Fancy came out of the darkened room and lured him on, a thing of flaming brightness. His mirror of vision was silver-clear, a flashing, dazzling palimpsest of imagery. Wonder and beauty walked with him, hand in hand, and all power was his. He tried to tell it to Joe, but Joe had visions of his own, infallible schemes whereby he would escape the slavery of laundry-work and become himself the owner of a great steam laundry.

"I tell yeh, Mart, they won't be no kids workin' in my laundry—not on yer life. An' they won't be no workin' a livin' soul after six P.M. You hear me talk! They'll be machinery enough an' hands enough to do it all in decent workin' hours, an' Mart, s'help me, I'll make yeh superintendent of the shebang—the whole of it, all of it. Now here's the scheme. I get on the water-wagon an' save my money for two years—save an' then—"

But Martin turned away, leaving him to tell it to the barkeeper, until that worthy was called away to furnish drinks to two farmers who, coming in, accepted Martin's invitation. Martin dispensed royal largess, inviting everybody up, farmhands, a stableman, and the gardener's assistant from the hotel, the barkeeper, and the furtive hobo who slid in like a shadow and like a shadow hovered at the end of the bar.

Chapter XVIII

MONDAY MORNING, Joe groaned over the first truck load of clothes to the washer.

"I say," he began.

"Don't talk to me," Martin snarled.

"I'm sorry, Joe," he said at noon, when they knocked off for dinner.

Tears came into the other's eyes.

"That's all right, old man," he said. "We're in hell, an' we can't help ourselves. An', you know, I kind of like you a whole lot. That's what made it hurt. I cottoned to you from the first."

Martin shook his hand.

"Let's quit," Joe suggested. "Let's chuck it, an' go hoboin'. I ain't never tried it, but it must be dead easy. An' nothin' to do. Just think of it, nothin' to do. I was sick once, typhoid, in the hospital, an' it was beautiful. I wish I'd get sick again."

The week dragged on. The hotel was full, and extra "fancy starch" poured in upon them. They performed prodigies of valor. They fought late each night under the electric lights, bolted their meals, and even got in a half hour's work before breakfast. Martin no longer took his cold baths. Every moment was drive, drive, drive, and Joe was the masterful shepherd of moments, herding them carefully, never losing one, counting them over like a miser counting gold, working on in a frenzy, toil-mad, a feverish machine, aided ably by that other machine that thought of itself as once having been one Martin Eden, a man.

But it was only at rare moments that Martin was able to think. The house of thought was closed, its windows boarded up, and he was its shadowy caretaker. He was a shadow. Joe was right. They were both shadows, and this was the unending limbo of toil. Or was it a dream? Sometimes, in the steaming, sizzling heat, as he swung the heavy irons back and forth over the white garments, it came to him that it was a dream. In a short while, or maybe after a thousand years or so, he would awake, in his little room with the ink-stained table, and take up his writing where he had left off the day before. Or maybe that was a dream, too, and the awakening would be the changing of the watches, when he would drop down out of his bunk in the lurching forecastle and go up on deck, under the tropic stars, and take the wheel and feel the cool tradewind blowing through his flesh.

Came Saturday and its hollow victory at three o'clock.

"Guess I'll go down an' get a glass of beer," Joe said, in the queer, monotonous tones that marked his week-end collapse.

Martin seemed suddenly to wake up. He opened the kit bag and oiled his wheel, putting graphite on the chain and adjusting the bearings. Joe was halfway down to the saloon when Martin passed by, bending low over the handle-bars, his legs driving the ninety-six gear with rhythmic strength, his face set for seventy miles of road and grade and dust. He slept in Oakland that night, and on Sunday covered the seventy miles back. And on Monday morning, weary, he began the new week's work, but he had kept sober.

A fifth week passed, and a sixth, during which he lived and toiled as a machine, with just a spark of something more in him, just a glimmering bit of soul, that compelled him, at each week-end, to scorch off the hundred and forty miles. But this was not rest. It was super-machinelike, and it helped to crush out the glimmering bit of soul that was all that was left him from former life. At the end of the seventh week, without intending it, too weak to resist, he drifted down to the village with Joe and drowned life and found life until Monday morning.

Again, at the week-ends, he ground out the one hundred and forty miles, obliterating the numbness of too great exertion by the numbness of still greater exertion. At the end of three months he went down a third time to the village with Joe. He forgot, and lived again, and, living, he saw, in clear illumination, the beast he was making of himself—not by the drink, but by the work. The drink was an effect, not a cause. It followed inevitably upon the work, as the night follows upon the day. Not by becoming a toil-beast could he win to the heights, was the message the whiskey whispered to him, and he nodded approbation. The whiskey was wise. It told secrets on itself.

He called for paper and pencil, and for drinks all around, and while they drank his very good health, he clung to the bar and scribbled.

"A telegram, Joe," he said. "Read it."

Joe read it with a drunken, quizzical leer. But what he read seemed to sober him. He looked at the other reproachfully, tears oozing into his eyes and down his cheeks.

"You ain't goin' back on me, Mart?" he queried hopelessly.

Martin nodded, and called one of the loungers to him to take the message to the telegraph office.

"Hold on," Joe muttered thickly. "Lemme think."

He held on to the bar, his legs wobbling under him, Martin's arm around him and supporting him, while he thought.

"Make that two laundrymen," he said abruptly. "Here, lemme fix it."

"What are you quitting for?" Martin demanded.

"Same reason as you."

"But I'm going to sea. You can't do that."

"Nope," was the answer, "but I can hobo all right, all right."

Martin looked at him searchingly for a moment, then cried: —

"By God, I think you're right! Better a hobo than a beast of toil. Why, man, you'll live. And that's more than you ever did before."

"I was in hospital, once," Joe corrected. "It was beautiful. Typhoid—did I tell you?"

While Martin changed the telegram to "two laundrymen," Joe went on: —

"I never wanted to drink when I was in hospital. Funny, ain't it? But when I've ben workin' like a slave all week, I just got to bowl up. Ever noticed that cooks drink like hell?—an' bakers, too? It's the work. They've sure got to. Here, lemme pay half of that telegram."

"I'll shake you for it," Martin offered.

"Come on, everybody drink," Joe called, as they rattled the dice and rolled them out on the damp bar.

Monday morning Joe was wild with anticipation. He did not mind his aching head, nor did he take interest in his work. Whole herds of moments stole away and were lost while their careless shepherd gazed out of the window at the sunshine and the trees.

"Just look at it!" he cried. "An' it's all mine! It's free. I can lie down under them trees an' sleep for a thousan' years if I want to. Aw, come on, Mart, let's chuck it. What's the good of waitin' another moment. That's the land of nothin' to do out there, an' I got a ticket for it—an' it ain't no return ticket, b'gosh!"

A few minutes later, filling the truck with soiled clothes for the washer, Joe spied the hotel manager's shirt. He knew its mark, and with a sudden glorious consciousness of freedom he threw it on the floor and stamped on it.

"I wish you was in it, you pig-headed Dutchman!" he shouted. "In it, an' right there where I've got you! Take that! an' that! an' that! damn you! Hold me back, somebody! Hold me back!"

Martin laughed and held him to his work. On Tuesday night the new laundrymen arrived, and the rest of the week was spent breaking them into the routine. Joe sat around and explained his system, but he did no more work.

"Not a tap," he announced. "Not a tap. They can fire me if they want to, but if they do, I'll quit. No more work in mine, thank you kindly. Me for the freight cars an' the shade under the trees. Go to it, you slaves! That's right. Slave an' sweat! Slave an' sweat! An' when you're dead, you'll rot the same as me, an' what's it matter how you live?—eh? Tell me that— what's it matter in the long run?"

On Saturday they drew their pay and came to the parting of the ways.

"They ain't no use in me askin' you to change your mind an' hit the road with me?" Joe asked hopelessly.

Martin shook his head. He was standing by his wheel, ready to start. They shook hands, and Joe held on to his for a moment, as he said:—

"I'm goin' to see you again, Mart, before you an' me die. That's straight dope. I feel it in my bones. Good-by, Mart, an' be good. I like you like hell, you know."

He stood, a forlorn figure, in the middle of the road, watching until Martin turned a bend and was gone from sight.

"He's a good Indian, that boy," he muttered. "A good Indian."

Then he plodded down the road himself, to the water-tank, where half a dozen empties lay on a side-track waiting for the up freight.

Chapter XIX

Ruth and her family were home again, and Martin, returned to Oakland, saw much of her. Having gained her degree, she was doing no more studying; and he, having worked all vitality out of his mind and body, was doing no writing. This gave them time for each other that they had never had before, and their intimacy ripened fast.

At first, Martin had done nothing but rest. He had slept a great deal, and spent long hours musing and thinking and doing nothing. He was like one recovering from some terrible bout of hardship. The first signs of reawakening came when he discovered more than languid interest in the daily paper. Then he began to read again—light novels, and poetry; and after several days more he was head over heels in his long-neglected Fiske. His splendid body and health made new vitality, and he possessed all the resiliency and rebound of youth.

Ruth showed her disappointment plainly when he announced that he was going to sea for another voyage as soon as he was well rested.

"Why do you want to do that?" she asked.

"Money," was the answer. "I'll have to lay in a supply for my next attack on the editors. Money is the sinews of war, in my case—money and patience."

"But if all you wanted was money, why didn't you stay in the laundry?"

"Because the laundry was making a beast of me. Too much work of that sort drives to drink."

She stared at him with horror in her eyes.

"Do you mean—?" she quavered.

It would have been easy for him to get out of it; but his natural impulse was for frankness, and he remembered his old resolve to be frank, no matter what happened.

"Yes," he answered. "Just that. Several times."

She shivered and drew away from him.

"No man that I have ever known did that—ever did that."

"Then they never worked in the laundry at Shelly Hot

Springs," he laughed bitterly. "Toil is a good thing. It is necessary for human health, so all the preachers say, and Heaven
knows I've never been afraid of it. But there is such a thing
as too much of a good thing, and the laundry up there is one
of them. And that's why I'm going to sea one more voyage.
It will be my last, I think, for when I come back, I shall break
into the magazines. I am certain of it."

She was silent, unsympathetic, and he watched her mood-
ily, realizing how impossible it was for her to understand
what he had been through.

"Some day I shall write it up—'The Degradation of Toil'
or the 'Psychology of Drink in the Working-class,' or something like that for a title."

Never, since the first meeting, had they seemed so far apart
as that day. His confession, told in frankness, with the spirit of
revolt behind, had repelled her. But she was more shocked by
the repulsion itself than by the cause of it. It pointed out to her
how near she had drawn to him, and once accepted, it paved
the way for greater intimacy. Pity, too, was aroused, and innocent, idealistic thoughts of reform. She would save this raw
young man who had come so far. She would save him
from the curse of his early environment, and she would save
him from himself in spite of himself. And all this affected her
as a very noble state of consciousness; nor did she dream that
behind it and underlying it were the jealousy and desire of
love.

They rode on their wheels much in the delightful fall
weather, and out in the hills they read poetry aloud, now one
and now the other, noble, uplifting poetry that turned one's
thoughts to higher things. Renunciation, sacrifice, patience,
industry, and high endeavor were the principles she thus indirectly preached—such abstractions being objectified in her
mind by her father, and Mr. Butler, and by Andrew Carnegie,
who, from a poor immigrant boy had arisen to be the book-
giver of the world.

All of which was appreciated and enjoyed by Martin. He
followed her mental processes more clearly now, and her soul
was no longer the sealed wonder it had been. He was on
terms of intellectual equality with her. But the points of disagreement did not affect his love. His love was more ardent

than ever, for he loved her for what she was, and even her physical frailty was an added charm in his eyes. He read of sickly Elizabeth Barrett, who for years had not placed her feet upon the ground, until that day of flame when she eloped with Browning and stood upright, upon the earth, under the open sky; and what Browning had done for her, Martin decided he could do for Ruth. But first, she must love him. The rest would be easy. He would give her strength and health. And he caught glimpses of their life, in the years to come, wherein, against a background of work and comfort and general well-being, he saw himself and Ruth reading and discussing poetry, she propped amid a multitude of cushions on the ground while she read aloud to him. This was the key to the life they would live. And always he saw that particular picture. Sometimes it was she who leaned against him while he read, one arm about her, her head upon his shoulder. Sometimes they pored together over the printed pages of beauty. Then, too, she loved nature, and with generous imagination he changed the scene of their reading—sometimes they read in closed-in valleys with precipitous walls, or in high mountain meadows, and, again, down by the gray sand-dunes with a wreath of billows at their feet, or afar on some volcanic tropic isle where waterfalls descended and became mist, reaching the sea in vapor veils that swayed and shivered to every vagrant wisp of wind. But always, in the foreground, lords of beauty and eternally reading and sharing, lay he and Ruth, and always in the background that was beyond the background of nature, dim and hazy, were work and success and money earned that made them free of the world and all its treasures.

"I should recommend my little girl to be careful," her mother warned her one day.

"I know what you mean. But it is impossible. He is not—"

Ruth was blushing, but it was the blush of maidenhood called upon for the first time to discuss the sacred things of life with a mother held equally sacred.

"Your kind." Her mother finished the sentence for her.

Ruth nodded.

"I did not want to say it, but he is not. He is rough, brutal, strong—too strong. He has not—"

She hesitated and could not go on. It was a new experience, talking over such matters with her mother. And again her mother completed her thought for her.

"He has not lived a clean life, is what you wanted to say."

Again Ruth nodded, and again a blush mantled her face.

"It is just that," she said. "It has not been his fault, but he has played much with—"

"With pitch?"

"Yes, with pitch. And he frightens me. Sometimes I am positively in terror of him, when he talks in that free and easy way of the things he has done—as if they did not matter. They do matter, don't they?"

They sat with their arms twined around each other, and in the pause her mother patted her hand and waited for her to go on.

"But I am interested in him dreadfully," she continued. "In a way he is my protégé. Then, too, he is my first boy friend— but not exactly friend; rather protégé and friend combined. Sometimes, too, when he frightens me, it seems that he is a bulldog I have taken for a plaything, like some of the 'frat' girls, and he is tugging hard, and showing his teeth, and threatening to break loose."

Again her mother waited.

"He interests me, I suppose, like the bulldog. And there is much good in him, too; but there is much in him that I would not like in—in the other way. You see, I have been thinking. He swears, he smokes, he drinks, he has fought with his fists (he has told me so, and he likes it; he says so). He is all that a man should not be—a man I would want for my—" her voice sank very low—"husband. Then he is too strong. My prince must be tall, and slender, and dark—a graceful, bewitching prince. No, there is no danger of my falling in love with Martin Eden. It would be the worst fate that could befall me."

"But it is not that that I spoke about," her mother equivocated. "Have you thought about him? He is so ineligible in every way, you know, and suppose he should come to love you?"

"But he does—already," she cried.

"It was to be expected," Mrs. Morse said gently. "How could it be otherwise with any one who knew you?"

"Olney hates me!" she exclaimed passionately. "And I hate Olney. I feel always like a cat when he is around. I feel that I must be nasty to him, and even when I don't happen to feel that way, why, he's nasty to me, anyway. But I am happy with Martin Eden. No one ever loved me before—no man, I mean, in that way. And it is sweet to be loved—that way. You know what I mean, mother dear. It is sweet to feel that you are really and truly a woman." She buried her face in her mother's lap, sobbing. "You think I am dreadful, I know, but I am honest, and I tell you just how I feel."

Mrs. Morse was strangely sad and happy. Her child-daughter, who was a bachelor of arts, was gone; but in her place was a woman-daughter. The experiment had succeeded. The strange void in Ruth's nature had been filled, and filled without danger or penalty. This rough sailor-fellow had been the instrument, and, though Ruth did not love him, he had made her conscious of her womanhood.

"His hand trembles," Ruth was confessing, her face, for shame's sake, still buried. "It is most amusing and ridiculous, but I feel sorry for him, too. And when his hands are too trembly, and his eyes too shiny, why, I lecture him about his life and the wrong way he is going about it to mend it. But he worships me, I know. His eyes and his hands do not lie. And it makes me feel grown-up, the thought of it, the very thought of it; and I feel that I am possessed of something that is by rights my own—that makes me like the other girls—and—and young women. And, then, too, I knew that I was not like them before, and I knew that it worried you. You thought you did not let me know that dear worry of yours, but I did, and I wanted to—'to make good,' as Martin Eden says."

It was a holy hour for mother and daughter, and their eyes were wet as they talked on in the twilight, Ruth all white innocence and frankness, her mother sympathetic, receptive, yet calmly explaining and guiding.

"He is four years younger than you," she said. "He has no place in the world. He has neither position nor salary. He is impractical. Loving you, he should, in the name of common sense, be doing something that would give him the right to marry, instead of paltering around with those stories of his and with childish dreams. Martin Eden, I am afraid, will never grow up. He does not take to responsibility and a man's work in the world like your father did, or like all our friends, Mr. Butler for one. Martin Eden, I am afraid, will never be a money-earner. And this world is so ordered that money is necessary to happiness—oh, no, not these swollen fortunes, but enough of money to permit of common comfort and decency. He—he has never spoken?"

"He has not breathed a word. He has not attempted to; but if he did, I would not let him, because, you see, I do not love him."

"I am glad of that. I should not care to see my daughter, my one daughter, who is so clean and pure, love a man like him. There are noble men in the world who are clean and true and manly. Wait for them. You will find one some day, and you will love him and be loved by him, and you will be happy with him as your father and I have been happy with each other. And there is one thing you must always carry in mind—"

"Yes, mother."

Mrs. Morse's voice was low and sweet as she said, "And that is the children."

"I—have thought about them," Ruth confessed, remembering the wanton thoughts that had vexed her in the past, her face again red with maiden shame that she should be telling such things.

"And it is that, the children, that makes Mr. Eden impossible," Mrs. Morse went on incisively. "Their heritage must be clean, and he is, I am afraid, not clean. Your father has told me of sailors' lives, and—and you understand."

Ruth pressed her mother's hand in assent, feeling that she really did understand, though her conception was of something vague, remote, and terrible that was beyond the scope of imagination.

"You know I do nothing without telling you," she began. "—Only, sometimes you must ask me, like this time. I wanted to tell you, but I did not know how. It is false modesty, I know it is that, but you can make it easy for me. Sometimes, like this time, you must ask me, you must give me a chance.

"Why, mother, you are a woman, too!" she cried exultantly, as they stood up, catching her mother's hands and standing erect, facing her in the twilight, conscious of a strangely sweet equality between them. "I should never have thought of you in that way if we had not had this talk. I had to learn that I was a woman to know that you were one, too."

"We are women together," her mother said, drawing her to her and kissing her. "We are women together," she repeated, as they went out of the room, their arms around each other's waists, their hearts swelling with a new sense of companionship.

"Our little girl has become a woman," Mrs. Morse said proudly to her husband an hour later.

"That means," he said, after a long look at his wife, "that means she is in love."

"No, but that she is loved," was the smiling rejoinder. "The experiment has succeeded. She is awakened at last."

"Then we'll have to get rid of him." Mr. Morse spoke briskly, in matter-of-fact, businesslike tones.

But his wife shook her head. "It will not be necessary. Ruth says he is going to sea in a few days. When he comes back, she will not be here. We will send her to Aunt Clara's. And, besides, a year in the East, with the change in climate, people, ideas, and everything, is just the thing she needs."

Chapter XX

THE DESIRE to write was stirring in Martin once more. Stories and poems were springing into spontaneous creation in his brain, and he made notes of them against the future time when he would give them expression. But he did not write. This was his little vacation; he had resolved to devote it to rest and love, and in both matters he prospered. He was soon spilling over with vitality, and each day he saw Ruth, at the moment of meeting, she experienced the old shock of his strength and health.

"Be careful," her mother warned her once again. "I am afraid you are seeing too much of Martin Eden."

But Ruth laughed from security. She was sure of herself, and in a few days he would be off to sea. Then, by the time he returned, she would be away on her visit East. There was a magic, however, in the strength and health of Martin. He, too, had been told of her contemplated Eastern trip, and he felt the need for haste. Yet he did not know how to make love to a girl like Ruth. Then, too, he was handicapped by the possession of a great fund of experience with girls and women who had been absolutely different from her. They had known about love and life and flirtation, while she knew nothing about such things. Her prodigious innocence appalled him, freezing on his lips all ardors of speech, and convincing him, in spite of himself, of his own unworthiness. Also he was handicapped in another way. He had himself never been in love before. He had liked women in that turgid past of his, and been fascinated by some of them, but he had not known what it was to love them. He had whistled in a masterful, careless way, and they had come to him. They had been diversions, incidents, part of the game men play, but a small part at most. And now, and for the first time, he was a suppliant, tender and timid and doubting. He did not know the way of love, nor its speech, while he was frightened at his loved one's clear innocence.

In the course of getting acquainted with a varied world, whirling on through the ever changing phases of it, he had learned a rule of conduct which was to the effect that when one played a strange game, he should let the other fellow play first. This had stood him in good stead a thousand times and trained him as an observer as well. He knew how to watch the thing that was strange, and to wait for a weakness, for a place of entrance, to divulge itself. It was like sparring for an opening in fist-fighting. And when such an opening came, he knew by long experience to play for it and to play hard.

So he waited with Ruth and watched, desiring to speak his love but not daring. He was afraid of shocking her, and he was not sure of himself. Had he but known it, he was following the right course with her. Love came into the world before articulate speech, and in its own early youth it had learned ways and means that it had never forgotten. It was in this old, primitive way that Martin wooed Ruth. He did not know he was doing it at first, though later he divined it. The touch of his hand on hers was vastly more potent than any word he could utter, the impact of his strength on her imagination was more alluring than the printed poems and spoken passions of a thousand generations of lovers. Whatever his tongue could express would have appealed, in part, to her judgment; but the touch of hand, the fleeting contact, made its way directly to her instinct. Her judgment was as young as she, but her instincts were as old as the race and older. They had been young when love was young, and they were wiser than convention and opinion and all the new-born things. So her judgment did not act. There was no call upon it, and she did not realize the strength of the appeal Martin made from moment to moment to her love-nature. That he loved her, on the other hand, was as clear as day, and she consciously delighted in beholding his love-manifestations— the glowing eyes with their tender lights, the trembling hands, and the never failing swarthy flush that flooded darkly under his sunburn. She even went farther, in a timid way inciting him, but doing it so delicately that he never suspected, and doing it half-consciously, so that she scarcely suspected herself. She thrilled with these proofs of her power that proclaimed her a woman, and she took an Eve-like delight in tormenting him and playing upon him.

Tongue-tied by inexperience and by excess of ardor, wooing unwittingly and awkwardly, Martin continued his approach by contact. The touch of his hand was pleasant to her, and something deliciously more than pleasant. Martin did not know it, but he did know that it was not distasteful to her. Not that they touched hands often, save at meeting and parting; but that in handling the bicycles, in strapping on the books of verse they carried into the hills, and in conning the pages of books side by side, there were opportunities for hand to stray against hand. And there were opportunities, too, for her hair to brush his cheek, and for shoulder to touch shoulder, as they leaned together over the beauty of the books. She smiled to herself at vagrant impulses which arose from nowhere and suggested that she rumple his hair; while he desired greatly, when they tired of reading, to rest his head in her lap and dream with closed eyes about the future that was to be theirs. On Sunday picnics at Shellmound Park and Schuetzen Park, in the past, he had rested his head on many laps, and, usually, he had slept soundly and selfishly while the girls shaded his face from the sun and looked down and loved him and wondered at his lordly carelessness of their love. To rest his head in a girl's lap had been the easiest thing in the world until now, and now he found Ruth's lap inaccessible and impossible. Yet it was right here, in his reticence, that the strength of his wooing lay. It was because of this reticence that he never alarmed her. Herself fastidious and timid, she never awakened to the perilous trend of their intercourse. Subtly and unaware she grew toward him and closer to him, while he, sensing the growing closeness, longed to dare but was afraid.

Once he dared, one afternoon, when he found her in the darkened living room with a blinding headache.

"Nothing can do it any good," she had answered his inquiries. "And besides, I don't take headache powders. Doctor Hall won't permit me."

"I can cure it, I think, and without drugs," was Martin's answer. "I am not sure, of course, but I'd like to try. It's simply massage. I learned the trick first from the Japanese. They are a race of masseurs, you know. Then I learned it all over again with variations from the Hawaiians. They call it *lomi-lomi*. It can accomplish most of the things drugs accomplish and a few things that drugs can't."

Scarcely had his hands touched her head when she sighed deeply.

"That is so good," she said.

She spoke once again, half an hour later, when she asked, "Aren't you tired?"

The question was perfunctory, and she knew what the answer would be. Then she lost herself in drowsy contemplation of the soothing balm of his strength. Life poured from the ends of his fingers, driving the pain before it, or so it seemed to her, until with the easement of pain, she fell asleep and he stole away.

She called him up by telephone that evening to thank him.

"I slept until dinner," she said. "You cured me completely, Mr. Eden, and I don't know how to thank you."

He was warm, and bungling of speech, and very happy, as he replied to her, and there was dancing in his mind, throughout the telephone conversation, the memory of Browning and of sickly Elizabeth Barrett. What had been done could be done again, and he, Martin Eden, could do it and would do it for Ruth Morse. He went back to his room and to the volume of Spencer's "Sociology" lying open on the bed. But he could not read. Love tormented him and overrode his will, so that, despite all determination, he found himself at the little ink-stained table. The sonnet he composed that night was the first of a love-cycle of fifty sonnets which was completed within two months. He had the "Love-sonnets from the Portuguese" in mind as he wrote, and he wrote under the best conditions for great work, at a climacteric of living, in the throes of his own sweet love-madness.

The many hours he was not with Ruth he devoted to the "Love-cycle," to reading at home, or to the public reading-rooms, where he got more closely in touch with the magazines of the day and the nature of their policy and content. The hours he spent with Ruth were maddening alike in promise and in inconclusiveness. It was a week after he cured her headache that a moonlight sail on Lake Merritt was proposed by Norman and seconded by Arthur and Olney. Martin was the only one capable of handling a boat, and he was pressed into service. Ruth sat near him in the stern, while the three young fellows lounged amidships, deep in a wordy wrangle over "frat" affairs.

The moon had not yet risen, and Ruth, gazing into the starry vault of the sky and exchanging no speech with Martin, experienced a sudden feeling of loneliness. She glanced at him. A puff of wind was heeling the boat over till the deck was awash, and he, one hand on tiller and the other on mainsheet, was luffing slightly, at the same time peering ahead to make out the near-lying north shore. He was unaware of her gaze, and she watched him intently, speculating fancifully about the strange warp of soul that led him, a young man with signal powers, to fritter away his time on the writing of stories and poems foredoomed to mediocrity and failure.

Her eyes wandered along the strong throat, dimly seen in the starlight, and over the firm-poised head, and the old desire to lay her hands upon his neck came back to her. The strength she abhorred attracted her. Her feeling of loneliness became more pronounced, and she felt tired. Her position on the heeling boat irked her, and she remembered the headache he had cured and the soothing rest that resided in him. He was sitting beside her, quite beside her, and the boat seemed to tilt her toward him. Then arose in her the impulse to lean against him, to rest herself against his strength—a vague, half-formed impulse, which, even as she considered it, mastered her and made her lean toward him. Or was it the heeling of the boat? She did not know. She never knew. She knew only that she was leaning against him and that the easement and soothing rest were very good. Perhaps it had been the boat's fault, but she made no effort to retrieve it. She leaned lightly against his shoulder, but she leaned, and she continued to lean when he shifted his position to make it more comfortable for her.

It was a madness, but she refused to consider the madness. She was no longer herself but a woman, with a woman's clinging need; and though she leaned ever so lightly, the need seemed satisfied. She was no longer tired. Martin did not speak. Had he, the spell would have been broken. But his reticence of love prolonged it. He was dazed and dizzy. He

could not understand what was happening. It was too wonderful to be anything but a delirium. He conquered a mad
desire to let go sheet and tiller and to clasp her in his arms.
His intuition told him it was the wrong thing to do, and he
was glad that sheet and tiller kept his hands occupied and
fended off temptation. But he luffed the boat less delicately,
spilling the wind shamelessly from the sail so as to prolong
the tack to the north shore. The shore would compel him to
go about, and the contact would be broken. He sailed with
skill, stopping way on the boat without exciting the notice of
the wranglers, and mentally forgiving his hardest voyages in
that they had made this marvellous night possible, giving him
mastery over sea and boat and wind so that he could sail with
her beside him, her dear weight against him on his shoulder.

When the first light of the rising moon touched the sail,
illuminating the boat with pearly radiance, Ruth moved away
from him. And, even as she moved, she felt him move away.
The impulse to avoid detection was mutual. The episode was
tacitly and secretly intimate. She sat apart from him with
burning cheeks, while the full force of it came home to her.
She had been guilty of something she would not have her
brothers see, nor Olney see. Why had she done it? She had
never done anything like it in her life, and yet she had been
moonlight-sailing with young men before. She had never desired to do anything like it. She was overcome with shame
and with the mystery of her own burgeoning womanhood.
She stole a glance at Martin, who was busy putting the boat
about on the other tack, and she could have hated him for
having made her do an immodest and shameful thing. And
he, of all men! Perhaps her mother was right, and she was
seeing too much of him. It would never happen again, she
resolved, and she would see less of him in the future. She
entertained a wild idea of explaining to him the first time
they were alone together, of lying to him, of mentioning casually the attack of faintness that had overpowered her just
before the moon came up. Then she remembered how they
had drawn mutually away before the revealing moon, and she
knew he would know it for a lie.

In the days that swiftly followed she was no longer herself
but a strange, puzzling creature, wilful over judgment and

scornful of self-analysis, refusing to peer into the future or to think about herself and whither she was drifting. She was in a fever of tingling mystery, alternately frightened and charmed, and in constant bewilderment. She had one idea firmly fixed, however, which insured her security. She would not let Martin speak his love. As long as she did this, all would be well. In a few days he would be off to sea. And even if he did speak, all would be well. It could not be otherwise, for she did not love him. Of course, it would be a painful half hour for him, and an embarrassing half hour for her, because it would be her first proposal. She thrilled deliciously at the thought. She was really a woman, with a man ripe to ask for her in marriage. It was a lure to all that was fundamental in her sex. The fabric of her life, of all that constituted her, quivered and grew tremulous. The thought fluttered in her mind like a flame-attracted moth. She went so far as to imagine Martin proposing, herself putting the words into his mouth; and she rehearsed her refusal, tempering it with kindness and exhorting him to true and noble manhood. And especially he must stop smoking cigarettes. She would make a point of that. But no, she must not let him speak at all. She could stop him, and she had told her mother that she would. All flushed and burning, she regretfully dismissed the conjured situation. Her first proposal would have to be deferred to a more propitious time and a more eligible suitor.

Chapter XXI

C AME a beautiful fall day, warm and languid, palpitant with the hush of the changing season, a California Indian summer day, with hazy sun and wandering wisps of breeze that did not stir the slumber of the air. Filmy purple mists, that were not vapors but fabrics woven of color, hid in the recesses of the hills. San Francisco lay like a blur of smoke upon her heights. The intervening bay was a dull sheen of molten metal, whereon sailing craft lay motionless or drifted with the lazy tide. Far Tamalpais, barely seen in the silver haze, bulked hugely by the Golden Gate, the latter a pale gold pathway under the westering sun. Beyond, the Pacific, dim and vast, was raising on its sky-line tumbled cloud-masses that swept landward, giving warning of the first blustering breath of winter.

The erasure of summer was at hand. Yet summer lingered, fading and fainting among her hills, deepening the purple of her valleys, spinning a shroud of haze from waning powers and sated raptures, dying with the calm content of having lived and lived well. And among the hills, on their favorite knoll, Martin and Ruth sat side by side, their heads bent over the same pages, he reading aloud from the love-sonnets of the woman who had loved Browning as it is given to few men to be loved.

But the reading languished. The spell of passing beauty all about them was too strong. The golden year was dying as it had lived, a beautiful and unrepentant voluptuary, and reminiscent rapture and content freighted heavily the air. It entered into them, dreamy and languorous, weakening the fibres of resolution, suffusing the face of morality, or of judgment, with haze and purple mist. Martin felt tender and melting, and from time to time warm glows passed over him. His head was very near to hers, and when wandering phantoms of breeze stirred her hair so that it touched his face, the printed pages swam before his eyes.

"I don't believe you know a word of what you are reading," she said once when he had lost his place.

He looked at her with burning eyes, and was on the verge of becoming awkward, when a retort came to his lips.

"I don't believe you know either. What was the last sonnet about?"

"I don't know," she laughed frankly. "I've already forgotten. Don't let us read any more. The day is too beautiful."

"It will be our last in the hills for some time," he announced gravely. "There's a storm gathering out there on the sea-rim."

The book slipped from his hands to the ground, and they sat idly and silently, gazing out over the dreamy bay with eyes that dreamed and did not see. Ruth glanced sidewise at his neck. She did not lean toward him. She was drawn by some force outside of herself and stronger than gravitation, strong as destiny. It was only an inch to lean, and it was accomplished without volition on her part. Her shoulder touched his as lightly as a butterfly touches a flower, and just as lightly was the counter-pressure. She felt his shoulder press hers, and a tremor run through him. Then was the time for her to draw back. But she had become an automaton. Her actions had passed beyond the control of her will—she never thought of control or will in the delicious madness that was upon her. His arm began to steal behind her and around her. She waited its slow progress in a torment of delight. She waited, she knew not for what, panting, with dry, burning lips, a leaping pulse, and a fever of expectancy in all her blood. The girdling arm lifted higher and drew her toward him, drew her slowly and caressingly. She could wait no longer. With a tired sigh, and with an impulsive movement all her own, unpremeditated, spasmodic, she rested her head upon his breast. His head bent over swiftly, and, as his lips approached, hers flew to meet them.

This must be love, she thought, in the one rational moment that was vouchsafed her. If it was not love, it was too shameful. It could be nothing else than love. She loved the man whose arms were around her and whose lips were pressed to hers. She pressed more tightly to him, with a snuggling movement of her body. And a moment later, tearing herself half out of his embrace, suddenly and exultantly she reached up and placed both hands upon Martin Eden's sunburnt neck.

So exquisite was the pang of love and desire fulfilled that she uttered a low moan, relaxed her hands, and lay half-swooning in his arms.

Not a word had been spoken, and not a word was spoken for a long time. Twice he bent and kissed her, and each time her lips met his shyly and her body made its happy, nestling movement. She clung to him, unable to release herself, and he sat, half supporting her in his arms, as he gazed with unseeing eyes at the blur of the great city across the bay. For once there were no visions in his brain. Only colors and lights and glows pulsed there, warm as the day and warm as his love. He bent over her. She was speaking.

"When did you love me?" she whispered.

"From the first, the very first, the first moment I laid eyes on you. I was mad for love of you then, and in all the time that has passed since then I have only grown the madder. I am maddest, now, dear. I am almost a lunatic, my head is so turned with joy."

"I am glad I am a woman, Martin—dear," she said, after a long sigh.

He crushed her in his arms again and again, and then asked:—

"And you? When did you first know?"

"Oh, I knew it all the time, almost from the first."

"And I have been as blind as a bat!" he cried, a ring of vexation in his voice. "I never dreamed it until just now, when I—when I kissed you."

"I didn't mean that." She drew herself partly away and looked at him. "I meant I knew you loved me almost from the first."

"And you?" he demanded.

"It came to me suddenly." She was speaking very slowly, her eyes warm and fluttery and melting, a soft flush on her cheeks that did not go away. "I never knew until just now when—you put your arms around me. And I never expected to marry you, Martin, not until just now. How did you make me love you?"

"I don't know," he laughed, "unless just by loving you, for I loved you hard enough to melt the heart of a stone, much less the heart of the living, breathing woman you are."

"This is so different from what I thought love would be," she announced irrelevantly.

"What did you think it would be like?"

"I didn't think it would be like this." She was looking into his eyes at the moment, but her own dropped as she continued, "You see, I didn't know what this was like."

He offered to draw her toward him again, but it was no more than a tentative muscular movement of the girdling arm, for he feared that he might be greedy. Then he felt her body yielding, and once again she was close in his arms and lips were pressed on lips.

"What will my people say?" she queried, with sudden apprehension, in one of the pauses.

"I don't know. We can find out very easily any time we are so minded."

"But if mamma objects? I am sure I am afraid to tell her."

"Let me tell her," he volunteered valiantly. "I think your mother does not like me, but I can win her around. A fellow who can win you can win anything. And if we don't—"

"Yes?"

"Why, we'll have each other. But there's no danger of not winning your mother to our marriage. She loves you too well."

"I should not like to break her heart," Ruth said pensively.

He felt like assuring her that mothers' hearts were not so easily broken, but instead he said, "And love is the greatest thing in the world."

"Do you know, Martin, you sometimes frighten me. I am frightened now, when I think of you and of what you have been. You must be very, very good to me. Remember, after all, that I am only a child. I never loved before."

"Nor I. We are both children together. And we are fortunate above most, for we have found our first love in each other."

"But that is impossible!" she cried, withdrawing herself from his arms with a swift, passionate movement. "Impossible for you. You have been a sailor, and sailors, I have heard, are—are—"

Her voice faltered and died away.

"Are addicted to having a wife in every port?" he suggested. "Is that what you mean?"

"Yes," she answered in a low voice.

"But that is not love." He spoke authoritatively. "I have been in many ports, but I never knew a passing touch of love until I saw you that first night. Do you know, when I said good night and went away, I was almost arrested."

"Arrested?"

"Yes. The policeman thought I was drunk; and I was, too—with love for you."

"But you said we were children, and I said it was impossible, for you, and we have strayed away from the point."

"I said that I never loved anybody but you," he replied. "You are my first, my very first."

"And yet you have been a sailor," she objected.

"But that doesn't prevent me from loving you the first."

"And there have been women—other women—oh!"

And to Martin Eden's supreme surprise, she burst into a storm of tears that took more kisses than one and many caresses to drive away. And all the while there was running through his head Kipling's line: *"And the Colonel's lady and Judy O'Grady are sisters under their skins."* It was true, he decided; though the novels he had read had led him to believe otherwise. His idea, for which the novels were responsible, had been that only formal proposals obtained in the upper classes. It was all right enough, down whence he had come, for youths and maidens to win each other by contact; but for the exalted personages up above on the heights to make love in similar fashion had seemed unthinkable. Yet the novels were wrong. Here was a proof of it. The same pressures and caresses, unaccompanied by speech, that were efficacious with the girls of the working-class, were equally efficacious with the girls above the working-class. They were all of the same flesh, after all, sisters under their skins; and he might have known as much himself had he remembered his Spencer. As he held Ruth in his arms and soothed her, he took great consolation in the thought that the Colonel's lady and Judy O'Grady were pretty much alike under their skins. It brought Ruth closer to him, made her possible. Her dear flesh was as anybody's flesh, as his flesh. There was no bar to their marriage. Class difference was the only difference, and class was extrinsic. It could be shaken off. A slave, he had read, had risen to the Roman purple. That being so, then he could rise to Ruth. Under her purity, and saintliness, and culture, and ethereal beauty of soul, she was, in things fundamentally human, just like Lizzie Connolly and all Lizzie Connollys. All that was possible of them was possible of her. She could love, and hate, maybe have hysterics; and she could certainly be jealous, as she was jealous now, uttering her last sobs in his arms.

"Besides, I am older than you," she remarked suddenly, opening her eyes and looking up at him, "three years older."

"Hush, you are only a child, and I am forty years older than you, in experience," was his answer.

In truth, they were children together, so far as love was concerned, and they were as naïve and immature in the expression of their love as a pair of children, and this despite the fact that she was crammed with a university education and that his head was full of scientific philosophy and the hard facts of life.

They sat on through the passing glory of the day, talking as lovers are prone to talk, marvelling at the wonder of love and at destiny that had flung them so strangely together, and dogmatically believing that they loved to a degree never attained by lovers before. And they returned insistently, again and again, to a rehearsal of their first impressions of each other and to hopeless attempts to analyze just precisely what they felt for each other and how much there was of it.

The cloud-masses on the western horizon received the descending sun, and the circle of the sky turned to rose, while the zenith glowed with the same warm color. The rosy light was all about them, flooding over them, as she sang, "Goodby, Sweet Day." She sang softly, leaning in the cradle of his arm, her hands in his, their hearts in each other's hands.

Chapter XXII

M RS. MORSE did not require a mother's intuition to read the advertisement in Ruth's face when she returned home. The flush that would not leave the cheeks told the simple story, and more eloquently did the eyes, large and bright, reflecting an unmistakable inward glory.

"What has happened?" Mrs. Morse asked, having bided her time till Ruth had gone to bed.

"You know?" Ruth queried, with trembling lips.

For reply, her mother's arm went around her, and a hand was softly caressing her hair.

"He did not speak," she blurted out. "I did not intend that it should happen, and I would never have let him speak—only he didn't speak."

"But if he did not speak, then nothing could have happened, could it?"

"But it did, just the same."

"In the name of goodness, child, what are you babbling about?" Mrs. Morse was bewildered. "I don't think I know what happened, after all. What did happen?"

Ruth looked at her mother in surprise.

"I thought you knew. Why, we're engaged, Martin and I."

Mrs. Morse laughed with incredulous vexation.

"No, he didn't speak," Ruth explained. "He just loved me, that was all. I was as surprised as you are. He didn't say a word. He just put his arm around me. And—and I was not myself. And he kissed me, and I kissed him. I couldn't help it. I just had to. And then I knew I loved him."

She paused, waiting with expectancy the benediction of her mother's kiss, but Mrs. Morse was coldly silent.

"It is a dreadful accident, I know," Ruth recommenced with a sinking voice. "And I don't know how you will ever forgive me. But I couldn't help it. I did not dream that I loved him until that moment. And you must tell father for me."

"Would it not be better not to tell your father? Let me see

Martin Eden, and talk with him, and explain. He will understand and release you."

"No! no!" Ruth cried, starting up. "I do not want to be
released. I love him, and love is very sweet. I am going to
marry him—of course, if you will let me."

"We have other plans for you, Ruth, dear, your father and
I—oh, no, no; no man picked out for you, or anything like
that. Our plans go no farther than your marrying some man
in your own station in life, a good and honorable gentleman,
whom you will select yourself, when you love him."

"But I love Martin already," was the plaintive protest.

"We would not influence your choice in any way; but you
are our daughter, and we could not bear to see you make a
marriage such as this. He has nothing but roughness and
coarseness to offer you in exchange for all that is refined and
delicate in you. He is no match for you in any way. He could
not support you. We have no foolish ideas about wealth, but
comfort is another matter, and our daughter should at least
marry a man who can give her that—and not a penniless adventurer, a sailor, a cowboy, a smuggler, and Heaven knows
what else, who, in addition to everything, is hare-brained and
irresponsible."

Ruth was silent. Every word she recognized as true.

"He wastes his time over his writing, trying to accomplish
what geniuses and rare men with college educations sometimes accomplish. A man thinking of marriage should be preparing for marriage. But not he. As I have said, and I know
you agree with me, he is irresponsible. And why should he
not be? It is the way of sailors. He has never learned to be
economical or temperate. The spendthrift years have marked
him. It is not his fault, of course, but that does not alter his
nature. And have you thought of the years of licentiousness
he inevitably has lived? Have you thought of that, daughter?
You know what marriage means."

Ruth shuddered and clung close to her mother.

"I have thought." Ruth waited a long time for the thought
to frame itself. "And it is terrible. It sickens me to think of it.
I told you it was a dreadful accident, my loving him; but I
can't help myself. Could you help loving father? Then it is the

same with me. There is something in me, in him—I never
knew it was there until to-day—but it is there, and it makes
me love him. I never thought to love him, but, you see, I
do," she concluded, a certain faint triumph in her voice.

They talked long, and to little purpose, in conclusion agreeing to wait an indeterminate time without doing anything.

The same conclusion was reached, a little later that night,
between Mrs. Morse and her husband, after she had made
due confession of the miscarriage of her plans.

"It could hardly have come otherwise," was Mr. Morse's
judgment. "This sailor-fellow has been the only man she was
in touch with. Sooner or later she was going to awaken anyway; and she did awaken, and lo! here was this sailor-fellow,
the only accessible man at the moment, and of course she
promptly loved him, or thought she did, which amounts to
the same thing."

Mrs. Morse took it upon herself to work slowly and indirectly upon Ruth, rather than to combat her. There would be
plenty of time for this, for Martin was not in position to
marry.

"Let her see all she wants of him," was Mr. Morse's advice.
"The more she knows him, the less she'll love him, I wager.
And give her plenty of contrast. Make a point of having
young people at the house. Young women and young men,
all sorts of young men, clever men, men who have done
something or who are doing things, men of her own class,
gentlemen. She can gauge him by them. They will show him
up for what he is. And after all, he is a mere boy of twenty-
one. Ruth is no more than a child. It is calf love with the pair
of them, and they will grow out of it."

So the matter rested. Within the family it was accepted that
Ruth and Martin were engaged, but no announcement was
made. The family did not think it would ever be necessary.
Also, it was tacitly understood that it was to be a long engagement. They did not ask Martin to go to work, nor to
cease writing. They did not intend to encourage him to mend
himself. And he aided and abetted them in their unfriendly
designs, for going to work was farthest from his thoughts.

"I wonder if you'll like what I have done!" he said to Ruth
several days later. "I've decided that boarding with my sister

is too expensive, and I am going to board myself. I've rented a little room out in North Oakland, retired neighborhood and all the rest, you know, and I've bought an oil-burner on which to cook."

Ruth was overjoyed. The oil-burner especially pleased her.

"That was the way Mr. Butler began his start," she said.

Martin frowned inwardly at the citation of that worthy gentleman, and went on: "I put stamps on all my manuscripts and started them off to the editors again. Then to-day I moved in, and to-morrow I start to work."

"A position!" she cried, betraying the gladness of her surprise in all her body, nestling closer to him, pressing his hand, smiling. "And you never told me! What is it?"

He shook his head.

"I meant that I was going to work at my writing." Her face fell, and he went on hastily. "Don't misjudge me. I am not going in this time with any iridescent ideas. It is to be a cold, prosaic, matter-of-fact business proposition. It is better than going to sea again, and I shall earn more money than any position in Oakland can bring an unskilled man.

"You see, this vacation I have taken has given me perspective. I haven't been working the life out of my body, and I haven't been writing, at least not for publication. All I've done has been to love you and to think. I've read some, too, but it has been part of my thinking, and I have read principally magazines. I have generalized about myself, and the world, my place in it, and my chance to win to a place that will be fit for you. Also, I've been reading Spencer's 'Philosophy of Style,' and found out a lot of what was the matter with me—or my writing, rather; and for that matter with most of the writing that is published every month in the magazines.

"But the upshot of it all—of my thinking and reading and loving—is that I am going to move to Grub Street. I shall leave masterpieces alone and do hack-work—jokes, paragraphs, feature articles, humorous verse, and society verse— all the rot for which there seems so much demand. Then there are the newspaper syndicates, and the newspaper short-story syndicates, and the syndicates for the Sunday supplements. I can go ahead and hammer out the stuff they want, and earn the equivalent of a good salary by it. There are free-lances, you know, who earn as much as four or five hundred a month. I don't care to become as they; but I'll earn a good living, and have plenty of time to myself, which I wouldn't have in any position.

"Then, I'll have my spare time for study and for real work. In between the grind I'll try my hand at masterpieces, and I'll study and prepare myself for the writing of masterpieces. Why, I am amazed at the distance I have come already. When I first tried to write, I had nothing to write about except a few paltry experiences which I neither understood nor appreciated. But I had no thoughts. I really didn't. I didn't even have the words with which to think. My experiences were so many meaningless pictures. But as I began to add to my knowledge, and to my vocabulary, I saw something more in my experiences than mere pictures. I retained the pictures and I found their interpretation. That was when I began to do good work, when I wrote 'Adventure,' 'Joy,' 'The Pot,' 'The Wine of Life,' 'The Jostling Street,' the 'Love-cycle,' and the 'Sea Lyrics.' I shall write more like them, and better; but I shall do it in my spare time. My feet are on the solid earth, now. Hack-work and income first, masterpieces afterward. Just to show you, I wrote half a dozen jokes last night for the comic weeklies; and just as I was going to bed, the thought struck me to try my hand at a triolet—a humorous one; and inside an hour I had written four. They ought to be worth a dollar apiece. Four dollars right there for a few afterthoughts on the way to bed.

"Of course it's all valueless, just so much dull and sordid plodding; but it is no more dull and sordid than keeping books at sixty dollars a month, adding up endless columns of meaningless figures until one dies. And furthermore, the hack-work keeps me in touch with things literary and gives me time to try bigger things."

"But what good are these bigger things, these master-pieces?" Ruth demanded. "You can't sell them."

"Oh, yes, I can," he began; but she interrupted.

"All those you named, and which you say yourself are good—you have not sold any of them. We can't get married on masterpieces that won't sell."

"Then we'll get married on triolets that will sell," he asserted stoutly, putting his arm around her and drawing a very unresponsive sweetheart toward him.

"Listen to this," he went on in attempted gayety. "It's not art, but it's a dollar.

> "He came in
>   When I was out,
> To borrow some tin
> Was why he came in,
>   And he went without;
> So I was in
>   And he was out."

The merry lilt with which he had invested the jingle was at variance with the dejection that came into his face as he finished. He had drawn no smile from Ruth. She was looking at him in an earnest and troubled way.

"It may be a dollar," she said, "but it is a jester's dollar, the fee of a clown. Don't you see, Martin, the whole thing is lowering. I want the man I love and honor to be something finer and higher than a perpetrator of jokes and doggerel."

"You want him to be like—say Mr. Butler?" he suggested.

"I know you don't like Mr. Butler," she began.

"Mr. Butler's all right," he interrupted. "It's only his indigestion I find fault with. But to save me I can't see any difference between writing jokes or comic verse and running a type-writer, taking dictation, or keeping sets of books. It is all a means to an end. Your theory is for me to begin with keeping books in order to become a successful lawyer or man of business. Mine is to begin with hack-work and develop into an able author."

"There is a difference," she insisted.

"What is it?"

"Why, your good work, what you yourself call good, you can't sell. You have tried,—you know that,—but the editors won't buy it."

"Give me time, dear," he pleaded. "The hack-work is only makeshift, and I don't take it seriously. Give me two years. I shall succeed in that time, and the editors will be glad to buy my good work. I know what I am saying; I have faith in myself. I know what I have in me; I know what literature is, now; I know the average rot that is poured out by a lot of little men; and I know that at the end of two years I shall be on the highroad to success. As for business, I shall never succeed at it. I am not in sympathy with it. It strikes me as dull, and stupid, and mercenary, and tricky. Anyway I am not adapted for it. I'd never get beyond a clerkship, and how could you and I be happy on the paltry earnings of a clerk? I want the best of everything in the world for you, and the only time when I won't want it will be when there is something better. And I'm going to get it, going to get all of it. The income of a successful author makes Mr. Butler look cheap. A 'best-seller' will earn anywhere between fifty and a hundred thousand dollars—sometimes more and sometimes less; but, as a rule, pretty close to those figures."

She remained silent; her disappointment was apparent.

"Well?" he asked.

"I had hoped and planned otherwise. I had thought, and I still think, that the best thing for you would be to study shorthand—you already know type-writing—and go into father's office. You have a good mind, and I am confident you would succeed as a lawyer."

Chapter XXIII

THAT RUTH had little faith in his power as a writer, did not alter her nor diminish her in Martin's eyes. In the breathing spell of the vacation he had taken, he had spent many hours in self-analysis, and thereby learned much of himself. He had discovered that he loved beauty more than fame, and that what desire he had for fame was largely for Ruth's sake. It was for this reason that his desire for fame was strong. He wanted to be great in the world's eyes: "to make good," as he expressed it, in order that the woman he loved should be proud of him and deem him worthy.

As for himself, he loved beauty passionately, and the joy of serving her was to him sufficient wage. And more than beauty he loved Ruth. He considered love the finest thing in the world. It was love that had worked the revolution in him, changing him from an uncouth sailor to a student and an artist; therefore, to him, the finest and greatest of the three, greater than learning and artistry, was love. Already he had discovered that his brain went beyond Ruth's, just as it went beyond the brains of her brothers, or the brain of her father. In spite of every advantage of university training, and in the face of her bachelorship of arts, his power of intellect over-shadowed hers, and his year or so of self-study and equipment gave him a mastery of the affairs of the world and art and life that she could never hope to possess.

All this he realized, but it did not affect his love for her, nor her love for him. Love was too fine and noble, and he was too loyal a lover for him to besmirch love with criticism. What did love have to do with Ruth's divergent views on art, right conduct, the French Revolution, or equal suffrage? They were mental processes, but love was beyond reason; it was superrational. He could not belittle love. He worshipped it. Love lay on the mountain-tops beyond the valley-land of reason. It was a sublimated condition of existence, the top-most peak of living, and it came rarely. Thanks to the school of scientific philosophers he favored, he knew the biological significance of love; but by a refined process of the same scientific reasoning he reached the conclusion that the human organism achieved its highest purpose in love, that love must not be questioned, but must be accepted as the highest guerdon of life. Thus, he considered the lover blessed over all creatures, and it was a delight to him to think of "God's own mad lover," rising above the things of earth, above wealth and judgment, public opinion and applause, rising above life itself and "dying on a kiss."

Much of this Martin had already reasoned out, and some of it he reasoned out later. In the meantime he worked, taking no recreation except when he went to see Ruth, and living like a Spartan. He paid two dollars and a half a month rent for the small room he got from his Portuguese landlady, Maria Silva, a virago and a widow, hard working and harsher tempered, rearing her large brood of children somehow, and drowning her sorrow and fatigue at irregular intervals in a gallon of the thin, sour wine that she bought from the corner grocery and saloon for fifteen cents. From detesting her and her foul tongue at first, Martin grew to admire her as he observed the brave fight she made. There were but four rooms in the little house—three, when Martin's was subtracted. One of these, the parlor, gay with an ingrain carpet and dolorous with a funeral card and a death-picture of one of her numerous departed babes, was kept strictly for company. The blinds were always down, and her barefooted tribe was never permitted to enter the sacred precinct save on state occasions. She cooked, and all ate, in the kitchen, where she likewise washed, starched, and ironed clothes on all days of the week except Sunday; for her income came largely from taking in washing from her more prosperous neighbors. Remained the bedroom, small as the one occupied by Martin, into which she and her seven little ones crowded and slept. It was an everlasting miracle to Martin how it was accomplished, and from her side of the thin partition he heard nightly every detail of the going to bed, the squalls and squabbles, the soft chattering, and the sleepy, twittering noises as of birds. Another source of income to Maria were her cows, two of them, which she milked night and morning and which gained a surreptitious livelihood from vacant lots and the grass that grew on either side the public sidewalks, attended always by one or

more of her ragged boys, whose watchful guardianship consisted chiefly in keeping their eyes out for the poundmen.

In his own small room Martin lived, slept, studied, wrote,
and kept house. Before the one window, looking out on the
tiny front porch, was the kitchen table that served as desk,
library, and type-writing stand. The bed, against the rear wall,
occupied two-thirds of the total space of the room. The table
was flanked on one side by a gaudy bureau, manufactured for
profit and not for service, the thin veneer of which was shed
day by day. This bureau stood in the corner, and in the opposite corner, on the table's other flank, was the kitchen—the
oil-stove on a dry-goods box, inside of which were dishes and
cooking utensils, a shelf on the wall for provisions, and a
bucket of water on the floor. Martin had to carry his water
from the kitchen sink, there being no tap in his room. On
days when there was much steam to his cooking, the harvest
of veneer from the bureau was unusually generous. Over the
bed, hoisted by a tackle to the ceiling, was his bicycle. At first
he had tried to keep it in the basement; but the tribe of Silva,
loosening the bearings and puncturing the tires, had driven
him out. Next he attempted the tiny front porch, until a
howling southeaster drenched the wheel a night-long. Then
he had retreated with it to his room and slung it aloft.

A small closet contained his clothes and the books he had
accumulated and for which there was no room on the table
or under the table. Hand in hand with reading, he had developed the habit of making notes, and so copiously did he make
them that there would have been no existence for him in the
confined quarters had he not rigged several clothes-lines
across the room on which the notes were hung. Even so, he
was crowded until navigating the room was a difficult task.
He could not open the door without first closing the closet
door, and *vice versa*. It was impossible for him anywhere to
traverse the room in a straight line. To go from the door to
the head of the bed was a zigzag course that he was never
quite able to accomplish in the dark without collisions. Having settled the difficulty of the conflicting doors, he had to
steer sharply to the right to avoid the kitchen. Next, he
sheered to the left, to escape the foot of the bed; but this
sheer, if too generous, brought him against the corner of the

table. With a sudden twitch and lurch, he terminated the sheer and bore off to the right along a sort of canal, one bank of which was the bed, the other the table. When the one chair in the room was at its usual place before the table, the canal was unnavigable. When the chair was not in use, it reposed on top of the bed, though sometimes he sat on the chair when cooking, reading a book while the water boiled, and even becoming skilful enough to manage a paragraph or two while steak was frying. Also, so small was the little corner that constituted the kitchen, he was able, sitting down, to reach anything he needed. In fact, it was expedient to cook sitting down; standing up, he was too often in his own way.

In conjunction with a perfect stomach that could digest anything, he possessed knowledge of the various foods that were at the same time nutritious and cheap. Pea-soup was a common article in his diet, as well as potatoes and beans, the latter large and brown and cooked in Mexican style. Rice, cooked as American housewives never cook it and can never learn to cook it, appeared on Martin's table at least once a day. Dried fruits were less expensive than fresh, and he had usually a pot of them, cooked and ready at hand, for they took the place of butter on his bread. Occasionally he graced his table with a piece of round-steak, or with a soup-bone. Coffee, without cream or milk, he had twice a day, in the evening substituting tea; but both coffee and tea were excellently cooked.

There was need for him to be economical. His vacation had consumed nearly all he had earned in the laundry, and he was so far from his market that weeks must elapse before he could hope for the first returns from his hack-work. Except at such times as he saw Ruth, or dropped in to see his sister Gertrude, he lived a recluse, in each day accomplishing at least three days' labor of ordinary men. He slept a scant five hours, and only one with a constitution of iron could have held himself down, as Martin did, day after day, to nineteen consecutive hours of toil. He never lost a moment. On the looking-glass were lists of definitions and pronunciations; when shaving, or dressing, or combing his hair, he conned these lists over. Similar lists were on the wall over the oil-stove, and they were similarly conned while he was engaged in cooking or in washing the dishes.

New lists continually displaced the old ones. Every strange or partly familiar word encountered in his reading was immediately jotted down, and later, when a sufficient number had been accumulated, were typed and pinned to the wall or looking-glass. He even carried them in his pockets, and reviewed them at odd moments on the street, or while waiting in butcher shop or grocery to be served.

He went farther in the matter. Reading the works of men who had arrived, he noted every result achieved by them, and worked out the tricks by which they had been achieved—the tricks of narrative, of exposition, of style, the points of view, the contrasts, the epigrams; and of all these he made lists for study. He did not ape. He sought principles. He drew up lists of effective and fetching mannerisms, till out of many such, culled from many writers, he was able to induce the general principle of mannerism, and, thus equipped, to cast about for new and original ones of his own, and to weigh and measure and appraise them properly. In similar manner he collected lists of strong phrases, the phrases of living language, phrases that bit like acid and scorched like flame, or that glowed and were mellow and luscious in the midst of the arid desert of common speech. He sought always for the principle that lay behind and beneath. He wanted to know how the thing was done; after that he could do it for himself. He was not content with the fair face of beauty. He dissected beauty in his crowded little bedroom laboratory, where cooking smells alternated with the outer bedlam of the Silva tribe; and, having dissected and learned the anatomy of beauty, he was nearer being able to create beauty itself.

He was so made that he could work only with understanding. He could not work blindly, in the dark, ignorant of what he was producing and trusting to chance and the star of his genius that the effect produced should be right and fine. He had no patience with chance effects. He wanted to know why and how. His was deliberate creative genius, and, before he began a story or poem, the thing itself was already alive in his brain, with the end in sight and the means of realizing that end in his conscious possession. Otherwise the effort was doomed to failure. On the other hand, he appreciated the chance effects in words and phrases that came lightly and eas-

ily into his brain, and that later stood all tests of beauty and
power and developed tremendous and incommunicable connotations. Before such he bowed down and marvelled, knowing that they were beyond the deliberate creation of any man.
And no matter how much he dissected beauty in search of the
principles that underlie beauty and make beauty possible, he
was aware, always, of the innermost mystery of beauty to
which he did not penetrate and to which no man had ever
penetrated. He knew full well, from his Spencer, that man
can never attain ultimate knowledge of anything, and that the
mystery of beauty was no less than that of life—nay, more—
that the fibres of beauty and life were intertwisted, and that
he himself was but a bit of the same nonunderstandable fabric, twisted of sunshine and star-dust and wonder.

In fact, it was when filled with these thoughts that he wrote
his essay entitled "Star-dust," in which he had his fling, not
at the principles of criticism, but at the principal critics. It
was brilliant, deep, philosophical, and deliciously touched
with laughter. Also it was promptly rejected by the magazines
as often as it was submitted. But having cleared his mind of
it, he went serenely on his way. It was a habit he developed,
of incubating and maturing his thought upon a subject, and
of then rushing into the type-writer with it. That it did not
see print was a matter of small moment with him. The writing of it was the culminating act of a long mental process, the
drawing together of scattered threads of thought and the final
generalizing upon all the data with which his mind was burdened. To write such an article was the conscious effort by
which he freed his mind and made it ready for fresh material
and problems. It was in a way akin to that common habit of
men and women troubled by real or fancied grievances, who
periodically and volubly break their long-suffering silence and
"have their say" till the last word is said.

Chapter XXIV

THE WEEKS passed. Martin ran out of money, and publishers' checks were far away as ever. All his important manuscripts had come back and been started out again, and his hack-work fared no better. His little kitchen was no longer graced with a variety of foods. Caught in the pinch with a part sack of rice and a few pounds of dried apricots, rice and apricots was his menu three times a day for five days handrunning. Then he started to realize on his credit. The Portuguese grocer, to whom he had hitherto paid cash, called a halt when Martin's bill reached the magnificent total of three dollars and eighty-five cents.

"For you see," said the grocer, "you no catcha da work, I losa da mon'."

And Martin could reply nothing. There was no way of explaining. It was not true business principle to allow credit to a strong-bodied young fellow of the working-class who was too lazy to work.

"You catcha da job, I let you have mora da grub," the grocer assured Martin. "No job, no grub. Thata da business." And then, to show that it was purely business foresight and not prejudice, "Hava da drink on da house—good friends justa da same."

So Martin drank, in his easy way, to show that he was good friends with the house, and then went supperless to bed.

The fruit store, where Martin had bought his vegetables, was run by an American whose business principles were so weak that he let Martin run a bill of five dollars before stopping his credit. The baker stopped at two dollars, and the butcher at four dollars. Martin added his debts and found that he was possessed of a total credit in all the world of fourteen dollars and eighty-five cents. He was up with his type-writer rent, but he estimated that he could get two months' credit on that, which would be eight dollars. When that occurred, he would have exhausted all possible credit.

The last purchase from the fruit store had been a sack of

potatoes, and for a week he had potatoes, and nothing but potatoes, three times a day. An occasional dinner at Ruth's helped to keep strength in his body, though he found it tantalizing enough to refuse further helping when his appetite was raging at sight of so much food spread before it. Now and again, though afflicted with secret shame, he dropped in at his sister's at meal-time and ate as much as he dared— more than he dared at the Morse table.

Day by day he worked on, and day by day the postman delivered to him rejected manuscripts. He had no money for stamps, so the manuscripts accumulated in a heap under the table. Came a day when for forty hours he had not tasted food. He could not hope for a meal at Ruth's, for she was away to San Rafael on a two weeks' visit; and for very shame's sake he could not go to his sister's. To cap misfortune, the postman, in his afternoon round, brought him five returned manuscripts. Then it was that Martin wore his overcoat down into Oakland, and came back without it, but with five dollars tinkling in his pocket. He paid a dollar each on account to the four tradesmen, and in his kitchen fried steak and onions, made coffee, and stewed a large pot of prunes. And having dined, he sat down at his table-desk and completed before midnight an essay which he entitled "The Dignity of Usury." Having typed it out, he flung it under the table, for there had been nothing left from the five dollars with which to buy stamps.

Later on he pawned his watch, and still later his wheel, reducing the amount available for food by putting stamps on all his manuscripts and sending them out. He was disappointed with his hack-work. Nobody cared to buy. He compared it with what he found in the newspapers, weeklies, and cheap magazines, and decided that his was better, far better, than the average; yet it would not sell. Then he discovered that most of the newspapers printed a great deal of what was called "plate" stuff, and he got the address of the association that furnished it. His own work that he sent in was returned, along with a stereotyped slip informing him that the staff supplied all the copy that was needed.

In one of the great juvenile periodicals he noted whole columns of incident and anecdote. Here was a chance. His paragraphs were returned, and though he tried repeatedly he never succeeded in placing one. Later on, when it no longer mattered, he learned that the associate editors and sub-editors augmented their salaries by supplying those paragraphs themselves. The comic weeklies returned his jokes and humorous verse, and the light society verse he wrote for the large magazines found no abiding-place. Then there was the newspaper storiette. He knew that he could write better ones than were published. Managing to obtain the addresses of two newspaper syndicates, he deluged them with storiettes. When he had written twenty and failed to place one of them, he ceased. And yet, from day to day, he read storiettes in the dailies and weeklies, scores and scores of storiettes, not one of which would compare with his. In his despondency, he concluded that he had no judgment whatever, that he was hypnotized by what he wrote, and that he was a self-deluded pretender.

The inhuman editorial machine ran smoothly as ever. He folded the stamps in with his manuscript, dropped it into the letter-box, and from three weeks to a month afterward the postman came up the steps and handed him the manuscript. Surely there were no live, warm editors at the other end. It was all wheels and cogs and oil-cups—a clever mechanism operated by automatons. He reached stages of despair wherein he doubted if editors existed at all. He had never received a sign of the existence of one, and from absence of judgment in rejecting all he wrote it seemed plausible that editors were myths, manufactured and maintained by office boys, typesetters, and pressmen.

The hours he spent with Ruth were the only happy ones he had, and they were not all happy. He was afflicted always with a gnawing restlessness, more tantalizing than in the old days before he possessed her love; for now that he did possess her love, the possession of her was far away as ever. He had asked for two years; time was flying, and he was achieving nothing. Again, he was always conscious of the fact that she did not approve what he was doing. She did not say so directly. Yet indirectly she let him understand it as clearly and definitely as she could have spoken it. It was not resentment with her, but disapproval; though less sweet-natured women might have resented where she was no more than disappointed. Her disappointment lay in that this man she had taken to mould, refused to be moulded. To a certain extent she had found his clay plastic, then it had developed stubbornness, declining to be shaped in the image of her father or of Mr. Butler.

What was great and strong in him, she missed, or, worse yet, misunderstood. This man, whose clay was so plastic that he could live in any number of pigeonholes of human existence, she thought wilful and most obstinate because she could not shape him to live in her pigeonhole, which was the only one she knew. She could not follow the flights of his mind, and when his brain got beyond her, she deemed him erratic. Nobody else's brain ever got beyond her. She could always follow her father and mother, her brothers and Olney; wherefore, when she could not follow Martin, she believed the fault lay with him. It was the old tragedy of insularity trying to serve as mentor to the universal.

"You worship at the shrine of the established," he told her once, in a discussion they had over Praps and Vanderwater. "I grant that as authorities to quote they are most excellent— the two foremost literary critics in the United States. Every school teacher in the land looks up to Vanderwater as the Dean of American criticism. Yet I read his stuff, and it seems to me the perfection of the felicitous expression of the inane. Why, he is no more than a ponderous bromide, thanks to Gelett Burgess. And Praps is no better. His 'Hemlock Mosses,' for instance, is beautifully written. Not a comma is out of place; and the tone—ah!—is lofty, so lofty. He is the best-paid critic in the United States. Though, Heaven forbid! he's not a critic at all. They do criticism better in England.

"But the point is, they sound the popular note, and they sound it so beautifully and morally and contentedly. Their reviews remind me of a British Sunday. They are the popular mouthpieces. They back up your professors of English, and your professors of English back them up. And there isn't an original idea in any of their skulls. They know only the established,—in fact, they are the established. They are weak minded, and the established impresses itself upon them as easily as the name of the brewery is impressed on a beer bottle. And their function is to catch all the young fellows attending the university, to drive out of their minds any glimmering originality that may chance to be there, and to put upon them the stamp of the established."

"I think I am nearer the truth," she replied, "when I stand by the established, than you are, raging around like an iconoclastic South Sea Islander."

"It was the missionary who did the image breaking," he laughed. "And unfortunately, all the missionaries are off among the heathen, so there are none left at home to break those old images, Mr. Vanderwater and Mr. Praps."

"And the college professors, as well," she added.

He shook his head emphatically. "No; the science professors should live. They're really great. But it would be a good deed to break the heads of nine-tenths of the English professors—little, microscopic-minded parrots!"

Which was rather severe on the professors, but which to Ruth was blasphemy. She could not help but measure the professors, neat, scholarly, in fitting clothes, speaking in well-modulated voices, breathing of culture and refinement, with this almost indescribable young fellow whom somehow she loved, whose clothes never would fit him, whose heavy muscles told of damning toil, who grew excited when he talked, substituting abuse for calm statement and passionate utterance for cool self-possession. They at least earned good salaries and were—yes, she compelled herself to face it—were gentlemen; while he could not earn a penny, and he was not as they.

She did not weigh Martin's words nor judge his argument by them. Her conclusion that his argument was wrong was reached—unconsciously, it is true—by a comparison of externals. They, the professors, were right in their literary judgments because they were successes. Martin's literary judgments were wrong because he could not sell his wares. To use his own phrase, they made good, and he did not make good. And besides, it did not seem reasonable that he should be right—he who had stood, so short a time before, in that same living room, blushing and awkward, acknowledging his introduction, looking fearfully about him at the bric-a-brac his swinging shoulders threatened to break, asking how long since Swinburne died, and boastfully announcing that he had read "Excelsior" and the "Psalm of Life."

Unwittingly, Ruth herself proved his point that she worshipped the established. Martin followed the processes of her thoughts, but forbore to go farther. He did not love her for what she thought of Praps and Vanderwater and English professors, and he was coming to realize, with increasing conviction, that he possessed brain-areas and stretches of knowledge which she could never comprehend nor know existed.

In music she thought him unreasonable, and in the matter of opera not only unreasonable but wilfully perverse.

"How did you like it?" she asked him one night, on the way home from the opera.

It was a night when he had taken her at the expense of a month's rigid economizing on food. After vainly waiting for him to speak about it, herself still tremulous and stirred by what she had just seen and heard, she had asked the question.

"I liked the overture," was his answer. "It was splendid."

"Yes, but the opera itself?"

"That was splendid too; that is, the orchestra was, though I'd have enjoyed it more if those jumping-jacks had kept quiet or gone off the stage."

Ruth was aghast.

"You don't mean Tetralani or Barillo?" she queried.

"All of them—the whole kit and crew."

"But they are great artists," she protested.

"They spoiled the music just the same, with their antics and unrealities."

"But don't you like Barillo's voice?" Ruth asked. "He is next to Caruso, they say."

"Of course I liked him, and I liked Tetralani even better. Her voice is exquisite—or at least I think so."

"But, but—" Ruth stammered. "I don't know what you mean, then. You admire their voices, yet say they spoiled the music."

"Precisely that. I'd give anything to hear them in concert, and I'd give even a bit more not to hear them when the orchestra is playing. I'm afraid I am a hopeless realist. Great singers are not great actors. To hear Barillo sing a love passage with the voice of an angel, and to hear Tetralani reply like another angel, and to hear it all accompanied by a perfect orgy of glowing and colorful music—is ravishing, most ravishing. I do not admit it. I assert it. But the whole effect is spoiled when I look at them—at Tetralani, five feet ten in her stocking feet and weighing a hundred and ninety pounds, and at Barillo, a scant five feet four, greasy-featured, with the chest of a squat, undersized blacksmith, and at the pair of them, attitudinizing, clasping their breasts, flinging their arms in the air like demented creatures in an asylum; and when I am expected to accept all this as the faithful illusion of a love-scene between a slender and beautiful princess and a handsome, romantic, young prince—why, I can't accept it, that's all. It's rot; it's absurd; it's unreal. That's what's the matter with it. It's not real. Don't tell me that anybody in this world ever made love that way. Why, if I'd made love to you in such fashion, you'd have boxed my ears."

"But you misunderstand," Ruth protested. "Every form of art has its limitations." (She was busy recalling a lecture she had heard at the university on the conventions of the arts.) "In painting there are only two dimensions to the canvas, yet you accept the illusion of three dimensions which the art of a painter enables him to throw into the canvas. In writing, again, the author must be omnipotent. You accept as perfectly legitimate the author's account of the secret thoughts of the heroine, and yet all the time you know that the heroine was alone when thinking these thoughts, and that neither the author nor any one else was capable of hearing them. And so with the stage, with sculpture, with opera, with every art form. Certain irreconcilable things must be accepted."

"Yes, I understood that," Martin answered. "All the arts have their conventions." (Ruth was surprised at his use of the word. It was as if he had studied at the university himself, instead of being ill-equipped from browsing at haphazard through the books in the library.) "But even the conventions must be real. Trees, painted on flat cardboard and stuck up on each side of the stage, we accept as a forest. It is a real enough convention. But, on the other hand, we would not accept a sea scene as a forest. We can't do it. It violates our senses. Nor would you, or, rather, should you, accept the

ravings and writhings and agonized contortions of those two
lunatics to-night as a convincing portrayal of love."

"But you don't hold yourself superior to all the judges of
music?" she protested.

"No, no, not for a moment. I merely maintain my right as
an individual. I have just been telling you what I think, in
order to explain why the elephantine gambols of Madame
Tetralani spoil the orchestra for me. The world's judges of
music may all be right. But I am I, and I won't subordinate
my taste to the unanimous judgment of mankind. If I don't
like a thing, I don't like it, that's all; and there is no reason
under the sun why I should ape a liking for it just because
the majority of my fellow-creatures like it, or make believe
they like it. I can't follow the fashions in the things I like or
dislike."

"But music, you know, is a matter of training," Ruth argued; "and opera is even more a matter of training. May it
not be—"

"That I am not trained in opera?" he dashed in.

She nodded.

"The very thing," he agreed. "And I consider I am fortunate in not having been caught when I was young. If I had,
I could have wept sentimental tears to-night, and the clown-
ish antics of that precious pair would have but enhanced the
beauty of their voices and the beauty of the accompanying
orchestra. You are right. It's mostly a matter of training. And
I am too old, now. I must have the real or nothing. An illusion that won't convince is a palpable lie, and that's what
grand opera is to me when little Barillo throws a fit, clutches
mighty Tetralani in his arms (also in a fit), and tells her how
passionately he adores her."

Again Ruth measured his thoughts by comparison of externals and in accordance with her belief in the established. Who
was he that he should be right and all the cultured world
wrong? His words and thoughts made no impression upon
her. She was too firmly entrenched in the established to have
any sympathy with revolutionary ideas. She had always been
used to music, and she had enjoyed opera ever since she was
a child, and all her world had enjoyed it, too. Then by what
right did Martin Eden emerge, as he had so recently emerged,

from his rag-time and working-class songs, and pass judgment on the world's music? She was vexed with him, and as she walked beside him she had a vague feeling of outrage. At the best, in her most charitable frame of mind, she considered the statement of his views to be a caprice, an erratic and uncalled-for prank. But when he took her in his arms at the door and kissed her good night in tender lover-fashion, she forgot everything in the outrush of her own love to him. And later, on a sleepless pillow, she puzzled, as she had often puzzled of late, as to how it was that she loved so strange a man, and loved him despite the disapproval of her people.

And next day Martin Eden cast hack-work aside, and at white heat hammered out an essay to which he gave the title, "The Philosophy of Illusion." A stamp started it on its travels, but it was destined to receive many stamps and to be started on many travels in the months that followed.

Chapter XXV

MARIA SILVA was poor, and all the ways of poverty were clear to her. Poverty, to Ruth, was a word signifying a not-nice condition of existence. That was her total knowledge on the subject. She knew Martin was poor, and his condition she associated in her mind with the boyhood of Abraham Lincoln, of Mr. Butler, and of other men who had become successes. Also, while aware that poverty was anything but delectable, she had a comfortable middle-class feeling that poverty was salutary, that it was a sharp spur that urged on to success all men who were not degraded and hopeless drudges. So that her knowledge that Martin was so poor that he had pawned his watch and overcoat did not disturb her. She even considered it the hopeful side of the situation, believing that sooner or later it would arouse him and compel him to abandon his writing.

Ruth never read hunger in Martin's face, which had grown lean and had enlarged the slight hollows in the cheeks. In fact, she marked the change in his face with satisfaction. It seemed to refine him, to remove from him much of the dross of flesh and the too animal-like vigor that lured her while she detested it. Sometimes, when with her, she noted an unusual brightness in his eyes, and she admired it, for it made him appear more the poet and the scholar—the things he would have liked to be and which she would have liked him to be. But Maria Silva read a different tale in the hollow cheeks and the burning eyes, and she noted the changes in them from day to day, by them following the ebb and flow of his fortunes. She saw him leave the house with his overcoat and return without it, though the day was chill and raw, and promptly she saw his cheeks fill out slightly and the fire of hunger leave his eyes. In the same way she had seen his wheel and watch go, and after each event she had seen his vigor bloom again.

Likewise she watched his toils, and knew the measure of the midnight oil he burned. Work! She knew that he outdid her, though his work was of a different order. And she was surprised to behold that the less food he had, the harder he worked. On occasion, in a casual sort of way, when she thought hunger pinched hardest, she would send him in a loaf of new baking, awkwardly covering the act with banter to the effect that it was better than he could bake. And again, she would send one of her toddlers in to him with a great pitcher of hot soup, debating inwardly the while whether she was justified in taking it from the mouths of her own flesh and blood. Nor was Martin ungrateful, knowing as he did the lives of the poor, and that if ever in the world there was charity, this was it.

On a day when she had filled her brood with what was left in the house, Maria invested her last fifteen cents in a gallon of cheap wine. Martin, coming into her kitchen to fetch water, was invited to sit down and drink. He drank her very good health, and in return she drank his. Then she drank to prosperity in his undertakings, and he drank to the hope that James Grant would show up and pay her for his washing. James Grant was a journeyman carpenter who did not always pay his bills and who owed Maria three dollars.

Both Maria and Martin drank the sour new wine on empty stomachs, and it went swiftly to their heads. Utterly differentiated creatures that they were, they were lonely in their misery, and though the misery was tacitly ignored, it was the bond that drew them together. Maria was amazed to learn that he had been in the Azores, where she had lived until she was eleven. She was doubly amazed that he had been in the Hawaiian Islands, whither she had migrated from the Azores with her people. But her amazement passed all bounds when he told her he had been on Maui, the particular island whereon she had attained womanhood and married. Kahului, where she had first met her husband,—he, Martin, had been there twice! Yes, she remembered the sugar steamers, and he had been on them—well, well, it was a small world. And Wailuku! That place, too! Did he know the head-luna of the plantation? Yes, and had had a couple of drinks with him.

And so they reminiscenced and drowned their hunger in the raw, sour wine. To Martin the future did not seem so dim. Success trembled just before him. He was on the verge of clasping it. Then he studied the deep-lined face of the toil-worn woman before him, remembered her soups and loaves of new baking, and felt spring up in him the warmest gratitude and philanthropy.

"Maria," he exclaimed suddenly. "What would you like to have?"

She looked at him, bepuzzled.

"What would you like to have now, right now, if you could get it?"

"Shoe alla da roun' for da childs—seven pairs da shoe."

"You shall have them," he announced, while she nodded her head gravely. "But I mean a big wish, something big that you want."

Her eyes sparkled good-naturedly. He was choosing to make fun with her, Maria, with whom few made fun these days.

"Think hard," he cautioned, just as she was opening her mouth to speak.

"Alla right," she answered. "I thinka da hard. I lika da house, dis house—all mine, no paya da rent, seven dollar da month."

"You shall have it," he granted, "and in a short time. Now wish the great wish. Make believe I am God, and I say to you anything you want you can have. Then you wish that thing, and I listen."

Maria considered solemnly for a space.

"You no 'fraid?" she asked warningly.

"No, no," he laughed, "I'm not afraid. Go ahead."

"Most verra big," she warned again.

"All right. Fire away."

"Well, den—" She drew a big breath like a child, as she voiced to the uttermost all she cared to demand of life. "I lika da have one milka ranch—good milka ranch. Plenty cow, plenty land, plenty grass. I lika da have near San Le-an; my sister liva dere. I sella da milk in Oakland. I maka da plentee mon. Joe an' Nick no runna da cow. Dey go-a to school. Bimeby maka da good engineer, worka da railroad. Yes, I lika da milka ranch."

She paused and regarded Martin with twinkling eyes.

"You shall have it," he answered promptly.

She nodded her head and touched her lips courteously to

the wine-glass and to the giver of the gift she knew would never be given. His heart was right, and in her own heart she appreciated his intention as much as if the gift had gone with it.

"No, Maria," he went on; "Nick and Joe won't have to peddle milk, and all the kids can go to school and wear shoes the whole year round. It will be a first-class milk ranch—everything complete. There will be a house to live in and a stable for the horses, and cow-barns, of course. There will be chickens, pigs, vegetables, fruit trees, and everything like that; and there will be enough cows to pay for a hired man or two. Then you won't have anything to do but take care of the children. For that matter, if you find a good man, you can marry and take it easy while he runs the ranch."

And from such largess, dispensed from his future, Martin turned and took his one good suit of clothes to the pawnshop. His plight was desperate for him to do this, for it cut him off from Ruth. He had no second-best suit that was presentable, and though he could go to the butcher and the baker, and even on occasion to his sister's, it was beyond all daring to dream of entering the Morse home so disreputably apparelled.

He toiled on, miserable and well-nigh hopeless. It began to appear to him that the second battle was lost and that he would have to go to work. In doing this he would satisfy everybody—the grocer, his sister, Ruth, and even Maria, to whom he owed a month's room rent. He was two months behind with his type-writer, and the agency was clamoring for payment or for the return of the machine. In desperation, all but ready to surrender, to make a truce with fate until he could get a fresh start, he took the civil service examinations for the Railway Mail. To his surprise, he passed first. The job was assured, though when the call would come to enter upon his duties nobody knew.

It was at this time, at the lowest ebb, that the smooth-running editorial machine broke down. A cog must have slipped or an oil-cup run dry, for the postman brought him one morning a short, thin envelope. Martin glanced at the upper left-hand corner and read the name and address of the *Transcontinental Monthly*. His heart gave a great leap, and he suddenly felt faint, the sinking feeling accompanied by a strange trembling of the knees. He staggered into his room and sat down on the bed, the envelope still unopened, and in that moment came understanding to him how people suddenly fall dead upon receipt of extraordinarily good news.

Of course this was good news. There was no manuscript in that thin envelope, therefore it was an acceptance. He knew the story in the hands of the *Transcontinental*. It was "The Ring of Bells," one of his horror stories, and it was an even five thousand words. And, since first-class magazines always paid on acceptance, there was a check inside. Two cents a word—twenty dollars a thousand; the check must be a hundred dollars. One hundred dollars! As he tore the envelope open, every item of all his debts surged in his brain— $3.85 to the grocer; butcher, $4.00 flat; baker, $2.00; fruit store, $5.00; total, $14.85. Then there was room rent, $2.50; another month in advance, $2.50; two months' type-writer, $8.00; a month in advance, $4.00; total, $31.85. And finally to be added, his pledges, plus interest, with the pawnbroker— watch, $5.50; overcoat, $5.50; wheel, $7.75; suit of clothes, $5.50 (60% interest, but what did it matter?)—grand total, $56.10. He saw, as if visible in the air before him, in illuminated figures, the whole sum, and the subtraction that followed and that gave a remainder of $43.90. When he had squared every debt, redeemed every pledge, he would still have jingling in his pockets a princely $43.90. And on top of that he would have a month's rent paid in advance on the type-writer and on the room.

By this time he had drawn the single sheet of type-written letter out and spread it open. There was no check. He peered into the envelope, held it to the light, but could not trust his eyes, and in trembling haste tore the envelope apart. There was no check. He read the letter, skimming it line by line, dashing through the editor's praise of his story to the meat of the letter, the statement why the check had not been sent. He found no such statement, but he did find that which made him suddenly wilt. The letter slid from his hand. His eyes went lack-lustre, and he lay back on the pillow, pulling the blanket about him and up to his chin.

Five dollars for "The Ring of Bells"—five dollars for five

thousand words! Instead of two cents a word, ten words for a cent! And the editor had praised it, too. And he would receive the check when the story was published. Then it was all poppycock, two cents a word for minimum rate and payment upon acceptance. It was a lie, and it had led him astray. He would never have attempted to write had he known that. He would have gone to work—to work for Ruth. He went back to the day he first attempted to write, and was appalled at the enormous waste of time—and all for ten words for a cent. And the other high rewards of writers, that he had read about, must be lies, too. His second-hand ideas of authorship were wrong, for here was the proof of it.

The *Transcontinental* sold for twenty-five cents, and its dignified and artistic cover proclaimed it as among the first-class magazines. It was a staid, respectable magazine, and it had been published continuously since long before he was born. Why, on the outside cover were printed every month the words of one of the world's great writers, words proclaiming the inspired mission of the *Transcontinental* by a star of literature whose first coruscations had appeared inside those self-same covers. And the high and lofty, heaven-inspired *Transcontinental* paid five dollars for five thousand words! The great writer had recently died in a foreign land—in dire poverty, Martin remembered, which was not to be wondered at, considering the magnificent pay authors receive.

Well, he had taken the bait, the newspaper lies about writers and their pay, and he had wasted two years over it. But he would disgorge the bait now. Not another line would he ever write. He would do what Ruth wanted him to do, what everybody wanted him to do—get a job. The thought of going to work reminded him of Joe—Joe, tramping through the land of nothing-to-do. Martin heaved a great sigh of envy. The reaction of nineteen hours a day for many days was strong upon him. But then, Joe was not in love, had none of the responsibilities of love, and he could afford to loaf through the land of nothing-to-do. He, Martin, had something to work for, and go to work he would. He would start out early next morning to hunt a job. And he would let Ruth know, too, that he had mended his ways and was willing to go into her father's office.

Five dollars for five thousand words, ten words for a cent, the market price for art. The disappointment of it, the lie of it, the infamy of it, were uppermost in his thoughts; and under his closed eyelids, in fiery figures, burned the "$3.85" he owed the grocer. He shivered, and was aware of an aching in his bones. The small of his back ached especially. His head ached, the top of it ached, the back of it ached, the brains inside of it ached and seemed to be swelling, while the ache over his brows was intolerable. And beneath the brows, planted under his lids, was the merciless "$3.85." He opened his eyes to escape it, but the white light of the room seemed to sear the balls and forced him to close his eyes, when the "$3.85" confronted him again.

Five dollars for five thousand words, ten words for a cent—that particular thought took up its residence in his brain, and he could no more escape it than he could the "$3.85" under his eyelids. A change seemed to come over the latter, and he watched curiously, till "$2.00" burned in its stead. Ah, he thought, that was the baker. The next sum that appeared was "$2.50." It puzzled him, and he pondered it as if life and death hung on the solution. He owed somebody two dollars and a half, that was certain, but who was it? To find it was the task set him by an imperious and malignant universe, and he wandered through the endless corridors of his mind, opening all manner of lumber rooms and chambers stored with odds and ends of memories and knowledge as he vainly sought the answer. After several centuries it came to him, easily, without effort, that it was Maria. With a great relief he turned his soul to the screen of torment under his lids. He had solved the problem; now he could rest. But no, the "$2.50" faded away, and in its place burned "$8.00." Who was that? He must go the dreary round of his mind again and find out.

How long he was gone on this quest he did not know, but after what seemed an enormous lapse of time, he was called back to himself by a knock at the door, and by Maria's asking if he was sick. He replied in a muffled voice he did not recognize, saying that he was merely taking a nap. He was surprised when he noted the darkness of night in the room. He had received the letter at two in the afternoon, and he realized that he was sick.

Then the "$8.00" began to smoulder under his lids again, and he returned himself to servitude. But he grew cunning. There was no need for him to wander through his mind. He had been a fool. He pulled a lever and made his mind revolve about him, a monstrous wheel of fortune, a merry-go-round of memory, a revolving sphere of wisdom. Faster and faster it revolved, until its vortex sucked him in and he was flung whirling through black chaos.

Quite naturally he found himself at a mangle, feeding starched cuffs. But as he fed he noticed figures printed on the cuffs. It was a new way of marking linen, he thought, until, looking closer, he saw "$3.85" on one of the cuffs. Then it came to him that it was the grocer's bill, and that these were his bills flying around on the drum of the mangle. A crafty idea came to him. He would throw the bills on the floor and so escape paying them. No sooner thought than done, and he crumpled the cuffs spitefully as he flung them upon an unusually dirty floor. Ever the heap grew, and though each bill was duplicated a thousand times, he found only one for two dollars and a half, which was what he owed Maria. That meant that Maria would not press for payment, and he resolved generously that it would be the only one he would pay; so he began searching through the cast-out heap for hers. He sought it desperately, for ages, and was still searching when the manager of the hotel entered, the fat Dutchman. His face blazed with wrath, and he shouted in stentorian tones that echoed down the universe, "I shall deduct the cost of those cuffs from your wages!" The pile of cuffs grew into a mountain, and Martin knew that he was doomed to toil for a thousand years to pay for them. Well, there was nothing left to do but kill the manager and burn down the laundry. But the big Dutchman frustrated him, seizing him by the nape of the neck and dancing him up and down. He danced him over the ironing tables, the stove, and the mangles, and out into the wash-room and over the wringer and washer. Martin was danced until his teeth rattled and his head ached, and he marvelled that the Dutchman was so strong.

And then he found himself before the mangle, this time receiving the cuffs an editor of a magazine was feeding from the other side. Each cuff was a check, and Martin went over them anxiously, in a fever of expectation, but they were all blanks. He stood there and received the blanks for a million years or so, never letting one go by for fear it might be filled out. At last he found it. With trembling fingers he held it to the light. It was for five dollars. "Ha! Ha!" laughed the editor across the mangle. "Well, then, I shall kill you," Martin said. He went out into the wash-room to get the axe, and found Joe starching manuscripts. He tried to make him desist, then swung the axe for him. But the weapon remained poised in mid-air, for Martin found himself back in the ironing room in the midst of a snow-storm. No, it was not snow that was falling, but checks of large denomination, the smallest not less than a thousand dollars. He began to collect them and sort them out, in packages of a hundred, tying each package securely with twine.

He looked up from his task and saw Joe standing before him juggling flat-irons, starched shirts, and manuscripts. Now and again he reached out and added a bundle of checks to the flying miscellany that soared through the roof and out of sight in a tremendous circle. Martin struck at him, but he seized the axe and added it to the flying circle. Then he plucked Martin and added him. Martin went up through the roof, clutching at manuscripts, so that by the time he came down he had a large armful. But no sooner down than up again, and a second and a third time and countless times he flew around the circle. From far off he could hear a childish treble singing: "Waltz me around again, Willie, around, around, around."

He recovered the axe in the midst of the Milky Way of checks, starched shirts, and manuscripts, and prepared, when he came down, to kill Joe. But he did not come down. Instead, at two in the morning, Maria, having heard his groans through the thin partition, came into his room, to put hot flat-irons against his body and damp cloths upon his aching eyes.

Chapter XXVI

MARTIN EDEN did not go out to hunt for a job in the morning. It was late afternoon before he came out of his delirium and gazed with aching eyes about the room. Mary, one of the tribe of Silva, eight years old, keeping watch, raised a screech at sight of his returning consciousness. Maria hurried into the room from the kitchen. She put her work-calloused hand upon his hot forehead and felt his pulse.

"You lika da eat?" she asked.

He shook his head. Eating was farthest from his desire, and he wondered that he should ever have been hungry in his life.

"I'm sick, Maria," he said weakly. "What is it? Do you know?"

"Grip," she answered. "Two or three days you alla da right. Better you no eat now. Bimeby plenty can eat, to-morrow can eat maybe."

Martin was not used to sickness, and when Maria and her little girl left him, he essayed to get up and dress. By a supreme exertion of will, with reeling brain and eyes that ached so that he could not keep them open, he managed to get out of bed, only to be left stranded by his senses upon the table. Half an hour later he managed to regain the bed, where he was content to lie with closed eyes and analyze his various pains and weaknesses. Maria came in several times to change the cold cloths on his forehead. Otherwise she left him in peace, too wise to vex him with chatter. This moved him to gratitude, and he murmured to himself, "Maria, you getta da milka ranch, all righta, all right."

Then he remembered his long-buried past of yesterday. It seemed a life-time since he had received that letter from the *Transcontinental*, a life-time since it was all over and done with and a new page turned. He had shot his bolt, and shot it hard, and now he was down on his back. If he hadn't starved himself, he wouldn't have been caught by La Grippe. He had been run down, and he had not had the strength to throw off the germ of disease which had invaded his system. This was what resulted.

"What does it profit a man to write a whole library and lose his own life?" he demanded aloud. "This is no place for me. No more literature in mine. Me for the counting-house and ledger, the monthly salary, and the little home with Ruth."

Two days later, having eaten an egg and two slices of toast and drunk a cup of tea, he asked for his mail, but found his eyes still hurt too much to permit him to read.

"You read for me, Maria," he said. "Never mind the big, long letters. Throw them under the table. Read me the small letters."

"No can," was the answer. "Teresa, she go to school, she can."

So Teresa Silva, aged nine, opened his letters and read them to him. He listened absently to a long dun from the type-writer people, his mind busy with ways and means of finding a job. Suddenly he was shocked back to himself.

" 'We offer you forty dollars for all serial rights in your story,' " Teresa slowly spelled out, " 'provided you allow us to make the alterations suggested.' "

"What magazine is that?" Martin shouted. "Here, give it to me!"

He could see to read, now, and he was unaware of the pain of the action. It was the *White Mouse* that was offering him forty dollars, and the story was "The Whirlpool," another of his early horror stories. He read the letter through again and again. The editor told him plainly that he had not handled the idea properly, but that it was the idea they were buying because it was original. If they could cut the story down one-third, they would take it and send him forty dollars on receipt of his answer.

He called for pen and ink, and told the editor he could cut the story down three-thirds if he wanted to, and to send the forty dollars right along.

The letter despatched to the letter-box by Teresa, Martin lay back and thought. It wasn't a lie, after all. The *White Mouse* paid on acceptance. There were three thousand words in "The Whirlpool." Cut down a third, there would be two thousand. At forty dollars that would be two cents a word. Pay on acceptance and two cents a word—the newspapers had told the truth. And he had thought the *White Mouse* a third-rater! It was evident that he did not know the magazines. He had deemed the *Transcontinental* a first-rater, and it paid a cent for ten words. He had classed the *White Mouse* as of no account, and it paid twenty times as much as the *Transcontinental* and also had paid on acceptance.

Well, there was one thing certain: when he got well, he would not go out looking for a job. There were more stories in his head as good as "The Whirlpool," and at forty dollars apiece he could earn far more than in any job or position. Just when he thought the battle lost, it was won. He had proved for his career. The way was clear. Beginning with the *White Mouse* he would add magazine after magazine to his growing list of patrons. Hack-work could be put aside. For that matter, it had been wasted time, for it had not brought him a dollar. He would devote himself to work, good work, and he would pour out the best that was in him. He wished Ruth was there to share in his joy, and when he went over the letters left lying on his bed, he found one from her. It was sweetly reproachful, wondering what had kept him away for so dreadful a length of time. He reread the letter adoringly, dwelling over her handwriting, loving each stroke of her pen, and in the end kissing her signature.

And when he answered, he told her recklessly that he had not been to see her because his best clothes were in pawn. He told her that he had been sick, but was once more nearly well, and that inside ten days or two weeks (as soon as a letter could travel to New York City and return) he would redeem his clothes and be with her.

But Ruth did not care to wait ten days or two weeks. Besides, her lover was sick. The next afternoon, accompanied by Arthur, she arrived in the Morse carriage, to the unqualified delight of the Silva tribe and of all the urchins on the street, and to the consternation of Maria. She boxed the ears of the Silvas who crowded about the visitors on the tiny front porch, and in more than usual atrocious English tried to apologize for her appearance. Sleeves rolled up from soap-flecked arms and a wet gunny-sack around her waist told of the task at which she had been caught. So flustered was she by two such grand young people asking for her lodger, that she for-

got to invite them to sit down in the little parlor. To enter
Martin's room, they passed through the kitchen, warm and
moist and steamy from the big washing in progress. Maria, in
her excitement, jammed the bedroom and bedroom-closet
doors together, and for five minutes, through the partly open
door, clouds of steam, smelling of soap-suds and dirt, poured
into the sick chamber.

Ruth succeeded in veering right and left and right again,
and in running the narrow passage between table and bed to
Martin's side; but Arthur veered too wide and fetched up
with clatter and bang of pots and pans in the corner where
Martin did his cooking. Arthur did not linger long. Ruth occupied the only chair, and having done his duty, he went outside and stood by the gate, the centre of seven marvelling
Silvas, who watched him as they would have watched a curiosity in a side-show. All about the carriage were gathered the
children from a dozen blocks, waiting and eager for some
tragic and terrible dénouement. Carriages were seen on their
street only for weddings and funerals. Here was neither marriage nor death; therefore, it was something transcending experience and well worth waiting for.

Martin had been wild to see Ruth. His was essentially a
love-nature, and he possessed more than the average man's
need for sympathy. He was starving for sympathy, which,
with him, meant intelligent understanding; and he had yet to
learn that Ruth's sympathy was largely sentimental and tactful, and that it proceeded from gentleness of nature rather
than from understanding of the objects of her sympathy. So
it was while Martin held her hand and gladly talked, that her
love for him prompted her to press his hand in return, and
that her eyes were moist and luminous at sight of his helplessness and of the marks suffering had stamped upon his
face.

But while he told her of his two acceptances, of his despair
when he received the one from the *Transcontinental*, and of
the corresponding delight with which he received the one
from the *White Mouse*, she did not follow him. She heard the
words he uttered and understood their literal import, but she
was not with him in his despair and his delight. She could
not get out of herself. She was not interested in selling stories

to magazines. What was important to her was matrimony. She was not aware of it, however, any more than she was aware that her desire that Martin take a position was the instinctive and preparative impulse of motherhood. She would have blushed had she been told as much in plain, set terms, and next, she might have grown indignant and asserted that her sole interest lay in the man she loved and her desire for him to make the best of himself. So, while Martin poured out his heart to her, elated with the first success his chosen work in the world had received, she paid heed to his bare words only, gazing now and again about the room, shocked by what she saw.

For the first time Ruth gazed upon the sordid face of poverty. Starving lovers had always seemed romantic to her, but she had had no idea how starving lovers lived. She had never dreamed it could be like this. Ever her gaze shifted from the room to him and back again. The steamy smell of dirty clothes, which had entered with her from the kitchen, was sickening. Martin must be soaked with it, Ruth concluded, if that awful woman washed frequently. Such was the contagiousness of degradation. When she looked at Martin, she seemed to see the smirch left upon him by his surroundings. She had never seen him unshaven, and the three days' growth of beard on his face was repulsive to her. Not alone did it give him the same dark and murky aspect of the Silva house, inside and out, but it seemed to emphasize that animal-like strength of his which she detested. And here he was, being confirmed in his madness by the two acceptances he took such pride in telling her about. A little longer and he would have surrendered and gone to work. Now he would continue on in this horrible house, writing and starving for a few more months.

"What is that smell?" she asked suddenly.

"Some of Maria's washing smells, I imagine," was the answer. "I am growing quite accustomed to them."

"No, no; not that. It is something else. A stale, sickish smell."

Martin sampled the air before replying.

"I can't smell anything else, except stale tobacco smoke," he announced.

"That's it. It is terrible. Why do you smoke so much, Martin?"

"I don't know, except that I smoke more than usual when I am lonely. And then, too, it's such a long-standing habit. I learned when I was only a youngster."

"It is not a nice habit, you know," she reproved. "It smells to heaven."

"That's the fault of the tobacco. I can afford only the cheapest. But wait until I get that forty-dollar check. I'll use a brand that is not offensive even to the angels. But that wasn't so bad, was it, two acceptances in three days? That forty-five dollars will pay about all my debts."

"For two years' work?" she queried.

"No, for less than a week's work. Please pass me that book over on the far corner of the table, the account book with the gray cover." He opened it and began turning over the pages rapidly. "Yes, I was right. Four days for 'The Ring of Bells,' two days for 'The Whirlpool.' That's forty-five dollars for a week's work, one hundred and eighty dollars a month. That beats any salary I can command. And, besides, I'm just beginning. A thousand dollars a month is not too much to buy for you all I want you to have. A salary of five hundred a month would be too small. That forty-five dollars is just a starter. Wait till I get my stride. Then watch my smoke."

Ruth misunderstood his slang, and reverted to cigarettes.

"You smoke more than enough as it is, and the brand of tobacco will make no difference. It is the smoking itself that is not nice, no matter what the brand may be. You are a chimney, a living volcano, a perambulating smoke-stack, and you are a perfect disgrace, Martin dear, you know you are."

She leaned toward him, entreaty in her eyes, and as he looked at her delicate face and into her pure, limpid eyes, as of old he was struck with his own unworthiness.

"I wish you wouldn't smoke any more," she whispered. "Please, for—my sake."

"All right, I won't," he cried. "I'll do anything you ask, dear love, anything; you know that."

A great temptation assailed her. In an insistent way she had caught glimpses of the large, easy-going side of his nature, and she felt sure, if she asked him to cease attempting to write, that he would grant her wish. In the swift instant that elapsed, the words trembled on her lips. But she did not utter them. She was not quite brave enough; she did not quite dare. Instead, she leaned toward him to meet him, and in his arms murmured:—

"You know, it is really not for my sake, Martin, but for your own. I am sure smoking hurts you; and besides, it is not good to be a slave to anything, to a drug least of all."

"I shall always be your slave," he smiled.

"In which case, I shall begin issuing my commands."

She looked at him mischievously, though deep down she was already regretting that she had not preferred her largest request.

"I live but to obey, your majesty."

"Well, then, my first commandment is, Thou shalt not omit to shave every day. Look how you have scratched my cheek."

And so it ended in caresses and love-laughter. But she had made one point, and she could not expect to make more than one at a time. She felt a woman's pride in that she had made him stop smoking. Another time she would persuade him to take a position, for had he not said he would do anything she asked?

She left his side to explore the room, examining the clothes-lines of notes overhead, learning the mystery of the tackle used for suspending his wheel under the ceiling, and being saddened by the heap of manuscripts under the table which represented to her just so much wasted time. The oil-stove won her admiration, but on investigating the food shelves she found them empty.

"Why, you haven't anything to eat, you poor dear," she said with tender compassion. "You must be starving."

"I store my food in Maria's safe and in her pantry," he lied. "It keeps better there. No danger of my starving. Look at that."

She had come back to his side, and she saw him double his arm at the elbow, the biceps crawling under his shirt-sleeve and swelling into a knot of muscle, heavy and hard. The sight repelled her. Sentimentally, she disliked it. But her pulse, her blood, every fibre of her, loved it and yearned for it, and, in the old, inexplicable way, she leaned toward him, not away from him. And in the moment that followed, when he crushed her in his arms, the brain of her, concerned with the superficial aspects of life, was in revolt; while the heart of her, the woman of her, concerned with life itself, exulted triumphantly. It was in moments like this that she felt to the uttermost the greatness of her love for Martin, for it was almost a swoon of delight to her to feel his strong arms about her, holding her tightly, hurting her with the grip of their fervor. At such moments she found justification for her treason to her standards, for her violation of her own high ideals, and, most of all, for her tacit disobedience to her mother and father. They did not want her to marry this man. It shocked them that she should love him. It shocked her, too, sometimes, when she was apart from him, a cool and reasoning creature. With him, she loved him—in truth, at times a vexed and worried love; but love it was, a love that was stronger than she.

"This La Grippe is nothing," he was saying. "It hurts a bit, and gives one a nasty headache, but it doesn't compare with break-bone fever."

"Have you had that, too?" she queried absently, intent on the heaven-sent justification she was finding in his arms.

And so, with absent queries, she led him on, till suddenly his words startled her.

He had had the fever in a secret colony of thirty lepers on one of the Hawaiian Islands.

"But why did you go there?" she demanded.

Such royal carelessness of body seemed criminal.

"Because I didn't know," he answered. "I never dreamed of lepers. When I deserted the schooner and landed on the beach, I headed inland for some place of hiding. For three days I lived off guavas, *ohia*-apples, and bananas, all of which grew wild in the jungle. On the fourth day I found the trail— a mere foot-trail. It led inland, and it led up. It was the way I wanted to go, and it showed signs of recent travel. At one place it ran along the crest of a ridge that was no more than a knife-edge. The trail wasn't three feet wide on the crest, and on either side the ridge fell away in precipices hundreds of feet deep. One man, with plenty of ammunition, could have held it against a hundred thousand.

"It was the only way in to the hiding-place. Three hours after I found the trail I was there, in a little mountain valley, a pocket in the midst of lava peaks. The whole place was terraced for taro-patches, fruit trees grew there, and there were eight or ten grass huts. But as soon as I saw the inhabitants I knew what I'd struck. One sight of them was enough."

"What did you do?" Ruth demanded breathlessly, listening, like any Desdemona, appalled and fascinated.

"Nothing for me to do. Their leader was a kind old fellow, pretty far gone, but he ruled like a king. He had discovered the little valley and founded the settlement—all of which was against the law. But he had guns, plenty of ammunition, and those Kanakas, trained to the shooting of wild cattle and wild pig, were dead shots. No, there wasn't any running away for Martin Eden. He stayed—for three months."

"But how did you escape?"

"I'd have been there yet, if it hadn't been for a girl there, a half-Chinese, quarter-white, and quarter-Hawaiian. She was a beauty, poor thing, and well educated. Her mother, in Honolulu, was worth a million or so. Well, this girl got me away at last. Her mother financed the settlement, you see, so the girl wasn't afraid of being punished for letting me go. But she made me swear, first, never to reveal the hiding-place; and I never have. This is the first time I have even mentioned it. The girl had just the first signs of leprosy. The fingers of her right hand were slightly twisted, and there was a small spot on her arm. That was all. I guess she is dead, now."

"But weren't you frightened? And weren't you glad to get away without catching that dreadful disease?"

"Well," he confessed, "I was a bit shivery at first; but I got used to it. I used to feel sorry for that poor girl, though. That made me forget to be afraid. She was such a beauty, in spirit as well as in appearance, and she was only slightly touched; yet she was doomed to lie there, living the life of a primitive savage and rotting slowly away. Leprosy is far more terrible than you can imagine it."

"Poor thing," Ruth murmured softly. "It's a wonder she let you get away."

"How do you mean?" Martin asked unwittingly.

"Because she must have loved you," Ruth said, still softly. "Candidly, now, didn't she?"

Martin's sunburn had been bleached by his work in the laundry and by the indoor life he was living, while the hunger and the sickness had made his face even pale; and across this pallor flowed the slow wave of a blush. He was opening his mouth to speak, but Ruth shut him off.

"Never mind, don't answer; it's not necessary," she laughed.

But it seemed to him there was something metallic in her laughter, and that the light in her eyes was cold. On the spur of the moment it reminded him of a gale he had once experienced in the North Pacific. And for the moment the apparition of the gale rose before his eyes—a gale at night, with a clear sky and under a full moon, the huge seas glinting coldly in the moonlight. Next, he saw the girl in the leper refuge and remembered it was for love of him that she had let him go.

"She was noble," he said simply. "She gave me life."

That was all of the incident, but he heard Ruth muffle a dry sob in her throat, and noticed that she turned her face away to gaze out of the window. When she turned it back to him, it was composed, and there was no hint of the gale in her eyes.

"I'm such a silly," she said plaintively. "But I can't help it. I do so love you, Martin, I do, I do. I shall grow more catholic in time, but at present I can't help being jealous of those ghosts of the past, and you know your past is full of ghosts.

"It must be," she silenced his protest. "It could not be otherwise. And there's poor Arthur motioning me to come. He's tired waiting. And now good-by, dear.

"There's some kind of a mixture, put up by the druggists, that helps men to stop the use of tobacco," she called back from the door, "and I am going to send you some."

The door closed, but opened again.

"I do, I do," she whispered to him; and this time she was really gone.

Maria, with worshipful eyes that none the less were keen to note the texture of Ruth's garments and the cut of them (a cut unknown that produced an effect mysteriously beautiful), saw her to the carriage. The crowd of disappointed urchins stared till the carriage disappeared from view, then transferred their stare to Maria, who had abruptly become the most important person on the street. But it was one of her progeny who blasted Maria's reputation by announcing that the grand visitors had been for her lodger. After that Maria dropped back into her old obscurity and Martin began to notice the respectful manner in which he was regarded by the small fry of the neighborhood. As for Maria, Martin rose in her estimation a full hundred per cent, and had the Portuguese grocer witnessed that afternoon carriage-call he would have allowed Martin an additional three-dollars-and-eighty-five-cents' worth of credit.

Chapter XXVII

THE SUN of Martin's good fortune rose. The day after Ruth's visit, he received a check for three dollars from a New York scandal weekly in payment for three of his triolets. Two days later a newspaper published in Chicago accepted his "Treasure Hunters," promising to pay ten dollars for it on publication. The price was small, but it was the first article he had written, his very first attempt to express his thought on the printed page. To cap everything, the adventure serial for boys, his second attempt, was accepted before the end of the week by a juvenile monthly calling itself *Youth and Age*. It was true the serial was twenty-one thousand words, and they offered to pay him sixteen dollars on publication, which was something like seventy-five cents a thousand words; but it was equally true that it was the second thing he had attempted to write and that he was himself thoroughly aware of its clumsy worthlessness.

But even his earliest efforts were not marked with the clumsiness of mediocrity. What characterized them was the clumsiness of too great strength—the clumsiness which the tyro betrays when he crushes butterflies with battering rams and hammers out vignettes with a war-club. So it was that Martin was glad to sell his early efforts for songs. He knew them for what they were, and it had not taken him long to acquire this knowledge. What he pinned his faith to was his later work. He had striven to be something more than a mere writer of magazine fiction. He had sought to equip himself with the tools of artistry. On the other hand, he had not sacrificed strength. His conscious aim had been to increase his strength by avoiding excess of strength. Nor had he departed from his love of reality. His work was realism, though he had endeavored to fuse with it the fancies and beauties of imagination. What he sought was an impassioned realism, shot through with human aspiration and faith. What he wanted was life as it was, with all its spirit-groping and soul-reaching left in.

He had discovered, in the course of his reading, two schools of fiction. One treated of man as a god, ignoring his earthly origin; the other treated of man as a clod, ignoring his heaven-sent dreams and divine possibilities. Both the god and the clod schools erred, in Martin's estimation, and erred through too great singleness of sight and purpose. There was a compromise that approximated the truth, though it flattered not the school of god, while it challenged the brute-savageness of the school of clod. It was his story, "Adventure," which had dragged with Ruth, that Martin believed had achieved his ideal of the true in fiction; and it was in an essay, "God and Clod," that he had expressed his views on the whole general subject.

But "Adventure," and all that he deemed his best work, still went begging among the editors. His early work counted for nothing in his eyes except for the money it brought, and his horror stories, two of which he had sold, he did not consider high work nor his best work. To him they were frankly imaginative and fantastic, though invested with all the glamour of the real, wherein lay their power. This investiture of the grotesque and impossible with reality, he looked upon as a trick—a skilful trick at best. Great literature could not reside in such a field. Their artistry was high, but he denied the worthwhileness of artistry when divorced from humanness. The trick had been to fling over the face of his artistry a mask of humanness, and this he had done in the half-dozen or so stories of the horror brand he had written before he emerged upon the high peaks of "Adventure," "Joy," "The Pot," and "The Wine of Life."

The three dollars he received for the triolets he used to eke out a precarious existence against the arrival of the *White Mouse* check. He cashed the first check with the suspicious Portuguese grocer, paying a dollar on account and dividing the remaining two dollars between the baker and the fruit store. Martin was not yet rich enough to afford meat, and he was on slim allowance when the *White Mouse* check arrived. He was divided on the cashing of it. He had never been in a bank in his life, much less been in one on business, and he had a naïve and childlike desire to walk into one of the big banks down in Oakland and fling down his indorsed check for forty dollars. On the other hand, practical common sense ruled that he should cash it with his grocer and thereby make an impression that would later result in an increase of credit. Reluctantly Martin yielded to the claims of the grocer, paying his bill with him in full, and receiving in change a pocketful of jingling coin. Also, he paid the other tradesmen in full, redeemed his suit and his bicycle, paid one month's rent on the type-writer, and paid Maria the overdue month for his room and a month in advance. This left him in his pocket, for emergencies, a balance of nearly three dollars.

In itself, this small sum seemed a fortune. Immediately on recovering his clothes he had gone to see Ruth, and on the way he could not refrain from jingling the little handful of silver in his pocket. He had been so long without money that, like a rescued starving man who cannot let the unconsumed food out of his sight, Martin could not keep his hand off the silver. He was not mean, nor avaricious, but the money meant more than so many dollars and cents. It stood for success, and the eagles stamped upon the coins were to him so many winged victories.

It came to him insensibly that it was a very good world. It certainly appeared more beautiful to him. For weeks it had been a very dull and sombre world; but now, with nearly all debts paid, three dollars jingling in his pocket, and in his mind the consciousness of success, the sun shone bright and warm, and even a rain-squall that soaked unprepared pedestrians seemed a merry happening to him. When he starved, his thoughts had dwelt often upon the thousands he knew were starving the world over; but now that he was feasted full, the fact of the thousands starving was no longer pregnant in his brain. He forgot about them, and, being in love, remembered the countless lovers in the world. Without deliberately thinking about it, *motifs* for love-lyrics began to agitate his brain. Swept away by the creative impulse, he got off the electric car, without vexation, two blocks beyond his crossing.

He found a number of persons in the Morse home. Ruth's two girl-cousins were visiting her from San Rafael, and Mrs. Morse, under pretext of entertaining them, was pursuing her plan of surrounding Ruth with young people. The campaign had begun during Martin's enforced absence, and was already in full swing. She was making a point of having at the house men who were doing things. Thus, in addition to the cousins Dorothy and Florence, Martin encountered two university professors, one of Latin, the other of English; a young army officer just back from the Philippines, one-time schoolmate of Ruth's; a young fellow named Melville, private secretary to Joseph Perkins, head of the San Francisco Trust Company; and finally of the men, a live bank cashier, Charles Hapgood, a youngish man of thirty-five, graduate of Stanford University, member of the Nile Club and the Unity Club, and a conservative speaker for the Republican Party during campaigns—in short, a rising young man in every way. Among the women was one who painted portraits, another who was a professional musician, and still another who possessed the degree of Doctor of Sociology and who was locally famous for her social settlement work in the slums of San Francisco. But the women did not count for much in Mrs. Morse's plan. At the best, they were necessary accessories. The men who did things must be drawn to the house somehow.

"Don't get excited when you talk," Ruth admonished Martin, before the ordeal of introduction began.

He bore himself a bit stiffly at first, oppressed by a sense of his own awkwardness, especially of his shoulders, which were up to their old trick of threatening destruction to furniture and ornaments. Also, he was rendered self-conscious by the company. He had never before been in contact with such exalted beings nor with so many of them. Hapgood, the bank cashier, fascinated him, and he resolved to investigate him at the first opportunity. For underneath Martin's awe lurked his assertive ego, and he felt the urge to measure himself with these men and women and to find out what they had learned from the books and life which he had not learned.

Ruth's eyes roved to him frequently to see how he was getting on, and she was surprised and gladdened by the ease with which he got acquainted with her cousins. He certainly did not grow excited, while being seated removed from him the worry of his shoulders. Ruth knew them for clever girls, superficially brilliant, and she could scarcely understand their praise of Martin later that night at going to bed. But he, on the other hand, a wit in his own class, a gay quizzer and

laughter-maker at dances and Sunday picnics, had found the
making of fun and the breaking of good-natured lances simple enough in this environment. And on this evening success
stood at his back, patting him on the shoulder and telling him
that he was making good, so that he could afford to laugh
and make laughter and remain unabashed.

Later, Ruth's anxiety found justification. Martin and Professor Caldwell had got together in a conspicuous corner, and
though Martin no longer wove the air with his hands, to
Ruth's critical eye he permitted his own eyes to flash and glitter too frequently, talked too rapidly and warmly, grew too
intense, and allowed his aroused blood to redden his cheeks
too much. He lacked decorum and control, and was in decided contrast to the young professor of English with whom
he talked.

But Martin was not concerned with appearances! He had
been swift to note the other's trained mind and to appreciate
his command of knowledge. Furthermore, Professor Caldwell
did not realize Martin's concept of the average English professor. Martin wanted him to talk shop, and, though he
seemed averse at first, succeeded in making him do it. For
Martin did not see why a man should not talk shop.

"It's absurd and unfair," he had told Ruth weeks before,
"this objection to talking shop. For what reason under the
sun do men and women come together if not for the exchange of the best that is in them? And the best that is in
them is what they are interested in, the thing by which they
make their living, the thing they've specialized on and sat up
days and nights over, and even dreamed about. Imagine Mr.
Butler living up to social etiquette and enunciating his views
on Paul Verlaine or the German drama or the novels of
D'Annunzio. We'd be bored to death. I, for one, if I must
listen to Mr. Butler, prefer to hear him talk about his law. It's
the best that is in him, and life is so short that I want the best
of every man and woman I meet."

"But," Ruth had objected, "there are the topics of general
interest to all."

"There, you mistake," he had rushed on. "All persons in
society, all cliques in society—or, rather, nearly all persons
and cliques—ape their betters. Now, who are the best bet-

ters? The idlers, the wealthy idlers. They do not know, as a rule, the things known by the persons who are doing something in the world. To listen to conversation about such things would mean to be bored, wherefore the idlers decree that such things are shop and must not be talked about. Likewise they decree the things that are not shop and which may be talked about, and those things are the latest operas, latest novels, cards, billiards, cocktails, automobiles, horse shows, trout fishing, tuna-fishing, big-game shooting, yacht sailing, and so forth—and mark you, these are the things the idlers know. In all truth, they constitute the shop-talk of the idlers. And the funniest part of it is that many of the clever people, and all the would-be clever people, allow the idlers so to impose upon them. As for me, I want the best a man's got in him, call it shop vulgarity or anything you please."

And Ruth had not understood. This attack of his on the established had seemed to her just so much wilfulness of opinion.

So Martin contaminated Professor Caldwell with his own earnestness, challenging him to speak his mind. As Ruth paused beside them she heard Martin saying:—

"You surely don't pronounce such heresies in the University of California?"

Professor Caldwell shrugged his shoulders. "The honest taxpayer and the politician, you know. Sacramento gives us our appropriations and therefore we kowtow to Sacramento, and to the Board of Regents, and to the party press, or to the press of both parties."

"Yes, that's clear; but how about you?" Martin urged. "You must be a fish out of the water."

"Few like me, I imagine, in the university pond. Sometimes I am fairly sure I am out of water, and that I should belong in Paris, in Grub Street, in a hermit's cave, or in some sadly wild Bohemian crowd, drinking claret,—dago-red they call it in San Francisco,—dining in cheap restaurants in the Latin Quarter, and expressing vociferously radical views upon all creation. Really, I am frequently almost sure that I was cut out to be a radical. But then, there are so many questions on which I am not sure. I grow timid when I am face to face with my human frailty, which ever prevents me from grasping

all the factors in any problem—human, vital problems, you
know."

And as he talked on, Martin became aware that to his own
lips had come the "Song of the Trade Wind":—

> "I am strongest at noon,
>   But under the moon
>   I stiffen the bunt of the sail."

He was almost humming the words, and it dawned upon
him that the other reminded him of the trade wind, of the
Northeast Trade, steady, and cool, and strong. He was equable, he was to be relied upon, and withal there was a certain
bafflement about him. Martin had the feeling that he never
spoke his full mind, just as he had often had the feeling that
the trades never blew their strongest but always held reserves
of strength that were never used. Martin's trick of visioning
was active as ever. His brain was a most accessible storehouse
of remembered fact and fancy, and its contents seemed ever
ordered and spread for his inspection. Whatever occurred in
the instant present, Martin's mind immediately presented associated antithesis or similitude which ordinarily expressed
themselves to him in vision. It was sheerly automatic, and his
visioning was an unfailing accompaniment to the living present. Just as Ruth's face, in a momentary jealousy, had called
before his eyes a forgotten moonlight gale, and as Professor
Caldwell made him see again the Northeast Trade herding the
white billows across the purple sea, so, from moment to moment, not disconcerting but rather identifying and classifying,
new memory-visions rose before him, or spread under his
eyelids, or were thrown upon the screen of his consciousness.
These visions came out of the actions and sensations of the
past, out of things and events and books of yesterday and last
week—a countless host of apparitions that, waking or sleeping, forever thronged his mind.

So it was, as he listened to Professor Caldwell's easy flow
of speech—the conversation of a clever, cultured man—that
Martin kept seeing himself down all his past. He saw himself
when he had been quite the hoodlum, wearing a "stiff-rim"

Stetson hat and a square-cut, double-breasted coat, with a certain swagger to the shoulders and possessing the ideal of being as tough as the police permitted. He did not disguise it to himself, nor attempt to palliate it. At one time in his life he had been just a common hoodlum, the leader of a gang that worried the police and terrorized honest, working-class householders. But his ideals had changed. He glanced about him at the well-bred, well-dressed men and women, and breathed into his lungs the atmosphere of culture and refinement, and at the same moment the ghost of his early youth, in stiff-rim and square-cut, with swagger and toughness, stalked across the room. This figure, of the corner hoodlum, he saw merge into himself, sitting and talking with an actual university professor.

For, after all, he had never found his permanent abiding place. He had fitted in wherever he found himself, been a favorite always and everywhere by virtue of holding his own at work and at play and by his willingness and ability to fight for his rights and command respect. But he had never taken root. He had fitted in sufficiently to satisfy his fellows but not to satisfy himself. He had been perturbed always by a feeling of unrest, had heard always the call of something from beyond, and had wandered on through life seeking it until he found books and art and love. And here he was, in the midst of all this, the only one of all the comrades he had adventured with who could have made themselves eligible for the inside of the Morse home.

But such thoughts and visions did not prevent him from following Professor Caldwell closely. And as he followed, comprehendingly and critically, he noted the unbroken field of the other's knowledge. As for himself, from moment to moment the conversation showed him gaps and open stretches, whole subjects with which he was unfamiliar. Nevertheless, thanks to his Spencer, he saw that he possessed the outlines of the field of knowledge. It was a matter only of time, when he would fill in the outline. Then watch out, he thought—ware shoal, everybody! He felt like sitting at the feet of the professor, worshipful and absorbent; but, as he listened, he began to discern a weakness in the other's judgments—a weakness so stray and elusive that he might not have caught it had it not been ever present. And when he did catch it, he leapt to equality at once.

Ruth came up to them a second time, just as Martin began to speak.

"I'll tell you where you are wrong, or, rather, what weakens your judgments," he said. "You lack biology. It has no place in your scheme of things.—Oh, I mean the real interpretative biology, from the ground up, from the laboratory and the test-tube and the vitalized inorganic right on up to the widest æsthetic and sociological generalizations."

Ruth was appalled. She had sat two lecture courses under Professor Caldwell and looked up to him as the living repository of all knowledge.

"I scarcely follow you," he said dubiously.

Martin was not so sure but what he had followed him.

"Then I'll try to explain," he said. "I remember reading in Egyptian history something to the effect that understanding could not be had of Egyptian art without first studying the land question."

"Quite right," the professor nodded.

"And it seems to me," Martin continued, "that knowledge of the land question, in turn, of all questions, for that matter, cannot be had without previous knowledge of the stuff and the constitution of life. How can we understand laws and institutions, religions and customs, without understanding, not merely the nature of the creatures that made them, but the nature of the stuff out of which the creatures are made? Is literature less human than the architecture and sculpture of Egypt? Is there one thing in the known universe that is not subject to the law of evolution?—Oh, I know there is an elaborate evolution of the various arts laid down, but it seems to me to be too mechanical. The human himself is left out. The evolution of the tool, of the harp, of music and song and dance, are all beautifully elaborated; but how about the evolution of the human himself, the development of the basic and intrinsic parts that were in him before he made his first tool or gibbered his first chant? It is that which you do not consider, and which I call biology. It is biology in its largest aspects.

"I know I express myself incoherently, but I've tried to hammer out the idea. It came to me as you were talking, so I was not primed and ready to deliver it. You spoke yourself of the human frailty that prevented one from taking all the factors into consideration. And you, in turn,—or so it seems to me,—leave out the biological factor, the very stuff out of which has been spun the fabric of all the arts, the warp and the woof of all human actions and achievements."

To Ruth's amazement, Martin was not immediately crushed, and that the professor replied in the way he did struck her as forbearance for Martin's youth. Professor Caldwell sat for a full minute, silent and fingering his watch chain.

"Do you know," he said at last, "I've had that same criticism passed on me once before—by a very great man, a scientist and evolutionist, Joseph Le Conte. But he is dead, and I thought to remain undetected; and now you come along and expose me. Seriously, though—and this is confession— I think there is something in your contention—a great deal, in fact. I am too classical, not enough up-to-date in the interpretative branches of science, and I can only plead the disadvantages of my education and a temperamental slothfulness that prevents me from doing the work. I wonder if you'll believe that I've never been inside a physics or chemistry laboratory? It is true, nevertheless. Le Conte was right, and so are you, Mr. Eden, at least to an extent—how much I do not know."

Ruth drew Martin away with her on a pretext; when she had got him aside, whispering:—

"You shouldn't have monopolized Professor Caldwell that way. There may be others who want to talk with him."

"My mistake," Martin admitted contritely. "But I'd got him stirred up, and he was so interesting that I did not think. Do you know, he is the brightest, the most intellectual, man I have ever talked with. And I'll tell you something else. I once thought that everybody who went to universities, or who sat in the high places in society, was just as brilliant and intelligent as he."

"He's an exception," she answered.

"I should say so. Whom do you want me to talk to now?— Oh, say, bring me up against that cashier-fellow."

Martin talked for fifteen minutes with him, nor could Ruth have wished better behavior on her lover's part. Not once did his eyes flash nor his cheeks flush, while the calmness and poise with which he talked surprised her. But in Martin's estimation the whole tribe of bank cashiers fell a few hundred per cent, and for the rest of the evening he labored under the impression that bank cashiers and talkers of platitudes were synonymous phrases. The army officer he found good-natured and simple, a healthy, wholesome young fellow, content to occupy the place in life into which birth and luck had flung him. On learning that he had completed two years in the university, Martin was puzzled to know where he had stored it away. Nevertheless Martin liked him better than the platitudinous bank cashier.

"I really don't object to platitudes," he told Ruth later; "but what worries me into nervousness is the pompous, smugly complacent, superior certitude with which they are uttered and the time taken to do it. Why, I could give that man the whole history of the Reformation in the time he took to tell me that the Union-Labor Party had fused with the Democrats. Do you know, he skins his words as a professional poker-player skins the cards that are dealt out to him. Some day I'll show you what I mean."

"I'm sorry you don't like him," was her reply. "He's a favorite of Mr. Butler's. Mr. Butler says he is safe and honest—calls him the Rock, Peter, and says that upon him any banking institution can well be built."

"I don't doubt it—from the little I saw of him and the less I heard from him; but I don't think so much of banks as I did. You don't mind my speaking my mind this way, dear?"

"No, no; it is most interesting."

"Yes," Martin went on heartily, "I'm no more than a barbarian getting my first impressions of civilization. Such impressions must be entertainingly novel to the civilized person."

"What did you think of my cousins?" Ruth queried.

"I liked them better than the other women. There's plenty of fun in them along with paucity of pretence."

"Then you did like the other women?"

He shook his head.

"That social-settlement woman is no more than a sociological poll-parrot. I swear, if you winnowed her out between the stars, like Tomlinson, there would be found in her not one original thought. As for the portrait-painter, she was a positive bore. She'd make a good wife for the cashier. And the musician woman! I don't care how nimble her fingers are, how perfect her technique, how wonderful her expression— the fact is, she knows nothing about music."

"She plays beautifully," Ruth protested.

"Yes, she's undoubtedly gymnastic in the externals of music, but the intrinsic spirit of music is unguessed by her. I asked her what music meant to her—you know I'm always curious to know that particular thing; and she did not know what it meant to her, except that she adored it, that it was the greatest of the arts, and that it meant more than life to her."

"You were making them talk shop," Ruth charged him.

"I confess it. And if they were failures on shop, imagine my sufferings if they had discoursed on other subjects. Why, I used to think that up here, where all the advantages of culture were enjoyed—" He paused for a moment, and watched the youthful shade of himself, in stiff-rim and square-cut, enter the door and swagger across the room. "As I was saying, up here I thought all men and women were brilliant and radiant. But now, from what little I've seen of them, they strike me as a pack of ninnies, most of them, and ninety per cent of the remainder as bores. Now there's Professor Caldwell—he's different. He's a man, every inch of him and every atom of his gray matter."

Ruth's face brightened.

"Tell me about him," she urged. "Not what is large and brilliant—I know those qualities; but whatever you feel is adverse. I am most curious to know."

"Perhaps I'll get myself in a pickle." Martin debated humorously for a moment. "Suppose you tell me first. Or maybe you find in him nothing less than the best."

"I attended two lecture courses under him, and I have known him for two years; that is why I am anxious for your first impression."

"Bad impression, you mean? Well, here goes. He is all the

fine things you think about him, I guess. At least, he is the
finest specimen of intellectual man I have met; but he is a
man with a secret shame.

"Oh, no, no!" he hastened to cry. "Nothing paltry nor vulgar. What I mean is that he strikes me as a man who has gone
to the bottom of things, and is so afraid of what he saw that
he makes believe to himself that he never saw it. Perhaps
that's not the clearest way to express it. Here's another way.
A man who has found the path to the hidden temple but has
not followed it; who has, perhaps, caught glimpses of the
temple and striven afterward to convince himself that it was
only a mirage of foliage. Yet another way. A man who could
have done things but who placed no value on the doing, and
who, all the time, in his innermost heart, is regretting that he
has not done them; who has secretly laughed at the rewards
for doing, and yet, still more secretly, has yearned for the
rewards and for the joy of doing."

"I don't read him that way," she said. "And for that matter,
I don't see just what you mean."

"It is only a vague feeling on my part," Martin temporized.
"I have no reason for it. It is only a feeling, and most likely it
is wrong. You certainly should know him better than I."

From the evening at Ruth's Martin brought away with him
strange confusions and conflicting feelings. He was disappointed in his goal, in the persons he had climbed to be with.
On the other hand, he was encouraged with his success. The
climb had been easier than he expected. He was superior to
the climb, and (he did not, with false modesty, hide it from
himself) he was superior to the beings among whom he had
climbed—with the exception, of course, of Professor Caldwell. About life and the books he knew more than they, and
he wondered into what nooks and crannies they had cast
aside their educations. He did not know that he was himself
possessed of unusual brain vigor; nor did he know that the
persons who were given to probing the depths and to thinking ultimate thoughts were not to be found in the drawing
rooms of the world's Morses; nor did he dream that such
persons were as lonely eagles sailing solitary in the azure sky
far above the earth and its swarming freight of gregarious life.

Chapter XXVIII

B UT SUCCESS had lost Martin's address, and her messengers no longer came to his door. For twenty-five days,
working Sundays and holidays, he toiled on "The Shame of
the Sun," a long essay of some thirty thousand words. It was
a deliberate attack on the mysticism of the Maeterlinck
school—an attack from the citadel of positive science upon
the wonder-dreamers, but an attack nevertheless that retained
much of beauty and wonder of the sort compatible with ascertained fact. It was a little later that he followed up the
attack with two short essays, "The Wonder-Dreamers" and
"The Yardstick of the Ego." And on essays, long and short,
he began to pay the travelling expenses from magazine to
magazine.

During the twenty-five days spent on "The Shame of the
Sun," he sold hack-work to the extent of six dollars and fifty
cents. A joke had brought in fifty cents, and a second one,
sold to a high-grade comic weekly, had fetched a dollar. Then
two humorous poems had earned two dollars and three dollars respectively. As a result, having exhausted his credit with
the tradesmen (though he had increased his credit with the
grocer to five dollars), his wheel and suit of clothes went back
to the pawnbroker. The type-writer people were again clamoring for money, insistently pointing out that according to
the agreement rent was to be paid strictly in advance.

Encouraged by his several small sales, Martin went back to
hack-work. Perhaps there was a living in it, after all. Stored
away under his table were the twenty storiettes which had
been rejected by the newspaper short-story syndicate. He read
them over in order to find out how not to write newspaper
storiettes, and so doing, reasoned out the perfect formula. He
found that the newspaper storiette should never be tragic,
should never end unhappily, and should never contain beauty
of language, subtlety of thought, nor real delicacy of sentiment. Sentiment it must contain, plenty of it, pure and noble,
of the sort that in his own early youth had brought his applause from "nigger heaven"—the "For-God-my-country-

777

and-the-Czar" and "I-may-be-poor-but-I-am-honest" brand of sentiment.

Having learned such precautions, Martin consulted "The Duchess" for tone, and proceeded to mix according to formula. The formula consists of three parts: (1) a pair of lovers are jarred apart; (2) by some deed or event they are reunited; (3) marriage bells. The third part was an unvarying quantity, but the first and second parts could be varied an infinite number of times. Thus, the pair of lovers could be jarred apart by misunderstood motives, by accident of fate, by jealous rivals, by irate parents, by crafty guardians, by scheming relatives, and so forth and so forth; they could be reunited by a brave deed of the man lover, by a similar deed of the woman lover, by change of heart in one lover or the other, by forced confession of crafty guardian, scheming relative, or jealous rival, by voluntary confession of same, by discovery of some unguessed secret, by lover storming girl's heart, by lover making long and noble self-sacrifice, and so on, endlessly. It was very fetching to make the girl propose in the course of being reunited, and Martin discovered, bit by bit, other decidedly piquant and fetching ruses. But marriage bells at the end was the one thing he could take no liberties with; though the heavens rolled up as a scroll and the stars fell, the wedding bells must go on ringing just the same. In quantity, the formula prescribed twelve hundred words minimum dose, fifteen hundred words maximum dose.

Before he got very far along in the art of the storiette, Martin worked out half a dozen stock forms, which he always consulted when constructing storiettes. These forms were like the cunning tables used by mathematicians, which may be entered from top, bottom, right, and left, which entrances consist of scores of lines and dozens of columns, and from which may be drawn, without reasoning or thinking, thousands of different conclusions, all unchallengably precise and true. Thus, in the course of half an hour with his forms, Martin could frame up a dozen or so storiettes, which he put aside and filled in at his convenience. He found that he could fill one in, after a day of serious work, in the hour before going to bed. As he later confessed to Ruth, he could almost do it in his sleep. The real work was in constructing the frames, and that was merely mechanical.

He had no doubt whatever of the efficacy of his formula, and for once he knew the editorial mind when he said positively to himself that the first two he sent off would bring checks. And checks they brought, for four dollars each, at the end of twelve days.

In the meantime he was making fresh and alarming discoveries concerning the magazines. Though the *Transcontinental* had published "The Ring of Bells," no check was forthcoming. Martin needed it, and he wrote for it. An evasive answer and a request for more of his work was all he received. He had gone hungry two days waiting for the reply, and it was then that he put his wheel back in pawn. He wrote regularly, twice a week, to the *Transcontinental* for his five dollars, though it was only semi-occasionally that he elicited a reply. He did not know that the *Transcontinental* had been staggering along precariously for years, that it was a fourth-rater, or a tenth-rater, without standing, with a crazy circulation that partly rested on petty bullying and partly on patriotic appealing, and with advertisements that were scarcely more than charitable donations. Nor did he know that the *Transcontinental* was the sole livelihood of the editor and the business manager, and that they could wring their livelihood out of it only by moving to escape paying rent and by never paying any bill they could evade. Nor could he have guessed that the particular five dollars that belonged to him had been appropriated by the business manager for the painting of his house in Alameda, which painting he performed himself, on weekday afternoons, because he could not afford to pay union wages and because the first scab he had employed had had a ladder jerked out from under him and been sent to the hospital with a broken collar-bone.

The ten dollars for which Martin had sold "Treasure Hunters" to the Chicago newspaper did not come to hand. The article had been published, as he had ascertained at the file in the Central Reading-room, but no word could he get from the editor. His letters were ignored. To satisfy himself that they had been received, he registered several of them. It was nothing less than robbery, he concluded—a cold-blooded steal; while he starved, he was pilfered of his merchandise, of his goods, the sale of which was the sole way of getting bread to eat.

Youth and Age was a weekly, and it had published two-thirds of his twenty-one-thousand-word serial when it went out of business. With it went all hopes of getting his sixteen dollars.

To cap the situation, "The Pot," which he looked upon as one of the best things he had written, was lost to him. In despair, casting about frantically among the magazines, he had sent it to *The Billow*, a society weekly in San Francisco. His chief reason for submitting it to that publication was that, having only to travel across the bay from Oakland, a quick decision could be reached. Two weeks later he was overjoyed to see, in the latest number on the news-stand, his story printed in full, illustrated, and in the place of honor. He went home with leaping pulse, wondering how much they would pay him for one of the best things he had done. Also, the celerity with which it had been accepted and published was a pleasant thought to him. That the editor had not informed him of the acceptance made the surprise more complete. After waiting a week, two weeks, and half a week longer, desperation conquered diffidence, and he wrote to the editor of *The Billow*, suggesting that possibly through some negligence of the business manager his little account had been overlooked.

Even if it isn't more than five dollars, Martin thought to himself, it will buy enough beans and pea-soup to enable me to write half a dozen like it, and possibly as good.

Back came a cool letter from the editor that at least elicited Martin's admiration.

"We thank you," it ran, "for your excellent contribution. All of us in the office enjoyed it immensely, and, as you see, it was given the place of honor and immediate publication. We earnestly hope that you liked the illustrations.

"On rereading your letter it seems to us that you are laboring under the misapprehension that we pay for unsolicited manuscripts. This is not our custom, and of course yours was unsolicited. We assumed, naturally, when we received your story, that you understood the situation. We can only deeply regret this unfortunate misunderstanding, and assure you of our unfailing regard. Again, thanking you for your kind contribution, and hoping to receive more from you in the near future, we remain, etc."

There was also a postscript to the effect that though *The Billow* carried no free list, it took great pleasure in sending him a complimentary subscription for the ensuing year.

After that experience, Martin typed at the top of the first sheet of all his manuscripts: "Submitted at your usual rate."

Some day, he consoled himself, they will be submitted at *my* usual rate.

He discovered in himself, at this period, a passion for perfection, under the sway of which he rewrote and polished "The Jostling Street," "The Wine of Life," "Joy," the "Sea Lyrics," and others of his earlier work. As of old, nineteen hours of labor a day was all too little to suit him. He wrote prodigiously, and he read prodigiously, forgetting in his toil the pangs caused by giving up his tobacco. Ruth's promised cure for the habit, flamboyantly labelled, he stowed away in the most inaccessible corner of his bureau. Especially during his stretches of famine he suffered from lack of the weed; but no matter how often he mastered the craving, it remained with him as strong as ever. He regarded it as the biggest thing he had ever achieved. Ruth's point of view was that he was doing no more than was right. She brought him the anti-tobacco remedy, purchased out of her glove money, and in a few days forgot all about it.

His machine-made storiettes, though he hated them and derided them, were successful. By means of them he redeemed all his pledges, paid most of his bills, and bought a new set of tires for his wheel. The storiettes at least kept the pot a-boiling and gave him time for ambitious work; while the one thing that upheld him was the forty dollars he had received from *The White Mouse*. He anchored his faith to that, and was confident that the really first-class magazines would pay an unknown writer at least an equal rate, if not a better one. But the thing was, how to get into the first-class magazines. His best stories, essays, and poems went begging among them, and yet, each month, he read reams of dull, prosy, inartistic stuff between all their various covers. If only one editor, he sometimes thought, would descend from his high seat of pride to write me one cheering line! No matter if my work is unusual, no matter if it is unfit, for prudential reasons, for their pages, surely there must be some sparks in it, somewhere, a few, to warm them to some sort of appreciation. And thereupon he would get out one or another of his manuscripts, such as "Adventure," and read it over and over in a vain attempt to vindicate the editorial silence.

As the sweet California spring came on, his period of plenty came to an end. For several weeks he had been worried by a strange silence on the part of the newspaper storiette syndicate. Then, one day, came back to him through the mail ten of his immaculate machine-made storiettes. They were accompanied by a brief letter to the effect that the syndicate was overstocked, and that some months would elapse before it would be in the market again for manuscripts. Martin had even been extravagant on the strength of those ten storiettes. Toward the last the syndicate had been paying him five dollars each for them and accepting every one he sent. So he had looked upon the ten as good as sold, and he had lived accordingly, on a basis of fifty dollars in the bank. So it was that he entered abruptly upon a lean period, wherein he continued selling his earlier efforts to publications that would not pay and submitting his later work to magazines that would not buy. Also, he resumed his trips to the pawnbroker down in Oakland. A few jokes and snatches of humorous verse, sold to the New York weeklies, made existence barely possible for him. It was at this time that he wrote letters of inquiry to the several great monthly and quarterly reviews, and learned in reply that they rarely considered unsolicited articles, and that most of their contents were written upon order by well-known specialists who were authorities in their various fields.

Chapter XXIX

IT WAS a hard summer for Martin. Manuscript readers and editors were away on vacation, and publications that ordinarily returned a decision in three weeks now retained his manuscript for three months or more. The consolation he drew from it was that a saving in postage was effected by the deadlock. Only the robber-publications seemed to remain actively in business, and to them Martin disposed of all his early efforts, such as "Pearl-diving," "The Sea as a Career," "Turtle-catching," and "The Northeast Trades." For these manuscripts he never received a penny. It is true, after six months' correspondence, he effected a compromise, whereby he received a safety razor for "Turtle-catching," and that *The Acropolis*, having agreed to give him five dollars cash and five yearly subscriptions for "The Northeast Trades," fulfilled the second part of the agreement.

For a sonnet on Stevenson he managed to wring two dollars out of a Boston editor who was running a magazine with a Matthew Arnold taste and a penny-dreadful purse. "The Peri and the Pearl," a clever skit of a poem of two hundred lines, just finished, white hot from his brain, won the heart of the editor of a San Francisco magazine published in the interest of a great railroad. When the editor wrote, offering him payment in transportation, Martin wrote back to inquire if the transportation was transferable. It was not, and so, being prevented from peddling it, he asked for the return of the poem. Back it came, with the editor's regrets, and Martin sent it to San Francisco again, this time to *The Hornet*, a pretentious monthly that had been fanned into a constellation of the first magnitude by the brilliant journalist who founded it. But *The Hornet's* light had begun to dim long before Martin was born. The editor promised Martin fifteen dollars for the poem, but, when it was published, seemed to forget about it. Several of his letters being ignored, Martin indicted an angry one which drew a reply. It was written by a new editor, who coolly informed Martin that he declined to be held respon-

sible for the old editor's mistakes, and that he did not think
much of "The Peri and the Pearl" anyway.

But *The Globe*, a Chicago magazine, gave Martin the most
cruel treatment of all. He had refrained from offering his "Sea
Lyrics" for publication, until driven to it by starvation. After
having been rejected by a dozen magazines, they had come to
rest in *The Globe* office. There were thirty poems in the collection, and he was to receive a dollar apiece for them. The
first month four were published, and he promptly received a
check for four dollars; but when he looked over the magazine,
he was appalled at the slaughter. In some cases the titles had
been altered: "Finis," for instance, being changed to "The
Finish," and "The Song of the Outer Reef" to "The Song of
the Coral Reef." In one case, an absolutely different title, a
misappropriate title, was substituted. In place of his own,
"Medusa Lights," the editor had printed, "The Backward
Track." But the slaughter in the body of the poems was terrifying. Martin groaned and sweated and thrust his hands
through his hair. Phrases, lines, and stanzas were cut out, in-
terchanged, or juggled about in the most incomprehensible
manner. Sometimes lines and stanzas not his own were substituted for his. He could not believe that a sane editor could
be guilty of such maltreatment, and his favorite hypothesis
was that his poems must have been doctored by the office
boy or the stenographer. Martin wrote immediately, begging
the editor to cease publishing the lyrics and to return them to
him. He wrote again and again, begging, entreating, threatening, but his letters were ignored. Month by month the
slaughter went on till the thirty poems were published, and
month by month he received a check for those which had
appeared in the current number.

Despite these various misadventures, the memory of the
White Mouse forty-dollar check sustained him, though he was
driven more and more to hack-work. He discovered a bread-
and-butter field in the agricultural weeklies and trade journals,
though among the religious weeklies he found he could easily
starve. At his lowest ebb, when his black suit was in pawn, he
made a ten-strike—or so it seemed to him—in a prize contest arranged by the County Committee of the Republican
Party. There were three branches of the contest, and he en-

tered them all, laughing at himself bitterly the while in that he was driven to such straits to live. His poem won the first prize of ten dollars, his campaign song the second prize of five dollars, his essay on the principles of the Republican Party the first prize of twenty-five dollars. Which was very gratifying to him until he tried to collect. Something had gone wrong in the County Committee, and, though a rich banker and a state senator were members of it, the money was not forthcoming. While this affair was hanging fire, he proved that he understood the principles of the Democratic Party by winning the first prize for his essay in a similar contest. And, moreover, he received the money, twenty-five dollars. But the forty dollars won in the first contest he never received.

Driven to shifts in order to see Ruth, and deciding that the long walk from north Oakland to her house and back again consumed too much time, he kept his black suit in pawn in place of his bicycle. The latter gave him exercise, saved him hours of time for work, and enabled him to see Ruth just the same. A pair of knee duck trousers and an old sweater made him a presentable wheel costume, so that he could go with Ruth on afternoon rides. Besides, he no longer had opportunity to see much of her in her own home, where Mrs. Morse was thoroughly prosecuting her campaign of entertainment. The exalted beings he met there, and to whom he had looked up but a short time before, now bored him. They were no longer exalted. He was nervous and irritable, what of his hard times, disappointments, and close application to work, and the conversation of such people was maddening. He was not unduly egotistic. He measured the narrowness of their minds by the minds of the thinkers in the books he read. At Ruth's home he never met a large mind, with the exception of Professor Caldwell, and Caldwell he had met there only once. As for the rest, they were numskulls, ninnies, superficial, dogmatic, and ignorant. It was their ignorance that astounded him. What was the matter with them? What had they done with their educations? They had had access to the same books he had. How did it happen that they had drawn nothing from them?

He knew that the great minds, the deep and rational

thinkers, existed. He had his proofs from the books, the books
that had educated him beyond the Morse standard. And he
knew that higher intellects than those of the Morse circle were
to be found in the world. He read English society novels,
wherein he caught glimpses of men and women talking politics
and philosophy. And he read of salons in great cities, even in
the United States, where art and intellect congregated. Foolishly, in the past, he had conceived that all well-groomed
persons above the working class were persons with power of
intellect and vigor of beauty. Culture and collars had gone
together, to him, and he had been deceived into believing
that college educations and mastery were the same things.

Well, he would fight his way on and up higher. And he
would take Ruth with him. Her he dearly loved, and he was
confident that she would shine anywhere. As it was clear to
him that he had been handicapped by his early environment,
so now he perceived that she was similarly handicapped. She
had not had a chance to expand. The books on her father's
shelves, the paintings on the walls, the music on the piano—
all was just so much meretricious display. To real literature,
real painting, real music, the Morses and their kind, were
dead. And bigger than such things was life, of which they
were densely, hopelessly ignorant. In spite of their Unitarian
proclivities and their masks of conservative broadmindedness,
they were two generations behind interpretative science: their
mental processes were mediæval, while their thinking on the
ultimate data of existence and of the universe struck him as
the same metaphysical method that was as young as the
youngest race, as old as the cave-man, and older—the same
that moved the first Pleistocene ape-man to fear the dark; that
moved the first hasty Hebrew savage to incarnate Eve from
Adam's rib; that moved Descartes to build an idealistic system of the universe out of the projections of his own puny
ego; and that moved the famous British ecclesiastic to de-
nounce evolution in satire so scathing as to win immediate
applause and leave his name a notorious scrawl on the page
of history.

So Martin thought, and he thought further, till it dawned
upon him that the difference between these lawyers, officers,
business men, and bank cashiers he had met and the members

of the working class he had known was on a par with the difference in the food they ate, clothes they wore, neighborhoods in which they lived. Certainly, in all of them was lacking the something more which he found in himself and in the books. The Morses had shown him the best their social position could produce, and he was not impressed by it. A pauper himself, a slave to the money-lender, he knew himself the superior of those he met at the Morses'; and, when his one decent suit of clothes was out of pawn, he moved among them a lord of life, quivering with a sense of outrage akin to what a prince would suffer if condemned to live with goatherds.

"You hate and fear the socialists," he remarked to Mr. Morse, one evening at dinner; "but why? You know neither them nor their doctrines."

The conversation had been swung in that direction by Mrs. Morse, who had been invidiously singing the praises of Mr. Hapgood. The cashier was Martin's black beast, and his temper was a trifle short where the talker of platitudes was concerned.

"Yes," he had said, "Charley Hapgood is what they call a rising young man—somebody told me as much. And it is true. He'll make the Governor's Chair before he dies, and, who knows? maybe the United States Senate."

"What makes you think so?" Mrs. Morse had inquired.

"I've heard him make a campaign speech. It was so cleverly stupid and unoriginal, and also so convincing, that the leaders cannot help but regard him as safe and sure, while his platitudes are so much like the platitudes of the average voter that—oh, well, you know you flatter any man by dressing up his own thoughts for him and presenting them to him."

"I actually think you are jealous of Mr. Hapgood," Ruth had chimed in.

"Heaven forbid!"

The look of horror on Martin's face stirred Mrs. Morse to belligerence.

"You surely don't mean to say that Mr. Hapgood is stupid?" she demanded icily.

"No more than the average Republican," was the retort, "or average Democrat, either. They are all stupid when they are not crafty, and very few of them are crafty. The only wise Republicans are the millionnaires and their conscious hench-men. They know which side their bread is buttered on, and they know why."

"I am a Republican," Mr. Morse put in lightly. "Pray, how do you classify me?"

"Oh, you are an unconscious henchman."

"Henchman?"

"Why, yes. You do corporation work. You have no working-class nor criminal practice. You don't depend upon wife-beaters and pickpockets for your income. You get your livelihood from the masters of society, and whoever feeds a man is that man's master. Yes, you are a henchman. You are interested in advancing the interests of the aggregations of capital you serve."

Mr. Morse's face was a trifle red.

"I confess, sir," he said, "that you talk like a scoundrelly socialist."

Then it was that Martin made his remark:—

"You hate and fear the socialists; but why? You know nei-ther them nor their doctrines."

"Your doctrine certainly sounds like socialism," Mr. Morse replied, while Ruth gazed anxiously from one to the other, and Mrs. Morse beamed happily at the opportunity afforded of rousing her liege lord's antagonism.

"Because I say Republicans are stupid, and hold that lib-erty, equality, and fraternity are exploded bubbles, does not make me a socialist," Martin said with a smile. "Because I question Jefferson and the unscientific Frenchmen who in-formed his mind, does not make me a socialist. Believe me, Mr. Morse, you are far nearer socialism than I who am its avowed enemy."

"Now you please to be facetious," was all the other could say.

"Not at all. I speak in all seriousness. You still believe in equality, and yet you do the work of the corporations, and the corporations, from day to day, are busily engaged in burying equality. And you call me a socialist because I deny equality, because I affirm just what you live up to. The Republicans are foes to equality, though most of them fight the battle against equality with the very word itself the slogan on their lips. In the name of equality they destroy equality. That was why I called them stupid. As for myself, I am an individualist. I believe the race is to the swift, the battle to the strong. Such is the lesson I have learned from biology, or at least think I have learned. As I said, I am an individualist, and individualism is the hereditary and eternal foe of socialism."

"But you frequent socialist meetings," Mr. Morse challenged.

"Certainly, just as spies frequent hostile camps. How else are you to learn about the enemy? Besides, I enjoy myself at their meetings. They are good fighters, and, right or wrong, they have read the books. Any one of them knows far more about sociology and all the other ologies than the average captain of industry. Yes, I have been to half a dozen of their meetings, but that doesn't make me a socialist any more than hearing Charley Hapgood orate made me a Republican."

"I can't help it," Mr. Morse said feebly, "but I still believe you incline that way."

Bless me, Martin thought to himself, he doesn't know what I was talking about. He hasn't understood a word of it. What did he do with his education, anyway?

Thus, in his development, Martin found himself face to face with economic morality, or the morality of class; and soon it became to him a grisly monster. Personally, he was an intellectual moralist, and more offending to him than platitudinous pomposity was the morality of those about him, which was a curious hotchpotch of the economic, the metaphysical, the sentimental, and the imitative.

A sample of this curious messy mixture he encountered nearer home. His sister Marian had been keeping company with an industrious young mechanic, of German extraction, who, after thoroughly learning the trade, had set up for himself in a bicycle-repair shop. Also, having got the agency for a low-grade make of wheel, he was prosperous. Marian had called on Martin in his room a short time before to announce her engagement, during which visit she had playfully inspected Martin's palm and told his fortune. On her next visit she brought Hermann von Schmidt along with her. Martin did the honors and congratulated both of them in language so easy and graceful as to affect disagreeably the peasant-mind of his sister's lover. This bad impression was further heightened by Martin's reading aloud the half-dozen stanzas of verse with which he had commemorated Marian's previous visit. It was a bit of society verse, airy and delicate, which he had named "The Palmist." He was surprised, when he finished reading it, to note no enjoyment in his sister's face. Instead, her eyes were fixed anxiously upon her betrothed, and Martin, following her gaze, saw spread on that worthy's asymmetrical features nothing but black and sullen disapproval. The incident passed over, they made an early departure, and Martin forgot all about it, though for the moment he had been puzzled that any woman, even of the working class, should not have been flattered and delighted by having poetry written about her.

Several evenings later Marian again visited him, this time alone. Nor did she waste time in coming to the point, upbraiding him sorrowfully for what he had done.

"Why, Marian," he chided, "you talk as though you were ashamed of your relatives, or of your brother at any rate."

"And I am, too," she blurted out.

Martin was bewildered by the tears of mortification he saw in her eyes. The mood, whatever it was, was genuine.

"But, Marian, why should your Hermann be jealous of my writing poetry about my own sister?"

"He ain't jealous," she sobbed. "He says it was indecent, ob—obscene."

Martin emitted a long, low whistle of incredulity, then proceeded to resurrect and read a carbon copy of "The Palmist."

"I can't see it," he said finally, proffering the manuscript to her. "Read it yourself and show me whatever strikes you as obscene—that was the word, wasn't it?"

"He says so, and he ought to know," was the answer, with a wave aside of the manuscript, accompanied by a look of loathing. "And he says you've got to tear it up. He says he won't have no wife of his with such things written about her which anybody can read. He says it's a disgrace, an' he won't stand for it."

"Now, look here, Marian, this is nothing but nonsense," Martin began; then abruptly changed his mind.

He saw before him an unhappy girl, knew the futility of attempting to convince her husband or her, and, though the whole situation was absurd and preposterous, he resolved to surrender.

"All right," he announced, tearing the manuscript into half a dozen pieces and throwing it into the waste-basket.

He contented himself with the knowledge that even then the original typewritten manuscript was reposing in the office of a New York magazine. Marian and her husband would never know, and neither himself nor they nor the world would lose if the pretty, harmless poem ever were published.

Marian, starting to reach into the waste-basket, refrained.

"Can I?" she pleaded.

He nodded his head, regarding her thoughtfully as she gathered the torn pieces of manuscript and tucked them into the pocket of her jacket—ocular evidence of the success of her mission. She reminded him of Lizzie Connolly, though there was less of fire and gorgeous flaunting life in her than in that other girl of the working class whom he had seen twice. But they were on a par, the pair of them, in dress and carriage, and he smiled with inward amusement at the caprice of his fancy which suggested the appearance of either of them in Mrs. Morse's drawing-room. The amusement faded, and he was aware of a great loneliness. This sister of his and the Morse drawing-room were milestones of the road he had travelled. And he had left them behind. He glanced affectionately about him at his few books. They were all the comrades left to him.

"Hello, what's that?" he demanded in startled surprise.

Marian repeated her question.

"Why don't I go to work?" He broke into a laugh that was only half-hearted. "That Hermann of yours has been talking to you."

She shook her head.

"Don't lie," he commanded, and the nod of her head affirmed his charge.

"Well, you tell that Hermann of yours to mind his own business; that when I write poetry about the girl he's keeping company with it's his business, but that outside of that he's got no say so. Understand?

"So you don't think I'll succeed as a writer, eh?" he went on. "You think I'm no good?—that I've fallen down and am a disgrace to the family?"

"I think it would be much better if you got a job," she said firmly, and he saw she was sincere. "Hermann says—"

"Damn Hermann!" he broke out good-naturedly. "What I want to know is when you're going to get married. Also, you find out from your Hermann if he will deign to permit you to accept a wedding present from me."

He mused over the incident after she had gone, and once or twice broke out into laughter that was bitter as he saw his sister and her betrothed, all the members of his own class and the members of Ruth's class, directing their narrow little lives by narrow little formulas—herd-creatures, flocking together and patterning their lives by one another's opinions, failing of being individuals and of really living life because of the childlike formulas by which they were enslaved. He summoned them before him in apparitional procession: Bernard Higginbotham arm in arm with Mr. Butler, Hermann von Schmidt cheek by jowl with Charley Hapgood, and one by one and in pairs he judged them and dismissed them—judged them by the standards of intellect and morality he had learned from the books. Vainly he asked: Where are the great souls, the great men and women? He found them not among the careless, gross, and stupid intelligences that answered the call of vision to his narrow room. He felt a loathing for them such as Circe must have felt for her swine. When he had dismissed the last one and thought himself alone, a late-comer entered, unexpected and unsummoned. Martin watched him and saw the stiff-rim, the square-cut, double-breasted coat and the swaggering shoulders, of the youthful hoodlum who had once been he.

"You were like all the rest, young fellow," Martin sneered. "Your morality and your knowledge were just the same as theirs. You did not think and act for yourself. Your opinions, like your clothes, were ready made; your acts were shaped by popular approval. You were cock of your gang because others acclaimed you the real thing. You fought and ruled the gang, not because you liked to—you know you really despised it,—but because the other fellows patted you on the shoulder.

You licked Cheese-Face because you wouldn't give in, and you wouldn't give in partly because you were abysmal brute and for the rest because you believed what every one about you believed, that the measure of manhood was the carnivorous ferocity displayed in injuring and marring fellow-creatures' anatomies. Why, you whelp, you even won other fellows' girls away from them, not because you wanted the girls, but because in the marrow of those about you, those who set your moral pace, was the instinct of the wild stallion and the bull-seal. Well, the years have passed, and what do you think about it now?"

As if in reply, the vision underwent a swift metamorphosis. The stiff-rim and the square-cut vanished, being replaced by milder garments; the toughness went out of the face, the hardness out of the eyes; and the face, chastened and refined, was irradiated from an inner life of communion with beauty and knowledge. The apparition was very like his present self, and, as he regarded it, he noted the student-lamp by which it was illuminated, and the book over which it pored. He glanced at the title and read, "The Science of Æsthetics." Next, he entered into the apparition, trimmed the student-lamp, and himself went on reading "The Science of Æsthetics."

Chapter XXX

O N A BEAUTIFUL FALL DAY, a day of similar Indian summer to that which had seen their love declared the year
before, Martin read his "Love-cycle" to Ruth. It was in the
afternoon, and, as before, they had ridden out to their favorite knoll in the hills. Now and again she had interrupted his
reading with exclamations of pleasure, and now, as he laid the
last sheet of manuscript with its fellows, he waited her judgment.

She delayed to speak, and at last she spoke haltingly, hesi-
tating to frame in words the harshness of her thought.

"I think they are beautiful, very beautiful," she said; "but
you can't sell them, can you? You see what I mean," she said,
almost pleaded. "This writing of yours is not practical. Something is the matter—maybe it is with the market—that prevents you from earning a living by it. And please, dear, don't
misunderstand me. I am flattered, and made proud, and all
that—I could not be a true woman were it otherwise—that
you should write these poems to me. But they do not make
our marriage possible. Don't you see, Martin? Don't think me
mercenary. It is love, the thought of our future, with which
I am burdened. A whole year has gone by since we learned
we loved each other, and our wedding day is no nearer. Don't
think me immodest in thus talking about our wedding, for
really I have my heart, all that I am, at stake. Why don't you
try to get work on a newspaper, if you are so bound up in
your writing? Why not become a reporter?—for a while, at
least?"

"It would spoil my style," was his answer, in a low, monotonous voice. "You have no idea how I've worked for
style."

"But those storiettes," she argued. "You called them hack-
work. You wrote many of them. Didn't they spoil your
style?"

"No, the cases are different. The storiettes were ground
out, jaded, at the end of a long day of application to style.
But a reporter's work is all hack from morning till night, is

the one paramount thing of life. And it is a whirlwind life, the life of the moment, with neither past nor future, and certainly without thought of any style but reportorial style, and that certainly is not literature. To become a reporter now, just as my style is taking form, crystallizing, would be to commit literary suicide. As it is, every storiette, every word of every storiette, was a violation of myself, of my self-respect, of my respect for beauty. I tell you it was sickening. I was guilty of sin. And I was secretly glad when the markets failed, even if my clothes did go into pawn. But the joy of writing the 'Love-cycle'! The creative joy in its noblest form! That was compensation for everything."

Martin did not know that Ruth was unsympathetic concerning the creative joy. She used the phrase—it was on her lips he had first heard it. She had read about it, studied about it, in the university in the course of earning her Bachelorship of Arts; but she was not original, not creative, and all manifestations of culture on her part were but harpings of the harpings of others.

"May not the editor have been right in his revision of your 'Sea Lyrics'?" she questioned. "Remember, an editor must have proved qualifications or else he would not be an editor."

"That's in line with the persistence of the established," he rejoined, his heat against the editor-folk getting the better of him. "What is, is not only right, but is the best possible. The existence of anything is sufficient vindication of its fitness to exist—to exist, mark you, as the average person unconsciously believes, not merely in present conditions, but in all conditions. It is their ignorance, of course, that makes them believe such rot—their ignorance, which is nothing more nor less than the henidical mental process described by Weininger. They think they think, and such thinkless creatures are the arbiters of the lives of the few who really think."

He paused, overcome by the consciousness that he had been talking over Ruth's head.

"I'm sure I don't know who this Weininger is," she retorted. "And you are so dreadfully general that I fail to follow you. What I was speaking of was the qualification of editors—"

"And I'll tell you," he interrupted. "The chief qualification of ninety-nine per cent of all editors is failure. They have failed as writers. Don't think they prefer the drudgery of the desk and the slavery to their circulation and to the business manager to the joy of writing. They have tried to write, and they have failed. And right there is the cursed paradox of it. Every portal to success in literature is guarded by those watch-dogs, the failures in literature. The editors, sub-editors, associate editors, most of them, and the manuscript-readers for the magazines and book-publishers, most of them, nearly all of them, are men who wanted to write and who have failed. And yet they, of all creatures under the sun the most unfit, are the very creatures who decide what shall and what shall not find its way into print—they, who have proved themselves not original, who have demonstrated that they lack the divine fire, sit in judgment upon originality and ge- nius. And after them come the reviewers, just so many more failures. Don't tell me that they have not dreamed the dream and attempted to write poetry or fiction; for they have, and they have failed. Why, the average review is more nauseating than cod-liver oil. But you know my opinion on the reviewers and the alleged critics. There are great critics, but they are as rare as comets. If I fail as a writer, I shall have proved for the career of editorship. There's bread and butter and jam, at any rate."

Ruth's mind was quick, and her disapproval of her lover's views was buttressed by the contradiction she found in his contention.

"But, Martin, if that be so, if all the doors are closed as you have shown so conclusively, how is it possible that any of the great writers ever arrived?"

"They arrived by achieving the impossible," he answered. "They did such blazing, glorious work as to burn to ashes those that opposed them. They arrived by course of miracle, by winning a thousand-to-one wager against them. They ar- rived because they were Carlyle's battle-scarred giants who will not be kept down. And that is what I must do; I must achieve the impossible."

"But if you fail? You must consider me as well, Martin."

"If I fail?" He regarded her for a moment as though the thought she had uttered was unthinkable. Then intelligence illumined his eyes. "If I fail, I shall become an editor, and you will be an editor's wife."

She frowned at his facetiousness—a pretty, adorable frown that made him put his arm around her and kiss it away.

"There, that's enough," she urged, by an effort of will withdrawing herself from the fascination of his strength. "I have talked with father and mother. I never before asserted myself so against them. I demanded to be heard. I was very undutiful. They are against you, you know; but I assured them over and over of my abiding love for you, and at last father agreed that if you wanted to, you could begin right away in his office. And then, of his own accord, he said he would pay you enough at the start so that we could get married and have a little cottage somewhere. Which I think was very fine of him—don't you?"

Martin, with the dull pain of despair at his heart, mechanically reaching for the tobacco and paper (which he no longer carried) to roll a cigarette, muttered something inarticulate, and Ruth went on.

"Frankly, though, and don't let it hurt you—I tell you, to show you precisely how you stand with him—he doesn't like your radical views, and he thinks you are lazy. Of course I know you are not. I know you work hard."

How hard, even she did not know, was the thought in Martin's mind.

"Well, then," he said, "how about my views? Do you think they are so radical?"

He held her eyes and waited the answer.

"I think them, well, very disconcerting," she replied.

The question was answered for him, and so oppressed was he by the grayness of life that he forgot the tentative proposition she had made for him to go to work. And she, having gone as far as she dared, was willing to wait the answer till she should bring the question up again.

She had not long to wait. Martin had a question of his own to propound to her. He wanted to ascertain the measure of her faith in him, and within the week each was answered. Martin precipitated it by reading to her his "The Shame of the Sun."

"Why don't you become a reporter?" she asked when he

had finished. "You love writing so, and I am sure you would succeed. You could rise in journalism and make a name for yourself. There are a number of great special correspondents. Their salaries are large, and their field is the world. They are sent everywhere, to the heart of Africa, like Stanley, or to interview the Pope, or to explore unknown Thibet."

"Then you don't like my essay?" he rejoined. "You believe that I have some show in journalism but none in literature?"

"No, no; I do like it. It reads well. But I am afraid it's over the heads of your readers. At least it is over mine. It sounds beautiful, but I don't understand it. Your scientific slang is beyond me. You are an extremist, you know, dear, and what may be intelligible to you may not be intelligible to the rest of us."

"I imagine it's the philosophic slang that bothers you," was all he could say.

He was flaming from the fresh reading of the ripest thought he had expressed, and her verdict stunned him.

"No matter how poorly it is done," he persisted, "don't you see anything in it?—in the thought of it, I mean?"

She shook her head.

"No, it is so different from anything I have read. I read Maeterlinck and understand him—"

"His mysticism, you understand that?" Martin flashed out.

"Yes, but this of yours, which is supposed to be an attack upon him, I don't understand. Of course, if originality counts—"

He stopped her with an impatient gesture that was not followed by speech. He became suddenly aware that she was speaking and that she had been speaking for some time.

"After all, your writing has been a toy to you," she was saying. "Surely you have played with it long enough. It is time to take up life seriously —*our* life, Martin. Hitherto you have lived solely your own."

"You want me to go to work?" he asked.

"Yes. Father has offered—"

"I understand all that," he broke in; "but what I want to know is whether or not you have lost faith in me?"

She pressed his hand mutely, her eyes dim.

"In your writing, dear," she admitted in a half-whisper.

"You've read lots of my stuff," he went on brutally. "What do you think of it? Is it utterly hopeless? How does it compare with other men's work?"

"But they sell theirs, and you—don't."

"That doesn't answer my question. Do you think that literature is not at all my vocation?"

"Then I will answer." She steeled herself to do it. "I don't think you were made to write. Forgive me, dear. You compel me to say it; and you know I know more about literature than you do."

"Yes, you are a Bachelor of Arts," he said meditatively; "and you ought to know."

"But there is more to be said," he continued, after a pause painful to both. "I know what I have in me. No one knows that so well as I. I know I shall succeed. I will not be kept down. I am afire with what I have to say in verse, and fiction, and essay. I do not ask you to have faith in that, though. I do not ask you to have faith in me, nor in my writing. What I do ask of you is to love me and have faith in love.

"A year ago I begged for two years. One of those years is yet to run. And I do believe, upon my honor and my soul, that before that year is run I shall have succeeded. You remember what you told me long ago, that I must serve my apprenticeship to writing. Well, I have served it. I have crammed it and telescoped it. With you at the end awaiting me, I have never shirked. Do you know, I have forgotten what it is to fall peacefully asleep. A few million years ago I knew what it was to sleep my fill and to awake naturally from very glut of sleep. I am awakened always now by an alarm clock. If I fall asleep early or late, I set the alarm accordingly; and this, and the putting out of the lamp, are my last conscious actions.

"When I begin to feel drowsy, I change the heavy book I am reading for a lighter one. And when I doze over that, I beat my head with my knuckles in order to drive sleep away. Somewhere I read of a man who was afraid to sleep. Kipling wrote the story. This man arranged a spur so that when unconsciousness came, his naked body pressed against the iron teeth. Well, I've done the same. I look at the time, and I resolve that not until midnight, or not until one o'clock, or two o'clock, or three o'clock, shall the spur be removed. And so it rowels me awake until the appointed time. That spur has been my bed-mate for months. I have grown so desperate that five and a half hours of sleep is an extravagance. I sleep four hours now. I am starved for sleep. There are times when I am light-headed from want of sleep, times when death, with its rest and sleep, is a positive lure to me, times when I am haunted by Longfellow's lines:—

> " 'The sea is still and deep;
> All things within its bosom sleep;
> A single step and all is o'er,
> A plunge, a bubble, and no more.'

"Of course, this is sheer nonsense. It comes from nervousness, from an overwrought mind. But the point is: Why have I done this? For you. To shorten my apprenticeship. To compel Success to hasten. And my apprenticeship is now served. I know my equipment. I swear that I learn more each month than the average college man learns in a year. I know it, I tell you. But were my need for you to understand not so desperate I should not tell you. It is not boasting. I measure the results by the books. Your brothers, to-day, are ignorant barbarians compared with me and the knowledge I have wrung from the books in the hours they were sleeping. Long ago I wanted to be famous. I care very little for fame now. What I want is you; I am more hungry for you than for food, or clothing, or recognition. I have a dream of laying my head on your breast and sleeping an æon or so, and the dream will come true ere another year is gone."

His power beat against her, wave upon wave; and in the moment his will opposed hers most she felt herself most strongly drawn toward him. The strength that had always poured out from him to her was now flowering in his impassioned voice, his flashing eyes, and the vigor of life and intellect surging in him. And in that moment, and for the moment, she was aware of a rift that showed in her certitude—a rift through which she caught sight of the real Martin Eden, splendid and invincible; and as animal-trainers have their moments of doubt, so she, for the instant, seemed to doubt her power to tame this wild spirit of a man.

"And another thing," he swept on. "You love me. But why do you love me? The thing in me that compels me to write is the very thing that draws your love. You love me because I am somehow different from the men you have known and might have loved. I was not made for the desk and counting-house, for petty business squabbling and legal jangling. Make me do such things, make me like those other men, doing the work they do, breathing the air they breathe, developing the point of view they have developed, and you have destroyed the difference, destroyed me, destroyed the thing you love. My desire to write is the most vital thing in me. Had I been a mere clod, neither would I have desired to write, nor would you have desired me for a husband."

"But you forget," she interrupted, the quick surface of her mind glimpsing a parallel. "There have been eccentric inventors, starving their families while they sought such chimeras as perpetual motion. Doubtless their wives loved them, and suffered with them and for them, not because of but in spite of their infatuation for perpetual motion."

"True," was the reply. "But there have been inventors who were not eccentric and who starved while they sought to invent practical things; and sometimes, it is recorded, they succeeded. Certainly I do not seek any impossibilities—"

"You have called it 'achieving the impossible,'" she interpolated.

"I spoke figuratively. I seek to do what men have done before me—to write and to live by my writing."

Her silence spurred him on.

"To you, then, my goal is as much a chimera as perpetual motion?" he demanded.

He read her answer in the pressure of her hand on his—the pitying mother-hand for the hurt child. And to her, just then, he was the hurt child, the infatuated man striving to achieve the impossible.

Toward the close of their talk she warned him again of the antagonism of her father and mother.

"But you love me?" he asked.

"I do! I do!" she cried.

"And I love you, not them, and nothing they do can hurt me." Triumph sounded in his voice. "For I have faith in your love, not fear of their enmity. All things may go astray in this world, but not love. Love cannot go wrong unless it be a weakling that faints and stumbles by the way."

Chapter XXXI

M ARTIN had encountered his sister Gertrude by chance
on Broadway—as it proved, a most propitious yet
disconcerting chance. Waiting on the corner for a car, she had
seen him first, and noted the eager, hungry lines of his face
and the desperate, worried look of his eyes. In truth, he was
desperate and worried. He had just come from a fruitless interview with the pawnbroker, from whom he had tried to
wring an additional loan on his wheel. The muddy fall
weather having come on, Martin had pledged his wheel some
time since and retained his black suit.

"There's the black suit," the pawnbroker, who knew his
every asset, had answered. "You needn't tell me you've gone
and pledged it with that Jew, Lipka. Because if you have—"

The man had looked the threat, and Martin hastened to
cry:—

"No, no; I've got it. But I want to wear it on a matter of
business."

"All right," the mollified usurer had replied. "And I want it
on a matter of business before I can let you have any more
money. You don't think I'm in it for my health?"

"But it's a forty-dollar wheel, in good condition," Martin
had argued. "And you've only let me have seven dollars on it.
No, not even seven. Six and a quarter; you took the interest
in advance."

"If you want some more, bring the suit," had been the reply that sent Martin out of the stuffy little den, so desperate
at heart as to reflect it in his face and touch his sister to pity.

Scarcely had they met when the Telegraph Avenue car
came along and stopped to take on a crowd of afternoon
shoppers. Mrs. Higginbotham divined from the grip on her
arm as he helped her on, that he was not going to follow her.
She turned on the step and looked down upon him. His haggard face smote her to the heart again.

"Ain't you comin'?" she asked.

The next moment she had descended to his side.

"I'm walking—exercise, you know," he explained.

"Then I'll go along for a few blocks," she announced. "Mebbe it'll do me good. I ain't ben feelin' any too spry these last few days."

Martin glanced at her and verified her statement in her general slovenly appearance, in the unhealthy fat, in the drooping shoulders, the tired face with the sagging lines, and in the heavy fall of her feet, without elasticity—a very caricature of the walk that belongs to a free and happy body.

"You'd better stop here," he said, though she had already come to a halt at the first corner, "and take the next car."

"My goodness!—if I ain't all tired a'ready!" she panted. "But I'm just as able to walk as you in them soles. They're that thin they'll bu'st long before you git out to North Oakland."

"I've a better pair at home," was the answer.

"Come out to dinner to-morrow," she invited irrelevantly. "Mr. Higginbotham won't be there. He's goin' to San Leandro on business."

Martin shook his head, but he had failed to keep back the wolfish, hungry look that leapt into his eyes at the suggestion of dinner.

"You haven't a penny, Mart, and that's why you're walkin'. Exercise!" She tried to sniff contemptuously, but succeeded in producing only a sniffle. "Here, lemme see."

And, fumbling in her satchel, she pressed a five-dollar piece into his hand. "I guess I forgot your last birthday, Mart," she mumbled lamely.

Martin's hand instinctively closed on the piece of gold. In the same instant he knew he ought not to accept, and found himself struggling in the throes of indecision. That bit of gold meant food, life, and light in his body and brain, power to go on writing, and—who was to say?—maybe to write something that would bring in many pieces of gold. Clear on his vision burned the manuscripts of two essays he had just completed. He saw them under the table on top of the heap of returned manuscripts for which he had no stamps, and he saw their titles, just as he had typed them—"The High Priests of Mystery," and "The Cradle of Beauty." He had never submitted them anywhere. They were as good as anything he had done in that line. If only he had stamps for them! Then the certitude of his ultimate success rose up in him, an able ally of hunger, and with a quick movement he slipped the coin into his pocket.

"I'll pay you back, Gertrude, a hundred times over," he gulped out, his throat painfully contracted and in his eyes a swift hint of moisture.

"Mark my words!" he cried with abrupt positiveness. "Before the year is out I'll put an even hundred of those little yellow-boys into your hand. I don't ask you to believe me. All you have to do is wait and see."

Nor did she believe. Her incredulity made her uncomfortable, and failing of other expedient, she said:—

"I know you're hungry, Mart. It's sticking out all over you. Come in to meals any time. I'll send one of the children to tell you when Mr. Higginbotham ain't to be there. An' Mart—"

He waited, though he knew in his secret heart what she was about to say, so visible was her thought process to him.

"Don't you think it's about time you got a job?"

"You don't think I'll win out?" he asked.

She shook her head.

"Nobody has faith in me, Gertrude, except myself." His voice was passionately rebellious. "I've done good work already, plenty of it, and sooner or later it will sell."

"How do you know it is good?"

"Because—" He faltered as the whole vast field of literature and the history of literature stirred in his brain and pointed the futility of his attempting to convey to her the reasons for his faith. "Well, because it's better than ninety-nine per cent of what is published in the magazines."

"I wish't you'd listen to reason," she answered feebly, but with unwavering belief in the correctness of her diagnosis of what was ailing him. "I wish't you'd listen to reason," she repeated, "an' come to dinner to-morrow."

After Martin had helped her on the car, he hurried to the post-office and invested three of the five dollars in stamps; and when, later in the day, on the way to the Morse home, he stopped in at the post-office to weigh a large number of long, bulky envelopes, he affixed to them all the stamps save three of the two-cent denomination.

It proved a momentous night for Martin, for after dinner
he met Russ Brissenden. How he chanced to come there,
whose friend he was or what acquaintance brought him, Martin did not know. Nor had he the curiosity to inquire about
him of Ruth. In short, Brissenden struck Martin as anæmic
and feather-brained, and was promptly dismissed from his
mind. An hour later he decided that Brissenden was a boor as
well, what of the way he prowled about from one room to
another, staring at the pictures or poking his nose into books
and magazines he picked up from the table or drew from the
shelves. Though a stranger in the house he finally isolated
himself in the midst of the company, huddling into a capacious Morris chair and reading steadily from a thin volume he
had drawn from his pocket. As he read, he abstractedly ran
his fingers, with a caressing movement, through his hair.
Martin noticed him no more that evening, except once when
he observed him chaffing with great apparent success with
several of the young women.

It chanced that when Martin was leaving, he overtook Brissenden already half down the walk to the street.

"Hello, is that you?" Martin said.

The other replied with an ungracious grunt, but swung
alongside. Martin made no further attempt at conversation,
and for several blocks unbroken silence lay upon them.

"Pompous old ass!"

The suddenness and the virulence of the exclamation startled Martin. He felt amused, and at the same time was aware
of a growing dislike for the other.

"What do you go to such a place for?" was abruptly flung
at him after another block of silence.

"Why do you?" Martin countered.

"Bless me, I don't know," came back. "At least this is my
first indiscretion. There are twenty-four hours in each day,
and I must spend them somehow. Come and have a drink."

"All right," Martin answered.

The next moment he was nonplussed by the readiness of
his acceptance. At home was several hours' hack-work waiting
for him before he went to bed, and after he went to bed there
was a volume of Weismann waiting for him, to say nothing
of Herbert Spencer's Autobiography, which was as replete for

him with romance as any thrilling novel. Why should he waste any time with this man he did not like? was his thought. And yet, it was not so much the man nor the drink as was it what was associated with the drink—the bright lights, the mirrors and dazzling array of glasses, the warm and glowing faces and the resonant hum of the voices of men. That was it, it was the voices of men, optimistic men, men who breathed success and spent their money for drinks like men. He was lonely, that was what was the matter with him; that was why he had snapped at the invitation as a bonita strikes at a white rag on a hook. Not since with Joe, at Shelly Hot Springs, with the one exception of the wine he took with the Portuguese grocer, had Martin had a drink at a public bar. Mental exhaustion did not produce a craving for liquor such as physical exhaustion did, and he had felt no need for it. But just now he felt desire for the drink, or, rather, for the atmosphere wherein drinks were dispensed and disposed of. Such a place was the Grotto, where Brissenden and he lounged in capacious leather chairs and drank Scotch and soda.

They talked. They talked about many things, and now Brissenden and now Martin took turn in ordering Scotch and soda. Martin, who was extremely strong-headed, marvelled at the other's capacity for liquor, and ever and anon broke off to marvel at the other's conversation. He was not long in assuming that Brissenden knew everything, and in deciding that here was the second intellectual man he had met. But he noted that Brissenden had what Professor Caldwell lacked— namely, fire, the flashing insight and perception, the flaming uncontrol of genius. Living language flowed from him. His thin lips, like the dies of a machine, stamped out phrases that cut and stung; or again, pursing caressingly about the in- choate sound they articulated, the thin lips shaped soft and velvety things, mellow phrases of glow and glory, of haunting beauty, reverberant of the mystery and inscrutableness of life; and yet again the thin lips were like a bugle, from which rang the crash and tumult of cosmic strife, phrases that sounded clear as silver, that were luminous as starry spaces, that epit- omized the final word of science and yet said something more—the poet's word, the transcendental truth, elusive and

without words which could express, and which none the less
found expression in the subtle and all but ungraspable connotations of common words. He, by some wonder of vision,
saw beyond the farthest outpost of empiricism, where was no
language for narration, and yet, by some golden miracle of
speech, investing known words with unknown significances,
he conveyed to Martin's consciousness messages that were incommunicable to ordinary souls.

Martin forgot his first impression of dislike. Here was the
best the books had to offer coming true. Here was an intelligence, a living man for him to look up to. "I am down in the
dirt at your feet," Martin repeated to himself again and again.

"You've studied biology," he said aloud, in significant allusion.

To his surprise Brissenden shook his head.

"But you are stating truths that are substantiated only by
biology," Martin insisted, and was rewarded by a blank stare.
"Your conclusions are in line with the books which you must
have read."

"I am glad to hear it," was the answer. "That my smatter-
ing of knowledge should enable me to short-cut my way to
truth is most reassuring. As for myself, I never bother to find
out if I am right or not. It is all valueless anyway. Man can
never know the ultimate verities."

"You are a disciple of Spencer!" Martin cried triumphantly.

"I haven't read him since adolescence, and all I read then
was his 'Education.' "

"I wish I could gather knowledge as carelessly," Martin
broke out half an hour later. He had been closely analyzing
Brissenden's mental equipment. "You are a sheer dogmatist,
and that's what makes it so marvellous. You state dogmatically the latest facts which science has been able to establish
only by *à posteriori* reasoning. You jump at correct conclusions. You certainly short-cut with a vengeance. You feel your
way with the speed of light, by some hyperrational process,
to truth."

"Yes, that was what used to bother Father Joseph, and
Brother Dutton," Brissenden replied. "Oh, no," he added; "I
am not anything. It was a lucky trick of fate that sent me to

a Catholic college for my education. Where did you pick up what you know?"

And while Martin told him, he was busy studying Brissenden, ranging from his long, lean, aristocratic face and drooping shoulders to the overcoat on a neighboring chair, its pockets sagged and bulged by the freightage of many books. Brissenden's face and long, slender hands were browned by the sun—excessively browned, Martin thought. This sunburn bothered Martin. It was patent that Brissenden was no outdoor man. Then how had he been ravaged by the sun? Something morbid and significant attached to that sunburn, was Martin's thought as he returned to a study of the face, narrow, with high cheek-bones and cavernous hollows, and graced with as delicate and fine an aquiline nose as Martin had ever seen. There was nothing remarkable about the size of the eyes. They were neither large nor small, while their color was a nondescript brown; but in them smouldered a fire, or, rather, lurked an expression dual and strangely contradictory. Defiant, indomitable, even harsh to excess, they at the same time aroused pity. Martin found himself pitying him he knew not why, though he was soon to learn.

"Oh, I'm a lunger," Brissenden announced, offhand, a little later, having already stated that he came from Arizona. "I've been down there a couple of years living on the climate."

"Aren't you afraid to venture it up in this climate?"

"Afraid?"

There was no special emphasis of his repetition of Martin's word. But Martin saw in that ascetic face the advertisement that there was nothing of which it was afraid. The eyes had narrowed till they were eagle-like, and Martin almost caught his breath as he noted the eagle beak with its dilated nostrils, defiant, assertive, aggressive. Magnificent, was what he commented to himself, his blood thrilling at the sight. Aloud, he quoted:—

> " 'Under the bludgeoning of Chance
> My head is bloody but unbowed.' "

"You like Henley," Brissenden said, his expression chang-

ing swiftly to large graciousness and tenderness. "Of course,
I couldn't have expected anything else of you. Ah, Henley! A
brave soul. He stands out among contemporary rhymesters—
magazine rhymesters—as a gladiator stands out in the midst
of a band of eunuchs."

"You don't like the magazines," Martin softly impeached.

"Do you?" was snarled back at him so savagely as to startle
him.

"I—I write, or, rather, try to write, for the magazines,"
Martin faltered.

"That's better," was the mollified rejoinder. "You try to
write, but you don't succeed. I respect and admire your failure. I know what you write. I can see it with half an eye, and
there's one ingredient in it that shuts it out of the magazines.
It's guts, and magazines have no use for that particular commodity. What they want is wish-wash and slush, and God
knows they get it, but not from you."

"I'm not above hack-work," Martin contended.

"On the contrary—" Brissenden paused and ran an insolent eye over Martin's objective poverty, passing from the
well-worn tie and the saw-edged collar to the shiny sleeves of
the coat and on to the slight fray of one cuff, winding up and
dwelling upon Martin's sunken cheeks. "On the contrary,
hack-work is above you, so far above you that you can never
hope to rise to it. Why, man, I could insult you by asking
you to have something to eat."

Martin felt the heat in his face of the involuntary blood,
and Brissenden laughed triumphantly.

"A full man is not insulted by such an invitation," he concluded.

"You are a devil," Martin cried irritably.

"Anyway, I didn't ask you."

"You didn't dare."

"Oh, I don't know about that. I invite you now."

Brissenden half rose from his chair as he spoke, as if with
the intention of departing to the restaurant forthwith.

Martin's fists were tight-clenched, and his blood was drumming in his temples.

"Bosco! He eats 'em alive! Eats 'em alive!" Brissenden exclaimed, imitating the *spieler* of a locally famous snake-eater.

"I could certainly eat you alive," Martin said, in turn running insolent eyes over the other's disease-ravaged frame.

"Only I'm not worthy of it?"

"On the contrary," Martin considered, "because the incident is not worthy." He broke into a laugh, hearty and wholesome. "I confess you made a fool of me, Brissenden. That I am hungry and you are aware of it are only ordinary phenomena, and there's no disgrace. You see, I laugh at the conventional little moralities of the herd; then you drift by, say a sharp, true word, and immediately I am the slave of the same little moralities."

"You were insulted," Brissenden affirmed.

"I certainly was, a moment ago. The prejudice of early youth, you know. I learned such things then, and they cheapen what I have since learned. They are the skeletons in my particular closet."

"But you've got the door shut on them now?"

"I certainly have."

"Sure?"

"Sure."

"Then let's go and get something to eat."

"I'll go you," Martin answered, attempting to pay for the current Scotch and soda with the last change from his two dollars and seeing the waiter bullied by Brissenden into putting that change back on the table.

Martin pocketed it with a grimace, and felt for a moment the kindly weight of Brissenden's hand upon his shoulder.

Chapter XXXII

PROMPTLY, the next afternoon, Maria was excited by Martin's second visitor. But she did not lose her head this time, for she seated Brissenden in her parlor's grandeur of respectability.

"Hope you don't mind my coming?" Brissenden began.

"No, no, not at all," Martin answered, shaking hands and waving him to the solitary chair, himself taking to the bed. "But how did you know where I lived?"

"Called up the Morses. Miss Morse answered the 'phone. And here I am." He tugged at his coat pocket and flung a thin volume on the table. "There's a book, by a poet. Read it and keep it." And then, in reply to Martin's protest: "What have I to do with books? I had another hemorrhage this morning. Got any whiskey? No, of course not. Wait a minute."

He was off and away. Martin watched his long figure go down the outside steps, and, on turning to close the gate, noted with a pang the shoulders, which had once been broad, drawn in now over the collapsed ruin of the chest. Martin got two tumblers, and fell to reading the book of verse, Henry Vaughn Marlow's latest collection.

"No Scotch," Brissenden announced on his return. "The beggar sells nothing but American whiskey. But here's a quart of it."

"I'll send one of the youngsters for lemons, and we'll make a toddy," Martin offered.

"I wonder what a book like that will earn Marlow?" he went on, holding up the volume in question.

"Possibly fifty dollars," came the answer. "Though he's lucky if he pulls even on it, or if he can inveigle a publisher to risk bringing it out."

"Then one can't make a living out of poetry?"

Martin's tone and face alike showed his dejection.

"Certainly not. What fool expects to? Out of rhyming, yes. There's Bruce, and Virginia Spring, and Sedgwick. They do very nicely. But poetry—do you know how Vaughn Marlow makes his living?—teaching in a boys' cramming-joint down

in Pennsylvania, and of all private little hells such a billet is
the limit. I wouldn't trade places with him if he had fifty years
of life before him. And yet his work stands out from the ruck
of the contemporary versifiers as a balas ruby among carrots.
And the reviews he gets! Damn them, all of them, the crass
manikins!"

"Too much is written by the men who can't write about
the men who do write," Martin concurred. "Why, I was appalled at the quantities of rubbish written about Stevenson
and his work."

"Ghouls and harpies!" Brissenden snapped out with click-
ing teeth. "Yes, I know the spawn—complacently pecking at
him for his Father Damien letter, analyzing him, weighing
him—"

"Measuring him by the yardstick of their own miserable
egos," Martin broke in.

"Yes, that's it, a good phrase,—mouthing and besliming
the True, and Beautiful, and Good, and finally patting him
on the back and saying, 'Good dog, Fido.' Faugh! 'The little
chattering daws of men,' Richard Realf called them the night
he died."

"Pecking at star-dust," Martin took up the strain warmly;
"at the meteoric flight of the master-men. I once wrote a
squib on them—the critics, or the reviewers, rather."

"Let's see it," Brissenden begged eagerly.

So Martin unearthed a carbon copy of "Star-dust," and
during the reading of it Brissenden chuckled, rubbed his
hands, and forgot to sip his toddy.

"Strikes me you're a bit of star-dust yourself, flung into a
world of cowled gnomes who cannot see," was his comment
at the end of it. "Of course it was snapped up by the first
magazine?"

Martin ran over the pages of his manuscript book.

"It has been refused by twenty-seven of them."

Brissenden essayed a long and hearty laugh, but broke
down in a fit of coughing.

"Say, you needn't tell me you haven't tackled poetry," he
gasped. "Let me see some of it."

"Don't read it now," Martin pleaded. "I want to talk with
you. I'll make up a bundle and you can take it home."

Brissenden departed with the "Love-cycle," and "The Peri and the Pearl," returning next day to greet Martin with:—

"I want more."

Not only did he assure Martin that he was a poet, but Martin learned that Brissenden also was one. He was swept off his feet by the other's work, and astounded that no attempt had been made to publish it.

"A plague on all their houses!" was Brissenden's answer to Martin's volunteering to market his work for him. "Love Beauty for its own sake," was his counsel, "and leave the magazines alone. Back to your ships and your sea—that's my advice to you, Martin Eden. What do you want in these sick and rotten cities of men? You are cutting your throat every day you waste in them trying to prostitute beauty to the needs of magazinedom. What was it you quoted me the other day?—Oh, yes, 'Man, the latest of the ephemera.' Well, what do you, the latest of the ephemera, want with fame? If you got it, it would be poison to you. You are too simple, too elemental, and too rational, by my faith, to prosper on such pap. I hope you never do sell a line to the magazines. Beauty is the only master to serve. Serve her and damn the multitude! Success! What in hell's success if it isn't right there in your Stevenson sonnet, which outranks Henley's 'Apparition,' in that 'Love-cycle,' in those sea-poems?

"It is not in what you succeed in doing that you get your joy, but in the doing of it. You can't tell me. I know it. You know it. Beauty hurts you. It is an everlasting pain in you, a wound that does not heal, a knife of flame. Why should you palter with magazines? Let beauty be your end. Why should you mint beauty into gold? Anyway, you can't; so there's no use in my getting excited over it. You can read the magazines for a thousand years and you won't find the value of one line of Keats. Leave fame and coin alone, sign away on a ship tomorrow, and go back to your sea."

"Not for fame, but for love," Martin laughed. "Love seems to have no place in your Cosmos; in mine, Beauty is the handmaiden of Love."

Brissenden looked at him pityingly and admiringly. "You are so young, Martin boy, so young. You will flutter high, but your wings are of the finest gauze, dusted with the fairest pigments. Do not scorch them. But of course you have scorched them already. It required some glorified petticoat to account for that 'Love-cycle,' and that's the shame of it."

"It glorifies love as well as the petticoat," Martin laughed.

"The philosophy of madness," was the retort. "So have I assured myself when wandering in hasheesh dreams. But beware. These bourgeois cities will kill you. Look at that den of traitors where I met you. Dry rot is no name for it. One can't keep his sanity in such an atmosphere. It's degrading. There's not one of them who is not degrading, man and woman, all of them animated stomachs guided by the high intellectual and artistic impulses of clams—"

He broke off suddenly and regarded Martin. Then, with a flash of divination, he saw the situation. The expression on his face turned to wondering horror.

"And you wrote that tremendous 'Love-cycle' to her—that pale, shrivelled, female thing!"

The next instant Martin's right hand had shot to a throttling clutch on his throat, and he was being shaken till his teeth rattled. But Martin, looking into his eyes, saw no fear there,—naught but a curious and mocking devil. Martin remembered himself, and flung Brissenden, by the neck, sidelong upon the bed, at the same moment releasing his hold.

Brissenden panted and gasped painfully for a moment, then began to chuckle.

"You had made me eternally your debtor had you shaken out the flame," he said.

"My nerves are on a hair-trigger these days," Martin apologized. "Hope I didn't hurt you. Here, let me mix a fresh toddy."

"Ah, you young Greek!" Brissenden went on. "I wonder if you take just pride in that body of yours. You are devilish strong. You are a young panther, a lion cub. Well, well, it is you who must pay for that strength."

"What do you mean?" Martin asked curiously, passing him a glass. "Here, down this and be good."

"Because—" Brissenden sipped his toddy and smiled appreciation of it. "Because of the women. They will worry you until you die, as they have already worried you, or else I was born yesterday. Now there's no use in your choking me; I'm

going to have my say. This is undoubtedly your calf love; but
for Beauty's sake show better taste next time. What under
heaven do you want with a daughter of the bourgeoisie?
Leave them alone. Pick out some great, wanton flame of a
woman, who laughs at life and jeers at death and loves one
while she may. There are such women, and they will love you
just as readily as any pusillanimous product of bourgeois-
sheltered life."

"Pusillanimous?" Martin protested.

"Just so, pusillanimous; prattling out little moralities that
have been prattled into them, and afraid to live life. They will
love you, Martin, but they will love their little moralities
more. What you want is the magnificent abandon of life, the
great free souls, the blazing butterflies and not the little gray
moths. Oh, you will grow tired of them, too, of all the female
things, if you are unlucky enough to live. But you won't live.
You won't go back to your ships and sea; therefore, you'll
hang around these pest-holes of cities until your bones are
rotten, and then you'll die."

"You can lecture me, but you can't make me talk back,"
Martin said. "After all, you have but the wisdom of your temperament, and the wisdom of my temperament is just as un-
impeachable as yours."

They disagreed about love, and the magazines, and many
things, but they liked each other, and on Martin's part it was
no less than a profound liking. Day after day they were together, if for no more than the hour Brissenden spent in Martin's stuffy room. Brissenden never arrived without his quart
of whiskey, and when they dined together down-town, he
drank Scotch and soda throughout the meal. He invariably
paid the way for both, and it was through him that Martin
learned the refinements of food, drank his first champagne,
and made acquaintance with Rhenish wines.

But Brissenden was always an enigma. With the face of an
ascetic, he was, in all the failing blood of him, a frank voluptuary. He was unafraid to die, bitter and cynical of all the
ways of living; and yet, dying, he loved life, to the last atom
of it. He was possessed by a madness to live, to thrill, "to
squirm my little space in the cosmic dust whence I came," as
he phrased it once himself. He had tampered with drugs and

done many strange things in quest of new thrills, new sensations. As he told Martin, he had once gone three days without water, had done so voluntarily, in order to experience the exquisite delight of such a thirst assuaged. Who or what he was, Martin never learned. He was a man without a past, whose future was the imminent grave and whose present was a bitter fever of living.

Chapter XXXIII

MARTIN was steadily losing his battle. Economize as he would, the earnings from hack-work did not balance expenses. Thanksgiving found him with his black suit in pawn and unable to accept the Morses' invitation to dinner. Ruth was not made happy by his reason for not coming, and the corresponding effect on him was one of desperation. He told her that he would come, after all; that he would go over to San Francisco, to the *Transcontinental* office, collect the five dollars due him, and with it redeem his suit of clothes.

In the morning he borrowed ten cents from Maria. He would have borrowed it, by preference, from Brissenden, but that erratic individual had disappeared. Two weeks had passed since Martin had seen him, and he vainly cudgelled his brains for some cause of offence. The ten cents carried Martin across the ferry to San Francisco, and as he walked up Market Street he speculated upon his predicament in case he failed to collect the money. There would then be no way for him to return to Oakland, and he knew no one in San Francisco from whom to borrow another ten cents.

The door to the *Transcontinental* office was ajar, and Martin, in the act of opening it, was brought to a sudden pause by a loud voice from within, which exclaimed:—

"But that is not the question, Mr. Ford." (Ford, Martin knew, from his correspondence, to be the editor's name.) "The question is, are you prepared to pay?—cash, and cash down, I mean? I am not interested in the prospects of the *Transcontinental* and what you expect to make it next year. What I want is to be paid for what I do. And I tell you, right now, the Christmas *Transcontinental* don't go to press till I have the money in my hand. Good day. When you get the money, come and see me."

The door jerked open, and the man flung past Martin with an angry countenance and went down the corridor, muttering curses and clenching his fists. Martin decided not to enter immediately, and lingered in the hallways for a quarter of an hour. Then he shoved the door open and walked in. It was a new experience, the first time he had been inside an editorial office. Cards evidently were not necessary in that office, for the boy carried word to an inner room that there was a man who wanted to see Mr. Ford. Returning, the boy beckoned him from halfway across the room and led him to the private office, the editorial sanctum. Martin's first impression was of the disorder and cluttered confusion of the room. Next he noticed a bewhiskered, youthful-looking man, sitting at a roll-top desk, who regarded him curiously. Martin marvelled at the calm repose of his face. It was evident that the squabble with the printer had not affected his equanimity.

"I—I am Martin Eden," Martin began the conversation. ("And I want my five dollars," was what he would have liked to say.)

But this was his first editor, and under the circumstances he did not desire to scare him too abruptly. To his surprise, Mr. Ford leaped into the air with a "You don't say so!" and the next moment, with both hands, was shaking Martin's hand effusively.

"Can't say how glad I am to see you, Mr. Eden. Often wondered what you were like."

Here he held Martin off at arm's length and ran his beaming eyes over Martin's second-best suit, which was also his worst suit, and which was ragged and past repair, though the trousers showed the careful crease he had put in with Maria's flat-irons.

"I confess, though, I conceived you to be a much older man than you are. Your story, you know, showed such breadth, and vigor, such maturity and depth of thought. A masterpiece, that story—I knew it when I had read the first half-dozen lines. Let me tell you how I first read it. But no; first let me introduce you to the staff."

Still talking, Mr. Ford led him into the general office, where he introduced him to the associate editor, Mr. White, a slender, frail little man whose hand seemed strangely cold, as if he were suffering from a chill, and whose whiskers were sparse and silky.

"And Mr. Ends, Mr. Eden. Mr. Ends is our business manager, you know."

Martin found himself shaking hands with a cranky-eyed,

bald-headed man, whose face looked youthful enough from
what little could be seen of it, for most of it was covered by
a snow-white beard, carefully trimmed—by his wife, who did
it on Sundays, at which times she also shaved the back of his
neck.

The three men surrounded Martin, all talking admiringly
and at once, until it seemed to him that they were talking
against time for a wager.

"We often wondered why you didn't call," Mr. White was
saying.

"I didn't have the carfare, and I live across the Bay," Martin
answered bluntly, with the idea of showing them his imperative need for the money.

Surely, he thought to himself, my glad rags in themselves
are eloquent advertisement of my need. Time and again,
whenever opportunity offered, he hinted about the purpose
of his business. But his admirers' ears were deaf. They sang
his praises, told him what they had thought of his story at
first sight, what they subsequently thought, what their wives
and families thought; but not one hint did they breathe of
intention to pay him for it.

"Did I tell you how I first read your story?" Mr. Ford said.
"Of course I didn't. I was coming west from New York, and
when the train stopped at Ogden, the train-boy on the new
run brought aboard the current number of the *Transcontinental*."

My God! Martin thought; you can travel in a Pullman
while I starve for the paltry five dollars you owe me. A
wave of anger rushed over him. The wrong done him by
the *Transcontinental* loomed colossal, for strong upon him
were all the dreary months of vain yearning, of hunger and
privation, and his present hunger awoke and gnawed at
him, reminding him that he had eaten nothing since the
day before, and little enough then. For the moment he saw
red. These creatures were not even robbers. They were
sneak-thieves. By lies and broken promises they had tricked
him out of his story. Well, he would show them. And a
great resolve surged into his will to the effect that he
would not leave the office until he got his money. He remembered, if he did not get it, that there was no way for

him to go back to Oakland. He controlled himself with an effort, but not before the wolfish expression of his face had awed and perturbed them.

They became more voluble than ever. Mr. Ford started anew to tell how he had first read "The Ring of Bells," and Mr. Ends at the same time was striving to repeat his niece's appreciation of "The Ring of Bells," said niece being a school-teacher in Alameda.

"I'll tell you what I came for," Martin said finally. "To be paid for that story all of you like so well. Five dollars, I believe, is what you promised me would be paid on publication."

Mr. Ford, with an expression on his mobile features of immediate and happy acquiescence, started to reach for his pocket, then turned suddenly to Mr. Ends, and said that he had left his money home. That Mr. Ends resented this, was patent; and Martin saw the twitch of his arm as if to protect his trousers pocket. Martin knew that the money was there.

"I am sorry," said Mr. Ends, "but I paid the printer not an hour ago, and he took my ready change. It was careless of me to be so short; but the bill was not yet due, and the printer's request, as a favor, to make an immediate advance, was quite unexpected."

Both men looked expectantly at Mr. White, but that gentleman laughed and shrugged his shoulders. His conscience was clean at any rate. He had come into the *Transcontinental* to learn magazine-literature, instead of which he had principally learned finance. The *Transcontinental* owed him four months' salary, and he knew that the printer must be appeased before the associate editor.

"It's rather absurd, Mr. Eden, to have caught us in this shape," Mr. Ford preambled airily. "All carelessness, I assure you. But I'll tell you what we'll do. We'll mail you a check the first thing in the morning. You have Mr. Eden's address, haven't you, Mr. Ends?"

Yes, Mr. Ends had the address, and the check would be mailed the first thing in the morning. Martin's knowledge of banks and checks was hazy, but he could see no reason why they should not give him the check on this day just as well as on the next.

"Then it is understood, Mr. Eden, that we'll mail you the check to-morrow?" Mr. Ford said.

"I need the money to-day," Martin answered stolidly.

"The unfortunate circumstances—if you had chanced here any other day," Mr. Ford began suavely, only to be interrupted by Mr. Ends, whose cranky eyes justified themselves in his shortness of temper.

"Mr. Ford has already explained the situation," he said with asperity. "And so have I. The check will be mailed—"

"I also have explained," Martin broke in, "and I have explained that I want the money to-day."

He had felt his pulse quicken a trifle at the business manager's brusqueness, and upon him he kept an alert eye, for it was in that gentleman's trousers pocket that he divined the *Transcontinental's* ready cash was reposing.

"It is too bad—" Mr. Ford began.

But at that moment, with an impatient movement, Mr. Ends turned as if about to leave the room. At the same instant Martin sprang for him, clutching him by the throat with one hand in such fashion that Mr. Ends' snow-white beard, still maintaining its immaculate trimness, pointed ceilingward at an angle of forty-five degrees. To the horror of Mr. White and Mr. Ford, they saw their business manager shaken like an Astrakhan rug.

"Dig up, you venerable discourager of rising young talent!" Martin exhorted. "Dig up, or I'll shake it out of you, even if it's all in nickels." Then, to the two affrighted onlookers: "Keep away! If you interfere, somebody's liable to get hurt."

Mr. Ends was choking, and it was not until the grip on his throat was eased that he was able to signify his acquiescence in the digging-up programme. All together, after repeated digs, his trousers pocket yielded four dollars and fifteen cents.

"Inside out with it," Martin commanded.

An additional ten cents fell out. Martin counted the result of his raid a second time to make sure.

"You next!" he shouted at Mr. Ford. "I want seventy-five cents more."

Mr. Ford did not wait, but ransacked his pockets, with the result of sixty cents.

"Sure that is all?" Martin demanded menacingly, possessing himself of it. "What have you got in your vest pockets?"

In token of his good faith, Mr. Ford turned two of his pockets inside out. A strip of cardboard fell to the floor from one of them. He recovered it and was in the act of returning it, when Martin cried:—

"What's that?—A ferry ticket? Here, give it to me. It's worth ten cents. I'll credit you with it. I've now got four dollars and ninety-five cents, including the ticket. Five cents is still due me."

He looked fiercely at Mr. White, and found that fragile creature in the act of handing him a nickel.

"Thank you," Martin said, addressing them collectively. "I wish you a good day."

"Robber!" Mr. Ends snarled after him.

"Sneak-thief!" Martin retorted, slamming the door as he passed out.

Martin was elated—so elated that when he recollected that *The Hornet* owed him fifteen dollars for "The Peri and the Pearl," he decided forthwith to go and collect it. But *The Hornet* was run by a set of clean-shaven, strapping young men, frank buccaneers who robbed everything and everybody, not excepting one another. After some breakage of the office furniture, the editor (an ex-college athlete), ably assisted by the business manager, an advertising agent, and the porter, succeeded in removing Martin from the office and in accelerating, by initial impulse, his descent of the first flight of stairs.

"Come again, Mr. Eden; glad to see you any time," they laughed down at him from the landing above.

Martin grinned as he picked himself up.

"Phew!" he murmured back. "The *Transcontinental* crowd were nanny-goats, but you fellows are a lot of prize-fighters."

More laughter greeted this.

"I must say, Mr. Eden," the editor of *The Hornet* called down, "that for a poet you can go some yourself. Where did you learn that right cross—if I may ask?"

"Where you learned that half-Nelson," Martin answered. "Anyway, you're going to have a black eye."

"I hope your neck doesn't stiffen up," the editor wished

solicitously. "What do you say we all go out and have a drink on it—not the neck, of course, but the little rough-house?"

"I'll go you if I lose," Martin accepted.

And robbers and robbed drank together, amicably agreeing that the battle was to the strong, and that the fifteen dollars for "The Peri and the Pearl" belonged by right to *The Hornet's* editorial staff.

Chapter XXXIV

Arthur remained at the gate while Ruth climbed Maria's front steps. She heard the rapid click of the type-writer, and when Martin let her in, found him on the last page of a manuscript. She had come to make certain whether or not he would be at their table for Thanksgiving dinner; but before she could broach the subject Martin plunged into the one with which he was full.

"Here, let me read you this," he cried, separating the carbon copies and running the pages of manuscript into shape. "It's my latest, and different from anything I've done. It is so altogether different that I am almost afraid of it, and yet I've a sneaking idea it is good. You be judge. It's an Hawaiian story. I've called it 'Wiki-Wiki.' "

His face was bright with the creative glow, though she shivered in the cold room and had been struck by the coldness of his hands at greeting. She listened closely while he read, and though he from time to time had seen only disapprobation in her face, at the close he asked:—

"Frankly, what do you think of it?"

"I—I don't know," she answered. "Will it—do you think it will sell?"

"I'm afraid not," was the confession. "It's too strong for the magazines. But it's true, on my word it's true."

"But why do you persist in writing such things when you know they won't sell?" she went on inexorably. "The reason for your writing is to make a living, isn't it?"

"Yes, that's right; but the miserable story got away with me. I couldn't help writing it. It demanded to be written."

"But that character, that Wiki-Wiki, why do you make him talk so roughly? Surely it will offend your readers, and surely that is why the editors are justified in refusing your work."

"Because the real Wiki-Wiki would have talked that way."

"But it is not good taste."

"It is life," he replied bluntly. "It is real. It is true. And I must write life as I see it."

She made no answer, and for an awkward moment they sat

silent. It was because he loved her that he did not quite understand her, and she could not understand him because he was so large that he bulked beyond her horizon.

"Well, I've collected from the *Transcontinental*," he said in an effort to shift the conversation to a more comfortable subject. The picture of the bewhiskered trio, as he had last seen them, mulcted of four dollars and ninety cents and a ferry ticket, made him chuckle.

"Then you'll come!" she cried joyously. "That was what I came to find out."

"Come?" he muttered absently. "Where?"

"Why, to dinner to-morrow. You know you said you'd recover your suit if you got that money."

"I forgot all about it," he said humbly. "You see, this morning the poundman got Maria's two cows and the baby calf, and—well, it happened that Maria didn't have any money, and so I had to recover her cows for her. That's where the *Transcontinental* fiver went—'The Ring of Bells' went into the poundman's pocket."

"Then you won't come?"

He looked down at his clothing.

"I can't."

Tears of disappointment and reproach glistened in her blue eyes, but she said nothing.

"Next Thanksgiving you'll have dinner with me in Delmonico's," he said cheerily; "or in London, or Paris, or anywhere you wish. I know it."

"I saw in the paper a few days ago," she announced abruptly, "that there had been several local appointments to the Railway Mail. You passed first, didn't you?"

He was compelled to admit that the call had come for him, but that he had declined it. "I was so sure—I am so sure—of myself," he concluded. "A year from now I'll be earning more than a dozen men in the Railway Mail. You wait and see."

"Oh," was all she said, when he finished. She stood up, pulling at her gloves. "I must go, Martin. Arthur is waiting for me."

He took her in his arms and kissed her, but she proved a passive sweetheart. There was no tenseness in her body, her arms did not go around him, and her lips met his without their wonted pressure.

She was angry with him, he concluded, as he returned from the gate. But why? It was unfortunate that the poundman had gobbled Maria's cows. But it was only a stroke of fate. Nobody could be blamed for it. Nor did it enter his head that he could have done aught otherwise than what he had done. Well, yes, he was to blame a little, was his next thought, for having refused the call to the Railway Mail. And she had not liked "Wiki-Wiki."

He turned at the head of the steps to meet the letter-carrier on his afternoon round. The ever recurrent fever of expectancy assailed Martin as he took the bundle of long envelopes. One was not long. It was short and thin, and outside was printed the address of *The New York Outview*. He paused in the act of tearing the envelope open. It could not be an acceptance. He had no manuscripts with that publication. Perhaps—his heart almost stood still at the wild thought— perhaps they were ordering an article from him; but the next instant he dismissed the surmise as hopelessly impossible.

It was a short, formal letter, signed by the office editor, merely informing him that an anonymous letter which they had received was enclosed, and that he could rest assured the *Outview's* staff never under any circumstances gave consideration to anonymous correspondence.

The enclosed letter Martin found to be crudely printed by hand. It was a hotchpotch of illiterate abuse of Martin, and of assertion that the "so-called Martin Eden" who was selling stories to magazines was no writer at all, and that in reality he was stealing stories from old magazines, typing them, and sending them out as his own. The envelope was postmarked "San Leandro." Martin did not require a second thought to discover the author. Higginbotham's grammar, Higginbotham's colloquialisms, Higginbotham's mental quirks and processes, were apparent throughout. Martin saw in every line, not the fine Italian hand, but the coarse grocer's fist, of his brother-in-law.

But why? he vainly questioned. What injury had he done Bernard Higginbotham? The thing was so unreasonable, so wanton. There was no explaining it. In the course of the week a dozen similar letters were forwarded to Martin by the editors of various Eastern magazines. The editors were behaving handsomely, Martin concluded. He was wholly unknown to them, yet some of them had even been sympathetic. It was evident that they detested anonymity. He saw that the malicious attempt to hurt him had failed. In fact, if anything came of it, it was bound to be good, for at least his name had been called to the attention of a number of editors. Sometime, perhaps, reading a submitted manuscript of his, they might remember him as the fellow about whom they had received an anonymous letter. And who was to say that such a remembrance might not sway the balance of their judgment just a trifle in his favor?

It was about this time that Martin took a great slump in Maria's estimation. He found her in the kitchen one morning, groaning with pain, tears of weakness running down her cheeks, vainly endeavoring to put through a large ironing. He promptly diagnosed her affliction as La Grippe, dosed her with hot whiskey (the remnants in the bottles for which Brissenden was responsible), and ordered her to bed. But Maria was refractory. The ironing had to be done, she protested, and delivered that night, or else there would be no food on the morrow for the seven small and hungry Silvas.

To her astonishment (and it was something that she never ceased from relating to her dying day), she saw Martin Eden seize an iron from the stove and throw a fancy shirt-waist on the ironing-board. It was Kate Flanagan's best Sunday waist, than whom there was no more exacting and fastidiously dressed woman in Maria's world. Also, Miss Flanagan had sent special instruction that said waist must be delivered by that night. As every one knew, she was keeping company with John Collins, the blacksmith, and, as Maria knew privily, Miss Flanagan and Mr. Collins were going next day to Golden Gate Park. Vain was Maria's attempt to rescue the garment. Martin guided her tottering footsteps to a chair, from where she watched him with bulging eyes. In a quarter of the time it would have taken her she saw the shirt-waist safely ironed, and ironed as well as she could have done it, as Martin made her grant.

"I could work faster," he explained, "if your irons were only hotter."

To her, the irons he swung were much hotter than she ever dared to use.

"Your sprinkling is all wrong," he complained next. "Here, let me teach you how to sprinkle. Pressure is what's wanted. Sprinkle under pressure if you want to iron fast."

He procured a packing-case from the woodpile in the cellar, fitted a cover to it, and raided the scrap-iron the Silva tribe was collecting for the junkman. With fresh-sprinkled garments in the box, covered with the board and pressed by the iron, the device was complete and in operation.

"Now you watch me, Maria," he said, stripping off to his undershirt and gripping an iron that was what he called "really hot."

"An' when he feenish da iron' he washa da wools," as she described it afterward. "He say, 'Maria, you are da greata fool. I showa you how to washa da wools,' an' he showa me, too. Ten minutes he maka da machine—one barrel, one wheel-hub, two poles, justa like dat."

Martin had learned the contrivance from Joe at the Shelly Hot Springs. The old wheel-hub, fixed on the end of the upright pole, constituted the plunger. Making this, in turn, fast to the spring-pole attached to the kitchen rafters, so that the hub played upon the woollens in the barrel, he was able, with one hand, thoroughly to pound them.

"No more Maria washa da wools," her story always ended. "I maka da kids worka da pole an' da hub an' da barrel. Him da smarta man, Mister Eden."

Nevertheless, by his masterly operation and improvement of her kitchen-laundry, he fell an immense distance in her regard. The glamour of romance with which her imagination had invested him faded away in the cold light of fact that he was an ex-laundryman. All his books, and his grand friends who visited him in carriages or with countless bottles of whiskey, went for naught. He was, after all, a mere workingman, a member of her own class and caste. He was more human and approachable, but he was no longer mystery.

Martin's alienation from his family continued. Following

upon Mr. Higginbotham's unprovoked attack, Mr. Hermann von Schmidt showed his hand. The fortunate sale of several storiettes, some humorous verse, and a few jokes gave Martin a temporary splurge of prosperity. Not only did he partially pay up his bills, but he had sufficient balance left to redeem his black suit and wheel. The latter, by virtue of a twisted crank-hanger, required repairing, and, as a matter of friendliness with his future brother-in-law, he sent it to Von Schmidt's shop.

The afternoon of the same day Martin was pleased by the wheel being delivered by a small boy. Von Schmidt was also inclined to be friendly, was Martin's conclusion from this unusual favor. Repaired wheels usually had to be called for. But when he examined the wheel, he discovered no repairs had been made. A little later in the day he telephoned his sister's betrothed, and learned that that person didn't want anything to do with him in "any shape, manner, or form."

"Hermann von Schmidt," Martin answered cheerfully, "I've a good mind to come over and punch that Dutch nose of yours."

"You come to my shop," came the reply, "an' I'll send for the police. An' I'll put you through, too. Oh, I know you, but you can't make no rough-house with me. I don't want nothin' to do with the likes of you. You're a loafer, that's what, an' I ain't asleep. You ain't goin' to do no spongin' off me just because I'm marryin' your sister. Why don't you go to work an' earn an honest livin', eh? Answer me that."

Martin's philosophy asserted itself, dissipating his anger, and he hung up the receiver with a long whistle of incredulous amusement. But after the amusement came the reaction, and he was oppressed by his loneliness. Nobody understood him, nobody seemed to have any use for him, except Brissenden, and Brissenden had disappeared, God alone knew where.

Twilight was falling as Martin left the fruit store and turned homeward, his marketing on his arm. At the corner an electric car had stopped, and at sight of a lean, familiar figure alighting, his heart leapt with joy. It was Brissenden, and in the fleeting glimpse, ere the car started up, Martin noted the overcoat pockets, one bulging with books, the other bulging with a quart bottle of whiskey.

Chapter XXXV

B RISSENDEN gave no explanation of his long absence, nor did Martin pry into it. He was content to see his friend's cadaverous face opposite him through the steam rising from a tumbler of toddy.

"I, too, have not been idle," Brissenden proclaimed, after hearing Martin's account of the work he had accomplished.

He pulled a manuscript from his inside coat pocket and passed it to Martin, who looked at the title and glanced up curiously.

"Yes, that's it," Brissenden laughed. "Pretty good title, eh? 'Ephemera'—it is the one word. And you're responsible for it, what of your *man*, who is always the erected, the vitalized inorganic, the latest of the ephemera, the creature of temperature strutting his little space on the thermometer. It got into my head and I had to write it to get rid of it. Tell me what you think of it."

Martin's face, flushed at first, paled as he read on. It was perfect art. Form triumphed over substance, if triumph it could be called where the last conceivable atom of substance had found expression in so perfect construction as to make Martin's head swim with delight, to put passionate tears into his eyes, and to send chills creeping up and down his back. It was a long poem of six or seven hundred lines, and it was a fantastic, amazing, unearthly thing. It was terrific, impossible; and yet there it was, scrawled in black ink across the sheets of paper. It dealt with man and his soul-gropings in their ultimate terms, plumbing the abysses of space for the testimony of remotest suns and rainbow spectrums. It was a mad orgy of imagination, wassailing in the skull of a dying man who half sobbed under his breath and was quick with the wild flutter of fading heart-beats. The poem swung in majestic rhythm to the cool tumult of interstellar conflict, to the onset of starry hosts, to the impact of cold suns and the flaming up of nebulæ in the darkened void; and through it all, unceasing and faint, like a silver shuttle, ran the frail, piping voice of man, a querulous chirp amid the screaming of planets and the crash of systems.

"There is nothing like it in literature," Martin said, when at last he was able to speak. "It's wonderful!—wonderful! It has gone to my head. I am drunken with it. That great, infinitesimal question—I can't shake it out of my thoughts. That questing, eternal, ever recurring, thin little wailing voice of man is still ringing in my ears. It is like the dead-march of a gnat amid the trumpeting of elephants and the roaring of lions. It is insatiable with microscopic desire. I know I'm making a fool of myself, but the thing has obsessed me. You are—I don't know what you are—you are wonderful, that's all. But how do you do it? How do you do it?"

Martin paused from his rhapsody, only to break out afresh.

"I shall never write again. I am a dauber in clay. You have shown me the work of the real artificer-artisan. Genius! This is something more than genius. It transcends genius. It is truth gone mad. It is true, man, every line of it. I wonder if you realize that, you dogmatist. Science cannot give you the lie. It is the truth of the sneer, stamped out from the black iron of the Cosmos and interwoven with mighty rhythms of sound into a fabric of splendor and beauty. And now I won't say another word. I am overwhelmed, crushed. Yes, I will, too. Let me market it for you."

Brissenden grinned. "There's not a magazine in Christendom that would dare to publish it—you know that."

"I know nothing of the sort. I know there's not a magazine in Christendom that wouldn't jump at it. They don't get things like that every day. That's no mere poem of the year. It's the poem of the century."

"I'd like to take you up on the proposition."

"Now don't get cynical," Martin exhorted. "The magazine editors are not wholly fatuous. I know that. And I'll close with you on the bet. I'll wager anything you want that 'Ephemera' is accepted either on the first or second offering."

"There's just one thing that prevents me from taking you." Brissenden waited a moment. "The thing is big—the biggest I've ever done. I know that. It's my swan song. I am almighty proud of it. I worship it. It's better than whiskey. It is what I dreamed of—the great and perfect thing—when I was a simple young man, with sweet illusions and clean ideals. And I've got it, now, in my last grasp, and I'll not have it pawed over and soiled by a lot of swine. No, I won't take the bet. It's mine. I made it, and I've shared it with you."

"But think of the rest of the world," Martin protested. "The function of beauty is joy-making."

"It's my beauty."

"Don't be selfish."

"I'm not selfish." Brissenden grinned soberly in the way he had when pleased by the thing his thin lips were about to shape. "I'm as unselfish as a famished hog."

In vain Martin strove to shake him from his decision. Martin told him that his hatred of the magazines was rabid, fanatical, and that his conduct was a thousand times more despicable than that of the youth who burned the temple of Diana at Ephesus. Under the storm of denunciation Brissenden complacently sipped his toddy and affirmed that everything the other said was quite true, with the exception of the magazine editors. His hatred of them knew no bounds, and he excelled Martin in denunciation when he turned upon them.

"I wish you'd type it for me," he said. "You know how a thousand times better than any stenographer. And now I want to give you some advice." He drew a bulky manuscript from his outside coat pocket. "Here's your 'Shame of the Sun.' I've read it not once, but twice and three times—the highest compliment I can pay you. After what you've said about 'Ephemera' I must be silent. But this I will say: when 'The Shame of the Sun' is published, it will make a hit. It will start a controversy that will be worth thousands to you just in advertising."

Martin laughed. "I suppose your next advice will be to submit it to the magazines."

"By all means no—that is, if you want to see it in print. Offer it to the first-class houses. Some publisher's reader may be mad enough or drunk enough to report favorably on it. You've read the books. The meat of them has been transmuted in the alembic of Martin Eden's mind and poured into 'The Shame of the Sun,' and one day Martin Eden will be famous, and not the least of his fame will rest upon that work. So you must get a publisher for it—the sooner the better."

Brissenden went home late that night; and just as he mounted the first step of the car, he swung suddenly back on Martin and thrust into his hand a small, tightly crumpled wad of paper.

"Here, take this," he said. "I was out to the races to-day, and I had the right dope."

The bell clanged and the car pulled out, leaving Martin wondering as to the nature of the crinkly, greasy wad he clutched in his hand. Back in his room he unrolled it and found a hundred-dollar bill.

He did not scruple to use it. He knew his friend had always plenty of money, and he knew also, with profound certitude, that his success would enable him to repay it. In the morning he paid every bill, gave Maria three months' advance on the room, and redeemed every pledge at the pawnshop. Next he bought Marian's wedding present, and simpler presents, suitable to Christmas, for Ruth and Gertrude. And finally, on the balance remaining to him, he herded the whole Silva tribe down into Oakland. He was a winter late in redeeming his promise, but redeemed it was, for the last, least Silva got a pair of shoes, as well as Maria herself. Also, there were horns, and dolls, and toys of various sorts, and parcels and bundles of candies and nuts that filled the arms of all the Silvas to overflowing.

It was with this extraordinary procession trooping at his and Maria's heels into a confectioner's in quest of the biggest candy-cane ever made, that he encountered Ruth and her mother. Mrs. Morse was shocked. Even Ruth was hurt, for she had some regard for appearances, and her lover, cheek by jowl with Maria, at the head of that army of Portuguese ragamuffins, was not a pretty sight. But it was not that which hurt so much as what she took to be his lack of pride and self-respect. Further, and keenest of all, she read into the incident the impossibility of his living down his working-class origin. There was stigma enough in the fact of it, but shamelessly to flaunt it in the face of the world—her world—was going too far. Though her engagement to Martin had been kept secret, their long intimacy had not been unproductive of

gossip; and in the shop, glancing covertly at her lover and his
following, had been several of her acquaintances. She lacked
the easy largeness of Martin and could not rise superior to
her environment. She had been hurt to the quick, and her
sensitive nature was quivering with the shame of it. So it was,
when Martin arrived later in the day, that he kept her present
in his breast-pocket, deferring the giving of it to a more propitious occasion. Ruth in tears—passionate, angry tears—
was a revelation to him. The spectacle of her suffering convinced him that he had been a brute, yet in the soul of him
he could not see how nor why. It never entered his head to
be ashamed of those he knew, and to take the Silvas out to a
Christmas treat could in no way, so it seemed to him, show
lack of consideration for Ruth. On the other hand, he did see
Ruth's point of view, after she had explained it; and he
looked upon it as a feminine weakness, such as afflicted all
women and the best of women.

Chapter XXXVI

"COME ON,—I'll show you the real dirt," Brissenden said to him, one evening in January.

They had dined together in San Francisco, and were at the Ferry Building, returning to Oakland, when the whim came to him to show Martin the "real dirt." He turned and fled across the water-front, a meagre shadow in a flapping over-coat, with Martin straining to keep up with him. At a whole-sale liquor store he bought two gallon-demijohns of old port, and with one in each hand boarded a Mission Street car, Martin at his heels burdened with several quart-bottles of whiskey.

If Ruth could see me now, was his thought, while he won-dered as to what constituted the real dirt.

"Maybe nobody will be there," Brissenden said, when they dismounted and plunged off to the right into the heart of the working-class ghetto, south of Market Street. "In which case you'll miss what you've been looking for so long."

"And what the deuce is that?" Martin asked.

"Men, intelligent men, and not the gibbering nonentities I found you consorting with in that trader's den. You read the books and you found yourself all alone. Well, I'm going to show you to-night some other men who've read the books, so that you won't be lonely any more.

"Not that I bother my head about their everlasting discus-sions," he said at the end of a block. "I'm not interested in book philosophy. But you'll find these fellows intelligences and not bourgeois swine. But watch out, they'll talk an arm off of you on any subject under the sun.

"Hope Norton's there," he panted a little later, resisting Martin's effort to relieve him of the two demijohns. "Nor-ton's an idealist—a Harvard man. Prodigious memory. Ide-alism led him to philosophic anarchy, and his family threw him off. Father's a railroad president and many times million-naire, but the son's starving in 'Frisco, editing an anarchist sheet for twenty-five a month."

Martin was little acquainted in San Francisco, and not at

all south of Market; so he had no idea of where he was being led.

"Go ahead," he said; "tell me about them beforehand. What do they do for a living? How do they happen to be here?"

"Hope Hamilton's there." Brissenden paused and rested his hands. "Strawn-Hamilton's his name—hyphenated, you know—comes of old Southern stock. He's a tramp—laziest man I ever knew, though he's clerking, or trying to, in a socialist coöperative store for six dollars a week. But he's a confirmed hobo. Tramped into town. I've seen him sit all day on a bench and never a bite pass his lips, and in the evening, when I invited him to dinner—restaurant two blocks away— have him say, 'Too much trouble, old man. Buy me a package of cigarettes instead.' He was a Spencerian like you till Kreis turned him to materialistic monism. I'll start him on monism if I can. Norton's another monist—only he affirms naught but spirit. He can give Kreis and Hamilton all they want, too."

"Who is Kreis?" Martin asked.

"His rooms we're going to. One time professor—fired from university—usual story. A mind like a steel trap. Makes his living any old way. I know he's been a street fakir when he was down. Unscrupulous. Rob a corpse of a shroud—anything. Difference between him and the bourgeoisie is that he robs without illusion. He'll talk Nietzsche, or Schopenhauer, or Kant, or anything, but the only thing in this world, not excepting Mary, that he really cares for, is his monism. Haeckel is his little tin god. The only way to insult him is to take a slap at Haeckel.

"Here's the hang-out." Brissenden rested his demijohn at the upstairs entrance, preliminary to the climb. It was the usual two-story corner building, with a saloon and grocery underneath. "The gang lives here—got the whole upstairs to themselves. But Kreis is the only one who has two rooms. Come on."

No lights burned in the upper hall, but Brissenden threaded the utter blackness like a familiar ghost. He stopped to speak to Martin.

"There's one fellow—Stevens—a theosophist. Makes a

pretty tangle when he gets going. Just now he's dish-washer
in a restaurant. Likes a good cigar. I've seen him eat in a ten-
cent hash-house and pay fifty cents for the cigar he smoked
afterward. I've got a couple in my pocket for him, if he shows
up.

"And there's another fellow—Parry—an Australian, a stat-
istician and a sporting encyclopædia. Ask him the grain output of Paraguay for 1903, or the English importation of
sheetings into China for 1890, or at what weight Jimmy Britt
fought Battling Nelson, or who was welter-weight champion
of the United States in '68, and you'll get the correct answer
with the automatic celerity of a slot-machine. And there's
Andy, a stone-mason, has ideas on everything, a good chess-
player; and another fellow, Harry, a baker, red hot socialist
and strong union man. By the way, you remember the Cooks'
and Waiters' strike—Hamilton was the chap who organized
that union and precipitated the strike—planned it all out in
advance, right here in Kreis's rooms. Did it just for the fun
of it, but was too lazy to stay by the union. Yet he could have
risen high if he wanted to. There's no end to the possibilities
in that man—if he weren't so insuperably lazy."

Brissenden advanced through the darkness till a thread of
light marked the threshold of a door. A knock and an answer
opened it, and Martin found himself shaking hands with
Kreis, a handsome brunette man, with dazzling white teeth,
a drooping black mustache, and large, flashing black eyes.
Mary, a matronly young blonde, was washing dishes in the
little back room that served for kitchen and dining room. The
front room served as bedchamber and living room. Overhead
was the week's washing, hanging in festoons so low that Martin did not see at first the two men talking in a corner. They
hailed Brissenden and his demijohns with acclamation, and,
on being introduced, Martin learned they were Andy and
Parry. He joined them and listened attentively to the description of a prize-fight Parry had seen the night before; while
Brissenden, in his glory, plunged into the manufacture of a
toddy and the serving of wine and whiskey-and-sodas. At his
command, "Bring in the clan," Andy departed to go the
round of the rooms for the lodgers.

"We're lucky that most of them are here," Brissenden whispered to Martin. "There's Norton and Hamilton; come on and meet them. Stevens isn't around, I hear. I'm going to get them started on monism if I can. Wait till they get a few jolts in them and they'll warm up."

At first the conversation was desultory. Nevertheless Martin could not fail to appreciate the keen play of their minds. They were men with opinions, though the opinions often clashed, and, though they were witty and clever, they were not superficial. He swiftly saw, no matter upon what they talked, that each man applied the correlation of knowledge and had also a deep-seated and unified conception of society and the Cosmos. Nobody manufactured their opinions for them; they were all rebels of one variety or another, and their lips were strangers to platitudes. Never had Martin, at the Morses', heard so amazing a range of topics discussed. There seemed no limit save time to the things they were alive to. The talk wandered from Mrs. Humphry Ward's new book to Shaw's latest play, through the future of the drama to reminiscences of Mansfield. They appreciated or sneered at the morning editorials, jumped from labor conditions in New Zealand to Henry James and Brander Matthews, passed on to the German designs in the Far East and the economic aspect of the Yellow Peril, wrangled over the German elections and Bebel's last speech, and settled down to local politics, the latest plans and scandals in the union labor party administration, and the wires that were pulled to bring about the Coast Seamen's strike. Martin was struck by the inside knowledge they possessed. They knew what was never printed in the newspapers—the wires and strings and the hidden hands that made the puppets dance. To Martin's surprise, the girl, Mary, joined in the conversation, displaying an intelligence he had never encountered in the few women he had met. They talked together on Swinburne and Rossetti, after which she led him beyond his depth into the by-paths of French literature. His revenge came when she defended Maeterlinck and he brought into action the carefully-thought-out thesis of "The Shame of the Sun."

Several other men had dropped in, and the air was thick with tobacco smoke, when Brissenden waved the red flag.

"Here's fresh meat for your axe, Kreis," he said; "a rose-white youth with the ardor of a lover for Herbert Spencer. Make a Haeckelite of him—if you can."

Kreis seemed to wake up and flash like some metallic, magnetic thing, while Norton looked at Martin sympathetically, with a sweet, girlish smile, as much as to say that he would be amply protected.

Kreis began directly on Martin, but step by step Norton interfered, until he and Kreis were off and away in a personal battle. Martin listened and fain would have rubbed his eyes. It was impossible that this should be, much less in the labor ghetto south of Market. The books were alive in these men. They talked with fire and enthusiasm, the intellectual stimulant stirring them as he had seen drink and anger stir other men. What he heard was no longer the philosophy of the dry, printed word, written by half-mythical demigods like Kant and Spencer. It was living philosophy, with warm, red blood, incarnated in these two men till its very features worked with excitement. Now and again other men joined in, and all followed the discussion with cigarettes going out in their hands and with alert, intent faces.

Idealism had never attracted Martin, but the exposition it now received at the hands of Norton was a revelation. The logical plausibility of it, that made an appeal to his intellect, seemed missed by Kreis and Hamilton, who sneered at Norton as a metaphysician, and who, in turn, sneered back at them as metaphysicians. *Phenomenon* and *noumenon* were bandied back and forth. They charged him with attempting to explain consciousness by itself. He charged them with word-jugglery, with reasoning from words to theory instead of from facts to theory. At this they were aghast. It was the cardinal tenet of their mode of reasoning to start with facts and to give names to the facts.

When Norton wandered into the intricacies of Kant, Kreis reminded him that all good little German philosophies when they died went to Oxford. A little later Norton reminded them of Hamilton's Law of Parsimony, the application of which they immediately claimed for every reasoning process of theirs. And Martin hugged his knees and exulted in it all. But Norton was no Spencerian, and he, too, strove for Martin's philosophic soul, talking as much at him as to his two opponents.

"You know Berkeley has never been answered," he said, looking directly at Martin. "Herbert Spencer came the nearest, which was not very near. Even the stanchest of Spencer's followers will not go farther. I was reading an essay of Saleeby's the other day, and the best Saleeby could say was that Herbert Spencer *nearly* succeeded in answering Berkeley."

"You know what Hume said?" Hamilton asked. Norton nodded, but Hamilton gave it for the benefit of the rest. "He said that Berkeley's arguments admit of no answer and produce no conviction."

"In his, Hume's, mind," was the reply. "And Hume's mind was the same as yours, with this difference: he was wise enough to admit there was no answering Berkeley."

Norton was sensitive and excitable, though he never lost his head, while Kreis and Hamilton were like a pair of cold-blooded savages, seeking out tender places to prod and poke. As the evening grew late, Norton, smarting under the repeated charges of being a metaphysician, clutching his chair to keep from jumping to his feet, his gray eyes snapping and his girlish face grown harsh and sure, made a grand attack upon their position.

"All right, you Haeckelites, I may reason like a medicine man, but, pray, how do you reason? You have nothing to stand on, you unscientific dogmatists with your positive science which you are always lugging about into places it has no right to be. Long before the school of materialistic monism arose, the ground was removed so that there could be no foundation. Locke was the man, John Locke. Two hundred years ago—more than that, even—in his 'Essay concerning the Human Understanding,' he proved the non-existence of innate ideas. The best of it is that that is precisely what you claim. To-night, again and again, you have asserted the non-existence of innate ideas.

"And what does that mean? It means that you can never know ultimate reality. Your brains are empty when you are born. Appearances, or phenomena, are all the content your minds can receive from your five senses. Then noumena, which are not in your minds when you are born, have no way of getting in—"

"I deny—" Kreis started to interrupt.

"You wait till I'm done," Norton shouted. "You can know only that much of the play and interplay of force and matter as impinges in one way or another on your senses. You see, I am willing to admit, for the sake of the argument, that matter exists; and what I am about to do is to efface you by your own argument. I can't do it any other way, for you are both congenitally unable to understand a philosophic abstraction.

"And now, what do you know of matter, according to your own positive science? You know it only by its phenomena, its appearances. You are aware only of its changes, or of such changes in it as cause changes in your consciousness. Positive science deals only with phenomena, yet you are foolish enough to strive to be ontologists and to deal with noumena. Yet, by the very definition of positive science, science is concerned only with appearances. As somebody has said, phenomenal knowledge cannot transcend phenomena.

"You cannot answer Berkeley, even if you have annihilated Kant, and yet, perforce, you assume that Berkeley is wrong when you affirm that science proves the non-existence of God, or, as much to the point, the existence of matter. — You know I granted the reality of matter only in order to make myself intelligible to your understanding. Be positive scientists, if you please; but ontology has no place in positive science, so leave it alone. Spencer is right in his agnosticism, but if Spencer—"

But it was time to catch the last ferry-boat for Oakland, and Brissenden and Martin slipped out, leaving Norton still talking and Kreis and Hamilton waiting to pounce on him like a pair of hounds as soon as he finished.

"You have given me a glimpse of fairyland," Martin said on the ferry-boat. "It makes life worth while to meet people like that. My mind is all worked up. I never appreciated idealism before. Yet I can't accept it. I know that I shall always be a realist. I am so made, I guess. But I'd like to have made a reply to Kreis and Hamilton, and I think I'd have had a word or two for Norton. I didn't see that Spencer was damaged any. I'm as excited as a child on its first visit to the circus. I see I must read up some more. I'm going to get hold of Saleeby. I still think Spencer is unassailable, and next time I'm going to take a hand myself."

But Brissenden, breathing painfully, had dropped off to sleep, his chin buried in a scarf and resting on his sunken chest, his body wrapped in the long overcoat and shaking to the vibration of the propellers.

Chapter XXXVII

THE FIRST THING Martin did next morning was to go counter both to Brissenden's advice and command. "The Shame of the Sun" he wrapped and mailed to *The Acropolis*. He believed he could find magazine publication for it, and he felt that recognition by the magazines would commend him to the book-publishing houses. "Ephemera" he likewise wrapped and mailed to a magazine. Despite Brissenden's prejudice against the magazines, which was a pronounced mania with him, Martin decided that the great poem should see print. He did not intend, however, to publish it without the other's permission. His plan was to get it accepted by one of the high magazines, and, thus armed, again to wrestle with Brissenden for consent.

Martin began, that morning, a story which he had sketched out a number of weeks before and which ever since had been worrying him with its insistent clamor to be created. Apparently it was to be a rattling sea story, a tale of twentieth-century adventure and romance, handling real characters, in a real world, under real conditions. But beneath the swing and go of the story was to be something else—something that the superficial reader would never discern and which, on the other hand, would not diminish in any way the interest and enjoyment for such a reader. It was this, and not the mere story, that impelled Martin to write it. For that matter, it was always the great, universal motif that suggested plots to him. After having found such a motif, he cast about for the particular persons and particular location in time and space wherewith and wherein to utter the universal thing. "Overdue" was the title he had decided for it, and its length he believed would not be more than sixty thousand words—a bagatelle for him with his splendid vigor of production. On this first day he took hold of it with conscious delight in the mastery of his tools. He no longer worried for fear that the sharp, cutting edges should slip and mar his work. The long months of intense application and study had brought their reward. He could now devote himself with sure hand to the larger phases of the thing he shaped; and as he worked, hour after hour, he felt, as never before, the sure and cosmic grasp with which he held life and the affairs of life. "Overdue" would tell a story that would be true of its particular characters and its particular events; but it would tell, too, he was confident, great vital things that would be true of all time, and all sea, and all life—thanks to Herbert Spencer, he thought, leaning back for a moment from the table. Ay, thanks to Herbert Spencer and to the master-key of life, evolution, which Spencer had placed in his hands.

He was conscious that it was great stuff he was writing. "It will go! It will go!" was the refrain that kept sounding in his ears. Of course it would go. At last he was turning out the thing at which the magazines would jump. The whole story worked out before him in lightning flashes. He broke off from it long enough to write a paragraph in his note-book. This would be the last paragraph in "Overdue"; but so thoroughly was the whole book already composed in his brain that he could write, weeks before he had arrived at the end, the end itself. He compared the tale, as yet unwritten, with the tales of the sea-writers, and he felt it to be immeasurably superior. "There's only one man who could touch it," he murmured aloud, "and that's Conrad. And it ought to make even him sit up and shake hands with me, and say, 'Well done, Martin, my boy.'"

He toiled on all day, recollecting, at the last moment, that he was to have dinner at the Morses'. Thanks to Brissenden, his black suit was out of pawn and he was again eligible for dinner parties. Down town he stopped off long enough to run into the library and search for Saleeby's books. He drew out "The Cycle of Life," and on the car turned to the essay Norton had mentioned on Spencer. As Martin read, he grew angry. His face flushed, his jaw set, and unconsciously his hand clenched, unclenched, and clenched again as if he were taking fresh grips upon some hateful thing out of which he was squeezing the life. When he left the car, he strode along the sidewalk as a wrathful man will stride, and he rang the Morse bell with such viciousness that it roused him to consciousness of his condition, so that he entered in good nature, smiling with amusement at himself. No sooner, however, was he inside than a great depression descended upon him. He fell from the height where he had been up-borne all day on the wings of inspiration. "Bourgeois," "trader's den"—Brissenden's epithets repeated themselves in his mind. But what of that? he demanded angrily. He was marrying Ruth, not her family.

It seemed to him that he had never seen Ruth more beautiful, more spiritual and ethereal and at the same time more healthy. There was color in her cheeks, and her eyes drew him again and again—the eyes in which he had first read immortality. He had forgotten immortality of late, and the trend of his scientific reading had been away from it; but here, in Ruth's eyes, he read an argument without words that transcended all worded arguments. He saw that in her eyes before which all discussion fled away, for he saw love there. And in his own eyes was love; and love was unanswerable. Such was his passionate doctrine.

The half hour he had with her, before they went in to dinner, left him supremely happy and supremely satisfied with life. Nevertheless, at table, the inevitable reaction and exhaustion consequent upon the hard day seized hold of him. He was aware that his eyes were tired and that he was irritable. He remembered it was at this table, at which he now sneered and was so often bored, that he had first eaten with civilized beings in what he had imagined was an atmosphere of high culture and refinement. He caught a glimpse of that pathetic figure of him, so long ago, a self-conscious savage, sprouting sweat at every pore in an agony of apprehension, puzzled by the bewildering minutiæ of eating-implements, tortured by the ogre of a servant, striving at a leap to live at such dizzy social altitude, and deciding in the end to be frankly himself, pretending no knowledge and no polish he did not possess.

He glanced at Ruth for reassurance, much in the same manner that a passenger, with sudden panic thought of possible shipwreck, will strive to locate the life-preservers. Well, that much had come out of it—love and Ruth. All the rest had failed to stand the test of the books. But Ruth and love had stood the test; for them he found a biological sanction. Love was the most exalted expression of life. Nature had been busy designing him, as she had been busy with all normal men, for the purpose of loving. She had spent ten thousand centuries—ay, a hundred thousand and a million centuries—upon the task, and he was the best she could do. She had made love the strongest thing in him, increased its power a myriad per cent with her gift of imagination, and sent him forth into the ephemera to thrill and melt and mate. His hand sought Ruth's hand beside him hidden by the table, and a warm pressure was given and received. She looked at him a swift instant, and her eyes were radiant and melting. So were his in the thrill that pervaded him; nor did he realize how much that was radiant and melting in her eyes had been aroused by what she had seen in his.

Across the table from him, cater-cornered, at Mr. Morse's right, sat Judge Blount, a local superior court judge. Martin had met him a number of times and had failed to like him. He and Ruth's father were discussing labor union politics, the local situation, and socialism, and Mr. Morse was endeavoring to twit Martin on the latter topic. At last Judge Blount looked across the table with benignant and fatherly pity. Martin smiled to himself.

"You'll grow out of it, young man," he said soothingly. "Time is the best cure for such youthful distempers." He turned to Mr. Morse. "I do not believe discussion is good in such cases. It makes the patient obstinate."

"That is true," the other assented gravely. "But it is well to warn the patient occasionally of his condition."

Martin laughed merrily, but it was with an effort. The day had been too long, the day's effort too intense, and he was deep in the throes of the reaction.

"Undoubtedly you are both excellent doctors," he said; "but if you care a whit for the opinion of the patient, let him tell you that you are poor diagnosticians. In fact, you are both suffering from the disease you think you find in me. As for me, I am immune. The socialist philosophy that riots half-baked in your veins has passed me by."

"Clever, clever," murmured the judge. "An excellent ruse in controversy, to reverse positions."

"Out of your mouth." Martin's eyes were sparkling, but he kept control of himself. "You see, Judge, I've heard your campaign speeches. By some henidical process—henidical, by the

way, is a favorite word of mine which nobody understands—
by some henidical process you persuade yourself that you believe in the competitive system and the survival of the strong,
and at the same time you indorse with might and main all
sorts of measures to shear the strength from the strong."

"My young man—"

"Remember, I've heard your campaign speeches," Martin
warned. "It's on record, your position on interstate commerce regulation, on regulation of the railway trust and Standard Oil, on the conservation of the forests, on a thousand
and one restrictive measures that are nothing else than socialistic."

"Do you mean to tell me that you do not believe in regulating these various outrageous exercises of power?"

"That's not the point. I mean to tell you that you are a
poor diagnostician. I mean to tell you that I am not suffering
from the microbe of socialism. I mean to tell you that it is
you who are suffering from the emasculating ravages of that
same microbe. As for me, I am an inveterate opponent of
socialism just as I am an inveterate opponent of your own
mongrel democracy that is nothing else than pseudo-socialism
masquerading under a garb of words that will not stand the
test of the dictionary.

"I am a reactionary—so complete a reactionary that my position is incomprehensible to you who live in a veiled lie of
social organization and whose sight is not keen enough to
pierce the veil. You make believe that you believe in the survival of the strong and the rule of the strong. I believe. That
is the difference. When I was a trifle younger,—a few months
younger,—I believed the same thing. You see, the ideas of
you and yours had impressed me. But merchants and traders
are cowardly rulers at best; they grunt and grub all their days
in the trough of money-getting, and I have swung back to
aristocracy, if you please. I am the only individualist in this
room. I look to the state for nothing. I look only to the
strong man, the man on horseback, to save the state from its
own rotten futility.

"Nietzsche was right. I won't take the time to tell you who
Nietzsche was, but he was right. The world belongs to the
strong—to the strong who are noble as well and who do not

wallow in the swine-trough of trade and exchange. The world belongs to the true noblemen, to the great blond beasts, to the noncompromisers, to the 'yes-sayers.' And they will eat you up, you socialists who are afraid of socialism and who think yourselves individualists. Your slave-morality of the meek and lowly will never save you.—Oh, it's all Greek, I know, and I won't bother you any more with it. But remember one thing. There aren't half a dozen individualists in Oakland, but Martin Eden is one of them."

He signified that he was done with the discussion, and turned to Ruth.

"I'm wrought up to-day," he said in an undertone. "All I want to do is to love, not talk."

He ignored Mr. Morse, who said:—

"I am unconvinced. All socialists are Jesuits. That is the way to tell them."

"We'll make a good Republican out of you yet," said Judge Blount.

"The man on horseback will arrive before that time," Martin retorted with good humor, and returned to Ruth.

But Mr. Morse was not content. He did not like the laziness and the disinclination for sober, legitimate work of this prospective son-in-law of his, for whose ideas he had no respect and of whose nature he had no understanding. So he turned the conversation to Herbert Spencer. Judge Blount ably seconded him, and Martin, whose ears had pricked at the first mention of the philosopher's name, listened to the judge enunciate a grave and complacent diatribe against Spencer. From time to time Mr. Morse glanced at Martin, as much as to say, "There, my boy, you see."

"Chattering daws," Martin muttered under his breath and went on talking with Ruth and Arthur.

But the long day and the "real dirt" of the night before were telling upon him; and, besides, still burning in his mind was what had made him angry when he read it on the car.

"What is the matter?" Ruth asked suddenly, alarmed by the effort he was making to contain himself.

"There is no god but the Unknowable, and Herbert Spencer is its prophet," Judge Blount was saying at that moment.

Martin turned upon him.

"A cheap judgment," he remarked quietly. "I heard it first in the City Hall Park, on the lips of a workingman who ought to have known better. I have heard it often since, and each time the clap-trap of it nauseates me. You ought to be ashamed of yourself. To hear that great and noble man's name upon your lips is like finding a dew-drop in a cesspool. You are disgusting."

It was like a thunderbolt. Judge Blount glared at him with apoplectic countenance, and silence reigned. Mr. Morse was secretly pleased. He could see that his daughter was shocked. It was what he wanted to do—to bring out the innate ruffi-anism of this man he did not like.

Ruth's hand sought Martin's beseechingly under the table, but his blood was up. He was inflamed by the intellectual pretence and fraud of those who sat in the high places. A Superior Court Judge! It was only several years before that he had looked up from the mire at such glorious entities and deemed them gods.

Judge Blount recovered himself and attempted to go on, addressing himself to Martin with an assumption of polite-ness that the latter understood was for the benefit of the la-dies. Even this added to his anger. Was there no honesty in the world?

"You can't discuss Spencer with me," he cried. "You do not know any more about Spencer than do his own country-men. But it is no fault of yours, I grant. It is just a phase of the contemptible ignorance of the times. I ran across a sample of it on my way here this evening. I was reading an essay by Saleeby on Spencer. You should read it. It is accessible to all men. You can buy it in any book-store or draw it from the public library. You would feel ashamed of your paucity of abuse and ignorance of that noble man compared with what Saleeby has collected on the subject. It is a record of shame that would shame your shame.

" 'The philosopher of the half-educated,' he was called by an academic philosopher who was not worthy to pollute the atmosphere he breathed. I don't think you have read ten pages of Spencer, but there have been critics, assumably more intelligent than you, who have read no more than you of Spencer, who publicly challenged his followers to adduce one single idea from all his writings—from Herbert Spencer's writings, the man who has impressed the stamp of his genius over the whole field of scientific research and modern thought; the father of psychology; the man who revolution-ized pedagogy, so that to-day the child of the French peasant is taught the three R's according to principles laid down by him. And the little gnats of men sting his memory when they get their very bread and butter from the technical application of his ideas. What little of worth resides in their brains is largely due to him. It is certain that had he never lived, most of what is correct in their parrot-learned knowledge would be absent.

"And yet a man like Principal Fairbanks of Oxford—a man who sits in an even higher place than you, Judge Blount—has said that Spencer will be dismissed by posterity as a poet and dreamer rather than a thinker. Yappers and blatherskites, the whole brood of them! ' "First Principles" is not wholly destitute of a certain literary power,' said one of them. And others of them have said that he was an industrious plodder rather than an original thinker. Yappers and blatherskites! Yappers and blatherskites!"

Martin ceased abruptly, in a dead silence. Everybody in Ruth's family looked up to Judge Blount as a man of power and achievement, and they were horrified at Martin's out-break. The remainder of the dinner passed like a funeral, the judge and Mr. Morse confining their talk to each other, and the rest of the conversation being extremely desultory. Then afterward, when Ruth and Martin were alone, there was a scene.

"You are unbearable," she wept.

But his anger still smouldered, and he kept muttering, "The beasts! The beasts!"

When she averred he had insulted the judge, he re-torted:—

"By telling the truth about him?"

"I don't care whether it was true or not," she insisted. "There are certain bounds of decency, and you had no license to insult anybody."

"Then where did Judge Blount get the license to assault truth?" Martin demanded. "Surely to assault truth is a more serious misdemeanor than to insult a pygmy personality such as the judge's. He did worse than that. He blackened the name of a great, noble man who is dead. Oh, the beasts! The beasts!"

His complex anger flamed afresh, and Ruth was in terror of him. Never had she seen him so angry, and it was all mystified and unreasonable to her comprehension. And yet, through her very terror ran the fibres of fascination that had drawn and that still drew her to him—that had compelled her to lean towards him, and, in that mad culminating moment, lay her hands upon his neck. She was hurt and outraged by what had taken place, and yet she lay in his arms and quivered while he went on muttering, "The beasts! The beasts!" And she still lay there when he said: "I'll not bother your table again, dear. They do not like me, and it is wrong of me to thrust my objectionable presence upon them. Besides, they are just as objectionable to me. Faugh! They are sickening. And to think of it, I dreamed in my innocence that the persons who sat in the high places, who lived in fine houses and had educations and bank accounts, were worth while!"

Chapter XXXVIII

"C OME ON, let's go down to the local."

So spoke Brissenden, faint from a hemorrhage of half an hour before—the second hemorrhage in three days. The perennial whiskey glass was in his hands, and he drained it with shaking fingers.

"What do I want with socialism?" Martin demanded.

"Outsiders are allowed five-minute speeches," the sick man urged. "Get up and spout. Tell them why you don't want socialism. Tell them what you think about them and their ghetto ethics. Slam Nietzsche into them and get walloped for your pains. Make a scrap of it. It will do them good. Discussion is what they want, and what you want, too. You see, I'd like to see you a socialist before I'm gone. It will give you a sanction for your existence. It is the one thing that will save you in the time of disappointment that is coming to you."

"I never can puzzle out why you, of all men, are a socialist," Martin pondered. "You detest the crowd so. Surely there is nothing in the canaille to recommend it to your æsthetic soul." He pointed an accusing finger at the whiskey glass which the other was refilling. "Socialism doesn't seem to save you."

"I'm very sick," was the answer. "With you it is different. You have health and much to live for, and you must be handcuffed to life somehow. As for me, you wonder why I am a socialist. I'll tell you. It is because socialism is inevitable; because the present rotten and irrational system cannot endure; because the day is past for your man on horseback. The slaves won't stand for it. They are too many, and willy-nilly they'll drag down the would-be equestrian before ever he gets astride. You can't get away from them, and you'll have to swallow the whole slave-morality. It's not a nice mess, I'll allow. But it's been a-brewing and swallow it you must. You are antediluvian anyway, with your Nietzsche ideas. The past is past, and the man who says history repeats itself is a liar. Of course I don't like the crowd, but what's a poor chap to do? We can't have the man on horseback, and anything is

preferable to the timid swine that now rule. But come on,
anyway. I'm loaded to the guards now, and if I sit here any
longer, I'll get drunk. And you know the doctor says—damn
the doctor! I'll fool him yet."

It was Sunday night, and they found the small hall packed
by the Oakland socialists, chiefly members of the working
class. The speaker, a clever Jew, won Martin's admiration at
the same time that he aroused his antagonism. The man's
stooped and narrow shoulders and weazened chest proclaimed him the true child of the crowded ghetto, and strong
on Martin was the age-long struggle of the feeble, wretched
slaves against the lordly handful of men who had ruled over
them and would rule over them to the end of time. To Martin
this withered wisp of a creature was a symbol. He was the
figure that stood forth representative of the whole miserable
mass of weaklings and inefficients who perished according to
biological law on the ragged confines of life. They were the
unfit. In spite of their cunning philosophy and of their antlike
proclivities for coöperation, Nature rejected them for the exceptional man. Out of the plentiful spawn of life she flung
from her prolific hand she selected only the best. It was by
the same method that men, aping her, bred race-horses and
cucumbers. Doubtless, a creator of a Cosmos could have devised a better method; but creatures of this particular Cosmos
must put up with this particular method. Of course, they
could squirm as they perished, as the socialists squirmed, as
the speaker on the platform and the perspiring crowd were
squirming even now as they counselled together for some
new device with which to minimize the penalties of living and
outwit the Cosmos.

So Martin thought, and so he spoke when Brissenden
urged him to give them hell. He obeyed the mandate, walking up to the platform, as was the custom, and addressing the
chairman. He began in a low voice, haltingly, forming into
order the ideas which had surged in his brain while the Jew
was speaking. In such meetings five minutes was the time al-
lotted to each speaker; but when Martin's five minutes were
up, he was in full stride, his attack upon their doctrines but
half completed. He had caught their interest, and the audience urged the chairman by acclamation to extend Martin's

time. They appreciated him as a foeman worthy of their intellect, and they listened intently, following every word. He spoke with fire and conviction, mincing no words in his attack upon the slaves and their morality and tactics and frankly alluding to his hearers as the slaves in question. He quoted Spencer and Malthus, and enunciated the biological law of development.

"And so," he concluded, in a swift résumé, "no state composed of the slave-types can endure. The old law of development still holds. In the struggle for existence, as I have shown, the strong and the progeny of the strong tend to survive, while the weak and the progeny of the weak are crushed and tend to perish. The result is that the strong and the progeny of the strong survive, and, so long as the struggle obtains, the strength of each generation increases. That is development. But you slaves—it is too bad to be slaves, I grant—but you slaves dream of a society where the law of development will be annulled, where no weaklings and inefficients will perish, where every inefficient will have as much as he wants to eat as many times a day as he desires, and where all will marry and have progeny—the weak as well as the strong. What will be the result? No longer will the strength and life-value of each generation increase. On the contrary, it will diminish. There is the Nemesis of your slave philosophy. Your society of slaves—of, by, and for, slaves—must inevitably weaken and go to pieces as the life which composes it weakens and goes to pieces.

"Remember, I am enunciating biology and not sentimental ethics. No state of slaves can stand—"

"How about the United States?" a man yelled from the audience.

"And how about it?" Martin retorted. "The thirteen colonies threw off their rulers and formed the Republic so-called. The slaves were their own masters. There were no more masters of the sword. But you couldn't get along without masters of some sort, and there arose a new set of masters—not the great, virile, noble men, but the shrewd and spidery traders and money-lenders. And they enslaved you over again—but not frankly, as the true, noble men would do with weight of their own right arms, but secretly, by spidery machinations and by wheedling and cajolery and lies. They have purchased your slave judges, they have debauched your slave legislatures, and they have forced to worse horrors than chattel slavery your slave boys and girls. Two million of your children are toiling to-day in this trader-oligarchy of the United States. Ten millions of you slaves are not properly sheltered nor properly fed.

"But to return. I have shown that no society of slaves can endure, because, in its very nature, such society must annul the law of development. No sooner can a slave society be organized than deterioration sets in. It is easy for you to talk of annulling the law of development, but where is the new law of development that will maintain your strength? Formulate it. Is it already formulated? Then state it."

Martin took his seat amidst an uproar of voices. A score of men were on their feet clamoring for recognition from the chair. And one by one, encouraged by vociferous applause, speaking with fire and enthusiasm and excited gestures, they replied to the attack. It was a wild night—but it was wild intellectually, a battle of ideas. Some strayed from the point, but most of the speakers replied directly to Martin. They shook him with lines of thought that were new to him; and gave him insights, not into new biological laws, but into new applications of the old laws. They were too earnest to be always polite, and more than once the chairman rapped and pounded for order.

It chanced that a cub reporter sat in the audience, detailed there on a day dull of news and impressed by the urgent need of journalism for sensation. He was not a bright cub reporter. He was merely facile and glib. He was too dense to follow the discussion. In fact, he had a comfortable feeling that he was vastly superior to these wordy maniacs of the working class. Also, he had a great respect for those who sat in the high places and dictated the policies of nations and newspapers. Further, he had an ideal, namely, of achieving that excellence of the perfect reporter who is able to make something—even a great deal—out of nothing.

He did not know what all the talk was about. It was not necessary. Words like *revolution* gave him his cue. Like a paleontologist, able to reconstruct an entire skeleton from one fossil bone, he was able to reconstruct a whole speech from the one word *revolution*. He did it that night, and he did it well; and since Martin had made the biggest stir, he put it all into his mouth and made him the arch-anarch of the show, transforming his reactionary individualism into the most lurid, red-shirt socialist utterance. The cub reporter was an artist, and it was a large brush with which he laid on the local color—wild-eyed long-haired men, neurasthenic and degenerate types of men, voices shaken with passion, clenched fists raised on high, and all projected against a background of oaths, yells, and the throaty rumbling of angry men.

Chapter XXXIX

OVER THE COFFEE, in his little room, Martin read next morning's paper. It was a novel experience to find himself head-lined, on the first page at that; and he was surprised to learn that he was the most notorious leader of the Oakland socialists. He ran over the violent speech the cub reporter had constructed for him, and, though at first he was angered by the fabrication, in the end he tossed the paper aside with a laugh.

"Either the man was drunk or criminally malicious," he said that afternoon, from his perch on the bed, when Brissenden had arrived and dropped limply into the one chair.

"But what do you care?" Brissenden asked. "Surely you don't desire the approval of the bourgeois swine that read the newspapers?"

Martin thought for a while, then said:—

"No, I really don't care for their approval, not a whit. On the other hand, it's very likely to make my relations with Ruth's family a trifle awkward. Her father always contended I was a socialist, and this miserable stuff will clinch his belief. Not that I care for his opinion—but what's the odds? I want to read you what I've been doing to-day. It's 'Overdue,' of course, and I'm just about halfway through."

He was reading aloud when Maria thrust open the door and ushered in a young man in a natty suit who glanced briskly about him, noting the oil-burner and the kitchen in the corner before his gaze wandered on to Martin.

"Sit down," Brissenden said.

Martin made room for the young man on the bed and waited for him to broach his business.

"I heard you speak last night, Mr. Eden, and I've come to interview you," he began.

Brissenden burst out in a hearty laugh.

"A brother socialist?" the reporter asked, with a quick glance at Brissenden that appraised the color-value of that cadaverous and dying man.

"And he wrote that report," Martin said softly. "Why, he is only a boy!"

"Why don't you poke him?" Brissenden asked. "I'd give a thousand dollars to have my lungs back for five minutes."

The cub reporter was a trifle perplexed by this talking over him and around him and at him. But he had been commended for his brilliant description of the socialist meeting and had further been detailed to get a personal interview with Martin Eden, the leader of the organized menace to society.

"You do not object to having your picture taken, Mr. Eden?" he said. "I've a staff photographer outside, you see, and he says it will be better to take you right away before the sun gets lower. Then we can have the interview afterward."

"A photographer," Brissenden said meditatively. "Poke him, Martin! Poke him!"

"I guess I'm getting old," was the answer. "I know I ought, but I really haven't the heart. It doesn't seem to matter."

"For his mother's sake," Brissenden urged.

"It's worth considering," Martin replied; "but it doesn't seem worth while enough to rouse sufficient energy in me. You see, it does take energy to give a fellow a poking. Besides, what does it matter?"

"That's right—that's the way to take it," the cub announced airily, though he had already begun to glance anxiously at the door.

"But it wasn't true, not a word of what he wrote," Martin went on, confining his attention to Brissenden.

"It was just in a general way a description, you understand," the cub ventured, "and besides, it's good advertising. That's what counts. It was a favor to you."

"It's good advertising, Martin, old boy," Brissenden repeated solemnly.

"And it was a favor to me—think of that!" was Martin's contribution.

"Let me see—where were you born, Mr. Eden?" the cub asked, assuming an air of expectant attention.

"He doesn't take notes," said Brissenden. "He remembers it all."

"That is sufficient for me." The cub was trying not to look worried. "No decent reporter needs to bother with notes."

"That was sufficient—for last night." But Brissenden was not a disciple of quietism, and he changed his attitude abruptly. "Martin, if you don't poke him, I'll do it myself, if I fall dead on the floor the next moment."

"How will a spanking do?" Martin asked.

Brissenden considered judicially, and nodded his head.

The next instant Martin was seated on the edge of the bed with the cub face downward across his knees.

"Now don't bite," Martin warned, "or else I'll have to punch your face. It would be a pity, for it is such a pretty face."

His uplifted hand descended, and thereafter rose and fell in a swift and steady rhythm. The cub struggled and cursed and squirmed, but did not offer to bite. Brissenden looked on gravely, though once he grew excited and gripped the whiskey bottle, pleading, "Here, just let me swat him once."

"Sorry my hand played out," Martin said, when at last he desisted. "It is quite numb."

He uprighted the cub and perched him on the bed.

"I'll have you arrested for this," he snarled, tears of boyish indignation running down his flushed cheeks. "I'll make you sweat for this. You'll see."

"The pretty thing," Martin remarked. "He doesn't realize that he has entered upon the downward path. It is not honest, it is not square, it is not manly, to tell lies about one's fellow-creatures the way he has done, and he doesn't know it."

"He has to come to us to be told," Brissenden filled in a pause.

"Yes, to me whom he has maligned and injured. My grocery will undoubtedly refuse me credit now. The worst of it is that the poor boy will keep on this way until he deteriorates into a first-class newspaper man and also a first-class scoundrel."

"But there is yet time," quoth Brissenden. "Who knows but what you may prove the humble instrument to save him. Why didn't you let me swat him just once? I'd like to have had a hand in it."

"I'll have you arrested, the pair of you, you b-b-big brutes," sobbed the erring soul.

"No, his mouth is too pretty and too weak." Martin shook

his head lugubriously. "I'm afraid I've numbed my hand in vain. The young man cannot reform. He will become eventually a very great and successful newspaper man. He has no conscience. That alone will make him great."

With that the cub passed out the door, in trepidation to the last for fear that Brissenden would hit him in the back with the bottle he still clutched.

In the next morning's paper Martin learned a great deal more about himself that was new to him. "We are the sworn enemies of society," he found himself quoted as saying in a column interview. "No, we are not anarchists but socialists." When the reporter pointed out to him that there seemed little difference between the two schools, Martin had shrugged his shoulders in silent affirmation. His face was described as bilaterally asymmetrical, and various other signs of degeneration were described. Especially notable were his thuglike hands and the fiery gleams in his blood-shot eyes.

He learned, also, that he spoke nightly to the workmen in the City Hall Park, and that among the anarchists and agitators that there inflamed the minds of the people he drew the largest audiences and made the most revolutionary speeches. The cub painted a high-light picture of his poor little room, its oil-stove and the one chair, and of the death's-head tramp who kept him company and who looked as if he had just emerged from twenty years of solitary confinement in some fortress dungeon.

The cub had been industrious. He had scurried around and nosed out Martin's family history, and procured a photograph of Higginbotham's Cash Store with Bernard Higginbotham himself standing out in front. That gentleman was depicted as an intelligent, dignified business man who had no patience with his brother-in-law's socialistic views, and no patience with the brother-in-law, either, whom he was quoted as characterizing as a lazy good-for-nothing who wouldn't take a job when it was offered to him and who would go to jail yet. Hermann von Schmidt, Marian's husband, had likewise been interviewed. He had called Martin the black sheep of the family and repudiated him. "He tried to sponge off of me, but I put a stop to that good and quick," Von Schmidt had said to the reporter. "He knows better than to come bumming around here. A man who won't work is no good, take that from me."

This time Martin was genuinely angry. Brissenden looked upon the affair as a good joke, but he could not console Martin, who knew that it would be no easy task to explain to Ruth. As for her father, he knew that he must be overjoyed with what had happened and that he would make the most of it to break off the engagement. How much he would make of it he was soon to realize. The afternoon mail brought a letter from Ruth. Martin opened it with a premonition of disaster, and read it standing at the open door when he had received it from the postman. As he read, mechanically his hand sought his pocket for the tobacco and brown paper of his old cigarette days. He was not aware that the pocket was empty or that he had even reached for the materials with which to roll a cigarette.

It was not a passionate letter. There were no touches of anger in it. But all the way through, from the first sentence to the last, was sounded the note of hurt and disappointment. She had expected better of him. She had thought he had got over his youthful wildness, that her love for him had been sufficiently worth while to enable him to live seriously and decently. And now her father and mother had taken a firm stand and commanded that the engagement be broken. That they were justified in this she could not but admit. Their relation could never be a happy one. It had been unfortunate from the first. But one regret she voiced in the whole letter, and it was a bitter one to Martin. "If only you had settled down to some position and attempted to make something of yourself," she wrote. "But it was not to be. Your past life had been too wild and irregular. I can understand that you are not to be blamed. You could act only according to your nature and your early training. So I do not blame you, Martin. Please remember that. It was simply a mistake. As father and mother have contended, we were not made for each other, and we should both be happy because it was discovered not too late." . . . "There is no use trying to see me," she said toward the last. "It would be an unhappy meeting for both of us, as well as for my mother. I feel, as it is, that I have caused

her great pain and worry. I shall have to do much living to
atone for it."

He read it through to the end, carefully, a second time,
then sat down and replied. He outlined the remarks he had
uttered at the socialist meeting, pointing out that they were
in all ways the converse of what the newspaper had put in his
mouth. Toward the end of the letter he was God's own lover
pleading passionately for love. "Please answer," he said, "and
in your answer you have to tell me but one thing. Do you
love me? That is all—the answer to that one question."

But no answer came the next day, nor the next. "Overdue"
lay untouched upon the table, and each day the heap of returned manuscripts under the table grew larger. For the first
time Martin's glorious sleep was interrupted by insomnia, and
he tossed through long, restless nights. Three times he called
at the Morse home, but was turned away by the servant who
answered the bell. Brissenden lay sick in his hotel, too feeble
to stir out, and, though Martin was with him often, he did
not worry him with his troubles.

For Martin's troubles were many. The aftermath of the cub
reporter's deed was even wider than Martin had anticipated.
The Portuguese grocer refused him further credit, while the
greengrocer, who was an American and proud of it, had
called him a traitor to his country and refused further dealings
with him—carrying his patriotism to such a degree that he
cancelled Martin's account and forbade him ever to attempt
to pay it. The talk in the neighborhood reflected the same
feeling, and indignation against Martin ran high. No one
would have anything to do with a socialist traitor. Poor Maria
was dubious and frightened, but she remained loyal. The children of the neighborhood recovered from the awe of the
grand carriage which once had visited Martin, and from safe
distances they called him "hobo" and "bum." The Silva tribe,
however, stanchly defended him, fighting more than one
pitched battle for his honor, and black eyes and bloody noses
became quite the order of the day and added to Maria's per-
plexities and troubles.

Once, Martin met Gertrude on the street, down in Oakland, and learned what he knew could not be otherwise—that
Bernard Higginbotham was furious with him for having

dragged the family into public disgrace, and that he had forbidden him the house.

"Why don't you go away, Martin?" Gertrude had begged.
"Go away and get a job somewhere and steady down. Afterwards, when this all blows over, you can come back."

Martin shook his head, but gave no explanations. How
could he explain? He was appalled at the awful intellectual
chasm that yawned between him and his people. He could
never cross it and explain to them his position,—the Nietzschean position, in regard to socialism. There were not words
enough in the English language, nor in any language, to make
his attitude and conduct intelligible to them. Their highest
concept of right conduct, in his case, was to get a job. That
was their first word and their last. It constituted their whole
lexicon of ideas. Get a job! Go to work! Poor, stupid slaves,
he thought, while his sister talked. Small wonder the world
belonged to the strong. The slaves were obsessed by their
own slavery. A job was to them a golden fetich before which
they fell down and worshipped.

He shook his head again, when Gertrude offered him
money, though he knew that within the day he would have
to make a trip to the pawnbroker.

"Don't come near Bernard now," she admonished him.
"After a few months, when he is cooled down, if you want
to, you can get the job of drivin' delivery-wagon for him. Any
time you want me, just send for me an' I'll come. Don't
forget."

She went away weeping audibly, and he felt a pang of sorrow shoot through him at sight of her heavy body and uncouth gait. As he watched her go, the Nietzschean edifice
seemed to shake and totter. The slave-class in the abstract was
all very well, but it was not wholly satisfactory when it was
brought home to his own family. And yet, if there was ever
a slave trampled by the strong, that slave was his sister Gertrude. He grinned savagely at the paradox. A fine Nietzscheman he was, to allow his intellectual concepts to be shaken by
the first sentiment or emotion that strayed along—ay, to be
shaken by the slave-morality itself, for that was what his pity
for his sister really was. The true noble men were above pity
and compassion. Pity and compassion had been generated in

the subterranean barracoons of the slaves and were no more
than the agony and sweat of the crowded miserables and
weaklings.

Chapter XL

"O VERDUE" still continued to lie forgotten on the table. Every manuscript that he had had out now lay under the table. Only one manuscript he kept going, and that was Brissenden's "Ephemera." His bicycle and black suit were again in pawn, and the type-writer people were once more worrying about the rent. But such things no longer bothered him. He was seeking a new orientation, and until that was found his life must stand still.

After several weeks, what he had been waiting for happened. He met Ruth on the street. It was true, she was accompanied by her brother, Norman, and it was true that they tried to ignore him and that Norman attempted to wave him aside.

"If you interfere with my sister, I'll call an officer," Norman threatened. "She does not wish to speak with you, and your insistence is insult."

"If you persist, you'll have to call that officer, and then you'll get your name in the papers," Martin answered grimly. "And now, get out of my way and get the officer if you want to. I'm going to talk with Ruth."

"I want to have it from your own lips," he said to her.

She was pale and trembling, but she held up and looked inquiringly.

"The question I asked in my letter," he prompted.

Norman made an impatient movement, but Martin checked him with a swift look.

She shook her head.

"Is all this of your own free will?" he demanded.

"It is." She spoke in a low, firm voice and with deliberation. "It is of my own free will. You have disgraced me so that I am ashamed to meet my friends. They are all talking about me, I know. That is all I can tell you. You have made me very unhappy, and I never wish to see you again."

"Friends! Gossip! Newspaper misreports! Surely such things are not stronger than love! I can only believe that you never loved me."

A blush drove the pallor from her face.

"After what has passed?" she said faintly. "Martin, you do not know what you are saying. I am not common."

"You see, she doesn't want to have anything to do with you," Norman blurted out, starting on with her.

Martin stood aside and let them pass, fumbling unconsciously in his coat pocket for the tobacco and brown papers that were not there.

It was a long walk to North Oakland, but it was not until he went up the steps and entered his room that he knew he had walked it. He found himself sitting on the edge of the bed and staring about him like an awakened somnambulist. He noticed "Overdue" lying on the table and drew up his chair and reached for his pen. There was in his nature a logical compulsion toward completeness. Here was something undone. It had been deferred against the completion of something else. Now that something else had been finished, and he would apply himself to this task until it was finished. What he would do next he did not know. All that he did know was that a climacteric in his life had been attained. A period had been reached, and he was rounding it off in workmanlike fashion. He was not curious about the future. He would soon enough find out what it held in store for him. Whatever it was, it did not matter. Nothing seemed to matter.

For five days he toiled on at "Overdue," going nowhere, seeing nobody, and eating meagrely. On the morning of the sixth day the postman brought him a thin letter from the editor of *The Parthenon*. A glance told him that "Ephemera" was accepted. "We have submitted the poem to Mr. Cartwright Bruce," the editor went on to say, "and he has reported so favorably upon it that we cannot let it go. As an earnest of our pleasure in publishing the poem, let me tell you that we have set it for the August number, our July number being already made up. Kindly extend our pleasure and our thanks to Mr. Brissenden. Please send by return mail his photograph and biographical data. If our honorarium is unsatisfactory, kindly telegraph us at once and state what you consider a fair price."

Since the honorarium they had offered was three hundred and fifty dollars, Martin thought it not worth while to telegraph. Then, too, there was Brissenden's consent to be gained. Well, he had been right, after all. Here was one magazine editor who knew real poetry when he saw it. And the price was splendid, even though it was for the poem of a century. As for Cartwright Bruce, Martin knew that he was the one critic for whose opinions Brissenden had any respect.

Martin rode down town on an electric car, and as he watched the houses and cross-streets slipping by he was aware of a regret that he was not more elated over his friend's success and over his own signal victory. The one critic in the United States had pronounced favorably on the poem, while his own contention that good stuff could find its way into the magazines had proved correct. But enthusiasm had lost its spring in him, and he found that he was more anxious to see Brissenden than he was to carry the good news. The acceptance of *The Parthenon* had recalled to him that during his five days' devotion to "Overdue" he had not heard from Brissenden nor even thought about him. For the first time Martin realized the daze he had been in, and he felt shame for having forgotten his friend. But even the shame did not burn very sharply. He was numb to emotions of any sort save the artistic ones concerned in the writing of "Overdue." So far as other affairs were concerned, he had been in a trance. For that matter, he was still in a trance. All this life through which the electric car whirred seemed remote and unreal, and he would have experienced little interest and less shock if the great stone steeple of the church he passed had suddenly crumbled to mortar-dust upon his head.

At the hotel he hurried up to Brissenden's room, and hurried down again. The room was empty. All luggage was gone.

"Did Mr. Brissenden leave any address?" he asked the clerk, who looked at him curiously for a moment.

"Haven't you heard?" he asked.

Martin shook his head.

"Why, the papers were full of it. He was found dead in bed. Suicide. Shot himself through the head."

"Is he buried yet?" Martin seemed to hear his voice, like some one else's voice, from a long way off, asking the question.

"No. The body was shipped East after the inquest. Lawyers engaged by his people saw to the arrangements."

"They were quick about it, I must say," Martin commented.

"Oh, I don't know. It happened five days ago."

"Five days ago?"

"Yes, five days ago."

"Oh," Martin said as he turned and went out.

At the corner he stepped into the Western Union and sent a telegram to *The Parthenon*, advising them to proceed with the publication of the poem. He had in his pocket but five cents with which to pay his carfare home, so he sent the message collect.

Once in his room, he resumed his writing. The days and nights came and went, and he sat at his table and wrote on. He went nowhere, save to the pawnbroker, took no exercise, and ate methodically when he was hungry and had something to cook, and just as methodically went without when he had nothing to cook. Composed as the story was, in advance, chapter by chapter, he nevertheless saw and developed an opening that increased the power of it, though it necessitated twenty thousand additional words. It was not that there was any vital need that the thing should be well done, but that his artistic canons compelled him to do it well. He worked on in the daze, strangely detached from the world around him, feeling like a familiar ghost among these literary trappings of his former life. He remembered that some one had said that a ghost was the spirit of a man who was dead and who did not have sense enough to know it; and he paused for the moment to wonder if he were really dead and unaware of it.

Came the day when "Overdue" was finished. The agent of the type-writer firm had come for the machine, and he sat on the bed while Martin, on the one chair, typed the last pages of the final chapter. "Finis," he wrote, in capitals, at the end, and to him it was indeed finis. He watched the type-writer carried out the door with a feeling of relief, then went over and lay down on the bed. He was faint from hunger. Food had not passed his lips in thirty-six hours, but he did not think about it. He lay on his back, with closed eyes, and did not think at all, while the daze or stupor slowly welled up, saturating his consciousness. Half in delirium, he began muttering aloud the lines of an anonymous poem Brissenden had been fond of quoting to him. Maria, listening anxiously outside his door, was perturbed by his monotonous utterance. The words in themselves were not significant to her, but the fact that he was saying them was. "I have done," was the burden of the poem.

> " 'I have done—
> Put by the lute.
> Song and singing soon are over
> As the airy shades that hover
> In among the purple clover.
> I have done—
> Put by the lute.
> Once I sang as early thrushes
> Sing among the dewy bushes;
> Now I'm mute.
> I am like a weary linnet,
> For my throat has no song in it;
> I have had my singing minute.
> I have done.
> Put by the lute.' "

Maria could stand it no longer, and hurried away to the stove, where she filled a quart-bowl with soup, putting into it the lion's share of chopped meat and vegetables which her ladle scraped from the bottom of the pot. Martin roused himself and sat up and began to eat, between spoonfuls reassuring Maria that he had not been talking in his sleep and that he did not have any fever.

After she left him he sat drearily, with drooping shoulders, on the edge of the bed, gazing about him with lack-lustre eyes that saw nothing until the torn wrapper of a magazine, which had come in the morning's mail and which lay unopened, shot a gleam of light into his darkened brain. It is *The Parthenon*, he thought, the August *Parthenon*, and it must contain "Ephemera." If only Brissenden were here to see!

He was turning the pages of the magazine, when suddenly he stopped. "Ephemera" had been featured, with gorgeous head-piece and Beardsley-like margin decorations. On one side of the head-piece was Brissenden's photograph, on the other side was the photograph of Sir John Value, the British Ambassador. A preliminary editorial note quoted Sir John Value as saying that there were no poets in America, and the publication of "Ephemera" was *The Parthenon's* "There, take that, Sir John Value!" Cartwright Bruce was described as the greatest critic in America, and he was quoted as saying that "Ephemera" was the greatest poem ever written in America. And finally, the editor's foreword ended with: "We have not yet made up our minds entirely as to the merits of "Ephemera"; perhaps we shall never be able to do so. But we have read it often, wondering at the words and their arrangement, wondering where Mr. Brissenden got them, and how he could fasten them together." Then followed the poem.

"Pretty good thing you died, Briss, old man," Martin murmured, letting the magazine slip between his knees to the floor.

The cheapness and vulgarity of it was nauseating, and Martin noted apathetically that he was not nauseated very much. He wished he could get angry, but did not have energy enough to try. He was too numb. His blood was too congealed to accelerate to the swift tidal flow of indignation. After all, what did it matter? It was on a par with all the rest that Brissenden had condemned in bourgeois society.

"Poor Briss," Martin communed; "he would never have forgiven me."

Rousing himself with an effort, he possessed himself of a box which had once contained type-writer paper. Going through its contents, he drew forth eleven poems which his friend had written. These he tore lengthwise and crosswise and dropped into the waste basket. He did it languidly, and, when he had finished, sat on the edge of the bed staring blankly before him.

How long he sat there he did not know, until, suddenly, across his sightless vision he saw form a long horizontal line of white. It was curious. But as he watched it grow in definiteness he saw that it was a coral reef smoking in the white

Pacific surges. Next, in the line of breakers, he made out a
small canoe, an outrigger canoe. In the stern he saw a young
bronzed god in scarlet hip-cloth, dipping a flashing paddle.
He recognized him. He was Moti, the youngest son of Tati,
the chief, and this was Tahiti, and beyond that smoking reef
lay the sweet land of Papara and the chief's grass house by
the river's mouth. It was the end of the day, and Moti was
coming home from the fishing. He was waiting for the rush
of a big breaker whereon to jump the reef. Then he saw himself, sitting forward in the canoe as he had often sat in the
past, dipping a paddle that waited Moti's word to dig in like
mad when the turquoise wall of the great breaker rose behind
them. Next, he was no longer an onlooker but was himself in
the canoe, Moti was crying out, they were both thrusting
hard with their paddles, racing on the steep face of the flying
turquoise. Under the bow the water was hissing as from a
steam jet, the air was filled with driven spray, there was a rush
and rumble and long-echoing roar, and the canoe floated on
the placid water of the lagoon. Moti laughed and shook the
salt water from his eyes, and together they paddled in to the
pounded-coral beach where Tati's grass walls through the co-
coanut-palms showed golden in the setting sun.

The picture faded, and before his eyes stretched the disorder of his squalid room. He strove in vain to see Tahiti again.
He knew there was singing among the trees and that the
maidens were dancing in the moonlight, but he could not see
them. He could see only the littered writing-table, the empty
space where the type-writer had stood, and the unwashed
window-pane. He closed his eyes with a groan, and slept.

Chapter XLI

H E SLEPT heavily all night, and did not stir until aroused by the postman on his morning round. Martin felt tired and passive, and went through his letters aimlessly. One thin envelope, from a robber magazine, contained a check for twenty-two dollars. He had been dunning for it for a year and a half. He noted its amount apathetically. The old-time thrill at receiving a publisher's check was gone. Unlike his earlier checks, this one was not pregnant with promise of great things to come. To him it was a check for twenty-two dollars, that was all, and it would buy him something to eat.

Another check was in the same mail, sent from a New York weekly in payment for some humorous verse which had been accepted months before. It was for ten dollars. An idea came to him, which he calmly considered. He did not know what he was going to do, and he felt in no hurry to do anything. In the meantime he must live. Also he owed numerous debts. Would it not be a paying investment to put stamps on the huge pile of manuscripts under the table and start them on their travels again? One or two of them might be accepted. That would help him to live. He decided on the investment, and, after he had cashed the checks at the bank down in Oakland, he bought ten dollars' worth of postage stamps. The thought of going home to cook breakfast in his stuffy little room was repulsive to him. For the first time he refused to consider his debts. He knew that in his room he could manufacture a substantial breakfast at a cost of from fifteen to twenty cents. But, instead, he went into the Forum Café and ordered a breakfast that cost two dollars. He tipped the waiter a quarter, and spent fifty cents for a package of Egyptian cigarettes. It was the first time he had smoked since Ruth had asked him to stop. But he could see now no reason why he should not, and besides, he wanted to smoke. And what did the money matter? For five cents he could have bought a package of Durham and brown papers and rolled forty cigarettes—but what of it? Money had no meaning to him now except what it would immediately buy. He was chartless and

rudderless, and he had no port to make, while drifting involved the least living, and it was living that hurt.

The days slipped along, and he slept eight hours regularly
every night. Though now, while waiting for more checks, he
ate in the Japanese restaurants where meals were served for
ten cents, his wasted body filled out, as did the hollows in his
cheeks. He no longer abused himself with short sleep, overwork, and overstudy. He wrote nothing, and the books were
closed. He walked much, out in the hills, and loafed long
hours in the quiet parks. He had no friends nor acquaintances, nor did he make any. He had no inclination. He was
waiting for some impulse, from he knew not where, to put
his stopped life into motion again. In the meantime his life
remained run down, planless, and empty and idle.

Once he made a trip to San Francisco to look up the "real
dirt." But at the last moment, as he stepped into the upstairs
entrance, he recoiled and turned and fled through the swarming ghetto. He was frightened at the thought of hearing philosophy discussed, and he fled furtively, for fear that some
one of the "real dirt" might chance along and recognize him.

Sometimes he glanced over the magazines and newspapers
to see how "Ephemera" was being maltreated. It had made a
hit. But what a hit! Everybody had read it, and everybody
was discussing whether or not it was really poetry. The local
papers had taken it up, and daily there appeared columns of
learned criticisms, facetious editorials, and serious letters from
subscribers. Helen Della Delmar (proclaimed with a flourish
of trumpets and rolling of tomtoms to be the greatest woman
poet in the United States) denied Brissenden a seat beside her
on Pegasus and wrote voluminous letters to the public, proving that he was no poet.

The Parthenon came out in its next number patting itself
on the back for the stir it had made, sneering at Sir John
Value, and exploiting Brissenden's death with ruthless commercialism. A newspaper with a sworn circulation of half a
million published an original and spontaneous poem by
Helen Della Delmar, in which she gibed and sneered at Brissenden. Also, she was guilty of a second poem, in which she
parodied him.

Martin had many times to be glad that Brissenden was

dead. He had hated the crowd so, and here all that was finest and most sacred of him had been thrown to the crowd. Daily the vivisection of Beauty went on. Every nincompoop in the land rushed into free print, floating their wizened little egos into the public eye on the surge of Brissenden's greatness. Quoth one paper: "We have received a letter from a gentleman who wrote a poem just like it, only better, some time ago." Another paper, in deadly seriousness, reproving Helen Della Delmar for her parody, said: "But unquestionably Miss Delmar wrote it in a moment of badinage and not quite with the respect that one great poet should show to another and perhaps to the greatest. However, whether Miss Delmar be jealous or not of the man who invented 'Ephemera,' it is certain that she, like thousands of others, is fascinated by his work, and that the day may come when she will try to write lines like his."

Ministers began to preach sermons against "Ephemera," and one, who too stoutly stood for much of its content, was expelled for heresy. The great poem contributed to the gayety of the world. The comic verse-writers and the cartoonists took hold of it with screaming laughter, and in the personal columns of society weeklies jokes were perpetrated on it to the effect that Charley Frensham told Archie Jennings, in confidence, that five lines of "Ephemera" would drive a man to beat a cripple, and that ten lines would send him to the bottom of the river.

Martin did not laugh; nor did he grit his teeth in anger. The effect produced upon him was one of great sadness. In the crash of his whole world, with love on the pinnacle, the crash of magazinedom and the dear public was a small crash indeed. Brissenden had been wholly right in his judgment of the magazines, and he, Martin, had spent arduous and futile years in order to find it out for himself. The magazines were all Brissenden had said they were and more. Well, he was done, he solaced himself. He had hitched his wagon to a star and been landed in a pestiferous marsh. The visions of Tahiti—clean, sweet Tahiti—were coming to him more frequently. And there were the low Paumotus, and the high Marquesas; he saw himself often, now, on board trading schooners or frail little cutters, slipping out at dawn through the reef at Papeete and beginning the long beat through the pearl-atolls to Nukahiva and the Bay of Taiohæ, where Tamari, he knew, would kill a pig in honor of his coming, and where Tamari's flower-garlanded daughters would seize his hands and with song and laughter garland him with flowers. The South Seas were calling, and he knew that sooner or later he would answer the call.

In the meantime he drifted, resting and recuperating after the long traverse he had made through the realm of knowledge. When *The Parthenon* check of three hundred and fifty dollars was forwarded to him, he turned it over to the local lawyer who had attended to Brissenden's affairs for his family. Martin took a receipt for the check, and at the same time gave a note for the hundred dollars Brissenden had let him have.

The time was not long when Martin ceased patronizing the Japanese restaurants. At the very moment when he had abandoned the fight, the tide turned. But it had turned too late. Without a thrill he opened a thin envelope from *The Millennium*, scanned the face of a check that represented three hundred dollars, and noted that it was the payment on acceptance for "Adventure." Every debt he owed in the world, including the pawnshop with its usurious interest, amounted to less than a hundred dollars. And when he had paid everything, and lifted the hundred-dollar note with Brissenden's lawyer, he still had over a hundred dollars in pocket. He ordered a suit of clothes from the tailor and ate his meals in the best cafés in town. He still slept in his little room at Maria's, but the sight of his new clothes caused the neighborhood children to cease from calling him "hobo" and "tramp" from the roofs of woodsheds and over back fences.

"Wiki-Wiki," his Hawaiian short story, was bought by *Warren's Monthly* for two hundred and fifty dollars. *The Northern Review* took his essay, "The Cradle of Beauty," and *Mackintosh's Magazine* took "The Palmist"—the poem he had written to Marian. The editors and readers were back from their summer vacations, and manuscripts were being handled quickly. But Martin could not puzzle out what strange whim animated them to this general acceptance of the things they had persistently rejected for two years. Nothing of his had been published. He was not known anywhere outside of Oakland, and in Oakland, with the few who thought they knew him, he was notorious as a red-shirt and a socialist. So there was no explaining this sudden acceptability of his wares. It was sheer jugglery of fate.

After it had been refused by a number of magazines, he had taken Brissenden's rejected advice and started "The Shame of the Sun" on the round of publishers. After several refusals, Singletree, Darnley & Co. accepted it, promising fall publication. When Martin asked for an advance on royalties, they wrote that such was not their custom, that books of that nature rarely paid for themselves, and that they doubted if his book would sell a thousand copies. Martin figured what the book would earn him on such a sale. Retailed at a dollar, on a royalty of fifteen per cent, it would bring him one hundred and fifty dollars. He decided that if he had it to do over again he would confine himself to fiction. "Adventure," one-fourth as long, had brought him twice as much from *The Millennium*. That newspaper paragraph he had read so long ago had been true, after all. The first-class magazines did pay on acceptance, and they paid well. Not two cents a word, but four cents a word, had *The Millennium* paid him. And, furthermore, they bought good stuff, too, for were they not buying his? This last thought he accompanied with a grin.

He wrote to Singletree, Darnley & Co., offering to sell out his rights in "The Shame of the Sun" for a hundred dollars, but they did not care to take the risk. In the meantime he was not in need of money, for several of his later stories had been accepted and paid for. He actually opened a bank account, where, without a debt in the world, he had several hundred dollars to his credit. "Overdue," after having been declined by a number of magazines, came to rest at the Meredith-Lowell Company. Martin remembered the five dollars Gertrude had given him, and his resolve to return it to her a hundred times over; so he wrote for an advance on royalties of five hundred dollars. To his surprise a check for that amount, accompanied by a contract, came by return mail. He cashed the check into five-dollar gold pieces and telephoned Gertrude that he wanted to see her.

She arrived at the house panting and short of breath from the haste she had made. Apprehensive of trouble, she had stuffed the few dollars she possessed into her hand-satchel; and so sure was she that disaster had overtaken her brother, that she stumbled forward, sobbing, into his arms, at the same time thrusting the satchel mutely at him.

"I'd have come myself," he said. "But I didn't want a row with Mr. Higginbotham, and that is what would have surely happened."

"He'll be all right after a time," she assured him, while she wondered what the trouble was that Martin was in. "But you'd best get a job first an' steady down. Bernard does like to see a man at honest work. That stuff in the newspapers broke 'm all up. I never saw 'm so mad before."

"I'm not going to get a job," Martin said with a smile. "And you can tell him so from me. I don't need a job, and there's the proof of it."

He emptied the hundred gold pieces into her lap in a glinting, tinkling stream.

"You remember that fiver you gave me the time I didn't have carfare? Well, there it is, with ninety-nine brothers of different ages but all of the same size."

If Gertrude had been frightened when she arrived, she was now in a panic of fear. Her fear was such that it was certitude. She was not suspicious. She was convinced. She looked at Martin in horror, and her heavy limbs shrank under the golden stream as though it were burning her.

"It's yours," he laughed.

She burst into tears, and began to moan, "My poor boy, my poor boy!"

He was puzzled for a moment. Then he divined the cause of her agitation and handed her the Meredith-Lowell letter which had accompanied the check. She stumbled through it, pausing now and again to wipe her eyes, and when she had finished, said: —

"An' does it mean that you come by the money honestly?"

"More honestly than if I'd won it in a lottery. I earned it."

Slowly faith came back to her, and she reread the letter carefully. It took him long to explain to her the nature of the transaction which had put the money into his possession, and longer still to get her to understand that the money was really hers and that he did not need it.

"I'll put it in the bank for you," she said finally.

"You'll do nothing of the sort. It's yours, to do with as you please, and if you won't take it, I'll give it to Maria. She'll know what to do with it. I'd suggest, though, that you hire a servant and take a good long rest."

"I'm goin' to tell Bernard all about it," she announced, when she was leaving.

Martin winced, then grinned.

"Yes, do," he said. "And then, maybe, he'll invite me to dinner again."

"Yes, he will—I'm sure he will!" she exclaimed fervently, as she drew him to her and kissed and hugged him.

Chapter XLII

ONE DAY Martin became aware that he was lonely. He was healthy and strong, and had nothing to do. The cessation from writing and studying, the death of Brissenden, and the estrangement from Ruth had made a big hole in his life; and his life refused to be pinned down to good living in cafés and the smoking of Egyptian cigarettes. It was true the South Seas were calling to him, but he had a feeling that the game was not yet played out in the United States. Two books were soon to be published, and he had more books that might find publication. Money could be made out of them, and he would wait and take a sackful of it into the South Seas. He knew a valley and a bay in the Marquesas that he could buy for a thousand Chili dollars. The valley ran from the horseshoe, land-locked bay to the tops of the dizzy, cloud-capped peaks and contained perhaps ten thousand acres. It was filled with tropical fruits, wild chickens, and wild pigs, with an occasional herd of wild cattle, while high up among the peaks were herds of wild goats harried by packs of wild dogs. The whole place was wild. Not a human lived in it. And he could buy it and the bay for a thousand Chili dollars.

The bay, as he remembered it, was magnificent, with water deep enough to accommodate the largest vessel afloat, and so safe that the South Pacific Directory recommended it as the best careening place for ships for hundreds of miles around. He would buy a schooner—one of those yacht-like, coppered crafts that sailed like witches—and go trading copra and pearling among the islands. He would make the valley and the bay his headquarters. He would build a patriarchal grass house like Tati's, and have it and the valley and the schooner filled with dark-skinned servitors. He would entertain there the factor of Taiohæ, captains of wandering traders, and all the best of the South Pacific riffraff. He would keep open house and entertain like a prince. And he would forget the books he had opened and the world that had proved an illusion.

To do all this he must wait in California to fill the sack

with money. Already it was beginning to flow in. If one of
the books made a strike, it might enable him to sell the whole
heap of manuscripts. Also he could collect the stories and the
poems into books, and make sure of the valley and the bay
and the schooner. He would never write again. Upon that he
was resolved. But in the meantime, awaiting the publication
of the books, he must do something more than live dazed and
stupid in the sort of uncaring trance into which he had fallen.

He noted, one Sunday morning, that the Bricklayers' Picnic
took place that day at Shell Mound Park, and to Shell Mound
Park he went. He had been to the working-class picnics too
often in his earlier life not to know what they were like, and
as he entered the park he experienced a recrudescence of all
the old sensations. After all, they were his kind, these working
people. He had been born among them, he had lived among
them, and though he had strayed for a time, it was well to
come back among them.

"If it ain't Mart!" he heard some one say, and the next moment a hearty hand was on his shoulder. "Where you ben all
the time? Off to sea? Come on an' have a drink."

It was the old crowd in which he found himself—the old
crowd, with here and there a gap, and here and there a new
face. The fellows were not bricklayers, but, as in the old days,
they attended all Sunday picnics for the dancing, and the
fighting, and the fun. Martin drank with them, and began to
feel really human once more. He was a fool to have ever left
them, he thought; and he was very certain that his sum of
happiness would have been greater had he remained with
them and let alone the books and the people who sat in the
high places. Yet the beer seemed not so good as of yore. It
didn't taste as it used to taste. Brissenden had spoiled him for
steam beer, he concluded, and wondered if, after all, the
books had spoiled him for companionship with these friends
of his youth. He resolved that he would not be so spoiled,
and he went on to the dancing pavilion. Jimmy, the plumber,
he met there, in the company of a tall, blond girl who
promptly forsook him for Martin.

"Gee, it's like old times," Jimmy explained to the gang that
gave him the laugh as Martin and the blonde whirled away in
a waltz. "An' I don't give a rap. I'm too damned glad to see

'm back. Watch 'm waltz, eh? It's like silk. Who'd blame any girl?"

But Martin restored the blonde to Jimmy, and the three of them, with half a dozen friends, watched the revolving couples and laughed and joked with one another. Everybody was glad to see Martin back. No book of his had been published; he carried no fictitious value in their eyes. They liked him for himself. He felt like a prince returned from exile, and his lonely heart burgeoned in the geniality in which it bathed. He made a mad day of it, and was at his best. Also, he had money in his pockets, and, as in the old days when he returned from sea with a pay-day, he made the money fly.

Once, on the dancing-floor, he saw Lizzie Connolly go by in the arms of a young workingman; and, later, when he made the round of the pavilion, he came upon her sitting by a refreshment table. Surprise and greetings over, he led her away into the grounds, where they could talk without shouting down the music. From the instant he spoke to her, she was his. He knew it. She showed it in the proud humility of her eyes, in every caressing movement of her proudly carried body, and in the way she hung upon his speech. She was not the young girl as he had known her. She was a woman, now, and Martin noted that her wild, defiant beauty had improved, losing none of its wildness, while the defiance and the fire seemed more in control. "A beauty, a perfect beauty," he murmured admiringly under his breath. And he knew she was his, that all he had to do was to say "Come," and she would go with him over the world wherever he led.

Even as the thought flashed through his brain he received a heavy blow on the side of his head that nearly knocked him down. It was a man's fist, directed by a man so angry and in such haste that the fist had missed the jaw for which it was aimed. Martin turned as he staggered, and saw the fist coming at him in a wild swing. Quite as a matter of course he ducked, and the fist flew harmlessly past, pivoting the man who had driven it. Martin hooked with his left, landing on the pivoting man with the weight of his body behind the blow. The man went to the ground sidewise, leaped to his feet, and made a mad rush. Martin saw his passion-distorted face and wondered what could be the cause of the fellow's anger. But while he wondered, he shot in a straight left, the weight of his body behind the blow. The man went over backward and fell in a crumpled heap. Jimmy and others of the gang were running toward them.

Martin was thrilling all over. This was the old days with a vengeance, with their dancing, and their fighting, and their fun. While he kept a wary eye on his antagonist, he glanced at Lizzie. Usually the girls screamed when the fellows got to scrapping, but she had not screamed. She was looking on with bated breath, leaning slightly forward, so keen was her interest, one hand pressed to her breast, her cheek flushed, and in her eyes a great and amazed admiration.

The man had gained his feet and was struggling to escape the restraining arms that were laid on him.

"She was waitin' for me to come back!" he was proclaiming to all and sundry. "She was waitin' for me to come back, an' then that fresh guy comes buttin' in. Let go o' me, I tell yeh. I'm goin' to fix 'm."

"What's eatin' yer?" Jimmy was demanding, as he helped hold the young fellow back. "That guy's Mart Eden. He's nifty with his mits, lemme tell you that, an' he'll eat you alive if you monkey with 'm."

"He can't steal her on me that way," the other interjected.

"He licked the Flyin' Dutchman, an' you know *him*," Jimmy went on expostulating. "An' he did it in five rounds. You couldn't last a minute against him. See?"

This information seemed to have a mollifying effect, and the irate young man favored Martin with a measuring stare.

"He don't look it," he sneered; but the sneer was without passion.

"That's what the Flyin' Dutchman thought," Jimmy assured him. "Come on, now, let's get outa this. There's lots of other girls. Come on."

The young fellow allowed himself to be led away toward the pavilion, and the gang followed after him.

"Who is he?" Martin asked Lizzie. "And what's it all about, anyway?"

Already the zest of combat, which of old had been so keen

and lasting, had died down, and he discovered that he was
self-analytical, too much so to live, single heart and single
hand, so primitive an existence.

Lizzie tossed her head.

"Oh, he's nobody," she said. "He's just ben keepin' company with me.

"I had to, you see," she explained after a pause. "I was
gettin' pretty lonesome. But I never forgot." Her voice sank
lower, and she looked straight before her. "I'd throw 'm
down for you any time."

Martin, looking at her averted face, knowing that all he had
to do was to reach out his hand and pluck her, fell to pondering whether, after all, there was any real worth in refined,
grammatical English, and, so, forgot to reply to her.

"You put it all over him," she said tentatively, with a laugh.

"He's a husky young fellow, though," he admitted generously. "If they hadn't taken him away, he might have given
me my hands full."

"Who was that lady friend I seen you with that night?" she
asked abruptly.

"Oh, just a lady friend," was his answer.

"It was a long time ago," she murmured contemplatively.
"It seems like a thousand years."

But Martin went no further into the matter. He led the
conversation off into other channels. They had lunch in the
restaurant, where he ordered wine and expensive delicacies
and afterward he danced with her and with no one but her,
till she was tired. He was a good dancer, and she whirled
around and around with him in a heaven of delight, her head
against his shoulder, wishing that it could last forever. Later
in the afternoon they strayed off among the trees, where, in
the good old fashion, she sat down while he sprawled on his
back, his head in her lap. He lay and dozed, while she fondled
his hair, looked down on his closed eyes, and loved him without reserve. Looking up suddenly, he read the tender advertisement in her face. Her eyes fluttered down, then they
opened and looked into his with soft defiance.

"I've kept straight all these years," she said, her voice so
low that it was almost a whisper.

In his heart Martin knew that it was the miraculous truth.

And at his heart pleaded a great temptation. It was in his power to make her happy. Denied happiness himself, why should he deny happiness to her? He could marry her and take her down with him to dwell in the grass-walled castle in the Marquesas. The desire to do it was strong, but stronger still was the imperative command of his nature not to do it. In spite of himself he was still faithful to Love. The old days of license and easy living were gone. He could not bring them back, nor could he go back to them. He was changed—how changed he had not realized until now.

"I am not a marrying man, Lizzie," he said lightly.

The hand caressing his hair paused perceptibly, then went on with the same gentle stroke. He noticed her face harden, but it was with the hardness of resolution, for still the soft color was in her cheeks and she was all glowing and melting.

"I did not mean that—" she began, then faltered. "Or anyway I don't care.

"I don't care," she repeated. "I'm proud to be your friend. I'd do anything for you. I'm made that way, I guess."

Martin sat up. He took her hand in his. He did it deliberately, with warmth but without passion; and such warmth chilled her.

"Don't let's talk about it," she said.

"You are a great and noble woman," he said. "And it is I who should be proud to know you. And I am, I am. You are a ray of light to me in a very dark world, and I've got to be straight with you, just as straight as you have been."

"I don't care whether you're straight with me or not. You could do anything with me. You could throw me in the dirt an' walk on me. An' you're the only man in the world that can," she added with a defiant flash. "I ain't taken care of myself ever since I was a kid for nothin'."

"And it's just because of that that I'm not going to," he said gently. "You are so big and generous that you challenge me to equal generousness. I'm not marrying, and I'm not— well, loving without marrying, though I've done my share of that in the past. I'm sorry I came here to-day and met you. But it can't be helped now, and I never expected it would turn out this way.

"But look here, Lizzie. I can't begin to tell you how much

I like you. I do more than like you. I admire and respect you.
You are magnificent, and you are magnificently good. But
what's the use of words? Yet there's something I'd like to do.
You've had a hard life; let me make it easy for you." (A joyous light welled into her eyes, then faded out again.) "I'm
pretty sure of getting hold of some money soon—lots of it."

In that moment he abandoned the idea of the valley and
the bay, the grass-walled castle and the trim, white schooner.
After all, what did it matter? He could go away, as he had
done so often, before the mast, on any ship bound anywhere.

"I'd like to turn it over to you. There must be something
you want—to go to school or business college. You might
like to study and be a stenographer. I could fix it for you. Or
maybe your father and mother are living—I could set them
up in a grocery store or something. Anything you want, just
name it, and I can fix it for you."

She made no reply, but sat, gazing straight before her, dry-
eyed and motionless, but with an ache in the throat which
Martin divined so strongly that it made his own throat ache.
He regretted that he had spoken. It seemed so tawdry what
he had offered her—mere money—compared with what she
offered him. He offered her an extraneous thing with which
he could part without a pang, while she offered him herself,
along with disgrace and shame, and sin, and all her hopes of
heaven.

"Don't let's talk about it," she said with a catch in her voice
that she changed to a cough. She stood up. "Come on, let's
go home. I'm all tired out."

The day was done, and the merrymakers had nearly all departed. But as Martin and Lizzie emerged from the trees they
found the gang waiting for them. Martin knew immediately
the meaning of it. Trouble was brewing. The gang was his
body-guard. They passed out through the gates of the park
with, straggling in the rear, a second gang, the friends that
Lizzie's young man had collected to avenge the loss of his
lady. Several constables and special police officers, anticipating trouble, trailed along to prevent it, and herded the two
gangs separately aboard the train for San Francisco. Martin
told Jimmy that he would get off at Sixteenth Street Station
and catch the electric car into Oakland. Lizzie was very quiet

and without interest in what was impending. The train pulled in to Sixteenth Street Station, and the waiting electric car could be seen, the conductor of which was impatiently clanging the gong.

"There she is," Jimmy counselled. "Make a run for it, an' we'll hold 'em back. Now you go! Hit her up!"

The hostile gang was temporarily disconcerted by the manœuvre, then it dashed from the train in pursuit. The staid and sober Oakland folk who sat upon the car scarcely noted the young fellow and the girl who ran for it and found a seat in front on the outside. They did not connect the couple with Jimmy, who sprang on the steps, crying to the motor-man:—

"Slam on the juice, old man, and beat it outa here!"

The next moment Jimmy whirled about, and the passengers saw him land his fist on the face of a running man who was trying to board the car. But fists were landing on faces the whole length of the car. Thus, Jimmy and his gang, strung out on the long, lower steps, met the attacking gang. The car started with a great clanging of its gong, and, as Jimmy's gang drove off the last assailants, they, too, jumped off to finish the job. The car dashed on, leaving the flurry of combat far behind, and its dumfounded passengers never dreamed that the quiet young man and the pretty working-girl sitting in the corner on the outside seat had been the cause of the row.

Martin had enjoyed the fight, with a recrudescence of the old fighting thrills. But they quickly died away, and he was oppressed by a great sadness. He felt very old—centuries older than those careless, care-free young companions of his other days. He had travelled far, too far to go back. Their mode of life, which had once been his, was now distasteful to him. He was disappointed in it all. He had developed into an alien. As the steam beer had tasted raw, so their companionship seemed raw to him. He was too far removed. Too many thousands of opened books yawned between them and him. He had exiled himself. He had travelled in the vast realm of intellect until he could no longer return home. On the other hand, he was human, and his gregarious need for companionship remained unsatisfied. He had found no new home. As the gang could not understand him, as his own family could not understand him, as the bourgeoisie could not understand him, so this girl beside him, whom he honored high, could not understand him nor the honor he paid her. His sadness was not untouched with bitterness as he thought it over.

"Make it up with him," he advised Lizzie, at parting, as they stood in front of the workingman's shack in which she lived, near Sixth and Market. He referred to the young fellow whose place he had usurped that day.

"I can't—now," she said.

"Oh, go on," he said jovially. "All you have to do is whistle and he'll come running."

"I didn't mean that," she said simply.

And he knew what she had meant.

She leaned toward him as he was about to say good night. But she leaned not imperatively, not seductively, but wistfully and humbly. He was touched to the heart. His large tolerance rose up in him. He put his arms around her, and kissed her, and knew that upon his own lips rested as true a kiss as man ever received.

"My God!" she sobbed. "I could die for you. I could die for you."

She tore herself from him suddenly and ran up the steps. He felt a quick moisture in his eyes.

"Martin Eden," he communed. "You're not a brute, and you're a damn poor Nietzscheman. You'd marry her if you could and fill her quivering heart full with happiness. But you can't, you can't. And it's a damn shame.

" 'A poor old tramp explains his poor old ulcers,' " he muttered, remembering his Henley. " 'Life is, I think, a blunder and a shame.' It is—a blunder and a shame."

Chapter XLIII

"THE SHAME OF THE SUN" was published in October. As Martin cut the cords of the express package and the half-dozen complimentary copies from the publishers spilled out on the table, a heavy sadness fell upon him. He thought of the wild delight that would have been his had this happened a few short months before, and he contrasted that delight that should have been with his present uncaring coldness. His book, his first book, and his pulse had not gone up a fraction of a beat, and he was only sad. It meant little to him now. The most it meant was that it might bring some money, and little enough did he care for money.

He carried a copy out into the kitchen and presented it to Maria.

"I did it," he explained, in order to clear up her bewilderment. "I wrote it in the room there, and I guess some few quarts of your vegetable soup went into the making of it. Keep it. It's yours. Just to remember me by, you know."

He was not bragging, not showing off. His sole motive was to make her happy, to make her proud of him, to justify her long faith in him. She put the book in the front room on top of the family Bible. A sacred thing was this book her lodger had made, a fetich of friendship. It softened the blow of his having been a laundryman, and though she could not understand a line of it, she knew that every line of it was great. She was a simple, practical, hard-working woman, but she possessed faith in large endowment.

Just as emotionlessly as he had received "The Shame of the Sun" did he read the reviews of it that came in weekly from the clipping bureau. The book was making a hit, that was evident. It meant more gold in the money sack. He could fix up Lizzie, redeem all his promises, and still have enough left to build his grass-walled castle.

Singletree, Darnley & Co. had cautiously brought out an edition of fifteen hundred copies, but the first reviews had started a second edition of twice the size through the presses; and ere this was delivered a third edition of five thousand had

889

been ordered. A London firm made arrangements by cable
for an English edition, and hot-footed upon this came the
news of French, German, and Scandinavian translations in
progress. The attack upon the Maeterlinck school could not
have been made at a more opportune moment. A fierce controversy was precipitated. Saleeby and Haeckel indorsed and
defended "The Shame of the Sun," for once finding themselves on the same side of a question. Crookes and Wallace
ranged up on the opposing side, while Sir Oliver Lodge attempted to formulate a compromise that would jibe with his
particular cosmic theories. Maeterlinck's followers rallied
around the standard of mysticism. Chesterton set the whole
world laughing with a series of alleged non-partisan essays on
the subject, and the whole affair, controversy and controver-
sialists, was well-nigh swept into the pit by a thundering
broadside from George Bernard Shaw. Needless to say the
arena was crowded with hosts of lesser lights, and the dust
and sweat and din became terrific.

"It is a most marvellous happening," Singletree, Darnley
& Co. wrote Martin, "a critical philosophic essay selling like
a novel. You could not have chosen your subject better, and
all contributory factors have been unwarrantedly propitious.
We need scarcely to assure you that we are making hay while
the sun shines. Over forty thousand copies have already been
sold in the United States and Canada, and a new edition of
twenty thousand is on the presses. We are overworked, trying
to supply the demand. Nevertheless we have helped to create
that demand. We have already spent five thousand dollars in
advertising. The book is bound to be a record-breaker.

"Please find herewith a contract in duplicate for your next
book which we have taken the liberty of forwarding to you.
You will please note that we have increased your royalties to
twenty per cent, which is about as high as a conservative publishing house dares go. If our offer is agreeable to you, please
fill in the proper blank space with the title of your book. We
make no stipulations concerning its nature. Any book on any
subject. If you have one already written, so much the better.
Now is the time to strike. The iron could not be hotter.

"On receipt of signed contract we shall be pleased to make
you an advance on royalties of five thousand dollars. You see,

we have faith in you, and we are going in on this thing big. We should like, also, to discuss with you the drawing up of a contract for a term of years, say ten, during which we shall have the exclusive right of publishing in book-form all that you produce. But more of this anon."

Martin laid down the letter and worked a problem in mental arithmetic, finding the product of fifteen cents times sixty thousand to be nine thousand dollars. He signed the new contract, inserting "The Smoke of Joy" in the blank space, and mailed it back to the publishers along with the twenty storiettes he had written in the days before he discovered the formula for the newspaper storiette. And promptly as the United States mail could deliver and return, came Singletree, Darnley & Co.'s check for five thousand dollars.

"I want you to come down town with me, Maria, this afternoon about two o'clock," Martin said, the morning the check arrived. "Or, better, meet me at Fourteenth and Broadway at two o'clock. I'll be looking out for you."

At the appointed time she was there; but *shoes* was the only clew to the mystery her mind had been capable of evolving, and she suffered a distinct shock of disappointment when Martin walked her right by a shoe-store and dived into a real estate office. What happened thereupon resided forever after in her memory as a dream. Fine gentlemen smiled at her benevolently as they talked with Martin and one another; a type-writer clicked; signatures were affixed to an imposing document; her own landlord was there, too, and affixed his signature; and when all was over and she was outside on the sidewalk, her landlord spoke to her, saying, "Well, Maria, you won't have to pay me no seven dollars and a half this month."

Maria was too stunned for speech.

"Or next month, or the next, or the next," her landlord said.

She thanked him incoherently, as if for a favor. And it was not until she had returned home to North Oakland and conferred with her own kind, and had the Portuguese grocer investigate, that she really knew that she was the owner of the little house in which she had lived and for which she had paid rent so long.

"Why don't you trade with me no more?" the Portuguese

grocer asked Martin that evening, stepping out to hail him when he got off the car; and Martin explained that he wasn't doing his own cooking any more, and then went in and had a drink of wine on the house. He noted it was the best wine the grocer had in stock.

"Maria," Martin announced that night, "I'm going to leave you. And you're going to leave here yourself soon. Then you can rent the house and be a landlord yourself. You've a brother in San Leandro or Haywards, and he's in the milk business. I want you to send all your washing back un-washed—understand?—unwashed, and to go out to San Leandro to-morrow, or Haywards, or wherever it is, and see that brother of yours. Tell him to come to see me. I'll be stopping at the Metropole down in Oakland. He'll know a good milk-ranch when he sees one."

And so it was that Maria became a landlord and the sole owner of a dairy, with two hired men to do the work for her and a bank account that steadily increased despite the fact that her whole brood wore shoes and went to school. Few persons ever meet the fairy princes they dream about; but Maria, who worked hard and whose head was hard, never dreaming about fairy princes, entertained hers in the guise of an ex-laundry-man.

In the meantime the world had begun to ask: "Who is this Martin Eden?" He had declined to give any biographical data to his publishers, but the newspapers were not to be denied. Oakland was his own town, and the reporters nosed out scores of individuals who could supply information. All that he was and was not, all that he had done and most of what he had not done, was spread out for the delectation of the public, accompanied by snapshots and photographs—the lat-ter procured from the local photographer who had once taken Martin's picture and who promptly copyrighted it and put it on the market. At first, so great was his disgust with the mag-azines and all bourgeois society, Martin fought against pub-licity; but in the end, because it was easier than not to, he surrendered. He found that he could not refuse himself to the special writers who travelled long distances to see him. Then again, each day was so many hours long, and, since he no longer was occupied with writing and studying, those hours had to be occupied somehow; so he yielded to what was to him a whim, permitted interviews, gave his opinions on literature and philosophy, and even accepted invitations of the bourgeoisie. He had settled down into a strange and comfortable state of mind. He no longer cared. He forgave everybody, even the cub reporter who had painted him red and to whom he now granted a full page with specially posed photographs.

He saw Lizzie occasionally, and it was patent that she regretted the greatness that had come to him. It widened the space between them. Perhaps it was with the hope of narrowing it that she yielded to his persuasions to go to night school and business college and to have herself gowned by a wonderful dressmaker who charged outrageous prices. She improved visibly from day to day, until Martin wondered if he was doing right, for he knew that all her compliance and endeavor was for his sake. She was trying to make herself of worth in his eyes—of the sort of worth he seemed to value. Yet he gave her no hope, treating her in brotherly fashion and rarely seeing her.

"Overdue" was rushed upon the market by the Meredith-Lowell Company in the height of his popularity, and being fiction, in point of sales it made even a bigger strike than "The Shame of the Sun." Week after week his was the credit of the unprecedented performance of having two books at the head of the list of best-sellers. Not only did the story take with the fiction-readers, but those who read "The Shame of the Sun" with avidity were likewise attracted to the sea-story by the cosmic grasp of mastery with which he had handled it. First, he had attacked the literature of mysticism, and had done it exceeding well; and, next, he had successfully supplied the very literature he had exposited, thus proving himself to be that rare genius, a critic and a creator in one.

Money poured in on him, fame poured in on him; he flashed, comet-like, through the world of literature, and he was more amused than interested by the stir he was making. One thing was puzzling him, a little thing that would have puzzled the world had it known. But the world would have puzzled over his bepuzzlement rather than over the little thing that to him loomed gigantic. Judge Blount invited him to dinner. That was the little thing, or the beginning of the little thing, that was soon to become the big thing. He had insulted Judge Blount, treated him abominably, and Judge Blount, meeting him on the street, invited him to dinner. Martin bethought himself of the numerous occasions on which he had met Judge Blount at the Morses' and when Judge Blount had not invited him to dinner. Why had he not invited him to dinner then? he asked himself. He had not changed. He was the same Martin Eden. What made the difference? The fact that the stuff he had written had appeared inside the covers of books? But it was work performed. It was not something he had done since. It was achievement accomplished at the very time Judge Blount was sharing this general view and sneering at his Spencer and his intellect. Therefore it was not for any real value, but for a purely fictitious value that Judge Blount invited him to dinner.

Martin grinned and accepted the invitation, marvelling the while at his complacence. And at the dinner, where, with their womenkind, were half a dozen of those that sat in high places, and where Martin found himself quite the lion, Judge Blount, warmly seconded by Judge Hanwell, urged privately that Martin should permit his name to be put up for the Styx—the ultra-select club to which belonged, not the mere men of wealth, but the men of attainment. And Martin declined, and was more puzzled than ever.

He was kept busy disposing of his heap of manuscripts. He was overwhelmed by requests from editors. It had been discovered that he was a stylist, with meat under his style. *The Northern Review*, after publishing "The Cradle of Beauty," had written him for half a dozen similar essays, which would have been supplied out of the heap, had not *Burton's Magazine*, in a speculative mood, offered him five hundred dollars each for five essays. He wrote back that he would supply the demand, but at a thousand dollars an essay. He remembered that all these manuscripts had been refused by the very magazines that were now clamoring for them. And their refusals had been cold-blooded, automatic, stereotyped. They had made him sweat, and now he intended to make them sweat. *Burton's Magazine* paid his price for five essays, and the remaining four, at the same rate, were snapped up by *Mackintosh's Monthly*, *The Northern Review* being too poor to stand the pace. Thus went out to the world "The High Priests of Mystery," "The Wonder-Dreamers," "The Yardstick of the Ego," "Philosophy of Illusion," "God and Clod," "Art and Biology," "Critics and Test-tubes," "Star-dust," and "The Dignity of Usury,"—to raise storms and rumblings and mutterings that were many a day in dying down.

Editors wrote to him telling him to name his own terms, which he did, but it was always for work performed. He refused resolutely to pledge himself to any new thing. The thought of again setting pen to paper maddened him. He had seen Brissenden torn to pieces by the crowd, and despite the fact that him the crowd acclaimed, he could not get over the shock nor gather any respect for the crowd. His very popularity seemed a disgrace and a treason to Brissenden. It made him wince, but he made up his mind to go on and fill the money-bag.

He received letters from editors like the following: "About a year ago we were unfortunate enough to refuse your collection of love-poems. We were greatly impressed by them at the time, but certain arrangements already entered into prevented our taking them. If you still have them, and if you will be kind enough to forward them, we shall be glad to publish the entire collection on your own terms. We are also prepared to make a most advantageous offer for bringing them out in book-form."

Martin recollected his blank-verse tragedy, and sent it instead. He read it over before mailing, and was particularly impressed by its sophomoric amateurishness and general worthlessness. But he sent it; and it was published, to the everlasting regret of the editor. The public was indignant and incredulous. It was too far a cry from Martin Eden's high standard to that serious bosh. It was asserted that he had never written it, that the magazine had faked it very clumsily, or that Martin Eden was emulating the elder Dumas and at the height of success was hiring his writing done for him. But when he explained that the tragedy was an early effort of his literary childhood, and that the magazine had refused to be happy unless it got it, a great laugh went up at the magazine's expense and a change in the editorship followed. The tragedy was never brought out in book-form, though Martin pocketed the advance royalties that had been paid.

Coleman's Weekly sent Martin a lengthy telegram, costing nearly three hundred dollars, offering him a thousand dollars an article for twenty articles. He was to travel over the United States, with all expenses paid, and select whatever topics interested him. The body of the telegram was devoted to hypothetical topics in order to show him the freedom of range that was to be his. The only restriction placed upon him was that he must confine himself to the United States. Martin sent his inability to accept and his regrets by wire "collect."

"Wiki-Wiki," published in *Warren's Monthly*, was an instantaneous success. It was brought out forward in a wide-margined, beautifully decorated volume that struck the holiday trade and sold like wildfire. The critics were unanimous in the belief that it would take its place with those two classics by two great writers, "The Bottle Imp" and "The Magic Skin."

The public, however, received the "Smoke of Joy" collection rather dubiously and coldly. The audacity and unconventionality of the storiettes was a shock to bourgeois morality and prejudice; but when Paris went mad over the immediate translation that was made, the American and English reading public followed suit and bought so many copies that Martin compelled the conservative house of Singletree, Darnley & Co. to pay a flat royalty of twenty-five per cent for a third book, and thirty per cent flat for a fourth. These two volumes comprised all the short stories he had written and which had received, or were receiving, serial publication. "The Ring of Bells" and his horror stories constituted one collection; the other collection was composed of "Adventure," "The Pot," "The Wine of Life," "The Whirlpool," "The Jostling Street," and four other stories. The Lowell-Meredith Company captured the collection of all his essays, and the Maxmillian Company got his "Sea Lyrics" and the "Love-cycle," the latter receiving serial publication in the *Ladies' Home Companion* after the payment of an extortionate price.

Martin heaved a sigh of relief when he had disposed of the last manuscript. The grass-walled castle and the white, coppered schooner were very near to him. Well, at any rate he had discovered Brissenden's contention that nothing of merit found its way into the magazines. His own success demonstrated that Brissenden had been wrong. And yet, somehow, he had a feeling that Brissenden had been right, after all. "The Shame of the Sun" had been the cause of his success more than the stuff he had written. That stuff had been merely incidental. It had been rejected right and left by the magazines. The publication of "The Shame of the Sun" had started a controversy and precipitated the landslide in his favor. Had there been no "Shame of the Sun" there would have been no landslide, and had there been no miracle in the go of "The Shame of the Sun" there would have been no landslide. Singletree, Darnley & Co. attested that miracle. They had brought out a first edition of fifteen hundred copies and been dubious of selling it. They were experienced publishers and no one had been more astounded than they at the success which had followed. To them it had been in truth a miracle. They never got over it, and every letter they wrote him reflected their reverent awe of that first mysterious happening. They did not attempt to explain it. There was no explaining it. It had happened. In the face of all experience to the contrary, it had happened.

So it was, reasoning thus, that Martin questioned the validity of his popularity. It was the bourgeoisie that bought his books and poured its gold into his money-sack, and from what little he knew of the bourgeoisie it was not clear to him how it could possibly appreciate or comprehend what he had written. His intrinsic beauty and power meant nothing to the hundreds of thousands who were acclaiming him and buying his books. He was the fad of the hour, the adventurer who had stormed Parnassus while the gods nodded. The hundreds of thousands read him and acclaimed him with the same brute non-understanding with which they had flung themselves on Brissenden's "Ephemera" and torn it to pieces—a wolf-rabble that fawned on him instead of fanging him. Fawn or fang, it was all a matter of chance. One thing he knew with absolute certitude: "Ephemera" was infinitely greater than anything he had done. It was infinitely greater than anything he had in him. It was a poem of centuries. Then the tribute the mob paid him was a sorry tribute indeed, for that same mob had wallowed "Ephemera" into the mire. He sighed heavily and with satisfaction. He was glad the last manuscript was sold and that he would soon be done with it all.

Chapter XLIV

Mr. Morse met Martin in the office of the Hotel Metropole. Whether he had happened there just casually, intent on other affairs, or whether he had come there for the direct purpose of inviting him to dinner, Martin never could quite make up his mind, though he inclined toward the second hypothesis. At any rate, invited to dinner he was by Mr. Morse—Ruth's father, who had forbidden him the house and broken off the engagement.

Martin was not angry. He was not even on his dignity. He tolerated Mr. Morse, wondering the while how it felt to eat such humble pie. He did not decline the invitation. Instead, he put it off with vagueness and indefiniteness and inquired after the family, particularly after Mrs. Morse and Ruth. He spoke her name without hesitancy, naturally, though secretly surprised that he had had no inward quiver, no old, familiar increase of pulse and warm surge of blood.

He had many invitations to dinner, some of which he accepted. Persons got themselves introduced to him in order to invite him to dinner. And he went on puzzling over the little thing that was becoming a great thing. Bernard Higginbotham invited him to dinner. He puzzled the harder. He remembered the days of his desperate starvation when no one invited him to dinner. That was the time he needed dinners, and went weak and faint for lack of them and lost weight from sheer famine. That was the paradox of it. When he wanted dinners, no one gave them to him, and now that he could buy a hundred thousand dinners and was losing his appetite, dinners were thrust upon him right and left. But why? There was no justice in it, no merit on his part. He was no different. All the work he had done was even at that time work performed. Mr. and Mrs. Morse had condemned him for an idler and a shirk and through Ruth had urged that he take a clerk's position in an office. Furthermore, they had been aware of his work performed. Manuscript after manuscript of his had been turned over to them by Ruth. They had read them. It was the very same work that had put his name in all the papers, and it was his name being in all the papers that led them to invite him.

One thing was certain: the Morses had not cared to have him for himself or for his work. Therefore they could not want him now for himself or for his work, but for the fame that was his, because he was somebody amongst men, and—why not?—because he had a hundred thousand dollars or so. That was the way bourgeois society valued a man, and who was he to expect it otherwise? But he was proud. He disdained such valuation. He desired to be valued for himself, or for his work, which, after all, was an expression of himself. That was the way Lizzie valued him. The work, with her, did not even count. She valued him, himself. That was the way Jimmy, the plumber, and all the old gang valued him. That had been proved often enough in the days when he ran with them; it had been proved that Sunday at Shell Mound Park. His work could go hang. What they liked, and were willing to scrap for, was just Mart Eden, one of the bunch and a pretty good guy.

Then there was Ruth. She had liked him for himself, that was indisputable. And yet, much as she had liked him she had liked the bourgeois standard of valuation more. She had opposed his writing, and principally, it seemed to him, because it did not earn money. That had been her criticism of his "Love-cycle." She, too, had urged him to get a job. It was true, she refined it to "position," but it meant the same thing, and in his own mind the old nomenclature stuck. He had read her all that he wrote—poems, stories, essays—"Wiki-Wiki," "The Shame of the Sun," everything. And she had always and consistently urged him to get a job, to go to work—good God! as if he hadn't been working, robbing sleep, exhausting life, in order to be worthy of her.

So the little thing grew bigger. He was healthy and normal, ate regularly, slept long hours, and yet the growing little thing was becoming an obsession. *Work performed*. The phrase haunted his brain. He sat opposite Bernard Higginbotham at a heavy Sunday dinner over Higginbotham's Cash Store, and it was all he could do to restrain himself from shouting out:—

"It was work performed! And now you feed me, when then

you let me starve, forbade me your house, and damned me because I wouldn't get a job. And the work was already done, all done. And now, when I speak, you check the thought un-uttered on your lips and hang on my lips and pay respectful attention to whatever I choose to say. I tell you your party is rotten and filled with grafters, and instead of flying into a rage you hum and haw and admit there is a great deal in what I say. And why? Because I'm famous; because I've a lot of money. Not because I'm Martin Eden, a pretty good fellow and not particularly a fool. I could tell you the moon is made of green cheese and you would subscribe to the notion, at least you would not repudiate it, because I've got dollars, mountains of them. And it was all done long ago; it was work performed, I tell you, when you spat upon me as the dirt under your feet."

But Martin did not shout out. The thought gnawed in his brain, an unceasing torment, while he smiled and succeeded in being tolerant. As he grew silent, Bernard Higginbotham got the reins and did the talking. He was a success himself, and proud of it. He was self-made. No one had helped him. He owed no man. He was fulfilling his duty as a citizen and bringing up a large family. And there was Higginbotham's Cash Store, that monument of his own industry and ability. He loved Higginbotham's Cash Store as some men loved their wives. He opened up his heart to Martin, showed with what keenness and with what enormous planning he had made the store. And he had plans for it, ambitious plans. The neighborhood was growing up fast. The store was really too small. If he had more room, he would be able to put in a score of labor-saving and money-saving improvements. And he would do it yet. He was straining every effort for the day when he could buy the adjoining lot and put up another two-story frame building. The upstairs he could rent, and the whole ground-floor of both buildings would be Higgin-botham's Cash Store. His eyes glistened when he spoke of the new sign that would stretch clear across both buildings.

Martin forgot to listen. The refrain of "Work performed," in his own brain, was drowning the other's clatter. The re-frain maddened him, and he tried to escape from it.

"How much did you say it would cost?" he asked suddenly.

His brother-in-law paused in the middle of an expatiation on the business opportunities of the neighborhood. He hadn't said how much it would cost. But he knew. He had figured it out a score of times.

"At the way lumber is now," he said, "four thousand could do it."

"Including the sign?"

"I didn't count on that. It'd just have to come, onc't the buildin' was there."

"And the ground?"

"Three thousand more."

He leaned forward, licking his lips, nervously spreading and closing his fingers, while he watched Martin write a check. When it was passed over to him, he glanced at the amount—seven thousand dollars.

"I—I can't afford to pay more than six per cent," he said huskily.

Martin wanted to laugh, but, instead, demanded:—

"How much would that be?"

"Lemme see. Six per cent—six times seven—four hundred an' twenty."

"That would be thirty-five dollars a month, wouldn't it?"

Higginbotham nodded.

"Then, if you've no objection, we'll arrange it this way." Martin glanced at Gertrude. "You can have the principal to keep for yourself, if you'll use the thirty-five dollars a month for cooking and washing and scrubbing. The seven thousand is yours if you'll guarantee that Gertrude does no more drudgery. Is it a go?"

Mr. Higginbotham swallowed hard. That his wife should do no more housework was an affront to his thrifty soul. The magnificent present was the coating of a pill, a bitter pill. That his wife should not work! It gagged him.

"All right, then," Martin said. "I'll pay the thirty-five a month, and—"

He reached across the table for the check. But Bernard Higginbotham got his hand on it first, crying:—

"I accept! I accept!"

When Martin got on the electric car, he was very sick and tired. He looked up at the assertive sign.

"The swine," he groaned. "The swine, the swine."

When *Mackintosh's Magazine* published "The Palmist," featuring it with decorations by Berthier and with two pictures by Wenn, Hermann von Schmidt forgot that he had called the verses obscene. He announced that his wife had inspired the poem, saw to it that the news reached the ears of a reporter, and submitted to an interview by a staff writer who was accompanied by a staff photographer and a staff artist. The result was a full page in a Sunday supplement, filled with photographs and idealized drawings of Marian, with many intimate details of Martin Eden and his family, and with the full text of "The Palmist" in large type, and republished by special permission of *Mackintosh's Magazine*. It caused quite a stir in the neighborhood, and good housewives were proud to have the acquaintance of the great writer's sister, while those who had not made haste to cultivate it. Hermann von Schmidt chuckled in his little repair shop and decided to order a new lathe. "Better than advertising," he told Marian, "and it costs nothing."

"We'd better have him to dinner," she suggested.

And to dinner Martin came, making himself agreeable with the fat wholesale butcher and his fatter wife—important folk, they, likely to be of use to a rising young man like Hermann von Schmidt. No less a bait, however, had been required to draw them to his house than his great brother-in-law. Another man at table who had swallowed the same bait was the superintendent of the Pacific Coast agencies for the Asa Bicycle Company. Him Von Schmidt desired to please and propitiate because from him could be obtained the Oakland agency for the bicycle. So Hermann von Schmidt found it a goodly asset to have Martin for a brother-in-law, but in his heart of hearts he couldn't understand where it all came in. In the silent watches of the night, while his wife slept, he had floundered through Martin's books and poems, and decided that the world was a fool to buy them.

And in his heart of hearts Martin understood the situation only too well, as he leaned back and gloated at Von Schmidt's head, in fancy punching it well-nigh off of him, sending blow after blow home just right—the chuckle-headed Dutchman! One thing he did like about him, however. Poor as he was, and determined to rise as he was, he nevertheless hired one servant to take the heavy work off of Marian's hands. Martin talked with the superintendent of the Asa agencies, and after dinner he drew him aside with Hermann, whom he backed financially for the best bicycle store with fittings in Oakland. He went further, and in a private talk with Hermann told him to keep his eyes open for an automobile agency and garage, for there was no reason that he should not be able to run both establishments successfully.

With tears in her eyes and her arms around his neck, Marian, at parting, told Martin how much she loved him and always had loved him. It was true, there was a perceptible halt midway in her assertion, which she glossed over with more tears and kisses and incoherent stammerings, and which Martin inferred to be her appeal for forgiveness for the time she had lacked faith in him and insisted on his getting a job.

"He can't never keep his money, that's sure," Hermann von Schmidt confided to his wife. "He got mad when I spoke of interest, an' he said damn the principal and if I mentioned it again, he'd punch my Dutch head off. That's what he said— my Dutch head. But he's all right, even if he ain't no business man. He's given me my chance, an' he's all right."

Invitations to dinner poured in on Martin; and the more they poured, the more he puzzled. He sat, the guest of honor, at an Arden Club banquet, with men of note whom he had heard about and read about all his life; and they told him how, when they had read "The Ring of Bells" in the *Transcontinental*, and "The Peri and the Pearl" in *The Hornet*, they had immediately picked him for a winner. My God! and I was hungry and in rags, he thought to himself. Why didn't you give me a dinner then? Then was the time. It was work performed. If you are feeding me now for work performed, why did you not feed me then when I needed it? Not one word in "The Ring of Bells," nor in "The Peri and the Pearl" has been changed. No; you're not feeding me now for work performed. You are feeding me because everybody else is feeding me and because it is an honor to feed me. You are feeding me now because you are herd animals; because you are part of the mob; because the one blind, automatic thought in the mob-mind just now is to feed me. And where does Martin Eden and the work Martin Eden performed come in in all this? he asked himself plaintively, then arose to respond cleverly and wittily to a clever and witty toast.

So it went. Wherever he happened to be—at the Press Club, at the Redwood Club, at pink teas and literary gatherings—always were remembered "The Ring of Bells" and "The Peri and the Pearl" when they were first published. And always was Martin's maddening and unuttered demand: Why didn't you feed me then? It was work performed. "The Ring of Bells" and "The Peri and the Pearl" are not changed one iota. They were just as artistic, just as worth while, then as now. But you are not feeding me for their sake, nor for the sake of anything else I have written. You're feeding me because it is the style of feeding just now, because the whole mob is crazy with the idea of feeding Martin Eden.

And often, at such times, he would abruptly see slouch in among the company a young hoodlum in square-cut coat and under a stiff-rim Stetson hat. It happened to him at the Gallina Society in Oakland one afternoon. As he rose from his chair and stepped forward across the platform, he saw stalk through the wide door at the rear of the great room the young hoodlum with the square-cut coat and stiff-rim hat. Five hundred fashionably gowned women turned their heads, so intent and steadfast was Martin's gaze, to see what he was seeing. But they saw only the empty centre aisle. He saw the young tough lurching down that aisle and wondered if he would remove the stiff-rim which never yet had he seen him without. Straight down the aisle he came, and up the platform. Martin could have wept over that youthful shade of himself, when he thought of all that lay before him. Across the platform he swaggered, right up to Martin, and into the foreground of Martin's consciousness disappeared. The five hundred women applauded softly with gloved hands, seeking to encourage the bashful great man who was their guest. And Martin shook the vision from his brain, smiled, and began to speak.

The Superintendent of Schools, good old man, stopped Martin on the street and remembered him, recalling seances in his office when Martin was expelled from school for fighting.

"I read your 'Ring of Bells' in one of the magazines quite a time ago," he said. "It was as good as Poe. Splendid, I said at the time, splendid!"

Yes, and twice in the months that followed you passed me on the street and did not know me, Martin almost said aloud. Each time I was hungry and heading for the pawnbroker. Yet it was work performed. You did not know me then. Why do you know me now?

"I was remarking to my wife only the other day," the other was saying, "wouldn't it be a good idea to have you out to dinner some time? And she quite agreed with me. Yes, she quite agreed with me."

"Dinner?" Martin said so sharply that it was almost a snarl.

"Why, yes, yes, dinner, you know—just pot luck with us, with your old superintendent, you rascal," he uttered nervously, poking Martin in an attempt at jocular fellowship.

Martin went down the street in a daze. He stopped at the corner and looked about him vacantly.

"Well, I'll be damned!" he murmured at last. "The old fellow was afraid of me."

Chapter XLV

K REIS came to Martin one day—Kreis, of the "real dirt"; and Martin turned to him with relief, to receive the glowing details of a scheme sufficiently wild-catty to interest him as a fictionist rather than an investor. Kreis paused long enough in the midst of his exposition to tell him that in most of his "Shame of the Sun" he had been a chump.

"But I didn't come here to spout philosophy," Kreis went on. "What I want to know is whether or not you will put a thousand dollars in on this deal?"

"No, I'm not chump enough for that, at any rate," Martin answered. "But I'll tell you what I will do. You gave me the greatest night of my life. You gave me what money cannot buy. Now I've got money, and it means nothing to me. I'd like to turn over to you a thousand dollars of what I don't value for what you gave me that night and which was beyond price. You need the money. I've got more than I need. You want it. You came for it. There's no use scheming it out of me. Take it."

Kreis betrayed no surprise. He folded the check away in his pocket.

"At that rate I'd like the contract of providing you with many such nights," he said.

"Too late." Martin shook his head. "That night was the one night for me. I was in paradise. It's commonplace with you, I know. But it wasn't to me. I shall never live at such a pitch again. I'm done with philosophy. I want never to hear another word of it."

"The first dollar I ever made in my life out of my philosophy," Kreis remarked, as he paused in the doorway. "And then the market broke."

Mrs. Morse drove by Martin on the street one day, and smiled and nodded. He smiled back and lifted his hat. The episode did not affect him. A month before it might have disgusted him, or made him curious and set him to speculating about her state of consciousness at that moment. But now it was not provocative of a second thought. He forgot about it the next moment. He forgot about it as he would have forgotten the Central Bank Building or the City Hall after having walked past them. Yet his mind was preternaturally active. His thoughts went ever around and around in a circle. The centre of that circle was "work performed"; it ate at his brain like a deathless maggot. He awoke to it in the morning. It tormented his dreams at night. Every affair of life around him that penetrated through his senses immediately related itself to "work performed." He drove along the path of relentless logic to the conclusion that he was nobody, nothing. Mart Eden, the hoodlum, and Mart Eden, the sailor, had been real, had been he; but Martin Eden! the famous writer, did not exist. Martin Eden, the famous writer, was a vapor that had arisen in the mob-mind and by the mob-mind had been thrust into the corporeal being of Mart Eden, the hoodlum and sailor. But it couldn't fool him. He was not that sun-myth that the mob was worshipping and sacrificing dinners to. He knew better.

He read the magazines about himself, and pored over portraits of himself published therein until he was unable to associate his identity with those portraits. He was the fellow who had lived and thrilled and loved; who had been easy-going and tolerant of the frailties of life; who had served in the forecastle, wandered in strange lands, and led his gang in the old fighting days. He was the fellow who had been stunned at first by the thousands of books in the free library, and who had afterward learned his way among them and mastered them; he was the fellow who had burned the midnight oil and bedded with a spur and written books himself. But the one thing he was not was that colossal appetite that all the mob was bent upon feeding.

There were things, however, in the magazines that amused him. All the magazines were claiming him. *Warren's Monthly* advertised to its subscribers that it was always on the quest after new writers, and that, among others, it had introduced Martin Eden to the reading public. *The White Mouse* claimed him; so did *The Northern Review* and *Mackintosh's Magazine*, until silenced by *The Globe*, which pointed triumphantly to its files where the mangled "Sea Lyrics" lay buried. *Youth and Age*, which had come to life again after having escaped paying its bills, put in a prior claim, which nobody but farmers' children ever read. The *Transcontinental* made a dignified and convincing statement of how it first discovered Martin Eden, which was warmly disputed by *The Hornet*, with the exhibit of "The Peri and the Pearl." The modest claim of Singletree, Darnley & Co. was lost in the din. Besides, that publishing firm did not own a magazine wherewith to make its claim less modest.

The newspapers calculated Martin's royalties. In some way the magnificent offers certain magazines had made him leaked out, and Oakland ministers called upon him in a friendly way, while professional begging letters began to clutter his mail. But worse than all this were the women. His photographs were published broadcast, and special writers exploited his strong, bronzed face, his scars, his heavy shoulders, his clear, quiet eyes, and the slight hollows in his cheeks like an ascetic's. At this last he remembered his wild youth and smiled. Often, among the women he met, he would see now one, now another, looking at him, appraising him, selecting him. He laughed to himself. He remembered Brissenden's warning and laughed again. The women would never destroy him, that much was certain. He had gone past that stage.

Once, walking with Lizzie toward night school, she caught a glance directed toward him by a well-gowned, handsome woman of the bourgeoisie. The glance was a trifle too long, a shade too considerative. Lizzie knew it for what it was, and her body tensed angrily. Martin noticed, noticed the cause of it, told her how used he was becoming to it and that he did not care anyway.

"You ought to care," she answered with blazing eyes. "You're sick. That's what's the matter."

"Never healthier in my life. I weigh five pounds more than I ever did."

"It ain't your body. It's your head. Something's wrong with your think-machine. Even I can see that, an' I ain't nobody."

He walked on beside her, reflecting.

"I'd give anything to see you get over it," she broke out impulsively. "You ought to care when women look at you that way, a man like you. It's not natural. It's all right enough for sissy-boys. But you ain't made that way. So help me, I'd be willing an' glad if the right woman came along an' made you care."

When he left Lizzie at night school, he returned to the Metropole.

Once in his rooms, he dropped into a Morris chair and sat staring straight before him. He did not doze. Nor did he think. His mind was a blank, save for the intervals when unsummoned memory pictures took form and color and radiance just under his eyelids. He saw these pictures, but he was scarcely conscious of them—no more so than if they had been dreams. Yet he was not asleep. Once, he roused himself and glanced at his watch. It was just eight o'clock. He had nothing to do, and it was too early for bed. Then his mind went blank again, and the pictures began to form and vanish under his eyelids. There was nothing distinctive about the pictures. They were always masses of leaves and shrub-like branches shot through with hot sunshine.

A knock at the door aroused him. He was not asleep, and his mind immediately connected the knock with a telegram, or letter, or perhaps one of the servants bringing back clean clothes from the laundry. He was thinking about Joe and wondering where he was, as he said, "Come in."

He was still thinking about Joe, and did not turn toward the door. He heard it close softly. There was a long silence. He forgot that there had been a knock at the door, and was still staring blankly before him when he heard a woman's sob. It was involuntary, spasmodic, checked, and stifled—he noted that as he turned about. The next instant he was on his feet.

"Ruth!" he said, amazed and bewildered.

Her face was white and strained. She stood just inside the door, one hand against it for support, the other pressed to her side. She extended both hands toward him piteously, and started forward to meet him. As he caught her hands and led her to the Morris chair he noticed how cold they were. He drew up another chair and sat down on the broad arm of it. He was too confused to speak. In his own mind his affair with Ruth was closed and sealed. He felt much in the same way that he would have felt had the Shelly Hot Springs Laundry suddenly invaded the Hotel Metropole with a whole week's washing ready for him to pitch into. Several times he was about to speak, and each time he hesitated.

"No one knows I am here," Ruth said in a faint voice, with an appealing smile.

"What did you say?" he asked.

He was surprised at the sound of his own voice.

She repeated her words.

"Oh," he said, then wondered what more he could possibly say.

"I saw you come in, and I waited a few minutes."

"Oh," he said again.

He had never been so tongue-tied in his life. Positively he did not have an idea in his head. He felt stupid and awkward, but for the life of him he could think of nothing to say. It would have been easier had the intrusion been the Shelly Hot Springs laundry. He could have rolled up his sleeves and gone to work.

"And then you came in," he said finally.

She nodded, with a slightly arch expression, and loosened the scarf at her throat.

"I saw you first from across the street when you were with that girl."

"Oh, yes," he said simply. "I took her down to night school."

"Well, aren't you glad to see me?" she said at the end of another silence.

"Yes, yes." He spoke hastily. "But wasn't it rash of you to come here?"

"I slipped in. Nobody knows I am here. I wanted to see you. I came to tell you I have been very foolish. I came because I could no longer stay away, because my heart compelled me to come, because—because I wanted to come."

She came forward, out of her chair and over to him. She rested her hand on his shoulder a moment, breathing quickly, and then slipped into his arms. And in his large, easy way, desirous of not inflicting hurt, knowing that to repulse this proffer of herself was to inflict the most grievous hurt a woman could receive, he folded his arms around her and held her close. But there was no warmth in the embrace, no caress in the contact. She had come into his arms, and he held her, that was all. She nestled against him, and then, with a change of position, her hands crept up and rested upon his neck. But his flesh was not fire beneath those hands, and he felt awkward and uncomfortable.

"What makes you tremble so?" he asked. "Is it a chill? Shall I light the grate?"

He made a movement to disengage himself, but she clung more closely to him, shivering violently.

"It is merely nervousness," she said with chattering teeth. "I'll control myself in a minute. There, I am better already."

Slowly her shivering died away. He continued to hold her, but he was no longer puzzled. He knew now for what she had come.

"My mother wanted me to marry Charley Hapgood," she announced.

"Charley Hapgood, that fellow who speaks always in platitudes?" Martin groaned. Then he added, "And now, I suppose, your mother wants you to marry me."

He did not put it in the form of a question. He stated it as a certitude, and before his eyes began to dance the rows of figures of his royalties.

"She will not object, I know that much," Ruth said.

"She considers me quite eligible?"

Ruth nodded.

"And yet I am not a bit more eligible now than I was when she broke our engagement," he meditated. "I haven't changed any. I'm the same Martin Eden, though for that matter I'm a bit worse—I smoke now. Don't you smell my breath?"

In reply she pressed her open fingers against his lips, placed them graciously and playfully, and in expectancy of the kiss that of old had always been a consequence. But there was no caressing answer of Martin's lips. He waited until the fingers were removed and then went on.

"I am not changed. I haven't got a job. I'm not looking for a job. Furthermore, I am not going to look for a job. And I still believe that Herbert Spencer is a great and noble man and that Judge Blount is an unmitigated ass. I had dinner with him the other night, so I ought to know."

"But you didn't accept father's invitation," she chided.

"So you know about that? Who sent him? Your mother?"
She remained silent.

"Then she did send him. I thought so. And now I suppose she has sent you."

"No one knows that I am here," she protested. "Do you think my mother would permit this?"

"She'd permit you to marry me, that's certain."

She gave a sharp cry. "Oh, Martin, don't be cruel. You have not kissed me once. You are as unresponsive as a stone. And think what I have dared to do." She looked about her with a shiver, though half the look was curiosity. "Just think of where I am."

"I could die for you! I could die for you!"—Lizzie's words were ringing in his ears.

"Why didn't you dare it before?" he asked harshly. "When I hadn't a job? When I was starving? When I was just as I am now, as a man, as an artist, the same Martin Eden? That's the question I've been propounding to myself for many a day— not concerning you merely, but concerning everybody. You see I have not changed, though my sudden apparent appreciation in value compels me constantly to reassure myself on that point. I've got the same flesh on my bones, the same ten fingers and toes. I am the same. I have not developed any new strength nor virtue. My brain is the same old brain. I haven't made even one new generalization on literature or philosophy. I am personally of the same value that I was when nobody wanted me. And what is puzzling me is why they want me now. Surely they don't want me for myself, for myself is the same old self they did not want. Then they must want me for something else, for something that is outside of me, for something that is not I! Shall I tell you what that something is? It is for the recognition I have received. That recognition is not I. It resides in the minds of others. Then again for the money I have earned and am earning. But that money is not I. It resides in banks and in the pockets of Tom, Dick, and Harry. And is it for that, for the recognition and the money, that you now want me?"

"You are breaking my heart," she sobbed. "You know I love you, that I am here because I love you."

"I am afraid you don't see my point," he said gently. "What

I mean is: if you love me, how does it happen that you love me now so much more than you did when your love was weak enough to deny me?"

"Forget and forgive," she cried passionately. "I loved you all the time, remember that, and I am here, now, in your arms."

"I'm afraid I am a shrewd merchant, peering into the scales, trying to weigh your love and find out what manner of thing it is."

She withdrew herself from his arms, sat upright, and looked at him long and searchingly. She was about to speak, then faltered and changed her mind.

"You see, it appears this way to me," he went on. "When I was all that I am now, nobody out of my own class seemed to care for me. When my books were all written, no one who had read the manuscripts seemed to care for them. In point of fact, because of the stuff I had written they seemed to care even less for me. In writing the stuff it seemed that I had committed acts that were, to say the least, derogatory. 'Get a job,' everybody said."

She made a movement of dissent.

"Yes, yes," he said; "except in your case you told me to get a position. The homely word *job*, like much that I have written, offends you. It is brutal. But I assure you it was no less brutal to me when everybody I knew recommended it to me as they would recommend right conduct to an immoral creature. But to return. The publication of what I had written, and the public notice I received, wrought a change in the fibre of your love. Martin Eden, with his work all performed, you would not marry. Your love for him was not strong enough to enable you to marry him. But your love is now strong enough, and I cannot avoid the conclusion that its strength arises from the publication and the public notice. In your case I do not mention royalties, though I am certain that they apply to the change wrought in your mother and father. Of course, all this is not flattering to me. But worst of all, it makes me question love, sacred love. Is love so gross a thing that it must feed upon publication and public notice? It would seem so. I have sat and thought upon it till my head went around."

"Poor, dear head." She reached up a hand and passed the fingers soothingly through his hair. "Let it go around no more. Let us begin anew, now. I loved you all the time. I know that I was weak in yielding to my mother's will. I should not have done so. Yet I have heard you speak so often with broad charity of the fallibility and frailty of humankind. Extend that charity to me. I acted mistakenly. Forgive me."

"Oh, I do forgive," he said impatiently. "It is easy to forgive where there is really nothing to forgive. Nothing that you have done requires forgiveness. One acts according to one's lights, and more than that one cannot do. As well might I ask you to forgive me for my not getting a job."

"I meant well," she protested. "You know that. I could not have loved you and not meant well."

"True; but you would have destroyed me out of your well-meaning.

"Yes, yes," he shut off her attempted objection. "You would have destroyed my writing and my career. Realism is imperative to my nature, and the bourgeois spirit hates realism. The bourgeoisie is cowardly. It is afraid of life. And all your effort was to make me afraid of life. You would have formalized me. You would have compressed me into a two-by-four pigeonhole of life, where all life's values are unreal, and false, and vulgar." He felt her stir protestingly. "Vulgarity—a hearty vulgarity, I'll admit—is the basis of bourgeois refinement and culture. As I say, you wanted to formalize me, to make me over into one of your own class, with your class-ideals, class-values, and class-prejudices." He shook his head sadly. "And you do not understand, even now, what I am saying. My words do not mean to you what I endeavor to make them mean. What I say is so much fantasy to you. Yet to me it is vital reality. At the best you are a trifle puzzled and amused that this raw boy, crawling up out of the mire of the abyss, should pass judgment upon your class and call it vulgar."

She leaned her head wearily against his shoulder, and her body shivered with recurrent nervousness. He waited for a time for her to speak, and then went on.

"And now you want to renew our love. You want us to be married. You want me. And yet, listen—if my books had not

been noticed, I'd nevertheless have been just what I am now.
And you would have stayed away. It is all those damned
books—"

"Don't swear," she interrupted.

Her reproof startled him. He broke into a harsh laugh.

"That's it," he said, "at a high moment, when what seems
your life's happiness is at stake, you are afraid of life in the
same old way—afraid of life and a healthy oath."

She was stung by his words into realization of the puerility
of her act, and yet she felt that he had magnified it unduly
and was consequently resentful. They sat in silence for a long
time, she thinking desperately and he pondering upon his
love which had departed. He knew, now, that he had not
really loved her. It was an idealized Ruth he had loved, an
ethereal creature of his own creating, the bright and luminous
spirit of his love-poems. The real bourgeois Ruth, with all the
bourgeois failings and with the hopeless cramp of the bourgeois psychology in her mind, he had never loved.

She suddenly began to speak.

"I know that much you have said is so. I have been afraid
of life. I did not love you well enough. I have learned to love
better. I love you for what you are, for what you were, for
the ways even by which you have become. I love you for the
ways wherein you differ from what you call my class, for your
beliefs which I do not understand but which I know I can
come to understand. I shall devote myself to understanding
them. And even your smoking and your swearing—they are
part of you and I will love you for them, too. I can still learn.
In the last ten minutes I have learned much. That I have
dared to come here is a token of what I have already learned.
Oh, Martin!—"

She was sobbing and nestling close against him.

For the first time his arms folded her gently and with sympathy, and she acknowledged it with a happy movement and
a brightening face.

"It is too late," he said. He remembered Lizzie's words. "I
am a sick man—oh, not my body. It is my soul, my brain. I
seem to have lost all values. I care for nothing. If you had
been this way a few months ago, it would have been different.
It is too late, now."

"It is not too late," she cried. "I will show you. I will prove to you that my love has grown, that it is greater to me than my class and all that is dearest to me. All that is dearest to the bourgeoisie I will flout. I am no longer afraid of life. I will leave my father and mother, and let my name become a by-word with my friends. I will come to you here and now, in free love if you will, and I will be proud and glad to be with you. If I have been a traitor to love, I will now, for love's sake, be a traitor to all that made that earlier treason."

She stood before him, with shining eyes.

"I am waiting, Martin," she whispered, "waiting for you to accept me. Look at me."

It was splendid, he thought, looking at her. She had redeemed herself for all that she had lacked, rising up at last, true woman, superior to the iron rule of bourgeois convention. It was splendid, magnificent, desperate. And yet, what was the matter with him? He was not thrilled nor stirred by what she had done. It was splendid and magnificent only intellectually. In what should have been a moment of fire, he coldly appraised her. His heart was untouched. He was unaware of any desire for her. Again he remembered Lizzie's words.

"I am sick, very sick," he said with a despairing gesture. "How sick I did not know till now. Something has gone out of me. I have always been unafraid of life, but I never dreamed of being sated with life. Life has so filled me that I am empty of any desire for anything. If there were room, I should want you, now. You see how sick I am."

He leaned his head back and closed his eyes; and like a child, crying, that forgets its grief in watching the sunlight percolate through the tear-dimmed films over the pupils, so Martin forgot his sickness, the presence of Ruth, everything, in watching the masses of vegetation, shot through hotly with sunshine that took form and blazed against the background of his eyelids. It was not restful, that green foliage. The sunlight was too raw and glaring. It hurt him to look at it, and yet he looked, he knew not why.

He was brought back to himself by the rattle of the doorknob. Ruth was at the door.

"How shall I get out?" she questioned tearfully. "I am afraid."

"Oh, forgive me," he cried, springing to his feet. "I'm not myself, you know. I forgot you were here." He put his hand to his head. "You see, I'm not just right. I'll take you home. We can go out by the servants' entrance. No one will see us. Pull down that veil and everything will be all right."

She clung to his arm through the dim-lighted passages and down the narrow stairs.

"I am safe now," she said, when they emerged on the sidewalk, at the same time starting to take her hand from his arm.

"No, no, I'll see you home," he answered.

"No, please don't," she objected. "It is unnecessary."

Again she started to remove her hand. He felt a momentary curiosity. Now that she was out of danger she was afraid. She was in almost a panic to be quit of him. He could see no reason for it and attributed it to her nervousness. So he restrained her withdrawing hand and started to walk on with her. Halfway down the block, he saw a man in a long overcoat shrink back into a doorway. He shot a glance in as he passed by, and, despite the high turned-up collar, he was certain that he recognized Ruth's brother, Norman.

During the walk Ruth and Martin held little conversation. She was stunned. He was apathetic. Once, he mentioned that he was going away, back to the South Seas, and, once, she asked him to forgive her having come to him. And that was all. The parting at her door was conventional. They shook hands, said good night, and he lifted his hat. The door swung shut, and he lighted a cigarette and turned back for his hotel. When he came to the doorway into which he had seen Norman shrink, he stopped and looked in in a speculative humor.

"She lied," he said aloud. "She made believe to me that she had dared greatly, and all the while she knew the brother that brought her was waiting to take her back." He burst into laughter. "Oh, these bourgeois! When I was broke, I was not fit to be seen with his sister. When I have a bank account, he brings her to me."

As he swung on his heel to go on, a tramp, going in the same direction, begged him over his shoulder.

"Say, mister, can you give me a quarter to get a bed?" were the words.

But it was the voice that made Martin turn around. The next instant he had Joe by the hand.

"D'ye remember that time we parted at the Hot Springs?" the other was saying. "I said then we'd meet again. I felt it in my bones. An' here we are."

"You're looking good," Martin said admiringly, "and you've put on weight."

"I sure have." Joe's face was beaming. "I never knew what it was to live till I hit hoboin'. I'm thirty pounds heavier an' feel tiptop all the time. Why, I was worked to skin an' bone in them old days. Hoboin' sure agrees with me."

"But you're looking for a bed just the same," Martin chided, "and it's a cold night."

"Huh? Lookin' for a bed?" Joe shot a hand into his hip pocket and brought it out filled with small change. "That beats hard graft," he exulted. "You just looked good; that's why I battered you."

Martin laughed and gave in.

"You've several full-sized drunks right there," he insinuated.

Joe slid the money back into his pocket.

"Not in mine," he announced. "No gettin' oryide for me, though there ain't nothin' to stop me except I don't want to. I've ben drunk once since I seen you last, an' then it was unexpected, bein' on an empty stomach. When I work like a beast, I drink like a beast. When I live like a man, I drink like a man—a jolt now an' again when I feel like it, an' that's all."

Martin arranged to meet him next day, and went on to the hotel. He paused in the office to look up steamer sailings. The *Mariposa* sailed for Tahiti in five days.

"Telephone over to-morrow and reserve a stateroom for me," he told the clerk. "No deck-stateroom, but down below, on the weather-side,—the port-side, remember that, the port-side. You'd better write it down."

Once in his room he got into bed and slipped off to sleep as gently as a child. The occurrences of the evening had made no impression on him. His mind was dead to impressions. The glow of warmth with which he met Joe had been most

fleeting. The succeeding minute he had been bothered by the
ex-laundryman's presence and by the compulsion of conversation. That in five more days he sailed for his loved South
Seas meant nothing to him. So he closed his eyes and slept
normally and comfortably for eight uninterrupted hours. He
was not restless. He did not change his position, nor did he
dream. Sleep had become to him oblivion, and each day that
he awoke, he awoke with regret. Life worried and bored him,
and time was a vexation.

Chapter XLVI

"SAY, JOE," was his greeting to his old-time working-mate next morning, "there's a Frenchman out on Twenty-eighth Street. He's made a pot of money, and he's going back to France. It's a dandy, well-appointed, small steam laundry. There's a start for you if you want to settle down. Here, take this; buy some clothes with it and be at this man's office by ten o'clock. He looked up the laundry for me, and he'll take you out and show you around. If you like it, and think it is worth the price—twelve thousand—let me know and it is yours. Now run along. I'm busy. I'll see you later."

"Now look here, Mart," the other said slowly, with kindling anger, "I come here this mornin' to see you. Savve? I didn't come here to get no laundry. I come here for a talk for old friends' sake, and you shove a laundry at me. I tell you what you can do. You can take that laundry an' go to hell."

He was starting to fling out of the room when Martin caught him by the shoulder and whirled him around.

"Now look here, Joe," he said; "if you act that way, I'll punch your head. And for old friends' sake I'll punch it hard. Savve?—you will, will you?"

Joe had clinched and attempted to throw him, and he was twisting and writhing out of the advantage of the other's hold. They reeled about the room, locked in each other's arms, and came down with a crash across the splintered wreckage of a wicker chair. Joe was underneath, with arms spread out and held and with Martin's knee on his chest. He was panting and gasping for breath when Martin released him.

"Now we'll talk a moment," Martin said. "You can't get fresh with me. I want that laundry business finished first of all. Then you can come back and we'll talk for old sake's sake. I told you I was busy. Look at that."

A servant had just come in with the morning mail, a great mass of letters and magazines.

"How can I wade through that and talk with you? You go and fix up that laundry, and then we'll get together."

"All right," Joe admitted reluctantly. "I thought you was turnin' me down, but I guess I was mistaken. But you can't lick me, Mart, in a stand-up fight. I've got the reach on you."

"We'll put on the gloves sometime and see," Martin said with a smile.

"Sure; as soon as I get that laundry going." Joe extended his arm. "You see that reach? It'll make you go a few."

Martin heaved a sigh of relief when the door closed behind the laundryman. He was becoming anti-social. Daily he found it a severer strain to be decent with people. Their presence perturbed him, and the effort of conversation irritated him. They made him restless, and no sooner was he in contact with them than he was casting about for excuses to get rid of them.

He did not proceed to attack his mail, and for a half hour he lolled in his chair, doing nothing, while no more than vague, half-formed thoughts occasionally filtered through his intelligence, or rather, at wide intervals, themselves constituted the flickering of his intelligence.

He roused himself and began glancing through his mail. There were a dozen requests for autographs—he knew them at sight; there were professional begging letters; and there were letters from cranks, ranging from the man with a working model of perpetual motion, and the man who demonstrated that the surface of the earth was the inside of a hollow sphere, to the man seeking financial aid to purchase the Peninsula of Lower California for the purpose of communist colonization. There were letters from women seeking to know him, and over one such he smiled, for enclosed was her receipt for pew-rent, sent as evidence of her good faith and as proof of her respectability.

Editors and publishers contributed to the daily heap of letters, the former on their knees for his manuscripts, the latter on their knees for his books—his poor disdained manuscripts that had kept all he possessed in pawn for so many dreary months in order to find them in postage. There were unexpected checks for English serial rights and for advance payments on foreign translations. His English agent announced the sale of German translation rights in three of his books, and informed him that Swedish editions, from which he could expect nothing because Sweden was not a party to the

Berne Convention, were already on the market. Then there was a nominal request for his permission for a Russian translation, that country being likewise outside the Berne Convention.

He turned to the huge bundle of clippings which had come in from his press bureau, and read about himself and his vogue, which had become a furore. All his creative output had been flung to the public in one magnificent sweep. That seemed to account for it. He had taken the public off its feet, the way Kipling had, that time when he lay near to death and all the mob, animated by a mob-mind thought, began suddenly to read him. Martin remembered how that same world-mob, having read him and acclaimed him and not understood him in the least, had, abruptly, a few months later, flung itself upon him and torn him to pieces. Martin grinned at the thought. Who was he that he should not be similarly treated in a few more months? Well, he would fool the mob. He would be away, in the South Seas, building his grass house, trading for pearls and copra, jumping reefs in frail outriggers, catching sharks and bonitas, hunting wild goats among the cliffs of the valley that lay next to the valley of Taiohæ.

In the moment of that thought the desperateness of his situation dawned upon him. He saw, cleared eyed, that he was in the Valley of the Shadow. All the life that was in him was fading, fainting, making toward death. He realized how much he slept, and how much he desired to sleep. Of old, he had hated sleep. It had robbed him of precious moments of living. Four hours of sleep in the twenty-four had meant being robbed of four hours of life. How he had grudged sleep! Now it was life he grudged. Life was not good; its taste in his mouth was without tang, and bitter. This was his peril. Life that did not yearn toward life was in fair way toward ceasing. Some remote instinct for preservation stirred in him, and he knew he must get away. He glanced about the room, and the thought of packing was burdensome. Perhaps it would be better to leave that to the last. In the meantime he might be getting an outfit.

He put on his hat and went out, stopping in at a gun-store, where he spent the remainder of the morning buying automatic rifles, ammunition, and fishing tackle. Fashions changed in trading, and he knew he would have to wait till he reached Tahiti before ordering his trade-goods. They could come up from Australia, anyway. This solution was a source of pleasure. He had avoided doing something, and the doing of anything just now was unpleasant. He went back to the hotel gladly, with a feeling of satisfaction in that the comfortable Morris chair was waiting for him; and he groaned inwardly, on entering his room, at sight of Joe in the Morris chair.

Joe was delighted with the laundry. Everything was settled, and he would enter into possession next day. Martin lay on the bed, with closed eyes, while the other talked on. Martin's thoughts were far away—so far away that he was rarely aware that he was thinking. It was only by an effort that he occasionally responded. And yet this was Joe, whom he had always liked. But Joe was too keen with life. The boisterous impact of it on Martin's jaded mind was a hurt. It was an aching probe to his tired sensitiveness. When Joe reminded him that sometime in the future they were going to put on the gloves together, he could almost have screamed.

"Remember, Joe, you're to run the laundry according to those old rules you used to lay down at Shelly Hot Springs," he said. "No overworking. No working at night. And no children at the mangles. No children anywhere. And a fair wage."

Joe nodded and pulled out a note-book.

"Look at here. I was workin' out them rules before breakfast this A.M. What d'ye think of them?"

He read them aloud, and Martin approved, worrying at the same time as to when Joe would take himself off.

It was late afternoon when he awoke. Slowly the fact of life came back to him. He glanced about the room. Joe had evidently stolen away after he had dozed off. That was considerate of Joe, he thought. Then he closed his eyes and slept again.

In the days that followed Joe was too busy organizing and taking hold of the laundry to bother him much; and it was not until the day before sailing that the newspapers made the announcement that he had taken passage on the *Mariposa*. Once, when the instinct of preservation fluttered, he went to a doctor and underwent a searching physical examination. Nothing could be found the matter with him. His heart and lungs were pronounced magnificent. Every organ, so far as the doctor could know, was normal and was working normally.

"There is nothing the matter with you, Mr. Eden," he said, "positively nothing the matter with you. You are in the pink of condition. Candidly, I envy you your health. It is superb. Look at that chest. There, and in your stomach, lies the secret of your remarkable constitution. Physically, you are a man in a thousand—in ten thousand. Barring accidents, you should live to be a hundred."

And Martin knew that Lizzie's diagnosis had been correct. Physically he was all right. It was his "think-machine" that had gone wrong, and there was no cure for that except to get away to the South Seas. The trouble was that now, on the verge of departure, he had no desire to go. The South Seas charmed him no more than did bourgeois civilization. There was no zest in the thought of departure, while the act of departure appalled him as a weariness of the flesh. He would have felt better if he were already on board and gone.

The last day was a sore trial. Having read of his sailing in the morning papers, Bernard Higginbotham, Gertrude, and all the family came to say good-by, as did Hermann von Schmidt and Marian. Then there was business to be transacted, bills to be paid, and everlasting reporters to be endured. He said good-by to Lizzie Connolly, abruptly, at the entrance to night school, and hurried away. At the hotel he found Joe, too busy all day with the laundry to have come to him earlier. It was the last straw, but Martin gripped the arms of his chair and talked and listened for half an hour.

"You know, Joe," he said, "that you are not tied down to that laundry. There are no strings on it. You can sell it any time and blow the money. Any time you get sick of it and want to hit the road, just pull out. Do what will make you the happiest."

Joe shook his head.

"No more road in mine, thank you kindly. Hoboin's all right, exceptin' for one thing—the girls. I can't help it, but I'm a ladies' man. I can't get along without 'em, and you've got to get along without 'em when you're hoboin'. The times I've passed by houses where dances an' parties was goin' on,

an' heard the women laugh, an' saw their white dresses and
smiling faces through the windows—Gee! I tell you them
moments was plain hell. I like dancin' an' picnics, an' walking
in the moonlight, an' all the rest too well. Me for the laundry,
and a good front, with big iron dollars clinkin' in my jeans. I
seen a girl already, just yesterday, and, d'ye know, I'm feelin'
already I'd just as soon marry her as not. I've ben whistlin' all
day at the thought of it. She's a beaut, with the kindest eyes
and softest voice you ever heard. Me for her, you can stack
on that. Say, why don't you get married with all this money
to burn? You could get the finest girl in the land."

Martin shook his head with a smile, but in his secret heart
he was wondering why any man wanted to marry. It seemed
an amazing and incomprehensible thing.

From the deck of the *Mariposa*, at the sailing hour, he saw
Lizzie Connolly hiding on the skirts of the crowd on the
wharf. Take her with you, came the thought. It is easy to be
kind. She will be supremely happy. It was almost a temptation one moment, and the succeeding moment it became a
terror. He was in a panic at the thought of it. His tired soul
cried out in protest. He turned away from the rail with a
groan, muttering, "Man, you are too sick, you are too sick."

He fled to his stateroom, where he lurked until the steamer
was clear of the dock. In the dining saloon, at luncheon, he
found himself in the place of honor, at the captain's right;
and he was not long in discovering that he was the great man
on board. But no more unsatisfactory great man ever sailed
on a ship. He spent the afternoon in a deck-chair, with closed
eyes, dozing brokenly most of the time, and in the evening
went early to bed.

After the second day, recovered from seasickness, the full
passenger list was in evidence, and the more he saw of the
passengers the more he disliked them. Yet he knew that he
did them injustice. They were good and kindly people, he
forced himself to acknowledge, and in the moment of acknowledgment he qualified—good and kindly like all the
bourgeoisie, with all the psychological cramp and intellectual
futility of their kind. They bored him when they talked with
him, their little superficial minds were so filled with emptiness; while the boisterous high spirits and the excessive en-

ergy of the younger people shocked him. They were never quiet, ceaselessly playing deck-quoits, tossing rings, promenading, or rushing to the rail with loud cries to watch the leaping porpoises and the first schools of flying fish.

He slept much. After breakfast he sought his deck-chair with a magazine he never finished. The printed pages tired him. He puzzled that men found so much to write about, and, puzzling, dozed in his chair. When the gong awoke him for luncheon, he was irritated that he must awaken. There was no satisfaction in being awake.

Once, he tried to arouse himself from his lethargy, and went forward into the forecastle with the sailors. But the breed of sailors seemed to have changed since the days he had lived in the forecastle. He could find no kinship with these stolid-faced, ox-minded bestial creatures. He was in despair. Up above nobody had wanted Martin Eden for his own sake, and he could not go back to those of his own class who had wanted him in the past. He did not want them. He could not stand them any more than he could stand the stupid first-cabin passengers and the riotous young people.

Life was to him like strong, white light that hurts the tired eyes of a sick person. During every conscious moment life blazed in a raw glare around him and upon him. It hurt. It hurt intolerably. It was the first time in his life that Martin had travelled first class. On ships at sea he had always been in the forecastle, the steerage, or in the black depths of the coal-hold, passing coal. In those days, climbing up the iron ladders from out the pit of stifling heat, he had often caught glimpses of the passengers, in cool white, doing nothing but enjoy themselves, under awnings spread to keep the sun and wind away from them, with subservient stewards taking care of their every want and whim, and it had seemed to him that the realm in which they moved and had their being was nothing else than paradise. Well, here he was, the great man on board, in the midmost centre of it, sitting at the captain's right hand, and yet vainly harking back to forecastle and stoke-hole in quest of the Paradise he had lost. He had found no new one, and now he could not find the old one.

He strove to stir himself and find something to interest him. He ventured the petty officers' mess, and was glad to get away. He talked with a quartermaster off duty, an intelligent man who promptly prodded him with the socialist propaganda and forced into his hands a bunch of leaflets and pamphlets. He listened to the man expounding the slave-morality, and as he listened, he thought languidly of his own Nietzsche philosophy. But what was it worth, after all? He remembered one of Nietzsche's mad utterances wherein that madman had doubted truth. And who was to say? Perhaps Nietzsche had been right. Perhaps there was no truth in anything, no truth in truth—no such thing as truth. But his mind wearied quickly, and he was content to go back to his chair and doze.

Miserable as he was on the steamer, a new misery came upon him. What when the steamer reached Tahiti? He would have to go ashore. He would have to order his trade-goods, to find a passage on a schooner to the Marquesas, to do a thousand and one things that were awful to contemplate. Whenever he steeled himself deliberately to think, he could see the desperate peril in which he stood. In all truth, he was in the Valley of the Shadow, and his danger lay in that he was not afraid. If he were only afraid, he would make toward life. Being unafraid, he was drifting deeper into the shadow. He found no delight in the old familiar things of life. The *Mariposa* was now in the northeast trades, and this wine of wind, surging against him, irritated him. He had his chair moved to escape the embrace of this lusty comrade of old days and nights.

The day the *Mariposa* entered the doldrums, Martin was more miserable than ever. He could no longer sleep. He was soaked with sleep, and perforce he must now stay awake and endure the white glare of life. He moved about restlessly. The air was sticky and humid, and the rain-squalls were unrefreshing. He ached with life. He walked around the deck until that hurt too much, then sat in his chair until he was compelled to walk again. He forced himself at last to finish the magazine, and from the steamer library he culled several volumes of poetry. But they could not hold him, and once more he took to walking.

He stayed late on deck, after dinner, but that did not help him, for when he went below, he could not sleep. This surcease from life had failed him. It was too much. He turned

on the electric light and tried to read. One of the volumes
was a Swinburne. He lay in bed, glancing through its pages,
until suddenly he became aware that he was reading with interest. He finished the stanza, attempted to read on, then
came back to it. He rested the book face downward on his
breast and fell to thinking. That was it. The very thing.
Strange that it had never come to him before. That was the
meaning of it all; he had been drifting that way all the time,
and now Swinburne showed him that it was the happy way
out. He wanted rest, and here was rest awaiting him. He
glanced at the open port-hole. Yes, it was large enough. For
the first time in weeks he felt happy. At last he had discovered
the cure of his ill. He picked up the book and read the stanza
slowly aloud:—

> " 'From too much love of living,
>   From hope and fear set free,
>   We thank with brief thanksgiving
>   Whatever gods may be
>   That no life lives forever;
>   That dead men rise up never;
>   That even the weariest river
>   Winds somewhere safe to sea.' "

He looked again at the open port. Swinburne had furnished the key. Life was ill, or, rather, it had become ill—an
unbearable thing. "That dead men rise up never!" That line
stirred him with a profound feeling of gratitude. It was the
one beneficent thing in the universe. When life became an
aching weariness, death was ready to soothe away to everlasting sleep. But what was he waiting for? It was time to go.

He arose and thrust his head out the port-hole, looking
down into the milky wash. The *Mariposa* was deeply loaded,
and, hanging by his hands, his feet would be in the water. He
could slip in noiselessly. No one would hear. A smother of
spray dashed up, wetting his face. It tasted salt on his lips,
and the taste was good. He wondered if he ought to write a
swan-song, but laughed the thought away. There was no
time. He was too impatient to be gone.

Turning off the light in his room so that it might not betray him, he went out the port-hole feet first. His shoulders stuck, and he forced himself back so as to try it with one arm down by his side. A roll of the steamer aided him, and he was through, hanging by his hands. When his feet touched the sea, he let go. He was in a milky froth of water. The side of the *Mariposa* rushed past him like a dark wall, broken here and there by lighted ports. She was certainly making time. Almost before he knew it, he was astern, swimming gently on the foam-crackling surface.

A bonita struck at his white body, and he laughed aloud. It had taken a piece out, and the sting of it reminded him of why he was there. In the work to do he had forgotten the purpose of it. The lights of the *Mariposa* were growing dim in the distance, and there he was, swimming confidently, as though it were his intention to make for the nearest land a thousand miles or so away.

It was the automatic instinct to live. He ceased swimming, but the moment he felt the water rising above his mouth the hands struck out sharply with a lifting movement. The will to live, was his thought, and the thought was accompanied by a sneer. Well, he had will,—ay, will strong enough that with one last exertion it could destroy itself and cease to be.

He changed his position to a vertical one. He glanced up at the quiet stars, at the same time emptying his lungs of air. With swift, vigorous propulsion of hands and feet, he lifted his shoulders and half his chest out of water. This was to gain impetus for the descent. Then he let himself go and sank without movement, a white statue, into the sea. He breathed in the water deeply, deliberately, after the manner of a man taking an anæsthetic. When he strangled, quite involuntarily his arms and legs clawed the water and drove him up to the surface and into the clear sight of the stars.

The will to live, he thought disdainfully, vainly endeavoring not to breathe the air into his bursting lungs. Well, he would have to try a new way. He filled his lungs with air, filled them full. This supply would take him far down. He turned over and went down head first, swimming with all his strength and all his will. Deeper and deeper he went. His eyes were open, and he watched the ghostly, phosphorescent trails of the darting bonita. As he swam, he hoped that they would not strike at him, for it might snap the tension of his will. But they did not strike, and he found time to be grateful for this last kindness of life.

Down, down, he swam till his arms and legs grew tired and hardly moved. He knew that he was deep. The pressure on his ear-drums was a pain, and there was a buzzing in his head. His endurance was faltering, but he compelled his arms and legs to drive him deeper until his will snapped and the air drove from his lungs in a great explosive rush. The bubbles rubbed and bounded like tiny balloons against his cheeks and eyes as they took their upward flight. Then came pain and strangulation. This hurt was not death, was the thought that oscillated through his reeling consciousness. Death did not hurt. It was life, the pangs of life, this awful, suffocating feeling; it was the last blow life could deal him.

His wilful hands and feet began to beat and churn about, spasmodically and feebly. But he had fooled them and the will to live that made them beat and churn. He was too deep down. They could never bring him to the surface. He seemed floating languidly in a sea of dreamy vision. Colors and radiances surrounded him and bathed him and pervaded him. What was that? It seemed a lighthouse; but it was inside his brain—a flashing, bright white light. It flashed swifter and swifter. There was a long rumble of sound, and it seemed to him that he was falling down a vast and interminable stairway. And somewhere at the bottom he fell into darkness. That much he knew. He had fallen into darkness. And at the instant he knew, he ceased to know.

JOHN BARLEYCORN

Chapter I

IT ALL came to me one election day. It was on a warm California afternoon, and I had ridden down into the Valley of the Moon from the ranch to the little village to vote yes and no to a host of proposed amendments to the Constitution of the State of California. Because of the warmth of the day I had had several drinks before casting my ballot, and divers drinks after casting it. Then I had ridden up through the vine-clad hills and rolling pastures of the ranch and arrived at the farmhouse in time for another drink and supper.

"How did you vote on the suffrage amendment?" Charmian asked.

"I voted for it."

She uttered an exclamation of surprise. For be it known, in my younger days, despite my ardent democracy, I had been opposed to woman suffrage. In my later and more tolerant years I had been unenthusiastic in my acceptance of it as an inevitable social phenomenon.

"Now just why did you vote for it?" Charmian asked.

I answered. I answered at length. I answered indignantly. The more I answered, the more indignant I became. (No; I was not drunk. The horse I had ridden was well-named "The Outlaw." I 'd like to see any drunken man ride her.)

And yet—how shall I say?—I was lighted up, I was feeling "good," I was pleasantly jingled.

"When the women get the ballot, they will vote for prohibition," I said. "It is the wives, and sisters, and mothers, and they only, who will drive the nails into the coffin of John Barleycorn—"

"But I thought you were a friend to John Barleycorn," Charmian interpolated.

"I am. I was. I am not. I never am. I am never less his friend than when he is with me and when I seem most his friend. He is the king of liars. He is the frankest truth-sayer. He is the august companion with whom one walks with the gods. He is also in league with the Noseless One. His way leads to truth naked, and to death. He gives clear vision, and

muddy dreams. He is the enemy of life, and the teacher of
wisdom beyond life's vision. He is a red-handed killer, and he
slays youth."

And Charmian looked at me, and I knew she wondered
where I had got it.

I continued to talk. As I say, I was lighted up. In my brain
every thought was at home. Every thought, in its little cell,
crouched ready-dressed at the door, like prisoners at midnight
waiting a jail-break. And every thought was a vision, bright-
imaged, sharp-cut, unmistakable. My brain was illuminated
by the clear, white light of alcohol. John Barleycorn was on
a truth-telling rampage, giving away the choicest secrets on
himself. And I was his spokesman. There moved the multitudes of memories of my past life, all orderly arranged like
soldiers in some vast review. It was mine to pick and choose.
I was a lord of thought, the master of my vocabulary and of
the totality of my experience, unerringly capable of selecting
my data and building my exposition. For so John Barleycorn
tricks and lures, setting the maggots of intelligence gnawing,
whispering his fatal intuitions of truth, flinging purple passages into the monotony of one's days.

I outlined my life to Charmian, and expounded the make-
up of my constitution. I was no hereditary alcoholic. I had
been born with no organic, chemical predisposition toward
alcohol. In this matter I was normal in my generation. Alcohol was an acquired taste. It had been painfully acquired.
Alcohol had been a dreadfully repugnant thing—more nauseous than any physic. Even now I did not like the taste of it.
I drank it only for its "kick." And from the age of five to that
of twenty-five, I had not learned to care for its kick. Twenty
years of unwilling apprenticeship had been required to make
my system rebelliously tolerant of alcohol, to make me, in the
heart and the deeps of me, desirous of alcohol.

I sketched my first contacts with alcohol, told of my first
intoxications and revulsions, and pointed out always the one
thing that in the end had won me over—namely, the accessibility of alcohol. Not only had it always been accessible, but
every interest of my developing life had drawn me to it. A
newsboy on the streets, a sailor, a miner, a wanderer in far
lands, always where men came together to exchange ideas, to

laugh and boast and dare, to relax, to forget the dull toil of tiresome nights and days, always they came together over alcohol. The saloon was the place of congregation. Men gathered to it as primitive men gathered about the fire of the squatting-place or the fire at the mouth of the cave.

I reminded Charmian of the canoe-houses from which she had been barred in the South Pacific, where the kinky-haired cannibals escaped from their womenkind and feasted and drank by themselves, the sacred precincts taboo to women under pain of death. As a youth, by way of the saloon I had escaped from the narrowness of women's influence into the wide free world of men. All ways led to the saloon. The thousand roads of romance and adventure drew together in the saloon, and thence led out and on over the world.

"The point is," I concluded my sermon, "that it is the accessibility of alcohol that has given me my taste for alcohol. I did not care for it. I used to laugh at it. Yet here I am, at the last, possessed with the drinker's desire. It took twenty years to implant that desire; and for ten years more that desire has grown. And the effect of satisfying that desire is anything but good. Temperamentally I am wholesome-hearted and merry. Yet when I walk with John Barleycorn I suffer all the damnation of intellectual pessimism.

"—But," I hastened to add (I always hasten to add), "—John Barleycorn must have his due. He does tell the truth. That is the curse of it. The so-called truths of life are not true. They are the vital lies by which life lives, and John Barleycorn gives them the lie."

"Which does not make toward life," Charmian said.

"Very true," I answered. "And that is the perfectest hell of it. John Barleycorn makes toward death. That is why I voted for the amendment to-day. I read back in my life and saw how the accessibility of alcohol had given me the taste for it. You see, comparatively few alcoholics are born in a generation. And by alcoholic I mean a man whose chemistry craves alcohol and drives him resistlessly to it. The great majority of habitual drinkers are born not only without desire for alcohol but with actual repugnance toward it. Not the first, nor the twentieth, nor the hundredth drink, succeeded in giving them the liking. But they learned, just as men learn to smoke;

though it is far easier to learn to smoke than to learn to drink. They learned because alcohol was so accessible. The women know the game. They pay for it—the wives and sisters and mothers. And when they come to vote they will vote for prohibition. And the best of it is that there will be no hardship worked on the coming generation. Not having access to alcohol, not being predisposed toward alcohol, it will never miss alcohol. It will mean life more abundant for the manhood of the young boys born and growing up—ay, and life more abundant for the young girls born and growing up to share the lives of the young men."

"Why not write all this up for the sake of the young men and women coming?" Charmian asked. "Why not write it so as to help the wives and sisters and mothers to the way they should vote?"

"The 'Memoirs of an Alcoholic.'" I sneered—or, rather, John Barleycorn sneered; for he sat with me there at table in my pleasant, philanthropic jingle, and it is a trick of John Barleycorn to turn the smile to a sneer without an instant's warning.

"No," said Charmian, ignoring John Barleycorn's roughness as so many women have learned to do. "You have shown yourself no alcoholic, no dipsomaniac, but merely an habitual drinker, one who has made John Barleycorn's acquaintance through long years of rubbing shoulders with him. Write it up and call it 'Alcoholic Memoirs.'"

Chapter II

Aᴺᴰ, ere I begin, I must ask the reader to walk with me in all sympathy; and, since sympathy is merely understanding, begin by understanding me and whom and what I write about. In the first place, I am a seasoned drinker. I have no constitutional predisposition for alcohol. I am not stupid. I am not a swine. I know the drinking game from A to Zed, and I have used my judgment in drinking. I never have to be put to bed. Nor do I stagger. In short, I am a normal, average man; and I drink in the normal, average way, as drinking goes. And this is the very point: I am writing of the effects of alcohol on the normal, average man. I have no word to say for or about the microscopically unimportant excessivist, the dipsomaniac.

There are, broadly speaking, two types of drinkers. There is the man whom we all know, stupid, unimaginative, whose brain is bitten numbly by numb maggots; who walks generously with wide-spread, tentative legs, falls frequently in the gutter, and who sees, in the extremity of his ecstasy, blue mice and pink elephants. He is the type that gives rise to the jokes in the funny papers.

The other type of drinker has imagination, vision. Even when most pleasantly jingled he walks straight and naturally, never staggers nor falls, and knows just where he is and what he is doing. It is not his body but his brain that is drunken. He may bubble with wit, or expand with good fellowship. Or he may see intellectual specters and phantoms that are cosmic and logical and that take the forms of syllogisms. It is when in this condition that he strips away the husks of life's healthiest illusions and gravely considers the iron collar of necessity welded about the neck of his soul. This is the hour of John Barleycorn's subtlest power. It is easy for any man to roll in the gutter. But it is a terrible ordeal for a man to stand upright on his two legs unswaying, and decide that in all the universe he finds for himself but one freedom, namely, the anticipating of the day of his death. With this man this is the hour of the white logic (of which more anon), when he knows that he may know only the laws of things—the meaning of things never. This is his danger hour. His feet are taking hold of the path that leads down into the grave.

All is clear to him. All these baffling head-reaches after immortality are but the panics of souls frightened by the fear of death, and cursed with the thrice-cursed gift of imagination. They have not the instinct for death; they lack the will to die when the time to die is at hand. They trick themselves into believing they will outwit the game and win to a future, leaving the other animals to the darkness of the grave or the annihilating heats of the crematory. But he, this man in the hour of his white logic, knows that they trick and outwit themselves. The one event happeneth to all alike. There is no new thing under the sun, not even that yearned-for bauble of feeble souls—immortality. But he knows, *he* knows, standing upright on his two legs unswaying. He is compounded of meat and wine and sparkle, of sun-mote and world-dust, a frail mechanism made to run for a span, to be tinkered at by doctors of divinity and doctors of physic, and to be flung into the scrap-heap at the end.

Of course, all this is soul-sickness, life-sickness. It is the penalty the imaginative man must pay for his friendship with John Barleycorn. The penalty paid by the stupid man is simpler, easier. He drinks himself into sottish unconsciousness. He sleeps a drugged sleep, and, if he dream, his dreams are dim and inarticulate. But to the imaginative man, John Barleycorn sends the pitiless, spectral syllogisms of the white logic. He looks upon life and all its affairs with the jaundiced eye of a pessimistic German philosopher. He sees through all illusions. He trans-values all values. God is bad, truth is a cheat, and life is a joke. From his calm-mad heights, with the certitude of a god, he beholds all life as evil. Wife, children, friends—in the clear, white light of his logic they are exposed as frauds and shams. He sees through them, and all that he sees is their frailty, their meagerness, their sordidness, their pitifulness. No longer do they fool him. They are miserable little egotisms, like all the other little humans, fluttering their May-fly life-dance of an hour. They are without freedom. They are puppets of chance. So is he. He realizes that. But there is one difference. He sees; he knows. And he knows his one freedom: he may anticipate the day of his death. All of which is not good for a man who is made to live and love and be loved. Yet suicide, quick or slow, a sudden spill or a gradual oozing away through the years, is the price John Barleycorn exacts. No friend of his ever escapes making the just, due payment.

Chapter III

I WAS five years old the first time I got drunk. It was on a hot day, and my father was plowing in the field. I was sent from the house, half a mile away, to carry to him a pail of beer. "And be sure you don't spill it," was the parting injunction.

It was, as I remember it, a lard pail, very wide across the top, and without a cover. As I toddled along, the beer slopped over the rim upon my legs. And as I toddled, I pondered. Beer was a very precious thing. Come to think of it, it must be wonderfully good. Else why was I never permitted to drink of it in the house? Other things kept from me by the grown-ups I had found good. Then this, too, was good. Trust the grown-ups. They knew. And anyway, the pail was too full. I was slopping it against my legs and spilling it on the ground. Why waste it? And no one would know whether I had drunk or spilled it.

I was so small that in order to negotiate the pail, I sat down and gathered it into my lap. First I sipped the foam. I was disappointed. The preciousness evaded me. Evidently it did not reside in the foam. Besides, the taste was not good. Then I remembered seeing the grown-ups blow the foam away before they drank. I buried my face in the foam and lapped the solid liquid beneath. It wasn't good at all. But still I drank. The grown-ups knew what they were about. Considering my diminutiveness, the size of the pail in my lap, and my drinking out of it with my breath held and my face buried to the ears in foam, it was rather difficult to estimate how much I drank. Also, I was gulping it down like medicine, in nauseous haste to get the ordeal over.

I shuddered when I started on, and decided that the good taste would come afterward. I tried several times more in the course of that long half-mile. Then, astounded by the quantity of beer that was lacking, and remembering having seen stale beer made to foam afresh, I took a stick and stirred what was left till it foamed to the brim.

And my father never noticed. He emptied the pail with the

wide thirst of the sweating plowman, returned it to me, and started up the plow. I endeavored to walk beside the horses. I remember tottering and falling against their heels in front of the shining share, and that my father hauled back on the lines so violently that the horses nearly sat down on me. He told me afterward that it was by only a matter of inches that I escaped disembowelling. Vaguely, too, I remember, my father carried me in his arms to the trees on the edge of the field, while all the world reeled and swung about me and I was aware of deadly nausea mingled with an appalling conviction of sin.

I slept the afternoon away under the trees, and when my father roused me at sundown it was a very sick little boy that got up and dragged wearily homeward. I was exhausted, oppressed by the weight of my limbs, and in my stomach was a harp-like vibration that extended to my throat and brain. My condition was like that of one who had gone through a battle with poison. In truth, I had been poisoned.

In the weeks and months that followed I had no more interest in beer than in the kitchen stove after it had burned me. The grown-ups were right. Beer was not for children. The grown-ups did n't mind it; but neither did they mind taking pills and castor oil. As for me, I could manage to get along quite well without beer. Yes, and to the day of my death I could have managed to get along quite well without it. But circumstance decreed otherwise. At every turn in the world in which I lived, John Barleycorn beckoned. There was no escaping him. All paths led to him. And it took twenty years of contact, of exchanging greetings and passing on with my tongue in my cheek, to develop in me a sneaking liking for the rascal.

Chapter IV

M Y NEXT BOUT with John Barleycorn occurred when I
was seven. This time my imagination was at fault, and
I was frightened into the encounter. Still farming, my family
had moved to a ranch on the bleak sad coast of San Mateo
County south of San Francisco. It was a wild, primitive countryside in those days; and often I heard my mother pride herself that we were old American stock and not immigrant Irish
and Italians like our neighbors. In all our section there was
only one other old American family.

One Sunday morning found me, how or why I cannot now
remember, at the Morrisey ranch. A number of young people
had gathered there from the nearer ranches. Besides, the old-
sters had been there, drinking since early dawn, and, some of
them, since the night before. The Morriseys were a huge
breed, and there were many strapping great sons and uncles,
heavy-booted, big-fisted, rough-voiced.

Suddenly there were screams from the girls and cries of
"Fight!" There was a rush. Men hurled themselves out of the
kitchen. Two giants, flush-faced, with graying hair, were
locked in each other's arms. One was Black Matt, who, everybody said, had killed two men in his time. The women
screamed softly, crossed themselves, or prayed brokenly, hiding their eyes and peeping through their fingers. But not I. It
is a fair presumption that I was the most interested spectator.
Maybe I would see that wonderful thing, a man killed. Anyway, I would see a man-fight. Great was my disappointment.
Black Matt and Tom Morrisey merely held on to each other
and lifted their clumsy-booted feet in what seemed a grotesque, elephantine dance. They were too drunk to fight.
Then the peacemakers got hold of them and led them back to
cement the new friendship in the kitchen.

Soon they were all talking at once, rumbling and roaring as
big-chested open-air men will when whisky has whipped their
taciturnity. And I, a little shaver of seven, my heart in my
mouth, my trembling body strung tense as a deer's on the
verge of flight, peered wonderingly in at the open door and

learned more of the strangeness of men. And I marveled at Black Matt and Tom Morrisey, sprawled over the table, arms about each other's necks, weeping lovingly.

The kitchen-drinking continued, and the girls outside grew timorous. They knew the drink game, and all were certain that something terrible was going to happen. They protested that they did not wish to be there when it happened, and some one suggested going to a big Italian rancho four miles away, where they could get up a dance. Immediately they paired off, lad and lassie, and started down the sandy road. And each lad walked with his sweetheart—trust a child of seven to listen and to know the love affairs of his countryside. And behold, I, too, was a lad with a lassie. A little Irish girl of my own age had been paired off with me. We were the only children in this spontaneous affair. Perhaps the oldest couple might have been twenty. There were chits of girls, quite grown up, of fourteen and sixteen, walking with their fellows. But we were uniquely young, this little Irish girl and I, and we walked hand in hand, and, sometimes, under the tutelage of our elders, with my arm around her waist. Only that was n't comfortable. And I was very proud, on that bright Sunday morning, going down the long bleak road among the sandhills. I, too, had my girl, and was a little man.

The Italian rancho was a bachelor establishment. Our visit was hailed with delight. The red wine was poured in tumblers for all, and the long dining-room was partly cleared for dancing. And the young fellows drank and danced with the girls to the strains of an accordeon. To me that music was divine. I had never heard anything so glorious. The young Italian who furnished it would even get up and dance, his arms around his girl, playing the accordeon behind her back. All of which was very wonderful for me, who did not dance, but who sat at a table and gazed wide-eyed at the amazingness of life. I was only a little lad, and there was so much of life for me to learn. As the time passed, the Irish lads began helping themselves to the wine, and jollity and high spirits reigned. I noted that some of them staggered and fell down in the dances, and that one had gone to sleep in a corner. Also, some of the girls were complaining and wanting to leave, and

others of the girls were titteringly complacent, willing for
anything to happen.

When our Italian hosts had offered me wine in a general
sort of way, I had declined. My beer experience had been
enough for me, and I had no inclination to traffic further in
the stuff nor in anything related to it. Unfortunately, one
young Italian, Peter, an impish soul, seeing me sitting solitary, stirred by a whim of the moment, half-filled a tumbler
with wine and passed it to me. He was sitting across the table
from me. I declined. His face grew stern, and he insistently
proffered the wine. And then terror descended upon me—a
terror which I must explain.

My mother had theories. First, she steadfastly maintained
that brunettes and all the tribe of dark-eyed humans were de-
ceitful. Needless to say, my mother was a blond. Next, she
was convinced that the dark-eyed Latin races were profoundly
sensitive, profoundly treacherous, and profoundly murderous.
Again and again, drinking in the strangeness and the fear-
someness of the world from her lips, I had heard her state
that if one offended an Italian, no matter how slightly and
unintentionally, he was certain to retaliate by stabbing one in
the back. That was her particular phrase—"stab you in the
back."

Now, although I had been eager to see Black Matt kill Tom
Morrisey that morning, I did not care to furnish to the
dancers the spectacle of a knife sticking in *my* back. I had not
yet learned to distinguish between facts and theories. My faith
was implicit in my mother's exposition of the Italian character. Besides, I had some glimmering inkling of the sacredness
of hospitality. Here was a treacherous, sensitive, murderous
Italian, offering me hospitality. I had been taught to believe
that if I offended him he would strike at me with a knife
precisely as a horse kicked out when one got too close to its
heels and worried it. Then, too, this Italian, Peter, had those
terrible black eyes I had heard my mother talk about. They
were eyes different from the eyes I knew, from the blues and
grays and hazels of my own family, from the pale and genial
blues of the Irish. Perhaps Peter had had a few drinks. At any
rate his eyes were brilliantly black and sparkling with deviltry.
They were the mysterious, the unknown, and who was I, a

seven-year-old, to analyze them and know their prankishness? In them I visioned sudden death, and I declined the wine half-heartedly. The expression in his eyes changed. They grew stern and imperious as he shoved the tumbler of wine closer.

What could I do? I have faced real death since in my life, but never have I known the fear of death as I knew it then. I put the glass to my lips, and Peter's eyes relented. I knew he would not kill me just then. That was a relief. But the wine was not. It was cheap, new wine, bitter and sour, made of the leavings and scrapings of the vineyards and the vats, and it tasted far worse than beer. There is only one way to take medicine, and that is to take it. And that is the way I took that wine. I threw my head back and gulped it down. I had to gulp again and hold the poison down, for poison it was to my child's tissues and membranes.

Looking back now, I can realize that Peter was astounded. He half-filled a second tumbler and shoved it across the table. Frozen with fear, in despair at the fate which had befallen me, I gulped the second glass down like the first. This was too much for Peter. He must share the infant prodigy he had discovered. He called Dominick, a young mustached Italian, to see the sight. This time it was a full tumbler that was given me. One will do anything to live. I gripped myself, mastered the qualms that rose in my throat, and downed the stuff.

Dominick had never seen an infant of such heroic caliber. Twice again he refilled the tumbler, each time to the brim, and watched it disappear down my throat. By this time my exploits were attracting attention. Middle-aged Italian laborers, old-country peasants who did not talk English and who could not dance with the Irish girls, surrounded me. They were swarthy and wild-looking; they wore belts and red shirts; and I knew they carried knives; and they ringed me around like a pirate chorus. And Peter and Dominick made me show off for them.

Had I lacked imagination, had I been stupid, had I been stubbornly mulish in having my own way, I should never have got in this pickle. And the lads and lassies were dancing, and there was no one to save me from my fate. How much I drank I do not know. My memory of it is of an age-long suffering of fear in the midst of a murderous crew, and of an

infinite number of glasses of red wine passing across the bare
boards of a wine-drenched table and going down my burning
throat. Bad as the wine was, a knife in the back was worse,
and I must survive at any cost.

Looking back with the drinker's knowledge, I know now
why I did not collapse stupefied upon the table. As I have
said, I was frozen, I was paralyzed, with fear. The only movement I made was to convey that never-ending procession of
glasses to my lips. I was a poised and motionless receptacle
for all that quantity of wine. It lay inert in my fear-inert stomach. I was too frightened, even, for my stomach to turn. So
all that Italian crew looked on and marveled at the infant phenomenon that downed wine with the *sang-froid* of an automaton. It is not in the spirit of braggadocio that I dare to assert
they had never seen anything like it.

The time came to go. The tipsy antics of the lads had led a
majority of the soberer-minded lassies to compel a departure.
I found myself at the door, beside my little maiden. She had
not had my experience, so she was sober. She was fascinated
by the titubations of the lads who strove to walk beside their
girls, and began to mimic them. I thought this a great game,
and I, too, began to stagger tipsily. But she had no wine to
stir up, while my movements quickly set the fumes rising to
my head. Even at the start, I was more realistic than she. In
several minutes I was astonishing myself. I saw one lad, after
reeling half a dozen steps, pause at the side of the road,
gravely peer into the ditch, and gravely, and after apparent
deep thought, fall into it. To me this was excruciatingly
funny. I staggered to the edge of the ditch, fully intending to
stop on the edge. I came to myself, in the ditch, in process of
being hauled out by several anxious-faced girls.

I did n't care to play at being drunk any more. There was
no more fun in me. My eyes were beginning to swim, and
with wide-open mouth I panted for air. A girl led me by the
hand on either side, but my legs were leaden. The alcohol I
had drunk was striking my heart and brain like a club. Had I
been a weakling of a child, I am confident that it would have
killed me. As it was, I know I was nearer death than any of
the scared girls dreamed. I could hear them bickering among
themselves as to whose fault it was; some were weeping—for

themselves, for me, and for the disgraceful way their lads had behaved. But I was not interested. I was suffocating, and I wanted air. To move was agony. It made me pant harder. Yet those girls persisted in making me walk, and it was four miles home. Four miles! I remember my swimming eyes saw a small bridge across the road an infinite distance away. In fact, it was not a hundred feet distant. When I reached it, I sank down and lay on my back panting. The girls tried to lift me, but I was helpless and suffocating. Their cries of alarm brought Larry, a drunken youth of seventeen, who proceeded to resuscitate me by jumping on my chest. Dimly I remember this, and the squalling of the girls as they struggled with him and dragged him away. And then I knew nothing, though I learned afterward that Larry wound up under the bridge and spent the night there.

When I came to, it was dark. I had been carried unconscious for four miles and been put to bed. I was a sick child, and, despite the terrible strain on my heart and tissues, I continually relapsed into the madness of delirium. All the content of the terrible and horrible in my child's mind spilled out. The most frightful visions were realities to me. I saw murders committed, and I was pursued by murderers. I screamed and raved and fought. My sufferings were prodigious. Emerging from such delirium, I would hear my mother's voice: "But the child's brain. He will lose his reason." And sinking back into delirium, I would take the idea with me and be immured in madhouses, and be beaten by keepers, and surrounded by screeching lunatics.

One thing that had strongly impressed my young mind was the talk of my elders about the dens of iniquity in San Francisco's Chinatown. In my delirium I wandered deep beneath the ground through a thousand of these dens, and behind locked doors of iron I suffered and died a thousand deaths. And when I would come upon my father, seated at table in these subterranean crypts, gambling with Chinese for great stakes of gold, all my outrage gave vent in the vilest cursing. I would rise in bed, struggling against the detaining hands, and curse my father till the rafters rang. All the inconceivable filth a child running at large in a primitive countryside may hear men utter, was mine; and though I had never dared utter such oaths, they now poured from me, at the top of my lungs, as I cursed my father sitting there underground and gambling with long-haired, long-nailed Chinamen.

It is a wonder that I did not burst my heart or brain that night. A seven-year-old child's arteries and nerve-centers are scarcely fitted to endure the terrific paroxysms that convulsed me. No one slept in the thin, frame farmhouse that night when John Barleycorn had his will of me. And Larry, under the bridge, had no delirium like mine. I am confident that his sleep was stupefied and dreamless, and that he awoke next day merely to heaviness and moroseness, and that if he lives to-day he does not remember that night, so passing was it as an incident. But my brain was seared forever by that experience. Writing now, thirty years afterward, every vision is as distinct, as sharp-cut, every pain as vital and terrible, as on that night.

I was sick for days afterward, and I needed none of my mother's injunctions to avoid John Barleycorn in the future. My mother had been dreadfully shocked. She held that I had done wrong, very wrong, and that I had gone contrary to all her teaching. And how was I, who was never allowed to talk back, who lacked the very words with which to express my psychology—how was I to tell my mother that it was her teaching that was directly responsible for my drunkenness? Had it not been for her theories about dark eyes and Italian character, I should never have wet my lips with the sour, bitter wine. And not until man-grown did I tell her the true inwardness of that disgraceful affair.

In those after-days of sickness, I was confused on some points, and very clear on others. I felt guilty of sin, yet smarted with a sense of injustice. It had not been my fault; yet I had done wrong. But very clear was my resolution never to touch liquor again. No mad dog was ever more afraid of water than was I of alcohol.

Yet the point I am making is that this experience, terrible as it was, could not in the end deter me from forming John Barleycorn's cheek-by-jowl acquaintance. All about me, even then, were the forces moving me toward him. In the first place, barring my mother, ever extreme in her views, it seemed to me all the grown-ups looked upon the affair with tolerant eyes. It was a joke, something funny that had happened. There was no shame attached. Even the lads and lassies giggled and snickered over their part in the affair, narrating with gusto how Larry had jumped on my chest and slept under the bridge, how So-and-So had slept out in the sandhills that night, and what had happened to the other lad who fell in the ditch. As I say, so far as I could see, there was no shame anywhere. It had been something ticklishly, devilishly fine—a bright and gorgeous episode in the monotony of life and labor on that bleak, fog-girt coast.

The Irish ranchers twitted me good-naturedly on my exploit, and patted me on the back until I felt that I had done something heroic. Peter and Dominick and the other Italians were proud of my drinking prowess. The face of morality was not set against drinking. Besides, everybody drank. There was not a teetotaler in the community. Even the teacher of our little country school, a graying man of fifty, gave us vacations on the occasions when he wrestled with John Barleycorn and was thrown. Thus there was no spiritual deterrence. My loathing for alcohol was purely physiological. I did n't like the damned stuff.

Chapter V

THIS PHYSICAL LOATHING for alcohol I have never got over. But I have conquered it. To this day I re-conquer it every time I take a drink. The palate never ceases to rebel, and the palate can be trusted to know what is good for the body. But men do not knowingly drink for the effect alcohol produces on the body. What they drink for is the brain-effect; and if it must come through the body, so much the worse for the body.

And yes, despite my physical loathing for alcohol, the brightest spots in my child life were the saloons. Sitting on the heavy potato wagons, wrapped in fog, feet stinging from inactivity, the horses plodding slowly along the deep road through the sandhills, one bright vision made the way never too long. The bright vision was the saloon at Colma, where my father, or whoever drove, always got out to get a drink. And I got out to warm by the great stove and get a soda cracker. Just one soda cracker, but a fabulous luxury. Saloons were good for something. Back behind the plodding horses, I would take an hour in consuming that one cracker. I took the smallest of nibbles, never losing a crumb, and chewed the nibble till it became the thinnest and most delectable of pastes. I never voluntarily swallowed this paste. I just tasted it, and went on tasting it, turning it over with my tongue, spreading it on the inside of one cheek, then on the inside of the other cheek, until, at the end, it eluded me and in tiny drops and oozelets slipped and dribbled down my throat. Horace Fletcher had nothing on me when it came to soda crackers.

I liked saloons. Especially I liked the San Francisco saloons. They had the most delicious dainties for the taking—strange breads and crackers, cheeses, sausages, sardines—wonderful foods that I never saw on our meager home-table. And once, I remember, a barkeeper mixed me a sweet temperance drink of syrup and soda water. My father did not pay for it. It was the barkeeper's treat, and he became my ideal of a good, kind man. I dreamed day dreams of him for years. Although I was seven years old at the time, I can see him now with undiminished clearness, though I never laid eyes on him but that one time. The saloon was south of Market Street in San Francisco. It stood on the west side of the street. As you entered, the bar was on the left. On the right, against the wall, was the free-lunch counter. It was a long, narrow room, and at the rear, beyond the beer kegs on tap, were small round tables and chairs. The barkeeper was blue-eyed, and had fair, silky hair peeping out from under a black silk skull-cap. I remember he wore a brown Cardigan jacket, and I know precisely the spot, in the midst of the array of bottles, from which he took the bottle of red-colored syrup. He and my father talked long, and I sipped my sweet drink and worshiped him. And for years afterward I worshiped the memory of him.

Despite my two disastrous experiences, here was John Barleycorn, prevalent and accessible everywhere in the community, luring and drawing me. Here were connotations of the saloon making deep indentations in a child's mind. Here was a child, forming its first judgments of the world, finding the saloon a delightful and desirable place. Stores, nor public buildings, nor all the dwellings of men ever opened their doors to me and let me warm by their fires or permitted me to eat the food of the gods from narrow shelves against the wall. Their doors were ever closed to me; the saloon's doors were ever open. And always and everywhere I found saloons, on highway and byway, up narrow alleys and on busy thoroughfares, bright-lighted and cheerful, warm in winter and in summer dark and cool. Yes, the saloon was a mighty fine place, and it was more than that.

By the time I was ten years old, my family had abandoned ranching and gone to live in the city. And here, at ten, I began on the streets as a newsboy. One of the reasons for this was that we needed the money. Another reason was that I needed the exercise. I had found my way to the free public library, and was reading myself into nervous prostration. On the poor-ranches on which I had lived there had been no books. In ways truly miraculous, I had been lent four books, marvelous books, and them I had devoured. One was the life of Garfield; the second, Paul du Chaillu's African travels; the third, a novel by Ouida with the last forty pages missing; and the fourth, Irving's "Alhambra." This last had been lent me by a school-teacher. I was not a forward child. Unlike Oliver Twist, I was incapable of asking for more. When I returned the "Alhambra" to the teacher I hoped she would lend me another book. And because she did not—most likely she deemed me unappreciative—I cried all the way home on the three-mile tramp from the school to the ranch. I waited and yearned for her to lend me another book. Scores of times I nerved myself almost to the point of asking her, but never quite reached the necessary pitch of effrontery.

And then came the city of Oakland, and on the shelves of that free-library I discovered all the great world beyond the skyline. Here were thousands of books as good as my four wonder-books, and some were even better. Libraries were not concerned with children in those days, and I had strange adventures. I remember, in the catalogue, being impressed by the title, "The Adventures of Peregrine Pickle." I filled an application blank and the librarian handed me the collected and entirely unexpurgated works of Smollett in one huge volume. I read everything, but principally history and adventure, and all the old travels and voyages. I read mornings, afternoons, and nights. I read in bed, I read at table, I read as I walked to and from school, and I read at recess while the other boys were playing. I began to get the "jerks." To everybody I replied: "Go away. You make me nervous."

And so, at ten, I was out on the streets, a newsboy. I had no time to read. I was busy getting exercise and learning how to fight, busy learning forwardness, and brass and bluff. I had an imagination and a curiosity about all things that made me plastic. Not least among the things I was curious about was the saloon. And I was in and out of many a one. I remember, in those days, on the east side of Broadway between Sixth and Seventh, from corner to corner, there was a solid block of saloons.

In the saloons life was different. Men talked with great voices, laughed great laughs, and there was an atmosphere of greatness. Here was something more than common every-day where nothing happened. Here life was always very live, and, sometimes, even lurid, when blows were struck, and blood was shed, and big policemen came shouldering in. Great moments, these, for me, my head filled with all the wild and valiant fighting of the gallant adventures on sea and land. There were no big moments when I trudged along the street throwing my papers in at doors. But in the saloons, even the sots, stupefied, sprawling across the tables or in the sawdust, were objects of mystery and wonder.

And more, the saloons were right. The city fathers sanctioned them and licensed them. They were not the terrible places I heard boys deem them who lacked my opportunities to know. Terrible they might be, but then that only meant they were terribly wonderful, and it is the terribly wonderful that a boy desires to know. In the same way pirates, and shipwrecks, and battles were terrible; and what healthy boy would n't give his immortal soul to participate in such affairs?

Besides, in saloons I saw reporters, editors, lawyers, judges, whose names and faces I knew. They put the seal of social approval on the saloon. They verified my own feeling of fascination in the saloon. They, too, must have found there that something different, that something beyond, which I sensed and groped after. What it was, I did not know; yet there it must be, for there men focused like buzzing flies about a honey pot. I had no sorrows, and the world was very bright, so I could not guess that what these men sought was forgetfulness of jaded toil and stale grief.

Not that I drank at that time. From ten to fifteen I rarely tasted liquor, but I was intimately in contact with drinkers and drinking places. The only reason I did not drink was because I did n't like the stuff. As the time passed, I worked as boy-helper on an ice-wagon, set up pins in a bowling-alley with a saloon attached, and swept out saloons at Sunday picnic grounds.

Big jovial Josie Harper ran a road-house at Telegraph Avenue and Thirty-ninth Street. Here for a year I delivered an evening paper, until my route was changed to the water-front and tenderloin of Oakland. The first month, when I collected Josie Harper's bill, she poured me a glass of wine. I was ashamed to refuse, so I drank it. But after that I watched the chance when she was n't around so as to collect from her barkeeper.

The first day I worked in the bowling-alley, the barkeeper,

according to custom, called us boys up to have a drink after we had been setting up pins for several hours. The others asked for beer. I said I 'd take ginger ale. The boys snickered, and I noticed the barkeeper favored me with a strange, searching scrutiny. Nevertheless he opened a bottle of ginger ale. Afterward, back in the alleys, in the pauses between games, the boys enlightened me. I had offended the barkeeper. A bottle of ginger ale cost the saloon ever so much more than a glass of steam beer; and it was up to me, if I wanted to hold my job, to drink beer. Besides, beer was food. I could work better on it. There was no food in ginger ale. After that, when I could n't sneak out of it, I drank beer and wondered what men found in it that was so good. I was always aware that I was missing something.

What I really liked in those days was candy. For five cents I could buy five "cannon-balls"—big lumps of the most delicious lastingness. I could chew and worry a single one for an hour. Then there was a Mexican who sold big slabs of brown chewing-taffy for five cents each. It required a quarter of a day properly to absorb one of them. And many a day I made my entire lunch off of one of those slabs. In truth, I found food there, but not in beer.

Chapter VI

BUT THE TIME was rapidly drawing near when I was to begin my second series of bouts with John Barleycorn. When I was fourteen, my head filled with the tales of the old voyagers, my vision with tropic isles and far sea-rims, I was sailing a small centerboard skiff around San Francisco Bay and on the Oakland Estuary. I wanted to go to sea. I wanted to get away from monotony and the commonplace. I was in the flower of my adolescence, a-thrill with romance and adventure, dreaming of wild life in the wild man-world. Little I guessed how all the warp and woof of that man-world was entangled with alcohol.

So, one day, as I hoisted sail on my skiff, I met Scotty. He was a husky youngster of seventeen, a runaway apprentice, he told me, from an English ship in Australia. He had just worked his way on another ship to San Francisco; and now he wanted to see about getting a berth on a whaler. Across the estuary, near where the whalers lay, was lying the sloop-yacht *Idler*. The caretaker was a harpooner who intended sailing next voyage on the whale ship *Bonanza*. Would I take him, Scotty, over in my skiff to call upon the harpooner?

Would I? Had n't I heard the stories and rumors about the *Idler*?—the big sloop that had come up from the Sandwich Islands where it had been engaged in smuggling opium. And the harpooner who was caretaker! How often had I seen him and envied him his freedom. He never had to leave the water. He slept aboard the *Idler* each night, while I had to go home upon the land to go to bed. The harpooner was only nineteen years old (and I have never had anything but his own word that he was a harpooner); but he had been too shining and glorious a personality for me ever to address as I paddled around the yacht at a wistful distance. Would I take Scotty, the runaway sailor, to visit the harpooner, on the opium-smuggler *Idler*? Would I!

The harpooner came on deck to answer our hail, and invited us aboard. I played the sailor and the man, fending off the skiff so that it would not mar the yacht's white paint, dropping the skiff astern on a long painter, and making the painter fast with two nonchalant half-hitches. We went below. It was the first sea-interior I had ever seen. The clothing on the wall smelled musty. But what of that? Was it not the sea-gear of men?—leather jackets lined with corduroy, blue coats of pilot cloth, sou'westers, sea-boots, oilskins. And everywhere was in evidence the economy of space—the narrow bunks, the swinging tables, the incredible lockers. There were the tell-tale compass, the sea-lamps in their gimbals, the blue-backed charts carelessly rolled and tucked away, the signal-flags in alphabetical order, and a mariner's dividers jammed into the woodwork to hold a calendar. At last I was living. Here I sat, inside my first ship, a smuggler, accepted as a comrade by a harpooner and a runaway English sailor who said his name was Scotty.

The first thing that the harpooner, aged nineteen, and the sailor, aged seventeen, did to show that they were men, was to behave like men. The harpooner suggested the eminent desirableness of a drink, and Scotty searched his pockets for dimes and nickels. Then the harpooner carried away a pink flask to be filled in some blind pig, for there were no licensed saloons in that locality. We drank the cheap rotgut out of tumblers. Was I any the less strong, any the less valiant, than the harpooner and the sailor? They were men. They proved it by the way they drank. Drink was the badge of manhood. So I drank with them, drink by drink, raw and straight, though the damned stuff could n't compare with a stick of chewing taffy or a delectable "cannonball." I shuddered and swallowed my gorge with every drink, though I manfully hid all such symptoms.

Divers times we filled the flask that afternoon. All I had was twenty cents, but I put it up like a man, though with secret regret at the enormous store of candy it could have bought. The liquor mounted in the heads of all of us, and the talk of Scotty and the harpooner was upon running the Easting down, gales off the Horn and pamperos off the Plate, lower topsail breezes, southerly busters, North Pacific gales, and of smashed whaleboats in the Arctic ice.

"You can't swim in that ice water," said the harpooner confidentially to me. "You double up in a minute and go down.

When a whale smashes your boat, the thing to do is to get your belly across an oar, so that when the cold doubles you you'll float."

"Sure," I said, with a grateful nod and an air of certitude that I, too, would hunt whales and be in smashed boats in the Arctic Ocean. And, truly, I registered his advice as singularly valuable information, and filed it away in my brain, where it persists to this day.

But I could n't talk—at first. Heavens! I was only fourteen, and had never been on the ocean in my life. I could only listen to the two sea-dogs, and show my manhood by drinking with them, fairly and squarely, drink and drink.

The liquor worked its will with me; the talk of Scotty and the harpooner poured through the pent space of the *Idler's* cabin and through my brain like great gusts of wide, free wind; and in imagination I lived my years to come and rocked over the wild, mad, glorious world on multitudinous adventures.

We unbent. Our inhibitions and taciturnities vanished. We were as if we had known each other for years and years, and we pledged ourselves to years of future voyagings together. The harpooner told of misadventures and secret shames. Scotty wept over his poor old mother in Edinburg—a lady, he insisted, gently born—who was in reduced circumstances, who had pinched herself to pay the lump sum to the shipowners for his apprenticeship, whose sacrificing dream had been to see him a merchantman officer and a gentleman, and who was heartbroken because he had deserted his ship in Australia and joined another as a common sailor before the mast. And Scotty proved it. He drew her last sad letter from his pocket and wept over it as he read it aloud. The harpooner and I wept with him, and swore that all three of us would ship on the whaleship *Bonanza*, win a big pay-day, and, still together, make a pilgrimage to Edinburg and lay our store of money in the dear lady's lap.

And, as John Barleycorn heated his way into my brain, thawing my reticence, melting my modesty, talking through me and with me and as me, my adopted twin brother and *alter ego*, I, too, raised my voice to show myself a man and an adventurer, and bragged in detail and at length of how I had crossed San Francisco Bay in my open skiff in a roaring southwester when even the schooner sailors doubted my exploit. Further, I—or John Barleycorn, for it was the same thing—told Scotty that he might be a deep sea sailor and know the last rope on the great deep sea ships, but that when it came to small-boat sailing I could beat him hands down and sail circles around him.

The best of it was that my assertion and brag were true. With reticence and modesty present, I could never have dared tell Scotty my small-boat estimate of him. But it is ever the way of John Barleycorn to loosen the tongue and babble the secret thought.

Scotty, or John Barleycorn, or the pair, was very naturally offended by my remarks. Nor was I loath. I could whip any runaway sailor seventeen years old. Scotty and I flared and raged like young cockerels, until the harpooner poured another round of drinks to enable us to forgive and make up. Which we did, arms around each other's necks, protesting vows of eternal friendship—just like Black Matt and Tom Morrisey, I remembered, in the ranch kitchen in San Mateo. And remembering, I knew that I was at last a man—despite my meager fourteen years—a man as big and manly as those two strapping giants who had quarreled and made up on that memorable Sunday morning of long ago.

By this time the singing stage was reached, and I joined Scotty and the harpooner in snatches of sea songs and chanties. It was here, in the cabin of the *Idler*, that I first heard "Blow the Man Down," "Flying Cloud," and "Whisky, Johnny, Whisky." Oh, it was brave. I was beginning to grasp the meaning of life. Here was no commonplace, no Oakland Estuary, no weary round of throwing newspapers at front doors, delivering ice, and setting up ninepins. All the world was mine, all its paths were under my feet, and John Barleycorn, tricking my fancy, enabled me to anticipate the life of adventure for which I yearned.

We were not ordinary. We were three tipsy young gods, incredibly wise, gloriously genial, and without limit to our powers. Ah!—and I say it now, after the years—could John Barleycorn keep one at such a height, I should never draw a sober breath again. But this is not a world of free freights.

One pays according to an iron schedule—for every strength the balanced weakness; for every high a corresponding low; for every fictitous god-like moment an equivalent time in reptilian slime. For every feat of telescoping long days and weeks of life into mad, magnificent instants, one must pay with shortened life, and, oft-times, with savage usury added.

Intenseness and duration are as ancient enemies as fire and water. They are mutually destructive. They cannot co-exist. And John Barleycorn, mighty necromancer though he be, is as much a slave to organic chemistry as we mortals are. We pay for every nerve Marathon we run, nor can John Barleycorn intercede and fend off the just payment. He can lead us to the heights, but he cannot keep us there, else would we all be devotees. And there is no devotee but pays for the mad dances John Barleycorn pipes.

Yet the foregoing is all in after-wisdom spoken. It was no part of the knowledge of the lad, fourteen years old, who sat in the *Idler's* cabin between the harpooner and the sailor, the air rich in his nostrils with the musty smell of men's sea-gear, roaring in chorus: "Yankee ship come down de ribber—Pull, my bully boys, pull!"

We grew maudlin, and all talked and shouted at once. I had a splendid constitution, a stomach that would digest scrap-iron, and I was still running my Marathon in full vigor when Scotty began to fail and fade. His talk grew incoherent. He groped for words and could not find them, while the ones he found his lips were unable to form. His poisoned consciousness was leaving him. The brightness went out of his eyes, and he looked as stupid as were his efforts to talk. His face and body sagged as his consciousness sagged. (A man cannot sit upright save by an act of will). Scotty's reeling brain could not control his muscles. All his correlations were breaking down. He strove to take another drink, and feebly dropped the tumbler on the floor. Then, to my amazement, weeping bitterly, he rolled into a bunk on his back and immediately snored off to sleep.

The harpooner and I drank on, grinning in a superior way to each other over Scotty's plight. The last flask was opened, and we drank it between us, to the accompaniment of Scotty's stertorous breathing. Then the harpooner faded away

into his bunk, and I was left alone, unthrown, on the field of
battle.

I was very proud, and John Barleycorn was proud with me.
I could carry my drink. I was a man. I had drunk two men,
drink for drink, into unconsciousness. And I was still on my
two feet, upright, making my way on deck to get air into my
scorching lungs. It was in this bout on the *Idler* that I discovered what a good stomach and a strong head I had for
drink—a bit of knowledge that was to be a source of pride
in succeeding years, and that ultimately I was to come to consider a great affliction. The fortunate man is the one who
cannot take more than a couple of drinks without becoming
intoxicated. The unfortunate wight is the one who can take
many glasses without betraying a sign; who *must* take numerous glasses in order to get the "kick."

The sun was setting when I came on the *Idler's* deck. There
were plenty of bunks below. I did not need to go home. But
I wanted to demonstrate to myself how much I was a man.
There lay my skiff astern. The last of a strong ebb was running out in channel in the teeth of an ocean breeze of forty
miles an hour. I could see the stiff whitecaps, and the suck
and run of the current was plainly visible in the face and
trough of each one.

I set sail, cast off, took my place at the tiller, the sheet in
my hand, and headed across channel. The skiff heeled over
and plunged into it madly. The spray began to fly. I was at
the pinnacle of exaltation. I sang "Blow the Man Down" as I
sailed. I was no boy of fourteen, living the mediocre ways of
the sleepy town called Oakland. I was a man, a god, and the
very elements rendered me allegiance as I bitted them to my
will.

The tide was out. A full hundred yards of soft mud intervened between the boat wharf and the water. I pulled up my
centerboard, ran full tilt into the mud, took in sail, and,
standing in the stern as I had often done at low tide, I began
to shove the skiff with an oar. It was then that my correlations began to break down. I lost my balance and pitched
headforemost into the ooze. Then, and for the first time, as I
floundered to my feet covered with slime, the blood running
down my arms from a scrape against a barnacled stake, I

knew that I was drunk. But what of it? Across the channel two strong sailormen lay unconscious in their bunks where I had drunk them. I *was* a man. I was still on my legs, if they *were* knee deep in mud. I disdained to get back into the skiff. I waded through the mud, shoving the skiff before me and yammering the chant of my manhood to the world.

I paid for it. I was sick for a couple of days, meanly sick, and my arms were painfully poisoned from the barnacle scratches. For a week I could not use them, and it was a torture to put on and take off my clothes.

I swore, "Never again!" The game was n't worth it. The price was too stiff. I had no moral qualms. My revulsion was purely physical. No exalted moments were worth such hours of misery and wretchedness. When I got back to my skiff, I shunned the *Idler*. I would cross the opposite side of the channel to go around her. Scotty had disappeared. The harpooner was still about, but him I avoided. Once, when he landed on the boat-wharf, I hid in a shed so as to escape seeing him. I was afraid he would propose some more drinking, maybe have a flask full of whisky in his pocket.

And yet—and here enters the necromancy of John Barleycorn—that afternoon's drunk on the *Idler* had been a purple passage flung into the monotony of my days. It was memorable. My mind dwelt on it continually. I went over the details, over and over again. Among other things, I had got into the cogs and springs of men's actions. I had seen Scotty weep about his own worthlessness and the sad case of his Edinburg mother who was a lady. The harpooner had told me terribly wonderful things of himself. I had caught a myriad enticing and inflammatory hints of a world beyond my world, and for which I was certainly as fitted as the two lads who had drunk with me. I had got behind men's souls. I had got behind my own soul and found unguessed potencies and greatnesses.

Yes, that day stood out above all my other days. To this day it so stands out. The memory of it is branded in my brain. But the price exacted was too high. I refused to play and pay, and returned to my cannonballs and taffy-slabs. The point is that all the chemistry of my healthy, normal body drove me away from alcohol. The stuff did n't agree with me. It was abominable. But despite this, circumstance was to

continue to drive me toward John Barleycorn, to drive me
again and again, until, after long years, the time should come
when I would look up John Barleycorn in every haunt of
men—look him up and hail him gladly as benefactor and
friend. And detest and hate him all the time. Yes, he is a
strange friend, John Barleycorn.

Chapter VII

I WAS barely turned fifteen, and working long hours in a cannery. Month in and month out, the shortest day I ever worked was ten hours. When to ten hours of actual work at a machine is added the noon hour; the walking to work and walking home from work; the getting up in the morning, dressing, and eating; the eating at night, undressing, and going to bed, there remains no more than the nine hours out of the twenty-four required by a healthy youngster for sleep. Out of those nine hours, after I was in bed and ere my eyes drowsed shut, I managed to steal a little time for reading.

But many a night I did not knock off work until midnight. On occasion I worked eighteen and twenty hours on a stretch. Once I worked at my machine for thirty-six consecutive hours. And there were weeks on end when I never knocked off work earlier than eleven o'clock, got home and in bed at half after midnight, and was called at half-past five to dress, eat, walk to work, and be at my machine at seven o'clock whistle blow.

No moments here to be stolen for my beloved books. And what had John Barleycorn to do with so strenuous, Stoic toil of a lad just turned fifteen? He had everything to do with it. Let me show you. I asked myself if this were the meaning of life—to be a work-beast? I knew of no horse in the city of Oakland that worked the hours I worked. If this were living, I was entirely unenamored of it. I remembered my skiff, lying idle and accumulating barnacles at the boat-wharf; I remembered the wind that blew every day on the bay, the sunrises and sunsets I never saw; the bite of the salt air in my nostrils, the bite of the salt water on my flesh when I plunged over-side; I remembered all the beauty and the wonder and the sense-delights of the world denied me. There was only one way to escape my deadening toil. I must get out and away on the water. I must earn my bread on the water. And the way of the water led inevitably to John Barleycorn. I did not know this. And when I did learn it, I was courageous enough not to retreat back to my bestial life at the machine.

I wanted to be where the winds of adventure blew. And the winds of adventure blew the oyster pirate sloops up and down San Francisco Bay, from raided oyster-beds and fights at night on shoal and flat, to markets in the morning against city wharves, where peddlers and saloon-keepers came down to buy. Every raid on an oyster-bed was a felony. The penalty was state imprisonment, the stripes and the lockstep. And what of that? The men in stripes worked a shorter day than I at my machine. And there was vastly more romance in being an oyster pirate or a convict than in being a machine slave. And behind it all, behind all of me with youth a-bubble, whispered Romance, Adventure.

So I interviewed my Mammy Jennie, my old nurse at whose black breast I had suckled. She was more prosperous than my folks. She was nursing sick people at a good weekly wage. Would she lend her "white child" the money? *Would she?* What she had was mine.

Then I sought out French Frank, the oyster pirate, who wanted to sell, I had heard, his sloop, the *Razzle Dazzle*. I found him lying at anchor on the Alameda side of the estuary, near the Webster Street bridge, with visitors aboard, whom he was entertaining with afternoon wine. He came on deck to talk business. He was willing to sell. But it was Sunday. Besides, he had guests. On the morrow he would make out the bill of sale and I could enter into possession. And in the meantime I must come below and meet his friends. They were two sisters, Mamie and Tess; a Mrs. Hadley, who chaperoned them; "Whisky" Bob, a youthful oyster pirate of sixteen; and "Spider" Healey, a black-whiskered wharf-rat of twenty. Mamie, who was Spider's niece, was called the Queen of the Oyster Pirates, and, on occasion, presided at their revels. French Frank was in love with her, though I did not know it at the time; and she steadfastly refused to marry him.

French Frank poured a tumbler of red wine from a big demijohn to drink to our transaction. I remembered the red wine of the Italian rancho, and shuddered inwardly. Whisky and beer were not quite so repulsive. But the Queen of the Oyster Pirates was looking at me, a part-emptied glass in her own hand. I had my pride. If I was only fifteen, at least I could not show myself any less a man than she. Besides, there were her sister, and Mrs. Hadley, and the young oyster pirate, and the whiskered wharf-rat, all with glasses in their hands. Was I a milk and water sop? No; a thousand times no, and a thousand glasses no. I downed the tumblerful like a man.

French Frank was elated by the sale, which I had bound with a twenty-dollar goldpiece. He poured more wine. I had learned my strong head and stomach, and I was certain I could drink with them in a temperate way and not poison myself for a week to come. I could stand as much as they; and besides, they had already been drinking for some time.

We got to singing. Spider sang "The Boston Burglar" and "Black Lulu." The Queen sang "Then I Wisht I were a Little Bird." And her sister Tess sang "Oh, Treat My Daughter Kind-i-ly." The fun grew fast and furious. I found myself able to miss drinks without being noticed or called to account. Also, standing in the companionway, head and shoulders out and glass in hand, I could fling the wine overboard.

I reasoned something like this: It is a queerness of these people that they like this vile-tasting wine. Well, let them. I cannot quarrel with their tastes. My manhood, according to their queer notions, must compel me to appear to like this wine. Very well. I shall so appear. But I shall drink no more than is unavoidable.

And the Queen began to make love to me, the latest recruit to the oyster pirate fleet, and no mere hand, but a master and owner. She went upon deck to take the air, and took me with her. She knew, of course, but I never dreamed, how French Frank was raging down below. Then Tess joined us, sitting on the cabin; and Spider, and Bob; and at the last, Mrs. Hadley and French Frank. And we sat there, glasses in hand, and sang, while the big demijohn went around; and I was the only strictly sober one.

And I enjoyed it as no one of them was able to enjoy it. Here, in this atmosphere of bohemianism, I could not but contrast the scene with my scene of the day before, sitting at my machine, in the stifling, shut-in air, repeating, endlessly repeating, at top speed, my series of mechanical motions. And here I sat now, glass in hand, in warm-glowing camaraderie, with the oyster pirates, adventurers who refused to be slaves to petty routine, who flouted restrictions and the law, who carried their lives and their liberty in their hands. And it was through John Barleycorn that I came to join this glorious company of free souls, unashamed and unafraid.

And the afternoon sea breeze blew its tang into my lungs, and curled the waves in mid-channel. Before it came the scow schooners, wing-and-wing, blowing their horns for the draw-bridges to open. Red-stacked tugs tore by, rocking the *Razzle Dazzle* in the waves of their wake. A sugar bark towed from the "boneyard" to sea. The sun-wash was on the crisping water, and life was big. And Spider sang:

> "Oh, it 's Lulu, black Lulu, my darling,
>   Oh, it 's where have you been so long?
> Been layin' in jail,
> A-waitin' for bail,
>   Till my bully comes rollin' along."

There it was, the smack and slap of the spirit of revolt, of adventure, of romance, of the things forbidden and done defiantly and grandly. And I knew that on the morrow I would not go back to my machine at the cannery. To-morrow I would be an oyster pirate, as free a freebooter as the century and the waters of San Francisco Bay would permit. Spider had already agreed to sail with me as my crew of one, and, also, as cook while I did the deck work. We would outfit our grub and water in the morning, hoist the big mainsail (which was a bigger piece of canvas than any I had ever sailed under), and beat our way out the estuary on the first of the sea breeze and the last of the ebb. Then we would slack sheets, and on the first of the flood run down the bay to the Asparagus Islands, where we would anchor miles off shore. And at last my dream would be realized: I would sleep upon the water. And next morning I would wake upon the water; and thereafter all my days and nights would be on the water.

And the Queen asked me to row her ashore in my skiff, when at sunset French Frank prepared to take his guests ashore. Nor did I catch the significance of his abrupt change of plan when he turned the task of rowing his skiff over to

Whisky Bob, himself remaining on board the sloop. Nor did I understand Spider's grinning side-remark to me: "Gee! There 's nothin' slow about *you*." How could it possibly enter my boy's head that a grizzled man of fifty should be jealous of me?

Chapter VIII

WE MET by appointment, early Monday morning, to complete the deal, in Johnny Heinhold's "Last Chance"—a saloon, of course, for the transactions of men. I paid the money over, received the bill of sale, and French Frank treated. This struck me as an evident custom, and a logical one—the seller, who receives the money, to wet a piece of it in the establishment where the trade was consummated. But to my surprise, French Frank treated the house. He and I drank, which seemed just; but why should Johnny Heinhold, who owned the saloon and waited behind the bar, be invited to drink? I figured it immediately that he made a profit on the very drink he drank. I could, in a way, considering that they were friends and shipmates, understand Spider and Whisky Bob being asked to drink; but why should the longshoremen, Bill Kelly and Soup Kennedy, be asked?

Then there was Pat, the Queen's brother, making a total of eight of us. It was early morning and all ordered whisky. What could I do, here in this company of big men, all drinking whisky? "Whisky," I said, with the careless air of one who had said it a thousand times. And such whisky! I tossed it down. A-r-r-r-gh! I can taste it yet.

And I was appalled at the price French Frank had paid—eighty cents. *Eighty cents!* It was an outrage to my thrifty soul. Eighty cents—the equivalent of eight long hours of my toil at the machine, gone down our throats and gone like that, in a twinkling, leaving only a bad taste in my mouth. There was no discussion but that French Frank was a waster.

I was anxious to be gone, out into the sunshine, out over the water to my glorious boat. But all hands lingered. Even Spider, my crew, lingered. No hint broke through my obtuseness of why they lingered. I have often thought since of how they must have regarded me, the newcomer being welcomed into their company, standing at bar with them, and not standing for a single round of drinks.

French Frank, who, unknown to me, had swallowed his chagrin since the day before, now that the money for the

Razzle Dazzle was in his pocket began to behave curiously toward me. I sensed the change in his attitude, saw the forbidding glitter in his eyes, and wondered. The more I saw of men, the queerer they became. Johnny Heinhold leaned across the bar and whispered in my ear: "He 's got it in for you. Watch out."

I nodded comprehension of his statement, and acquiescence in it, as a man should nod who knows all about men. But secretly I was perplexed. Heavens! How was I, who had worked hard and read books of adventure, and who was only fifteen years old, who had not dreamed of giving the Queen of the Oyster Pirates a second thought, and who did not know that French Frank was madly and Latinly in love with her—how was I to guess that I had done him shame? And how was I to guess that the story of how the Queen had thrown him down on his own boat, the moment I hove in sight, was already the gleeful gossip of the waterfront? And by the same token, how was I to guess that her brother Pat 's offishness with me was anything else than temperamental gloominess of spirit?

Whisky Bob got me aside a moment. "Keep your eyes open," he muttered. "Take my tip. French Frank 's ugly. I 'm going up river with him to get a schooner for oystering. When he gets down on the beds, watch out. He says he 'll run you down. After dark, any time he 's around, change your anchorage and douse your riding light. Savve?"

Oh, certainly, I savve'd. I nodded my head, and as one man to another thanked him for his tip; and drifted back to the group at the bar. No; I did not treat. I never dreamed that I was expected to treat. I left with Spider, and my ears burn now as I try to surmise the things they must have said about me.

I asked Spider, in an off-hand way, what was eating French Frank. "He 's crazy jealous of you," was the answer. "Do you think so?" I stalled, and dismissed the matter as not worth thinking about.

But I leave it to any one—the swell of my fifteen-years-old manhood at learning that French Frank, the adventurer of fifty, the sailor of all the seas of all the world, was jealous of me—and jealous over a girl most romantically named the

Queen of the Oyster Pirates. I had read of such things in books, and regarded them as personal probabilities of a distant maturity. Oh, I felt a rare young devil, as we hoisted the big mainsail that morning, broke out anchor, and filled away close-hauled on the three-mile beat to windward out into the bay.

Such was my escape from the killing machine-toil, and my introduction to the oyster pirates. True, the introduction had begun with drink, and the life promised to continue with drink. But was I to stay away from it for such reason? Wherever life ran free and great, there men drank. Romance and adventure seemed always to go down the street locked arm in arm with John Barleycorn. To know the two, I must know the third. Or else I must go back to my free-library books and read of the deeds of other men and do no deeds of my own save slave for ten cents an hour at a machine in a cannery.

No; I was not to be deterred from this brave life on the water by the fact that the water-dwellers had queer and expensive desires for beer and wine and whisky. What if their notions of happiness included the strange one of seeing me drink? When they persisted in buying the stuff and thrusting it upon me, why, I would drink it. It was the price I would pay for their comradeship. And I did n't have to get drunk. I had not got drunk the Sunday afternoon I arranged to buy the *Razzle Dazzle*, despite the fact that none of the rest was sober. Well, I could go on into the future that way, drinking the stuff when it gave them pleasure that I should drink it, but carefully avoiding over-drinking.

Chapter IX

GRADUAL as was my development as a heavy drinker among the oyster pirates, the real heavy drinking came suddenly and was the result, not of desire for alcohol, but of an intellectual conviction.

The more I saw of the life, the more I was enamored of it. I can never forget my thrills, the first night I took part in a concerted raid, when we assembled on board the *Annie*— rough men, big and unafraid, and weazened wharf rats, some of them ex-convicts, all of them enemies of the law and meriting jail, in sea-boots and sea-gear, talking in gruff, low voices, and "Big" George with revolvers strapped about his waist to show that he meant business.

Oh, I know, looking back, that the whole thing was sordid and silly. But I was not looking back in those days when I was rubbing shoulders with John Barleycorn and beginning to accept him. The life was brave and wild, and I was living the adventure I had read so much about.

Nelson, "Young Scratch" they called him to distinguish him from "Old Scratch," his father, sailed in the sloop *Reindeer*, partners with one "Clam." Clam was a dare-devil, but Nelson was a reckless maniac. He was twenty years old, with the body of a Hercules. When he was shot in Benicia, a couple of years later, the coroner said he was the greatest-shouldered man he had ever seen laid on a slab.

Nelson could not read nor write. He had been "dragged" up by his father on San Francisco Bay, and boats were second nature with him. His strength was prodigious, and his reputation along the waterfront for violence was anything but savory. He had Berserker rages and did mad, terrible things. I made his acquaintance the first cruise of the *Razzle Dazzle*, and saw him sail the *Reindeer* in a blow and dredge oysters all around the rest of us as we lay at two anchors, troubled with fear of going ashore.

He was some man, this Nelson; and when, passing by the Last Chance saloon, he spoke to me, I felt very proud. But try to imagine my pride when he promptly asked me in to have a drink. I stood at bar and drank a glass of beer with him, and talked manfully of oysters, and boats, and of the mystery of who had put the load of buckshot through the *Annie's* mainsail.

We talked and lingered at the bar. It seemed to me strange that we lingered. We had had our beer. But who was I to lead the way outside when great Nelson chose to lean against the bar? After a few minutes, to my surprise, he asked me to have another drink, which I did. And still we talked, and Nelson evinced no intention of leaving the bar.

Bear with me while I explain the way of my reasoning and of my innocence. First of all, I was very proud to be in the company of Nelson, who was the most heroic figure among the oyster pirates and bay adventurers. Unfortunately for my stomach and mucous membranes, Nelson had a strange quirk of nature that made him find happiness in treating me to beer. I had no moral disinclination for beer, and just because I did n't like the taste of it and the weight of it was no reason I should forego the honor of his company. It was his whim to drink beer, and to have me drink beer with him. Very well, I would put up with the passing discomfort.

So we continued to talk at bar, and to drink beer ordered and paid for by Nelson. I think, now, when I look back upon it, that Nelson was curious. He wanted to find out just what kind of a gink I was. He wanted to see how many times I 'd let him treat without offering to treat in return.

After I had drunk half-a-dozen glasses, my policy of temperateness in mind, I decided that I had had enough for that time. So I mentioned that I was going aboard the *Razzle Dazzle*, then lying at the city wharf a hundred yards away.

I said good-by to Nelson, and went on down the wharf. But John Barleycorn, to the extent of six glasses, went with me. My brain tingled and was very much alive. I was uplifted by my sense of manhood. I, a truly-true oyster pirate, was going aboard my own boat after hobnobbing in the Last Chance with Nelson, the greatest oyster pirate of us all. Strong in my brain was the vision of us leaning against the bar and drinking beer. And curious it was, I decided, this whim of nature that made men happy in spending good money for beer for a fellow like me who did n't want it.

As I pondered this, I recollected that several times other men, in couples, had entered the Last Chance, and first one, then the other, had treated to drinks. I remembered, on the drunk on the *Idler*, how Scotty and the harpooner and myself had raked and scraped dimes and nickels with which to buy the whisky. Then came my boy code: when on a day a fellow gave another a "cannonball" or a chunk of taffy, on some other day he would expect to receive back a cannonball or a chunk of taffy.

That was why Nelson had lingered at the bar. Having bought a drink, he had waited for me to buy one. *I had let him buy six drinks and never once offered to treat.* And he was the great Nelson! I could feel myself blushing with shame. I sat down on the stringer-piece of the wharf and buried my face in my hands. And the heat of my shame burned up my neck and into my cheeks and forehead. I have blushed many times in my life, but never have I experienced so terrible a blush as that one.

And sitting there on the stringer-piece in my shame, I did a great deal of thinking and trans-valuing of values. I had been born poor. Poor I had lived. I had gone hungry on occasion. I had never had toys nor playthings like other children. My first memories of life were pinched by poverty. The pinch of poverty had been chronic. I was eight years old when I wore my first little undershirt actually sold in a store across the counter. And then it had been only one little undershirt. When it was soiled I had to return to the awful home-made things until it was washed. I had been so proud of it that I insisted on wearing it without any outer garment. For the first time I mutinied against my mother—mutinied myself into hysteria, until she let me wear the store undershirt so all the world could see.

Only a man who has undergone famine can properly value food; only sailors and desert-dwellers know the meaning of fresh water. And only a child, with a child's imagination, can come to know the meaning of things it has been long denied. I early discovered that the only things I could have were those I got for myself. My meager childhood developed meagerness. The first things I had been able to get for myself had been cigarette pictures, cigarette posters, and cigarette albums. I had not had the spending of the money I earned, so I traded "extra" newspapers for these treasures. I traded duplicates with the other boys, and circulating, as I did, all about town, I had greater opportunities for trading and acquiring.

It was not long before I had complete every series issued by every cigarette manufacturer—such as the Great Race Horses, Parisian Beauties, Women of All Nations, Flags of All Nations, Noted Actors, Champion Prize Fighters, etc. And each series I had three different ways: in the card from the cigarette package, in the poster, and in the album.

Then I began to accumulate duplicate sets, duplicate albums. I traded for other things that boys valued and which they usually bought with money given them by their parents. Naturally, they did not have the keen sense of values that I had, who was never given money to buy anything. I traded for postage stamps, for minerals, for curios, for birds' eggs, for marbles (I had a more magnificent collection of agates than I have ever seen any other boy possess—and the nucleus of the collection was a handful worth at least three dollars which I had kept as security for twenty cents I loaned to a messenger-boy who was sent to reform school before he could redeem them).

I'd trade anything and everything for anything else, and turn it over in a dozen more trades until it was transmuted into something that was worth something. I was famous as a trader. I was notorious as a miser. I could even make a junk man weep when I had dealings with him. Other boys called me in to sell for them their collections of bottles, rags, old iron, grain and gunny sacks, and five-gallon oil-cans—ay, and gave me a commission for doing it.

And this was the thrifty, close-fisted boy, accustomed to slave at a machine for ten cents an hour, who sat on the stringer-piece and considered the matter of beer at five cents a glass and gone in a moment with nothing to show for it. I was now with men I admired. I was proud to be with them. Had all my pinching and saving brought me the equivalent of one of the many thrills which had been mine since I came among the oyster pirates? Then what was worth while—money or thrills? These men had no horror of squandering a nickel, or many nickels. They were magnificently careless of money, calling up eight men to drink whisky at ten cents a glass, as French Frank had done. Why, Nelson had just spent sixty cents on beer for the two of us.

Which was it to be? I was aware that I was making a grave decision. I was deciding between money and men, between niggardliness and romance. Either I must throw overboard all my old values of money and look upon it as something to be flung about wastefully, or I must throw overboard my comradeship with those men whose peculiar quirks made them care for strong drink.

I retraced my steps up the wharf to the Last Chance where Nelson still stood outside. "Come on and have a beer," I invited. Again we stood at bar and drank and talked, but this time it was I who paid—ten cents! A whole hour of my labor at a machine for a drink of something I did n't want and which tasted rotten. But it was n't difficult. I had achieved a concept. Money no longer counted. It was comradeship that counted. "Have another," I said. And we had another, and I paid for it. Nelson, with the wisdom of the skilled drinker, said to the barkeeper, "Make mine a small one, Johnny." Johnny nodded and gave him a glass that contained only a third as much as the glasses we had been drinking. Yet the charge was the same—five cents.

By this time I was getting nicely jingled, so such extravagance did n't hurt me much. Besides, I was learning. There was more in this buying of drinks than mere quantity. I got my finger on it. There was a stage when the beer did n't count at all, but just the spirit of comradeship of drinking together. And, ha!—another thing! I, too, could call for small beers and minimize by two-thirds the detestable freightage with which comradeship burdened one.

"I had to go aboard to get some money," I remarked casually, as we drank, in the hope Nelson would take it as an explanation of why I had let him treat six consecutive times.

"Oh, well, you did n't have to do that," he answered. "Johnny 'll trust a fellow like you—won't you, Johnny?"

"Sure," Johnny agreed, with a smile.

"How much you got down against me?" Nelson queried.

Johnny pulled out the book he kept behind the bar, found

Nelson's page, and added up the account of several dollars. At once I became possessed with a desire to have a page in that book. Almost it seemed the final badge of manhood.

After a couple more drinks, for which I insisted on paying, Nelson decided to go. We parted true comradely, and I wandered down the wharf to the *Razzle Dazzle*. Spider was just building the fire for supper.

"Where 'd you get it?" he grinned up at me through the open companion.

"Oh, I 've been with Nelson," I said carelessly, trying to hide my pride.

Then an idea came to me. Here was another one of them. Now that I had achieved my concept, I might as well practice it thoroughly. "Come on," I said, "up to Johnny's and have a drink."

Going up the wharf, we met Clam coming down. Clam was Nelson's partner, and he was a fine, brave, handsome, mustached man of thirty—everything, in short, that his nickname did not connote. "Come on," I said, "and have a drink." He came. As we turned into the Last Chance, there was Pat, the Queen's brother, coming out.

"What's your hurry?" I greeted him. "We 're having a drink. Come on along." "I 've just had one," he demurred. "What of it?—we 're having one now," I retorted. And Pat consented to join us, and I melted my way into his good graces with a couple of glasses of beer. Oh! I was learning things that afternoon about John Barleycorn. There was more in him than the bad taste when you swallowed him. Here, at the absurd cost of ten cents, a gloomy, grouchy individual, who threatened to become an enemy, was made into a good friend, even genial, his looks were kindly, and our voices mellowed together as we talked water-front and oyster-bed gossip.

"Small beer for me, Johnny," I said, when the others had ordered schooners. Yet I said it like the accustomed drinker, carelessly, casually, as a sort of spontaneous thought that had just occurred to me. Looking back, I am confident that the only one there who guessed I was a tyro at bar-drinking was Johnny Heinhold.

"Where 'd he get it?" I overheard Spider confidentially ask Johnny.

"Oh, he 's been sousin' here with Nelson all afternoon," was Johnny's answer.

I never let on that I 'd heard, but *proud*? Ay, even the bar-keeper was giving me commendation as a man. *"He 's been sousin' here with Nelson all afternoon."* Magic words! The accolade delivered by a barkeeper with a beer glass!

I remembered that French Frank had treated Johnny the day I bought the *Razzle Dazzle*. The glasses were filled, and we were ready to drink. "Have something yourself, Johnny," I said, with an air of having intended to say it all the time but of having been a trifle remiss because of the interesting conversation I had been holding with Clam and Pat.

Johnny looked at me with quick sharpness, divining, I am positive, the strides I was making in my education, and poured himself whisky from his private bottle. This hit me for a moment on my thrifty side. He had taken a ten-cent drink when the rest of us were drinking five-cent drinks! But the hurt was only for a moment. I dismissed it as ignoble, remembered my concept, and did not give myself away.

"You 'd better put me down in the book for this," I said, when we had finished the drink. And I had the satisfaction of seeing a fresh page devoted to my name and a charge penciled for a round of drinks amounting to thirty cents. And I glimpsed, as through a golden haze, a future wherein that page would be much-charged, and crossed off, and charged again.

I treated a second time around, and then, to my amazement, Johnny redeemed himself in that matter of the ten-cent drink. He treated us a round from behind the bar, and I decided that he had arithmetically evened things up handsomely.

"Let 's go around to the St. Louis House," Spider suggested, when we got outside. Pat, who had been shoveling coal all day, had gone home, and Clam had gone upon the *Reindeer* to cook supper.

So around Spider and I went to the St. Louis House—my first visit—a huge barroom, where perhaps fifty men, mostly

longshoremen, were congregated. And there I met Stew Kennedy for the second time, and Bill Kelly. And Smith, of the
Annie, drifted in—he of the belt-buckled revolvers. And Nelson showed up. And I met others, including the Vigy brothers, who ran the place, and, chiefest of all, Joe Goose, with
the wicked eyes, the twisted nose, and the flowered vest, who
played the harmonica like a roystering angel and went on the
most atrocious tears that even the Oakland water-front could
conceive of and admire.

As I bought drinks—others treated as well—the thought
flickered across my mind that Mammy Jennie was n't going
to be repaid much on her loan out of that week's earnings of
the *Razzle Dazzle*. "But what of it?" I thought, or rather,
John Barleycorn thought it for me. "You 're a man and you
're getting acquainted with men. Mammy Jennie does n't
need the money as promptly as all that. She is n't starving.
You know that. She 's got other money in bank. Let her wait,
and pay her back gradually."

And thus it was I learned another trait of John Barleycorn.
He inhibits morality. Wrong conduct that it is impossible for
one to do sober, is done quite easily when one is not sober.
In fact, it is the only thing one can do, for John Barleycorn's
inhibition rises like a wall between one's immediate desires
and long-learned morality.

I dismissed my thought of debt to Mammy Jennie and proceeded to get acquainted at the trifling expense of some trifling money and a jingle that was growing unpleasant. Who
took me on board and put me to bed that night I do not
know, but I imagine it must have been Spider.

Chapter X

AND SO I won my manhood's spurs. My status on the water-front and with the oyster pirates became immediately excellent. I was looked upon as a good fellow, as well as no coward. And somehow, from the day I achieved that concept sitting on the stringer-piece of the Oakland City Wharf, I have never cared much for money. No one has ever considered me a miser since, while my carelessness of money is a source of anxiety and worry to some that know me.

So completely did I break with my parsimonious past that I sent word home to my mother to call in the boys of the neighborhood and give to them all my collections. I never even cared to learn what boys got what collections. I was a man, now, and I made a clean sweep of everything that bound me to my boyhood.

My reputation grew. When the story went around the water-front of how French Frank had tried to run me down with his schooner, and of how I had stood on the deck of the *Razzle Dazzle*, a cocked double-barreled shotgun in my hands, steering with my feet and holding her to her course, and compelled him to put up his wheel and keep away, the water-front decided that there was something to me despite my youth. And I continued to show what was in me. There were the times I brought the *Razzle Dazzle* in with a bigger load of oysters than any other two-man craft; there was the time when we raided far down in Lower Bay and mine was the only craft back at daylight to the anchorage off Asparagus Island; there was the Thursday night we raced for market and I brought the *Razzle Dazzle* in without a rudder, first of the fleet, and skimmed the cream of the Friday morning trade; and there was the time I brought her in from Upper Bay under a jib, when Scotty burned my mainsail. (Yes; it was Scotty of the *Idler* adventure. Irish had followed Spider on board the *Razzle Dazzle*, and Scotty, turning up, had taken Irish's place).

But the things I did on the water only partly counted. What completed everything and won for me the title of

"Prince of the Oyster Beds," was that I was a good fellow ashore with my money, buying drinks like a man. I little dreamed that the time would come when the Oakland waterfront, which had shocked me at first, would be shocked and annoyed by the deviltry of the things I did.

But always the life was tied up with drinking. The saloons are poor men's clubs. Saloons are congregating places. We engaged to meet one another in saloons. We celebrated our good fortune or wept our grief in saloons. We got acquainted in saloons.

Can I ever forget the afternoon I met "Old Scratch," Nelson's father? It was in the Last Chance. Johnny Heinhold introduced us. That Old Scratch was Nelson's father was noteworthy enough. But there was more to it than that. He was owner and master of the scow-schooner *Annie Mine*, and some day I might ship as a sailor with him. Still more, he was romance. He was a blue-eyed, yellow-haired, raw-boned Viking, big-bodied and strong-muscled despite his age. And he had sailed the seas in ships of all nations in the old savage sailing days.

I had heard many weird tales about him, and worshiped him from a distance. It took the saloon to bring us together. Even so, our acquaintance might have been no more than a handgrip and a word—he was a laconic old fellow—had it not been for the drinking.

"Have a drink," I said, with promptitude, after the pause which I had learned good form in drinking dictates. Of course, while we drank our beer, which I had paid for, it was incumbent on him to listen to me and to talk to me. And Johnny, like a true host, made the tactful remarks that enabled us to find mutual topics of conversation. And of course, having drunk my beer, Captain Nelson must now buy beer in turn. This led to more talking, and Johnny drifted out of the conversation to wait on other customers.

The more beer Captain Nelson and I drank the better we got acquainted. In me he found an appreciative listener, who, by virtue of book-reading, knew much about the sea-life he had lived. So he drifted back to his wild young days, and spun many a rare yarn for me, while we downed beer, treat by treat, all through a blessed summer afternoon. And it was only John Barleycorn that made possible that long afternoon with the old sea dog.

It was Johnny Heinhold who secretly warned me across the bar that I was getting pickled and advised me to take small beers. But as long as Captain Nelson drank large beers, my pride forbade anything else than large beers. And not until the skipper ordered his first small beer did I order one for myself. Oh, when we came to a lingering fond farewell, I was drunk. But I had the satisfaction of seeing Old Scratch as drunk as I. My youthful modesty scarcely let me dare believe that the hardened old bucaneer was even drunker.

And afterwards, from Spider, and Pat, and Clam, and Johnny Heinhold, and others, came the tips that Old Scratch liked me and had nothing but good words for the fine lad I was. Which was the more remarkable, because he was known as a savage, cantankerous old cuss who never liked anybody. (His very nickname, "Scratch," arose from a Berserker trick of his, in fighting, of tearing off his opponent's face). And that I had won to his friendship, all thanks were due to John Barleycorn. I have given the incident merely as an example of the multitudinous lures and draws and services by which John Barleycorn wins his followers.

Chapter XI

AND STILL there arose in me no desire for alcohol, no chemical demand. In years and years of heavy drinking, drinking did not beget the desire. Drinking was the way of the life I led, the way of the men with whom I lived. While away on my cruises on the bay, I took no drink along; and while out on the bay the thought of the desirableness of a drink never crossed my mind. It was not until I tied the *Razzle Dazzle* up to the wharf and got ashore in the congregating places of men, where drink flowed, that the buying of drinks for other men, and the accepting of drinks from other men, devolved upon me as a social duty and a manhood rite.

Then, too, there were the times, lying at the city wharf or across the estuary on the sandpit, when the Queen, and her sister, and her brother Pat, and Mrs. Hadley came aboard. It was my boat. I was host, and I could only dispense hospitality in the terms of their understanding of it. So I would rush Spider, or Irish, or Scotty, or whoever was my crew, with the can for beer and the demijohn for red wine. And again, lying at the wharf disposing of my oysters, there were dusky twilights when big policemen and plain clothes men stole on board. And because we lived in the shadow of the police, we opened oysters and fed them to them with squirts of pepper sauce, and rushed the growler or got stronger stuff in bottles.

Drink as I would, I could n't come to like John Barleycorn. I valued him extremely well for his associations, but not for the taste of him. All the time I was striving to be a man amongst men, and all the time I nursed secret and shameful desires for candy. But I would have died before I 'd let anybody guess it. I used to indulge in lonely debauches, on nights when I knew my crew was going to sleep ashore. I would go up to the Free Library, exchange my books, buy a quarter's worth of all sorts of candy that chewed and lasted, sneak aboard the *Razzle Dazzle*, lock myself in the cabin, go to bed, and lie there long hours of bliss, reading and chewing candy. And those were the only times I felt that I got my real money's worth. Dollars and dollars, across the bar, could n't buy the satisfaction that twenty-five cents did in a candy store. As my drinking grew heavier, I began to note more and more that it was in the drinking bouts the purple passages occurred. Drunks were always memorable. At such times things happened. Men like Joe Goose dated existence from drunk to drunk. The longshoremen all looked forward to their Saturday night drunk. We of the oyster boats waited until we had disposed of our cargoes before we got really started, though a scattering of drinks and a meeting of a chance friend sometimes precipitated an accidental drunk.

In ways, the accidental drunks were the best. Stranger and more exciting things happened at such times. As, for instance, the Sunday when Nelson and French Frank and Captain Spink stole the stolen salmon boat from Whisky Bob and Nicky the Greek. Changes had taken place in the personnel of the oyster boats. Nelson had got into a fight with Bill Kelly on the *Annie* and was carrying a bullet-hole through his left hand. Also, having quarreled with Clam and broken partnership, Nelson had sailed the *Reindeer*, his arm in a sling, with a crew of two deep-water sailors, and he had sailed so madly as to frighten them ashore. Such was the tale of his recklessness they spread, that no one on the water-front would go out with Nelson. So the *Reindeer*, crewless, lay across the estuary at the sandpit. Beside her lay the *Razzle Dazzle* with a burned mainsail and with Scotty and me on board. Whisky Bob had fallen out with French Frank and gone on a raid "up river" with Nicky the Greek.

The result of this raid was a brand new Columbia River salmon boat, stolen from an Italian fisherman. We oyster pirates were all visited by the searching Italian, and we were convinced, from what we knew of their movements, that Whisky Bob and Nicky the Greek were the guilty parties. But where was the salmon boat? Hundreds of Greek and Italian fishermen, up river and down bay, had searched every slough and tule patch for it. When the owner despairingly offered a reward of fifty dollars, our interest increased and the mystery deepened.

One Sunday morning, old Captain Spink paid me a visit. The conversation was confidential. He had just been fishing in his skiff in the old Alameda ferry slip. As the tide went down, he had noticed a rope tied to a pile under water and leading downward. In vain he had tried to heave up what was fast on the other end. Farther along, to another pile, was a similar rope, leading downward and unheavable. Without doubt, it was the missing salmon boat. If we restored it to its rightful owner there was fifty dollars in it for us. But I had queer ethical notions about honor amongst thieves, and declined to have anything to do with the affair.

But French Frank had quarreled with Whisky Bob, and Nelson was also an enemy. (Poor Whisky Bob!—without viciousness, good-natured, generous, born weak, raised poorly, with an irresistible chemical demand for alcohol, still prosecuting his vocation of bay pirate, his body was picked up, not long afterward, beside a dock where it had sunk full of gunshot wounds). Within an hour after I had rejected Captain Spink's proposal, I saw him sail down the estuary on board the *Reindeer* with Nelson. Also, French Frank went by on his schooner.

It was not long ere they sailed back up the estuary, curiously side by side. As they headed in for the sandpit, the submerged salmon boat could be seen, gunwales awash and held up from sinking by ropes fast to the schooner and the sloop. The tide was half out, and they sailed squarely in on the sand, grounding in a row with the salmon boat in the middle.

Immediately Hans, one of French Frank's sailors, was into a skiff and pulling rapidly for the north shore. The big demijohn in the stern-sheets told his errand. They could n't wait a moment to celebrate the fifty dollars they had so easily earned. It is the way of the devotees of John Barleycorn. When good fortune comes, they drink. When they have no fortune they drink to the hope of good fortune. If fortune be ill, they drink to forget it. If they meet a friend, they drink. If they quarrel with a friend and lose him, they drink. If their love-making be crowned with success, they are so happy they needs must drink. If they be jilted, they drink for the contrary reason. And if they have n't anything to do at all, why they take a drink, secure in the knowledge that when they have taken a sufficient number of drinks the maggots will start crawling in their brains and they will have their hands full with things to do. When they are sober they want to drink; and when they have drunk they want to drink more.

Of course, as fellow comrades, Scotty and I were called in for the drinking. We helped to make a hole in that fifty dollars not yet received. The afternoon, from just an ordinary, common, summer, Sunday afternoon, became a gorgeous, purple afternoon. We all talked and sang and ranted and bragged, and ever French Frank and Nelson sent more drinks around. We lay in full sight of the Oakland water-front, and the noise of our revels attracted friends. Skiff after skiff crossed the estuary and hauled up on the sandpit, while Hans' work was cut out for him—ever to row back and forth for more supplies of booze.

Then Whisky Bob and Nicky the Greek arrived, sober, indignant, outraged in that their fellow pirates had raised their plant. French Frank, aided by John Barleycorn, orated hypocritically about virtue and honesty, and, despite his fifty years, got Whisky Bob out on the sand and proceded to lick him. When Nicky the Greek jumped in with a short-handled shovel to Whisky Bob's assistance, short work was made of him by Hans. And of course, when the bleeding remnants of Bob and Nicky were sent packing in their skiff, the event must needs be celebrated in further carousal.

By this time, our visitors being numerous, we were a large crowd compounded of many nationalities and diverse temperaments, all aroused by John Barleycorn, all restraints cast off. Old quarrels revived, ancient hates flared up. Fight was in the air. And whenever a longshoreman remembered something against a scow-schooner sailor, or vice versa, or an oyster pirate remembered or was remembered, a fist shot out and another fight was on. And every fight was made up in more rounds of drinks, wherein the combatants, aided and abetted by the rest of us, embraced each other and pledged undying friendship.

And of all times, Soup Kennedy selected this time to come and retrieve an old shirt of his, left aboard the *Reindeer* from the trip he sailed with Clam. He had espoused Clam's side of the quarrel with Nelson. Also, he had been drinking in the St. Louis House, so that it was John Barleycorn who led him

to the sandpit in quest of his old shirt. A few words started
the fray. He locked with Nelson in the cockpit of the *Reindeer*, and in the mix-up barely escaped being brained by an
iron bar wielded by irate French Frank—irate because a two-
handed man had attacked a one-handed man. (If the *Reindeer*
still floats, the dent of the iron bar remains in the hard-wood
rail of her cockpit.)

But Nelson pulled his bandaged hand, bullet-perforated,
out of its sling, and, held by us, wept and roared his Berserker
belief that he could lick Soup Kennedy one-handed. And we
let them loose on the sand. Once, when it looked as if Nelson
were getting the worst of it, French Frank and John Barleycorn sprang unfairly into the fight. Scotty protested and
reached for French Frank, who whirled upon him and fell on
top of him in a pummeling clinch after a sprawl of twenty
feet across the sand. In the course of separating these two,
half-a-dozen fights started amongst the rest of us. These fights
were finished, one way or the other, or we separated them
with drinks, while all the time Nelson and Soup Kennedy
fought on. Occasionally we returned to them and gave advice,
such as, when they lay exhausted in the sand, unable to strike
a blow, "Throw sand in his eyes." And they threw sand in
each other's eyes, recuperated and fought on to successive ex-
haustions.

And now, of all this that is squalid, and ridiculous, and
bestial, try to think what it meant to me, a youth not yet
sixteen, burning with the spirit of adventure, fancy-filled with
tales of bucaneers and sea-rovers, sacks of cities and conflicts
of armed men, and imagination-maddened by the stuff I had
drunk. It was life raw and naked, wild and free—the only life
of that sort which my birth in time and space permitted me
to attain. And more than that. It carried a promise. It was the
beginning. From the sandpit the way led out through the
Golden Gate to the vastness of adventure of all the world,
where battles would be fought, not for old shirts and over
stolen salmon boats, but for high purposes and romantic
ends.

And because I told Scotty what I thought of his letting an
old man like French Frank get away with him, we, too,
brawled and added to the festivity of the sandpit. And Scotty

threw up his job as crew, and departed in the night with a pair of blankets belonging to me. During the night, while the oyster pirates lay stupefied in their bunks, the schooner and the *Reindeer* floated on the high water and swung about to their anchors. The salmon boat, still filled with rocks and water, rested on the bottom.

In the morning, early, I heard wild cries from the *Reindeer*, and tumbled out in the chill gray to see a spectacle that made the water-front laugh for days. The beautiful salmon boat lay on the hard sand, squashed flat as a pancake, while on it were perched French Frank's schooner and the *Reindeer*. Unfortunately two of the *Reindeer's* planks had been crushed in by the stout oak stem of the salmon boat. The rising tide had flowed through the hole and just awakened Nelson by getting into his bunk with him. I lent a hand, and we pumped the *Reindeer* out and repaired the damage.

Then Nelson cooked breakfast, and while we ate we considered the situation. He was broke. So was I. The fifty dollars' reward would never be paid for that pitiful mess of splinters on the sand beneath us. He had a wounded hand and no crew. I had a burned mainsail and no crew. "What d 'ye say you and me?" Nelson queried. "I 'll go you," was my answer. And thus I became partners with "Young Scratch" Nelson, the wildest, maddest of them all. We borrowed the money for an outfit of grub from Johnny Heinhold, filled our water-barrels, and sailed away that day for the oyster-beds.

Chapter XII

N OR have I ever regretted those months of mad deviltry I put in with Nelson. He *could* sail, even if he did frighten every man that sailed with him. To steer to miss destruction by an inch or an instant was his joy. To do what everybody else did not dare attempt to do was his pride. Never to reef down was his mania, and in all the time I spent with him, blow high or low, the *Reindeer* was never reefed. Nor was she ever dry. We strained her open and sailed her open and sailed her open continually. And we abandoned the Oakland water-front and went wider afield for our adventures.

And all this glorious passage in my life was made possible for me by John Barleycorn. And this is my complaint against John Barleycorn. Here I was, thirsting for the wild life of adventure, and the only way for me to win to it was through John Barleycorn's mediation. It was the way of the men who lived the life. Did I wish to live the life, I must live it the way they did. It was by virtue of drinking that I gained that partnership and comradeship with Nelson. Had I drunk only the beer he paid for, or had I declined to drink at all, I should never have been selected by him as a partner. He wanted a partner who would meet him on the social side, as well as the work side, of life.

I abandoned myself to the life, and developed the misconception that the secret of John Barleycorn lay in going on mad drunks, rising through the successive stages that only an iron constitution could endure to final stupefaction and swinish unconsciousness. I did not like the taste, so I drank for the sole purpose of getting drunk, of getting hopelessly, helplessly drunk. And I, who had saved and scraped, traded like a Shylock and made junkmen weep; I, who had stood aghast when French Frank, at a single stroke, spent eighty cents for whisky for eight men; I turned myself loose with a more lavish disregard for money than any of them.

I remember going ashore one night with Nelson. In my pocket was one hundred and eighty dollars. It was my intention, first, to buy me some clothes, after that some drinks. I needed the clothes. All I possessed were on me, and they were as follows: a pair of sea-boots that providentially leaked the water out as fast as it ran in, a pair of fifty-cent overalls, a forty-cent cotton shirt, and a sou'wester. I had no hat, so I had to wear the sou'wester, and it will be noted that I have listed neither underclothes nor socks. I did n't own any.

To reach the stores where clothes could be bought, we had to pass a dozen saloons. So I bought me the drinks first. I never got to the clothing stores. In the morning, broke, poisoned, but contented, I came back on board, and we set sail. I possessed only the clothes I had gone ashore in, and not a cent remained of the one hundred and eighty dollars. It might well be deemed impossible, by those who have never tried it, that in twelve hours a lad can spend all of one hundred and eighty dollars for drinks. I know otherwise.

And I had no regrets. I was proud. I had shown them I could spend with the rest of them. Amongst strong men I had proved myself strong. I had clinched again, as I had often clinched, my right to the title of "Prince." Also, my attitude may be considered, in part, as a reaction from my childhood's meagerness and my childhood's excessive toil.

Possibly my inchoate thought was: Better to reign among booze-fighters, a prince, than to toil twelve hours a day at a machine for ten cents an hour. There are no purple passages in machine toil. But if the spending of one hundred and eighty dollars in twelve hours is n't a purple passage, then I 'd like to know what is.

Oh, I skip much of the details of my trafficking with John Barleycorn during this period, and shall only mention events that will throw light on John Barleycorn's ways. There were three things that enabled me to pursue this heavy drinking: first, a magnificent constitution far better than the average; second, the healthy, open-air life on the water; and third, the fact that I drank irregularly. While out on the water, we never carried any drink along.

The world was opening up to me. Already I knew several hundred miles of the waterways of it, and of the towns and cities and fishing hamlets on the shores. Came the whisper to range farther. I had not found it yet. There was more behind.

But even this much of the world was too wide for Nelson. He wearied for his beloved Oakland water-front, and when he elected to return to it we separated in all friendliness.

I now made the old town of Benicia, on the Carquinez Straits, my headquarters. In a cluster of fishermen's arks, moored in the tules on the water-front, dwelt a congenial crowd of drinkers and vagabonds, and I joined them. I had longer spells ashore, between fooling with salmon fishing and making raids up and down bay and rivers as a deputy fish patrolman, and I drank more and learned more about drinking. I held my own with any one, drink for drink; and often drank more than my share to show the strength of my manhood. When, on a morning, my unconscious carcass was disentangled from the nets on the drying-frames, whither I had stupidly, blindly crawled the night before; and when the water-front talked it over with many a giggle and laugh and another drink, I was proud indeed. It was an exploit.

And when I never drew a sober breath, on one stretch, for three solid weeks, I was certain I had reached the top. Surely, in that direction, one could go no farther. It was time for me to move on. For always, drunk or sober, at the back of my consciousness something whispered that this carousing and bay-adventuring was not all of life. This whisper was my good fortune. I happened to be so made that I could hear it calling, always calling, out and away over the world. It was not canniness on my part. It was curiosity, desire to know, an unrest and a seeking for things wonderful that I seemed somehow to have glimpsed or guessed. What was this life for, I demanded, if this were all? No; there was something more, away and beyond. (And, in relation to my much later development as a drinker, this whisper, this promise of the things at the back of life, must be noted, for it was destined to play a dire part in my later wrestlings with John Barleycorn.)

But what gave immediacy to my decision to move on, was a trick John Barleycorn played me—a monstrous, incredible trick that showed abysses of intoxication hitherto undreamed. At one o'clock in the morning, after a prodigious drunk, I was tottering aboard a sloop at the end of the wharf, intending to go to sleep. The tides sweep through Carquinez Straits as in a mill-race, and the full ebb was on when I stumbled overboard. There was nobody on the wharf, nobody on the sloop. I was borne away by the current. I was not startled. I thought the misadventure delightful. I was a good swimmer, and in my inflamed condition the contact of the water with my skin soothed me like cool linen.

And then John Barleycorn played me his maniacal trick. Some maundering fancy of going out with the tide suddenly obsessed me. I had never been morbid. Thoughts of suicide had never entered my head. And now that they entered, I thought it fine, a splendid culmination, a perfect rounding off of my short but exciting career. I, who had never known girl's love, nor woman's love, nor the love of children; who had never played in the wide joy-fields of art, nor climbed the star-cool heights of philosophy, nor seen with my eyes more than a pin-point's surface of the gorgeous world; I decided that this was all, that I had seen all, lived all, been all, that was worth while, and that now was the time to cease. This was the trick of John Barleycorn, laying me by the heels of my imagination and in a drug-dream dragging me to death.

Oh, he was convincing. I had really experienced all of life, and it did n't amount to much. The swinish drunkenness in which I had lived for months (this was accompanied by the sense of degradation and the old feeling of conviction of sin) was the last and best, and I could see for myself what it was worth. There were all the broken-down old bums and loafers I had bought drinks for. That was what remained of life. Did I want to become like them? A thousand times no; and I wept tears of sweet sadness over my glorious youth going out with the tide. (And who has not seen the weeping-drunk, the melancholic drunk? They are to be found in all the barrooms, if they can find no other listener telling their sorrows to the barkeeper, who is paid to listen.)

The water was delicious. It was a man's way to die. John Barleycorn changed the tune he played in my drink-maddened brain. Away with tears and regret. It was a hero's death, and by the hero's own hand and will. So I struck up my death-chant and was singing it lustily, when the gurgle and splash of the current-riffles in my ears reminded me of my more immediate situation.

Below the town of Benicia, where the *Solano* wharf projects, the straits widen out into what bay-farers call the "Bight of Turner's Shipyard." I was in the shore-tide that swept under the *Solano* wharf and on into the bight. I knew of old the power of the suck which developed when the tide swung around the end of Dead Man's Island and drove straight for the wharf. I did n't want to go through those piles. It would n't be nice, and I might lose an hour in the bight on my way out with the tide.

I undressed in the water and struck out with a strong, single-overhand stroke, crossing the current at right angles. Nor did I cease until, by the wharf-lights, I knew I was safe to sweep by the end. Then I turned over and rested. The stroke had been a telling one, and I was a little time in recovering my breath.

I was elated, for I had succeeded in avoiding the suck. I started to raise my death-chant again—a purely extemporized farrago of a drug-crazed youth. "Don't sing . . . yet," whispered John Barleycorn. "The *Solano* runs all night. There are railroad men on the wharf. They will hear you, and come out in a boat and rescue you, and you don't want to be rescued." I certainly did n't. What? Be robbed of my hero's death? Never. And I lay on my back in the starlight, watching the familiar wharf-lights go by, red and green and white, and bidding sad, sentimental farewell to them, each and all.

When I was well clear, in mid-channel, I sang again. Sometimes I swam a few strokes, but in the main I contented myself with floating and dreaming long drunken dreams. Before daylight, the chill of the water and the passage of the hours had sobered me sufficiently to make me wonder what portion of the Straits I was in, and also to wonder if the turn of the tide would n't catch me and take me back ere I had drifted out into San Pablo Bay.

Next I discovered that I was very weary and very cold, and quite sober, and that I did n't in the least want to be drowned. I could make out the Selby Smelter on the Contra Costa shore and the Mare Island lighthouse. I started to swim for the Solano shore, but was too weak and chilled, and made so little headway, and at the cost of so painful effort that I gave it up and contented myself with floating, now and then giving a stroke to keep my balance in the tide-rips which were increasing their commotion on the surface of the water. And I knew fear. I was sober, now, and I did n't want to die. I discovered scores of reasons for living. And the more reasons I discovered, the more liable it seemed that I was going to drown anyway.

Daylight, after I had been four hours in the water, found me in a parlous condition in the tide-rips off Mare Island light, where the swift ebbs from Vallejo Straits and Carquinez Straits were fighting with each other, and where, at that particular moment, they were fighting the flood tide setting up against them from San Pablo Bay. A stiff breeze had sprung up, and the crisp little waves were persistently lapping into my mouth, and I was beginning to swallow salt water. With my swimmer's knowledge, I knew the end was near. And then the boat came—a Greek fisherman running in for Vallejo; and again I had been saved from John Barleycorn by my constitution and physical vigor.

And in passing, let me note that this maniacal trick John Barleycorn played me is nothing uncommon. An absolute statistic of the percentage of suicides due to John Barleycorn would be appalling. In my case, healthy, normal, young, full of the joy of life, the suggestion to kill myself was unusual; but it must be taken into account that it came on the heels of a long carouse, when my nerves and brain were fearfully poisoned, and that the dramatic, romantic side of my imagination, drink-maddened to lunacy, was delighted with the suggestion. And yet, the older, more morbid drinkers, more jaded with life and more disillusioned, who kill themselves, do so usually after a long debauch, when their nerves and brains are thoroughly poison-soaked.

Chapter XIII

S O I LEFT BENICIA, where John Barleycorn had nearly got me, and ranged wider afield in pursuit of the whisper from the back of life to come and find. And wherever I ranged, the way lay along alcohol-drenched roads. Men still congregated in saloons. They were the poorman's clubs, and they were the only clubs to which I had access. I could get acquainted in saloons. I could go into a saloon and talk with any man. In the strange towns and cities I wandered through, the only place for me to go was the saloon. I was no longer a stranger in any town the moment I had entered a saloon.

And right here let me break in with experiences no later than last year. I harnessed four horses to a light trap, took Charmian along, and drove for three months and a half over the wildest mountain parts of California and Oregon. Each morning I did my regular day's work of writing fiction. That completed, I drove on through the middle of the day and the afternoon to the next stop. But the irregularity of occurrence of stopping places, coupled with widely varying road conditions, made it necessary to plan, the day before, each day's drive and my work. I must know when I was to start driving in order to start writing in time to finish my day's output. Thus, on occasion, when the drive was to be long, I would be up and at my writing by five in the morning. On easier driving days I might not start writing till nine o'clock.

But how to plan? As soon as I arrived in a town, and put the horses up, on the way from the stable to the hotel I dropped into the saloons. First thing, a drink—oh, I wanted the drink, but also it must not be forgotten that, because of wanting to know things, it was in this very way I had learned to want a drink. Well, the first thing, a drink. "Have something yourself," to the barkeeper. And then, as we drink, my opening query about roads and stopping-places on ahead.

"Let me see," the barkeeper will say, "there 's the road across Tarwater Divide. That used to be good. I was over it three years ago. But it was blocked this spring. . . . Say, I 'll tell you what. I 'll ask Jerry—" And the barkeeper turns and addresses some men sitting at a table or leaning against the bar farther along, and who may be Jerry, or Tom, or Bill. "Say, Jerry, how about the Tarwater road? You was down to Wilkins last week."

And while Bill or Jerry or Tom is beginning to unlimber his thinking and speaking apparatus, I suggest that he join us in the drink. Then discussions arise about the advisability of this road or that, what the best stopping places may be, what running time I may expect to make, where the best trout streams are, and so forth, in which other men join, and which are punctuated with more drinks.

Two or three more saloons, and I accumulate a warm jingle and come pretty close to knowing everybody in town, all about the town, and a fair deal about the surrounding country. I know the lawyers, editors, business men, local politicians, and the visiting ranchers, hunters, and miners, so that by evening, when Charmian and I stroll down the main street and back, she is astounded by the number of my acquaintances in that totally strange town.

And thus is demonstrated a service John Barleycorn renders, a service by which he increases his power over men. And over the world, wherever I have gone, during all the years, it has been the same. It may be a cabaret in the Latin Quarter, a café in some obscure Italian village, a boozing-ken in sailor-town, and it may be up at the club over Scotch and soda; but always it will be where John Barleycorn makes fellowship that I get immediately in touch, and meet, and know. And in the good days coming, when John Barleycorn will have been banished out of existence along with the other barbarians, some other institution than the saloon will have to obtain, some other congregating place of men where strange men and stranger men may get in touch, and meet, and know.

But to return to my narrative. When I turned my back on Benicia, my way led through saloons. I had developed no moral theories against drinking, and I disliked as much as ever the taste of the stuff. But I had grown respectfully suspicious of John Barleycorn. I could not forget that trick he had played on me—on *me*, who did not want to die. So I continued to drink, and to keep a sharp eye on John Barleycorn, resolved to resist all future suggestions of self-destruction.

In strange towns I made immediate acquaintances in the saloons. When I hoboed, and had n't the price of a bed, a saloon was the only place that would receive me and give me a chair by the fire. I could go into a saloon and wash up, brush my clothes, and comb my hair. And saloons were always so damnably convenient. They were everywhere in my western country.

I could n't go into the dwellings of strangers that way. Their doors were not open to me; no seats were there for me by their fires. Also, churches and preachers I had never known. And from what I did n't know I was not attracted toward them. Besides, there was no glamour about them, no haze of romance, no promise of adventure. They were the sort with whom things never happened. They lived and remained always in the one place, creatures of order and system, narrow, limited, restrained. They were without greatness, without imagination, without camaraderie. It was the good fellows, easy and genial, daring, and, on occasion, mad, that I wanted to know—the fellows, generous-hearted and handed, and not rabbit-hearted.

And here is another complaint I bring against John Barleycorn. It is these good fellows that he gets—the fellows with the fire and the go in them, who have bigness, and warmness, and the best of the human weaknesses. And John Barleycorn puts out the fire, and soddens the agility, and, when he does not more immediately kill them or make maniacs of them, he coarsens and grossens them, twists and malforms them out of the original goodness and fineness of their natures.

Oh!—and I speak out of later knowledge—heaven forefend me from the most of the average run of male humans who are not good fellows—the ones cold of heart and cold of head who don't smoke, drink, nor swear, nor do much of anything else that is brave, and resentful, and stinging, because in their feeble fibers there has never been the stir and prod of life to well over its boundaries and be devilish and daring. One does n't meet these in saloons, nor rallying to lost causes, nor flaming on the adventure-paths, nor loving as God's own mad lovers. They are too busy keeping their feet dry, conserving their heart-beats, and making unlovely life-successes of their spirit-mediocrity.

And so I draw the indictment home to John Barleycorn. It is just these, the good fellows, the worth while, the fellows with the weakness of too much strength, too much spirit, too much fire and flame of fine devilishness, that he solicits and ruins. Of course, he ruins weaklings; but with them, the worst we breed, I am not here concerned. My concern is that it is so much of the best we breed whom John Barleycorn destroys. And the reason why these best are destroyed is because John Barleycorn stands on every highway and byway, accessible, law-protected, saluted by the policeman on the beat, speaking to them, leading them by the hand to the places where the good fellows and daring ones foregather and drink deep. With John Barleycorn out of the way, these daring ones would still be born, and they would do things instead of perishing.

Always I encountered the camaraderie of drink. I might be walking down the track to the water-tank to lie in wait for a passing freight-train, when I would chance upon a bunch of "alki-stiffs." An alki-stiff is a tramp who drinks druggist's alcohol. Immediately, with greeting and salutation, I am taken into the fellowship. The alcohol, shrewdly blended with water, is handed to me, and soon I am caught up in the revelry, with maggots crawling in my brain and John Barleycorn whispering to me that life is big, and that we are all brave and fine—free spirits sprawling like careless gods upon the turf and telling the two-by-four, cut-and-dried, conventional world to go hang.

Chapter XIV

B ACK IN OAKLAND from my wanderings, I returned to the water-front and renewed my comradeship with Nelson, who was now on shore all the time and living more madly than before. I, too, spent my time on shore with him, only occasionally going for cruises of several days on the bay to help out on short-handed scow-schooners.

The result was that I was no longer reinvigorated by periods of open-air abstinence and healthy toil. I drank every day, and whenever opportunity offered I drank to excess; for I still labored under the misconception that the secret of John Barleycorn lay in drinking to bestiality and unconsciousness. I became pretty thoroughly alcohol-soaked during this period. I practically lived in saloons; became a barroom loafer, and worse.

And right here was John Barleycorn getting me in a more insidious though no less deadly way than when he nearly sent me out with the tide. I had a few months still to run before I was seventeen; I scorned the thought of a steady job at anything; I felt myself a pretty tough individual in a group of pretty tough men; and I drank because these men drank and because I had to make good with them. I had never had a real boyhood, and in this, my precocious manhood, I was very hard and woefully wise. Though I had never known girl's love even, I had crawled through such depths that I was convinced absolutely that I knew the last word about love and life. And it was n't a pretty knowledge. Without being pessimistic, I was quite satisfied that life was a rather cheap and ordinary affair.

You see, John Barleycorn was blunting me. The old stings and prods of the spirit were no longer sharp. Curiosity was leaving me. What did it matter what lay on the other side of the world? Men and women, without doubt, very much like the men and women I knew; marrying and giving in marriage and all the petty run of petty human concerns; and drinks, too. But the other side of the world was a long way to go for a drink. I had but to step to the corner and get all I wanted at Joe Vigy's. Johnny Heinhold still ran the Last Chance. And there were saloons on all the corners and between the corners.

The whispers from the back of life were growing dim as my mind and body soddened. The old unrest was drowsy. I might as well rot and die here in Oakland as anywhere else. And I should have so rotted and died and not in very long order either, at the pace John Barleycorn was leading me, had the matter depended wholly on him. I was learning what it was to have no appetite. I was learning what it was to get up shaky in the morning, with a stomach that quivered, with fingers touched with palsy, and to know the drinker's need for a stiff glass of whisky neat in order to brace up. (Oh! John Barleycorn is a wizard dopester. Brain and body, scorched and jangled and poisoned, return to be tuned up by the very poison that caused the damage.)

There is no end to John Barleycorn's tricks. He had tried to inveigle me into killing myself. At this period he was doing his best to kill me at a fairly rapid pace. But not satisfied with that, he tried another dodge. He very nearly got me, too, and right there I learned a lesson about him—became a wiser, a more skilful drinker. I learned there were limits to my gorgeous constitution, and that there were no limits to John Barleycorn. I learned that in a short hour or two he could master my strong head, my broad shoulders and deep chest, put me on my back, and with a devil's grip on my throat proceed to choke the life out of me.

Nelson and I were sitting in the Overland House. It was early in the evening, and the only reason we were there was because we were broke and it was election time. You see, in election time local politicians, aspirants for office, have a way of making the rounds of the saloons to get votes. One is sitting at a table, in a dry condition, wondering who is going to turn up and buy him a drink, or if his credit is good at some other saloon and if it 's worth while to walk that far to find out, when suddenly the saloon doors swing wide and enters a bevy of well-dressed men, themselves usually wide and exhaling an atmosphere of prosperity and fellowship.

They have smiles and greetings for everybody—for you, without the price of a glass of beer in your pocket, for the

timid hobo who lurks in the corner and who certainly has n't
a vote but who may establish a lodging-house registration.
And do you know, when these politicians swing wide the
doors and come in, with their broad shoulders, their deep
chests, and their generous stomachs which cannot help making them optimists and masters of life, why, you perk right
up. It 's going to be a warm evening after all, and you know
you 'll get a souse started at the very least. And—who
knows?—the gods may be kind, other drinks may come, and
the night culminate in glorious greatness. And the next thing
you know, you are lined up at the bar, pouring drinks down
your throat and learning the gentlemen's names and the offices which they hope to fill.

It was during this period, when the politicians went their
saloon rounds, that I was getting bitter bits of education and
having illusions punctured—I, who had pored and thrilled
over "The Rail-Splitter," and "From Canal Boy to President."
Yes, I was learning how noble politics and politicians are.

Well, on this night, broke, thirsty, but with the drinker's
faith in the unexpected drink, Nelson and I sat in the Overland House waiting for something to turn up, especially
politicians. And there entered Joe Goose—he of the un-
quenchable thirst, the wicked eyes, the crooked nose, the
flowered vest.

"Come on, fellows—free booze—all you want of it. I did
n't want you to miss it."

"Where?" we wanted to know.

"Come on. I'll tell you as we go along. We have n't a minute to lose." And as we hurried up town, Joe Goose explained. "It 's the Hancock Fire Brigade. All you have to do
is wear a red shirt and a helmet, and carry a torch. They 're
going down on a special train to Haywards to parade."

(I think the place was Haywards. It may have been San
Leandro or Niles. And, to save me, I can't remember whether
the Hancock Fire Brigade was a Republican or a Democratic
organization. But anyway, the politicians who ran it were
short of torch-bearers, and anybody who would parade could
get drunk if he wanted to.)

"The town 'll be wide open," Joe Goose went on. "Booze?
It 'll run like water. The politicians have bought the stocks of

the saloons. There 'll be no charge. All you got to do is walk right up and call for it. We 'll raise hell."

At the hall, on Eighth Street near Broadway, we got into the firemen's shirts and helmets, were equipped with torches, and, growling because we were n't given at least one drink before we started, were herded aboard the train. Oh, those politicians had handled our kind before. At Haywards there were no drinks either. Parade, first, and earn your booze, was the order of the night.

We paraded. Then the saloons were opened. Extra bar-keepers had been engaged, and the drinkers jammed six deep before every drink-drenched and unwiped bar. There was no time to wipe the bar, nor wash glasses, nor do anything save fill glasses. The Oakland water-front can be real thirsty on occasion.

This method of jamming and struggling in front of the bar was too slow for us. The drink was ours. The politicians had bought it for us. We 'd paraded and earned it, had n't we? So we made a flank attack around the end of the bar, shoved the protesting barkeepers aside, and helped ourselves to bottles.

Outside, we knocked the necks of the bottles off against the concrete curbs, and drank. Now Joe Goose and Nelson had learned discretion with straight whisky, drunk in quantity. I had n't: I still labored under the misconception that one was to drink all he could get—especially when it did n't cost anything. We shared our bottles with others, and drank a good portion ourselves, while I drank most of all. And I did n't like the stuff. I drank it as I had drunk beer at five, and wine at seven. I mastered my qualms and downed it like so much medicine. And when we wanted more bottles, we went into other saloons where the free drink was flowing, and helped ourselves.

I have n't the slightest idea of how much I drank—whether it was two quarts or five. I do know that I began the orgy with half-pint draughts and with no water afterward to wash the taste away and to dilute the whisky.

Now the politicians were too wise to leave the town filled with drunks from the water-front of Oakland. When train time came, there was a round-up of the saloons. Already I was feeling the impact of the whisky. Nelson and I were hustled out of a saloon, and found ourselves in the very last rank of a disorderly parade. I struggled along heroically, my correlations breaking down, my legs tottering under me, my head swimming, my heart pounding, my lungs panting for air.

My helplessness was coming on so rapidly that my reeling brain told me I would go down and out and never reach the train if I remained at the rear of the procession. I left the ranks and ran down a pathway beside the road under broad-spreading trees. Nelson pursued me, laughing. Certain things stand out, as in memories of nightmare. I remember those trees especially, and my desperate running along under them, and how, every time I fell, roars of laughter went up from the other drunks. They thought I was merely antic drunk. They did not dream that John Barleycorn had me by the throat in a death-clutch. But I knew it. And I remember the fleeting bitterness that was mine as I realized that I was in a struggle with death and that these others did not know. It was as if I were drowning before a crowd of spectators who thought I was cutting up tricks for their entertainment.

And running there under the trees, I fell and lost consciousness. What happened afterward, with one glimmering exception, I had to be told. Nelson, with his enormous strength, picked me up and dragged me on and aboard the train. When he had got me into a seat, I fought and panted so terribly for air that even with his obtuseness he knew I was in a bad way. And right there, at any moment, I know now, I might have died. I often think it is the nearest to death I have ever been. I have only Nelson's description of my behavior to go by.

I was scorching up, burning alive internally, in an agony of fire and suffocation, and I wanted air. I madly wanted air. My efforts to raise a window were vain, for all the windows in the car were screwed down. Nelson had seen drink-crazed men, and thought I wanted to throw myself out. He tried to restrain me, but I fought on. I seized some man's torch and smashed the glass.

Now there were pro-Nelson and anti-Nelson factions on the Oakland water-front, and men of both factions, with more drink in them than was good, filled the car. My smashing of the window was the signal for the anti's. One of them reached for me, and dropped me, and started the fight, of all of which I have no knowledge save what was told me afterward, and a sore jaw next day from the blow that put me out. The man who struck me went down across my body, Nelson followed him, and they say there were few unbroken windows in the wreckage of the car that followed as the free-for-all fight had its course.

This being knocked cold and motionless was perhaps the best thing that could have happened to me. My violent struggles had only accelerated my already dangerously accelerated heart, and increased the need for oxygen in my suffocating lungs.

After the fight was over and I came to, I did not come to myself. I was no more myself than a drowning man is who continues to struggle after he has lost consciousness. I have no memory of my actions, but I cried "Air! Air!" so insistently, that it dawned on Nelson that I did not contemplate self-destruction. So he cleared the jagged glass from the window ledge and let me stick my head and shoulders out. He realized, partially, the seriousness of my condition, and held me by the waist to prevent me from crawling farther out. And for the rest of the run in to Oakland I kept my head and shoulders out, fighting like a maniac whenever he tried to draw me inside.

And here my one glimmering streak of true consciousness came. My sole recollection, from the time I fell under the trees until I awoke the following evening, is of my head out the window, facing the wind caused by the train, cinders striking and burning and blinding me, while I breathed with will. All my will was concentrated on breathing—on breathing the air in the hugest lung-full gulps I could, pumping the greatest amount of air into my lungs in the shortest possible time. It was that or death, and I was a swimmer and diver and I knew it; and in the most intolerable agony of prolonged suffocation, during those moments I was conscious, I faced the wind and the cinders and breathed for life.

All the rest is a blank. I came to the following evening, in a water-front lodging-house. I was alone. No doctor had been called in. And I might well have died there, for Nelson and the others, deeming me merely "sleeping off my drunk," had let me lie there in a comatose condition for seventeen hours. Many a man, as every doctor knows, has died of the sudden impact of a quart or more of whisky. Usually one reads of them so dying, strong drinkers, on account of a wager. But I did n't know . . . then. And so I learned; and by no virtue nor prowess, but simply through good fortune and constitution. Again my constitution had triumphed over John Barleycorn. I had escaped from another death-pit, dragged myself through another morass, and perilously acquired the discretion that would enable me to drink wisely for many another year to come.

Heavens! That was twenty years ago, and I am still very much and wisely alive; and I have seen much, done much, lived much, in that intervening score of years; and I shudder when I think how close a shave I ran, how near I was to missing that splendid fifth of a century that has been mine. And, oh, it was n't John Barleycorn's fault that he did n't get me that night of the Hancock Fire Brigade.

Chapter XV

I̲T̲ W̲A̲S̲ during the early winter of 1892 that I resolved to go
to sea. My Hancock Fire Brigade experience was very little
responsible for this. I still drank and frequented saloons—
practically lived in saloons. Whisky was dangerous, in my
opinion, but not wrong. Whisky was dangerous, like other
dangerous things in the natural world. Men died of whisky;
but then, too, fishermen were capsized and drowned, hoboes
fell under trains and were cut to pieces. To cope with winds
and waves, railroad trains, and barrooms, one must use judgment. To get drunk after the manner of men was all right,
but one must do it with discretion. No more quarts of whisky
for me.

What really decided me to go to sea was that I had caught
my first vision of the death-road which John Barleycorn maintains for his devotees. It was not a clear vision, however, and
there were two phases of it, somewhat jumbled at the time.
It struck me, from watching those with whom I associated,
that the life we were living was more destructive than that
lived by the average man.

John Barleycorn, by inhibiting morality, incited to crime.
Everywhere I saw men doing, drunk, what they would never
dream of doing sober. And this was n't the worst of it. It was
the penalty that must be paid. Crime was destructive. Saloon-
mates I drank with, who were good fellows and harmless,
sober, did most violent and lunatic things when they were
drunk. And then the police gathered them in and they vanished from our ken. Sometimes I visited them behind the bars
and said good-by ere they journeyed across the bay to put on
the felon's stripes. And time and again I heard the one explanation: *If I had n't been drunk I would n't a-done it.* And
sometimes, under the spell of John Barleycorn, the most
frightful things were done—things that shocked even my
case-hardened soul.

The other phase of the death-road was that of the habitual
drunkards, who had a way of turning up their toes without
apparent provocation. When they took sick, even with trifling

afflictions that any ordinary man could pull through, they just pegged out. Sometimes they were found unattended and dead in their beds; on occasion their bodies were dragged out of the water; and sometimes it was just plain accident, as when Bill Kelly, unloading cargo while drunk, had a finger jerked off, which, under the circumstances, might just as easily have been his head.

So I considered my situation and knew that I was getting into a bad way of living. It made toward death too quickly to suit my youth and vitality. And there was only one way out of this hazardous manner of living and that was to get out. The sealing-fleet was wintering in San Francisco Bay, and in the saloons I met skippers, mates, hunters, boat-steerers, and boat-pullers. I met the seal-hunter, Pete Holt, and agreed to be his boat-puller and to sign on any schooner he signed on. And I had to have half-a-dozen drinks with Pete Holt there and then to seal our agreement.

And at once awoke all my old unrest that John Barleycorn had put to sleep. I found myself actually bored with the saloon-life of the Oakland water-front, and wondered what I had ever found fascinating in it. Also, with this death-road concept in my brain, I began to grow afraid that something would happen to me before sailing day, which was set for some time in January. I lived more circumspectly, drank less deeply, and went home more frequently. When drinking grew too wild, I got out. When Nelson was in his maniacal cups, I managed to get separated from him.

On the twelfth of January, 1893, I was seventeen, and the twentieth of January I signed before the shipping commissioner the articles of the *Sophie Sutherland*, a three topmast sealing schooner bound on a voyage to the coast of Japan. And of course we had to drink on it. Joe Vigy cashed my advance note, and Pete Holt treated, and I treated, and Joe Vigy treated, and other hunters treated. Well, it was the way of men, and who was I, just turned seventeen, that I should decline the way of life of these fine, chesty, man-grown men?

Chapter XVI

THERE WAS NOTHING to drink on the *Sophie Sutherland*, and we had fifty-one days of glorious sailing, taking the southern passage in the northeast trades to Bonin Islands. This isolated group, belonging to Japan, had been selected as the rendezvous of the Canadian and American sealing-fleets. Here they filled their water-barrels and made repairs before starting on the hundred days' harrying of the seal-herd along the northern coasts of Japan to Behring Sea.

Those fifty-one days of fine sailing and intense sobriety had put me in splendid fettle. The alcohol had been worked out of my system, and from the moment the voyage began I had not known the desire for a drink. I doubt if I even thought once about a drink. Often, of course, the talk in the forecastle turned on drink, and the men told of their more exciting or humorous drunks, remembering such passages more keenly, with greater delight, than all the other passages of their adventurous lives.

In the forecastle, the oldest man, fat and fifty, was Louis. He was a broken skipper. John Barleycorn had thrown him, and he was winding up his career where he had begun it, in the forecastle. His case made quite an impression on me. John Barleycorn did other things beside kill a man. He had n't killed Louis. He had done much worse. He had robbed him of power and place and comfort, crucified his pride, and condemned him to the hardship of the common sailor that would last as long as his healthy breath lasted, which promised to be for a long time.

We completed our run across the Pacific, lifted the volcanic peaks, jungle-clad, of the Bonin Islands, sailed in among the reefs to the land-locked harbor, and let our anchor rumble down where lay a score or more of sea-gipsies like ourself. The scents of strange vegetation blew off the tropic land. Aborigines, in queer outrigger canoes, and Japanese, in queerer sampans, paddled about the bay and came aboard. It was my first foreign land; I had won to the other side of the world,

and I would see all I had read in the books come true. I was
wild to get ashore.

Victor and Axel, a Swede and a Norwegian, and I planned
to keep together. (And so well did we, that for the rest of the
cruise we were known as the "Three Sports.") Victor pointed
out a pathway that disappeared up a wild canyon, emerged
on a steep, bare lava-slope, and thereafter appeared and disappeared, ever climbing, among the palms and flowers. We
would go over that path, he said, and we agreed, and we
would see beautiful scenery, and strange native villages, and
find Heaven alone knew what adventure at the end. And Axel
was keen to go fishing. The three of us agreed to that, too.
We would get a sampan, and a couple of Japanese fishermen
who knew the fishing grounds, and we would have great
sport. As for me, I was keen for anything.

And then, our plans made, we rowed ashore over the banks
of living coral and pulled our boat up the white beach of coral
sand. We walked across the fringe of beach under the co-
coanut palms and into the little town, and found several
hundred riotous seamen from all the world, drinking prodigiously, singing prodigiously, dancing prodigiously—and all
on the main street to the scandal of a helpless handful of Japanese police.

Victor and Axel said we 'd have a drink before we started
on our long walk. Could I decline to drink with these two
chesty shipmates? Drinking together, glass in hand, put the
seal on comradeship. It was the way of life. Our teetotaler
owner-captain was laughed at, and sneered at, by all of us
because of his teetotalism. I did n't in the least want a drink,
but I did want to be a good fellow and a good comrade. Nor
did Louis' case deter me, as I poured the biting, scorching
stuff down my throat. John Barleycorn had thrown Louis to
a nasty fall, but I was young. My blood ran full and red; I
had a constitution of iron; and—well, youth ever grins scorn-
fully at the wreckage of age.

Queer, fierce, alcoholic stuff it was that we drank. There
was no telling where or how it had been manufactured—
some native concoction, most likely. But it was hot as fire,
pale as water, and quick as death with its kick. It had been
filled into empty "square-face" bottles which had once con-

tained Holland gin and which still bore the fitting legend: "Anchor Brand." It certainly anchored us. We never got out of the town. We never went fishing in the sampan. And though we were there ten days, we never trod that wild path along the lava-cliffs and among the flowers.

We met old acquaintances from other schooners, fellows we had met in the saloons of San Francisco before we sailed. And each meeting meant a drink; and there was much to talk about; and more drinks; and songs to be sung; and pranks and antics to be performed; until the maggots of imagination began to crawl, and it all seemed great and wonderful to me, these lusty, hard-bitten sea-rovers, of whom I made one, gathered in wassail on a coral strand. Old lines about knights at table in the great banquet-halls, and of those above the salt and below the salt, and of Vikings feasting fresh from sea and ripe for battle, came to me; and I knew that the old times were not dead and that we belonged to that self-same ancient breed.

By mid-afternoon Victor went mad with drink, and wanted to fight everybody and everything. I have since seen lunatics in the violent wards of asylums that seemed to behave in no wise different from Victor's way, save that perhaps he was more violent. Axel and I interfered as peace-makers, were roughed and jostled in the mix-ups, and finally, with infinite precaution and intoxicated cunning, succeeded in inveigling our chum down to the boat and in rowing him aboard our schooner.

But no sooner did Victor's feet touch the deck, than he began to clean up the ship. He had the strength of several men, and he ran amuck with it. I remember especially one man whom he got into the chain-boxes but failed to damage through inability to hit him. The man dodged and ducked, and Victor broke the knuckles of both his fists against the huge links of the anchor chain. By the time we dragged him out of that, his madness had shifted to the belief that he was a great swimmer, and the next moment he was overboard and demonstrating his ability by floundering like a sick porpoise and swallowing much salt water.

We rescued him, and by the time we got him below, undressed, and into his bunk, we were wrecks ourselves. But

Axel and I wanted to see more of shore, and away we went, leaving Victor snoring. It was curious, the judgment passed on Victor by his shipmates, drinkers themselves. They shook their heads disapprovingly and muttered: "A man like that ought n't to drink." Now Victor was the smartest sailor and best-tempered shipmate in the forecastle. He was an all-around splendid type of seaman; his mates recognized his worth, and respected him and liked him. Yet John Barleycorn metamorphosed him into a violent lunatic. And that was the very point these drinkers made. They knew that drink—and drink with a sailor is always excessive—made them mad, but only mildly mad. Violent madness was objectionable because it spoiled the fun of others and often culminated in tragedy. From their standpoint, mild madness was all right. But from the standpoint of the whole human race, is not all madness objectionable? And is there a greater maker of madness of all sorts than John Barleycorn?

But to return. Ashore, snugly ensconced in a Japanese house of entertainment, Axel and I compared bruises, and over a comfortable drink talked of the afternoon's happenings. We liked the quietness of that drink and took another. A shipmate dropped in, several shipmates dropped in, and we had more quiet drinks. Finally, just as we had engaged a Japanese orchestra, and as the first strains of the *samisens* and *taikos* were rising, through the paper-walls came a wild howl from the street. We recognized it. Still howling, disdaining doorways, with bloodshot eyes and wildly waving muscular arms, Victor burst upon us through the fragile walls. The old amuck rage was on him, and he wanted blood, anybody's blood. The orchestra fled; so did we. We went through doorways, and we went through paper-walls—anything to get away.

And after the place was half wrecked, and we had agreed to pay the damage, leaving Victor partly subdued and showing symptoms of lapsing into a comatose state, Axel and I wandered away in quest of a quieter drinking-place. The main street was a madness. Hundreds of sailors rollicked up and down. Because the chief of police with his small force was helpless, the Governor of the colony had issued orders to the captains to have all their men on board by sunset.

What! To be treated in such fashion! As the news spread among the schooners, they were emptied. Everybody came ashore. Men who had had no intention of coming ashore, climbed into the boats. The unfortunate governor's *ukase* had precipitated a general debauch for all hands. It was hours after sunset, and the men wanted to see anybody try to put them on board. They went around inviting the authorities to try to put them on board. In front of the governor's house they were gathered thickest, bawling sea-songs, circulating square-faces, and dancing uproarious Virginia reels and old-country dances. The police, including the reserves, stood in little forlorn groups, waiting for the command the governor was too wise to issue. And I thought this saturnalia was great. It was like the old days of the Spanish Main come back. It was license; it was adventure. And I was part of it, a chesty sea-rover along with all these other chesty sea-rovers among the paper houses of Japan.

The governor never issued the order to clear the streets, and Axel and I wandered on from drink to drink. After a time, in some of the antics, getting hazy myself, I lost him. I drifted along, making new acquaintances, downing more drinks, getting hazier and hazier. I remember, somewhere, sitting in a circle with Japanese fishermen, kanaka boat-steerers from our own vessels, and a young Danish sailor fresh from cowboying in the Argentine and with a penchant for native customs and ceremonials. And with due and proper and most intricate Japanese ceremonial, we of the circle drank *sake*, pale, mild, and lukewarm, from tiny porcelain bowls.

And, later, I remember the runaway apprentices—boys of eighteen and twenty, of middle class English families, who had jumped their ships and apprenticeships in various ports of the world and drifted into the forecastles of the sailing schooners. They were healthy, smooth-skinned, clear-eyed, and they were young—youths like me, learning the way of their feet in the world of men. And they *were* men. No mild *sake* for them, but square-faces illicitly refilled with corrosive fire that flamed through their veins and burst into conflagrations in their heads. I remember a melting song they sang, the refrain of which was:

> 'T is but a little golden ring,
> I give it to thee with pride,
> Wear it for your mother's sake
> When you are on the tide.

They wept over it as they sang it, the graceless young scamps who had all broken their mothers' prides, and I sang with them, and wept with them, and luxuriated in the pathos and the tragedy of it, and struggled to make glimmering inebriated generalizations on life and romance. And one last picture I have, standing out very clear and bright in the midst of vagueness before and blackness afterward. We—the apprentices and I—are swaying and clinging to one another under the stars. We are singing a rollicking sea-song, all save one who sits on the ground and weeps; and we are marking the rhythm with waving square-faces. From up and down the street come far choruses of sea-voices similarly singing, and life is great, and beautiful, and romantic, and magnificently mad.

And next, after the blackness, I open my eyes in the early dawn to see a Japanese woman, solicitously anxious, bending over me. She is the port-pilot's wife, and I am lying in her doorway. I am chilled and shivering, sick with the after sickness of debauch. And I feel lightly clad. Those rascals of runaway apprentices! They have acquired the habit of running away. They have run away with my possessions. My watch is gone. My few dollars are gone. My coat is gone. So is my belt. And yes, my shoes.

And the foregoing is a sample of the ten days I spent in the Bonin Islands. Victor got over his lunacy, rejoined Axel and me, and after that we caroused somewhat more discreetly. And we never climbed that lava path among the flowers. The town and the square-faces were all we saw.

One who has been burned by fire must preach about the fire. I might have seen and healthily enjoyed a whole lot more of the Bonin Islands, if I had done what I ought to have done. But, as I see it, it is not a matter of what one ought to do, or ought not to do. It is what one *does* do. That is the everlasting, irrefragable fact. I did just what I did. I did what all those men did in the Bonin Islands. I did what millions of men over the world were doing at that particular point in time. I did it because the way led to it, because I was only a human boy, a creature of my environment, and neither an anemic nor a god. I was just human, and I was taking the path in the world that men took—men whom I admired, if you please; full-blooded men, lusty, breedy, chesty men, free spirits and anything but niggards in the way they foamed life away.

And the way was open. It was like an uncovered well in a yard where children play. It is small use to tell the brave little boys toddling their way along into knowledge of life that they must n't play near the uncovered well. They *will* play near it. Any parent knows that. And we know that a certain percentage of them, the livest and most daring, will fall into the well. The thing to do—we all know it—is to cover up the well. The case is the same with John Barleycorn. All the no-saying and no-preaching in the world will fail to keep men, and youths growing into manhood, away from John Barleycorn when John Barleycorn is everywhere accessible, and where John Barleycorn is everywhere the connotation of manliness, and daring, and great-spiritedness.

The only rational thing for the twentieth century folk to do is to cover up the well; to make the twentieth century in truth the twentieth century, and to relegate to the nineteenth century and all the preceding centuries the things of those centuries, the witch-burnings, the intolerances, the fetiches, and, not least among such barbarisms, John Barleycorn.

Chapter XVII

NORTH WE RACED from the Bonin Islands to pick up the seal-herd, and north we hunted it for a hundred days into frosty, wintry weather and into and through vast fogs which hid the sun from us for a week at a time. It was wild and heavy work off the Siberian coast, without a drink or thought of drink. Then we sailed south to Yokohama, with a big catch of skins in our salt and a heavy pay-day coming.

I was eager to be ashore and see Japan, but the first day was devoted to ship's work, and not until evening did we sailors land. And here, by the very system of things, by the way life was organized and men transacted affairs, John Barleycorn reached out and tucked my arm in his. The captain had given money for us to the hunters, and the hunters were waiting in a certain Japanese public house for us to come and get it. We rode to the place in rickshaws. Our own crowd had taken possession of it. Drink was flowing. Everybody had money, and everybody was treating. After the hundred days of hard toil and absolute abstinence, in the pink of physical condition, bulging with health, overspilling with spirits that had been long pent by discipline and circumstance, of course we would have a drink or two. And after that we would see the town.

It was the old story. There were so many drinks to be drunk, and as the warm magic poured through our veins and mellowed our voices and affections we knew it was no time to make invidious distinctions—to drink with this shipmate and to decline to drink with that shipmate. We were all shipmates who had been through stress and storm together, who had pulled and hauled on the same sheets and tackles, relieved one another's wheels, lain out side by side on the same jib-boom when she was plunging into it and looked to see who was missing when she cleared and lifted. So we drank with all, and all treated, and our voices rose, and we remembered a myriad kindly acts of comradeship, and forgot our fights and wordy squabbles, and knew one another for the best fellows in the world.

Well, the night was young when we arrived in that public house, and for all of that first night that public house was what I saw of Japan—a drinking place which was very like a drinking place at home or anywhere else over the world.

We lay in Yokohama harbor for two weeks, and about all we saw of Japan was its drinking places where sailors congregated. Occasionally, some one of us varied the monotony with a more exciting drunk. In such fashion I managed a real exploit by swimming off to the schooner one dark midnight and going soundly to sleep while the water-police searched the harbor for my body and brought my clothes out for identification.

Perhaps it was for things like that, I imagined, that men got drunk. In our little round of living what I had done was a noteworthy event. All the harbor talked about it. I enjoyed several days of fame among the Japanese boatmen and ashore in the pubs. It was a red letter event. It was an event to be remembered and narrated with pride. I remember it to-day, twenty years afterward, with a secret glow of pride. It was a purple passage, just as Victor's wrecking of the tea house in the Bonin Islands and my being looted by the runaway apprentices were purple passages.

The point is that the charm of John Barleycorn was still a mystery to me. I was so organically a non-alcoholic that alcohol itself made no appeal; the chemical reactions it produced in me were not satisfying because I possessed no need for such chemical satisfaction. I drank because the men I was with drank, and because my nature was such that I could not permit myself to be less of a man than other men at their favorite pastime. And I still had a sweet tooth, and on privy occasions when there was no man to see, bought candy and blissfully devoured it.

We hove up anchor to a jolly chanty, and sailed out of Yokohama harbor for San Francisco. We took the northern passage, and with the stout west wind at our back made the run across the Pacific in thirty-seven days of brave sailing. We still had a big pay-day coming to us, and for thirty-seven days, without a drink to addle our mental processes, we incessantly planned the spending of our money.

The first statement of each man—ever an ancient one

in homeward-bound forecastles—was: "No boarding-house sharks in mine." Next, in parentheses, was regret at having spent so much money in Yokohama. And after that, each man proceeded to paint his favorite phantom. Victor, for instance, said that immediately he landed in San Francisco he would pass right through the water-front and the Barbary Coast, and put an advertisement in the papers. His advertisement would be for board and room in some simple working-class family. "Then," said Victor, "I shall go to some dancing-school for a week or two, just to meet and get acquainted with the girls and fellows. Then I 'll get the run of the different dancing-crowds, and be invited to their homes, and to parties, and all that, and with the money I 've got I can last out till next January when I 'll go sealing again."

No; he was n't going to drink. He knew the way of it, particularly his way of it, wine in, wit out, and his money would be gone in no time. He had his choice, based on bitter experience, between three days' debauch among the sharks and harpies of the Barbary Coast and a whole winter of wholesome enjoyment and sociability, and there was n't any doubt of the way he was going to choose.

Said Axel Gunderson, who did n't care for dancing and social functions: "I 've got a good pay-day. Now I can go home. It is fifteen years since I 've seen my mother and all the family. When I pay off I shall send my money home to wait for me. Then I 'll pick a good ship bound for Europe, and arrive there with another pay-day. Put them together, and I 'll have more money than ever in my life before. I 'll be a prince at home. You have n't any idea how cheap everything is in Norway. I can make presents to everybody, and spend my money like what would seem to them a millionaire, and live a whole year there before I 'd have to go back to sea."

"The very thing I 'm going to do," declared Red John. "It 's three years since I 've received a line from home and ten years since I was there. Things are just as cheap in Sweden, Axel, as in Norway, and my folks are real country folks and farmers. I 'll send my pay-day home and ship on the same ship with you for around the Horn. We 'll pick a good one."

And as Axel Gunderson and Red John painted the pastoral delights and festive customs of their respective countries, each fell in love with the other's home place, and they solemnly pledged to make the journey together, and to spend, together, six months in the one's Swedish home and six months in the other's Norwegian home. And for the rest of the voyage they could hardly be pried apart, so infatuated did they become with discussing their plans.

Long John was not a home-body. But he was tired of the forecastle. No boarding-house sharks in his. He, too, would get a room in a quiet family, and he would go to a navigation school and study to be a captain. And so it went. Each man swore that for once he would be sensible and not squander his money. No boarding-house sharks, no sailor-town, no drink, was the slogan of our forecastle.

The men became stingy. Never was there such economy. They refused to buy anything more from the slop-chest. Old rags had to last, and they sewed patch upon patch, turning out what are called "homeward-bound patches" of the most amazing dimensions. They saved on matches, even, waiting till two or three were ready to light their pipes from the same match.

As we sailed up the San Francisco water-front, the moment the port doctors passed us the boarding-house runners were alongside in whitehall boats. They swarmed on board, each drumming for his own boarding-house, and each with a bottle of free whisky inside his shirt. But we waved them grandly and blasphemously away. We wanted none of their boarding-houses and none of their whisky. We were sober, thrifty sailormen, with better use for our money.

Came the paying off before the Shipping Commissioner. We emerged upon the sidewalk, each with a pocketful of money. About us, like buzzards, clustered the sharks and harpies. And we looked at each other. We had been seven months together, and our paths were separating. One last farewell rite of comradeship remained. (Oh, it was the way, the custom). "Come on, boys," said our sailing-master. There stood the inevitable adjacent saloon. There were a dozen saloons all around. And when we had followed the sailing-master into the one of his choice, the sharks were thick on the sidewalk outside. Some of them even ventured inside, but we would have nothing to do with them.

There we stood at the long bar—the sailing-master, the mates, the six hunters, the six boat-steerers, and the five boat-pullers. There were only five of the last, for one of our number had been dropped overboard, with a sack of coal at his feet, between two snow squalls in a driving gale off Cape Jerimo. There were nineteen of us, and it was to be our last drink together. With seven months of men's work in the world, blow high, blow low, behind us, we were looking on each other for the last time. We knew it, for sailors' ways go wide. And the nineteen of us drank the sailing-master's treat. Then the mate looked at us with eloquent eyes and called for another round. We liked the mate just as well as the sailing-master, and we liked them both. Could we drink with one, and not the other?

And Pete Holt, my own hunter (lost next year in the *Mary Thomas* with all hands), called a round. The time passed, the drinks continued to come on the bar, our voices rose, and the maggots began to crawl. There were six hunters, and each insisted, in the sacred name of comradeship, that all hands drink with him just once. There were six boat-steerers and five boat-pullers and the same logic held with them. There was money in all our pockets, and our money was as good as any man's, and our hearts were as free and generous.

Nineteen rounds of drinks. What more would John Barleycorn ask in order to have his will with men? They were ripe to forget their dearly cherished plans. They rolled out of the saloon and into the arms of the sharks and harpies. They did n't last long. From two days to a week saw the end of their money and saw them being carted by the boarding-house master on board outward-bound ships. Victor was a fine body of a man, and through a lucky friendship managed to get into the life-saving service. He never saw the dancing-school nor placed his advertisement for a room in a working-class family. Nor did Long John win to navigation-school. By the end of the week he was a transient lumper on a river steamboat. Red John and Axel did not send their pay-days home to the old country. Instead, and along with the rest, they were scattered on board sailing ships bound for the four quarters of the globe, where they had been placed by the boarding-house masters and where they were working out advance money which they had neither seen nor spent.

What saved me was that I had a home and people to go to. I crossed the bay to Oakland, and, among other things, took a look at the death-road. Nelson was gone—shot to death while drunk and resisting the officers. His partner in that affair was lying in prison. Whisky Bob was gone. Old Cole, Old Smoudge and Bob Smith were gone. Another Smith, he of the belted guns and the *Annie*, was drowned. French Frank, they said, was lurking up river, afraid to come down because of something he had done. Others were wearing stripes in San Quentin or Folsom. Big Alec, the King of the Greeks, whom I had known well in the old Benicia days, and with whom I had drunk whole nights through, had killed two men and fled to foreign parts. Fitzsimmons, with whom I had sailed on the Fish Patrol, had been stabbed in the lung through the back and had died a lingering death from tuberculosis. And so it went, a very lively and well-patronized road, and, from what I knew of all of them, John Barleycorn was responsible, with the sole exception of Smith of the *Annie*.

Chapter XVIII

MY INFATUATION for the Oakland water-front was quite dead. I did n't like the looks of it nor the life. I did n't care for the drinking, nor the vagrancy of it, and I wandered back to the Oakland Free Library and read the books with greater understanding. Then, too, my mother said I had sown my wild oats and it was time I settled down to a regular job. Also, the family needed the money. So I got a job at the jute mills—a ten-hour day at ten cents an hour. Despite my increase in strength and general efficiency, I was receiving no more than when I worked in the cannery several years before. But, then, there was a promise of a raise to a dollar and a quarter a day after a few months.

And here, so far as John Barleycorn is concerned, began a period of innocence. I did not know what it was to take a drink from month end to month end. Not yet eighteen years old, healthy and with labor-hardened but unhurt muscles, like any young animal I needed diversion, excitement, something beyond the books and the mechanical toil.

I strayed into Young Men's Christian Associations. The life there was healthful and athletic, but too juvenile. For me it was too late. I was not boy, nor youth, despite my paucity of years. I had bucked big with men. I knew mysterious and violent things. I was from the other side of life so far as concerned the young men I encountered in the Y. M. C. A. I spoke another language, possessed a sadder and more terrible wisdom. (When I come to think it over, I realize, now, that I have never had a boyhood.) At any rate, the Y. M. C. A. young men were too juvenile for me, too unsophisticated. This I would not have minded, could they have met me and helped me mentally. But I had got more out of the books than they. Their meager physical experiences, plus their meager intellectual experiences, made a negative sum so vast that it overbalanced their wholesome morality and healthful sports.

In short, I could n't play with the pupils of a lower grade. All the clean splendid young life that was theirs was denied me—thanks to my earlier tutelage under John Barleycorn. I knew too much too young. And yet, in the good time coming, when alcohol is eliminated from the needs and the institutions of men, it will be the Y. M. C. A., and similar unthinkably better and wiser and more virile congregating places, that will receive the men who now go to saloons to find themselves and one another. In the meantime, we live today, here and now, and we discuss to-day, here and now.

I was working ten hours a day in the jute mills. It was humdrum machine-toil. I wanted life. I wanted to realize myself in other ways than at a machine for ten cents an hour. And yet I had had my fill of saloons. I wanted something new. I was growing up. I was developing unguessed and troubling potencies and proclivities. And at this very stage, fortunately, I met Louis Shattuck and we became chums.

Louis Shattuck, without one vicious trait, was a real innocently devilish young fellow who was quite convinced that he was a sophisticated town-boy. And I was n't a town-boy at all. Louis was handsome, and graceful, and filled with love for the girls. With him it was an exciting and all-absorbing pursuit. I did n't know anything about girls. I had been too busy being a man. This was an entirely new phase of existence which had escaped me. And when I saw Louis say good-by to me, raise his hat to a girl of his acquaintance, and walk on by her side down the sidewalk, I was made excited and envious. I, too, wanted to play this game.

"Well—there 's only one thing to do," said Louis, "and that is, you must get a girl."

Which is more difficult than it sounds. Let me show you, at the expense of a slight going aside. Louis did not know girls in their home life. He had the entrée to no girl's home. And of course, I, a stranger in this new world, was similarly circumstanced. But further, Louis and I were unable to go to dancing-schools, or to public dances, which were very good places for getting acquainted. We did n't have the money. He was a blacksmith's apprentice, and was earning but slightly more than I. We both lived at home and paid our way. When we had done this, and bought our cigarettes, and the inevitable clothes and shoes, there remained to each of us, for personal spending, a sum that varied between seventy cents and a dollar for the week. We whacked this up, shared it, and sometimes loaned all of what was left of it when one of us needed it for some more gorgeous girl-adventure, such as car-fare out to Blair's Park and back—twenty cents, bang, just like that; and ice-cream for two—thirty cents; or tamales, which came cheaper and which for two cost only twenty cents.

I did not mind this money meagerness. The disdain for money I had learned from the oyster pirates had never left me. I did n't care over-weeningly for it for personal gratification; and in my philosophy I completed the circle, finding myself as equable with the lack of a ten-cent piece as I was with the squandering of scores of dollars in calling all men and hangers-on up to the bar to drink with me.

But how to get a girl? There was no girl's home to which Louis could take me and where I might be introduced to girls. I knew none. And Louis' several girls he wanted for himself; and anyway, in the very human nature of boys' and girls' ways, he could n't turn any of them over to me. He did persuade them to bring girlfriends for me; but I found them weak sisters, pale and ineffectual alongside the choice specimens he had.

"You 'll have to do like I did," he said finally. "I got these by getting them. You'll have to get one the same way."

And he initiated me. It must be remembered that Louis and I were hard situated. We really had to struggle to pay our board and maintain a decent appearance. We met each other in the evening, after the day's work, on the street corner, or in a little candy store on a side street, our sole frequenting place. Here we bought our cigarettes, and, occasionally, a nickel's worth of "red-hots." (Oh, yes; Louis and I unblushingly ate candy—all we could get. Neither of us drank. Neither of us ever went into a saloon.)

But the girl. In quite primitive fashion, as Louis advised me, I was to select her and make myself acquainted with her. We strolled the streets in the early evenings. The girls, like us, strolled in pairs. And strolling girls *will* look at strolling boys who look. (And to this day, in any town, city, or village, in which I, in my middle age, find myself, I look on with the eye trained of old experience, and watch the sweet game played by the strolling boys and girls who just *must* stroll when the spring and summer evenings call.)

The trouble was that in this Arcadian phase of my history, I, who had come through, case-hardened, from the other side of life, was timid and bashful. Again and again Louis nerved me up. But I did n't know girls. They were strange and wonderful to me after my precocious man's life. I failed of the bold front and the necessary forwardness when the crucial moment came.

Then Louis would show me how—a certain, eloquent glance of eye, a smile, a daring, lifted hat, a spoken word, hesitancies, giggles, coy nervousness, and, behold, Louis acquainted and nodding me up to be introduced. But, when we paired off to stroll along boy and girl together, I noted that Louis had invariably picked the good-looker and left to me the little lame sister.

I improved, of course, after experiences too numerous to enter upon, so that there were divers girls to whom I could lift my hat and who would walk beside me in the early evenings. But girl's love did not immediately come to me. I was excited, interested, and I pursued the quest. And the thought of drink never entered my mind. Some of Louis' and my adventures have since given me serious pause when casting sociological generalizations. But it was all good and innocently youthful, and I learned one generalization, biological rather than sociological, namely, that the "Colonel's lady and Judy O'Grady are sisters under their skins."

And before long I learned girl's love, all the dear fond deliciousness of it, all the glory and the wonder. I shall call her Haydee. She was between fifteen and sixteen. Her little skirt reached her shoe-tops. We sat side by side in a Salvation Army meeting. She was not a convert, nor was her aunt, who sat on the other side of her and who, visiting from the country, where at that time the Salvation Army was not, had dropped in to the meeting for half an hour out of curiosity. And Louis sat beside me and observed—I do believe he did no more than observe, because Haydee was not his style of girl.

We did not speak, but in that great half-hour we glanced shyly at each other, and shyly avoided or as shyly returned and met each other's glances more than several times. She had a slender oval face. Her brown eyes were beautiful. Her nose was a dream, as was her sweet-lipped, petulant-hinting mouth. She wore a tam o'shanter, and I thought her brown hair the prettiest shade of brown I had ever seen. And from that single experience of half an hour I have ever since been convinced of the reality of love at first sight.

All too soon the aunt and Haydee departed. (This is permissible at any stage of a Salvation Army meeting.) I was no longer interested in the meeting, and after an appropriate interval of a couple of minutes or less, started to leave with Louis. As we passed out, at the back of the hall a woman recognized me with her eyes, arose, and followed me. I shall not describe her. She was of my own kind and friendship of the old time on the water-front. When Nelson was shot, he had died in her arms, and she knew me as his one comrade. And she must tell me how Nelson had died, and I did want to know; so I went with her across the width of life from dawning boy's love for a brown-haired girl in a tam o'shanter back to the old sad savagery I had known.

And when I had heard the tale, I hurried away to find Louis, fearing that I had lost my first love with the first glimpse of her. But Louis was dependable. Her name was— Haydee. He knew where she lived. Each day she passed the blacksmith-shop where he worked, going to or from the Lafayette school. Further, he had seen her on occasion with Ruth, another schoolgirl; and, still further, Nita, who sold us red-hots at the candy store, was a friend of Ruth. The thing to do was to go around to the candy store and see if we could get Nita to give a note to Ruth to give to Haydee. If that could be arranged, all I had to do was write the note.

And it so happened. And in stolen half-hours of meeting I came to know all the sweet madness of boy's love and girl's love. So far as it goes it is not the biggest love in the world, but I do dare to assert that it is the sweetest. Oh, as I look back on it! Never did girl have more innocent boy-lover than I who had been so wicked-wise and violent beyond my years. I did n't know the first thing about girls. I, who had been hailed Prince of the Oyster Pirates, who could go anywhere in the world as a man amongst men; who could sail boats,

lay aloft in black and storm, or go into the toughest hang-
outs in sailor town and play my part in any rough-house that
started or call all hands to the bar—I did n't know the first
thing I might say or do with this slender little chit of a girl-
woman whose scant skirt just reached her shoe-tops and who
was as abysmally ignorant of life, as I was, or thought I was,
profoundly wise.

I remember we sat on a bench in the starlight. There was
fully a foot of space between us. We slightly faced each other,
our near elbows on the back of the bench; and once or twice
our elbows just touched. And all the time, deliriously happy,
talking in the gentlest and most delicate terms that might not
offend her sensitive ears, I was cudgeling my brains in an
effort to divine what I was expected to do. What did girls
expect of boys, sitting on a bench and tentatively striving to
find out what love was? What did she expect me to do? Was
I expected to kiss her? Did she expect me to try? And if she
did expect me, and I did n't, what would she think of me?

Ah, she was wiser than I—I know it now—the little innocent girl-woman in her shoe-top skirt. She had known boys
all her life. She encouraged me in the ways a girl may. Her
gloves were off and in one hand, and I remember, lightly and
daringly, in mock reproof for something I had said, how she
tapped my lips with a tiny flirt of those gloves. I was like to
swoon with delight. It was the most wonderful thing that had
ever happened to me. And I remember yet the faint scent that
clung to those gloves and that I breathed in the moment they
touched my lips.

Then came the agony of apprehension and doubt. Should
I imprison in my hand that little hand with the dangling,
scented gloves which had just tapped my lips? Should I dare
to kiss her there and then, or slip my arm around her waist?
Or dared I even sit closer?

Well, I did n't dare. I did nothing. I merely continued to
sit there and love with all my soul. And when we parted that
evening I had not kissed her. I do remember the first time I
kissed her, on another evening, at parting—a mighty moment, when I took all my heart of courage and dared. We
never succeeded in managing more than a dozen stolen meetings, and we kissed perhaps a dozen times—as boys and girls

kiss, briefly and innocently, and wonderingly. We never went anywhere—not even to a matinée. We once shared together five cents' worth of red-hots. But I have always fondly believed that she loved me. I know I loved her; and I dreamed day dreams of her for a year and more, and the memory of her is very dear.

Chapter XIX

W HEN I WAS with folk who did not drink, I never thought of drinking. Louis did not drink. Neither he nor I could afford it; but, more significant than that, we had no desire to drink. We were healthy, normal, non-alcoholic. Had we been alcoholic, we would have drunk whether or not we could have afforded it.

Each night, after the day's work, washed up, clothes changed and supper eaten, we met on the street corner or in the little candy store. But the warm, fall weather passed, and on bitter nights of frost or damp nights of drizzle the street corner was not a comfortable meeting place. And the candy store was unheated. Nita, or whoever waited on the counter, between waitings lurked in a back living-room that was heated. We were not admitted to this room, and in the store it was as cold as out-of-doors.

Louis and I debated the situation. There was only one solution: the saloon, the congregating place of men, the place where men hobnobbed with John Barleycorn. Well do I remember the damp and draughty evening, shivering without overcoats because we could not afford them, that Louis and I started out to select our saloon. Saloons are always warm and comfortable. Now Louis and I did not go into this saloon because we wanted a drink. Yet we knew that saloons were not charitable institutions. A man could not make a lounging place of a saloon without occasionally buying something over the bar.

Our dimes and nickels were few. We could ill spare any of them when they were so potent in buying carfare for oneself and a girl. (We never paid carfare when by ourselves, being content to walk.) So, in this saloon, we desired to make the most of our expenditure. We called for a deck of cards and sat down at a table and played euchre for an hour, in which time Louis treated once, and I treated once, to beer—the cheapest drink, ten cents for two. Prodigal! How we grudged it!

We studied the men who came into the place. They seemed

all middle-aged and elderly workmen, most of them Germans, who flocked by themselves in old-acquaintance groups, and with whom we could have only the slightest contacts. We voted against that saloon, and went out cast-down with the knowledge that we had lost an evening and wasted twenty cents for beer that we did n't want.

We made several more tries on succeeding nights, and at last found our way into the National, a saloon on Tenth and Franklin. Here was a more congenial crowd. Here Louis met a fellow or two he knew, and here I met fellows I had gone to school with when a little lad in knee pants. We talked of old days, and of what had become of this fellow, and what that fellow was doing now, and of course we talked it over drinks. They treated, and we drank. Then, according to the code of drinking, we had to treat. It hurt, for it meant forty to fifty cents a clatter.

We felt quite enlivened when the short evening was over; but at the same time we were bankrupt. Our week's spending-money was gone. We decided that that was the saloon for us, and we agreed to be more circumspect thereafter in our drink-buying. Also, we had to economize for the rest of the week. We did n't even have carfare. We were compelled to break an engagement with two girls from West Oakland with whom we were attempting to be in love. They were to meet us up town the next evening, and we had n't the carfare necessary to take them home. Like many others financially embarrassed, we had to disappear for a time from the gay whirl—at least until Saturday night pay-day. So Louis and I rendezvoused in a livery stable, and with coats buttoned and chattering teeth played euchre and casino until the time of our exile was over.

Then we returned to the National Saloon and spent no more than we could decently avoid spending for the comfort and warmth. Sometimes we had mishaps, as when one got stuck twice in succession in a five-handed game of Sancho Pedro for the drinks. Such a disaster meant anywhere between twenty-five to eighty cents, just according to how many of the players ordered ten-cent drinks. But we could temporarily escape the evil effects of such disaster by virtue of an account we ran behind the bar. Of course, this only set back the day of reckoning and seduced us into spending more than we would have spent on a cash basis. (When I left Oakland suddenly for the adventure-path the following spring, I well remember I owed that saloon keeper one dollar and seventy cents. Long after, when I returned, he was gone. I still owe him that dollar and seventy cents, and if he should chance to read these lines I want him to know that I 'll pay on demand.)

The foregoing incident of the National Saloon I have given in order again to show the lure, or draw, or compulsion, toward John Barleycorn in society as at present organized with saloons on all the corners. Louis and I were two healthy youths. We did n't want to drink. We could n't afford to drink. And yet we were driven by the circumstances of cold and rainy weather to seek refuge in a saloon, where we had to spend part of our pitiful dole for drink. It will be urged by some critics that we might have gone to the Y. M. C. A., to night school, and to the social circles and homes of young people. The only reply is that we did n't. That is the irrefragable fact. We did n't. And to-day, at this moment, there are hundreds of thousands of boys like Louis and me doing just what Louis and I did, with John Barleycorn, warm and comfortable, beckoning and welcoming, tucking their arms in his and beginning to teach them his mellow ways.

Chapter XX

THE JUTE MILLS failed of its agreement to increase my pay to a dollar and a quarter a day, and I, a free-born American boy whose direct ancestors had fought in all the wars from the old pre-Revolutionary Indian wars down, exercised my sovereign right of free contract by quitting the job.

I was still resolved to settle down, and I looked about me. One thing was clear. Unskilled labor did n't pay. I must learn a trade, and I decided on electricity. The need for electricians was constantly growing. But how to become an electrician? I had n't the money to go to a technical school or university; besides, I did n't think much of schools. I was a practical man in a practical world. Also, I still believed in the old myths which were the heritage of the American boy when I was a boy.

A canal boy could become a president. Any boy, who took employment with any firm, could, by thrift, energy, and sobriety, learn the business and rise from position to position until he was taken in as a junior partner. After that the senior partnership was only a matter of time. Very often—so ran the myth—the boy, by reason of his steadiness and application, married his employer's daughter. By this time I had been encouraged to such faith in myself in the matter of girls that I was quite certain I would marry my employer's daughter. There was n't a doubt of it. All the little boys in the myths did it as soon as they were old enough.

So I bade farewell forever to the adventure-path, and went out to the power-plant of one of our Oakland street-railways. I saw the superintendent himself, in a private office so fine that it almost stunned me. But I talked straight up. I told him I wanted to become a practical electrician, that I was unafraid of work, that I was used to hard work, and that all he had to do was look at me to see I was fit and strong. I told him that I wanted to begin right at the bottom and work up, that I wanted to devote my life to this one occupation and this one employment.

The superintendent beamed as he listened. He told me that

I was the right stuff for success, and that he believed in encouraging American youth that wanted to rise. Why, employers were always on the lookout for young fellows like me, and alas, they found them all too rarely. My ambition was fine and worthy, and he would see to it that I got my chance. (And as I listened with swelling heart, I wondered if it was his daughter I was to marry.)

"Before you can go out on the road and learn the more complicated and higher details of the profession," he said, "you will, of course, have to work in the car house with the men who install and repair the motors. (By this time I was sure that it was his daughter, and I was wondering how much stock he might own in the company.)

"But," he said, "as you yourself so plainly see, you could n't expect to begin as a helper to the car house electricians. That will come when you have worked up to it. You will really begin at the bottom. In the car house your first employment will be sweeping up, washing the windows, keeping things clean. And after you have shown yourself satisfactory at that, then you may become a helper to the car house electricians."

I did n't see how sweeping and scrubbing a building was any preparation for the trade of electrician; but I did know that in the books all the boys started with the most menial tasks and by making good ultimately won to the ownership of the whole concern.

"When shall I come to work?" I asked, eager to launch on this dazzling career.

"But," said the superintendent, "as you and I have already agreed, you must begin at the bottom. Not immediately can you in any capacity enter the car house. Before that you must pass through the engine room as an oiler."

My heart went down slightly and for the moment, as I saw the road lengthen between his daughter and me; then it rose again. I would be a better electrician with knowledge of steam engines. As an oiler in the great engine room I was confident that few things concerning steam would escape me. Heavens! My career shone more dazzling than ever.

"When shall I come to work?" I asked gratefully.

"But," said the superintendent, "you could not expect to

enter immediately into the engine room. There must be preparation for that. And through the fire room, of course. Come,
you see the matter clearly, I know. And you will see that even
the mere handling of coal is a scientific matter and not to be
sneezed at. Do you know that we weigh every pound of coal
we burn? Thus, we learn the value of the coal we buy; we
know to a tee the last penny of cost of every item of production, and we learn which firemen are the most wasteful, which
firemen, out of stupidity or carelessness, get the least out of
the coal they fire." The superintendent beamed again. "You
see how very important the little matter of coal is, and by as
much as you learn of this little matter you will become that
much better a workman—more valuable to us, more valuable
to yourself. Now, are you prepared to begin?"

"Any time," I said valiantly. "The sooner the better."

"Very well," he answered. "You will come to-morrow
morning at seven o'clock."

I was taken out and shown my duties. Also, I was told the
terms of my employment—a ten-hour day, every day in the
month including Sundays and holidays, with one day off each
month, with a salary of thirty dollars a month. It was n't exciting. Years before, at the cannery, I had earned a dollar a
day for a ten-hour day. I consoled myself with the thought
that the reason my earning capacity had not increased with
my years and strength was because I had remained an unskilled laborer. But it was different now. I was beginning to
work for skill, for a trade, for career and fortune and the superintendent's daughter.

And I was beginning in the right way—right at the beginning. That was the thing. I was passing coal to the firemen,
who shoveled it into the furnaces where its energy was transformed into steam, which, in the engine room, was transformed into the electricity with which the electricians worked.
This passing of coal was surely the very beginning . . . unless
the superintendent should take it into his head to send me to
work in the mines from which the coal came in order to get
a completer understanding of the genesis of electricity for
street railways.

Work! I, who had worked with men, found that I did n't
know the first thing about real work. A ten-hour day! I had

to pass coal for the day and night shifts, and, despite working through the noon-hour, I never finished my task before eight at night. I was working a twelve- to thirteen-hour day, and I was n't being paid overtime as in the cannery.

I might as well give the secret away right here. I was doing the work of two men. Before me, one mature able-bodied laborer had done the day shift and another equally mature able-bodied laborer had done the night shift. They had received forty dollars a month each. The superintendent, bent on an economical administration, had persuaded me to do the work of both men for thirty dollars a month. I thought he was making an electrician of me. In truth and fact, he was saving fifty dollars a month operating expenses to the company.

But I did n't know I was displacing two men. Nobody told me. On the contrary, the superintendent warned everybody not to tell me. How valiantly I went at it that first day. I worked at top speed, filling the iron wheelbarrow with coal, running it on the scales and weighing the load, then trundling it into the fire room and dumping it on the plates before the fires.

Work! I did more than the two men whom I had displaced. They had merely wheeled in the coal and dumped it on the plates. But while I did this for the day coal, the night coal I had to pile against the wall of the fire room. Now the fire room was small. It had been planned for a night coal-passer. So I had to pile the night coal higher and higher, buttressing up the heap with stout planks. Toward the top of the heap I had to handle the coal a second time, tossing it up with a shovel.

I dripped with sweat, but I never ceased from my stride, though I could feel exhaustion coming on. By ten o'clock in the morning, so much of my body's energy had I consumed, I felt hungry and snatched a thick double-slice of bread and butter from my dinner pail. This I devoured, standing, grimed with coal dust, my knees trembling under me. By eleven o'clock, in this fashion, I had consumed my whole lunch. But what of it? I realized that it would enable me to continue working through the noon hour. And I worked all afternoon. Darkness came on, and I worked under the electric lights. The day fireman went off and the night fireman came on. I plugged away.

At half-past eight, famished, tottering, I washed up, changed my clothes, and dragged my weary body to the car. It was three miles to where I lived, and I had received a pass with the stipulation that I could sit down as long as there were no paying passengers in need of a seat. As I sank into a corner outside seat I prayed that no passenger might require my seat. But the car filled up, and, half way in, a woman came on board, and there was no seat for her. I started to get up, and to my astonishment found that I could not. With the chill wind blowing on me, my spent body had stiffened into the seat. It took me the rest of the run in to unkink my complaining joints and muscles and get into a standing position on the lower step. And when the car stopped at my corner I nearly fell to the ground when I stepped off.

I hobbled two blocks to the house and limped into the kitchen. While my mother started to cook I plunged into bread and butter; but before my appetite was appeased, or the steak fried, I was sound asleep. In vain my mother strove to shake me awake enough to eat the meat. Failing in this, with the assistance of my father she managed to get me to my room, where I collapsed dead asleep on the bed. They undressed me and covered me up. In the morning came the agony of being awakened. I was terribly sore, and worst of all my wrists were swelling. But I made up for my lost supper, eating an enormous breakfast, and when I hobbled to catch my car I carried a lunch twice as big as the one the day before.

Work! Let any youth just turned eighteen try to out-shovel two man-grown coal-shovelers. Work! Long before midday I had eaten the last scrap of my huge lunch. But I was resolved to show them what a husky young fellow determined to rise could do. The worst of it was that my wrists were swelling and going back on me. There are few who do not know the pain of walking on a sprained ankle. Then imagine the pain of shoveling coal and trundling a loaded wheelbarrow with two sprained wrists.

Work! More than once I sank down on the coal where no

one could see me, and cried with rage, and mortification, and exhaustion, and despair. That second day was my hardest, and all that enabled me to survive it and get in the last of the night coal at the end of thirteen hours was the day fireman, who bound both my wrists with broad leather straps. So tightly were they buckled that they were like slightly flexible plaster casts. They took the stresses and pressures which thitherto had been borne by my wrists, and they were so tight that there was no room for the inflammation to rise in the sprains.

And in this fashion I continued to learn to be an electrician. Night after night I limped home, fell asleep before I could eat my supper, and was helped into bed and undressed. Morning after morning, always with huger lunches in my dinner pail, I limped out of the house on my way to work.

I no longer read my library books. I made no dates with the girls. I was a proper work-beast. I worked, and ate, and slept, while my mind slept all the time. The whole thing was a nightmare. I worked every day, including Sunday, and I looked far ahead to my one day off at the end of a month, resolved to lie abed all that day and just sleep and rest up.

The strangest part of this experience was that I never took a drink nor thought of taking a drink. Yet I knew that men under hard pressure almost invariably drank. I had seen them do it, and in the past had often done it myself. But so sheerly non-alcoholic was I that it never entered my mind that a drink might be good for me. I instance this to show how entirely lacking from my make-up was any predisposition toward alcohol. And the point of this instance is that later on, after more years had passed, contact with John Barleycorn at last did induce in me the alcoholic desire.

I had often noticed the day fireman staring at me in a curious way. At last, one day, he spoke. He began by swearing me to secrecy. He had been warned by the superintendent not to tell me, and in telling me he was risking his job. He told me of the day coal-passer and the night coal-passer, and of the wages they had received. I was doing for thirty dollars a month what they had received eighty dollars for doing. He would have told me sooner, the fireman said, had he not been so certain that I would break down under the work and quit.

As it was, I was killing myself, and all to no good purpose. I was merely cheapening the price of labor, he argued, and keeping two men out of a job.

Being an American boy, and a proud American boy, I did not immediately quit. This was foolish of me, I know; but I resolved to continue the work long enough to prove to the superintendent that I could do it without breaking down. Then I would quit, and he would realize what a fine young fellow he had lost.

All of which I faithfully and foolishly did. I worked on until the time came when I got in the last of the night coal by six o'clock. Then I quit the job of learning electricity by doing more than two men's work for a boy's wages, went home, and proceeded to sleep the clock around.

Fortunately, I had not stayed by the job long enough to injure myself—though I was compelled to wear straps on my wrists for a year afterward. But the effect of this work orgy in which I had indulged was to sicken me with work. I just would n't work. The thought of work was repulsive. I did n't care if I never settled down. Learning a trade could go hang. It was a whole lot better to royster and frolic over the world in the way I had previously done. So I headed out on the adventure-path again, starting to tramp East by beating my way on the railroads.

Chapter XXI

BUT BEHOLD! As soon as I went out on the adventure-path I met John Barleycorn again. I moved through a world of strangers, and the act of drinking together made one acquainted with men and opened the way to adventures. It might be in a saloon with jingled townsmen, or with a genial railroad man well lighted up and armed with pocket flasks, or with a bunch of alki-stiffs in a hang-out. Yes; and it might be in a prohibition state, such as Iowa was in 1894, when I wandered up the main street of Des Moines and was variously invited by strangers into various blind pigs—I remember drinking in barber-shops, plumbing establishments, and furniture stores.

Always it was John Barleycorn. Even a tramp, in those halcyon days, could get most frequently drunk. I remember, inside the prison at Buffalo, how some of us got magnificently jingled, and how, on the streets of Buffalo after our release, another jingle was financed with pennies begged on the main-drag.

I had no call for alcohol, but when I was with those who drank I drank with them. I insisted on traveling or loafing with the livest, keenest men, and it was just these live, keen ones that did most of the drinking. They were the more comradely men, the more venturous, the more individual. Perhaps it was too much temperament that made them turn from the commonplace and humdrum to find relief in the lying and fantastic sureties of John Barleycorn. Be that as it may, the men I liked best, desired most to be with, were invariably to be found in John Barleycorn's company.

In the course of my tramping over the United States I achieved a new concept. As a tramp, I was behind the scenes of society—ay, and down in the cellar. I could watch the machinery work. I saw the wheels of the social machine go around, and I learned that the dignity of manual labor wasn't what I had been told it was by the teachers, preachers, and politicians. The men without trades were helpless cattle. If one learned a trade, he was compelled to belong to a union

in order to work at his trade. And his union was compelled
to bully and slug the employers' unions in order to hold up
wages or hold down hours. The employers' unions likewise
bullied and slugged. I could n't see any dignity at all. And
when a workman got old, or had an accident, he was thrown
into the scrap-heap like any worn-out machine. I saw too
many of this sort who were making anything but dignified
ends of life.

So my new concept was that manual labor was undignified,
and that it did n't pay. No trade for me, was my decision,
and no superintendent's daughter. And no criminality, I also
decided. That would be almost as disastrous as to be a laborer. Brains paid, not brawn, and I resolved never again to
offer my muscles for sale in the brawn market. Brain, and
brain only, would I sell.

I returned to California with the firm intention of developing my brain. This meant school education. I had gone
through the grammar school long ago, so I entered the Oakland High School. To pay my way, I worked as a janitor. My
sister helped me, too; and I was not above mowing anybody's
lawn or taking up and beating carpets when I had half a day
to spare. I was working to get away from work, and I buckled
down to it with a grim realization of the paradox.

Boy and girl love was left behind, and along with it, Haydee and Louis Shattuck, and the early evening strolls. I had
n't the time. I joined the Henry Clay Debating Society. I was
received into the homes of some of the members, where I met
nice girls whose skirts reached the ground. I dallied with little
home clubs wherein we discussed poetry and art and the nu-
ances of grammar. I joined the socialist local, where we studied and orated political economy, philosophy, and politics. I
kept half-a-dozen membership cards working in the free library and did an immense amount of collateral reading.

And for a year and a half on end I never took a drink nor
thought of taking a drink. I had n't the time, and I certainly
did not have the inclination. Between my janitor-work, my
studies, and innocent amusements such as chess, I had n't a
moment to spare. I was discovering a new world, and such
was the passion of my exploration that the old world of John
Barleycorn held no inducements for me.

Come to think of it, I did enter a saloon. I went to see Johnny Heinhold in the Last Chance, and I went to borrow money. And right here is another phase of John Barleycorn. Saloon-keepers are notoriously good fellows. On an average they perform vastly greater generosities than do business men. When I simply had to have ten dollars, desperate, with no place to turn, I went to Johnny Heinhold. Several years had passed since I had been in his place or spent a cent across his bar. And when I went to borrow the ten dollars I did n't buy a drink, either. And Johnny Heinhold let me have the ten dollars, without security or interest.

More than once, in the brief days of my struggle for an education, I went to Johnny Heinhold to borrow money. When I entered the university, I borrowed forty dollars from him, without interest, without security, without buying a drink. And yet—and here is the point, the custom and the code—in the days of my prosperity, after the lapse of years, I have gone out of my way by many a long block to spend across Johnny Heinhold's bar deferred interest on the various loans. Not that Johnny Heinhold asked me to do it or expected me to do it. I did it, as I have said, in obedience to the code I had learned along with all the other things connected with John Barleycorn. In distress, when a man has no other place to turn, when he has n't the slightest bit of security which a savage-hearted pawnbroker would consider, he can go to some saloon keeper he knows. Gratitude is inherently human. When the man so helped has money again, depend upon it that a portion will be spent across the bar of the saloon keeper who befriended him.

Why, I recollect the early days of my writing career, when the small sums of money I earned from the magazines came with tragic irregularity, while at the same time I was staggering along with a growing family—a wife, children, a mother, a nephew, and my Mammy Jennie and her old husband fallen on evil days. There were two places at which I could borrow money; a barber shop and a saloon. The barber charged me five per cent. per month in advance. That is to say, when I borrowed one hundred dollars, he handed me ninety-five. The other five dollars he retained as advance interest for the first month. And on the second month I paid him five dollars more, and continued so to do each month until I made a ten-strike with the editors and lifted the loan.

The other place to which I came in trouble was the saloon. This saloon keeper I had known by sight for a couple of years. I had never spent my money in his saloon, and even when I borrowed from him I did n't spend any money. Yet never did he refuse me any sum I asked of him. Unfortunately, before I became prosperous, he moved away to another city. And to this day I regret that he is gone. It is the code I have learned. The right thing to do, and the thing I 'd do right now did I know where he is, would be to drop in on occasion and spend a few dollars across his bar for old sake's sake and gratitude.

This is not to exalt saloon keepers. I have written it to exalt the power of John Barleycorn, and to illustrate one more of the myriad ways by which a man is brought in contact with John Barleycorn, until in the end he finds he cannot get along without him.

But to return to the run of my narrative. Away from the adventure-path, up to my ears in study, every moment occupied, I lived oblivious to John Barleycorn's existence. Nobody about me drank. If any had drunk, and had they offered it to me, I surely would have drunk. As it was, when I had spare moments I spent them playing chess, or going with nice girls who were themselves students, or in riding a bicycle whenever I was fortunate enough to have it out of the pawnbroker's possession.

What I am insisting upon all the time is this: in me was not the slightest trace of alcoholic desire, and this despite the long and severe apprenticeship I had served under John Barleycorn. I had come back from the other side of life to be delighted with this Arcadian simplicity of student youths and student maidens. Also, I had found my way into the realm of the mind, and I was intellectually intoxicated. Alas! as I was to learn at a later period, intellectual intoxication, too, has its katzenjammer.

Chapter XXII

THREE YEARS was the time required to go through high school. I grew impatient. Also, my schooling was becoming financially impossible. At such rate I could not last out, and I did greatly want to go to the state university. When I had done a year of high school, I decided to attempt a short cut. I borrowed the money and paid to enter the senior class of a "cramming joint" or academy. I was scheduled to graduate right into the university at the end of four months, thus saving two years.

And how I did cram! I had two years' new work to do in a third of a year. For five weeks I crammed, until simultaneous quadratic equations and chemical formulas fairly oozed from my ears. And then the master of the academy took me aside. He was very sorry, but he was compelled to give me back my tuition fee and to ask me to leave the school. It was n't a matter of scholarship. I stood well in my classes, and did he graduate me into the university he was confident that in that institution I would continue to stand well. The trouble was that tongues were gossiping about my case. What! In four months accomplish two years' work! It would be a scandal, and the universities were becoming severer in their treatment of accredited prep schools. He could n't afford such a scandal, therefore I must gracefully depart.

I did. And I paid back the borrowed money, and gritted my teeth, and started to cram by myself. There were three months yet before the university entrance-examinations. Without laboratories, without coaching, sitting in my bedroom, I proceeded to compress that two years' work into three months and to keep reviewed on the previous year's work.

Nineteen hours a day I studied. For three months I kept this pace, only breaking it on several occasions. My body grew weary, my mind grew weary, but I stayed with it. My eyes grew weary and began to twitch, but they did not break down. Perhaps, toward the last, I got a bit dotty. I know that at the time I was confident I had discovered the formula for squaring the circle; but I resolutely deferred the working of it out until after the examinations. Then I would show them.

Came the several days of the examinations, during which time I scarcely closed my eyes in sleep, devoting every moment to cramming and reviewing. And when I turned in my last examination paper I was in full possession of a splendid case of brain-fag. I did n't want to see a book. I did n't want to think nor to lay eyes on anybody who was liable to think.

There was but one prescription for such a condition, and I gave it to myself—the adventure-path. I did n't wait to learn the result of my examinations. I stowed a roll of blankets and some cold food into a borrowed whitehall boat and set sail. Out of the Oakland Estuary I drifted on the last of an early morning ebb, caught the first of the flood up bay, and raced along with a spanking breeze. San Pablo Bay was smoking, and the Carquinez Straits off the Selby Smelter were smoking, as I picked up ahead and left astern the old landmarks I had first learned with Nelson in the unreefed *Reindeer*.

Benicia showed before me. I opened the bight of Turner's Shipyard, rounded the *Solano* wharf, and surged along abreast of the patch of tules and the clustering fishermen's-arks where in the old days I had lived and drunk deep.

And right here something happened to me, the gravity of which I never dreamed for many a long year to come. I had no intention of stopping at Benicia. The tide favored, the wind was fair and howling—glorious sailing for a sailor. Bull Head and Army Points showed ahead, marking the entrance to Suisun Bay, which I know was smoking. And yet, when I laid eyes on those fishing-arks lying in the water-front tules, without debate, on the instant, I put down my tiller, came in on the sheet, and headed for the shore. On the instant, out of the profound of my brain-fag, I knew what I wanted. I wanted to drink. I wanted to get drunk.

The call was imperative. There was no uncertainty about it. More than anything else in the world, my frayed and frazzled mind wanted surcease from weariness in the way it knew surcease would come. And right here is the point. For the first time in my life I consciously, deliberately desired to get drunk. It was a new, a totally different manifestation of John Barleycorn's power. It was not a body need for alcohol. It was a mental desire. My overworked and jaded mind wanted to forget.

And here the point is drawn to its sharpest. Granted my prodigious brain-fag, nevertheless, had I never drunk in the past, the thought would never have entered my mind to get drunk now. Beginning with physical intolerance for alcohol, for years drinking only for the sake of comradeship and because alcohol was everywhere on the adventure-path, I had now reached the stage where my brain cried out, not merely for a drink, but for a drunk. And had I not been so long used to alcohol, my brain would not have so cried out. I should have sailed on past Bull Head, and in the smoking white of Suisun Bay, and in the wine of wind that filled my sail and poured through me, I should have forgotten my weary brain and rested and refreshed it.

So I sailed in to shore, made all fast, and hurried up among the arks. Charley Le Grant fell on my neck. His wife, Lizzie, folded me to her capacious breast. Billy Murphy, and Joe Lloyd, and all the survivors of the old guard, got around me and their arms around me. Charley seized the can and started for Jorgensen's saloon across the railroad tracks. That meant beer. I wanted whisky, so I called after him to bring a flask.

Many times that flask journeyed across the railroad tracks and back. More old friends of the old free and easy times dropped in, fishermen, Greeks, and Russians, and French. They took turns in treating, and treated all around in turn again. They came and went, but I stayed on and drank with all. I guzzled, I swilled. I ran the liquor down and joyed as the maggots mounted in my brain.

And Clam came in, Nelson's partner before me, handsome as ever, but more reckless, half insane, burning himself out with whisky. He had just had a quarrel with his partner on the sloop *Gazelle*, and knives had been drawn, and blows struck, and he was bent on maddening the fever of the memory with more whisky. And while we downed it, we remembered Nelson and that he had stretched out his great shoulders for the last long sleep in this very town of Benicia; and we wept over the memory of him, and remembered only the good things of him, and sent out the flask to be filled and drank again.

They wanted me to stay over, but through the open door I could see the brave wind on the water, and my ears were filled with the roar of it. And while I forgot that I had plunged into the books nineteen hours a day for three solid months, Charley Le Grant shifted my outfit into a big Columbia River salmon boat. He added charcoal and a fisherman's brazier, a coffee pot and frying-pan, and the coffee and the meat, and a black bass fresh from the water that day.

They had to help me down the rickety wharf and into the salmon boat. Likewise they stretched my boom and sprit until the sail set like a board. Some feared to set the sprit; but I insisted, and Charley had no doubts. He knew me of old, and knew that I could sail as long as I could see. They cast off my painter. I put the tiller up, filled away before it, and with dizzy eyes checked and steadied the boat on her course and waved farewell.

The tide had turned, and the fierce ebb, running in the teeth of a fiercer wind, kicked up a stiff, upstanding sea. Suisun Bay was white with wrath and sea-lump. But a salmon boat can sail, and I knew how to sail a salmon boat. So I drove her into it, and through it, and across, and maundered aloud and chanted my disdain for all the books and schools. Cresting seas filled me a foot or so with water, but I laughed at it sloshing about my feet, and chanted my disdain for the wind and the water. I hailed myself a master of life, riding on the back of the unleashed elements, and John Barleycorn rode with me. Amid dissertations on mathematics and philosophy and spoutings and quotations, I sang all the old songs learned in the days when I went from the cannery to the oyster boats to be a pirate—such songs as: "Black Lulu," "Flying Cloud," "Treat My Daughter Kind-i-ly," "The Boston Burglar," "Come All You Rambling Gambling Men," "I Wisht I Was a Little Bird," "Shenandoah," and "Ranzo, Boys, Ranzo."

Hours afterward, in the fires of sunset, where the Sacramento and the San Joaquin tumble their muddy floods together, I took the New York Cut-Off, skimmed across the smooth land-locked water past Black Diamond, on into the San Joaquin, and on to Antioch, where, somewhat sobered and magnificently hungry, I laid alongside a big potato sloop that had a familiar rig. Here were old friends aboard, who fried my black bass in olive oil. Then, too, there was a meaty fisherman's stew, delicious with garlic, and crusty Italian bread without butter, and all washed down with pint mugs of thick and heady claret.

My salmon boat was a-soak, but in the snug cabin of the sloop dry blankets and a dry bunk were mine; and we lay and smoked and yarned of old days, while overhead the wind screamed through the rigging and taut halyards drummed against the mast.

Chapter XXIII

M Y CRUISE in the salmon boat lasted a week, and I returned ready to enter the university. During the
week's cruise I did not drink again. To accomplish this I was
compelled to avoid looking up old friends, for as ever the
adventure-path was beset with John Barleycorn. I had wanted
the drink that first day, and in the days that followed I did
not want it. My tired brain had recuperated. I had no moral
scruples in the matter. I was not ashamed nor sorry because
of that first day's orgy at Benicia, and I thought no more
about it, returning gladly to my books and studies.

Long years were to pass ere I looked back upon that day
and realized its significance. At the time, and for a long time
afterward, I was to think of it only as a frolic. But still later,
in the slough of brain-fag and intellectual weariness, I was to
remember and know the craving for the anodyne that resides
in alcohol.

In the meantime, after this one relapse at Benicia, I went
on with my abstemiousness, primarily because I did n't want
to drink. And next, I was abstemious because my way led
among books and students, where no drinking was. Had I
been out on the adventure-path, I should as a matter of
course have been drinking. For that is the pity of the adventure-path, which is one of John Barleycorn's favorite stamp-
ing-grounds.

I completed the first half of my freshman year, and in January of 1897 took up my course for the second half. But the
pressure from lack of money, plus a conviction that the university was not giving me all that I wanted in the time I could
spare for it, forced me to leave. I was not very disappointed.
For two years I had studied, and in those two years, what
was far more valuable, I had done a prodigious amount of
reading. Then, too, my grammar had improved. It is true, I
had not yet learned that I must say "It is I"; but I no longer
was guilty of the double negative in writing, though still
prone to that error in excited speech.

I decided immediately to embark on my career. I had four

preferences: first, music; second, poetry; third, the writing of philosophic, economic, and political essays; and, fourth, and last, and least, fiction writing. I resolutely cut out music as impossible, settled down in my bedroom, and tackled my second, third and fourth choices simultaneously. Heavens, how I wrote! Never was there a creative fever such as mine from which the patient escaped fatal results. The way I worked was enough to soften my brain and send me to a mad-house. I wrote, I wrote everything—ponderous essays, scientific and sociological, short stories, humorous verse, verse of all sorts from triolets and sonnets to blank verse tragedy and elephantine epics in Spenserian stanzas. On occasion I composed steadily, day after day, for fifteen hours a day. At times I forgot to eat, or refused to tear myself away from my passionate outpouring in order to eat.

And then there was the matter of typewriting. My brother-in-law owned a machine which he used in the daytime. In the night I was free to use it. That machine was a wonder. I could weep now as I recollect my wrestlings with it. It must have been a first model in the year one of the typewriter era. Its alphabet was all capitals. It was informed with an evil spirit. It obeyed no known laws of physics, and overthrew the hoary axiom that like things performed to like things produce like results. I 'll swear that machine never did the same thing in the same way twice. Again and again it demonstrated that unlike actions produce like results.

How my back used to ache with it! Prior to that experience, my back had been good for every violent strain put upon it in a none too gentle career. But that typewriter proved to me that I had a pipe-stem for a back. Also, it made me doubt my shoulders. They ached as with rheumatism after every bout. The keys of that machine had to be hit so hard that to one outside the house it sounded like distant thunder or some one breaking up the furniture. I had to hit the keys so hard that I strained my first fingers to the elbows, while the ends of my fingers were blisters burst and blistered again. Had it been my machine I 'd have operated it with a carpenter's hammer.

The worst of it was that I was actually typing my manuscripts at the same time I was trying to master that machine.

It was a feat of physical endurance and a brain storm combined to type a thousand words, and I was composing thousands of words every day which just had to be typed for the waiting editors.

Oh, between the writing and the typewriting I was well a-weary. I had brain- and nerve-fag, and body-fag as well, and yet the thought of drink never suggested itself. I was living too high to stand in need of an anodyne. All my waking hours, except those with that infernal typewriter, were spent in a creative heaven. And along with this I had no desire for drink, because I still believed in many things—in the love of all men and women in the matter of man and woman love; in fatherhood; in human justice; in art—in the whole host of fond illusions that keep the world turning around.

But the waiting editors elected to keep on waiting. My manuscripts made amazing round-trip records between the Pacific and the Atlantic. It might have been the weirdness of the typewriting that prevented the editors from accepting at least one little offering of mine. I don't know, and goodness knows the stuff I wrote was as weird as its typing. I sold my hard-bought school books for ridiculous sums to second-hand bookmen. I borrowed small sums of money wherever I could, and suffered my old father to feed me with the meager returns of his failing strength.

It did n't last long, only a few weeks, when I had to surrender and go to work. Yet I was unaware of any need for the drink-anodyne. I was not disappointed. My career was retarded, that was all. Perhaps I did need further preparation. I had learned enough from the books to realize that I had touched only the hem of knowledge's garment. I still lived on the heights. My waking hours, and most of the hours I should have used for sleep, were spent with the books.

Chapter XXIV

OUT IN THE COUNTRY, at the Belmont Academy, I went to work in a small, perfectly appointed steam laundry. Another fellow and myself did all the work from sorting and washing to ironing the white shirts, collars and cuffs, and the "fancy starch" of the wives of the professors. We worked like tigers, especially as summer came on and the academy boys took to the wearing of duck trousers. It consumes a dreadful lot of time to iron one pair of duck trousers. And there were so many pairs of them. We sweated our way through long sizzling weeks at a task that was never done; and many a night, while the students snored in bed, my partner and I toiled on under the electric light at steam mangle or ironing board.

The hours were long, the work was arduous, despite the fact that we became past masters in the art of eliminating waste motion. And I was receiving thirty dollars a month and board—a slight increase over my coal-shoveling and cannery days, at least to the extent of board, which cost my employer little (we ate in the kitchen), but which was to me the equivalent of twenty dollars a month. My robuster strength of added years, my increased skill, and all I had learned from the books, were responsible for this increase of twenty dollars. Judging by my rate of development, I might hope before I died to be a night watchman for sixty dollars a month, or a policeman actually receiving a hundred dollars with pickings.

So relentlessly did my partner and I spring into our work throughout the week that by Saturday night we were frazzled wrecks. I found myself in the old familiar work-beast condition, toiling longer hours than the horses toiled, thinking scarcely more frequent thoughts than horses think. The books were closed to me. I had brought a trunkful to the laundry, but found myself unable to read them. I fell asleep the moment I tried to read; and if I did manage to keep my eyes open for several pages, I could not remember the contents of those pages. I gave over attempts on heavy study, such as jurisprudence, political economy, and biology, and tried

lighter stuff, such as history. I fell asleep. I tried literature,
and fell asleep. And finally, when I fell asleep over lively novels, I gave up. I never succeeded in reading one book in all
the time I spent in the laundry.

And when Saturday night came, and the week's work was
over until Monday morning, I knew only one desire besides
the desire to sleep, and that was to get drunk. This was the
second time in my life that I had heard the unmistakable call
of John Barleycorn. The first time it had been because of
brain-fag. But I had no overworked brain now. On the contrary, all I knew was the dull numbness of a brain that was
not worked at all. That was the trouble. My brain had become so alert and eager, so quickened by the wonder of the
new world the books had discovered to it, that it now suffered all the misery of stagnancy and inaction.

And I, the long-time intimate of John Barleycorn, knew
just what he promised me—maggots of fancy, dreams of
power, forgetfulness, anything and everything save whirling
washers, revolving mangles, humming centrifugal wringers,
and fancy starch and interminable processions of duck trousers moving in steam under my flying iron. And that 's it.
John Barleycorn makes his appeal to weakness and failure, to
weariness and exhaustion. He is the easy way out. And he is
lying all the time. He offers false strength to the body, false
elevation to the spirit, making things seem what they are not
and vastly fairer than what they are.

But it must not be forgotten that John Barleycorn is protean. As well as to weakness and exhaustion, does he appeal
to too much strength, to superabundant vitality, to the ennui
of idleness. He can tuck in his arm the arm of any man in any
mood. He can throw the net of his lure over all men. He
exchanges new lamps for old, the spangles of illusion for the
drabs of reality, and in the end cheats all who traffic with
him.

I did n't get drunk, however, for the simple reason that it
was a mile and a half to the nearest saloon. And this, in turn,
was because the call to get drunk was not very loud in my
ears. Had it been loud, I would have traveled ten times the
distance to win to the saloon. On the other hand, had the
saloon been just around the corner, I should have got drunk.

As it was, I would sprawl out in the shade on my one day of rest and dally with the Sunday papers. But I was too weary even for their froth. The comic supplement might bring a pallid smile to my face, and then I would fall asleep.

Although I did not yield to John Barleycorn while working in the laundry, a certain definite result was produced. I had heard the call, felt the gnaw of desire, yearned for the anodyne. I was being prepared for the stronger desire of later years.

And the point is that this development of desire was entirely in my brain. My body did not cry out for alcohol. As always, alcohol was repulsive to my body. When I was bodily weary from shoveling coal, the thought of taking a drink had never flickered into my consciousness. When I was brain-wearied after taking the entrance examinations to the university, I promptly got drunk. At the laundry, I was suffering physical exhaustion again, and physical exhaustion that was not nearly as profound as that of the coal-shoveling. But there was a difference. When I went coal-shoveling, my mind had not yet awakened. Between that time and the laundry my mind had found the kingdom of the mind. While shoveling coal, my mind was somnolent. While toiling in the laundry, my mind, informed and eager to do and be, was crucified.

And whether I yielded to drink, as at Benicia, or whether I refrained, as at the laundry, in my brain the seeds of desire for alcohol were germinating.

Chapter XXV

AFTER THE LAUNDRY, my sister and her husband grub-staked me into the Klondike. It was the first gold rush into that region, the early fall rush of 1897. I was twenty-one years old, and in splendid physical condition. I remember, at the end of the twenty-eight-mile portage across Chilkoot from Dyea Beach to Lake Linderman, I was packing up with the Indians and outpacking many an Indian. The last pack into Linderman was three miles. I back-tripped it four times a day, and on each forward trip carried one hundred and fifty pounds. This means that over the worst trails I daily traveled twenty-four miles, twelve of which were under a burden of one hundred and fifty pounds.

Yes, I had let career go hang, and was on the adventure-path again in quest of fortune. And of course, on the adventure-path, I met John Barleycorn. Here were the chesty men again, rovers and adventurers, and while they did n't mind a grub famine, whisky they could not do without. Whisky went over the trail, while the flour lay cached and untouched by the trail-side.

As good fortune would have it, the three men in my party were not drinkers. Therefore I did n't drink save on rare occasions and disgracefully when with other men. In my personal medicine chest was a quart of whisky. I never drew the cork till six months afterward, in a lonely camp, where, without anesthetics, a doctor was compelled to operate on a man. The doctor and the patient emptied my bottle between them and then proceeded to the operation.

Back in California a year later, recovering from scurvy, I found that my father was dead and that I was the head and the sole bread-winner of a household. When I state that I had passed coal on a steamship from Behring Sea to British Columbia, and traveled in the steerage from there to San Francisco, it will be understood that I brought nothing back from the Klondike but my scurvy.

Times were hard. Work of any sort was difficult to get. And work of any sort was what I had to take, for I was still an unskilled laborer. I had no thought of career. That was over and done with. I had to find food for two mouths beside my own and keep a roof over our heads—yes, and buy a winter suit, my one suit being decidedly summery. I had to get some sort of work immediately. After that, when I had caught my breath, I might think about my future.

Unskilled labor is the first to feel the slackness of hard times, and I had no trades save those of sailor and laundryman. With my new responsibilities I did n't dare go to sea, and I failed to find a job at laundrying. I failed to find a job at anything. I had my name down in five employment bureaus. I advertised in three newspapers. I sought out the few friends I knew who might be able to get me work; but they were either uninterested or unable to find anything for me.

The situation was desperate. I pawned my watch, my bicycle, and a mackintosh of which my father had been very proud and which he had left to me. It was and is my sole legacy in this world. It had cost fifteen dollars, and the pawnbroker let me have two dollars on it. And—oh, yes—a waterfront comrade of earlier years drifted along one day with a dress suit wrapped in newspapers. He could give no adequate explanation of how he had come to possess it, nor did I press for an explanation. I wanted the suit myself. No; not to wear. I traded him a lot of rubbish which, being unpawnable, was useless to me. He peddled the rubbish for several dollars, while I pledged the dress suit with my pawnbroker for five dollars. And for all I know, the pawnbroker still has the suit. I had never intended to redeem it.

But I could n't get any work. Yet I was a bargain in the labor market. I was twenty-two years old, weighed one hundred and sixty-five pounds stripped, every pound of which was excellent for toil; and the last traces of my scurvy were vanishing before a treatment of potatoes chewed raw. I tackled every opening for employment. I tried to become a studio model, but there were too many fine-bodied young fellows out of jobs. I answered advertisements of elderly invalids in need of companions. And I almost became a sewing machine agent, on commission, without salary. But poor people don't buy sewing machines in hard times, so I was forced to forego that employment.

Of course, it must be remembered that along with such frivolous occupations, I was trying to get work as wop, lumper, and roustabout. But winter was coming on, and the surplus labor army was pouring into the cities. Also, I, who had romped along carelessly through the countries of the world and the kingdom of the mind, was not a member of any union.

I sought odd jobs. I worked days, and half-days, at anything I could get. I mowed lawns, trimmed hedges, took up carpets, beat them, and laid them again. Further, I took the civil service examinations for mail carrier and passed first. But alas, there was no vacancy, and I must wait. And while I waited, and in between the odd jobs I managed to procure, I started to earn ten dollars by writing a newspaper account of a voyage I had made, in an open boat down the Yukon, of nineteen hundred miles in nineteen days. I did n't know the first thing about the newspaper game, but I was confident I 'd get ten dollars for my article.

But I did n't. The first San Francisco newspaper to which I mailed it never acknowledged receipt of the manuscript, but held on to it. The longer it held on to it, the more certain I was that the thing was accepted.

And here is the funny thing. Some are born to fortune, and some have fortune thrust upon them. But in my case I was clubbed into fortune, and bitter necessity wielded the club. I had long since abandoned all thought of writing as a career. My honest intention in writing that article was to earn ten dollars. And that was the limit of my intention. It would help to tide me along until I got steady employment. Had a vacancy occurred in the post office at that time, I should have jumped at it.

But the vacancy did not occur, nor did a steady job; and I employed the time between odd jobs with writing a twenty-one-thousand-word serial for the "Youth's Companion." I turned it out and typed it in seven days. I fancy that was what was the matter with it, for it came back.

It took some time for it to go and come, and in the meantime I tried my hand at short stories. I sold one to the *Overland Monthly* for five dollars. The *Black Cat* gave me forty dollars for another. The *Overland Monthly* offered me seven dollars and a half, pay on publication, for all the stories I should deliver. I got my bicycle, my watch, and my father's mackintosh out of pawn and rented a typewriter. Also, I paid up the bills I owed to the several groceries that allowed me a small credit. I recall the Portuguese groceryman who never permitted my bill to go beyond four dollars. Hopkins, another grocer, could not be budged beyond five dollars.

And just then came the call from the post office to go to work. It placed me in a most trying predicament. The sixty-five dollars I could earn regularly every month was a terrible temptation. I could n't decide what to do. And I 'll never be able to forgive the postmaster of Oakland. I answered the call, and I talked to him like a man. I frankly told him the situation. It looked as if I might win out at writing. The chance was good, but not certain. Now, if he would pass me by and select the next man on the eligible list, and give me a call at the next vacancy—

But he shut me off with: "Then you don't want the position?"

"But I do," I protested. "Don't you see, if you will pass me over this time—"

"If you want it you will take it," he said coldly.

Happily for me, the cursed brutality of the man made me angry.

"Very well," I said. "I won't take it."

Chapter XXVI

HAVING BURNED my one ship, I plunged into writing. I am afraid I always was an extremist. Early and late I was at it—writing, typing, studying grammar, studying writing and all the forms of writing, and studying the writers who succeeded in order to find out how they succeeded. I managed on five hours' sleep in the twenty-four, and came pretty close to working the nineteen waking hours left to me. My light burned till two and three in the morning, which led a good neighbor woman into a bit of sentimental Sherlock Holmes deduction. Never seeing me in the daytime, she concluded that I was a gambler, and that the light in my window was placed there by my mother to guide her erring son home.

The trouble with the beginner at the writing game is the long, dry spells, when there is never an editor's check and everything pawnable is pawned. I wore my summer suit pretty well through that winter, and the following summer experienced the longest, dryest spell of all, in the period when salaried men are gone on vacation and manuscripts lie in editorial offices until vacation is over.

My difficulty was that I had no one to advise me. I did n't know a soul who had written or who had ever tried to write. I did n't even know one reporter. Also, to succeed at the writing game, I found I had to unlearn about everything the teachers and professors of literature of the high school and university had taught me. I was very indignant about this at the time; though now I can understand it. They did not know the trick of successful writing in the years of 1895 and 1896. They knew all about "Snow Bound" and "Sartor Resartus"; but the American editors of 1899 did not want such truck. They wanted the 1899 truck, and offered to pay so well for it that the teachers and professors of literature would have quit their jobs could they have supplied it.

I struggled along, stood off the butcher and the grocer, pawned my watch and bicycle and my father's mackintosh, and I worked. I really did work, and went on short commons of sleep. Critics have complained about the swift education one of my characters, Martin Eden, achieved. In three years, from a sailor with a common school education, I made a successful writer of him. The critics say this is impossible. Yet I was Martin Eden. At the end of three working years, two of which were spent in high school and the university and one spent at writing, and all three in studying immensely and intensely, I was publishing stories in magazines such as the *Atlantic Monthly*, was correcting proofs of my first book (issued by Houghton, Mifflin Co.), was selling sociological articles to *Cosmopolitan* and *McClure's*, had declined an associate editorship proffered me by telegraph from New York City, and was getting ready to marry.

Now the foregoing means work, especially the last year of it, when I was learning my trade as a writer. And in that year, running short on sleep and tasking my brain to its limit, I neither drank nor cared to drink. So far as I was concerned, alcohol did not exist. I did suffer from brain-fag on occasion, but alcohol never suggested itself as an ameliorative. Heavens! Editorial acceptances and checks were all the amelioratives I needed. A thin envelope from an editor in the morning's mail was more stimulating than half-a-dozen cocktails. And if a check of decent amount came out of the envelope, such incident in itself was a whole drunk.

Furthermore, at that time in my life I did not know what a cocktail was. I remember, when my first book was published, several Alaskans who were members of the Bohemian Club entertained me one evening at the club in San Francisco. We sat in most wonderful leather chairs, and drinks were ordered. Never had I heard such an ordering of liqueurs and of highballs of particular brands of Scotch. I did n't know what a liqueur or a highball was, and I did n't know that "Scotch" meant whisky. I knew only poor men's drinks, the drinks of the frontier and of sailor-town—cheap beer and cheaper whisky that was just called whisky and nothing else. I was embarrassed to make a choice, and the waiter nearly collapsed when I ordered claret as an after-dinner drink.

Chapter XXVII

As I SUCCEEDED with my writing, my standard of living rose and my horizon broadened. I confined myself to writing and typing a thousand words a day, including Sundays and holidays; and I still studied hard, but not so hard as formerly. I allowed myself five and one-half hours of actual sleep. I added this half-hour because I was compelled. Financial success permitted me more time for exercise. I rode my wheel more, chiefly because it was permanently out of pawn; and I boxed and fenced, walked on my hands, jumped high and broad, put the shot and tossed the caber, and went swimming. And I learned that more sleep is required for physical exercise than for mental exercise. There were tired nights, bodily, when I slept six hours; and on occasion of very severe exercise I actually slept seven hours. But such sleep orgies were not frequent. There was so much to learn, so much to be done, that I felt wicked when I slept seven hours. And I blessed the man who invented alarm clocks.

And still no desire to drink. I possessed too many fine faiths, was living at too keen a pitch. I was a socialist, intent on saving the world, and alcohol could not give me the fervors that were mine from ideas and ideals. My voice, on account of my successful writing, had added weight, or so I thought. At any rate, my reputation as a writer drew me audiences that my reputation as a speaker never could have drawn. I was invited before clubs and organizations of all sorts to deliver my message. I fought the good fight, and went on studying and writing, and was very busy.

Up to this time I had had a very restricted circle of friends. But now I began to go about. I was invited out, especially to dinner; and I made many friends and acquaintances whose economic lives were easier than mine had been. And many of them drank. In their own houses they drank and offered me drink. They were not drunkards any of them. They just drank temperately, and I drank temperately with them as an act of comradeship and accepted hospitality. I did not care for it, neither wanted it nor did not want it, and so small was the

impression made by it that I do not remember my first cocktail nor my first Scotch highball.

Well, I had a house. When one is asked into other houses,
he naturally asks others into his house. Behold the rising standard of living. Having been given drink in other houses, I
could expect nothing else of myself than to give drink in my
own house. So I laid in a supply of beer and whisky and table
claret. Never since that has my house not been well supplied.

And still, through all this period, I did not care in the
slightest for John Barleycorn. I drank when others drank, and
with them, as a social act. And I had so little choice in the
matter that I drank whatever they drank. If they elected
whisky, then whisky it was for me. If they drank root beer or
sarsaparilla, I drank root beer or sarsaparilla with them. And
when there were no friends in the house, why, I did n't drink
anything. Whisky decanters were always in the room where I
wrote, and for months and years I never knew what it was,
when by myself, to take a drink.

When out at dinner, I noticed the kindly, genial glow of
the preliminary cocktail. It seemed a very fitting and gracious
thing. Yet so little did I stand in need of it, with my own
high intensity and vitality, that I never thought it worth while
to have a cocktail before my own meal when I ate alone.

On the other hand, I well remember a very brilliant man,
somewhat older than I, who occasionally visited me. He liked
whisky, and I recall sitting whole afternoons in my den,
drinking steadily with him, drink for drink, until he was
mildly lighted up and I was slightly aware that I had drunk
some whisky. Now why did I do this? I don't know, save that
the old schooling held, the training of the old days and
nights, glass in hand, with men, the drinking ways of drink
and drinkers.

Besides, I no longer feared John Barleycorn. Mine was that
most dangerous stage when a man believes himself John Barleycorn's master. I had proved it to my satisfaction in the long
years of work and study. I could drink when I wanted, refrain
when I wanted, drink without getting drunk, and to cap
everything I was thoroughly conscious that I had no liking
for the stuff. During this period I drank precisely for the same
reason I had drunk with Scotty and the harpooner and with

the oyster pirates—because it was an act performed by men
with whom I wanted to behave as a man. These brilliant ones,
these adventurers of the mind, drank. Very well. There was
no reason I should not drink with them,—I who knew so
confidently that I had nothing to fear from John Barleycorn.

And the foregoing was my attitude of mind for years. Occasionally I got well jingled, but such occasions were rare. It
interfered with my work, and I permitted nothing to interfere
with my work. I remember, when spending several months in
the East End of London, during which time I wrote a book
and adventured much amongst the worst of the slum classes,
that I got drunk several times and was mightily wroth with
myself because it interfered with my writing. Yet these very
times were because I was out on the adventure-path, where
John Barleycorn is always to be found.

Then, too, with the certitude of long training and unholy
intimacy, there were occasions when I engaged in drinking-
bouts with men. Of course, this was on the adventure-path in
various parts of the world, and it was a matter of pride. It is
a queer man-pride that leads one to drink with men in order
to show as strong a head as they. But this queer man-pride is
no theory. It is a fact.

For instance, a wild band of young revolutionists invited
me as the guest of honor to a beer bust. It is the only technical beer bust I ever attended. I did not know the true inwardness of the affair when I accepted. I imagined that the
talk would be wild and high, that some of them might drink
more than they ought, and that I would drink discreetly. But
it seemed these beer busts were a diversion of these high-
spirited young fellows whereby they whiled away the tedium
of existence by making fools of their betters. As I learned
afterward, they had got their previous guest of honor, a brilliant young radical, unskilled in drinking, quite pipped.

When I found myself with them, and the situation dawned
on me, up rose my queer man-pride. I 'd show them, the
young rascals. I 'd show them who was husky and chesty,
who had the vitality and the constitution, the stomach and
the head, who could make most of a swine of himself and
show it least. These unlicked cubs who thought they could
out-drink *me*!

You see, it was an endurance test, and no man likes to give another best. Faugh! It was steam beer. I had learned more expensive brews. Not for years had I drunk steam beer; but when I had, I had drunk with men, and I guessed I could show these youngsters some ability in beer-guzzling. And the drinking began, and I had to drink with the best of them. Some of them might lag, but the guest of honor was not permitted to lag.

And all my austere nights of midnight oil, all the books I had read, all the wisdom I had gathered, went glimmering before the ape and tiger in me that crawled up from the abysm of my heredity, atavistic, competitive and brutal, lustful with strength and desire to outswine the swine.

And when the session broke up I was still on my feet, and I walked erect, unswaying—which was more than can be said of some of my hosts. I recall one of them in indignant tears on the street corner, weeping as he pointed out my sober condition. Little he dreamed the iron clutch, born of old training, with which I held to my consciousness in my swimming brain, kept control of my muscles and my qualms, kept my voice unbroken and easy and my thoughts consecutive and logical. Yes, and mixed up with it all I was privily a-grin. They had n't made a fool of me in that drinking bout. And I was proud of myself for the achievement. Darn it, I am still proud, so strangely is man compounded.

But I did n't write my thousand words next morning. I was sick, poisoned. It was a day of wretchedness. In the afternoon I had to give a public speech. I gave it, and I am confident it was as bad as I felt. Some of my hosts were there in the front rows to mark any signs on me of the night before. I don't known what signs they marked, but I marked signs on them and took consolation in the knowledge that they were just as sick as I.

Never again, I swore. And I have never been inveigled into another beer bust. For that matter, that was my last drinking bout of any sort. Oh, I have drunk ever since, but with more wisdom, more discretion, and never in a competitive spirit. It is thus the seasoned drinker grows seasoned.

To show that at this period in my life drinking was wholly a matter of companionship, I remember crossing the Atlantic in the old *Teutonic*. It chanced, at the start, that I chummed with an English cable operator and a younger member of a Spanish shipping firm. Now the only thing they drank was "horse's neck"—a long, soft, cool drink with an apple peel or an orange peel floating in it. And for that whole voyage I drank horse's necks with my two companions. On the other hand, had they drunk whisky, I should have drunk whisky with them. From this it must not be concluded that I was merely weak. I did n't care. I had no morality in the matter. I was strong with youth, and unafraid, and alcohol was an utterly negligible question so far as I was concerned.

Chapter XXVIII

NOT YET was I ready to tuck my arm in John Barleycorn's. The older I got, the greater my success, the more money I earned, the wider was the command of the world that became mine and the more prominently did John Barleycorn bulk in my life. And still I maintained no more than a nodding acquaintance with him. I drank for the sake of sociability, and when alone I did not drink. Sometimes I got jingled, but I considered such jingles the mild price I paid for sociability.

To show how unripe I was for John Barleycorn, when, at this time, I descended into my slough of despond, I never dreamed of turning to John Barleycorn for a helping hand. I had life troubles and heart troubles which are neither here nor there in this narrative. But, combined with them, were intellectual troubles which are indeed germane.

Mine was no uncommon experience. I had read too much positive science and lived too much positive life. In the eagerness of youth I had made the ancient mistake of pursuing Truth too relentlessly. I had torn her veils from her, and the sight was too terrible for me to stand. In brief, I lost my fine faiths in pretty well everything except humanity, and the humanity I retained faith in was a very stark humanity indeed.

This long sickness of pessimism is too well known to most of us to be detailed here. Let it suffice to state that I had it very bad. I meditated suicide coolly, as a Greek philosopher might. My regret was that there were too many dependent directly upon me for food and shelter for me to quit living. But that was sheer morality. What really saved me was the one remaining illusion—the PEOPLE.

The things I had fought for and burned my midnight oil for, had failed me. Success—I despised it. Recognition—it was dead ashes. Society, men and women above the ruck and the muck of the water-front and the forecastle—I was appalled by their unlovely mental mediocrity. Love of woman—it was like all the rest. Money—I could sleep in only one bed at a time, and of what worth was an income of a hundred

porterhouses a day when I could eat only one? Art, culture—
in the face of the iron facts of biology such things were ridiculous, the exponents of such things only the more ridiculous.

From the foregoing it can be seen how very sick I was. I
was born a fighter. The things I had fought for had proved
not worth the fight. Remained the PEOPLE. My fight was
finished, yet something was left still to fight for—the
PEOPLE.

But while I was discovering this one last tie to bind me to
life, in my extremity, in the depths of despond, walking in
the valley of the shadow, my ears were deaf to John Barleycorn. Never the remotest whisper arose in my consciousness
that John Barleycorn was the anodyne, that he could lie me
along to live. One way only was uppermost in my thought—
my revolver, the crashing eternal darkness of a bullet. There
was plenty of whisky in the house—for my guests. I never
touched it. I grew afraid of my revolver—afraid during the
period in which the radiant, flashing vision of the PEOPLE
was forming in my mind and will. So obsessed was I with the
desire to die, that I feared I might commit the act in my sleep,
and I was compelled to give my revolver away to others who
were to lose it for me where my subconscious hand might not
find it.

But the PEOPLE saved me. By the PEOPLE was I handcuffed to life. There was still one fight left in me, and here
was the thing for which to fight. I threw all precaution to the
winds, threw myself with fiercer zeal into the fight for socialism, laughed at the editors and publishers who warned me
and who were the sources of my hundred porterhouses a day,
and was brutally careless of whose feelings I hurt and of how
savagely I hurt them. As the "well-balanced radicals" charged
at the time, my efforts were so strenuous, so unsafe and un-
sane, so ultra-revolutionary, that I retarded the socialist development in the United States by five years. In passing, I
wish to remark, at this late date, that it is my fond belief that
I accelerated the socialist development in the United States by
at least five minutes.

It was the PEOPLE, and no thanks to John Barleycorn,
who pulled me through my long sickness. And when I was
convalescent, came the love of woman to complete the cure

and lull my pessimism asleep for many a long day, until John Barleycorn again awoke it. But, in the meantime, I pursued Truth less relentlessly, refraining from tearing her last veils aside even when I clutched them in my hand. I no longer cared to look upon Truth naked. I refused to permit myself to see a second time what I had once seen. And the memory of what I had that time seen I resolutely blotted from my mind.

And I was very happy. Life went well with me. I took delight in little things. The big things I declined to take too seriously. I still read the books, but not with the old eagerness. I still read the books to-day, but never again shall I read them with that old glory of youthful passion when I harked to the call from over and beyond that whispered me on to win to the mystery at the back of life and behind the stars.

The point of this chapter is that, in the long sickness that at some time comes to most of us, I came through without any appeal for aid to John Barleycorn. Love, socialism, the PEOPLE—healthful figments of man's mind—were the things that cured and saved me. If ever a man was not a born alcoholic, I believe that I am that man. And yet . . . well, let the succeeding chapters tell their tale, for in them will be shown how I paid for my previous quarter of a century of contact with ever-accessible John Barleycorn.

Chapter XXIX

AFTER MY LONG SICKNESS my drinking continued to be convivial. I drank when others drank and I was with them. But, imperceptibly, my need for alcohol took form and began to grow. It was not a body need. I boxed, swam, sailed, rode horses, lived in the open an arrantly healthful life, and passed life insurance examinations with flying colors. In its inception, now that I look back upon it, this need for alcohol was a mental need, a nerve need, a good-spirits need. How can I explain?

It was something like this. Physiologically, from the standpoint of palate and stomach, alcohol was, as it had always been, repulsive. It tasted no better than beer did when I was five, than bitter claret did when I was seven. When I was alone, writing or studying, I had no need for it. But—I was growing old, or wise, or both, or senile as an alternative. When I was in company I was less pleased, less excited, with the things said and done. Erstwhile worth-while fun and stunts seemed no longer worth while; and it was a torment to listen to the insipidities and stupidities of women, to the pompous, arrogant sayings of the little half-baked men. It is the penalty one pays for reading the books too much, or for being oneself a fool. In my case it does not matter which was my trouble. The trouble itself was the fact. The condition of the fact was mine. For me the life, and light, and sparkle of human intercourse were dwindling.

I had climbed too high among the stars, or, maybe, I had slept too hard. Yet I was not hysterical nor in any way overwrought. My pulse was normal. My heart was an amazement of excellence to the insurance doctors. My lungs threw the said doctors into ecstasies. I wrote a thousand words every day. I was punctiliously exact in dealing with all the affairs of life that fell to my lot. I exercised in joy and gladness. I slept at night like a babe. But—

Well, as soon as I got out in the company of others I was driven to melancholy and spiritual tears. I could neither laugh with nor at the solemn utterances of men I esteemed ponderous asses; nor could I laugh with nor at, nor engage in my old-time lightsome persiflage, with the silly superficial chatterings of women, who, underneath all their silliness and softness, were as primitive, direct, and deadly in their pursuit of biological destiny as the monkey women were before they shed their furry coats and replaced them with the furs of other animals.

And I was not pessimistic. I swear I was not pessimistic. I was merely bored. I had seen the same show too often, listened too often to the same songs and the same jokes. I knew too much about the box-office receipts. I knew the cogs of the machinery behind the scenes so well, that the posing on the stage, and the laughter and the song, could not drown the creaking of the wheels behind.

It does n't pay to go behind the scenes and see the angel-voiced tenor beat his wife. Well, I 'd been behind, and I was paying for it. Or else I was a fool. It is immaterial which was my situation. The situation is what counts, and the situation was that social intercourse for me was getting painful and difficult. On the other hand, it must be stated that on rare occasions, on very rare occasions, I did meet rare souls, or fools like me, with whom I could spend magnificent hours among the stars, or in the paradise of fools. I was married to a rare soul, or a fool, who never bored me and who was always a source of new and unending surprise and delight. But I could not spend all my hours solely in her company. Nor would it have been fair, nor wise, to compel her to spend all her hours in my company. Besides, I had written a string of successful books, and society demands some portion of the recreative hours of a fellow that writes books. And any normal man, of himself and his needs, demands some hours of his fellow man.

And now we begin to come to it. How to face social intercourse with the glamour gone? John Barleycorn! The ever-patient one had waited a quarter of a century and more for me to reach my hand out in need of him. His thousand tricks had failed, thanks to my constitution and good luck, but he had more tricks in his bag. A cocktail or two, or several, I found, cheered me up for the foolishness of foolish people. A cocktail, or several, before dinner, enabled me to laugh whole-heartedly at things which had long since ceased being laughable. The cocktail was a prod, a spur, a kick, to my jaded mind and bored spirits. It recrudesced the laughter and the song, and put a lilt into my own imagination so that I could laugh and sing and say foolish things with the liveliest of them, or platitudes with verve and intensity to the satisfaction of the pompous mediocre ones who knew no other way to talk.

A poor companion without a cocktail, I became a very good companion with one. I achieved a false exhilaration, drugged myself to merriment. And the thing began so imperceptibly, that I, old intimate of John Barleycorn, never dreamed whither it was leading me. I was beginning to call for music and wine; soon I should be calling for madder music and more wine.

It was at this time I became aware of waiting with expectancy for the pre-dinner cocktail. I *wanted* it, and I was *conscious* that I wanted it. I remember, while war-corresponding in the Far East, of being irresistibly attracted to a certain home. Besides accepting all invitations to dinner, I made a point of dropping in almost every afternoon. Now, the hostess was a charming woman, but it was not for her sake that I was under her roof so frequently. It happened that she made by far the finest cocktail procurable in that large city where drink-mixing on the part of the foreign population was indeed an art. Up at the club, down at the hotels, and in other private houses, no such cocktails were created. Her cocktails were subtle. They were masterpieces. They were the least repulsive to the palate and carried the most "kick." And yet, I desired her cocktails only for sociability's sake, to key myself to sociable moods. When I rode away from that city, across hundreds of miles of rice-fields and mountains, and through months of campaigning, and on with the victorious Japanese into Manchuria, I did not drink. Several bottles of whisky were always to be found on the backs of my pack-horses. Yet I never broached a bottle for myself, never took a drink by myself, and never knew a desire to take such a drink. Oh, if a white man came into my camp, I opened a bottle and we drank together according to the way of men, just as he would open a bottle and drink with me if I came into his camp. I carried that whisky for social purposes, and I so charged it up in my expense account to the newspaper for which I worked.

Only in retrospect can I mark the almost imperceptible growth of my desire. There were little hints then that I did not take, little straws in the wind that I did not see, little incidents the gravity of which I did not realize.

For instance, for some years it had been my practice each winter to cruise for six or eight weeks on San Francisco Bay. My stout sloop yacht, the *Spray*, had a comfortable cabin and a coal stove. A Korean boy did the cooking, and I usually took a friend or so along to share the joys of the cruise. Also, I took my machine along and did my thousand words a day. On the particular trip I have in mind, Cloudesley and Toddy came along. This was Toddy's first trip. On previous trips Cloudesley had elected to drink beer; so I had kept the yacht supplied with beer and had drunk beer with him.

But on this cruise the situation was different. Toddy was so nicknamed because of his diabolical cleverness in concocting toddies. So I brought whisky along—a couple of gallons. Alas! Many another gallon I bought, for Cloudesley and I got into the habit of drinking a certain hot toddy of huge dimensions that actually tasted delicious going down and that carried the most exhilarating kick imaginable.

I *liked* those toddies. I grew to look forward to the making of them. We drank them regularly, one before breakfast, one before dinner, one before supper, and a final one when we went to bed. We never got drunk. But I will say that four times a day we were very genial. And when, in the middle of the cruise, Toddy was called back to San Francisco on business, Cloudesley and I saw to it that the Korean boy mixed toddies regularly for us according to formula.

But that was only on the boat. Back on the land, in my house, I took no before-breakfast eye-opener, no bed-going nightcap. And I have n't drunk hot toddies since, and that was many a year ago. But the point is, I *liked* those toddies. The geniality of which they were provocative was marvelous.

They were eloquent proselyters for John Barleycorn in their small insidious way. They were tickles of the something destined to grow into daily and deadly desire. And I did n't know, never dreamed—I, who had lived with John Barleycorn for so many years and laughed at all his unavailing attempts to win me.

Chapter XXX

PART OF THE PROCESS of recovering from my long sickness was to find delight in little things, in things unconnected with books and problems, in play, in games of tag in the swimming pool, in flying kites, in fooling with horses, in working out mechanical puzzles. As a result, I grew tired of the city. On the ranch, in the Valley of the Moon, I found my paradise. I gave up living in cities. All the cities held for me were music, the theater, and Turkish baths.

And all went well with me. I worked hard, played hard, and was very happy. I read more fiction and less fact. I did not study a tithe as much as I had studied in the past. I still took an interest in the fundamental problems of existence, but it was a very cautious interest; for I had burned my fingers that time I clutched at the veils of Truth and rent them from her. There was a bit of lie in this attitude of mine, a bit of hypocrisy; but the lie and the hypocrisy were those of a man desiring to live. I deliberately blinded myself to what I took to be the savage interpretation of biological fact. After all, I was merely forswearing a bad habit, foregoing a bad frame of mind. And I repeat, I was very happy. And I add, that in all my days, measuring them with cold, considerative judgment, this was, far and away beyond all other periods, the happiest period of my life.

But the time was at hand, rimeless and reasonless so far as I can see, when I was to begin to pay for my score of years of dallying with John Barleycorn. Occasionally guests journeyed to the ranch and remained a few days. Some did not drink. But to those who did drink, the absence of all alcohol on the ranch was a hardship. I could not violate my sense of hospitality by compelling them to endure this hardship. I ordered in a stock . . . for my guests.

I was never interested enough in cocktails to know how they were made. So I got a barkeeper in Oakland to make them in bulk and ship them to me. When I had no guests I did n't drink. But I began to notice, when I finished my morning's work, that I was glad if there were a guest, for then I could drink a cocktail with him.

Now I was so clean of alcohol that even a single cocktail was provocative of pitch. A single cocktail would glow the mind and tickle a laugh for the few minutes prior to sitting down to table and starting the delightful process of eating. On the other hand, such was the strength of my stomach, of my alcoholic resistance, that the single cocktail was only the glimmer of a glow, the faintest tickle of a laugh. One day a friend frankly and shamelessly suggested a second cocktail. I drank the second one with him. The glow was appreciably longer and warmer, the laughter deeper and more resonant. One does not forget such experiences. Sometimes I almost think that it was because I was so very happy that I started on my real drinking.

I remember one day Charmian and I took a long ride over the mountains on our horses. The servants had been dismissed for the day, and we returned late at night to a jolly chafing-dish supper. Oh, it was good to be alive that night while the supper was preparing, the two of us alone in the kitchen. I, personally, was at the top of life. Such things as the books and ultimate truth did not exist. My body was gloriously healthy, and healthily tired from the long ride. It had been a splendid day. The night was splendid. I was with the woman who was my mate, picnicking in gleeful abandon. I had no troubles. The bills were all paid, and a surplus of money was rolling in on me. The future ever widened before me. And right there, in the kitchen, delicious things bubbled in the chafing dish, our laughter bubbled, and my stomach was keen with a most delicious edge of appetite.

I felt so good, that somehow, somewhere, in me arose an insatiable greed to feel better. I was so happy that I wanted to pitch my happiness even higher. And I knew the way. Ten thousand contacts with John Barleycorn had taught me. Several times I wandered out of the kitchen to the cocktail bottle, and each time I left it diminished by one man's size cocktail. The result was splendid. I was n't jingled, I was n't lighted up; but I was warmed, I glowed, my happiness was pyramided. Munificent as life was to me, I added to that munificence. It was a great hour—one of my greatest. But I paid for it, long afterwards, as you shall see. One does not forget such experiences, and, in human stupidity, cannot be brought to realize that there is no immutable law which decrees that same things shall produce same results. For they don't, else would the thousandth pipe of opium be provocative of similar delights to the first, else would one cocktail, instead of several, produce an equivalent glow after a year of cocktails.

One day, just before I ate midday dinner, after my morning's writing was done, when I had no guest, I took a cocktail by myself. Thereafter, when there were no guests, I took this daily pre-dinner cocktail. And right there John Barleycorn had me. I was beginning to drink regularly. I was beginning to drink alone. And I was beginning to drink, not for hospitality's sake, not for the sake of the taste, but for the effect of the drink.

I *wanted* that daily pre-dinner cocktail. And it never crossed my mind that there was any reason I should not have it. I paid for it. I could pay for a thousand cocktails each day if I wanted. And what was a cocktail—one cocktail—to me who on so many occasions for so many years had drunk inordinate quantities of stiffer stuff and been unharmed?

The program of my ranch life was as follows: Each morning, at eight-thirty, having been reading or correcting proofs in bed since four or five, I went to my desk. Odds and ends of correspondence and notes occupied me till nine, and at nine sharp, invariably, I began my writing. By eleven, sometimes a few minutes earlier or later, my thousand words were finished. Another half hour at cleaning up my desk, and my day's work was done, so that at eleven-thirty I got into a hammock under the trees with my mail bag and the morning newspaper. At twelve-thirty I ate dinner and in the afternoon I swam and rode.

One morning, at eleven-thirty, before I got into the hammock, I took a cocktail. I repeated this on subsequent mornings, of course, taking another cocktail just before I ate at twelve-thirty. Soon I found myself, seated at my desk in the midst of my thousand words, looking forward to that eleven-thirty cocktail.

At last, now, I was thoroughly conscious that I desired alcohol. But what of it? I was n't afraid of John Barleycorn. I had associated with him too long. I was wise in the matter of drink. I was discreet. Never again would I drink to excess. I knew the dangers and the pitfalls of John Barleycorn, the various ways by which he had tried to kill me in the past. But all that was past, long past. Never again would I drink myself to stupefaction. Never again would I get drunk. All I wanted, and all I would take, was just enough to glow and warm me, to kick geniality alive in me and put laughter in my throat and stir the maggots of imagination slightly in my brain. Oh, I was thoroughly master of myself, and of John Barleycorn.

Chapter XXXI

BUT THE SAME STIMULUS to the human organism will not continue to produce the same response. By and by I discovered there was no kick at all in one cocktail. One cocktail left me dead. There was no glow, no laughter tickle. Two or three cocktails were required to produce the original effect of one. And I wanted that effect. I drank my first cocktail at eleven-thirty when I took the morning's mail into the hammock, and I drank my second cocktail an hour later just before I ate. I got into the habit of crawling out of the hammock ten minutes earlier so as to find time and decency for two more cocktails ere I ate. This became schedule—three cocktails in the hour that intervened between my desk and dinner. And these were two of the deadliest drinking habits: regular drinking and solitary drinking.

I was always willing to drink when any one was around. I drank by myself when no one was around. Then I made another step. When I had for guest a man of limited drinking caliber, I took two drinks to his one—one drink with him, the other drink without him and of which he did not know. I *stole* that other drink, and, worse than that, I began the habit of drinking alone when there was a guest, a man, a comrade, with whom I could have drunk. But John Barleycorn furnished the extenuation. It was a wrong thing to trip a guest up with excess of hospitality and get him drunk. If I persuaded him, with his limited caliber, into drinking up with me, I'd surely get him drunk. What could I do but steal that every second drink, or else deny myself the kick equivalent to what he had got out of half the number?

Please remember, as I recite this development of my drinking, that I am no fool, no weakling. As the world measures such things, I am a success—I dare say a success more conspicuous than the success of the average successful man, and a success that required a pretty fair amount of brains and will power. My body is a strong body. It has survived where weaklings died like flies. And yet these things which I am relating happened to my body and to me. I am a fact. My drinking is a fact. My drinking is a thing that has happened, and is no theory nor speculation; and, as I see it, it but lays the emphasis on the power of John Barleycorn—a savagery that we still permit to exist, a deadly institution that lingers from the mad old brutal days and that takes its heavy toll of youth and strength and high spirit, and of very much of all of the best we breed.

To return. After a boisterous afternoon in the swimming pool, followed by a glorious ride on horseback over the mountains or up or down the Valley of the Moon, I found myself so keyed and splendid that I desired to be more highly keyed, to feel more splendid. I knew the way. A cocktail before supper was not the way. Two or three, at the very least, was what was needed. I took them. Why not? It was living. I had always dearly loved to live. This also became part of the daily schedule.

Then, too, I was perpetually finding excuses for extra cocktails. It might be the assembling of a particularly jolly crowd; a touch of anger against my architect or against a thieving stone-mason working on my barn; the death of my favorite horse in a barbed wire fence; or news of good fortune in the morning mail from my dealings with editors and publishers. It was immaterial what the excuse might be, once the desire had germinated in me. The thing was: I *wanted* alcohol. At last, after a score and more of years of dallying and of not wanting, now I wanted it. And my strength was my weakness. I required two, three, or four drinks to get an effect commensurate with the effect the average man got out of one drink.

One rule I observed. I never took a drink until my day's work of writing a thousand words was done. And, when done, the cocktails reared a wall of inhibition in my brain between the day's work done and the rest of the day of fun to come. My work ceased from my consciousness. No thought of it flickered in my brain till next morning at nine o'clock when I sat at my desk and began my next thousand words. This was a desirable condition of mind to achieve. I conserved my energy by means of this alcoholic inhibition. John Barleycorn was not so black as he was painted. He did a fellow many a good turn, and this was one of them.

And I turned out work that was healthful, and wholesome, and sincere. It was never pessimistic. The way to life I had learned in my long sickness. I knew the illusions were right, and I exalted the illusions. Oh, I still turn out the same sort of work, stuff that is clean, alive, optimistic, and that makes toward life. And I am always assured by the critics of my superabundant and abounding vitality, and of how thoroughly I am deluded by these very illusions I exploit.

And while on this digression, let me repeat the question I have repeated to myself ten thousand times. *Why did I drink?* What need was there for it? I was happy. Was it because I was too happy? I was strong. Was it because I was too strong? Did I possess too much vitality? I don't know why I drank. I cannot answer, though I can voice the suspicion that ever grows in me. I had been in too familiar contact with John Barleycorn through too many years. A left-handed man, by long practice, can become a right-handed man. Had I, a non-alcoholic, by long practice, become an alcoholic?

I was so happy! I had won through my long sickness to the satisfying love of woman. I earned more money with less endeavor. I glowed with health. I slept like a babe. I continued to write successful books, and in sociological controversy I saw my opponents confuted with the facts of the times that daily reared new buttresses to my intellectual position. From day's end to day's end I never knew sorrow, disappointment, nor regret. I was happy all the time. Life was one unending song. I begrudged the very hours of blessed sleep because by that much was I robbed of the joy that would have been mine had I remained awake. And yet I drank. And John Barleycorn, all unguessed by me, was setting the stage for a sickness all his own.

The more I drank the more I was required to drink to get an equivalent effect. When I left the Valley of the Moon, and went to the city and dined out, a cocktail served at table was a wan and worthless thing. There was no pre-dinner kick in it. On my way to dinner I was compelled to accumulate the kick—two cocktails, three, and, if I met some fellows, four or five, or six, it did n't matter within several. Once, I was in a rush. I had no time decently to accumulate the several drinks. A brilliant idea came to me. I told the barkeeper to mix me a double cocktail. Thereafter, whenever I was in a hurry, I ordered double cocktails. It saved time.

One result of this regular heavy drinking was to jade me. My mind grew so accustomed to spring and liven by artificial means, that without artificial means it refused to spring and liven. Alcohol become more and more imperative in order to meet people, in order to become sociably fit. I had to get the kick and the hit of the stuff, the crawl of the maggots, the genial brain glow, the laughter tickle, the touch of devilishness and sting, the smile over the face of things, ere I could join my fellows and make one with them.

Another result was that John Barleycorn was beginning to trip me up. He was thrusting my long sickness back upon me, inveigling me into again pursuing Truth and snatching her veils away from her, tricking me into looking reality stark in the face. But this came on gradually. My thoughts were growing harsh again, though they grew harsh slowly.

Sometimes warnings crossed my mind. Where was this steady drinking leading? But trust John Barleycorn to silence such questions. "Come on and have a drink and I 'll tell you all about it," is his way. And it works. For instance, the following is a case in point, and one which John Barleycorn never wearied of reminding me:

I had suffered an accident which required a ticklish operation. One morning, a week after I had come off the table, I lay on my hospital bed, weak and weary. The sunburn of my face, what little of it could be seen through a scraggly growth of beard, had faded to a sickly yellow. My doctor stood at my bedside on the verge of departure. He glared disapprovingly at the cigarette I was smoking.

"That's what you ought to quit," he lectured. "It will get you in the end. Look at me."

I looked. He was about my own age, broad-shouldered, deep-chested, eyes sparkling, and ruddy-cheeked with health. A finer specimen of manhood one would not ask.

"I used to smoke," he went on. "Cigars. But I gave even them up. And look at me."

The man was arrogant, and rightly arrogant, with conscious well-being. And within a month he was dead. It was no accident. Half-a-dozen different bugs of long scientific names had attacked and destroyed him. The complications were astonishing and painful, and for days before he died the screams of agony of that splendid manhood could be heard for a block around. He died screaming.

"You see," said John Barleycorn. "He took care of himself. He even stopped smoking cigars. And that 's what he got for it. Pretty rotten, eh? But the bugs will jump. There 's no fore-fending them. Your magnificent doctor took every precaution, yet they got him. When the bug jumps you can't tell where it will land. It may be you. Look what he missed. Will you miss all I can give you, only to have a bug jump on you and drag you down? There is no equity in life. It 's all a lottery. But I put the lying smile on the face of life and laugh at the facts. Smile with me and laugh. You 'll get yours in the end, but in the meantime laugh. It 's a pretty dark world. I illuminate it for you. It 's a rotten world, when things can happen such as happened to your doctor. There 's only one thing to do; take another drink and forget it."

And of course I took another drink for the inhibition that accompanied it. I took another drink every time John Barleycorn reminded me of what had happened. Yet I drank rationally, intelligently. I saw to it that the quality of the stuff was of the best. I sought the kick and the inhibition, and avoided the penalties of poor quality and of drunkenness. It is to be remarked, in passing, that when a man begins to drink rationally and intelligently he betrays a grave symptom of how far along the road he has traveled.

But I continued to observe my rule of never taking my first drink of the day until the last word of my thousand words was written. On occasion, however, I took a day's vacation from my writing. At such times, since it was no violation of my rule, I did n't mind how early in the day I took that first drink. And persons who have never been through the drinking game wonder how the drinking habit grows!

Chapter XXXII

WHEN the *Snark* sailed on her long cruise from San Francisco there was nothing to drink on board. Or, rather, we were all of us unaware that there was anything to drink, nor did we discover it for many a month. This sailing with a "dry" boat was malice aforethought on my part. I had played John Barleycorn a trick. And it showed that I was listening ever so slightly to the faint warnings that were beginning to arise in my consciousness.

Of course, I veiled the situation to myself and excused myself to John Barleycorn. And I was very scientific about it. I said that I would drink only while in ports. During the dry sea-stretches my system would be cleansed of the alcohol that soaked it, so that when I reached a port I should be in shape to enjoy John Barleycorn more thoroughly. His bite would be sharper, his kick keener and more delicious.

We were twenty-seven days on the traverse between San Francisco and Honolulu. After the first day out, the thought of a drink never troubled me. This I take to show how intrinsically I am not an alcoholic. Sometimes, during the traverse, looking ahead and anticipating the delightful *lanai* luncheons and dinners of Hawaii (I had been there a couple of times before), I thought, naturally, of the drinks that would precede those meals. I did not think of those drinks with any yearning, with any irk at the length of the voyage. I merely thought they would be nice and jolly, part of the atmosphere of a proper meal.

Thus, once again I proved to my complete satisfaction that I was John Barleycorn's master. I could drink when I wanted, refrain when I wanted. Therefore I would continue to drink when I wanted.

Some five months were spent in the various islands of the Hawaiian group. Being ashore, I drank. I even drank a bit more than I had been accustomed to drink in California prior to the voyage. The people in Hawaii seemed to drink a bit more, on the average, than the people in more temperate latitudes. I do not intend the pun, and can awkwardly revise the statement to "latitudes more distant from the equator." Yet Hawaii is only sub-tropical. The deeper I got into the tropics the deeper I found men drank, the deeper I drank myself.

From Hawaii we sailed for the Marquesas. The traverse occupied sixty days. For sixty days we never raised land, a sail, nor a steamer smoke. But early in those sixty days, the cook, giving an overhauling to the galley, made a find. Down in the bottom of a deep locker he found a dozen bottles of angelica and muscatel. These had come down from the kitchen cellar of the ranch along with the home-preserved fruits and jellies. Six months in the galley-heat had effected some sort of a change in the thick sweet wine—brandied it, I imagine.

I took a taste. Delicious! And thereafter, once each day, at twelve o'clock, after our observations were worked up and the *Snark's* position charted, I drank half a tumbler of the stuff. It had a rare kick to it. It warmed the cockles of my geniality and put a fairer face on the truly fair face of the sea. Each morning, below, sweating out my thousand words, I found myself looking forward to that twelve o'clock event of the day.

The trouble was I had to share the stuff, and the length of the traverse was doubtful. I regretted that there were not more than a dozen bottles. And when they were gone I even regretted that I had shared any of it. I was thirsty for the alcohol, and eager to arrive in the Marquesas.

So it was that I reached the Marquesas the possessor of a real, man's size thirst. And in the Marquesas were several white men, a lot of sickly natives, much magnificent scenery, plenty of trade rum, an immense quantity of absinthe, but neither whisky nor gin. The trade rum scorched the skin of one's mouth. I know, because I tried it. But I had ever been plastic, and I accepted the absinthe. The trouble with the stuff was that I had to take such inordinate quantities in order to feel the slightest effect.

From the Marquesas I sailed with sufficient absinthe in ballast to last me to Tahiti, where I outfitted with Scotch and American whisky, and thereafter there were no dry stretches between ports. But please do not misunderstand. There was no drunkenness, as drunkenness is ordinarily understood— no staggering and rolling around, no befuddlement of the

senses. The skilled and seasoned drinker, with a strong constitution, never descends to anything like that. He drinks to
feel good, to get a pleasant jingle, and no more than that.
The things he carefully avoids are the nausea of over-drinking, the after-effect of over-drinking, the helplessness and loss
of pride of over-drinking.

What the skilled and seasoned drinker achieves is a discreet
and canny semi-intoxication. And he does it by the twelvemonth around without any apparent penalty. There are
hundreds of thousands of men of this sort in the United
States to-day, in clubs, hotels, and in their own homes—men
who are never drunk, and who, though most of them will
indignantly deny it, are rarely sober. And all of them fondly
believe, as I fondly believed, that they are beating the game.

On the sea-stretches I was fairly abstemious; but ashore I
drank more. I seemed to need more, anyway, in the tropics.
This is a common experience, for the excessive consumption
of alcohol in the tropics by white men is a notorious fact. The
tropics is no place for white-skinned men. Their skin-pigment
does not protect them against the excessive white light of the
sun. The ultra-violet rays, and other high-velocity and invisible rays from the upper end of the spectrum, rip and tear
through their tissues, just as the X-ray ripped and tore
through the tissues of so many laboratory experimenters before they learned the danger.

White men in the tropics undergo radical changes of nature. They become savage, merciless. They commit monstrous
acts of cruelty that they would never dream of committing in
their original temperate climate. They become nervous, irritable, and less moral. And they drink as they never drank before. Drinking is one form of the many forms of degeneration
that set in when white men are exposed too long to too much
white light. The increase of alcoholic consumption is automatic. The tropics is no place for a long sojourn. They seem
doomed to die anyway, and the heavy drinking expedites the
process. They don't reason about it. They just do it.

The sun-sickness got me, despite the fact that I had been in
the tropics only a couple of years. I drank heavily during this
time, but right here I wish to forestall misunderstanding. The
drinking was not the cause of the sickness, nor of the aban-

donment of the voyage. I was strong as a bull, and for many months I fought the sun-sickness that was ripping and tearing my surface and nervous tissues to pieces. All through the New Hebrides and the Solomons and up among the atolls on the Line, during this period, under a tropic sun, rotten with malaria, and suffering from a few minor afflictions such as Biblical leprosy with the silvery skin, I did the work of five men.

To navigate a vessel through the reefs and shoals and passages and unlighted coasts of the coral seas is a man's work in itself. I was the only navigator on board. There was no one to check me up on the working out of my observations, nor any one with whom I could advise in the ticklish darkness among uncharted reefs and shoals. And I stood all watches. There was no seaman on board whom I could trust to stand a mate's watch. I was mate as well as captain. Twenty-four hours a day were the watches I stood at sea, catching cat-naps when I might. Third, I was doctor. And let me say right here that the doctor's job on the *Snark* at that time was a man's job. All on board suffered from malaria—the real, tropical malaria that can kill in three months. All on board suffered from perforating ulcers and from the maddening itch of *ngari ngari*. A Japanese cook went insane from his too numerous afflictions. One of my Polynesian sailors lay at death's door with blackwater fever. Oh, yes, it was a full man's job, and I dosed and doctored, and pulled teeth, and dragged my patients through mild little things like ptomaine poisoning.

Fourth, I was a writer. I sweated out my thousand words a day, every day, except when the shock of fever smote me, or a couple of nasty squalls smote the *Snark*, in the morning. Fifth, I was a traveler and a writer, eager to see things and to gather material into my note books. And, sixth, I was master and owner of the craft that was visiting strange places where visitors are rare and where visitors are made much of. So here I had to hold up the social end, entertain on board, be entertained ashore by planters, traders, governors, captains of war vessels, kinky-headed cannibal kings, and prime ministers sometimes fortunate enough to be clad in cotton under shirts.

Of course I drank. I drank with my guests and hosts. Also, I drank by myself. Doing the work of five men, I thought, entitled me to drink. Alcohol was good for a man who overworked. I noted its effect on my small crew, when, breaking their backs and hearts at heaving up anchor in forty fathoms, they knocked off gasping and trembling at the end of half an hour and had new life put into them by stiff jolts of rum. They caught their breaths, wiped their mouths, and went to it again with a will. And when we careened the *Snark* and had to work in the water to our necks between shocks of fever, I noted how raw trade-rum helped the work along.

And here again we come to another side of many-sided John Barleycorn. On the face of it, he gives something for nothing. Where no strength remains he finds new strength. The wearied one rises to greater effort. For the time being there is an actual accession of strength. I remember passing coal on an ocean steamer through eight days of hell, during which time we coal-passers were kept to the job by being fed whisky. We toiled half drunk all the time. And without the whisky we could not have passed the coal.

This strength John Barleycorn gives is not fictitious strength. It is real strength. But it is manufactured out of the sources of strength, and it must ultimately be paid for, and with interest. But what weary human will look so far ahead? He takes this apparently miraculous accession of strength at its face value. And many an overworked business and professional man, as well as a harried common laborer, has traveled John Barleycorn's death-road because of this mistake.

Chapter XXXIII

I WENT to Australia to go into hospital and get tinkered up, after which I planned to go on with the voyage. And during the long weeks I lay in hospital, from the first day I never missed alcohol. I never thought about it. I knew I should have it again when I was on my feet. But when I regained my feet I was not cured of my major afflictions. Naaman's silvery skin was still mine. The mysterious sun-sickness, which the experts of Australia could not fathom, still ripped and tore my tissues. Malaria still festered in me and put me on my back in shivering delirium at the most unexpected moments, among other things compelling me to cancel a double lecture tour which had been arranged.

So I abandoned the *Snark* voyage and sought a cooler climate. The day I came out of hospital I took up drinking again as a matter of course. I drank wine at meals. I drank cocktails before meals. I drank Scotch highballs when anybody I chanced to be with was drinking them. I was so thoroughly the master of John Barleycorn, I could take up with him or let go of him whenever I pleased, just as I had done all my life.

After a time, for cooler climate, I went down to southernmost Tasmania in forty-three South. And I found myself in a place where there was nothing to drink. It did n't mean anything. I did n't drink. It was no hardship. I soaked in the cool air, rode horseback, and did my thousand words a day save when the fever shock came in the morning.

And for fear that the idea may still lurk in some minds that my preceding years of drinking were the cause of my disabilities, I here point out that my Japanese cabin-boy, Nakata, still with me, was rotten with fever, as was Charmian, who in addition was in the slough of a tropical neurasthenia that required several years of temperate climate to cure, and that neither she nor Nakata drank or ever had drunk.

When I returned to Hobart Town, where drink was obtainable, I drank as of old. The same when I arrived back in Australia. On the contrary, when I sailed from Australia on a tramp steamer commanded by an abstemious captain, I took no drink along, and had no drink for the forty-three days' passage. Arrived in Ecuador, squarely under the equatorial sun, where the humans were dying of yellow fever, smallpox, and the plague, I promptly drank again—every drink of every sort that had a kick in it. I caught none of these diseases. Neither did Charmian nor Nataka, who did not drink.

Enamored of the tropics, despite the damage done me, I stopped in various places, and was a long while getting back to the splendid, temperate climate of California. I did my thousand words a day, traveling or stopping over, suffered my last faint fever shock, saw my silvery skin vanish and my sun-torn tissues healthily knit again, and drank as a broad-shouldered, chesty man may drink.

Chapter XXXIV

BACK ON THE RANCH, in the Valley of the Moon, I resumed my steady drinking. My program was no drink in the morning; first drink-time came with the completion of my thousand words. Then, between that and the midday meal, were drinks numerous enough to develop a pleasant jingle. Again, in the hour preceding the evening meal, I developed another pleasant jingle. Nobody ever saw me drunk, for the simple reason that I never was drunk. But I did get a jingle twice each day; and the amount of alcohol I consumed every day, if loosed in the system of one unaccustomed to drink, would have put such a one on his back and out.

It was the old proposition. The more I drank, the more I was compelled to drink in order to get an effect. The time came when cocktails were inadequate. I had neither the time in which to drink them nor the space to accommodate them. Whisky had a more powerful jolt. It gave quicker action with less quantity. Bourbon or rye, or cunningly aged blends, constituted the pre-midday drinking. In the late afternoon it was Scotch and soda.

My sleep, always excellent, now became not quite so excellent. I had been accustomed to read myself back to sleep when I chanced to awake. But now this began to fail me. When I had read two or three of the small hours away and was as wide awake as ever, I found that a drink furnished the soporific effect. Sometimes two or three drinks were required.

So short a period of sleep then intervened before early morning rising, that my system did not have time to work off the alcohol. As a result I awoke with mouth parched and dry, with a slight heaviness of head, and with a mild nervous palpitation in the stomach. In fact I did not feel good. I was suffering from the morning sickness of the steady, heavy drinker. What I needed was a pick-me-up, a bracer. Trust John Barleycorn, once he has broken down a man's defenses! So it was a drink before breakfast to put me right for breakfast—the old poison of the snake that has bitten one! Another custom, begun at this time, was that of the pitcher of water by the bed-side to furnish relief to my scorched and sizzling membranes.

I achieved a condition in which my body was never free from alcohol. Nor did I permit myself to be away from alcohol. If I traveled to out-of-the-way places, I declined to run the risk of finding them dry. I took a quart, or several quarts, along in my grip. In the past I had been amazed by other men guilty of this practice. Now I did it myself unblushingly. And when I got out with the fellows, I cast all rules by the board. I drank when they drank, what they drank, and in the same way they drank.

I was carrying a beautiful alcoholic conflagration around with me. The thing fed on its own heat and flamed the fiercer. There was no time, in all my waking time, that I did n't want a drink. I began to anticipate the completion of my daily thousand words by taking a drink when only five hundred words were written. It was not long until I prefaced the beginning of the thousand words with a drink.

The gravity of this I realized too well. I made new rules. Resolutely I would refrain from drinking until my work was done. But a new and most diabolical complication arose. The work refused to be done without drinking. It just could n't be done. I had to drink in order to do it. I was beginning to fight now. I had the craving at last, and it was mastering me. I would sit at my desk and dally with pad and pen, but words refused to flow. My brain could not think the proper thoughts because continually it was obsessed with the one thought that across the room in the liquor cabinet stood John Barleycorn. When, in despair, I took my drink, at once my brain loosened up and began to roll off the thousand words.

In my town house, in Oakland, I finished the stock of liquor and wilfully refused to purchase more. It was no use, because, unfortunately, there remained in the bottom of the liquor cabinet a case of beer. In vain I tried to write. Now beer is a poor substitute for strong waters; besides, I did n't like beer; yet all I could think of was that beer so singularly accessible in the bottom of the cabinet. Not until I had drunk a pint of it did the words begin to reel off, and the thousand were reeled off to the tune of numerous pints. The worst of it was that the beer caused me severe heart-burn; but despite the discomfort I soon finished the case.

The liquor cabinet was now bare. I did not replenish it. By truly heroic perseverance, I finally forced myself to write the daily thousand words without the spur of John Barleycorn. But all the time I wrote I was keenly aware of the craving for a drink. And as soon as the morning's work was done, I was out of the house and away down-town to get my first drink. Merciful goodness!—if John Barleycorn could get such sway over me, a non-alcoholic, what must be the sufferings of the true alcoholic, battling against the organic demands of his chemistry while those closest to him sympathize little, understand less, and despise and deride him!

Chapter XXXV

$\mathbf{B}$UT THE FREIGHT has to be paid. John Barleycorn began to collect, and he collected not so much from the body as from the mind. The old long sickness, which had been purely an intellectual sickness, recrudesced. The old ghosts, long laid, lifted their heads again. But they were different and more deadly ghosts. The old ghosts, intellectual in their inception, had been laid by a sane and normal logic. But now they were raised by the White Logic of John Barleycorn, and John Barleycorn never lays the ghosts of his raising. For this sickness of pessimism, caused by drink, one must drink further in quest of the anodyne that John Barleycorn promises but never delivers.

How to describe this White Logic to those who have never experienced it? It is perhaps better first to state how impossible such a description is. Take Hasheesh Land, for instance, the land of enormous extensions of time and space. In past years I have made two memorable journeys into that far land. My adventures there are seared in sharpest detail on my brain. Yet I have tried vainly, with endless words, to describe any tiny particular phase to persons who have not traveled there.

I use all the hyperbole of metaphor, and tell what centuries of time and profounds of unthinkable agony and horror can obtain in each interval of all the intervals between the notes of a quick jig played quickly on the piano. I talk for an hour, elaborating that one phase of Hasheesh Land, and at the end I have told them nothing. And when I cannot tell them this one thing of all the vastness of terrible and wonderful things, I know I have failed to give them the slightest concept of Hasheesh Land.

But, let me talk with some other traveler in that weird region, and at once am I understood. A phrase, a word, conveys instantly to his mind what hours of words and phrases could not convey to the mind of the non-traveler. So it is with John Barleycorn's realm where the White Logic reigns. To those untraveled there, the traveler's account must always seem unintelligible and fantastic. At the best, I may only beg of the untraveled ones to strive to take on faith the narrative I shall relate.

For there are fatal intuitions of truth that reside in alcohol. Philip sober vouches for Philip drunk in this matter. There seem to be various orders of truth in this world. Some sorts of truth are truer than others. Some sorts of truth are lies, and these sorts are the very ones that have the greatest use-value to life that desires to realize and live. At once, O un-traveled reader, you see how lunatic and blasphemous is the realm I am trying to describe to you in the language of John Barleycorn's tribe. It is not the language of your tribe, all of whose members resolutely shun the roads that lead to death and tread only the roads that lead to life. For there are roads and roads, and of truth there are orders and orders. But have patience. At least, through what seems no more than verbal yammerings, you may, perchance, glimpse faint far vistas of other lands and tribes.

Alcohol tells truth, but its truth is not normal. What is normal is healthful. What is healthful tends toward life. Normal truth is a different order, and a lesser order, of truth. Take a dray horse. Through all the vicissitudes of its life, from first to last, somehow, in unguessably dim ways, it must believe that life is good; that the drudgery in harness is good; that death, no matter how blind-instinctively apprehended, is a dread giant; that life is beneficent and worth-while; that, in the end, with fading life, it will not be knocked about and beaten and urged beyond its sprained and spavined best; that old age, even, is decent, dignified, and valuable, though old age means a ribby scarecrow in a hawker's cart, stumbling a step to every blow, stumbling dizzily on through merciless servitude and slow disintegration to the end—the end, the apportionment of its parts (of its subtle flesh, its pink and springy bone, its juices and ferments, and all the sensateness that informed it), to the chicken farm, the hide-house, the glue-rendering works, and the bone-meal fertilizer factory. To the last stumble of its stumbling end this dray horse must abide by the mandates of the lesser truth that is the truth of life and that makes life possible to persist.

This dray horse, like all other horses, like all other animals including man, is life-blinded and sense-struck. It will live, no matter what the price. The game of life is good, though all of life may be hurt, and though all lives lose the game in the end. This is the order of truth that obtains, not for the universe, but for the live things in it if they for a little space will endure ere they pass. This order of truth, no matter how erroneous it may be, is the sane and normal order of truth, the rational order of truth that life must believe in order to live.

To man, alone among the animals, has been given the awful privilege of reason. Man, with his brain, can penetrate the intoxicating show of things and look upon a universe brazen with indifference toward him and his dreams. He can do this, but it is not well for him to do it. To live, and live abundantly, to sting with life, to be alive (which is to be what he is), it is good that man be life-blinded and sense-struck. What is good is true. And this is the order of truth, lesser though it be, that man must know and guide his actions by, with unswerving certitude that it is absolute truth and that in the universe no other order of truth can obtain. It is good that man should accept at face value the cheats of sense and snares of flesh, and through the fogs of sentiency pursue the lures and lies of passion. It is good that he shall see neither shadows nor futilities, nor be appalled by his lusts and rapacities.

And man does this. Countless men have glimpsed that other and truer order of truth and recoiled from it. Countless men have passed through the long sickness and lived to tell of it and deliberately to forget it to the end of their days. They lived. They realized life, for life is what they were. They did right.

And now comes John Barleycorn with the curse he lays upon the imaginative man who is lusty with life and desire to live. John Barleycorn sends his White Logic, the argent messenger of truth beyond truth, the antithesis of life, cruel and bleak as interstellar space, pulseless and frozen as absolute zero, dazzling with the frost of irrefragable logic and unforgettable fact. John Barleycorn will not let the dreamer dream, the liver live. He destroys birth and death, and dissipates to mist the paradox of being, until his victim cries out, as in "The City of Dreadful Night": "Our life 's a cheat, our death a black abyss." And the feet of the victim of such dreadful intimacy take hold of the way of death.

Chapter XXXVI

B ACK to personal experiences and the effects in the past of John Barleycorn's White Logic on me. On my lovely ranch in the Valley of the Moon, brain-soaked with many months of alcohol, I am oppressed by the cosmic sadness that has always been the heritage of man. In vain do I ask myself why I should be sad. My nights are warm. My roof does not leak. I have food galore for all the caprices of appetite. Every creature-comfort is mine. In my body are no aches nor pains. The good old flesh-machine is running smoothly on. Neither brain nor muscle is overworked. I have land, money, power, recognition from the world, a consciousness that I do my meed of good in serving others, a mate whom I love, children that are of my own fond flesh. I have done, and am doing, what a good citizen of the world should do. I have built houses, many houses, and tilled many a hundred acres. And as for trees, have I not planted a hundred thousand? Everywhere, from any window of my house, I can gaze forth upon these trees of my planting, standing valiantly erect and aspiring toward the sun.

My life has indeed fallen in pleasant places. Not a hundred men in a million have been so lucky as I. Yet, with all this vast good fortune, am I sad. And I am sad because John Barleycorn is with me. And John Barleycorn is with me because I was born in what future ages will call the dark ages before the ages of rational civilization. John Barleycorn is with me because in all the unwitting days of my youth John Barleycorn was accessible, calling to me and inviting me on every corner and on every street between the corners. The pseudo-civilization into which I was born permitted everywhere licensed shops for the sale of soul-poison. The system of life was so organized that I (and millions like me) was lured and drawn and driven to the poison shops.

Wander with me through one mood of the myriad of moods of sadness into which one is plunged by John Barleycorn. I ride out over my beautiful ranch. Between my legs is a beautiful horse. The air is wine. The grapes on a score of

rolling hills are red with autumn flame. Across Sonoma
Mountain wisps of sea fog are stealing. The afternoon sun
smoulders in the drowsy sky. I have everything to make me
glad I am alive. I am filled with dreams and mysteries. I am
all sun and air and sparkle. I am vitalized, organic. I move, I
have the power of movement, I command movement of the
live thing I bestride. I am possessed with the pomps of being,
and know proud passions and inspirations. I have ten thousand august connotations. I am a king in the kingdom of
sense, and trample the face of the uncomplaining dust. . . .

And yet, with jaundiced eye I gaze upon all the beauty and
wonder about me, and with jaundiced brain consider the pitiful figure I cut in this world that endured so long without me
and that will again endure without me. I remember the men
who broke their hearts and their backs over this stubborn soil
that now belongs to me. As if anything imperishable could
belong to the perishable! These men passed. I, too, shall pass.
These men toiled, and cleared, and planted, gazed with aching eyes, while they rested their labor-stiffened bodies, on
these same sunrises and sunsets, at the autumn glory of the
grape, and at the fog-wisps stealing across the mountain. And
they are gone. And I know that I, too, shall some day, and
soon, be gone.

Gone? I am going now. In my jaw are cunning artifices of
the dentists which replace the parts of me already gone. Never
again will I have the thumbs of my youth. Old fights and
wrestlings have injured them irreparably. That punch on the
head of a man whose very name is forgotten, settled this
thumb finally and forever. A slip-grip at catch-as-catch-can
did for the other. My lean runner's stomach has passed into
the limbo of memory. The joints of the legs that bear me up
are not so adequate as they once were, when, in wild nights
and days of toil and frolic, I strained and snapped and rup-
tured them. Never again can I swing dizzily aloft and trust all
the proud quick that is I to a single rope-clutch in the driving
blackness of storm. Never again can I run with the sled-dogs
along the endless miles of Arctic trail.

I am aware that within this disintegrating body which has
been dying since I was born I carry a skeleton; that under the
rind of flesh which is called my face is a bony, noseless death's

head. All of which does not shudder me. To be afraid is to be
healthy. Fear of death makes for life. But the curse of the
White Logic is that it does not make one afraid. The world-
sickness of the White Logic makes one grin jocosely into the
face of the Noseless One and to sneer at all the phantasmagoria of living.

I look about me as I ride, and on every hand I see the
merciless and infinite waste of natural selection. The White
Logic insists upon opening the long-closed books, and by
paragraph and chapter states the beauty and wonder I behold
in terms of futility and dust. About me is murmur and hum,
and I know it for the gnat-swarm of the living, piping for a
little space its thin plaint of troubled air.

I return across the ranch. Twilight is on, and the hunting-
animals are out. I watch the piteous tragic play of life feeding
on life. Here is no morality. Only in man is morality, and
man created it—a code of action that makes toward living
and that is of the lesser order of truth. Yet all this I knew
before, in the weary days of my long sickness. These were the
greater truths that I so successfully schooled myself to forget;
the truths that were so serious that I refused to take them
seriously, and played with gently, O so gently, as sleeping
dogs at the back of consciousness which I did not care to
waken. I did but stir them, and let them lie. I was too wise,
too wicked wise, to wake them. But now White Logic willy
nilly wakes them for me, for White Logic, most valiant, is
unafraid of all the monsters of the earthly dream.

"Let the doctors of all the schools condemn me," White
Logic whispers as I ride along. "What of it? I am truth. You
know it. You cannot combat me. They say I make for death.
What of it? It is truth. Life lies in order to live. Life is a
perpetual lie-telling process. Life is a mad dance in the do-
main of flux, wherein appearances in mighty tides ebb and
flow, chained to the wheels of moons beyond our ken. Appearances are ghosts. Life is ghost land, where appearances
change, transfuse, permeate each the other and all the others,
that are, that are not, that always flicker, fade, and pass, only
to come again as new appearances, as other appearances. You
are such an appearance, composed of countless appearances
out of the past. All an appearance can know is mirage. You

know mirages of desire. These very mirages are the unthinkable and incalculable congeries of appearances that crowd in upon you and form you out of the past, and that sweep you on to dissemination into other unthinkable and incalculable congeries of appearances to people the ghost land of the future. Life is apparitional, and passes. You are an apparition. Through all the apparitions that preceded you and that compose the parts of you, you rose gibbering from the evolutionary mire, and gibbering you will pass on, interfusing, permeating the procession of apparitions that will succeed you."

And of course it is all unanswerable, and as I ride along through the evening shadows I sneer at that Great Fetish which Comte called the world. And I remember what another pessimist of sentiency has uttered: "Transient are all. They, being born, must die; and, being dead, are glad to be at rest."

But here through the dusk comes one who is not glad to be at rest. He is a workman on the ranch, an old man, an immigrant Italian. He takes his hat off to me in all servility, because, forsooth, I am to him a lord of life. I am food to him, and shelter, and existence. He has toiled like a beast all his days, and lived less comfortably than my horses in their deep-strawed stalls. He is labor-crippled. He shambles as he walks. One shoulder is twisted higher than the other. His hands are gnarled claws, repulsive, horrible. As an apparition he is a pretty miserable specimen. His brain is as stupid as his body is ugly.

"His brain is so stupid that he does not know he is an apparition," the White Logic chuckles to me. "He is sense-drunk. He is the slave of the dream of life. His brain is filled with superrational sanctions and obsessions. He believes in a transcendent over-world. He has listened to the vagaries of the prophets, who have blown for him the sumptuous bubble of Paradise. He feels inarticulate affinities with self-conjured non-realities. He sees penumbral visions of himself titubating fantastically through days and nights of space and stars. Beyond the shadow of any doubt he is convinced that the universe was made for him, and that it is his destiny to live forever in the immaterial and supersensuous realms he and his kind have builded of the stuff of semblance and deception.

"But you, who have opened the books and who share my awful confidence—you know him for what he is, brother to you and the dust, a cosmic joke, a sport of chemistry, a garmented beast that arose out of the ruck of screaming beastliness by virtue and accident of two opposable great toes. He is brother as well to the gorilla and the chimpanzee. He thumps his chest in anger, and roars and quivers with cataleptic ferocity. He knows monstrous, atavistic promptings, and he is composed of all manner of shreds of abysmal and forgotten instincts."

"Yet he dreams he is immortal," I argue feebly. "It is vastly wonderful for so stupid a clod to bestride the shoulders of time and ride the eternities."

"Pah!" is the retort. "Would you then shut the books and exchange places with this thing that is only an appetite and a desire, a marionette of the belly and the loins?"

"To be stupid is to be happy," I contend.

"Then your ideal of happiness is a jelly-like organism floating in a tideless, tepid, twilight sea, eh?"

—Oh, the victim cannot combat John Barleycorn!

"One step removed from the annihilating bliss of Buddha's Nirvana," the White Logic adds. "Oh, well, here 's the house. Cheer up and take a drink. We know, we illuminated, you and I, all the folly and the farce."

And in my book-walled den, the mausoleum of the thoughts of men, I take my drink, and other drinks, and roust out the sleeping dogs from the recesses of my brain and halloo them on over the walls of prejudice and law and through all the cunning labyrinths of superstition and belief.

"Drink," says the White Logic. "The Greeks believed that the gods gave them wine so that they might forget the miserableness of existence. And remember what Heine said."

Well do I remember that flaming Jew's "With the last breath all is done: joy, love, sorrow, macaroni, the theater, lime-trees, raspberry drops, the power of human relations, gossip, the barking of dogs, champagne."

"Your clear white light is sickness," I tell the White Logic. "You lie."

"By telling too strong a truth," he quips back.

"Alas, yes, so topsyturvy is existence," I acknowledge sadly.

"Ah, well, Liu Ling was wiser than you," the White Logic girds. "You remember him?"

I nod my head—Liu Ling, a hard drinker, one of the group of bibulous poets who called themselves the Seven Sages of the Bamboo Grove and who lived in China many an ancient century ago.

"It was Liu Ling," prompts the White Logic, "who declared that to a drunken man the affairs of this world appear but as so much duckweed on a river. Very well. Have another Scotch, and let semblance and deception become duckweed on a river."

And while I pour and sip my Scotch, I remember another Chinese philosopher, Chuang Tzu, who, four centuries before Christ, challenged this dreamland of the world, saying: "How then do I know but that the dead repent of having previously clung to life? Those who dream of the banquet, wake to lamentation and sorrow. Those who dream of lamentation and sorrow, wake to join the hunt. While they dream, they do not know that they dream. Some will even interpret the very dream they are dreaming; and only when they awake do they know it was a dream. . . . Fools think they are awake now, and flatter themselves they know if they are really princes or peasants. Confucius and you are both dreams; and I who say you are dreams—I am but a dream myself.

"Once upon a time, I, Chuang Tzu, dreamt I was a butterfly, fluttering hither and thither, to all intents and purposes a butterfly. I was conscious only of following my fancies as a butterfly, and was unconscious of my individuality as a man. Suddenly, I awaked, and there I lay, myself again. Now I do not know whether I was then a man dreaming I was a butterfly, or whether I am now a butterfly dreaming I am a man."

Chapter XXXVII

"COME," says the White Logic, "and forget these Asian dreamers of old time. Fill your glass and let us look at the parchments of the dreamers of yesterday who dreamed their dreams on your own warm hills."

I pore over the abstract of title of the vineyard called Tokay on the rancho called Petaluma. It is a sad long list of the names of men, beginning with Manuel Micheltoreno, one time Mexican "Governor, Commander-in-Chief, and Inspector of the Department of the Californias," who deeded ten square leagues of stolen Indian land to Colonel Don Mariano Guadalupe Vallejo for services rendered his country and for moneys paid by him for ten years to his soldiers.

Immediately this musty record of man's land-lust assumes the formidableness of a battle—the quick struggling with the dust. There are deeds of trust, mortgages, certificates of release, transfers, judgments, foreclosures, writs of attachment, orders of sale, tax liens, petitions for letters of administration, and decrees of distribution. It is like a monster ever unsubdued, this stubborn land that drowses in this Indian summer weather and that survives them all, the men who scratched its surface and passed.

Who was this James King of William, so curiously named? The oldest surviving settler in the Valley of the Moon knows him not. Yet only sixty years ago he loaned Mariano G. Vallejo eighteen thousand dollars on security of certain lands including the vineyard yet to be and to be called Tokay. Whence came Peter O'Connor, and whither vanished, after writing his little name of a day on the woodland that was to become a vineyard? Appears Louis Csomortanyi, a name to conjure with. He lasts through several pages of this record of the enduring soil.

Comes old American stock, thirsting across the Great American Desert, mule-backing across the Isthmus, wind-jamming around the Horn, to write brief and forgotten names where ten thousand generations of wild Indians are equally forgotten—names like Halleck, Hastings, Swett, Tait,

Denman, Tracy, Grimwood, Carlton, Temple. There are no
names like those to-day in the Valley of the Moon.

The names begin to appear fast and furiously, flashing from
legal page to legal page and in a flash vanishing. But ever the
persistent soil remains for others to scrawl themselves across.
Come the names of men of whom I have vaguely heard but
whom I have never known. Kohler and Frohling—who built
the great stone winery on the vineyard called Tokay, but who
built upon a hill up which other vinyardists refused to haul
their grapes. So Kohler and Frohling lost the land; the earthquake of 1906 threw down the winery; and I now live in its
ruins.

La Motte—he broke the soil, planted vines and orchards,
instituted commercial fish-culture, built a mansion renowned
in its day, was defeated by the soil, and passed. And my name
of a day appears. On the site of his orchards and vineyards,
of his proud mansion, of his very fish ponds, I have scrawled
myself with a hundred thousand eucalyptus trees.

Cooper and Greenlaw—on what is called the Hill Ranch
they left two of their dead, "Little Lillie" and "Little David,"
who rest to-day inside a tiny square of hand-hewn palings.
Also, Cooper and Greenlaw in their time cleared the virgin
forest from three fields of forty acres. To-day I have those
three fields sown with Canada peas, and in the spring they
shall be plowed under for green manure.

Haska—a dim legendary figure of a generation ago, who
went back up the mountain and cleared six acres of brush in
the tiny valley that took his name. He broke the soil, reared
stone walls and a house, and planted apple trees. And already
the site of the house is undiscoverable, the location of the
stone walls may be deduced from the configuration of the
landscape, and I am renewing the battle, putting in Angora
goats to browse away the brush that has overrun Haska's
clearing and choked Haska's apple trees to death. So I, too,
scratch the land with my brief endeavor and flash my name
across a page of legal script ere I pass and the page grows
musty.

"Dreamers and ghosts," the White Logic chuckles.

"But surely the striving was not altogether vain," I contend.

"It was based on illusion and is a lie."

"A vital lie," I retort.

"And pray what is a vital lie but a lie?" the White Logic challenges. "Come. Fill your glass and let us examine these vital liars who crowd your bookshelves. Let us dabble in William James a bit."

"A man of health," I say. "From him we may expect no philosopher's stone, but at least we shall find a few robust tonic things to which to tie."

"Rationality gelded to sentiment," the White Logic grins. "At the end of all his thinking he still clung to the sentiment of immortality. Facts transmuted in the alembic of hope into terms of faith. The ripest fruit of reason the stultification of reason. From the topmost peak of reason James teaches to cease reasoning and to have faith that all is well and will be well—the old, oh, ancient old, acrobatic flip of the metaphysicians whereby they reasoned reason quite away in order to escape the pessimism consequent upon the grim and honest exercise of reason.

"Is this flesh of yours you? Or is it an extraneous something possessed by you? Your body—what is it? A machine for converting stimuli into reactions. Stimuli and reactions are remembered. They constitute experience. Then you are in your consciousness these experiences. You are at any moment what you are thinking at that moment. Your I is both subject and object; it predicates things of itself and is the things predicated. The thinker is the thought, the knower is what is known, the possessor is the things possessed.

"After all, as you know well, man is a flux of states of consciousness, a flow of passing thoughts, each thought of self another self, a myriad thoughts, a myriad selves, a continual becoming but never being, a will-of-the-wisp flitting of ghosts in ghostland. But this, man will not accept of himself. He refuses to accept his own passing. He will not pass. He will live again if he has to die to do it.

"He shuffles atoms and jets of light, remotest nebulæ, drips of water, prick-points of sensation, slime-oozings and cosmic bulks, all mixed with pearls of faith, love of woman, imagined dignities, frightened surmises, and pompous arrogances, and of the stuff builds himself an immortality to startle the heavens and baffle the immensities. He squirms on his dunghill, and like a child lost in the dark among goblins, calls to the gods that he is their younger brother, a prisoner of the quick that is destined to be as free as they—monuments of egotism reared by the epiphenomena; dreams and the dust of dreams, that vanish when the dreamer vanishes and are no more when he is not.

"It is nothing new, these vital lies men tell themselves, muttering and mumbling them like charms and incantations against the powers of Night. The voodoos and medicine men and the devil-devil doctors were the fathers of metaphysics. Night and the Noseless One were ogres that beset the way of light and life. And the metaphysicians would win by if they had to tell lies to do it. They were vexed by the brazen law of the Ecclesiast that men die like the beasts of the field and their end is the same. Their creeds were their schemes, their religions their nostrums, their philosophies their devices, by which they half-believed they would outwit the Noseless One and the Night.

"Bog-lights, vapors of mysticism, psychic overtones, soul orgies, wailings among the shadows, weird gnosticisms, veils and tissues of words, gibbering subjectivisms, gropings and maunderings, ontological fantasies, pan-psychic hallucinations—this is the stuff, the phantasms of hope, that fills your book shelves. Look at them, all the sad wraiths of sad mad men and passionate rebels—your Schopenhauers, your Strindbergs, your Tolstois and Nietzsches.

"Come. Your glass is empty. Fill and forget."

I obey, for my brain is now well a-crawl with the maggots of alcohol, and as I drink to the sad thinkers on my shelves I quote Richard Hovey:

> "Abstain not! Life and Love, like night and day,
>   Offer themselves to us on their own terms,
>   Not ours. Accept their bounty while ye may,
>   Before we be accepted by the worms."

"I will cap you," cries the White Logic.

"No," I answer, while the maggots madden me. "I know you for what you are, and I am unafraid. Under your mask of hedonism you are yourself the Noseless One and your way leads to the Night. Hedonism has no meaning. It, too, is a lie, at best the coward's smug compromise—"

"Now will I cap you!" the White Logic breaks in.

> "But if you would not this poor life fulfil,
> Lo, you are free to end it when you will,
> Without the fear of waking after death."

And I laugh my defiance; for now, and for the moment, I know the White Logic to be the arch-impostor of them all, whispering his whispers of death. And he is guilty of his own unmasking, with his own genial chemistry turning the tables on himself, with his own maggots biting alive the old illusions, resurrecting and making to sound again the old voice from beyond of my youth, telling me again that still are mine the possibilities and powers which life and the books had taught me did not exist.

And the dinner-gong sounds to the reversed bottom of my glass. Jeering at the White Logic, I go out to join my guests at table, and with assumed seriousness to discuss the current magazines and the silly doings of the world's day, whipping every trick and ruse of controversy through all the paces of paradox and persiflage. And, when the whim changes, it is most easy and delightfully disconcerting to play with the respectable and cowardly bourgeois fetishes and to laugh and epigram at the flitting god-ghosts and the debaucheries and follies of wisdom.

The clown's the thing! The clown! If one must be a philosopher, let him be Aristophanes. And no one at the table thinks I am jingled. I am in fine fettle, that is all. I tire of the labor of thinking, and, when the table is finished, start practical jokes and set all playing at games, which we carry on with bucolic boisterousness.

And when the evening is over and good night said, I go back through my book-walled den to my sleeping porch and to myself and to the White Logic which, undefeated, has never left me. And as I fall to fuddled sleep I hear Youth crying, as Harry Kemp heard it:

"I heard Youth calling in the night:
'Gone is my former world-delight;
For there is naught my feet may stay;
The morn suffuses into day,
It dare not stand a moment still
But must the world with light fulfil.
More evanescent than the rose
My sudden rainbow comes and goes
Plunging bright ends across the sky—
Yea, I am Youth because I die!' "

Chapter XXXVIII

THE FOREGOING is a sample roaming with the White Logic through the dusk of my soul. To the best of my power I have striven to give the reader a glimpse of a man's secret dwelling when it is shared with John Barleycorn. And the reader must remember that this mood, which he has read in a quarter of an hour, is but one mood of the myriad moods of John Barleycorn, and that the procession of such moods may well last the clock around through many a day and week and month.

My alcoholic reminiscences draw to a close. I can say, as any strong, chesty drinker can say, that all that leaves me alive to-day on the planet is my unmerited luck—the luck of chest, and shoulders, and constitution. I dare to say that a not large percentage of youths, in the formative stage of fifteen to seventeen, could have survived the stress of heavy drinking that I survived between my fifteenth and seventeenth years; that a not large percentage of men could have punished the alcohol I have punished in my manhood years and lived to tell the tale. I survived, through no personal virtue, but because I did not have the chemistry of a dipsomaniac and because I possessed an organism unusually resistant to the ravages of John Barleycorn. And, surviving, I have watched the others die, not so lucky, down all the long sad road.

It was my unmitigated and absolute good fortune, good luck, chance, call it what you will, that brought me through the fires of John Barleycorn. My life, my career, my joy in living, have not been destroyed. They have been scorched, it is true; but, like the survivors of forlorn hopes, they have by unthinkably miraculous ways come through the fight to marvel at the tally of the slain.

And like such a survivor of old red War who cries out, "Let there be no more war!" so I cry out, "Let there be no more poison-fighting by our youths!" The way to stop war is to stop it. The way to stop drinking is to stop it. The way China stopped the general use of opium was by stopping the cultivation and importation of opium. The philosophers, priests,

and doctors of China could have preached themselves breathless against opium for a thousand years, and the use of
opium, so long as opium was ever-accessible and obtainable,
would have continued unabated. We are so made, that is all.
We have with great success made a practice of not leaving
arsenic and strychnine, and typhoid and tuberculosis germs,
lying around for our children to be destroyed by. Treat John
Barleycorn the same way. Stop him. Don't let him lie around,
licensed and legal, to pounce upon our youth. Not of alcoholics nor for alcoholics do I write, but for our youths, for
those who possess no more than the adventure-stings and the
genial predispositions, the social man-impulses, which are
twisted all awry by our barbarian civilization which feeds
them poison on all the corners. It is the healthy, normal boys,
now born or being born, for whom I write.

It was for this reason, more than any other, and more ardently than any other, that I rode down into the Valley of the
Moon, all a-jingle, and voted for equal suffrage. I voted that
women might vote, because I knew that they, the wives and
mothers of the race, would vote John Barleycorn out of existence and back into the historical limbo of our vanished customs of savagery. If I thus seem to cry out as one hurt, please
remember that I have been sorely bruised and that I do dislike
the thought that any son or daughter of mine or yours should
be similarly bruised.

The women are the true conservators of the race. The men
are the wastrels, the adventure-lovers and gamblers, and in
the end it is by their women that they are saved. About man's
first experiment in chemistry was the making of alcohol, and
down all the generations to this day man has continued to
manufacture and drink it. And there has never been a day
when the women have not resented man's use of alcohol,
though they have never had the power to give weight to their
resentment. The moment women get the vote in any community, the first thing they proceed to do, or try to do, is to
close the saloons. In a thousand generations to come men of
themselves will not close the saloons. As well expect the morphine victims to legislate the sale of morphine out of existence.

The women know. They have paid an incalculable price of

sweat and tears for man's use of alcohol. Ever jealous for the race, they will legislate for the babes of boys yet to be born; and for the babes of girls, too, for they must be the mothers, wives, and sisters of these boys.

And it will be easy. The only ones that will be hurt will be the topers and seasoned drinkers of a single generation. I am one of these, and I make solemn assurance, based upon long traffic with John Barleycorn, that it won't hurt me very much to stop drinking when no one else drinks and when no drink is obtainable. On the other hand, the overwhelming proportion of young men are so normally non-alcoholic, that, never having had access to alcohol, they will never miss it. They will know of the saloon only in the pages of history, and they will think of the saloon as a quaint old custom similar to bull-baiting and the burning of witches.

Chapter XXXIX

O F COURSE, no personal tale is complete without bringing the narrative of the person down to the last moment. But mine is no tale of a reformed drunkard. I was never a drunkard, and I have not reformed.

It chanced, some time ago, that I made a voyage of one hundred and forty-eight days in a windjammer around the Horn. I took no private supply of alcohol along, and, though there was no day of those one hundred and forty-eight days that I could not have got a drink from the captain, I did not take a drink. I did not take a drink because I did not desire a drink. No one else drank on board. The atmosphere for drinking was not present, and in my system there was no organic need for alcohol. My chemistry did not demand alcohol.

So there arose before me a problem, a clear and simple problem: *This is so easy, why not keep it up when you get back on land?* I weighed this problem carefully. I weighed it for five months, in a state of absolute non-contact with alcohol. And out of the data of past experience, I reached certain conclusions.

In the first place, I am convinced that not one man in ten thousand, or in a hundred thousand, is a genuine, chemical dipsomaniac. Drinking, as I deem it, is practically entirely a habit of mind. It is unlike tobacco, or cocaine, or morphine, or all the rest of the long list of drugs. The desire for alcohol is quite peculiarly mental in its origin. It is a matter of mental training and growth, and it is cultivated in social soil. Not one drinker in a million began drinking alone. All drinkers begin socially, and this drinking is accompanied by a thousand social connotations such as I have described out of my own experience in the first part of this narrative. These social connotations are the stuff of which the drink habit is largely composed. The part that alcohol itself plays is inconsiderable, when compared with the part played by the social atmosphere in which it is drunk. The human is rarely born these days, who, without long training in the social relations of drinking, feels the irresistible chemical propulsion of his system toward alcohol. I do assume that such rare individuals are born, but I have never encountered one.

On this long, five-months' voyage, I found that among all my bodily needs not the slightest shred of a bodily need for alcohol existed. But this I did find: my need was mental and social. When I thought of alcohol, the connotation was fellowship. When I thought of fellowship, the connotation was alcohol. Fellowship and alcohol were Siamese twins. They always occurred linked together.

Thus, when reading in my deck-chair or when talking with others, practically any mention of any part of the world I knew instantly aroused the connotation of drinking and good fellows. Big nights and days and moments, all purple passages and freedoms, thronged my memory. "Venice" stares at me from the printed page, and I remember the café tables on the sidewalks. "The Battle of Santiago," some one says, and I answer, "Yes, I 've been over the ground." But I do not see the ground, nor Kettle Hill, nor the Peace Tree. What I see is the Café Venus, on the plaza of Santiago, where one hot night I talked long and drank deep with a dying consumptive.

The East End of London, I read, or some one says; and first of all, under my eyelids, leap the visions of the shining pubs, and in my ears echo the calls for "two of bitter" and "three of Scotch." The Latin Quarter—at once I am in the student cabarets, bright faces and keen spirits around me, sipping cool, well-dripped absinthe while our voices mount and soar in Latin fashion as we settle God and art and democracy and the rest of the simple problems of existence.

In a pampero off the River Plate, we speculate, if we are disabled, of running in to Buenos Ayres, the "Paris of America," and I have visions of bright congregating-places of men, of the jollity of raised glasses, and of song and cheer and the hum of genial voices. When we have picked up the Northeast Trades in the Pacific, we try to persuade our dying captain to run for Honolulu, and while I persuade I see myself again drinking cocktails on the cool *lanais*, and fizzes out at Waikiki where the surf rolls in. Some one mentions the way wild ducks are cooked in the restaurants of San Francisco, and at once I am transported to the light and clatter of many tables, where I gaze at old friends across the golden brims of long-stemmed Rhine-wine glasses.

And so I pondered my problem. I should not care to revisit all these fair places of the world except in the fashion I visited them before. *Glass in hand!* There is a magic in the phrase. It means more than all the words in the dictionary can be made to mean. It is a habit of mind to which I have been trained all my life. It is now part of the stuff that composes me. I like the bubbling play of wit, the chesty laughs, the resonant voices of men, when, glass in hand, they shut the gray world outside and prod their brains with the fun and folly of an accelerated pulse.

No, I decided; I shall take my drink on occasion. With all the books on my shelves, with all the thoughts of the thinkers shaded by my particular temperament, I decided coolly and deliberately that I should continue to do what I had been trained to want to do. I would drink—but, oh, more skil-fully, more discreetly, than ever before. Never again would I be a peripatetic conflagration. Never again would I invoke the White Logic. I had learned how not to invoke him.

The White Logic now lies decently buried alongside the Long Sickness. Neither will afflict me again. It is many a year since I laid the Long Sickness away; his sleep is sound. And just as sound is the sleep of the White Logic. And yet, in conclusion, I can well say that I wish my forefathers had banished John Barleycorn before my time. I regret that John Barleycorn flourished everywhere in the system of society in which I was born, else I should not have made his acquaintance, and I was long trained in his acquaintance.

THE END

ESSAYS

Essays

How I Became a Socialist 1117

The Scab 1121

Jack London on "The Jungle" 1137

Revolution 1147

How I Became a Socialist

IT IS QUITE FAIR to say that I became a Socialist in a fashion somewhat similar to the way in which the Teutonic pagans became Christians—it was hammered into me. Not only was I not looking for Socialism at the time of my conversion, but I was fighting it. I was very young and callow, did not know much of anything, and though I had never even heard of a school called "Individualism," I sang the pæan of the strong with all my heart.

This was because I was strong myself. By strong I mean that I had good health and hard muscles, both of which possessions are easily accounted for. I had lived my childhood on California ranches, my boyhood hustling newspapers on the streets of a healthy Western city, and my youth on the ozone-laden waters of San Francisco Bay and the Pacific Ocean. I loved life in the open, and I toiled in the open, at the hardest kinds of work. Learning no trade, but drifting along from job to job, I looked on the world and called it good, every bit of it. Let me repeat, this optimism was because I was healthy and strong, bothered with neither aches nor weaknesses, never turned down by the boss because I did not look fit, able always to get a job at shovelling coal, sailorizing, or manual labor of some sort.

And because of all this, exulting in my young life, able to hold my own at work or fight, I was a rampant individualist. It was very natural. I was a winner. Wherefore I called the game, as I saw it played, or thought I saw it played, a very proper game for MEN. To be a MAN was to write man in large capitals on my heart. To adventure like a man, and fight like a man, and do a man's work (even for a boy's pay)— these were things that reached right in and gripped hold of me as no other thing could. And I looked ahead into long vistas of a hazy and interminable future, into which, playing what I conceived to be MAN'S game, I should continue to travel with unfailing health, without accidents, and with muscles ever vigorous. As I say, this future was interminable. I could see myself only raging through life without end like one of Nietzsche's *blond beasts*, lustfully roving and conquering by sheer superiority and strength.

As for the unfortunates, the sick, and ailing, and old, and maimed, I must confess I hardly thought of them at all, save that I vaguely felt that they, barring accidents, could be as good as I if they wanted to real hard, and could work just as well. Accidents? Well, they represented FATE, also spelled out in capitals, and there was no getting around FATE. Napoleon had had an accident at Waterloo, but that did not dampen my desire to be another and later Napoleon. Further, the optimism bred of a stomach which could digest scrap iron and a body which flourished on hardships did not permit me to consider accidents as even remotely related to my glorious personality.

I hope I have made it clear that I was proud to be one of Nature's strong-armed noblemen. The dignity of labor was to me the most impressive thing in the world. Without having read Carlyle, or Kipling, I formulated a gospel of work which put theirs in the shade. Work was everything. It was sanctification and salvation. The pride I took in a hard day's work well done would be inconceivable to you. It is almost inconceivable to me as I look back upon it. I was as faithful a wage slave as ever capitalist exploited. To shirk or malinger on the man who paid me my wages was a sin, first, against myself, and second, against him. I considered it a crime second only to treason and just about as bad.

In short, my joyous individualism was dominated by the orthodox bourgeois ethics. I read the bourgeois papers, listened to the bourgeois preachers, and shouted at the sonorous platitudes of the bourgeois politicians. And I doubt not, if other events had not changed my career, that I should have evolved into a professional strike-breaker, (one of President Eliot's American heroes), and had my head and my earning power irrevocably smashed by a club in the hands of some militant trades-unionist.

Just about this time, returning from a seven months' voyage before the mast, and just turned eighteen, I took it into my head to go tramping. On rods and blind baggages I fought my way from the open West, where men bucked big and the job hunted the man, to the congested labor centres of the East, where men were small potatoes and hunted the job for all they were worth. And on this new *blond-beast* adventure I found myself looking upon life from a new and totally different angle. I had dropped down from the proletariat into what sociologists love to call the "submerged tenth," and I was startled to discover the way in which that submerged tenth was recruited.

I found there all sorts of men, many of whom had once been as good as myself and just as *blond-beastly*; sailor-men, soldier-men, labor-men, all wrenched and distorted and twisted out of shape by toil and hardship and accident, and cast adrift by their masters like so many old horses. I battered on the drag and slammed back gates with them, or shivered with them in box cars and city parks, listening the while to life-histories which began under auspices as fair as mine, with digestions and bodies equal to and better than mine, and which ended there before my eyes in the shambles at the bottom of the Social Pit.

And as I listened my brain began to work. The woman of the streets and the man of the gutter drew very close to me. I saw the picture of the Social Pit as vividly as though it were a concrete thing, and at the bottom of the Pit I saw them, myself above them, not far, and hanging on to the slippery wall by main strength and sweat. And I confess a terror seized me. What when my strength failed? when I should be unable to work shoulder to shoulder with the strong men who were as yet babes unborn? And there and then I swore a great oath. It ran something like this: *All my days I have worked hard with my body, and according to the number of days I have worked, by just that much am I nearer the bottom of the Pit. I shall climb out of the Pit, but not by the muscles of my body shall I climb out. I shall do no more hard work, and may God strike me dead if I do another day's hard work with my body more than I absolutely have to do.* And I have been busy ever since running away from hard work.

Incidentally, while tramping some ten thousand miles through the United States and Canada, I strayed into Niagara Falls, was nabbed by a fee-hunting constable, denied the right to plead guilty or not guilty, sentenced out of hand to thirty days' imprisonment for having no fixed abode and no visible

means of support, handcuffed and chained to a bunch of men
similarly circumstanced, carted down country to Buffalo, registered at the Erie County Penitentiary, had my head clipped
and my budding mustache shaved, was dressed in convict
stripes, compulsorily vaccinated by a medical student who
practised on such as we, made to march the lock-step, and
put to work under the eyes of guards armed with Winchester
rifles—all for adventuring in *blond-beastly* fashion. Concerning further details deponent sayeth not, though he may hint
that some of his plethoric national patriotism simmered down
and leaked out of the bottom of his soul somewhere—at
least, since that experience he finds that he cares more for men
and women and little children than for imaginary geographical lines.

*   *   *

To return to my conversion. I think it is apparent that my
rampant individualism was pretty effectively hammered out of
me, and something else as effectively hammered in. But, just
as I had been an individualist without knowing it, I was now
a Socialist without knowing it, withal, an unscientific one. I
had been reborn, but not renamed, and I was running around
to find out what manner of thing I was. I ran back to California and opened the books. I do not remember which ones
I opened first. It is an unimportant detail anyway. I was already It, whatever It was, and by aid of the books I discovered that It was a Socialist. Since that day I have opened
many books, but no economic argument, no lucid demonstration of the logic and inevitableness of Socialism affects me as
profoundly and convincingly as I was affected on the day
when I first saw the walls of the Social Pit rise around me and
felt myself slipping down, down, into the shambles at the
bottom.

The Scab

IN A COMPETITIVE society, where men struggle with one another for food and shelter, what is more natural than that generosity, when it diminishes the food and shelter of men other than he who is generous, should be held an accursed thing? Wise old saws to the contrary, he who takes from a man's purse takes from his existence. To strike at a man's food and shelter is to strike at his life; and in a society organized on a tooth-and-nail basis, such an act, performed though it may be under the guise of generosity, is none the less menacing and terrible.

It is for this reason that a laborer is so fiercely hostile to another laborer who offers to work for less pay or longer hours. To hold his place, (which is to live), he must offset this offer by another equally liberal, which is equivalent to giving away somewhat from the food and shelter he enjoys. To sell his day's work for $2, instead of $2.50, means that he, his wife, and his children will not have so good a roof over their heads, so warm clothes on their backs, so substantial food in their stomachs. Meat will be bought less frequently and it will be tougher and less nutritious, stout new shoes will go less often on the children's feet, and disease and death will be more imminent in a cheaper house and neighborhood.

Thus the generous laborer, giving more of a day's work for less return, (measured in terms of food and shelter), threatens the life of his less generous brother laborer, and at the best, if he does not destroy that life, he diminishes it. Whereupon the less generous laborer looks upon him as an enemy, and, as men are inclined to do in a tooth-and-nail society, he tries to kill the man who is trying to kill him.

When a striker kills with a brick the man who has taken his place, he has no sense of wrong-doing. In the deepest holds of his being, though he does not reason the impulse, he has an ethical sanction. He feels dimly that he has justification, just as the home-defending Boer felt, though more sharply, with each bullet he fired at the invading English. Behind every brick thrown by a striker is the selfish will "to live" of himself, and the slightly altruistic will "to live" of his family. The family group came into the world before the State group, and society, being still on the primitive basis of tooth and nail, the will "to live" of the State is not so compelling to the striker as is the will "to live" of his family and himself.

In addition to the use of bricks, clubs, and bullets, the selfish laborer finds it necessary to express his feelings in speech. Just as the peaceful country-dweller calls the sea-rover a "pirate," and the stout burgher calls the man who breaks into his strong-box a "robber," so the selfish laborer applies the opprobrious epithet "scab" to the laborer who takes from him food and shelter by being more generous in the disposal of his labor power. The sentimental connotation of "scab" is as terrific as that of "traitor" or "Judas," and a sentimental definition would be as deep and varied as the human heart. It is far easier to arrive at what may be called a technical definition, worded in commercial terms, as, for instance, that *a scab is one who gives more value for the same price than another*.

The laborer who gives more time or strength or skill for the same wage than another, or equal time or strength or skill for a less wage, is a scab. This generousness on his part is hurtful to his fellow-laborers, for it compels them to an equal generousness which is not to their liking, and which gives them less of food and shelter. But a word may be said for the scab. Just as his act makes his rivals compulsorily generous, so do they, by fortune of birth and training, make compulsory his act of generousness. He does not scab because he wants to scab. No whim of the spirit, no burgeoning of the heart, leads him to give more of his labor power than they for a certain sum.

It is because he cannot get work on the same terms as they that he is a scab. There is less work than there are men to do work. This is patent, else the scab would not loom so large on the labor-market horizon. Because they are stronger than he, or more skilled, or more energetic, it is impossible for him to take their places at the same wage. To take their places he must give more value, must work longer hours or receive a smaller wage. He does so, and he cannot help it, for his will "to live" is driving him on as well as they are being driven on by their will "to live"; and to live he must win food and shelter, which he can do only by receiving permission to work from some man who owns a bit of land or a piece of machinery. And to receive permission from this man, he must make the transaction profitable for him.

Viewed in this light, the scab, who gives more labor power for a certain price than his fellows, is not so generous after all. He is no more generous with his energy than the chattel slave and the convict laborer, who, by the way, are the almost perfect scabs. They give their labor power for about the minimum possible price. But, within limits, they may loaf and malinger, and, as scabs, are exceeded by the machine, which never loafs and malingers and which is the ideally perfect scab.

It is not nice to be a scab. Not only is it not in good social taste and comradeship, but, from the standpoint of food and shelter, it is bad business policy. Nobody desires to scab, to give most for least. The ambition of every individual is quite the opposite, to give least for most; and, as a result, living in a tooth-and-nail society, battle royal is waged by the ambitious individuals. But in its most salient aspect, that of the struggle over the division of the joint product, it is no longer a battle between individuals, but between groups of individuals. Capital and labor apply themselves to raw material, make something useful out of it, add to its value, and then proceed to quarrel over the division of the added value. Neither cares to give most for least. Each is intent on giving less than the other and on receiving more.

Labor combines into its unions, capital into partnerships, associations, corporations, and trusts. A group-struggle is the result, in which the individuals, as individuals, play no part. The Brotherhood of Carpenters and Joiners, for instance, serves notice on the Master Builders' Association that it demands an increase of the wage of its members from $3.50 a day to $4, and a Saturday half-holiday without pay. This means that the carpenters are trying to give less for more. Where they received $21 for six full days, they are endeavoring to get $22 for five days and a half,—that is, they will work half a day less each week and receive a dollar more.

Also, they expect the Saturday half-holiday to give work to one additional man for each eleven previously employed. This last affords a splendid example of the development of the group idea. In this particular struggle the individual has no chance at all for life. The individual carpenter would be crushed like a mote by the Master Builders' Association, and like a mote the individual master builder would be crushed by the Brotherhood of Carpenters and Joiners.

In the group-struggle over the division of the joint product, labor utilizes the union with its two great weapons, the strike and the boycott; while capital utilizes the trust and the association, the weapons of which are the black-list, the lock-out, and the scab. The scab is by far the most formidable weapon of the three. He is the man who breaks strikes and causes all the trouble. Without him there would be no trouble, for the strikers are willing to remain out peacefully and indefinitely so long as other men are not in their places, and so long as the particular aggregation of capital with which they are fighting is eating its head off in enforced idleness.

But both warring groups have reserve weapons. Were it not for the scab, these weapons would not be brought into play. But the scab takes the place of the striker, who begins at once to wield a most powerful weapon, terrorism. The will "to live" of the scab recoils from the menace of broken bones and violent death. With all due respect to the labor leaders, who are not to be blamed for volubly asseverating otherwise, terrorism is a well-defined and eminently successful policy of the labor unions. It has probably won them more strikes than all the rest of the weapons in their arsenal. This terrorism, however, must be clearly understood. It is directed solely against the scab, placing him in such fear for life and limb as to drive him out of the contest. But when terrorism gets out of hand and inoffensive non-combatants are injured, law and order threatened, and property destroyed, it becomes an edged tool that cuts both ways. This sort of terrorism is sincerely deplored by the labor leaders, for it has probably lost them as many strikes as have been lost by any other single cause.

The scab is powerless under terrorism. As a rule, he is not so good nor gritty a man as the men he is displacing, and he lacks their fighting organization. He stands in dire need of stiffening and backing. His employers, the capitalists, draw their two remaining weapons, the ownership of which is debatable, but which they for the time being happen to control. These two weapons may be called the political and judicial machinery of society. When the scab crumples up and is ready to go down before the fists, bricks, and bullets of the labor group, the capitalist group puts the police and soldiers into the field, and begins a general bombardment of injunctions. Victory usually follows, for the labor group cannot withstand the combined assault of gatling guns and injunctions.

But it has been noted that the ownership of the political and judicial machinery of society is debatable. In the Titanic struggle over the division of the joint product, each group reaches out for every available weapon. Nor are they blinded by the smoke of conflict. They fight their battles as coolly and collectedly as ever battles were fought on paper. The capitalist group has long since realized the immense importance of controlling the political and judicial machinery of society. Taught by gatlings and injunctions, which have smashed many an otherwise successful strike, the labor group is beginning to realize that it all depends upon who is behind and who is before the gatlings and the injunctions. And he who knows the labor movement knows that there is slowly growing up and being formulated a clear and definite policy for the capture of the political and judicial machinery.

This is the terrible spectre which Mr. John Graham Brooks sees looming portentously over the twentieth century world. No man may boast a more intimate knowledge of the labor movement than he; and he reiterates again and again the dangerous likelihood of the whole labor group capturing the political machinery of society. As he says in his recent book:[1] "It is not probable that employers can destroy unionism in the United States. Adroit and desperate attempts will, however, be made, if we mean by unionism the undisciplined and aggressive fact of vigorous and determined organizations. If capital should prove too strong in this struggle, the result is easy to predict. The employers have only to convince organized labor that it cannot hold its own against the capitalist manager, and the whole energy that now goes to the union will turn to an aggressive political socialism. It will not be the

[1] *The Social Unrest*. Macmillan Company.

harmless sympathy with increased city and state functions which trade unions already feel; it will become a turbulent political force bent upon using every weapon of taxation against the rich."

This struggle not to be a scab, to avoid giving more for less and to succeed in giving less for more, is more vital than it would appear on the surface. The capitalist and labor groups are locked together in desperate battle, and neither side is swayed by moral considerations more than skin-deep. The labor group hires business agents, lawyers, and organizers, and is beginning to intimidate legislators by the strength of its solid vote; and more directly, in the near future, it will attempt to control legislation by capturing it bodily through the ballot-box. On the other hand, the capitalist group, numerically weaker, hires newspapers, universities, and legislatures, and strives to bend to its need all the forces which go to mould public opinion.

The only honest morality displayed by either side is white-hot indignation at the iniquities of the other side. The striking teamster complacently takes a scab driver into an alley, and with an iron bar breaks his arms, so that he can drive no more, but cries out to high Heaven for justice when the capitalist breaks his skull by means of a club in the hands of a policeman. Nay, the members of a union will declaim in impassioned rhetoric for the God-given right of an eight-hour day, and at the time be working their own business agent seventeen hours out of the twenty-four.

A capitalist such as Collis P. Huntington, and his name is Legion, after a long life spent in buying the aid of countless legislatures, will wax virtuously wrathful, and condemn in unmeasured terms "the dangerous tendency of crying out to the Government for aid" in the way of labor legislation. Without a quiver, a member of the capitalist group will run tens of thousands of pitiful child-laborers through his life-destroying cotton factories, and weep maudlin and constitutional tears over one scab hit in the back with a brick. He will drive a "compulsory" free contract with an unorganized laborer on the basis of a starvation wage, saying, "Take it or leave it," knowing that to leave it means to die of hunger, and in the next breath, when the organizer entices that laborer into a union, will storm patriotically about the inalienable right of all men to work. In short, the chief moral concern of either side is with the morals of the other side. They are not in the business for their moral welfare, but to achieve the enviable position of the non-scab who gets more than he gives.

But there is more to the question than has yet been discussed. The labor scab is no more detestable to his brother laborers than is the capitalist scab to his brother capitalists. A capitalist may get most for least in dealing with his laborers, and in so far be a non-scab; but at the same time, in his dealings with his fellow-capitalists, he may give most for least and be the very worst kind of scab. The most heinous crime an employer of labor can commit is to scab on his fellow-employers of labor. Just as the individual laborers have organized into groups to protect themselves from the peril of the scab laborer, so have the employers organized into groups to protect themselves from the peril of the scab employer. The employers' federations, associations, and trusts are nothing more nor less than unions. They are organized to destroy scabbing amongst themselves and to encourage scabbing amongst others. For this reason they pool interests, determine prices, and present an unbroken and aggressive front to the labor group.

As has been said before, nobody likes to play the compulsorily generous rôle of scab. It is a bad business proposition on the face of it. And it is patent that there would be no capitalist scabs if there were not more capital than there is work for capital to do. When there are enough factories in existence to supply, with occasional stoppages, a certain commodity, the building of new factories by a rival concern, for the production of that commodity, is plain advertisement that that capital is out of a job. The first act of this new aggregation of capital will be to cut prices, to give more for less,—in short to scab, to strike at the very existence of the less generous aggregation of capital the work of which it is trying to do.

No scab capitalist strives to give more for less for any other reason than that he hopes, by undercutting a competitor and driving that competitor out of the market, to get that market and its profits for himself. His ambition is to achieve the day when he shall stand alone in the field both as buyer and seller,—when he will be the royal non-scab, buying most for least, selling least for most, and reducing all about him, the small buyers and sellers, (the consumers and the laborers), to a general condition of scabdom. This, for example, has been the history of Mr. Rockefeller and the Standard Oil Company. Through all the sordid villanies of scabdom he has passed, until to-day he is a most regal non-scab. However, to continue in this enviable position, he must be prepared at a moment's notice to go scabbing again. And he is prepared. Whenever a competitor arises, Mr. Rockefeller changes about from giving least for most and gives most for least with such a vengeance as to drive the competitor out of existence.

The banded capitalists discriminate against a scab capitalist by refusing him trade advantages, and by combining against him in most relentless fashion. The banded laborers, discriminating against a scab laborer in more primitive fashion, with a club, are no more merciless than the banded capitalists.

Mr. Casson tells of a New York capitalist who withdrew from the Sugar Union several years ago and became a scab. He was worth something like twenty millions of dollars. But the Sugar Union, standing shoulder to shoulder with the Railroad Union and several other unions, beat him to his knees till he cried "Enough." So frightfully did they beat him that he was obliged to turn over to his creditors his home, his chickens, and his gold watch. In point of fact, he was as thoroughly bludgeoned by the Federation of Capitalist Unions as ever scab workman was bludgeoned by a labor union. The intent in either case is the same,—to destroy the scab's producing power. The labor scab with concussion of the brain is put out of business, and so is the capitalist scab who has lost all his dollars down to his chickens and his watch.

But the rôle of scab passes beyond the individual. Just as individuals scab on other individuals, so do groups scab on other groups. And the principle involved is precisely the same as in the case of the simple labor scab. A group, in the nature of its organization, is often compelled to give most for least, and, so doing, to strike at the life of another group. At the present moment all Europe is appalled by that colossal scab, the United States. And Europe is clamorous with agitation for a Federation of National Unions to protect her from the United States. It may be remarked, in passing, that in its prime essentials this agitation in no wise differs from the trade-union agitation among workmen in any industry. The trouble is caused by the scab who is giving most for least. The result of the American scab's nefarious actions will be to strike at the food and shelter of Europe. The way for Europe to protect herself is to quit bickering among her parts and to form a union against the scab. And if the union is formed, armies and navies may be expected to be brought into play in fashion similar to the bricks and clubs in ordinary labor struggles.

In this connection, and as one of many walking delegates for the nations, M. Leroy-Beaulieu, the noted French economist, may well be quoted. In a letter to the Vienna *Tageblatt*, he advocates an economic alliance among the Continental nations for the purpose of barring out American goods, an economic alliance, in his own language, *"which may possibly and desirably develop into a political alliance."*

It will be noted, in the utterances of the Continental walking delegates, that, one and all, they leave England out of the proposed union. And in England herself the feeling is growing that her days are numbered if she cannot unite for offence and defence with the great American scab. As Andrew Carnegie said some time ago, "The only course for Great Britain seems to be reunion with her grandchild or sure decline to a secondary place, and then to comparative insignificance in the future annals of the English-speaking race."

Cecil Rhodes, speaking of what would have obtained but for the pig-headedness of George III, and of what will obtain when England and the United States are united, said, *"No cannon would . . . be fired on either hemisphere but by permission of the English race."* It would seem that England, fronted by the hostile Continental Union and flanked by the great American scab, has nothing left but to join with the scab and play the historic labor rôle of armed Pinkerton. Granting the words of Cecil Rhodes, the United States would be enabled to scab without let or hindrance on Europe, while England, as professional strike-breaker and policeman, destroyed the unions and kept order.

All this may appear fantastic and erroneous, but there is in it a soul of truth vastly more significant than it may seem. Civilization may be expressed to-day in terms of trade-unionism. Individual struggles have largely passed away, but group-struggles increase prodigiously. And the things for which the groups struggle are the same as of old. Shorn of all subtleties and complexities, the chief struggle of men, and of groups of men, is for food and shelter. And, as of old they struggled with tooth and nail, so to-day they struggle with teeth and nails elongated into armies and navies, machines, and economic advantages.

Under the definition that a scab is *one who gives more value for the same price than another*, it would seem that society can be generally divided into the two classes of the scabs and the non-scabs. But on closer investigation, however, it will be seen that the non-scab is a vanishing quantity. In the social jungle, everybody is preying upon everybody else. As in the case of Mr. Rockefeller, he who was a scab yesterday is a non-scab to-day, and to-morrow may be a scab again.

The woman stenographer or bookkeeper who receives forty dollars per month where a man was receiving seventy-five is a scab. So is the woman who does a man's work at a weaving-machine, and the child who goes into the mill or factory. And the father, who is scabbed out of work by the wives and children of other men, sends his own wife and children to scab in order to save himself.

When a publisher offers an author better royalties than other publishers have been paying him, he is scabbing on those other publishers. The reporter on a newspaper, who feels he should be receiving a larger salary for his work, says so, and is shown the door, is replaced by a reporter who is a scab; whereupon, when the belly-need presses, the displaced reporter goes to another paper and scabs himself. The minister who hardens his heart to a call, and waits for a certain congregation to offer him say $500 a year more, often finds himself scabbed upon by another and more impecunious minister; and the next time it is *his* turn to scab while a brother minister is hardening his heart to a call. The scab is everywhere. The professional strike-breakers, who as a class receive large wages, will scab on one another, while scab unions are even formed to prevent scabbing upon scabs.

There are non-scabs, but they are usually born so, and are protected by the whole might of society in the possession of their food and shelter. King Edward is such a type, as are all individuals who receive hereditary food-and-shelter privileges,—such as the present Duke of Bedford, for instance, who yearly receives $75,000 from the good people of London because some former king gave some former ancestor of his the market privileges of Covent Garden. The irresponsible rich are likewise non-scabs,—and by them is meant that coupon-clipping class which hires its managers and brains to invest the money usually left it by its ancestors.

Outside these lucky creatures, all the rest, at one time or another in their lives, are scabs, at one time or another are engaged in giving more for a certain price than any one else. The meek professor in some endowed institution, by his meek suppression of his convictions, is giving more for his salary than gave the other and more outspoken professor whose chair he occupies. And when a political party dangles a full dinner-pail in the eyes of the toiling masses, it is offering more for a vote than the dubious dollar of the opposing party. Even a money-lender is not above taking a slightly lower rate of interest and saying nothing about it.

Such is the tangle of conflicting interests in a tooth-and-nail society that people cannot avoid being scabs, are often made so against their desires, and are often unconsciously made so. When several trades in a certain locality demand and receive an advance in wages, they are unwittingly making scabs of their fellow-laborers in that district who have received no advance in wages. In San Francisco the barbers, laundry-workers, and milk-wagon drivers received such an advance in wages. Their employers promptly added the amount of this advance to the selling price of their wares. The price of shaves, of washing, and of milk went up. This reduced the purchasing power of the unorganized laborers, and, in point of fact, reduced their wages and made them greater scabs.

Because the British laborer is disinclined to scab,—that is, because he restricts his output in order to give less for the wage he receives,—it is to a certain extent made possible for the American capitalist, who receives a less restricted output from his laborers, to play the scab on the English capitalist. As a result of this, (of course combined with other causes), the American capitalist and the American laborer are striking at the food and shelter of the English capitalist and laborer.

The English laborer is starving to-day because, among other things, he is not a scab. He practises the policy of "ca' canny," which may be defined as "go easy." In order to get most for least, in many trades he performs but from one-fourth to one-sixth of the labor he is well able to perform. An instance of this is found in the building of the Westinghouse Electric Works at Manchester. The British limit per man was 400 bricks per day. The Westinghouse Company imported a "driving" American contractor, aided by half a dozen "driving" American foremen, and the British bricklayer swiftly attained an average of 1800 bricks per day, with a maximum of 2500 bricks for the plainest work.

But the British laborer's policy of "ca' canny," which is the very honorable one of giving least for most, and which is likewise the policy of the English capitalist, is nevertheless frowned upon by the English capitalist, whose business existence is threatened by the great American scab. From the rise of the factory system, the English capitalist gladly embraced the opportunity, wherever he found it, of giving least for most. He did it all over the world whenever he enjoyed a market monopoly, and he did it at home with the laborers employed in his mills, destroying them like flies till prevented, within limits, by the passage of the Factory Acts. Some of the proudest fortunes of England to-day may trace their origin to the giving of least for most to the miserable slaves of the factory towns. But at the present time the English capitalist is outraged because his laborers are employing against him precisely the same policy he employed against them, and which he would employ again did the chance present itself.

Yet "ca' canny" is a disastrous thing to the British laborer. It has driven ship-building from England to Scotland, bottle-making from Scotland to Belgium, flint-glass-making from England to Germany, and to-day is steadily driving industry after industry to other countries. A correspondent from

Northampton wrote not long ago: "Factories are working half and third time. . . . There is no strike, there is no real labor trouble, but the masters and men are alike suffering from sheer lack of employment. Markets which were once theirs are now American." It would seem that the unfortunate British laborer is 'twixt the devil and the deep sea. If he gives most for least, he faces a frightful slavery such as marked the beginning of the factory system. If he gives least for most, he drives industry away to other countries and has no work at all.

But the union laborers of the United States have nothing of which to boast, while, according to their trade-union ethics, they have a great deal of which to be ashamed. They passionately preach short hours and big wages, the shorter the hours and the bigger the wages the better. Their hatred for a scab is as terrible as the hatred of a patriot for a traitor, of a Christian for a Judas. And in the face of all this, they are as colossal scabs as the United States is a colossal scab. For all of their boasted unions and high labor ideals, they are about the most thoroughgoing scabs on the planet.

Receiving $4.50 per day, because of his proficiency and immense working power, the American laborer has been known to scab upon scabs (so called) who took his place and received only $0.90 per day for a longer day. In this particular instance, five Chinese coolies, working longer hours, gave less value for the price received from their employer than did one American laborer.

It is upon his brother laborers overseas that the American laborer most outrageously scabs. As Mr. Casson has shown, an English nail-maker gets $3 per week, while an American nail-maker gets $30. But the English worker turns out 200 pounds of nails per week, while the American turns out 5500 pounds. If he were as "fair" as his English brother, other things being equal, he would be receiving, at the English worker's rate of pay, $82.50. As it is, he is scabbing upon his English brother to the tune of $79.50 per week. Dr. Schultze-Gaevernitz has shown that a German weaver produces 466 yards of cotton a week at a cost of .303 per yard, while an American weaver produces 1200 yards at a cost of .02 per yard.

But, it may be objected, a great part of this is due to the more improved American machinery. Very true, but none the less a great part is still due to the superior energy, skill, and willingness of the American laborer. The English laborer is faithful to the policy of "ca' canny." He refuses point-blank to get the work out of a machine that the New World scab gets out of a machine. Mr. Maxim, observing a wasteful hand-labor process in his English factory, invented a machine which he proved capable of displacing several men. But workman after workman was put at the machine, and without exception they turned out neither more nor less than a workman turned out by hand. They obeyed the mandate of the union and went easy, while Mr. Maxim gave up in despair. Nor will the British workman run machines at as high speed as the American, nor will he run so many. An American workman will "give equal attention simultaneously to three, four, or six machines or tools, while the British workman is compelled by his trade union to limit his attention to one, so that employment may be given to half a dozen men."

But, for scabbing, no blame attaches itself anywhere. With rare exceptions, all the people in the world are scabs. The strong, capable workman gets a job and holds it because of his strength and capacity. And he holds it because out of his strength and capacity he gives a better value for his wage than does the weaker and less capable workman. Therefore he is scabbing upon his weaker and less capable brother workman. He is giving more value for the price paid by the employer.

The superior workman scabs upon the inferior workman because he is so constituted and cannot help it. The one, by fortune of birth and upbringing, is strong and capable; the other, by fortune of birth and upbringing, is not so strong nor capable. It is for the same reason that one country scabs upon another. That country which has the good fortune to possess great natural resources, a finer sun and soil, unhampering institutions, and a deft and intelligent labor class and capitalist class is bound to scab upon a country less fortunately situated. It is the good fortune of the United States that is making her the colossal scab, just as it is the good fortune of one man to be born with a straight back while his brother is born with a hump.

It is not good to give most for least, not good to be a scab. The word has gained universal opprobrium. On the other hand, to be a non-scab, to give least for most, is universally branded as stingy, selfish, and unchristian-like. So all the world, like the British workman, is 'twixt the devil and the deep sea. It is treason to one's fellows to scab, it is unchristian-like not to scab.

Since to give least for most, and to give most for least, are universally bad, what remains? Equity remains, which is to give like for like, the same for the same, neither more nor less. But this equity, society, as at present constituted, cannot give. It is not in the nature of present-day society for men to give like for like, the same for the same. And so long as men continue to live in this competitive society, struggling tooth and nail with one another for food and shelter, (which is to struggle tooth and nail with one another for life), that long will the scab continue to exist. His will "to live" will force him to exist. He may be flouted and jeered by his brothers, he may be beaten with bricks and clubs by the men who by superior strength and capacity scab upon him as he scabs upon them by longer hours and smaller wages, but through it all he will persist, giving a bit more of most for least than they are giving.

"The Jungle"

"At first, this Earth, a stage so gloomed with woe
You all but sicken at the shifting of the scenes.
And yet be patient. Our Playwright may show
In some fifth Act what this Wild Drama means."

WHEN JOHN BURNS, the great English labor leader and present member of the Cabinet, visited Chicago, he was asked by a reporter for his opinion of that city. "Chicago," he answered, "is a pocket edition of hell." Some time later, when Burns was going aboard his steamer to sail to England, he was approached by another reporter, who wanted to know if he had yet changed his opinion of Chicago. "Yes, I have," was the prompt reply. "My present opinion is that hell is a pocket edition of Chicago."

Possibly Upton Sinclair was of the same opinion when he selected Chicago for the scene of his novel of industry, "The Jungle." At any rate, he selected the greatest industrial city in the country, the one city of the country that is ripest industrially, that is the most perfect specimen of jungle-civilization to be found. One cannot question the wisdom of the author's choice, for Chicago certainly is industrialism incarnate, the storm-center of the conflict between capital and labor, a city of street battles and blood, with a class-conscious capitalist organization and a class-conscious workman organization, where the school teachers are formed into labor unions and are affiliated with the hod carriers and bricklayers of the American Federation of Labor, where the very office clerks rain office furniture out of the windows of the sky-scrapers upon the heads of the police who are trying to deliver scab meat in a beef strike, and where practically as many policemen as strikers are carried away in the ambulances.

This, then, is the scene of Upton Sinclair's novel, Chicago, the industrial jungle of twentieth century civilization. And right here it may be just as well to forestall the legions who will rise up and say that the book is untrue. In the first place, Upton Sinclair himself says: "The book is a true book, true in substance and in detail, an exact and faithful picture of the life with which it deals."

Nevertheless, and in spite of the intrinsic evidence of truth, there will be many who will call "The Jungle" a tissue of lies, and first among them may be expected the Chicago newspapers. They are quick to resent the bald truth about their beloved city. Not more than three months ago, a public speaker, in New York City, instancing extreme cases of the smallness of wage in the Chicago sweat shops, spoke of women receiving ninety cents per week. He was promptly called a liar by the Chicago newspapers—all except one paper, that really investigated, and that found not only many who were receiving no more than ninety cents per week, but found some receiving as low as fifty cents per week.

For that matter, when the New York publishers of "The Jungle" first read it, they sent it on to the editor of one of the largest Chicago newspapers, and that gentleman's written opinion was that Upton Sinclair was "the damndest liar in the United States." Then the publishers called Upton Sinclair upon the carpet. He gave his authorities. The publishers were still dubious—no doubt worried by visions of bankrupting libel suits. They wanted to make sure. They sent a lawyer to Chicago to investigate. And after a week or so the lawyer's report came back to the effect that Sinclair had left the worst untold.

Then the book was published, and here it is, a story of human destruction, of poor broken cogs in the remorseless grind of the industrial machine. It is essentially a book of to-day. It is alive and warm. It is brutal with life. It is written of sweat and blood, and groans and tears. It depicts, not what man ought to be, but what man is compelled to be in this, our world, in the twentieth century. It depicts, not what our country ought to be, nor what our country seems to be to those who live in softness and comfort far from the labor-ghetto, but it depicts what our country really is, the home of oppression and injustice, a nightmare of misery, an inferno of suffering, a jungle wherein wild beasts eat and are eaten.

and set to work. Jurgis was the one workingman in a thousand. There were men in that crowd who had stood there
every day for a month. They were of the nine hundred and
ninety-nine.

Jurgis was prosperous. He was getting seventeen and one-
half cents per hour, and just then it happened that he worked
many hours. The next thing he did needed no urging from
President Roosevelt. With the joy of youth in his blood and
the cornucopia of prosperity spilling over him, he got married. "It was the supreme hour of ecstacy in the life of one of
God's gentlest creatures, the wedding feast and the joy trans-
figuration of little Ona Lukozaite."

Jurgis worked on the killing floor, wading through the
steaming blood that flowed upon the floor, with a street
sweeper's broom sweeping the smoking entrails into a trap as
fast as they were drawn from the carcasses of the steers. But
he did not mind. He was wildly happy. He proceeded to buy
a house—on the installment plan.

Why pay rent when one could buy a house for less? That
was what the advertisement asked. "And why, indeed?" was
what Jurgis asked. There were quite a number in the combined families of Jurgis and Ona, and they studied the house
proposition long and carefully, and then paid all their old
country savings (three hundred dollars) down, agreeing to
pay twelve dollars per month until the balance of twelve
hundred was paid. Then the house would be theirs. Until
such time, according to the contract that was foisted on them,
they would be renters. Failure to pay an installment would
lose for them all they had already paid. And in the end they
lost the three hundred dollars and the rent and interest they
had paid, because the house was built, not as a home, but as
a gamble on misfortune, and resold many times to just such
simple folk as they.

In the meantime Jurgis worked and learned. He began to
see things and to understand. He saw "How there were portions of the work which determined the pace of the rest, and
for these they had picked out men whom they paid high
wages, and whom they changed frequently. This was called
'speeding up the gang,' and if any man could not keep up
with the pace, there were hundreds outside begging to try."

For a hero, Upton Sinclair did not select an American-born man, who, through the mists of Fourth of July oratory and campaign spellbinding, sees clearly in a way the ferocious facts of the American workingman's life. Upton Sinclair made no such mistake. He selected a foreigner, a Lithuanian, fleeing from the oppression and injustice of Europe and dreaming of liberty and freedom and equal rights with all men in the pursuit of happiness.

This Lithuanian was one Jurgis (pronounced Yoorghis), a young giant, broad of back, spilling over with vigor, passionately enamored of work, ambitious, a workingman in a thousand. He was the sort of a man that can set a work-pace that is heart-breaking and soul-killing to the men who work beside him and who must keep his pace despite the fact that they are weaklings compared with him.

In short, Jurgis was "the sort the bosses like to get hold of, the sort they make it a grievance they cannot get hold of." Jurgis was indomitable. This was because of his mighty muscles and superb health. No matter what the latest misfortune that fell upon him, he squared his shoulders and said, "Never mind, I will work harder." That was his clarion cry, his Excelsior! "Never mind, I will work harder!" He had no thought of the time to come when his muscles would not be so mighty, nor his health so superb, and when he would not be able to work harder.

On his second day in Chicago he stood in the crowd at the gates of the packing-houses. "All day long these gates were besieged by starving and penniless men; they came, literally, by the thousands every single morning, fighting with each other for a chance for life. Blizzards and cold made no difference to them, they were always on hand; they were on hand two hours before the sun rose, an hour before the work began. Sometimes their faces froze, sometimes their feet a· their hands—but still they came, for they had no other p' to go."

But Jurgis stood only half an hour in this crowd. H⸳ shoulders, his youth and health and unsullied marked him out in the crowd like a virgin in the many hags. For he was a labor-virgin, his magni⸍ yet unbroken by toil, and he was quickly picked ⸜

He saw that "the bosses grafted off the men, and they grafted off each other, while the superintendents grafted off the bosses. Here was Durham's, owned by a man who was trying to make as much money of it as he could, and did not care in the least how he did it; and underneath, ranged in ranks and grades like an army, were managers, superintendents and foremen, each man driving the man next below him and trying to squeeze out of him as much work as possible. And all the men of the same rank were pitted against each other; the accounts of each were kept separately, and every man lived in terror of losing his job if another made a better record than he. There was no loyalty or decency anywhere about it, there was no place in it where a man counted for anything against a dollar. The man who told tales and spied upon his fellow creatures would rise; but the man who minded his own business and did his work—why, they would 'speed him up' till they had worn him out, and then they would throw him into the gutter."

And why should the bosses have any care for the men. There were always plenty more. "One day Durham advertised in the paper for two hundred men to cut ice; and all that day the homeless and starving of the city came trudging through the snow from all of its two hundred square miles. That night forty score of them crowded into the station house of the stockyards district—they filled the rooms, sleeping on each other's laps, toboggan fashion, and they piled on top of one another in the corridors, till the police shut the doors and left some to freeze outside. On the morrow, before daybreak, there were three thousand at Durham's, and the police reserves had to be sent for to quell the riot. Then Durham's bosses picked out twenty of the biggest," and set them to work.

And the *accident* began to loom big to Jurgis. He began to live in fear of the accident. The thing, terrible as death, that was liable to happen any time. One of his friends, Mikolas, a beef-boner, had been laid up at home twice in three years with blood poisoning, once for three months and once for seven months.

Also, Jurgis saw how the "speeding up" made the accident more imminent. "In the winter time, on the killing floor, one was apt to be covered with blood, and it would freeze solid. The men would tie up their feet in newspapers and old sacks, and these would be soaked in blood and frozen. All of them that used knives were unable to wear gloves, and their arms would be white with frost, and their hands would grow numb, and then of course there would be accidents." Now and then, when the bosses were not looking, the men, for very relief from the cold, would plunge their feet and ankles into the steaming carcasses of the fresh-killed steers.

Another thing that Jurgis saw, and gathered from what was told him, was the procession of the nationalities. At one time "the workers had all been Germans. Afterwards, as cheaper labor came, these Germans had moved away. The next had been the Irish. The Bohemians had come then, and after them the Poles. The people had come in hordes; and old Durham had squeezed them tighter and tighter, speeding them up and grinding them to pieces. The Poles had been driven to the wall by the Lithuanians, and now the Lithuanians were giving way to the Slovaks. Who there was poorer and more misera-ble than the Slovaks, there was no telling; but the packers would find them, never fear. It was easy to bring them, for wages were really much higher, and it was only when it was too late that the poor people found out that everything else was higher, too."

Then there was the lie of society, or the countless lies, for Jurgis to learn. The food was adulterated, the milk for the children was doctored, the very insect-powder for which Jur-gis paid twenty-five cents was adulterated and harmless to in-sects. Under his house was a cesspool containing the sewage of fifteen years. "Jurgis went about with his soul full of sus-picion; he understood that he was environed by hostile pow-ers that were trying to get his money. The storekeepers plas-tered up their windows with all sorts of lies to entice him, the very fences by the wayside, the lamp-posts and telegraph poles were pasted over with lies. The great corporation that employed him lied to him, and lied to the whole country— from top to bottom it was nothing but one gigantic lie."

Work became slack, and Jurgis worked part time and learned what the munificent pay of seventeen and one-half cents per hour really meant. There were days when he worked no more than two hours, and days when there was no work at all. But he managed to average nearly six hours a day, which meant six dollars per week.

Then came to Jurgis that haunting thing of the labor world, the accident. It was only an injured ankle. He worked on it till he fainted. After that he spent three weeks in bed, went to work on it again too soon, and went back to bed for two months. By that time everybody in the combined families had to get to work. The children sold papers on the streets. Ona sewed hams all day long, and her cousin, Marija, painted cans. And little Stanislovas worked on a marvelous machine that almost did all the work. All Stanislovas had to do was to place an empty lard-can every time the arm of the machine reached out to him.

"And so was decided the place in the universe for little Stanislovas, and his destiny till the end of his days. Hour after hour, day after day, year after year, it was fated that he should stand on a certain square-foot of floor from seven in the morning until noon, and again from half-past twelve to half-past five, making never a motion and thinking never a thought, save for the setting of lard-cans." And for this he received something like three dollars per week, which was his proper share of the total earnings of the million and three-quarters of child laborers in the United States. And his wages a little more than paid the interest on the house.

And Jurgis lay on his back, helpless, starving, in order that the payments and interest on the house should be met. Because of this, when he got on his feet again he was no longer the finest-looking man in the crowd. He was thin and haggard, and he looked miserable. His old job was gone, and he joined the crowd at the gate, morning after morning, striving to keep to the front and to look eager.

"The peculiar bitterness of all this was that Jurgis saw so plainly the meaning of it. In the beginning he had been fresh and strong, and he had gotten a job the first day; but now he was second-hand, a damaged article, so to speak, and they did not want him. They had got the best out of him—they had worn him out, with their speeding up and their carelessness, and now they had thrown him away."

The situation was now desperate. Several of the family lost

their jobs, and Jurgis, as a last resort, descended into the inferno of the fertilizer-works and went to work. And then came another accident, of a different sort. Ona, his wife, was vilely treated by her foreman (too vilely treated for narration here), and Jurgis thrashed the foreman and was sent to jail. Both he and Ona lost their jobs.

In the working-class world, disasters do not come singly. The loss of the house followed the loss of the jobs. Because Jurgis had struck a boss he was blacklisted in all the packing-houses and could not even get back his job in the fertilizer works. The family was broken up, and its members went their various ways to living hell. The lucky ones died, such as Jurgis' father, who died of blood-poisoning, contracted by working in chemicals, and Jurgis' little son, Antanas, who was drowned in the street. (And in this connection I wish to say that this last is a fact. I have personally talked with a man in Chicago, a charity-worker, who buried the child drowned in the streets of Packingtown.)

And Jurgis, under the ban of the blacklist, mused thus: "There was no justice, there was no right, anywhere in it—it was only force, it was tyranny, the will and the power, reckless and unrestrained. They had ground him beneath their heel, they had devoured all his substance, they had murdered his old father, they had broken and wrecked his wife, they had crushed and cowed his whole family. And now they were through with him. They had no further use for him."

"The men gazed on him with pitying eyes—poor devil, he was blacklisted. He stood as much chance of getting a job in Packingtown as of being chosen Mayor of Chicago. They had his name on a secret list in every office, big and little, in the place. They had his name in St. Louis and New York, in Omaha and Boston, in Kansas City and St. Joseph. He was condemned and sentenced without trial and without appeal; he could never work for the packers again."

Nor does "The Jungle" end here. Jurgis lives to get on the inside of the rottenness and corruption of the industrial and political machinery; and of all that he sees and learns nothing less than the book itself can tell.

It is a book well worth the reading, and it is a book that

may well make history, as "Uncle Tom's Cabin" made history. For that matter, there are large chances that it may prove to be the "Uncle Tom's Cabin" of wage slavery. It is dedicated, not to a Huntington nor to a Carnegie, but to the Workingmen of America. It has truth and power, and it has behind it in the United States over four hundred thousand men and women who are striving to give it a wider hearing than any book has been given in fifty years. Not only may it become one of the "great sellers," but it is very likely to become the greatest seller. And yet, such is the strangeness of modern life, "The Jungle" may be read by the hundreds of thousands and by the millions of copies and yet not be listed as a "best seller" in the magazines. The reason for this will be that it will be read by the working-class, as it has already been read by hundreds of thousands of the working-class. Dear masters, would it not be wise to read for once the literature that all your working-class is reading?

Revolution

"The present is enough for common souls,
Who, never looking forward, are indeed
Mere clay, wherein the footprints of their age
Are petrified forever."

I RECEIVED a letter the other day. It was from a man in Arizona. It began, "Dear Comrade." It ended, "Yours for the Revolution." I replied to the letter, and my letter began, "Dear Comrade." It ended, "Yours for the Revolution." In the United States there are 400,000 men, of men and women nearly 1,000,000, who begin their letters "Dear Comrade," and end them "Yours for the Revolution." In Germany there are 3,000,000 men who begin their letters "Dear Comrade" and end them "Yours for the Revolution"; in France, 1,000,000 men; in Austria, 800,000 men; in Belgium, 300,000 men; in Italy, 250,000 men; in England, 100,000 men; in Switzerland, 100,000 men; in Denmark, 55,000 men; in Sweden, 50,000 men; in Holland, 40,000 men; in Spain, 30,000 men—comrades all, and revolutionists.

These are numbers which dwarf the grand armies of Napoleon and Xerxes. But they are numbers not of conquest and maintenance of the established order, but of conquest and revolution. They compose, when the roll is called, an army of 7,000,000 men, who, in accordance with the conditions of to-day, are fighting with all their might for the conquest of the wealth of the world and for the complete overthrow of existing society.

There has never been anything like this revolution in the history of the world. There is nothing analogous between it and the American Revolution or the French Revolution. It is unique, colossal. Other revolutions compare with it as asteroids compare with the sun. It is alone of its kind, the first world-revolution in a world whose history is replete with revolutions. And not only this, for it is the first organized movement of men to become a world movement, limited only by the limits of the planet.

This revolution is unlike all other revolutions in many respects. It is not sporadic. It is not a flame of popular discontent, arising in a day and dying down in a day. It is older than the present generation. It has a history and traditions, and a martyr-roll only less extensive possibly than the martyr-roll of Christianity. It has also a literature a myriad times more imposing, scientific, and scholarly than the literature of any previous revolution.

They call themselves "comrades," these men, comrades in the socialist revolution. Nor is the word empty and meaning-less, coined of mere lip service. It knits men together as brothers, as men should be knit together who stand shoulder to shoulder under the red banner of revolt. This red banner, by the way, symbolizes the brotherhood of man, and does not symbolize the incendiarism that instantly connects itself with the red banner in the affrighted bourgeois mind. The comradeship of the revolutionists is alive and warm. It passes over geographical lines, transcends race prejudice, and has even proved itself mightier than the Fourth of July, spread-eagle Americanism of our forefathers. The French socialist workingmen and the German socialist workingmen forget Al-sace and Lorraine, and, when war threatens, pass resolutions declaring that as workingmen and comrades they have no quarrel with each other. Only the other day, when Japan and Russia sprang at each other's throats, the revolutionists of Japan addressed the following message to the revolutionists of Russia: "Dear Comrades—Your government and ours have recently plunged into war to carry out their imperialistic tendencies, but for us socialists there are no boundaries, race, country, or nationality. We are comrades, brothers and sis-ters, and have no reason to fight. Your enemies are not the Japanese people, but our militarism and so-called patriotism. Patriotism and militarism are our mutual enemies."

In January, 1905, throughout the United States the social-ists held mass-meetings to express their sympathy for their struggling comrades, the revolutionists of Russia, and, more to the point, to furnish the sinews of war by collecting money and cabling it to the Russian leaders.

The fact of this call for money, and the ready response, and the very wording of the call, make a striking and practical demonstration of the international solidarity of this world revolution: "Whatever may be the immediate results of the present revolt in Russia, the socialist propaganda in that country has received from it an impetus unparalleled in the history of modern class wars. The heroic battle for freedom is being fought almost exclusively by the Russian working-class under the intellectual leadership of Russian socialists, thus once more demonstrating the fact that the class-conscious workingmen have become the vanguard of all liberating movements of modern times."

Here are 7,000,000 comrades in an organized, international, world-wide, revolutionary movement. Here is a tremendous human force. It must be reckoned with. Here is power. And here is romance—romance so colossal that it seems to be beyond the ken of ordinary mortals. These revolutionists are swayed by great passion. They have a keen sense of personal right, much of reverence for humanity, but little reverence, if any at all, for the rule of the dead. They refuse to be ruled by the dead. To the bourgeois mind their unbelief in the dominant conventions of the established order is startling. They laugh to scorn the sweet ideals and dear moralities of bourgeois society. They intend to destroy bourgeois society with most of its sweet ideals and dear moralities, and chiefest among these are those that group themselves under such heads as private ownership of capital, survival of the fittest, and patriotism—even patriotism.

Such an army of revolution, 7,000,000 strong, is a thing to make rulers and ruling classes pause and consider. The cry of this army is, "No quarter! We want all that you possess. We will be content with nothing less than all that you possess. We want in our hands the reins of power and the destiny of mankind. Here are our hands. They are strong hands. We are going to take your governments, your palaces, and all your purpled ease away from you, and in that day you shall work for your bread even as the peasant in the field or the starved and runty clerk in your metropolises. Here are our hands. They are strong hands."

Well may rulers and ruling classes pause and consider. This is revolution. And, further, these 7,000,000 men are not an army on paper. Their fighting strength in the field is 7,000,000. To-day they cast 7,000,000 votes in the civilized countries of the world.

Yesterday they were not so strong. To-morrow they will be still stronger. And they are fighters. They love peace. They are unafraid of war. They intend nothing less than to destroy existing capitalist society and to take possession of the whole world. If the law of the land permits, they fight for this end peaceably, at the ballot-box. If the law of the land does not permit, and if they have force meted out to them, they resort to force themselves. They meet violence with violence. Their hands are strong and they are unafraid. In Russia, for instance, there is no suffrage. The government executes the revolutionists. The revolutionists kill the officers of the government. The revolutionists meet legal murder with assassination.

Now here arises a particularly significant phase which would be well for the rulers to consider. Let me make it concrete. I am a revolutionist. Yet I am a fairly sane and normal individual. I speak, and I *think*, of these assassins in Russia as "my comrades." So do all the comrades in America, and all the 7,000,000 comrades in the world. Of what worth an organized, international, revolutionary movement if our comrades are not backed up the world over! The worth is shown by the fact that we do back up the assassinations by our comrades in Russia. They are not disciples of Tolstoy, nor are we. We are revolutionists.

Our comrades in Russia have formed what they call "The Fighting Organization." This Fighting Organization accused, tried, found guilty, and condemned to death, one Sipiaguin, Minister of Interior. On April 2 he was shot and killed in the Maryinsky Palace. Two years later the Fighting Organization condemned to death and executed another Minister of Interior, Von Plehve. Having done so, it issued a document, dated July 29, 1904, setting forth the counts of its indictment of Von Plehve and its responsibility for the assassination. Now, and to the point, this document was sent out to the socialists of the world, and by them was published everywhere in the magazines and newspapers. The point is, not that the socialists of the world were unafraid to do it, not that they dared to do it, but that they did it as a matter of routine, giving publication to what may be called an official document of the international revolutionary movement.

These are high lights upon the revolution—granted, but they are also facts. And they are given to the rulers and the ruling classes, not in bravado, not to frighten them, but for them to consider more deeply the spirit and nature of this world revolution. The time has come for the revolution to demand consideration. It has fastened upon every civilized country in the world. As fast as a country becomes civilized, the revolution fastens upon it. With the introduction of the machine into Japan, socialism was introduced. Socialism marched into the Philippines shoulder to shoulder with the American soldiers. The echoes of the last gun had scarcely died away when socialist locals were forming in Cuba and Porto Rico. Vastly more significant is the fact that of all the countries the revolution has fastened upon, on not one has it relaxed its grip. On the contrary, on every country its grip closes tighter year by year. As an active movement it began obscurely over a generation ago. In 1867, its voting strength in the world was 30,000. By 1871, its vote had increased to 100,000. Not till 1884 did it pass the half-million point. By 1889, it had passed the million point. It had then gained momentum. In 1892 the socialist vote of the world was 1,798,391; in 1893, 2,585,898; in 1895, 3,033,718; in 1898, 4,515,591; in 1902, 5,253,054; in 1903, 6,285,374; and in the year of our Lord 1905 it passed the seven-million mark.

Nor has this flame of revolution left the United States untouched. In 1888, there were only 2,068 socialist votes. In 1902, there were 127,713 socialist votes. And in 1904, 435,040 socialist votes were cast. What fanned this flame? Not hard times. The first four years of the twentieth century were considered prosperous years, yet in that time more than 300,000 men added themselves to the ranks of the revolutionists, flinging their defiance in the teeth of bourgeois society and taking their stand under the blood-red banner. In the state of the writer, California, one man in twelve is an avowed and registered revolutionist.

One thing must be clearly understood. This is no spontaneous and vague uprising of a large mass of discontented and miserable people—a blind and instinctive recoil from hurt.

On the contrary, the propaganda is intellectual; the movement is based upon economic necessity and is in line with
social evolution; while the miserable people have not yet revolted. The revolutionist is no starved and diseased slave in
the shambles at the bottom of the social pit, but is, in the
main, a hearty, well-fed workingman, who sees the shambles
waiting for him and his children and recoils from the descent.
The very miserable people are too helpless to help themselves.
But they are being helped, and the day is not far distant when
their numbers will go to swell the ranks of the revolutionists.

Another thing must be clearly understood. In spite of the
fact that middle-class men and professional men are interested
in the movement, it is nevertheless a distinctly working-class
revolt. The world over, it is a working-class revolt. The workers of the world, as a class, are fighting the capitalists of the
world, as a class. The so-called great middle class is a growing
anomaly in the social struggle. It is a perishing class (wily
statisticians to the contrary), and its historic mission of buffer
between the capitalist- and working-classes has just about
been fulfilled. Little remains for it but to wail as it passes into
oblivion, as it has already begun to wail in accents Populistic
and Jeffersonian-Democratic. The fight is on. The revolution
is here now, and it is the world's workers that are in revolt.

Naturally the question arises: Why is this so? No mere
whim of the spirit can give rise to a world revolution. Whim
does not conduce to unanimity. There must be a deep-seated
cause to make 7,000,000 men of the one mind, to make them
cast off allegiance to the bourgeois gods and lose faith in so
fine a thing as patriotism. There are many counts of the indictment which the revolutionists bring against the capitalist
class, but for present use only one need be stated, and it is a
count to which capital has never replied and can never reply.

The capitalist class has managed society, and its management has failed. And not only has it failed in its management,
but it has failed deplorably, ignobly, horribly. The capitalist
class had an opportunity such as was vouchsafed no previous
ruling class in the history of the world. It broke away from
the rule of the old feudal aristocracy and made modern society. It mastered matter, organized the machinery of life, and
made possible a wonderful era for mankind, wherein no crea-

ture should cry aloud because it had not enough to eat, and wherein for every child there would be opportunity for education, for intellectual and spiritual uplift. Matter being mastered, and the machinery of life organized, all this was possible. Here was the chance, God-given, and the capitalist class failed. It was blind and greedy. It prattled sweet ideals and dear moralities, rubbed its eyes not once, nor ceased one whit in its greediness, and smashed down in a failure as tremendous only as was the opportunity it had ignored.

But all this is like so much cobwebs to the bourgeois mind. As it was blind in the past, it is blind now and cannot see nor understand. Well, then, let the indictment be stated more definitely, in terms sharp and unmistakable. In the first place, consider the caveman. He was a very simple creature. His head slanted back like an orang-utan's and he had but little more intelligence. He lived in a hostile environment, the prey of all manner of fierce life. He had no inventions nor artifices. His natural efficiency for food-getting was, say, 1. He did not even till the soil. With his natural efficiency of 1, he fought off his carnivorous enemies and got himself food and shelter. He must have done all this, else he would not have multiplied and spread over the earth and sent his progeny down, generation by generation, to become even you and me.

The caveman, with his natural efficiency of 1, got enough to eat most of the time, and no caveman went hungry all the time. Also, he lived a healthy, open-air life, loafed and rested himself, and found plenty of time in which to exercise his imagination and invent gods. That is to say, he did not have to work all his waking moments in order to get enough to eat. The child of the caveman (and this is true of the children of all savage peoples) had a childhood, and by that is meant a happy childhood of play and development.

And now, how fares modern man? Consider the United States, the most prosperous and most enlightened country of the world. In the United States there are 10,000,000 people living in poverty. By poverty is meant that condition in life in which, through lack of food and adequate shelter, the mere standard of working efficiency cannot be maintained. In the United States there are 10,000,000 people who have not enough to eat. In the United States, because they have not enough to eat, there are 10,000,000 people who cannot keep the ordinary measure of strength in their bodies. This means that these 10,000,000 people are perishing, are dying, body and soul, slowly, because they have not enough to eat. All over this broad, prosperous, enlightened land, are men, women, and children who are living miserably. In all the great cities, where they are segregated in slum ghettos by hundreds of thousands and by millions, their misery becomes beastliness. No caveman ever starved as chronically as they starve, ever slept as vilely as they sleep, ever festered with rottenness and disease as they fester, nor ever toiled as hard and for as long hours as they toil.

In Chicago there is a woman who toiled sixty hours per week. She was a garment worker. She sewed buttons on clothes. Among the Italian garment workers of Chicago, the average weekly wage of the dressmakers is 90 cents, but they work every week in the year. The average weekly wage of the pants finishers is $1.31, and the average number of weeks employed in the year is 27.85. The average yearly earnings of the dressmakers is $37.00, of the pants finishers, $42.41. Such wages means no childhood for the children, beastliness of living, and starvation for all.

Unlike the caveman, modern man cannot get food and shelter whenever he feels like working for it. Modern man has first to find the work, and in this he is often unsuccessful. Then misery becomes acute. This acute misery is chronicled daily in the newspapers. Let several of the countless instances be cited.

In New York City lived a woman, Mary Mead. She had three children: Mary, one year old; Johanna, two years old; Alice, four years old. Her husband could find no work. They starved. They were evicted from their shelter at 160 Steuben Street. Mary Mead strangled her baby, Mary, one year old; strangled Alice, four years old; failed to strangle Johanna, two years old, and then herself took poison. Said the father to the police: "Constant poverty had driven my wife insane. We lived at No. 160 Steuben Street until a week ago, when we were dispossessed. I could get no work. I could not even make enough to put food into our mouths. The babies grew ill and weak. My wife cried nearly all the time."

"So overwhelmed is the Department of Charities with tens of thousands of applications from men out of work that it finds itself unable to cope with the situation."—*New York Commercial*, January 11, 1905.

In a daily paper, because he cannot get work in order to get something to eat, modern man advertises as follows:—

"Young man, good education, unable to obtain employment, will sell to physician and bacteriologist for experimental purposes all right and title to his body. Address for price, box 3466, *Examiner*."

"Frank A. Mallin went to the central police station Wednesday night and asked to be locked up on a charge of vagrancy. He said he had been conducting an unsuccessful search for work for so long that he was sure he must be a vagrant. In any event, he was so hungry he must be fed. Police Judge Graham sentenced him to ninety days' imprisonment."—*San Francisco Examiner*.

In a room at the Soto House, 32 Fourth Street, San Francisco, was found the body of W. G. Robbins. He had turned on the gas. Also was found his diary, from which the following extracts are made:—

"March 3.—No chance of getting anything here. What will I do?

"March 7.—Cannot find anything yet.

"March 8.—Am living on doughnuts at five cents a day.

"March 9.—My last quarter gone for room rent.

"March 10.—God help me. Have only five cents left. Can get nothing to do. What next? Starvation or—? I have spent my last nickel to-night. What shall I do? Shall it be steal, beg, or die? I have never stolen, begged, or starved in all my fifty years of life, but now I am on the brink—death seems the only refuge.

"March 11.—Sick all day—burning fever this afternoon. Had nothing to eat to-day or since yesterday noon. My head, my head. Good-by, all."

How fares the child of modern man in this most prosperous of lands? In the city of New York 50,000 children go hungry to school every morning. From the same city on January 12, a press despatch was sent out over the country of a case reported by Dr. A. E. Daniel, of the New York Infirmary for Women and Children. The case was that of a babe, eighteen months old, who earned by its labor fifty cents per week in a tenement sweat-shop.

"On a pile of rags in a room bare of furniture and freezing cold, Mrs. Mary Gallin, dead from starvation, with an emaciated baby four months old crying at her breast, was found this morning at 513 Myrtle Avenue, Brooklyn, by Policeman McConnon of the Flushing Avenue Station. Huddled together for warmth in another part of the room were the father, James Gallin, and three children ranging from two to eight years of age. The children gazed at the policeman much as ravenous animals might have done. They were famished, and there was not a vestige of food in their comfortless home."—*New York Journal*, January 2, 1902.

In the United States 80,000 children are toiling out their lives in the textile mills alone. In the South they work twelve-hour shifts. They never see the day. Those on the night shift are asleep when the sun pours its life and warmth over the world, while those on the day shift are at the machines before dawn and return to their miserable dens, called "homes," after dark. Many receive no more than ten cents a day. There are babies who work for five and six cents a day. Those who work on the night shift are often kept awake by having cold water dashed in their faces. There are children six years of age who have already to their credit eleven months' work on the night shift. When they become sick, and are unable to rise from their beds to go to work, there are men employed to go on horseback from house to house, and cajole and bully them into arising and going to work. Ten per cent of them contract active consumption. All are puny wrecks, distorted, stunted, mind and body. Elbert Hubbard says of the child-laborers of the Southern cotton-mills:—

"I thought to lift one of the little toilers to ascertain his weight. Straightaway through his thirty-five pounds of skin and bones there ran a tremor of fear, and he struggled forward to tie a broken thread. I attracted his attention by a touch, and offered him a silver dime. He looked at me dumbly from a face that might have belonged to a man of sixty, so furrowed, tightly drawn, and full of pain it was. He did not reach for the money—he did not know what it was.

There were dozens of such children in this particular mill. A physician who was with me said that they would all be dead probably in two years, and their places filled by others—there were plenty more. Pneumonia carries off most of them. Their systems are ripe for disease, and when it comes there is no rebound—no response. Medicine simply does not act—nature is whipped, beaten, discouraged, and the child sinks into a stupor and dies."

So fares modern man and the child of modern man in the United States, most prosperous and enlightened of all countries on earth. It must be remembered that the instances given are instances only, but that they can be multiplied myriads of times. It must also be remembered that what is true of the United States is true of all the civilized world. Such misery was not true of the caveman. Then what has happened? Has the hostile environment of the caveman grown more hostile for his descendants? Has the caveman's natural efficiency of 1 for food-getting and shelter-getting diminished in modern man to one-half or one-quarter?

On the contrary, the hostile environment of the caveman has been destroyed. For modern man it no longer exists. All carnivorous enemies, the daily menace of the younger world, have been killed off. Many of the species of prey have become extinct. Here and there, in secluded portions of the world, still linger a few of man's fiercer enemies. But they are far from being a menace to mankind. Modern man, when he wants recreation and change, goes to the secluded portions of the world for a hunt. Also, in idle moments, he wails regretfully at the passing of the "big game," which he knows in the not distant future will disappear from the earth.

Nor since the day of the caveman has man's efficiency for food-getting and shelter-getting diminished. It has increased a thousand fold. Since the day of the caveman, matter has been mastered. The secrets of matter have been discovered. Its laws have been formulated. Wonderful artifices have been made, and marvellous inventions, all tending to increase tremendously man's natural efficiency of 1 in every food-getting, shelter-getting exertion, in farming, mining, manufacturing, transportation, and communication.

From the caveman to the hand-workers of three genera-

tions ago, the increase in efficiency for food- and shelter-getting has been very great. But in this day, by machinery, the
efficiency of the hand-worker of three generations ago has in
turn been increased many times. Formerly it required 200
hours of human labor to place 100 tons of ore on a railroad
car. To-day, aided by machinery, but two hours of human
labor is required to do the same task. The United States Bureau of Labor is responsible for the following table, showing
the comparatively recent increase in man's food- and shelter-
getting efficiency:

	Machine Hours.	Hand Hours.
Barley (100 bushels)	9	211
Corn (50 bushels shelled, stalks, husks, and blades cut into fodder)	34	228
Oats (160 bushels)	28	265
Wheat (50 bushels)	7	160
Loading ore (loading 100 tons iron ore on cars)	2	200
Unloading coal (transferring 200 tons from canal-boats to bins 400 feet distant)	20	240
Pitchforks (50 pitchforks, 12-inch tines) . .	12	200
Plough (one landside plough, oak beams and handles)	3	118

According to the same authority, under the best conditions
for organization in farming, labor can produce 20 bushels of
wheat for 66 cents, or 1 bushel for $3^1/3$ cents. This was done on a
bonanza farm of 10,000 acres in California, and was the average
cost of the whole product of the farm. Mr. Carroll D. Wright
says that to-day 4,500,000 men, aided by machinery, turn out a
product that would require the labor of 40,000,000 men if
produced by hand. Professor Herzog, of Austria, says that
5,000,000 people with the machinery of to-day, employed
at socially useful labor, would be able to supply a population of 20,000,000 people with all the necessaries and small
luxuries of life by working $1^1/2$ hours per day.

This being so, matter being mastered, man's efficiency for
food- and shelter-getting being increased a thousand fold over
the efficiency of the caveman, then why is it that millions of

modern men live more miserably than lived the caveman? This is the question the revolutionist asks, and he asks it of the managing class, the capitalist class. The capitalist class does not answer it. The capitalist class cannot answer it.

If modern man's food- and shelter-getting efficiency is a thousand fold greater than that of the caveman, why, then, are there 10,000,000 people in the United States to-day who are not properly sheltered and properly fed? If the child of the caveman did not have to work, why, then, to-day, in the United States, are 80,000 children working out their lives in the textile factories alone? If the child of the caveman did not have to work, why, then, to-day, in the United States, are there 1,752,187 child-laborers?

It is a true count in the indictment. The capitalist class has mismanaged, is to-day mismanaging. In New York City 50,000 children go hungry to school, and in New York City there are 1320 millionnaires. The point, however, is not that the mass of mankind is miserable because of the wealth the capitalist class has taken to itself. Far from it. The point really is that the mass of mankind is miserable, not for want of the wealth taken by the capitalist class, *but for want of the wealth that was never created*. This wealth was never created because the capitalist class managed too wastefully and irrationally. The capitalist class, blind and greedy, grasping madly, has not only not made the best of its management, but made the worst of it. It is a management prodigiously wasteful. This point cannot be emphasized too strongly.

In face of the facts that modern man lives more wretchedly than the caveman, and that modern man's food- and shelter-getting efficiency is a thousand fold greater than the caveman's, no other solution is possible than that the management is prodigiously wasteful.

With the natural resources of the world, the machinery already invented, a rational organization of production and distribution, and an equally rational elimination of waste, the able-bodied workers would not have to labor more than two or three hours per day to feed everybody, clothe everybody, house everybody, educate everybody, and give a fair measure of little luxuries to everybody. There would be no more material want and wretchedness, no more children toiling out their lives, no more men and women and babes living like beasts and dying like beasts. Not only would matter be mastered, but the machine would be mastered. In such a day incentive would be finer and nobler than the incentive of to-day, which is the incentive of the stomach. No man, woman, or child would be impelled to action by an empty stomach. On the contrary, they would be impelled to action as a child in a spelling match is impelled to action, as boys and girls at games, as scientists formulating law, as inventors applying law, as artists and sculptors painting canvases and shaping clay, as poets and statesmen serving humanity by singing and by statecraft. The spiritual, intellectual, and artistic uplift consequent upon such a condition of society would be tremendous. All the human world would surge upward in a mighty wave.

This was the opportunity vouchsafed the capitalist class. Less blindness on its part, less greediness, and a rational management, were all that was necessary. A wonderful era was possible for the human race. But the capitalist class failed. It made a shambles of civilization. Nor can the capitalist class plead not guilty. It knew of the opportunity. Its wise men told it of the opportunity, its scholars and its scientists told it of the opportunity. All that they said is there to-day in the books, just so much damning evidence against it. It would not listen. It was too greedy. It rose up (as it rises up to-day), shamelessly, in our legislative halls, and declared that profits were impossible without the toil of children and babes. It lulled its conscience to sleep with prattle of sweet ideals and dear moralities, and allowed the suffering and misery of mankind to continue and to increase. In short, the capitalist class failed to take advantage of the opportunity.

But the opportunity is still here. The capitalist class has been tried and found wanting. Remains the working-class to see what it can do with the opportunity. "But the working-class is incapable," says the capitalist class. "What do you know about it?" the working-class replies. "Because you have failed is no reason that we shall fail. Furthermore, we are going to have a try at it, anyway. Seven millions of us say so. And what have you to say to that?"

And what can the capitalist class say? Grant the incapacity

of the working-class. Grant that the indictment and the argument of the revolutionists are all wrong. The 7,000,000 revolutionists remain. Their existence is a fact. Their belief in their capacity, and in their indictment and their argument, is a fact. Their constant growth is a fact. Their intention to destroy present-day society is a fact, as is also their intention to take possession of the world with all its wealth and machinery and governments. Moreover, it is a fact that the working-class is vastly larger than the capitalist class.

The revolution is a revolution of the working-class. How can the capitalist class, in the minority, stem this tide of revolution? What has it to offer? What does it offer? Employers' associations, injunctions, civil suits for plundering of the treasuries of the labor-unions, clamor and combination for the open shop, bitter and shameless opposition to the eight-hour day, strong efforts to defeat all reform child-labor bills, graft in every municipal council, strong lobbies and bribery in every legislature for the purchase of capitalist legislation, bayonets, machine-guns, policemen's clubs, professional strike-breakers, and armed Pinkertons—these are the things the capitalist class is dumping in front of the tide of revolution, as though, forsooth, to hold it back.

The capitalist class is as blind to-day to the menace of the revolution as it was blind in the past to its own God-given opportunity. It cannot see how precarious is its position, cannot comprehend the power and the portent of the revolution. It goes on its placid way, prattling sweet ideals and dear moralities, and scrambling sordidly for material benefits.

No overthrown ruler or class in the past ever considered the revolution that overthrew it, and so with the capitalist class of to-day. Instead of compromising, instead of lengthening its lease of life by conciliation and by removal of some of the harsher oppressions of the working-class, it antagonizes the working-class, drives the working-class into revolution. Every broken strike in recent years, every legally plundered trades-union treasury, every closed shop made into an open shop, has driven the members of the working-class directly hurt over to socialism by hundreds and thousands. Show a workingman that his union fails, and he becomes a revolutionist. Break a strike with an injunction or bankrupt a union with a civil suit, and the workingmen hurt thereby listen to the siren song of the socialist and are lost forever to the *political capitalist* parties.

Antagonism never lulled revolution, and antagonism is about all the capitalist class offers. It is true, it offers some few antiquated notions which were very efficacious in the past, but which are no longer efficacious. Fourth-of-July liberty in terms of the Declaration of Independence and of the French Encyclopedists is scarcely apposite to-day. It does not appeal to the workingman who has had his head broken by a policeman's club, his union treasury bankrupted by a court decision, or his job taken away from him by a labor-saving invention. Nor does the Constitution of the United States appear so glorious and constitutional to the workingman who has experienced a bull pen or been unconstitutionally deported from Colorado. Nor are this particular workingman's hurt feelings soothed by reading in the newspapers that both the bull pen and the deportation were preëminently just, legal, and constitutional. "To hell, then, with the Constitution!" says he, and another revolutionist has been made—by the capitalist class.

In short, so blind is the capitalist class that it does nothing to lengthen its lease of life, while it does everything to shorten it. The capitalist class offers nothing that is clean, noble, and alive. The revolutionists offer everything that is clean, noble, and alive. They offer service, unselfishness, sacrifice, martyrdom—the things that sting awake the imagination of the people, touching their hearts with the fervor that arises out of the impulse toward good and which is essentially religious in its nature.

But the revolutionists blow hot and blow cold. They offer facts and statistics, economics and scientific arguments. If the workingman be merely selfish, the revolutionists show him, mathematically demonstrate to him, that his condition will be bettered by the revolution. If the workingman be the higher type, moved by impulses toward right conduct, if he have soul and spirit, the revolutionists offer him the things of the soul and the spirit, the tremendous things that cannot be measured by dollars and cents, nor be held down by dollars and cents. The revolutionist cries out upon wrong and injustice, and preaches righteousness. And, most potent of all, he sings the eternal song of human freedom—a song of all lands and all tongues and all time.

Few members of the capitalist class see the revolution. Most of them are too ignorant, and many are too afraid to see it. It is the same old story of every perishing ruling class in the world's history. Fat with power and possession, drunken with success, and made soft by surfeit and by cessation of struggle, they are like the drones clustered about the honey vats when the worker-bees spring upon them to end their rotund existence.

President Roosevelt vaguely sees the revolution, is frightened by it, and recoils from seeing it. As he says: "Above all, we need to remember that any kind of class animosity in the political world is, if possible, even more wicked, even more destructive to national welfare, than sectional, race, or religious animosity."

Class animosity in the political world, President Roosevelt maintains, is wicked. But class animosity in the political world is the preachment of the revolutionists. "Let the class wars in the industrial world continue," they say, "but extend the class war to the political world." As their leader, Eugene V. Debs, says: "So far as this struggle is concerned, there is no good capitalist and no bad workingman. Every capitalist is your enemy and every workingman is your friend."

Here is class animosity in the political world with a vengeance. And here is revolution. In 1888 there were only 2000 revolutionists of this type in the United States; in 1900 there were 127,000 revolutionists; in 1904, 435,000 revolutionists. Wickedness of the President Roosevelt definition evidently flourishes and increases in the United States. Quite so, for it is the revolution that flourishes and increases.

Here and there a member of the capitalist class catches a clear glimpse of the revolution, and raises a warning cry. But his class does not heed. President Eliot of Harvard raised such a cry: "I am forced to believe there is a present danger of socialism never before so imminent in America in so dangerous a form, because never before imminent in so well organized a form. The danger lies in the obtaining control of the trades-unions by the socialists." And the capitalist employers, instead of giving heed to the warnings, are perfecting their strike-breaking organization and combining more strongly than ever for a general assault upon that dearest of all things to the trades-unions,—the closed shop. In so far as this assault succeeds, by just that much will the capitalist class shorten its lease of life. It is the old, old story, over again and over again. The drunken drones still cluster greedily about the honey vats.

Possibly one of the most amusing spectacles of to-day is the attitude of the American press toward the revolution. It is also a pathetic spectacle. It compels the onlooker to be aware of a distinct loss of pride in his species. Dogmatic utterance from the mouth of ignorance may make gods laugh, but it should make men weep. And the American editors (in the general instance) are so impressive about it! The old "divide-up," "men-are-*not*-born-free-and-equal" propositions are enunciated gravely and sagely, as things white-hot and new from the forge of human wisdom. Their feeble vaporings show no more than a schoolboy's comprehension of the nature of the revolution. Parasites themselves on the capitalist class, serving the capitalist class by moulding public opinion, they, too, cluster drunkenly about the honey vats.

Of course, this is true only of the large majority of American editors. To say that it is true of all of them would be to cast too great obloquy upon the human race. Also, it would be untrue, for here and there an occasional editor does see clearly—and in his case, ruled by stomach-incentive, is usually afraid to say what he thinks about it. So far as the science and the sociology of the revolution are concerned, the average editor is a generation or so behind the facts. He is intellectually slothful, accepts no facts until they are accepted by the majority, and prides himself upon his conservatism. He is an instinctive optimist, prone to believe that what ought to be, is. The revolutionist gave this up long ago, and believes not that what ought to be, is, but what is, is, and that it may not be what it ought to be at all.

Now and then, rubbing his eyes vigorously, an editor catches a sudden glimpse of the revolution and breaks out in naïve volubility, as, for instance, the one who wrote the following in the *Chicago Chronicle*: "American socialists are revolutionists. They know that they are revolutionists. It is high time that other people should appreciate the fact." A white-hot, brand-new discovery, and he proceeded to shout it out from the housetops that we, forsooth, were revolutionists. Why, it is just what we have been doing all these years—shouting it out from the housetops that we are revolutionists, and stop us who can.

The time should be past for the mental attitude: "Revolution is atrocious. Sir, there is no revolution." Likewise should the time be past for that other familiar attitude: "Socialism is slavery. Sir, it will never be." It is no longer a question of dialectics, theories, and dreams. There is no question about it. The revolution is a fact. It is here now. Seven million revolutionists, organized, working day and night, are preaching the revolution—that passionate gospel, the Brotherhood of Man. Not only is it a cold-blooded economic propaganda, but it is in essence a religious propaganda with a fervor in it of Paul and Christ. The capitalist class has been indicted. It has failed in its management and its management is to be taken away from it. Seven million men of the working-class say that they are going to get the rest of the working-class to join with them and take the management away. The revolution is here, now. Stop it who can.

SACRAMENTO RIVER,
March, 1905.

Chronology

1876   Jack London born January 12 in San Francisco and named John Griffith Chaney. Mother, Flora Wellman, had been deserted by her common-law husband, William Chaney, an itinerant astrologer, when he learned she was pregnant. Jack is nursed by Virginia (Jennie) Prentiss for eight months. On September 7, Flora Wellman marries John London, a widower with two daughters, Eliza and Ida.

1876–85   Family lives precariously in various communities and on various farms in the San Francisco Bay region. Flora London gives music lessons and conducts séances. Jack is looked after by his stepsister, Eliza, nine years his senior, until her marriage to Captain James H. Shepard in 1884.

1886–90   Family moves to Oakland. The Oakland Public Library gives Jack his· first real access to books. Helps support family by delivering newspapers, sweeping saloon floors, setting up pins in a bowling alley, and other odd jobs.

1891–92   Graduates from grammar school. After working several months in a cannery, borrows $300 from Jennie Prentiss to buy a sloop, the *Razzle Dazzle*, and becomes an oyster pirate on San Francisco Bay. Later is hired by "the other side," the California Fish Patrol.

1893   In January, signs up for a voyage on the sealer *Sophia Sutherland* (the *Ghost* of *The Sea-Wolf*) and spends seven months at sea, visiting the Bonin Islands and Yokohama. On return, works ten hours a day in a jute mill, for ten cents an hour. His article about a typhoon off the Japanese coast wins a contest conducted by the *San Francisco Morning Call* for best descriptive essay.

1894   Works in a power plant. In April joins Kelly's Army of the unemployed (the western branch of Coxey's Army) on its march to Washington. Drops out at Hannibal, Missouri, in late May. Arrested for vagrancy in late June, spends thirty days in Erie County (New York) Penitentiary. Later tells his adventures in *The Road* (1907).

1895–96   Attends Oakland High School for a year, preparing for
          admission to the University of California at Berkeley.
          Writes for the school magazine, joins the Socialist Party,
          and meets Mabel Applegarth, the Ruth Morse of *Martin
          Eden*. Gains local notoriety as the "boy Socialist" of Oak-
          land.

1896–97   Attends the university during the fall. Quits and attempts
          unsuccessfully to support himself by writing, then works
          in a steam laundry.

1897–98   In July, London and his brother-in-law, Captain James
          Shepard, join the Klondike gold rush. Spends the winter
          in a cabin near Henderson's Creek, south of Dawson City,
          and is stricken with scurvy. Leaves Klondike in early June,
          rafting down the Yukon River to its mouth and thence by
          steamer to San Francisco. Arrives home in July to discover
          that John London has died the previous October.

1898–99   Tries again to write for a living. Sells his first story, "To
          the Man on Trail," to the *Overland Monthly* of San Fran-
          cisco for five dollars. It appears in January 1899. In Au-
          gust 1899 the *Atlantic Monthly* (a maker of reputations)
          accepts his "An Odyssey of the North" and pays him $120.
          In the fall meets Anna Strunsky, the Kempton of *The
          Kempton-Wace Letters* (1903).

1900   *The Son of the Wolf*, London's first book, a collection of
          his Klondike tales, is published by Houghton, Mifflin Co.
          on April 7, the day he marries Elizabeth (Bess) Maddern.
          They settle in Oakland.

1901   Joan London born. London receives 245 votes as Socialist
          candidate for mayor of Oakland. Second volume of Klon-
          dike stories, *The God of His Fathers*, is published by
          McClure, Phillips & Co.

1902   London and his family move to the Piedmont Hills in the
          Bay Area. Establishes close friendship with George Ster-
          ling (the Russ Brissenden of *Martin Eden*). First novel, *A
          Daughter of the Snows*, is published by J. B. Lippincott Co.
          Spends six weeks during the summer in the East End of
          London collecting material for *The People of the Abyss*. Sec-
          ond daughter, Bess (Becky) London, born.

1903   *The Kempton-Wace Letters* (epistolary dialogue on love co-authored with Anna Strunsky) published anonymously by The Macmillan Co. *The Call of the Wild*, for which London sold the book rights for $2000, is published by Macmillan with great success. Begins *The Sea-Wolf*, falls in love with Charmian Kittredge, and separates from Bess London. *The People of the Abyss* is published by Macmillan.

1904   Travels as a correspondent to Japan and Korea to report on the Russo-Japanese War for William Randolph Hearst's newspaper syndicate. *The Sea-Wolf*, published by Macmillan, is a best-seller.

1905   Receives 981 votes as Socialist candidate for mayor of Oakland in March election. *War of the Classes* (sociological essays) is published by Macmillan. Lectures at Bowdoin and Harvard. Buys ranch near Glen Ellen in the Sonoma Valley in June. Is divorced by Bess London and on November 19 marries Charmian Kittredge.

1906   Begins building the schooner *Snark* to sail around the world. *White Fang* is published by Macmillan; works on *The Iron Heel* and *The Road*.

1907   Charmian and Jack London sail in April for the South Seas. The voyage lasts twenty-seven months, with the *Snark* calling at Hawaii, the Marquesas, Tahiti, and the Solomons. *The Road* published by Macmillan.

1908   *The Iron Heel* published by Macmillan.

1909   London forced to leave the *Snark* in the Solomons because of illness; recovers in Sydney, Australia, and returns to Glen Ellen in July. *Martin Eden* published by Macmillan. Devotes energies to building Beauty Ranch.

1910   Expands ranch to 1100 acres and hires stepsister Eliza Shepard as business manager. Begins construction of Wolf House, a mansion designed to stand "a thousand years." Birth and death of daughter, Joy. Occasional visits to Carmel artists' colony. Buys story plots from Sinclair Lewis. *Burning Daylight* is published by Macmillan.

1911   Drives four-horse carriage with Charmian to Oregon and back. Supports the Mexican Revolution in his writings. *South Sea Tales* published by Macmillan.

1912   Spends two months with Charmian in New York City prior to five-month voyage from Baltimore to Seattle around Cape Horn aboard a four-masted barque.

1913   Intensifies work on Beauty Ranch and writes *The Little Lady of the Big House*. Has an appendectomy in July. Is warned by surgeon that his kidneys are deteriorating. *John Barleycorn* is published by The Century Co., and Macmillan publishes *The Valley of the Moon*. Wolf House destroyed by fire, cause unknown.

1914   In April sails with Charmian from Galveston to Vera Cruz to report on the Mexican Revolution for *Collier's*. His articles no longer support the revolution. Two months later he is forced to return home by a severe attack of dysentery complicated by pleurisy. *The Strength of the Strong* is published by Macmillan.

1915   Suffers from acute rheumatism and spends five months in Hawaii in effort to improve health. Two fantasy fictions, *The Scarlet Plague* and *The Star Rover*, are published by Macmillan.

1916   In Hawaii from January until late July. Resigns from Socialist Party in March "because of its lack of fire and fight, and its loss of emphasis on the class struggle." Hospitalized with rheumatism in September. Dies November 22 from an attack of acute "gastro-intestinal type of uremia," and possibly a self-induced drug overdose.

Note on the Texts

Modern editors face an apparent dilemma in selecting texts for a reprinting of the works of Jack London because of differences between the first periodical and book versions. Familiarity with London's lifelong practice as an author, however, and with American publishing conventions of the time, supports the selection of the first book edition of a London story, novel, or essay as invariably the most authoritative version. To earn his living as a writer, London was forced to publish his novels and stories initially in magazines. And in order to reach the highly profitable magazine market, he had to accept the magazine editors' conventional privilege to tailor material for the specific needs of their journals: to omit profanity; to cut material considered overlong for the space provided; and to divide paragraphs too lengthy for the double-column format of most magazines.

But London controlled the book publication of his material. Although in some instances the book version of a London work is very similar to its periodical version, in the great majority of instances there is considerable difference. For example, the Macmillan text of *The Road* contains a number of brief passages not in the *Cosmopolitan Magazine* version and also often differs in wording, paragraphing, and punctuation. In making up a book, it appears, London did not rely on tear sheets or proof of the periodical appearances of the contents of the book; rather he used a copy of the original typescript. Thus, book publication in a sense "restored" the work to its author's intent.

The editorial principle, therefore, adopted for this reprinting of London's works has been to rely upon the first book edition text. (London is not known to have revised any work after its first book appearance.) This text has been compared to that of its first periodical appearance, and has been found in each case to be more authoritative than the periodical text.

The following is a list of the works included here, in order of their appearance in this volume, giving first periodical and book publication dates. Where necessary, or where they are of sufficient interest, differences between periodical and book texts are noted.

THE PEOPLE OF THE ABYSS
  No periodical publication.
  (New York: Macmillan, 1903).
  The Macmillan edition contains a large number of photographs which are omitted from this republication of *The People of the Abyss*. Although the photographs are of some interest (London himself took many of them during his stay in the East End), they were added to the volume after its composition and are thus not integral to the work. The text contains no specific references to the photographs, many of which illustrate scenes not mentioned in the text. This republication preserves the quotation mark usage of the Macmillan edition in which double quote marks are used for dialogue and single marks are frequently used for emphasis. Also preserved is London's use of brackets to gloss East End dialect.

THE ROAD
  Cosmopolitan Magazine, 43 (May 1907), 17–22; (June 1907), 142–50; (July 1907), 263–70; (Aug. 1907), 373–80; (Sept. 1907), 513–18; (Oct. 1907), 643–48; 44 (Dec. 1907), 190–97; (March 1908), 417–23.
  (New York: Macmillan, 1907).
  The Macmillan edition contains a number of illustrations which are omitted from this republication of *The Road*. The *Cosmopolitan* serialization of *The Road* does not contain "Road-Kids and Gay-Cats," which appears in the Macmillan edition for the first time. Also omitted in the *Cosmopolitan* is a passage from "Pinched" (pp. 239.16–19), in which London describes sucking out his prison vaccination, and a number of minor passages from "Bulls." The *Cosmopolitan* text contains many minor variations in punctuation and paragraphing from the Macmillan text.

THE IRON HEEL
  No periodical publication.
  (New York: Macmillan, 1908).
  Maintained in this republication of *The Iron Heel* is the practice in the Macmillan edition of printing as footnotes the notes by "Anthony Meredith" to Avis Everhard's memoir.

MARTIN EDEN
  Pacific Monthly, 20 (Sept. 1908), 234–54; (Oct. 1908), 402–18; (Nov. 1908), 486–504; (Dec. 1908), 621–40; 21 (Jan. 1909), 33–46;

(Feb. 1909), 166–76; (March 1909), 258–72; (April 1909), 420–29; (May 1909), 530–44; (June 1909), 637–52; 22 (July 1909), 85–95; (Aug. 1909), 190–206; (Sept. 1909), 300–17.
(New York: Macmillan, 1909).
There are occasional minor variations in punctuation and wording between the *Pacific Monthly* and Macmillan texts. In the *Pacific Monthly*, the *Transcontinental Monthly* is called the *Occidental Review*; omitted from the *Pacific Monthly* are two passages describing some of the shady practices of the *Transcontinental Review*: 749.13–25 and 779.17–33.

JOHN BARLEYCORN
The Saturday Evening Post, 185 (March 15, 1913), –5, 50–53; (March 22, 1913), 18–20, 44–46; (March 29, 1913), 21–23, 56–58; (April 5, 1913), 23–25, 54; (April 12, 1913), 22–24, 48–49; (April 19, 1913), 25–27, 65–66; (April 26, 1913), 23–25, 42–43; (May 3, 1913), 24–25, 78–79.
(New York: The Century Co., 1913).
Omitted from this republication of *John Barleycorn* are the illustrations which appeared in the Century Co. first edition. The *Saturday Evening Post* text of *John Barleycorn* differs from that in the Century Co. edition in paragraphing and punctuation; a number of minor passages are also omitted in the *Saturday Evening Post*. London's stylistic habit of opening a paragraph with a conjunction was much revised in the *Saturday Evening Post*.

"HOW I BECAME A SOCIALIST"
Comrade, 2 (March 1903), 122–23.
War of the Classes (New York: Macmillan, 1905).

"THE SCAB"
Atlantic Monthly, 93 (Jan. 1904), 54–63.
War of the Classes (New York: Macmillan, 1905).

"JACK LONDON ON 'THE JUNGLE'"
New York Evening Journal (Aug. 6, 1906), 2.
Wilshire's Magazine, 11 (Jan. 1907), 24–25.
The *New York Evening Journal* text omits the last four paragraphs (1144.19–1145.17) of the essay, and differs slightly in wording and punctuation from *Wilshire's Magazine*. The first printing of *Novels and Social Writings* reproduced the *New York Evening Journal* version; the second printing replaces this with the *Wilshire's Magazine* version, with the omission of a brief "Editor's Note."

"Revolution"
   Contemporary Review, 93 (Jan. 1908), 17–31.
   Revolution and Other Essays (New York: Macmillan, 1910).
   Omitted in the *Contemporary Review* is 1153.36–1154.32.

The standards for American English continue to fluctuate and in some ways were different in earlier periods from what they are now. In nineteenth-century writings, for example, a word might be spelled in more than one way, even in the same work. Commas could be used expressively to suggest the movements of voice, and capitals were sometimes meant to give significances to a word beyond those it might have in its uncapitalized form. Works printed in the first decade of the twentieth century have many of the same characteristics. Since modernization would remove these effects, this volume has preserved the spelling, punctuation, capitalization, and wording of the editions reprinted here.

The present edition is concerned only with representing the texts of these first editions; it does not attempt to reproduce features of the typographic design such as the display capitalization of chapter openings. Footnotes within the text are by London. Open contractions are retained when they appear in the original edition. Typographical errors have been corrected. The following is a list of those errors, cited by page and line numbers: 96.1, Hamstead; 135.28, waded,; 167.18, Country; 212.11, softly,; 317.5, Johnson's Arm; 328.3, Do; 420.16–17, destribution; 421.27, protelariat; 445.32, alternations; 492.5, striken; 492.25, second; 513.39, us,; 573.12, trignometry; 610.18, an; 620.3, again; 629.22, Marion; 745.19, journeymen; 767.26, Melville; 818.4, Thankgiving; 856.37, nothing; 871.8, *Parthenon's*.; 877.19, did not; 887.31, others; 888.28, can't; 888.30, Henly; 892.7, your're; 954.19, Smollet; 975.4, Idler; 1005.37, too; 1098.7, proceded; 1098.14, Compte; 1139.1, Amerian; 1140.40, try.; 1141.1, that the; 1151.21, 1,000,000. Errors corrected third printing: 957.38, yatch's.

Notes

In the notes below, the numbers refer to page and line of the present volume (the line count includes chapter headings). No note is made for material included in a standard desk reference book. Notes printed at the foot of pages within the text are by the author.

THE PEOPLE OF THE ABYSS

1.1 THE PEOPLE OF THE ABYSS] London uses "East End" and "West End" to designate both geographical area and social reality. The Thames flows through London from west to east, dividing the city into distinctive districts related to their position on or near the river. The West End in 1902 included the political center of the country (Parliament, Whitehall, and Buckingham Palace); the great parks (Hyde, Green, and Kensington); theatres, hotels, and restaurants (many of them located in and around Trafalgar Square, Leicester Square, and Piccadilly); and the better shops and business establishments. Downriver from this area, east of Trafalgar Square and following the Strand and other main thoroughfares paralleling the river, were first St. Paul's Cathedral and the City (the financial center of England), then the Tower of London, and finally the East End, which was made up of the boroughs (among others) of Whitechapel, Hackney, Bethnal Green, and Stepney. Here life was dominated by the proximity of the docks and by the presence of immigrant groups from every quarter of the globe. In the early twentieth century, "West End" symbolized the well-to-do and fashionable, "East End" the poor and degraded.

Jack London was in England from approximately early August to late September 1902. During this time he not only experienced the events recorded in *The People of the Abyss* but also had access to a large collection of published material dealing with the condition of the deprived and working classes of Great Britain and of the East End of London in particular. Many of the authorities he cites and quotes in *The People of the Abyss* are obscure figures whose writings usually appeared in ephemeral pamphlets and periodicals. These writers have, whenever possible, been identified in the notes.

2.1–17 The chief . . . me."] "A Parable" (1843), ll.33–44.

5.27–35 "The workhouses . . . provided."] "Hard Times in London," *Independent*, 55 (Jan. 8, 1903), 73.

7.7 Thomas Ashe] (1836–89) A minor poet and editor.

8.4 Ludgate Circus] A major intersection, with the Strand to the west and St. Paul's Cathedral to the east.

8.7   Cook's Cheapside branch]   In the City of London.

9.4−5   American consul-general]   In 1902, H. Clay Evans.

11.30   Petticut Lane]   Petticoat Lane, or Middlesex Street (just east of the City), was famous for its second-hand wares sold from street stalls.

12.9   Highbury Vale]   A working-class neighborhood directly north of the East End.

15.6   Thorold Rogers]   James Edwin Thorold Rogers (1823−90) was Professor of Political Economy at Oxford and a prolific writer on social and economic subjects. His most well-known work was *Six Centuries of Work and Wages: The History of English Labour* (1884).

17.26   Old Sleuth]   A detective in the popular dime novel series *Old Sleuth Library*, published in the 1880s by George Munro.

19.3−10 The poor . . . melody.]   "The Symphony" (1875), ll.21−28.

23.3−6   After . . . shake?]   Verse 43 of Edward FitzGerald's *The Rubáiyát of Omar Khayyám* (1859).

23.11−12 Pool . . . Limehouse]   The Upper and Lower Pool of London are sections of the Thames; Limehouse is an East End dock area adjacent to the Lower Pool.

25.15   Wapping]   An East End district west of the West India Docks.

28.35   A. C. Pigou]   Arthur C. Pigou (1877−1959), an economist who believed that society was responsible for and should bear the costs of unemployment, poor housing, and poor health.

30.3−5   I . . . London.]   As a very young man in 1841, T. H. Huxley worked as an apprentice physician in the East End district of Rotherhithe.

31.15−16 Sir William Thisleton-Dyer]   (1843−1928) The director of the Royal Gardens at Kew from 1885 to 1905.

35.3−6   The beasts . . . by.]   "The Symphony" (1875), ll.35−38.

35.8   Mile End Road]   A main thoroughfare of the East End, running east-west as a continuation of Whitechapel Road.

35.10   Fra Lippo Lippi]   An apparent allusion to Robert Browning's "Fra Lippo Lippi" (1855). In that poem, however, though Lippi is poor and hungry as a boy, there are no lines describing the possible effect on him of a puff of wind.

35.14−15 pro-Boer meetings]   The Boer War, which lasted from October 1899 to May 1902, had increasingly attracted the opposition of English socialists.

36.17−18 Leman . . . Alley]   The general area is the East End district of Spitalfields, just east of Liverpool Street Station.

37.34   "grindery"]   The various materials and tools used by shoemakers.

38.20   Arthur . . . Jago"]   (1863–1945) The novel, *A Child of the Jago* (1896), is set in the East End borough of Bethnal Green.

39.9   Doré]   Gustave Doré was famous for his engravings for Dante's *Inferno*.

41.3–4   From . . . out.]   Job 24:12.

42.13–20   Kipling's . . . service.]   Lines 29–32 of "The Galley-Slave," *Departmental Ditties* (1890).

45.13   Poplar Workhouse]   Poplar is a district directly east of White-chapel.

50.28–29   four . . . oakum]   Oakum is loose fiber which is obtained by unraveling ("picking") old rope. Picking oakum is traditionally a prison and workhouse activity.

54.5–6   stands . . . parade]   Edward VII was crowned on August 9, 1902, but parades in honor of the event began several weeks earlier.

54.15   Roberts . . . Egypt]   General Roberts commanded English forces in India and Afghanistan during the 1870s and 80s; the British occupied Egypt in 1882.

56.3–9   The old . . . year.]   From chapter IV, book III, of Carlyle's *Sartor Resartus* (1836).

57.36   peg]   As London later notes (p. 73.28–29), the "peg" is argot for any place where free meals may be obtained.

62.29   'towny']   A resident of London who is not from the East End.

64.1   Stratford spike]   The reference is to Stratford East, a district in the easternmost region of the East End, not to Stratford-upon-Avon.

69.3–7   I . . . work]   "The Method of Nature" (1841).

69.37–70.1   well-dressed women]   The more expensive streetwalkers frequented the Piccadilly area.

70.19–21   St. James . . . Park.]   The heart of fashionable London, with many clubs and government buildings.

77.21   Life Guards]   The various Guards regiments were noted for the height of their soldiers.

82.19–20   Alhambra ballets]   The Alhambra Palace, a London music hall, was famous for its "ballets" featuring girls in scanty costumes.

82.23   Hotel Cecil]   One of the largest London hotels, on the Embankment, near Waterloo Bridge.

84.3–30 And . . . day.] 1 Samuel 8:9–18.

85.25 King's watermen] Sailors on the royal barges.

85.33–36 Spens . . . Roberts] Named are Maj.-Gen. James Spens (1853–1934), who served in South Africa; Viscount Plumer (1857–1934), who led the Matabele relief force in the Boer War; Lt.-Gen. Robert Broadwood (1862–1917), who served in Egypt and South Africa; Maj.-Gen. Charles Duncan Cooper (1849–1929), who relieved Ookiep during the Boer War; Col. Henry Malthias (1850–1914), who led the charge of the Gordon Highlanders at the Battle of Dargai, Northwest Frontier, India, in 1895; Brig.-Gen. Sir Henry Grey Dixon (1850–1933), the commander-in-chief in South Africa, 1899–1900; General Sir Alfred Gaselee (1844–1918), who served in various Indian wars; Admiral Sir Edward Seymour (1840–1929), who served in China during 1898–1901; Earl Kitchener (1850–1916), who recaptured Khartoum, in the Sudan, in 1896; and Lord Roberts (1832–1914), who was commander-in-chief in India from 1885 to 1893.

93.28 Dan Burns] London undoubtedly means John Elliot Burns (1858–1943), one of the early leaders of the Trades Union Congress in Great Britain.

93.29–30 Walter Besant's novels] Sir Walter Besant (1836–1901) wrote both historical fiction and novels dealing with the East End, of which his *All Sorts and Conditions of Men* (1882) is the best known.

94.18 'Great Dock Strike'] Of London dock workers in 1889.

95.3 Queen's Bounty nurses] More fully, Queen Anne's Bounty, a fund established by Queen Anne for the aid of poor clergymen but later extended to the poor in general.

96.27 Jude the Obscure] An allusion to the central figure in Thomas Hardy's *Jude the Obscure* (1895), a poor stone cutter who goes to Oxford in search of knowledge.

96.34–35 "For . . . tragedy."] A loose paraphrase of a passage from chapter IV, book III, of Thomas Carlyle's *Sartor Resartus* (1836): "That there should be one man die ignorant who had capacity for knowledge, this I call a tragedy."

97.3s6–8 Ill . . . supplied.] "The Deserted Village" (1770), ll.51–56.

100.9 'bean-feasters'] British slang for employees on an outing paid for by their employers.

104.3–11 These . . . purse.] From section IV of Crane's short story "Death and the Child" (1898).

113.8 Robert Blatchford] (1851–1943) Socialist journalist best known for his tract *Merrie England* (1893).

113.9—10   Mile End Waste]   An open space off Mile End Road.

119.12   Lesser London]   Areas of London under the control of the London County Council.

121.16   Lord Londonderry]   The Marquess of Londonderry (1852—1915) was active in educational and philanthropic matters during this period.

122.29   Thomas Holmes]   (1846—1918) The author of *Pictures and Problems from London's Police Courts* (1900).

124.3—10   It . . . poor.]   "Locksley Hall Sixty Years After" (1886), ll.217—24.

124.24—25   "London . . . Border"]   To the east of the East End and in the county of Essex.

125.39   Charles Booth]   (1840—1916) A shipowner and writer on social problems who also edited the massive *Life and Labour of the People in London* (1891—97).

127.3   Devonshire . . . Grove]   Not in the East End but rather in a working-class section near Paddington Station, north of the West End.

127.28   Bishop Wilkinson]   Thomas E. Wilkinson (?—1914), Bishop of Zululand in 1870 and rector of a City of London church in the 1880s.

128.5—6   St. James's Hall]   A fashionable concert hall off Piccadilly.

128.6   Rev. Hugh Price Hughes]   (1847—1902) An evangelical clergyman and writer on London social problems.

131.30—31   Rev. Stopford Brooke]   (1832—1916) Curate of Kensington Church from 1860 to 1863 and a prolific writer on religious and literary subjects.

136.17   'Hobo . . . jail]   The portion of a prison where minor offenders are kept in a large cage.

140.40—141.1   Childe Roland]   An allusion to Robert Browning's "Childe Roland to the Dark Tower Came" (1855).

142.32—33   Leman . . . Piccadilly]   Streets frequented by prostitutes, from working-class Leman Street to fashionable Piccadilly.

146.9—10   Luton Guardians]   Luton is about thirty miles north of London; its "Guardians" are a board elected to administer the poor law of the district.

146.25   Sir A. Forwood]   Sir Arthur Forwood (1836—1898), Member of Parliament from Lancastershire from 1858 to his death.

146.37   Philippines]   Philippine natives were in revolt (from 1899 to early 1902) against the American occupation of the islands.

147.31 George Haw] The figures are derived from Haw's *No Room to Live: The Plaint of Overcrowded London* (1900).

148.13—17 Arlidge . . . ceases."] John T. Arlidge (1822—99), author of a number of tracts on industrial diseases.

150.7 Vaughan Nash] (1861—1932) A newspaperman who wrote on industrial matters.

152.30—31 Britannia lock-keeper] One of the locks on the Regent's Canal, which runs through central London and the East End.

153.39 Stalybridge] An industrial town east of Manchester.

156.28—29 Frank Cavilla] Cavilla's murder of his wife and children was reported in the London *Times* from September 3 to 9, 1902; his trial was reported on October 23, 1902.

163.6—8 Late . . . docks.] London has walked directly south from the Bethnal Green district of the East End to the London Docks on the Thames.

163.16 'nightly . . . Strand] An allusion to the prevalence of street-walkers on these streets.

166.18—19 Fen Country] A low-lying area of mideastern England, chiefly in Lincolnshire.

168.12—169.2 Wilde . . . dismissal."] From Wilde's letter to the editor of the *Daily Chronicle*, May 27, 1897; in *The Letters of Oscar Wilde* (1963).

171.30 Rowntree] Benjamin S. Rowntree (1871—1954) wrote frequently on agricultural employment.

173.3—8 Sometimes . . . animal.] From Wilde's *The Soul of Man Under Socialism* (1895).

177.40 Dr. Barnardo] Thomas J. Barnardo (1845—1905) founded in 1867 an East End mission for destitute children. In 1882 he began sending such children to Canada.

179.5 Edward Atkinson] (1827—1905) American industrialist and economist who wrote prolifically on economic subjects.

THE ROAD

185.1 THE ROAD] London's account of his tramp adventures are often undated and are also in mixed chronological order. The experiences, however, date from two specific periods in London's life—the summer of 1892, when he was 16, and the six months from April to October, 1894. During 1892, London became a member of a gang of youths who frequently rode trains as hoboes from Sacramento to Reno and back. These adventures are the basis for the chapters "Road-Kids and Gay-Cats" and "Confession" in

The Road. In early 1894, London decided to join Charles T. Kelly's Industrial Army, a western branch of Jacob Coxey's similar group. (Coxey had organized his Army of the unemployed in Ohio for a march on Washington to protest hard times and to demand government inflation of the currency.) He missed the departure of the Army from Oakland on April 6, 1894, but caught up with its rear guard on April 17 on the Continental Divide, and then with the Army itself at Council Bluffs on April 19. He remained with the Army until late May. These experiences appear in "Hoboes That Pass in the Night" and "Two Thousand Stiffs."

After leaving Kelly's Army and spending some days with an aunt near Chicago, London visited New York City. It was while on a trip from New York to view Niagara Falls that London was arrested for vagrancy in late June, 1894, and spent 30 days in the Erie County Penitentiary ("Pinched" and "The Pen"). On release from jail, London tramped in the East from Harrisburg to Washington to Boston and Vermont ("Pictures" and "Bulls"). In mid-September, he went to Montreal and from there hoboed across Canada to Vancouver ("Holding Her Down"). In Vancouver, he got a job as a coal stoker on a steamer which returned him to San Francisco in early October.

Railroading and tramping have been two of the richest sources of American slang, and London liberally sprinkles *The Road* with argot. Much of this he explains immediately, and the meaning of a good deal of the remainder is clear from its context. Only those expressions and terms whose meaning may still be unclear have been annotated below.

186.2   Josiah Flynt]   The pen name of Josiah Flynt Willard (1869–1907), who wrote frequently about his tramping experiences in the United States.

186.3   *Blowed . . . Glass*]   Genuine and first-rate, from liquor bottles with the brand name blown in the glass.

188.1–6   "Speakin' . . . die."]   Rudyard Kipling (1896).

189.19   hitting . . . piece"]   Begging for change.

190.13   blind baggage]   As London notes elsewhere in *The Road*, a blind baggage is a baggage car which can only be opened from its side doors; hence, its end platform is a protected place for hoboes as long as the train is in motion.

196.1   "lime-juicer"]   A British ship, from the custom of requiring British sailors to eat limes to prevent scurvy.

202.19   rods]   See London's account of riding the rods on pp. 210ff.

203.14   "jerk"]   A short branch rail line.

204.3–4   In . . . wept.]   Psalms 137:1.

228.20–21   Ormuz . . . Ind]   Poetical terms for, respectively, the East and India.

231.1   "fly-cop"]   A detective in street clothing.

232.33   hard times]   The Wall Street collapse of June 1893 led to a depression which lasted until 1898.

235.40–236.1   Rocklyn . . . Newcastle.]   The town is Black Rock, now a suburb of Buffalo.

238.11   Fra Lippo Lippi]   In Browning's poem (ll.94–99), Lippi renounced all the trappings of life when he entered the monastery.

238.32–33   Kipling's . . . Lungtungpen]   In Kipling's comic story "The Taking of Lungtungpen" (1888), a number of British soldiers strip naked in order to cross a stream and take an Indian town.

240.35–36   Childe . . . bore.]   An allusion to the closing lines of Browning's "Childe Roland to the Dark Tower Came." A "slug-horn" is a buglelike instrument.

242.29   Lexow Committee]   The commission chaired by Clarence Lexow (1852–1910) which in 1894 investigated corruption in the New York City police department.

253.7   "oryide"]   Drunkard, derived from "hoary-eyed."

257.17   October 15, 1894]   A mistake for September 15, 1894.

258.38–39   "wind . . . world"]   Kipling's "Sestina of the Tramp-Royal."

274.21   "smoudge"]   A rough, unkempt person, often a beggar.

274.31–32   Benicia . . . Port Costa]   Towns on either side of the Carquinez Straits, which connect San Pablo Bay (the northern portion of San Francisco Bay) and the Sacramento River.

277.6–7   Rio Vista]   About twenty-five miles upstream on the Sacramento River.

277.39   'hog,']   Behaving swinishly, that is niggardly, toward hoboes.

278.6   'punk']   A cheap bread.

285.18–19   *chechaquos*]   The Klondike term for newcomers.

285.24   "prushun"]   Derived from *Prussian*; a boy who travels with an older tramp, often begs for him, and is presumed to be homosexually involved with him.

285.35–36   *blond beasts* . . . Nietzsche]   London's term for the Nietzschean idea of the übermensch or superman.

292.21   diary]   London's diary, from April 6 to May 31, is published in *Jack London on the Road: The Tramp Diary and Other Hobo Writings*, ed. Richard W. Etulain (Logan: Utah State Univ. Pr., 1979).

294.19–20   Colonel . . . Baker]   George Speed, a hatter, led the Sacramento unit of Kelly's Army; William Baker was one of the organizers of the San Francisco segment.

298.12–13   Dr. Jordan's . . . it?"]   David Starr Jordan (1851–1931) was a scientist and president of Stanford University; the quotation is from his "The Stability of Truth," *Popular Science Monthly*, 50 (March 1897), 646.

304.38–39   pee-wee]   A game played with marbles.

305.38   Blackwell's Island]   The site of the New York City prison, an island in the East River off midtown Manhattan.

306.29   name . . . papers]   London, as the "boy socialist of Oakland," had several stories written about him in Bay Area newspapers in early 1896.

307.19   Prisoner . . . stunt]   An allusion to Byron's poem "The Prisoner of Chillon" (1816), which deals with a Swiss patriot imprisoned for many years in the fortress of Chillon, on Lake Geneva.

311.14–15   making . . . down.]   The dice holder was winning each bet and letting his winnings accumulate as the next bet.

THE IRON HEEL

325.24   Blind Tom]   Thomas Bethune (1849–1908), a self-taught blind pianist and composer.

329.30–32   As . . . knowledge.]   A summary of Spencer's definition of the "knowable" in his *First Principles* (1862).

333.4   Dr. Jordan . . . it]   See note 298.12–13.

334.8   "My . . . is,"]   Poem by Sir Edward Dyer (1540–1607).

345.2   Austin Lewis]   A San Francisco attorney (1865–1944) and close friend of London's.

346.37   Henry van Dyke]   (1852–1933) A clergyman, popular moralist, and Professor of English at Princeton University; the quotation is from Van Dyke's essay "Property and Theft," in which he attacks the use of the Bible to support socialist ideas.

356.38   'red . . . fang']   An echo of Tennyson's "Nature, red in tooth and claw," stanza 56, "In Memoriam" (1850).

358.37   socialist vote]   London's figures are those of votes cast for socialist candidates in all elections in the years he cites.

365.37   George F. Baer]   A protege of J. P. Morgan, Baer (1842–1914) played a major role in breaking the coal miners' strike of 1902.

367.12   *Outlook*]   The article is Jocelyn Lewis' "Was It Worth While?"

Outlook, 83 (Aug. 10, 1906), 902–904; London relied on many of its details for his account of the case of Jackson's arm.

379.29   mass-plays]   The tactic (outlawed around the turn of the century) of dropping a number of men behind the line of scrimmage to form a wall of blockers for the ball carrier.

393.31–396.12   "I . . . say—"]   London borrowed most of Bishop More-land's speech verbatim from a 1901 article by Frank Harris, "The Bishop of London and Public Morality," in which Harris ironically attributed these sentiments to a pillar of the British religious establishment. When challenged by Harris to explain his unacknowledged use of this material, London replied that he had copied the passage from a socialist newspaper which had itself copied it from Harris' article without noting its source or its ironic character.

395.26–396.4   "The . . . tears.' "]   Wilde's sonnet, "Easter Day," appears in his *Poems* (1881).

406.26–27   Joshua . . . Gibeon]   Joshua 10:12.

408.33–35   Twice . . . unconstitutional.]   London refers to the Supreme Court decisions which led to the passage in 1913 of the 16th Amendment giving Congress the right to levy a tax on income.

421.37   Lucien Sanial]   Sanial (1836–1928) was a prominent socialist journalist and sociologist.

424.24–26   Even . . . combination.]   Cited by London are: James J. Hill (1838–1916), who controlled the Great Northern system, including the Northern Pacific; Jacob H. Schiff (1847–1920), head of the Kuhn, Loeb financial empire, which controlled the Pennsylvania Railroad; E. H. Harriman (1848–1909), controller of the Union Pacific from the mid-1880s and the Southern Pacific from about 1900; Henry Clay Frick (1849–1919), principally a steel capitalist; Benjamin B. Odell (1854–1926), Republican governor of New York, 1900–1904; Jay Gould (1836–1892), long active in railway financing; and William H. Moore (1848–1923), leader of a syndicate which was in control of the Rock Island Railroad.

433.32   Farley]   James Farley, known as the King of the Strike Breakers, flourished in this role during the first decade of the twentieth century.

476.3–4   When . . . mixtures]   In the history of gunpowder manufacture, mechanical or dry mixing of the ingredients was supplanted by chemical or "wet" mixing because wet mixing was both safer and produced a better blend.

483.22–23   Fighting . . . Revolution]   The full name was Fighting Organization of the Party of Socialists-Revolutionists. These militant terrorists were formed in 1902 and played a major role in the Russian Revolution of 1905.

488.30   flash . . . explosion.]   London models this event on the famous
Haymarket Square bomb explosion of May 1886 in which several Chicago
policemen were killed. The event provided the opportunity for the arrest and
eventual execution of several Anarchist leaders.

492.38–45   Then . . . murder.]   William D. (Big Bill) Haywood and
Charles H. Moyer were accused in late 1905 of murdering Frank R. Steunen-
berg, a former governor of Idaho. The two labor leaders were arrested in
Colorado and "kidnapped" to Idaho; they were acquitted of the crime in
1907.

496.12   lights of Alcatraz]   Alcatraz Island was a U.S. Army prison from
1886 to 1934 and a Federal penitentiary from 1934 to 1963.

497.15   Once . . . ranch;]   The "writer friend" is of course London and
the ranch is his Beauty Ranch.

497.29   Spreckels]   The great California entrepreneurial family (founded
by Claus Spreckels, 1828–1908), with large sugar beet and cane holdings in
California and Hawaii.

497.34   state . . . feeble-minded]   The California Home for the Feeble-
Minded at Glen Ellen.

500.4–6   S.L.P. . . . S.P.]   The Socialist Labor Party, the principal
American socialist organization during the 1880s and 1890s, had a long history
of factionalism. One such dissident group combined with a faction of the Social Democratic Party (led by Eugene Debs) to form the Socialist Party in 1901.

505.31–32   gaseous . . . Haeckel]   The materialist Ernst Haeckel defines
God in his *The Riddle of the Universe* (1900) as a gaseous vertebrate.

510.14   Cabañas]   A town in Pinar del Rio province of Cuba.

524.38   John Burns]   See note 93.28.

528.18   air-line]   The most direct rail route between two points.

550.14   Pullman]   The model town south of Chicago founded by George
M. Pullman for the manufacture of his sleeping cars.

MARTIN EDEN

560.21   Iseult]   In *Tristram of Lyonesse* (1882).

579.20   penitent form]   The bench for penitents in a communion service.

588.35   bean-feast]   See note 100.9.

592.20   Temescal]   A working-class section of north Oakland.

594.32–35   "Norrie's . . . Marshall]   Named by London are *Epitome of
Navigation* by J. W. Norie (not Norrie) (1772–1843) and *American Practical
Navigator* by Nathaniel Bowditch (1773–1838). Thornton S. Lecky

(1838–1902) and Charles H. Marshall (1792–1865) wrote many books on navigation.

605.17–19   Madam . . . Science."]   *The Secret Doctrine* (1888), by Madame Helena Blavatsky (1831–91), an explanation of the religion of Theosophy; *Progress and Poverty* (1879), by Henry George (1839–97), a defense of the single-tax notion of land reform; *The Quintessence of Socialism* (1889), by Albert Schäffle (1831–1903); and *History of the Warfare of Science with Theology in Christendom* (1896), by Andrew D. White (1832–1918).

606.9   Gayley's . . . Myths"]   Charles Mills Gayley (1858–1932), *The Classic Myths in English Literature* (1893).

616.28   "The Princess,"]   The poem (1847) by Tennyson.

619.17–18   Browning . . . souls.]   The allusion is to Browning's "A Light Woman" (1855), l.45.

621.21   nigger heaven]   The highest portion of a theater balcony.

652.36   Romanes]   George John Romanes (1848–94), an English biologist.

657.27–28   'Whan . . . soote']   The first line of the Prologue to Chaucer's *Canterbury Tales*.

660.12–15   What's . . . thing?]   Spencer's definition of the law of evolution, from his *First Principles* (1862), is that evolution is "an integration of matter and concomitant dissipation of motion, during which the matter passes from an incoherent homogeneity to a definite coherent heterogeneity, and during which the retained motion undergoes a parallel transformation."

669.24–25   'In Memoriam . . . Hall,"]   The contrast is between the high-minded religiosity of Tennyson's "In Memoriam" (1850) and the more socially grounded themes of his "Locksley Hall" (1842).

681.29   'ape . . . die']   From stanza 118 of Tennyson's "In Memoriam."

682.15   Fiske]   John Fiske (1842–1901), the American popularizer of evolutionary ideas and the author of *Outlines of Cosmic Philosophy* (1874).

712.29–30   "Love . . . Portuguese"]   Elizabeth Barrett Browning, *Sonnets from the Portuguese* (1850).

712.39   Lake Merritt]   The large lake near the center of Oakland.

720.22–23   Kipling's . . . *skins.*"]   "The Ladies" (1896).

738.19   Vanderwater]   As is revealed by Martin's reference (just below) to Vanderwater as "the Dean of American Criticism," the figure is modeled on William Dean Howells (1837–1920), the foremost critic of the age.

738.25–26   bromide . . . Burgess]   Gelett Burgess (1866–1951) popularized the term "bromide" in his *Are You a Bromide?* (1906) to signify a bore.

745.35   head-luna]   Hawaiian for chief overseer.

747.40   *Transcontinental Monthly*]   Here and in chapter XXXIII London tells of his sale of "To the Man on Trail" to the *Overland Monthly* and of his attempts to obtain payment for the story.

749.18–21   world's . . . covers]   The allusion is to Bret Harte (1836–1902), who contributed some of his famous stories to the *Overland Monthly* and who edited the magazine from 1868 to 1871.

754.24   *White Mouse*]   One of London's earliest major sales was of his horror story "A Thousand Deaths" to the magazine *The Black Cat* in 1899.

760.27–28   secret . . . Islands]   London also used much of the account of a Hawaiian leper colony which follows in his story "Koolau the Leper" (1909). London visited a Hawaiian leper colony in 1907.

764.11   *Youth and Age*]   *Youth's Companion*, to which London contributed considerable early work. London identifies the magazine as a monthly here, but on 780.5 he correctly notes that it is a weekly.

767.26–27   Hapgood . . . cashier]   The Macmillan text reads "Melville, the bank cashier," but since London at 767.5–7 identifies Melville as a private secretary and Hapgood as a cashier, and since Hapgood the cashier is clearly intended in this passage and in those which follow, this obvious slip has been corrected to "Hapgood, the bank cashier."

773.15   Joseph Le Conte]   Le Conte (1823–1901) was an extremely popular teacher of science at the University of California and the author of *Evolution and Its Relation to Religious Thought* (1888).

774.22   skins the cards]   Slides the cards off the top of a pack one by one.

775.2–3   winnowed . . . Tomlinson]   In Kipling's poem "Tomlinson" (1891), l.83, the Devil asks that the dilettante Tomlinson be winnowed out " 'twixt star and star" to "sieve his proper worth."

778.3–4   "The Duchess"]   The pseudonym of Mrs. Margaret Hungerford (1855–97), the author of extremely popular sentimental romances.

780.12   *The Billow*]   The San Francisco *Wave*; Frank Norris was on its staff from 1896 to 1898.

783.28–30   *The Hornet . . . it*]   *The Wasp.* The "brilliant journalist" is undoubtedly Ambrose Bierce, who though he did not found the magazine did edit it from 1881 to 1886.

786.34–37   British . . . history]   Bishop Samuel Wilberforce (1805–73), who viciously attacked Darwinism during his famous Oxford debate with T. H. Huxley in 1860.

793.20   "The Science of Æsthetics."]   The work (1872) by Henry N. Day (1808–90).

795.31–32   henidical . . . Weininger] Otto Weininger (1880–1903) coined the term "henid" in his *Sex and Character* (1906) to designate the early stage of a perception in which there is little precise understanding of the phenomenon perceived.

800.8–12   Longfellow's . . . more.']   *The Golden Legend* (1873), part v, ll.358–61.

806.2   Russ Brissenden] London's portrait of George Sterling (1869–1926), the San Francisco minor poet and Bohemian. Sterling's first book of poems, *The Testimony of the Suns* (1903), made a considerable stir.

809.35–36   " 'Under . . . unbowed.' "]   W. E. Henley, "Invictus" (1888).

812.20–21   Henry Vaughn Marlow]   Undoubtedly the American philo-sophical poet William Vaughn Moody (1869–1910), whose *Poems* appeared in 1901.

813.13   Father Damien letter]   In 1890 Robert Louis Stevenson published his celebrated "Father Damien: An Open Letter," in which he defended Fa-ther Damien's practices as the head of a Hawaiian leper colony against the attacks of a Mr. Hyde, a Presbyterian missionary.

813.20   Richard Realf]   Realf (1834–78) was a minor poet who commit-ed suicide in San Francisco.

837.7   Strawn-Hamilton]   Frank Strawn-Hamilton, a celebrated figure in turn-of-the-century San Francisco for his combination of socialist idealism and panhandling.

837.15   Kreis]   Nathan L. Greist, whose rooms on Market Street London often visited for philosophical discussions.

839.23–24   Bebel's last speech]   August Bebel (1840–1913), a German socialist political leader.

845.30–31   Saleeby's . . . Life"]   Caleb W. Saleeby (1878–1940), a pro-lific British writer on scientific subjects. His *The Cycle of Life* appeared in 1904.

851.13   Fairbanks]   Andrew Fairbairn (1838–1912), a writer on religious subjects and Principal of Mansfield College, Oxford, from 1886 to 1902.

874.27   Helen Della Delmar] Undoubtedly Ella Wheeler Wilcox (1850–1919), a popular sentimental poet.

877.19–20   first-class . . . acceptance]   The Macmillan text contains a "not" after "did," the *Pacific Monthly* text does not. Since the intent of the sentence is to confirm Martin Eden's earlier belief that first-class magazines pay on acceptance, I have emended the Macmillan text by omitting the "not."

881.32   steam beer]   A cheap form of beer especially popular in California.

888.29–31 " 'A poor . . . shame.'] The concluding lines of Henley's poem "Waiting," from *In Hospital* (1887).

896.19–20 "The Bottle . . . Skin."] The works by Robert Louis Stevenson and Honoré de Balzac.

919.24 oryide] See note 253.7.

923.1 Berne Convention] The international copyright agreement of 1886.

923.10 Kipling . . . death] Kipling became seriously ill with pneumonia during the winter of 1898–99 in New York.

929.15–22 " 'From . . . sea' "] Swinburne's "The Garden of Proserpine" (1866).

JOHN BARLEYCORN

935.3–4 Valley . . . village] London is riding down from his Beauty Ranch in the Sonoma Valley (also called Valley of the Moon) to Glen Ellen.

935.11 suffrage amendment] California passed a women's suffrage amendment to its constitution in November, 1911.

952.28 Horace Fletcher] Fletcher (1849–1919) was an American nutrition expert who advocated the slow mastication of food.

953.39 Paul . . . travels] Chaillu (1831–1903) was the author of *Explorations and Adventures in Equatorial Africa* (1861) and similar works.

956.9 steam beer] See note 881.32.

968.9 "boneyard"] An anchorage for derelict ships.

973.23 Benicia] See note 274.31–32.

984.24 rushed the growler] To fetch beer from a saloon in a pail.

993.40 *Solano* wharf] The wharf for the ferryboat *Solano*, which crossed the Carquinez Strait.

994.35–37 Contra . . . shore,] Contra Costa and Solano counties face each other across the Carquinez Strait; Mare Island, a shipyard, is on the northwestern edge of the strait.

1008.30 *Sophie Sutherland*] London means the *Sophia* (not *Sophie*) *Sutherland*.

1012.24–25 *samisens* and *taikos*] Japanese musical instruments; the first resembles a lute, the second is a small drum.

1018.1–2 boarding-house sharks] Hucksters who attempt to allure returning sailors into free-and-easy waterfront boarding houses.

1018.6   Barbary Coast]   The waterfront saloon and brothel area of San Francisco.

1025.26—27   "Colonel's . . . skins"]   See note 720.22—23.

1030.35—36   Sancho Pedro]   A card game.

1042.36   katzenjammer]   Hangover.

1056.2   wop]   Slang of the time for an unskilled laborer, not necessarily of Italian background.

1058.29   "Snow . . . Resartus"]   The works by John Greenleaf Whittier and Thomas Carlyle, published in 1866 and 1836 respectively.

1059.26—27   Bohemian Club]   Founded in 1872 as a club for those interested in the arts; by the turn of the century it also contained many wealthy San Franciscans. London became a member in 1904.

1071.16   Cloudesley]   Cloudesley Johns, a California writer and one of London's closest friends for many years.

1085.6—7   Biblical . . . skin]   The so-called white leprosy of the Old Testament was in fact leucoderma, a loss of skin pigment.

1087.7—8   Naaman's silvery skin]   2 Kings 5.27; Naaman was stricken with a leprosy as "white as snow."

1094.38—39   "The City . . . abyss."]   From section XVI of the poem (1880) by James Thomson (1834—82).

1095.17—20   trees . . . sun.]   London reforested a good deal of the Beauty Ranch with groves of eucalyptus trees.

1096.29   catch-as-catch-can]   A form of wrestling in which any grip is permissible.

1098.13—14   Great . . . world.]   August Comte (1798—1857), the founder of philosophical positivism, designated the earliest stage of human belief—in which each object was held to have a will of its own—as "fetishism."

1100.1   Liu Ling]   A third-century Chinese poet.

1100.13—31   Chuang Tzu . . . man."]   The Taoist philosopher whose work was translated under the title *Chuang Tzu* by Herbert Giles in 1889. London quotes from chapter 11 of this translation.

1101.7   rancho . . . Petaluma]   The Rancho Petaluma, with headquarters across the Sonoma Mountains from London's Beauty Ranch, was founded by General Mariano Vallejo (1808—90) in the early nineteenth century.

1101.8   Manuel Micheltoreno]   Micheltorena (not Micheltoreno) was governor of Alta California from 1842 to 1845.

1101.23   James . . . William]   King (1822–56) was a San Francisco news-paperman and banker.

1103.4–5   William James]   In the passage which follows London alludes to the two extremes of James's work and thought: his scientific study of the mind in *Principles of Psychology* (1890) and his study of the human interest in the supernatural in *The Varieties of Religious Experience* (1902).

1104.30–34   Hovey . . . worms."]   From Hovey's "Quatrains," in the collection by Bliss Carman and Richard Hovey (1864–1900), *Last Songs from Vagabondia* (1901).

1105.37–1106.10   Kemp . . . die!' "]   From "The Cry of Youth" by the minor American poet (1883–1960); the poem appeared initially in the *American Magazine* of October, 1912, and was collected in Kemp's *The Cry of Youth* (1914).

1111.17   Battle of Santiago]   One of the chief battles of the Spanish-American War.

ESSAYS

1118.1   Nietzsche's *blond beasts*]   See note 285.35–36.

1118.32–33   President . . . heroes]   Charles William Eliot (1834–1926), president of Harvard College from 1869 to 1909. In a much-noted speech of 1902—published in *Cassier's Magazine*, 23 (Jan. 1903), 434–40—Eliot attacked a number of union practices, including violence against scabs.

1118.38   rods . . . baggages]   For "rods," see note 202.19; for "blind baggages," see note 190.13.

1119.12–13   battered . . . gates]   Hobo slang for begging on the street and at back doors.

1128.18   Mr. Casson]   Herbert N. Casson (1869–?), a prolific author of articles and books on American business history.

1129.14   M. Leroy-Beaulieu]   Paul Leroy-Beaulieu (1843–1916).

1132.29   Factory Acts]   The parliamentary acts of 1802, 1816, and 1833 set certain minimum conditions for factory employment.

1133.36–37   Dr. Schultze-Gaevernitz]   Gerhart Schulze- (not Schultze-) Gaevernitz (1864–1943), author of *The Cotton Trade in England and on the Continent* (1895).

1134.7   Mr. Maxim]   Hiram Maxim (1840–1916), American inventor.

1148.22–23   Japan . . . throats]   The Russian-Japanese War of 1904.

1148.32–34   January . . . Russia]   The Russian revolution of 1905 broke

out on 22 January with the shooting down of protesting workers outside the
Winter Palace, in St. Petersburg.

1150.27–28   Fighting Organization]   See note 483.22–23.

1151.21   100,000]   The Macmillan text reads "1,000,000," the *Contemporary Review* "100,000." The context makes it clear that "100,000" is intended.

1158.30   Carroll D. Wright]   See p. 434.

1162.15–16   unconstitutionally . . . Colorado.]   See note 497.38–45.

1163.12–17   Roosevelt . . . animosity."]   From Theodore Roosevelt's
Second Annual Message to Congress, December, 1902; in Roosevelt's *Works*
(1926), XV, 149.

CATALOGING INFORMATION

London, Jack, 1876–1916.
  Novels and social writings.

  (The Library of America)
  Contents: The people of the abyss—The road—The iron heel—Martin
Eden—John Barleycorn—Essays.
  I. Pizer, Donald.   II. Title.   III. The people of the abyss. 1982.
IV. The road. 1982.   V. The iron heel. 1982.
VI. Martin Eden. 1982.   VII. John Barleycorn. 1982.   VIII. Series: The
Library of America.
PS3523.046A6   1982C   813'.52   82–6940
ISBN 0–940450–06–2

This book is set in 10 point Linotron Galliard, a face designed for photocomposition by Matthew Carter and based on the sixteenth-century face Granjon. The paper is Olin Nyalite and conforms to guidelines adopted by the Committee on Book Longevity of the Council on Library Resources. The binding material is Brillianta, a 100% rayon cloth made by Van Heek-Scholco Textielfabrieken, Holland. Composition by Haddon Craftsmen, Inc. and The Clarinda Company. Printing and binding by R. R. Donnelley & Sons Company. Designed by Bruce Campbell.

THE LIBRARY OF AMERICA SERIES

1. Herman Melville, *Typee, Omoo, Mardi* (1982)
2. Nathaniel Hawthorne, *Tales and Sketches* (1982)
3. Walt Whitman, *Poetry and Prose* (1982)
4. Harriet Beecher Stowe, *Three Novels* (1982)
5. Mark Twain, *Mississippi Writings* (1982)
6. Jack London, *Novels and Stories* (1982)
7. Jack London, *Novels and Social Writings* (1982)
8. William Dean Howells, *Novels 1875–1886* (1982)
9. Herman Melville, *Redburn, White-Jacket, Moby-Dick* (1983)
10. Nathaniel Hawthorne, *Novels* (1983)
11. Francis Parkman, *France and England in North America* vol. I, (1983)
12. Francis Parkman, *France and England in North America* vol. II, (1983)
13. Henry James, *Novels 1871–1880* (1983)
14. Henry Adams, *Novels, Mont Saint Michel, The Education* (1983)
15. Ralph Waldo Emerson, *Essays and Lectures* (1983)
16. Washington Irving, *History, Tales and Sketches* (1983)
17. Thomas Jefferson, *Writings* (1984)
18. Stephen Crane, *Prose and Poetry* (1984)
19. Edgar Allan Poe, *Poetry and Tales* (1984)
20. Edgar Allan Poe, *Essays and Reviews* (1984)
21. Mark Twain, *The Innocents Abroad, Roughing It* (1984)
22. Henry James, *Essays, American & English Writers* (1984)
23. Henry James, *European Writers & The Prefaces* (1984)
24. Herman Melville, *Pierre, Israel Potter, The Confidence-Man, Tales & Billy Budd* (1985)
25. William Faulkner, *Novels 1930–1935* (1985)
26. James Fenimore Cooper, *The Leatherstocking Tales* vol. I, (1985)
27. James Fenimore Cooper, *The Leatherstocking Tales* vol. II, (1985)
28. Henry David Thoreau, *A Week, Walden, The Maine Woods, Cape Cod* (1985)
29. Henry James, *Novels 1881–1886* (1985)
30. Edith Wharton, *Novels* (1986)
31. Henry Adams, *History of the United States during the Administrations of Jefferson* (1986)
32. Henry Adams, *History of the United States during the Administrations of Madison* (1986)
33. Frank Norris, *Novels and Essays* (1986)
34. W. E. B. Du Bois, *Writings* (1986)
35. Willa Cather, *Early Novels and Stories* (1987)
36. Theodore Dreiser, *Sister Carrie, Jennie Gerhardt, Twelve Men* (1987)
37. Benjamin Franklin, *Writings* (1987)
38. William James, *Writings 1902–1910* (1987)
39. Flannery O'Connor, *Collected Works* (1988)
40. Eugene O'Neill, *Complete Plays 1913–1920* (1988)
41. Eugene O'Neill, *Complete Plays 1920–1931* (1988)
42. Eugene O'Neill, *Complete Plays 1932–1943* (1988)
43. Henry James, *Novels 1886–1890* (1989)
44. William Dean Howells, *Novels 1886–1888* (1989)
45. Abraham Lincoln, *Speeches and Writings 1832–1858* (1989)
46. Abraham Lincoln, *Speeches and Writings 1859–1865* (1989)
47. Edith Wharton, *Novellas and Other Writings* (1990)
48. William Faulkner, *Novels 1936–1940* (1990)
49. Willa Cather, *Later Novels* (1990)
50. Ulysses S. Grant, *Personal Memoirs and Selected Letters* (1990)
51. William Tecumseh Sherman, *Memoirs* (1990)